MY LIFE
AND LOVES

MY LIFE
AND LOVES

Frank Harris

EDITED AND WITH AN INTRODUCTION BY

JOHN F. GALLAGHER

FOREWORD TO THE NEW EDITION BY

ANTHONY BURGESS

GROVE WEIDENFELD

NEW YORK

Copyright © 1925 by Frank Harris
Copyright © 1953 by Nellie Harris
Copyright © 1963 by Arthur Leonard Ross as executor of the Frank Harris Estate
Foreword to the new edition copyright © 1991 by Anthony Burgess

All rights reserved.

No part of this book may be reproduced,
stored in a retrieval system, or transmitted
in any form, by any means, including mechanical,
electronic, photocopying, recording, or otherwise,
without prior written permission of the publisher.

Published by Grove Weidenfeld
A division of Grove Press, Inc.
841 Broadway
New York, NY 10003–4793

Quotations on pages 958–963 are from *The Economic Consequences
of the Peace* by John Maynard Keynes. Copyright, 1920, by Harcourt,
Brace & World, Inc.; renewed, 1948, by Lydia Lopokova Keynes, and
reprinted by permission of the publishers.

Library of Congress Cataloging-in-Publication Data

Harris, Frank, 1855–1931.
    My life and loves / Frank Harris : edited by John F. Gallagher.—
1st ed.
        p.   cm.
    Originally published: Paris, 1922–1927.
    Includes index.
    ISBN 0–8021–5161–2
    1. Harris, Frank, 1855–1931—Biography. 2. Authors, English—19th
century—Biography. 3. Authors, English—20th century—Biography.
4. Men authors, English—Sexual behavior. I. Gallagher, John F.
II. Title.
PR4759.H37Z5   1991
828'.91209—dc20
[B]   91–20044
                                                                              CIP

Manufactured in the United States of America

Printed on acid-free paper

First American Edition 1963
First Black Cat Edition 1964
First Evergreen Edition 1991

10 9 8 7 6 5 4 3 2 1

Acknowledgments

I am most indebted to Mr. Arthur Leonard Ross, Literary Executor of the Frank Harris Estate, not only for the privilege of editing *My Life and Loves,* but also for his advice and endless patience.

I owe a special debt to Lyle Blair, my former colleague at the Michigan State University Press, for his encouragement and constructive criticism.

I am grateful to Mr. Richard Chapin, Librarian, Mr. Henry Koch, Associate Librarian, and the staff of the Michigan State University Library for their time, assistance, and facilities; to Mr. Richard Vosper, Director of Libraries, University of Kansas, for the loan of Frank Harris' annotated copies of *My Life and Loves*; to Mrs. Ann Bowden of The Humanities Research Center, University of Texas, for co-operation in verifying the manuscript of the last volume; and to Professor C. L. Cline, University of Texas, for his advice, as well as his aid in identifying obscure (to me) figures of the late nineteenth century.

I am obliged to Mrs. Jane Hovde for her invaluable research, to Ruth Hein for tracking down and translating the German quotations, and to Marcia Page for typing and collating a formidable manuscript.

Finally, my especial obligation to my wife and family, who have suffered with me through the long period of editing.

J.F.G.

Contents

Foreword

SIR KINGSLEY AMIS has called his memoirs an allobiography, meaning a life story which deals more with others than himself. It is a useful neologism, as perhaps might be the description of Frank Harris's rambling and shambling monster as a phallobiography. Perhaps for the first time in English letters the author's phallus marches forward in the vanguard of the author himself. A comparison with Giovanni Giacomo Casanova's memoirs is probably not in order, since in that book the author presents a human totality, an engagement in the art of love of the lover's entire personality, with wit, affection, and elegance. Frank Harris wrote in a period when it was possible to be vulgar and to confuse a physical sexual candor with the telling of the whole truth. Vulgarity was not a vice of the eighteenth century, though an engaging bawdiness has often been confused with it. Vulgarity characterizes the modern age, of which Harris was first a precursor and later a sad inhabitant, and it is increasingly abetted by the techniques of publicity. Harris, as a self-publicist, was inevitably a prey to its seductions, but unlike our advertising pundits, he was not really aware of it. He saw himself as a shining exemplar of the verities.

The essence of vulgarity is dissociation. It sees the human complex as capable of fission. Our television commercials concentrate on man solely as a consumer and appeal to his appetites. The intellect, the capacity for rational choice, the aesthetic instinct are rigidly omitted from the human image; greed alone is the object of appeal. The same selectiveness is at work in the contemporary fixation on physical allure and even physical health. The building of pectoral muscles and the gratification of the clitoris with a vibrator are not immoral, but they are certainly vulgar. The vulgarity is emphasized by the use of homely abbreviations like "pecs" and "clit," which reduce noble parts of the body to toys that can be played with. To call the female pudenda a "pussy," as Harris frequently does, is as much an evasion as to call it, as the eighteenth-century pornographers did, "the bower of bliss," but at least the more orotund term raises it to a paradisal level, while the other is a childish reduction, a nursery animalization that is ignoble.

Harris began his sexual life in America, after some preliminary investigations on British soil, and it would probably be unjust to suggest that the vulgarity in him was an American endowment. If you want the best vulgarity, the culture of the United States, which is both material and evangelical, will gladly provide it. Vulgarity of language, as much in the other sundered colonies as in the mother of revolution, is a rebuke to the stiff system of the homeland. Harris was against stiffness, except in a basic physical region, and there was a great deal of the American in him. And yet, like an American, he could not resist the temptation of reversion; no one loves a lord more than an American, and the snob in Harris anticipates the snob in the Astor family and the egregious Sir Henry ("Chips") Channon.

It is probably unfair to corroborate the vulgar, and near-illiterate, view of Frank Harris as an autopornographer. *My Life and Loves* was sought after in Paris bookshops as *Tropic of Cancer* and *Ulysses* were during the age of unpermissiveness. Harris, in being titularly titillating, was after sales, and he cannot be blamed. But it was an aspect of his vulgarity, a vice that often touches hypocrisy, to excuse his revelations in terms of a salutary candor. We have heard from a best-selling dealer in sex and violence asseverations about the nobility of showing up the horrors of the world. This is best left to moral evangelists who are poorly paid; in rich purveyors of pulp fiction it has a hollow ring. But there is a sense in which Harris was quite sincere in wishing to combat the antimacassared excesses of Victorian puritanism. The trouble was, and always will be, that sexual candor is ill served by the bald notation of sexual acts. Probably that plural is out of order. Harris's sexuality was straightforwardly masculine, and each sexual act he describes is a more or less exact replica of the previous one. The mechanics of sex are easily described, but they convey little because the ecstasies of congress represent an oceanic experience akin to the raptures of the mystic. Only skilled poets can express the bliss of orgasm, and they rarely think it worthwhile to do so, though the earl of Rochester has some fine lines. Virgil was content to describe sexual excitement as *flamma nota*—"the fire that everybody knows about and which I need not delineate more exactly"—and Shakespeare took metaphorical fire from the classical poets. In going too far, Harris was embarrassingly vulgar; he indulged in dissociation very grossly. Even the most hardened of us cannot read him without a blush of shame.

It is useful to compare Harris with his friend Oscar Wilde. Wilde was the victim of bitter, and highly hypocritical, sexual persecution, but he could not be arraigned on the ground of propagandizing for his alleged vice. He kept his erotic life separate from his art. He was never vulgar; indeed, he execrated vulgarity as a mortal sin. It was to Harris's credit that he perceived the literary greatness of Wilde, and perhaps his best book is his life of the Irish master, despite the inaccuracies and the appalling style. It has, of course, been superseded by Richard Ellmann's biography, scholarly, definitive, and very much the product of an age of tolerance, but it was brave, and it predisposes us to think well of Harris. Indeed, Harris's devotion to Shakespeare and Jesus

Christ stands well in his favor. He knew what greatness was and where it lay. The trouble was that he was inclined to believe that he had a touch of it himself. His arrogance is insufferable, and it has a sexual provenance. Men who do well with women like to think of themselves as world conquerors. Harris conquered a small area of Victorian England. He was a fine editor, conceivably a great one, and his libertarian instincts were admirable. But he was coarse, quarrelsome, self-opinionated. He was, in a word, no gentleman.

Nor, for that matter, was George Bernard Shaw, who understood him probably better than any other man of letters of the late Victorian time. Indeed, there is something Shavian about Harris's refusal to truckle to received opinion. While Shaw dived into deep trouble by refusing to support the Great War, Harris anticipated him by denouncing British imperialism in South Africa. He even attacked General Charles Gordon, so great an icon of the conquering British virtues that Edward Elgar had once contemplated the composition of a Gordon Symphony. But while Shaw's wit and wholly ironic megalomania sweetened his outrageousness, Harris had no instrument of debate or invective other than a brutish truculence.

He was not a gentleman, nor did he look like one. Like many sexual conquerors, he was ugly, undersized, even simian-browed. He dressed flashily, like a bookmaker. He was no asset to an upper-class dinner party. As Wilde said, "Frank Harris has been received in all the great houses—once." But Max Beerbohm called him "the best talker in London," an amazing assertion when one thinks of the brilliance of Oscar himself. He possessed a voice of great beauty and power. This is puzzling, since on the evidence of his lauding Sir Arthur Sullivan to the heavens and finding Sir Henry Wood as superb as Arturo Toscanini, as well as the coarseness of his literary style, he seems to have had an insensitive ear. He admits to a bad French accent (and a haziness about genders), but Karl Marx, hearing his German, said it was *echt deutsch.* His ability to learn languages was allied to a prodigious memory for the best that had ever been thought or said. This book is crammed with citations from poets as well as prose writers which Harris has not troubled to check. Where he goes wrong is usually on discardable morphemes; he gets his Shakespeare and Goethe and Heine substantially right. He had the acumen to doubt the value of his gift. A head crammed with the words of others often has difficulty in generating words of its own. It was a gift that was an after-dinner conversational asset, as well as invaluable for putting down the pseudo-learned. Cambridge professors could burble generalities about Shakespeare, but Harris could quote chapter and verse. It was not a gift that denoted high intelligence, and Harris's intelligence, as opposed to self-serving shrewdness, is always in doubt.

In fact, where he conquered outside the sexual field it was through force of personality more than the power of dialectic or epigram. There was something elemental about him—swarthy, hirsute, pulsating with sexual energy. Naturally he made his appeal more to the young and inexperienced than to the mature and achieved. With the young, dogmatic bullying used to be accepted as the right of the sage or guru. The young fed his self-esteem and justified an immense egotism. He had some difficulty with the mature and established. One of the more embarrassing moments in this chronicle comes when he dares question Robert Browning about his erotic life. Harris was genuinely puzzled when Browning took offense. When Harris dared the theater with a mediocre play, he presumed to lecture Shaw on dramaturgy. Shaw was good-humored, as he nearly always was, but he rightly deplored the impertinence. The impertinence was a mark of immaturity. Harris never really grew up.

He wrote fiction as well as drama and was unlucky enough to receive laudations from critics who should have known better. The tales that he published in the *Fortnightly Review* and later (1894) collected as *Elder Conklin and Other Stories* are, to the present-day reader, acceptable magazine fodder, but the literary element—skill with the choice of words, a sharp ear for dialogue, the telling image—is minimal. It was especially unfortunate that George Meredith, a very considerable novelist, overpraised *Montes the Matador*, a very inconsiderable exercise in the exotic. Harris was confirmed in the opinion of his own greatness; he never tried to improve; he saw no point in pursuing the search for perfection that so agonized Henry James. His attitude to James is the gravest of the testimonies against him. "One day someone sent me a thin book of James's, begging me to read it and to give some account of what he thought a master-work. . . . It was a story of two children, a little boy and girl, who had been corrupted, if I remember aright, by some teacher or governess. They were a foul pair, carefully presented: lifelike, but not alive, a study in child viciousness—worse than worthless, because not even natural. I never read another line of Henry James." Harris's prose style certainly reads as if he never did.

A man who had no doubt of the greatness of Shakespeare might be expected to appreciate the verbal contortions of James; it is only through doing strange things with language that a writer can mirror the convolutions of the human brain. But Harris, and this may be somewhat to his credit, saw Shakespeare as a great prophet or messiah, certainly a supreme humanitarian, and was inclined to underestimate his art. Shakespeare as a secular Christ, or Christ as a holy Shakespeare, dominated Harris's thinking. The Christ tales came during the Great War—"The Miracle of the Stigmata," "The Holy Man," and "The King of the Jews"—but *The Man Shakespeare and His Tragic Life Story* was published in 1909. It is the cause of one more anachronism in Joyce's *Ulysses*, for it seems to be mentioned in the Irish National Library on June 16, 1904. Joyce, in his own fanciful narrative about Shakespeare's willed cuck-oldry, seems to owe something to Harris. His book is far from scholarly, but it is vital, loving, and demotic. Shakespeare is no longer a preserve of the professors; he is a suffering human being and very much a man of the people. Harris performed a useful task in relating Shakespeare's work to his life, and since Harris's day, genuine scholars like Leslie Hotson and Caroline Spurgeon have been ready to take such a relationship further, though more soberly. Where Harris's book is monstrous is in its implied identification of subject and author. The subjects of his more considerable writing are all men unjustly crucified.

One of these, of course, was Wilde. In Harris's version of Wilde's Calvary, Lord Alfred Douglas is the Judas. This role has been more or less confirmed by Ellmann's biography, but the supporters and, indeed, adorers of "Bosie" wished to scratch out Harris's eyes. Douglas was an undoubted Adonis or Narcissus, but a very mediocre poet, yet there are still not lacking those who would rate him as high as Shelley. Harris told what looks like the truth, and his assessment of Douglas seems just, as both man and artist. His excoriation of the little golden-haired Judas is not balanced by an uncritical evaluation of the betrayed genius, and this did not please Robert Ross and the other canonizing Wildeans. Harris's *Oscar Wilde* is, I think, a fair and even exciting book, though no biographical masterpiece. It has, somewhere in the shadows, that property of self-identification which Harris's large ego insisted upon. From 1910 onward this ego swelled in proportion to the diminution of Harris's standing as a writer and an editor. By 1920 he had become not merely a neglected man of letters but a penurious one. The publication of *My Life and Loves* in five successive volumes, which was intended to restore his fortunes, failed to do so very miserably, and Harris himself became one of the great ruined geniuses who had been scorned, scourged, and crucified. England was to blame, that philistine plutocracy of hippic gorgers who sneered at living writers and revered them nominally when they were safely dead. Success had come too early to Harris.

It is not really possible to exaggerate his importance as an editor, first of the *Evening News*, at the age of twenty-seven, then of the *Fortnightly Review*, three years later, eventually, as owner as well, of the *Saturday Review*. Fine editors are probably rarer than fine authors, certainly in England, and probably Harris can be matched only by Charles Dickens and Ford Madox Ford in a métier that primarily demands flair. With the *Fortnightly Review* Harris was not merely an efficient editor but a magnanimous one. Frederic Chapman, of Chapman and Hall, the publishers, was in charge of it and was a typically British obscurantist. "He hated poetry and thought it should be paid for at the ordinary rates. When he found that I was giving my salary in payment to his contributors, I fell in his esteem. To give Swinburne fifty pounds for a poem seemed to him monstrous. . . . And if he disliked art and literature, he hated the social movement of the time with a hatred peculiarly English; he looked upon a socialist as a sort of low thief, and pictured a communist as one who had his hand always in his neighbor's pocket." One's heart goes out wholly to Harris in his effort to liberalize English journalism; one rejoices when he is able to buy the *Saturday Review* and shape it to his will, or the will of the progressive zeitgeist.

Harris tempted Bernard Shaw away from his post as music critic for the *World*—certainly not appreciating the greatness of this musical journalism, the best in all history—and installed him as drama critic. "I wrote to him that music was not the forte of the man who had written *Widowers' Houses*. . . ."

H. G. Wells joined as fiction reviewer; Robert Bontine Cunninghame Graham wrote fine fiction and travel sketches; Joseph Conrad's *Almayer's Folly* was discovered. "I have written pages about Conrad, not columns," said Wells, "and I have praised him to the skies. Will you stand it?" Harris replied: "First-rate. . . . [A] great reviewer should be a star-finder and not a fault-finder." It is on the strength of his editorial acumen that Harris deserves his place among the prophets of modernism. He was generous to the new, as Ford was. Whether literature can still advance through literary journals seems doubtful, but the fin de siècle situation is to be remembered with awe and homage. Harris, unfortunately, was less than wholehearted in his promotion of literary talent. That large ego got in the way. As soon as the *Saturday Review* was launched, Harris felt impelled to rush off to Cape Town to protest about the Jameson Raid in the Transvaal. He could not leave public affairs alone; he considered himself a little too large for what Woodrow Wilson called "mere literature."

His various editorial positions brought him into the world of affairs and into contact with those whom that world considered to be great men. Great women, too. He writes of Queen Victoria with the assumed authority of one who knew her; his anecdotes have the assurance of a personal contact which he never achieved. He loves scandal, especially when it concerns the dour gillie John Brown, and his obsession with the physical comes out in "As a girl even, she was far too broad for her height, and particularly short-necked. In her old age she was very stout, so stout that for ten years before she died, she had to be watched in her sleep continually by one of her women, for fear her head should roll on one side and she should choke, her neck was so short." As for the prince of Wales, Harris preens himself on a kind of diffident intimacy. He reaches him through the society belles of the time—ladies like Mrs. Vyner ("an intimate friend of the Prince of Wales . . . an extraordinary woman") and her daughter, Lady Alwynne Compton. He always drops names like disdainful half crowns on his way to his goal. He persuades the prince to give his name to the Damien Fund for the cure of leprosy. The prince at first associates Harris only with dirty stories, but he is soon persuaded that his influence can further the liquidation of "one of the vilest diseases that afflict humanity." The duke of Norfolk asks Harris how much he should give to the fund, and Harris replies: "You must remember that as the first Catholic in the realm, your gift will certainly not be surpassed; the more you give, the more others will give." Of course, the episode is not complete without a whiff of scandal. The saint of the lepers, Father Damien, is rumored to have contracted the disease through "carnal love." The prince is astounded and sends for Harris "hot-foot." Harris puts things right. "In spite of the comparative failure of the scheme, it made the Prince of Wales like me better, and certainly turned Sir Francis Knollys, who was nominally the head of the Prince's household and his most trusted adviser, into a really close friend." Harris makes many "really close" friends in high places, but he still ends his chronicle in seclusion and poverty.

Harris in his great days sees high life and even partakes of it. He joins in the gorging and swilling, but there is a salvatory instinct in his abhorrence of excess. His account of the splashing in the green and glutinous turtle soup of the lord mayor's banquet is a small masterpiece of disgust. You can smell the odor of the Corona-Coronas as the port is circulated; see the well-filled shirtfronts gleaming under the chandeliers. He is both drawn to the bon vivant, best exemplified in His Royal Highness, and repelled by him. Typically, it is in some small detail, always highly physical, that he sees the prospect of the redemption of the Victorian sybarites. The cigarette replaces the cigar, cuts down the postcenal time of male sodality with the widdershins passage of the port, brings the sexes together. Oscar Wilde also saw in the cigarette an emblem of a kind of ascetic elegance—the type of the best pleasures, exquisite and unsatisfying. To mention Harris's mention of the change in smoking habits is, of course, highly trivial. "Harrisian" would be a better term. One of Harris's virtues is his concern with discardable minutiae.

It is always more edifying to read Harris on small particularities than to endure his gaseous generalizations. At the beginning of his memoirs, after his denunciation of those "Rebels and Lovers of the Ideal" in America who have accused him of obscenity and sedition, he sermonizes unbecomingly: "One thing certain: we deserve the misery into which we have fallen. The laws of this world are inexorable and don't cheat! Where, when, how have we gone astray? The malady is as wide as civilization which fortunately narrows the enquiry to time." And then: "Ever since our conquest of natural forces began, towards the end of the eighteenth century, and material wealth increased by leaps and bounds, our conduct has deteriorated. Up to that time we had done the Gospel of Christ mouth honor at least; and had to some slight extent shown consideration if not love to our fellowmen. . . ." We are weary already and want the sex to begin, sex being glossed as the love so lamentably missing from our lives. But since Harris has assumed the preacher's tone, we are entitled to ask a diffident question about his theology.

He is always borrowing from *King Lear* the term "God's spies," signifying a select group of souls that look on human conduct and invoke a transcendental moral system for the judging of it. Harris evidently considers himself one of those, but his God appears to be metaphorical. "In truth," he says in Volume V, "we men are called and chosen to a purpose higher than our consciousness, and the creative impulse, if not God, is at least a conscious striving to reach the highest. And we must cooperate with this impulse and do our best to make this life worth living for all and so turn men and women into ideals and this earthly pilgrimage of ours into a sacred achievement." This is windy, unworthy verbiage, but one can glimpse through its thin mist a hint of Shavian vitalism, the life-force Shaw borrowed from Samuel Butler rather than Henri Bergson. That "conscious striving to reach the highest" recalls the infernal discussion in *Man and Superman*. It sits rather strangely with Harris's devotion to Christ.

He devotes a chapter to "Jesus, the Christ," according him at least as much space as Lord Randolph Churchill. Typically he gets into his subject through a page of name-dropping. He meets Ernest Renan, author of an acclaimed *Vie de Jésus*, and casually puts him right on a point of language. "[S]trange that I had never thought of that before; where did you get the idea?" And Harris smiles, forbearing to tell the great scholar how fundamentally useless his researches have been. Then we have the gospel according to Frank. Ever the editor, he blue-pencils the Lord's Prayer. "I should prefer simply: 'Give and forgive.' " But without accepting either Christ's divinity or an eschatological sanction for human conduct, he approves the doctrine of love: "Is it not plain . . . that the Good is imperishable and Divine and must ultimately conquer even in this world?" Having secularized Christ, he has no difficulty in making Shakespeare his natural successor. He quotes "I say unto you, love your enemies, bless them that curse you, do good to them that hate you, and pray for them which despitefully use you and persecute you." Bigheartedly, the aging man of sorrows, Harris gives his imprimatur to that, adding that Shakespeare "saw its everlasting truth and found a reason for it and so added a coping stone to the divine Temple of Humanity." He cites a passage from *Timon of Athens* about the hate that does harm to the heart. He forgives his enemies. And then, being Harris, he discusses kissing.

There is something engaging about his divagations on the higher morality. There is something touching about a Victorian optimism carried into the age between two great wars. "Paul preached Faith, Hope, and Love, but he had no faith such as we have, no hope so well-founded as ours. Think of what we have done in the last hundred years, and forecast, if you will, the transcendent future. Tennyson's words recur to me:

> For I looked into the future far as human eye could see,
> Saw the wonders of the world and all the rapture that would be.

Citing, as always, from memory, he does not get those lines from *Locksley Hall* quite right ("dipt," not "looked"; "Vision," not "wonders"; "wonder," not "rapture"), but we accept the greathearted trust in progress, though retrogression was to characterize the age that Harris did not live to see. Wells saw it and gave a dying cry of exasperation: "You fools, you damned fools!" Take him for all in all, Frank Harris was a man, like Hamlet's father, and if we shall not look upon his like again, that is because he was very much a man of his time. Unlike his great contemporaries, he did not have the transcendental qualities which defeat time. He is only marginally part of fin de siècle history, but, a rather leaky boat, he carried some of its great literary figures from nameless islets to the haven of metropolitan notice. That is no small thing.

It is highly ironic that his huge autobiography should for so long have been sought after for its sleazy erotic revelations. These one can now skip; they are embarrassing rather than enlightening. It was always a mistake to evaluate his book in terms appropriate to Chaucer or Rabelais or Henry Miller. Miller, anyway, does not fit into that holistic picture which accepted sex and excretion as inescapable aspects of life. Miller is all sex; sex is discardable in Harris.

The value of *My Life and Loves* is, to use Amis's term again, more allobiographical than autobiographical. We are not greatly interested in Harris, except as a skilled but essentially journalistic purveyor of news from a lost world. It is the portraits that count, as also the just gibes. "Edmund Gosse, knighted for mediocrity in England, writes about 'the brutality of *La Garçonne* and the foul chaos of *Ulysses*,' though both Victor Marguerite and James Joyce are children of light, above his understanding." One half thanks him for that. He was praising Joyce for the wrong reasons. "And the new paganism, with its creed of self-development, is just as emphatic: we see its first fruits in Anatole France and Verlaine, in *La Garçonne* of Marguerite, in the *Ulysses* of James Joyce, and in this *Life* of mine." No, no, no—he just did not understand. His intelligence, though far above the level of Henry Miller, was insufficient to grasp the nature of literary values. Words, to him, were journalistic counters; they lacked overtones; he did not see that literature was the exploitation of language above the level of an editorial or a review. Ergo, his book is not literature.

It is as a manipulator on the margins of history that he is most memorable. Dead though he is, he is still everywhere. I write these lines in the principality of Monaco, which Harris claimed to know well. Indeed, I write them in the Sporting Club, which Harris claimed to have founded as a means of cleansing the casino of its ill fame as a mere "gambling house." He asked Prince Albert to appoint him as secretary. He was offered a thousand pounds a year. "I said that would suit me excellently; I made out the whole thing—constitution, articles and all. . . ." But the wily prince "sold the whole idea of the Sporting Club, as constituted by me, to Camille Blanc . . . and so cheated me." Harris concludes this episode, piously, with "Verily, *The children of this world are wiser in their generation than the children of Light!*" It is pleasant to think of Harris as one of the latter; he seems to be almost archetypally of this world.

So much so that Vincent Brome felt compelled to entitle his biography *Frank Harris: The Life and Loves of a Scoundrel.* Hesketh Pearson, another Shakespeare addict, and no more scholarly than Harris, began by admiring the man and ended by assuming that he had got on "through the blackmailing of men and the seduction of women." It was, as was to be expected, Bernard Shaw who saw him most clearly and forgave his faults most charitably, summing him up as "a man of splendid visions, unreasonable expectations, fierce appetites which he was unable to relate to anything except to romantic literature. . . . It is hardly an exaggeration to say that he ultimately quarrelled with everybody but Shakespear. . . ." Harris has no official epitaph, but Shaw devised a typically generous one for him: "Here lies a man of letters who hated cruelty and injustice and bad art, and never spared them in his own interest. R.I.P." We may as well leave it at that.

—ANTHONY BURGESS
1991

Introduction

Had Frank Harris died in 1914—he was then about sixty years of age—he would be known to us first as the incomparable editor of the *Saturday Review* and friend of Oscar Wilde, and then as a writer. We would grant him his position in *fin-de-siècle* London, the London that was "dying into a dance,/An agony of trance," and we would enjoy his moral and social eccentricities, much as we do those of Swinburne, Whistler, and Wilde. We would be amused by his rags to riches story and we would like his standing up to Cecil Rhodes and the British government in support of the Boers. His last public act would have been a brave one—going to Brixton Prison in the cause of a free press. His tidy legacy of short stories and his great biography of Wilde would have kept his memory alive.

But the memory of Frank Harris, insofar as it now exists, is drawn from his last fifteen years, and it comes to most of us second-hand. His books have been out of print in England and America for almost thirty years.* Because of its erotic passages, *My Life and Loves* has long been "must" reading for tourists in Paris, where it has been in print. Unfortunately, such readers have rarely been disposed to read more than the erotic parts, and there is no gainsaying the impression they have taken away of Harris as a "sexual gymnast," as S. N. Behrman so trimly labels him. This simple notion of Harris as a sex enthusiast, as well as a bit of a liar and a cheat, now even dominates the capsule sketches he is conceded in encyclopedias, biographical dictionaries, and the like.

It is to be doubted whether anyone who ever knew Harris was neutral about him. Until the middle twenties, chances are his followers outnumbered his detractors. In 1923 Hesketh Pearson could idolize him in this fashion:

Frank Harris is the most dynamic writer alive. . . . His appeal is to the men and women who have lived, not drifted through life; or to those who have the instinct, without the actual experience, of life's sensations. That is why he

---

* *Oscar Wilde: His Life and Confessions* was republished by the Michigan State University Press in 1959. The University of Chicago Press has just reissued Harris' novel, *The Bomb*, with an introduction by John Dos Passos.

doesn't appeal to our so-called literary artists. He has no conscious style of expression. The style is the man. . . .

. . . He is indeed a monster according to all conventional standards, but his monstrosity only offends the shallow people who simply aren't worth propitiating. . . . All the higher wisdom we poor mortals enjoy comes from the few choice spirits who stand outside and above the common law.*

By 1931, when Harris died, the consensus had moved the other way, with the two camps more widely divided than ever, and this led to one-dimensional writing about him. Typical of one extreme is E. Merrill Root's *Frank Harris, A Biography,*** a muddle-headed, proselytizing appreciation of Harris; at the other extreme is Vincent Brome's obsessively destructive *Frank Harris: The Life and Loves of a Scoundrel,*† the biography of the straw man who had been erected and struck him down with such relish every so often the last thirty years. Now and then a Hesketh Pearson hazarded his way across no man's land to the other camp, supporting his new view with all the fervor with which he had served the old. Pearson in 1956 blamed his youthful naïveté (although he was thirty-six years old when he wrote *Men and Mummers*) for the favorable impression Harris had made on him earlier:

How this undersized, low-browed, flashily dressed, ill-featured fellow managed to achieve the position he had in the journalistic world of his time was a mystery to everyone, if not to himself. No doubt the blackmailing of men and the seduction of women had something to do with his success. . . .††

But George Bernard Shaw, who kept Harris as a friend for forty years, writes of him with candor and understanding.

Harris suffered deeply from repeated disillusions and disappointments. Like Hedda Gabler he was tormented by a sense of the sordidness in the commonplace realities which form so much of the stuff of life, and was not only disappointed in people who did nothing splendid, but savagely contemptuous of people who did not want to have anything splendid done. . . .

Frank, too, was a man of splendid visions, unreasonable expectations, fierce appetites which he was unable to relate to anything except to romantic literature, and especially to the impetuous rhetoric of Shakespear. It is hardly an exaggeration to say that he ultimately quarrelled with everybody but Shakespear. . . .

. . . He blazed through London like a comet, leaving a trail of deeply annoyed persons behind him, and like a meteor through America. . . . Then he retired to Nice and became a sort of literary sage. . . . He impressed many young bloods in revolt against *bourgeois* civilization as a great man, as I have reason to know; for when they came my way afterwards I had to be careful not to shock them by the slightest levity in discussing him. . . .

* *Men and Mummers,* New York, 1923.
** New York, 1947.
† New York, 1959. Almost all the reviewers who took notice of this book did so uncritically, generally saying that Brome had produced as good a book as could be written about a rascal such as Harris.
††*The Listener,* July 5, 1956.

I think I know pretty well all the grievances his detractors had against him; but if I had to write his epitaph it should run, *"Here lies a man of letters who hated cruelty and injustice and bad art, and never spared them in his own interest. R.I.P."**

In large measure, Harris' reputation is the price he paid for his arrogance. As an editor of leading journals, he was neither urbane nor discreet. He ran over or shouted down anyone who stood in his way or merely differed with him, and he frequently wrote with a similar lack of finesse. He patronized the English for their prudery and neglect of artists; he attacked institutions like General "Chinese" Gordon; he piled scorn on friends who did not flaunt their friendship with Wilde as he did. He was blessed, or cursed, with a singular insensitivity, a blindness to decorum, which would let him, for example, ask Robert Browning whether he had learned all the passion revealed in *James Lee's Wife* from one woman— and then be puzzled why Browning took offense. Oscar Wilde came near the mark in saying, "Frank Harris has been received in all the great houses —once!" As Shaw told him, he was a social buccaneer, expecting others to honor the proprieties while he offended against them. But the editor of the *Fortnightly* and of the *Saturday Review* couldn't be ignored.

Harris could act thus with impunity as long as he had a prestigious journal behind him, or as long as there was the threat that he might transform a *Candid Friend* or *Vanity Fair* into one. Not until he yielded up *Pearson's* in 1922, when he also published *My Life and Loves,* did he make himself vulnerable to the basest kind of charge. Those he had outraged were able to pull him down, and keep him down. Then his cry became, "They flee from me that sometimes did me seek."

Max Beerbohm in one of his cartoons called Harris "the best talker in London." He doubtless was that, outshining even Oscar Wilde. His voice was a magnificent instrument on which he played a matchless rhetoric. He could, when he chose, make the most ordinary observation sound rare. But Harris was not content to say the ordinary thing, nor need he have been. His prodigious memory let him quote freely from everything he had read, and he was well read; he knew the people who counted in government, society, and the arts, and was privy to the spiciest gossip of the day; and he was "radical" in politics and morals, which could give an agreeable shock value to his utterances.

But Harris was not only a talker; he was a presence, short, swarthy, heavily mustached, and intense. He dominated every gathering, behaving like the cynosure, and he spared no pains to assure that he was. An ego of mighty proportions governed him; it was nourished only by attention and applause.

It was unfortunate that he won encomiums from eminent critics for his first fiction, *Elder Conklin and Other Stories*** and *Montes the Matador*

* From Shaw's postscript to Harris' *Bernard Shaw* (New York, 1931).
** London, 1894, but the stories had been published earlier in the *Fortnightly Review*.

and Other Stories,* for, his notions of his genius confirmed, he was not prompted to work at further improving his fiction. These stories were the best he would write; neither his novels more than a decade later nor the short stories he wrote as much as twenty years after showed development in technique or characterization. Instead Harris came to rely for his effects on exotic settings and novel situations. But he behaved for the rest of his life as one who had already achieved immortality. Harris was "happily free from modesty," Mencken said. He could not concede he had not fulfilled the promise of *Elder Conklin* and *Montes*; the fault must lie with the critics, whose faculties had not kept pace with his art. There was no limit to Harris' self-esteem. Indeed, after his run-of-the-mill play, *Mr. and Mrs. Daventry* (1899–1900), had been successfully produced, he took Shaw to task for a lack of dramatic vision and art. In a most extraordinary feat of self-deception, he could regard his inept *Joan la Romée*** as superior in conception and execution to *Saint Joan,* and he had the temerity to tell Shaw so.

His critics unwittingly injured him again by so unreservedly touting *The Man Shakespeare and His Tragic Life Story,*† which, though it was an original and for its time exciting effort, was hardly a significant work. In giving Shakespeare back to the people, he was shrewd in insight and often exciting, but he wrote a book for the amateur. He did not rout the scholars, who did not even take him seriously, H. L. Mencken to the contrary. Not even the years, as one would expect, provided Harris with anything like a proper perspective on *The Man Shakespeare.*

Oscar Wilde, by all odds Harris' best book, failed to get the praise and attention it deserved because of its "unfairness" to Lord Alfred Douglas and because of attacks that bordered on the hysterical by some of Wilde's "defenders" such as Robert Ross and Robert Sherard. A reader today can appreciate Douglas' being discomfited by it, but it is hard to understand the shrewish behavior of the others toward Harris. They must have resented his writing something less than a pure panegyric to Wilde.

None of the books †† and none of the journals‡ Harris edited in Eng-

---

* London, 1900; many of these stories, and in particular *Montes,* which Meredith had praised so extravagantly, had been published earlier in periodicals.
** New York and London, 1926.
† London, 1909.
†† *Shakespeare and His Love* (London, 1910); *The Women of Shakespeare* (London, 1911); *Unpath'd Waters* (London, 1913); *Great Days* (London, 1914); *The Yellow Ticket and Other Stories* (London, 1914); *England or Germany* (New York, 1915); *Contemporary Portraits* (London, 1915); *Love in Youth* (New York, 1916); *Contemporary Portraits, Second Series* (New York, 1919); *Contemporary Portraits, Third Series* (New York, 1920); *Contemporary Portraits, Fourth Series* (New York, 1923); *Undream'd of Shores* (New York, 1924); *Latest Contemporary Portraits* (New York, 1927); *My Reminiscences as a Cowboy* (New York, 1930); *Confessional* (New York, 1930); *Pantopia,* (New York, 1930); *Bernard Shaw* (New York, 1931).
‡ *Hearth and Home* (1911–12); *Modern Society* (1913–14); *Pearson's* (1916–22); *View of Truth* (1927–28).

land and America after 1910 were critical or financial successes. By 1920 he was neglected and distressingly poor. But his soul had fed long on the praise rendered him so many years before by George Meredith, T. H. Huxley, Coventry Patmore, Ernest Dowson, and Arnold Bennett, and his self-esteem had grown into megalomania. So it had always been with artists in England, he reasoned; they were neglected, when they were not mistreated, until a place was found for them in Westminster Abbey. Had anyone before *The Man Shakespeare* truly understood or appreciated that great heart, or sensed that Shakespeare's message—forgiveness and "lovingkindness"—was essentially one with Christ's? Christ, Shakespeare, and Goethe—and Harris himself—were "God's spies."*

Harris' identification with his hero in *The Man Shakespeare* is as evident as his admiration and love for him. The fascination with Christ became evident about 1915 in stories such as *The Miracle of the Stigmata, The Holy Man,* and *The King of the Jews.* In *Contemporary Portraits*—and the superior tone of them is what so many readers take exception to—Harris' judgments on his subjects all too often sound Olympian; it is obvious that Harris regarded only the greatest figures as his equals. After the first two volumes of *My Life and Loves* had been not only unappreciated but assailed, the identification with Christ and Shakespeare became most pronounced.

All this should not be taken to imply that Harris was a fool. He was, on the contrary, a vital and notable personality, a resourceful entrepreneur, and a gifted writer; his achievements seem small only when they are gauged against his conception of them. Unconnected and unknown, he euchred his way to the editorship of the *Evening News* at twenty-seven; he won the editorship of the *Fortnightly Review* at thirty and breathed new life into that journal; and he became editor and owner of the moribund *Saturday Review* at thirty-eight, making it perhaps the best journal ever published in London. He mingled familiarly with royalty and peers of the realm, he had easy access to most of the political and social figures of his day, and he earned the esteem of fellow writers. He became recognized as an epicure and connoisseur, and he was a lover of many beautiful women. Busts were done of him by Jo Davidson and Gaudier-Brzeska; Oscar Wilde dedicated *An Ideal Husband* to him.** He was a generous and indulgent friend to most men, devoid of meanness and pettiness, though he had hurt many persons through his crudity and indiscretion. His most serious shortcoming was his insistent ego, which annoyed many people to the point of blinding them to everything else about him.

Harris tried with *My Life and Loves* to write the most honest autobiography ever written. Honest confessions had been attempted before,

---

* *King Lear,* Lear to Cordelia, Act V, Scene iii: "And take upon's the mystery of things/As if we were God's spies."
** The dedication reads: "To Frank Harris, a slight tribute to his power and distinction as an artist, his chivalry and nobility as a friend."

most notably by Rousseau, who failed so wonderfully, giving us instead an anguished account of how the world tried to corrupt and ruin him. But no man has the self-knowledge to write an "honest" autobiography, and he cannot be objective about what he does know. Any autobiography thus says more and less than the author intended. In this, autobiography of course resembles all other kinds of writing, the difference being that it is a rare autobiographer who admits it.

Harris did not admit it.* Indeed, as a professed "truth-seeker" he looked upon himself as a most dispassionate observer. His writing reveals him to be nothing of the sort. As a product of the nineteenth century, he was a deeply committed man, and he could no more be neutral about anything than could Whistler or Randolph Churchill. Such persons reacted almost chemically to men, events, and ideas, and it was the way each reacted that gave him his remarkable individuality. And the last quarter of the nineteeth century was the age of transition, when the old order was changed for the new, when there was so much to react to. Rarely in the hearts and minds of men has there been such a struggle between respect for tradition and sympathy for change. Harris' rendering of that struggle in *My Life and Loves,* typical because of its subjectivity, is an enlightening social document.

Those who take Harris simply at face value as he discloses himself in *My Life and Loves*—and it seems inconceivable that any reader could do that in these days of psychoanalysis—may find his vanity and stridency and boldness about sex unpalatable. But it must be urged in Harris' defense that he did not intend to write a conventional, discreet memoir, in which a self-effacing author squares accounts with society on its own terms, and which is therefore more admired for its art and restraint than for anything else. Harris was several decades ahead of his time in writing the sort of confession yielded up to a psychiatrist, who encourages the patient to cast inhibitions to the wind so that root matters may be dealt with. It is indeed difficult not to admire Harris, however grudgingly, for the fearlessness with which he let his ego take over, and for his courage in speaking about his desires and secret vices. It is remarkable that he was not indiscreet regarding sex in anything else he ever wrote. The fact that we may not like him because of what we learn may mean we would not care for anyone about whom we knew so much.

Volumes I and II of *My Life and Loves* proceed in a fairly straightforward chronological manner; Harris' strength in narrative makes these volumes the best written, as well as the most engrossing. Volumes III and IV are more episodic, though they are roughly chronological in arrange-

---

* After Volume I had been attacked for the inaccuracy of some dates and statements, Harris admitted he could be at fault at times because he was writing wholly from memory. Yet, he maintained, though "I am no longer a trustworthy witness; [I am] yet more honest, I dare swear, than any Rousseau or Casanova of them all." (Foreword to Volume II)

ment. Volume V is almost purely episodic, having been written to fill gaps in the earlier volumes. Harris' discouragement with the reception of the first two volumes doubtless accounts for the carelessness and lack of finish in the other volumes, particularly the last.

The subject matter in *My Life and Loves* falls under four headings—adventure, ideas, men and events, and sex—but, no matter what his subject, Harris' person and his vanity permeate every page. If many of his exploits (other than sexual) as a youth in America and London seem extraordinary, it should be borne in mind that he was an extraordinary as well as a vain man. The occasions when his account is open to challenge are noted in footnotes to the text. The instances when Harris' meetings or exchanges with anyone of significance have been challenged are also noted.*

Harris was not a philosopher, nor a highly sophisticated thinker; therefore his philosophizing, especially about immortality, politics, and sex, leave much to be desired, not only in profundity, but also in interest.

He had, however, a great talent for portraiture. His *Contemporary Portraits*, all five series, are exciting reading. Especially in the first two volumes of *My Life and Loves,* his sketches of Professor Byron Smith, Emerson, Carlyle, Ruskin, Wagner, and Maupassant serve as fine diversions in the narrative. In his recounting of events, Harris reveals a good sense of drama; he makes those events come alive for the reader. In sum, the story of Harris making his way in the world and his observations on persons and events provide us with a splendid piece of social, political, and literary history.

Harris determined in writing his autobiography that he would not only avoid the trap of self-pity into which Rousseau had fallen, but would also add a new dimension to autobiography—sex. No autobiography, he believed, could be "honest" unless it dealt with this primary influence.**
But Harris fails in that, with few exceptions, the passages in *My Life and*

* Harris' acquaintance with many famous persons has been challenged frequently, and a few persons have asked why, if he knew these persons, they never wrote about him. Many did, though not more extensively than of other persons they knew who were incidental to their work. Many more famous people perhaps wrote *to* Harris than about him. Alice of Monaco, for example, a steady correspondent, addressed Harris as, "My dear dear friend" and "Ever yours in deep & true affection"; at least eighteen letters, a wedding invitation, and a telegram were written by Winston Churchill to Harris; and Shaw in one unpublished letter teases Harris for having "married a lady in Park Lane and spent all her money consorting with Randolph Churchill and Edouard Sept."

** Ernest Dewey reports that he once complimented Harris on *Oscar Wilde,* saying it was the best biography he had read, excepting perhaps Boswell's *Johnson.* Harris replied that Boswell's *Johnson* "was lopsided and incomplete. There wasn't one word in the book about Johnson's love-life. How can you give an understandable picture of any man or woman without even mentioning the phase of life that has the greatest of all influences?" But Harris' discomfiture with talking about sex in such bold terms is reflected in his frequent need to sublimate the mere animalistic act into something intellectual or aesthetic—sometimes amusingly so.

Loves that deal with sex do not provide special insight into his character or its formation. Most of these passages are also artistic failures in that they lack individuality. The persons involved in them are sticks, not figures; *anyone* could have had such experiences. Yet the use of the pronoun "I" and the succession of intimate details provide the illusion that they are revelatory about Harris alone.

There is the question of whether Harris invented sex episodes in the hope of increasing sales or heightening effect, or whether his memory played him false in recalling details. It does not seem likely that a man who could accurately quote at length, say, from Swinburne's *Anactoria* and from Macaulay's essay on history fifty years after reading them would find it difficult to remember the faces and anatomies of women. And those persons still alive who knew him best deny there was any necessity for invention by him.

I have attempted to identify each person and event mentioned by Harris, so that the reader will have sufficient information to read intelligently and appreciatively. Events such as the Ashanti War and the Bradlaugh incident, which may be wholly obscure to the reader, I have explained at greater length, as I have Harris' relations with certain people, such as Carlyle and Wagner. I have also attempted to identify each quotation made by Harris, although a few have eluded identification.

The text for the first four volumes of this edition of *My Life and Loves* is based on Harris' personal copies of the original, privately printed edition, which has his marginal corrections in his own hand. The typesetting for this private printing was chaotic. If Harris ever did read the galley proofs for these volumes, he was a careless proofreader. In his personal copies, with few exceptions, Harris' marginal alterations and notes dealt only with what he would have deleted in an expurgated version of *My Life and Loves*. I have, therefore, made slight changes in capitalization and punctuation, and in Americanizing the spelling.

The fifth volume, as it was published in Paris in 1958, is apparently not authentic, the chapters and portions of chapters having been rearranged and including materials of doubtful origin. The fifth volume, as it appears here, has been checked against Harris' final typescript which is in the possession of the Humanities Research Center of the University of Texas.

JOHN F. GALLAGHER

Volume

I

Foreword

To the Story of
My Life and Loves

Go, soul, the body's guest,
Upon a thankless errand:
Fear not to touch the best,
The Truth shall be thy warrant.*
Sir Walter Raleigh

HERE IN THE BLAZING HEAT of an American August, amid the hurry and scurry of New York, I sit down to write my final declaration of Faith, as a preface or foreword to the story of my life. Ultimately it will be read in the spirit in which it has been written and I ask no better fortune. My journalism during the war and after the armistice brought me prosecutions from the federal government. The authorities at Washington accused me of sedition, and though the third postmaster general, ex-Governor Dockery,** of Missouri who was chosen by the department as judge, proclaimed my innocence and assured me I should not be prosecuted again, my magazine (*Pearson's*) was time and again held up in the post, and its circulation reduced thereby to one-third. I was brought to ruin by the illegal persecution of President Wilson and his arch-assistant Burleson,† and was laughed at when I asked for compensation. The American government, it appears, is too poor to pay for its dishonorable blunders.

I record the shameful fact for the benefit of those Rebels and Lovers of the Ideal who will surely find themselves in a similar plight in future emergencies. For myself I do not complain. On the whole I have received better treatment in life than the average man and more loving-kindness than I perhaps deserved. I make no complaint.

If America had not reduced me to penury I should probably not have

* The opening lines of *The Lie.*
** Alexander M. Dockery (1845–1926), twenty-sixth governor of Missouri, 1901–05; third assistant Postmaster General, 1930.
† A. S. Burleson (1863–1937), Postmaster General.

written this book as boldly as the ideal demanded. At the last push of Fate (I am much nearer seventy than sixty) we are all apt to sacrifice something of Truth for the sake of kindly recognition by our fellows and a peaceful ending. Being that "wicked animal," as the French say, "who defends himself when he is attacked," I turn at length to bay, without any malice, I hope, but also without any fear such as might prompt compromise. I have always fought for the Holy Spirit of Truth and have been, as Heine said he was, a brave soldier in the Liberation War of Humanity: now one fight more, the best and the last.

There are two main traditions of English writing: the one of perfect liberty, that of Chaucer and Shakespeare, completely outspoken, with a certain liking for lascivious details and witty smut, a man's speech; the other emasculated more and more by Puritanism and since the French Revolution, gelded to tamest propriety; for that upheaval brought the illiterate middle-class to power and insured the domination of girl readers. Under Victoria, English prose literally became half childish, as in stories of "Little Mary," or at best provincial, as anyone may see who cares to compare the influence of Dickens, Thackeray and Reade* in the world with the influence of Balzac, Flaubert and Zola.

Foreign masterpieces such as *Les Contes Drolatiques* and *L'Assommoir* were destroyed in London as obscene by a magistrate's order; even the Bible and Shakespeare were expurgated and all books dolled up to the prim decorum of the English Sunday-school. And America with unbecoming humility worsened the disgraceful, brainless example.

All my life I have rebelled against this old maid's canon of deportment, and my revolt has grown stronger with advancing years.

In the foreword to *The Man Shakespeare*, I tried to show how the Puritanism that had gone out of our morals had gone into the language, enfeebling English thought and impoverishing English speech.

At long last I am going back to the old English tradition. I am determined to tell the truth about my pilgrimage through this world, the whole truth and nothing but the truth, about myself and others, and I shall try to be at least as kindly to others as to myself.

Bernard Shaw assures me that no one is good enough or bad enough to tell the naked truth about himself, but I am beyond good and evil in this respect.

French literature is there to give the cue and inspiration; it is the freest of all in discussing matters of sex and chiefly by reason of its constant preoccupation with all that pertains to passion and desire, it has become the world literature to men of all races.

"Women and love," Edmond de Goncourt** writes in his journal, "al-

---

* Charles Reade (1814–84), author of *The Cloister and the Hearth*; discussed further in Vol. II.

** (1822–1896), French novelist and critic; his estate furnished the funds for the *Prix Goncourt*.

ways constitute the subject of conversation wherever there is a meeting of intellectual people socially brought together by eating and drinking. Our talk at dinner was at first smutty (*polisonne*) and Tourgueneff listened to us with the open-mouthed wonder (*l'étonnement un peu meduse*) of a barbarian who only makes love (*fait l'amour*) very naturally (*très naturellement*)."

Whoever reads this passage carefully will understand the freedom I intend to use. But I shall not be tied down even to French conventions. Just as in painting, our knowledge of what the Chinese and Japanese have done, has altered our whole conception of the art, so the Hindoos and Burmese too have extended our understanding of the art of love. I remember going with Rodin through the British Museum and being surprised at the time he spent over the little idols and figures of the South Sea Islanders: "Some of them are trivial," he said, "but look at that, and that, and that—sheer masterpieces that anyone might be proud of—lovely things!"

Art has become coextensive with humanity, and some of my experiences with so-called savages may be of interest even to the most cultured Europeans.

I intend to tell what life has taught me, and if I begin at the A.B.C. of love, it is because I was brought up in Britain and the United States; I shall not stop there.

Of course I know the publication of such a book will at once justify the worst that my enemies have said about me. For forty years now I have championed nearly all the unpopular causes, and have thus made many enemies; now they will all be able to gratify their malice while taking credit for prevision. In itself the book is sure to disgust the "unco guid" and the mediocrities of every kind who have always been unfriendly to me. I have no doubt, too, that many sincere lovers of literature who would be willing to accept such license as ordinary French writers use will condemn me for going beyond this limit. Yet there are many reasons why I should use perfect freedom in this last book.

First of all, I made hideous blunders early in life, and saw worse blunders made by other youths, out of sheer ignorance; I want to warn the young and impressionable against the shoals and hidden reefs of life's ocean and chart, so to speak, at the very beginning of the voyage when the danger is greatest, the "unpath'd waters."

On the other hand I have missed indescribable pleasures because the power to enjoy and to give delight is keenest early in life, while the understanding of both how to give and how to receive pleasure comes much later, when the faculties are already on the decline.

I used to illustrate the absurdity of our present system of educating the young by a quaint simile. "When training me to shoot," I said, "my earthly father gave me a little single-barreled gun, and when he saw that I had learned the mechanism and could be trusted, he gave me a double-barreled shotgun. After some years I came into possession of a magazine gun which could shoot half a dozen times if necessary without reloading, my efficiency increasing with my knowledge.

"My Creator, or Heavenly Father, on the other hand, when I was wholly without experience and had only just entered my teens, gave me, so to speak, a magazine gun of sex, and hardly had I learned its use and enjoyment when he took it away from me forever, and gave me in its place a double-barreled gun: after a few years, he took that away and gave me a single-barreled gun with which I was forced to content myself for the best part of my life.

"Towards the end the old single-barrel began to show signs of wear and age; sometimes it would go off too soon, sometimes it missed fire and shamed me, do what I would."

I want to teach youths how to use their magazine gun of sex so that it may last for years, and when they come to the double-barrel, how to take such care that the good weapon will do them liege service right into their fifties, and the single-barrel will then give them pleasure up to three score years and ten.

Moreover, not only do I desire in this way to increase the sum of happiness in the world while decreasing the pains and disabilities of men, but I wish also to set an example and encourage other writers to continue the work that I am sure is beneficent, as well as enjoyable.

W. L. George* in *A Novelist on Novels* writes: "If a novelist were to develop his characters evenly, the three-hundred-page novel might extend to five hundred, the additional two hundred pages would be made up entirely of the sex preoccupations of the characters. There would be as many scenes in the bedroom as in the drawing room, probably more, as more time is passed in the sleeping apartment. The additional two hundred pages would offer pictures of the sex side of the characters and would compel them to become alive: at present they often fail to come to life because they only develop, say, five sides out of six. . . . Our literary characters are lop-sided because their ordinary traits are fully portrayed while their sex life is cloaked, minimized or left out. . . . Therefore the characters in modern novels are all false. They are megalocephalous and emasculate. English women speak a great deal about sex. . . . It is a cruel position for the English novel. The novelist may discuss anything but the main preoccupation of life . . . we are compelled to pad out with murder, theft and arson which, as everybody knows, are perfectly moral things to write about."

> Pure is the snow—till mixed with mire—
> But never half so pure as fire.

There are greater reasons than any I have yet given why the truth should be told boldly. The time has come when those who are, as Shakespeare

---

* (1882–1926), an English novelist who served with the French Army during the First World War. He wrote *A Bed of Roses* (1911) and *The City of Light* (1912), among other novels. *A Novelist on Novels* was published in London in 1918.

called them, "God's Spies," having learned the mystery of things, should be called to counsel, for the ordinary political guides have led mankind to disaster: blind leaders of the blind!

Over Niagara we have plunged, as Carlyle predicted, and as every one with vision must have foreseen, and now like driftwood we move round and round the whirlpool impotently without knowing whither or why.

One thing certain: we deserve the misery into which we have fallen. The laws of this world are inexorable and don't cheat! Where, when, how have we gone astray? The malady is as wide as civilization which fortunately narrows the enquiry to time.

Ever since our conquest of natural forces began, towards the end of the eighteenth century, and material wealth increased by leaps and bounds, our conduct has deteriorated. Up to that time we had done the Gospel of Christ mouth honor at least; and had to some slight extent shown consideration if not love to our fellowmen: we did not give tithes to charity; but we did give petty doles till suddenly science appeared to reinforce our selfishness with a new message: progress comes through the blotting out of the unfit, we were told, and self-assertion was preached as a duty: the idea of the Super-man came into life and the Will to Power, and thereby Christ's teaching of love and pity and gentleness was thrust into the background.

At once we men gave ourselves over to wrong-doing and our iniquity took monstrous forms.

The creed we professed and the creed we practiced were poles apart. Never I believe in the world's history was there such confusion in man's thought about conduct, never were there so many different ideals put forward for his guidance. It is imperatively necessary for us to bring clearness into this muddle and see why we have gone wrong and where.

For the World War is only the last of a series of diabolical acts which have shocked the conscience of humanity. The greatest crimes in recorded time have been committed during the last half century almost without protest by the most civilized nations, nations that still call themselves Christian. Whoever has watched human affairs in the last half century must acknowledge that our progress has been steady hellward.

The hideous massacres and mutilations of tens of thousands of women and children in the Congo Free State without protest on the part of Great Britain, who could have stopped it all with one word, is surely due to the same spirit that directed the abominable blockade (continued by both England and America long after the armistice) which condemned hundreds and thousands of women and children of our own kith and kin to death by starvation. The unspeakable meanness and confessed fraud of the Peace of Versailles with its tragic consequences from Vladivostok to London and finally the shameless, dastardly war waged by all the Allies and by America on Russia, for money, show us that we have been assisting at the overthrow of morality itself and returning to the ethics of the wolf and the polity of the Thieves' Kitchen.

And our public acts as nations are paralleled by our treatment of our fellows within the community. For the small minority the pleasures of living have been increased in the most extraordinary way while the pains and sorrows of existence have been greatly mitigated, but the vast majority even of civilized peoples have hardly been admitted to any share in the benefits of our astounding material progress. The slums of our cities show the same spirit we have displayed in our treatment of the weaker races. It is no secret that over fifty per cent of English volunteers in the war were below the pigmy physical standard required and about one-half of our American soldiers were morons with the intelligence of children under twelve years of age: *vae victis* has been our motto, with the most appalling results. Clearly we have come to the end of a period and must take thought about the future.

The religion that directed or was supposed to direct our conduct for nineteen centuries has been finally discarded. Even the divine spirit of Jesus was thrown aside by Nietzsche as one throws the hatchet after the helve, or to use the better German simile, the child was thrown out with the bathwater. The silly sex-morality of Paul has brought discredit upon the whole Gospel. Paul was impotent, boasted indeed that he had no sexual desires, wished that all men were even as he was in this respect, just as the fox in the fable who had lost his tail wished that all other foxes should be mutilated in the same way in order to attain his perfection.

I often say that the Christian churches were offered two things: the spirit of Jesus and the idiotic morality of Paul, and they all rejected the highest inspiration and took to their hearts the incredibly base and stupid prohibition. Following Paul, we have turned the goddess of love into a fiend and degraded the crowning impulse of our being into a capital sin; yet everything high and ennobling in our nature springs directly out of the sexual instinct.

Grant Allen* says rightly: "Its alliance is wholly with whatever is purest and most beautiful within us. To it we owe our love of bright colors, graceful form, melodious sound, rhythmic motion. To it we owe the evolution of music, of poetry, of romance, of *belles lettres,* of painting, of sculpture, of decorative art, of dramatic entertainment. To it we owe the entire existence of our aesthetic sense which in the last resort is a secondary sex-attribute. From it springs the love of beauty, around it all beautiful arts circle as their center. Its subtle aroma pervades all literature. And to it we owe the paternal, maternal and marital relations, the growth of affections, the love of little pattering feet and baby laughter."

And this scientific statement is incomplete: not only is the sexual instinct the inspiring force of all art and literature; it is also our chief teacher of

---

* (1848–1899). A Canadian novelist who emigrated to England. His most successful book was *The Woman Who Did* (1895), an attack on the double standard of morality. Harris devotes a sketch to Allen in *Contemporary Portraits, Fourth Series,* and describes him as a "charming" devotee of free thinking and free love.

gentleness and tenderness, making loving-kindness an ideal and so warring against cruelty and harshness and that misjudging of our fellows which we men call justice. To my mind, cruelty is the one diabolic sin which must be wiped out of life and made impossible.

Paul's condemnation of the body and its desires is in direct contradiction to the gentle teaching of Jesus and is in itself idiotic. I reject Paulism as passionately as I accept the Gospel of Christ. In regard to the body, I go back to the pagan ideals, to Eros and Aphrodite and

> The fair humanities of old religion.*

Paul and the Christian churches have dirtied desire, degraded women, debased procreation, vulgarized and vilified the best instinct in us.

> Priests in black gowns are going their rounds,
> And binding with briars, my joys and desires.**

And the worst of it all is that the highest function of man has been degraded by foul words so that it is almost impossible to write the body's hymn of joy as it should be written. The poets have been almost as guilty in this respect as the priests: Aristophanes and Rabelais are ribald, dirty, Boccaccio cynical, while Ovid leers cold-bloodedly and Zola, like Chaucer, finds it difficult to suit language to his desires. Walt Whitman is better, though often merely commonplace. The Bible is the best of all, but not frank enough even in the noble song of Solomon which now and then by sheer imagination manages to convey the ineffable!

We are beginning to reject Puritanism and its unspeakable, brainless pruderies; but Catholicism is just as bad. Go to the Vatican Gallery and the great Church of St. Peter in Rome and you will find the fairest figures of ancient art clothed in painted tin, as if the most essential organs of the body were disgusting and had to be concealed.

I say the body is beautiful and must be lifted and dignified by our reverence: I love the body more than any Pagan of them all and I love the soul and her aspirations as well; for me the body and the soul are alike beautiful, all dedicate to Love and her worship.

I have no divided allegiance and what I preach today amid the scorn and hatred of men will be universally accepted tomorrow; for in my vision, too, a thousand years are as one day.

We must unite the soul of Paganism, the love of beauty and art and literature with the soul of Christianity and its human loving-kindness in a new synthesis which shall include all the sweet and gentle and noble impulses in us.

* The intelligible forms of ancient poets, / The fair humanities of old religion, etc. S. T. Coleridge, *Wallenstein,* Part I "Piccolomini," Act II, scene 4. Translated from Schiller.

** William Blake, *The Garden of Love,* last two lines.

What we all need is more of the spirit of Jesus: we must learn at length with Shakespeare: "Pardon's the word for all!"*

I want to set this Pagan-Christian ideal before men as the highest and most human, too.

Now one word to my own people and their peculiar shortcomings. Anglo-Saxon domineering combativeness is the greatest danger to humanity in the world today. Americans are proud of having blotted out the Red Indian and stolen his possessions and of burning and torturing Negroes in the sacred name of equality. At all cost we must get rid of our hypocrisies and falsehoods and see ourselves as we are—a domineering race, vengeful and brutal, as exemplified in Haiti; we must study the inevitable effects of our soulless, brainless selfishness as shown in the World War.

The Germanic ideal, which is also the English and American ideal, of the conquering male that despises all weaker and less intelligent races and is eager to enslave or annihilate them must be set aside. A hundred years ago, there were only fifteen millions of English and American folk; today there are nearly two hundred millions, and it is plain that in another century or so they will be the most numerous, as they are already by far the most powerful race on earth.

The most numerous folk hitherto, the Chinese, has set a good example by remaining within its own boundaries, but these conquering, colonizing Anglo-Saxons threaten to overrun the earth and destroy all other varieties of the species man. Even now we annihilate the Red Indian because he is not subservient, while we are content to degrade the Negro who doesn't threaten our domination.

Is it wise to desire only one flower in this garden of a world? Is it wise to blot out the better varieties while preserving the inferior?

And the Anglo-Saxon ideal for the individual is even baser and more inept. Intent on satisfying his own conquering lust, he has compelled the female of the species to an unnatural chastity of thought and deed and word. He has made of his wife a meek upper-servant or slave (*die Hausfrau*), who has hardly any intellectual interests and whose spiritual being only finds a narrow outlet in her mother-instincts. The daughter he has labored to degrade into the strangest sort of two-legged tame fowl ever imagined: she must seek a mate while concealing or denying all her strongest sex-feelings; in fine, she should be as cold-blooded as a frog and as wily and ruthless as an Apache on the war-path.

The ideal he has set before himself is confused and confusing: really he desires to be healthy and strong while gratifying all his sexual appetites. The highest type, however, the English gentleman, has pretty constantly in mind the individualistic ideal of what he calls an "all-round man," a man whose body is harmoniously developed and brought to a comparatively high state of efficiency.

* *Cymbeline*, Act V, scene 5.

He has no inkling of the supreme truth that every man and woman possesses some small facet of the soul which reflects life in a peculiar way or, to use the language of religion, sees God as no other soul born into the world can ever see Him.

It is the first duty of every individual to develop all his faculties of body, mind and spirit as completely and harmoniously as possible; but it is a still higher duty for each of us to develop our special faculty to the uttermost consistent with health; for only by so doing shall we attain to the highest self-consciousness or be able to repay our debt to humanity. No Anglo-Saxon, so far as I know, has ever advocated this ideal or dreamed of regarding it as a duty. In fact, no teacher so far has even thought of helping men and women to find out the particular power which constitutes their essence and inbeing and justifies their existence. And so nine men and women out of ten go through life without realizing their own special nature: they cannot lose their souls, for they have never found them.

For every son of Adam, for every daughter of Eve, this is the supreme defeat, the final disaster. Yet no one, so far as I know, has ever warned of the danger or spoken of this ideal.

That's why I love this book in spite of all its shortcomings and all its faults: it is the first book ever written to glorify the body and its passionate desires and the soul as well and its sacred, climbing sympathies.

Give and forgive, I always say, is the supreme lesson of life.

I only wish I had begun the book five years ago, before I had been half-drowned in the brackish flood of old age and become conscious of failing memory; but notwithstanding this handicap, I have tried to write the book I have always wanted to read, the first chapter in the Bible of Humanity.

Hearken to good counsel:

> Live out your whole free life, while yet on earth,
> Seize the quick Present, prize your one sure boon:
> Though brief, each day a golden sun has birth;
> Though dim, the night is gemmed with stars and moon.

Chapter I

My Life and Loves

MEMORY is the Mother of the Muses, the prototype of the artist. As a rule she selects and relieves out the important, omitting what is accidental or trivial. Now and then, however, she makes mistakes, like all other artists. Nevertheless, I take memory in the main as my guide.

I was born on the 14th of February, 1855, and named James Thomas, after my father's two brothers; my father was in the navy, a lieutenant in command of a revenue cutter or gunboat, and we children saw him only at long intervals.

My earliest recollection is being danced on the foot of my father's brother James, the captain of an Indiaman, who paid us a visit in the south of Kerry when I was about two. I distinctly remember repeating a hymn by heart for him, my mother on the other side of the fireplace, prompting: then I got him to dance me a little more, which was all I wanted. I remember my mother telling him I could read, and his surprise.

The next memory must have been about the same time; I was seated on the floor screaming when my father came in and asked: "What's the matter?"

"It's only Master Jim," replied the nurse crossly; "he's just screaming out of sheer temper, Sir. Look, there's not a tear in his eye."

A year or so later, it must have been, I was proud of walking up and down a long room while my mother rested her hand on my head and called me her walking stick.

Later still I remember coming to her room at night. I whispered to her and then kissed her, but her cheek was cold and she didn't answer, and I woke the house with my shrieking—she was dead. I felt no grief, but something gloomy and terrible in the sudden cessation of the usual household activities.

A couple of days later I saw her coffin carried out, and when the nurse told my sister and me that we would never see our mother again I was surprised merely and wondered why.

My mother died when I was nearly four and soon after we moved to Kingstown near Dublin. I used to get up in the night with my sister Annie, four years my senior, and go foraging for bread and jam or sugar. One morning about daybreak I stole into the nurse's room and saw a man beside her in bed, a man with a red mustache. I drew my sister in and she too saw him. We crept out again without waking them. My only emotion was surprise, but next day the nurse denied me sugar on my bread and butter, and I said: "I'll tell!" I don't know why; I had no inkling then of modern journalism.

"Tell what?" she asked.

"There was a man in your bed last night," I replied.

"Hush, hush!" she said, and gave me the sugar.

After that I found all I had to do was to say "I'll tell!" to get whatever I wanted. My sister even wished to know one day what I had to tell, but I would not say. I distinctly remember my feeling of superiority over her because she had not sense enough to exploit the sugar mine.

When I was between four and five, I was sent with Annie to a girls' boarding school in Kingstown kept by a Mrs. Frost. I was put in the class with the oldest girls on account of my proficiency in arithmetic, and I did my best at it because I wanted to be with them, though I had no conscious reason for my preference. I remember how the nearest girl used to lift me up and put me in my high-chair and how I would hurry over the sums set in compound long division and proportion; for as soon as I had finished, I would drop my pencil on the floor and then turn around and climb down out of my chair, ostensibly to get it, but really to look at the girls' legs. Why? I couldn't have said.

I was at the bottom of the class and the legs got bigger and bigger towards the end of the long table and I preferred to look at the big ones.

As soon as the girl next to me missed me she would move her chair back and call me. I'd pretend to have just found my slate pencil which, I said, had rolled; and she'd lift me back into my high-chair.

One day I noticed a beautiful pair of legs on the other side of the table near the top. There must have been a window behind the girl, for her legs up to the knees were in full light. They filled me with emotion, giving me an indescribable pleasure. They were not the thickest legs, which surprised me. Up to that moment I had thought it was the thickest legs I liked best but now I saw that several girls, three anyway, had bigger legs; but none like hers, so shapely, with such slight ankles and tapering lines. I was enthralled and at the same time a little scared.

I crept back into my chair with one idea in my little head: could I get close to those lovely legs and perhaps touch them—breathless expectancy! I knew I could hit my slate pencil and make it roll up between the files of legs. Next day I did this and crawled right up till I was close to the legs that made my heart beat in my throat and yet give me a strange delight. I put out my hand to touch them. Suddenly the thought came that the girl would simply be frightened by my touch and pull her legs back and I should be discovered and—I was frightened.

I returned to my chair to think and soon found the solution. Next day I again crouched before the girl's legs, choking with emotion. I put my pencil near her toes and reached round between her legs with my left hand as if to get it, taking care to touch her calf. She shrieked and drew back her legs, holding my hand tight between them, and cried: "What are you doing there?"

"Getting my pencil," I said humbly. "It rolled."

"There it is," she said, kicking it with her foot.

"Thanks," I replied, overjoyed, for the feel of her soft legs was still on my hand.

"You're a funny little fellow," she said. But I didn't care. I had had my first taste of paradise and the forbidden fruit—authentic heaven!

I have no recollection of her face—it seemed pleasant, that's all I remember. None of the girls made any impression on me but I can still recall the thrill of admiration and pleasure her shapely limbs gave me.

I record this incident at length because it stands alone in my memory and because it shows that sex feeling may manifest itself in early childhood.

One day about 1890 I had Meredith, Walter Pater and Oscar Wilde* dining with me in Park Lane and the time of sex-awakening was discussed. Both Pater and Wilde spoke of it as a sign of puberty. Pater thought it began about thirteen or fourteen and Wilde to my amazement set it as late as sixteen. Meredith alone was inclined to put it earlier.

"It shows sporadically," he said, "and sometimes before puberty."

I recalled the fact that Napoleon tells how he was in love before he was five years old with a schoolmate called Giacominetta, but even Meredith laughed at this and would not believe that any real sex feeling could show itself so early. To prove the point I gave my experience as I have told it here and brought Meredith to pause. "Very interesting," he thought, "but peculiar!"

"In her abnormalities," says Goethe, "nature reveals her secrets." Here is an abnormality, perhaps as such, worth noting.

I hadn't another sensation of sex till nearly six years later when I was eleven, since which time such emotions have been almost incessant.

My exaltation to the oldest class in arithmetic got me into trouble by bringing me into relations with the head-mistress, Mrs. Frost, who was very cross and seemed to think that I should spell as correctly as I did sums. When she found I couldn't, she used to pull my ears and got into the habit of digging her long thumb nail into my ear till it bled. I didn't mind the smart; in fact, I was delighted, for her cruelty brought me the pity of the elder girls who used to wipe my ears with their pocket-handkerchiefs and say that old Frost was a beast and a cat.

* George Meredith (1828–1909); Harris talks about him at length in vols. I, II. Pater (1839–94). Wilde (1854–1900), of whom Harris has written a fascinating, vastly underrated biography; it is perhaps Harris' best work.

One day my father sent for me and I went with a petty officer to his vessel in the harbor. My right ear had bled onto my collar. As soon as my father noticed it and saw the older scars he got angry and took me back to the school and told Mrs. Frost what he thought of her and her punishments.

Immediately afterwards, it seems to me, I was sent to live with my eldest brother Vernon, ten years older than myself, who was in lodgings with friends in Galway while going to college.

There I spent the next five years, which passed leaving a blank. I learned nothing in those years except how to play "tag," "hide and seek," "footer" and "ball." I was merely a healthy, strong little animal without an ache or pain or trace of thought.

Then I remember an interlude at Belfast where Vernon and I lodged with an old Methodist who used to force me to go to church with him and drew on a little black skull-cap during the service, which filled me with shame and made me hate him. There is a period in life when everything peculiar or individual excites dislike and is in itself an offense.

I learned here to "mitch" and lie simply to avoid school and to play, till my brother found I was coughing, and having sent for a doctor, was informed that I had congestion of the lungs; the truth being that I played all day and never came home for dinner, seldom indeed before seven o'clock, when I knew Vernon would be back. I mention this incident because, while confined to the house, I discovered under the old Methodist's bed a set of doctor's books with colored plates of the insides and pudenda of men and women. I devoured all the volumes, and bits of knowledge from them stuck to me for many a year. Curiously enough, the main sex fact was not revealed to me then, but in talks a little later with boys of my own age.

I learned nothing in Belfast but rules of games and athletics. My brother Vernon used to go to a gymnasium every evening and exercise and box. To my astonishment he was not among the best; so while he was boxing I began practicing this and that, drawing myself up till my chin was above the bar, and repeating this till one evening Vernon found I could do it thirty times running: his praise made me proud.

About this time, when I was ten or so, we were all brought together in Carrickfergus. My brothers and sisters then first became living, individual beings to me. Vernon was going to a bank as a clerk and was away all day. Willie, six years older than I was, and Annie, and Chrissie, two years my junior, went to the same day-school, though the girls went to the girls' entrance and had women teachers. Willie and I were in the same class; though he had grown to be taller than Vernon, I could beat him in most of the lessons. There was, however, one important branch of learning in which he was easily the best in the school. The first time I heard him recite *The Battle of Ivry* by Macaulay, I was carried off my feet. He made gestures and his voice altered so naturally that I was lost in admiration.

That evening my sisters and I were together and we talked of Willie's talent. My eldest sister was enthusiastic, which I suppose stirred envy and emulation in me. I got up and imitated him and to my sisters' surprise I knew the whole poem by heart. "Who taught you?" Annie wanted to know, and when she heard that I had learned it just from hearing Willie recite it once, she was astonished and must have told our teacher; for the next afternoon he asked me to follow Willie and told me I was very good. From this time on the reciting class was my chief education. I learned every boy's piece and could imitate them all perfectly, except one red-haired rascal who could recite *The African Chief* better than anyone else, better even than the master. It was pure melodrama but Red-head was a born actor and swept us all away by the realism of his impersonation. Never shall I forget how the boy rendered the words:

> Look, feast thy greedy eyes on gold,
>> Long kept for sorest need;
> Take it, thou askest sums untold
>> And say that I am freed.

> Take it; my wife the long, long day
>> Weeps by the cocoa-tree,
> And my young children leave their play
>> And ask in vain for me.*

I haven't seen or heard the poem these fifty odd years. It seems tawdry stuff to me now; but the boy's accents were of the very soul of tragedy and I realized clearly that I couldn't recite that poem as well as he did. He was inimitable. Every time his accents and manner altered; now he did these verses wonderfully, at another time those, so that I couldn't ape him; always there was a touch of novelty in his intense realization of the tragedy. Strange to say, it was the only poem he recited at all well.

An examination came and I was the first in the school in arithmetic and first too in elocution. Vernon even praised me, while Willie slapped me and got kicked on the shins for his pains. Vernon separated us and told Willie he should be ashamed of hitting one only half as big as he was. Willie lied promptly, saying I had kicked him first. I disliked Willie, I hardly know why, save that he was a rival in the school life.

After this Annie began to treat me differently and now I seemed to see her as she was and was struck by her funny ways. She wished both Chrissie and myself to call her "Nita"; it was short for Anita, she said, which was the stylish French way of pronouncing Annie. She hated "Annie"—it was "common and vulgar"; I couldn't make out why.

One evening we were together and she had undressed Chrissie for bed, when she opened her own dress and showed us how her breasts had grown while Chrissie's still remained small; and indeed "Nita's" were ever so much larger and prettier and round like apples. Nita let us touch them gently and was evidently very proud of them. She sent Chrissie to bed in

---

* An eight-stanza poem by William Cullen Byrant. Harris quotes it accurately.

the next room while I went on learning a lesson beside her. Nita left the room to get something, I think, when Chrissie called me and I went into the bedroom wondering what she wanted. She wished me to know that her breasts would grow too and be just as pretty as Nita's. "Don't you think so?" she asked, and taking my hand put it on them. And I said, "Yes," for indeed I liked her better than Nita, who was all airs and graces and full of affectations.

Suddenly Nita called me, and Chrissie kissed me whispering: "Don't tell her," and I promised. I always liked Chrissie and Vernon. Chrissie was very clever and pretty, with dark curls and big hazel eyes, and Vernon was a sort of hero and always very kind to me.

I learned nothing from this happening. I had hardly any sex-thrill with either sister, indeed, nothing like so much as I had had five years before, through the girl's legs in Mrs. Frost's school; and I record the incident here chiefly for another reason. One afternoon about 1890, Aubrey Beardsley* and his sister Mabel, a very pretty girl, had been lunching with me in Park Lane. Afterwards we went into the park. I accompanied them as far as Hyde Park Corner. For some reason or other I elaborated the theme that men of thirty or forty usually corrupted young girls, and women of thirty or forty in turn corrupted youths.

"I don't agree with you," Aubrey remarked. "It's usually a fellow's sister who gives him his first lessons in sex. I know it was Mabel here who first taught me."

I was amazed at his outspokenness. Mabel flushed crimson and I hastened to add:

"In childhood girls are far more precocious. But these little lessons are usually too early to matter." He wouldn't have it, but I changed the subject resolutely and Mabel told me some time afterwards that she was very grateful to me for cutting short the discussion. "Aubrey," she said, "loves all sex things and doesn't care what he says or does."

I had seen before that Mabel was pretty. I realized that day when she stooped over a flower that her figure was beautifully slight and round. Aubrey caught my eye at the moment and remarked maliciously, "Mabel was my first model, weren't you, Mabs? I was in love with her figure," he went on judicially. "Her breasts were so high and firm and round that I took her as my ideal." She laughed, blushing a little, and rejoined, "Your figures, Aubrey, are not exactly ideal."

I learned from this little discussion that most men's sisters are just as precocious as mine were and just as likely to act as teachers in matters of sex.

From about this time on the individualities of people began to impress me definitely. Vernon suddenly got an appointment in a bank at Armagh

* (1872–98). His rise as an illustrator was meteoric; among the books he illustrated were *Morte d'Arthur* and *Salome,* and he helped found the *Yellow Book,* a magazine, in 1894. He, with Wilde, was a leader of the "Decadents" in the 1890's.

and I went to live with him there, in lodgings. The lodging-house keeper I disliked: she was always trying to make me keep hours and rules, and I was as wild as a homeless dog; but Armagh was wonder city to me. Vernon made me a day-boy at the Royal School: it was my first big school; I learned all the lessons very easily and most of the boys and all the masters were kind to me. The great mall or park-like place in the centre of the town delighted me; I had soon climbed nearly every tree in it, tree climbing and reciting being the two sports in which I excelled.

When we were at Carrickfergus my father had had me on board his vessel and had matched me at climbing the rigging against a cabin boy, and though the sailor was first at the cross-trees, I caught him on the descent by jumping at a rope and letting it slide through my hands, almost at falling speed to the deck. I heard my father tell this afterwards with pleasure to Vernon, which pleased my vanity inordinately and increased, if that were possible, my delight in showing off.

For another reason my vanity had grown beyond measure. At Carrick-fergus I had got hold of a book on athletics belonging to Vernon and had there learned that if you went into the water up to your neck and threw yourself boldly forward and tried to swim, you would swim; for the body is lighter than the water and floats.

The next time I went down to bathe with Vernon, instead of going on the beach in the shallow water and wading out, I went with him to the end of the pier. When he dived in, I went down the steps. As soon as he came up to the surface I cried, "Look! I can swim too!" and I boldly threw myself forward and, after a moment's dreadful sinking and spluttering, did in fact swim. When I wanted to get back I had a moment of appalling fear: "Could I turn around?" The next moment I found it quite easy to turn and I was soon safely back on the steps again.

"When did you learn to swim?" asked Vernon, coming out beside me. "This minute," I replied. As he was surprised, I told him I had read it all in his book and made up my mind to venture the very next time I bathed. A little time afterwards I heard him tell this to some of his men friends in Armagh, and they all agreed that it showed extraordinary courage, for I was small for my age and always appeared even younger than I was.

Looking back, I see that many causes combined to strengthen the vanity in me which had already become inordinate and in the future was destined to shape my life and direct its purposes. Here in Armagh everything conspired to foster my besetting sin. I was put among boys of my age, I think in the lower fourth. The form-master, finding that I knew no Latin, showed me a Latin grammar and told me I'd have to learn it as quickly as possible, for the class had already begun to read Caesar. He showed me the first declension *mensa* as the example, and asked me if I could learn it by the next day. I said I would, and as luck would have it, the mathematical master passing at the moment, the form-master told him I was backward and should be in a lower form.

"He's very good indeed at figures," the mathematical master rejoined. "He might be in the Upper Division."

"Really!" exclaimed the form-master. "See what you can do," he said to me. "You may find it possible to catch up. Here's a Caesar too; you may as well take it with you. We have done only two or three pages."

That evening I sat down to the Latin grammar, and in an hour or so had learned all the declensions and nearly all the adjectives and pronouns. Next day I was trembling with hope of praise and if the form-master had encouraged me or said one word of commendation, I might have distinguished myself in the class work, and so changed perhaps my whole life, but the next day he had evidently forgotten all about my backwardness. By dint of hearing the other boys answer I got a smattering of the lessons, enough to get through them without punishment, and soon a good memory brought me among the foremost boys, though I took no interest in learning Latin.

Another incident fed my self-esteem and opened to me the world of books. Vernon often went to a clergyman's who had a pretty daughter, and I too was asked to their evening parties. The daughter found out I could recite and at once it became the custom to get me to recite some poem everywhere we went. Vernon bought me the poems of Macaulay and Walter Scott and I had soon learned them all by heart. I used to declaim them with infinite gusto: at first my gestures were imitations of Willie's: but Vernon taught me to be more natural and I bettered his teaching. No doubt my small stature helped the effect and the Irish love of rhetoric did the rest; but everyone praised me and the showing off made me very vain and—a more important result—the learning of new poems brought me to the reading of novels and books of adventure. I was soon lost in this new world: though I played at school with the other boys, in the evening I never opened a lesson-book. Instead, I devoured Lever and Mayne Reid, Marryat* and Fenimore Cooper with unspeakable delight.

I had one or two fights at school with boys of my own age. I hated fighting, but I was conceited and combative and strong and so got to fisticuffs twice or three times. Each time, as soon as an elder boy saw the scrimmage, he would advise us, after looking on for a round or two, to stop and make friends. The Irish are supposed to love fighting better than eating; but my school days assure me, however, that they are not nearly so combative, or perhaps, I should say, so brutal, as the English.

In one of my fights a boy took my part and we became friends. His name was Howard and we used to go on long walks together. One day I wanted him to meet Strangways, the Vicar's son, who was fourteen but silly, I thought. Howard shook his head: "He wouldn't want to know me," he said. "I am a Roman Catholic." I still remember the feeling of horror his confession called up in me: "A Roman Catholic! Could anyone as nice as Howard be a Catholic?"

* Charles James Lever (1806–72); Thomas Mayne Reid (1818–83); Frederick Marryat (1792–1848). All were English writers of adventure novels.

I was thunderstruck and this amazement has always illumined for me the abyss of Protestant bigotry, but I wouldn't break with Howard, who was two years older than I and who taught me many things. He taught me to like Fenians, though I hardly knew what the word meant. One day I remember he showed me posted on the court house a notice offering £5000 sterling as reward to anyone who would tell the whereabouts of James Stephen,* the Fenian head-centre. "He's travelling all over Ireland," Howard whispered. "Everybody knows him," adding with gusto, "but no one would give the head-centre away to the dirty English." I remember thrilling to the mystery and chivalry of the story. From that moment, head-centre was a sacred symbol to me as Howard.

One day we met Strangways and somehow or other began talking of sex. Howard knew all about it and took pleasure in enlightening us both. It was Cecil Howard who first initiated Strangways and me, too, in self-abuse. In spite of my novel reading, I was still at eleven too young to get pleasure from the practice; but I was delighted to know how children were made and a lot of new facts about sex. Strangways had hair about his private parts, as indeed Howard had, also, and when he rubbed himself and the orgasm came, a sticky, milky fluid spirted from Strangway's cock, which Howard told us was the man's seed, which must go right into the woman's womb to make a child.

A week later Strangways astonished us both by telling how he had made up to the nursemaid of his younger sisters and got into her bed at night. The first time she wouldn't let him do anything, it appeared, but, after a night or two, he managed to touch her sex and assured us it was all covered with silky hairs. A little later he told us how she had locked her door and how the next day he had taken off the lock and got into bed with her again. At first she was cross, or pretended to be, he said, but he kept on kissing and begging her, and bit by bit she yielded, and he touched her sex again. "It was a slit," he said. A few nights later, he told us he had put his prick into her and, "Oh! by gum, it was wonderful, wonderful!"

"But how did you do it?" we wanted to know, and he gave us his whole experience.

"Girls love kissing," he said, "and so I kissed and kissed her and put my leg on her, and her hand on my cock and I kept touching her breasts and her cunny (that's what she calls it) and at last I got on her between her legs and she guided my prick into her cunt (God, it was wonderful!) and now I go with her every night and often in the day as well. She likes her cunt touched, but very gently," he added; "she showed me how to do it with one finger like this," and he suited the action to the word.

Strangways in a moment became to us not only a hero but a miracle-

---

* (1825–1901). After being wounded in Ballingarry in 1848, he escaped to France and then to America, where he helpd found the Fenian Brotherhood. He returned to Ireland and was forced to flee again in 1865. Allowed to return to Dublin in 1886, he died there.

man; we pretended not to believe him in order to make him tell us the truth and we were almost crazy with breathless desire.

I got him to invite me up to the vicarage and I saw Mary the nurse-girl there, and she seemed to me almost a woman and spoke to him as "Master Will" and he kissed her, though she frowned and said, "Leave off" and "Behave yourself," very angrily; but I felt that her anger was put on to prevent my guessing the truth. I was aflame with desire and when I told Howard, he, too, burned with lust, and took me out for a walk and questioned me all over again, and under a haystack in the country we gave ourselves to a bout of frigging, which for the first time thrilled me with pleasure.

All the time we were playing with ourselves, I kept thinking of Mary's hot slit, as Strangways had described it, and, at length, a real orgasm came and shook me; the imagining had intensified my delight.

Nothing in my life up to that moment was comparable in joy to that story of sexual pleasure as described, and acted for us, by Strangways.

My Father

Father was coming; I was sick with fear: he was so strict and loved to punish. On the ship he had beaten me with a strap because I had gone forward and listened to the sailors talking smut: I had feared him and disliked him ever since I saw him once come aboard drunk.

It was the evening of a regatta at Kingstown. He had been asked to lunch on one of the big yachts. I heard the officers talking of it. They said he was asked because he knew more about tides and currents along the coast than anyone, more even than the fishermen. The racing skippers wanted to get some information out of him. Another added, "He knows the slants of the wind off Howth Head, ay, and the weather, too, better than anyone living!" All agreed he was a first rate sailor, "One of the best, the very best if he had a decent temper—the little devil."

"D'ye mind when he steered the gig in that race for all? Won? Av course he won, he has always won—ah! He's a great little sailor an' he takes care of the men's food, too, but he has the divil's own temper—an' that's the truth."

That afternoon of the regatta, he came up the ladder quickly and stumbled, smiling as he stepped down to the deck. I had never seen him like that; he was grinning and walking unsteadily: I gazed at him in amazement. An officer turned aside and as he passed me he said to another: "Drunk as a lord." Another helped my father down to his cabin and came up five minutes afterwards: "He's snoring: he'll soon be all right: it's that champagne they give him, and all that praising him and pressing him to give them tips for this and that."

"No, no!" cried another. "It's not the drink; he only gets drunk when he hasn't to pay for it," and all of them grinned; it was true, I felt, and I despised the meanness inexpressibly.

I hated them for seeing him, and hated him—drunk and talking thick and staggering about; an object of derision and pity!—my "governor," as Vernon called him; I despised him.

And I recalled other griefs I had against him. A Lord of the Admiralty had come aboard once; father was dressed in his best; I was very young: it was just after I had learned to swim in Carrickfergus. My father used to make me undress and go in and swim round the vessel every morning after my lessons.

That morning I had come up as usual at eleven and a strange gentleman and my father were talking together near the companion. As I appeared my father gave me a frown to go below, but the stranger caught sight of me and laughing called me. I came to them and the stranger was surprised on hearing I could swim. "Jump in, Jim!" cried my father, "and swim round."

Nothing loath, I ran down the ladder, pulled off my clothes and jumped in. The stranger and my father were above me smiling and talking; my father waved his hand and I swam round the vessel. When I got back, I was about to get on the steps and come aboard when my father said:

"No, no, swim on round till I tell you to stop."

Away I went again quite proud, but when I got round the second time I was tired; I had never swum so far and I had sunk deep in the water and a little spray of wave had gone into my mouth; I was very glad to get near the steps, but as I stretched out my hand to mount them, my father waved his hand.

"Go on, go on," he cried, "till you're told to stop!"

I went on; but now I was very tired and frightened as well, and as I got to the bow the sailors leant over the bulwark and one encouraged me: "Go slow, Jim; you'll get round all right." I saw it was big Newton, the stroke-oar of my father's gig, but just because of his sympathy I hated my father the more for making me so tired and so afraid.

When I got round the third time, I swam very slowly and let myself sink very low, and the stranger spoke for me to my father, and then he himself told me to "come up."

I came eagerly, but a little scared at what my father might do, but the stranger came over to me, saying: "He's all blue; that water's very cold, Captain; someone should give him a good towelling."

My father said nothing but: "Go down and dress," adding, "get warm."

The memory of my fear made me see that he was always asking me to do too much, and I hated him who could get drunk and shame me and make me run races up the rigging with the cabin boys who were grown men and could beat me. I disliked him.

I was too young then to know that it was probably the habit of command which prevented him from praising me. Yet I knew in a half-conscious way that he was proud of me because I was the only one of his children who never got sea-sick.

A little later he arrived in Armagh and the following week was wretched: I had to come straight home from school every day, and go out for a long walk with the "governor," and he was not a pleasant companion. I couldn't let myself go with him as with a chum; I might in the heat of talk use some word or tell him something and get into an awful row. So I walked beside him silently, taking heed as to what I should say in answer to his simplest question. There was no companionship.

In the evening he used to send me to bed early, even before nine o'clock, though Vernon always let me stay up with him reading till eleven or twelve o'clock. One night I went up to my bedroom on the next floor, but returned almost at once to get a book and have a read in bed, which was a rare treat to me. I was afraid to go into the sitting room; but crept into the dining room where there were a few books, though not so interesting as those in the parlor; the door between the two rooms was ajar. Suddenly I heard my father say:

"He's a little Fenian."

"Fenian," repeated Vernon, in amazement. "Really, Governor, I don't believe he knows the meaning of the word; he's only just eleven, you must remember."

"I tell you," broke in my father, "he talked of James Stephen, the Fenian head-centre, today, with wild admiration. He's a Fenian, all right, but how did he catch it?"

"I'm sure I don't know," replied Vernon. "He reads a great deal and is very quick: I'll find out about it."

"No, no!" said my father. "The thing is to cure him. He must go to some school in England; that'll cure him."

I waited to hear no more but got my book and crept upstairs. So because I loved the Fenian head-centre I must be a Fenian.

"How stupid father is," was my summing up, but England tempted me, England—life was opening out.

It was at the Royal School in the summer after my sex-experience with Strangways and Howard that I first began to notice dress. A boy in the sixth form named Milman had taken a liking to me, and though he was five years older than I was, he often went with Howard and myself for walks. He was a stickler for dress, said that no one but "cads" (a name I learned from him for the first time) and common folk would wear a made-up tie: he gave me one of his scarves and showed me how to make a running lover's knot in it. On another occasion he told me that only "cads" would wear trousers frayed or repaired. Was it Milman's talk that made me self-conscious or my sex awakening through Howard and Strangways? I couldn't say, but at this time I had a curious and prolonged experience. My brother Vernon, hearing me once complain of my dress, got me three suits of clothes, one in black with an Eton jacket for best and a tall hat and the others in tweeds. He gave me shirts, too, and ties, and I began to take great care of my appearance. At our evening parties the girls and young women (Vernon's friends) were kinder to me than ever, and I found myself wondering whether I really looked "nice," as they said.

I began to wash and bathe carefully and brush my hair to regulation smoothness (only "cads" used pomatum, Milman said), and when I was asked to recite, I would pout and plead prettily that I did not want to, just in order to be pressed.

Sex was awakening in me at this time but was still indeterminate, I imagine. Two motives ruled me for over six months: I was always wondering how I looked and watching to see if people liked me. I used to try to speak with the accent used by the "best people," and on coming into a room I prepared my entrance. Someone, I think it was Vernon's sweetheart, Monica, said that I had an energetic profile, so I always sought to show my profile. In fact, for some six months, I was more a girl than a boy, with all a girl's self-consciousness and manifold affectations and sentimentalities: I often used to think that no one cared for me really and I would weep over my unloved loneliness.

Whenever later as a writer I wished to picture a young girl, I had only to go back to this period in my consciousness in order to attain the peculiar viewpoint of the girl.

Chapter II

Life in an English Grammar School

IF I TRIED MY BEST, it would take a year to describe the life in that English grammar school at R . . . . I had always been perfectly happy in every Irish school and especially in the Royal School at Armagh. Let me give one difference as briefly as possible. When I whispered in the classroom in Ireland, the master would frown at me and shake his head; ten minutes later I was talking again, and he'd hold up an admonitory finger; the third time he'd probably say, "Stop talking, Harris; don't you see you're disturbing your neighbor?" Half an hour later in despair he'd cry, "If you still talk, I'll have to punish you."

Ten minutes afterwards: "You're incorrigible, Harris; come up here," and I'd have to go and stand beside his desk for the rest of the morning, and even this light punishment did not happen more than twice a week, and as I came to be head of my class, it grew rarer.

In England, the procedure was quite different. "That new boy there is talking; take 300 lines to write out and keep quiet."

"Please, Sir," I'd pipe up—"Take 500 lines and keep quiet."

"But, Sir"—in remonstrance.

"Take a thousand lines and if you answer again, I'll send you to the Doctor"—which meant I'd get a caning or a long talking to.

The English masters one and all ruled by punishment; consequently I was indoors writing out lines almost every day, and every half-holiday for the first year. Then my father, prompted by Vernon, complained to the Doctor that writing out lines was ruining my handwriting.

After that I was punished by lines to learn by heart; the lines quickly grew into pages, and before the end of the first half year it was found that I knew the whole school history of England by heart through these punishments. Another remonstrance from my father and I was given lines of Vergil to learn. Thank God! that seemed worth learning and the story of Ulysses and Dido on "the wild sea-banks" became a series of living pictures to me, not to be dimmed, even so long as I live.

That English school for a year and a half was to me a brutal prison with stupid daily punishments. At the end of that time I was given a seat by myself, thanks to the mathematical master; but that's another story.

The two or three best boys of my age in England were far more advanced than I was in Latin and had already waded through half the Greek grammar, which I had not begun, but I was better in mathematics than any one in the whole lower school. Because I was behind the English standard in languages, the form-master took me to be stupid and called me "stupid," and as a result I never learned a Latin or Greek lesson in my two and a half years in grammar school. Nevertheless, thanks to the punishment of having to learn Vergil and Livy by heart, I was easily the best of my age in Latin, too, before the second year was over.

I had an extraordinary verbal memory. The Doctor, I remember, once mouthed out some lines of *Paradise Lost* and told us in his pompous way that Lord Macaulay knew *Paradise Lost* by heart from beginning to end. I asked: "Is that hard, Sir?" "When you've learned half of it," he replied, "you'll understand how hard! Lord Macaulay was a genius," and he emphasized the "Lord" again.

A week later when the Doctor again took the school in literature, I said at the end of the hour: "Please, Sir, I know *Paradise Lost* by heart"; he tested me, and I remember how he looked at me afterwards from head to foot, as if asking himself where I had put all the learning. This "piece of impudence," as the older boys called it, brought me several cuffs and kicks from boys in the sixth, and much ill will from many others.

All English school life was summed up for me in the "fagging." There was "fagging" in the Royal School in Armagh, but it was kindly. If you wanted to get out of it for a long walk with a chum, you had only to ask one of the sixth and you got permission to skip it.

But in England the rule was rhadamanthine; the fags' names on duty were put up on a blackboard, and if you were not on time, ay, and servile to boot, you'd get a dozen from an ash plant on your behind, and not laid on perfunctorily and with distaste, as the Doctor did it, but with vim, so that I had painful weals on my backside and couldn't sit down for days without a smart.

The fags, too, being young and weak, were very often brutally treated just for fun. On Sunday mornings in summer, for instance, we had an hour longer in bed. I was one of the half-dozen juniors in the big bedroom; there were two older boys in it, one at each end, presumably to keep order; but in reality to teach lechery and corrupt their younger favorites. If the mothers of England knew what goes on in the dormitories of these boarding schools throughout England, they would all be closed, from Eton and Harrow, upwards or downwards, in a day. If English fathers even had brains enough to understand that the fires of sex need no stoking in boyhood, they, too, would protect their sons from the foul abuse. But I shall come back to this. Now I wish to speak of the cruelty.

Every form of cruelty was practiced on the younger, weaker and more nervous boys. I remember one Sunday morning the half-dozen older boys pulled one bed along the wall and forced all seven younger boys underneath it, beating with sticks any hand or foot that showed. One little fellow cried that he couldn't breathe, and at once the gang of tormentors began stuffing up all the apertures, saying that they would make a "Black Hole" of it. There were soon cries and strugglings under the bed, and at length one of the youngest began shrieking, so that the torturers ran away from the prison, fearing lest some master should hear.

One wet Sunday afternoon in midwinter, a little nervous "mother's darling" from the West Indies, who always had a cold and was always sneaking near the fire in the big schoolroom, was caught by two of the fifth and held near the flames. Two more brutes pulled his trousers tight over his bottom, and the more he squirmed and begged to be let go, the nearer the flames he was pushed, till suddenly the trousers split apart scorched through; and as the little fellow tumbled forward screaming, the torturers realized that they had gone too far. The little "nigger," as he was called, didn't tell how he came to be so scorched but took his fortnight in sick bay as a respite.

We read of a fag at Shrewsbury who was thrown into a bath of boiling water by some older boys because he liked to take his bath very warm; but this experiment turned out badly, for the little fellow died and the affair could not be hushed up, though it was finally dismissed as a regrettable accident.

The English are proud of the fact that they hand a good deal of the school discipline to the older boys: they attribute this innovation to Arnold of Rugby and, of course, it is possible, if the supervision is kept up by a genius, that it may work for good and not for evil; but usually it turns the school into a forcing-house of cruelty and immorality. The older boys establish the legend that only sneaks would tell anything to the masters, and they are free to give rein to their basest instincts.

The two monitors in our big bedroom were a strapping big fellow named Dick F. . . . , who tired all the little boys by going into their beds and making them frig him till his semen came. The little fellows all hated to be covered by his filthy slime, but had to pretend to like doing as he told them, and usually he insisted on frigging them by way of exciting himself. Dick only picked me out once or twice, but I managed to catch his semen on his own night-shirt, and so after calling me a "dirty little devil," he left me alone.

The other monitor was Jones, a Liverpool boy of about seventeen, very backward in lessons but very strong, the "Cock" of the school at fighting. He used always to go to one young boy's bed, whom he favored in many ways. Henry H. . . used to be able to get off any fagging and he never let out what Jones made him do at night, but in the long run he got to be chums with another fellow and it all came out. Henry's chum one day let the cat out of the bag. It appeared that Jones used to make the little fellow take his sex in his mouth and frig and suck him at the same time. But one evening he had brought up some butter and smeared it over his prick and gradually inserted it into Henry's anus and this came to be his ordinary practice. But this night he had forgotten the butter, and when he found a certain resistance, he thrust violently forward, causing extreme pain and making his pathic bleed. Henry screamed, and so after an interval of some weeks or months, the whole procedure came to be known.

If there had been no big boys as monitors, there would still have been a certain amount of solitary frigging; from twelve to thirteen on, most boys, and girls, too, practice self-abuse from time to time on some slight provocation; but the practice doesn't often become habitual unless it is fostered by one's elders and practiced mutually. In Ireland it is sporadic; in England perpetual, and in English schools it often led to downright sodomy, as in this instance.

In my own case there were two restraining influences, and I wish to dwell on both as a hint to parents. I was a very eager little athlete; thanks to instructions and photographs in a book on athletics belonging to Vernon, I found out how to jump and how to run. To jump high, one had to take but a short run from the side and straighten oneself horizontally as one cleared the bar. By constant practice I could at thirteen walk under the bar and then jump it. I soon noticed that if I frigged myself the night before, I could not jump so well, the consequence being that I restrained myself, and never frigged save on Sunday, and soon managed to omit the practice three Sundays out of four.

Since I came to understanding, I have always been grateful to that exercise for this lesson in self-restraint. Besides, one of the boys was always frigging himself: even in school he kept his right hand in his trousers pocket and continued the practice. All of us knew that he had torn a hole in his pocket so that he could play with his cock; but none of the masters ever noticed anything. The little fellow grew gradually paler and paler until he took to crying in a corner, and unaccountable nervous trembling shook him for a quarter of an hour at a time. At length, he was taken away by his parents: what became of him afterwards, I don't know, but I do know that till he was taught self-abuse, he was one of the quickest boys of his age at lessons and given like myself to much reading.

This object lesson in consequences had little effect on me at the time; but later it was useful as a warning. Such teaching may have affected the Spartans, as we read that they taught their children temperance by showing them a drunken helot; but I want to lay stress on the fact I was first taught self-control by a keen desire to excel in jumping and running, and as soon as I found that I couldn't run as fast or jump as high after practicing self-abuse, I began to restrain myself, and in return this had a most potent effect on my will power.

I was over thirteen when a second and still stronger restraining influence made itself felt, and strangely enough this influence grew through my very desire for girls and curiosity about them.

The story marks an epoch in my life. We were taught singing at school, and when it was found that I had a good alto voice and a very good ear, I was picked to sing solos, both in school and in the church choir. Before every church festival there was a good deal of practice with the organist, and girls from neighboring houses joined in our classes. One girl alone sang alto and she and I were separated from the other boys and girls; the upright piano was put across the corner of the room and we two sat or stood behind it, almost out of sight of all the other singers, the organist, of course, being seated in front of the piano. The girl E. . . . , who sang alto with me, was about my own age; she was very pretty, or seemed so to me, with golden hair and blue eyes, and I always made up to her as well as I could, in my boyish way. One day while the organist was explaining something, E. . . . stood up on the chair and leant over the back of the piano to hear better or see more. Seated in my chair behind her, I caught sight of her legs, for her dress rucked up behind as she leaned over; at once my breath stuck in my throat. Her legs were lovely, I thought, and the temptation came to touch them; for no one could see.

I got up immediately and stood by the chair she was standing on. Casually I let my hand fall against her left leg. She didn't draw her leg away or seem to feel my hand, so I touched her more boldly. She never moved, though now I knew she must have felt my hand. I began to slide my hand up her leg and suddenly my fingers felt the warm flesh on her thigh where the stocking ended above the knee. The feel of her warm flesh made me literally choke with emotion: my hand went on up, warmer and warmer, when suddenly I touched her sex; there was soft down on it. The heart-pulse throbbed in my throat. I have no words to describe the intensity of my sensations.

Thank God, E. . . . did not move or show any sign of distaste. Curiosity was stronger even than desire in me and I felt her sex all over, and at once the idea came into my head that it was like a fig (the Italians, I learned later, called it familiarly *fica*); it opened at my touches and I inserted my finger gently, as Strangways had told me that Mary had taught him to do; still E. . . . did not move. Gently I rubbed the front part of her sex with my finger. I could have kissed her a thousand times out of gratitude.

Suddenly, as I went on, I felt her move, and then again; plainly she was showing me where my touch gave her most pleasure: I could have died for her in thanks; again she moved and I could feel a little mound or small button of flesh right in the front of her sex, above the junction of the inner lips; of course it was her clitoris. I had forgotten all the old Methodist doctor's books till that moment; this fragment of long forgotten knowledge came back to me: gently I rubbed the clitoris and at once she pressed down on my finger for a moment or two. I tried to insert my finger into the vagina; but she drew away at once and quickly, closing her sex as if hurt, so I went back to caressing her tickler.

Suddenly the miracle ceased. The cursed organist had finished his explanation of the new plain chant, and as he touched the first notes on the piano, E. . . . drew her legs together; I took away my hand and she stepped down from the chair. "You darling, darling," I whispered, but she frowned, and then just gave me a smile out of the corner of her eye to show me she was not displeased.

Ah, how lovely, how seductive she seemed to me now, a thousand times lovelier and more desirable than ever before. As we stood up to sing again, I whispered to her: "I love you, love you, dear, dear!"

I can never express the passion of gratitude I felt to her for her goodness, her sweetness in letting me touch her sex. E. . . . it was who opened the Gates of Paradise to me and let me first taste the hidden mysteries of sexual delight. Still after more than fifty years I feel the thrill of the joy she gave me by her response, and the passionate reverence of my gratitude is still alive in me.

This experience with E. . . . had the most important and unlooked for results. The mere fact that girls could feel sex-pleasure "just as boys do" increased my liking for them and lifted the whole sexual intercourse to a higher plane in my thought. The excitement and pleasure were so much more intense than anything I had experienced before that I resolved to keep myself for this higher joy. No more self-abuse for me; I knew something infinitely better. One kiss was better, one touch of a girl's sex.

That kissing and caressing a girl should inculcate self-restraint is not taught by our spiritual guides and masters; but it is nevertheless true. Another cognate experience came at this time to reinforce the same lesson. I had read all Scott, and his heroine Di Vernon* made a great impression on me. I resolved now to keep all my passion for some Di Vernon in the future. Thus the first experiences of passion and the reading of a love story completely cured me of the bad habit of self-abuse.

Naturally, after this first divine experience, I was on edge for a second and keen as a questing hawk. I could not see E. . . . till the next music lesson—a week to wait; but even such a week comes to an end, and once more we were imprisoned in our solitude behind the piano; but though I whispered all the sweet and pleading words I could imagine, E. . . . did nothing but frown refusal and shake her pretty head. This killed for the moment all my faith in girls: why did she act so? I puzzled my brain for a reasonable answer and found none. It was part of the damned inscrutability of girls, but at the moment it filled me with furious anger. I was savage with disappointment.

"You're mean!" I whispered to her at long last, and I would have said more if the organist hadn't called on me for a solo, which I sang very badly, so badly indeed that he made me come from behind the piano and thus abolished even the chance of future intimacies. Time and time again I cursed organist and girl, but I was always alert for a similiar experience.

* A sports-loving heroine in *Rob Roy*.

As dog fanciers say of hunting dogs, "I had tasted blood and could never afterwards forget the scent of it."

Twenty-five years or more later, I dined with Frederic Chapman,* the publisher of the *Fortnightly Review,* which I was then editing; he asked me some weeks afterwards, had I noticed a lady, and described her dress to me, adding, "She was very curious about you. As soon as you came into the room she recognized you and has asked me to tell her if you recognized her; did you?"

I shook my head. "I'm near-sighted, you know," I said, "and therefore to be forgiven, but when did she know me?"

He replied, "As a boy at school; she said you would remember her by her Christian name of E. . . ."

"Of course I do," I cried. "Oh, please tell me her name and where she lives. I'll call on her. I want (and then reflection came to suggest prudence) to ask her some questions," I added, lamely.

"I can't give you her name or address," he replied. "I promised her not to, but she's long been happily married, I was to tell you."

I pressed him, but he remained obstinate, and on second thought I came to see that I had no right to push myself on a married woman who did not wish to renew acquaintance with me, but oh! I longed to see her and hear from her own lips the explanation of what to me at the time seemed her inexplicable, cruel change of attitude.

As a man, of course, I know she may have had a very good reason indeed, and her mere name still carries a glamour about it for me, and unforgettable fascination.

My father was always willing to encourage self-reliance in me: indeed, he tried to make me act as a man while I was still a mere child. The Christmas holidays only lasted for four weeks; it was cheaper for me, therefore, to take lodgings in some neighboring town rather than return to Ireland. Accordingly, the headmaster received the request to give me some seven pounds for my expenses and he did so, adding moreover much excellent advice.

My first holiday I spent in the watering-place of Rhyl in North Wales because a chum of mine, Evan Morgan, came from the place and told me he'd make it interesting for me. And in truth he did a good deal to make me like the people and love the place. He introduced me to three or four girls, among whom I took a great fancy to one Gertrude Hanniford. Gertie was over fifteen, tall and pretty, I thought, with long plaits of chestnut hair; one of the best companions possible. She would kiss me willingly but whenever I tried to touch her more intimately, she would wrinkle up her nose with "Don't!" or "Don't be dirty!"

One day I said to her reproachfully: "You'll make me couple 'dirty' with 'Gertie' if you go on using it so often." Bit by bit she grew tamer, though all too slowly for my desires; but luck was eager to help me.

* (1823–95).

One evening late we were together on some high ground behind the town when suddenly there came a great glare in the sky, which lasted two or three minutes: the next moment we were shaken by a sort of earthquake accompanied by a dull thud.

"An explosion!" I cried, "on the railway: let's go and see!" And away we set off for the railway. For a hundred yards or so Gertie was fast as I was; but after the first quarter of a mile I had to hold in so as not to leave her. Still for a girl she was very fast and strong. We found a footpath alongside the railway, for we found running over the wooden ties very slow and dangerous. We had covered a little over a mile when we saw the blaze in front of us and a crowd of figures moving about before the glare.

In a few minutes we were opposite three or four blazing railway carriages and the wreck of an engine.

"How awful!" cried Gertie. "Let's get over the fence," I replied, "and go close!" The next moment I had thrown myself on the wooden paling and half-vaulted, half-clambered over it. But Gertie's skirts prevented her from imitating me. As she stood in dismay, a great thought came to me. "Step on the low rail, Gertie," I cried, "and then on the upper one, and I'll lift you over. Quick!"

At once she did as she was told, and while she stood with a foot on each rail hesitating, and her hand on my head to steady herself, I put my right hand and arm between her legs, and pulling her at the same moment towards me with my left hand, I lifted her over safely, but my arm was in her crotch, and when I withdrew it, my right hand stopped on her sex and began to touch it.

It was larger than E. . . .'s and had more hairs and was just as soft, but she did not give me time to let it excite me so intensely.

"Don't!" she exclaimed angrily. "Take your hand away!" And slowly, reluctantly I obeyed, trying to excite her first. As she still scowled, "Come quick!" I cried, and taking her hand, drew her over to the blazing wreck.

In a little while we learned what had happened: a goods train loaded with barrels of oil had been at the top of the siding: it began to glide down of its own weight and ran into the Irish Express on its way from London to Holyhead. When the two met, the oil barrels were hurled over the engine of the express train, caught fire on the way and poured in flame over the first three carriages, reducing them and their unfortunate inmates to cinders in a very short time. There were a few persons burned and singed in the fourth and fifth carriages, but not many. Open-eyed, we watched the gang of workmen lift out charred things like burnt logs, rather than men and women, and lay them reverently in rows alongside the rails: about forty bodies, if I remember rightly, were taken out of that holocaust.

Suddenly Gertie realized that it was late and quickly hand in hand we made our way home: "They will be angry with me," said Gertie, "for being so late; it's after midnight." "When you tell them what you've seen," I replied, "they won't wonder why we waited!" As we parted I said, "Gertie, dear, I want to thank you—" "What for?" she said shortly. "You know," I said cunningly. "It was so kind of you—" She made a face at me and ran up the steps into her house.

Slowly I returned to my lodgings, only to find myself the hero of the house when I told the story in the morning.

That experience in common made Gertie and myself great friends. She used to kiss and say I was sweet: once she even let me see her breasts when I told her a girl (I did not say who it was) had shown hers to me once: her breasts were nearly as large as my sister's and very pretty. Gertie even let me touch her legs right up to the knee; but as soon as I tried to go further, she would pull down her dress with a frown. Still I was always going higher, making progress; persistence brings one closer to any goal; but alas, it was near the end of Christmas holidays and though I returned to Rhyl at Easter, I never saw Gertie again.

When I was just over thirteen I tried mainly out of pity to get up a revolt of the fags, and at first had a partial success, but some of the little fellows talked and as a ringleader I got a trouncing. The monitors threw me down on my face on a long desk; one sixth-form boy sat on my head and another on my feet, and a third, it was Jones, laid on with an ash plant. I bore it without a groan but I can never describe the storm of rage and hate that boiled in me. Do English fathers really believe that such work is a part of education? It made me murderous. When they let me up, I looked at Jones and if looks could kill, he'd have had short shrift. He tried to hit me but I dodged the blow and went out to plot revenge.

Jones was the head of the cricket first eleven in which I too was given a place just for my bowling. Vernon of the sixth was the chief bowler, but I was second, the only boy in the lower school who was in the eleven at all. Soon afterwards a team from some other school came over to play us: the rival captains met before the tent, all on their best behavior; for some reason, Vernon not being ready or something, I was given the new ball. A couple of the masters stood near. Jones lost the toss and said to the rival captain very politely, "If you're ready, Sir, we'll go out." The other captain bowed smiling. My chance had come:

"I'm not going to play with you, you brute!" I cried and dashed the ball in Jones' face.

He was very quick and throwing his head aside, escaped the full force of the blow; still the seam of the new ball grazed his cheekbone and broke the skin: everyone stood amazed: only people who know the strength of English conventions can realize the sensation. Jones himself did not know what to do but took out his handkerchief to mop the blood, the skin being just broken. As for me, I walked away by myself. I had broken the supreme law of our schoolboy honor: never to give away our dissensions to a master, still less to boys and masters from another school; I had sinned in public, too, and before everyone; I'd be universally condemned.

The truth is, I was desperate, dreadfully unhappy, for since the breakdown of the fags' revolt the lower boys had drawn away from me and the older boys never spoke to me if they could help it; and then it was always as "Pat."

I felt myself an outcast and was utterly lonely and miserable, as only despised outcasts can be. I was sure, too, I should be expelled and knew my father would judge me harshly; he was always on the side of the authorities and masters. However, the future was not to be as gloomy as my imagination pictured it.

The mathematical master was a young Cambridge man of perhaps six and twenty, Stackpole by name: I had asked him one day about a problem in algebra and he had been kind to me. On returning to the school this fatal afternoon about six, I happened to meet him on the edge of the playing field and by a little sympathy he soon drew out my whole story.

"I want to be expelled. I hate the beastly school," was my cry. All the charm of the Irish schools was fermenting in me: I missed the kindliness of boy to boy and of the masters to the boys; above all the imaginative fancies of fairies and "the little people" which had been taught us by our nurses, and though only half believed in, yet enriched and glorified life—all this was lost to me. My head in especial was full of stories of banshees and fairy queens and heroes, half due to memory, half to my own shaping, which made me a desirable companion to Irish boys and only got me derision from the English.

"I wish I had known that you were being fagged," Stackpole said when he had heard all. "I can easily remedy that," and he went with me to the schoolroom and then and there erased my name from the fags' list and wrote in my name in the first mathematical division.

"There," he said with a smile, "you are now in the upper school where you belong. I think," he added, "I had better go and tell the Doctor what I've done. Don't be downhearted, Harris," he added; "it'll all come right."

Next day the sixth did nothing except cut out my name from the list of the first eleven: I was told that Jones was going to thrash me, but I startled my informant by saying: "I'll put a knife into him if he lays a hand on me: you can tell him so."

In fact, however, I was half sent to Coventry, and what hurt me most was that it was the boys of the lower school who were the coldest to me, the very boys for whom I had been fighting. That gave me a bitter foretaste of what was to happen to me again and again all through my life.

The partial boycotting of me didn't affect me much; I went for long walks in the beautiful park of Sir. W. W. . . . near the school.

I have said many harsh things here of English school life, but for me it had two great redeeming features: the one was the library, which was open to every boy, and the other the physical training of the playing fields, the various athletic exercises and the gymnasium. The library to me for some months meant Walter Scott. How right George Eliot was to speak of him as "making the joy of many a young life." Certain scenes of his made ineffaceable impressions on me, though unfortunately not always his best work. The wrestling match between the Puritan, Balfour of Burleigh,* and the soldier was one of my beloved passages. Another favorite page was approved, too, by my maturer judgment, the brave suicide of the little atheist apothecary in the *Fair Maid of Perth.*** But Scott's finest work, such as the character painting of old Scotch servants, left me cold. Dickens I never could stomach, either as a boy or in later life. His *Tale of Two Cities* and *Nicholas Nickleby* seemed to me then about the best, and I've never had any desire since to revise my judgment after reading *David Copperfield* in my student days and finding men painted by a name or phrase or gesture, women by their modesty, and souls by some silly catch-word; "the mere talent of the caricaturist," I said to myself, "at his best another Hogarth."

Naturally, the romances and tales of adventure were all swallowed whole; but few affected me vitally: *The Chase of the White Horse* by Mayne Reid, lives with me still because of the love scenes with the Spanish heroine, and Marryat's *Peter Simple,†* which I read a hundred times and could read again tomorrow; for there is better character painting in Chucks, the boatswain, than in all Dickens, in my poor opinion. I remember being astounded ten years later when Carlyle spoke of Marryat with contempt. I knew he was unfair, just as I am probably unfair to Dickens: after all, even Hogarth has one or two good pictures to his credit, and no one survives even three generations without some merit.

In my two years I read every book in the library, and half a dozen are still beloved by me.

I profited, too, from all games and exercises. I was no good at cricket; I was short-sighted and caught some nasty knocks through an unsuspected astigmatism; but I had an extraordinary knack of bowling, which, as I have stated, put me in the first eleven. I liked football and was good at it. I took the keenest delight in every form of exercise: I could jump and run better than almost any boy of my age, and in wrestling and a little later in boxing, was among the best in the school. In the gymnasium, too, I practiced assiduously; I was so eager to excel that the teacher was continually advising me to go slow. At fourteen I could pull myself up with my right hand till my chin was above the bar.

In all games the English have a high ideal of fairness and courtesy. No one ever took an unfair advantage of another and courtesy was a law. If another school sent a team to play us at cricket or football, the victors always cheered the vanquished when the game was over, and it was a rule for the captain to thank the captain of the visitors for his kindness in coming and for the good game he had given us. This custom obtained, too, in

* Correctly "Burley," in *Old Mortality* (1816).
** *St. Valentine's Day: or The Fair Maid of Perth* (1828).
† (1834); his most widely read novel (English schoolboys still read it) is *Mr. Midshipman Easy*. It attacks philosophy and democracy and parodies the hero as Scott presented him.

the Royal Schools in Ireland that were founded for the English garrison, but I couldn't help noting that these courtesies were not practiced in ordinary Irish schools. It was for years the only thing in which I had to admit the superiority of John Bull.

The ideal of a gentleman is not a very high one. Emerson says somewhere that the evolution of the gentleman is the chief spiritual product of the last two or three centuries; but the concept, it seems to me, dwarfs the ideal. A "gentleman" to me is a thing of some parts but no magnitude: one should be a gentleman and much more: a thinker, guide or artist.

English custom in the games taught me the value and need of courtesy, and athletics practiced assiduously did much to steel and strengthen my control of all my bodily desires: they gave my mind and reason the mastery of me. At the same time they taught me the laws of health and the necessity of obeying them.

I found out that by drinking little at meals I could reduce my weight very quickly and was thereby enabled to jump higher than ever; but when I went on reducing I learned that there was a limit beyond which, if I persisted, I began to lose strength: athletics taught me what the French call the *juste milieu,* the middle path of moderation.

When I was about fourteen I discovered that to think of love before going to sleep was to dream of it during the night. And this experience taught me something else; if I repeated any lesson just before going to sleep, I knew it perfectly next morning; the mind, it seems, works even during unconsciousness. Often since, I have solved problems during sleep in mathematics and in chess that have puzzled me during the day.

Chapter III

School Days in England

IN MY THIRTEENTH YEAR the most important experience took place of my schoolboy life. Walking out one day with a West Indian boy of sixteen or so, I admitted that I was going to be "confirmed" in the Church of England. I was intensely religious at this time and took the whole rite with appalling seriousness. "Believe and thou shalt be saved" rang in my ears day and night, but I had no happy conviction. Believe what? "Believe in Me, Jesus." Of course I believe; then I should be happy, and I was not happy.

"Believe not" and eternal damnation and eternal torture follow. My soul revolted at the iniquity of the awful condemnation. What became of the myriads who had not heard of Jesus? It was all a horrible puzzle to me; but the radiant figure and sweet teaching of Jesus just enabled me to believe and resolve to live as he had lived, unselfishly—purely. I never liked that word "purely" and used to relegate it to the darkest background of my thought. But I would try to be good—I'd try at least!

"Do you believe all the fairy stories in the Bible?" my companion asked.

"Of course I do," I replied. "It's the Word of God, isn't it?"

"Who is God?" asked the West Indian.

"He made the world," I added, "all this wonder," and with a gesture I included earth and sky.

"Who made God?" asked my companion.

I turned away stricken: in a flash I saw I had been building on a word taught me: "who made God?" I walked away alone, up the long meadow by the little brook, my thoughts in a whirl: story after story that I had accepted were now to me "fairy stories." Jonah hadn't lived three days in a whale's belly. A man couldn't get down a whale's throat. The Gospel of Matthew began with Jesus' pedigree, showing that he had been born of the seed of David through Joseph, his father, and in the very next chapter you are told that Joseph wasn't his father; but the Holy Ghost. In an hour the whole fabric of my spiritual beliefs lay in ruins about me: I believed none of it, not a jot, nor a tittle: I felt as though I had been stripped naked to the cold.

Suddenly a joy came to me: if Christianity was all lies and fairy tales like Mohammedanism, then the prohibitions of it were ridiculous and I could kiss and have any girl who would yield to me. At once I was partially reconciled to my spiritual nakedness: there was compensation.

The loss of my belief was for a long time very painful to me. One day I told Stackpole of my infidelity, and he recommended me to read Butler's *Analogy** and keep an open mind. Butler finished what the West Indian had begun and in my thirst for some certainty I took up a course of deeper reading. In Stackpole's rooms one day I came across a book of Huxley's Essays;** in an hour I had swallowed them and proclaimed myself an "agnostic"; that's what I was; I knew nothing surely, but was willing to learn.

I aged ten years mentally in the next six months: I was always foraging for books to convince me and at length got hold of Hume's argument against miracles.† That put an end to all my doubts, satisfied me finally. Twelve years later, when studying philosophy in Goettingen, I saw that Hume's reasoning was not conclusive, but for the time I was cured. At midsummer I refused to be confirmed. For weeks before, I had been reading the Bible for the most incredible stories in it and the smut, which I retailed at night to the delight of the boys in the big bedroom.

This year as usual I spent the midsummer holidays in Ireland. My father had made his house with my sister Nita where Vernon happened to be sent by his bank. This summer was passed in Ballybay, in County Monaghan, I think. I remember little or nothing about the village save that there was a noble series of reed-fringed lakes near the place which gave good duck and snipe shooting to Vernon in the autumn.

These holidays were memorable to me for several incidents. A conversation began one day at dinner between my sister and my eldest brother about making up to girls and winning them. I noticed with astonishment that my brother Vernon was very deferential to my sister's opinion on the matter, so I immediately got hold of Nita after the lunch and asked her to explain to me what she meant by "flattery."

"You said all girls like flattery. What did you mean?"

"I mean," she said, "they all like to be told they are pretty, that they have good eyes or good teeth or good hair, as the case may be, or that they

---

* Bishop Joseph Butler (1692–1725), *The Analogy of Religion, Natural and Revealed, to the Constitution and Course of Nature.* The *Analogy* is a defense of Christianity against deism. Butler argues that Christian tenets are sufficiently probable to justify faith in them.

** Thomas Henry Huxley (1825–95). Since Harris was thirteen at the time, the year was 1868. Apparently Harris is referring to the essay "Science and Christian Tradition," which specifically treats agnosticism, but that essay was not published until 1889. Harris is writing from memory, however; he may be referring to *Man's Place in Nature* (1863), or to *Lay Sermons, Addresses and Reviews* (1870).

† David Hume (1711–76). The essay "Of Miracles," is from his *Enquiry concerning Human Understanding* (1748).

are tall and nicely made. They all like their good points noticed and praised."

"Is that all?" I asked. "Oh no!" she said, "they all like their dress noticed too and especially their hat; if it suits their face, if it's very pretty and so forth. All girls think that if you notice their clothes you really like them, for most men don't."

"Number two," I said to myself. "Is there anything else?"

"Of course," she said, "you must say that the girl you are with is the prettiest girl in the room or in town—in fact, is quite unlike any other girl, superior to all the rest, the only girl in the world for you. All women like to be the only girl in the world for as many men as possible."

"Number three," I said to myself: "Don't they like to be kissed?" I asked.

"That comes afterwards," said my sister. "Lots of men begin with kissing and pawing you about before you even like them. That puts you off. Flattery first of looks and dress, then devotion, and afterwards the kissing comes naturally."

"Number four!" I went over these four things again and again to myself and began trying them even on the older girls and women about me and soon found that they all had a better opinion of me almost immediately.

I remember practicing my new knowledge first on the younger Miss Raleigh whom, I thought, Vernon liked. I just praised her as my sister had advised: first her eyes and hair (she had very pretty blue eyes). To my astonishment she smiled on me at once; accordingly I went on to say she was the prettiest girl in town and suddenly she took my head in her hands and kissed me, saying, "You're a dear boy!"

But my experience was yet to come. There was a very good looking man whom I met two or three times at parties; I think his name was Tom Connolly: I'm not certain, though I ought not to forget it; for I can see him as plainly as if he were before me now; five feet ten or eleven, very handsome, with shaded violet eyes. Everybody was telling a story about him that had taken place on his visit to the Viceroy in Dublin. It appeared that the Vicereine had a very pretty French maid and Tom Connolly made up to the maid. One night the Vicereine was taken ill and sent her husband upstairs to call the maid. When the husband knocked at the maid's door, saying that his wife wanted her, Tom Connolly replied in a strong voice: "It's unfriendly of you to interrupt a man at such a time."

The Viceroy, of course, apologized immediately and hurried away, but like a fool he told the story to his wife, who was very indignant, and next day at breakfast she put an *aide-de-camp* on her right and Tom Connolly's place far down the table. As usual, Connolly came in late and the moment he saw the arrangement of the places, he took it all in and went over to the *aide-de-camp*.

"Now, young man," he said, "you'll have many opportunities later, so give me my place," and forthwith turned him out of his place and took his seat by the Vicereine, though she would barely speak to him.

At length Tom Connolly said to her: "I wouldn't have thought it of you, for you're so kind. Fancy blaming a poor young girl the first time she yields to a man!"

This response made the whole table roar and established Connolly's fame for impudence throughout Ireland.

Everyone was talking of him and I went about after him all through the gardens and whenever he spoke, my large ears were cocked to hear any word of wisdom that might fall from his lips. At length he noticed me and asked me why I followed him about.

"Everybody says you can win any woman you like, Mr. Connolly," I said half-ashamed. "I want to know how you do it, what you say to them."

"Faith, I don't know," he said, "but you're a funny little fellow. What age are you to be asking such questions?"

"I'm fourteen," I said boldly.

"I wouldn't have given you fourteen, but even fourteen is too young; you must wait." So I withdrew but still kept within earshot.

I heard him laughing with my eldest brother over my question and so imagined that I was forgiven, and the next day or the day after, finding me as assiduous as ever, he said:

"You know, your question amused me, and I thought I would try to find an answer to it, and here is one. When you can put a stiff penis in her hand and weep profusely the while, you're getting near any woman's heart. But don't forget the tears." I found the advice a counsel of perfection; I was unable to weep at such a moment, but I never forgot the words.*

There was a large barracks of Irish constabulary in Ballybay and the sub-inspector was a handsome fellow of five feet nine or ten named Walter Raleigh. He used to say that he was a descendant of the famous courtier of Queen Elizabeth, and he pronounced his name "Rolly," and assured us that his illustrious namesake had often spelt it in this way, which showed that he must have pronounced it as if written with an *o*. The reason I mention Raleigh here is that his sisters and mine were great friends and he came in and out of our house almost as if it were his own.

Every evening, when Vernon and Raleigh had nothing better to do, they cleared away the chairs in our back parlor, put on boxing gloves and had a set to. My father used to sit in a corner and watch them. Vernon was lighter and smaller, but quicker; still I used to think that Raleigh did not put out his full strength against him.

One of the first evenings when Vernon was complaining that Raleigh hadn't come in or sent, my father said: "Why not try Joe?" (My nickname!) In a jiffy I had the gloves on and got my first lesson from Vernon, who taught me at least how to hit straight and then how to guard and side-step. I was very quick and strong for my size, but for some time Vernon hit me very lightly. Soon, however, it became difficult for him to hit me at all; and

---

* Though Harris tells a funny story superbly, he usually misses its humor. There's little doubt that he took this advice to heart and did his best to squeeze out tears.

then I sometimes got a heavy blow that floored me. But with constant practice I improved rapidly and after a fortnight or so put on the gloves once with Raleigh. His blows were very much heavier and staggered me even to guard them, so I got accustomed to duck or side-step or slip every blow aimed at me while hitting back with all my strength. One evening when Vernon and Raleigh both had been praising me, I told them of Jones and how he bullied me; he had really made my life a misery to me. He never met me outside the school without striking or kicking me and his favorite name for me was "bog-trotter!" His attitude, too, affected the whole school: I had grown to hate him as much as I feared him.

They both thought I could beat him; but I described him as very strong and finally Raleigh decided to send for two pairs of four-ounce gloves, or fighting gloves, and use these with me to give me confidence. In the first half hour with the new gloves, Vernon did not hit me once and I had to acknowledge that he was stronger and quicker even than Jones. At the end of the holidays they both made me promise to slap Jones' face the very first time I saw him in the school.

On returning to school we always met in the big school room. When I entered the room there was silence. I was dreadfully excited and frightened, I don't know why, but fully resolved: "He can't kill me," I said to myself a thousand times; still I was in a trembling funk inwardly though composed enough in outward seeming. Jones and two others of the sixth stood in front of the empty fireplace: I went up to them. Jones nodded, "How d'ye do, Pat?"

"Fairly," I said, "but why do you take all the room?" and I jostled him aside; he immediately pushed me hard and I slapped his face, as I had promised. The elder boys held him back or the fight would have taken place then and there. "Will you fight?" he barked at me and I replied, "As much as you like, bully!" It was arranged that the fight should take place on the next afternoon, which happened to be a Wednesday and half-holiday. From three to six would give us time enough. That evening Stackpole asked me to his room and told me he would get the Doctor to stop the fight if I wished; I assured him it had to be and I preferred to have it settled.

"I'm afraid he's too old and strong for you," said Stackpole; I only smiled.

Next day the ring was made at the top of the playing field behind the haystack so that we could not be seen from the school. All the sixth and nearly all the school stood behind Jones; but Stackpole, while ostensibly strolling about, was always close to me. I felt very grateful to him: I don't know why, but his presence took away from my loneliness. At first the fight was almost a boxing-match. Jones shot out his left hand, my head slipped it and I countered with my right in his face: a moment later he rushed me but I ducked and side-stepped and hit him hard on the chin. I could feel the astonishment of the school in the dead silence.

"Good, good!" cried Stackpole behind me. "That's the way." And indeed it was the "way" of the fight in every round except one. We had been hard at it for some eight or ten minutes when I felt Jones getting weaker or losing his breath: at once I went in attacking with all my might, when suddenly, as luck would have it, I caught a right swing just under the left ear and was knocked clean off my feet: he could hit hard enough, that was clear. As I went into the middle of the ring for the next round, Jones peered at me.

"You got that, didn't ye, Pat?"

"Yes," I replied, "but I'll beat you black and blue for it," and the fight went on. I had made up my mind, lying on the ground, to strike only at his face. He was short and strong and my body blows didn't seem to make any impression on him; but if I could blacken all his face, the masters and especially the Doctor would understand what had happened.

Again and again Jones swung, first with right hand and then with his left, hoping to knock me down again; but my training had been too varied and complete and the knock-down blow had taught me the necessary caution. I ducked his swings, or side-stepped them and hit him right and left in the face till suddenly his nose began to bleed, and Stackpole cried out behind me in huge excitement: "That's the way, that's the way; keep on peppering him."

As I turned to smile at him, I found that a lot of the fags, former chums of mine, had come round to my corner and now were all smiling encouragement at me and bold exhortations to "give it him hard."

I then realized for the first time that I had only to keep on and be careful and the victory would be mine. A cold, hard exultation took the place of nervous excitement in me, and when I struck, I tried to cut with my knuckles, as Raleigh had once shown me.

The bleeding of Jones' nose took some time to stop and as soon as he came into the middle of the ring, I started it again with another right-hander. After this round his seconds and backers kept him so long in his corner that at length, on Stackpole's whispered advice, I went over and said to him: "Either fight or give in: I'm catching cold." He came out at once and rushed at me full of fight, but his face was all one bruise and his left eye nearly closed. Every chance I got, I struck at the right eye till it was in an even worse condition.

It is strange to me since that I never once felt pity for him and offered to stop: the truth is, he had bullied me so relentlessly and continually, had wounded my pride so often in public that even at the end I was filled with cold rage against him. I noticed everything: I saw that a couple of the sixth went away towards the school-house and afterwards returned with Shaddy, the second master. As they came round the haystack, Jones came out into the ring; he struck savagely right and left as I came within striking distance, but I slipped in outside his weaker left and hit him as hard as I could, first right, then left on the chin and down he went on his back.

At once there was a squeal of applause from the little fellows in my corner and I saw that Stackpole had joined Shaddy near Jones' corner. Suddenly Shaddy came right up to the ringside and spoke, to my astonishment, with a certain dignity.

"This fight must stop now," he said loudly. "If another blow is struck or word said, I'll report the disobedience to the Doctor." Without a word I went and put on my coat and waistcoat and collar, while his friends of the sixth escorted Jones to the schoolhouse.

I had never had so many friends and admirers in my life as came up to me then to congratulate me and testify to their admiration and good will. The whole lower school was on my side, it appeared, and had been from the outset, and one or two of the sixth, Herbert in especial, came over and praised me warmly. "A great fight," said Herbert, "and now perhaps we'll have less bullying; at any rate," he added humorously, "no one will want to bully you: you're a pocket professional; where did you learn to box?"

I had sense enough to smile and keep my own counsel. Jones didn't appear in school that night: indeed, for days after he was kept in sick bay upstairs. The fags and lower school boys brought me all sorts of stories how the doctor had come and said "he feared erysipelas; the bruises were so large and Jones must stay in bed and in the dark!" and a host of other details.

One thing was quite clear; my position in the school was radically changed. Stackpole spoke to the Doctor and I got a seat by myself in his classroom and only went to the form-master for special lessons; Stackpole became more than ever my teacher and friend.

When Jones first appeared in the school, we met in the sixth room while waiting for the Doctor to come in. I was talking with Herbert; Jones came in and nodded to me: I went over and held out my hands but said nothing. Herbert's nod and smile showed me I had done right. "Bygones should be bygones," he said in English fashion. I wrote the whole story to Vernon that night, thanking him, you may be sure, and Raleigh for the training and encouragement they had given me.

My whole outlook on life was permanently altered: I was cock-a-hoop and happy. One night I got thinking of E. . . . and for the first time in months practiced onanism. But next day I felt heavy and resolved that belief or no belief, self-restraint was a good thing for the health. All the next Christmas holidays spent in Rhyl I tried to get intimate with some girl, but failed. As soon as I tried to touch even their breasts, they drew away. I liked girls fully formed and they all thought, I suppose, that I was too young and too small: if they had only known!

One more incident belongs in this thirteenth year and is worthy perhaps of record. Freed of the bullying and senseless cruelty of the older boys who for the most part, still siding with Jones, left me severely alone, the restraints of school life began to irk me. "If I were free," I said to myself, "I'd go after E. . . . or some other girl and have a great time; as it is, I can do nothing, hope for nothing." Life was stale, flat and unprofitable to me. Besides, I had read nearly all the books I thought worth reading in the school library, and time hung heavy on my hands; I began to long for liberty as a caged bird.

What was the quickest way out? I knew that my father as a captain in the navy could give me or get me a nomination so that I might become a midshipman. Of course I'd have to be examined before I was fourteen; but I knew I could win a high place in any test.

The summer vacation, after I was thirteen on the fourteenth of February, I spent at home in Ireland, as I have told, and from time to time bothered my father to get me the nomination. He promised he would, and I took his promise seriously. All the autumn I studied carefully the subjects I was to be examined in, and from time to time wrote to my father, reminding him of his promise. But he seemed unwilling to touch on the matter in his letters, which were mostly filled with Biblical exhortations that sickened me with contempt for his brainless credulity. My unbelief made me feel immeasurably superior to him.

Christmas came and I wrote him a serious letter. I flattered him, saying that I knew his word was sacred: but the time-limit was at hand and I was getting nervous, lest some official delay might make me pass the prescribed limit of age. I got no reply: I wrote to Vernon, who said he would do his best with the governor. The days went on, the fourteenth of February came and went: I was fourteen. That way of escape into the wide world was closed to me by my father. I raged in hatred of him.

How was I to get free? Where should I go? What should I do? One day in an illustrated paper in '68 I read of the discovery of diamonds in the Cape, and then of the opening of the diamond fields. That prospect tempted me and I read all I could about South Africa, but one day I found that the cheapest passage to the Cape cost fifteen pounds and I despaired. Shortly afterwards I read that a steerage passage to New York could be had for five pounds; that amount seemed to me possible to get; for there was a prize of ten pounds for books to be given to the second in the mathematical scholarship exam that would take place in the summer. I thought I could win that, and I set myself to study mathematics harder than ever.

The result was—but I shall tell the result in its proper place. Meanwhile I began reading about America and soon learned of the buffalo and Indians on the Great Plains, and a myriad entrancing romantic pictures opened to my boyish imagining. I wanted to see the world and I had grown to dislike England; its snobbery, though I had caught the disease, was loathsome, and worse still, its spirit of sordid self-interest. The rich boys were favored by all the masters, even by Stackpole; I was disgusted with English life as I saw it. Yet there were good elements in it which I could not but see, which I shall try to indicate later.

Towards the middle of this winter term it was announced that at midsummer, besides a scene from a play of Plautus to be given in Latin, the trial scene of *The Merchant of Venice* would also be played—of course, by boys of the fifth and sixth form only, and rehearsals immediately began. Naturally I took out *The Merchant of Venice* from the school library and in one day knew it by heart. I could learn good poetry by a single careful reading; bad poetry or prose was much harder.

Nothing in the play appealed to me except Shylock and the first time I heard Fawcett of the sixth recite the part, I couldn't help grinning. He repeated the most passionate speeches like a lesson, in a singsong, monotonous voice. For days I went about spouting Shylock's defiance and one day, as luck would have it, Stackpole heard me. We had become great friends: I had done all algebra with him and was now devouring trigonometry, resolved to do conic sections afterwards, and then the calculus. Already there was only one boy who was my superior and he was captain of the sixth, Gordon, a big fellow of over seventeen, who intended to go to Cambridge with the eighty pound mathematical scholarship that summer.

Stackpole told the head that I would be a good Shylock; Fawcett to my amazement didn't want to play the Jew: he found it difficult even to learn the part, and finally it was given to me. I was particularly elated, for I felt that I could make a great hit.

One day my sympathy with the bullied got me a friend. The vicar's son, Edwards, was a nice boy of fourteen who had grown rapidly and was not strong. A brute of sixteen in the upper fifth was twisting his arm and hitting him on the writhen muscle and Edwards was trying hard not to cry. "Leave him alone, Johnson," I said. "Why do you bully?" "You ought to have a taste of it," he cried, letting Edwards go, however.

"Don't try it on me if you're wise," I retorted.

"Pat would like us to speak to him," he sneered and turned away. I shrugged my shoulders.

Edwards thanked me warmly for rescuing him and I asked him to come for a walk. He accepted and our friendship began, a friendship memorable for bringing me one novel and wonderful experience.

The vicarage was a large house with a good deal of ground about it. Edwards had some sisters but they were too young to interest me; the French governess, on the other hand, Mlle. Lucille, was very attractive with her black eyes and hair and quick, vivacious manner. She was of medium height and not more than eighteen. I made up to her at once and tried to talk French with her from the beginning. She was very kind to me and we got on together at once. She was lonely, I suppose, and I began well by telling her she was the prettiest girl in the whole place and the finest. She translated finest, I remember, as *la plus chic*.

The next half-holiday Edwards went into the house for something. I told her I wanted a kiss, and she said:

"You're only a boy, *mais gentil*," and she kissed me. When my lips dwelt on hers, she took my head in her hands, pushed it away and looked at me with surprise.

"You are a strange boy," she said musingly.

The next holiday I spent at the vicarage. I gave her a little French love letter I had copied from a book in the school library, and I was delighted when she read it and nodded at me, smiling, and tucked it away in her bodice. "Near her heart," I said to myself, but I had no chance even for a kiss, for Edwards always hung about. But late one afternoon he was called away by his mother for something and my opportunity came.

We usually sat in a sort of rustic summerhouse in the garden. This afternoon Lucille was seated, leaning back in an armchair right in front of the door, for the day was sultry-close, and when Edwards went, I threw myself on the doorstep at her feet: her dress clung to her form, revealing the outlines of her thighs and breasts seductively. I was wild with excitement. Suddenly I noticed her legs were apart; I could see her slim ankles. Pulses awoke throbbing in my forehead and throat: I begged for a kiss and got on my knees to take it: she gave me one; but when I persisted, she repulsed me, saying:

"*Non, non! Sois sage!*"

As I returned to my seat reluctantly, the thought came, "Put your hand up her clothes"; I felt sure I could reach her sex. She was seated on the edge of the chair and leaning back. The mere idea shook and scared me: but what can she do, I thought: she can only get angry. I thought again of all possible consequences: the example with E. . . . came to encourage and hearten me. I leaned round and knelt in front of her, smiling, begging for a kiss, and as she smiled in return, I put my hand boldly right up her clothes on her sex. I felt the soft hairs and the form of it in breathless ecstasy; but I scarcely held it when she sprang upright. "How dare you?" she cried, trying to push my hand away.

My sensations were too overpowering for words or act; my life was in my fingers; I held her cunt. A moment later I tried to touch her gently with my middle finger as I had touched E. . . . : 'twas a mistake: I no longer held her sex and at once Lucille whirled round and was free.

"I have a good mind to strike you," she cried. "I'll tell Mrs. Edwards," she snorted indignantly. "You're a bad, bad boy and I thought you nice. I'll never be kind to you again: I hate you!" She fairly stamped with anger.

I went to her, my whole being one prayer. "Don't spoil it all," I cried. "You hurt so when you are angry, dear."

She turned to me hotly. "I'm really angry, angry," she panted, "and you're a hateful rude boy and I don't like you any more," and she turned away again, shaking her dress straight. "Oh, how could I help it?" I began. "You're so pretty, oh, you are wonderful, Lucille!"

"Wonderful," she repeated, sniffing disdainfully, but I saw she was mollified.

"Kiss me," I pleaded, "and don't be cross."

"I'll never kiss you again," she replied quickly; "you can be sure of that." I went on begging, praising, pleading for ever so long, till at length she took my head in her hands, saying:

"If you'll promise never to do that again, never, I'll give you a kiss and try to forgive you."

"I can't promise," I said, "it was too sweet; but kiss me and I'll try to be good."

She kissed me a quick peck and pushed me away.

"Didn't you like it?" I whispered, "I did awfully. I can't tell you how I thrilled: oh, thank you, Lucille, thank you, you are the sweetest girl in the world, and I shall always be grateful to you, you dear!"

She looked down at me musingly, thoughtfully; I felt I was gaining ground.

"You are lovely there," I ventured in a whisper. "Please dear, what do you call it? I saw *chat* once: is that right, 'pussy?' "

"Don't talk of it," she cried impatiently. "I hate to think—"

"Be kind, Lucille," I pleaded. "You'll never be the same to me again: you were pretty before, chic and provoking, but now you're sacred. I don't love you, I adore you, reverence you, darling! May I say 'pussy?' "

"You're a strange boy," she said at length, "but you must never do that again; it's nasty and I don't like it. I—"

"Don't say such things!" I cried, pretending indignation. "You don't know what you're saying—nasty! Look, I'll kiss the fingers that have touched your pussy," and I suited the action to the word.

"Oh, don't," she cried and caught my hand in hers, "don't!" But somehow she leaned against me at the same time and left her lips on mine. Bit by bit my right hand went down to her sex again, this time on the outside of her dress, but at once she tore herself away and would not let me come near her again. My insane desire had again made me blunder. Yet she had half yielded, I knew, and that consciousness set me thrilling with triumph and hope, but alas! at that moment we heard Edwards shout to us as he left the house to rejoin us.

This experience had two immediate and unlooked for consequences: first of all, I could not sleep that night for thinking of Lucille's sex. When I fell asleep I dreamed of Lucille, dreamed that she had yielded to me and I was pushing my sex into hers; but there was some obstacle and while I was pushing, pushing, my seed spirted in an orgasm of pleasure—and at once I awoke and putting down my hand, found that I was still coming: the sticky, hot, milklike sperm was all over my hairs and prick.

I got up and washed and returned to bed; the cold water had quieted me; but soon by thinking of Lucille and her soft, hot, hairy "pussy," I grew randy again and in this state fell asleep. Again I dreamed of Lucille and again I was trying, trying in vain to get into her when again the spasm of pleasure overtook me; I felt my seed spirting hot and—I awoke.

But lo! when I put my hand down, there was no seed, only a little moisture just at the head of my sex—nothing more. Did it mean that I could only give forth seed once? I tested myself at once; while picturing Lucille's sex, its soft hot roundness and hairs, I caressed my sex, moving my hand faster up and down till soon I brought on the orgasm of pleasure and felt distinctly the hot thrills as if my seed were spirting, but nothing came, hardly even the moisture.

Next morning I tested myself at the high jump and found I couldn't clear the bar at an inch lower than usual. I didn't know what to do: why had I indulged so foolishly?

But next night the dream of Lucille came back again, and again I awoke after an acute spasm of pleasure, all wet with my own seed. What was I to do? I got up and washed and put cold water in a sponge on my testicles and all chilled crawled back into bed. But imagination was master. Time and again the dream came and awakened me. In the morning I felt exhausted, and washed-out and needed no test to assure me that I was physically below par.

That same afternoon I picked up by chance a little piece of whipcord and at once it occurred to me that if I tied this hard cord around my penis, as soon as the organ began to swell and stiffen in excitement, the cord would grow tight and awake me with the pain.

That night I tied up Tommy and gave myself up to thoughts of Lucille's private parts: as soon as my sex stood and grew stiff, the whipcord hurt dreadfully and I had to apply cold water at once to reduce my unruly member to ordinary proportions. I returned to bed and went to sleep: I had a short sweet dream of Lucille's beauties, but then awoke in agony. I got up quickly and sat on the cold marble slab of the washstand. That acted more speedily than even the cold water: why? I didn't learn the reason for many a year.

The cord was effective, did all I wanted: after this experience I wore it regularly and within a week was again able to walk under the bar and afterwards jump it, able to pull myself up with one hand till my chin was above the bar. I had conquered temptation and once more was captain of my body.

The second unsuspected experience was also a direct result, I believe, of my sex awakening with Lucille and the intense sex-excitement. At all events it came just after the love passages with her that I have described and *post hoc* is often *propter hoc*.

I had never yet noticed the beauties of nature; indeed, whenever I came across descriptions of scenery in my reading, I always skipped them as wearisome. Now of a sudden, in a moment, my eyes were unsealed to natural beauties. I remember the scene and my rapt wonder as if it were yesterday. It was a bridge across the Dee near Overton in full sunshine; on my right the river made a long curve, swirling deep under a wooded height, leaving a little tawny sand bank half bare just opposite to me: on my left both banks, thickly wooded, drew together and passed round a curve out of sight. I was entranced and speechless—enchanted by the sheer color-beauty of the scene—sunlit water there and shadowed here, reflecting the gorgeous vesture of the wooded height. And when I left the place and came out again and looked at the adjoining cornfields, golden against the green of the hedgerows and scattered trees, the colors took on a charm I had never noticed before: I could not understand what had happened to me.

It was the awakening of sex-life in me, I believe, that first revealed to me the beauty of inanimate nature.

A night or two later I was ravished by a moon nearly at the full that flooded our playing field with ivory radiance, making the haystack in the corner a thing of supernal beauty.

Why had I never before seen the wonder of the world, the sheer loveliness of nature all about me? From this time on I began to enjoy descriptions of scenery in the books I read, and began, too, to love landscapes in painting.

Thank goodness! the miracle was accomplished, at long last, and my life enriched, ennobled, transfigured as by the bounty of God! From that day on I began to live an enchanted life, for at once I tried to see beauty everywhere and at all times of day and night caught glimpses that ravished me with delight and turned my being into a hymn of praise and joy.

Faith had left me, and with faith, hope in heaven or indeed in any future existence: saddened and fearful, I was as one in prison with an undetermined sentence; but now in a moment the prison had become a paradise, the walls of the actual had fallen away into frames of entrancing pictures. Dimly I became conscious that if this life were sordid and mean, petty and unpleasant, the fault was in myself and in my blindness. I began then for the first time to understand that I myself was a magician and could create my own fairyland, ay, and my own heaven, transforming this world into the throne-room of a god!

This joy and this belief I want to impart to others more than almost anything else, for this has been to me a new Gospel of courage and resolve and certain reward, a man's creed teaching that as you grow in wisdom and courage and kindness, all good things are added unto you.

I find that I am outrunning my story and giving here a stage of thought and belief that only became mine much later; but the beginning of my individual soul-life was this experience, that I had been blind to natural beauty and now could see; this was the root and germ, so to speak, of the later faith that guided all my mature life, filling me with courage and spilling over into hope and joy ineffable.

Very soon the first command of it came to my lips almost every hour: "Blame your own blindness! Always blame yourself!"

Chapter IV

From School to America

EARLY IN JANUARY there was a dress rehearsal of the trial scene of *The Merchant of Venice*. The grandee of the neighborhood who owned the great park, Sir. W. W. W., some M. P.'s, notably a Mr. Whalley,* who had a pretty daughter and lived in the vicinity, and the vicar and his family were invited, and others whom I did not know; but with the party from the vicarage came Lucille.

The big schoolroom had been arranged as a sort of theatre and the estrada at one end, where the head-master used to throne it on official occasions, was converted into a makeshift stage and draped by a big curtain that could be drawn back or forth at will.

The Portia was a very handsome lad of sixteen named Herbert, gentle and kindly, yet redeemed from effeminacy by the fact that he was the fleetest sprinter in the school and could do the hundred yards in eleven and a half seconds. The Duke was, of course, Jones; and the merchant, Antonio, a big fellow named Vernon; and I had got Edwards the part of Bassanio; and a pretty boy in the fourth form was taken as Nerissa. So far as looks went the cast was passable; but the Duke recited his lines as if they had been imperfectly learned and so the trial scene opened badly. But the part of Shylock suited me intimately and I had learned how to recite. Now before E. . . . and Lucille, I was set on doing better than my best. When my cue came, I bowed low before the Duke and then bowed again to left and right of him in silence and formally, as if I, the outcast Jew, were saluting the whole court; then in a voice that at first I simply made slow and clear and hard, I began the famous reply:

> I have possessed your Grace of what I purpose;
> And by our Holy Sabbath have I sworn
> To have the due and forfeit of my bond.

I don't expect to be believed; but nevertheless I am telling the bare truth when I say that in my impersonation of Shylock I brought in the very

* George Hammond Whalley (1813– ?); sent to Commons from Peterborough, 1852–53, 1859.

piece of "business" that made Henry Irving's* Shylock fifteen years later "ever memorable," according to the papers.

When at the end, baffled and beaten, Shylock gives in:

> I pray you, give me leave to go from hence,
> I am not well: send the deed after me,
> And I will sign it,

the Duke says, "Get thee gone, but do it," and Gratiano insults the Jew— the only occasion, I think, when Shakespeare allows the beaten to be insulted by a gentleman.

On my way to the door as Shylock I stopped, bent low before the Duke's dismissal; but at Gratiano's insult, I turned slowly round, while drawing myself up to my full height and scanning him from head to foot.

Irving used to return all across the stage, and folding his arms on his breast, look down on him with measureless contempt.

When, fifteen years later, Irving, at the Garrick Club one night after supper asked me what I thought of this new "business," I replied that if Shylock had done what he did, Gratiano would probably have spat in his face and then kicked him off the stage. Shylock complains that the Christians spat upon his gaberdine.

My boyish, romantic reading of the part, however, was essentially the same as Irving's, and Irving's reading was cheered in London to the echo because it was a rehabilitation of the Jew; and the Jew rules the roost today in all the cities of Europe.

At my first words I could feel the younger members of the audience look about as if to see if such reciting as mine was proper and permitted, then one after the other gave in to the flow and flood of passion. When I had finished everyone cheered, Whalley and Lady W. . . . enthusiastically, and to my delight, Lucille as well.

After the rehearsal, everyone crowded about me. "Where did you learn?" "Who taught you?" At length Lucille came. "I knew you were someone," she said in her pretty way (*quelqu'un*), "but it was extraordinary! You'll be a great actor, I'm sure."

"And yet you deny me a kiss," I whispered, taking care no one should hear.

"I deny you nothing," she replied, turning away, leaving me transfixed with hope and assurance of delight. "Nothing," I said to myself, "nothing means everything"; a thousand times I said it over to myself in an ecstasy.

That was my first happy night in England. Mr. Whalley congratulated me and introduced me to his daughter, who praised me enthusiastically, and best of all, the Doctor said, "We must make you stage manager, Harris, and I hope you'll put some of your fire into the other actors."

To my astonishment my triumph did me harm with the boys. Some

---

* (1838–1905); the noted actor, whom Harris mentions frequently.

sneered, while all agreed that I did it to show off. Jones and the sixth began the boycott again. I didn't mind much, for I had heavier disappointments and dearer hopes.

The worst was I found it difficult to see Lucille in the bad weather; indeed, I hardly caught a glimpse of her the whole winter. Edwards asked me frequently to the vicarage; she might have made half a dozen meetings but she would not, and I was sick at heart with disappointment and the regret of unfulfilled desire. It was March or April before I was alone with her in her schoolroom at the vicarage. I was too cross with her to be more than polite. Suddenly she said: "*Vous me boudez.*" I shrugged my shoulders.

"You don't like me," I began, "so what's the use of my caring?"

"I like you a great deal," she said, "but—"

"No, no," I said, shaking my head. "If you really liked me, you wouldn't avoid me and—"

"Perhaps it's because I like you too much—"

"Then you'd make me happy," I broke in.

"Happy," she repeated. "How can I?"

"By letting me kiss you, and—"

"Yes, and—" she repeated significantly.

"What harm does it do you?" I asked.

"What harm?" she repeated. "Don't you know it's wrong? One should only do that with one's husband; you know that."

"I don't know anything of the sort," I cried. "That's silly. We don't believe that today."

"I believe it," she said gravely.

"But if you didn't, you'd let me?" I cried. "Say that, Lucille. That would be almost as good, for it would show you liked me a little."

"You know I like you a great deal," she replied.

"Kiss me then," I said. "There's no harm in that." And when she kissed me I put my hand over her breasts; they thrilled me, they were so elastic-firm; and in a moment my hand slid down her body, but she drew away at once, quietly but with resolve.

"No, no," she said, half smiling.

"Please," I begged.

"I can't," she said, shaking her head. "I mustn't. Let us talk of other things. How is the play getting on?" But I could not talk of the play as she stood there before me. For the first time I divined through her clothes nearly all the beauties of her form. The bold curves of hip and breast tantalized me and her face was expressive and defiant.

How was it I had never noticed all the details before? Had I been blind? Or did Lucille dress to show off her figure? Certainly her dresses were arranged to display the form more than English dresses, but I too had become more curious, more observant. Would life go on showing me new beauties I had not even imagined?

My experience with E. . . . and Lucille made the routine of school life almost intolerable to me. I could only force myself to study by reminding myself of the necessity of winning the second prize in the mathematical scholarship, which would give me ten pounds and ten pounds would take me to America.

Soon after the Christmas holidays I had taken the decisive step. The examination in winter was not nearly so important as the one that ended the summer term, but it had been epoch-making to me. My punishments having compelled me to learn two or three books of Vergil by heart and whole chapters of Caesar and Livy, I had come to some knowledge of Latin: in the examination I had beaten not only all my class, but thanks to trigonometry and Latin and history, all the two next classes as well. As soon as the school reassembled I was put in the upper fifth. All the boys were from two to three years older than I was, and they all made cutting remarks about me to each other and avoided speaking to "Pat." All this strengthened my resolution to get to America as soon as I could.

Meanwhile I worked as I had never worked, at Latin and Greek as well as mathematics, but chiefly at Greek, for there I was backward: by Easter I had mastered the grammar—irregular verbs and all—and was about the first in the class. My mind, too, through my religious doubts and gropings and through the reading of the thinkers had grown astonishingly: one morning I construed a piece of Latin that had puzzled the best in the class and the Doctor nodded at me approvingly. Then came the step I spoke of as decisive.

The morning prayers were hardly over one bitter morning when the Doctor rose and gave out the terms of the scholarship exam at midsummer, the winner to get eighty pounds a year for three years at Cambridge, and the second ten pounds with which to buy books. "All boys," he added, "who wish to go in for this scholarship will now stand up and give their names." I thought only Gordon would stand up, but when I saw Johnson get up and Fawcett and two or three others, I too got up. A sort of derisive growl went through the school; but Stackpole smiled at me and nodded his head as much as to say, "They'll see," and I took heart of grace and gave my name very distinctly. Somehow I felt that the step was decisive.

I liked Stackpole and this term he encouraged me to come to his rooms to talk whenever I felt inclined, and as I had made up my mind to use all the half-holidays for study, this association did me a lot of good and his help was invaluable.

One day when he had just come into his room, I shot a question at him and he stopped, came over to me and put his arm on my shoulder as he answered. I don't know how I knew; but by some instinct I felt a caress in the apparently innocent action. I didn't like to draw away or show him I objected; but I buried myself feverishly in the trigonometry and he soon moved away.

When I thought of it afterwards I recalled the fact that his marked liking for me began after my fight with Jones. I had often been on the point of confessing to him my love-passages; but now I was glad I had kept them strenuously to myself, for day by day I noticed that his liking for me grew, or rather his compliments and flatteries increased. I hardly knew what to do: working with him and in his room was a godsend to me; yet at the same time I didn't like him much or admire him really.

In some ways he was curiously dense. He spoke of the school life as the happiest of all and the healthiest; a good moral tone here, he would say, no lying, cheating or scandal, much better than life outside. I used to find it difficult not to laugh in his face. Moral tone indeed! When the Doctor came down out of temper, it was usually accepted among the boys that he had had his wife in the night and was therefore a little below par physically.

Though a really good mathematical scholar and a first rate teacher, patient and painstaking, with a gift of clear exposition, Stackpole seemed to me stupid and hidebound and soon I found that by laughing at his compliments, I could balk his desire to lavish on me his unwelcome caresses.

Once he kissed me but my amused smile made him blush while he muttered shamefacedly, "You're a queer lad!" At the same time I knew quite well that if I encouraged him, he would take further liberties.

One day he talked of Jones and Henry H. . . . He had evidently heard something of what had taken place in our bedroom; but I pretended not to know what he meant and when he asked me whether none of the big boys had made up to me, I ignored big Fawcett's smutty excursions and said, "No," adding that I was interested in girls and not in dirty boys. For some reason or other Stackpole seemed to me younger than I was and not twelve years older, and I had no real difficulty in keeping him within the bounds of propriety till the math exam.

I was asked once whether I thought that "Shaddy," as we called the housemaster, had ever had a woman. The idea of "Shaddy" as a virgin filled us with laughter; but when one spoke of him as a lover, it was funnier still. He was a man about forty, tall and fairly strong: he had a degree from some college in Manchester, but to us little snobs he was a bounder because he had not been to either Oxford or Cambridge. He was fairly capable, however.

But for some reason or other he had a down on me and I grew to hate him and was always thinking of how I might hurt him. My new habit of forcing myself to watch and observe everything came to my aid. There were five or six polished oak steps up to the big bedroom where fourteen of us slept. "Shaddy" used to give us half an hour to get into bed and then would come up, and standing just inside the door under the gaslight would ask us, "Have you all said your prayers?" We all answered: "Yes, Sir"; then would come his, "Goodnight, boys," and our stereotyped reply, "Goodnight, Sir."

He would then turn out the light and go downstairs to his room. The oak steps outside were worn in the middle and I had noticed that as one goes downstairs one treads on the very edge of each step.

One day "Shaddy" had maddened me by giving me one hundred lines of Vergil to learn by heart for some trifling peccadillo. That night, having provided myself with a cake of brown Windsor soap, I ran upstairs before the other boys and rubbed the soap freely on the edge of the two top steps, and then went on to undress.

When "Shaddy" put out the light and stepped down to the second step, there was a slip and then a great thud as he half slid, half fell to the bottom. In a moment, for my bed was nearest the door, I had sprung up, opened the door and made incoherent exclamations of sympathy as I helped him to get up.

"I've hurt my hip," he said, putting his hand on it. He couldn't account for his fall.

Grinning to myself as I went back, I rubbed the soap off the top step with my handkerchief and got into bed again, where I chuckled over the success of my stratagem. He had only got what he richly deserved, I said to myself.

At length the long term wore to its end; the exam was held and after consulting Stackpole I was very sure of the second prize. "I believe," he said one day, "that you'd rather have the second prize than the first." "Indeed I would," I replied without thinking.

"Why," he asked, "why?" I only just restrained myself in time or I'd have given him the true reason. "You'll come nearer winning the scholarship," he said at length, "than any of them guesses."

After the exams came the athletic games, much more interesting than the beastly lessons. I won two first prizes and Jones four, but I gained fifteen "seconds," a record, I believe, for according to my age I was still in the lower school.

I was fully aware of the secret of my success and, strange to say, it did not increase but rather diminished my conceit. I won, not through natural advantages but by will power and practice. I should have been much prouder had I succeeded through natural gifts. For instance, there was a boy named Reggie Miller, who at sixteen was five feet ten in height, while I was still under five feet: do what I would, he could jump higher than I could, though he only jumped up to his chin, while I could jump the bar above my head. I believed that Reggie could easily practice and then out-jump me still more. I had yet to learn in life that the resolved will to succeed was more than any natural advantage. But this lesson only came to me later. From the beginning I was taking the highway to success in everything by strengthening my will even more than my body. Thus, every handicap in natural deficiency turns out to be an advantage in life to the brave soul, whereas every natural gift is surely a handicap. Demosthenes had a difficulty in his speech; practicing to overcome this made him the greatest of orators.

The last day came at length and at eleven o'clock all the school and a goodly company of guests and friends gathered in the schoolroom to hear the results of the examinations and especially the award of the scholarships. Though most of the boys were early at the great blackboard where the official figures were displayed, I didn't even go near it till one little boy told me shyly: "You're ahead of your form and sure of your remove."

I found this to be true, but wasn't even elated. A Cambridge professor, it appeared, had come down in person to announce the result of the math scholarship.

He made a rather long talk, telling us that the difficulty of deciding had been unusually great, for there was practical equality between two boys: indeed, he might have awarded the scholarship to Number Nine (my number) and not to Number One on the sheer merit of the work, but when he found that the one boy was under fifteen while the other was eighteen and ready for the university, he felt it only right to take the view of the headmaster and give the scholarship to the older boy, for the younger one was very sure to win it next year and even next year he would still be too young for university life. He therefore gave the scholarship to Gordon and the second prize of ten pounds to Harris. Gordon stood up and bowed his thanks while the whole school cheered and cheered again: then the examiner called on me. I had taken in the whole situation. I wanted to get away with all the money I could and as soon as I could. My cue was to make myself unpleasant: accordingly, I got up and thanked the examiner, saying that I had no doubt of his wish to be fair. "But," I added, "had I known the issue was to be determined by age, I should not have entered. Now I can only say that I will never enter again," and I sat down.

The sensation caused by my little speech was a thousand times greater than I had expected. There was a breathless silence and mute expectancy. The Cambridge professor turned to the head of the school and talked with him very earnestly, with visible annoyance, indeed, and then rose again.

"I must say," he began, "I have to say," repeating himself, "that I have the greatest sympathy with Harris. I was never in so embarrassing a position. I must leave the whole responsibility with the headmaster. I can't do anything else, unfortunately!" and he sat down, evidently annoyed.

The Doctor got up and made a long hypocritical speech. It was one of those difficult decisions one is forced sometimes to make in life: he was sure that everyone would agree that he had tried to act fairly, and so far as he could make it up to the younger boy, he certainly would; he hoped next year to award him the scholarship with as good a heart as he now gave him his check; and he fluttered it in the air.

The masters all called me and I went up to the platform and accepted the check, smiling with delight, and when the Cambridge professor shook hands with me and would have further excused himself, I whispered shyly, "It's all right, Sir, I'm glad that you decided as you did." He laughed aloud with pleasure, put his arm round my shoulder and said:

"I'm obliged to you; you're certainly a good loser, or winner, perhaps I ought to have said, and altogether a remarkable boy. Are you really under sixteen?" I nodded smiling, and the rest of the prize-giving went off without further incident, save that when I appeared on the platform to get the form prize of books, he smiled pleasantly at me and led the cheering.

I've described the whole incident, for it illustrates to me the English desire to be fair: it is really a guiding impulse in them, on which one may reckon, and so far as my experience goes, it is perhaps stronger in them than in any other race. If it were not for their religious hypocrisies, childish conventions and above all, their incredible snobbishness, their love of fair play alone would make them the worthiest leaders of humanity. All this I felt then as a boy as clearly as I see it today.

I knew that the way of my desire was open to me. Next morning I asked to see the head; he was very amiable; but I pretended to be injured and disappointed. "My father," I said, "reckons, I think, on my success and I'd like to see him before he hears the bad news from anyone else. Would you please give me the money for my journey and let me go today? It isn't very pleasant for me to be here now."

"I'm sorry," said the Doctor (and I think he was sorry), "of course I'll do anything I can to lighten your disappointment. It's very unfortunate but you must not be downhearted. Professor S. . . . . says that your papers ensure your success next year, and I—well, I'll do anything in my power to help you."

I bowed: "Thank you, Sir. Can I go today? There's a train to Liverpool at noon."

"Certainly, certainly, if you wish it," he said. "I'll give orders immediately," and he cashed the check for ten pounds as well, with only a word that it was nominally to be used to buy books with, but he supposed it did not matter seriously.

By noon I was in the train for Liverpool with fifteen pounds in my pocket, five pounds being for my fare to Ireland. I was trembling with excitement and delight; at length I was going to enter the real world and live as I wished to live. I had no regrets, no sorrows. I was filled with lively hopes and happy presentiments.

As soon as I got to Liverpool, I drove to the Adelphi Hotel and looked up the steamers and soon found one that charged only four pounds for a steerage passage to New York, and to my delight this steamer was starting next day about two o'clock. By four o'clock I had booked my passage and paid for it. The clerk said something or other about bedding, but I paid no attention. For just on entering his office I had seen an advertisement of *The Two Roses,** a "romantic drama" to be played that night, and I was determined to get a seat and see it. Do you know what courage that act required? More than was needed to cut loose from everyone I loved and go to America. For my father was a Puritan of the Puritans and had often spoken of the theatre as the "open door to hell."

* A comedy in three acts by J. Albery. It was produced in London on June 4, 1870.

I had lost all belief in hell or heaven, but a cold shiver went through me as I bought my ticket and time and again in the next four hours I was on the point of forfeiting it without seeing the play. What if my father was right? I couldn't help the fear that came over me like a vapor.

I was in my seat as the curtain rose and sat for three hours enraptured; it was just a romantic love-story, but the heroine was lovely and affectionate and true and I was in love with her at first sight. When the play was over I went into the street, resolved to keep myself pure for some girl like the heroine: no moral lesson I have received before or since can compare with that given me by that first night in a theatre. The effect lasted for many a month and made self-abuse practically impossible to me ever afterwards. The preachers may digest this fact at their leisure.

The next morning I had a good breakfast at the Adelphi Hotel and before ten I was on board the steamer, had stowed away my trunk and taken my station by my sleeping place traced in chalk on the deck. About noon the doctor came round, a young man of good height with a nonchalant manner, reddish hair, Roman nose and easy, unconventional ways.

"Whose is this berth?" he asked, pointing to mine.

"Mine, Sir," I replied.

"Tell your father or mother," he said curtly, "that you must have a mattress like this," and he pointed to one, "and two blankets," he added.

"Thank you, Sir," I said and shrugged my shoulders at his interference. In another hour he came round again.

"Why is there no mattress here and no blanket?" he asked.

"Because I don't need 'em," I replied.

"You must have them," he barked. "It's the rule, d'ye understand?" and he hurried on with his inspection. In half an hour he was back again.

"You haven't the mattress yet," he snarled.

"I don't want a mattress," I replied.

"Where's your father or mother?" he asked.

"Haven't got any," I retorted.

"Do they let children like you go to America?" he cried. "What age are you?"

I was furious with him for exposing my youth there in public before everyone. "How does it matter to you?" I asked disdainfully, "You are not responsible for me, thank God!"

"I am though," he said, "to a certain degree, at least. Are you really going to America on your own?"

"I am," I rejoined casually and rudely.

"What to do?" was his next query.

"Anything I can get," I replied.

"Hm," he muttered, "I must see to this."

Ten minutes later he returned again. "Come with me," he said, and I followed him to his cabin—a comfortable stateroom with a good berth on the right of the door as you entered, and a good sofa opposite.

"Are you really alone?" he asked.

I nodded, for I was a little afraid he might have the power to forbid me to go and I resolved to say as little as possible.

"What age are you?" was his next question.

"Sixteen." I lied boldly.

"Sixteen!" he repeated. "You don't look it but you speak as if you had been well educated." I smiled; I had already measured the crass ignorance of the peasants in the steerage.

"Have you any friends in America?" he asked.

"What do you want to question me for?" I demanded. "I've paid for my passage and I'm doing no harm."

"I want to help you," he said. "Will you stay here until we draw out and I get a little time?"

"Certainly," I said, "I'd rather be here than with those louts, and if I might read your books—"

I had noticed that there were two little oak bookcases, one on each side of the washing stand, and smaller books and pictures scattered about.

"Of course you may," he rejoined, and threw open the door of the bookcase. There was a Macaulay staring at me.

"I know his poetry," I said, seeing that the book contained his essays and was written in prose. "I'd like to read this."

"Go ahead," he said smiling, "in a couple of hours I'll be back." When he returned he found me curled upon his sofa, lost in fairyland. I had just come to the end of the essay on Clive and was breathless. "You like it?" he asked. "I should just think I did," I replied. "It's better even than his poetry," and suddenly I closed the book and began to recite:

With all his faults, and they were neither few nor small, only one cemetery was worthy to contain his remains. In the Great Abbey—*

The doctor took the book from me where I held it.

"Are you reciting from Clive?" he asked.

"Yes, I said, "but the essay on Warren Hastings is just as good," and I began again:

He looked like a great man, and not like a bad one. A person small and emaciated, yet deriving dignity from a carriage which, while it indicated deference to the Court, indicated also habitual self-possession and self-respect. A high and intellectual forehead, a brow pensive but not gloomy, a mouth of inflexible decision, a face on which was written as legibly as under the great picture in the Council Chamber of Calcutta, *Mens aequa in arduis:* such was the aspect with which the great proconsul presented himself to his judges.

* This quotation is also from *Warren Hastings* (see below). Harris renders the first sentence precisely, but the second sentence actually runs: "In that temple of silence and reconciliation, where the enmities of twenty generations lie buried, in the Great Abbey . . ."

"Have you learned all this by heart?" cried the doctor, laughing.

"I don't have to learn stuff like that," I replied. "One reading is enough." He stared at me.

"I was surely right in bringing you down here," he began. "I wanted to get you a berth in the intermediate, but there's no room: if you could put up with that sofa, I'd have the steward make up a bed for you on it."

"Oh, would you?" I cried. "How kind of you; and you'll let me read your books?" "Every one of 'em," he replied, adding, "I only wish I could make as good use of them."

The upshot of it was that in an hour he had drawn some of my story from me and we were great friends. His name was Keogh. "Of course he's Irish," I said to myself as I went to sleep that night, "no one else would have been so kind."

The ordinary man will think I am bragging here about my memory. He's mistaken. Swinburne's memory especially for poetry was far, far better than mine, and I have always regretted the fact that a good memory often prevents one thinking for oneself. I shall come back to this belief of mine when I later explain how want of books gave me whatever originality I possess. A good memory and books at command are two of the greatest dangers of youth and form by themselves a terrible handicap, but like all gifts, a good memory is apt to make you friends among the unthinking, especially when you are very young.

As a matter of fact, Doctor Keogh went about bragging of my memory and power of reciting until some of the cabin passengers became interested in the extraordinary schoolboy. The outcome was that I was asked to recite one evening in the first cabin, and afterwards a collection was taken up for me and a first-class passage paid and about twenty dollars over and above was given to me. Besides, an old gentleman offered to adopt me and play second father to me, but I had not got rid of one father to take on another, so I kept as far away from him as I decently could.

I am again, however, running ahead of my story. The second evening of the voyage, the sea got up a little and there was a great deal of sickness. Doctor Keogh was called out of his cabin and while he was away, someone knocked at the door. I opened it and found a pretty girl.

"Where's the doctor?" she asked. I told her he had been called to a cabin passenger.

"Please tell him," she said, "when he returns, that Jessie Kerr, the chief engineer's daughter, would like to see him."

"I'll go after him now if you wish, Miss Jessie," I said. "I know where he is."

"It isn't important," she rejoined, "but I feel giddy, and he told me he could cure it."

"Coming up on the deck is the best cure," I declared. "The fresh air will soon blow the sick feeling away. You'll sleep like a top and tomorrow morning you'll be all right. Will you come?" She consented readily and in ten minutes admitted that the slight nausea had disappeared in the sharp breeze. As we walked up and down the dimly lighted deck I had now and then to support her, for the ship was rolling a little under a sou-wester. Jessie told me something about herself, how she was going to New York to spend some months with an elder married sister and how strict her father was. In return she had my whole story and could hardly believe I was only sixteen. Why, she was over sixteen and she could never have stood up and recited piece after piece as I did in the cabin; she thought it "wonderful."

Before she went down, I told her she was the prettiest girl on board, and she kissed me and promised to come up the next evening and have another walk. "If you've nothing better to do," she said at parting, "you might come forward to the little promenade deck of the second cabin and I'll get one of the men to arrange a seat in one of the boats for us." "Of course," I promised gladly, and spent the next afternoon with Jessie in the stern sheets of the great launch where we were out of sight of everyone, and out of hearing as well.

There we were, tucked in with two rugs and cradled, so to speak, between sea and sky, while the keen air whistling past increased our sense of solitude. Jessie, though rather short, was a very pretty girl with large hazel eyes and fair complexion.

I soon got my arm around her and kept kissing her till she told me she had never known a man so greedy of kisses as I was. It was delicious flattery to me to speak of me as a man, and in return I raved about her eyes and mouth and form; caressing her left breast, I told her I could divine the rest and knew she had a lovely body. But when I put my hand up her clothes, she stopped me when I got just above her knee and said:

"We'd have to be engaged before I could let you do that. Do you really love me?"

Of course I swore I did, but when she said she'd have to tell her father that we were engaged to be married, cold shivers went down my back.

"I can't marry for a long time yet," I said. "I'll have to make a living first and I'm not very sure where I'll begin." But she had heard that an old man wished to adopt me and everyone said that he was very rich and even her father admitted that I'd be "well-fixed."

Meanwhile my right hand was busy. I had got my fingers to her warm flesh between the stockings and the drawers and was wild with desire: soon, mouth on mouth, I touched her sex.

What a gorgeous afternoon we had! I had learned enough now to go slow and obey what seemed to be her moods. Gently, gently, I caressed her sex with my finger till it opened and she leaned against me and kissed me of her own will, while her eyes turned up and her whole being was lost in thrills of ecstasy. When she asked me to stop and take my hand away, I did her bidding at once and was rewarded by being told that I was a "dear boy" and "a sweet," and soon the embracing and caressing began again. She moved now in response to my lascivious touchings, and when the ecstasy came on her, she clasped me close and kissed me passionately with hot lips and afterward in my arms wept a little, and then pouted that she was cross with me for being so naughty. But her eyes gave themselves to me even while she tried to scold.

The dinner bell rang and she said she'd have to go, and we made a meeting for afterwards on the top deck; but as she was getting up she yielded again to my hand with a little sigh and I found her sex all wet, wet!

She got down out of the boat by the main rigging and I waited a few moments before following her. At first our caution seemed likely to be rewarded, chiefly, I have thought since, because everyone believed me to be too young and too small to be taken seriously. But everything is quickly known on seaboard, at least by the sailors.

I went down to Dr. Keogh's cabin, once more joyful and grateful, as I had been with E. . . . My fingers were like eyes gratifying my curiosity, and the curiosity was insatiable. Jessie's thighs were smooth and firm and round: I took delight in recalling the touch of them, and her bottom was firm like warm marble. I wanted to see her naked and study her beauties one after the other. Her sex, too, was wonderful, fuller even than Lucille's, and her eyes were finer. Oh, life was a thousand times better than school. I thrilled with joy and passionate wild hopes—perhaps Jessie would let me, perhaps—I was breathless.

Our walk on deck that evening was not so satisfactory: the wind had gone down and there were many other couples and the men all seemed to know Jessie, and it was Miss Kerr here, and Miss Kerr there, till I was cross and disappointed. I couldn't get her to myself save at moments, but then I had to admit she was as sweet as ever and her Aberdeen accent even was quaint and charming to me.

I got some long kisses at odd moments and just before we went down I drew her behind a boat in the davits and was able to caress her little breasts; and when she turned her back to me to go, I threw my arms round her hips and drew them against me, and she leant her head back over her shoulder and gave me her mouth with dying eyes. The darling! Jessie was apt at all love's lessons.

The next day was cloudy and rain threatened, but we were safely ensconced in the boat by two o'clock, as soon as lunch was over, and we hoped no one had seen us. An hour passed in caressings and fondlings, in love's words and love's promises; I had won Jessie to touch my sex and her eyes seemed to deepen as she caressed it.

"I love you, Jessie. Won't you let it touch yours?"

She shook her head. "Not here, not in the open," she whispered and then, "Wait a little till we get to New York, dear," and our mouths sealed the compact.

Then I asked her about New York and her sister's house, and we were discussing where we should meet, when a big head and beard showed above the gunwale of the boat and a deep Scotch voice said: "I want ye, Jessie, I've been luiking everywhere for ye."

"Awright, father," she said. "I'll be down in a minute."

"Come quick," said the voice as the head disappeared.

"I'll tell him we love each other and he won't be angry for long," whispered Jessie; but I was doubtful. As she got up to go my naughty hand went up her dress behind and felt her warm, smooth buttocks. Ah, the poignancy of the ineffable sensations; her eyes smiled over her shoulder at me and she was gone—and the sunlight with her.

I still remember the sick disappointment as I sat in the boat alone. Life then, like school, had its chagrins, and as the pleasures were keener, the balks and blights were bitterer. For the first time in my life vague misgivings came over me, a heartshaking suspicion that everything delightful and joyous in life had to be paid for—I wouldn't harbor the fear. If I had to pay, I'd pay; after all, the memory of the ecstasy could never be taken away, while the sorrow was fleeting. And that faith I still hold.

Next day the chief steward allotted me a berth in a cabin with an English midshipman of seventeen going out to join his ship in the West Indies. William Ponsonby was not a bad sort, but he talked of nothing but girls from morning till night and insisted that Negresses were better than white girls: they were far more passionate, he said.

He showed me his sex; excited himself before me, while assuring me he meant to have a Miss Le Breton, a governess, who was going out to take up a position in Pittsburgh.

"But suppose you put her in the family way?" I asked.

"That's not my funeral," was his answer, and seeing that the cynicism shocked me, he went on to say there was no danger if you withdraw in time. Ponsonby never opened a book and was astoundingly ignorant: he didn't seem to care to learn anything that hadn't to do with sex. He introduced me to Miss Le Breton the same evening. She was rather tall, with fair hair and blue eyes, and she praised my reciting. To my wonder she was a woman and pretty, and I could see by the way she looked at Ponsonby that she was more than a little in love with him. He was above middle height, strong and good tempered, and that was all I could see in him.

Miss Jessie kept away the whole evening, and when I saw her father on the "upper deck," he glowered at me and went past without a word. That night I told Ponsonby my story, or part of it, and he declared he would find a sailor to carry a note to Jessie next morning if I'd write it.

Besides, he proposed we should occupy the cabin alternate afternoons; for example, he'd take it next day and I must not come near it, and if at any time one of us found the door locked, he was to respect his chum's privacy. I agreed to it all with enthusiasm and went to sleep in a fever of hope. Would Jessie risk her father's anger and come to me? Perhaps she would: at any rate I'd write and ask her and I did. In one hour the same sailor came back with her reply. It ran like this: "Dear love, father is mad, we shall have to take great care for two or three days; as soon as it's safe, I'll come—your loving Jess," with a dozen crosses for kisses.

That afternoon, without thinking of my compact with Ponsonby, I went to our cabin and found the door locked: at once our compact came into my head and I went quickly away. Had he succeeded so quickly? And was she with him in bed? The half-certainty made my heart beat.

That evening Ponsonby could not conceal his success, but as he used it partly to praise his mistress, I forgave him.

"She has the prettiest figure you ever saw," he declared, "and is really a dear. We had just finished when you came to the door. I said it was some mistake and she believed me. She wants me to marry her, but I can't marry. If I were rich, I'd marry quick enough. It's better than risking some foul disease," and he went on to tell about one of his colleagues, John Lawrence, who got black pox, as he called syphilis, caught from a Negress.

"He didn't notice it for three months," Ponsonby went on, "and it got into his system; his nose got bad and he was invalided home, poor devil. Those black girls are foul," he continued; "they give everyone the clap and that's bad enough, I can tell you; they're dirty devils." His ruttish sorrows didn't interest me much, for I had made up my mind never at any time to go with any prostitute.

I came to several such uncommon resolutions on board that ship, and I may set down the chief of them here very briefly. First of all, I resolved that I would do every piece of work given to me as well as I could so that no one coming after me could do it better. I had found out at school in the last term that if you gave your whole mind and heart to anything, you learned it very quickly and thoroughly. I was sure even before the trial that my first job would lead me straight to fortune. I had seen men at work and knew it would be easy to beat any of them. I was only eager for the trial.

I remember one evening I had waited for Jessie and she never came, and just before going to bed, I went up into the bow of the ship where one was alone with the sea and sky, and swore to myself this great oath, as I called it in my romantic fancy: whatever I undertook to do, I would do it to the uttermost in me.

If I have had any successes in life or done any good work, it is due in great part to that resolution.

I could not keep my thoughts from Jessie; if I tried to put her out of my head, I'd get a little note from her, or Ponsonby would come, begging me to leave him the cabin the whole day: at length in despair I begged her for her address in New York, for I feared to lose her forever in that maelstrom. I added that I would always be in my cabin alone from one to half past, if she could ever come.

That day she didn't come and the old gentleman who said he would adopt me got hold of me, told me he was a banker and would send me to Harvard, the university near Boston; from what the doctor had said of me, he hoped I would do great things. He was really kind and tried to be sympathetic, but he had no idea that what I wanted chiefly was to prove myself, to justify my own high opinion of my powers in the open fight of life. I didn't want help and I absolutely resented his protective airs.

Next day in the cabin came a touch on the door and Jessie, all flustered, was in my arms. "I can only stay a minute," she cried. "Father is dreadful, says you are only a child and won't have me engage myself and he watches me from morning to night. I could only get away now because he had to go down to the machine-room."

Before she had finished, I locked the cabin door.

"Oh, I must go," she cried. "I must really; I only came to give you my address in New York; here it is," and she handed me the paper that I put at once in my pocket. And then I put both my arms under her clothes and my hands were on her warm hips, and I was speechless with delight; in a moment my right hand came round in front and as I touched her sex our lips clung together and her sex opened at once, and my finger began to caress her and we kissed and kissed again. Suddenly her lips got hot and while I was still wondering why, her sex got wet and her eyes began to flutter and turn up. A moment or two later she tried to get out of my embrace.

"Really, dear, I'm frightened: he might come and make a noise and I'd die; please let me go now; we'll have lots of time in New York"—but I could not bear to let her go. "He'd never come here where there are two men," I said, "never. He might find the wrong one," and I drew her to me, but seeing she was only half-reassured, I said, while lifting her dress, "Let mine just touch yours, and I'll let you go"; and the next moment my sex was against hers and almost in spite of herself she yielded to the throbbing warmth of it; but, when I pushed in, she drew away and down on it a little and I saw anxiety in her eyes that had grown very dear to me.

At once I stopped and put away my sex and let her clothes drop. "You're such a sweet, Jess," I said, "who could deny you anything; in New York then, but now one long kiss."

She gave me her mouth at once and her lips were hot. I learned that morning that, when a girl's lips grow hot, her sex is hot first and she is ready to give herself and ripe for the embrace.

Chapter V

The Great New World

A STOLEN KISS AND FLEETING CARESS as we met on the deck at night were all I had of Jessie for the rest of the voyage. One evening land lights flickering in the distance drew crowds to the deck; the ship began to slow down. The cabin passengers went below as usual, but hundreds of immigrants sat up as I did and watched the stars slide down the sky till at length dawn came with silver lights and startling revelations.

I can still recall the thrills that overcame me when I realized the great waterways of that land-locked harbor and saw Long Island Sound stretching away on one hand like a sea and the magnificent Hudson River with its palisades on the other, while before me was the East River, nearly a mile in width. What an entrance to a new world! A magnificent and safe ocean port which is also the meeting place of great water paths into the continent.

No finer site could be imagined for a world capital. I was entranced with the spacious grandeur, the manifest destiny of this Queen City of the Waters.

The Old Battery was pointed out to me and Governor's Island and the prison and where the bridge was being built to Brooklyn: suddenly Jessie passed on her father's arm and shot me one radiant, lingering glance of love and promise.

I remember nothing more till we landed and the old banker came up to tell me he had had my little box taken from the "H's" where it belonged and put with his luggage among the "S's."

"We are going," he added, "to the Fifth Avenue Hotel a way uptown in Madison Square: we'll be comfortable there," and he smiled self-complacently. I smiled too, and thanked him; but I had no intention of going in his company. I went back to the ship and thanked Doctor Keogh with all my heart for his great goodness to me; he gave me his address in New York, and incidentally I learned from him that if I kept the key of my trunk, no one could open it or take it away; it would be left in charge of the customs till I called for it.

In a minute I was back in the long shed on the dock and had wandered nearly to the end when I perceived the stairs. "Is that the way into the town?" I asked and a man replied, "Sure." One quick glance around to see that I was not noticed and in a moment I was down the stairs and out in the street. I raced straight ahead of me for two or three blocks and then asked and was told that Fifth Avenue was right in front. As I turned up Fifth Avenue, I began to breathe freely; "No more fathers for me." The old greybeard who had bothered me was consigned to oblivion without regret. Of course, I know now that he deserved better treatment. Perhaps, indeed, I should have done better had I accepted his kindly, generous help, but I'm trying to set down the plain, unvarnished truth, and here at once I must say that children's affections are much slighter than most parents imagine. I never wasted a thought on my father; even my brother Vernon, who had always been kind to me and fed my inordinate vanity, was not regretted: the new life called me: I was in a flutter of expectancy and hope.

Some way up Fifth Avenue I came into the great square and saw the Fifth Avenue Hotel, but I only grinned and kept right on till at length I reached Central Park. Near it, I can't remember exactly where, but I believe it was near where the Plaza Hotel stands today, there was a small wooden house with an outhouse at the other end of the lot. While I stared a woman came out with a bucket and went across to the outhouse. In a few moments she came back again and noticed me looking over the fence.

"Would you please give me a drink?" I asked. "Sure I will," she replied with a strong Irish brogue; "come right in," and I followed her into the kitchen.

"You're Irish," I said, smiling at her. "I am," she replied, "how did ye guess?" "Because I was born in Ireland, too," I retorted. "You were not!" she cried emphatically, more for pleasure than to contradict. "I was born in Galway," I went on, and at once she became very friendly and poured me out some milk warm from the cow; and when she heard I had had no breakfast and saw I was hungry, she pressed me to eat and sat down with me and soon heard my whole story, or enough of it to break out in wonder again and again.

In turn she told me how she had married Mike Mulligan, a longshoreman who earned good wages and was a good husband but took a drop too much now and again, as a man will when tempted by one of "thim saloons." It was the saloons, I learned, that were the ruination of all the best Irishmen and "they were the best men anyway, an'—an'—"; and the kindly, homely talk flowed on, charming me.

When the breakfast was over and the things cleared away, I rose to go with many thanks, but Mrs. Mulligan wouldn't hear of it. "Ye're a child," she said, "an' don't know New York; it's a terrible place and you must wait till Mike comes home an'—"

"But I must find some place to sleep," I said. "I have money."

"You'll sleep here," she broke in decisively, "and Mike will put ye on yer feet; sure he knows New York like his pocket, an' yer as welcome as the flowers in May, an'—"

What could I do but stay and talk and listen to all sorts of stories about New York, and "toughs" that were "hard cases" and "gunmen" and "wimmin that were worse—bad scran to them."

In due time Mrs. Mulligan and I had dinner together, and after dinner I got her permission to go into the Park for a walk, but "mind now and be home by six or I'll send Mike after ye," she added, laughing.

I walked a little way in the park and then started down town again to the address Jessie had given me near the Brooklyn Bridge. It was a mean street, I thought, but I soon found Jessie's sister's house and went to a nearby restaurant and wrote a little note to my love, that she could show if need be, saying that I proposed to call on the eighteenth, or two days after the ship we had come in was due to return to Liverpool. After that duty, which made it possible for me to hope all sorts of things on the eighteenth, nineteenth, or twentieth, I sauntered over to Fifth Avenue and made my way uptown again. At any rate I was spending nothing in my present lodging.

When I returned that night I was presented to Mike: I found him a big, good looking Irishman who thought his wife a wonder and all she did perfect. "Mary," he said, winking at me, "is one of the best cooks in the wurrld and if it weren't that she's down on a man when he has a drop in him, she'd be the best gurrl on God's earth. As it is, I married her, and I've never been sorry, have I, Mary?" "Ye've had no cause, Mike Mulligan."

Mike had nothing particular to do next morning and so he promised he would go and get my little trunk from the custom house. I gave him the key. He insisted as warmly as his wife that I should stay with them till I got work: I told him how eager I was to begin and Mike promised to speak to his chief and some friends and see what could be done.

Next morning I got up about five-thirty as soon as I heard Mike stirring, and went down Seventh Avenue with him till he got on the horse-car for down town and left me. About seven-thirty to eight o'clock a stream of people began walking down town to their offices. On several corners were bootblack shanties. One of them happened to have three customers in it and only one bootblack.

"Won't you let me help you shine a pair or two?" I asked. The bootblack looked at me. "I don't mind," he said and I seized the brushes and went to work. I had done the two just as he finished the first: he whispered to me "halves" as the next man came in and he showed me how to use the polishing rag or cloth. I took off my coat and waistcoat and went to work with a will; for the next hour and a half we both had our hands full. Then the rush began to slack off, but not before I had taken just over a dollar and a half. Afterwards we had a talk, and Allison, the bootblack, told me he'd be glad to give me work any morning on the same terms. I assured him I'd be there and do my best till I got other work. I had earned three shillings and had found out I could get good board for three dollars a week, so in a couple of hours I had earned my living. The last anxiety left me.

Mike had a day off, so he came home for dinner at noon and he had great news. They wanted men to work under water in the iron caissons of Brooklyn Bridge and they were giving from five to ten dollars a day.

"Five dollars," cried Mrs. Mulligan. "It must be dangerous or unhealthy or somethin'—sure, you'd never put the child to work like that."

Mike excused himself, but the danger, if danger there was, appealed to me almost as much as the big pay: my only fear was that they'd think me too small or too young. I had told Mrs. Mulligan I was sixteen, for I didn't want to be treated as a child, and now I showed her the eighty cents I had earned that morning bootblacking and she advised me to keep on at it and not go to work under the water; but the promised five dollars a day won me.

Next morning Mike took me to Brooklyn Bridge soon after five o'clock to see the contractor; he wanted to engage Mike at once but shook his head over me. "Give me a trial," I pleaded; "you'll see I'll make good." After a pause, "O.K.," he said; "four shifts have gone down already under-handed: you may try."

I've told about the work and its dangers at some length in my novel, *The Bomb,** but here I may add some details just to show what labor has to suffer.

In the bare shed where we got ready, the men told me no one could do the work for long without getting the "bends"; the "bends" were a sort of convulsive fit that twisted one's body like a knot and often made you an invalid for life. They soon explained the whole procedure to me. We worked, it appeared, in a huge bell-shaped caisson of iron that went to the bottom of the river and was pumped full of compressed air to keep the water from entering it from below: the top of the caisson is a room called the "material chamber," into which the stuff dug out of the river passes up and is carted away. On the side of the caisson is another room, called the "air-lock," into which we were to go to be "compressed." As the compressed air is admitted, the blood keeps absorbing the gasses of the air till the tension of the gasses in the blood becomes equal to that in the air: when this equilibrium has been reached, men can work in the caisson for hours without serious discomfort, if sufficient pure air is constantly pumped in. It was the foul air that did the harm, it appeared. "If they'd pump in good air, it would be O.K.; but that would cost a little time and trouble, and men's lives are cheaper." I saw that the men wanted to warn me thinking I was too young, and accordingly I pretended to take little heed.

When we went into the "air-lock" and they turned on one air-cock after another of compressed air, the men put their hands to their ears and I soon imitated them, for the pain was very acute. Indeed, the drums of the ears are often driven in and burst if the compressed air is brought in too quickly. I found that the best way of meeting the pressure was to keep swallowing

* (London, 1908; New York, 1909); it has the Haymarket riots as its background. Dedicated to Princess Alice of Monaco.

air and forcing it up into the middle ear, where it acted as an air-pad on the inner side of the drum and so lessened the pressure from the outside.

It took about half an hour or so to "compress" us and that half an hour gave me lots to think about. When the air was fully compressed, the door of the air-lock opened at a touch and we all went down to work with pick and shovel on the gravelly bottom. My headache soon became acute. The six of us were working naked to the waist in a small iron chamber with a temperature of about 180° Fahrenheit:* in five minutes the sweat was pouring from us, and all the while we were standing in icy water that was only kept from rising by the terrific air pressure. No wonder the headaches were blinding. The men didn't work for more than ten minutes at a time, but I plugged on steadily, resolved to prove myself and get constant employment; only one man, a Swede named Anderson, worked at all as hard. I was overjoyed to find that together we did more than the four others.

The amount done each week was estimated, he told me, by an inspector. Anderson was known to the contractor and received half a wage extra as head of our gang. He assured me I could stay as long as I liked, but he advised me to leave at the end of a month: it was too unhealthy: above all, I mustn't drink and should spend all my spare time in the open. He was kindness itself to me, as indeed were all the others. After two hours' work down below we went up into the air-lock room to get gradually "decompressed," the pressure of air in our veins having to be brought down gradually to the usual air pressure. The men began to put on their clothes and passed round a bottle of schnapps; but though I was soon as cold as a wet rat and felt depressed and weak to boot, I would not touch the liquor. In the shed above I took a cupful of hot cocoa with Anderson, which stopped the shivering, and I was soon able to face the afternoon's ordeal.

I had no idea one could feel so badly when being "decompressed" in the air-lock, but I took Anderson's advice and got into the open as soon as I could, and by the time I had walked home in the evening and changed, I felt strong again; but the headache didn't leave me entirely and the earache came back every now and then, and to this day a slight deafness reminds me of that spell of work under water.

I went into Central Park for half an hour; the first pretty girl I met reminded me of Jessie: in one week I'd be free to see her and tell her I was making good and she'd keep her promise, I felt sure; the mere hope led me to fairyland. Meanwhile nothing could take away the proud consciousness that with my five dollars I had earned two weeks' living in a day: a month's work would make me safe for a year.

When I returned I told the Mulligans I must pay for my board, saying "I'd feel better, if you'll let me," and finally they consented, although Mrs. Mulligan thought three dollars a week too much. I was glad when it was settled and went to bed early to have a good sleep. For three or four days things went fairly well with me, but on the fifth or sixth day we came on a

* Obviously an uncorrected typographical error.

spring of water, or "gusher," and were wet to the waist before the air pressure could be increased to cope with it. As a consequence, a dreadful pain shot through both my ears: I put my hands to them tight and sat still a little while. Fortunately, the shift was almost over and Anderson came with me to the horse-car. "You'd better knock off," he said. "I've known 'em go deaf from it."

The pain had been appalling, but it was slowly diminishing and I was resolved not to give in. "Could I get a day off?" I asked Anderson. He nodded, "Of course: you're the best in the shift, the best I've ever seen, a great little pony."

Mrs. Mulligan saw at once something was wrong and made me try her household remedy—a roasted onion cut in two and clapped tight on each ear with a flannel bandage. It acted like magic: in ten minutes I was free of pain; then she poured in a little warm sweet oil and in an hour I was walking in the park as usual. Still, the fear of deafness was on me and I was very glad when Anderson told me he had complained to the boss and we were to get an extra thousand feet of pure air. It would make a great difference, Anderson said, and he was right, but the improvement was not sufficient.*

One day, just as the "decompression" of an hour and a half was ending, an Italian named Manfredi fell down and writhed about, knocking his face on the floor till the blood spurted from his nose and mouth. When we got him into the shed, his legs were twisted like plaited hair. The surgeon had him taken to the hospital. I made up my mind that a month would be enough for me.

At the end of the first week, I got a note from Jessie saying that her father was going on board that afternoon and she could see me the next evening. I went and was introduced to Jessie's sister who, to my surprise, was tall and large but without a trace of Jessie's good looks.

"He's younger than you, Jess," she burst out laughing. A week earlier I'd have been hurt to the soul, but I had proved myself, so I said simply, "I'm earning five dollars a day, Mrs. Plummer, and money talks." Her mouth fell open in amazement. "Five dollars," she repeated, "I'm so sorry, I—I—"

"There, Maggie," Jessie broke in, "I told you, you had never seen anyone like him; you'll be great friends yet. Now come and we'll have a walk," she added, and out we went.

To be with her even in the street was delightful and I had a lot to say, but making love in a New York street on a summer evening is difficult and I was hungry to kiss and caress her freely. Jessie, however, had thought of a way: if her sister and husband had theatre tickets, they'd go out and we'd

---

* In Germany I have since learned the state requires that ten times as much pure air must be supplied as we had, and in consequence the serious illnesses which with us amounted to eighty per cent in three months have been reduced to eight. Paternal government, it appears, has certain good points. (F.H.)

be alone in the apartment; it would cost two dollars, however, and she thought that a lot. I was delighted: I gave her the bills and arranged to be with her next night before eight o'clock. Did Jessie know what was going to happen? Even now I'm uncertain, though I think she guessed.

Next night I waited till the coast was clear and then hurried to the door. As soon as we were alone in the little parlor and I had kissed her, I said, "Jessie, I want you to undress. I'm sure your figure is lovely, but I want to know it."

"Not at once, eh?" she pouted. "Talk to me first. I want to know how you are," and I drew her to the big armchair and sat down with her in my arms. "What am I to tell you?" I asked, while my hand went up her dress to her warm thighs and sex. She frowned, but I kissed her lips and with a movement or two stretched her out on me so that I could use my finger easily. At once, her lips grew hot and I went on kissing and caressing till her eyes closed and she gave herself to the pleasure. Suddenly she wound herself upon me and gave me a big kiss. "You don't talk," she said.

"I can't," I exclaimed, making up my mind. "Come," and I lifted her to her feet and took her into the bedroom. "I'm crazy for you," I said; "take off your clothes, please." She resisted a little, but when I began loosening her dress, she helped me and took it off. Her knickers, I noticed, were new. They soon fell off and she stood in her chemise and black stockings.

"That's enough, isn't it," she said, "Mr. Curious," and she drew the chemise tight about her.

"No," I cried, "beauty must unveil, please!" The next moment the chemise, slipping down, caught for a moment on her hips and then slid circling round her feet.

Her nakedness stopped my heart; desire blinded me: my arms went round her, straining her soft form to me: in a moment I had lifted her onto the bed, pulling the bed clothes back at the same time. The foolish phrase of being in bed together deluded me: I had no idea that she was more in my power just lying on the edge of the bed; in a moment I had torn off my clothes and boots and got in beside her. Our warm bodies lay together, a thousand pulses beating in us; soon I separated her legs and, lying on her, tried to put my sex into hers, but she drew away almost at once. "O-O, it hurts," she murmured, and each time I tried to push my sex in her, her "O's" of pain stopped me.

My wild excitement made me shiver; I could have struck her for drawing away; but soon I noticed that she let my sex touch her clitoris with pleasure and I began to use my cock as a finger, caressing her with it. In a moment or two I began to move it more quickly, and as my excitement grew to the height, I again tried to slip it into her pussy, and now, as her love-dew came, I got my sex in a little way, which gave me inexpressible pleasure; but when I pushed to go further, she drew away again with a sharp cry of pain. At the same moment my orgasm came on for the first time and seed like milk spirted from my sex. The pleasure-thrill was almost unbearably keen; I could have screamed with the pang of it, but Jessie cried out: "Oh, you're wetting me," and drew away with a frightened, "Look, look!" And there, sure enough, on her round white thighs were patches of crimson blood. "Oh! I'm bleeding," she cried. "What have you done?"

"Nothing," I answered, a little sulky, I'm afraid, at having my indescribable pleasure cut short, "Nothing"; and in a moment I had got out of bed, and taking my handkerchief soon wiped away the tell-tale traces.

But when I wanted to begin again, Jessie would not hear of it at first. "No, no," she said. "You've really hurt me, Jim (my Christian name, I had told her, was James), and I'm scared; please be good." I could only do her will until a new thought struck me. At any rate, I could see her now and study her beauties one by one, and so still lying by her I began kissing her left breast and soon the nipple grew a little stiff in my mouth. Why, I didn't know and Jessie said she didn't, but she liked it when I said her breasts were lovely, and indeed they were, small and firm, while the nipples pointed straight out. Suddenly, the thought came, surprising me: it would have been much prettier if the circle surrounding the nipples had been rose-red, instead of merely amber-brown. I was thrilled by the bare idea. But her flanks and belly were lovely; the navel like a curled sea-shell, I thought, and the triangle of silky brown hairs on the Mount of Venus seemed to me enchanting, but Jessie kept covering her beauty-place. "It's ugly," she said, "please boy," but I went on caressing it and soon I was trying to slip my sex in again; though Jessie's "O's" of pain began at once and she begged me to stop.

"We must get up and dress," she said; "they'll soon be back," so I had to content myself with just lying in her arms with my sex touching hers. Soon she began to move against my sex, and to kiss me, and then she bit my lips just as my sex slipped into hers again; she left it in for a long moment and then as her lips grew hot: "It's so big," she said "but you're a dear." The moment after she cried: "We must get up, boy! If they caught us, I'd die of shame." When I tried to divert her attention by kissing her breasts, she pouted, "That hurts, too. Please, boy, stop and don't look," she added as she tried to rise, covering her sex the while with her hand, and pulling a frowning face. Though I told her she was mistaken and her sex was lovely, she persisted in hiding it, and in truth her breasts and thighs excited me more, perhaps because they were in themselves more beautiful.

I put my hand on her hip; she smiled, "Please, boy," and as I moved away to give her room, she got up and stood by the bed, a perfect little figure in rosy, warm outline. I was entranced, but the cursed critical faculty was awake. As she turned, I saw she was too broad for her height; her legs were too short, her hips too stout. It all chilled me a little. Should I ever find perfection?*

Ten minutes later she had rearranged the bed and we were seated in the

* In truth, a bit of it in virtually every woman he ever knew, as we shall see.

sitting room, but to my wonder Jessie didn't want to talk over our experience. "What gave you the most pleasure?" I asked. "All of it," she said, "you naughty dear; but don't let's talk of it."

I told her I was going to work for a month, but I couldn't talk to her; my hand was soon up her clothes again, playing with her sex and caressing it, and we had to move apart hurriedly when we heard her sister at the door.

I didn't get another evening alone with Jessie for some time. I asked for it often enough, but Jessie made excuses and her sister was very cold to me. I soon found out that it was by her advice that Jessie guarded herself. Jessie confessed that her sister accused her of letting me "act like a husband. She must have seen a stain on my chemise," Jessie added, "when you made me bleed, you naughty boy; anyway, something gave her the idea, and now you must be good."

That was the conclusion of the whole matter. If I had known as much then as I knew ten years later, neither the pain nor her sister's warnings could have dissuaded Jessie from giving herself to me. Even at the time I felt that a little more knowledge would have made me the arbiter.

The desire to have Jessie completely to myself again was one reason why I gave up the job at the bridge as soon as the month was up. I had over a hundred and fifty dollars clear in my pocket and I had noticed that though the pains in my ears soon ceased, I had become a little hard of hearing. The first morning I wanted to lie in bed and have one great lazy day, but I awoke at five as usual, and it suddenly occurred to me that I should go down and see Allison, the bootblack, again. I found him busier than ever and I had soon stripped off and set to work. About ten o'clock we had nothing to do, so I told him of my work under water; he boasted that his "stand" brought him in about four dollars a day: there wasn't much to do in the afternoons, but from six to seven again he usually earned something more.

I was welcome to come and work with him any morning on halves and I thought it well to accept his offer.

That very afternoon I took Jessie for a walk in the park, but when we had found a seat in the shade she confessed that her sister thought we ought to be engaged, and as soon as I got steady work we could be married. "A woman wants a home of her own," she said, "and oh, boy! I'd make it so pretty! And we'd go out to the theatres and have a gay old time."

I was horrified; married at my age, no sir! It seemed absurd to me, and with Jessie! I saw she was pretty and bright, but she knew nothing, never had read anything: I couldn't marry her. The idea made me snort. But she was dead in earnest, so I agreed to all she said, only insisting that first I must get regular work; I'd buy the engagement ring too: but first we must have another great evening. Jessie didn't know whether her sister would go out, but she'd see. Meanwhile we kissed and kissed and her lips grew hot and my hand got busy, and then we walked again, on and on, and finally went into the great museum.

Here I got one of the shocks of my life. Suddenly, Jessie stopped before a picture representing, I think, Paris choosing the goddess of beauty, Paris being an ideal figure of youthful manhood.

"Oh, isn't he splendid!" cried Jessie. "Just like you," she added with feminine wit, pouting out her lips as if to kiss me. If she hadn't made the personal application, I might not have realized the absurdity of the comparison. But Paris had long, slim legs while mine were short and stout, and his face was oval and his nose straight, while my nose jutted out with broad, scenting nostrils.

The conviction came to me in a flash: I was ugly with irregular features, sharp eyes and short squat figure. The certainty overpowered me: I had learned before that I was too small to be a great athlete, now I saw that I was ugly to boot: my heart sank: I cannot describe my disappointment and disgust.

Jessie asked what was the matter and at length I told her. She wouldn't have it. "You've a lovely white skin," she cried, "and you're quick and strong: no one would call you ugly! The idea!" But the knowledge was in me indisputable, never to leave me again for long. It even led me to some erroneous inferences then and there. For example, it seemed clear to me that if I had been tall and handsome like Paris, Jessie would have given herself to me in spite of her sister; but further knowledge of women makes me inclined to doubt this. They have a luscious eye for good looks in the male, naturally; but other qualities, such as strength and dominant self-confidence, have an even greater attraction for the majority, especially for those who are richly endowed sexually. I am inclined to think that it was her sister's warnings and her own matter-of-fact hesitation before the irrevocable that induced Jessie to withhold her sex from complete abandonment. But the pleasure I had experienced with her made me keener than ever and more enterprising. The conviction of my ugliness, too, made me resolve to develop my mind and all other faculties as much as I could.

Finally I saw Jessie home and had a great hug and long kiss and was told she had had a bully afternoon and we made another appointment.

I worked at bootblacking every morning and soon got some regular customers, notably a young, well dressed man who seemed to like me. Either Allison or he himself told me his name was Kendrick and he came from Chicago. One morning he was very silent and absorbed. At length I said, "Finished," and "Finished," he repeated after me. "I was thinking of something else," he explained. "Intent," I said smiling. "A business deal," he explained, "but why do you say intent?" "The Latin phrase came into my head," I replied without thinking, *"Intentique ore tenebant,* Vergil says."

"Good God!" he cried. "Fancy a bootblack quoting Vergil. You're a strange lad; what age are you?" "Sixteen," I replied. "You don't look it," he said, "but now I must hurry; one of these days we'll have a talk." I smiled, "Thank you, Sir," and away he hastened.

The very next day he was in still greater haste. "I must get down town," he said. "I'm late already. Just give me a rub or two"; he cried impatiently, "I must catch that train." And he fumbled with some bills in his hand. "It's all right," I said, and smiling added: "Hurry! I'll be here tomorrow." He smiled and went off without paying, taking me at my word.

The next day I strolled down town early, for Allison had found that a stand and lean-to were to be sold on the corner of Thirteenth Street and Seventh Avenue, and as he was known, he wanted me to go and have a look at the business done from seven to nine. The Dago who wished to sell out and go back to Dalmatia wanted three hundred dollars for the outfit, asserting that the business brought in four dollars a day. He had not exaggerated unduly, I found, and Allison was hot that we should buy it together and go fifty-fifty. "You'll make five or six dollars a day at it," he said, "if the Dago makes four. It's one of the good pitches and with three dollars a day coming in, you'll soon have a stand of your own."

While we were discussing it, Kendrick came up and took his accustomed seat. "What were you so hot about?" he asked, and as Allison smiled, I told him. "Three dollars a day seems good," he said, "but bootblacking's not your game. How would you like to come to Chicago and have a place as night clerk in my hotel? I've got one with my uncle," he added, "and I think you'd make good."

"I'd do my best," I replied, the very thought of Chicago and the Great West drawing me. "Will you let me think it over?"

"Sure, sure!" he replied. "I don't go back till Friday; that gives you three days to decide."

Allison stuck to his opinion that a good stand would make more money; but when I talked it over with the Mulligans, they were both in favor of the hotel. I saw Jessie that same evening and told her of the "stand" and begged for another evening, but she stuck to it that her sister was suspicious and cross with me and would not leave us alone again. Accordingly, I said nothing to her of Chicago.

I had always noticed that sexual pleasure is in its nature profoundly selfish. So long as Jessie yielded to me and gave me delight, I was attracted to her; but as soon as she denied me, I became annoyed and dreamed of more pliant beauties. I was rather pleased to leave her without even a word; "That'll teach her!" my wounded vanity whispered; "She deserves to suffer a little for disappointing me."

But parting with the Mulligans was really painful: Mrs. Mulligan was a dear, kind woman who would have mothered the whole race if she could, one of those sweet Irish women whose unselfish deeds and thoughts are the flowers of our sordid, human life. Her husband, too, was not unworthy of her, very simple and straight and hard-working, without a mean thought in him, a natural prey to good fellowship and songs and poteen.

On Friday afternoon I left New York for Chicago with Mr. Kendrick. The country seemed to me very bare, harsh and unfinished, but the great distances enthralled me; it was indeed a land to be proud of, every broad acre of it spoke of the future and suggested hope.

My first round, so to speak, with American life was over. What I had learned in it remains with me still. No people is so kind to children and no life so easy for the handworkers; the hewers of wood and drawers of water are better off in the United States than anywhere else on earth. To this one class, and it is by far the most numerous class, the American democracy more than fulfills its promises. It levels up the lowest in a most surprising way. I believed then with all my heart what so many believe today, that all deductions made, it was on the whole the best civilization yet known among men.

In time deeper knowledge made me modify this opinion more and more radically. Five years later I was to see Walt Whitman, the noblest of all Americans, living in utter poverty at Camden, dependent upon English admirers for a change of clothes or a sufficiency of food; and Poe had suffered in the same way.

Bit by bit the conviction was forced upon me that if the American democracy does much to level up the lowest class, it is still more successful in leveling down the highest and best. No land on earth is so friendly to the poor illiterate toilers, no land so contemptuous-cold to the thinkers and artists, the guides of humanity. What help is there here for men of letters and artists, for the seers and prophets? Such guides are not wanted by the idle rich and are ignored by the masses, and after all, the welfare of the head is more important even than that of the body and feet.

What will become of those who stone the prophets and persecute the teachers? The doom is written in flaming letters on every page of history.

Chapter VI

Life in Chicago

THE FREMONT HOUSE, Kendrick's hotel, was near the Michigan Street depot. In those days, when Chicago had barely 300,000 inhabitants, it was a hotel of the second class. Mr. Kendrick had told me that his uncle, a Mr. Cotton, really owned the House, but left him the chief share in the management, adding, "What uncle says, goes always." In the course of time, I understood the nephew's loyalty, for Mr. Cotton was really kindly and an able man of business. My duties as night clerk were simple: from eight at night till six in the morning, I was master in the office and had to apportion bedrooms to the incoming guests, and give bills and collect the moneys due from the outgoing public. I set myself at once to learn the good and bad points of the hundred odd bedrooms in the house and the arrival and departure times of all the night trains. When guests came in, I met them at the entrance, found out what they wanted and told this or that porter or bellboy to take them to their rooms. However curt or irritable they were, I always tried to smooth them down and soon found I was succeeding. In a week Mr. Kendrick told me that he had heard golden opinions of me from a dozen visitors. "You have a dandy night clerk," he was told, "Spares no pains . . . pleasant manners . . . knows everything . . . *some* clerk; yes, sir!"

My experience in Chicago assured me that if one does his very best, he comes to success in business in comparatively short time; so few do all they can. Going to bed at six, I was up every day at one o'clock for dinner, as it was called, and after dinner I got into the habit of going into the billiard room, at one end of which was a large bar. By five o'clock or so, the billiard room was crowded and there was no one to superintend things, so I spoke to Mr. Kendrick about it and took the job on my own shoulders. I had little to do but induce newcomers to await their turn patiently and to mollify old customers who expected to find tables waiting for them. The result of a little courtesy and smiling promises was so marked that at the end of the very first month the bookkeeper, a man named Curtis, told me with a grin that I was to get sixty dollars a month and not forty dollars, as I had supposed. Needless to say the extra pay simply quickened my desire to make myself useful. But now I found my way up barred by two superiors; the bookkeeper was one and the steward, a dry, taciturn westerner named Payne, was the other. Payne bought everything and had control of the dining room and waiters, while Curtis ruled the office and the bellboys. I was really under Curtis, but my control of the billiard room gave me a sort of independent position.

I soon made friends with Curtis, got into the habit of dining with him, and when he found that my handwriting was very good, he gave me the day book to keep and in a couple of months had taught me bookkeeping while entrusting me with a good deal of it. He was not lazy, but most men of forty like to have a capable assistant. By Christmas that year I was keeping all the books except the ledger and I knew, as I thought, the whole business of the hotel.

The dining room, it seemed to me, was very badly managed; but as luck would have it, I was first to get control of the office. As soon as Curtis found that I could safely be trusted to do his work, he began going out at dinner time and often stayed away the whole day. About New Year he was away for five days and confided in me when he returned that he had been on a "bust." He wasn't happy with his wife, it appeared, and he used to drink to drown her temper. In February he was away for ten days, but as he had given me the key of the safe I kept everything going. One day Kendrick found me in the office working and wanted to know about Curtis: "How long has he been away?" "A day or two," I replied. Kendrick looked at me and asked for the ledger. "It's written right up!" he exclaimed; "Did you do it?" I had to say I did, but at once I sent a bellboy for Curtis. The boy didn't find him at his house and next day I was brought up before Mr. Cotton. I couldn't deny that I had kept the books and Cotton soon saw that I was shielding Curtis out of loyalty. When Curtis came in next day, he gave the whole show away; he was half-drunk still and rude to boot. He had been unwell, he said, but his work was in order. He was "fired" there and then by Mr. Cotton and that evening Kendrick asked me to keep things going properly till he could persuade his uncle that I was trustworthy and older than I looked.

In a couple of days I saw Mr. Cotton and Mr. Kendrick together. "Can you keep the books and be night clerk and take care of the billiard room?" Mr. Cotton asked me sharply.

"I think so," I replied. "I'll do my best." "Hm!" he grunted. "What pay do you think you ought to have?"

"I'll leave that to you, Sir," I said. "I shall be satisfied whatever you give me."

"The devil you will," he said grumpily; "Suppose I said keep on at your present rate?"

I smiled, "O.K., Sir."

"Why do you smile?" he asked.

"Because, Sir, pay like water tends to find its level!"

"What the devil d'ye mean by 'its level'?"

"The level," I went on, "is surely the market price; sooner or later it'll rise towards that and I can wait."

His keen grey eyes suddenly bored into me. "I begin to think you're much older than you look, as my nephew here tells me," he said. "Put yourself down at a hundred a month for the present and in a little while we'll perhaps find the 'level,' " and he smiled. I thanked him and went out to my work.

It seemed as if incidents were destined to crowd my life. A day or so after this the taciturn steward, Payne, came and asked me if I'd go out with him to dinner and some theatre or other. I had not had a day off in five or six months, so I said, "Yes." He gave me a great dinner at a famous French restaurant (I forget the name now) and wanted me to drink champagne. But I had already made up my mind not to touch any intoxicating liquor till I was twenty-one, and so I told him simply that I had taken the pledge. He beat about the bush a great deal, but at length said that as I was bookkeeper in place of Curtis, he hoped we should get along as he and Curtis had done. I asked him just what he meant, but he wouldn't speak plainly, which excited my suspicions. A day or two afterwards I got into talk with a butcher in another quarter of the town and asked him what he would supply seventy pounds of beef and fifty pounds of mutton for, daily for a hotel. He gave me a price so much below the price Payne was paying that my suspicions were confirmed. I was tremendously excited. In my turn I invited Payne to dinner and led up to the subject. At once he said, "Of course there's a 'rake-off,' and if you'll hold in with me, I'll give you a third, as I gave Curtis. The 'rake-off' don't hurt anyone," he went on, "for I buy below market price." Of course I was all ears and eager interest when he admitted that the 'rake-off' was on everything he bought and amounted to about 20 per cent of the cost. By this he changed his wages from two hundred dollars a month into something like two hundred dollars a week.

As soon as I had all the facts clear, I asked the nephew to dine with me and laid the situation before him. I had only one loyalty—to my employers and the good of the ship. To my astonishment he seemed displeased at first. "More trouble," he began; "Why can't you stick to your own job and leave the others alone? What's in a commission after all?" When he came to understand what the commission amounted to and that he himself could do the buying in half an hour a day, he altered his tone. "What will my uncle say now?" he cried and went off to tell the owner his story. There was a tremendous row two days later for Mr. Cotton was a business man and went to the butchers we dealt with and ascertained for himself how important the "rake-off" really was. When I was called into the uncle's room, Payne tried to hit me; but he found it easier to receive than to give punches and that "the damned kid" was not a bit afraid of him.

Curiously enough, I soon noticed that the "rake-off" had had the secondary result of giving us an inferior quality of meat; whenever the butcher was left with a roast he could not sell, he used to send it to us, confident that Payne wouldn't quarrel about it. The Negro cook declared that the meat now was far better, all that could be desired, in fact, and our customers too were not slow to show their appreciation.

One other change the discharge of Payne brought about; it made me master of the dining room. I soon picked a smart waiter and put him as chief over the rest and together we soon improved the waiting and discipline among the waiters out of all comparison. For over a year I worked eighteen hours out of the twenty-four and after the first six months or so I got one hundred and fifty dollars a month and saved practically all of it.

Some experiences in this long, icy-cold winter in Chicago enlarged my knowledge of American life and particularly of life on the lowest level. I had been about three months in the hotel when I went out one evening for a sharp walk, as I usually did, about seven o'clock. It was bitterly cold; a western gale raked the streets with its icy teeth, the thermometer was about ten below zero. I had never imagined anything like the cold. Suddenly I was accosted by a stranger, a small man with red moustache and stubbly, unshaven beard.

"Say, mate, can you help a man to a meal?" The fellow was evidently a tramp: his clothes shabby and dirty; his manner servile with a backing of truculence. I was kindly and not critical. Without a thought I took my roll of bills out of my pocket. I meant to take off a dollar bill. As the money came to view the tramp with a pounce grabbed at it, but caught my hand as well. Instinctively I held on to my roll like grim Death, but while I was still under the shock of surprise, the hobo hit me viciously in the face and plucked at the bills again. I hung on all the tighter, and angry now, struck the man in the face with my left fist. The next moment we had clenched and fallen. As luck and youth would have it, I fell on top. At once I put out all my strength, struck the fellow hard in the face and at the same time tore my bills away. The next moment I was on my feet with my roll deep in my pocket and both fists ready for the next assault. To my astonishment, the hobo picked himself up and said confidently:

"I'm hungry, weak, or you wouldn't have downed me so easy." And then he went on with what to me seemed incredible impudence: "You should peel me off a dollar at least for hittin' me like that," and he stroked his jaw as if to ease the pain.

"I've a good mind to give you in charge," said I, suddenly realizing that I had the law on my side.

"If you don't cash up," barked the hobo, "I'll call the cops and say you've grabbed my wad."

"Call away," I cried; "we'll see who'll be believed."

But the hobo knew a better trick. In a familiar wheedling voice he began again: "Come, young fellow, you'll never miss one dollar and I'll put you

wise to a good many things here in Chicago. You had no business to pull
out a wad like that in a lonely place to tempt a hungry man."

"I was going to help you," I said hesitatingly.

"I know," replied my weird acquaintance, "but I prefer to help myself,"
and he grinned. "Take me to a hash-house: I'm hungry and I'll put you
wise to many things; you're a tenderfoot and show it."

Clearly the hobo was master of the situation and somehow or other his
whole attitude stirred my curiosity.

"Where are we to go?" I asked. "I don't know any restaurant near here
except the Fremont House."

"Hell," cried the hobo, "only millionaires and fools go to hotels. I follow
my nose for grub," and he turned on his heel and led the way without another word down a side street and into a German dive set out with bare
wooden tables and sanded floor.

Here he ordered hash and hot coffee, and when I came to pay I was
agreeably surprised to find that the bill was only forty cents and we could
talk in our corner undisturbed as long as we liked.

In ten minutes' chat the hobo had upset all my preconceived ideas and
given me a host of new and interesting thoughts. He was a man of some
reading, if not of education, and the violence of his language attracted me
almost as much as the novelty of his point of view.

All rich men were thieves, all workmen sheep and fools, was his creed.
The workmen did the work, created the wealth, and the employers robbed
them of nine-tenths of the product of their labor and so got rich. It all
seemed simple. The tramp never meant to work; he lived by begging and
went wherever he wanted to go.

"But how do you get about?" I cried.

"Here in the middle west," he replied, "I steal rides in freight cars and
box-cars and on top of coal wagons; in the real west and south I get inside
the cars and ride, and when the conductor turns me off I wait for the next
train. Life is full of happenings—some of 'em painful," he added, thoughtfully rubbing his jaw again.

He appeared to be a tough little man whose one object in life was to
avoid work, and in spite of himself, he worked hard in order to do nothing.

The experience had a warning, quickening effect on me. I resolved to
save all I could.

When I stood up to go the hobo grinned amicably: "I guess I've earned
that dollar?"

I could not help laughing. "I guess you have," I replied, but took care to
turn aside as I stripped off the bill.

"So long," said the tramp as we parted at the door and that was all the
thanks I ever got.

Another experience of this time told a sadder story. One evening a girl
spoke to me: she was fairly well dressed and as we came under a gas lamp,
I saw she was good looking with a tinge of nervous anxiety in her face.

"I don't buy love," I warned her, "but how much do you generally get?"

"From one dollar to five," she replied; "but tonight I want as much as I can get."

"I'll give you five," I replied; "but you must tell me all I want to know."

"All right," she said eagerly, "I'll tell all I know; it's not much," she added bitterly. "I'm not twenty yet, but you'd have taken me for more, now wouldn't you?"

"No," I replied, "you look about eighteen." In a few minutes we were climbing the stairs of a tenement house. The girl's room was poorly furnished and narrow, a hall bedroom just the width of the corridor, perhaps six feet by eight. As soon as she had taken off her thick coat and hat, she hastened out of the room, saying she'd be back in a minute. In the silence I thought I heard her running up the stairs; a baby somewhere near cried; and then silence again, till she opened the door, drew my head to her and kissed me. "I like you," she said, "though you're funny."

"Why funny?" I asked.

"It's a scream," she said, "to give five dollars to a girl and never touch her, but I'm glad, for I was tired tonight and anxious."

"Why anxious?" I queried, "and why did you go out if you were tired?"

"Got to," she replied through tightly closed lips. "You don't mind if I leave you again for a moment?" she added, and before I could answer she was out of the room again. When she returned in five minutes I had grown impatient and put on my overcoat and hat.

"Goin'?" she asked in surprise.

"Yes," I replied; "I don't like this empty cage while you go off to someone else."

"Someone else," she repeated, and then as if desperate, "It's my baby if you must know: a friend takes care of her when I'm out or working."

"Oh, you poor thing," I cried. "Fancy you with a baby at this life!"

"I wanted a baby," she cried defiantly. "I wouldn't be without her for anything! I always wanted a baby: there's lots of girls like that."

"Really?" I cried astounded. "Do you know her father?" I went on.

"Of course I do," she retorted. "He's working in the stockyards; he's tough and won't keep sober."

"I suppose you'd marry him if he would go straight?" I asked.

"Any girl would marry a decent feller!" she replied.

"You're pretty," I said.

"D'ye think so?" she asked eagerly, pushing her hair back from the sides of her head. "I used to be but now—this life—" and she shrugged her shoulders expressively.

"You don't like it?" I asked.

"No," she cried, "though when you get a nice feller, it's not so bad; but they're scarce," she went on bitterly, "and generally when they're nice, they've no bucks. The nice fellers are all poor or old," she added reflectively.

I had had the best part of her wisdom, so I stripped off a five-dollar bill and gave it to her. "Thanks," she said, "you're a dear and if you want to come an' see me at any time, just come an' I'll try to give you a good time." —Away I went. I had had my first talk with a prostitute and in her room! The idea that a girl could want a baby was altogether new to me; her temptations very different from a boy's, very!

For the greater part of my first year in Chicago I had no taste of love: I was often tempted by this chambermaid or that, but I knew that I should lose prestige if I yielded and I simply put it all out of my head resolvedly, as I had abjured drink. But towards the beginning of the summer temptation came to me in a new guise. A Spanish family, named Vidal, stopped at the Fremont House.

Señor Vidal was like a French officer, middle height, trim figure, very dark, with grey moustache waving up at the ends. His wife, motherly but stout, with large dark eyes and small features; a cousin, a man of about thirty, rather tall with a small black moustache, like a tooth brush, I thought, and sharp imperious ways. At first I did not notice the girl who was talking to her Indian maid. I understood at once that the Vidals were rich and gave them the best rooms. "All communicating—except yours," I added, turning to the young man; "It is on the other side of the corridor, but large and quiet." A shrug and contemptuous nod was all I got for my pains from Señor Arriga. As I handed the keys to the bellboy, the girl threw back her black mantilla.

"Any letters for us?" she asked quietly. For a minute I stood dumbfounded, enthralled, then, "I'll see," I muttered and went to the rack, but only to give myself a countenance. I knew there were none.

"None, I'm sorry to say," I smiled, watching the girl as she moved away.

"What's the matter with me?" I said to myself angrily. "She's nothing wonderful, this Miss Vidal; pretty, yes, and dark, with fine dark eyes, but nothing extraordinary." It would not do; I was shaken in a new way and would not admit it even to myself. In fact, the shock was so great that my head took sides against heart and temperament at once, as if alarmed. "All Spaniards are dark," I said to myself, trying to depreciate the girl and so regain self-control, "besides, her nose is beaked a little." But there was no conviction in my criticism. As soon as I recalled the proud grace of carriage and the magic of her glance, the fever-fit shook me again; for the first time my heart had been touched.

Next day I found out that the Vidals had come from Spain and were on their way to their hacienda near Chihuahua in northern Mexico. They meant to rest in Chicago for three or four days because Señora Vidal had heart trouble and couldn't stand much fatigue. I discovered besides that Señor Arriga was either courting his cousin or betrothed to her, and at once I sought to make myself agreeable to the man. Señor Arriga was a fine billiards player and I took the nearest way to his heart by reserving for him the best table, getting him a fair opponent and complimenting him upon his skill. The next day Arriga opened his heart to me: "What is there to do in this dull hole?" Did I know of any amusement? Any pretty women?

I could do nothing but pretend to sympathize and draw him out, and this I easily accomplished, for Señor Arriga loved to boast of his name and position in Mexico and his conquests. "Ah, you should have seen her as I led her in the *baile* (dance)—an angel!" and he kissed his fingers gallantly.

"As pretty as your cousin?" I ventured. Señor Arriga flashed a sharp suspicious glance at me, but apparently reassured by my frankness, went on:

"In Mexico we never talk of members of our family," he warned. "The Señorita is pretty, of course, but very young; she has not the charm of experience, the caress of—I know so little American, I find it difficult to explain."

But I was satisfied. "He doesn't love her," I said to myself; "loves no one except himself."

In a thousand little ways I took occasion to commend myself to the Vidals. Every afternoon they drove out and I took care they should have the best buggy and the best driver and was at pains to find out new and pretty drives, though goodness knows the choice was limited. The beauty of the girl grew on me in an extraordinary way; yet it was the pride and reserve in her face that fascinated me more even than her great dark eyes or fine features or splendid coloring. Her figure and walk were wonderful, I thought. I never dared to seek epithets for her eyes, or mouth, or neck. Her first appearance in evening dress was a revelation to me; she was my idol, enskied and sacred.

It is to be presumed that the girl saw how it was with me and was gratified. She made no sign, betrayed herself in no way, but her mother noticed that she was always eager to go downstairs to the lounge and missed no opportunity of making some inquiry at the desk.

"I want to practice my English," the girl said once, and the mother smiled: "*Los ojos,* you mean your eyes, my dear," and added to herself: "But why not? Youth . . ." and sighed for her own youth now foregone, and the petals already fallen.

One little talk I got with my goddess; she came to the office to ask about reserving a Pullman drawing room for El Paso. I undertook at once to see to everything, and when the dainty little lady added in her funny accent: "We have so many baggage, twenty-six bits," I said as earnestly as if my life depended on it, "Please trust me. I shall see to everything. I only wish," I added, "I could do more for you."

"That's kind," said the coquette, "very kind," looking full at me. Emboldened by despair at her approaching departure, I added: "I'm so sorry you're going. I shall never forget you, never."

Taken aback by my directness, the girl laughed saucily, "*Never* means a week, I suppose."

"You will see," I went on hurriedly, as if driven, as indeed I was. "If I thought I should not see you again and soon, I should not want to live."

"A declaration," she laughed merrily, still looking me brightly in the face.

"Not of independence," I cried, "but of—" as I hesitated between "affection" and "love," the girl put her finger to her lips.

"Hush, hush," she said gravely, "you are too young to take vows and I must not listen"; but seeing my face fall, she added, "You have been very kind. I shall remember my stay in Chicago with pleasure," and she stretched out her hand. I took it and held it treasuring every touch.

Her look and the warmth of her fingers I garnered up in my heart as purest treasure.

As soon as she had gone and the radiance with her, I cudgeled my brains to find some pretext for another talk. "She goes tomorrow," hammered in my brain and my heartache choked me, almost prevented me from thinking. Suddenly the idea of flowers came to me. I'd buy a lot. No; everyone would notice them and talk. A few would be better. How many? I thought and thought.

When they came into the lounge next day ready to start, I was watching my opportunity, but the girl gave me a better one than I could have picked. She waited till her father and Arriga had left the hall and then came over to the desk.

"You have ze checks?" she asked.

"Everything will be given you at the train," I said, "but I have these for you. Please accept them!" and I handed her three splendid red rosebuds, prettily tied up with maiden hair fern.

"How kind," she exclaimed, coloring, "and how pretty," she added, looking at the roses. "Just three?"

"One for your hair," I said, with love's cunning, "one for your eyes and one for your heart—will you remember?" I added in a low voice intensely.

She nodded and then looked up sparkling. "As long—as ze flowers last," she laughed, and was back with her mother.

I saw them into the omnibus and got kind words from all the party, even from Señor Arriga, but cherished most her look and word as she went out of the door.

Holding it open for her, I murmured as she passed, for the others were within hearing: "I shall come soon."

The girl stopped at once, pretending to look at the tag on a trunk the porter was carrying. "El Paso is far away," she sighed, "and the hacienda ten leagues further on. When shall we arrive—when?" she added, glancing up at me.

"When?" was the significant word to me for many a month; her eyes had filled it with meaning.

I've told of this meeting with Miss Vidal at length because it marked an epoch in my life; it was the first time that love had cast her glamor over me, making beauty superlative, intoxicating. The passion rendered it easier for me to resist ordinary temptation, for it taught me there was a whole gorgeous world in love's kingdom that I had never imagined, much less explored. I had scarcely a lewd thought of Gloria. It was not till I saw her bared shoulders in evening dress that I stripped her in imagination and went almost wild in uncontrollable desire. Would she ever kiss me? What was she like undressed? My imagination was still untutored: I could picture her breasts better than her sex, and I made up my mind to examine the next girl I was lucky enough to see naked much more precisely.

At the back of my mind was the fixed resolve to go to Chihuahua somehow or other in the near future and meet my charmer again, and that resolve in due course shaped my life anew.

In early June that year three strangers came to the hotel, all cattlemen I was told, of a new sort: Reece and Dell and Ford, the "Boss," as he was called. Reece was a tall dark Englishman or rather Welshman, always dressed in brown leather riding boots, Bedford cord breeches and dark tweed cutaway coat: he looked a prosperous gentleman farmer; Dell was almost a copy of him in clothes, about middle height and sturdier—in fact an ordinary Englishman. The Boss was fully six feet tall, taller even than Reece, with a hatchet-thin, bronzed face and eagle profile—evidently a Western cattleman from head to foot. The head-waiter told me about them, and as soon as I saw them I had them transferred to a shady-cool table and saw that they were well waited on.

A day or two afterwards we had made friends and a little later Reece got me measured for two pairs of cord breeches and had promised to teach me how to ride. They were cow-punchers, he said, with his strong English accent, and were going down to the Rio Grande to buy cattle and drive 'em back to market in Kansas City. Cattle, it appeared, could be bought in South Texas for a dollar a head or less and fetched from fifteen to twenty dollars each in Chicago.

"Of course we don't always get through unscathed," Reece remarked. "The plains Indians—Cherokees, Blackfeet and Sioux—take care of that; one herd in two gets through and that pays big."

I found they had brought up a thousand head of cattle from their ranch near Eureka, Kansas, and a couple of hundred head of horses.

To cut a long story short, Reece fascinated me; he told me that Chihuahua was the Mexican province just across the Rio Grande from Texas, and at once I resolved to go on the trail with these cow-punchers, if they'd take me. In two or three days Reece told me I shaped better at riding than anyone he had ever seen, though he added, "When I saw your thick, short legs I thought you'd never make much of a hand at it." But I was strong and had grown nearly six inches in my year in the States and I turned in my toes as Reece directed and hung on to the English saddle by the grip of my knees till I was both tired and sore. In a fortnight Reece made me put five-cent pieces between my knees and the saddle and keep them there when galloping or trotting.

This practice soon made a rider of me so far as the seat was concerned, and I had already learned that Reece was a pastmaster in the deeper mysteries of the art, for he told me he used to ride colts in the hunting field in England; and "That's how you learn to know horses," he added significantly.

One day I found out that Dell knew some poetry, literature, too, and economics, and that won me completely; when I asked them would they take me with them as a cowboy, they told me I'd have to ask the Boss, but there was no doubt he'd consent; and he consented, after one sharp glance.

Then came my hardest task: I had to tell Mr. Kendrick and Mr. Cotton that I must leave. They were more than astonished: at first they took it to be a little trick to extort a raise in salary: when they saw it was sheer boyish adventure-lust, they argued with me but finally gave in. I promised to return to them as soon as I got back to Chicago or got tired of cow-punching. I had nearly eighteen hundred dollars saved, which, by Mr. Cotton's advice, I transferred to a Kansas City bank he knew well.

Life on the Trail

On the tenth of June we took a train to Kansas City, the gate at that time of the "wild west." In Kansas City I became aware of three more men belonging to the outfit: Bent, Charlie, and Bob, the Mexican. Charlie, to begin with the least important, was a handsome American youth, blue eyed and fair haired, over six feet in height, very strong, careless, light hearted: I always thought of him as a big, kind, Newfoundland dog, rather awkward but always well meaning. Bent was ten years older, a war veteran, dark, saturnine, purposeful; five feet nine or ten in height with muscles of whipcord and a mentality that was curiously difficult to fathom. Bob, the most peculiar and original man I had ever met up to that time, was a little dried up Mexican, hardly five feet three in height, half Spaniard, half Indian, I believe, who might be thirty or fifty and who seldom opened his mouth, except to curse all Americans in Spanish. Even Reece admitted that Bob could ride "above a bit" and knew more about cattle than anyone else in this world. Reece's admiration directed my curiosity to the little man and I took every opportunity of talking to him and of giving him cigars, a courtesy so unusual that at first he was half inclined to resent it.

It appeared that these three men had been left in Kansas City to dispose of another herd of cattle and to purchase stores needed at the ranch. They were all ready, so the next day we rode out of Kansas City, about four o'clock in the morning, our course roughly south by west. Everything was new and wonderful to me. In three days we had finished with roads and farmstead and we were on the open prairie; in two or three days more, the prairie became the great plains, which stretched four or five thousand miles from north to south with a breadth of some seven hundred. The plains wore buffalo grass and sage brush for a garment, and little else, save in the river bottoms, trees like the cottonwood; everywhere rabbits, prairie chicken, deer and buffalo abounded.

We covered about thirty miles a day: Bob sat in the wagon and drove the four mules, while Bent and Charlie made us coffee and biscuits in the morning and cooked us sow-belly and any game we might bring in for dinner or supper. There was a small keg of rye whisky on the wagon, but we kept it for snake-bite or some emergency.

I became the hunter to the outfit, for it was soon discovered that by some sixth sense I could always find my way back to the wagon on a bee-line, and only Bob of the whole party possessed the same instinct. Bob explained it by muttering, "No Americano!" The instinct itself, which has stood me in good stead more times than I can count, is in essence inexplicable: I feel the direction; the vague feeling is strengthened by observing the path of the sun and the way the halms of grass lean, and the bushes grow. But it made me a valuable member of the outfit, instead of a mere parasite midway between master and man, and it was the first step to Bob's liking, which taught me more than all the other haps of my early life. I had bought a shotgun and a Winchester rifle and revolver in Kansas City, and Reece had taught me how to get weapons that would fit me, and this fact helped to make me a fair shot almost at once. Soon, to my grief, I found that I would never be a great shot, for Bob and Charlie and even Dell could see things far beyond my range of vision. I was short-sighted, in fact, through astigmatism, and even glasses, I discovered later, could not clear my blurred sight.

It was the second or third disappointment of my life, the others being the conviction of my personal ugliness and the fact that I should always be too short and small to be a great fighter or athlete.

As I went on in life, I discovered more serious disabilities, but they only strengthened my deep-seated resolve to make the most of any qualities I might possess; and meanwhile my life was divinely new and strange and pleasureful.

After breakfast, about five o'clock in the morning, I would ride away from the wagon till it was out of sight and then abandon myself to the joy of solitude, with no boundary between plain and sky. The air was brisk and dry, as exhilarating as champagne, and even when the sun reached the zenith and became blazing hot, the air remained lightsome and invigorating. Mid-Kansas is two thousand odd feet above sea-level and the air is so dry that an animal when killed dries up without stinking; and in a few months the hide's filled with mere dust. Game was plentiful: hardly an hour would elapse before I had got half a dozen ruffed grouse or a deer, and then I would walk my pony back to the midday camp, with perhaps a new wild-flower in my hand whose name I wished to learn.

After the midday meal I used to join Bob in the wagon and learn some

Spanish words or phrases from him or question him about his knowledge of cattle. In the first week we became great friends. I found, to my astonishment, that Bob was just as voluble in Spanish as he was tongue-tied in English, and his command of Spanish oaths, objurgations and indecencies was astounding. Bob despised all things American with an unimaginable ferocity and this interested me by its apparent unreason.

Once or twice on the way down we had a race; but Reece on a big Kentucky thoroughbred called Shiloh won easily. He told me, however, that there was a young mare called Blue Devil at the ranch which was as fast as Shiloh and of rare stay and stamina. "You can have her, if you can ride her," he threw out carelessly and I determined to win the "Devil" if I could.

In about ten days we reached the ranch near Eureka; it was set in five thousand acres of prairie, a big frame dwelling that would hold twenty men; but it wasn't nearly so well built as the great brick stable, the pride of Reece's eye, which would house forty horses and provide half a dozen with good loose boxes besides, in the best English style.

The house and stable were situated on a long billowy rise, perhaps three hundred yards away from a good-sized creek, which I soon christened Snake Creek, for snakes of all sizes simply swarmed in the brush and woodland of the banks. The big sitting room of the ranch was decorated with revolvers and rifles of a dozen different kinds, and pictures, strange to say, cut out of the illustrated papers; the floor was covered with buffalo and bear rugs, and rarer skins of mink and beaver hung here and there on the wooden walls. We got to the ranch late one night and I slept in a room with Dell, he taking the bed while I rolled myself in a rug on the couch. I slept like a top and next morning was out before sunrise to take stock, so to speak. An Indian lad showed me the stable, and as luck would have it, Blue Devil in a loose box, all to herself and very uneasy.

"What's the matter with her?" I asked, and the Indian told me she had rubbed her ear raw where it joins the head and the flies had got on it and plagued her; I went to the house and got Peggy, the mulatto cook, to fill a bucket with warm water, and with this bucket and a sponge I entered the loose box. Blue Devil came for me and nipped my shoulder, but as soon as I clapped the sponge with warm water on her ear, she stopped biting and we soon became friends. That same afternoon I led her out in front of the ranch saddled and bridled, got on her and walked her off as quiet as a lamb. "She's yours," said Reece, "but if she ever gets your foot in her mouth, you'll know what pain is!"

It appeared that that was a little trick she had, to tug and tug at the reins till the rider let them go loose, and then at once she would twist her head round, get the rider's toes in her mouth and bite like a fiend. No one she disliked could mount her, for she fought like a man with her forefeet, but I never had any difficulty with her, and she saved my life more than once. Like most feminine creatures, she responded immediately to kindness and was faithful to affection.

I'm compelled to notice that if I tell the other happenings in this eventful year at as great length as I've told the incidents of the fortnight that brought me from Chicago to the ranch at Eureka, I'd have to devote at least a volume to them; so I prefer to assure my readers that one of these days, if I live, I'll publish my novel *On the Trail*,* which gives the whole story in great detail. Now I shall content myself with saying that two days after reaching the ranch we set out, ten men strong and two wagons filled with our clothes and provender and dragged by four mules each, to cover the twelve hundred miles to southern Texas or New Mexico, where we hoped to buy five thousand or six thousand head of cattle at a dollar a head and drive them to Kansas City, the nearest train point.

When we got on the great trail a hundred miles from Fort Dodge, the days passed in absolute monotony. After sunset a light breeze usually sprang up to make the night pleasantly cool and we would sit and chat about the camp fire for an hour or two. Strange to say, the talk usually turned to bawd or religion or the relations of capital and labor. It was curious how eagerly these rough cattlemen would often discuss the mysteries of this unintelligible world, and as a militant skeptic I soon got a reputation among them, for Dell usually backed me up, and his knowledge of books and thinkers seemed to us extraordinary.

These constant evening discussions, this perpetual arguing, had an unimaginable effect on me. I had no books with me and I was often called on to deal with two or three different theories in a night; I had to think out the problems for myself, and usually I thought them out when hunting by myself in the daytime. It was as a cow-puncher that I taught myself how to think—a rare art among men and seldom practiced. Whatever originality I possess comes from the fact that in youth, while my mind was in process of growth, I was confronted with important modern problems and forced to think them out for myself and find some reasonable answer to the questionings of half a dozen different minds.

For example, Bent asked one night what the proper wage should be [for] the ordinary workman. I could only answer that the workman's wage should increase at least in measure as the productivity of labor increased; but I could not then see how to approach this ideal settlement. When I read Herbert Spencer ten years later in Germany, I was delighted to find that I had divined the best of his sociology and added to it materially. His idea that the amount of individual liberty in a country depends on "the pressure from the outside" I knew to be only half true. Pressure from the outside is one factor, but not even the most important: the centripetal force in the society itself is often much more powerful: how else can one explain the fact that during the World War liberty almost disappeared in these States, in spite of the First Amendment to the Constitution. At all times, indeed, there is much less regard for liberty here than in England, or even in Germany, or France: one has only to think of prohibition to admit this. The

* (London and New York, 1930).

pull towards the center in every country is in direct proportion to the masses, and accordingly the herd-feeling in America is unreasonably strong.

If we were not arguing or telling smutty stories, Bent would be sure to get out cards, and the gambling instinct would keep the boys busy till the stars paled in the eastern sky.

One incident I must relate here, for it broke the monotony of the routine in a curious way.

Our fire at night was made up of buffalo "chips," as the dried excrement was called, and Peggy had asked me, as I got up the earliest, always to replenish the fire before riding away. One morning I picked up a chip with my left hand and, as luck would have it, disturbed a little prairie rattlesnake that had been attracted probably by the heat of the camp fire. As I lifted the chip, the snake struck me on the back of my thumb, then coiled up in a flash and began to rattle. Angered, I put my right foot on him and killed him, and at the same moment bit out the place on my thumb where I had been stung; and then, still unsatisfied, rubbed my thumb in the red embers, especially above the wound. I paid little further attention to the matter; it seemed to me that the snake was too small to be very poisonous; but on returning to the wagon to wake Peggy, he cried out and called the Boss and Reece and Dell and was manifestly greatly perturbed, and even anxious. Reece, too, agreed with him that the bite of the little prairie rattlesnake was just as venomous as that of his big brother of the woods.

The Boss produced a glass of whisky and told me to drink it: I didn't want to take it, but he insisted and I drank it off. "Did it burn?" he asked. "No; 'twas just like water!" I replied, and noticed that the Boss and Reece exchanged a meaning look.

At once the Boss declared I must walk up and down, and each taking an arm, they walked me solemnly round and round for half an hour. At the end of that time I was half asleep: the Boss stopped and gave me another jorum of whisky; for a moment it awakened me, then I began to get numb again and deaf. Again they gave me whisky; I revived, but in five minutes I sagged down and begged them to let me sleep.

"Sleep be d . . . . d!" cried the Boss. "You'd never wake. Pull yourself together," and again I was given whisky. Then, dimly I began to realize that I must use my will power and so I started to jump about and shake off the overpowering drowsiness. Another two or three drinks of whisky and much frisking about occupied the next couple of hours, when suddenly I became aware of a sharp, intense pang of pain in my left thumb.

"Now you can sleep," said the Boss, "if you're minded to; I guess whisky has wiped out the rattler!"

The pain in my burnt thumb was acute: I found, too, I had a headache for the first time in my life. Peggy gave me hot water to drink and the headache soon disappeared. In a day or two I was as well as ever, thanks to the vigorous regimen of the Boss. In the course of a single year we lost two young men just through the little prairie snakes that seemed so insignificant.

The days passed quickly till we came near the first towns in southern Texas. Then every man wanted his arrears of salary from the Boss and proceeded to shave and doll up in wildest excitement. Charlie was like a madman. Half an hour after reaching the chief saloon in the town, everyone of them save Bent was crazy drunk and intent on finding some girl with whom to spend the night. I didn't even go to the saloon with them and begged Charlie in vain not to play the fool. "That's what I live for," he shouted, and raced off.

I had got accustomed to spend all my spare time with Reece, Dell, Bob or the Boss, and from all of them I learned a good deal. In a short time I had exhausted the Boss and Reece; but Dell and Bob each in his own way was richly equipped, and while Dell introduced me to literature and economics, Bob taught me some of the mysteries of cow-punching and the peculiar morals of Texan cattle. Every little herd of those half-wild animals had its own leader, it appeared, and followed him fanatically. When we brought together a few different bunches in our corral, there was confusion worse confounded, till after much hooking and some fighting a new leader would be chosen, whom all would obey. But sometimes we lost five or six animals in the mellay. I found Bob could ride his pony in among the half-savage brutes and pick out the future leader for them. Indeed, at the great sports held near Taos, he went in on foot where many herds had been corralled and led out the leader amid the triumphant cheers of his compatriots who challenged *los Americanos* to emulate that feat. Bob's knowledge of cattle was uncanny and all I know I learned from him.

For the first week or so, Reece and the Boss were out all day buying cattle; Reece would generally take Charlie and Jack Freeman, young Americans, to drive his purchase home to the big corral, while the Boss called indifferently first on one and then on another to help him. Charlie was the first to lay off: he had caught a venereal disease the very first night and had to lie up for more than a month. One after the other, all the younger men fell to the same plague. I went into the nearest town and consulted doctors and did what I could for them; the cure was often slow, for they would drink again to drown care and several in this way made the disease chronic. I could never understand the temptation; to get drunk was bad enough, but in that state to go with some dirty greaser woman, or half-breed prostitute, was incomprehensible to me.

Naturally I enquired about the Vidals; but no one seemed to have heard of them, and though I did my best, the weeks passed without my finding a trace of them. I wrote, however, to the address Gloria had given me before leaving Chicago so that I might be able to forward any letters; but I had left Texas before I heard from her; indeed, her letter reached me in the Fremont House when I got back to Chicago. She simply told me that they had crossed the Rio Grande and had settled in their hacienda on the other side, where perhaps, she added coyly, I would pay them a visit some day. I wrote thanking her and assuring her that her memory transfigured the world for me—which was the bare truth: I took infinite pains to put this letter into good Spanish, though I fear that in spite of Bob's assistance it had a dozen faults. But I'm outrunning my story.

Rapidly the herd was got together. Early in July we started northwards driving before us some six thousand head of cattle which certainly hadn't cost five thousand dollars. That first year everything went well with us; we only saw small bands of plains Indians and we were too strong for them. The Boss had allowed me to bring five hundred head of cattle on my own account: he wished to reward me, he said, for my incessant hard work, but I was sure it was Reece and Dell who put the idea into his head.

The fact that some of the cattle were mine made me a most watchful and indefatigable herdsman. More than once my vigilance, sharpened by Bob's instinct, made a difference to our fortunes. When we began to skirt the Indian territory, Bob warned me that a small band or even a single Indian might try some night to stampede the herd. About a week later, I noticed that the cattle were uneasy: "Indians!" said Bob when I told him the signs. That night I was off duty, but was on horseback circling round as usual, when about midnight, I saw a white figure leap from the ground with an unearthly yell. The cattle began to run together, so I threw my rifle up and fired at the Indian, and though I didn't hit him, he thought it better to drop the sheet and decamp. In five minutes we had pacified the cattle again and nothing unfortunate happened that night or indeed till we reached Wichita, which was then the outpost of civilization. In ten days more we were in Kansas City entraining, though we sold a fourth of our cattle there at about fifteen dollars a head. We reached Chicago about the first of October and put the cattle in the yards about the Michigan Street depot. Next day we sold more than half the herd, and I was lucky enough to get a purchaser at fifteen dollars a head for three hundred of my beasts. If it hadn't been for the Boss, who held out for three cents a pound, I should have sold all I had. As it was, I came out with more than five thousand dollars in the bank and felt myself another Croesus. My joy, however, was shortlived.

Of course I stayed in the Fremont and was excellently received. The management had slipped back a good deal, I thought, but I was glad that I was no longer responsible and could take my ease in my inn. My six months on the trail had marked my very being. It made a workman of me, and above all, it taught me that tense resolution, will power, was the most important factor of success in life. I made up my mind to train my will by exercise as I would train a muscle, and each day I proposed to myself a new test. For example, I liked potatoes, so I resolved not to eat one for a week, or again I foreswore coffee that I loved for a month, and I was careful to keep to my determination. I had noticed a French saying that intensified my decision, *Celui qui veut, celui-là peut:* "He who wills, can." My mind should govern me, not my appetites, I decided.

Chapter VII

The Great Fire of Chicago

I WISH I COULD PERSUADE MYSELF that I was capable of picturing the events of the week after we reached Chicago.

We arrived, if I remember rightly, on a Wednesday and put our cattle and horses in the stockyards near the Michigan Street depot. As I have related, we sold on Thursday and Friday about three-fifths of the cattle. I wanted to sell all, but followed the judgment of the Boss and sold three hundred head, and put a little over five thousand dollars in my banking account.

On Saturday night the alarm bells began to ring and awoke me. I slipped into my breeches, shirt and boots, and a youthful curiosity exciting me, I raced downstairs, got Blue Devil from the stable and rode out to the fire. I was infinitely impressed by the rapidity with which the firemen acted and the marvelous efficiency of the service. Where in England there would have been perhaps half a dozen fire-engines, the Americans sent fifty, but they all found work and did it magnificently. At one o'clock the fire was out and I returned to the hotel through two or three miles of uninjured streets. Of course, I told Reece and Ford all about it the next day. To my astonishment, no one seemed to pay attention; a fire was so common a thing in the wooden shanties on the outskirts of American towns that nobody cared to listen to my epic.

Next night, Sunday, the alarm bell began ringing about eleven o'clock: I was still dressed in my best. I changed into my working clothes, I do not know why, put my belt about me with a revolver in it and again took out the mare and rode to the fire. When still a quarter of a mile away, I realized that this fire was much more serious than that of the previous night: first of all, a gale of wind was blowing right down on the town. Then, when I wondered why there were so few fire engines, I was told that there were two other fires, and the man with whom I talked did not scruple to ascribe them to a plot and determination to burn the town down! "Them damned foreign anarchists are at the bottom of it"; he said, "three fires do not start on the very outskirts of the town with a gale of wind blowing, without some reason."

And indeed, it looked as if he were right. In spite of all the firemen could do, the fire spread with incredible rapidity. In half an hour I saw they were not going to master it soon or easily, and I rode back to get Reece, who had told me that he would have come with me the previous night if he had known where the fire was. When I got back to the hotel, Reece had gone out on his own and so had Dell and the Boss. I went back to the fire. It had caught on in the most extraordinary way. The wooden streets now were all blazing; the fire was swallowing block after block and the heat was so tremendous that the fire engines could not get within two hundred yards of the blaze. The roar of the fire was unearthly.

Another thing I noticed almost immediately: the heat was so terrific that the water decomposed into its elements and the oxygen gas in the water burned vehemently on its own account. The water, in fact, added fuel to the flames. As soon as I made sure of this, I saw that the town was doomed and walked my pony back a block or two to avoid flying sparks.

This must have been about three or four o'clock in the morning. I had gone back about three blocks when I came across a man talking to a group of men at the corner of a street. He was the one man of insight and sense I met that night. He seemed to me a typical, downeast Yankee: he certainly talked like one. The gist of his speech was as follows:

"I want you men to come with me right now to the mayor and tell him to give orders to blow up at least two blocks deep all along this side of the town; then, if we drench the houses on the other side, the flames will be stopped: there's no other way."

"That's sense," I cried, "that's what ought to be done at once. There's no other way of salvation; for the heat is disintegrating the water and the oxygen in the water is blazing fiercely, adding fuel to the flames."

"Gee! That's what I've been preaching for the last hour," he cried.

A little later fifty or sixty citizens went to the mayor, but he protested that he had not power to blow up houses and evidently, too, shirked the responsibility. He decided however to call in some of the councilmen and see what could be done. Meanwhile I went off and wandered towards the Randolph Street bridge and there saw a scene that appalled me.

Some men had caught a thief, they said, plundering one of the houses and they proceeded to string the poor wretch up to a lamp-post.

In vain I pleaded for his life, declared that he ought to be tried, that it was better to let off ten guilty men than hang one innocent one, but my foreign accent robbed my appeal, I think, of any weight; and before my eyes the man was strung up. It filled me with rage: it seemed a dreadful thing to have done: the cruelty of the executioners, the hard purpose of them, shut me away from my kin. Later I was to see these men from a better angle.

By the early morning the fire had destroyed over a mile deep of the town and was raging with unimaginable fury. I went down on the lake shore just before daybreak. The scene was one of indescribable magnificence: there were probably a hundred and fifty thousand homeless men, women and children grouped along the lake shore. Behind us roared the fire: it spread like a red sheet right up to the zenith above our heads, and from there was borne over the sky in front of us by long streamers of fire like rockets; vessels four hundred yards out in the bay were burning fiercely, and we were, so to speak, roofed and walled by flame. The danger and uproar were indeed terrifying and the heat, even in this October night, almost unbearable.

I wandered along the lake shore, noting the kind way in which the men took care of the women and children. Nearly every man was able to erect some kind of shelter for his wife and babies, and everyone was willing to help his neighbor. While working at one shelter for a little while, I said to the man I wished I could get a drink.

"You can get one," he said, "right there," and he pointed to a sort of makeshift shanty on the beach. I went over and found that a publican had managed to get four barrels down on the beach and had rigged up a sort of low tent above them; on one of the barrels he had nailed his shingle, and painted on it were the words, "What do you think of our hell? No drinks less than a dollar!" The wild humor of the thing amused me infinitely and the man certainly did a roaring trade.

A little later it occurred to me that our cattle might possibly burn, so I went out and hurried back to the Michigan Street stockyards. An old Irishman was in charge of the yard, but though he knew me perfectly well, he refused to let me take out a steer. The cattle were moving about wildly, evidently in a state of intense excitement. I pleaded with the man and begged him, and at length tied my mare up to the lamp-post at the corner and went back and got into the stockyard when he wasn't looking. I let down two or three of the bars and the next moment started the cattle through the opening. They went crazy wild and choked the gateway. In five minutes there were ten or twelve dead cattle in the entrance and the rest had to go over them. Suddenly, just as I got through the gap, the mad beasts made a rush and carried away the rails on both sides of the gateway. The next moment I was knocked down and I had just time to drag myself through the fence and so avoid their myriad trampling heels.

A few minutes later I was on Blue Devil, trying to get the cattle out of the town and on to the prairie. The herd broke up at almost every corner, but I managed to get about six hundred head right out into the country.

I drove them on the dead run for some miles. By this time it was daybreak and at the second or third farmhouse I came to I found a farmer willing to take in the cattle. I bargained with him a little and at length told him I would give him a dollar a head if he kept them for the week or so we might want to leave them with him. In two minutes he brought out his son and an Irish helper and turned the cattle back and into his pasture. There were six hundred and seventy-six of them, as near as I could count, out of practically two thousand head.

By the time I had finished the business and returned to the hotel, it was almost noon and as I could get nothing to eat I wandered out again to see the progress of the fire. Already I found that relief trains were being sent in with food from all neighboring towns and this was the feature of the next week in starving Chicago.

Strangely enough, at that time the idea was generally accepted that a man or woman could only live three days without food. It was years before Dr. Tanner showed the world that a man could fast for forty days or more. Everyone I met acted as if he believed that if he were fully three days without food, he must die incontinently. I laughed at the idea, which seemed to me absurd, but so strong was the universal opinion and the influence of the herd-sentiment, that on the third day I too felt particularly empty and thought I had better take my place in the bread line. There were perhaps five thousand in front of me and there were soon fifty or sixty thousand behind me. We were five deep moving to the depot where the bread trains were discharging, one after the other. When I got pretty close to the food wagons, I noticed that the food supply was coming to an end, and next moment I noticed something else.

Again and again women and girls came into our bread line and walked through the lines of waiting men, who, mark you, really believed they were going to die that night if they could not get food; but instead of objecting, they one and all made way for the women and girls and encouraged them: "Go right on, Madam, take all you want. This way, Missee, you won't be able to carry much, I'm afraid"—proof on proof, it seemed to me, of courage, good humor and high self-abnegation. I went into that bread line an Irish boy and came out of it a proud American, but I did not get any bread that night or the next. In fact, my first meal was made when I ran across Reece on the Friday or Saturday after: Reece, as usual, had fallen on his feet and found a hotel where they had provisions—though at famine prices.

He insisted that I should come with him and soon got me my first meal. In return, I told him and Ford of the cattle I had saved. They were, of course, delighted and determined next day to come out and retrieve them. "One thing is certain," said Ford; "six hundred head of cattle are worth as much today in Chicago as fifteen hundred head were worth before the fire, so we hain't lost much."

Next day I led Reece and the Boss straight to the farmer's place, but to my surprise he told me that I had agreed to give him two dollars a head, whereas I had bargained with him for only one dollar. His son backed up the farmer's statement and the Irish helper declared that he was sorry to disagree with me, but I was mistaken; it was two dollars I had said. They little knew the sort of men they had to deal with. "Where are the cattle?" Ford asked, and we went down to the pasture where they were penned. "Count them, Harris," said Ford, and I counted six hundred and twenty head. Fifty odd had disappeared, but the farmer wanted to persuade me that I had counted wrongly.

Ford went about and soon found a rough lean-to stable where there were thirty more head of Texan cattle. These were driven up and soon disappeared in the herd; Reece and I began to move the herd towards the entrance. The farmer declared he would not let us go, but Ford looked at him a little while and then said very quietly, "You have stolen enough cattle to pay you. If you bother with us, I will make meat of you—see!—cold meat," and the farmer moved aside and kept quiet.

That night we had a great feast, and the day after Ford announced that he had sold the whole of the cattle to two hotel proprietors and got nearly as much money as if we had not lost a hoof.

My five thousand dollars became six thousand five hundred.

The courage shown by the common people in the fire, the wild humor coupled with the consideration for the women, had won my heart. This is the greatest people in the world, I said to myself, and was proud to feel at one with them.

Chapter VIII

Back on the Trail

PROMPTED BY DELL, before leaving Chicago I bought some books for the winter evenings, notably Mill's *Political Economy;** Carlyle's *Heroes and Hero Worship* and *Latter Day Pamphlets;* Col. Hay's *Dialect Poems,*** too, and three medical books, and took them down with me to the ranch. We had six weeks of fine weather, during which I broke in horses under Reece's supervision, and found out that gentleness and especially carrots and pieces of sugar were the direct way to the heart of the horse; discovered, too, that a horse's bad temper and obstinacy were nearly always due to fear. A remark of Dell that a horse's eye had magnifying power and that the poor, timid creatures saw men as trees walking, gave me the clue and soon I was gratified by Reece's saying that I could "gentle" horses as well as anyone on the ranch, excepting Bob.

As winter drew down and the bitter frost came, outdoor work almost ceased. I read from morning till night and not only devoured Mill, but saw through the fallacy of his wage-fund theory. I knew from my own experience that the wages of labor depended primarily on the productivity of labor. I liked Mill for his humanitarian sympathies with the poor; but I realized clearly that he was a second-rate intelligence, just as I felt pretty sure that Carlyle was one of the immortals. I took Carlyle in small doses: I wanted to think for myself. After the first chapters I tried to put down first, chapter by chapter, what I thought or knew about the subject treated, and am still inclined to believe that that is a good way to read in order to estimate what the author has taught you.

Carlyle was the first dominant influence in my life and one of the most important: I got more from him than from any other writer. His two or three books, learned almost by heart, taught me that Dell's knowledge was skimpy and superficial, and I was soon Sir Oracle among the men on all deep subjects. For the medical books, too, turned out to be excellent and

---

* Either Mill's *Essays on Some Unsettled Questions of Political Economy* (1831–44), or his *Principles of Political Economy* (1848).

** John Hay (1838–1905), Secretary of State, 1898–1905. Harris is doubtless referring to Hay's *Pike County Ballads and Other Pieces* (1871).

gave me almost the latest knowledge on all sex-matters. I was delighted to put all my knowledge at the disposal of the boys, or rather to show off to them how much I knew.

That fall brought me to grief: early in October I was taken by ague, "chills and fever," as it was called. I suffered miseries, and though Reece induced me to ride all the same and spend most of the daytime in the open, [I] lost weight till I learned that arsenic was a better specific even than quinine. Then I began to mend, but, off and on, every fall and spring afterwards, so long as I stayed in America, I had to take quinine and arsenic to ward off the debilitating attacks.

I was very low indeed when we started down the trail; the Boss being determined, as he said, to bring up two herds that summer. Early in May he started north from near San Anton' with some five thousand head, leaving Reece, Dell, Bob, Peggy the Cook, Bent, Charlie and myself to collect another herd. I never saw the Boss again—I understood, however, from Reece's cursing that he had got through safely, sold the cattle at a good price and made off with all the proceeds, though he owed Reece and Dell more than one-half.

Charlie's love-adventure that ended so badly did not quiet him for long. In our search for cheap cattle we had gone down nearly to the Rio Grande, and there, in a little half-Mexican town, Charlie met his fate.

As it happened, I had gone to the saloon with him on his promise that he would only drink one glass, and though the glass would be full of forty-rod whisky, I knew it would have only a passing effect on Charlie's superb strength. But it excited him enough to make him call up all the girls for a drink: they all streamed laughing to the bar, all save one. Naturally Charlie went after her and found a very pretty blond girl, who had a strain of Indian blood in her, it was said. At first she didn't yield to Charlie's invitation, so he turned away angrily, saying:

"You don't want to drink probably because you want to cure yourself, or because you're ugly where women are usually beautiful." Answering the challenge, the girl sprang to her feet, tore off her jacket and in a moment was naked to her boots and stockings.

"Am I ugly?" she cried, pushing out her breasts, "Or do I look ill, you fool!" and whirled around to give us the back view!

She certainly had a lovely figure with fair youthful breasts and peculiarly full bottom and looked the picture of health. The full cheeks of her bottom excited me intensely, I didn't know why: therefore it didn't surprise me when Charlie, with a half-articulate shout of admiration, picked her up bodily in his arms and carried her out of the room.

When I remonstrated with him afterwards, he told me he had a sure way of knowing whether the girl, Sue, was diseased or not.

I contradicted him and found that this was his infallible test: as soon as he was alone with a girl, he pulled out ten or twenty dollars, as the case might be, and told her to keep the money. "I'll not give you any more in any case," he would add. "Now tell me, dear, if you are ill and we'll have a last drink and then I'll go. If she's ill she's sure to tell you—see!" and he laughed triumphantly.

"Suppose she doesn't know she's ill?" I asked. But he replied: "They always know and they'll tell the truth when their greed is not against you."

For some time it looked as if Charlie had enjoyed his beauty without any evil consequences, but a month or so later he noticed a lump in his right groin and soon afterwards a syphilitic sore showed itself just under the head of his penis. We had already started northwards but I had to tell Charlie the plain truth.

"Then it's serious," he cried in astonishment, and I replied:

"I'm afraid so, but not if you take it in time and go under a rigorous regimen."

Charlie did everything he was told to do and always bragged that gonorrhea was much worse, as it is certainly more painful than syphilis; but the disease in time had its revenge.

As he began to get better on the trail, thanks to the good air, regular exercise and absence of drink, he became obstreperous from time to time and I at any rate forgot about his ailment.

The defection of the Boss made a serious difference to us; Reece and Dell with three or four Mexicans and Peggy went on slowly buying cattle; but Bob and Bent put a new scheme into my head. Bent was always preaching that the Boss's defection had ruined Reece and that if I would put in, say five thousand dollars, I could be Reece's partner and make a fortune with him. Bob, too, was keen on this and told me incidentally that he could get cattle from the Mexicans for nothing. I had a talk with Reece who said he'd have to be content with buying three thousand head, for cattle had gone up in price twofold and the Boss's swindle had crippled him. If I would pay Bent's, Charlie's and Bob's wages, he'd be delighted, he said, to join forces with me; on Bob's advice, I consented and with his help I managed to secure three thousand head for little more than three thousand dollars. And this is how we managed it.

For some reason or other, perhaps because I had learnt a few words of Spanish, Bob had taken a fancy to me and was always willing to help me, except when he was mad with drink. He now assured me that if I would go with him down the Rio Grande a hundred miles or so, he'd get me a thousand head of cattle for nothing. I consented, for Bent, too, and Charlie were on Bob's side.

The next morning before sunrise we started out and rode steadily to the southeast. We carried enough food for two or three days. Bob saw to that without any question, but generally he brought us about eight o'clock near some house or other where we could get food and shelter. His knowledge of the whole frontier was as uncanny as his knowledge of cattle.

On the fourth or fifth day about nine in the morning he stopped us by a little wooded height looking over a gorge of the river. To the left the river spread out almost to a shallow lake; and one did not need to be told that a little lower down there must be one or more fords where cattle could cross almost without wetting themselves.

Bob got off his horse in a clump of cottonwood trees, which he said was a good place to camp without being seen. I asked him where the cattle were and he told me "across the river." Within two or three miles, it appeared, there was a famous hacienda with great herds. As soon as it got dark, he proposed to go across and find out all about it and bring us the news. We were to be careful not to be seen and he hoped that we would not even make a fire, but would lie close till he returned.

We were more than willing, and when we got tired of talking, Bent produced an old deck of cards and we would play draw poker or euchre or casino for two or three hours. The first night passed quickly enough. We had been in the saddle for ten hours a day for four or five days and slept a dreamless sleep. Bob did not return that day or the next and on the third day Bent began to curse him, but I felt sure he had good reason for the delay and so waited with what patience I could muster. On the third night he was suddenly with us, just as if he had come out of the earth.

"Welcome back," I cried. "Everything right?"

"Everything," he said. "It was no good coming sooner; they have brought some cattle within four miles of the river; the orders are to keep 'em away seven or eight miles, so that they could not be driven across without rousing the whole country; but Don José is very rich and carefree and there is a herd of fifteen hundred that will suit us, not three miles from the river in a fold of the prairie guarded only by two men whom I'll make so very drunk that they'll hear nothing till next morning. A couple of bottles of aguardiente will do the buzness, and I'll come back for you tomorrow night by eight or nine o'clock."

It all turned out as Bob had arranged. The next night he came to us as soon as it was dark. We rode some two miles down the river to a ford, splashed through the rivulets of water and came out on the Mexican side. In single file and complete silence we followed Bob at a lope for perhaps twenty minutes, when he put up his hand and we drew down to a walk. There below us, between two waves of prairie, were the cattle.

In a few words Bob told Bent and Charlie what they were to do. Bent was to stay behind and shoot in case they were followed—unlikely but always possible. Charlie and I were to move the cattle towards the ford, quietly all the way if we could, but if we were pursued, then as hard as we could drive them.

For the first half hour all went according to program. Charlie and I moved the cattle together and drove them over the waves of prairie towards the river; it all seemed as easy as eating and we had begun to push the cattle into a fast walk, when suddenly there was a shot in front and a sort of stampede!

At once Charlie shot out on the left as I shot out on the right, and using our whips, we quickly got the herd into motion again, the rear ranks forcing the front ones on; the cattle were soon pressed into a shuffling trot and the difficulty seemed overcome. Just at that moment I saw two or three bright flames half a mile away on the other side of Charlie and suddenly I heard the zip of a bullet pass my own head and turning, saw pretty plainly a man riding fifty yards away from me. I took very careful aim at his horse and fired and was delighted to see horse and man come down and disappear. I paid no further attention to him and kept on forcing the pace of the cattle. But Charlie was very busily engaged for two or three minutes because the fusillade was kept up from behind till he was joined by Bent and shortly afterwards by Bob. We were all now driving the cattle as hard as they could go, straight towards the ford. The shots behind us continued and even grew more frequent, but we were not further molested till three-quarters of an hour later, [when] we reached the Rio Grande and began urging the cattle across the ford. There progress was necessarily slow. We could scarcely have got across had it not been that about the middle Bob came up and made his whip and voice a perfect terror to the beasts in the rear.

When we got them out on the other side I began to turn them westwards towards our wooded knoll. The next moment Bob was beside me shouting: "Straight ahead, straight ahead; they are following us and we shall have to fight. You get on with the herd always straight north and I'll bring Charlie back to the bank so as to hold 'em off."

Boylike, I said I would rather go and fight, but he said: "You go on. If Charlie's killed no matter. I want you." And I had perforce to do what the little devil ordered.

When Texan cattle have been brought up together, the largest herd can be driven like a small bunch. They have their leader and they follow him religiously and so one man can drive a thousand head with very little trouble.

For two or three miles I kept them on the trot and then I let them gradually get down to a walk. I did not want to lose any more of them; some fat cows had already died in their tracks through being driven so fast.

About two o'clock in the morning I passed a log-house and soon an American rode up beside me and wanted to know who I was, where I had brought the cattle from and where I was going. I told him the owner was behind me, that the boys and I were driving them straight ahead because some greasers had been interfering with us.

"That's the shooting I heard," he said. "You have driven them across the river, haven't you?"

"I've driven them from the river," I replied; "some of them were getting a drink."

I could feel him grin, though I was not looking at him.

"I guess I'll see your friends pretty soon," he said, "but this raiding is bad business. Them greasers'll come across and give me trouble. We border-folk don't want a fuss hatched up by you foreigners!"

I placated him as well as I could; at first [I] was unsuccessful. He didn't say much, but he evidently intended to come with me to the end because wherever I rode, I found him right behind the herd when I returned.

Day had broken when I let the cattle halt for the first time. I reckoned I had gone twelve miles from the ford and the beasts were foot-sore and very tired, more and more of them requiring the whip in order to keep up even a walk. I bunched them together and came back to my saturnine acquaintance.

"You are young to be at this game," he said. "Who is your boss?"

"I don't keep a boss," I answered, taking him in with hostile scrutiny. He was a man of about forty, tall and lean, with an enormous quid of tobacco in his left cheek—a typical Texan.

His bronco interested me; instead of being an Indian pony of thirteen hands or so, it was perhaps fifteen and a half and looked to be three-quarters bred.

"A good horse you have there," I said.

"The best in the hull country," he replied, "easy."

"That's only your conceit," I retorted. "The mare I am on right now can give him a hundred yards a mile."

"You don't want to risk any money on that, do you?" he remarked.

"Oh, yes," I smiled.

"Well, we can try it out one of these days, but here comes your crowd," and indeed, although I had not expected them, in five minutes Bent and Bob and Charlie rode up.

"Get the cattle going," cried Bob, as he came within earshot. "We must go on. The Mexicans have gone back but they will come right after us again. Who is this?" he added, ranging up beside the Texan.

"My name is Locker," said my acquaintance; "and I guess your raiding will set the whole border boiling. Can't you buy cattle decently, like we all have to?"

"How do you know how decently we paid for them?" cried Bent, thrusting forward his brown face like a weasel's, his dog teeth showing.

"I guess Mr. Locker is all right," I cried laughing. "I propose he should help us and take two or three hundred head as payment, or the value of them—"

"Now you're talking," said Locker. "I call that sense. There is a herd of mine about a mile further on; if two or three hundred of your Jose steers join it, I can't hinder 'em; but I'd rather have dollars; cash is scarce!"

"Are they herded?" asked Bob.

"Sure," replied Locker. "I am too near the river to let any cattle run round loose, though nobody has interfered with me in the last ten years."

Bob and I began moving the cattle on leaving Bent with Locker to con-clude the negotiations. In an hour we had found Locker's herd that must have numbered at least six thousand head and were guarded by three herdsmen.

Locker and Bent had soon come to a working agreement. Locker, it turned out, had another herd some distance to the east, from which he could draw three or four herdsmen. He had also a couple of boys, sons of his, whom he could send to rouse some of the neighboring farmers, if the need was urgent. It turned out that we had done well to be generous to him, for he knew the whole of the countryside like a book and was a good friend in our need.

Late in the afternoon, Locker was informed by one of his sons, a youth of about sixteen, that twenty Mexicans had crossed the river and would be up to us in a short time. Locker sent him after the younger boy to round up as many Texans as possible, but before they could be collected, a bunch of greasers, twenty or so in number, rode up and demanded the return of the cattle. Bent and Locker put them off, and as luck would have it, while they were arguing, three or four Texans came up, and one of them, a man of about forty years of age named Rossiter, took control of the whole dispute. He told the Mexican leader, who said he was Don Luis, a son of Don José, that if he stayed any longer he would probably be arrested and put in prison for raiding American territory and threatening people.

The Mexican seemed to have a good deal of pluck and declared that he would not only threaten but carry out his threat. Rossiter told him to wade right in. The loud talk began again, and a couple more Texans came up and the Mexican leader, realizing that unless he did something at once he would be too late, started to circle round the cattle, no doubt thinking that if he did something his superior numbers would scare us.

In five minutes the fight had begun. In ten more it was all over. Nothing could stand against the deadly shooting of the Westerners. In five minutes one or two of the Mexicans had been killed and several wounded; half a dozen horses had gone down; it was perfectly evident that the eight or ten of us were more than a match for the twenty Mexicans, for except Don Luis, none of them seemed to have any stomach for the work, and Luis got a bullet through his arm in the first five minutes. Finally they drew off threatening and yelling and we saw no more of them.

After the battle we all adjourned to Locker's and had a big drink. Nobody took the fight seriously; whipping greasers was nothing to brag about; but Rossiter thought that a claim should be made against the Mexican Government for raiding United States territory; said he was going to draw up the papers and send them to the state district attorney at Austin. The proposal was received with whoops and cheers. The idea of punishing the Mexicans for getting shot trying to recapture their own cattle appealed to us Americans as something intensely humorous. All the Texans gave their names solemnly as witnesses, and Rossiter swore he would draw up the document. Years afterwards Bent, whom I met by chance, told me that Rossiter had got forty thousand dollars on that claim.

Three days later we began to move our cattle eastward to join Reece and Dell. I gave one hundred dollars as a reward to Locker's two boys who had helped us from start to finish most eagerly.

A week or so later we got back to the main camp. Reece and Dell had their herd ready and fat. After a talk we resolved to go each on his own and join afterwards for the fall and winter on the ranch, if it pleased us. We took three weeks to get our bunch of cattle into condition and so began driving north in July. I spent every night in the saddle and most of the day, even though the accursed fever was shaking me.

All went well with us at first; I promised my three lieutenants a third share in the profits and a small wage besides; they were as keen as mustard and did all men could do. As soon as we reached the latitude of the Indian territory our troubles began. One wild night Indians who wore sheets and had smeared their hands with phosphorus, stampeded the cattle, and though the boys did wonders, we lost nearly a thousand head and some hundred horses, all of them broken in carefully.

It was a serious loss, but not irreparable. The plains Indians, however, were as persistent that summer as mosquitoes. I never went out after game but they tried to cut me off, and once at least nothing but the speed and stamina of Blue Devil saved me. I had to give up serious shooting and depend on luck bringing us near game. Gradually the Indians following us grew more numerous and bolder. We were attacked at nightfall and daybreak three or four days running and the half-wild cattle began to get very scarey.

Bob did not conceal his anxiety. "Bad Injuns! Very mean Injuns!" One afternoon they followed us openly; there were at one time over a hundred in view; evidently they were getting ready for a serious attack. Bob's genius got us a respite. While Charlie was advising a pitched battle, Bob suddeny remembered that there was a scrub-oak forest some five miles further on to our right that would give us a refuge. Charlie and Bent, the best shots, lay down and began to shoot and soon made the Indians keep out of sight. In three hours we reached the scrub-oak wood and the bay or bight in it where Bob said the cattle would be safe; for nothing could get through scrub-oak, and as soon as we had driven the cattle deep into the bay and brought our wagon to the centre, on the arc of the bight, so to speak, no Indians could stampede the cattle without blotting us out first. For the moment we were safe, and as luck would have it, the water in a little creek nearby was drinkable. Still, we were besieged by over a hundred Indians and those odds were heavy, as even Bob admitted.

Days passed and the siege continued: the Indians evidently meant to tire us out and get the herd, and our tempers didn't improve under the enforced idleness and vigilance. One evening Charlie was sprawling at the fire, taking up more than his share of it, when Bent, who had been looking after the cattle, came in. "Take up your legs, Charlie," he said roughly; "you don't want the whole fire." Charlie didn't hear, or paid no attention:

Bent threw himself down on Charlie's long limbs. With a curse Charlie pushed him off: the next moment Bent had hurled himself on Charlie and had shoved his head down in the fire. After a short struggle Charlie got free and in spite of all I could do, struck Bent.

Bent groped for his gun at once, but Charlie was at him striking and swinging like a wild man and Bent had to meet the attack.

Till the trial came, everyone would have said that Charlie was far and away the better man, younger, too, and astonishingly powerful. But Bent evidently was no novice at the game. He side stepped Charlie's rush and hit out straight and hard and Charlie went down, but was up again like a flash and went for his man in a wild rush: soon he was down again and everyone realized that sooner or later Bent must win. Fighting, however, has a large element of chance in it, and as luck would have it just when Bent seemed most certain of winning, one of Charlie's wild swings caught him on the point of the jaw, and to our amazement he went down like a log and could not be brought to for some ten minutes. It was the first time I had seen this blow, and naturally we all exaggerated the force of it, not knowing that a light blow up against the chin jars the spinal cord and knocks any man insensible. In fact, in many cases, such a blow results in partial paralysis and life-long weakness.

Charlie was inclined to brag of his victory, but Bob told him the truth; and on reflection Bent's purpose and fighting power made the deeper impression on all of us, and he himself took pains next day to warn Charlie. "Don't get in my way again," he said to him dryly, "or I'll make meat of you."

The dire menace in his hard face was convincing. "Oh, hell," replied Charlie, "who wants to get in your way!"

Reflection teaches me that all the worst toughs on the border in my time were ex-soldiers: it was the Civil War that had bred those men to violence and the use of the revolver; it was the Civil War that produced (the "Wild Bills" and Bents who forced)* the good humored westerners to hold life cheaply and to use their guns instead of fists.

One evening we noticed a large increase in the force of Indians besieging us: one chief, too, on a piebald mustang appeared to be urging an immediate attack, and soon we found some of the "braves" stealing down the creek to outflank us, while a hundred others streamed past us at four hundred yards' distance, firing wildly. Bob and I went under the creek banks to stop the flankers, while Bent and Charlie and Jo brought down more than one horse and man and taught the band of Indians that a direct attack would surely cost them many lives.

Still there were only five of us and a chance bullet or two might make the odds against us desperate.

Talking it over, we came to the conclusion that one man should ride to Fort Dodge for help, and I was selected as the lightest, save Bob, and al-

* An addition made by Harris in his copy of Volume I.

together the worst shot, besides being the only man who would certainly find his way. Accordingly, I brought up Blue Devil at once, took some pounds of jerked beef with me and a goat water-skin I had bought in Taos; a girth and stirrups quickly turned a blanket into a makeshift light saddle and I was ready.

It was Bob's uncanny knowledge both of the trail and of Indian ways that gave me my chance. All the rest advised me to go north out of our bay and then ride for it. He advised me to go south where the large body of Indians had stationed themselves. "They'll not look for you there," he said, "and you may get through unseen; half an hour's riding more will take you round them; then you have one hundred and fifty miles north on the trail—you may pick up a herd—and then one hundred and twenty miles straight west. You ought to be in Dodge in five days and back here in five more; you'll find us," he added significantly. The little man padded Blue Devil's hoofs with some old garments he cut up and insisted on leading her away round the bight, and far to the south, and I verily believe beyond the Indian camp.

There he took off the mare's pads, while I tightened the girths and started to walk, keeping the mare between me and the Indians and my ears cocked for the slightest sound. But I heard nothing and saw nothing and in an hour more had made the round and was on the trail for the north, determined in my own mind to do the two or three hundred miles in four days at most. On the fourth day I got twenty troopers from the fort with Lieutenant Winder and was leading them in a bee-line to our refuge. We got there in six days, but in the meantime the Indians had been busy.

They cut a way through the scrub-oak brush that we regarded as impassable and stampeded the cattle one morning just at dawn, and our men were only able to herd off about six or seven hundred head and protect them in the extreme north corner of the bend. The Indians had all drawn off the day before I arrived with the U.S. Cavalry troopers. Next morning we began the march northwards and I had no difficulty in persuading Lieutenant Winder to give us his escort for the next four or five days.

A week later we reached Wichita, where we decided to rest for a couple of days, and there we encountered another piece of bad luck. Ever since he had caught syphilis, Charlie seemed to have lost his gay temper: he became gloomy and morose and we could do nothing to cheer him up. The very first night he had to be put to bed at the gambling saloon in Wichita, where he had become speechlessly drunk. And next day he was convinced that he had been robbed of his money by the man who kept the bank and went about swearing that he would get even with him at all costs. By the evening he had infected Bent and Joe with his insane determination, and finally I went along hoping to save him, if I could, from some disaster.

Already I had asked Bob to get another herdsman and drive the cattle steadily towards Kansas City: he consented, and for hours before we went to the saloon, Bob had been trekking north. I intended to rejoin him some five or six miles further on and drive slowly for the rest of the night. Somehow or other, I felt that the neighborhood was unhealthy for us.

The gambling saloon was lighted by three powerful oil lamps: two over the faro table and one over the bar. Jo stationed himself at the bar while Bent and Charlie went to the table. I walked about the room trying to play the indifferent among the twenty or thirty men scattered about. Suddenly, about ten o'clock, Charlie began disputing with the banker: they both rose, the banker drawing a big revolver from the table drawer in front of him. At the same moment Charlie struck the lamp above him and I saw him draw his gun just as all the lights went out (leaving us in pitch darkness).*

I ran to the door and was carried through it in a sort of mad stampede. A minute afterwards Bent joined me and then Charlie came rushing out at top speed with Jo hard after him. In a moment we were at the corner of the street where we had left our ponies and were off: one or two shots followed; I thought we had got off scot free, but I was mistaken.

We had ridden hell for leather about an hour when Charlie without apparent reason pulled up and swaying, fell out of his saddle: his pony stopped dead and we all gathered round the wounded man.

"I'm finished," said Charlie in a weak voice, "but I've got my money back and I want you to send it to my mother in Pleasant Hill, Missouri. It's about a thousand dollars, I guess."

"Are you badly hurt?" I asked.

"He drilled me through the stomach first go off," Charlie said, pointing, "and I guess I've got it at least twice more through the lungs: I'm done."

"What a pity, Charlie!" I cried; "you'll get more than a thousand dollars from your share of the cattle: I've told Bob that I intend to share equally with all of you. This money must go back, but the thousand shall be sent to your mother, I promise you."

"Not on your life!" cried the dying man, lifting himself up on one elbow. "This is my money: it shan't go back to that oily sneak thief!" The effort had exhausted him; even in the dim light we could see that his face was drawn and grey: he must have understood this himself, for I could just hear his last words: "Goodbye, boys!" His head fell back, his mouth opened: the brave boyish spirit was gone.

I couldn't control my tears: the phrase came to me: "I better could have lost a better man," for Charlie was at heart a good fellow!

I left Bent to carry back the money and arrange for Charlie's burial, leaving Jo to guard the body: in an hour I was again with Bob and had told him everything. Ten days later we were in Kansas City, where I was surprised by unexpected news.

My second brother, Willie, six years older than I was, had come out to America and hearing of me in Kansas, had located himself in Lawrence as a real estate agent; he wrote asking me to join him. This quickened my determination to have nothing more to do with cow-punching. Cattle, too,

* An addition made by Harris in his own copy.

we found, had fallen in price and we were lucky to get ten dollars a head for our bunch, which made a poor showing from the fact that the Indians had netted all the best. There was about six thousand dollars to divide: Jo got five hundred dollars and Bent, Bob, Charlie's mother and myself divided the rest. Bob told me I was a fool: I should keep it all and go down south again; but what had I gained by my two years of cow-punching? I had lost money* and caught malarial fever; I had won a certain knowledge of ordinary men and their way of living and had got more than a smattering of economics and of medicine; but I was filled with an infinite disgust for a merely physical life. What was I to do now? I'd see Willie and make up my mind.

* According to earlier figures, he had made money. This must be an incomplete accounting.

Chapter IX

Student Life and Love

THAT RAILWAY JOURNEY to Lawrence, Kansas, is as vivid to me now as if it had taken place yesterday; yet it all happened more than fifty years ago. It was a blazing hot day and in the seat opposite to me was an old grey-haired man who appeared to be much troubled by the heat: he moved about restlessly, mopped his forehead, took off his vest and finally went out, probably to the open observation platform, leaving a couple of books on his seat. I took one of them up heedlessly—it was *The Life and Death of Jason,* by William Morris. I read a page or two, was surprised by the easy flow of the verse, but not gripped, so I picked up the other volume: *Laus Veneris: Poems and Ballads* by Algernon Charles Swinburne. It opened at the *Ancatoria,* and in a moment I was carried away, entranced as no poetry before or since has ever entranced me. Venus herself spoke in the lines:

> Alas! that neither rain nor snow nor dew
> Nor all cold things can purge me wholly through,
> Assuage me nor allay me, nor appease,
> Till supreme sleep shall bring me bloodless ease,
> Till Time wax faint in all her periods,
> Till Fate undo the bondage of the Gods
> To lay and slake and satiate me all through,
> Lotus and Lethe on my lips like dew,
> And shed around and over and under me
> Thick darkness and the insuperable sea.*

I haven't seen the poem since and there may be verbal inaccuracies in my version, but the music and passion of the verses enthralled me; and when I came to *The Leper,* the last stanzas brought hot tears to my eyes; and in the *Garden of Proserpine,* I heard my own soul speaking with divine if hopeless assurance. Was there ever such poetry? Even the lighter verses were charming:

> Remembrance may recover
> And time bring back to time

* In the fifth line "her" should read "his."

> The name of your first lover,
> The ring of my first rhyme:
>
> But rose-leaves of December,
> The storms of June shall fret;
> The day that you remember,
> The day that I forget.*

And then the gay defiance:

> In the teeth of the glad salt weather,
> In the blown wet face of the sea;
> While three men hold together,
> Their Kingdoms are less by three.**

And the divine songs to Hugo and to Whitman and the superb *Dedication,* the last verse of it a miracle:

> Though the many lights dwindle to one light,
> There is help if the Heavens have one;
> Though the stars be discrowned of the sunlight
> And the earth dispossessed of the Sun:
> They have moonlight and sleep for repayment
> When refreshed as a bride and set free;
> With stars and sea-winds in her raiment
> Night sinks on the sea.

My very soul was taken; I had no need to read them twice: I've never seen them twice; I shall not forget them so long as this machine lasts. They flooded my eyes with tears, my heart with passionate admiration. In this state the old gentleman came back and found me, a cowboy to all appearance, lost, tear-drowned in Swinburne.

"I think that's my book," he said calling me back to dull reality.

"Surely," I replied bowing; "but what magnificent poetry, and I never heard of Swinburne before."

"This is his first book, I believe," said the old gentleman, "but I'm glad you like his verses."

"Like," I cried, "who could help adoring them?" and I let myself go to recite the *Prosperpine:*

> From too much love of living,
> From hope and fear set free,
> We thank with brief thanksgiving
> Whatever Gods may be

* The sixth stanza from *Rococo*. Harris erred in remembering the eight lines as two stanzas. In line six, "storms" should read "frosts," and in line eight, "forget" should read "forgot."

** From *A Song in Time of Order*. Harris errs only in the first line, which should read ". . . of the hard glad weather."

That no life lives forever,
That dead men rise up never,
That even the weariest river
Winds somewhere safe to sea.

"Why, you've learned it by heart!" cried the old man in wonder.

"Learned," I repeated, "I know half the book by heart: if you had stayed away another half hour, I'd have known it all," and I went on reciting for the next ten minutes.

"I never heard of such a thing in my life," he cried. "Fancy a cowboy who learns Swinburne by merely reading him. It's astounding! Where are you going?"

"To Lawrence," I replied.

"We're almost there," he added, and then, "I wish you would let me give you the book. I can easily get another copy and I think it ought to be yours." I thanked him with all my heart and in a few minutes more got down at Lawrence station, then as now far outside the little town, clasping my Swinburne in my hand.

I record this story not to brag of my memory, for all gifts are handicaps in life, but to show how kind western Americans were to young folk, and because the irresistible, unique appeal of Swinburne to youth has never been set forth before, so far as I know.

In a comfortable room at the Eldridge House, in the chief street of Lawrence, I met my brother. Willie seemed woefully surprised by my appearance. "You're as yellow as a guinea, but how you've grown," he cried. "You may be tall, but you look ill, very ill!"*

He was the picture of health and even better looking than I had remembered him: a man of five feet ten or so, with good figure and very handsome dark face: hair, small moustache, and goatee beard jet black; straight thin nose and superb long hazel eyes with black lashes: he might have stood for the model of a Greek god, were it not that his forehead was narrow and his eyes set close.

In three months he had become enthusiastically American. "America is the greatest country in the world"; he assured me from an abysmal ignorance, "any young man who works can make money here; if I had a little capital I'd be a rich man in a very few years; it's some capital I need, nothing more." Having drawn my story out of me, especially the last phase when I divided up with the boys, he declared I must be mad. "With five thousand dollars," he cried, "I could be rich in three years, a millionaire in ten. You must be mad; don't you know that everyone is for himself in this world? Good gracious! I never heard of such insanity: if I had only known!"

For some days I watched him closely and came to believe that he was perfectly suited to his surroundings, eminently fitted to succeed in them.

* Harris was only five feet six at maturity.

He was an earnest Christian, I found, who had been converted and baptized in the Baptist Church; he had a fair tenor voice and led the choir; he swallowed all the idiocies of the incredible creed, but drew some valuable moral sanctions from it; he was a teetotaler and didn't smoke; a Nazarene, too, determined to keep chaste, as he called a state of abstinence from women; and weekly indulgence in self-abuse which he tried to justify as inevitable.

The teaching of Jesus himself had little or no practical effect on him; he classed it all together as counsels of an impossible perfection and, like the vast majority of Americans, he accepted a childish Pauline-German morality, while despising the duty of forgiveness and scorning the Gospel of Love.

A few days after our first meeting, Willie proposed to me that I should lend him a thousand dollars and he would give me twenty-five per cent for the use of the money. When I exclaimed against the usurious rate, twelve per cent being the state limit, he told me he could lend a million dollars, if he had it, at from three to five per cent a month on perfect security. "So you see," he wound up, "that I can easily afford to give you two hundred and fifty dollars a year for the use of your thousand: one can buy real estate here to pay fifty per cent a year; the country is only just beginning to be developed," and so forth and so on in the wildest optimism: the end of it being that he got my thousand dollars, leaving me with barely five hundred. But as I could live in a good boarding house for four dollars a week, I reckoned that at the worst I had one carefree year before me, and if Willie kept his promise, I would be free to do whatever I wanted to do for years to come.

It was written that I was to have another experience in Lawrence much more important than anything to do with my brother. "Coming events cast their shadows before," is a poetic proverb, singularly inept; great events arrive unheralded, were truer.

One evening I went to a political meeting at Liberty Hall near my hotel. Senator Ingalls* was going to speak, and a Congressman on the Granger movement, the first attempt of the western farmers to react politically against the exploitation of Wall Street. The hall was packed: just behind me sat a man between two pretty grey-eyed girls. The man's face attracted me at first sight: I should be able to picture him, for even as I write his face comes before me as vividly as if the many long years that separate us were but the momentary closing of my eyes. Mentally, I can, even today, reproduce a perfect portrait of him and need only add the coloring and expression. The large eyes were hazel and set far apart under the white, overhanging brow; the hair and whiskers were chestnut-brown, tinged with auburn; but it was the eyes that drew and fascinated me, for they were luminous as no other eyes that I have ever seen; frank too, and kind, kind always.

* Senator John James Ingalls (1833–1900); he practiced law in Atchinson beginning in 1860; he was a Senator from 1873 until 1891.

But his dress, a black frock coat, with low stand-up white collar and a narrow black silk tie, excited my snobbish English contempt. Both the girls, sisters evidently, were making up to him for all they were worth, or so it seemed to my jaundiced, envious eyes.

Senator Ingalls made the usual kind of speech: the farmers were right to combine, but the money lords were powerful, and after all farmers and bankers alike were Americans—Americans first and last and all the time! (Great cheering!) The Congressman followed with the same brand of patriotic piffle and then cries arose from all parts of the hall for Professor Smith! I heard eager whispering behind me, and turning half-round, guessed that the good looking young man was Professor Smith, for his two girl admirers were persuading him to go on the platform and fascinate the audience.

In a little while he went up amid great applause; a good figure of a man, rather tall, about five feet ten, slight with broad shoulders. He began to speak in a thin tenor voice: "There is a manifest conflict of interests," he said, "between the manufacturing eastern states that demanded a high tariff on all imports and the farming west that wants cheap goods and cheap rates of transport.

"In essence, it's a mere matter of arithmetic, a mathematical problem, demanding a compromise; for every country should establish its own manufacturing industries and be self-supporting. The obvious reform is indicated; the Federal government should take over the railways and run them for the farmers, while competition among American manufacturers would ultimately reduce prices."

No one in the hall seemed to understand this "obvious reform," but the speech called forth a hurricane of cheers, and I concluded that there was a great many students from the state university in the audience.

I don't know what possessed me, but when Smith returned to his seat behind me between the two girls and they praised him to the skies, I got up and walked to the platform. I was greeted with a tempest of laughter and must have cut a ludicrous figure. I was in cow-puncher's dress as modified by Reece and Dell; I wore loose Bedford cord breeches, knee-high brown boots and a sort of buckskin shirt and jacket combined that tucked into my breeches. But rains and sun had worked their will on the buckskin, which had shrunk down my neck and up my arms.

Spurred on by the laughter, I went up the four steps on the platform and walked over to the mayor, who was chairman. "May I speak?" I asked.

"Sure," he replied; "your name?"

"My name is Harris," I answered, and the mayor manifestly regarding me as a great joke, announced that a Mr. Harris wished to address the meeting, and he hoped the audience would give him a fair hearing, even if his doctrines happened to be peculiar. As I faced him, the spectators shrieked with laughter: the house fairly rocked. I waited a full minute and then began. "How like Americans and Democrats," I said, "to judge a man by the clothes he wears and the amount of hair he has on his face or the dollars in his jeans!"

There was instantaneous silence, the silence of surprise, at least, and I went on to show what I had learned from Mill, that open competition was the law of life, another name for the struggle for existence; that each country should concentrate its energies on producing the things it was best fitted to produce and trade these off against the products of other nations; this was the great economic law, the law of the territorial division of labor.

"Americans should produce corn and wheat and meat for the world," I said, "and exchange these products for the cheapest English woolen goods and French silks and Irish linen. This would enrich the American farmer, develop all the waste American land, and be a thousand times better for the whole country than taxing all consumers with high import duties to enrich a few eastern manufacturers who were too inefficient to face the open competition of Europe. The American farmers," I went on, "should organize with the laborers, for their interests are identical, and fight the eastern manufacturer, who is nothing but a parasite living on the brains and work of better men."

And then, I wound up: "This common sense program won't please your Senators or your Congressmen, who prefer cheap claptrap to thought, or your super-fine Professors, who believe the war of classes is 'a mere arithmetical problem' (and I imitated the professor's thin voice), but it may nevertheless be accepted by the American farmer tired of being milked by the Yankee manufacturer, and it should stand as the first chapter in the new Granger gospel."

I bowed to the mayor and turned away, but the audience broke into cheers, and Senator Ingalls came over and shook my hand, saying he hoped to know me better, and the cheering went on till I had gotten back to my place and resumed my seat. A few minutes later and I was touched on the back by Professor Smith. As I turned round, he said smiling, "You gave me a good lesson: I'll never make a public speaker and what I said doubtless sounded inconsequent and absurd; but if you'd have a talk with me, I think I could convince you that my theory will hold water."

"I've no doubt you could," I broke in, heartily ashamed of having made fun of a man I didn't know; "I didn't grasp your meaning, but I'd be glad to have a talk with you."

"Are you free tonight?" he went on; I nodded. "Then come with me to my rooms. These ladies live out of town and we'll put them in their buggy and then be free. This is Mrs. . . . . . ," he added, presenting me to the stouter lady, "and this, her sister, Miss Stephens." I bowed and out we went, I keeping myself resolutely in the background till the sisters had driven away: then we set off together to Professor Smith's rooms for our talk.

If I could give you a complete account of that talk, this poor page would glow with wonder and admiration, all merged in loving reverence. We talked, or rather Smith talked, for I soon found he knew infinitely more than I did, was able indeed to label my creed as that of Mill, "a bourgeois English economist," he called him with smiling disdain.

Ever memorable to me, sacred indeed, that first talk with the man who was destined to reshape my life and inspire it with some of his own high purpose. He introduced me to the communism of Marx and Engels and easily convinced me that land and its products, coal and oil, should belong to the whole community, which should also manage all industries for the public benefit.

My breath was taken away by his mere statement of the case and I thrilled to the passion in his voice and manner, though even then I wasn't wholly convinced. Whatever topic we touched on, he illumined; he knew everything, it seemed to me, German and French and could talk Latin and classic Greek as fluently as English. I had never imagined such scholarship, and when I recited some verses of Swinburne as expressing my creed, he knew them too, and his pantheistic hymn to Hertha as well. And he wore his knowledge lightly as the mere garment of his shining spirit! And how handsome he was, like a sun-god! I had never seen anyone who could at all compare with him.

Day had dawned before we had done talking: he told me he was the professor of Greek in the state university and hoped I would come and study with him when the schools opened again in October. "To think of you as a cowboy," he said, "is impossible. Fancy a cowboy knowing books of Vergil and poems of Swinburne by heart; it's absurd: you must give your brains a chance and study."

"I've too little money," I said, beginning to regret my loan to my brother.

"I told you I am a Socialist," Smith retorted smiling. "I have three or four thousand dollars in the bank; take half of it and come to study," and his luminous eyes held me: it was true, after all; my heart swelled, jubilant there were noble souls in this world who took little thought of money and lived for better things than gold.

"I won't take your money," I said, with tears burning. "Every herring should hang by its own head in these democratic days; but if you think enough of me to offer such help, I'll promise to come, though I fear you'll be disappointed when you find how little I know, how ignorant I am. I've not been in school since I was fourteen."

"Come, we'll soon make up for the time lost," he said. "By the bye, where are you staying?"

"The Eldridge House," I replied.

He brought me to the door and we parted; as I turned to go, I saw the tall, slight figure and the radiant eyes, and I went away into a new world that was the old, feeling as if I were treading on air.

Once more my eyes had been opened as at Overton Bridge to the beauties of nature; but now to the splendor of an unique spirit. What luck!

I cried to myself, to meet such a man! It really seemed to me as if some god were following me with divine gifts!

And then the thought came: This man has chosen and called you very much as Jesus called his disciples: "Come, and I will make you fishers of men!" Already I was dedicated heart and soul to the new gospel.

But even that meeting with Smith, wherein I reached the topmost height of golden hours, was set off, so to speak, by another happening of this wonder-week. At the next table to me in the dining room I had already remarked once or twice a little, middle-aged, weary looking man who often began his breakfast with a glass of boiling water and followed it up with a baked apple drowned in rich cream. Brains, too, or sweetbreads he would eat for dinner, and rice, not potatoes: when I looked surprised, he told me he had been up all night and had a weak digestion. Mayhew, he said, was his name, and explained that if I ever wanted a game of faro or euchre or indeed anything else, he'd oblige me. I smiled; I could ride and shoot, I replied, but I was no good at cards.

The day after my talk with Smith, Mayhew and I were both late for supper: I sat long over a good meal and as he rose, he asked me if I would come across the street and see his "lay-out." I went willingly enough, having nothing to do. The gambling saloon was on the first floor of a building nearly opposite the Eldridge House: the place was well kept and neat, thanks to a colored bartender and waiter and a nigger for all work. The long room, too, was comfortably furnished and very brightly lit—altogether an attractive place.

As luck would have it, while he was showing me around, a lady came in. Mayhew after a word or two introduced me to her as his wife. Mrs. Mayhew was then a woman of perhaps twenty-eight or thirty, with tall, lissom, slight figure and interesting rather than pretty face: her features were all good, her eyes even were large and blue-grey; she would have been lovely if her coloring had been more pronounced. Give her golden hair or red or black and she would have been a beauty; she was always tastefully dressed and had appealing, ingratiating manners. I soon found that she loved books and reading, and as Mayhew said he was going to be busy, I asked if I might see her home. She consented smiling and away we went. She lived in a pretty frame house standing alone in a street that ran parallel to Massachusetts Street, nearly opposite to a large and ugly church.

As she went up the steps to the door, I noticed that she had fine, neat ankles and I divined shapely limbs. While she was taking off her light cloak and hat, the lifting of her arms stretched her bodice and showed small, round breasts: already my blood was lava and my mouth parched with desire.

"You look at me strangely!" she said, swinging round from the long mirror with a challenge on her parted lips. I made some inane remark: I couldn't trust myself to speak frankly; but natural sympathy drew us together. I told her I was going to be a student, and she wanted to know whether I could dance. I told her I could not, and she promised to teach me: "Lily Robins, a neighbor's girl, will play for us any afternoon. Do you know the steps?" She went on, and when I said, "No," she got up from the sofa, held up her dress and showed me the three polka steps, which she said were waltz steps, too, only taken on a glide.

"What pretty ankles you have!" I ventured, but she appeared not to hear me. We sat on and on and I learned that she was very lonely: Mr. Mayhew away every night and nearly all day and nothing to do in that little dead-and-alive place. "Will you let me come in for a talk sometimes?" I asked.

"Whenever you wish," was her answer. As I rose to go and we were standing opposite to each other by the door, I said: "You know, Mrs. Mayhew, in Europe when a man brings a pretty woman home, she rewards him with a kiss."

"Really?" she scoffed, smiling; "that's not a custom here."

"Are you less generous than they are?" I asked, and the next moment I had taken her face in my hands and kissed her on the lips.

She put her hands on my shoulders and left her eyes on mine. "We're going to be friends," she said; "I felt it when I saw you: don't stay away too long!"

"Will you see me tomorrow afternoon?" I asked. "I want that dance lesson!"

"Surely," she replied. "I'll tell Lily in the morning." And once more our hands met: I tried to draw her to me for another kiss; she held back with a smiling, "Tomorrow afternoon!"

"Tell me your name" I begged, "so that I may think of it."

"Lorna," she replied, "you funny boy!" I went my way with pulses hammering, blood aflame and hope in my heart.

Next morning I called again upon Smith but the pretty servant ("Rose," she said her name was), told me that he was nearly always at Judge Stephens', "five or six miles out," she thought it was. "They always come for him in a buggy," she added. So I said I'd write and make an appointment, and I did write and asked him to let me see him next morning.

That same morning Willie recommended to me a pension kept by a Mrs. Gregory, an English woman, the wife of an old Baptist clergyman, who would take good care of me for four dollars a week. Immediately I went with him to see her and was delighted to find that she lived only about a hundred yards from Mrs. Mayhew, on the opposite side of the street. Mrs. Gregory was a large, motherly woman, evidently a lady, who had founded this boarding house to provide for a rather reckless husband and two children, a big pretty girl, Kate, and a lad a couple of years younger. Mrs. Gregory was delighted with my English accent, I believe, and showed me special favor at once by giving me a large outside room with its own entrance and steps into the garden.

In an hour I had paid my bill at the Eldridge House and had moved in.

I showed a shred of prudence by making Willie promise Mrs. Gregory that he would turn up each Saturday with the five dollars for my board; the dollar extra was for the big room.

In due course I shall tell how he kept his promise and discharged his debt to me. For the moment everything was easily, happily settled. I went out and ordered a decent suit of ordinary tweeds and dressed myself up in my best blue suit to call upon Mrs. Mayhew after lunch. The clock crawled, but on the stroke of three I was at her door: a colored maid admitted me.

"Mrs. Mayhew," she said in her pretty singing voice, "will be down right soon: I'll go and call Miss Lily."

In five minutes Miss Lily appeared, a dark slip of a girl with shining black hair, wide, laughing mouth, temperamental thick, red lips, and grey eyes fringed with black lashes; she had hardly time to speak to me when Mrs. Mayhew came in. "I hope you two'll be great friends," she said prettily. "You're both about the same age," she added.

In a few minutes Miss Lily was playing a waltz on the Steinway and with my arm around the slight, flexible waist of my inamorata I was trying to waltz. But alas! after a turn or two I became giddy and in spite of all my resolutions had to admit that I should never be able to dance.

"You have got very pale," Mrs. Mayhew said, "you must sit down on the sofa a little while." Slowly the giddiness left me; before I had entirely recovered Miss Lily with kindly words of sympathy had gone home, and Mrs. Mayhew brought me in a cup of excellent coffee; I drank it down and was well at once.

"You should go in and lie down," said Mrs. Mayhew, still full of pity. "See," and she opened a door, "there's the guest bedroom all ready." I saw my chance and went over to her. "If you'd come too," I whispered, and then, "The coffee has made me quite well: won't you, Lorna, give me a kiss? You don't know how often I said your name last night, you dear!" And in a moment I had again taken her face and put my lips on hers.

She gave me her lips this time and my kiss became a caress; but in a little while she drew away and said, "Let's sit and talk; I want to know all you are doing." So I seated myself beside her on the sofa and told her all my news. She thought I would be comfortable with the Gregorys. "Mrs. Gregory is a good woman," she added, "and I hear the girl's engaged to a cousin: do you think her pretty?"

"I think no one pretty but you, Lorna," I said, and I pressed her head down on the arm of the sofa and kissed her. Her lips grew hot: I was certain. At once I put my hand down on her sex; she struggled a little at first, which I took care should bring our bodies closer, and when she ceased struggling I put my hands up her dress and began caressing her sex: it was hot and wet, as I knew it would be, and opened readily.

But in another moment she took the lead. "Some one might find us here," she whispered. "I've let the maid go: come up to my bedroom," and she took me upstairs. I begged her to undress: I wanted to see her figure; but she only said, "I have no corsets on; I don't often wear them in the house. Are you sure you love me, dear?"

"You know I do!" was my answer. The next moment I lifted her on to the bed, drew up her clothes, opened her legs and was in her. There was no difficulty and in a moment or two I came, but went right on poking passionately; in a few minutes her breath went and came quickly and her eyes fluttered and she met my thrusts with sighs and nippings of her sex. My second orgasm took some time and all the while Lorna became more and more responsive, till suddenly she put her hands on my bottom and drew me to her forcibly while she moved her sex up and down awkwardly to meet my thrusts with a passion I had hardly imagined. Again and again I came and the longer the play lasted the wilder was her excitement and delight. She kissed me hotly, foraging and thrusting her tongue into my mouth. Finally she pulled up her chemise to get me further into her and, at length, with little sobs, she suddenly got hysterical and, panting wildly, burst into a storm of tears.

That stopped me: I withdrew my sex and took her in my arms and kissed her; at first she clung to me with choking sighs and streaming eyes, but, as soon as she had won a little control, I went to the toilette and brought her a sponge of cold water and bathed her face and gave her some water to drink—that quieted her. But she would not let me leave her even to arrange my clothes.

"Oh, you great, strong dear," she cried, with her arms clasping me. "Oh, who would have believed such intense pleasure possible: I never felt anything like it before; how could you keep on so long? Oh, how I love you, you wonder and delight.

"I am all yours," she added gravely. "You shall do what you like with me: I am your mistress, your slave, your plaything, and you are my god and my love! Oh, darling! Oh!"

There was a pause while I smiled at her extravagant praise, then suddenly she sat up and got out of bed. "You wanted to see my figure"; she exclaimed, "here it is, I can deny you nothing; I only hope it may please you," and in a moment or two she showed herself nude from head to stocking.

As I had guessed, her figure was slight and lissom, with narrow hips, but she had a great bush of hair on her Mount of Venus and her breasts were not so round and firm as Jessie's: still she was very pretty and well-formed with the *fines attaches* (slender wrists and ankles), which the French are so apt to overestimate. They think that small bones indicate a small sex; but I have found the exceptions are very numerous, even if there is such a rule.

After I had kissed her breasts and navel and praised her figure, she disappeared in the bathroom, but was soon with me again on the sofa which we had left an hour or so before.

"Do you know," she began, "my husband assured me that only the strongest young man could go twice with a woman in one day? I believed him; aren't we women fools? You must have come a dozen times!"

"Not half that number," I replied, smiling.

"Aren't you tired?" was her next question. "Even I have a little headache," she added. "I never was so wrought up; at the end it was so intense; but you must be tired out."

"No," I replied, "I feel no fatigue, indeed, I feel the better for our joy ride!"

"But surely you're an exception!" she went on. "Most men have finished in one short spasm and leave the woman utterly unsatisfied, just excited and no more."

"Youth," I said, "that, I believe, makes the chief difference."

"Is there any danger of a child?" she went on. "I ought to say 'hope,'" she added bitterly, "for I'd love to have a child, your child," and she kissed me.

"When were you ill last?" I asked.

"About a fortnight ago," she replied. "I often thought that that had something to do with it."

"Why?" I asked. "Tell [the] truth," I warned her, and she began.

"I'll tell you anything; I thought the time had something to do with it, for soon after I am well each month, my 'pussy,' that's what we call it, often burns and itches intolerably; but, after a week or so, I'm not bothered any more till next time. Why is that?" she added.

"Two things I ought to explain to you," I said. "Your seed is brought down into your womb by the menstrual blood; it lives there a week or ten days and then dies, and with its death your desires decrease and the chance of impregnation. But near the next monthly period, say within three days, there is a double danger again; for the excitement may bring your seed down before the usual time, and in any case my seed will live in your womb about three days, so if you wish to avoid pregnancy, wait for ten days after your monthly flow is finished and stop, say four days before you expect it again; then the danger of getting a child is very slight."

"Oh, you wise boy!" she laughed. "Don't you see you are skipping the time I most desire you, and that's not kind to either of us, is it?"

"There's still another way of evasion," I said, "get me to withdraw before I come the first time, or get up immediately and syringe yourself with water thoroughly; water kills my seed as soon as it touches it."

"But how will that help if you go on half a dozen times more?" she asked.

"Doctors say," I replied, "that what comes from me afterward is not virile enough to impregnate a woman: I'll explain the process to you if you like; but you can take it, the fact is as I state it."

"When did you learn all this?" she asked.

"It has been my most engrossing study," I laughed, "and by far the most pleasureful!"

"You dear, dear," she cried. "I must kiss you for that."

"Do you know you kiss wonderfully?" she went on reflectingly. "With a lingering touch of the inside of the lips and then the thrust of the tongue: that's what excited me so the first time," and she sighed, as if delighted with the memory.

"You didn't seem excited," I said half reproachfully, "for when I wanted another kiss, you drew away and said 'Tomorrow'! Why are women so coquettish, so perverse?" I added, remembering Lucille and Jessie.

"I think it is that we wish to be sure of being desired," she replied, "and a little, too, that we want to prolong the joy of it, the delight of being wanted, really wanted! It is so easy for us to give and so exquisite to feel a man's desire pursuing us! Ah, how rare it is," she sighed passionately, "and how quickly lost! You'll soon tire of your mistress," she added, "now that I am all yours and thrill only for you," and she took my head in her hands and kissed me passionately, regretfully.

"You kiss better than I do, Lorna! Where did you acquire the art, Madame?" I asked. "I fear that you have been a naughty, naughty girl!"

"If you only knew the truth," she exclaimed, "if you only knew how girls long for a lover and burn and itch in vain and wonder why men are so stupid and cold and dull as not to see our desire.

"Don't we try all sorts of tricks? Aren't we haughty and withdrawn at one moment and affectionate, tender, loving at another? Don't we conceal the hook with every sort of bait, only to watch the fish sniff at it and turn away. Ah, if you knew—I feel a traitor to my sex even in telling you— if you guessed how we angle for you and how clever we are, how full of wiles. There's an expression I once heard my husband use which described us women exactly, or nine out of ten of us. I wanted to know how he kept the office warm all night: he said, we damp down the furnaces, and explained the process. That's it, I cried to myself, I'm a damped-down furnace: that's surely why I keep hot ever so long! Did you imagine," she asked, turning her flower-face all pale with passion half aside, "that I took off my hat that first day before the glass and turned slowly round with it held above my head, by chance? You dear innocent! I knew the movement would show my breasts and slim hips and did it deliberately, hoping it would excite you, and how I thrilled when I saw it did.

"Why did I show you the bed in that room," she added, "and leave the door ajar when I came back here to the sofa but to tempt you, and how heart-glad I was to feel your desire in your kiss. I was giving myself before you pushed my head back on the sofa-arm and disarranged all my hair!" she added, pouting and patting it with her hands to make sure it was in order.

"You were astonishingly masterful and quick," she went on, "how did you know that I wished you to touch me then? Most men would have gone on kissing and fooling, afraid to act decisively. You must have had a lot of experience? You naughty lad!"

"Shall I tell you the truth?" I said. "I will, just to encourage you to be frank with me. You are the first woman I have ever spent my seed in or had properly."

"Call it improperly, for God's sake," she cried laughing aloud with joy, "you darling virgin, you! Oh! how I wish I was sixteen again and you were my first lover. You would have made me believe in God. Yet you are my first lover," she added quickly. "I have only learned the delight and ecstasy of love in your arms."

Our love-talk lasted for hours till suddenly I guessed it was late and looked at my watch; it was nearly seven-thirty: I was late for supper, which started at half-past six!

"I must go," I exclaimed, "or I'll get nothing to eat."

"I could give you supper," she added, "my lips, too, that long for you and —and—but you know." She added regretfully, "He might come in and I want to know you better first before seeing you together; a young god and a man!—and the man God's likeness, yet so poor an imitation!"

"Don't, don't," I said, "you'll make life harder for yourself—"

"Harder," she repeated with a sniff of contempt. "Kiss me, my love, and go if you must. Shall I see you tomorrow? There!" she cried as with a curse, "I've given myself away: I can't help it; oh, how I want you always: how I shall long for you and count the dull dreary hours! Go, go or I'll never let you—" and she kissed and clung to me to the door.

"Sweet—tomorrow!" I said, and tore off.

Of course it is manifest that my liaison with Mrs. Mayhew had little or nothing to do with love. It was demoniac youthful sex-urge in me and much the same hunger in her, and as soon as the desire was satisfied my judgment of her was as impartial, cool as if she had always been indifferent to me. But with her I think there was a certain attachment and considerable tenderness. In intimate relations between the sexes it is rare indeed that the man gives as much to love as the woman.

Chapter X

Some Study, More Love

SUPPER AT THE GREGORYS' was almost over when I entered the dining room: Kate and her mother and father and the boy Tommy were seated at the end of the table, taking their meal. The dozen guests had all finished and disappeared. Mrs. Gregory hastened to rise and Kate got up to follow her mother into the neighboring kitchen.

"Please don't get up!" I cried to the girl. "I'd never forgive myself for interrupting you. I'll wait on myself or on you," I added smiling, "if you wish anything."

She looked at me with hard, indifferent eyes and sniffed scornfully. "If you sit there," she said, pointing to the other end of the table, "I'll bring your supper; do you take coffee or tea?"

"Coffee, please," I answered, and took the seat indicated, at once making up my mind to be cold to her while winning the others. Soon the boy began asking me had I ever seen any Indians—"In war-paint and armed, I mean," he added eagerly.

"Yes, and shot at them, too," I replied smiling.

Tommy's eyes gleamed. "Oh, tell us!" he panted, and I knew I could always count on one good listener!

"I've lots to tell, Tommy," I said. "But now I must eat my supper at express rate, or your sister'll be angry—" I added, as Kate came in with some steaming food: she pulled a face and shrugged her shoulders with contempt.

"Where do you preach?" I asked the grey-haired father. "My brother says you're really eloquent."

"Never eloquent," he replied deprecatingly, "but sometimes very earnest, perhaps, especially when some event of the day comes to point the Gospel story." He talked like a man of fair education and I could see he was pleased at being drawn to the front.

Then Kate brought me fresh coffee, and Mrs. Gregory came in and continued her meal; and the talk became interesting, thanks to Mr. Gregory, who couldn't help saying how the fire in Chicago had stimulated Christianity in his hearers and given him a great text. I mentioned casually that I had been in the fire and told of Randolph Street Bridge and the hanging and what else I saw there and on the lake-front that unforgettable Monday morning.

At first Kate went in and out of the room, removing dishes as if she were not concerned in the story, but when I told of the women and girls half-naked at the lakeside, while the flames behind us reached the zenith in a red sheet that kept throwing flame-arrows ahead and started the ships burning on the water in front of us, she, too, stopped to listen.

At once I caught my cue, to be liked and admired by all the rest, but indifferent, cold to her. I rose, as if her standing enthralled had interrupted me, and said: "I'm sorry to keep you: I've talked too much, forgive me!" and betook myself to my room in spite of the protests and prayers to continue of all the rest. Kate just flushed, but said nothing.

She attracted me greatly: she was infinitely desirable, very good looking and very young (only sixteen, her mother said later), and her great hazel eyes were almost as exciting as her pretty mouth or large lips and good height. She pleased me intimately, but I resolved to win her altogether and felt I had begun well: at any rate, she would think about me and my coldness.

I spent the evening in putting out my half-dozen books, not forgetting my medical treatises, and then slept the deep sleep of sex recuperation.

The next morning I called on Smith again, where he lived with the Reverend Mr. Kellogg, who was the Professor of English History in the university, Smith said. Kellogg was a man of about forty, stout and well kept, with a faded wife of about the same age. Rose, the pretty servant, let me in; I had a smile and warm word of thanks for her: she was astonishingly pretty, the prettiest girl I had seen in Lawrence: medium height and figure with quite lovely face and an exquisite rose-leaf skin! She smiled at me; evidently my admiration pleased her.

.Smith, I found, had got books for me, Latin and Greek-English dictionaries, a Tacitus, too, and Xenophon's *Memorabilia* with a Greek grammar: I insisted on paying for them all and he began to talk. Tacitus he just praised for his superb phrases and the great portrait of Tiberius—"perhaps the greatest historical portrait ever painted in words." I had a sort of picture of King Edward the Fourth in my romantic head, but didn't venture to trot it out. But soon, Smith passed to Xenophon and his portrait of Socrates as compared with that of Plato. I listened all ears while he read out a passage from Xenophon, painting Socrates with little human touches: I got him to translate every word literally and had a great lesson, resolving, when I got home, I'd learn the whole page by heart. Smith was more than kind to me: he said I'd be able to enter the junior class and thus have only two years to graduation. If Willie gave me back even five hundred dollars, I'd be able to get through without care or work.

Then Smith told me how he had gone to Germany after his American university: how he had studied there and then worked in Athens at ancient

Greek for another year till he could talk classic Greek as easily as German. "There were a few dozen professors and students," he said, "who met regularly and talked nothing but classic Greek: they were always trying to make the modern tongue just like the old." He gave me a translation of *Das Kapital* of Marx, and in fifty ways inspired and inspirited me to renewed effort.

I came back to the Gregorys' for dinner and discussed in my own mind whether I should go to Mrs. Mayhew's, as I had promised, or work at Greek. I decided to work and then and there made a vow always to prefer work, a vow more honored in the breach, I fear, than in the observance. But at least I wrote to Mrs. Mayhew, excusing myself, and promising her the next afternoon. I set myself to learn by heart the two pages in the *Memorabilia*.

That evening I sat near the end of the table; the head of it was taken by the university professor of physics, a dull pedant!

Every time Kate came near me I was ceremoniously polite: "Thank you, very much! It is very kind of you!" and not a word more. As soon as I could, I went to my room to work.

Next day at three o'clock I knocked at Mrs. Mayhew's: she opened the door herself. I cried, "How kind of you!" and once in the room drew her to me and kissed her time and time again: she seemed cold and numb.

For some moments she didn't speak, then: "I feel as if I had passed through fever," she said, putting her hands through her hair, lifting it in a gesture I was to know well in the days to come. "Never promise again if you don't come; I thought I should go mad: waiting is a horrible torture! Who kept you—some girl?" and her eyes searched mine.

I excused myself; but her intensity chilled me. At the risk of alienating my girl readers, I must confess this was the effect her passion had on me. When I kissed her, her lips were cold. But by the time we had got upstairs, she had thawed. She shut the door after us gravely and began: "See how ready I am for you!" and in a moment she had thrown back her robe and stood before me naked. She tossed the garment on a chair; it fell on the floor. She stooped to pick it up with her bottom toward me: I kissed her soft bottom and caught her up by it with my hand on her sex.

She turned her head over her shoulder: "I've washed and scented myself for you, Sir: how do you like the perfume? and how do you like this bush of hair?" and she touched her mount with a grimace. "I was so ashamed of it as a girl: I used to shave it off, that's what made it grow so thick, I believe. One day my mother saw it and made me stop shaving. Oh! how ashamed of it I was: it's animal, ugly,—don't you hate it? Oh, tell the truth!" she cried, "Or rather, don't; tell me you love it."

"I love it," I exclaimed, "because it's yours!"

"Oh, you dear lover," she smiled, "you always find the right word, the flattering salve for the sore!"

"Are you ready for me," I asked, "ripe-ready, or shall I kiss you first and caress pussy?"

"Whatever you do will be right," she said. "You know I am rotten-ripe, soft and wet for you always!"

All this while I was taking off my clothes; now I too was naked.

"I want you to draw up your knees," I said: "I want to see the Holy of Holies, the shrine of my idolatry."

At once she did as I asked. Her legs and bottom were well-shaped without being statuesque: but her clitoris was much more than the average button: it stuck out fully half an inch and the inner lips of her vulva hung down a little below the outer lips. I knew I should see prettier pussies. Kate's was better shaped, I felt sure, and the heavy, madder-brown lips put me off a little.

The next moment I began caressing her red clitoris with my hot, stiff organ: Lorna sighed deeply once or twice and her eyes turned up; slowly I pushed my prick in to the full and drew it out again to the lips, then in again, and I felt her warm love-juice gush as she drew up her knees even higher to let me further in. "Oh, it's divine," she sighed, "better even than the first time," and, when my thrusts grew quick and hard as the orgasm shook me, she writhed down on my prick as I withdrew, as if she would hold it, and as my seed spirted into her, she bit my shoulder and held her legs tight as if to keep my sex in her. We lay a few moments bathed in bliss. Then, as I began to move again to sharpen the sensation, she half rose on her arm. "Do you know," she said, "I dreamed yesterday of getting on you and doing it to you, do you mind if I try?"

"No, indeed!" I cried. "Go to it, I am your prey!" She got up smiling and straddled kneeling across me, and put my cock into her pussy and sank down on me with a deep sigh. She tried to move up and down on my organ and at once came up too high and had to use her hand to put my Tommy in again; then she sank down on it as far as possible. "I can sink down all right," she cried, smiling at the double meaning, "but I cannot rise so well! What fools we women are, we can't master even the act of love; we are so awkward!"

"Your awkwardness, however, excites me," I said.

"Does it?" she cried. "Then I'll do my best," and for some time she rose and sank rhythmically; but, as her excitement grew, she just let herself lie on me and wiggled her bottom till we both came. She was flushed and hot and I couldn't help asking her a question.

"Does your excitement grow to a spasm of pleasure," I asked, "or do you go on getting more and more excited continually?"

"I get more and more excited," she said, "till the other day with you, for the first time in my life, the pleasure became unbearably intense and I was hysterical, you wonder-lover!"

Since then I have read lascivious books in half a dozen languages and they all represent women coming to an orgasm in the act, as men do, followed by a period of content; which only shows that the books are all written by men, and ignorant, insensitive men at that. The truth is: hardly one married woman in a thousand is ever brought to her highest pitch of feeling; usually, just when she begins to feel, her husband goes to sleep. If the majority of husbands satisfied their wives occasionally, the woman's revolt would soon move to another purpose: women want above all a lover who lives to excite them to the top of their bent. As a rule, men through economic conditions marry so late that they have already half-exhausted their virile power before they marry. And when they marry young, they are so ignorant and self-centered that they imagine their wives must be satisfied when they are. Mrs. Mayhew told me that her husband had never excited her, really. She denied that she had ever had any real acute pleasure from his embraces.

"Shall I make you hysterical again?" I asked, out of boyish vanity. "I can, you know!"

"You mustn't tire yourself!" she warned. "My husband taught me long ago that when a woman tires a man, he gets a distaste for her, and I want your love, your desire, dear, a thousand times more even than the delight you give me—"

"Don't be afraid," I broke in. "You are sweet; you couldn't tire me; turn sideways and put your left leg up, and I'll just let my sex caress your clitoris back and forth gently; every now and then I'll let it go right in until our hairs meet." I kept on this game perhaps half an hour until she first sighed and sighed and then made awkward movements with her pussy which I sought to divine and meet as she wished, when suddenly she cried:

"Oh! Oh! Hurt me, please! hurt me, or I'll bite you! Oh God, oh, oh," panting, breathless till again the tears poured down!

"You darling," she sobbed. "How you can love! Could you go on forever?"

For answer, I put her hand on my sex. "Just as naughty as ever," she exclaimed, "and I am choking, breathless, exhausted! Oh, I'm sorry," she went on, "but we should get up, for I don't want my help to know or guess: niggers talk—"

I got up and went to the windows; one gave on the porch, but the other directly on the garden. "What are you looking at?" she asked, coming to me.

"I was just looking for the best way to get out if ever we were surprised," I said. "If we leave this window open I can always drop into the garden and get away quickly."

"You would hurt yourself," she cried.

"Not a bit of it," I answered. "I could drop half as far again without injury; the only thing is, I must have boots on and trousers, or those thorns of yours would gip!"

"You boy," she exclaimed laughing. "I think after your strength and passion, it is your boyishness I love best"—and she kissed me again and again.

"I must work," I warned her; "Smith has given me a lot to do."

"Oh, my dear," she said, her eyes filling with tears, "that means you won't come tomorrow or," she added hastily, "even the day after?"

"I can't possibly," I declared. "I have a good week's work in front of me; but you know I'll come the first afternoon I can make myself free and I'll let you know the day before, sweet!"

She looked at me with tearful eyes and quivering lips. "Love is its own torment!" she sighed, while I dressed and got away quickly.

The truth was I was already satiated. Her passion held nothing new in it: she had taught me all she could and had nothing more in her, I thought; while Kate was prettier and much younger and a virgin. Why shouldn't I confess it? It was Kate's virginity that attracted me irresistibly: I pictured her legs to myself, her hips and thighs . . .

The next few days passed in reading the books Smith had lent me, especially *Das Kapital,* the second book of which, with its frank exposure of the English factory system, was simply enthralling. I read some of Tacitus, too, and Xenophon with a crib, and learned a page of Greek every day by heart, and whenever I felt tired of work I laid siege to Kate. That is, I continued my plan of campaign. One day I called her brother into my room and told him true stories of buffalo hunting and of fighting with Indians; another day I talked theology with the father or drew the dear mother out to tell of her girlish days in Cornwall. "I never thought I'd come to work like this in my old age, but then children take all and give little; I was no better as a girl, I remember,"—and I got a scene of her brief courtship!

I had won the whole household long before I said a word to Kate beyond the merest courtesies. A week or so passed like this till one day I held them all after dinner while I told the story of our raid into Mexico. I took care, of course, that Kate was out of the room. Towards the end of my tale, Kate came in: at once I hastened to end abruptly, and after excusing myself, went into the garden.

Half an hour later I saw she was in my room tidying up; I took thought and then went up the outside steps. As soon as I saw her I pretended surprise. "I beg your pardon," I said. "I'll just get a book and go at once; please don't let me disturb you!" and I pretended to look for the book.

She turned sharply and looked at me fixedly. "Why do you treat me like this!" she burst out, shaking with indignation.

"Like what?" I repeated, pretending surprise.

"You know quite well," she went on angrily, hastily. "At first I thought it was chance, unintentional; now I know you mean it. Whenever you are talking or telling a story, as soon as I come into the room you stop and hurry away as if you hated me. Why? Why?" she cried with quivering lips. "What have I done to make you dislike me so?" and the tears gathered in her lovely eyes.

I felt the moment had come: I put my hands on her shoulders and looked with my whole soul into her eyes. "Did you never guess, Kate, that it might be love, not hate?" I asked.

"No, no!" she cried, the tears falling. "Love does not act like that!"

"Fear to miss love does, I can assure you," I cried. "I thought at first that you disliked me and already I had begun to care for you" (my arms went round her waist and I drew her to me), "to love you and want you. Kiss me, dear," and at once she gave me her lips, while my hand got busy on her breasts and then went down of itself to her sex.

Suddenly she looked at me gaily, brightly, while heaving a big sigh of relief. "I'm glad, glad!" she said. "If you only knew how hurt I was and how I tortured myself; one moment I was angry, then I was sad. Yesterday I made up my mind to speak, but today I said to myself, I'll just be obstinate and cold as he is and now—" and of her own accord she put her arms round my neck and kissed me—"you are a dear, dear! Anyway, I love you!"

"You mustn't give me those bird-pecks!" I exclaimed. "Those are not kisses: I want your lips to open and cling to mine," and I kissed her while my tongue darted into her mouth and I stroked her sex gently. She flushed, but at first didn't understand; then suddenly she blushed rosy red as her lips grew hot and she fairly ran from the room.

I exulted: I knew I had won: I must be very quiet and reserved and the bird would come to the lure; I felt exultingly certain!

Meanwhile I spent nearly every morning with Smith: golden hours! Always, always before we parted, he showed me some new beauty or revealed some new truth: he seemed to me the most wonderful creature in this strange, sunlit world. I used to hang entranced on his eloquent lips! (Strange! I was sixty-five before I found such a hero-worshiper as I was to Smith, who was only four or five and twenty!) He made me know all the Greek dramatists: Aeschylus, Sophocles and Euripides and put them for me in a truer light than English or German scholars have set them yet. He knew that Sophocles was the greatest, and from his lips I learned every chorus in the *Oedipus Rex* and *Colonnus* before I had completely mastered the Greek grammar; indeed, it was the supreme beauty of the literature that forced me to learn the language. In teaching me the choruses, he was careful to point out that it was possible to keep the measure and yet mark the accent too: in fact, he made classic Greek a living language to me, as living as English. And he would not let me neglect Latin: in the first year with him I knew poems of Catullus by heart, almost as well as I knew Swinburne. Thanks to Professor Smith, I had no difficulty in entering the junior class at the university; in fact, after my first three or four months' work [I] was easily the first in the class, which included Ned Stephens, the brother of Smith's inamorata. I soon discovered that Smith was heels over head in love with Kate Stephens, shot through the heart, as Mercutio would say, with a fair girl's blue eye!

And small wonder, for Kate was lovely; a little above middle height with slight, rounded figure and most attractive face: the oval, a thought long, rather than round, with dainty, perfect features, lit up by a pair of superlative grey-blue eyes, eyes by turns delightful and reflective and appealing, that mirrored a really extraordinary intelligence. She was in the senior class and afterwards for years held the position of Professor of Greek in the university. I shall have something to say of her in a later volume of this history, for I met her again in New York nearly fifty years later. But in 1872 or '73, her brother Ned, a handsome lad of eighteen who was in my class, interested me more. The only other member of the senior class of this time was a fine fellow, Ned Bancroft, who later came to France with me to study.

At this time, curiously enough, Kate Stephens was by way of being engaged to Ned Bancroft; but already it was plain that she was in love with Smith, and my outspoken admiration of Smith helped her, I hope, as I am sure it helped him, to a better mutual understanding. Bancroft accepted the situation with extraordinary self-sacrifice, losing neither Smith's nor Kate's friendship: I have seldom seen nobler self-abnegation; indeed, his high-mindedness in this crisis was what first won my admiration and showed me his other fine qualities.

Almost in the beginning I had serious disquietude: every little while Smith was ill and had to keep [to] his bed for a day or two. There was no explanation of this illness, which puzzled me and caused me a certain anxiety.

One day in midwinter there was a new development. Smith was in doubt how to act and confided in me. He had found Professor Kellogg, in whose house he lived, trying to kiss the pretty help, Rose, entirely against her will. Smith was emphatic on this point: the girl was struggling angrily to free herself, when by chance he interrupted them.

I relieved Smith's solemn gravity a little by roaring with laughter. The idea of an old professor and clergyman trying to win a girl by force filled me with amusement: "What a fool the man must be!" was my English judgment; Smith took the American high moral tone at first.

"Think of his disloyalty to his wife in the same house," he cried, "and then the scandal if the girl talked, and she is sure to talk!"

"Sure not to talk," I corrected. "Girls are afraid of the effect of such revelations; besides a word from you asking her to shield Mrs. Kellogg will ensure her silence."

"Oh, I cannot advise her," cried Smith. "I will not be mixed up in it: I told Kellogg at the time, I must leave the house, yet I don't know where to go! It's too disgraceful of him! His wife is really a dear woman!"

For the first time I became conscious of a rooted difference between Smith and myself: his high moral condemnation on very insufficient data seemed to me childish, but no doubt many of my readers will think my tolerance a proof of my shameless libertinism! However, I jumped at the opportunity of talking to Rose on such a scabrous matter and at the same time solved Smith's difficulty by proposing that he should come and take room and board with the Gregorys—a great stroke of practical diplomacy on my part, or so it appeared to me; for thereby I did the Gregorys, Smith and myself an immense, an incalculable service. Smith jumped at the idea, asked me to see about it at once and let him know, and then rang for Rose.

She came half-scared, half-angry, on the defensive, I could see; so I spoke first, smiling. "Oh Rose," I said, "Professor Smith has been telling me of your trouble; but you ought not to be angry: for you are so pretty that no wonder a man wants to kiss you; you must blame your lovely eyes and mouth."

Rose laughed outright: she had come expecting reproof and found sweet flattery.

"There's only one thing, Rose," I went on. "The story would hurt Mrs. Kellogg if it got out and she's not very strong, so you must say nothing about it, for her sake. That's what Professor Smith wanted to say to you." I added.

"I'm not likely to tell," cried Rose. "I'll soon forget all about it, but I guess I'd better get another job: he's liable to try again, though I gave him a good, hard slap," and she laughed merrily.

"I'm so glad for Mrs. Kellogg's sake," said Smith gravely, "and if I can help you get another place, please call upon me."

" I guess I'll have no difficulty," answered Rose flippantly, with a shade of dislike of the professor's solemnity. "Mrs. Kellogg will give me a good character," and the healthy young minx grinned, "besides I'm not sure but I'll go stay home a spell. I'm fed up with working and would like a holiday, and mother wants me—"

"Where do you live, Rose?" I asked with a keen eye for future opportunities.

"On the other side of the river," she replied, "next door to Elder Conklin's, where your brother boards," she added smiling.

When Rose went I begged Smith to pack his boxes, for I would get him the best room at the Gregorys' and assured him it was really large and comfortable and would hold all his books, etc.; and off I went to make my promise good. On the way, I set myself to think how I could turn the kindness I was doing the Gregorys to the advantage of my love. I decided to make Kate a partner in the good deed, or at least a herald of the good news. So when I got home I rang the bell in my room, and as I had hoped Kate answered it. When I heard her footsteps I was shaking, hot with desire, and now I wish to describe a feeling I then began to notice in myself. I longed to take possession of the girl, so to speak, abruptly, ravish her in fact, or at least thrust both hands up her dress at once and feel her bottom and sex altogether; but already I knew enough to realize certainly that girls prefer gentle and courteous approaches. Why? Of the fact I am sure. So I said, "Come in, Kate," gravely. "I want to ask you whether the best bedroom is still free, and if you'd like Professor Smith to have it, if I could get him to come here?"

"I'm sure, Mother would be delighted," she exclaimed.

"You see," I went on, "I'm trying to serve you all I can, yet you don't even kiss me of your own accord." She smiled, and so I drew her to the bed and lifted her up on it. I saw her glance and answered it: "The door is shut, dear," and half lying on her, I began kissing her passionately, while my hands went up her clothes to her sex. To my delight she wore no drawers, but at first she kept her legs tight together frowning. "Love denies nothing, Kate," I said gravely; slowly she drew her legs apart, half-pouting, half-smiling, and let me caress her sex. When her love-juice came, I kissed her and stopped. "It's dangerous here," I said, "that door you came in is open; but I must see your lovely limbs," and I turned up her dress. I hadn't exaggerated; she had limbs like a Greek statue and her triangle of brown hair lay in little silky curls on her belly and then—the sweetest cunny in the world. I bent down and kissed it.

In a moment Kate was on her feet, smoothing her dress down. "What a boy you are," she exclaimed, "but that's partly why I love you; oh, I hope you'll love me half as much. Say you will, Sir, and I'll do anything you wish!"

"I will," I replied, "but oh, I'm glad you want love; can you come to me tonight? I want a couple of hours with you uninterrupted."

"This afternoon," she said, "I'll say I'm going for a walk and I'll come to you, dear! They are all resting then or out and I shan't be missed."

I could only wait and think. One thing was fixed in me, I must have her, make her mine before Smith came: he was altogether too fascinating, I thought, to be trusted with such a pretty girl; but I was afraid she would bleed and I did not want to hurt her this first time, so I went out and bought a syringe and a pot of cold cream which I put beside my bed.

Oh, how that dinner lagged! Mrs. Gregory thanked me warmly for my kindness to them all (which seemed to me pleasantly ironical!) and Mr. Gregory followed her lead; but at length everyone had finished and I went to my room to prepare. First I locked the outside door and drew down the blinds: then I studied the bed and turned it back and arranged a towel along the edge; happily the bed was just about the right height! Then I loosened my trousers, unbuttoned the front and pulled up my shirt: a little later Kate put her lovely face in at the door and slipped inside. I shot the bolt and began kissing her; girls are strange mortals; she had taken off her corset, just as I had put a towel handy. I lifted up her clothes and touched her sex, caressing it gently while kissing her: in a moment or two her love-milk came.

I lifted her up on the bed, pushed down my trousers, anointed my prick with the cream and then, parting her legs and getting her to pull her knees up, I drew her bottom to the edge of the bed: she frowned at that, but I explained quickly: "It may give a little pain, at first, dear: and I want to give you as little as possible," and I slipped the head of my cock gently, slowly into her. Even greased, her pussy was very tight and at the very entrance I felt the obstacle, her maidenhead, in the way; I lay on her and kissed her and let her or Mother Nature help me.

As soon as Kate found that I was leaving it to her, she pushed forward boldly and the obstacle yielded. "O—O!" she cried, and then pushed forward again roughly and my organ went in her to the hilt and her clitoris must have felt my belly. Resolutely, I refrained from thrusting or withdrawing for a minute or two and then drew out slowly to her lips and, as I pushed Tommy gently in again, she leaned up and kissed me passionately. Slowly, with extremest care, I governed myself and pushed in and out with long slow thrusts, though I longed, longed to plunge it in hard and quicken the strokes as much as possible; but I knew from Mrs. Mayhew that the long, gentle thrusts and slow withdrawals were the aptest to excite a woman's passion and I was determined to win Kate.

In two or three minutes, she had again let down a flow of love-juice, or so I believed, and I kept right on with the love-game, knowing that the first experience is never forgotten by a girl and resolved to keep on to dinner-time if necessary to make her first love-joust ever memorable to her. Kate lasted longer than Mrs. Mayhew; I came ever so many times, passing ever more slowly from orgasm to orgasm before she began to move to me; but at length her breath began to get shorter and shorter and she held me to her violently, moving her pussy the while up and down harshly against my man-root. Suddenly she relaxed and fell back: there was no hysteria; but plainly I could feel the mouth of her womb fasten on my cock as if to suck it. That excited me fiercely and for the first time I indulged in quick, hard thrusts till a spasm of intensest pleasure shook me and my seed spirted or seemed to spirt for the sixth or seventh time.

When I had finished kissing and praising my lovely partner and drew away, I was horrified; the bed was a sheet of blood and some had gone on my pants: Kate's thighs and legs even were all incarnadined, making the lovely ivory white of her skin, one red. You may imagine how softly I used [a] towel on her legs and sex before I showed her the results of our love-passage. To my astonishment she was unaffected. "You must take the sheet away and burn it," she said, "or drop it in the river: I guess it won't be the first."

"Did it hurt much?" I asked.

"At first a good deal," she replied, "but soon the pleasure overpowered the smart and I would not even forget the pain. I love you so. I am not even afraid of consequences with you: I trust you absolutely and love to trust you and run whatever risks you wish."

"You darling!" I cried, "I don't believe there will be any consequences;

but I want you to go to the basin and use this syringe. I'll tell you why afterwards."

At once she went over to the basin. "I feel funny, weak," she said, "as if I were—I can't describe it—shaky on my legs. I'm glad now I don't wear drawers in summer, they'd get wet." Her ablutions completed and the sheet withdrawn and done up in paper, I shot back the bolt and we began our talk. I found her intelligent and kindly but ignorant and ill-read; still she was not prejudiced and was eager to know all about babies and how they were made. I told her what I had told Mrs. Mayhew and something more: how my seed was composed of tens of thousands of tadpole-shaped animalculae. Already in her vagina and womb these infinitely little things had a race: they could move nearly an inch in an hour and the strongest and quickest got up first to where her egg was waiting in the middle of her womb. My little tadpole, the first to arrive, thrust his head into her egg and thus having accomplished his work of impregnation, perished, love and death being twins.

The curious thing was that this indescribably small tadpole should be able to transmit all the qualities of all his progenitors in certain proportions; no such miracle was ever imagined by any religious teacher. More curious still, the living foetus in the womb passes in nine months through all the chief changes that the human race has gone through in countless aeons of time in its progress from the tadpole to the man. Till the fifth month the foetus is practically a four-legged animal.

I told her that it was accepted today that the weeks occupied in the womb in any metamorphosis correspond exactly to the ages it occupied in reality. Thus it was upright, a two-legged animal, ape and then man in the womb for the last three months, and this corresponded nearly to one-third of man's whole existence on this earth. Kate listened, enthralled, I thought, till she asked me suddenly:

"But what makes one child a boy and another a girl?"

"The nearest we've come to a law on the matter," I said, "is contained in the so-called law of contraries: that is, if the man is stronger than the woman, the children will be mostly girls; if the woman is greatly younger or stronger, the progeny will be chiefly boys. This bears out the old English proverb: "Any weakling can make a boy, but it takes a man to make a girl.""

Kate laughed and just then a knock came to the door. "Come in!" I cried, and then [the] colored maid came in with a note. "A lady's just been and left it," said Jenny. I saw it was from Mrs. Mayhew, so I crammed it into my pocket, saying regretfully: "I must answer it soon." Kate excused herself and after a long, long kiss went to prepare supper, while I read Mrs. Mayhew's note, which was short, if not exactly sweet:

"Eight days and no Frank, and no news; you cannot want to kill me: come today if possible.

Lorna."

I replied at once, saying I would come on the morrow, that I was so busy I didn't know where to turn, but would be with her sure on the morrow and I signed "Your Frank."

That afternoon at five o'clock Smith came and I helped to arrange his books and make him comfy.

Chapter XI

At the Age of Eighteen

Venus toute entière a sa proie attachée

I MEANT to write nothing but the truth in these pages, yet now I'm conscious that my memory has played a trick on me. It is in an artist what painters call foreshortening: events, that is, which took months to happen, it crushes together into days, passing, so to speak, from mountain top to mountain top of feeling, and so the effect of passion is heightened by the partial elimination of time. I can do nothing more than warn my readers that in reality some of the love-passages I shall describe were separated by weeks and sometimes by months, that the nuggets of gold were occasional "finds" in a desert.

After all, it cannot matter to my "gentle readers," and my good readers will have already divined the fact, that when you crush eighteen years into nine* chapters, you must leave out all sorts of minor happenings while recording chiefly the important—fortunately these carry the message.

It was with my knowledge as with my passions. Day after day I worked feverishly: whenever I met a passage such as the building of the bridge in Caesar, I refused to burden my memory with the dozens of new words because I thought, and still think, Latin comparatively unimportant: the nearest to a great man the Latins ever produced being Tacitus or Lucretius. No sensible person would take the trouble to master a language in order to gain acquaintance with the second-rate. But new words in Greek were precious to me like new words in English, and I used to memorize every passage studded with them, save choruses like that of the birds in Aristophanes, where he names birds unfamiliar to me in life.

Smith, I found, knew all such words in both languages. I asked him one day and he admitted that he had read everything in ancient Greek, following the example of Hermann,** the famous German scholar, and he believed he knew almost every word.

I did not desire any such pedantic perfection. I make no pretension to

---

* Actually ten.
** Johann Gottfried Jakob Hermann (1772–1848), Professor of Elocution and Poetry at Leipzig.

scholarship of any sort, and indeed learning of any kind leaves me indifferent, unless it leads to a fuller understanding of beauty, or that widening of the spirit by sympathy that is another name for wisdom. But what I wish to emphasize here is that in the first year with Smith I learned by heart dozens of choruses from the Greek dramatists and the whole of the *Apologia* and *Crito* of Plato, having guessed then, and still believe, that the *Crito* is a model short story, more important than any of even Plato's speculations. Plato and Sophocles! It was worthwhile spending five years of hard labor to enter into their intimacy and make them sister-spirits of one's soul. Didn't Sophocles give me Antigone, the prototype of the new woman for all time, in her sacred rebellion against hindering laws and thwarting conventions, the eternal model of that dauntless assertion of love that is beyond and above sex, the very heart of the divine!

And the Socrates of Plato led me to that high place where man becomes God, having learned obedience to law and the cheerful acceptance of death; but even there I needed Antigone, the twin sister of Bazaroff,* at least as much, realizing intuitively that my life-work, too, would be chiefly in revolt, and that the punishment Socrates suffered and Antigone dared would almost certainly be mine; for I was fated to meet worse opponents; after all, Creon was only stupid, whereas Sir Thomas Horridge** was malevolent to boot, and Woodrow Wilson unspeakable!

Again I am outrunning my story by half a century!

But in what I have written of Sophocles and Plato the reader will divine, I hope, my intense love and admiration for Smith, who led me, as Vergil led Dante, into the ideal world that surrounds our earth as with illimitable spaces of purple sky, wind-swept and star-sown!

If I could tell what Smith's daily companionship now did for me, I would hardly need to write this book; for, like all I have written, some of the best of it belongs as much to him as to me. In his presence for the first year and a half I was merely a sponge, absorbing now this truth, now that, hardly conscious of an original impulse. Yet all the time, too, as will be seen, I was advising him and helping him from my knowledge of life. Our relation was really rather that of a small, practical husband with some wise and infinitely learned Aspasia!† I want to say here in contempt of probability that in all our years of intimacy, living together for over three years side by side, I never found a fault in him of character or of sympathy, save the one that drew him to his death.

Now I must leave him for the moment and turn again to Mrs. Mayhew. Of course, I went to her that next afternoon even before three. She met me without a word, so gravely that I did not even kiss her, but began explaining what Smith was to me and how I could not do enough for him

---

* The nihilistic medical student in Turgenev's *Fathers and Sons*.
** An English judge (1857–1938) who jailed Harris for contempt of court.
† A Greek courtesan, famous for her wit and culture, who was a lifelong companion of Pericles.

who was everything to my mind, as she was (God help me!) to my heart
and body; and I kissed her cold lips, while she shook her head sadly.

"We have a sixth sense, we women, when we are in love," she began. "I
feel a new influence in you; I scent danger in the air you bring with you:
don't ask me to explain: I can't; but my heart is heavy and cold as death.
If you leave me, there'll be a catastrophe: the fall from such a height of
happiness must be fatal. If you can feel pleasure away from me, you no
longer love me. I feel none except in having you, seeing you, thinking of you
—none! Oh, why can't you love like a woman loves! No! like I love: it would
be heaven; for you and you alone satisfy the insatiable; you leave me bathed
in bliss, sighing with satisfaction, happy as the Queen in Heaven!"

"I have much to tell you, new things to say," I began in haste.

"Come upstairs," I broke in, interrupting myself. "I want to see you as
you are now, with the color in your cheeks, the light in your eyes, the
vibration in your voice, come!"

And she came like a sad sybil. "Who gave you the tact," she began while
we were undressing, "the tact to praise always?"

I seized her and stood naked against her, body to body. "What new
things have you to tell me?" I asked, lifting her into the bed and getting in
beside her, cuddling up to her warmer body.

"There's always something new in my love," she cried, cupping my face
with her slim hands and taking my lips with hers.

"Oh, how I desired you yesternoon, for I took the letter to your house
myself and heard you talking in your room, perhaps with Smith," she
added, sounding my eyes with hers. "I'm longing to believe it; but, when
I heard your voice, or imagined I did, I felt the lips of my sex open and
shut and then it began to burn and itch intolerably. I was on the point of
going in to you, but, instead, turned and hurried away, raging at you and
at myself—"

"I will not let you even talk such treason," I cried, separating her soft
thighs, as I spoke, and sliding between them. In a moment my sex was in
her and we were one body, while I drew it out slowly and then pushed it
in again, her naked body straining to mine.

"Oh," she cried, "as you draw out, my heart follows your sex in fear of
losing it and as you push in again, it opens wide in ecstasy and wants you
all, all—" and she kissed me with hot lips.

"Here is something new," she exclaimed, "food for your vanity from my
love! Mad as you make me with your love-thrusts, for at one moment I am
hot and dry with desire, the next moment wet with passion, bathed in love,
I could live with you all my life without having you, if you wished it, or if
it would do you good. Do you believe me?"

"Yes," I replied, continuing the love-game, but occasionally withdrawing
to rub her clitoris with my sex and then slowly burying him in her cunt
again to the hilt.

"We women have no souls but love," she said faintly, her eyes dying as she spoke.

"I torture myself to think of some new pleasure for you, and yet you'll leave me, I feel you will, for some silly girl who can't feel a tithe of what I feel or give you what I give—" She began here to breathe quickly. "I've been thinking how to give you more pleasure; let me try. Your seed, darling, is dear to me: I don't want it in my sex; I want to feel you thrill and so I want your sex in my mouth, I want to drink your essence and I will—" and suiting the action to the word, she slipped down in the bed and took my sex in her mouth and began rubbing it up and down till my seed spirted in long jets, filling her mouth while she swallowed it greedily.

"Now do I love you, Sir!" she exclaimed, drawing herself upon me again and nestling against me. "Wait till some girl does that to you and you'll know she loves you to distraction or, better still, to self-destruction."

"Why do you talk of any other girl?" I chided her. "I don't imagine you going with another man; why should you torment yourself just as causelessly?"

She shook her head. "My fears are prophetic," she sighed. "I'm willing to believe it hasn't happened yet, though—Ah, God, the torturing thought! The mere dread of you going with another drives me crazy; I could kill her, the bitch: why doesn't she get a man of her own? How dare she even look at you?" and she clasped me tightly to her. Nothing loath, I pushed my sex into her again and began the slow movement that excited her so quickly and me so gradually for, even while using my skill to give her the utmost pleasure, I could not help comparing and I realized surely enough that Kate's pussy was smaller and firmer and gave me infinitely more pleasure; still I kept on for her delight. And now again she began to pant and choke and, as I continued ploughing her body and touching her womb with every slow thrust, she began to cry inarticulately with little short cries growing higher in intensity till suddenly she squealed like a shot rabbit and then shrieked with laughter, breaking down in a storm of sighs and sobs and floods of tears.

As usual, her intensity chilled me a little; for her paroxysm aroused no corresponding heat in me, tending even to check my pleasure by the funny, irregular movements she made.

Suddenly, I heard steps going away from the door, light, stealing steps: who could it be? The servant? or—?

Lorna had heard them, too, and though still panting and swallowing convulsively, she listened intently, while her great eyes wandered in thought. I knew I could leave the riddle to her: it was my task to reassure and caress her.

I got up and went over to the open window for a breath of air and suddenly I saw Lily run quickly across the grass and disappear in the next house: so she was the listener! When I recalled Lorna's gasping cries, I smiled to myself. If Lily tried to explain them to herself, she would have an uneasy hour, I guessed.

When Lorna had dressed, and she dressed quickly and went downstairs hastily to convince herself, I think, that her darky had not spied on her, I waited in the sitting room. I must warn Lorna that my "studies" would only allow me to give one day a week to our pleasures.

"Oh," she cried, turning pale as I explained, "didn't I know it!"

"But Lorna," I pleaded, "didn't you say you could do without me altogether if 'twas for my good?"

"No, no, no! a thousand times no!" she cried. "I said if you were with me always, I could do without passion; but this starvation fare once a week! Go, go," she cried, "or I'll say something I'll regret. Go!" and she pushed me out of the door, and thinking it better in view of the future, I went.

The truth is, I was glad to get away; novelty is the soul of passion. There's an old English proverb: "Fresh cunt, fresh courage." On my way home I thought oftener of the slim, dark figure of Lily than of the woman, every hill and valley of whose body was now familiar to me, whereas Lily with her narrow hips and straight flanks must have a tiny sex. I thought, "D . . n Lily," and I hastened to Smith.

We went down to supper together and I introduced Smith to Kate: they were just polite; but when she turned to me she scanned me curiously, her brows lifting in a gesture of, "I know what I know," which was to become familiar to me in the sequel.

After supper I had a long talk with Smith in his room, a heart to heart talk which altered our relations.

I have already mentioned that Smith got ill every fortnight or so. I had no inkling of the cause, no notion of the scope of the malady. This evening he grew reminiscent and told me everything.

He had thought himself very strong, it appeared, till he went to Athens to study. There he worked prodigiously, and almost at the beginning of his stay came to know a Greek girl of a good class who talked Greek with him and finally gave herself to him passionately.* Being full of youthful vigor

---

* Here is where a controversy had its beginning. A. I. Tobin, in an introduction to *The Love Life of Byron Caldwell Smith* (Antigone Press, New York, 1930), says that Smith's successor at the University of Kansas, by maliciously reporting that Smith had had an affair in Athens, hoped by discrediting Smith, to gain permanent possession of his chair in Greek. Tobin implies there is no reason to believe this. Kate Stephens remained true to Smith after his death, never marrying, carefully preserving his every letter to her; and in time, when Harris wrote *My Life and Loves,* she, with the aid of Gerrit and Mary Caldwell Smith, published the *Lies and Libels of Frank Harris.* This latter book demonstrates that Harris was mistaken as to dates of occurrences in Lawrence (reminiscent of the attacks on Harris by Carlyle's lateral descendants); and Miss Stephens on occasion even denied that Harris was at all close to Smith. It is not to make a special case of pleading for Harris to remember that he is relying on his memory for the most part for dates, and that it is very much a matter of the word of one person against that of another.

always quickened by vivid imaginings, he told me that he usually came the first time almost as soon as he entered and that, in order to give his partner pleasure, he had to come two or three times and this drained and exhausted him. He admitted that he had abandoned himself to this fierce love-play day after day in and out of season. When he returned to the United States, he tried to put his Greek girl out of his head; but in spite of all he could do, he had love-dreams that came to an orgasm and ended in emissions of seed about once a fortnight. And after a year or so these fortnightly emissions gave him intense pains in the small of his back which lasted some twenty-four hours, evidently till some more seed had been secreted. I could not imagine how a fortnightly emission could weaken and distress a young man of Smith's vigor and health; but as soon as I had witnessed his suffering, I set my wits to work and told him of the trick by which I had brought my wet dreams to an end in the English school.

Smith at once consented to try my remedy, and as the fortnight was about up, I went at once in search of a whipcord and tied up his unruly member for him night after night. For some days the remedy worked; then he went out and spent the afternoon and night at Judge Stevens' and he was ill again. Of course, there had been no connection: indeed, in my opinion, it would have been much better for Smith if there had been; but the pro-

---

It should also be realized, as is clear in the prefaces to these volumes, that Harris is more interested in characterizing someone properly than in giving a factual record. On one occasion he complains about his being unable at times to distinguish between what he saw and what he was told. This is not on his part an admission of lying, but a plea for the reader to be reasonably tolerant with his recollection.

The case of Byron Caldwell Smith is an extremely engrossing one. The young Smith must have been an extraordinary person to affect Miss Stephens and Harris the way he did, as well as a D. O. Kellogg, who published *A Young Scholar's Letters* (Putnam, New York, 1897), Smith's letters from Germany to his mother and father. One gains from both collections of Smith's letters the impression of an industrious young man in love with learning. His letters to his home were nevertheless pompous, and they had about them the epicene quality of much nineteenth-century scholarly prose. That is to say, Smith embodied in his letters the attitudes he believed became a scholar. He was proper, correct, and, if these letters reveal him at all in his entirety, a bit of a wet fish. Yet one can see how an untutored boy could come to admire such achievement in so young a scholar, and how the scholar would have warmed to such an eager, receptive mind; and how a college girl would fall in love with him.

Smith's letters to Miss Stephens reveal him as conventional and gentlemanly in his sentiments: his passion was not that of a Hero for Leander. Yet his image was held tight to by Miss Stephens for the rest of her life, and Harris' imputing an affair to him—which today would not be tantamount to throwing aspersions on a man's character—brought lightning down on Harris' head. It is evident from the letters that Miss Stephens was one girl Harris met who was not won over by him, for Smith had to explain to her that he wrote a letter to Harris out of ordinary courtesy, and that he disapproved of Harris' morals.

The dispute, then, cannot be settled here. But Harris' portrait of Smith, if he did slip now and then on accuracy, makes Smith a man, and a likeable one at that. One cannot say so much for what Smith's friends would have him be. In any event, Smith owes his being remembered to Harris, without whom he would long ago have been forgotten.

pinquity of the girl he loved and, of course, the kissings that are always allowed to engaged couples by American custom took place unchecked, and when he went to sleep his dreaming ended in an orgasm. The worst of it was that my remedy having prevented his dreaming from reaching a climax for eighteen or twenty days, he dreamed a second time and had a second wet dream, which brought him to misery and even intenser pain than usual.

I combatted the evil with all the wit I possessed. I got Ned Stephens to lend the Professor a horse; I had Blue Devil out and we went riding two or three times a week. I got boxing gloves, too, and soon either Ned or I had a bout with Smith every day: gradually these exercises improved his general health, and when I could tie on the whipcord every night for a month or so, he put on weight and gained strength surprisingly.

The worst of it was that this improvement in health always led to a day or two spent with his betrothed, which undid all the good. I advised him to marry and then control himself vigorously; but he wanted to get well first and be his vigorous self again. I did all I knew to help him, but for a long time I had no suspicion that an occasional wet dream could have serious consequences. We used to make fun of them as schoolboys: how could I imagine—but as it is the finest, most highly strung natures that are most apt to suffer in this way, I will tell what happened step by step. Suffice it to say here that he was in better health when staying with me at the Gregorys' than he had been before and I continually hoped for a permanent improvement.

After our talk that first night in Gregorys', I went downstairs to the dining room, hoping to find Kate alone. I was lucky: she had persuaded her mother, who was tired, to go to bed and was just finishing her tidying up.

"I want to see you, Kate," I said, trying to kiss her. She drew her head aside: "That's why you've kept away all afternoon, I suppose," and she looked at me with a side-long glance. An inspiration came to me. "Kate," I exclaimed, "I had to be fitted for my new clothes!"

"Forgive me," she cried at once, that excuse being valid. "I thought, I feared—oh, I'm suspicious without reason, I know—am jealous without cause. There! I confess!" and the great hazel eyes turned on me full of love.

I played with her breasts, whispering, "When am I to see you naked, Kate? I want to; when?"

"You've seen most of me!" and she laughed joyously.

"All right," I said, turning away," if you are resolved to make fun of me and be mean to me—"

"Mean to you!" she cried, catching me and swinging me round. "I could easier be mean to myself. I'm glad you want to see me, glad and proud, and tonight, if you'll leave your door open, I'll come to you: mean, oh—" and she gave me her soul in a kiss.

"Isn't it risky?" I asked.

"I tried the stairs this afternoon," she glowed. "They don't creak: no one will hear, so don't sleep or I'll surprise you." By way of sealing the compact, I put my hand up her clothes and caressed her sex: it was hot and soon opened to me.

"There now, Sir, go," she smiled, "or you'll make me very naughty and I have a lot to do!"

"How do you mean 'naughty'," I said; "tell me what you feel, please!"

"I feel my heart beating," she said, "and, and—oh! wait till tonight and I'll try to tell you, dear," and she pushed me out of the door.

For the first time in my life I notice here that the writer's art is not only inferior to reality in keenness of sensation and emotion, but also more same, monotonous even, because of showing the tiny, yet ineffable differences of the same feeling which difference of personality brings with it. I seem to be repeating to myself in describing Kate's love after Mrs. Mayhew's, making the girl's feeling a fainter replica of the woman's. In reality the two were completely different. Mrs. Mayhew's feelings, long repressed, flamed with the heat of an afternoon in July or August, while in Kate's one felt the freshness and cool of a summer morning, shot through with the suggestion of heat to come. And this comparison, even, is inept, because it leaves out the account the effect of Kate's beauty, the great hazel eyes, the rosied skin, the superb figure. Besides, there was a glamor of the spirit about Kate: Lorna Mayhew would never give me a new note that didn't spring from passion; in Kate I felt a spiritual personality and the thrill of undeveloped possibilities. And still, using my utmost skill, I haven't shown my reader the enormous superiority of the girl and her more unselfish love. But I haven't finished yet.

Smith had given me *The Mill on the Floss* to read; I had never tried George Eliot before and I found that this book almost deserved Smith's praise. I had read till about one o'clock when my heart heard her; or was it some thrill of expectance? The next moment my door opened and she came in with the mane of hair about her shoulders and a long dressing gown reaching to her stocking feet. I got up like a flash, but she had already closed the door and bolted it. I drew her to the bed and stopped her from throwing off the dressing-gown. "Let me take off your stockings first," I whispered. "I want you all imprinted on me!"

The next moment she stood there naked, the flickering flame of the candle throwing quaint arabesques of light on her ivory body. I gazed and gazed: from the navel down she was perfect; I turned her round and the back, too, the bottom, even, was faultless, though large: but alas! the breasts were far too big for beauty, too soft to excite! I must think only of the bold curve of her hips, I reflected, the splendor of the firm thighs, the flesh of which had the hard outline of marble, and her—sex. I put her on the bed and opened her thighs: her pussy was ideally perfect.

At once I wanted to get into her; but she pleaded: "Please, dear, come into bed, I'm cold and want you." So in I got and began kissing her.

Soon she grew warm and I pulled off my night-shirt and my middle finger was caressing her sex that opened quickly. "E—E," she said, drawing in her breath quickly, "It still hurts." I put my sex gently against hers, moving it up and down slowly till she drew up her knees to let me in; but, as soon as the head entered, her face puckered a little with pain and, as I had had a long afternoon, I was the more inclined to forbear, and accordingly I drew away and took place beside her.

"I cannot bear to hurt you," I said. "Love's pleasure must be natural."

"You're sweet!" she whispered. "I'm glad you stopped, for it shows you really care for me and not just for the pleasure," and she kissed me lovingly.

"Kate, reward me," I said, "by telling me just what you felt when I first had you," and I put her hand on my hot stiff sex to encourage her.

"It's impossible," she said, flushing a little. "There was such a throng of new feelings; why, this evening, waiting in bed for the time to pass and thinking of you, I felt a strange prickling sensation in the inside of my thighs that I never felt before and now"—and she hid her glowing face against my neck, "I feel it again!

"Love is funny, isn't it?" she whispered the next moment. "Now the pricking sensation is gone and the front part of my sex burns and itches. Oh! I must touch it!"

"Let me," I cried, and, in a moment, I was on her, working my organ up and down on her clitoris, the porch, so to speak, of Love's temple. A little later she herself sucked the head into her hot, dry pussy and then closed her legs as if in pain to stop me going further; but I began to rub my sex up and down on her tickler, letting it slide right in every now and then, till she panted and her love-juice came and my weapon sheathed itself in her naturally. I soon began the very slow and gentle in-and-out movements which increased her excitement steadily while giving her more and more pleasure, till I came and immediately she lifted my chest up from her breasts with both hands and showed me her glowing face. "Stop, boy," she gasped, "please, my heart's fluttering so! I came too, you know, just with you," and indeed I felt her trembling all over convulsively.

I drew out and for safety's sake got her to use the syringe, having already explained its efficacy to her: she was adorably awkward and, when she had finished, I took her to bed again and held her to me, kissing her. "So you really love me, Kate!"

"Really," she said, "you don't know how much! I'll try never to suspect anything or to be jealous again." She went on, "It's a hateful thing, isn't it? But I want to see your classroom: would you take me up once to the university?"

"Why, of course," I cried. "I should be only too glad; "I'll take you tomorrow afternoon. Or better still," I added, "come up the hill at four o'clock and I'll meet you at the entrance."

And so it was settled and Kate went back to her room as noiselessly as she had come.

The next afternoon I found her waiting in the university hall ten minutes before the hour, for our lectures beginning at the hour always stopped after forty-five minutes to give us time to be punctual at any other classroom. After showing her everything of interest, we walked home together laughing and talking, when, a hundred yards from Mrs. Mayhew's, we met that lady, face to face. I don't know how I looked, for being a little short-sighted, I hadn't recognized her till she was within ten yards of me; but her glance pierced me. She bowed with a look that took us both in. I lifted my hat and we passed on.

"Who's that?" exclaimed Kate, "What a strange look she gave us!"

"She's the wife of a gambler," I replied as indifferently as I could. "He gives me work now and then," I went on, strangely forecasting the future. Kate looked at me, probing, then, "I don't mind. I'm glad she's quite old!"

"As old as both of us put together!" I retorted traitorously, and we went in.

These love-passages with Mrs. Mayhew and Kate, plus my lessons and my talks with Smith, fairly represent my life's happenings for this whole year from seventeen to eighteen, with this solitary qualification, that my afternoons with Lorna became less and less agreeable to me. But now I must relate happenings that again affected my life.

I hadn't been four months with the Gregorys when Kate told me that my brother Willie had ceased to pay my board for me more than a fortnight. She added sweetly, "It doesn't matter, dear, but I thought you ought to know and I'd hate anyone to hurt you, so I took it on myself to tell you." I kissed her, said it was sweet of her and went to find Willie. He made excuses, voluble but not convincing, and ended up by giving me a check while begging me to tell Mrs. Gregory that he, too, would come and board with her.

The incident set me thinking. I made Kate promise to tell me if he ever failed again to pay what was due, and I used the happening to excuse myself to Lorna. I went to see her and told her that I must think at once of earning my living. I had still some five hundred dollars left, but I wanted to be before-hand with need; besides, it gave me a good excuse for not visiting her even weekly. "I must work!" I kept repeating, though I was ashamed of the lie.

"Don't whip me, dear!" she pleaded. "My impotence to help you is painful enough; give me time to think. I know Mayhew is quite well off: give me a day or two, but come to me when you can. You see, I've no pride where you are concerned: I just beg like a dog for kind treatment for my love's sake. I wouldn't have believed that I could be so transformed. I was always so proud: my husband calls me 'proud and cold'—me cold! It's true I shiver when I hear your voice, but it's the shivering of fever. When you came in just now unexpectedly and kissed me waves of heat swept over me: my womb moved inside me. I never felt that till I had loved you and now, of course, my sex burns—I wish I were cold: a cold woman could rule the world.

"But no! I wouldn't change. Just as I never wished to be a man, never. Though other girls used to say they would like to change their sex, I, never! And since I've been married, less than ever. What's a man? His love is over before ours begins."

"Really?" I broke in grinning.

"Not you, my beloved!" she cried. "Oh, not you; but then you are more than a man! Come, don't let us waste time in talk. Now I have you, take me to our Heaven. I'm ready, 'ripe-ready' is your word: I go to our bed as to an altar. If I'm only to have you even less than once a week, don't come again for ten days: I shall be well again then and you can surely come to me a few days running. I want to reach the heights and hug the illusion, cramming one hot week with bliss and then death for a fortnight. What rags we women are! Come, dear, I will be your sheath and you shall be the sword and drive right into me.

"But I'll help you," she cried suddenly. "Was it that girl told you, you owed money for food?" I nodded and she glowed. "Oh, I'll help, never fear! I never liked that girl: she's brazen and conceited and—oh! Why did you walk with her?"

"She wanted to see the university," I said, "and I could not well refuse her."

"Oh, pay her," she cried, "but don't walk with her; she's a common thing. Fancy her mentioning money to you, my dear!"

That same evening I got a note from Lorna, saying her husband wanted to see me.

I met the little man in the sitting room and he proposed that I should come to his rooms every evening after supper and sit in a chair near the door reading, but with a Colt's revolver handy so that no one could rob him and get away with the plunder.

"I'd feel safer," he ended up, "and my wife tells me you're a sure shot and used to a wild life. What do you say? I'd give you sixty dollars a month and more than half the time you'd be free before midnight."

"It's very kind of you," I exclaimed with hot cheeks, "and very kind of Mrs. Mayhew, too: I'll do it and I beg you to believe that no one will bother you and get away with a whole skin," and so it was settled.

Aren't women wonderful! In half a day she had solved my difficulty and I found the hours spent in Mayhew's gambling rooms were more valuable than I had dreamed. The average man reveals himself in gaming more than in love or drink, and I was astonished to discover that many of the so-called best citizens had a flutter with Mayhew from time to time. I don't believe that they had a fair deal; he won too constantly for that; but it was none of my business so long as the clients accepted the results; and he often showed kindness by giving back a few dollars after he had skinned a man of all he possessed.

Naturally, the fact that I was working with her husband threw me more into Mrs. Mayhew's society: twice or so a week I had to spend the afternoon with her, and the constraint irked me. Kate, too, objected to my visits: she had seen me go into Mrs. Mayhew's and I think divined the rest, for at first she was cold to me and drew away even from my kisses. "You've chilled me," she cried. "I don't think I shall ever love you again entirely." But when I got into her . . . really excited her, she suddenly kissed me fervently, and her glorious eyes had heavy tears in them.

"Why do you cry, dear?" I asked.

"Because I cannot make you mine as I am all yours!" she cried. "Oh!" she went on, clutching me to her, "I think the pleasure is increased by the dreadful fear and the hate—oh, love me and me only, love mine!" Of course I promised fidelity, but I was surprised to feel that my desire for Kate, too, was beginning to cool.

The arrangement with the Mayhews came to an unexpected and untimely end. Mayhew now and then had a tussle with another gambler, and after I had been with him about three months, a gambler from Denver had a great contest with him and afterwards proposed that they should join forces and Mayhew should come to Denver. "More money to be made there in a week," he declared, "than in Lawrence in a month." Finally he persuaded Mayhew, who was wise enough to say nothing to his wife till the whole arrangement was fixed. She raved but could do nothing save give in, and so we had to part. Mayhew gave me one hundred dollars as a bonus, and Lorna one unforgettable, astonishing afternoon which I must now try to describe.

I did not go near the Mayhew's the day after this gift, leaving Lorna to suppose that I looked upon everything as ended. But the day after that I got a word from her, an imperious, "Come at once; I must see you!"

Of course I went, though reluctantly.

As soon as I entered the room she rose from the sofa and came to me. "If I get you work in Denver, will you come out?"

"How could I?" I asked in absolute astonishment. "You know I'm bound here to the university and then I want to go into a law office as well. Besides, I could not leave Smith: I've never known such a teacher; I don't believe his equal can be found anywhere."

She nodded her head. "I see," she sighed. "I suppose it's impossible; but I must see you," she cried. "If I haven't the hope—what do I say—the certainty of seeing you again, I shan't go. I'd rather kill myself! I'll be a servant and stay with you, my darling, and take care of you! I don't care what I do so long as we are together. I'm nearly crazed with fear that I shall lose you."

"It's all a question of money," I said quietly, for the idea of her staying behind scared me stiff. "If I can earn money, I'd love to go to Denver in my holidays. It must be gorgeous there in summer, six thousand odd feet above sea-level. I'd delight in it."

"If I send you the money, you'll come?"

I made a face. "I can't take money from—a love" (I said 'love' instead of 'woman': it was not ugly), I went on, "but Smith says he can get me work and I have still a little. I'll come in the holidays."

"Holy days they'll be to me!" she said solemnly, and then with quick change of mood, "I'll make a beautiful room for our love in Denver; but you must come for Christmas, I could not wait till midsummer. Oh, how I shall ache for you—ache!"

"Come upstairs," I coaxed and she came, and we went to the bed. I found her mad with desire, but after I had brought her in an hour to hysteria and she lay in my arms crying, she suddenly said, "He promised to come home early this afternoon, and I said I'd have a surprise for him. When he finds us together like this, it'll be a surprise, won't it?"

"But you're mad!" I cried, getting out of bed in a flash. "I shall never be able to visit you in Denver if we have a row here!"

"That's true," she said as if in a dream, "that's true. It's a pity: I'd love to have seen his foolish face stretched to wonder; but you're right. Hurry!" she cried, and was out of the room in a twinkling.

When she returned, I was dressed.

"Go downstairs and wait for me," she commanded, "on our sofa. If he knocks, open the door to him. That'll be a surprise, though not so great a one as I had planned," she added laughing shrilly.

"Are you going without kissing me?" she cried when I was at the door. "Well, go, it's all right, go, for if I felt your lips again, I might keep you."

I went downstairs and in a few moments she followed me. "I can't bear you to go!" she cried. "How partings hurt!" she whispered. "Why should we part again, love mine?" and she looked at me with rapt eyes.

"This life holds nothing worth having but love. Let us make love deathless, you and I, going together to death. What do we lose? Nothing! This world is an empty shell! Come with me, love, and we'll meet death together!"

"Oh, I want to do such a lot of things first," I exclaimed. "Death's empire is eternal, but this brief task of life, the adventure of it, the change of it, the huge possibilities of it beckon me. I can't leave it."

"The change!" she cried with dilating nostrils, while her eyes darkened, "the change!"

"You are determined to misunderstand me," I cried. "Is not every day a change?"

"I am weary," she cried, "and beaten. I can only beg you not to forget your promise to come—ah!" and she caught and kissed me on the mouth. "I shall die with your name on my lips," she said, and turned to bury her face in the sofa cushion. I went: what else was there to do?

I saw them off at the station. Lorna had made me promise to write often, and swore she would write every day, and she did send me short notes daily for a fortnight. Then came gaps ever lengthening: "Denver society was pleasant and a Mr. Wilson, a student, was assiduous: he comes every day," she wrote. Excuses finally, little hasty notes, and in two months her letters were formal, cold; in three months they had ceased altogether.

The break did not surprise me. I had taught her that youth was the first requisite in a lover for a woman of her type. She had doubtless put my precepts into practice: Mr. Wilson was probably as near the ideal as I was, and very much nearer to hand.

The passions of the sense demand propinquity and satisfaction and nothing is more forgetful than pleasures of the flesh. If Mrs. Mayhew had given me a little, I had given her even less of my better self.

Chapter XII

Hard Times and New Loves

So far I had had more good fortune than falls to the lot of most youths starting in life; now I was to taste ill luck and be tried as with fire. I had been so taken up with my own concerns that I had hardly given a thought to public affairs; now I was forced to take a wider view.

One day Kate told me that Willie was heavily in arrears: he had gone back to Deacon Conklin's to live on the other side of the Kaw River and I had naturally supposed that he had paid up everything before leaving. I found that he owed the Gregorys sixty dollars on his own account, and more than that on mine.

I went across to him really enraged. If he had warned me, I should not have minded so much; but to leave the Gregorys to tell me made me positively dislike him, and I did not know then the full extent of his selfishness. Years later my sister told me that he had written time and again to my father and got money from him, alleging that it was for me and that I was studying and couldn't earn anything. "Willie kept us poor, Frank," she told me, and I could only bow my head; but if I had known this fact at the time, it would have changed my relations with Willie.

As it was, I found him in the depths. Carried away by his optimism, he had bought real estate in 1871 and 1872, mortgaged it for more than he gave, and as the boom continued, he had repeated this game time and again till on paper and in paper he reckoned he had made a hundred thousand dollars. This he had told me and I was glad of it for his sake, unfeignedly glad.

It was easy to see that the boom and inflation period had been based at first on the extraordinary growth of the country through the immigration and trade that had followed the Civil War. But the Franco-German war had wasted wealth prodigiously, deranged trade, too, and diverted commerce into new channels. First France and then England felt the shock: London had to call in moneys lent to American railways and other enterprises. Bit by bit even American optimism was overcome, for immigration in 1871 and 1872 fell off greatly and the foreign calls for cash exhausted our banks. The crash came in 1873; nothing like it was seen again in these states till the slump of 1907, which led to the founding of the Federal Reserve Bank.

Willie's fortune melted almost in a moment: this mortgage and that had to be met and could only be met by forced sales, with no buyers except at minimum values. When I talked to him, he was almost in despair; no money; no property: all lost; the product of three years' hard work and successful speculation all swept away. Could I help him? If not, he was ruined. He told me he had drawn all he could from my father: naturally I promised to help him; but first I had to pay the Gregorys, and to my astonishment he begged me to let him have the money instead. "Mrs. Gregory and all of 'em like you," he pleaded. "They can wait, I cannot; I know of a purchase that could be made that would make me rich again!"

I realized then that he was selfish through and through, conscienceless in egotistic greed. I gave up my faint hope that he would ever repay me: henceforth he was a stranger to me and one that I did not even respect, though he had some fine, ingratiating qualities.

I left him to walk across the river and in a few blocks met Rose. She looked prettier than ever and I turned and walked with her, praising her beauty to the skies, and indeed she deserved it; short green sleeves, I remember, set off her exquisite, plump, white arms. I promised her some books and made her say she would read them; indeed, I was astonished by the warmth of her gratitude. She told me it was sweet of me, gave me her eyes, and we parted the best of friends, with just a hint of warmer relationship in the future.

That evening I paid the Gregorys Willie's debt and my own and did not send him the balance of what I possessed, as I had promised, but instead a letter telling him I had preferred to cancel his debt to the Gregorys.

Next day he came and assured me he had promised moneys on the strength of my promise, had bought a hundred crates, too, of chickens to ship to Denver, and had already an offer from the mayor of Denver at double what he had given. I read the letters and wire he showed me and let him have four hundred dollars, which drained me and kept me poor for months; indeed, till I brought off the deal with Dingwall, which I am about to relate, and which put me on my feet again in comfort.

I should now tell of Willie's misadventure with his carload of chickens: it suffices here to say that he was cheated by his purchaser and that I never saw a dollar of all I had loaned him.

Looking back, I understand that it was probably the slump of 1873 that induced the Mayhews to go to Denver; but after they left, I was at a loose end for some months. I could not get work, though I tried everything: I was met everywhere with the excuse, "Hard times! Hard times!" At length I took a place as waiter in the Eldridge House, the only job I could find that left most of the forenoon free for the university. Smith disliked this new departure of mine and told me he would soon find me a better post; and Mrs. Gregory was disgusted and resentful—partly out of snobbishness, I think. From this time on I felt her against me, and gradually she undermined my influence with Kate. I soon knew I had fallen in public esteem, too, but not for long.

One day in the fall Smith introduced me to a Mr. Rankin, the cashier of the First National Bank, who handed over to me at once the letting of Liberty Hall, the one hall in the town large enough to accommodate a thousand people: it had a stage, too, and so could be used for theatrical performances. I gave up my work in the Eldridge House and instead used to sit in the box office of the hall from two every afternoon till seven, and did my best to let it advantageously to the advance agents of the various traveling shows or lecturers. I received sixty dollars a month for this work and one day got an experience which has modified my whole life, for it taught me how money is made in this world and can be made by any intelligent man.

One afternoon the advance agent of the Hatherly Minstrels came into my room and threw down his card.

"This old one-hoss shay of a town," he cried; "should wear grave-clothes."

"What's the matter?" I asked.

"Matter!" he repeated scornfully. "I don't believe there's a place in the hull God d——d town big enough to show our double-crown bills! Not one: not a place. I meant to spend ten thousand dollars here in advertising the great Hatherly Minstrels, the best show on earth. They'll be here for a hull fortnight, and, by God, you won't take my money. You don't want money in this dead and alive hole!"

The fellow amused me: he was so convinced and outspoken that I took to him. As luck would have it, I had been at the university till late that day and had not gone to the Gregorys for dinner: I was healthily hungry. I asked Mr. Dingwall whether he had dined.

"No, Sir," was his reply. "Can one dine in this place?"

"I guess so," I replied. "If you'll do me the honor of being my guest, I'll take you to a good porterhouse steak at least," and I took him across to the Eldridge House, a short distance away, leaving a young friend, Will Thomson, a doctor's son whom I knew, in my place.

I gave Dingwall the best dinner I could and drew him out. He was indeed "a live wire," as he phrased it, and suddenly, inspired by his optimism, the idea came to me that if he would deposit the ten thousand dollars he had talked of, I could put up boardings on all the vacant lots in Massachusetts Street and make a good thing out of exhibiting the bills of the various traveling shows that visited Lawrence. It wasn't the first time I had been asked to help advertise this or that entertainment. I put forward my idea timidly, yet Dingwall took it up at once. "If you can find good security, or a good surety," he said, "I'll leave five thousand dollars with you. I've no right to, but I like you and I'll risk it."

I took him across to Mr. Rankin, the banker, who listened to me benevolently and finally said he'd go surety that I'd exhibit a thousand bills for a fortnight all down the chief street on boardings to be erected at once, on condition that Mr. Dingwall paid five thousand dollars in advance; and he gave Mr. Dingwall a letter to that effect, and then told me pleasantly he held five thousand and some odd dollars at my service.

Dingwall took the next train west, leaving me to put up boardings in a month, after getting first of all permission from the lot owners. To cut a long story short, I got permission from a hundred lot owners in a week through my brother Willie, who as an estate agent knew them all. Then I made a contract with a little English carpenter and put the boardings up and got the bills all posted three days before the date agreed upon. Hatherly's Minstrels had a great fortnight and everyone was content. From that time on I drew about fifty dollars a week as my profit from letting the boardings, in spite of the slump.

Suddenly Smith got a bad cold: Lawrence is nearly a thousand feet above sea-level and in winter can be as icy as the Pole. He began to cough, a nasty little, dry, hacking cough. I persuaded him to see a doctor and then to have a consultation, the result being that the specialists all diagnosed tuberculosis and recommended immediate change to the milder east. For some reason or other, I believe because an editorial post on the *Press* in Philadelphia was offered to him, he left Lawrence hastily and took up his residence in the Quaker City.

His departure had notable results for me. First of all, the spiritual effect astonished me. As soon as he went, I began going over all he had taught me, especially in economics and metaphysics. Bit by bit I came to the conclusion that his Marxian communism was only half the truth and probably the least important half. His Hegelianism, too, which I have hardly mentioned, was pure moonshine in my opinion, extremely beautiful at moments, as the moon is when silvering purple clouds. "History is the development of the spirit in time; nature is the projection of the idea in space," sounds wonderful, but it's moonshine, and not very enlightening.

In the first three months of Smith's absence, my own individuality sprang upright like a sapling that has long been bent almost to breaking, so to speak, by a superincumbent weight, and I began to grow with a sort of renewed youth. Now, for the first time, when about nineteen years of age, I came to deal with life in my own way and under this name, Frank.

As soon as I returned from the Eldridge House to lodge with the Gregorys again, Kate showed herself just as kind to me as ever. She would come to my bedroom twice or thrice a week and was always welcome, but again and again I felt that her mother was intent on keeping us apart as much as possible, and at length she arranged that Kate should pay a visit to some English friends who were settled in Kansas City. Kate postponed the visit several times, but at length she had to yield to her mother's entreaties and advice. By this time my boardings were bringing me in a good deal, and so I promised to accompany Kate and spend the whole night with her in some Kansas City hotel.

We got to the hotel about ten and bold as brass I registered as Mr. and Mrs. William Wallace and went up to our room with Kate's luggage, my heart beating in my throat. Kate, too, was "all of a quiver," as she confessed to me a little later, but what a night we had! Kate resolved to show me all her love and gave herself to me passionately, but she never took the initiative, I noticed, as Mrs. Mayhew used to do.

At first I kissed her and talked a little, but as soon as she had arranged her things, I began to undress her. When her chemise fell, all glowing with my caressings, she asked, "You really like that?" and she put her hand over her sex, standing there naked like a Greek Venus. "Naturally," I exclaimed, "and these, too," and I kissed and sucked her nipples until they grew rosy-red.

"Is it possible to do it—standing up?" she asked, in some confusion. "Of course," I replied. "Let's try! But what put that into your head?"

"I saw a man and a girl once behind the church near our house," she whispered, "and I wondered how—" and she blushed rosily. As I got into her, I felt difficulty: her pussy was really small and this time seemed hot and dry: I felt her wince and, at once, withdrew. "Does it still hurt, Kate?" I asked.

"A little at first," she replied. "But I don't mind," she hastened to add, "I like the pain!"

By way of answer, I slipped my arms around her, under her bottom, and carried her to the bed. "I will not hurt you tonight," I said, "I'll make you give down your love-juice first and then there'll be no pain."

A few kisses and she sighed: "I'm wet now," and I got into bed and put my sex against hers.

"I'm going to leave everything to you," I said, "but please don't hurt yourself." She put her hand down to my sex and guided it in, sighing a little with satisfaction as bit by bit it slipped home.

After the first ecstasy, I got her to use the syringe while I watched her curiously. When she came back to bed, "No danger now," I cried, "no danger; my love is queen!"

"You darling lover!" she cried, her eyes wide, as if in wonder. "My sex throbs and itches and oh! I feel prickings on the inside of my thighs: I want you dreadfully, Frank," and she stretched out as she spoke, drawing up her knees.

I got on top of her and softly, slowly let my sex slide into her and then began the love-play. When my second orgasm came, I indulged myself with quick, short strokes, though I knew that she preferred the long slow movement, for I was resolved to give her every sensation this golden night. When she felt me begin again the long slow movement she loved, she sighed two or three times and putting her hands on my buttocks, drew me close but otherwise made little sign of feeling for perhaps half an hour. I kept right on; the slow movement now gave me but little pleasure: it was rather a task than a joy; but I was resolved to give her a feast. I don't know how long the bout lasted, but once I withdrew and began rubbing her clitoris and the front of her sex, and panting she nodded her head and rubbed herself ecstatically against my sex, and after I had begun the slow movement again, "Please, Frank!" she gasped, "I can't stand more: I'm going crazy—choking!"

Strange to say, her words excited me more than the act: I felt my spasm coming and roughly, savagely I thrust in my sex at the same time, kneeling between her legs so as to be able to play back and forth on her tickler as well. "I'll ravish you!" I cried and gave myself to the keen delight. As my seed spirted, she didn't speak, but lay there still and white; I jumped out of the bed, got a spongeful of cold water and used it on her forehead.

At once, to my joy, she opened her eyes. "I'm sorry," she gasped, and took a drink of water, "but I was so tired, I must have slept. You dear heart!" When I had put down the sponge and glass, I slipped into her again and in a little while she became hysterical: "I can't help crying, Frank, love," she sighed. "I'm so happy, dear. You'll always love me? Won't you? Sweet!" Naturally, I reassured her with promises of enduring affection and many kisses. Finally, I put my left arm round her neck and so fell asleep with my head on her soft breast.

In the morning we ran another course, though, sooth to say, Kate was more curious than passionate.

"I want to study you!" she said, and took my sex in her hands and then my balls. "What are they for?" she asked, and I had to explain that that was where my seed was secreted. She made a face, so I added, "You have a similar manufactory, my dear, but it's inside you, the ovaries they are called, and it takes them a month to make one egg, whereas my balls make millions in an hour. I often wonder why?"

After getting Kate an excellent breakfast, I put her in a cab and she reached her friend's house just at the proper time, but the girl friend could never understand how they had missed each other at the station.

I returned to Lawrence the same day, wondering what fortune had in store for me! I was soon to find out that life could be disagreeable.

The University of Kansas had been established by the first western outwanderers and like most pioneers they had brains and courage; and accordingly they put in the statutes that there should be no religious teaching of any kind in the university; still less should religion ever be exalted into a test or qualification.

But in due course Yankees from New England swarmed out to prevent Kansas from being made into a slave-state, and these Yankees were all fanatical so-called Christians belonging to every known sect, but all distinguished, or rather deformed, by an intolerant bigotry in matters of religion and sex. Their honesty was by no means so pronounced: each sect had to have its own professor: thus history got an Episcopalian clergyman who knew no history, and Latin a Baptist who, when Smith greeted him in Latin, could only blush and beg him not to expose his shameful ignorance; the lady who taught French was a joke but a good Methodist, I believe; and so forth and so on: education degraded by sectarian jealousies.

As soon as Professor Smith left the university, the faculty passed a resolution establishing "college chapel" in imitation of an English university custom. At once I wrote to the faculty, protesting and citing the statutes of the founders. The faculty did not answer my letter and instituted roll call instead of chapel; and when they got all the students assembled for roll call, they had the doors locked and began prayers, ending with a hymn.

After the roll call, I got up and walked to the door and tried in vain to open it. Fortunately, the door on this side of the hall was only a makeshift structure of thin wooden planks. I stepped back a pace or two and appealed again to the professors seated on the platform. When they paid no heed, I ran and jumped with my foot against the lock. It sprang and the door flew open with a crash.

Next day by a unanimous vote of the faculty, I was expelled from the university and was free to turn all my attention to law. Judge Stephens told me he would bring action on my behalf against the faculty, if I wished, and felt sure he'd get damages and reinstate me. But the university without Smith meant less than nothing to me, and why should I waste time fighting brainless bigots? I little knew then that that would be the main work of my life; but this first time I left my enemies the victory and the field, as I probably shall at long last.

I made up my mind to study law, and as a beginning induced Barker of Barker & Sommerfeld to let me study in his law office. I don't remember how I got to know them, but Barker, an immensely fat man, was a famous advocate and very kind to me, for no apparent reason. Sommerfeld was a tall, fair, German-looking Jew, peculiarly inarticulate, almost tongue-tied, indeed, in English; but an excellent lawyer and a kindly, honest man who commanded the respect of all the Germans and Jews in Douglas County, partly because his fat little father had been one of the earliest settlers in Lawrence and one of the most successful tradesmen. He kept a general provision store and had been kind to his compatriots in their early struggling days.

It was an admirable partnership. Sommerfeld had the clients and prepared the briefs, while Barker did the talking in court with a sort of invincible good humor, which I never saw equalled save in the notorious Englishman, Bottomley.* Barker before a jury used to exude good nature and common sense and thus gain even bad cases. Sommerfeld I'll tell more about in due time.

A little later I got depressing news from Smith: his cough had not diminished and he missed our companionship. There was a hopelessness in the letter which hurt my very heart, but what could I do? I could only

* Horatio Bottomley (1860–1933), English journalist and financier.

keep on working hard at law, while using every spare moment to increase my income by adding to my boardings in two senses.

One evening I almost ran into Lily. Kate was still away in Kansas City, so I stopped eagerly enough to have a talk, for Lily had always interested me. After the first greetings she told me she was going home. "They are all out, I believe," she added. At once I offered to accompany her and she consented. It was early in summer but already warm, and when we went into the parlor and Lily took a seat on the sofa, her thin white dress defined her slim figure seductively.

"What do you do," she asked mischievously, "now that dear Mrs. Mayhew's gone? You must miss her!" she added suggestively.

"I do," I confessed boldly. "I wonder if you'd have pluck enough to tell me the truth," I went on.

"Pluck?" She wrinkled her forehead and pursed her large mouth.

"Courage, I mean," I said.

"Oh, I have courage," she rejoined.

"Did you ever come upstairs to Mrs. Mayhew's bedroom," I asked, "when I had gone up for a book?" The black eyes danced and she laughed knowingly.

"Mrs. Mayhew said that she had taken you upstairs to bathe your poor head after dancing," she retorted disdainfully, "but I don't care: it's nothing to do with me what you do!"

"It has too," I went on, carrying the war into her country.

"How?" she asked.

"Why the first day you went away and left me, though I was really ill," I said, "so I naturally believed that you disliked me, though I thought you lovely!"

"I'm not lovely," she said. "My mouth's too big and I'm too slight."

"Don't malign yourself," I replied earnestly; "that's just why you are seductive and excite a man."

"Really?" she cried, and so the talk went on, while I cudgelled my brains for an opportunity but found none, and all the while was in fear lest her father and mother should return. At length, angry with myself, I got up to go on some pretext and she accompanied me to the stoop. I said good-bye on the top step and then jumped down by the side with a prayer in my heart that she'd come a step or two down, and she did. There she stood, her hips on a level with my mouth; in a moment my hands went up her dress, the right to her sex, the left to her bottom behind to hold her. The thrill as I touched her half-fledged sex was almost painful in intensity. Her first movement brought her sitting down on the step above me and at once my finger was busy in her slit.

"How dare you!" she cried, but not angrily. "Take your hand away!"

"Oh, how lovely your sex is!" I exclaimed, as if astounded. "Oh, I must see it and have you, you miracle of beauty," and my left hand drew down her head for a long kiss while my middle finger still continued its caress.

Of a sudden her lips grew hot and at once I whispered, "Won't you love me, dear? I want you so: I'm burning and itching with desire. (I knew she was!) Please; I won't hurt you and I'll take care. Please, love, no one will know," and the end of it was that right there on the porch I drew her to me and put my sex against hers and began the rubbing of her tickler and front part of her sex that I knew would excite her. In a moment she came and her love-dew wet my sex and excited me terribly; but I kept on frigging her with my man-root while restraining myself from coming by thinking of other things, till she kissed me of her own accord and suddenly moving forward pushed my prick right into her pussy.

To my astonishment, there was no obstacle, no maidenhead to break through, though her sex itself was astonishingly small and tight. I didn't scruple then to let my seed come, only withdrawing to the lips and rubbing her clitoris the while, and, as soon as my spirting ceased, my root glided again into her and continued the slow in-and-out movement till she panted with her head on my shoulder and asked me to stop. I did as she wished, for I knew I had won another wonderful mistress.

We went into the house again, for she insisted I should meet her father and mother, and, while we were waiting, she showed me her lovely tiny breasts, scarcely larger than small apples, and I became aware of something childish in her mind which matched the childish outlines of her lovely, half-formed hips and pussy.

"I thought that you were in love with Mrs. Mayhew," she confessed, "and I couldn't make out why she made such funny noises. But now I know," she added, "you naughty dear, for I felt my heart fluttering just now and I was nearly choking."

I don't know why, but that ravishing of Lily made her dear to me. I resolved to see her naked and to make her thrill to ecstasy as soon as possible, and then and there we made a meeting place on the far side of the church, whence I knew I could bring her to my room at the Gregorys in a minute; and then I went home, for it was late and I didn't particularly want to meet her folks.

The next night I met Lily by the church and took her to my room. She laughed aloud with delight as we entered, for indeed she was almost like a boy of bold, adventurous spirit. She confessed to me that my challenge of her pluck had pleased her intimately.

"I never took a 'dare'!" she cried in her American slang, tossing her head.

"I'll give you two," I whispered, "right now: the first is, I dare you to strip naked as I'm going to do, and I'll tell you the other when we're in bed."

Again she tossed her little blue-black head. "Pooh," she cried, "I'll be undressed first," and she was. Her beauty made my pulses hammer and parched my mouth. No one could help admiring her: she was very slight, with tiny breasts, as I have said, flat belly and straight flanks and hips: her triangle was only brushed in, so to speak, with fluffy soft hairs, and, as I held her naked body against mine, the look and feel of her exasperated my desire. I still admired Kate's riper, richer, more luscious outlines: her figure was nearer my boyish ideal; but Lily represented a type of adolescence destined to grow on me mightily. In fact, as my youthful virility decreased, my love of opulent feminine charms diminished and grew more and more to love slender, youthful outlines with the signs of sex rather indicated than pronounced. What an all-devouring appetite Rubens confesses with the great, hanging breasts and uncouth fat pink bottoms of his Venuses!

I lifted Lily on the bed and separated her legs to study her pussy. She made a face at me; but, as I rubbed my hot sex against her little button that I could hardly see, she smiled and lay back contentedly. In a minute or two, her love-juice came and I got into bed on her and slipped my root into her small cunt; even when the lips were wide open, it was closed to the eye and this and her slim nakedness excited me uncontrollably. I continued the slow movements for a few minutes; but once she moved her sex quickly down on mine as I drew out to the lips, and gave me an intense thrill. I felt my seed coming and I let myself go in short, quick thrusts that soon brought on my spasm of pleasure and I lifted her little body against mine and crushed my lips on hers: she was strangely tantalizing, exciting like strong drink.

I took her out of bed and used the syringe in her, explaining its purpose, and then went to bed again and gave her the time of her life! Lying between her legs but side by side an hour later, I dared her to tell me how she had lost her maidenhead. I had to tell her first what it was. She maintained stoutly that "no feller" had ever touched her except me and I believed her, for she admitted having caressed herself ever since she was ten; at first she could not even get her forefinger into her pussy she told me. "What are you now?" I asked.

"I shall be sixteen next April," was her reply.

About eleven o'clock she dressed and went home, after making another appointment with me.

The haste of this narrative has many unforeseen drawbacks: it makes it appear as if I had had conquest after conquest and little or no difficulty in my efforts to win love. In reality, my half-dozen victories were spread out over nearly as many years, and time and again I met rebuffs and refusals quite sufficient to keep even my conceit in decent bounds. But I want to emphasize the fact that success in love, like success in every department of life, falls usually to the tough man unwearied in pursuit. Chaucer was right when he makes his Old Wyfe of Bath confess,

> And by a close attendance and attention
> Are we caught, more or less the truth to mention.

It is not the handsomest man or the most virile who has the most success with women, though both qualities smooth the way, but that man who pursues the most assiduously, flatters them most constantly, and always insists on taking the girl's "no" for consent, her reproofs for endearments, and even a little crossness for a new charm.

Above all, it is necessary to push forward after every refusal, for as soon as a girl refuses, she is apt to regret and may grant then what she expressly denied the moment before. Yet I could give dozens of instances where assiduity and flattery, love-books and words were all ineffective, so much so that I should never say with Shakespeare, "He's not a man who cannot win a woman." I have generally found, too, that the easiest to win were the best worth winning for me, for women have finer senses for suitability in love than any man.

Now for an example of one of my many failures, which took place when I was still a student and had a fair opportunity to succeed.

It was a custom in the university for every professor to lecture for forty-five minutes, thus leaving each student fifteen minutes at least free to go back to his private classroom to prepare for the next lecture. All the students took turns to use these classrooms for their private pleasure. For example, from eleven forty-five to noon each day I was supposed to be working in the junior classroom, and no student would interfere with me or molest me in any way.

One day, a girl Fresher, Grace Weldon by name, the daughter of the owner of the biggest department store in Lawrence, came to Smith when Miss Stephens and I were with him, about the translation of a phrase or two in Xenophon.

"Explain it to Miss Weldon, Frank!" said Smith, and in a few moments I had made the passage clear to her. She thanked me prettily, and I said, "If you ever want anything I can do, I'll be happy to make it clear to you, Miss Weldon; I'm in the junior classroom from eleven forty-five to noon, always."

She thanked me and a day or two later came to me in the classroom with another puzzle, and so our acquaintance ripened. Almost at once she let me kiss her, but as soon as I tried to put my hand up her clothes, she stopped me. We were friends for nearly a year, close friends, and I remember trying all I knew one Saturday, when I spent the whole day with her in our classroom till dusk came, and I could not get her to yield.

The curious thing was, I could not even soothe the smart to my vanity with the belief that she was physically cold. On the contrary, she was very passionate, but she had simply made up her mind and would not change.

That Saturday in the classroom she told me if she yielded she would hate me: I could see no sense in this, even though I was to find out later what a terrible weapon the confessional is as used by Irish Catholic priests. To commit a sin is easy; to confess it to your priest is for many women an absolute deterrent.

A few days later, I think, I got a letter from Smith that determined me to go to Philadelphia as soon as my boardings provided me with sufficient money. I wrote and told him I'd come and cheered him up. I had not long to wait.

Early that fall Bradlaugh* came to lecture in Liberty Hall on the French Revolution—a giant of a man with a great head, rough-hewn, irregular features and stentorian voice: no better figure of a rebel could be imagined. I knew he had been an English private soldier for a dozen years, but I soon found that, in spite of his passionate revolt against the Christian religion and all its cheap moralistic conventions he was a convinced individualist and saw nothing wrong in the despotism of money which had already established itself in Britain, though condemned by Carlyle at the end of his *French Revolution* as the vilest of all tyrannies.

Bradlaugh's speech taught me that a notorious and popular man, earnest, and gifted, too, and intellectually honest, might be fifty years before his time in one respect and fifty years behind the best opinion of the age in another province of thought. In the great conflict of our day between the "Haves" and the "Have-nots," Bradlaugh played no part whatever. He wasted his great powers in a vain attack on the rotten branches of the Christian tree, while he should have assimilated the spirit of Jesus and used it to gild his loyalty to truth.

About this time, Kate wrote that she would not be back for some weeks: she declared she was feeling another woman. I felt tempted to write, "So am I, stay as long as you please," but instead I wrote an affectionate, tempting letter, for I had a real affection for her, I discovered.

When she returned a few weeks later, I felt as if she were new and unknown and I had to win her again; but as soon as my hand touched her sex, the strangeness disappeared and she gave herself to me with renewed zest.

I teased her to tell me just what she felt and at length she consented. "Begin with the first time," I begged, "and then tell what you felt in Kansas City."

"It will be very hard," she said. "I'd rather write it for you."

"That'll do just as well," I replied, and here is the story she sent me the next day.

"I think the first time you had me," she began, "I felt more curiosity than desire: I had so often tried to picture it all to myself. When I saw your sex I was astonished, for it looked very big to me and I wondered whether you could really get it into my sex, which I knew was just big enough for my finger to go in. Still I did want to feel your sex pushing into me, and your kisses and the touch of your hand on my sex made me even more eager. When you slipped the head of your sex into mine, it hurt dreadfully; it was almost like a knife cutting into me, but the pain for some reason seemed to excite me and I pushed forward so as to get you further in me; I think that's what broke my maidenhead. At first I was disappointed because I felt no

---

* Charles Bradlaugh (1833–91), an Englishman, a freethinker and a political extremist.

thrill, only the pain; but, when my sex became all wet and open and yours could slip in and out easily, I began to feel real pleasure. I liked the slow movement best; it excited me to feel the head of your sex just touching the lips of mine and, when you pushed in slowly all the way, it gave me a gasp of breathless delight: when you drew your sex out, I wanted to hold it in me. And the longer you kept on, the more pleasure you gave me. For hours afterwards, my sex was sensitive; if I rubbed it ever so gently, it would begin to itch and burn.

"But that night in the hotel at Kansas City I really wanted you and the pleasure you gave me then was much keener than the first time. You kissed and caressed me for a few minutes and I soon felt my love-dew coming and the button of my sex began to throb. As you thrust your shaft in and out of me, I felt a strange sort of pleasure: every little nerve on the inside of my thighs and belly seemed to thrill and quiver; it was almost a feeling of pain. At first the sensation was not so intense, but, when you stopped and made me wash, I was shaken by quick, short spasms in my thighs, and my sex was burning and throbbing; I wanted you more than ever.

"When you began the slow movement again, I felt the same sensations in my thighs and belly, only more keenly, and, as you kept on, the pleasure became so intense that I could scarcely bear it. Suddenly you rubbed your sex against mine and my button began to throb; I could almost feel it move. Then you began to move your sex quickly in and out of me; in a moment I was breathless with emotion and I felt so faint and exhausted that I suppose I fell asleep for a few minutes, for I knew nothing more till I felt the cold water trickling down my face. When you began again, you made me cry, perhaps because I was all dissolved in feeling and too, too happy. Ah, love is divine: isn't it?"

Kate was really of the highest woman-type, mother and mistress in one. She used to come down and spend the night with me oftener than ever and one one of these occasions she found a new word for her passion. She declared she felt her womb move in yearning for me when I talked my best or recited poetry to her in what I had christened her holy week. Kate it was who taught me first that women could be even more moved and excited by words than by deeds. Once, I remember, when I had talked sentimentally, she embraced me of her own accord and we had each other with wet eyes.

Another effect of Smith's absence was important, for it threw me a good deal with Miss Stephens. I soon found that she had inherited the best of her father's brains and much of his strength of character. If she had married Smith, she might have done something noteworthy; as it was, she was very attractive and well-read as a girl and would have made Smith, I am sure, a most excellent wife.

Once and once only I tried to hint to her that her sweetness to Smith might do him harm physically; but the suspicion of reproof made her angry and she evidently couldn't or wouldn't understand what I meant without a physical explanation, which she would certainly have resented. I had to leave her to what she would have called her *daimon,* for she was as prettily pedantic as Tennyson's Princess, or any other mid-Victorian heroine.

Her brother, Ned, too, I came to know pretty well. He was a tall, handsome youth with fine grey eyes; a good athlete, but of commonplace mind.

The father was the most interesting of the whole family, were it only for his prodigious conceit. He was of noble appearance: a large, handsome head with silver grey hairs setting off a portly figure well above middle height. In spite of his assumption of superiority, I felt him hide-bound in thought, for he accepted all the familiar American conventions, believing, or rather knowing, that the American people, "the good old New England stock in particular, were the salt of the earth, the best breed to be seen anywhere."

It showed his brains that he tried to find a reason for this belief. "English oak is good," he remarked one day sententiously, "but American hickory is tougher still. Reasonable, too, this belief of mine," he added, "for the last glacial period skinned all the good soil off of New England and made it bitterly hard to get a living; and the English who came out for conscience sake were the pick of the Old Country; and they were forced for generations to scratch a living out of the poorest kind of soil with the worst climate in the world, and hostile Indians all round to sharpen their combativeness and weed out the weaklings and wastrels."

There was a certain amount of truth in his contention, but this was the nearest to an original thought I ever heard him express; and his intense patriotic fervor moved me to doubt his intelligence.

I was delighted to find that Smith rated him just as I did: "A first rate lawyer, I believe," was his judgment; "a sensibile, kindly man."

"A little above middle height," I interpreted; and Smith added smiling, "And considerably above average weight: he would never have done anything notable in literature or thought."

As the year wore on, Smith's letters called for me more and more insistently and at length I went to join him in Philadelphia.

Chapter XIII

New Experiences:
Emerson, Walt Whitman, Bret Harte

SMITH MET ME at the station. He was thinner than ever and the wretched little cough shook him very often in spite of some lozenges that the doctor had given him to suck. I began to be alarmed about him, and I soon came to the belief that the damp climate of the Quaker City was worse for him than the thin, dry Kansas air. But he believed in his doctors!

He boarded with a pleasant Puritan family in whose house he had also got me a room, and at once we resumed the old life. But now I kept constant watch on him and insisted on rigorous self-restraint, tying up his unruly organ every night carefully with thread, which was still more efficient (and painful) than the whipcord. But now he didn't improve quickly: it was a month before I could find any of the old vigor in him; but soon afterwards the cough diminished and he began to be his bright self again.

One of our first evenings I described to him the Bradlaugh lecture in much the same terms I have used in this narrative. Smith asked: "Why don't you write it? You ought to: the *Press* would take it. You've given me an extraordinary, life-like portrait of a great man, blind, so to speak, in one eye, a sort of Cyclops. If he had been a Communist, how much greater he'd have been."

I ventured to disagree and we were soon at it hammer and tongs. I wanted to see both principles realized in life, individualism and socialism, the centrifugal as well as the centripetal force, and was convinced that the problem was how to bring these opposites to a balance which would ensure an approximation of justice and make for the happiness of all.

Smith, on the other hand, argued at first as an out-and-out Communist and follower of Marx, but he was too fair minded to shut his eyes for long to the obvious. Soon he began congratulating me on my insight, declaring I had written a new chapter in economics.

His conversion made me feel that I was at long last his equal as a thinker. In any field where his scholarship didn't give him too great an advantage, I was no longer a pupil but an equal, and his quick recognition of the fact increased, I believe, our mutual affection. Though infinitely better read, he put me forward in every company with the rarest generosity, asserting that I had discovered new laws in sociology. For months we lived very happily together, but his Hegelianism defied all my attacks: it corresponded too intimately with the profound idealism of his own character.

As soon as I had written out the Bradlaugh story, Smith took me down to the *Press* office and introduced me to the chief editor, a Captain Forney:* indeed, the paper then was usually called "Forney's Press," though already some spoke of it as the *Philadelphia Press*. Forney liked my portrait of Bradlaugh and engaged me as a reporter on the staff and occasional descriptive writer at fifty dollars a week, which enabled me to save all the money coming to me from Lawrence.

One day Smith talked to me of Emerson and confessed he had got an introduction to him and had sent it on to the philosopher with a request for an interview. He had wished me to accompany him to Concord. I consented, but without any enthusiasm: Emerson was then an unknown name to me. Smith read me some of his poetry and praised it highly, though I could get little or nothing out of it. When young men now show me a similar indifference, my own experience makes it easy for me to excuse them. They know not what they do! is the explanation and excuse for all of us.

One bright fall day Smith and I went over to Concord and next day visited Emerson. He received us in the most pleasant, courteous way, made us sit, and composed himself to listen. Smith went off at score, telling him how greatly he had influenced his life and helped him with brave encouragement. The old man smiled benignantly and nodded his head, ejaculating from time to time, "Yes, yes!" Gradually Smith warmed to his work and wanted to know why Emerson had never expressed his views on sociology or on the relations between capital and labor. Once or twice the old gentleman cupped his ear with his hand, but all he said was, "Yes, yes!" or "I think so," with the same benevolent smile.

I guessed at once that he was deaf, but Smith had no inkling of the fact, for he went on probing, probing, while Emerson answered pleasant nothings quite irrelevantly. I studied the great man as closely as I could. He looked about five feet nine or ten in height, very thin, attenuated even, and very scrupulously dressed. His head was narrow, though long, his face bony; a long, high, somewhat beaked nose was the feature of his countenance. A good conceit of himself, I concluded, and considerable will power, for the chin was well-defined and large. But I got nothing more than this; and from his clear, steadfast grey eyes I got an intense impression of kindness and good will, and—why shouldn't I say it?—of sweetness even, as of a soul lifted high above earth's carking cares and strugglings.

"A nice old fellow," I told myself, "but deaf as a post."

Many years later his deafness became to me the symbol and explanation of his genius. He had always lived "the life removed" and kept himself un-

* John Wien Forney (1817–81).

spotted from the world: that explains both his narrowness of sympathy and the height to which he grew! His narrow, pleasantly smiling face comes back to me whenever I hear his name mentioned.

But at the time I was indignant with his deafness and out of temper with Smith because he didn't notice it and seemed somehow to make himself cheap. When we went away, I cried: "The old fool is as deaf as a post!"

"Ah, that was the explanation then of his stereotyped smile and peculiar answers," cried Smith. "How did you divine it?"

"He put his hand to his ear more than once," I replied.

"So he did," Smith exclaimed. "How foolish of me not to have drawn the obvious inference!"

It was in this fall, I believe, that the Gregorys went off to Colorado. I felt the loss of Kate a good deal at first, but she had made no deep impression on my mind, and the new life in Philadelphia and my journalistic work left me but little time for regrets; and as she never wrote to me, following doubtless her mother's advice, she soon drifted out of my memory. Moreover, Lily was quite as interesting a lover and Lily too had begun to pall on me. The truth is, the fever of desire in youth is a passing malady that intimacy quickly cures. Besides, I was already in pursuit of a girl in Philadelphia who kept me a long time at arm's length, and when she yielded I found her figure commonplace and her sex so large and loose that she deserves no place in this chronicle. She was modest, if you please, and no wonder. I have always since thought that modesty is the proper fig leaf of ugliness.

In the spring of this year, 1875, I had to return to Lawrence on business connected with my boardings. In several cases the owners of the lots refused to allow me to keep up the boardings unless they had a reasonable share in the profits. Finally I called them all together and came to an amicable agreement to divide twenty-five per cent of my profit among them, year by year.

I had also to go through my examination and get admitted to the bar. I had already taken out my first naturalization papers and Judge Bassett of the district court appointed the lawyers Barker and Hutchings to examine me. The examination was a mere form. They each asked me three simple questions, I answered them, and we adjourned to the Eldridge House for supper and they drank my health in champagne. I was notified by Judge Bassett that I had passed the examination and told to present myself for admission on the twenty-fifth of June, I think, 1875.

To my surprise, the court was half full. Judge Stephens even was present, whom I had never seen in court before. About eleven the judge informed the audience that I had passed a satisfactory examination and had taken out my first papers in due form, and unless some lawyer wished first to put questions to me to test my capacity, he proposed to call me within the bar. To my astonishment, Judge Stephens rose.

"With the permission of the court," he said, "I'd like to put some ques-

tions to this candidate who comes to us with high university commendation."
(No one had heard of my expulsion, though he knew of it.) He then began
a series of questions which soon plumbed the depths of my abysmal ignorance. I didn't know what an action of account was at old English common
law: I don't know now, nor do I want to. I had read Blackstone carefully
and a book on Roman law, Chitty on evidence, too, and someone on con-
tracts—half a dozen books, and that was all. For the first two hours Judge
Stephens just exposed my ignorance: it was a very warm morning and my
conceit was rubbed raw when Judge Bassett proposed an adjournment for
dinner. Stephens consented and we all rose. To my surprise Barker and
Hutchings and half a dozen other lawyers came round to encourage me.
"Stephens is just showing off," said Hutchings. "I myself couldn't have
answered half his questions!" Even Judge Bassett sent for me to his room
and practically told me I had nothing to fear, so I returned at two o'clock,
resolved to do my best and at all costs to keep smiling.

The examination continued in a crowded court till four o'clock and then
Judge Stephens sat down. I had done better in this session, but my examiner
had caught me in a trap on a moot point in the law of evidence, and I
could have kicked myself. But Hutchings rose as the senior of my two examiners who had been appointed by the court, and said simply that now
he repeated the opinion he had already had the honor to convey to Judge
Bassett, that I was a fit and proper person to practice law in the state of
Kansas.

"Judge Stephens," he added, "has shown us how widely read he is in
English common law, but some of us knew that before, and in any case his
erudition should not be made a purgatory to candidates. It looks," he went
on, "as if he wished to punish Mr. Harris for his superiority to all his classmates.

"Impartial persons in this audience will admit," he concluded, "that Mr.
Harris has come brilliantly out of an exceedingly severe test; and I have the
pleasant task of proposing, your Honor, that he now be admitted within
the bar, though he may not be able to practice till he becomes a full citizen
two years hence."

Everyone expected that Barker would second this proposal, but while
he was rising, Judge Stephens began to speak.

"I desire," he said, "to second that proposal, and I think I ought to explain why I subjected Mr. Harris to a severe examination in open court.
Since I came to Kansas from the state of New York twenty-five years ago,
I have been asked a score of times to examine one candidate or another.
I always refused. I did not wish to punish western candidates by putting
them against our eastern standards. But here at long last appears a candidate who has won honor in the university, to whom, therefore, a stiff examination in open court can only be a vindication; and accordingly I
examined Mr. Harris as if he had been in the state of New York; for surely

Kansas too has come of age and its inhabitants cannot wish to be humored as inferiors.

"This whole affair," he went on, "reminds me of a story told in the east of a dog fancier. The father lived by breeding and training bull dogs. One day he got an extraordinary promising pup and the father and son used to hunker down, shake their arms at the pup and thus encourage him to seize hold of their coat sleeves and hang on. While engaged in this game once, the bull-pup, grown bold by constant praise, sprang up and seized the father by the nose. Instinctively, the old man began to choke him off, but the son exclaimed, 'Don't, father, don't for God's sake! It may be hard on you, but it'll be the making of the pup.' So my examination, I thought, might be hard on Mr. Harris, but it would be the making of him."

The court roared and I applauded merrily. Judge Stephens continued. "I desire, however, to show myself not an enemy but a friend of Mr. Harris, whom I have known for some years. Mr. Hutchings evidently thinks that Mr. Harris must wait two years in order to become a citizen of the United States. I am glad from my reading of the statute laws of my country to be able to assure him that Mr. Harris need not wait a day. The law says that if a minor has lived three years in any state, he may on coming of age choose to become a citizen of the United States; and if Mr. Harris chooses to be one of us, he can be admitted at once as a citizen; and if your Honor approve, be allowed also to practice law tomorrow."

He sat down amid great applause, in which I joined most heartily. So on that day I was admitted to practice law as a full fledged citizen. Unluckily for me, when I asked the clerk of the court for my full papers, he gave me the certificate of my admission to practice law in Lawrence, saying that as this could only be given a citizen, it in itself was sufficient.

Forty odd years later the government of Woodrow Wilson refused to accept this plain proof of my citizenship and thus put me to much trouble by forcing me to get naturalized again!

But at the moment in Lawrence I was all cock-a-hoop and forthwith took a room on the same first floor where Barker & Sommerfeld had their offices and put out my shingle.

I have told this story of my examination at great length because I think it shows as in a glass the amenities and deep kindness of the American character.

A couple of days later I was again in Philadelphia.

Towards the end of this year, 1875, I believe, or the beginning of 1876, Smith drew my attention to an announcement that Walt Whitman, the poet, was going to speak in Philadelphia on Thomas Paine, the notorious infidel, who, according to Washington, had done more to secure the independence of the United States than any other man. Smith determined to go to the meeting, and if Whitman could rehabilitate Paine against the venomous attacks of Christian clergymen who asserted without contradiction that Paine was a notorious drunkard and of the loosest character, he would induce Forney to let him write an exhaustive and forceful defence of Paine in the *Press*.

I felt pretty sure that such an article would never appear, but I would not pour cold water on Smith's enthusiasm. The day came, one of those villainous days common enough in Philadelphia in every winter: the temperature was about zero with snow falling whenever the driving wind permitted. In the afternoon Smith finally determined that he must not risk it and asked me to go in his stead. I consented willingly, and he spent some hours in reading to me the best of Whitman's poetry, laying especial stress, I remember, on *When Lilacs Last in the Dooryard Bloom'd*. He assured me again and again that Whitman and Poe were the two greatest poets these States had ever produced, and he hoped I would be very nice to the great man.

Nothing could be more depressing than the aspect of the hall that night: ill-lit and half-heated, with perhaps thirty persons scattered about in a space that would have accommodated a thousand. Such was the reception America accorded to one of its greatest spirits, though that view of the matter did not strike me for many a year.

I took my seat in the middle of the first row, pulled out my notebook and made ready. In a few minutes Whitman came on the platform from the [left] to say just what he had to say, neither more nor [less].* He walked slowly, stiffly, which made me grin, for I did not then know that he had had a stroke of paralysis, and I thought his peculiar walk a mere pose. Besides, his clothes were astonishingly ill fitting and ill suited to his figure. He must have been nearly six feet in height and strongly made; yet he wore a short jacket which cocked up behind in the perkiest way. Looked at from the front, his white collar was wide open and discovered a tuft of grey hairs, while his trousers that corkscrewed about his legs had parted company with his vest and disclosed a margin of dingy white shirt. His appearance filled me—poor little English snob that I was—with contempt: he recalled to my memory irresistibly an old Cochin-China rooster I had seen when a boy; it stalked across the farmyard with the same slow, stiff gait and carried a stubby tail cocked up behind.

Yet a second look showed me Whitman as a fine figure of a man with something arresting in the perfect simplicity and sincerity of voice and manner. He arranged his notes in complete silence and began to speak very slowly, often pausing for a better word or to consult his papers. Sometimes hesitating and repeating himself—clearly an unpracticed speaker who disdained any semblance of oratory. He told us simply that in his youth he had met and got to know very well a certain colonel in the army who had known Thomas Paine intimately. This colonel had assured him more than once that all the accusations against Paine's habits and character were false—a

* These lines are jumbled in the text of the volume Harris first had privately printed; what appears here is a meshing of that and the expurgated text, published in the 1920's in the United States.

mere outcome of Christian bigotry. Paine would drink a glass or two of wine at dinner like all well-bred men of that day; but he was very moderate and in the last ten years of his life, the colonel asserted, Paine never once drank to excess. The colonel cleared Paine, too, of looseness of morals in much the same decisive way, and finally spoke of him as invariably well conducted, of witty speech and a vast fund of information, a most interesting and agreeable companion. And the colonel was an unimpeachable witness, Whitman assured us, a man of the highest honor and most scrupulous veracity.

Whitman spoke with such uncommon slowness that I was easily able to take down the chief sentences in longhand: he was manifestly determined to say just what he had to say, neither more nor less, which made an impression of singular sincerity and truthfulness.

When he had finished, I went up on the platform to see him near at hand and draw him out if possible. I showed him my card of the *Press* and asked him if he would kindly sign and thus authenticate the sentences on Paine he had used in his address.

"Aye, aye!" was all he said; but he read the half dozen sentences carefully, here and there correcting a word.

I thanked him and said Professor Smith, an editor of the *Press,* had sent me to get a word-for-word report of his speech, for he purposed writing an article in the *Press* on Paine, whom he greatly admired.

"Aye, aye!" ejaculated Whitman from time to time while his clear grey eyes absorbed all that I said. I went on to assure him that Smith had a profound admiration for him (Whitman), thought him the greatest American poet and regretted deeply that he was not well enough to come out that night and make his personal acquaintance.

"I'm sorry, too," said Whitman slowly, "for your friend Smith must have something large in him to be so interested in Paine and me." Perfectly simple and honest Walt Whitman appeared to me, even in his self-estimate an authentic great man!

I had nothing more to say, so hastened home to show Smith Whitman's boyish signature and to give him a description of the man. The impression Whitman left on me was one of transparent simplicity and sincerity: not a mannerism in him, not a trace of affectation, a man simply sure of himself, most careful in speech, but careless of appearance and curiously, significantly free of all afterthoughts or regrets. A new type of personality which, strangely enough, has grown upon me more and more with the passing of the years and now seems to me to represent the very best in America, the large unruffled soul of that great people manifestly called and chosen to exert an increasingly important influence on the destinies of mankind. I would die happily if I could believe that America's influence would be anything like as manful and true and clear-eyed as Whitman's in guiding humanity; but alas! . . .

It would be difficult to convey to European readers any just notion of the horror and disgust with which Walt Whitman was regarded at that time in the United States on account merely of the sex poems in *Leaves of Grass*. The poems to which objection could be taken don't constitute five per cent of the book, and my objection to them is that in any normal man love and desire take up a much larger proportion of life than five per cent. Moreover, the expression of passion is tame in the extreme. Nothing in *Leaves of Grass* can compare with half a dozen passages in the Songs of Solomon: think of the following verse:

I sleep, but my heart waketh: it is the voice of my beloved that knocketh, saying, Open to me, my sister, my love, my dove, my undefiled: for my head is filled with dew, and my locks with the drops of the night . . .

My beloved put in his hand by the hole of the door, and my bowels were moved for him.

And then the phrases:* "her lips are like a thread of scarlet** . . . her love like an army with banners";† but American Puritanism is more timid even than its purblind teachers.

It was commonly said at the time that Whitman had led a life of extraordinary self-indulgence: rumor attributed to him half a dozen illegitimate children and perverse tastes to boot. I think such statements exaggerated or worse: they are no more to be trusted than the stories of Paine's drunkenness. At any rate, Horace Traubell†† later declared to me that Whitman's life was singularly clean, and his own letter to John Addington Symonds‡ must be held to have disproved the charge of homosexuality. But I dare swear he loved more than once not wisely but too well, or he would not have risked the reprobation of the *unco guid*. In any case, it is to his honor that he dared to write plainly in America of the joys of sexual intercourse. Emerson, as Whitman himself tells us, did his utmost all one long afternoon to dissuade him from publishing the sex-poems, but fortunately all his arguments served only to confirm Whitman in his purpose. From certain querulous complaints later, it is plain that Whitman was too ignorant to gauge the atrocious results to himself and his reputation of his daring, but the same ignorance that allowed him to use scores of vile neologism in this one instance stood him in good stead. It was right of him to speak plainly of sex; accordingly he set down the main facts, disdainful of the best opinion of his time. And he was justified; in the long run it will be plain to all that

---

* Read "then" as "also," for Harris does not quote the following lines in proper sequence. Indeed, the lines quoted above fall within the compass of the ellipsis marks here.

** *Thy* lips are like a thread of scarlet, and thy speech is comely," etc.

† "Thou art beautiful, O my love, as Tirgah, comely as Jerusalem, *terrible as* an army with banners."

†† (1858–1919); American author and Whitman's literary executor.

‡ (1840–93); English scholar; his *Renaissance in Italy* (six volumes, 1875–86) is a classic.

he thus put the seal of the Highest upon his judgment. What can we think, and what will the future think, of Emerson's condemnation of Rabelais, whom he dared to liken to a dirty little boy who scribbles indecencies in public places and then runs away, and his contemptuous estimate of Shakespeare as a ribald playwright, when in good sooth he was "the reconciler" whom Emerson wanted to acclaim and had not the brains to recognize?

Whitman was the first of great men to write frankly about sex and five hundred years hence that will be his singular and supreme distinction.

Smith seemed permanently better, though, of course, for the moment disappointed because his careful eulogy of Paine never appeared in the *Press,* so one day I told him I'd have to return to Lawrence to go on with my law work, though Thomson, the doctor's son, kept all my personal affairs in good order and informed me of every happening. Smith at this time seemed to agree with me, though not enthusiastically, and I was on the point of starting when I got a letter from Willie, telling me that my eldest brother, Vernon, was in a New York hospital, having just tried to commit suicide, and I should go to see him.

I went at once and found Vernon in a ward in bed. The surgeon told me that he had tried to shoot himself and that the ball had struck the jaw-bone at such an angle that it went all round his head and was taken out just above his left ear: "It stunned him and that was all; he can go out almost any day now."

The first glance showed me the old Vernon. He cried, "Still a failure, you see, Joe: could not even kill myself, though I tried!" I told him I had renamed myself Frank; he nodded amicably, smiling.

I cheered him up as well as I could, got lodgings for him, took him out of the hospital, found work for him, too, and after a fortnight saw that I could safely leave him. He told me that he regretted having taken so much money from my father: "Your share, I'm afraid, and Nita's, but why did he give it to me? He might just as well have refused me years ago as let me strip him, but I was a fool and always shall be about money. Happy go lucky, I can take no thought for the morrow."

That fortnight showed me that Vernon had only the veneer of a gentleman; at heart he was as selfish as Willie but without Willie's power of work. I had overestimated him wildly as a boy, thought him noble and well read; but Smith's real nobility, culture and idealism showed me that Vernon was hardly silver-gilt. He had nice manners and [a] good temper and that was about all.

I stopped at Philadelphia on my way to Lawrence just to tell Smith all I owed him, which the association with Vernon had made clear to me. We had a great night and then for the first time he advised me to go to Europe to study and make myself a teacher and guide of men. I assured him he overestimated me because I had an excellent verbal memory, but he declared that I had unmistakable originality and fairness of judgment, and above all, a driving power of will that he had never seen equaled. "Whatever you make up your mind to do," he concluded, "you will surely accomplish, for you are inclined to under-rate yourself." At the time I laughed, saying he didn't even guess at my unlimited conceit, but his words and counsel sank into my mind and in due course exercised a decisive, shaping influence on my life.

I returned to Lawrence, put up a sofa-bed in my law room and went to the Eldridge House nearby for my meals. I read law assiduously and soon had a few clients, "hard cases" for the most part, sent to me, I found, by Judge Stephens and Barker, eager to foist nuisances on a beginner.

An old mulatto woman kept our offices tidy and clean for a few dollars monthly from each of us, and one night I was awakened by her groans and cries. She lived in a garret up two flights of stairs and was evidently suffering from indigestion and very much frightened, as colored folk are apt to be when anything ails them. "I'm gwine to die!" she told me a dozen times. I treated her with whisky and warm water, heated on my little gas-heater, and sat with her till at length she fell asleep. She declared next day I had saved her life and she'd never forget it. "Nebber, fo' sure!" I laughed at her and forgot all about it.

Every afternoon I went over to Liberty Hall for an hour or so to keep in touch with events, though I left the main work to Will Thomson. One day I was delighted to find that Bret Harte was coming to lecture for us: his subject: "The Argonauts of '49." I got some of his books from the bookstore kept by a lame man named Crew, I think, on Massachusetts Street, and read him carefully. His poetry did not make much impression on me—mere verse, I thought it; but *The Outcasts of Poker Flat* and other stories seemed to me almost masterpieces in spite of their romantic coloring and tinge of melodrama. Especially the description of Oakhurst, the gambler, stuck in my mind: it will be remembered that when crossing the "divide," Oakhurst advised the party of outcasts to keep on traveling till they reached a place of safety. But he did not press his point: he decided it was hopeless, and then came Bret Harte's extraordinary painting phrase: "Life to Oakhurst was at best an uncertain sort of game and he recognized the usual percentage in favor of the dealer."* There is more humor and insight in the one sentence than in all the ridiculously overpraised works of Mark Twain.

One afternoon I was alone in the box office of Liberty Hall when Rose came in, as pretty as ever. I was delighted to renew our acquaintance and more delighted still to find that she would like tickets for Bret Harte's lecture. "I didn't know that you cared for reading, Rose," I said, a little surprised.

"Professor Smith and you would make anybody read," she cried; "at any rate you started me." I gave her the tickets and engaged to take her for

---

* Correctly, "With him [Oakhurst] life was at best an uncertain game, and he recognized the usual percentage in favor of the dealer."

a buggy ride next day. I felt sure Rose liked me, but she soon surprised me by showing a stronger virtue than I usually encountered.

She kissed me when I asked her in the buggy, but told me at the same time that she didn't care much for kissing. "All men," she said, "are after a girl for the same thing; it's sickening; they all want kisses and try to touch you and say they love you; but they can't love and I don't want their kisses."

"Rose, Rose," I said, "you mustn't be too hard on us: we're different from you girls and that's all."

"How do you mean?" she asked.

"I mean that mere desire," I said, "just the wish to kiss and enjoy you, strikes the man first, but behind that lust is often a good deal of affection, and sometimes a deep and sacred tenderness comes to flower; whereas the girl begins with the liking and affection and learns to enjoy the kissing and caressing afterwards."

"I see," she rejoined quietly. "I think I understand: I am glad to believe that."

Her unexpected depth and sincerity impressed me and I continued: "We men may be so hungry that we will eat very poor fruit greedily because it's at hand, but that doesn't prove that we don't prefer good and sweet and nourishing food when we can get it."

She let her eyes dwell on mine. "I see," she said, "I see!"

And then I went on to tell her how lovely she was and how she had made a deathless impression on me, and I ventured to hope she liked me a little and would yet be good to me and come to care for me; and I was infinitely pleased to find that this was the right sort of talk, and I did my best in the new strain. Three or four times a week I took her out in a buggy and in a little while I had taught her how to kiss and won her to confess that she cared for me, loved me, indeed, and bit by bit she allowed me the little familiarities of love.

One day I took her out early for a picnic and said, "I'll play Turk and you must treat me," and I stretched myself out on a rug under a tree. She entered into the spirit of the game with zest, brought me food, and at length, as she stood close beside me, I couldn't control myself; I put my hand up her dress on her firm legs and sex. Next moment I was kneeling beside her. "Love me, Rose," I begged, "I want you so: I'm hungry for you, dear!"

She looked at me gravely with wide open eyes. "I love you too," she said, "but oh! I'm afraid. Be patient with me!" she added, like a little girl. I was patient but persistent and I went on caressing her till her hot lips told me that I had really excited her.

My fingers informed me that she had a perfect sex and her legs were wonderfully firm and tempting; and in her yielding there was the thrill of a conscious yielding out of affection for me, which I find is hard to express. I soon persuaded her to come next day to my office. She came about four o'clock and I kissed and caressed her and at length in the dusk got her to strip. She had the best figure I had ever seen and that made me like her more than I would have thought possible; but I soon found when I got into her that she was not nearly as passionate as Kate even, to say nothing of Lily. She was a cool mistress but would have made a wonderful wife, being all self-sacrifice and tender, thoughtful affection. I have still a very warm corner in my heart for that lovely child-woman and am rather ashamed of having seduced her, for she was never meant to be a plaything or pastime.

But incurably changeable, I had Lily a day or two afterwards and sent Rose a collection of books instead of calling on her. Still I took her out every week till I left Lawrence and grew to esteem her more and more.

Lily, on the other hand, was a born "daughter of the game," to use Shakespeare's phrase, and tried to become more and more proficient at it: she wanted to know when and how she gave me the most pleasure, and really did her best to excite me. Besides, she soon developed a taste in hats and dresses, and when I paid for a new outfit, she would dance with delight. She was an entertaining, light companion, too, and often found odd little naughty phrases that amused me. Her pet aversion was Mrs. Mayhew: she called her always "the Pirate," because she said Lorna only liked "stolen goods" and wanted every man "to walk the plank into her bedroom." Lily insisted that Lorna could cry whenever she wished, but had no real affection in her, and her husband filled Lily with contempt. "A well-matched pair," she exclaimed one day, "a mare and a mule, and the mare, as men say, in heat—all wet," and she wrinkled her little nose in disgust.

At the Bret Harte lecture both Rose and Lily had seats and they both understood that I would go and talk with the great man afterwards.

I expected to get a great deal from the lecture and Harte's advance agent had arranged that the hero of the evening should receive me in the Eldridge House after the address.

I was to call for him at the hotel and take him across to the hall. When I called, a middle-sized man came to meet me with a rather good looking, pleasant smile and introspective, musing eyes. Harte was in evening dress that suited his slight figure, and as he seemed disinclined to talk, I took him across to the hall at once and hastened round to the front to note his entrance. He walked quite simply to the desk, arranged his notes methodically and began in a plain, conversational tone, "The Argonauts," and he repeated it, "The Argonauts of '49."

I noticed that there was no American nasal twang in his accent, but with the best of will, I can give no account of the lecture, just as I can give no portrait of the man. I recall only one phrase, but think it probably the best. Referring to the old-timers crossing the great plains, he said, "I am going to tell you of a new crusade, a crusade without a cross, an exodus without a prophet!"

I met him ten years later in London when I had more self-confidence and much deeper understanding both of talent and genius, but I could never get anything of value out of Bret Harte, in spite of the fact that I had then and still keep a good deal of admiration for his undoubted talent. In London later I did my best to draw him out, to get him to say what he thought of life, death and the undiscovered country, but he either murmured commonplaces or withdrew into his shell of complete but apparently thoughtful silence.

The monotonous work and passionate interludes of my life were suddenly arrested by a totally unexpected happening. One day Barker came into my little office and stood there hiccoughing from time to time. "Did I know any remedy for hiccoughs?" I only knew a drink of cold water usually stopped it.

"I've drunk every sort of thing," he said, "but I reckon I'll give it rest and go home and if it continues send for the doctor!" I could only acquiesce. Next day I heard he was worse and in bed. A week later Sommerfeld told me I ought to call on poor Barker, for he was seriously ill.

That same afternoon I called and was horrified at the change: the constant hiccoughing had shaken all the unwieldy mass of flesh from his bones; the skin of his face was flaccid, the bony outline showing under the thin folds. I pretended to think he was better and attempted to congratulate him, but he did not even try to deceive himself. "If they can't stop it, it'll stop me," he said, "but no one ever heard of a man dying of hiccoughs, and I'm not forty yet."

The news came a few days later that he was dead—that great fat man!*

His death changed my whole life, though I didn't dream at the time it could have any effect upon me. One day I was in court arguing a case before Judge Bassett. Though I liked the man, he exasperated me that day by taking what I thought was a wrong view. I put my point in every light I could, but he wouldn't come round and finally gave the case against me.

"I shall take this case to the Supreme Court at my own expense," I explained bitterly, "and have your decision reversed."

"If you want to waste your time and money," he remarked pleasantly, "I can't hinder you."

I went out of the court and suddenly found Sommerfeld beside me.

"You fought that case very well," he said, "and you'll win it in the Supreme Court, but you shouldn't have told Bassett so, in his own—"

"Domain," I suggested, and he nodded.

When we got to our floor and I turned towards my office, he asked, "Won't you come in and smoke a cigar? I'd like a talk."

Sommerfeld's cigars were uniformly excellent, and I followed him very willingly into his big, quiet office at the back that looked over some empty

---

* A. I. Tobin and Elmer Gertz, in *Frank Harris, A Study in Black and White* (Chicago, 1931), state that George J. Barker, who represented Harris in two minor lawsuits, died in 1912, not 1875, of diabetes. This Barker was not a partner of Summerfeld [sic], nor is there any court record of Harris appearing as a counsel. The records do reveal, however, that Harris was admitted to the bar in Lawrence on June 22, 1875.

lots. I was not a bit curious, for a talk with Sommerfeld usually meant a rather silent smoke. This time, however, he had something to say and said it very abruptly.

"Barker's gone," he remarked in the air, and then: "Why shouldn't you come in here and take his place?"

"As your partner?" I exclaimed.

"Sure," he replied, "I'll make out the briefs in the cases as I did for Barker and you'll argue them in court. For instance," he added in his slow way, "there is a decision of the Supreme Court of the State of Ohio that decides your case today almost in your words, and if you had cited it you'd have convinced Bassett," and he turned and read out the report.

"The state of Ohio," he went on, "is one of the four states, as you know (I didn't know it), that have adopted the New York code—New York, Ohio, Kansas and California"—he proceeded, "the four states in a line across the continent; no one of these high courts will contradict the other. So you can be sure of your verdict. Well, what do you say?" he concluded.

"I shall be delighted," I replied at once. "Indeed, I am proud to work with you: I could have wished no better fortune."

He held out his hand silently and the thing was settled. Sommerfeld smoked a while in silence and then remarked casually, "I used to give Barker a hundred dollars a week for his household expenses: will that suit you?"

"Perfectly, perfectly," I cried. "I only hope I shall earn it and justify your good opinion."

"You are a better advocate than Barker even now," he said, "but you have one drawback." He hesitated.

"Please go on," I cried, "don't be afraid! I can stand any criticism and profit by it—I hope."

"Your accent is a little English, isn't it?" he said. "And that prejudices both judge and jury against you, especially the jury: if you had Barker's accent, you'd be the best pleader in the state."

"I'll get the accent," I exclaimed. "You're dead right: I had already felt the need of it, but I was obstinate. Now I'll get it, you may bet on that, get it within a week." And I did.

There was a lawyer in the town named Hoysradt who had had a fierce quarrel with my brother Willie. He had the most pronounced western American accent I had ever heard, and I set myself the task every morning and evening of imitating Hoysradt's accent and manner of speech. I made it a rule, too, to use the slow western enunciation in ordinary speech, and in a week no one would have taken me for anyone but an American.

Sommerfeld was delighted and told me he had fuller confidence in me than ever and from that time on our accord was perfect, for the better I knew him, the more highly I esteemed him. He was indeed able, hard-working, truthful and honest—a compact of all the virtues, but so modest and inarticulate that he was often his own worst enemy.

Chapter XIV

Law Work and Sophy

NOW BEGAN FOR ME a most delightful time. Sommerfeld relieved me of nearly all the office work: I had only to get up the speeches, for he prepared the cases for me. My income was so large that I only slept in my office-room for convenience sake, or rather for my lechery's sake.

I kept a buggy and horse at a livery stable and used to drive Lily or Rose out nearly every day. As Rose lived on the other side of the river, it was easy to keep the two separate, and indeed neither of them ever dreamed of the other's existence. I had a very soft spot in my heart for Rose: her beauty of face and form always excited and pleased me and her mind, too, grew quickly through our talks and the books I gave her. I'll never forget her joy when I first bought a small bookcase and sent it to her home one morning, full of books I thought she would like and ought to read.

In the evening she came straight to my office, told me it was the very thing she had most wanted, and she let me study her beauties one by one; but when I turned her round and kissed her bottom, she wanted me to stop. "You can't possibly like or admire that," was her verdict.

"Indeed I do," I cried, but I confessed to myself that she was right, her bottom was adorably dimpled but it was a little too fat, and the line underneath it was not perfect. One of her breasts, too, was prettier than the other, though both were small and stuck out boldly: my critical sense would find no fault with her triangle or her sex; the lips of it were perfect, very small and rose-red and her clitoris was like a tiny, tiny button. I often wished it were half an inch long like Mrs. Mayhew's. Only once in our intercourse did I try to bring her to ecstasy and only half succeeded; consequently, I used simply to have her just to enjoy myself, and only now and then went on to a second orgasm so as really to warm her to the love-play; Rose was anything but sensual, though invariably sweet and an excellent companion. How she could be so affectionate though sexually cold was always a puzzle to me.

Lily, as I have said, was totally different: a merry little grig and born child of Venus: now and then she gave me a really poignant sensation. She was always deriding Mrs. Mayhew, but curiously enough, she was very much like her in many intimate ways—a sort of understudy of the older and more passionate woman, with a child's mischievous gaiety to boot and a childish joy in living.

But a great and new sensation was now to come into my life. One evening a girl without a hat on and without knocking came into my office. Sommerfeld had gone home for the night and I was just putting my things straight before going out. She took my breath; she was astoundingly good looking, very dark with great, black eyes and slight girlish figure. "I'm Topsy," she announced and stood there smiling, as if the mere name told enough.

"Come in," I said, "and take a seat: I've heard of you!" And I had.

She was a privileged character in the town: she rode on the street-cars and railroads, too, without paying. Those who challenged her were all "poor white trash," she said, and some man was always eager to pay for her. She never hesitated to go up to any man and ask him for a dollar or even five dollars—and invariably got what she wanted: her beauty was as compelling to men as her scornful aloofness. I had often heard of her as "that d . . . . d pretty nigger girl!" but I could see no trace of any Negro characteristic in her pure loveliness. She took the seat and said with a faint southern accent I found pleasing, "You' name Harris?"

"That's my name," I replied smiling.

"You here instead of Barker?" she went on. "He sure deserve to die hicuppin': pore white trash!"

"What's your real name?" I asked.

"They call me 'Topsy'," she replied, "but ma real true name is Sophy, Sophy Beveridge. You was very kind to my mother who lives upstairs. Yes," she went on defiantly, "she's my mother and a mighty good mother, too, and don't you fergit it," she added, tossing her head in contempt of my astonishment.

"Your father must have been white," I couldn't help remarking, for I couldn't couple Topsy with the old octoroon, do what I would. She nodded, "He was white all right: that is, his skin was," and she got up and wandered about the office as if it belonged to her.

"I'll call you 'Sophy,'" I said, for I felt a passionate revolt of injured pride in her. She smiled at me with pleasure.

I didn't know what to do. I must not go with a colored girl, though I could see no sign of black blood in Sophy, and certainly she was astonishingly good looking, even in her simple sprigged gown. As she moved about I could not but remark the lithe panther-like grace of her and her little breasts stuck out against the thin cotton garment with a most provocative allurement. My mouth was parching when she swung round on me. "You ondressing me," she said smiling, "and I'se glad, 'cause my mother likes you and I loves her—sure pop!"

There was something childish, direct, innocent, even, about her frankness that fascinated me, and her good looks made sunshine in the darkening room.

"I like you, Sophy," I said, "but anyone would have done as much for your mother as I did. She was ill!"

"Hoo!" she snorted indignantly. "Most white folk would have let her die right there on the stairs. I know them: they'd have been angry with her for groaning. I hate 'em!" And her great eyes glowered.

She came over to me in a flash:

"If you'd been an American, I could never have come to you, never! I'd rather have died, or saved and stole and paid you—" the scorn in her voice was bitter with hate: evidently the Negro question had a side I had never realized.

"But you're different," she went on, "an' I just came—" and she paused, lifting her great eyes to mine with an unspoken offer in their lingering regard.

"I'm glad," I said lamely, staving off the temptation, "and I hope you'll come again soon and we'll be great friends—eh, Sophy?" and I held out my hand smiling; but she pouted and looked at me with reproach or appeal or disappointment in her eyes. I could not resist: I took her hand and drew her to me and kissed her on the lips, slipping my right hand the while up to her left breast. It was as firm as India rubber: at once I felt my sex stand up and throb: resolve and desire fought in me, but I was accustomed to make my will supreme.

"You are the loveliest girl in Lawrence," I said, "but I must really go now. I have an appointment and I'm late."

She smiled enigmatically as I seized my hat and went, not stopping even to shut or lock the office door.

As I walked up the street, my thoughts and feelings were all in a whirl. "Did I want her? Should I have her? Would she come again?

"Oh, Hell! women are the very devil and he's not so black as he's painted! Black?"

That night I was awakened by a loud knocking at my office door; I sprang up and opened without thinking and at once Sophy came in laughing.

"What is it?" I cried, half asleep still.

"I'se tired waiting," she answered cheekily, "and anyways I just came." I was about to remonstrate with her when she cried: "You go right to bed," and she took my head in her hands and kissed me.

My wish to resist died out of me. "Come quickly!" I said, getting into bed and watching her as she stripped. In a hand's turn she had undressed to her chemise. "I reckon this'll do," she said coquettishly.

"Please take it off," I cried, and the next moment she was in my arms naked. As I touched her sex, she wound her arms round my neck and kissed me greedily with hot lips. To my astonishment her sex was well formed and very small: I had always heard that Negroes had far larger genitals than white people; but the lips of Sophy's sex were thick and firm. "Have you ever been had, Sophy?" I asked.

"No, sir!" she replied. "I liked you because you never came after me and you was so kind and I thot that I'd be sure to do it sometime, so I'd rather let you have me than anyone else. I don't like colored men," she added, "and the white men all look down on me and despise me and I—I love you," she whispered, burying her face on my neck.

"It'll hurt you at first, Sophy, I'm afraid," but she stilled all scruples with, "Shucks, I don't care. If I gives you pleasure, I'se satisfied," and she opened her legs, stretching herself as I got on her. The next moment my sex was caressing her clitoris and of herself she drew up her knees and suddenly with one movement brought my sex into hers and against the maiden barrier. Sophy had no hesitation: she moved her body lithely against me and the next moment I had forced the passage and was in her. I waited a little while and then began the love game. At once Sophy followed my movements, lifting her sex up to me as I pushed in and depressing it to hold me as I withdrew. Even when I quickened, she kept time and so gave me the most intense pleasure, thrill on thrill, and, as I came and my seed spirted into her, the muscle inside her vagina gripped my sex, heightening the sensation to an acute pang; she even kissed me more passionately than any other girl, licking the inside of my lips with her hot tongue. When I went on again with the slow in-and-out movements, she followed in perfect time and her trick of bending her sex down on mine as I withdrew and gripping it at the same time excited me madly; soon, of her own accord, she quickened while gripping and thrilling me till again we both spent together in an ecstasy.

"You're a perfect wonder," I cried to her then, panting in my turn, "but how did you learn so quickly?"

"I loves you," she said, "so I do whatever I think you'd like then I likes that too, see?" And her lovely face glowed against mine.

I got up to show her the use of the syringe and found we were in a bath of blood. In a moment she had stripped the sheet off. "I'll wash that in the morning," she said laughing, while doubling it into a ball and throwing it in the corner. I turned the gas on full: never was there a more seductive figure. Her skin was darkish, it is true, but not darker than that of an ordinary Italian or Spanish girl, and her form had a curious attraction for me: her breasts, small and firm as elastic, stood out provocatively: her hips, however, were narrower than even Lily's, though the cheeks of her bottom were full; her legs, too, were well-rounded, not a trace of the sticks of the negro; her feet even were slender and high arched.

"You are the loveliest girl I've ever seen!" I cried as I helped to put in the syringe and wash her sex.

"You're mah man," she said proudly, "an' I want to show you that I can love better than any white trash; they only give themselves airs!"

"You are white," I cried, "don't be absurd!"

She shook her little head. "If you knew," she said. "When I was a girl, a child, old white men, the best in town, used to say dirty words to me in the street and try to touch me—the beasts!" I gasped: I had had no idea of such contempt and persecution.

When we were back in bed together: "Tell me, Sophy dear, how you learned to move with me in time as you do and give me such thrills?"

"Hoo!" she cried, gurgling with pleased joy. "That's easy to tell. I was scared you didn't like me, so this afternoon I went to wise old niggah woman and ask her how to make man love you really! She told me to go right to bed with you and do that," and she smiled.

"Nothing more?" I asked.

Her eyes opened brightly. "Shu!" she cried. "If you want to do love again, I show you!" The next moment, I was in her and now she kept even better time than at first and somehow or other the thick, firm lips of her sex seemed to excite me more than anyone had ever excited me. Instinctively the lust grew in me and I quickened and as I came to the short, hard strokes, she suddenly slipped her legs together under me and closing them tightly held my sex as in a firm grip and then began "milking" me—no other word conveys the meaning—with extraordinary skill and speed, so that, in a moment, I was gasping and choking with the intensity of the sensation and my seed came in hot jets while she continued the milking movement, tireless, indefatigible!

"What a marvel you are," I exclaimed as soon as I got breath enough to speak, "the best bedfellow I've ever had; wonderful, you dear, you!"

All glowing with my praise, she wound her arms about my neck and mounted me as Lorna Mayhew had done once; but what a difference! Lorna was so intent on gratifying her own lust that she often forgot my feelings altogether and her movements were awkward in the extreme; but Sophy thought only of me and, whereas Lorna was always slipping my sex out of her sheath, Sophy in some way seated herself on me and then began rocking her body back and forth while lifting it a little at each churning movement, so that my sex in the grip of her firm, thick lips had a sort of double movement. When she felt me coming as I soon did, she twirled half round on my organ half a dozen times with a new movement and then began rocking herself again, so that my seed was dragged out of me, so to speak, giving me indescribably acute, almost painful sensations. I was breathless, thrilling with her every movement.

"Had you any pleasure, Sophy?" I asked as soon as we were lying side by side again.

"Shuah!" she said smiling. "You're very strong, and you," she asked, "were you pleased?"

"Great God," I cried, "I felt as if all the hairs of my head were traveling down my backbone like an army! You are extraordinary, you dear!"

"Keep me with you, Frank," she whispered. "If you want me, I'll do anything, everything for you: I never hoped to have such a lover as you. Oh, this child's real glad her breasties and sex please you. You taught me that word, instead of the nasty word all white folks use. 'Sex' is a good word, very good!" and she crowed with delight.

"What do colored people call it?" I asked. "Coozie," she replied smiling, "Coozie. Good word too, very good!"

Long years later I heard an American story which recalled Sophy's performance vividly.

An engineer with a pretty daughter had an assistant who showed extraordinary qualities as a machinist and was quiet and well behaved to boot. The father introduced his helper to his daughter and the match was soon arranged. After the marriage, however, the son-in-law drew away and it was in vain that the father-in-law tried to guess the reason of the estrangement. At length he asked his son-in-law boldly for the reason. "I meant right, Bill," he began earnestly, "but if I've made a mistake I'll be sorry. Warn't the goods accordin' to specification? Warn't she a virgin?"

"It don't matter nothin'!" replied Bill frowning.

"Treat me fair, Bill," cried the father. "War she a virgin?"

"How can I tell?" exclaimed Bill. "All I can say is, I never know'd a virgin before that had that cinder-shifting movement."

Sophy was the first to show me the "cinder-shifting" movement, and she surely was a virgin!

As a mistress Sophy was perfection perfected and the long lines and slight curves of her lovely body came to have a special attraction for me as the very highest of the pleasure-giving type.

Lily first and then Rose were astonished and perhaps a little hurt at the sudden cooling off of my passion for them. From time to time I took Rose out or sent her books, and I had Lily anywhere, anywhen; but neither of them could compare with Sophy as a bedfellow, and her talk even fascinated me more the better I knew her. She had learned life from the streets, from the animal side first, but it was astonishing how quickly she grew in understanding: love is the only magical teacher! In a fortnight her speech was better than Lily's; in a month she talked as well as any of the American girls I had had; her desire of knowledge and her sponge-like ease of acquirement were always surprising me. She had a lovelier figure than even Rose and ten times the seduction even of Lily: she never hesitated to take my sex in her hand and caress it; she was a child of nature, bold with an animal's boldness and had besides a thousand endearing familiarities. I had only to hint a wish for her to gratify it. Sophy was the pearl of all the girls I met in this first stage of my development and I only wish I could convey to the reader a suggestion of her quaint, enthralling caresses. My admiration of Sophy cleansed me of any possible disdain I might otherwise have had of the Negro people, and I am glad of it; for else I might have closed my heart against the Hindu and so missed the best part of my life's experiences.

I have had a great artist make the sketch of her back which I reproduce at the end of this chapter; it conveys something of the strange vigor and nerve-force of her lovely firm body.

But it was written that as soon as I reached ease and content, the fates would reshuffle the cards and deal me another hand.

First of all, there came a letter from Smith telling me how he had had a bed wetting one night and had caught a severe cold. The cough then had returned and he was losing weight and heart. He had come to the conclusion, too, that I had reached, that the moist air of Philadelphia was doing him harm, and the doctors now were beginning to urge him to go to Denver, Colorado, all the foremost specialists agreeing that mountain air was the best for his lung-weakness. If I couldn't come to him, I must wire him and he'd stop in Lawrence to see me on on his way west, he had much to say—.

A couple of days later he was in the Eldridge House and I went to see him. His appearance shocked me: he had grown spectre thin and the great eyes seemed to burn like lamps in his white face. I knew at once that he was doomed and could scarcely control my tears.

We passed the whole day together and when he heard how I spent my days in casual reading and occasional speaking and my Topsy-turvey nights, he urged me to throw up the law and go to Europe to make myself a real scholar and thinker. But I could not give up Sophy and my ultra-pleasant life. So I resisted, told him he overrated me: I'd easily be the best advocate in the state, I said, and make a lot of money and then I'd go back and do Europe and study as well.

He warned me that I must choose between God and Mammon; I retorted lightly that Mammon and my senses gave me much that God denied. "I'll serve both," I cried, but he shook his head.

"I'm finished, Frank," he declared at length, "but I'd regret life less if I knew that you would take up the work I once hoped to accomplish. Won't you?"

I couldn't resist his appeal. "All right," I said, after choking down my tears, "give me a few months and I'll go, round the world first and then to Germany to study."

He drew me to him and kissed me on the forehead: I felt it as a sort of consecration.

A day or so afterwards he took train for Denver and I felt as if the sun had gone out of my life.

I had little to do in Lawrence at this time except read at large and I began to spend a couple of hours every day in the town library. Mrs. Trask, the librarian, was the widow of one of the early settlers who had been brutally murdered during the Quantrell raid, when Missourian bandits "shot up" the little town of Lawrence in a last attempt to turn Kansas into a slave-owning state.

Mrs. Trask was a rather pretty little woman who had been made librarian to compensate her in some sort for the loss of her husband. She was well read in American literature and I often took her advice as to my choice of books. She liked me, I think, for she was invariably kind to me and I owe her many pleasant hours and some instruction.

After Smith had gone west I spent more and more time in the library, for my law work was becoming easier to me every hour. One day, about a month after Smith had left, I went into the library and could find nothing enticing to read. Mrs. Trask happened to be passing and I asked her, "What am I to read?"

"Have you read any of that?" she replied, pointing to Bohn's edition of Emerson in two volumes. "He's good!"

"I saw him in Concord," I said, "but he was deaf and made little impression on me."

"He's the greatest American thinker," she retorted, "and you ought to read him."

Automatically I took down the volume and it opened of itself at the last page of Emerson's advice to the scholars of Dartmouth College. Every word is still printed on my memory: I can see the left-hand page and read again that divine message. I make no excuse for quoting it almost word for word:

Gentlemen, I have ventured to offer you these considerations upon the scholar's place and hope, because I thought that standing, as many of you now do, on the threshold of this College, girt and ready to go and assume tasks, public and private, in your country, you would not be sorry to be admonished of those primary duties of the intellect whereof you will seldom hear from the lips of your new companions. You will hear every day the maxims of a low prudence. You will hear that the first duty is to get land and money, place and name. 'What is this Truth you seek? What is this beauty?' men will ask, with derision. If nevertheless God have called any of you to explore truth and beauty, be bold, be firm, be true. When you shall say, 'As others do, so will I: I renounce, I am sorry for it, my early visions: I must eat the good of the land and let learning and romantic expectations go, until a more convenient season'; —then dies the man in you; then once more perish the buds of art, and poetry, and science, as they have died already in a thousand thousand men. The hour of that choice is the crisis of your history, and see that you hold yourself fast by the intellect. It is this domineering temper of the sensual world that creates the extreme need of the priests of science. . . . Be content with a little light, so it be your own. Explore and explore. Be neither chided nor flattered out of your position of perpetual inquiry. Neither dogmatize nor accept another's dogmatism. Why should you renounce your right to traverse the star-lit deserts of truth, for the premature comforts of an acre, house, and barn? Truth also has its roof, and bed, and board. Make yourself necessary to the world, and mankind will give you bread, and if not store of it, yet such as shall not take away your property in all men's affections, in art, in nature, and in hope.*

The truth of it shocked me: "Then perish the buds of art and poetry and science in you as they have perished already in a thousand thousand men!" That explained why it was that there was no Shakespeare, no Bacon, no

---

* From "Literary Ethics," An Oration delivered before the Literary Societies of Dartmouth College, July 24, 1838. Only a few punctuation marks have been added or altered.

Swinburne in America, where, according to population and wealth, there should be dozens.

There flashed on me the realization of the truth, that just because wealth was easy to get here, it exercised an incomparable attraction and in its pursuit "perished a thousand thousand" gifted spirits who might have steered humanity to new and nobler accomplishment.

The question imposed itself: "Was I too to sink to fatness, wallow in sensuality, degrade myself for a nerve-thrill?"

"No!" I cried to myself, "ten thousand times, no! No! I'll go and seek the star-lit deserts of Truth or die on the way!"

I closed the book, and with it and the second volume of it in my hand, went to Mrs. Trask.

"I want to buy this book," I said. "It has a message for me that I must never forget!"

"I'm glad," said the little lady smiling. "What is it?"

I read her a part of the passage. "I see," she exclaimed, "but why do you want the books?"

"I want to take them with me," I said. "I mean to leave Lawrence at once and go to Germany to study!"

"Good gracious!" she cried. "How can you do that? I thought you were a partner of Sommerfeld's; you can't go at once!"

"I must," I said. "The ground burns under my feet. If I don't go now, I shall never go. I'll be out of Lawrence tomorrow!"

Mrs. Trask threw up her hands and remonstrated with me: such quick decisions were dangerous; "why should I be in such a hurry?"

I repeated time and again. "If I don't go at once, I shall never go. The ignoble pleasure will grow sweeter and sweeter to me and I shall sink gradually and drown in the mud-honey of life."

Finally seeing I was adamant and my mind fixed, she sold me the books at full price and, with some demur, then she added,

"I almost wish I had never recommended Emerson to you!" and the dear lady looked distressed.

"Never regret that!" I cried. "I shall remember you as long as I live because of that and always be grateful to you. Professor Smith told me I ought to go, but it needed the word of Emerson to give me the last push! The buds of poetry and science and art shall not perish in me as they have 'perished already in a thousand thousand men!' Thanks to you!" I added warmly, "all my best heart-thanks: you have been to me the messenger of high fortune."

I clasped her hands, wished to kiss her, foolishly feared to hurt her, and so contented myself with a long kiss on her hand and went out at once to find Sommerfeld.

He was in the office and forthwith I told him the whole story, how Smith had tried to persuade me and how I had resisted till this page of Emerson had convinced me. "I am sorry to leave you in the lurch," I explained, "but I must go and go at once."

He told me it was madness: I could study German right there in Lawrence; he would help me with it gladly. "You mustn't throw away a livelihood just for a word," he cried. "It is madness. I never heard a more insane decision!"

We argued for hours: I couldn't convince him any more than he could persuade me. He tried his best to get me to stay two years, at any rate, and then go with full pockets. "You can easily spare two years," he cried; but I retorted, "Not even two days: I'm frightened of myself."

When he found that I wanted the money to go round the world with first, he saw a chance of delay, and said I must give him some time to find out what was coming to me. I told him I trusted him utterly (as indeed I did) and could only give him the Saturday and Sunday, for I'd go on the Monday at the latest. He gave in at last and was very kind.

I got a dress and a little hat for Lily, and lots of books besides a chinchilla cape for Rose, and broke the news to Lily next morning, keeping the afternoon for Rose. To my astonishment I had most trouble with Lily: she would not hear any reason. "There is no reason in it," she cried again and again, and then she broke down in a storm of tears. "What will become of me?" she sobbed. "I always hoped you'd marry me," she confessed at last, "and now you go away for nothing, nothing—on a wild-goose chase—to study," she added, in a tone of absolute disdain, "just as if you couldn't study here!"

"I'm too young to marry, Lily," I said, "and—"

"You were not too young to make me love you," she broke in, "and now what shall I do? Even mamma said that we ought to be engaged, and I want you so—oh, oh—" and again the tears fell in a shower.

I could not help saying at last that I would think it all over and let her know, and away I went to Rose. Rose heard me out in complete silence, and then with her eyes on mine in lingering affection, she said, "Do you know, I've been afraid often of some decision like this. I said to myself a dozen times: 'Why should he stay here? The wider world calls him,' and if I feel inclined to hate my work because it prevents my studying, what must it be for him in that horrible court, fighting day after day? I always knew I should lose you, dear!" she added, "but you were the first to help me to think and read, so I must not complain. Do you go soon?"

"On Monday," I replied, and her dear eyes grew sombre and her lips quivered.

"You'll write?" she asked. "Please do, Frank! No matter what happens, I shall never forget you: you've helped me, encouraged me more than I can say. Did I tell you, I've got a place in Crew's bookstore? When I said I had learned to love books from you, he was glad and said, 'If you get to know them as well as he did, or half as well, you'll be invaluable'; so you see, I am following in your footsteps, as you are following in Smith's."

"If you knew how glad I am that I've really helped and not hurt you, Rose!" I said sadly, for Lily's accusing voice was still in my ears.

"You couldn't hurt anyone," she exclaimed, almost as if she divined my remorse. "You are so gentle and kind and understanding."

Her words were balm to me and she walked with me to the bridge, where I told her she would hear from me on the morrow. I wanted to know what she would think of the books and cape. The last thing I saw of her was her hand raised, as if in benediction.

I kept the Sunday morning for Sommerfeld and my friend Will Thomson and the rest of the day for Sophy.

Sommerfeld came to the offices before nine and told me the firm owed me three thousand dollars. I didn't wish to take it. Could not believe he had meant to go halves with me, but he insisted and paid me.

"I don't agree with your sudden determination," he said, "perhaps because it was sudden, but I've no doubt you'll do well at anything you take up. Let me hear from you now and again, and if you ever need a friend, you know where to find me!"

As we shook hands I realized that parting could be as painful as the tearing asunder of flesh.

Will Thomson, I found, was eager to take over the boardings and my position in Liberty Hall. He had brought his father with him, and after much bargaining I conveyed everything I could over to him for three thousand five hundred dollars; and so after four years' work I had just the money I had had in Chicago four years earlier!

I dined in the Eldridge House and then went back to the office to meet Sophy, who was destined to surprise me more even than Lily or Rose; "I'm coming with you," she announced coolly, "if you're not ashamed to have me along; you goin' Frisco—so far away—" she pleaded, divining my surprise and unwillingness.

"Of course, I'll be delighted," I said, "but—" I simply could not refuse her.

She gurgled with joy and drew out her purse. "I've four hundred dollars," she said proudly, "and that'll take this child a long way."

I made her put her money away and promise me she wouldn't spend a cent of her money while we were together; and then I told her how I wished to dress her when we got to Denver, for I wanted to stop there for a couple of days to see Smith, who had written approving of everything I did and adding, to my heart's joy, that he was much better.

On the Monday morning Sophy and I started westwards.* She had had the tact to go to the depot first so that no one in Lawrence ever coupled our

* It is doubted by Tobin and Gertz in their *Frank Harris: A Study in Black and White*, that Harris went to Europe by way of the Orient. Indeed, they maintain that Harris borrowed money from Smith to get to Ohio, and that he somehow got from there across the Atlantic. No passport was issued to Harris to leave the United States either by a western or eastern port. We only know he did get to the Continent and then to London.

names. Sommerfeld and Judge Bassett saw me off at the depot and wished me "All luck!" And so the second stage of my life came to an end.

Sophy was a lively sweet companion; after leaving Topeka, she came boldly into my compartment and did not leave me again. May I confess it? I'd rather she had stayed in Lawrence, I wanted the adventure of being alone, and there was a girl in the train whose long eyes held mine as I passed her seat, and I passed it often. I'd have spoken to her if Sophy had not been with me.

When we got to Denver, I called on Smith, leaving Sophy in the hotel. I found him better but divined that the cursed disease was only taking breath, so to speak, before the final assault. He came back with me to my hotel, and as soon as he saw Sophy he declared I must go back with him: he had forgotten to give me something I must have. I smiled at Sophy, to whom Smith was very courteous-kind, and accompanied him. As soon as we were in the street, Smith began in horror, "Frank, she's a colored girl: you must leave her at once or you'll make dreadful trouble for yourself later."

"How did you know she was colored?" I asked.

"Look at her nails," he cried, "and her eyes: no Southerner would be in doubt for a moment. You must leave her at once, please!"

"We are going to part at Frisco," I said. And when he pressed me to send her back at once, I refused. I would not put such shame upon her, and even now I'm sure I was right in that resolve.

Smith was sorry but kind to me and so we parted forever.

He had done more for me than any other man, and now after fifty years I can only confess my incommensurable debt to him, and the hot tears come into my eyes now, as they came when our hands met for the last time. He was the dearest, sweetest, noblest spirit of a man I have met in this earthly pilgrimage. *Ave atque vale.*

As the time drew on to the day when the boat was to start, Sophy grew thoughtful. I got her a pretty corn-colored dress than set off her beauty as golden sunlight a lovely woodland, and when she thanked and hugged me, I wanted to put my hand up her clothes, for she made a mischievous, naughty remark that amused me and reminded me we had driven all the previous day and I had not had her. To my surprise she stopped me. "I've not washed since we came in," she explained.

"Do you wash so often?"

"Shuah," she replied, fixing me.

"Why?" I asked, searching her regard.

"Because I'm afraid of nigger-smell," she flung out passionately.

"What nonsense!" I exclaimed.

"Tain't either," she contradicted me angrily. "My mother took me once to Negro-church, and I near choked. I never went again, I just couldn't. When they get hot, they stink—pah!" and she shook her head and made a face in utter disgust and contempt.

"That's why you goin' to leave me," she added after a long pause, with tears in her voice. "If it wasn't for that damned nigger blood in me, I'd never leave you: I'd just go on with you as servant or anything. Ah God, how I love you and how lonely this Topsy'll be," and the tears ran down her quivering face. "If I were only all white or all black," she sobbed. "I'm so unhappy!" My heart bled for her.

If it had not been for the memory of Smith's disdain, I would have given in and taken her with me. As it was, I could only do my best to console her by saying, "A couple of years, Sophy, and I'll return; they'll pass quickly. I'll write you often, dear!"

But Sophy knew better and when the last night came, she surpassed herself. It was warm and we went early to bed. "It's my night dear!" she said. "You just let me show you, you dear! I didn't want you to go after any whitish girl in those islands till you get to China and you won't go with those yellow, slit-eyed girls—that's why I love you so, because you keep yourself for those you like—but you're naughty to like so many, ma man!" —and she kissed me with passion. She let me have her almost without response but, after the first orgasm, she gripped my sex and milked me, and, afterwards, mounting me made me thrill again and again till I was speechless and, like children, we fell asleep in each other's arms, weeping for the parting on the morrow.

I said "Good-bye!" at the hotel and went on board the steamer by myself, my eyes set on the Golden Gate into the great Pacific and the hopes and hazards of the new life. At length I was to see the world: what would I find in it? I had no idea then that I should find little or much in exact measure to what I brought, and it is now the saddest part of these confessions that on this first trip round the world I was so untutored, so thoughtless, that I got practically nothing out of my long journeying.

Like Odysseus, I saw many cities of men; but scenes seldom enrich the spirit. Yet one or two places made a distinct impression on me, young and hard though I was: Sydney Bay and Heights, Hong Kong, too, but above all, the old Chinese gate leading into the Chinese city of Shanghai so close to the European town and so astonishingly different. Kioto, too, imprinted itself on my memory, and the Japanese men and girls that ran naked out of their hot baths in order to see whether I was really white all over.

I learned nothing worth recalling till I came to Table Bay and saw the long line of Table Mountain four thousand feet above me, a cliff cutting the sky with an incomparable effect of dignity and grandeur. I stayed in Cape Town a month or so, and by good luck I got to know Jan Hofmeyr* there, who taught me what good fellows the Boers really were and how highly the English Premier Gladstone was esteemed for giving freedom to them after Majuba.** "We look on him with reverence," said my friend Hofmeyr, "as the embodied conscience of England." But alas! England

* (1845–1909).
** Where a British force of 500 men was routed by Boer troops in 1881.

could not stomach Majuba and had to spend blood and treasure later to demonstrate the manhood of the Boers to the world. But thank God, England then gave freedom and self-government again to South Africa and so atoned for her shameful "concentration camps." Thanks to Jan Hofmeyr, I got to know and esteem the South African Boer even on this first short acquaintance.

When I went round the world for the second time twenty years later, I tried to find the Hofmeyrs of every country and so learned all manner of things worthful and strange that I shall tell of, I hope, at the end of my next volume. The only short cut to knowledge is through intercourse with wise and gifted men.

Now I must confess something of my first six months of madness and pleasure in Paris, and then speak of England again and Thomas Carlyle and his incomparable influence upon me, and so lead you, gentle reader, to my later 'prentice years in Germany and Greece.

There in Athens I learned new sex-secrets which may perchance interest even the Philistines, though they can be learned in Paris as well, and will be set forth simply in the second volume of these "confessions," which will tell the whole "art of love," as understood in Europe, and perhaps contain my second voyage round the world and the further instruction in the great art which I received from the adepts of the East—unimaginable refinements, for they have studied the body as deeply as the soul.

Chapter XV

Europe and the Carlyles

I RETURNED to Europe, touching at Bombay and getting just a whiff of the intoxicating perfume of that wonderland with its noble, though sad, spiritual teaching, which is now beginning, through the Rig Veda, to inform the best European thought.

I stopped also at Alexandria and ran up to Cairo for a week to see the great Mosques. I admired their splendid rhetoric, but fell in love with the desert and its pyramids, and above all the sphinx and her eternal questioning of sense and outward things. Thus by easy, memorable stages that included Genoa and Florence and their storied palaces and churches and galleries, I came at length to Paris.

I distrust first impressions of great places or events or men. Who could describe the deathless fascination of the mere name and first view of Paris to the young student or artist of another race! If he has read and thought, he will be in a fever; tears in his eyes, heart thrilling with joyful expectancy, he will wander into that world of wonders!

I got to the station early one summer morning and sent my baggage by *fiacre* to the Hotel Meurice in the rue Rivoli, the same old hotel that Lever* the novelist has praised, and then I got into a little Victoria and drove to the Place de la Bastille. The obvious café life of the people did not appeal to me, but when I saw the glory springing from the Column of July, tears flooded my eyes, for I recalled Carlyle's description of the taking of the prison.**

I paid the *cocher* and wandered up the rue Rivoli, past the Louvre, past the blackened walls with the sightless windows of the Tuileries palace—a regret in their desolate appeal, and so to the Place de la Grève with its memories of the guillotine and the great revolution, now merged in the Place de la Concorde. Just opposite I could distinguish the gilt dome of the Church of the Invalides where the body of Napoleon lies as he desired:

* Irish novelist, editor, and diplomat of English parentage. He caricatured the military and Irish society to great effect in his books. *Charles O'Malley,* which dealt with college life at Dublin, was his first and perhaps most widely read novel.
** In his *French Revolution,* of course.

"On the banks of the Seine, in the midst of that French people I have loved so passionately!"

And there were the horses of Marly* champing at the entrance to the Champs Elysées and at the far end of the long hill, the Arch! The words came to my lips:

> Up the long dim road where thundered
> The army of Italy onward
> By the great pale arch of the Star.

It was the deep historic sense of this great people that first won me, and their loving admiration of their poets and artists and guides. I can never describe the thrill it gave me to find on a small house a marble plaque recording the fact that poor De Musset** had once lived there, and another on the house wherein he died. Oh, how right the French are to have a Place Malherbe, an Avenue Victor Hugo, an Avenue de la Grande Armée, too, and an Avenue de l'Impératrice as well, though it has since been changed prosaically into the Avenue du Bois de Boulogne.

From the Place de la Concorde I crossed the Seine and walked down the quays to the left and soon passed the Conciergerie and Ste. Chapelle with its gorgeous painted glass-windows of a thousand years ago; and there before me, on the Île de la Cité, the twin towers of Notre Dame caught my eyes and breath; and finally, early in the afternoon, I turned up the Boul' Mich and passed the Sorbonne, and then somehow or other lost myself in the old rue St. Jacques that Dumas père and other romance-writers had described for me a thousand times.

A little tired at length, having left the Luxembourg gardens far behind with their statues, which I promised myself soon to study more closely, I turned into a little wine shop-restaurant kept by a portly and pleasant lady, whose name, I soon learned, was Marguerite. After a most excellent meal I engaged a large room on the first floor looking on the street for forty francs a month, and if a friend should come to live with me, why, Marguerite promised, with a large smile, to put in another bed for an additional ten francs monthly, and supply us besides with coffee in the morning and whatever meals we wanted at most reasonable prices. There I lived gaudy, golden days for some three heavenly weeks.

I threw myself on French like a glutton and this was my method, which I don't recommend but simply record, though it brought me to understand everything said by the end of the first week. I spent five whole days on the grammar, learning all the verbs, especially the auxiliary and irregular verbs by heart, till I knew them as I knew my alphabet. I then read Hugo's *Hernani* with a dictionary in another long day of eighteen hours, and the next evening went to the gallery in the Comédie Française to see the play

---

* Statues by Guillaume Coustou (1677–1746) that once stood at the Chateau Marly-le-Roi which was built for Louis XIV.

** Alfred de Musset (1810–57), poet, dramatist, and novelist.

acted by Sarah Bernhardt as Doña Sol and Mounet-Sully* as Hernani. For a while the rapid speech and strange accent puzzled me, but after the first act I began to understand what was said on the stage, and after the second act I caught every word; and to my delight, when I came out into the streets, I understood everything said to me. After that golden night with Sarah's grave *trainante* voice in my ears, I made rapid because unconscious progress.

Next day in the restaurant I picked up a dirty, torn copy of *Madame Bovary* that lacked the first eighty pages. I took it to my room and swallowed it in a couple of breathless hours, realizing at once that it was a masterwork, but marking a hundred and fifty new words to turn out in my pocket dictionary afterwards. I learned these words carefully by heart and have never given myself any trouble about French since.

What I know of it, and I know it fairly well now, has come from reading and speaking it for thirty odd years. I still make mistakes in it, chiefly of gender, I regret to say, and my accent is that of a foreigner; but taking it by and large I know it and its literature, and speak it better than most foreigners, and that suffices me.

After some three weeks Ned Bancroft came from the States to live with me. He was never particularly sympathetic to me and I cannot account for our companionship, save by the fact that I was peculiarly heedless and full of human, unreflecting kindness. I have said little of Ned Bancroft, who was in love with Kate Stephens before she fell for Professor Smith; but I have just recorded the unselfish way he withdrew while keeping intact his friendship both for Smith and the girl. I thought that very fine of him.

He left Lawrence and the university shortly after we first met and by "pull" obtained a good position on the railroad at Columbus, Ohio.

He was always writing to me to come to visit him, and on my return from Philadelphia, in 1875, I think, I stopped at Columbus and spent a couple of days with him. As soon as he heard that I had gone to Europe and had reached Paris, he wrote to me that he wished I had asked him to come with me; and so I wrote setting forth my purpose, and at once he threw up his good prospects of riches and honor and came to me in Paris. We lived together for some six months. He was a tall, strong fellow, with pale face and grey eyes; a good student, an honorable, kindly, very intelligent man; but we envisaged life from totally different sides, and the longer we were together, the less we understood each other.

In everything we were antiposed; he should have been an Englishman, for he was a born aristocrat with imperious, expensive tastes, while I had really become a western American, careless of dress or food or position, intent only on acquiring knowledge and, if possible, wisdom, in order to reach greatness.

The first evening we dined at Marguerite's and spent the night talking

* (1841–1916); at one time the principal actor of the Comédie Française. He was a tragedian of the first rank, and he was especially admired for his *Oedipus*.

and swapping news. The very next afternoon Ned would go into Paris and we dined in a swell restaurant on the Grand Boulevard. A few tables away a tall, splendid looking brunette of perhaps thirty was dining with two men: I saw soon that Ned and she were exchanging looks and making signs. He told me he intended to go home with her. I remonstrated, but he was as obstinate as Charlie, and when I told him of the risks, he said he'd never do it again, but this time he couldn't get out of it. "I'll pay the bill at once," I said, "and let's go," but he would not; desire was alight in him and a feeling of false shame hindered him from taking my advice. Half an hour later the lady made a sign and he went out with the party, and when she entered her Victoria he got in with her, the pair on the sidewalk, he said, bursting into laughter as he and the woman drove away together.

Next morning he was back with me early, only saying that he had enjoyed himself hugely and was not even afraid. Her rooms were lovely, he declared; he had to give her a hundred francs; the bath and toilette arrangements were those of a queen; there was no danger. And he treated me to as wild a theory as Charlie had cherished: told me that the great *cocottes* who make heaps of money took as much care of themselves as gentlemen. "Go with a common prostitute and you'll catch something; go with a real top-notcher and she's sure to be all right!" And perfectly at ease he went to work with a will.

Bancroft's way of learning French, even, was totally different from mine. He went at the grammar and syntax and mastered them; he could write excellent French at the end of four months, but spoke it very haltingly and with a ferocious American accent. When I told him I was going to hear Taine* lecture on the philosophy of art and the ideal in art, he laughed at me; but I believe I got more from Taine than he got from his more exact knowledge of French. When I came to know Taine and was able to call on him and talk to him, Bancroft, too, wanted to know him. I brought them together, but clearly Taine was not impressed, for Ned out of false shame hardly opened his mouth. But I learned a good deal from Taine, and one illustration of his abides with me as giving a true and vivid conception of art and its ideal. In a lecture he pointed out to his students that a lion was not a running beast, but a great jaw set on four powerful springs of short, massive legs. The artist, he went on, seizing the *idea* of the animal, may exaggerate the size and strength of the jaw a little, emphasize, too, the springing power in his loins and legs and the tearing strength of his front paws and claws; but if he lengthened his legs or diminished his jaw, he would denaturalize the true *idea* of the beast and would produce an abortion. The ideal, however, should only be indicated. Taine's talks, too, on literature and the importance of the environment even on great men all made [a] profound impression on me. After listening to him for some time I began to see my way up more clearly. I shall never forget, too, some of his thought inspiring words. Talking one day of the Convent of Monte Cassino, where a hundred generations of students, freed from all the sordid cares of

* Hippolyte Adolphe Taine (1828–93), noted French historian, philosopher, critic.

existence, had given night and day to study and thought, and had preserved besides the priceless manuscripts of long past ages and so paved the way for a renascence of learning and thought, he added gravely:

"I wonder whether science will ever do as much for her votaries as religion has done for hers: in other words, I wonder will there ever be a laic Monte Cassino!"

Taine was a great teacher and I owe him much kindly encouragement and even enlightenment.

I add this last word, because his French freedom of speech came as pure spring water to my thirsty soul. A dozen of us were grouped about him one day talking, when one student with a remarkable gift for vague thought and highfalutin' rhetoric wanted to know what Taine thought of the idea that all the worlds and planets and solar systems were turning round one axis and moving to some divine fulfillment (accomplishment). Taine, who always disliked windy rhetoric, remarked quietly, "The only axis in my knowledge round which everything moves to some accomplishment is a woman's cunt (*le con d'une femme*)." They laughed, but not as if the bold word had astonished them. He used it when it was needed, as I have often heard Anatole France use it since, and no one thought anything of it.

In spite of the gorgeous installation of his brunette, Ned at the end of a week found out how blessed are those described in Holy Writ, who fished all night and caught nothing. He had caught a dreadful gonorrhea and was forbidden spirits or wine or coffee till he got well. Exercise, too, was only to be taken in small doses, so it happened that when I went out he had to stay home, and the outlook on the rue St. Jacques was anything but exhilarating. This naturally increased his desire to get about and see things, and as soon as he began to understand spoken French and to speak a little, he chafed against the confinement and a room without a bath. He longed for the centre, for the opera and the boulevards, and nothing would do but we should take rooms in the heart of Paris. He would borrow money from his folks, he said.

Like a fool I was willing, and so we took rooms one day in a quiet street just behind the Madeleine, at ten times the price we were paying Marguerite. I soon found that my money was melting, but the life was very pleasant. We often drove in the Bois, went frequently to the opera, the theatres and music-halls and appraised, too, the great restaurants, the Café Anglais and the Trois Frères, as if we had been millionaires.

As luck would have it, Ned's venereal disease and the doctors became a heavy additional expense that I could ill afford. Suddenly one day I realized that I had only six hundred dollars in the bank: at once I made up my mind to stop and make a fresh start. I told my resolution to Bancroft: he asked me to wait. "He had written to his people for money," he said, "he would soon pay his debt to me," but that wasn't what I wanted. I felt that I had got off the right road because of him and was angry with myself for having wasted my substance in profligate living, and worst of all, in silly luxury and brainless showing off.

I declared I was ill and was going to England at once. I must make a new start and accumulate some more money, and a few mornings later I bade Bancroft good-bye and crossed the channel and went on to my sister and father in Tenby, arriving there in a severe shivering fit with a bad headache and every symptom of ague.

I was indeed ill and played out. I had taken double doses of life and literature, had swallowed all the chief French writers from Rabelais and Montaigne to Flaubert, Zola and Balzac, passing by Pascal and Vauvenargues,* Renan and Hugo—a glutton's feast for six months. Then, too, I had nosed out this artist's studio and that, had spent hours watching Rodin at work and more hours comparing this painter's model with that, these breasts and hips with those.

My love of plastic beauty nearly brought me to grief at least once, and perhaps I had better record the incident, though it rather hurt my vanity at the time. One day I called at Manet's old studio, which was rented now by an American painter named Alexander.** He had real power as a craftsman, but only a moderate brain and was always trying by beauty or something remarkable in his model to make up for his own want of originality. On this visit I noticed an extraordinary sketch of a young girl standing where childhood and womanhood meet: she had cut her hair short and her chestnut-dark eyes lent her a startling distinction.

"You like it?" asked Alexander. "She has the most perfect figure I have ever seen."

"I like it," I replied. "I wonder whether the magic is in the model or in your brush?"

"You'll soon see," he retorted, a little piqued. "She's due here already," and almost as he spoke, she came in with quick, alert steps. She was below medium height, but evidently already a woman. Without a word she went behind the screen to undress, when Alexander said, "Well?" I had to think a moment or two before answering.

"God and you have conspired together!" I exclaimed, and indeed his brush had surpassed itself. He had caught and rendered a childish innocence in expression that I had not remarked, and he had blocked in the features with superb *brio*.

"It is your best work to date," I went on, "and almost anyone would have signed it."

At this moment the model emerged with a sheet about her, and probably because of my praise, Alexander introduced me to Mlle. Jeanne and said I was a distinguished American writer. She nodded to me saucily, flashing white teeth at me, mounted the estrade, threw off the sheet and took up her

---

* (1715–47), known for his *Réflexions et Maximes*.
** John White Alexander (1856–1915); best known for his portraits, especially those of women.

pose—all in a moment. I was carried off my feet; the more I looked, the more perfections I discovered. Needless to say, I told her so in my best French, with a hundred similes. Alexander also I conciliated by begging him to do no more to the sketch but sell it to me and do another. Finally he took four hundred and fifty francs for it and in an hour had made another sketch.

My purchase had convinced Mlle. Jeanne that I was a young millionaire, and when I asked her if I might accompany her to her home, she consented more than readily. As a matter of fact, I took her for a drive in the Bois de Boulogne and from there to dinner in a private room at the Café Anglais. During the meal I had got to like her: she lived with her mother, Alexander had told me; though by no means prudish, still less virginal, she was not a *coureuse*. I thought I might risk connection; but when I got her to take off her clothes and began to caress her sex, she drew away and said quite as a matter of course: "Why not *faire minette?*"

When I asked her what she meant, she told me frankly: "We women do not get excited in a moment as you men do; why not kiss me and tongue me there for a few minutes, then I shall have enjoyed myself and shall be ready."

I'm afraid I made rather a face, for she remarked coolly: "Just as you like, you know. I prefer in a meal the *hors-d'oeuvres* to the *pièce de resistance* like a good many other women: indeed, I often content myself with the *hors-d'oeuvres* and don't take any more. Surely you understand that a woman goes on getting more and more excited for an hour or two and no man is capable of bringing her to the highest pitch of enjoyment while pleasing himself."

"I'm able," I said stubbornly. "I can go on all night if you please me, so we should skip appetizers."

"No, no!" she replied, laughing, "let us have a banquet then, but begin with the lips and tongue!"

The delay, the bandying to and fro of argument, and above all the idea of kissing and tonguing her sex, had brought me to coolness and reason. Was I not just as foolish as Bancroft if I yielded to her—an unknown girl?

I replied finally, "No, little lady, your charms are not for me," and I took my seat again at the table and poured myself out some wine. I had the ordinary English or American youth's repugnance to what seemed like degradation, never guessing that Jeanne was giving me the second lesson in the noble art of seduction, of which my sister had taught me long ago the rudiments.

The next time I was offered *minette* I had grown wiser and made no scruples, but that's another story. The fact is that my first visit to Paris I kept perfectly chaste, thanks in part to the example of Ned's blunder; thanks, too, to my dislike of going with any girl sexually whom I didn't really care for, and I didn't care for Jeanne. She was too imperious, and imperiousness in a girl is the quality I most dislike, perhaps because I suffer from an overdose of the humor. At any rate, it was not sexual indulgence that broke my health in Paris, but my passionate desire to learn that had cut down my hours of sleep and exasperated my nerves. I took cold and had a dreadful recurrence of malaria. I wanted rest and time to breathe and think.

The little house in a side street in the lovely Welsh watering-place was exactly the haven of rest I needed. I soon got well and strong and for the first time learned to know my father. He came for long walks with me, though he was over sixty. After his terrible accident seven years before (he slipped and fell thirty feet into a drydock while his ship was being repaired), one side of his hair and moustache had turned white and the other remained jet-black. I was astonished first by his vigor: he thought nothing of a ten mile walk, and on one of our excursions I asked him why he had not given me the nomination I wanted as a midshipman.

He was curiously silent and waved the subject aside with, "The Navy for you? No!" and he shook his head. A few days afterwards, however, he came back to the subject of his own accord.

"You asked me," he began, "why I didn't send you the nomination for the midshipman's examination. Now I'll tell you. To get on in the British Navy and make a career in it, you should either be well-born or well-off: you were neither. For a youth without position or money, there are only two possible roads up: servility or silence, and you were incapable of both."

"Oh, Governor, how true and how wise of you," I cried, "but why, why didn't you tell me? I'd have understood then as well as now and thought the more of you for thwarting me."

"You forget," he went on, "that I had trained myself in the other road of silence: it is difficult for me even now to express myself." And he went on with bitterness in voice and accent, "They drove me to silence: if you knew what I endured before I got my first step as lieutenant. If it hadn't been that I was determined to marry your mother, I could never have swallowed the countless humiliations of my brainless superiors! What would have happened to you I saw as in a glass. You were extraordinarily quick, impulsive and high-tempered. Don't you know that brains and energy and will power are hated by all the wastrels, and in this world they are everywhere in the vast majority. Some lieutenant or captain would have taken an instantaneous dislike to you that would have grown on every manifestation of your superiority: he would have laid traps for you of insubordination and insolence, probably for months, and then in some port where he was powerful, he would have brought you before a court martial and you would have been dismissed from the Navy in disgrace, and perhaps your whole life ruined. The British Navy is the worst place in the world for genius."

That scene began my reconciliation with my father; one more experience completed it.

I got wet through on one of our walks and next day had lumbago. I went to a pleasant Welsh doctor I had become acquainted with and he gave me a bottle of belladonna mixture for external use. "I haven't got a proper poison bottle," he added, "and I've no business to give you this." (It is forbidden to dispense poisons in Great Britain, save in rough octagonal bottles which betray the nature of their contents to the touch.)

"I'll not drink it," I said laughing.

"Well, if you do," he said, "don't send for me, for there's more than enough here to kill a dozen men!" I took the bottle and curiously enough we talked belladonna and its effects for some minutes. Richards (that was his name) promised to send me a black draught the same evening, and he assured me that my lumbago would soon be cured, and he was right: but the cure was not effected as he thought it would be.

My sister had a girl of all work at this time called Eliza, Eliza Gibby, if I remember rightly. Lizzie, as we called her, was a slight red haired girl of perhaps eighteen with really large chestnut-brown eyes and a cheeky pug nose, and freckled neck and arms. I really don't know what induced me first to make up to her, but soon I was kissing her; when I wanted to touch her sex, however, she drew away, confiding to me that she was afraid of the possible consequences. I explained to her immediately that I would with-draw after the first spasm, and then there would be no more risk. She trusted me, and one night she came to my room in her night dress. I took it off with many kisses and was really astounded by her ivory white skin and almost perfect girlish form. I laid her on the edge of my bed, put her knees comfortable under my armpits and began to rub her clitoris: in a moment the brown eyes turned up and I ventured to slip in the head of my sex; to my surprise, there was no maidenhead to break through and soon my sex had slipt into the tightest cunt I had ever met. Very soon I played Onan and like that Biblical hero "spilt my seed upon the ground"—which in my case was a carpet. Then I got into bed with her and practiced the whole art of love as I understood it at that time. A couple of hours of it brought me four or five orgasms and Lizzie a couple of dozen, to judge by hurried breathings, inarticulate cries, and long kissings that soon became mouthings.

Lizzie was what most men would have thought a perfect bedfellow, but I missed Sophy's science and Sophy's passionate determination to give me the utmost thrill conceivable. Still in a dozen pleasant nights we became great friends and I began to notice that, by working in and out very slowly, I could after the first orgasm go on indefinitely without spending again. Alas! I had no idea at the time that this control simply marked the first de-crease of my sexual power. If I had only known, I would have cut out all the Lizzies that infested my life and reserved myself for the love that was to oust the mere sex urge.

Next door to us lived a doctor's widow with two daughters, the eldest a medium-sized girl with large head and good grey eyes, hardly to be called pretty, though all girls were pretty enough to excite me for the next ten years or more. This eldest girl was called Molly, a pet name for Maria. Her sister Kathleen was far more attractive physically: she was rather tall and slight, with a lithe grace of figure that was intensely provocative. Yet, though I noted all Kathleen's feline witchery, I fell prone for Molly. She seemed to me both intelligent and witty: she had read widely, too, and knew both French and German. She was as far above all the American girls I had met in knowledge of books and art as she was inferior to the best of them in bodily beauty. For the first time my mind was excited and interested and I thought I was in love, and one late afternoon or early evening on Castle Hill I told her I loved her and we became engaged. Oh, the sweet folly of it all! When she asked me how we should live, what I intended to do, I had no answer ready, save the perfect self-confidence of the man who had already proved himself in the struggle of life. Fortunately for me, that didn't seem very convincing to her. She admitted that she was three years older than I was, and if she had said four, she would have been nearer the truth; and she was quite certain that I would not find it so easy to win in England as in America: she underrated both my brains and my strength of will. She confided to me that she had a hundred a year of her own, but that, of course, was wholly inadequate. So, though she kissed me freely and allowed me a score of little privacies, she was resolved not to give herself completely. Her distrust of my ability and her delightfully piquant reserve heightened my passion, and once I won her consent to an immediate marriage. At her best, Molly was astonishingly intelligent and frank. One night alone together in our sitting-room, which my father and sister left to us, I tried my best to get her to give herself to me. But she shook her head. "It would not be right, dear, till we are married," she persisted.

"Suppose we were on a desert island," I said, "and no marriage [were] possible?"

"My darling," she said, kissing me on the mouth and laughing aloud, "don't you know, I should yield then without your urging: you dear! I want you, Sir, perhaps more than you want me." But she wore closed drawers and I didn't know how to unbutton them at the sides; and though she grew intensely and quickly excited, I could not break down the final barrier. In any case, before I could win, Fate used her shears decisively.

One morning I reproached Lizzie for not bringing me up a black draught Doctor Richards had promised to send me. "It's on the mantlepiece in the dining-room," I said, "but don't trouble, I'll get it myself," and I ran down as I was. An evening or two later I left the belladonna mixture the doctor had made up for me on the chimney piece. Like the black draught, it was dark brown in color and in a similar bottle.

Next morning Lizzie woke me and offered me a glassful of dark liquid. "Your medicine," she said, and, half asleep still, I told her to leave the breakfast tray on the table by my bed, and then drained the glass she offered to me. The taste awoke me; the drink had made my whole mouth and throat dry. I sprang out of bed and went to the looking glass. Yes! Yes! The pupils of my eyes were unnaturally distended: had she given me the whole draught of belladonna, instead of black draught? I still heard her on the stairs, but why waste time in asking her? I went over to the table, poured out cup after cup of tea and drained them; then I ran down to the dining-room, where my sister and father were at breakfast. I poured out their tea and drank cups full of it in silence: then I asked my sister to get me mustard and warm water and met my father's question with a brief explanation and request. "Go to Dr. Richards and tell him to come at once. I've drunk the belladonna mixture by mistake; there's no time to lose." My father was already out of the house! My sister brought me the mustard and I mixed a strong dose with hot water and took it as an emetic, but it didn't work. I went upstairs to my bedroom again and put my fingers down my throat over the bath: I retched and retched, but nothing came: plainly the stomach was paralyzed. My sister came in crying. "I'm afraid there's no hope, Nita," I said. "The Doctor told me there was enough to kill a dozen men, and I've drunk it all fasting; but you've always been good and kind to me, dear, and death is nothing."

She was sobbing terribly, so to give her something to do, I asked her to fetch me a kettle full of hot water. She vanished downstairs to get it and I stood before the glass to make up my accounts with my own soul. I knew now it was the belladonna I had taken, all of it on an empty stomach: no chance; in ten minutes I should be insensible, in a few hours dead. Dead! Was I afraid? I recognized with pride that I was not one whit afraid or in any doubt. Death is nothing but an eternal sleep, nothing! Yet I wished that I could have had time to prove myself and show what was in me! Was Smith right? Could I indeed have become one of the best heads in the world? Could I have been with the really great ones, had I lived? No one could tell now, but I made up my mind, as at the time of the rattlesnake bite, to do my best to live. All this time I was drinking cold water: now my sister brought the jug of warm water, saying, "It may make you throw up, dear," and I began drinking it in long draughts. Bit by bit I felt it more difficult to think, so I kissed my sister, saying, "I had better get into bed while I can walk, as I'm rather heavy!" And then as I got into bed, I said, "I wonder whether I shall be carried out next feet foremost while they chant the *Miserere*! Never mind, I've had a great draught of life and I'm ready to go if I must!"

At this moment Dr. Richards came in. "Now, how, how in Goodness' name, man, after our talk and all, how did ye come to take it?" His fussiness and strong Welsh accent made me laugh.

"Give me the stomach pump, Doctor, for I'm full of liquid to the gullet," I cried. I took the tube and pushed it down, sitting up in bed, and he depressed it, but only a brownish stream came: I had absorbed most of the belladonna. That was nearly my last conscious thought, only in myself I determined to keep thinking as long as I could. I heard the doctor say, "I'll give him opium—a large dose," and I smiled to myself at the thought that the narcotic opium and the stimulant belladonna would alike induce unconsciousness, the one by exciting the heart's action, the other by slackening it.

Many hours afterwards I awoke: it was night, candles were burning, and Dr. Richards was leaning over me. "Do you know me?" he asked, and at once I answered: "Of course I know you, Richards," and I went on jubilant to say, "I'm saved: I've won through. Had I been going to die, I should never have recovered consciousness."

To my astonishment, his brow wrinkled and he said, "Drink this and then go to sleep again quietly: it's all right," and he held a glass of whitish liquid to my lips.

I drained the glass and said joyously. "Milk! How funny you should give me milk; that's not prescribed in any of your books." He told me afterwards it was castor oil he had given me and I had mistaken it for milk. I somehow felt that my tongue was running away with me even before he laid his hand on my forehead to quiet me, saying, "There please! Don't talk, rest! Please!" and I pretended to obey him, but couldn't make out why he shut me up. I could not recall my words either—why?

A dreadful thought shook me suddenly: had I been talking nonsense? My father's face, too, appeared to be dreadfully perturbed while I was speaking.

"Could one think sanely and yet talk like a madman? What an appalling fate!" I resolved in that case to use my revolver on myself as soon as I knew that my state was hopeless: that thought gave me peace and I turned at once to compose myself. In a few minutes more I was fast asleep.

The next time I awoke, it was again night and again the doctor was beside me and my sister. "Do you know me?" he asked again, and again I replied, "Of course I know you, and Sis here as well."

"That's great," he cried joyously. "Now you'll soon be well again."

"Of course I shall," I cried joyously. "I told you that before, but you seemed hurt; did I wander in my mind?"

"There, there," he cried, "don't excite yourself, and you'll soon be well again!"

"Was it a near squeak?" I asked.

"You must know it was," he replied. "You took sixty grains of belladonna fasting, and the books give at most a quarter of a grain for a dose and declare one grain to be generally fatal. I shall never be able to brag of your case in the medical journals," he went on smiling, "for no one would ever believe that a heart could go on galloping far too fast to count, but certainly two hundred odd times a minute for thirty odd hours, without bursting. You've been tested," he concluded, "as no one was ever tested before and have come back safe! But now sleep again," he said. "Sleep is nature's restorative."

Next morning I awoke rested but very weak: the doctor came in and sponged me in warm water and changed my linen: my night-shirt and a great part of the sheet were quite brown. "Can you make water?" he asked, handing me a bed-dish. I tried and at once succeeded.

"The wonder is complete!" he cried. "I'll bet you have cured your lumbago too," and, indeed, I was completely free of pain.

That evening or the next my father and I had a great heart-to-heart talk. I told him all my ambitions and he tried to persuade me to take one hundred pounds a year from him to continue my studies. I told him I couldn't, though I was just as grateful. "I'll get work as soon as I am strong," I said; but his unselfish affection shook my very soul, and when he told me that my sister, too, had agreed he should make me the allowance, I could only shake my head and thank him. That evening I went to bed early and he came and sat with me: he said that the doctor advised that I should take a long rest. Strange colored lights kept sweeping across my sight every time I shut my eyes, so I asked him to lie beside me and hold my hand. At once he lay down beside me, and with his hand in mine, I soon fell asleep and slept like a log till seven next morning. I awoke perfectly well and refreshed and was shocked to see that my father's face was strangely drawn and white, and when he tried to get off the bed, he nearly fell. I saw then that he had lain all the night through on the brass edge of the bed rather than risk disturbing me to give him more room. From that time to the end of his noble and unselfish life, some twenty-five years later, I had only praise and admiration for him.

As soon as I began to take note of things, I remarked that Lizzie no longer came near my room. One day I asked my sister what had become of her. To my astonishment, my sister broke out in passionate dislike of her. "While you were lying unconscious," she cried, "and the doctor was taking your pulse every few minutes, evidently frightened, he asked me could he get a prescription made up at once. He wanted to inject morphia, he said, to stop or check the racing of your heart. He wrote the prescription and I sent Lizzie with it and told her to be as quick as she could, for your life might depend on it. When she didn't come back in ten minutes, I got the doctor to write it out again and sent father with it. He brought it back in double-quick time. Hours passed and Lizzie didn't return: she had gone out before ten and didn't get back till it was almost one. I asked her where she had been. Why she hadn't got back sooner? She replied coolly that she had been listening to the band. I was so shocked and angry I would not keep her another moment. I sent her away at once. Think of it! I have no patience with such heartless brutes!"

Lizzie's callousness seemed to me even stranger than it seemed to my sister. I have often noticed that girls are less considerate of others than even boys, unless their affections are engaged, but I certainly thought I had half won Lizzie at least! However, the fact is so peculiar that I insert it here for what it may be worth.

During my convalescence, which lasted three months, Molly went for a visit to some friends. At the time I regretted it: now looking back I have no doubt she went away to free herself from an engagement she thought ill-advised. Missing her, I went about with her younger, prettier, sister Kathleen, who was more sensuous and more affectionate than Molly.

A little later, Molly went to Dresden to stay with an elder married sister: thence she wrote to me to set her free, and I consented as a matter of course very willingly. Indeed, I had already more real affection for Kathleen than Molly had ever called to life in me.

As I got strong again I came to know a young Oxford man who professed to be astonished at my knowledge of literature, and one day he came to me with the news that Grant Allen, the writer, had thrown up his job as professor of literature at Brighton College. "Why should you not apply for it: it's about two hundred pounds a year, and they can do no worse than refuse you."

I wrote to Taine at once, telling him of the position and my illness and asking him to send me a letter of recommendation, if he thought I was fit. By return post I got a letter from him recommending me in the warmest way. This letter I sent on to Dr. Bigge, the head-master, together with one from Professor Smith of Lawrence, and Dr. Bigge answered by asking me to come to Brighton to see him. Within twenty-four hours I went and was accepted forthwith, though he thought I looked too young to keep discipline. He soon realized that his fears were merely imaginary, I could have kept order in a cage of hyenas.

A long book would not exhaust my year as a master in Brighton College, but only two or three happenings require notice here as affecting my character and its growth. First of all, I found in every class of thirty lads five or six of real ability, and in the whole school three or four of astonishing minds, well graced, too, in manners and spirit. But six out of ten were both stupid and obstinate, and these I left wholly to their own devices.

Dr. Bigge warned me by a report of my work exhibited on the notice board of the sixth form, that while some of my scholars displayed great improvement, the vast majority showed none at all. I went to see him immediately and handed him my written resignation to take place at any moment he pleased. "I cannot bother with the fools who don't even wish to learn," I said, "but I'll do anything for the others."

Most of the abler boys liked me, I believe, and a little characteristic incident came to help me. There was a form-master named Wolverton, an Oxford man and son of a well-known archdeacon, who sometimes went out with me to the theatre or the roller-skating rink in West Street. One night at the rink he drew my attention to a youth in a straw hat, going out accompanied by a woman.

"Look at that," said Wolverton, "there goes So-and-So in our colors and with a woman! Did you see him?"

"I didn't pay much attention," I replied, "but surely there's nothing unusual in a sixth form boy trying his wings outside the nest."

At the next masters' meeting, to my horror Wolverton related the circumstance and ended up by declaring that unless the boy could give the name of the woman, he should be expelled. He called upon me as a witness to the fact.

I got up at once and said that I was far too short-sighted to distinguish the boy at half the distance, and I refused to be used in the matter in any way.

Dr. Bigge thought the offense very grave. "The morals of a boy," he declared, "were the most important part of his education. The matter must be probed to the bottom: he thought that on reflection I would not deny that I had seen a college boy that night in colors and in suspicious company."

I thereupon got up and freed my soul; the whole crew seemed to me mere hypocrites.

"In the Doctor's own House," I said, "where I take evening preparation, I could give him a list of boys who are known as lovers, notorious even, and so long as this vice is winked at throughout the school, I shall be no party to persecuting anybody for yielding to legitimate and natural passion." I had hardly got out the last words when Cotteril, the son of the Bishop of Edinburgh, got up and called upon me to free his House from any such odious and unbearable suspicion.

I retorted immediately that there was a pair in his house known as "the inseparables," and went on to state that my quarrel was with the whole boarding-house system, and not with individual masters who, I was fain to believe, did their best.

The vice-principal, Dr. Newton, was the only one who even recognized my good motives: he came away from the meeting with me and advised me to consult with his wife. After this I was practically boycotted by the masters: I had dared to say in public what Wolverton and others of them had admitted to me in private a dozen times.

Mrs. Newton, the vice-principal's wife, was one of the leaders of Brighton society: she was what the French called *une maitresse femme,* and a born leader in any society. She advised me to form girls' classes in literature for the half-holidays each week; was good enough to send out the circulars and lend her drawing-room for my first lectures. In a week I had fifty pupils who paid me half a crown a lesson, and I soon found myself drawing ten pounds a week in addition to my pay. I saved every penny and thus came in a year to monetary freedom.

At every crisis in my life I have been helped by good friends who have aided me out of pure kindness at cost of time and trouble to themselves. Smith helped me in Lawrence and Mrs. Newton at Brighton out of bountiful human sympathy.

Before this I had got to know a man named Harold Hamilton, manager of the London & County Bank, I think, at Brighton. It amused him to see how quickly and regularly my balance grew; soon I confided my plans to him and my purpose: he was all sympathy. I lent him books and his daughter Ada was assiduous at all my lectures.

In the nick of time for me the war broke out between Chili and Peru: Chilean bonds dropped from 90 to 60. I saw Hamilton and assured him that Chili, if left alone, could beat all South America: he advised me to wait and see. A little later Bolivia threw in her lot with Peru, and Chilean bonds fell to 43 or 44. At once I went to Hamilton and asked him to buy Chileans for all I possessed on a margin of three or four. After much talk he did what I wished on a margin of ten: a fortnight later came the news of the first Chilean victory, and Chileans jumped to 60 odd and continued to climb steadily. I sold at over 80 and thus netted from my first five hundred pounds over two thousand pounds and by Christmas was free once more to study with a mind at ease. Hamilton told me that he had followed my lead a little later but had made more from a larger investment.

The most important happening at Brighton I must now relate. I have already told in a pen-portrait of Carlyle, published by Austin Harrison* in the *English Review* some twelve years ago, how I went one Sunday morning and called upon my hero, Thomas Carlyle, in Chelsea. I told there, too, how on more than one Sunday I used to meet him on his morning walk along the Chelsea embankment, and how once at least he talked to me of his wife and admitted his impotence.

I only gave a summary of a few talks in my portrait of him, for the traits did not call for strengthening by repetition, but here I am inclined to add a few details, for everything about Carlyle at his best is of enduring interest!

When I told him how I had been affected by reading Emerson's speech to the students of Dartmouth College and how it had in a way forced me to give up my law-practice and go to Europe to study, he broke in excitedly:

"I remember well reading that very page to my wife and saying that nothing like it for pure nobility had been heard since Schiller went silent. It had a great power with it. . . . And so that started you off and changed your way of life? . . . I don't wonder . . . It was a great call."

After that Carlyle seemed to like me. At our final parting, too, when I was going to Germany to study and he wished me "Godspeed and Good speed! on the way that lies before ye," he spoke again of Emerson and the sorrow he had felt on parting with him; deep, deep sorrow and regret, and he added, laying his hands on my shoulders, "Sorrowing most of all that they should see his face no more forever." I remembered the passage and cried:

"Oh, Sir, I should have said that, for mine is the loss, mine the unspeakable misfortune now," and through my tears I saw that his eyes, too, were full.

He had just given me a letter to Froude,** "good, kindly Froude," who, he was sure, would help me in any way of commendation to some literary

* (1873–1928).
** J. A. Froude, (1818–94), distinguished nineteenth-century historian and editor of Carlyle's *Reminiscences* and Mrs. Carlyle's *Letters*.

position, "if I have gone as is most likely," and in due time Froude did help me, as I shall tell in the proper place.

My pen-portrait of Carlyle* was ferociously attacked by a kinsman, Alexander Carlyle, who evidently believed that I had got my knowledge of Carlyle's weakness from Froude's revelations** in 1904. But luckily for me, Sir Charles Jessel† remembered a dinner in the Garrick Club given by him in 1886 or 1887, at which both Sir Richard Quain†† and myself were present. Jessel recalled distinctly that I had that evening told the story of Carlyle's impotence as explaining the sadness of his married life and had then asserted that the confession came to me from Carlyle himself.

At that dinner Sir Richard Quain said that he had been Mrs. Carlyle's physician and that he would tell me later exactly what Mrs. Carlyle had confessed to him. Here is Quain's account as he gave it to me that night in a private room at the Garrick. He said:

"I had been a friend of the Carlyles for years: he was a hero to me, one of the wisest and best of men: she was singularly witty and worldly-wise and pleased me even more than the sage. One evening I found her in great pain on the sofa: when I asked her where the pain was, she indicated her lower belly and I guessed at once that it must be some trouble connected with the change of life.

"I begged her to go up to her bedroom and I would come in a quarter of an hour and examine her, assuring her the while that I was sure I could give her almost immediate relief. She went upstairs. In about ten minutes I asked her husband, would he come with me? He replied in his broadest Scotch accent, always a sign of emotion with him:

" 'I'll have naething to do with it. Ye must arrange it yerselves.'

"Thereupon I went upstairs and knocked at Mrs. Carlyle's bedroom door: no reply; I tried to enter: the door was locked, and unable to get an answer, I went downstairs in a huff and flung out of the house.

"I stayed away for a fortnight, but when I went back one evening I was horrified to see how ill Mrs. Carlyle looked, stretched out on the sofa, and as pale as death. 'You're worse?' I asked.

---

* In *The English Review,* February, 1911, Harris reported a conversation held with Carlyle in 1878, in which Carlyle confessed his marriage had never been consummated. Froude had previously reopened the subject of Carlyle's impotence in 1903, in reply to attacks on him by J. Creichton-Browne, a physician, and Alexander Carlyle, who maintained that Froude, in editing *Reminiscences,* had misinterpreted Carlyle, as he had Jane Carlyle's letters in his life of Carlyle. The veracity of Harris's "pen-portrait" and his account of Richard Quain's revelations about Jane Carlyle are questioned by many scholars, as well as by Carlyle's lateral kin. Alexander Carlyle questions Harris's ever having met Carlyle. The truth of Harris's, let alone Froude's, assertions about Carlyle certainly cannot be resolved here, or perhaps anywhere. It is a question of whose word one is inclined to accept.

** *My Relations with Carlyle* (London, 1903).

† (1824–83), English jurist.

†† (1800–87), distinguished surgeon who left about 75,000 pounds to University College, London, "for the promotion and encouragement . . . of general education . . . and natural science."

" 'Much worse and weaker!' she replied.

" 'You naughty, obstinate creature!' I cried. 'I'm your friend and your doctor and anything but a fool: I'm sure I can cure you in double-quick time, and you prefer to suffer. It's stupid of you and worse.—Come up now at once and think of me only as your doctor,' and I half lifted, half helped her to the door: I supported her up the stairs and at the door of her room she said:

" 'Give me ten minutes, Doctor, and I'll be ready. I promise you I won't lock the door again.'

"With that assurance I waited and in ten minutes knocked and went in.

"Mrs. Carlyle was lying on the bed with a woolly-white shawl round her head and face. I thought it absurd affectation in an old married woman, so I resolved on drastic measures: I turned the light full on, then I put my hand under her dress and with one toss threw it right over her head. I pulled her legs apart, dragged her to the edge of the bed and began inserting the speculum in her vulva: I met an obstacle—I looked—and immediately sprang up. 'Why, you're a virgo intacta!' (an untouched virgin), I exclaimed.

"She pulled the shawl from her head and said: 'What did you expect?'

" 'Anything but that,' I cried, 'in a woman married these five and twenty years.'

"I soon found out the cause of her trouble and cured it or rather did away with it: that night she rested well and was her old gay, mutinous self when I called next day.

"A little later she told me her story.

" 'After the marriage,' she said, 'Carlyle was strange and out of sort, very nervous, he seemed, and irritable. When we reached the house, we had supper and about eleven o'clock I said I would go to bed, being rather tired: he nodded and grunted something. I put my hands on his shoulders as I passed him and said, "Dear, do you know that you haven't kissed me once, all day—this day of days!" and I bent down and laid my cheek against his. He kissed me, but said: "You women are always kissing—I'll be up soon!" Forced to be content with that, I went upstairs, undressed and got into bed: he hadn't even kissed me of his own accord, the whole day!

" 'A little later he came up, undressed and got into bed beside me. I expected him to take me in his arms and kiss and caress me.

" 'Nothing of the sort, he lay there, jiggling like.' ("I guessed what she meant," said Quain, "the poor devil in a blue funk was frigging himself . . .") 'I thought for some time,' Mrs. Carlyle went on, 'one moment I wanted to kiss and caress him; the next moment I felt indignant. Suddenly it occurred to me that in all my hopes and imaginings of a first night I had never got near the reality: silent the man lay there jiggling, jiggling. Suddenly I burst out laughing: it was too wretched! too absurd!

" 'At once he got out of bed with the one scornful word, "Woman!" and went into the next room: he never came back to my bed.

" 'Yet he's one of the best and noblest men in the world, and if he had been more expansive and told me oftener that he loved me, I could easily have forgiven him any bodily weakness; silence is love's worst enemy, and after all, he never really made me jealous, save for a short time with Lady Ashburnham.* I suppose I've been as happy with him as I could have been without anyone, yet—'

"That's my story," said Quain in conclusion, "and I make you a present of it: even in the Elysian Fields I shall be content to be in the Carlyles' company. They were a great pair!"

Just one more scene. When I told Carlyle how I had made some twenty-five hundred pounds in the year, and told him besides how a banker offered me almost the certainty of a great fortune if I would buy with him a certain coal-wharf at Tunbridge Wells (it was Hamilton's pet scheme), he was greatly astonished. "I want to know," I went on, "if you think I'll be able to do good work in literature; if so, I'll do my best. Otherwise I ought to make money and not waste time in making myself another second-rate writer."

"No one can tell you that," said Carlyle slowly. "You'll be lucky if you reach the knowledge of it yourself before ye die! I thought my Frederick was great work: yet the other day you said I had buried him under the dozen volumes, and you may be right; but have I ever done anything that will live?"

"Sure," I broke in, heartsore at my gibe, "sure. Your *French Revolution* must live and the *Heroes and Hero Worship,* and *Latter Day Pamphlets* and—and—"

"Enough," he cried; "you're sure?"

"Quite, quite sure," I repeated.

Then he said, "You can be equally sure of your own place; for we can all reach the heights we are able to oversee."

* Correctly, Lady Harriet Montagu Ashburton (died 1857), first wife of William Bingham Baring, 2nd Lord Ashburton.

Afterword

To the Story of
My Life's Story

I HAD HARDLY WRITTEN "Finis" at the end of this book when the faults in it, faults both of omission and commission, rose in swarms and robbed me of my joy in the work.

It will be six or seven years at least before I shall know whether the book is good and life-worthy or not, and yet need drives me to publish it at once.

Did not Horace require nine years to judge his work?

I, therefore, want the reader to know my intention; I want to give him the key, so to speak, to this chamber of my soul.

First of all I wished to destroy, or at least to qualify, the universal opinion that love in youth is all romance and idealism. The masters all paint it crowded with roses of illusion: Juliet is only fourteen; Romeo, having lost his love, refuses life; Goethe follows Shakespeare in his Mignon and Marguerite; even the great humorist Heine and the so-called realist Balzac adopt the same convention. Yet to me it is absolutely untrue in regard to the male in boyhood and early youth, say from thirteen to twenty: the sex urge, the lust of the flesh, was so overwhelming in me that I was conscious only of desire. When the rattlesnake's poison bag is full, he strikes at everything that moves, even the blades of grass; the poor brute is blinded and in pain with the overplus. In my youth I was blind, too, through excess of semen.

I often say that I was thirty-five years of age before I saw an ugly woman, that is, a woman whom I didn't desire. In early puberty, all women tempted me; and all girls still more poignantly.

From twenty to twenty-three, I began to distinguish qualities of the mind and heart and soul; to my amazement, I preferred Kate to Lily, though Lily gave me keener sensations; Rose excited me very little, yet I knew she was of rarer, finer quality than even Sophy, who seemed to me an unequalled bedfellow.

From that time on the charm of spirit, heart and soul, drew me with ever-increasing magnetism, overpowering the pleasures of the senses, though plastic beauty exercises as much fascination over me today as it did fifty years ago. I never knew the illusion of love, the rose-mist of passion, till I was twenty-seven, and I was intoxicated with it for years; but that story will be for my second volume.

Now strange to say, my loves till I left America just taught me as much of the refinements of passion as is commonly known in these States.

France and Greece made me wise to all that Europe has to teach; that deeper knowledge, too, is for the second volume, in which I shall relate how a French girl surpassed Sophy's art, as far as Sophy surpassed Rose's ingenuous yielding.

But it was not till I was over forty and had made my second journey round the world that I learned in India and Burma all the high mysteries of sense and the profounder artistry of the immemorial East. I hope to tell it all in a third volume, together with my vision of European and world politics. Then I may tell in a fourth volume of my breakdown in health and how I won it back again and how I found a pearl of woman and learned from her what affection really means, the treasures of tenderness, sweet-thoughted wisdom and self-abnegation that constitute the woman's soul. Vergil may lead Dante through Hell and Purgatory: it is Beatrice alone who can show him Paradise and guide him to the Divine. Having learned the wisdom of women—to absorb and not to reason—having experienced the irresistible might of gentleness and soul-subduing pity, I may tell of my beginnings in literature and art, and how I won to the front and worked with my peers and joyed in their achievements, always believing my own to be better. Without this blessed conviction, how could I ever have undergone the labor or endured the shame or faced the loneliness of the Garden, or carried the cross of my own Crucifixion; for every artist's life begins in joy and hope and ends in the shrouding shadows of doubt and defeat and the chill of everlasting night.

In these books, as in my life, there should be a crescendo of interest and understanding. I shall win the ears of men first and their senses, and later their minds and hearts and finally their souls; for I shall show them all the beautiful things I have discovered in Life's pilgrimage, all the sweet and loveable things, too, and so encourage and cheer them and those aftercomers, my peers, whose sounding footsteps already I seem to hear; and I shall say as little as may be of defeats and downfalls and disgraces save by way of warning, for it is courage men need most in life, courage and loving-kindness.

It is not written in the Book of Fate that he who gives most receives most, and do we not all, if we would tell the truth, win more love than we give. Are we not all debtors to the overflowing bounty of God?

FRANK HARRIS.

The Catskill Mts., this 25th day of August, 1922.

Volume

II

Foreword

to
Volume II

THE FIRST VOLUME of my autobiography was condemned savagely from one end of the English-speaking world to the other and especially by self-styled men of letters and journalists. One would have said that I had taken the bread out of their mouths, they made such an outcry. Strangely enough, the anathemas were louder and bitterer in England than in America; but what touched me more nearly, there were two notable exceptions. Bernard Shaw wrote that he could have defended the book had it not been for the illustrations, which were for the most part photographs of pretty, naked girls*—at worst inoffensive, I should have thought. Mencken, however, the best of American critics, went further than Shaw and declared boldly in print that the sex-urge, being the chief emotion in a healthy boy, should be described plainly; at the same time expressing his belief that if I pictured my later life in London as frankly, it would be a great human document.

Two righteous in two hundred millions. I hadn't expected a much larger proportion and their quality gives me hope. To alter long-established convention is difficult and dangerous and requires time. It is now some fifty years since some of us began to question the benefits of vaccination. Alfred Russel Wallace,** Bernard Shaw and others have written and spoken against it; but the authorities, doctor-driven, made this inoculation with cow-pox compulsory and answered our reasonable arguments with force and various punishments. Yet we had right and reason on our side. Take one fact: in 1914, the last year for which we have official figures, there were four deaths from small-pox registered in Great Britain and six deaths from vaccination; to say nothing of the dozens that were not accurately reported,

---

* The deluxe edition had scattered at random through it rose-tinted photographs of unclad girls, some coy, none indecent, all of them pretty. The photographs were not of the women Harris speaks of in these volumes, but professional models. Harris' idea was to make the books attractive, if only to leaf through, and to a great extent he succeeded.

** (1819–91), the renowned naturalist whose work on natural selection supported but modified Darwin's. He wrote *Forty-five Years of Registration Statistics,* proving vaccination to be both useless and dangerous (London: W. E. Allen, 1885).

owing to the prepossession of the ordinary medical attendant. One such fact, you would think, would give any one pause. But you have men of sense and learning like Sir Henry Maine* writing that "compulsory vaccination (inoculation with cow-pox) is in the utmost danger," not because there are more deaths year after year in Great Britain from the remedy than there are from the disease but, if you please, because of "the gradual establishment of the masses in power," which is, he adds, "of the blackest omen for all legislation founded on scientific opinion." By "scientific opinion" in this case he means doctors' fees!

The childish unreason of the world fills me with fear for the future of humanity. On all sides I still hear idiotic defenses of the World War in spite of its fifty millions of untimely deaths and the consequent misery and impoverishment of our whole generation. The lying slogan, "the war to end war," has not even put an end to armaments or munition-makers. The old lies are as popular as ever and pass uncontradicted, almost unquestioned.

Science is giving us every day new powers, and with the decline of religion our morality has positively diminished, not to say disappeared. The nations are growing daily stronger and more selfish. The struggle between the nations for world empire may be said to have had its first act in the World War. It looks as if the United States and the English Confederation were sure to emerge as the most powerful; with Russia next in the race. But if the combative spirit in the individual is not repressed, there may yet be wars of annihilation wherein the present races of men may be blotted out. It is our task to form if we can a new religion or at least a new morality. And the new moral laws must be laws of health and laws of reason. We have been told a good deal about our duty to our neighbor; but first we must learn our duty to ourselves and we must study our bodies at least as carefully as our minds.

The English and American people have enormous, preponderant power, power of numbers, power of wealth, power of almost unassailable position; but who does not see that their strength is out of all proportion to their brains. They are at the head of the industrial world; but they have no corresponding position in the world of science, or art or literature. We must copy the Germans and endow scientific research; we must copy the French and endow the arts and we must certainly imitate them by freeing literature from the silly prohibitions of an outworn Puritanism. That at least is my most mature opinion, and accordingly I have taken it on myself to set the example in this field. Does anyone imagine that we can hope to produce a greater Balzac while respecting the conventions of the Sunday School and using euphemisms such as our "little Mary"?

Everyone admits today that painters and sculptors should be free to represent the naked human figure, but the moment a writer claims similar

---

* (1822–88); an historian whose best work was on the origin and development of legal and social institutions.

freedom he is boycotted and disgraced, his books are seized and burned and he may think himself lucky if he escapes fine and imprisonment. Yet the evil results of this ostrich policy are surely plain enough and well enough known. In this volume, in which I propose to tell the intimate history of half a dozen famous contemporaries, the three greatest and most famous died in the flower of manhood of syphilis and two of the three were English. In the World War more than one in four of our American officers had suffered or was suffering from this foul disease. It is bred and fostered by secrecy and prudery: Voltaire knew that "when modesty goes out of manners, (moeurs, Lat: mores) it goes into speech."

No one need read our books unless they wish to; the conventicles and churches will always be able to signify their disapprobation; but why should they be allowed to make of their prejudice a law and punish others for not rejoicing in their blindness? No one can answer Milton's plea in favor of always letting "truth grapple with falsehood."

In this matter the time-spirit is with me and all the highest authorities. In France Flaubert was prosecuted for writing and publishing *Madame Bovary*; but a generation later the *Nana* of Zola passed unpersecuted and a generation later still *La garçonne* of Victor Marguerite* was published freely.

In England too there is progress, but it is backward. Thirty years ago Burton** was allowed to publish his *Arabian Nights* privately, and send it through the post; today he would be imprisoned for the crime. Yet the greatest writers are all in favor of freedom. I want the unprejudiced to consider a few of the undoubted authorities.

One evening after dinner Goethe read to Eckermann† several scenes from *Hanswurst's Hochzeit,* or *John Sausage's Marriage,* written or at least begun in the poet's prime; Eckermann compares it with *Faust* for creative vigor and freedom; but adds at once that it goes "beyond all limits"; and he can not even give any excerpt to show its force and freedom. Goethe himself admits that he cannot publish it in Germany. "In Paris I would have been able to publish it," he adds, "but not in Frankfort or Weimar."

This shows sufficiently what Goethe's opinion on free speech was; for the limits in Germany were and are far wider than in England or America. Let me quote another and equally great writer. Here is a small part of what

---

* (1866–1942). He collaborated with his brother, Paul (1860–1918), on several books, among them *Histoire de la guerre de 1870–1871* (1903). The collaboration dissolved in 1907. *La garçonne* (1922), translated as *The Bachelor Girl,* deals with homosexuality.

** Sir Richard Francis Burton (1821–1890), noted soldier, explorer of the White Nile (with poor, neglected Speke), and translator of the unexpurgated *Arabian Nights,* as well as the author of a book on pederasty. The *Arabian Nights* is not yet on the open stacks even of university libraries, though it is hardly shocking.

† Johann Peter Eckermann (1792–1854), Goethe's Boswell in *Conversations with Goethe.*

Montaigne wrote on this subject, and Montaigne, as Sainte-Beuve* declares, is "the wisest of all Frenchmen"; I use Florio's** translation:

Non pudeat dicere quod non pudeat sentire—"Let us not be ashamed to speak what we shame not to think . . . For my part I am resolved to dare speak whatsoever I dare do. And am displeased with thoughts not to be published. The worst of my actions or conditions seem not so ugly unto me as I finde it both ugly and base not to dare to avouch them . . ." And again: "Both wee and they (men and women) are capable of a thousand more hurtfull and unnaturall corruptions than is lust or lasciviousness. But wee frame vices and weigh sinnes not according to their nature but according to our interest . . ." And still in the same chapter: "What monstrous beaste is this whom his delights displease . . ." And finally: "Few I know will snarle at the liberty of my writings that have not more cause to snarle at their thoughts-looseness."†

And not only are the greatest German and French writers on my side but also the best Americans. I have already more than once adduced Whitman's faith and practice on this subject. In spite of a strange inarticulateness I regard him as the greatest of all Americans; but Poe is continually classed with him and accordingly I am eager to give Poe's considered opinion. Here are his words:

If any ambitious man have a fancy to revolutionize at one effort the universal world of human thought, human opinion, and human sentiment, the opportunity is his own—the road to immortal renown lies straight, open, and unencumbered before him. All that he has to do is to write and publish a very little book. Its title should be simple—a few plain words—*My Heart Laid Bare*. But this little book must be true to its title.

Now, is it not singular that, with the rabid thirst for notoriety which distinguishes so many of mankind—so many, too, who care not a fig what is thought of them after death, there should not be found one man having sufficient hardihood to write this little book? To write, I say. There are ten thousand men who, if the book were once written, would laugh at the notion of being disturbed by its publication during their life, and who could not even conceive why they should object to its being published after their death. But to write it—there is the rub. No man dare write it. No man ever will dare write it. No man could write it, even if he dared. The paper would shrivel and blaze at every touch of the fiery pen!

I wonder did even Poe realize how difficult it is to tell the truth about oneself. It is not merely a question of fear, as he seems to think; the paper might shrivel and I should not care a jot. German-American mediocrities might go on prating of my "literary and moral suicide," and the American authorities might go on making bonfires of my books in public, while saving

---

* Charles Augustin Sainte-Beuve (1804–69), French literary critic.
** John Florio (c.1553–1625), an Englishman of Italian-Protestant parentage, and a tutor at Oxford. His translation of Montaigne, from which he draws his fame, appeared in 1603.
† The quotations are from *Essays*, Book III, Ch. 5, "On Some Verses of Vergil."

from the flames copies enough to fill their pockets or gratify their taste in private. What would it matter to me? But is my attempt futile? That's the question. Is it possible truly to mirror in words the whole soul of man and this magical incomprehensible mystery of a world?

I thought that if I used Truth and described the intense sex-urge of my youth simply, at the same time showing how passionately eager I have always been to learn and grow at all costs, that at any rate the porch of the temple would be significant and appealing.

My first volume taught me that Truth was a mortal enemy of Beauty. I remember once measuring the distance between the pillars of the Parthenon on the Acropolis and finding that it was never exactly the same; the pillars looked to be of equal size and at an equal distance one from the other; but it was all a delusion of our seeing and the rhythmic beauty of the colonnade is surely due to inexactitude.

Was this why Goethe wrote *Wahrheit und Dichtung**—*Fact and Fiction Out of My Life?* He saw that he could not write the naked truth and accordingly admitted the poetry?

Should I follow his example?

His autobiography is dull, even tedious; yet if he had tried to tell the truth, how fascinating it would have been. We should have known Frederika and Mignon and Madame Von Stein** and a host of other passionate women to the heart's core; even his cook-wife would have thrown new light on what was prosaic in him and German-sentimental. We should have known Goethe infinitely better and he was well worth knowing. As he himself said:

> Willst du ins Unendliche schreiten,
> Geh nur in Endlichen nach allen Seiten.†

As soon as I first read it, I knew that this was my life's motto. The fact is we men cannot deal with absolutes. Truth is not for us; pure Light we cannot even see; but a nearer and ever nearer approximation to truth should be our endeavor.

One would have thought that the World War showed the danger of our ordinary aggressive Ideal clearly enough; yet the World War and its many millions of young and vigorous lives all lost is no worse than the hating,

---

* Correctly, *Dichtung und Wahrheit* (1811–32), his literary autobiography.

** Friederike Brion, a clergyman's daughter whom Goethe loved as a boy, and who inspired some of his early poetry.

Mignon: a member of the roving theatrical company in the autobiographical *Wilhelm Meister's Lehrjahre:* her songs are a high point in German romantic poetry.

Charlotte von Stein, a young widow Goethe loved for ten years while he was privy counsellor to the duke of Weimar. She is credited with helping his development as a writer.

† One of Goethe's rhymed proverbs:
> If you would step into the infinite,
> Just go to the finite's every side.

snarling and snapping of these dachshunds, poodles and bulldogs that are now making of Europe a hell on earth! And America, the America of Whitman and Lincoln, will stand aside forsooth and fill her pockets and see injustice done!

> To man propose this test
> Thy body at its best
> How far shall that project thy Soul
> On its lone way?*

What hope is there for humanity save in confession and reform; in truth and in love. We must construct a new ideal of life and build for ourselves a new faith: the arrogant, combative, prudish ideal of the past must be finally discredited and discarded.

And if all the ways of love are beautiful to me, why should I not say so? All the girls and women I have met and loved have taught me something; they have been to me the charm and the wonder, the mystery and the romance of life. I have been from the Cape to Cairo; and from Vladikavkas to Vladivostock; but one girl has taught me more than I could find in two continents. There is more to learn and love in one woman's spirit than in all the oceans. And their bodies are as fascinating—thank God!—as their souls. And all the lessons they have taught me have been of gentleness and generosity, of loving-kindness and tender pity, of flower-soft palms and clinging lips, and the perfume of their flesh is sweeter than all the scents of Araby, and they are gracious-rich in giving as crowned queens. All that is amiable and sweet and good in life, all that ennobles and chastens, I have won from women. Why should I not sing their praises or at least show my gratitude by telling of the subtle intoxication of their love that has made my life an entrancing romance?

The soul of life to me has always been love of women and admiration of great men.

For many years only two men appealed to me as guides in life's labyrinth, Jesus and Shakespeare; twin spirits of intensest appeal; then in maturity others like Goethe and Heine, Leopardi, Keats and Blake, Nietzsche, Wagner and Cervantes, Cézanne, Monet, Rodin and a host of others; my contemporaries who taught me that they too shared my striving and were proud of their singular achievement: this admiration of great men and especially of great artists is the other side of my religion.

In the world I have made many friends and found kindness at least equal to my own; sunny days of joy and nights moonlit with mystery and no foe to be found anywhere save ignorance, no enemy save corsets, prohibitions

---

* The quotation is from Browning's *Rabbi Ben Ezra:*
> To man, propose this test—
> Thy body at its best,
> How far can that project thy soul on its lone way?

and conventions, no boredom save hypocrisy and want of thought, no God save my own love of the highest, no devil except my own appalling limitations in sympathy and feeling.

Yet the "unco guid"* tell me that this honest attempt of mine to relate in simplest words the story of my earthly pilgrimage will do harm and not good, corrupt and not fortify. They lie and they know it, or the population of the world would diminish as rapidly as it is increasing.

But one warning I must give: this, my second volume, will not be so exact and painfully true as the first for several reasons. First of all, as soon as my fears of life, the dread that I might not be able to earn a good living, had been blotted out by my success as a youth in the United States, life itself grew more fascinating to me. I realized that I could fashion it, almost at will, could travel or study as I pleased and so could develop myself almost as I wished. True, I had learned that I had dreadful, natural limitations; I could never be a great athlcte, I was not big enough; nor a first-rate shot, my eyes were astigmatic; but I believed that within certain narrow limits I could do a great deal with myself and assuredly improve my mind and heart out of recognition. I resolved to do this; but first of all I wished to keep my word to Professor Smith and spend three or four years studying in Germany and afterwards at least one year at the University of Athens; a scholar I must be, even if I were never to be learned.

Alas! life in my *Lehrjahre* was infinitely interesting to me, so I took few notes and must now trust my memory, even for important facts.

It is a paradox that may serve as a truth that an excellent memory is the source of much falsehood. In talking to my friend Professor Churton Collins** once, I found that his extraordinary and minute exactitude came from a bad memory; he could not pin a date or a fact or a line of poetry in his head and so was compelled to verify all his statements. On the other hand, I had a most excellent memory, as I have said, especially for words; but even as a young man I had found out that my memory, even of poetry or prose, was often vitiated by time. Now and then my memory altered this word or that in a poem, sometimes bettering the original; but more often debasing the word-value in favor of extra sonority. My one natural endowment, a very strong and resonant bass voice, injured my memory.

As I came to maturity I found that my memory suffered in a different way; it began to color incidents dramatically. For example, I had been told a story by someone, it lay dormant in me for years; suddenly some striking fact called back the tale and I told it as if I had been present and it was fulfilled with dramatic effects, far beyond the first narration.

I am no longer a trustworthy witness; yet more honest, I dare swear, than

* See the Burns' poem of that title.
** John Churton Collins (1848–1908), professor of English literature at Birmingham, and a prominent critic. His *Dean Swift* (1893) and his *Essays in Poetry and Criticism* (1905) are his best works.

any Rousseau or Casanova of them all. Hamlet declares he could accuse himself of dreadful faults, but takes care never to hint even at the wild sensuality and mad, baffled jealousy which he pours out in floods on his unhappy mother, who, for love of lewdness, stands to him for his faithless mistress. I intend to accuse myself of all my worst faults, for already I notice that my mind is so confirmed a partisan that if I don't put in all the shadows, there will be little likeness to humanity in my self-colored portrait. To write one's life truthfully one should keep a complete diary and record, not only facts; but motives—fears, hopes and imaginings—day by day at very considerable length. It is altogether too late for me to begin such a work; but from today on (November 22nd, 1923) I propose to keep such a careful record that when I come to this last lap of the race I may be able to put down the true truth in every particular. Yet no man's mind can mirror truth perfectly.

But whether I can tell the truth or not does not alter the fact that I mean even in this second volume to keep as near the truth as I can.

The soul of the first volume was the insane sex-urge of healthy youth and the desire to learn and grow and become someone of note in life. The inspiration of this second volume is the realization of the virtue of chastity, or, if you will, of total abstinence from all sex-pleasure for years and its effect not only upon character but upon the mind, and especially upon the creative power.

In the first period I cultivated my will a little now and then in order to make my body subservient to my intelligence; in the second period I reaped enormous benefits from this discipline.

I never dreamed then that one day in my old age I should sing the praises of chastity; but clearly enough I see now that chastity is the mother of many virtues. There's a story of Balzac that illustrates my meaning, I think it's told by Gautier.* The great novelist came in one day with a gloomy face. "What's the matter?" asked Gautier.

"Matter enough," replied Balzac; "another masterpiece lost to French literature!"

"What do you mean?" cried Gautier.

"I had a wet dream last night," Balzac replied, "and consequently shall not be able to conceive any good story for at least a fortnight; yet I could certainly write a masterpiece in that time."

I found out that the chastity must not be continued too long or one would become too susceptible to mere sensuous pleasure; the semen, so to say, would get into one's blood and affect the healthy current of one's life. But to feel drained for a fortnight after one orgasm and unable to create any thing worth while proves to demonstrate that Balzac, like Shakespeare, must have been of poor virility. Didn't Shakespeare cry at thirty-four or -five:

* Théophile Gautier (1811–72), French poet and novelist.

> Past reason hunted and no sooner had
> Past reason hated,*

an experience that few healthy men reach before fifty-five and some of us, thank God, never reach at all.

But self-control or chastity must be practiced by all who wish to realize the highest in themselves or indeed who wish to reach vigorous old age.

There are other experiences of this kind that I think just as interesting and important as Balzac's, which I propose to record in this self-history. For example, besides the merits of chastity, I was also to learn that my pleasure in the embrace was not my chief object: as love entered my life I found that the keenest thrill of ecstasy could only be reached through the delight given to your partner. Again in this I resembled Montaigne: "Verily, the pleasure I do others in this sport, both more sweetly tickle my imagination, than that is done unto me."

In this volume I shall not be as contemptuous of convention as I was in the first; but I propose to use such freedom of speech as may be necessary, and certainly as much as Chaucer and the best Frenchmen use.

After all, the final proof of the pudding is in the eating. If anyone can write as true a record of his time or paint such deep and intimate portraits of great men as I have painted, without using equal freedom of speech, he may condemn me. If no one has or can, then I am justified and in time shall be praised and my example followed.

* Sonnet CXXIX:

> Past reason hunted; and no sooner had,
> Past reason hated, as a swallowed bait, etc.

Chapter I

Skobelef*

WHEN THE RUSSIAN-TURKISH WAR broke out in the early summer of 1877, I knew at once how my summer must be spent: I had to find out by experience what modern war was like, and to learn it while getting a sight of Russia and the Balkans and perhaps Turkey seduced me: I must get to the front immediately.

With the intuition that now and then comes to English journalists when writing about war, the name of Skobelef, the conqueror of Turkestan, had been blazoned about in half a dozen sheets and had captured my Celtic fancy. I sat down and wrote to him at once in English and French, asking him to allow me to see him at work and to chronicle his doings against the Turks for some American journals. I had already got the consent of two to act as correspondent and [a] promise to pay twenty dollars a column for everything they accepted, which seemed to me, in my utter ignorance, fair enough pay. In June I was in Moscow staying at the Slavianski Bazaar and had written again to Skobelef, begging for a meeting. I soon found out, however, to my astonishment, that Skobelef was not to be commander-in-chief; [he] had indeed no official position and had gone to the seat of war, hoping to make himself useful.

The first official position he had, and this after the passing of the Danube and the investment of Plevna, was as a sort of assistant** to General Dragomirof.† But neither envy nor jealousy could keep that soaring spirit down for long. Wherever he went in the camp he was a marked man: the first thing I heard about him was an obscene jest he had made when they brought him a mare after a horse had been killed under him: "It's the female's business, you think, to be mounted by a man," he was reported to have said.

* Major General Mikhail Dimitrievich Skobelef (1843–82).
** Not quite: Skobelef had command of the 8th Corps at the crossing of the Danube; he was a lieutenant-general in command of the 16th Division at the investment of Plevna.
† General Michael Ivanovich Dragomirof (1830–1905). He commanded the 14th Division at the crossing of the Danube. After reverses at Plevna, he, with other generals, suggested a retreat into Rumania.

His contempt of convention pleased me hugely. In a few days I got presented to him and thanked him in my best, carefully prepared French for the *mot*—a shrug of the shoulders and a gleam of amusement in his eyes satisfied me. He would have been more or less than human if he could have resisted my enthusiastic admiration. Years later I was telling Lord Wolseley* about it and he said, "It all reminds me of Stanley** in my Ashanti campaign.† He came up and asked me to be allowed to accompany me: I was the only person he wanted to know, he said; but he was so self-assured and cool that I told him to go to the proper officer who had charge of the correspondents. From time to time afterwards I noticed him, always pretty close to me; but one day we fell into a sort of ambush and were almost surrounded by the savages. As their fire slackened I remarked a man in grey some forty yards in front of me and to the right; the savages were creeping round him, dodging from tree to tree, and he was in the utmost danger; but he paid no attention to them, shooting very successfully at those in front: his coolness and splendid marksmanship fascinated me. Our troops came up and the savages broke and fled. I could not resist going over to see who the marksman was. I found it was my very independent American:†† he bowed and I had to ask: 'Didn't you see that the blacks had surrounded you?'

" 'To tell the truth, General,' he remarked, brushing his knee, 'I was so occupied with the gentlemen in front that I paid no attention to the others.'

"From that moment on we were friends," Wolseley concluded, "much I imagine as Skobelef and you became friends; courage in a common danger quickly breaks down all barriers."

However that may be, Skobelef and I soon became friends. The rich humanity in him and contempt of convention were irresistibly attractive to me; and there was something ingenuous, young in him, which made him accept my enthusiastic admiration, my hero-worship, if you will, without afterthought. I have noticed this *naiveté* since in other great men of action. In person Skobelef was above middle height, broad and strong; the lower face was concealed by a thick wavy moustache, beard and whiskers all coquettishly brushed away from the center; the forehead was both broad and high, the nose thick and of Jewish type, the eyes grey and keen; nothing remarkable in the face; the impetuosity of his character showed itself in

* Lord Garnet Joseph Wolseley (1833–1913), who served in the Crimean and China wars and in the Indian Mutiny of 1857. As a field marshal he modernized the training of the British army.

** Sir Henry Morton Stanley (1841–1904), journalist and explorer, commissioned by the *New York Herald* to accompany the British expedition to Ashanti.

† Ashanti was part of the Gold Coast. The Ashanti War of 1873–74 followed the transfer of territory to the British from the Dutch.

†† Stanley was born in Wales, but after shipping as a cabinboy to New Orleans, he served in the Confederate Army and in the U.S. Navy before he joined the *New York Herald*. Surely he must have *seemed* an American.

quick abrupt movements; he always appeared ready to strike; yet underneath there was much kindness in him and a fund of good humor.

It was mid-August when he got his first real chance: he had declared a week before that the key of Plevna was a certain fort. "If we had that," he said, "we could make it hot for Osman."* By what influence he got command of a large force, I don't know, but probably through the Emperor Alexander** himself, of whom Skobelef always spoke with liking.

The troops for the assault had to cross a stream and then climb the steep glacis: it had rained heavily the night before and the long slope was slippery. As the Russians began to toil up, the Turkish fire became deafening; but at first was not effective. When the Russians however got three quarters way up, they simply lay down in files. A moment's pause for thought and Skobelef galloped into the meadow, crossed the river and was soon among the fallen Russians. Naturally I was at his heels. Here the Turkish fire was diabolical; I noticed that it had cut down all the bushes near us to a certain height; I couldn't understand why; but Skobelef read the riddle almost immediately; swinging his horse round, he galloped back and gave orders that the men should advance in lines with a hundred yards or so between each line. When the first wave of men reached their fallen comrades, it too seemed to lie down—the Turkish fire was extraordinarily deadly; but the next wave got through and lined up close to the fortress; the third wave again got blotted out; but the fourth pressed on and joined the first line; at once Skobelef galloped up the glacis again and himself led the assault amid the frantic cheers of the men now racing to the redoubt. In his haste Skobelef fell into the ditch and had to be helped free of his horse; but though he was badly shaken and bruised and the officers begged him to go back, he wouldn't listen to them, and as we entered the fort, we saw the Turks stampeding down the other side.

A glance at the wall made the Turkish rifle practice clear to me: in order not to expose themselves, the Turkish soldiers had simply placed their rifles on the embrasures and fired away. About five hundred yards down the hill the bullets rained about four feet from the ground. This was the death-zone; a few hundred yards further down the bullets went into the air, three hundred yards higher up they whistled harmlessly overhead. When galloping up the slope Skobelef had noticed that the danger-zone was very narrow and at once seized the whole position and dealt with it victoriously.

But he had reckoned without his leaders. As soon as he had distributed the Russian soldiers in the fort, he sent for reinforcements; but none came, no word of answer even to his entreaties. He had won Plevna—the commanding position of the redoubt now would have been clear to a child, but he had lost heavily and had not men enough to sustain an attack in force. The night began to draw down; it was after three o'clock before we got

---

* (1832–1900), a Turkish pasha and field-marshal. The Russians lost 30,000 men assaulting his position at Plevna.
** Alexander II; he reigned from 1855–81.

settled in the fort and darkness came slowly, but it came; time and again Skobelef sent for reinforcements; at length he received the information that none could be spared.

We were told afterwards that the Tzar himself had urged the general to send the reinforcements but was assured that none could be spared, though it was sun-clear that out of two hundred thousand troops on the field it would have been easy to detach twenty thousand, and a quarter of that force sent to Skobelef would have won Plevna that day in August.

When Skobelef was convinced that no help would be sent, he seemed stunned with the disappointment; then rage possessed him, his whole face quivered, tears rolled down his cheeks unheeded while he raved in contempt of his superiors: "The grand dukes hate me," he cried, "and the general staff because I win victories, but who is to hinder them coming in force themselves and getting the credit—who cares for the credit so long as the work's done—oh damn them, damn them and their mean jealousy; they can't spare even five thousand men, the liars and curs!"

That night a couple of his officers sat with him and we all drank and discussed probabilities. As it turned out, Skobelef read his adversary Osman more correctly than any of us.

"When we don't shell them in the morning," he said, "Osman must come to the conclusion that we are weak and he'll feel us out with an early attack; then we shall have to prepare to get out; but if I had five thousand men and fifty field guns—just what I asked for—I could win Plevna by noon: Osman would have to surrender. The silly envy of our commanders will cost Russia half a million lives and prolong the war six months!" Skobelef taught me that putting yourself in your adversary's place was the essence of generalship. I remember when we were alone he turned to me.

"Don't report anything of all this," he said. "No Russian would expose Russian shame; it is as if our mother were in fault, and I don't want the d——d Germans to sneer. Ah, if I could only get a chance against them, I'd show them that our Russian soldiers are the best in the world, incomparable—" and he went on to give instance after instance of their hardihood and contempt of death.

It fell out almost exactly as Skobelef had foreseen; but later. It was long after noon when the Turkish soldiers attacked; we had difficulty in holding our own; an hour later Osman threw thirty thousand men more at us and we had to retreat; in an hour the retreat was a stampede and for hours driblets of broken men came limping, staggering and cursing into their previous quarters.

Next day Skobelef kept to his rooms. I noticed at once that his reputation had grown immensely: his own officers all knew what he had accomplished and when officers from other commands came to him, they all showed themselves aware of his supreme ability. The fine thing about him was that all the respect and indeed adulation had not the slightest effect on him;

when we met afterwards he always treated me with a certain kindly intimacy.

Of course nothing could save Plevna: army corps after army corps joined the Russian force, the Turkish communications were cut, Plevna was surrounded: months later Osman surrendered and was nobly received by Skobelef, whom everybody hailed now as the hero of Plevna. Osman riding at the head of his garrison of nearly 100,000 men was a fine sight: he was small and pale and had one arm in a sling from a recent wound, and as he passed at the head of his staff through the Russian ranks, the Russians, led by Skobelef himself, cheered and cheered him again in the noblest way. War is almost worth waging when it brings such honorable distinction to the beaten.

But though I learned a good deal in the war, I'm not here to compete with the professional historian. I want to picture Skobelef, who was, with Roberts,* the best general I ever met; and the contrast between the two makes them both more interesting. Neither of them was highly intelligent. In the Boer War, Roberts went to church every Sunday and observed all ordinary customs. He was a sincere Christian and followed the lead of his wife in all social affairs. At first he took Kitchener** at his face value, and even when at Paardeberg he was forced to realise his nonentity as a soldier, he kept his knowledge to himself for so long that he gave some support to the Kitchener myth. Skobelef, on the other hand, was altogether free of every form of snobbism; indeed, he had a certain sympathy with contempt of discipline and all social observances; some part of "the return to truth" of the nihilists had got into his blood; he hated all insincerities and in so far seemed to me a bigger man than Roberts. In insight and speed of stroke they were very much alike.

In the days of inaction that followed the taking and abandonment of the fort, I won Skobelef to tell me of his early life. With huge amusement he confessed that at fourteen or fifteen he was after every pretty girl he came near. One day an uncle found him trying to embrace a young servant in the house; she had just pushed the boy away when the uncle came on the scene. He said quietly, "You ought to be proud to be kissed, my girl, by the young baron."

"I had no more difficulty," Skobelef said simply, "the news spread through the house like wildfire, and I had no more refusals."

Nothing ever brought the true meaning of serfdom more clearly before

* Frederick Sleigh Roberts (1832–1914), Earl of Kandahar, Pretoria, and Waterford, and a field-marshal. He headed the British forces in South Africa during the Boer War and in 1901 succeeded Lord Wolseley as commander-in-chief of the British Army.
** Horatio Herbert Kitchener (1850–1916), a field-marshal. Kitchener was Robert's chief-of-staff during the Paardeberg campaign and succeeded him as commander-in-chief of the British Army in 1900. Kitchener took over the War office at the outbreak of war in 1914. He was lost with all other hands off the Orkneys when the H.M.S. *Southampton* struck a mine.

me than this little incident. It was as illuminating as a phrase of Kropotkin*
later, when in his *Memoirs of a Revolutionist* he tells of the "Oriental
practices" in the corps of pages and the countless immoralities and devilish
cruelties that reigned during serfdom. Some facts tell volumes. When a
soldier or servant was punished by flogging, if he died under the knout, the
full tale of lashes was inflicted on his unsentient corpse. And marriage
among the serfs was often arranged by the master without any regard for
love or individual preference.

"Did you go often with your pretty maid?" I asked.

"Continually," Skobelef laughed, "and when it wasn't that one, it was
one of the others. I had them all, every girl and woman in the place from
thirteen to fifty, but I liked the older ones best," he added meditatively. "If
I had not had to go to school, I'd have killed myself with them; as it was I
weakened myself so that now, at about forty, I'm practically impotent.
Since I was five and twenty it takes some extraordinary circumstance, such
as a drinking bout, to bring me up to the scratch!"

"Good God!" I cried. "What a dreadful fate!" Till then I had no idea
that the patrimony of sex-pleasure was so limited. "You must have been
angry with yourself and regretted your early indulgences terribly?" I
probed.

"No," he replied, "No! I've had a pretty good time on the whole; and if
I took double mouthfuls as a boy, as the French say, I have now many
sweet memories. Oh, in Petersburg as a young man I had golden hours;
there I met veritable passion, desire to match my own, and an understanding of life, a resolve to do great things and not be hampered by conventions—I remember my love let me have her, one day, in her dressing room,
when everyone was ready to go driving; and they called and called her—
Ah, life's victorious moments are *all* we get!"

The whole confession was out of my very heart, only I was resolved to
be wiser and make the pleasure last longer.

Two little scenes of this campaign made an impression on me. It was
after the capture of a town called Lovtcha, I think: Skobelef and his staff
came upon a lot of wounded Turks who had been dumped on the wayside
by their comrades days before, men dying and dead, the wounded curled
up in a hundred attitudes. Skobelef told the interpreter to ask them what
they'd like before being taken to the field hospital; they all asked for food,
but one big Turk with head all bandaged up asked for a cigarette. At once
Skobelef leant down from his horse and offered his own cigarette case. The
Turk took it, an officer gave him a match, and he puffed out the smoke with
an air of ineffable content. And then by way of return he undid the knot of
his bandage and began to unwind the dirty linen that covered his head. In

---

* Peter Alexeivich Kropotkin (1842–1921). He was of noble birth and inherited
the title of "Prince." He entered the Corps of Pages at 15 and served in it for five
years, after which he joined the army. At 25 he entered the university, joined the
revolutionary party, and soon became a nihilist. His *Memoirs* were published in 1900.

spite of Skobelef's gesture and prayer not to do it, he went on, and as the last fold was plucked loose, in spite of the sticky blood, the man's half-jaw fell on his chest. The other half had evidently been taken off by a shell—a most horrible sight—but the Turk smiled, held his half-jaw up and began winding on the linen bandage again. When he had secured it, in went the cigarette again into his mouth and he smiled up at us his liveliest gratitude. "Fine men," said Skobelef, "great soldiers!" And they were—and are!

One more scene. As an Englishman I managed to get down to Adrianople long before the Russian troops. I wanted to see Constantinople and the Turks before resuming work. At one station, I forget its name, I had to stay a day or two. The caravanserai was a miserable makeshift: one morning I heard that some Russian prisoners had been brought in and I went out and found a line of them outside the station sitting on benches and guarded by half a dozen Turks; one gigantic Turk marched up and down in front of the poor captives, scowling and muttering. I told the interpreter who was with me to go off and find a Turkish officer or the Russians would be murdered; he ran off at once. Suddenly the big Turk stopped in front of a bearded Russian at one end of the line, seized him by the beard and hair, wrenched his mouth open, and spat down his throat—I never saw such a gesture of hate and savage rage. My blood boiled, but I could do nothing except pray for the coming of some officer. Fortunately one came in time, and the poor Russians were saved.

I never saw Skobelef after that fall, but he remains to me as a splendid memory and I shall tell now of his end. I was praising him one day in London when a Russian officer who was in the Russian embassy told me how he died.

"You know he was our hero," he began. "There are more photographs of Skobelef in our peasant homes throughout Russia than even of the Tzar. And his end was wonderful: he had come to Moscow to review a couple of army corps; as usual, after the review, when he was very severe on some officers, he asked a lot of us junior ones to dine with him in the Slavianski Bazaar; to take away the sting of his sharp criticism, I fancy. Of course we all turned up, proud as peacocks at being asked, and we had a great feast.

"Afterwards someone suggested that we should adjourn to Madame X's, who had a house in a neighboring street. Nothing loath, Skobelef, to our astonishment, consented and we all went round, picked our girls and disappeared into bedrooms. After midnight I heard a mad screaming, and just as I was I opened my door and found in the passage the girl Skobelef had chosen. 'The General is dead!' she cried.

" 'Dead!' I yelled. 'What do you mean? Lead the way,' and back she took me, sobbing hysterically, to her bedroom. There lay Skobelef, motionless, with eyes wide open, staring at the ceiling; I called him, put my hand and then my ear on his heart. It had stopped. I looked at the girl. 'It wasn't my fault' she cried. 'Really, it wasn't!'

"I hastened back to my bedroom and dressed myself hurriedly; already every officer was up; we went to the keeper of the brothel and said we must take the general at once back to the Slaviansky Bazaar, his hotel. But the keeper said, 'It's forbidden: the police regulation prevents it; you must first get permission!' At once a couple of us rushed downstairs and drove to the police headquarters, but even there we could do nothing. Only the governor of Moscow, it seemed, could give us the permission. So off we raced to the palace. As ill-luck would have it, the governor was at his villa outside the town, so we had to take a droshky and drive like mad. At about three in the morning we knocked him up, got the necessary permission, and hurried back to the brothel.

"The General was cold and stiff: it was incredibly difficult to dress him, but it had to be done; and then my friend took him by one arm and I by the other and we half-led, half-carried him out to the carriage. Neither of us had thought of the time. Alas! It was already day and to our astonishment the news had got out and the streets were crowded with people. As soon as they saw us half-carrying Skobelef, they all knelt down on the sidewalk and in the street, the dear people, and crossing themselves began to pray for the rest of his soul!*

"It was through a kneeling crowd that we took our hero to the Slaviansky Bazaar and laid him on his bed. And the piety of the Russian people is such, its admiration of greatness so profound, that the story has never got out or been in print. Do you wonder that some of us always think of our fatherland as Holy Russia?"

As I listened to this story, the great words of Blake came into my mind, the final word for all of us mortals:

> And throughout all Eternity
> I forgive you, you forgive me:
> As our dear Redeemer said
> This is the wine and this is the bread.**

* The usual account is that Skobelef died of heart disease in a Moscow hotel.
** From Blake's *Notebook*, "My spectre around me." (*Complete Writings of William Blake*, Geoffrey Keynes, editor, London, 1957.)

Chapter II

How I Came to Know Shakespeare
and German Student Customs

WHY I WENT TO HEIDELBERG and not to Berlin to study I can't say; there was a touch of romance in the name which probably drew me. I had over fifteen hundred pounds in the bank and thought it would keep me five years and allow me to return to the States to begin my life's work with at least a thousand pounds in my pocket. But was I going back to America? I had to confess to myself that the malarial fever in the States daunted me; besides I liked England better and so put off any decision. Already the proverb influenced me: not to cross a river till you come to it.

Heidelberg fascinated me; I loved its beauty, the great forest-clad hills about it, its river, its ruined castle, its plain, business-like university, its Cafe Leer, its bookshops—everything. I went to the Hotel de l'Europe for a week and found it expensive; but the Rhine wines are delicious and not dear: the Marcobrunner and Liebfraumilch of ten years of age taught me what scent and flavor wine could possess.

On the river I got to know a couple of young Americans, Treadwell by name, with whom I soon struck up a friendship. I had gone to the riverside hoping to get a boat for a row: a stalwart young fellow was just paying for his canoe. "*Kann ich?*" I hesitated, pointing to his skiff. "*Ja wohl!*" was the loud genial answer. "But you're an Englishman?" he added in English. "American rather," I replied, and my acquaintance soon confided to me that he and his younger brother had been brought up in a German school and that he was studying chemistry and was already an assistant of the celebrated Professor Bunsen,* the man who first discovered the chemical composition of the stars and the inventor of the spectroscope. Here were wonders! I was on fire to learn more, to meet Bunsen. "Could I?" "Surely!" I thrilled.

This elder Treadwell was a personable fellow, perhaps five feet nine in height and evidently vigorous, clean-shaven, with strong features and alert expression; but I soon discovered that in spite of his knowledge of quanti-

---

*Robert Wilhelm von Bunsen (1811–1899); inventor of the Bunsen burner; but his greatest achievements were in spectrum analysis.

tative and qualitative analysis, he was not intellectual in my understanding of the word. His younger brother, who had just entered the university to continue the study of philology, pleased me more. He was about my own size and learned already in Latin and Greek, German and French; thoughtful, too, with indwelling grey eyes. "A fine mind," I concluded, "though immature," and we soon became friends. Through him I went to live in a pension where he and his brother boarded and where my living cost me less than a pound a week. The living was excellent because the pension was kept by a large motherly Englishwoman, widow of a German professor, who was a *maitresse femme* of the wisest and kindliest.

There I met a Mr. Onions* who had won all sorts of honors in Oxford and who soon became a sort of pal, for he, too, loved literature as I did and seemed to me inconceivably clever; for he wrote brilliant Latin and Greek verses and in three months had mastered German, though he didn't speak it well. Onions confessed that he studied German three of four hours every morning, so I did the same and gave three or four more hours to it every afternoon. One day he astonished and pleased me by saying that I must have a genius for languages, for my German was already better than his. At any rate I spoke it more fluently; for I talked it whenever I got the opportunity while he was rather silent.

Naturally young Treadwell introduced me to the university; I took all his lectures and worked night and day to the limiting of sleep and exercise. In three months I spoke German fluently and correctly and had read Lessing,** Schiller, Heine's *Lieder,* and all the ordinary novels, especially *Soll und Haben.*†

But I had not won much from the university lectures. I had heard one set of lectures on the Greek verb; but after two months the professor was still enmeshed in Sanskrit, and as I did not know a word of Sanskrit or its significance, I found it difficult to follow him. I was indeed continually reminded of Heine's experience. He had been hearing lectures on universal history, he tells us, but after three years' assiduous attendance he gave them up, for the professor had not yet reached the time of Sesostris.

Kuno Fischer†† was at this time perhaps the most popular professor in Heidelberg: he had announced a series of lectures on Shakespeare and Goethe and the *aula* was crammed not only by students, but by ladies and gentlemen from the town. Fischer had a face like a bulldog's and his nose had been split in a duel, which increased the likeness; he began by calling Shakespeare and Goethe the twin flowers of the Germanic race; I was still English enough to think the phrase almost a blasphemy, so I rubbed my feet loudly on the floor as a sign of disapproval or disagreement (*ich scharrte*).

---

* Charles Talbut Onions (1873–   ), on the editorial staff of the Oxford English Dictionary and editor of the *Shorter OED*.
** Gotthold Ephraim Lessing (1729–81), dramatist and critic.
† By Gustav Freytag (1816–95).
†† (1824–1907), professor of philosophy and German literature at Heidelberg.

Fischer paused in utter surprise (it was the first time, he told me afterwards, that he had ever been so interrupted): then, putting a manifest constraint on himself, he said: "If the gentleman who disagrees with me so emphatically will wait till I have finished, I will ask him to state the ground of his disapproval." There was applause throughout the audience at this and the men who were in my neighborhood glared at me in angry surprise.

Fischer went on to say that "the very name of Shakespeare showed his Teutonic ancestry; he was as German as Goethe."

I smiled to myself, but I could not deny that the rest of the lecture was interesting, though the professor hardly attempted to realize either man. At the end he contrasted their schooling and congratulated his hearers on the fact that Goethe had enjoyed far superior educational opportunities and had turned them to brilliant account. The audience applauded enthusiastically as he sat down. Fischer, however, rose again immediately and holding out his hand for silence added: "If the critic who made his disagreement at the beginning of my lecture so manifest now desires to explain, I'm sure we will hear him willingly."

I got up and stammered a little, as if embarrassed, while asking the audience and the professor to excuse my faulty German. But as a Welsh Celt, I said, "What I feel is that the eloquent Professor is overpraising the Teutons and especially their superior education. Superior!" I repeated; "Shakespeare has given us the drama of first love in *Romeo and Juliet* and of mature passion in *Antony and Cleopatra,* of jealousy in *Othello,* the malady of thought in *Hamlet* and madness in *Lear;* and against these Goethe has given *Faust* alone as a proof of his 'superior' advantages!

"But 'Shake' and 'speare' are Teuton, we are told. Now English is an amalgam of low German and of French; but curiously enough, all the higher words are French and only the poor monosyllables are Teuton; for example, mutton is French while "sheep" or "schaf" is pure German. I had always imagined," I added after a pause, "that 'Shakespeare' was plainly taken from the French and was a manifest corruption of 'Jacques Pierre' " —at this the audience began to titter and Fischer, entering into the joke, clapped his hands, smiling. Naturally, my effect achieved, I sat down at once.

As I was leaving the hall Fischer's servant came and told me the professor would like to see me in his room; of course I followed him at once and Fischer met me laughing. "*Ein genialer Streich!* A genial invention," he said, "and no worse than many of our etymologies," and then seriously, "You made an admirable defence of Shakespeare, though I think Goethe has a good deal more to his credit than *Faust.*"

This is what I remember of the beginning of a talk destined to alter my whole life. When I told Fischer of the to me incomprehensible lectures on the Greek verb and other similar difficulties, he asked about my studies and then told me that most of the American students in Germany were not sufficiently well-grounded in Latin and Greek to make the most of the advantages offered them in a German university. Finally, he advised me strongly to shave off my moustache and go for a year into a gymnasium —school again for me, at twenty odd! My whole nature revolted wildly; yet Fischer was insistent and persuasive. He asked me to his house, introduced me to a Professor Ihne,* who had been a teacher of the Kaiser's children or something very honorable, and who talked excellent English. He agreed with Fischer and Fischer won the day by remarking: "Harris has brains; his speech taught us all that, and you'll agree that the more talent he has, the more necessary is a thorough grounding." The end of it was that I consented, left my boarding-house, went to live with a family, attended the gymnasium regularly and buried myself in Latin and Greek for eight or ten months, during which I worked on an average twelve hours a day.

In four or five months I was among the best in the gymnasium: indeed, only one boy was indisputably above me. When a Latin theme was set, he used to write 'Livy' or 'Tacitus' or 'Caesar' at the head and never used an idiom or a word that he could not show in the special author he was imitating. Twice a week at least the professor used to read out his essay to us, emphasizing the most characteristic sentences. Of course I became friends with the youth, Carl Schurz;** I was resolved to find out how he had gained such mastery. He said, " 'Twas easy"; he had begun with Caesar, and after reading a page tried to turn it back into Caesar's language; his Latin, he soon found, was all wrong, a mere mishmash, so he began to learn all the peculiar phrases in his daily lesson in Caesar; gradually he discovered that every writer had his own peculiar way of speaking, and even his own vocabulary.

That gave me the cue. I went home and took up my Shakespeare. I had already noticed similarities between *Hamlet* and *Macbeth;* now I began to read for them and incidentally learned all the poetic passages by heart. Soon I began to catch the accent of Shakespeare's voice, hear when he spoke from the heart, and when from the lips; glimpses of his personality grew upon me, and one day I sat down to rewrite *Hamlet,* using my memory and thought. When I came to the scene in which Hamlet reproaches his guilty mother, I became aware of a Shakespeare I had dimly suspected. Visualizing the scene I saw at once how impossible it would be to write it. No man could possibly reproach his mother in that way. Hamlet was using the language of sex-jealousy:* my mother's infidelity would never have maddened me. I could not judge her temptation or my father's faults towards her. His goodness would make her sinning the more incomprehensible, and Hamlet's mother does not attempt to justify herself or explain. The ray of light came, inevitable, soul-revealing: Shakespeare was painting

---

* Professor Wilhelm Ihne (1821–1902), a German historian. He went to England as a private tutor in 1847 and after two years of teaching became headmaster of a school at Liverpool. He returned to Germany in 1863 and in his last years was at Heidelberg. He was not a tutor to the Kaiser's children.

** But this is neither Carl Schurz (1829–1906), who was by now an American statesman, nor his son, Carl Lincoln Schurz (1871–1924) who did not study at Heidelberg until 1900.

his own jealousy, and was raging not at his mother's sin, but at his love's betrayal; 'twas clear, every outburst reeked with sex. Who was it that had deceived Shakespeare and crazed him with jealousy? Who? The riddle began to intrigue me.

In the long vacation which I spent in Fluelen on the Lake of Lucerne, I read and reread Shakespeare. It was his *Richard the Second* that revealed him to me unmistakably; Richard was so plainly a younger, more unstable Hamlet, just as Posthumus and Prospero were older, staider Hamlets. I hugged myself for the discovery; why hadn't everyone seen the truth? Time and again I read him and all manner of sidelights fell on the page, till the very fashion of his soul became familiar to me.

Long before Tyler's* book appeared and discovered Queen Elizabeth's maid of honor, Mary Fitton, as Shakespeare's mistress, I knew that in 1596 he had fallen in love with a dark gipsy [sic], with fair skin, who treated him with disdain and was both witty and loose. Why else should he let Rosaline be thus minutely described in *Romeo and Juliet,* though she never appears on the stage, while there's not a word of bodily description about Juliet, the heroine?

In the same year, too, he revised *Love's Labour's Lost* at Christmas to be played at Court, and the heroine was Rosaline again, and every character in the piece describes her physically; and Shakespeare himself as Biron rages against his love for "a whitely wanton with two pitch balls in her face for eyes!" I could not but see, too, that she was the Dark Lady of the *Sonnets*—probably some lady of the court, I used to say, who looked down on Shakespeare from the height of aristocratic birth and breeding.

Strange to say, I did not at that time go on to identify her with "false Cressid" or with Cleopatra. I did not get as far as this till I fell across Tyler's book years later and saw that he had confined Shakespeare's passion to the "three years" spoken of in the sonnets. I knew then that Shakespeare had loved his gipsy, Mary Fitton, from the end of 1596 on; and I soon came to see that the story told in the sonnets was told also in his plays of that period; and finally I was forced to realize that "false Cressid" and the gipsy Cleopatra were also portraits of Mary Fitton, whom he loved for twelve years down to 1608, when she married and left London for good.

I shall always remember those great months spent in Fluelen, when I climbed all the mountains about the lake and twice walked over the St. Gothard and lived with "gentle Shakespeare's" sweet spirit and noble fairness of mind.

One important result this discovery of Shakespeare had upon me; it strengthened my self-esteem enormously. I picked up Coleridge's essays on Shakespeare and saw that his Puritanism had blinded him to the truth

---

* Thomas Tyler (1826–1902). In 1886, Tyler and a collaborator, W. A. Harrison, intimated that Mary Fitton was the "Dark Lady" of the *Sonnets*. Tyler elaborated the idea in his edition of *Shakespeare's Sonnets* (1890), and replied to his critics in *The Herbert-Fitton Theory: A Reply* (1898). Harris doubtless refers to this last work.

and I began to think that in time I might write something memorable. When the time came to go back to work I returned to Heidelberg, entered again at the university and resolved to read no more Latin except Tacitus and Catullus. I knew there were beautiful descriptions in Vergil, but I didn't like the language and saw no reason for prolonging my study of it in seminar if I could get out of it.

My next lesson in German life was peculiar. I was walking in one of the side streets with an English boy of fourteen or so who was living with Professor Ihne, when we met a tall young corps-student who pushed me roughly off the sidewalk into the street. "What a rude brute," I said to my companion.

"No, no!" the boy cried in wild excitement, "All he did was to *rempeln* you!"

"What does that mean?" I asked.

"It's his way of asking you, will you fight?"

"All right," I cried, and ran back after my rude gentleman. As I came up he stopped.

"Did you push me on purpose?" I asked.

"I believe I did," he replied haughtily.

"Then guard yourself," I said, and next moment I had thrown my stick into the gutter and hit him as hard as I could on the jaw. He went down like a log and lay where he fell. Just as I bent over him to see whether he was really hurt, there poured out from all the near-by shops a crowd of excited Germans. One, I remember, was a stout butcher who ran across the street and caught hold of my left arm: "Run and fetch the police," he cried to his assistant; "I'll hold him."

"Let go!" I said to him. "He told me he had pushed me on purpose."

"I saw you," exclaimed the butcher. "You hit him with the stick; how else could you have knocked him senseless?"

"If you don't let go," I said, "and keep your hands to yourself, I'll show you."

And as he tried to increase his grip, I pushed him into proper position with my left arm, at the same time hitting him as hard as I could on the point of the jaw with my free right hand. Down he went like a sackfull of coal; the crowd gave way with much loud cursing and my little companion and myself went on our way.

"How strong you must be!" was his first remark.

"Not especially," I replied, mock modest, "but I know where to hit and how to hit."

I thought the matter finished and done with, for I had seen the student get up hugging his jaw and knew there was no serious damage; but next morning I was in my rooms reading when six German policemen came to the door and took me away with them to a judge. He questioned me and I answered; the case against me would have been dismissed, I was told, had it not been for the butcher's lie that he saw me strike the student with my stick and the stick was found to be loaded. No German of that time could believe that a blow with the fist of a rather small man could be so effective. The student's face was bound up as if his jaw had been broken. The result was I was bound over to come up for trial; and in due time I was tried and convicted of *groben Unfugs auf der Strasse,* or, as one would say in English, "a rude assault on the street," and sentenced to six weeks in Carcer and dismissal from the university.

Chapter III

German Student Life and Pleasure

MY LIFE IN CARCER, the student prison, was simply amusing. Thanks to my "tips" to the jailors and Kuno Fischer's kind words about me to the authorities, I saw friends who visited me from ten in the morning till seven at night; and after that I had lights in my room and could read or write till midnight. My friends, especially my English and American friends, took pleasure in bringing with them all sorts of delicacies, and so my meals ordered from a near-by restaurant became feasts. I used to let down a stout string from my barred window and draw up bottles of Rhine wine; in fact, I lived like a "fighting cock," to use the good English phrase, and had nothing to complain of save want of exercise. But the detention strengthened curiously my dislike of what men speak of as justice. At the trial the student whom I had knocked down told the truth, that he had pushed me rudely and on purpose off the sidewalk without any provocation; but the judge tried to believe the butcher, who swore that I had used my stick on the student, though he admitted that I had struck him with my fist. The boy who accompanied me told the exact truth; everyone expected I'd get off with a caution, but my ignorance of German insults and how to accept them got me six weeks' confinement. And when I came out, I had to leave Heidelberg and was not allowed even to finish the lectures I had paid for. I had already been turned out of the University of Kansas and now out of Heidelberg. But Kuno Fischer and other professors remained my very good friends. Fischer advised me to go to Goettingen, "a purely German university," and hear the lectures of Lotze,* who was, he said, among the best German philosophers of the time, and he gave me letters that ensured my immediate admission.

Goettingen had many and special attractions for me, partly because it was famous for the best German in accent and in choice of words, partly because Bismarck and Heine had studied there—and already both these men were throned high in my admiration—Bismarck for qualities of character, Heine for intellect and humor. Already the essence of my religion was to learn to know great men and if possible understand their virtues and powers. So I migrated to Goettingen. But before telling of anything that

---

* Rudolph Hermann Lotze (1817–1881), who helped found the science of physiological psychology in combating the doctrine of "vitalism."

happened to me there, I must say something of my amusements in the summer months I had passed in Heidelberg.

I had tasted all the English and German pleasures: I had rowed on the river nearly every day keeping myself physically fit, and had taken long walks to the Koenigstuhl and all over the neighboring hills. I had learned a good deal of German music through going to the opera at Mannheim and hearing my American fellow student, Waldstein, praise Wagner and the other masters by the hour, while exemplifying their work at the same time on his piano. I had a fair acquaintance with German poetry and novels, though I had resolved not to try to read Goethe till I knew German as well as I knew English, and strange to say, I underrated Heine, in spite of the fact that I knew half his poems by heart and took delight in his *Reisebilder*. But the German opinion of the time placed Schiller infinitely higher and I sucked in the nonsense dutifully. Indeed, it was years before I placed Heine as far above Schiller in thought as the poet is generally above the rhetorician: and it took years more before I began to couple Heine with Goethe; and [a] quarter of a century passed before I realized that Heine was a better writer of prose than even Goethe and the greatest humorist that ever lived. Common opinion about great men is so wildly beside the mark that even I could not free myself from its bondage for half a lifetime. My steadily growing admiration of Heine has often made me excuse the false estimates of other men and taught me to be more patient of their misjudgings than I otherwise should have been. I was over fifty years of age myself before I began to recognize the myriad manifestations of genius with immediate certitude. I thank fortune that I wrote none of my portraits till I had climbed the height.

But I began my acquaintance with Wagner and Bach, Mozart and Beethoven, Schiller and Heine here in Heidelberg and was delighted to find my heaven lit by such radiant new stars.

My sex-life in Heidelberg was not by any means so rich. While I was learning the language I had few opportunities of flirting and I had already found out that my tongue was my best recommendation to girls.

Before I begin to tell of my sex experiences in Heidelberg, I must relate an incident that was vital with results for me. While a master at Brighton College I had got to know Dr. Robson Roose* quite intimately, and when dining at his house with men only one evening, the conversation came on circumcision. I was astonished when a surgeon who was present declared that the small proportion of Jews who were syphilized owed their comparative immunity to circumcision, which hardened the skin of the man's sex. "Syphilis is only caught through the abrasion of the cuticle," he explained. "Harden the cuticle by exposure and you make it more difficult to catch the disease. All the morality of the Old Testament," he continued, "is hygienic: the Mosaic laws of morals were all laws of health."

"It would be wise, then, for all of us to get circumcised?" I asked, laugh-

---

* Dr. Edward Charles Robson Roose (1848–1905), a fashionable physician.

ing; and he replied: "If I were a lawgiver I would make it one of the first commandments." Immediately I made up my mind to get circumcised. I felt sure, too, that the hardening of the cuticle would prolong the act, and already I had begun to notice that in my case the act was usually too quickly finished. Moreover, my power of repeating it was decreasing year by year and in the same proportion the desire to prolong the pleasure was growing keener; for in this, too, I was like Montaigne, who had to admit in that wonderful fifth chapter of the third book that he was "faulty in suddaineness" and had "to stay the fleeting pleasure and delay it with preambles." He loved to lie, as he puts it, "at Racke and Manger," for these "snatches and away marre the grace of it."

As soon, then, as my work at Brighton College was finished I went to bed and was circumcised. Though the surgeon had assured me that I'd feel no pain, I felt a good deal, and for ten days after was in misery many times each day, for a chance touch of my organ caused me acute suffering. During my first summer months in Heidelberg my prepuce contracted so that the act would have been difficult besides being painful, and this compulsory chastity taught me the most important lesson of my life.

It taught me that absolutely complete chastity enabled me to work longer hours than I had ever worked: it was impossible to tire myself; in fact, I was endowed, so to speak, with an intense energy that made study a pleasure and with a vivid clearness of understanding such as I had never before experienced. At first I thought there must be some virtue in the climate; but one wet-dream made me realize that the power was in the pent-up semen. I began to make up my mind to sacrifice many pleasures in the future in order to keep this intense energy and sense of abounding vigor. I recognized that I had been all too often the spoil of opportunity and very frequently had sought pleasure when I was not even really in love. Time and again, too, I had given myself out of false vanity when I would rather have restrained myself. In fine, I began at this time to make up my mind only to sacrifice my strength when I was really attracted, or better still, only then when I was deeply in love. I would cease playing the fool, I resolved; I had acted the giddy idiot who squanders his patrimony without any understanding of its value; I would now turn over a new leaf and make an art of life.

How had I been so blind, so foolish! I realized that I had already seriously diminished my capital of vigor, so to speak. In Brighton I had found it difficult to have two embraces in succession, whereas five years before at eighteen there was hardly any limit set. I resolved to restrain myself rigorously and get back to my former vigor, if indeed it were in any way possible.

From this time on I date my *Lehrjahre,* as the Germans call the prentice-years. I came to see later that I owed my salvation to the chance of circumcision, or as my vanity put it, to the desire to make myself as perfect as possible, which was the reason why I had undergone the pain of the operation.

A word of Goethe came to me fraught with significance to mark this crisis: *In der Beherrschung zeigt sich erst der Meister* (In self-control the master reveals himself.)

Two experiences at Heidelberg illustrate for me this new attitude towards life.

I had met a rather pretty girl on the river bank one day; began a conversation with her and accompanied her to her house, where, she told me, she lived with a sister. It was getting dark and in a shady place I kissed her, and when she kissed me, warmly my naughty hand found its way up her clothes, and I found her sex ready for the embrace.

Already this fact warned and chilled me: I was resolved never to go with any public woman; determined to pay, but restrain myself. In the sitting-room she introduced me to her elder sister, who was chatting with a stout student who had just called.

We all fraternized quickly. I soon ordered a bottle of Rhine-wine; the student preferred beer and soon betrayed himself as a most enthusiastic admirer of Kuno Fischer. Suddenly he said, "You know, Marthe and I are great friends," and he indicated the elder sister, "and I came here tonight to make love to her."

"Go to it," I said. "I won't balk you: if I disturb you, I'll go."

"You don't disturb us, does he Marthe?" and he suited the action to the word by getting up and leading the girl to the sofa at the side of the room.

"Go into the bedroom!" cried my girl, Kätchen, and Marthe followed her advice.

They were ten minutes gone, but their proximity seemed to affect Kätchen, who kissed me, again and again, passionately.

When the student returned he threw four marks on the table, kissed his girl perfunctorily, saying, "I leave one for the *Bier*," and then addressed me, "Are you coming?" which gave me my chance. I turned to Kätchen, gave her ten marks, kissed her hands and her eyes and followed the student out of the house. I had escaped without being too rude, for Kätchen thanked me warmly for the gold piece and begged me with eyes and lips to return whenever I could, but—I could not stand the student or his talk. There was something so common, so animal in the whole performance that I hastened to say "Good night" to him and take thought by myself. I was frankly disgusted; quite clearly I saw then for the first time that there must be some admiration, some spiritual attraction, or the act would leave me cold. If the fellow had even admired the girl's figure, I said to myself, or her pretty Gretchen face, it would have redeemed the business; but this coupling like animals, brutalized by the four marks thrown on the table, and the curt leave taking—No! It was disgusting and a stain on the name of love.

And now for a better and more memorable experience.

I had gone to balls twice or three times in the Heidelberg because a friend wished me to accompany him or to complete a gay party. I seldom went of my own accord because dancing made me excessively giddy, as I have already related. But at one ball I was introduced to a Miss Betsy C., an English girl of a good type, very well dressed and extraordinarily pretty, though very small. She stood out among the large German fräuleins like a moss-rose wrapped in a delicate greenery to heighten her entrancing color, and at once I told her this and assured her that she had the most magnificent dark eyes I had ever seen; for bashfulness I had never felt, and I knew that praise was as the breath of life to every woman. We became friends at once, but to my disappointment, she told me she was going next day to Frankfort, where some friends would meet her the day after to accompany her back to England. Before I thought of what I was letting myself in for, I told her I would love to go to Frankfort with her and show her Goethe's birth-place and the Goethe-Haus; would she accept my escort? Would she? The great brown eyes danced with the thought of adventure and companion-ship—I was in for it—was this my next-born resolution of restraint? Was this my first essay in making an art of my life?

Yet I didn't even think of excusing myself: Bessie was too pretty and too alluring, with a quiet humor that appealed to me intensely. A big German girl passed us and Bessie, looking at her arms, said, "I never knew what 'mottled' was before. I've seen advertisements of 'mottled soap'; but 'mottled' arms! They're not pretty, are they?" Bessie was worse than pretty; under medium height but rounded in entrancing curves to beauty; her face piquant; the dark eyes now gleaming in malice, now deep in self-revealing; her arms exquisite and the small mounds of white breasts half hidden, half discovered by the lacy dress. No wonder I asked, "What time is your train? Shall I take you to the *Bahnhof?*"

"We'll meet at the station," she said, with a glint in her eye, "but you must be very kind and good!" Had she ever given herself? Did this last admonition mean she would not yield to me? I was in a fever but resolved to be amiable as well as bold.

Next morning we met at the station and had a great talk; and at Frankfort I drove with her straight to the best hotel, walked boldly to the desk and ordered two good rooms communicating; and signed the register Mr. and Mrs. Harris.

We were shown rooms on the second floor: our English appearance had got us the best in the house, and as my luck would have it, the second smaller bedroom had the key and bolt, so that I could reckon at least on a fair chance. But at once I opened the door between the rooms and helped her with her outside wraps and then, taking her head in my hands, kissed her on the mouth. At once, almost, her lips grew warm, which seemed to me the best omen. I said to her, "You'll knock when you're ready, won't you? Or come in to me?"

She smiled, reassured by my withdrawal, and nodded gaily, "I'll call!"

I spent the whole day with her and talked my best, telling her of Goethe's many love affairs and of Gretchen-Frederika. After dinner we went out for a walk and then returned to the hotel and went up to our bedrooms.

I went into my room and closed the door, my heart throbbing heavily, my mouth all parched as in fever. I must cheat time, I said to myself, and so I put on my best suit of pajamas, a sort of white stuff with threads of gold in it. And then I waited for the summons, but none came. I looked at my watch: it was twenty minutes since we parted; I must give her half an hour at least. "Would she call me?" She had said she would. "Would she yield easily?" Again, as my imagination recalled her wilful, mutinous face and lovely eyes, my heart began to thump! At last the half hour was up; should I go in? Yes, I would, and I walked over to the door and listened—not a sound. I turned the handle; the room was entirely in the dark. I moved quickly to the lights and turned them on: there she was in bed, with only her little face showing and the great eyes. In a second I was by her side.

"You promised to call me," I said.

"Put out the light!" she begged. Without making any reply I pulled down the clothes and got in beside her. "You'll be good!" she pouted.

"I'll try," was my noncommittal answer, and I slipped my left arm under her and drew her lips to mine. I was thrilled by the slightness and warmth of her, and at first I just took her mouth and held her close to the heat of my body. In a moment or two her lips grew hot and I put my hand down to lift her nightie: "No, no!" she resisted, pouting. "You promised to be good."

"There's nothing bad in this," I said, persevering, and the next moment I had my hand on her sex. With a sigh she resigned herself and gave her lips. After caressing her for a minute or two her sex opened and I could move her legs apart, so at once I put her hand on my sex. My excitement was so intense that I felt a good deal of pain; but I was past caring for pain. In a moment I was between her legs with my sex caressing her sex; the great eyes closed, but as I sought to enter her she shrank back with a cry of pain: "Oo, oo! It's terrible—please stop; oh, you said you'd be good." Of course I kissed her, smiling, and went back to the caressing. Naturally, in a few minutes I was again trying to enter paradise; but at once the cries of pain began again and the entreaties to stop and be good and I'll love you so. She was so pretty in her entreating that I said: "Let me see, and if I hurt you, I'll stop," and drew down in the bed to look. The fools are always saying that one sex of a woman is very like another; it is absolutely false; they are as different as mouths and this I was looking at was one of the most lovely I had ever seen. As she lay there before me I could not help exclaiming, "You dear, pocket Venus!" She was so dainty-small, but the damage done was undeniable; there was blood on her sex and a spot of blood on one lovely little round thigh; and at the same moment I noticed that my infernal prepuce had shrunk and now hurt me dreadfully, compressing my sex with a ring of iron. For some obscure reason, half of pity, half of affection for the little beauty, I moved and lay beside her as at first, saying: "I'll do whatever you wish; I love you so much, I hate to hurt you so."

"Oh, you great dear," she cried, and her arms went round my neck and she kissed me of her own accord a hundred times. A little later I lifted her upon me, naked body to naked body, and was ravished by the sheer beauty of her.

I must have spent an hour in fondling and caressing her; continually I discovered new beauties in her; time and again I pushed her nightie up to her neck, delighting in the plastic beauty of her figure; but Bessie showed no wish to see me or excite me. Why? Girls are a strange folk, I decided, but I soon found she was as greedy of praise as could be, so I told her what an impression she had made at the ball and how a dozen students had asked me to introduce them, saying she was the queen of the evening. At length she fell asleep in my arms and I must have slept, too, for it was four in the morning before I awoke, turned out the lights and crept to my own room. I had acted unselfishly, spared Bessie: to give her merely pain for my thrill of pleasure would not have been fair, I thought; I was rather pleased with myself.

When I awoke in the morning, I hastened to her, but found she was getting up and did not want to be disturbed; she'd be ready before me, she said, and she wished to see the town and shops before her friends came for her at two o'clock. I followed her wishes, bolted the door between our rooms, took her for a drive, gave her lunch, said "Good-bye" afterwards. When I assured her that nothing had been done, she said that I was a darling, promised to write and kissed me warmly; but I felt a shade of reticence in her, a something of reserve too slight to be defined, and on the train back to Heidelberg I put my fears down to fancy. But though I wrote to her English address I received no answer. Had I lost her through sparing her? What a puzzle women were! Was Vergil right with his *spretae injuria formae?* the hatred that comes in them if their beauty is not triumphant? Do they forgive anything sooner than self-control? I was angry with myself and resolved not to be such an unselfish fool next time.

Chapter IV

Goethe, William I, Bismarck, Wagner

I had long been aware that there was something rotten in the core of our social system. I had seen that while immense fortunes were accumulating, the working classes, the creators of wealth, were steeped in the most abject poverty. (Disraeli)

MY LIFE AT GÖTTINGEN at first was all work: study from morning till night; I grudged even the time to bathe and dress myself, and instead of walking a couple of hours a day for exercise, I got into the habit of sprinting a hundred yards or so twice a day, and once at least daily would trot for about half a mile. I thus managed to keep physically fit.

Besides working at German I read philosophy, the Greek thinkers and above all Plato:

> . . . The divine One
> If one reads the Gods aright
> By their motions as they shine on
> In an endless trail of Light.*

And then the English thinkers, such as Hobbes, Locke and Hume, and the French, especially Pascal and Joubert,** and of course the Germans with Kant, the master of modern skepticism, and Schopenhauer, whose ordinary essays show greatness of mind and soul. All these men, I saw, are moments in the growth of human thought, and I turned away from the speculations, feeling that I included most of them in my own development.

One incident of this life may be worth recording: Lotze, the famous philosopher who preached a God immanent in every form of life, remarked

---

* Elizabeth Barrett Browning, from *Wine of Cyprus*, XIII:
> And my Plato, the divine one,—
> If men know that gods aright
> By their motions as they shine on
> With a glorious trail of light.

** Joseph Joubert (1754–1824). His posthumously published *Pensées* (1842) on literature, morals, politics, and theology were widely read and admired.

once in seminar that the *via media* of Aristotle was the first and greatest discovery in morals. I disagreed with him, and when he asked me for my reasons, I said that the *via media* belonged to statics, whereas morals were a part of dynamics. A bottle of wine might do me good and make another man drunk: the moral path was never a straight or middle line between extremes, as Aristotle imagined, but the resultant of two forces, a curve, therefore, always making towards one side or the other. As one's years increase, after thirty or so, the curve should set towards abstinence.

> Stirb und Werde!
> Denn wenn Du das nicht hast
> Bist Du nur ein trüber Gast
> Auf der dunklen Erde.*

Lotze made a great fuss about this; asked me, indeed, to lecture to the class on laws of morals, and I talked one afternoon on all the virtues of chastity. It must be remembered that I was years older than the majority of the students.

My student life in the walled town was all in extremes: by turns sterile and fruitful. I learned German thoroughly; wasted a year indeed on Gothic, and Old High German and Middle High German, too, till I knew German as well as I knew English, and the *Niebelungenlied* better than I knew Chaucer. Twice I went on public platforms and spoke in great meetings and no one suspected that I was a foreigner—all vanity and waste of time, as I had to learn later.

But at length I read Goethe, everything he had written, in chronological order, and so came into the modern world by the noblest entrance and stood breathless, enthralled by the Pisgah heights and the vision of what may come when men learn to develop their minds as some, even now, know how to develop their bodies. This was Goethe's supreme gift to men; he taught the duty of self-development to each of us and it is the first and chief duty; he preached culture as a creed, and even to those of us who had felt it beforehand and acted on it, his example was an inspiration. Later I saw that if Goethe had only had Whitman's pluck and had published the naughty poems and dramas that Eckermann tells us about and the true story of his life, he would have stood to the modern world as Shakespeare

---

*Und so lang du das nicht hast,
Dieses: Stirb und werde
Bist du nur ein trüber Gast
Auf der dunklen Erde.

(And unless you master this—
This: die and become [be transfigured]
You are but a shadowy guest
On the dark earth.)

Goethe, "Selige Sehnsucht" ("Holy Yearning"), published in *Westöstlicher Divan* (1819).

Note Harris' rather considerable misquoting here.

stood to the feudal world, the sacred guide of men for centuries and centuries.

But alas! He, too, was a snob and loved the dignities and flatteries, if not the empty ceremonials, of a provincial German court. Fancy a great man and one of the wisest of men content to sit on that old feudal wall in court attire and dangle buckled shoes and silken hose in the eyes of the passers by beneath him. Oh, Beethoven was right in his revolt when he crammed his hat down on his head as the Gross-Herzog drove by, while Goethe stood on the roadside, hat in hand, bowing. When Beethoven's brother put on his card *Gutsbesitzer* (land-owner), Beethoven put on his card *Hirnbesitzer* (brain-owner): the brainowner cannot be proud of being a landowner.

Goethe had not sufficient reverence for his own genius, and though well-off, did not make the best of his astounding gifts. He should have visited England and France early in life and spent at least two years there. If Goethe had known Blake, he might have won to the heights earlier and understood that he must give his own spirit the richest nourishment; for surely Blake's first songs would have shown him that even a Goethe had worthy competitors and thereby would have rendered the tedious *Wanderjahre* that were not, alas! spent in travel, altogether impossible; for even at sixteen Blake had reached magic of expression. In describing eventide he writes:

> . . . Let thy west wind sleep on
> The lake; speak silence with thy glimmering eyes
> And wash the dusk with silver . . .*

This "natural magic," as Matthew Arnold called it, is the one quality which Goethe's poetry never showed. Yet though consciously seeking the utmost self-development, how high Goethe grew even in the thin soil of Weimar.

As a lyric poet he ranks with the greatest of all time; no one has ever written a more poignant dramatic lyric than the appeal of Gretchen** to the Madonna; and Mignon's confession is of the same supreme quality. Heine says that Goethe has written the best lyrics in all literature, and Heine knew. But it was Goethe the thinker who won my heart; phrases of his, couplets even, seemed to me pure divination. There is one word about him that I envy. When Emerson was confronted by his insight into botany and into biology, he found the true word for the great German: "Surely the spirit that made the world, confided itself more to this man than to any other."

In sociology, too, Goethe deserves the high praise of Carlyle, and not mainly even for the discovery of the "open secret" that too great individual

---

* From *To the Evening Star.*
** The heroine of the first part of *Faust.*

liberty leads inevitably to slavery (Coleridge saw as far as that and writes of those who

> Wear the name of Freedom
> Graven on a heavier chain,*

but because he (Goethe) was the first to draw the line between socialism and individualism and apportion to each its true place in the modern industrial world. I make no scruple of reproducing the passage here for the second time; it has never, so far as I know, been quoted by any sociologist or even noticed; and I had arrived at the same conclusion years before reading the fragment of the play *Prometheus,* that contains the deepest piece of practical insight to be found anywhere.

"What then is yours?" Epimetheus asks; and the answer of Prometheus comes like a flash—

> "The sphere that my activity can fill, no more, no less."

In other words, every department of industry that the individual can control should be left to him; but all those where the individual has abdicated, all joint stock and limited liability companies, should be nationalized or municipalized; in other words, should be taken over by the community to be managed in the interest of all. Joint stock company's management has every fault of state or municipal management and none of their many virtues and advantages, as Stanley Jevons** proved in a memorable essay now nearly forgotten.

In this magnificent *aperçu* Goethe was a hundred years before his time, and considering that in the first years of the nineteenth century modern industry was in the cradle, so to speak, and gave scarcely a sign of its rapid and portentous development, Goethe's insight seems to me above praise. Of course he saw, too, that the land and its inherent products, such as oil and coal, should belong to the community.

It should teach us all the inestimable value of the seer and thinker that Goethe, though far removed from the main current of industrial life, should have found the true solution of the social problem a full century before any of the belauded European statemen! What a criticism of democracy in the bare fact!

I owe more to Goethe than to any other teacher: Carlyle came first and then Goethe. Carlyle, who only knew two men in the world worthy of respect, the workman and the thinker, the two iron chords out of which he struck heroic melody; and Goethe, who saw even further and was the first to recognize that the artist was the greatest of the sons of men: his destiny

---

* From *France, an Ode:*
> . . . wear the name
> Of Freedom, graven on a heavier chain!
** (1835–82). He demonstrated that value is derived from utility in his *Theory of Political Economy*.

the most arduous, prefiguring as it does, the ceaseless mother-labor of creation, the desire which is the soul of life to produce and produce, ever reaching outward and upward to a larger and more conscious vision; and when the critics complain that Goethe was too self-centered, they forget how he organized relief for the starving weavers, or worked night after night to save the huts of Thuringen peasants from fire.

And his creative work is of the best: his Mephistopheles is perhaps too generalized, just as Hamlet is too individual, to rank with Don Quixote or Falstaff; but look at his women, his Gretchen, Mignon and Philina;* only Shakespeare's Cleopatra and perhaps his Sonnet-Love are of the same quality.

I am annoyed whenever I hear Homer, who is not as great as our Walter Scott, placed among the first of men: to me the sacred ones are Jesus, Shakespeare and Goethe; even Cervantes and Dante, though of the same high lineage, are hardly of the same stature; for Cervantes has given us, strange to say, no new type of woman, and Dante is singer rather than creators; whereas Goethe and Shakespeare are supreme singers as well as creators; and on the Head of the Crucified One climb the crowns of the world.

For my own part and speaking merely personally, I would find a place for Balzac and Heine even in that high company; and who would dare to exclude Rembrandt, Beethoven and Wagner?

One small point which differentiates Goethe from Shakespeare: Shakespeare followed Jesus in insisting on repentance, whereas Goethe will have no sorrow for sin: what is past, is past, he says peremptorily, and tears are a waste of time: train yourself so that you will not fall twice into the same pit; and go forward boldly. The counsel is of high courage: yet sorrow, too, is the soul's purification.

But what a counselor is this Goethe:

> Einen Blick in's Buch hinein
> Und zwei in's Leben
> Das muss die rechte Form
> Dem Geiste geben.**

In Göttingen I learned a good many of the peculiarities of German university life and spent more time on the *Pauk-boden* (duelling-ground) and with the corps-students than in socialist meetings. Thanks to my excellent German, I was admitted everywhere as a German and soon discovered the cause of the extraordinary superiority of the German students in almost every department of life. I think [even] the discovery of value

---

* A character in *Wilhelm Meister*.
** A glance into the book
And two into life:
That will give the proper shape
To the spirit.

because it enabled me to predict the colossal development of German industry and German wealth twenty years before it took place.

The Emperor of Germany of that time,* the grandfather of the present man, must have had a rarely good head or he would never have found a Bismarck and given him almost royal power. But his wisdom was shown, I am inclined to think, just as clearly in another field. Desirous above all things of strengthening his army, he called Wilhelm von Humboldt, the brother of the famous scientist, Alexander,** to counsel. What should be done with the ever increasing number of students who year by year entered the army? Von Humboldt recommended that they should form a class apart as volunteers and be subjected to only one year's training instead of three. At first the old Kaiser would not hear of it: they would be inferior, he thought, to the ordinary soldier in drill and discipline. "All my soldiers must be as good as possible," was his final word. Von Humboldt assured him that the volunteers for one year would soon constitute the pick of the recruits, and he argued and pleaded for his conviction with such fervor that at length the old Emperor yielded. Von Humboldt said that a certain proportion, twenty per cent at any rate, of the volunteers would become non-commissioned officers before their year was over; and the Emperor agreed that if this happened, the experiment must be regarded as successful. Of course the first volunteers knew what was expected of them and more than fifty per cent of them gained the coveted distinction. All through the army the smartest soldiers were the one-year volunteers. It was even said later that the smartest non-commissioned officers were for the most part volunteers, but that is not generally believed, for the German is very proud of his non-commissioned officers and with good reason; for they serve 16 years with the colors, and as they are rewarded afterwards with good positions on the railways, or in the post-office or the police, and indeed may even rise to esteem as gentlemen, they form the most remarkable class in any army. I have known a good many German non-commissioned officers who had learned to speak both English and French fluently and correctly while still serving.

But not only was the whole spirit and mind and discipline of the army enormously vivified by the competition of the educated volunteers; but the institution exercised in turn the most wonderful effect upon the teaching and learning in the schools; and this has never been noticed so far as I know. The middle and lower-middle classes in Germany wished their sons to become one-year volunteers, and so fathers, mothers and sisters urged their sons and brothers to study and learn so as to gain this huge step in the social hierarchy.

* William I (1797–1888).
** Wilhelm von Humboldt (1767–1835), philologist and statesman and at one time first minister of Public Instruction.
Alexander von Humboldt (1769–1859); he helped found modern geography and meteorology with his studies of isotherms and magnetic declination.

In turn this inspired the masters and professors in the *Gymnasien* and *Real-Schulen,* and these teachers took immediate advantage of the new spirit in the scholars: the standard of the final examination in the *Gymnasien—das Abiturienten-Examen,* or "the going-away" examination—was put higher and higher year by year till it reached the limit set by human nature. The level of this examination now is about the level of second-honors in Oxford or Cambridge, far above the graduation standard of American universities. There are perhaps a thousand such students in Great Britain year by year, against the hundred thousand in German universities, some of whom are going on to further heights.

I don't for a moment mean to suggest that all these hundred thousand German students are the intellectual equals of the thousand honor men of the English universities; they may be on the same level of knowledge, but the best thousand from Oxford and Cambridge are at least as intelligent as the best thousand from German universities. Genius has little or nothing to do with learning; but what I do assert is that the number of cultivated and fairly intelligent men in Germany is ten times larger than it is in England. Many Englishmen are proud of their ignorance: how often have I heard in later life, "I never could learn languages; French, a beastly tongue to pronounce, I know a few words of, but German is absolutely beyond me: yet I know something of horses and I'm supposed to be pretty useful at banking," and so forth. I've heard an English millionaire, ennobled for his wealth, boast that he had only two books in his house: one "the guid book" meaning the Bible that he never opened, and the other his check book.

One scene which will show the enormous difference between the two peoples is bitten into my memory as with vitriol. In order to get special lessons in Old German, I spent a semester in the house of a professor in a Gymnasium; he had a daughter and two sons, the younger, Wilhelm, an excellent scholar, while Heinrich, the elder, was rather dull or slow. The father was a big, powerful man with a great voice and fiercely imperious temper: a sort of Bismarck; he was writing a book on comparative grammar. Night after night, he gave me an hour's lesson; I prepared it carefully not to excite his irritability and soon we became real friends. Duty was his religion, sweetened by love of his daughter, who was preparing to be a teacher. My bedroom was on the second floor in the back; but often, after I had retired and was lying in bed reading, I heard outbursts of voice from the sitting room downstairs. I soon found out that after my lesson and an hour or two given to his daughter, the professor would go through his lessons with Heinrich. One summer's night I had been reading in my room when I was startled by a terrible row. Without thinking I ran downstairs and into the sitting-room. Mary was trying to comfort her father, who was marching up and down the room with the tears pouring from his eyes: "To think of that stupid lout being a son of mine; look at him!" Heinrich, with a very red face and tousled hair, sat with his books at the table, sullen and angry: "*Ei* with the optative is beyond him," cried the professor, "and he's fifteen!"

"*Ei* with the optative was beyond me at sixteen," I laughed, hoping to allay the storm. The boy threw me a grateful look, but the father would not be appeased.

"His whole future depends on his work," he shouted. "He ought to be in *Secunda* next year and he hasn't a chance, not a chance!"

"Oh, come," I said, "you know you told me once that when Heinrich learned anything, he never forgot it, whereas I forget as easily as I learn; you can't have it both ways."

"That's what I tell my father," said Mary, and the storm gradually blew over.

But as the time of the examination approached, similar scenes were of almost nightly occurrence; I've seen the professor working passionately with Heinrich at one and two o'clock in the morning, the whole family on pins and needles because of one boy's slowness of apprehension.

The ordinary German is not by any means a genius, but as a rule he has had to learn a good deal and knows how to learn whatever he wishes; whereas the ordinary Englishman or American is almost inconceivably ignorant, and if he happens to have succeeded in life in spite of his limitations, he is all too apt to take pride in his ignorances. I know Englishmen and women who have spent twenty years in France and know nothing of French beyond a few ordinary phrases. It must be admitted that the Englishman is far worse than the American in this respect; the American is ashamed of ignorance.

In mental things the German is, so to speak, a trained athlete in comparison with an Englishman, and as soon as he comes into competition with him, he is conscious of his superiority and naturally loves to prove and display it. Time and again towards the end of the nineteenth century, English manufacturers grieving over the loss of the South American markets have shown me letters in Spanish and Portuguese written by German "drummers" that they could not get equalled by any English agents: "We are beaten by their knowledge," was the true summing up and plaint. And in the first ten years of the twentieth century the German's pride in his unhoped-for quick success in commerce and industry intensified his efforts, and at the same time his contempt of his easily beaten rivals.

In the spacious days of Elizabeth, Englishmen and Englishwomen too of the best class were eager to learn and prized learning perhaps above its value; the Queen herself knew four or five languages fairly well, better than any English sovereign since. One other fact that an Englishman should always keep before him: the population of Great Britain at the end of the sixteenth century was roughly five millions; at the end of the nineteenth it was some forty-five millions, or nine times as many; yet three-fourths of all the schools today in England for higher education were there in the days of Elizabeth. That fact and all it involves explains to me the efflorescence of genius in the earlier, greater age: the population has grown nine-fold, the educated class had not doubled its numbers, and certainly has not grown in appreciation or understanding of genius.

I am the more inclined to preach from this text because it suggests the true meaning of the World War, which England has steadily refused to learn. When from 1900 to 1910 she saw herself overtaken by Germany, not only in the production of steel, but also of iron and coal, England ought to have learned what her contempt of learning and love of sport were costing her, and have put her house in order in the high sense of the word. For a hundred years now she has been sending some of her ablest sons to govern India. She ought to have learned from Machiavelli that every possession of the Romans not colonized by Latins was a source of weakness in time of war. England ought to withdraw from India and Egypt as soon as possible and concentrate all her forces on developing her own colonies, who will always trade with her for sentimental reasons and by compulsion of habit. The Canadian buys six times as much of English goods as the American, and the Australian spends twenty times more on English products than on German, in spite of the superior qualities of the German output. The worst of it is that the English guides and leaders do not even yet grasp the truth.

But at the time the growth of Germany and its eager intellectual life only confirmed me in the belief that by nationalizing the land and socializing the chief industries such as railways, gas and water companies, which are too big for the individual to manage, one could not only lift the mass of the English people to a far higher level, but at the same time intensify their working power. It would surely be wise to double the wages of the workman when you could thereby increase the productivity of his labor. Moreover the nationalization of the railways, gas, water and mining companies would give five millions of men and women steady and secure employment and sufficient wages to ensure decent conditions of life; five millions of workmen more could be employed on the land in life-leases, and in this way Great Britain might be made self-supporting and her power and wealth enormously increased.

I tell all this because I resolved to make myself a social reformer and began to practice extempore speaking for at least half an hour daily.

From Goettingen after three semesters I went to Berlin; it was time; I needed the stimulus of the theatre and galleries of art and the pulsing life of a great city. But there was something provincial in Berlin; I called it a *Welt-dorf,* a world-village; yet I learned a good deal there: I heard Bismarck speak several times and carried away deathless memories of him as an authentic great man. In fact, I came to see that if he had not been born a Junker in a privileged position and had not become a corps-student to boot, he might have been as great a social reformer as Carlyle himself. As it was, he made Germany almost a model state. He was accused in the Reichstag one day by a socialist of having learned a good deal from Lassalle;* he stalked forth at once and annihilated his critic by declaring that he would think very little of anyone who had had the privilege of knowing that extraordinary man and had not learned from him. It was Bismarck, I believe, who was responsible for the first steps towards socializing German industries; Bismarck who established the land-banks to lend money on reasonable terms to the farmers; Bismarck too who dared first to nationalize some German railways and municipalize gas and water companies; and provide for the extension by the state of the canal system.

Under his beneficent despotism, too, the municipalities of Germany became instruments of progress; slums disappeared from Berlin and the housing of the poor excited the admiration of even casual foreign visitors; his labor-bureaus, providing suitable employment, were copied timidly forty years later in London. It is not too much to say that he practically eradicated poverty in Germany.

The great minister himself anticipated that his attempts to lift the lowest class to a decent level would hem industrial progress and make it more difficult for the captains of industry to amass riches, but in this he was completely mistaken. He had given help and hope to the very poor, and this stimulus to the most numerous class vivified the industry of the whole nation; the productivity of labor increased enormously: German workmen became the most efficient in the world, and in the decade before the great war, the chief industries of steel and iron, which twenty years before were not half so productive as those of Great Britain, became three and four fold more productive, and showing larger profits, made competition practically impossible. The vivifying impulse reached even to the shipping, and while it became necessary for the British government to help finance the Cunard line, the Hamburg-America became the chief steamship line of the world and made profits that turned English shippers green with envy: immigration into Germany reached a million a year, exceeding even that into the United States. And this astounding development of industry and wealth was not due to natural advantages, as in the United States, but simply to wise, humane government and to better schooling. Every officer on a German liner spoke at least French and English as well as German, whereas not one English or French officer in a hundred understood any language save his own.

Looking over the unparalleled growth of the country and its prodigious productivity and wealth, it is hardly to be wondered at that the ruler ascribed the astonishing prosperity to his own wisdom and foresight. It really appeared that Germany in a single generation had sprung from the position of a second rate power to the headship of the modern world. And

* Ferdinand Lassalle (1825–64), a German socialist who was imprisoned in 1848 for revolutionary activities. Later, when Bismarck and the Prussian Liberals were fiercely opposing each other, he proposed a third party which would work for political and economic emancipation. He died in a duel over a woman, which George Meredith immortalized in *The Tragic Comedians* (1880).

already in the early eighties, the future development could be foreseen. I spent one month of my holidays in Düsseldorf and Essen and was struck on all hands by the trained and cultured intelligence of the directors and foremen of the chief industries. The labor saving appliances alone reminded me of the best industries in the United States; but here there was a far wider and yet a specialized intelligence. Someday soon the whole story will be told properly, but even now in 1924 it's clear that the rival nations, instead of following Germany and bettering Bismarck's example, are·resolved on degrading, dismembering and punishing her. It makes one almost despair of humanity.

After Goettingen and Berlin, I went to Munich, drawn by the theatre and Opera-House, by Ernst Possart,* the greatest Shylock I ever saw and assuredly the best-graced, all-round actor, except the elder Coquelin,** who ruled the stage and was perfection perfected. And the music at Munich was as good as the acting: Heinrich Vogl† and his wife were both excellent interpreters and through them, as I have told, I came to know Richard Wagner. In my fourth volume of *Contemporary Portraits* I've done my best to picture him in his habit as he lived; but I left out half-consciously two or three features which it seemed to me hardly right to publish just when I had learned in 1922 that Cosima Wagner†† was still alive. Here I may be franker. In my "portrait" I left it half in doubt as to the person who was the Isolde, or inspiring soul, of that wonderful duo of love which is the second act of *Tristan*. Of course there is no doubt whatever that Mathilde von Wesendonck‡ was Wagner's Isolde; he wrote it to her in so many words: "Throughout eternity I shall owe it to you that I was able to create Tristan."

In her widowhood Mathilde retired to Traunblick near Traunsee in the Bavarian Alps, and I might have seen her there in the wonderful summer of 1880 which I spent in Salzburg; but hardly anyone knew her importance in Wagner's life till after her death in 1902, when she left instructions to publish the 150 letters he had written her and the famous journal in the form of letters to her, which he wrote in Venice immediately after their separation. He found a great word for her. "Your caresses crown my life,"

---

* Ernst Ritter Possart (1841–1921); he was also a producer and director.

** Benoit Constant Coquelin (1841–1909). One of his great sucesses was *Cyrano de Bergerac*. He toured America early in the twentieth century with Sarah Bernhardt; he published several books on the French theatre.

† (1845–1900); a Wagnerian tenor; he composed the opera *Der Fremdling* (1899).

†† (1837–1930). An illegitimate child of Liszt, who later legitimized her birth and provided generously for her. She bore Von Bülow and Wagner two children each. Her marriage to Wagner was a happy one, and Wagner composed the *Siegfried Idyll* for her as a surprise. She conducted the Bayreuth festivals after Wagner died. (Wagner left his first wife, Wilhelmina Planer, in 1866, after thirty years of marriage.)

‡ (1828–1902); Wagner's one-time mistress. A series of songs by Wagner, "The Wesendonck Lieder," is named for her.

he wrote. "They are the joy-roses of love that flower my crown of thorns;" and Mathilde deserved even this praise: she was, as he said, always kind and wise, and above even her lover in living always on the heights. He complained one day to her that Liszt, his best friend, did not fully understand him. "There could be no ideal friendship," he added, "between men." At once she recalled him to his better self: "After all, Liszt is the one man most nearly on your level. Don't allow yourself to underrate him. I know a great phrase he once used about you: 'I esteem men according to their treatment of Wagner.' What more could you want?" And her charming poetic word for their days of loving intimacy: "The heart-Sundays of my life." If ever a man was blest in his passions, it was Richard Wagner.

And yet here, too, when at his best he shows the yellow streak. In 1865, six years after the parting with Mathilde, he allowed Madame von Bülow to write—it is true: "In the name of his Majesty, the King of Bavaria," to Mathilde, to ask her for a portfolio of articles and sketches which Wagner in the days of their intimacy had confided to her keeping. Naturally Mathilde wrote in reply directly to Wagner, giving him a list of everything in the portfolio, and adding finely: "I pray you to tell me *what* manuscripts you want and whether *you* wish me to send them?" In the cult of love women are nearly always nobler and finer than the best of men: Wagner's answer that the King wanted to publish the things did not excuse him for having allowed Cosima to crow over her great rival. But in publishing Wagner's letters to her and his Venice journal, Mathilde got even with Cosima; yet again Cosima was not to be outdone. She had left Von Bülow* for Wagner, preferring, as someone said, "God to his Prophet"; but she, too, could reach the heights. Meeting Von Bülow years later, who said to her by way of reconciliation, "After all I forgive you," she replied finely; "it isn't a question of forgiveness, but one of understanding." And now, in face of the revelation of 1902 of Wagner's letters to Mathilde, she first wrote saying that "the Master desired these sheets to be destroyed" (*der Meister wünschte beiliegende Blätter vernichtet*); but when she found that they were sure to be published in spite of her opposition, she not only consented graciously to their publication in German, but added fourteen letters from Mathilde von Wesendonck, which she had found among Wagner's papers. The whole story, I think, is of curious human interest.

Cosima was Wagner's equal and deserved all his praise of her as "intellectually superior even to Liszt"; but whoever studies Wagner's life will, I think, admit that it was Mathilde who wove the first joy-roses in his crown of thorns, and she it was who helped him to his supreme achievement. The *Ring* and *Parsifal,* he used to contend later, constituted his greatest message; and Cosima was the true partner of his soul who gave

---

* Hans von Bülow (1830–94). Wagner helped his career as a pianist and conductor; indeed, Von Bülow conducted the first performances of *Tristan* and *Der Meistersinger*. The friendship broke up over Cosima.

him happiness and golden days; but there can be no doubt that Mathilde was the Rachel of his prime and the inspiration of all his noblest, artistic masterpieces.

Years later, he wrote the whole truth. "It is quite clear to me that I shall never again invent anything new. With Mathilde my life came to flower and left in me such a wealth of ideas that I have since had merely to return to the treasure-house and pick whatever I wish to develop . . . She is and remains my first and only love; with her I reached the zenith: those divine years hold all the sweetness of my life." She was the inspiring genius, not only of *Tristan* but of the *Meistersinger,* and it would not be difficult to prove that the finest moment in *Parsifal* was due to Wagner's intercourse with her. She came at the right time in his life. After all, he was well over fifty before Cosima joined him.

Wagner's life rests on three persons: on Mathilde von Wesendonck, King Ludwig* and on Cosima Liszt. In my "portrait" I said little of Cosima, but she was undoubtedly the chief person in his later life. His life with her in Tribschen from 1866 to 1872 was not only the happiest period of his existence but highly productive. The birth of the son, whom he boldly christened "Siegfried" (*den ich kühn 'Siegfried' nennen konnte*) was to him a consecration. Instead of living with a woman like his wife, who continually urged him to compromise with all conventions because she didn't believe in him and was incapable of appraising his genius at its true worth, he had now a better head and completer understanding than even Liszt's— "*Eine unerhört seltsam begabte Frau! Liszts wunderbares Ebenbild nur intellektuel uber ihm stehend*" (a singularly gifted woman; Liszt over again though intellectually his superior)—to encourage and sustain him.

In his delight, Wagner worked his hardest. For years he wrote from eight in the morning till five in the afternoon. In these happy fruitful years in Tribschen he completed the *Meistersinger,* perhaps his most characteristic work! He finished *Siegfried* also and composed nearly all the *Götterdämmerung.* Then, too, he wrote his best work, his Beethoven. In Tribschen he even began to publish the final edition of his works, and at length came the victory of 1870 to add a sort of consecration to his happiness. At long last the Germany he loved had come to honor and glory among men; now he too would live long and make the German stage worthy of the German people. He was really as affectionate as he was passionate, and his whole nature expanded in this atmosphere of well-being, encouragement and reverence. He took on the tone and manner of a great personage; he could not brook contradiction or criticism, not even from a Nietzsche, and this attitude brought with it blunders. If we mortals don't keep our eyes on the earth, we are apt to stumble.

Talking one day about *der Fliegende Holländer,* he said he had heard the story from a sailor on his memorable voyage from Riga to London

* (1845–86).

thirty-five years before. I could not help interrupting: "I thought you took the splendid redemption of the hero by love from Heine, Master?"*

"It was all told me by a sailor," he repeated. "Heine took the salvation of the hero by love from a Dutch theatre piece."

But there is no such Dutch theatre piece. It was excusable in Wagner, you may say, to have been misled in this instance; he took the story from Heine, but he believed that Heine himself had borrowed it. But there is no such explanation possible in regard to the legend of *Tannhäuser*. Wagner maintained always that he had taken the story from a simple *Volkslegent* (*aus dem Volksbuch und dem schlichten Tannhäuserlied*); but there is no such *Volksbuch,* no such legend. It's all from Heine. And when one day I talked with passionate admiration of Heine and placed him with Goethe far above Schiller, Wagner wouldn't have it. "*Sie schwärmen*—You are misled by admiration," he said. "Heine was only a simple lyric poet (*ein Lyriker*), but Schiller was a great dramatic genius."

He owed to Heine's genius the finest things in all the German legends which he set to music, and I think in the future his denial of Heine, though little known now, will be about the greatest blot on Wagner's character, which in many respects was noble. It shows him so much smaller, less sincere even than Beethoven, and with none of that magic of loving-comprehension which our Shakespeare lavished even on his rival Chapman.** That Wagner could pretend elaborately in such a case always seems to me to relegate him to a place below the very highest. Why will the men of genius who illumine our life keep such spots to mar their radiance?

---

* Harris' veracity about this meeting, which some contend never occurred, may be questioned. Inquiries made of the Munich police and the University of Munich reveal that Wagner lived in Munich from November 6 to 22, 1880, at 80 Brienner-strasse; and that Harris was in Munich from January 7 to May 13, 1881, part of the time at the same address. The police say that other reports on Harris may exist, and the university states that records on auditors were not kept until 1891. At the worst, Harris nearly met Wagner and must have manufactured his accounts from conversations with persons who had recently been with Wagner. At best, Harris did not register with the municipal authorities until he had been in Munich for six weeks, or those records were misplaced. Indeed, lacking records for Harris' whereabouts between April 10 and 17, the Munich police believe the lapse can be "explained by the theory that he delayed announcing his move to the new apartment." Credence may ultimately depend on one's prejudices.

** George Chapman (1559?–1634), whose translation of Homer Keats panegyrized in a sonnet.

Chapter V

Athens and the English Language

I SHALL NEVER BE ABLE to describe natural beauty, though I know scenes so lovely that the mere memory of them brings tears to my eyes; and in the same way there are two cities, Athens and Rome, which I can never attempt to describe: they must be seen and studied to be realized. The impression of Athens is as simple as that of Rome is complex. The beauty of the human body is the first impression: the majesty of the man's figure and the sensuous appeal of the woman's are what Athens gives immediately; while Rome is the epitome of a dozen different civilizations and makes a dozen dissimiliar appeals.

The second night I was in Athens there was nearly a full moon; all over the sky were small white cloudlets on the intense blue, like silver shields reflecting the radiance. I had nothing to do so I walked across the square where the barracks of a palace stands and went up the Acropolis through the Proplyaea. As I stood before the Parthenon its sheer beauty sang itself to me like exquisite verse; I spent the night there going to and fro from the Caryatides of the Erechtheum to the frieze of the Temple, to the Wingless Victory, and back again. As dawn came and the first shafts of light struck the Parthenon I stood with clasped hands, my soul one quiver of admiration and reverence for the spirit of beauty I saw incorporated there.

Athens is pure pagan and its temples, like its poems, appeal to the deepest humanity in us. These buildings do not lead the eye from pinnacle to pinnacle into the infinite, as the spires of a Gothic temple do: the temple here is the frame, so to speak, for exquisite white forms of men and women against a background of deep blue. This is the room where noble men and women meet: Pericles and Phidias, Socrates and Aspasia; here the great poet Sophocles, himself a model of beauty, walks among graceful girl-women with their apple-breasts and rounded firm hips. Here is the deification of humanity; and this religion appeals to me more profoundly than any other both in its sensuousness and in its nobility. Here are the loveliest bodies in the world to be kissed and here too the courage that smiles at Death; and I recall the words of Socrates in the Crito: "Let us go then whither the God leads,"* the highest in us being our God and guide!

*Leave me then, Crito, to fulfill the will of God, and to follow whither he leads. (Jowett).

Is there anything higher? In Socrates we seem to touch the zenith of humanity, but the commandment of Jesus is sweeter still: we men all need forgiveness, all need affection, and it is more blessed even to give love than to receive it. But paganism is the first religion and this Athens is its birthplace, its altar and home.

Oscar Wilde told me once that he was conscious of his genius as a schoolboy and quite certain he would be a great poet before he left Trinity, Dublin for Oxford. I had attained some originality at five and twenty when I saw Shakespeare as clearly as I saw him at forty, but I was long past thirty before I thought it possible that I might make myself a great writer. I was always painfully conscious that I had no writing talent, always used to repeat what Balzac said of himself: "*sans génie je suis flambe*" (if I haven't genius I have nothing). When I resolved to go to Greece from Munich I felt I had been studying languages long enough, and the great classic writers and heroes did not impress me much. Except Socrates, none of them came near my ideal. Sophocles, I saw, repeated himself; his *Electra* was a bad copy of his *Antigone* and he ended his *Ajax* with a political pamphlet in favor of Athens; he was a master of language and not of life or art, and I had lost time over him. Then there was no Roman at all except Tacitus and Catullus, the poet lover of Clodia-Lesbia, and of course Caesar, who was almost the ideal of the writer and man of action. My four years of hard study had not brought me much; the couple of months with Skobelef were richer in food for the spirit, for they strengthened my ideal of vigorous life lived in contempt of conventions.

I sent on my luggage and went through the mountains on foot to Innsbruck and thence took train to Venice. It was an astonishing experience. For the first time I came to see the value of the abnormal: water-streets gave the place unique distinction; the Bridge of Sighs was more memorable than any number of Brooklyn Bridges or even Waterloo Bridges; Marlowe's great phrase came back to me often: "I am myself alone!" Singularity is distinction.

I did a fortnight's hard work at Italian and could make myself understood and understand everything said to me, but when I went to the people's theatre where the Venetian dialect was spoken, I could not understand it at all and at first felt out of it; yet I had been able to understand everything in the *Münchener Volkstheater!* In a week or so, however, after reading *I promessi Sposi* and a good deal of Dante, I became able to follow the Venetian slang and in a low cabaret caught glimpses of common Venetian life. Everywhere the working classes are the most idiosyncratic and consequently the best worth knowing.

But I was longing for Greece, so I took a Florio boat and started. There was a Signor Florio on board and we became friends; he brought out some wonderful Marsala and taught me that there was at least one Italian wine worth drinking. From Florio I heard a good deal of Sicily and resolved on my way back to stop in Palermo or Syracuse to study it.

On the ship was a little lame Greek child; the mother was taking it back to Athens to be operated on; she seemed very despondent; I found out it was because the father had gone to the States and had not written since and the mother had not money enough for the operation. How much would it cost? Five hundred drachmae: as luck would have it, I had just a little over that sum about me. I gave it to the mother and told her to cheer up. She cried a great deal and kissed my hand. I don't know why I gave the money; it left me short; I couldn't drink much wine, had to make a bottle last two days. At the end of the voyage my bill for extras and tips took everything I had, and when we reached the Piraeus I found I had no money to pay the boatmen for taking me and my luggage to the railway station. How I cursed my foolish liberality. What business had I to be generous? That evening I went into the cabin and studied the passengers; I picked out a youngish man; he looked like a Jew but his nose was straight. I went up to him, told him of my dilemma, and asked him to lend me some money. He smiled, took out his pocket-book, and showed me notes of five hundred and a thousand drachmae. "May I take this?" I asked, and touched a thousand drachmae note. "Certainly," he said, "with pleasure." "Give me your card, please," I went on, "and in a week, as soon as I can get money from London, I'll repay you; I'm going to the Hotel Grand Bretagne. It's good, isn't it?" "It's supposed to be," he rejoined, "for the rich English all go there, but I'd prefer the Hotel d'Athènes." "I'll take your tip," I said, and shook hands. That night I slept in a room looking across the Palace-Square to the Acropolis.

The gentleman who lent me the money was a Mr. Constantine, the owner, if I remember rightly, of the gas-works in the Piraeus. When I wrote to my London bank for money, they sent it [to] me on condition I could get myself identified. That condition took me to the British Embassy and made me acquainted with the First Secretary Raikes,* who was kind enough to identify me without further to do. I gave a dinner to Constantine and had him meet Raikes and other friends of mine and repaid him the money with a thousand thanks. Constantine and I remained friends for many a year.

In the Hotel d'Athènes a number of students used to meet once a week in the evening and discuss everything connected with the Greek language, literature, art and life.

The students were mostly men of a good deal of capacity pursuing post-graduate courses. They came from the Italian school, the French school and the German school, but no English or Americans fraternized with us, though, I remember, Raikes visited us about once a month: he was not only chief attaché or something more in the English Embassy, but also the brother of the postmaster general. We called him "Long Raikes" because

---

* Arthur Stewart Raikes (1856–1925), attaché in Athens, 1880. He also served as diplomatic secretary in national capitals in Europe, South America, and the United States.

he was about six feet five. I used to think that Raikes would do something memorable in life, for he had a curiously fair mind, though it was not what you would call dynamic.

There was the German Lolling* too, who later became the head of the Archaeological Institute in Berlin, if I am not mistaken, and who wrote the famous Baedeker guide-book to Greece.

Then there was an Italian, a sort of assistant curator of the Pitti Gallery, in Florence, and an astonishing Frenchman, a man of perhaps forty or forty-five, with a fine presence and magnificent head, who spoke almost every European language excellently and with a perfect accent—the only Frenchman I ever saw, indeed, the only foreigner who spoke English so that you could not tell he was not an Englishman. I have forgotten his name, but we called him the Baron.

I remember one evening Raikes brought in Mr. Bryce,** afterwards Lord Bryce, who was then about to make his first tour through Greece. A couple of Greek professors from the university used to come pretty regularly; one of them I christened Plato and the nickname stuck. I have forgotten his real name; he had charming manners and was extraordinarily intelligent and well-read in all sorts of out-of-the-way subjects. For instance, he knew South Africa and especially Cape Colony almost as well as I did, though he had never set foot in the country. I came into the room rather late one evening and was told by the chairman, Lolling, that they had had an interesting discussion on various European languages and had settled some points to their entire satisfaction.

Everyone agreed, he said, that Italian was the most musical language, Spanish having been ruled out because of its harsh gutturals. German, it was decided, was the best instrument for abstract thought, and indeed the largest vehicle in a general way. French was considered to be the best language for diplomacy, being very precise and simple and having an extensive popularity from one end of Christendom to the other. Such were some of the general conclusions.

"All very interesting," I said, "but where on earth do you put English?"

"English," the German replied, "is very simple and logical, of course, but almost without grammatical construction or any rules of pronunciation. Therefore its claims have not been put forward very strongly, but we shall be glad to hear you on this subject, if you wish to say anything."

Of course I took the bull by the horns at once and began by saying it would be easy to prove that English was the most musical of all the languages mentioned, at which there was a shout of amused laughter. Signor Manzoni, the Italian, wanted to know whether I was serious; he thought

* H. Gerhardus Lolling (1848–94).
** Lord James Bryce (1838–1922). He wrote the classic *The American Commonwealth* (1888) and *Modern Democracies* (1921), and was ambassador to the United States (1907–1913).

it would be easy to demonstrate that English was the most cacophonous of European tongues.

"Let me first make my point," I interjected. "Why do you say Italian is the most musical of all languages?"

"Because of our beautiful open vowel sounds," he replied, "and we have no harsh gutturals or sibilants."

"But English has got your five pure vowel sounds," I replied, "and many more; English has six or seven different sounds for *o* and four or five different sounds for *a;* in fact, we have about twenty vowel sounds to your five. Is it really your contention that the fewer the instruments in an orchestra, the more divine is the music?"

"I see your point," said Manzoni. "I didn't think of it before. It is a good point, but you must admit that your English *s*'s are even a greater disqualification than the German gutturals."

"We avoid the sibilants," I replied, "as much as we can, though I do admit that the *s* is a danger in English, just as the guttural is in German; but the point is, you must admit, that we have a larger orchestra of vowel sounds than any other European lagnuage, and you must also admit that we have had the greatest poets in the world to use them. You can hardly then question the result as to the best music, for I know you would admit at once that the most complex music is pretty sure to be the finest."

"I seize your argument," he replied thoughtfully. "It would have been truer to say that you English have the finest orchestra and we Italians the finest string quintet in the world."

"Let us leave it at that," I exclaimed, laughing. "But if you care for my opinion, I can assure you that there are cadences in English verse so subtle and so musical that I put it above all other verse in the world, above even the best of Goethe. Think of the over-praised Greek, of Euripides, for example, who puts the caesura invariably in the second foot: his music is as mechanical as a treadmill. And no one tells you of that; all praise him, scholars and poets alike:

> And Euripides, the human,
> With his droppings of warm tears
> And his touches of things common
> Till they rise to touch the spheres.*

"Besides, this matter is being decided in another way. A century ago only about fifteen millions of people spoke English; now nearly two hundred millions of the most rapidly increasing population in the world speak English; in another century there will be four or five hundred millions speaking

---

* Elizabeth Barrett Browning, from *Wine of Cyprus, XII:*
> Our Euripides, the Human,
> With his droppings of warm tears,
> And his touches of things common
> Till they rose to touch the spheres.

it; the only competitor we have really is Russian, and Russian will be in a secondary place as soon as Australia and the great plateau of Central Africa are filled with English-speaking people. The verdict of humanity will be in favor of English as the language of the most progressive and most numerous people in the world. And I am inclined to believe that this judgment by results is pretty good judgment." (A year or so later I remember Turgenief saying once that he infinitely preferred Russian to German or to French, though he spoke both languages excellently. He insisted that Russian was far richer, a far finer instrument than German, and, "it is already much more widely spread," was his final argument.)

"The survival," said the Baron, "may be of the fittest, but the fittest is not always the best or highest. In spite of your arguments, and they are excellent, I regard the conclusions come to before you renewed the discussion as nearer the truth in many essentials. I still think Italian more musical than English: you cannot believe that your English "critcher" is as musical as *creatura* (he pronounced it in four syllables); and French is a better language for diplomacy than English, with finer shades of courtesy, more exact shades, I mean, of amiable converse. We French have fifty different ways of ending our letters; contrast them with 'Yours sincerely,' 'Yours truly,' 'Yours faithfully.' It seems to me that in all matters of politeness we have the full orchestra and you have nothing but the banjo, the cymbals and the drum!"

"The question," I replied, "is surely susceptible of proof. Give me any of the expressions with which you close your letters and I will undertake to render them into English without difficulty, giving the very shade of meaning you wish to have conveyed."

"Pardon," he retorted, "but you would not even be able to translate *amitiés!* The shade between love and friendship would slip through the large English mesh and be lost."

"We can say, 'your loving friend,' " I said, "or, 'your friend and lover,' or 'your affectionate friend,' the matter is perfectly simple."

The discussion became general for a few minutes. They all gave me phrases they thought would be difficult to translate into English, but they were all easily convertible, and I resumed the discussion by saying: "Let me give one English instance and see how you would translate it. I shall not excogitate a phrase out of my inner consciousness; I will simply give a well-known passage of Ruskin's in which he praises Venetian painters and ask you to translate it.

'Venice taught these men,' he said, 'to love another style of beauty; broad-chested and level-browed like her horizons; thighed and shouldered like her billows; footed like her stealing foam; bathed in clouds of golden hair like her sunset.'

"Now, Baron, don't be in a hurry to translate into French 'thighed and shouldered like her billows' or 'footed like her stealing foam.'

"I think you will find it hard to translate that sentence into even a page of any modern language, and in translating it I am sure you will lose the poetry of it, the beauty of it, or at least some part of the poetry and beauty; whereas you admit that I have been able to translate your French and German examples into their equivalent English pretty easily."

"Tell us," said Lolling, "what you really thing about the English language."

Flattered by the appeal, I did my best to sum up like a judge.

"It was Max Müller,"* I said, "or one of the German philologists—it may have been Karl Werner—who put me on the track by saying that English had more names of things, was richer in substantives than any other language, the observant habit of the people, the sense of the facts of life being very strong in Englishmen.

"English has shed almost all grammatical forms, it seems to me, in the struggle for existence. It is more simple, more logical than any other modern language. It can be used more easily by uneducated people than any other tongue, more easily even than French, and that quality gives it its fitness for spreading over the world. Its real weakness in sound is, as the Baron knows, the habit of accenting the first syllable, which tends to shorten all words, and the sibilant, which should be avoided as far as possible. The worst weakness of English in structure was, strange to say, in a people so given to action, its paucity of verbs.

"But here the poets have come to the rescue and have turned the present participles into verbs, as in the passage I quoted from Ruskin;** and they have also managed to turn nouns into verbs: 'She cupped her face with her hand'; 'he bottled up his wrath'; 'he legged it away.' These are just instances to show how the richness of English nouns is converted into the astonishing, unexpected richness of English in painting verbs. All modern European languages have painting adjectives and epithets at hand with all the colors of the palette; but we are alone in being able to use present participles that are half-adjectives and half-verbs, and to convert even nouns into verbs, and so lend both pictorial beauty and speed to the tongue almost at will.

"Though I have great liking for classic Greek, the Greek of Plato and Sophocles, I still think the language of Shakespeare and Keats the most beautiful in the world. That is why I resent the way it is prostituted and degraded by the users. The aristocracy of England has degraded the tongue into a few shibboleths of snobbery. It's 'awfully' this and 'awfully' that; she is a 'high-stepper', and 'high-stepper' becomes a portmanteau adjective of

---

* Friedrich Max Müller (1823–1900). After being educated in Germany, he went to Oxford as the first professor of philology and became a British citizen. His translation of the *Rig-Veda,* commissioned by the East India Company, is still standard.

** No present participles appear in the quotation, the part participles are used as adjectives.

the next generation of snobs who would fence themselves away from the middle classes, not by excellence of speech, but by idiotic shibboleths. The English aristocrat degrades his language as much as the corner-boy whose one adjective is 'bloody.'

"Oh! That English aristocracy: how it dwarfs the ideal! It knows a good deal about outward things, about the body and men's dress and social observances and trivial courtesies; but alas, it knows very little about the mind, and nothing about the soul—nothing. What aristocrat in England ever thought of training his faculties of thought, as lots of schoolboys train their muscles, to almost perfect vigor and beauty, knowing instinctively that no muscle must be overdeveloped, but all should be kept in perfect harmony. Yet even here the Hindu Yogi knows more about the muscles of the heart and stomach and intestines, the most important parts of the body.

"No Englishman thinks it disgraceful today to be completely ignorant of German, French, Italian, and Russian and the special achievements of these peoples in thought and art and literature—"

"True, true," exclaimed the Baron, interrupting me, "and it needs saying; but what do you mean by the 'soul' exactly, and how can one train that?"

"I know very little about it myself, I must confess," I replied, "but I got just a whiff of it as I came through India, and I have always promised myself to go back and spend six months or a year in assimilating the wisdom of the East. Gautama Buddha always impresses me as one of the noblest of men, and where a single tree grows to the sky, the soil and climate, too, must be worth studying. But we've gone far afield and gotten far away from our theme."

"Let me just say one word," the Baron broke in. "I think France in almost every way finer than England, nearer the ideal. Every Frenchman of any intelligence loves the things of the mind—art and literature—and tries to speak French as purely and as well as possible, whereas in England there is no class that seems to care for the finest heritage of the race in the same way. And what airs the English aristocrat gives himself. He's hardly human. Have you noticed that the only people who don't come to our meetings are the English students? And yet they need cosmopolitan education more than any other race."

Athens holds many of the deathless memories of my life. I was looking at the figures on the parapet of the Temple to the Wingless Victory one day when I suddenly noticed that the dress was drawn tight about the breast just to outline the exquisite beauty of the curve—sheer sensuality in the artist. Thirty years later I asked Rodin what he thought, and he declared that the Greek gods of the Parthenon are as undisguisedly sensual as any figures in plastic art.

I met yet another person in this life at the Hotel d'Athènes who deserves perhaps to be remembered. One day a tall good-looking Englishman was introduced to me by the manager of the hotel. "This is Major Geary, Mr.

Harris. I've told the Major," he went on, "that you know more about Athens, and indeed about all Greece, than any one of my acquaintances, and he wishes to ask you some questions."

"I'll be glad to answer so far as I can," I said, for Major Geary was good-looking and evidently of good class, tall and of course well-set-up, tho' he told me he had left the Royal Artillery some years before and was now in Armstrong's.

"The fact is," he began, "I've been sent out to sell some of our guns, and I want to ask someone who knows how I should set to work. A man at our Embassy advised me to go the King first."

"That would do you no good," I replied. "Do you know Tricoupis,* the Prime Minister? You can surely get a letter to him and that will be the best door to his confidence."

Geary thanked me and followed my advice; a little later we lunched together and I found him an admirable host with, strange to say, a rare knowledge of English poetry. Shakespeare he knew very little about, but a great part of English lyric poetry was at his finger's ends, and he showed astonishing taste and knowledge.

Geary's delight in poetry drew us together, and one morning he asked me to go with him to meet Tricoupis and some of the ministers and support the Armstrong proposition. Briefly, it was that the English firm would give a much larger and longer credit than either Krupp or Creusot would give. I went with him the more willingly, for I was eager to meet Tricoupis, who had written in a masterly way the *History of the Revolution.***

But at the meeting Tricoupis was all business and I could get no private or confidential speech with him. Towards the end of the sitting, Geary pulled out a magnificent gold watch which had been given to him by his comrades when he left the Royal Artillery; it was engraved, if I remember rightly, with the arms of the artillery in jewels. As Tricoupis would not force a decision on his colleagues, he was the more courteous to Geary and expressed his admiration of the watch. Geary at once took it off the chain and showed it to him; the next man leaned forward to look, and the watch passed down the table, while Tricoupis assured Major Geary that his proposal would be seriously considered and answered within a week or so. As he rose, Geary exclaimed, smiling, "And my watch!" But the watch was not forthcoming and no one seemed to know what had become of it. Tricoupis frowned, evidently disgusted. "Gentlemen," he said, at length, "if Major Geary's watch is not forthcoming, I'll get the police in and have us all searched."

"No, no!" Geary broke in, knowing that the commission he hoped to get from selling cannons was much more important than the watch. "I'd rather

---

* Charilaos Trikoupis (1832–1896), Greek statesman.
** But it was Spyridon Trikoupis (1788–1873), father of the prime minister, who wrote a *History of the Greek Revolution,* and he was dead by this time.

lose the watch; please, no police among gentlemen and in your house; I couldn't hear of it!"

"It's very kind of you," responded Tricoupis. "I'm sure the watch was pocketed by mistake and now the man who took it is ashamed to give it up publicly; suppose we put out the lights, and as my colleagues file out the man who has the watch can slip it on that little table by the door, where the buhl clock now stands, and no one will be any the wiser."

"First rate," cried Geary. "It takes genius," and he bowed to the Premier, "to hit on so admirable a solution."

The lights were all turned out and the ministers filed out of the room in almost complete silence. We heard them in the hall and then the house-door closed.

"Now," said Tricoupis, "we'll find your watch, Major," and he turned up the gas; but there was no watch on the table and—the buhl clock too had disappeared.

A week later, I believe, the watch was found through Tricoupis' efforts and returned to the Major, but I don't think Geary brought off Armstrong's deal. I tell the story because it is eminently characteristic of the Greece I knew and loved, loved in spite of its poverty, which was the cause of the somewhat low business morality of an exceedingly intelligent people.

When I knew Athens thoroughly and could speak modern Greek fluently I went with some friends, a German student and an Italian, on foot through Greece. We went to Thebes and Delphi and climbed Parnassus, and finally I went on by myself to Janina; and then returning visited Corinth, Sparta and Mycenae, where I was lucky enough to be among the first to see the astounding head of the Hermes of Praxiteles, surely the most beautiful face in plastic art, for no Venus, whether of Melos or Cnidos, possesses his superb intellectual appeal. It is curious that though love is the woman's province and love is the deepest emotion in life, yet the profoundest expressions, even of love, are not hers. And yet I cannot believe that she is man's inferior, and surely she is sufficiently articulate! It's a mystery for the future to solve, or some wiser man than I am.

Chapter VI

Love in Athens; and "The Sacred Band"

I HAD BEEN in the Hotel d'Athènes a week or so when I noticed a pretty girl on the stairs: she charmed by eyes. A chambermaid told me she was Mme. M— and had the next bedroom to mine. Then I discovered that her mother, a Mme. D—, had the big sitting-room on the first floor. I don't know how I made the mother's acquaintance, but she was kindly and easy of approach, and I found she had a son, Jacques D—, in the Corps des Pages, whom I came to know intimately in Paris some years later, as I shall relate in due course.* The daughter and I soon became friends; she was a very pretty girl in the early twenties. The D—s were of pure Greek stock, but they came from Marseilles and spoke French as well as modern Greek. The girl had been married to a Scot a couple of years before I met her; he was now in Britain somewhere, she said. She would hardly speak of her marriage; it was the mother who told me it had been a tragic failure.

In the freedom from fixed hours of study, my long habit of virtue weighed on me and Mme. M— was extraordinarily good looking: slight and rather tall with a Greek face of the best type, crowned with a mass of black hair. I have never seen larger or more beautiful dark eyes, and her slight figure had a lissom grace that was intensely provocative. Her name was Eirene, or "Peace," and she soon allowed me to use it. In three days I told her I loved her, and indeed I was taken as by storm. We went out together for long walks: one day we visited the Acropolis and she was delighted to learn from me all about the "Altar of the Gods." Another day we went down into the Agora, or market-place, and she taught me something of modern Greek life and customs. One day an old woman greeted us as lovers, and when Mme. M— shook her head and said *"ouk éstiv"* (it is not so), she shook her finger and said, "He's afire and you'll catch fire, too."

At first Mme. M— would not yield to me at all, but after a month or so of assiduity and companionship, I was able to steal a kiss or an embrace

* In the fifth volume Harris reveals him to be Jacques Damala, Sarah Bernhardt's husband for a short time.

and came slowly day by day, little by little, nearer to the goal. An accident helped me one day: shall I ever forget it? We had been all through the town together and only returned as the evening was drawing in. When we came to the first floor I opened the door of their sitting-room very quietly. As luck would have it, the screen before the door had been pushed aside and there on the sofa at the far side of the room I saw her mother in the arms of a Greek officer. I drew the door to slowly, so that the girl coming behind might see, and then closed it noiselessly.

As we turned off towards our bedrooms on the left, I saw that her face was glowing. At her door I stopped her. "My kiss," I said, and as in a dream she kissed me: *l'heure du berger* had struck.

"Won't you come to me tonight?" I whispered. "That door leads into my room." She looked at me with that inscrutable woman's glance, and for the first time her eyes gave themselves. That night I went to bed early and moved away the sofa, which on my side barred her door. I tried the lock but found it closed on her side, worse luck!

As I lay in bed that night about eleven o'clock, I heard and saw the handle of the door move. At once I blew out the light, but the blinds were not drawn and the room was alight with moonshine. "May I come in?" she asked.

"May you?" I was out of bed in a jiffy and had taken her adorable soft round form in my arms. "You darling sweet," I cried, and lifted her into my bed. She had dropped her dressing-gown, had only a nightie on, and in one moment my hands were all over her lovely body. The next moment I was with her in bed and on her, but she moved aside and away from me.

"No, let's talk," she said.

I began kissing her, but acquiesced, "Let's talk."

To my amazement, she began: "Have you read Zola's latest book, *Nana?*"

"Yes," I replied.

"Well," she said, "you know what the girl did to Nana?"

"Yes," I replied, with sinking heart.

"Well," she went on, "why not do that to me? I'm desperately afraid of getting a child; you would be too in my place; why not love each other without fear?" A moment's thought told me that all roads lead to Rome and so I assented and soon I slipped down between her legs. "Tell me please how to give you most pleasure," I said, and gently I opened the lips of her sex and put my lips on it and my tongue against her clitoris. There was nothing repulsive in it; it was another and more sensitive mouth. Hardly had I kissed it twice when she slid lower down in the bed with a sigh, whispering, "That's it; that's heavenly!"

Thus encouraged I naturally continued: soon her little lump swelled out so that I could take it in my lips and each time I sucked it, her body moved convulsively, and soon she opened her legs further and drew them up to let me in to the uttermost. Now I varied the movement by tonguing the rest of her sex and thrusting my tongue into her as far as possible; her movements quickened and her breathing grew more and more spasmodic, and when I went back to the clitoris again and took it in my lips and sucked it while pushing my forefinger back and forth into her sex, her movements became wilder and she began suddenly to cry in French, "Oh, c'est fou! Oh, c'est fou! Oh! Oh!" And suddenly she lifted me up, took my head in both her hands, and crushed my mouth with hers, as if she wanted to hurt me.

The next moment my head was between her legs again and the game went on. Little by little I felt that my finger rubbing the top of her sex while I tongued her clitoris gave her the most pleasure, and after another ten minutes of this delightful practice she cried: "Frank, Frank, stop! Kiss me! Stop and kiss me, I can't stand any more, I am rigid with passion and want to bite or pinch you."

Naturally I did as I was told and her body melted itself against mine while our lips met. "You dear," she said, "I love you so, and oh how wonderfully you kiss."

"You've taught me," I said. "I'm your pupil."

While we were together my sex was against hers and seeking an entry; each time it pushed in, she drew away; at length she said: "I'd love to give myself to you, dear, but I'm frightened."

"You need not be," I assured her. "If you let me enter, I'll withdraw before my seed comes and there'll be no danger." But do what I would, say what I would, that first night she would not yield to me in the usual way.

I knew enough about women to know that the more I restrained myself and left her to take the initiative, the greater would be my reward. A few days later I took her up Mount Lycabettus and showed her "all the kingdoms of the spirit," as I used to call Athens and the surroundings. She wanted to know about ancient Greek literature. "Was it better than modern French literature?"

"Yes and no; it was altogether different."

She confessed she could not understand Homer, but when I recited choruses from the *Oedipus Rex,* she understood them; and the great oath in Demosthenes' speech, "Not by those who first faced death at Marathon" —and the noble summing up brought tears to her eyes—"Now by your judgment you will either drive our accusers out over land and over sea, houseless and homeless, or you will give to us a sure release from all danger in the peace of the eternal silence." On hearing this, she kissed me of her own accord.

As we were walking that afternoon down the long slope of Lycabettus, "You don't want me any more?" she said, suddenly. "Men are such selfish creatures; if you don't do all they want at once, they draw away."

"You don't believe a word of that," I interrupted. "When have I drawn away? I'm awaiting your good pleasure. I didn't want to bother you perpetually, that's all. If you could see me watching the handle of your door every night—"

"Some night soon it will turn," she said, and slipped her hand through my arm. "I don't like to decide important things when I am all a quiver with feeling, but I've thought over all you said and I want to believe you, to trust you—see?" And her eyes were one promise.

Luckily, when the handle of her door did turn, I was on the watch and took her in my arms before she had crossed the threshold, and the love-game she had taught me went on for a long time. At length wearied and all dissolved in sensation, she lay in my arms and my sex throbbing hot was against hers, seeking, seeking its sheath. Luckily I did not force matters but let the contact plead for me. At length she whispered, "I hate to deny you; will you do what you promised?"

"Surely," I said.

"And there's no danger?"

"None," I replied. "I give you my word of honor," and the next moment she relaxed in my arms and let me have my will. Slowly I penetrated, bit by bit, and she leaned to me with greedy mouth, kissing me. It was divine, but oh, so brief: a few thrusts and I was compelled to withdraw to keep my word.

"Oh, it was heavenly," she sighed as I took up my spirting semen on my handkerchief, "but I like your mouth best: why is that? Your tongue excites me terribly: why?" she asked, and then, "Let's talk!"

But I said, "No dear! let's begin. Now there's no risk; I can go with you as much as we like without danger. I'll explain it to you afterwards, but take my word and let's enjoy ourselves."

The next moment I was in her again and the great game went on with renewed vigor. Again and again she came to an ecstasy and at length as I mounted high up so as to excite her more, she suddenly cried out: "Oh, oh, que c'est fou, fou, fou," and she bit my shoulder and then burst into tears.

Naturally I took her in my arms and began to kiss her; our first great love-duet was over. From that night on she had no secrets from me, no reticences, and bit by bit she taught me all she felt in the delirium of love: she told me she could not tell which gave her most pleasure, but I soon learned that she preferred me to begin by kissing her sex for ten or fifteen minutes and then to complete the orgasm with my sex used rather violently.

All the English schoolboy stories of some fancied resemblance between the mouth and the sex of the woman, and the nose and sex of the man, I found invariably false. Eirene had rather a large mouth and a very small pretty sex, whereas the girl with the largest sex and thickest lips I ever met had a small thin mouth. Similarly with the man. I'm sure there's no relation whatever between the sex and the feature of the face.

An exquisite mistress, Eirene, with a girl's body, small, round breasts, and a mouth I never grew tired of. Often afterwards, instead of walks, we adjourned to my room and spent the afternoon in love's games. Sometimes her mother came to her door and she would laugh and hug me; once or twice her brother came to mine, but we lay in each other's arms and let the foolish outside world knock. But we always practiced the game she had been the first to teach me; for some reason or other I learned more about women through it and the peculiar ebb and flow of their sensuality than the natural love-play had taught me; it gives the key, so to speak, to a woman's heart and senses, and to the man this is the chief reward, as wise old Montaigne knew, who wrote of "standing at rack and manger before the meal."

I was always trying to win confessions from my girl friends about their first experiences in sensuality, but save in the case of some few French-women, actresses for the most part, I was not very successful. What the reason is, others must explain, but I found girls strangely reticent on the subject. Time and again when in bed with Eirene I tried to get her to tell me, and at long last she confessed to one adventure.

When she was about twelve she had a French governess in Marseilles, and one day this lady came into the bathroom, telling her she had been a long time bathing, and offering to help her dry herself. "I noticed," said Eirene, "that she looked at me intently and it pleased me. When I got out she wrapped the robe about me and then sat down and took me on her knees and began to dry me. As she touched me often there I opened my legs and she touched me very caressingly, and then of a sudden she kissed me passionately on the mouth and left me. I liked her very much. She was a dear, really clever and kind."

"Did she ever dry you again?" I asked.

Eirene laughed. "You want to know too much, sir," was all she would say.

When I returned to Athens at the end of the summer, I took rooms in the people's quarter and lived very cheaply. Soon Eirene came to visit me again and we went often to the Greek theatre and I read Theocritus with her on many afternoons; but she gave me nothing new and in the spring I decided to return by way of Constantinople and the Black Sea to Vienna, for I felt that my *Lehrjahre*—"prentice-years"—were drawing to an end; and Paris beckoned, and London.

One of the last evenings we were together Eirene wanted to know what I liked best in her.

"You've a myriad good qualities," I began. "You are good-tempered and reasonable always, to say nothing of your lovely eyes and lithe slight figure. But why do you ask?"

"My husband used to say I was bony," she replied. "He made me dreadfully unhappy, tho' I tried my best to please him. I didn't feel much with him at first and that word 'bony' hurt terribly."

"Don't you know," I said, "[on] one of our first meetings, when you got out of bed to go to your room, I lifted up your nightie and saw the outline of your curving thighs and hips; it has always seemed to me one of the loveliest contours I've ever seen. If I had been a sculptor I'd have modeled it long ago—'bony,' indeed; the man didn't deserve you: put him out of your head."

"I have," she said, "for we women have only room for one, and you've put yourself in my heart. I'm glad you don't think me bony, but fancy you caring for a curve of flesh so much. Men are funny things. No woman would so over-prize a mere outline—your praise and his blame both show the same spirit."

"Yet desire is born of admiration," I corrected.

"My desire is born of yours," she replied. "But a woman's love is better and different: it is of the heart and soul."

"But the body gives the key," I said, "and makes intimacy divine!"

I found several unlooked for and unimaginable benefits in this mouth-worship. First of all, I could give pleasure to any extent without exhausting or even tiring myself. It thus enabled me to atone completely and make up for my steadily decreasing virility. Secondly, I discovered that by teaching me the most sensitive parts of the woman, I was able even in the ordinary way to give my mistresses more and keener pleasure than ever before. I had all the joy of coming into a new kingdom of delight with increased vigor. Moreover, as I have said, it taught me to know every woman more intimately than I had known any up to that time, and I soon found that they liked me better than even in the first flush of inexhaustible youth.

Later I learned other devices but none so important as this first discovery which showed me once for all how superior art is to nature.

The Sacred Band

For I doubt not through the ages one increasing purpose runs
And the thoughts of men are widened by the process of the suns.*

After studying in Athens for some months, I heard of a club where university professors and some students met and talked classic Greek. A mistake or even an awkwardness of expression was anathema, and out of this reverence for the language of Plato and Sophocles there grew a desire to make the modern tongue resemble the old one as nearly as possible. It was impossible to bring back into common use the elaborate syntax; the subtle, shading particles too were lost forever; but it was sought to use words in their old meaning so exactly that even today Xenophon could read the daily paper in Athens and understand it without difficulty.

This assimilation was only possible because the spoken language of the

* Tennyson's *Locksley Hall:*
      Yet I doubt not through the ages one increasing purpose runs,
      And the thoughts of men are widened with the process of the suns.

Greeks, *é koiné diàlektos,* had for many centuries existed side by side with the literary tongue. The spoken dialect had been preserved in the New Testament and in the Church services, and so it came easy for learned and enthusiastic Grecians to keep the language of the common people as like that of Plato as possible; and the race is so extraordinarily intelligent that even the peasant, who has always called a horse *alogos* (the brainless one), knows that *ippos* is a finer word for the same animal. And though the common pronunciation is not exactly that of classic times, still it is a great deal nearer the antique pronunciation than any English or even Erasmic imitation. The modern Greek does use his accents correctly, and anyone who has learned to do that by ear can appreciate the cadence of classic Greek poetry and prose far more perfectly than any scholar who only reads for the rhythm of long and short syllables.

I think it was Raikes told a story that illustrated a side of this Greek ambition for me. Professor Blackie,* a well-known Scotch [sic] historian and Philhellene, came out to Athens on a visit and spoke in the Piraeus. Raikes went to hear him with a distinguished university professor who was one of the leaders of the Hellenic movement. After listening to Blackie for a while, the Greek professor turned to Raikes and said, "I had no idea that English sounded so well."

"But he's speaking modern Greek," said Raikes.

"Good God!" cried the professor, "I'd never have guessed that; I've not understood a single word of it."

One experience of this time I must relate shortly, for it had an enormous, a disproportionate influence on my whole outlook and way of reading the past. Everyone knows that Plutarch was born at Chaeroneia, and in my wanderings on foot through Attica I stayed for some days in a peasant's house on the plain.

When Philip of Macedon and Alexander, his son, afterwards called the Great, invaded Attica, they came almost as barbarians and the city of Thebes had to bear the first shock. Plutarch tells how three hundred Theban youths of the best families came together and took a solemn oath that they would put a stop to Philip's astonishing carrer of conquest or die in the attempt. The forces met at Chaeroneia,** and Philip's new order, the famous phalanx, carried all before it. In vain the three hundred youths dashed themselves against it; time and again they were beaten back and the phalanx drove on. In the bed of a river, the "Sacred Band," as they were called, *ó îeros lôchos,* made their supreme effort and perished to the last man; and after the battle, we are told, the noble three hundred were buried in one grave by their parents in Thebes. The course of the river, Plutarch says, was turned aside so that they might all be interred on the very spot where their final assault had failed.

---

* Professor John Stuart Blackie (1809–95), a professor of Greek at the University of Edinburgh; he was especially known for his translation of Aeschylus.
** In 388 B.C.

Everyone knows that in our day there was a gigantic marble lion at Chaeroneia. The Turks in their time had heard that there was money in it, so they blew it up to get the treasure, but they found nothing, and no one could understand what the lion of Chaeroneia was doing in the center of a deserted plain, far away from any village.

At a big meeting of the Classic Greek Society, I declared my belief that the lion of Chaeroneia was an excellent specimen of antique work carved in classic times. I believed it had been erected over the barrow of the "Sacred Band," and if excavations were carried out, I felt sure that the grave of the heroes would be discovered. Greek patriotism took fire at the suggestion; a banker and friend offered to defray the expenses and we went up to Chaeroneia to begin the work. There was no river at Chaeroneia, but a shallow brook, the Thermodon, was a couple of hundred yards away from the fragments of the lion. On studying the ground closely, I was insistent that a long grass-grown depression in the ground near the lion should be laid open first, arguing always that the lion would prove to have been erected on the grave itself; and soon the barrow was discovered.

Four stone walls a foot or so broad and six feet or so in height had been built in the form of an elongated square, resting on the shingle of an old river bed, and therein like sardines we found the bodies, or rather, the skeletons of the "Sacred Band." The first thing we noticed was the terrible wounds sustained in the conflict; here, for example, was a skeleton with three ribs smashed on one side while the head of the spear that killed him was jammed between a rib and the backbone; another had his backbone broken by a vigorous spear-thrust and one side of his head beaten in as well. The next thing that struck us was that the teeth in all the skeletons were excellently preserved and in almost perfect order. Clearly our inferiority in this respect must be due to our modern, cooked food.

We counted two hundred and ninety-seven skeletons, and in one corner there was a little pile of ashes, evidently of the three who had survived longest and were finally cremated. At one side of the oblong enclosure there was a solid piece of masonry some ten feet square, plainly the pedestal of the lion which was placed there *couchant,* looking away over the bodies of the dead towards Thebes in eternal remembrance of the heroism of the youths who had given their lives in defence of their fatherland. A "Sacred Band," indeed!

So, the poetic legend that this modern historian and that could not even take seriously was found to be strictly and exactly true, a transcript of the facts. It all helped to make the work of the writer precious to me and vivified the past for me in such a way that I began to read other books, and notably the New Testament, in a different spirit. German scholars had taught me that Jesus was a mythical figure: his teaching a mish-mash of various traditions and religions and myths. He was not an historical personage in any way, they declared; the three synoptic Gospels were all compiled from 50 to 80 years after the events, and John was certainly later still.

The story of the "Sacred Band" led me to use my brain on the person of Jesus as I had already used it on Shakespeare; and soon I found indubitable proof that Jesus was not only an historical personage, but could be studied in his words and works and realized in his habit as he lived. Tacitus and Josephus both were witnesses to his existence, and if the passage in Josephus has been added to, that of Tacitus is untouched and absolutely convincing: "A certain fellow called Jesus" (Quidam Jesu) did certainly live and teach in Jerusalem and was there crucified as the "King of the Jews" and "Son of God!"

Not God or King to me in any superhuman sense, but flesh and bone, a man among men, though a sacred guide and teacher of the highest. As I read, the scales fell from my eyes, and I saw that this Jesus was blood-brother to Shakespeare: both weak in body: Jesus could not carry His Cross and was supposed to have died in the first few hours of agony; both too, called "gentle"; both of incomparable speed and depth of thought and sweet loving-kindness of character. Read the Arthur of *King John* speaking to his executioner,

> Are you sick, Hubert? You look pale today:
> In sooth, I would you were a little sick,
> That I might sit all night and watch with you.
> I warrant I love you more than you do me,*

and then recall the sacred words, "Suffer little children to come unto me and forbid them not; for of such is the kingdom of heaven!"

Surely these two men are of the same divine spirit.

In courage Jesus was the greater and accordingly came to a more dreadful end and to a loftier fame; but Shakespeare insists on the need of repentance and absolute forgiveness just as Jesus did: "Pardon's the word for all." My life was enriched by finding another sacred guide, but alas! I yielded to the new influence very reluctantly, and it was many years before the knowledge of the Christ began even to modify my character. But this gradual interpenetration is the dominant impulse in the next twenty years of my life and bit by bit led me to attempt that synthesis of paganism and the spirit of Jesus, which, it seems to me, must constitute the essential elements at least of "the religion of the future!" For what is the spirit of Jesus but the certainty that God is just goodness and must be loved by all of us mortals!

The first duty of man or woman is purely pagan: each of us should develop all his faculties of body and mind and soul as harmoniously as possible. He should, too, secure the highest enjoyment possible from his gifts; but when he has thus, so to speak, reached the zenith of his accomplishment, he should study how to give the utmost possible help to his fellow-men and make "the new commandment" of Jesus the chief purpose of his life.

* Act IV, scene 1.

Alas! To "love one another" is a most difficult rule, unless we can remember that it is just to love what is good and to forgive the veiling faults. The best way to this all-comprehending love, I feel, is by dint of pity— "good pity," Shakespeare calls it, and "sacred pity," "holy pity" even, for it leads, he knew, to pardon and forgiveness. And this pity must needs result in redressing the worst injustices of life, and, above all, in leveling up the awful inequality that gives one child everything in unimaginable superfluity and denies to another just as gifted and healthy even decent conditions of living. The handicap of the rich and great is just as poisonously bad as the handicap of the poor that stunts the frame and impoverishes the blood. It is pity and loving sympathy that may amend in time the worst diseases of society. One would think that the knowledge of natural laws and the control of natural resources, while increasing enormously the productivity of labor, would of necessity improve the position of the laborer. So far that has not been the case: the greater power given us by the thinker and man of science has merely increased the inequality between the possessors and the hordes of the dispossessed. If that process continues, the race is doomed; but already those of us who have reached a certain plane of thought, even though they have found riches easy or hard to acquire, are on the side of the poor.

John Stuart Mill thought the remedy lay in heavy succession duties and it may be that this is the most practical way of attack; indeed, it looks as if it were, though I prefer the nationalization of the land and public utilities, such as railways and water and gas companies. Yet the succession duties in England since the World War have remained without serious objection at something like thirty-three per cent of the great inheritances. One thing is certain, in one way or other the worst inequalities must be ended. The over-great individual liberty in England has led to the practical enslavement and degradation of the working classes. In 1837 only ten per cent of recruits were below five feet-six in height; in 1915 seventy per cent were below that height and even fifty per cent could not pass the puny physical standard required.

Having learned in life both what riches can give and what poverty gives, I have always stood in favor of the poor. The leveling up process is the most important task of our politicians, and they should be classed according to the help they give to this reform of reforms.

But after the World War and the misery which the hateful so-called peace of Versailles has brought upon Europe, other fears for the future of humanity must invade the soul. Pity, that angel of the world, must be cultivated and taught, or life for us short-sighted, selfish animals will become impossible. Will not some young noble-minded man start a new "Sacred Band" that will struggle for humanity and the rights of man as valiantly as those Theban youths struggled for the liberty and safety of Greece? Or must we come to the despair sung by Sophocles in his *Oedipus of Colonos:*

> Who breathes must suffer and who thinks must mourn
> And he alone is blest who n'er was born.*

But, everyone is asking, does this rebirth of paganism, which is mainly due to the progress of science, hold any hope, any consolation, in presence of the awful mystery of death? It must be admitted that here the fates are almost silent. We no longer believe, it is true, as the Greek did, that it would have been better for us never to have been born. We are proud of our inheritance of life, can already see how it may be bettered in a thousand ways, but hope beyond the grave there is none. Yet we English and Americans have the highest word and the most consoling yet heard among men.

Meredith's noble couplet is higher than the best of Sophocles:

> Into the breast that bears the rose
> Shall I, with shuddering, fall?**

These seventy years or so of life are all we've got, but, as Goethe says, we can fill them, if we will, with great deeds and greater dreams. Goethe and Meredith: I have compared them before: I love them both.

> . . . Both are cupbearers undying
> Of the wine that's meant for souls!†

---

* From a chorus about two-thirds through the play; whether this is Harris' own rendering of the lines is not known.
** From the "Ode to the Spirit of Earth in Autumn."
† Elizabeth Barrett Browning, from *Wine of Cyprus, XII:*
>   These were cup-bearers undying,
> *etc.*

Chapter VII

Holidays and Irish Virtue!

I WENT BY SHIP from Athens to Constantinople and admired, as every one must, the superb position of the city; like New York, a queen of many waters. But I was coming away without having learned much when, as my luck would have it, I fell into talk with a German, a student of Byzantine architecture who raved to me of St. Sophia, took me to see it, played guide and expositor of all its beauties time and again, till at length the scales fell from my eyes and I too saw that it was perhaps as he said, "The greatest church in the world," thought I could never like the outside as much as the inside. The bold arches and the immense sweep of pillars and the mosaics, frescoes, and inscriptions on the walls give an unique impression of splendor and grandeur combined, a union of color and form, singular in magnificence.

Devout Turks were always worshiping Mahomet in the church and here and there on the pavement schools were being held; but on the walls the older frescoes representing the Crucified One were everywhere, showing through the Mahometan paint or plaster, and the impression left on me was that the Cross everywhere was slowly but surely triumphing over the Crescent. In time I came to see that St. Sophia was a greater achievement even than the Parthenon, and learned in this way that the loftier Spirit usually finds in Time the nobler body.

My German friend took me too, to the Church of the Saviour, which he called "the gem of Byzantine work," and indeed the mosaics, at least of the fourteenth century, were richer and more varied than anything I have since seen, even in Palermo.

We had a wild passage through the Black Sea and neither Varna nor the Danube wiped out the sense of discomfort.

But Belgrade with its citadel pleased me intimately, and Buda with Pesth across the great bridge caught my fancy, its fortress hill reminding me of the Acropolis; but Vienna won my heart. The old Burg Theater with actors and actresses as good as those of Paris, the noble Opera-House with the best music in Europe, and the Belvedere with its gorgeous Venetian pictures, and the wonderful Armory, all appealed to me intensely! Then too there was the Court and the military pageants of the Hofburg, and the great library, and above all the rich kindly life of the people in the Wurstelprater, the stout German carpet, so to speak, illumined with a thousand colors of Slav and Semite, Bohemian and Polish embroidery, till even the gypsies seemed to add the touches of barbarism and superstition needed to fringe and set off the gorgeous fabric. In many-sided appeal, Vienna seemed to me richer even than Paris; and Pauline Lucca,* exquisite singer at once and [a] beautiful charming person, became to my imagination the genius of the city, with Billroth,** the great doctor, as symbol of the science on which the whole life was builded [sic]. I find it hard to forgive the barbarian Wilson for maiming and impoverishing a nobler corporate life than he and his compatriots are able to produce. It takes a thousand years to make a Vienna and fortunately for us no one man can utterly destroy it.

After spending some months in Vienna, I realized that the Danube was the great patrimony which the Viennese had left unexploited. Vienna should be the greatest port in southwestern Europe, but the Austrians haven't dredged and developed the noble stream as they should have done. Will they now, in poverty and misery, repair the fault? It is still time—always time, thank goodness!

Why did I leave Vienna? Because I had met a girl who attracted me, a cafe-dancer who was returning for a rest to her home in Salzburg, and who talked to me so much of Salzburg, the birthplace of Mozart—"the most beautiful city in the world," she called it—that I had to go and visit it with Marie for guide.

Marie, Marie Kirschner was her real name, and I have tried to sketch her in my story, *A Mad Love,* for indeed she was the best type of German, or perhaps I should say Austrian. To me she represented Vienna and its charms quite exquisitely. She had a perfect girl's figure, kept slight and lithe with constant exercise, for she danced at least an hour every day to keep up to the mark, as she said. Marie had a piquant, intelligent face with a *nez retroussé* as cheeky as her light hazel eyes; best of all, she was curiously frank about her sexual experiences and won my heart by telling me, one of the first evenings, how she had been seduced willingly enough, because of her curiosity, by an old banker of Buda-Pesth when she was barely thirteen. "He gave my mother and me enough to live on comfortably for six years or more and let me learn dancing. Otto died in his sleep or he'd have done more for us; he was really kind and I had grown to care for him, though he was a poor lover. However, he left us the house and furniture and I was already earning a fair living—"

"And since then?" I asked.

Marie tossed her head. "*Qui a bu, boira,*" she said. "Isn't love a part of

---

* Pauline Lucca (1841–1908), an Austrian operatic soprano of Italian descent; she toured the United States in 1872–74.

** Albert Christian Theodor Billroth (1829–94), a pioneer surgeon and renown teacher at the University of Vienna.

life and the best part? Even the illusion of love is worth more than anything else, and now and then hope tempts me, as I believe I tempt you. Oh, if we could see Salzburg and the Berchtesgaden and the Geiereck together; what a perfect summer we might have, in most lovely surroundings!"

"It's impossible," I said, "to give you an unforgettable memory; you've had so many lovers!"

"Never fear a number," she replied, smiling. "The great majority leave us nothing worth remembering; men know little about love. Why till now, my old banker's the best memory I have: he was really affectionate *und hätte mich auf den Händen tragen mögen* (he would have carried me in his hands)"—a German expression meaning "he took every care of me"— and "He taught me a lot too; oh, Otto was a dear," and with this assurance I took Marie to Salzburg.

I had never even heard Salzburg mentioned before among the beautiful cities of Europe, but I found by chance that Wilkie,* the Scottish painter, had used something like the right words to describe it. He said that "If the old town of Edinburgh with its castle on a rock were planted in the Trossachs and had a broad swift river like the Tay flowing between the houses of the town, it might resemble Salzburg." Salzburg itself is set amongst mountains and nearby are numberless scenes of romantic beauty: the Traunsee to the east, and the Chiemsee with the King of Bavaria's wonderful palace to the west; while to the south across the Bavarian border is Berchtesgaden, one of the most beautiful regions in Europe. Here is the Untersberg, nearly 7000 feet in height, with the famous Kolowrat caverns containing ice-masses that look like great waterfalls suddenly frozen; and on the eastern side, the Geiereck with the cliffs and precipices that have earned it its name. Marie was an incomparable guide, of the sweetest temper, a born companion and as good a lover as a man. Better indeed in that she made all the preliminaries of love fascinating: Marie was the first to tell me that my voice was musical—a delight to hear—exceedingly powerful, yet resonant and sweet. "I'd rather hear you recite than anyone," she said. "No actor was ever your equal; and your face too: I love the courage in it and the amazing life in it."

Marie was a born flatterer and found new compliments continually. Every day she discovered some new trait to praise, but goodness and sweetness of nature are not dramatic or interesting. I did my best forty years later to picture Marie in *A Mad Love,* and trying to find some fault to make her human, hit upon the fact that she would give her lips readily to any one who touched her heart, even tho' she didn't love him. But—I've not done her goodness justice. Time and again she reminded me of Browning's wonderful verses:

> Teach me only teach, love,
> As I ought!

* Sir David Wilkie (1785–1841).

> I will speak thy speech, love,
>   Think thy thought.
> Meet if thou require it
>   Both demands
> Laying flesh and spirit
>   In thy hands.*

But after six weeks or so I began to feel tired. Eirene's passion had weakened me, and charming, faultless as Marie was, I wanted to learn something new, and I had for the time being at least exhausted German. When we returned from the lovely country and its exquisite walks and drives, I bought Marie a gorgeous picture of Leopold's fairy palace on the Chiemsee and fairly ran away to Florence for the fall.

There I worked at Italian first and then at the pictures and the art-life. And now my education in art, always growing, took in the mosaics at Ravenna, and in Milan I came upon a small collection of Visconti armor of the fourteenth and fifteenth centuries, some suits of which I managed to secure for very small sums. Before the American demand began to grow imperious in the middle eighties, good suits of armor cost very little. I bought a gold inlaid suit complete for £100 that I sold five years later in London for £5,000; and the dealer got £15,000 for it.

Italy appears to have taught most visitors a great deal. It taught me very little, but one experience in Milan was valuable. I got to know Lamperti,** the great teacher of singing, and his German wife; and from Lamperti I learned a good deal about *il bel canto* and that culture of the voice for which Italy is famous. Lamperti wanted to teach me his art; he tried my voice and assured me that I'd have a great career, for without training I could sing two notes lower than were ever written. "Your patrimony is in your throat," he used to say, but I assured him it was in my head, and the career of a *basso profundo* did not appeal to me, though I believe I might have made a good actor. Lamperti had a fund of interesting anecdotes about singers and musicians, and he was the first to tell me that my rooted dislike of the piano came from a good ear. "You have "absolute pitch,' " he said, "an extraordinary ear and a great voice. It's a sin not to cultivate your voice," but I had more important things to cultivate—at least that was my conviction. I've often thought since what a different life I might have had,

---

* From Browning's *A Woman's Last Word:*
> Teach me, only teach, Love!
>   As I ought
> I will speak thy speech, Love
>   Think thy thought—
>
> Meet, if thou require it,
>   Both demands,
> Laying flesh and spirit
>   In thy hands

** Francesco Lamperti (1813–92) wrote a famous work on singing.

had I taken Lamperti's advice and used his teaching, but at the time I never even considered it.

I picked up whatever I could about music. I read Leopardi morning, noon, and night, for his profound pessimism appealed to me intensely, even in the flower of youth.* He says to his heart:

> . . . non val cosa nessuna
> I moti tuoi, ne di sospiri e degna
> La terra. Amaro e noia
> La vita, altro mai nulla, e fango e il mondo.**

I learned there in Florence for the first time the lesson that Whistler afterwards taught everyone who had ears to hear, that there was no such thing as an artistic period or an artistic people, that great artists were sporadic products, like all other great men, that in fact genius was as rare as talent is common. But I had then no idea that the world is always suffering from want of genius to direct it, and that reverence for it and love of it is always a forecast of its possession. But one amusing experience of this time in Florence may find a place here.

I had read a good deal of Italian when a friend one day asked me had I read Ariosto.† Strange to say, I had passed him over, though I had read a good deal of Tasso†† and some of the moderns and been disappointed. But Ariosto! What had he done? Well, my friend recited his first sonnet on beauty and the riches of love and lent me the book which contained also this lively and witty story.

It seems there was a painter whose name Ariosto had forgotten (*non mi ricordo il nome*), who always painted the devil as a beautiful young man with lovely eyes and thick dark hair. His feet, too, were well-shaped and there were no horns on his head; in everything he was as lovable and as fair as an angel of God.

Not wishing to be outdone in courtesy, the devil came once just before daybreak to the painter when he was sleeping and told him to ask whatever he most desired and his wish would be granted him.

Now the poor painter had a lovely wife and lived in jealous ecstasies, extremes of doubt and fear; consequently, he begged the devil to show him how he could guard against any infidelity on the part of his wife.

---

* Giacomo Leopardi (1798–1837), an Italian poet whose despondency must have sprung from hopeless, painful invalidism.
** From *To Himself:*
  Now you shall rest forever, my tired heart.
  The lost illusion is dead that I believed eternal.
  It died. I know that, not only is the hope of cherished illusions extinguished, but even the desire for them. All your palpitations are worth nothing, nor is the world worth your sighs. Life has never been other than bitterness and boredom, and the earth is a bog.
† (1474–1533), author of *Orlando Furioso.*
†† (1544–95).

The devil at once put a ring on his finger, assuring him that so long as his finger was in this ring, he could make his mind easy, for there would be no cause for even a shadow of suspicion.

Glad at heart the painter woke up to find his finger in his wife's sex (*it dito ha nella fica all moglier*).

Even afterwards the name of Ariosto had a meaning to me and significance, for he goes on to say that he isn't sure of the efficacy of the cure: if the woman took it into her head to give herself and deceive the man, she would accomplish even the impossible—a purely Latin view of the matter.

I returned to Paris, and in the early spring of 1881 I went out to live in Argenteuil. I don't remember why I went to Argenteuil, but I took an apartment in a villa on the river and there I passed a great summer. I worked hard at French and came to speak it with fluency and fair correctness, but I did not attempt to master it as I had mastered German, though French literature and French art too of the nineteenth century appealed to me infinitely more than the German literature or art of the same period. It was at Argenteuil in this spring that I read Balzac through and quickly came to the conviction that he was the greatest of all modern Frenchmen, the only one indeed who has enlarged our conception of French genius and added a story to the noble building designed and decorated by Montaigne. Balzac is one of the choice and master spirits of the world, but not intellectual enough, or perhaps not dreamer enough, to be in the foremost file and help to steer humanity. In spite of his prodigious creative faculty, he has added no new generic figure to the Pantheon. He knew women profoundly; but even his Baronne Hulot* has not the significance of Goethe's Gretchen.

This year in Paris was made memorable to me also by meeting Turgenief, as I've told in my "snapshot" of him. I knew then that he was a great man, but I did not put him nearly as high as I did later. Far and away the greatest Russian writer, I see now that by his creation of Bazarof, the realist, he ranks among the leaders and guides of men: a greater artist even than Balzac, though not so productive, perhaps because artistic productivity depends on living a great part of one's life amongst one's own compatriots.

In this summer too I met Guy de Maupassant at dinner, thanks to Blanche Macchetta,** and our acquaintance began, which was destined to grow year by year more intimate, till his tragic death some ten years later. At the time I thought him at least as great as Turgenief: now I know better.

* A character in *La Cousine Bette*.
** (1853–98). Altogether an extraordinary person, the daughter of Senator Tucker of Virginia. She went to Milan, studied singing, and married an Italian. She was published under the pseudonym of Blanche Roosevelt and wrote three novels of which *The Copper Queen, A Romance of Today and Yesterday* (1866) was the most widely read, as well as *The Home Life of H. W. Longfellow* (1882), *Life and Reminiscences of Gustave Doré* (1885), and *Verdi: Milan and "Othello"* (1887).

I got to know, too, the handsome Jew journalist Catulle Mendes,* surely one of the most wonderful improvisatori ever seen. He could write you a poem like Hugo or De Musset in a few minutes; could imitate any and every master of French prose or verse with equal ease and astounding mastery. Ever afterwards he was to me the perfect model of the man of talent without a touch of genius that might have ennobled or destroyed his unique gift of words. At the time I could only admire him, though I felt that something was lacking in him. His nickname in Paris hit off his beauty of person perfectly—*un Christ de Bordel!*

I had a memorable summer in Paris. In spite of a want of introductions, I came to know this man and that, here a writer on the *Figaro,* there an artist, and they introduced me to others.

Towards the end of the summer I made up my mind to go to Ireland again and study the country and conditions for myself. A little while before, Disraeli had spoken of the cloud in Ireland no larger than a man's hand that might yet develop into a great storm. The increasing power of the Land League,** the growth of the court for fixing rents,† the advent to power of Parnell, made me eager to study the problem for myself; and so I crossed from Holyhead to Dublin and gazed again at scenes familiar to me in boyhood. From the beginning I went to all the Nationalist meetings, and I suppose it was only natural that my strong bias in favor of Irish freedom should have been strengthened.

Still, I went too to Trinity College, Dublin, and got an independent scholarly view that found some good points occasionally even in the castle and English domination. Of course I went to Galway and equally of course to Kerry, where my mother was buried, and I may as well give here the only independent judgment I ever heard of her. A famous Plymouth brother†† was lecturing once and I went up to him afterwards to inform myself more exactly on some point of his strange creed. As soon as he saw my card he said, "I knew some Harrises well once in Kerry, a Captain and Mrs. Harris; you don't come from that stock, I presume."

"Indeed I do!" I exclaimed, and it turned out that he knew both my father and mother very well indeed. As may be imagined, I was intensely interested, particularly when I found that my religious friend was a gentleman with a very good head of his own and a judgment free at least from ordinary bias. He spoke of my father's energy, though clearly he did not like him particularly; but my mother to him was a saint of the sweetest dis-

---

* (1841–1909), poet, critic, and novelist. He founded the *Revue fantaisiste* and also wrote for the *Parnasse contemporain.*

** An agrarian organization founded in Ireland in 1879 to fight for Home Rule.

† The Irish resented the high rents and the evictions of tenants for not paying arrears; the courts were increasingly resorted to for adjudication.

†† An anti-ritualistic sect founded in Ireland in the 19th century, which regarded the scripture as the only true guide to religion. The name came from Plymouth, England, where many groups of the Brethren sprang up.

position and very good-looking, "a thousand times too good for her domineering, little husband. I had a very great admiration for her," he went on. "Though I was younger, I was really pained to hear of her death. You lost a good mother in her, my friend," was his summing up, and curiously enough, my own childish recollections corroborated the impression he gave of her sweet kindliness of nature. My father too when he spoke of her, which was very seldom, always laid stress on the fact that it was difficult to make her angry: "a very sweet and gentle nature" which her eldest son, Vernon, had inherited.

The thing I noticed most in Ireland was the way it rained, and the poverty of the wretched land impressed me the more, the more I studied it. The moral influence of the Catholic Church too was to be seen everywhere in the splendid physique of the people, and I was fated to experience its vigor very sharply. It was at Ballinasloe that I was surprised by the sheer loveliness of the innkeeper's daughter. I had been walking and working hard for some time and was minded to take it easy for a week or so when I came to his inn. The girl captivated me. She hadn't much to do and they liked to hire their jaunting-car to me, and I got into the habit of taking Molly (Margaret was her name) with me everywhere as a guide. Her mother had long been dead and the father found enough to do in his bar, while an elder sister took charge of the house. So Molly and I spent a good deal of time together: I made up to her from the beginning. Naturally I kissed her as soon as I could and as often as I got the chance; and when I told her I loved her, I found she took it much more seriously than I did. "You wouldn't be after marrying me," she said. "You'd be ashamed of me over there in London and Paris and Vienna." My boxes showed labels that were known to everyone in the house.

"You're an angel," I replied, "but I have a lot to do before I can think of marrying"; still the kissing and caressing went on continually.

I got into the habit of taking my dinner in my sitting-room, for there was seldom anyone in the public dining-room, and when my things were cleared away and I sat reading, Molly would come in and we'd talk like lovers. One evening I asked her why she didn't come to me in bed after everyone was asleep; to my amazement she said she'd love to and I made her promise to come that very night, scarcely daring to believe in my good fortune. About eleven I heard the pattering of bare feet, and as I opened the door that gave into my sitting-room, there was Molly with nothing but a red Indian shawl over her nightie. In bed together I kissed and kissed her and she responded, but as soon as I tried further she held me off: "Sure, you wouldn't be doing anything like that."

"You don't care for me much or you wouldn't deny me," was my retort.

"Indeed I would; you must be good for I love to cuddle you," and she slipped her arms round me and held me to her till I grew almost crazy with desire. At first I smiled to myself: a few nights of preliminaries and nature would be too strong, but I had reckoned without my host.

I have not even described Molly and yet I shall always see her as she stood before me nude that first night. She was as tall as I was and splendidly formed, of the mother-type with large breasts and hips. She held her head turned away, as if she did not want to see me while I perused her naked charms. But her flower face was finer even than her figure: the great grey eyes shaded with long black lashes that curled up, while masses of very dark hair fell to her waist. Curiously enough, her skin was as fair as that of a blonde. When she turned, half-smiling, half-fearful, to me, "Have you seen enough now," I drew down the nightie I had half round her neck.

"I could look a long time without ever having enough, you beauty!"

"Sure, I'm like everybody else and my cousin Anne Moriarty's the beauty, with her golden hair!"

"Nothing like so beautiful as you!" For answer, I kissed her. "You'll catch cold; you'll come to-morrow?" She nodded and I went to bed in a fever. I had failed absolutely, but I was in no hurry and ultimate failure was unthinkable.

The next night I began by showing her the syringe and explaining its use. She would hardly hear me out, so I began kissing her sex till she sobbed breathless in my arms; but still she wouldn't let me come to the natural act.

"Please not; be good now!"

"But why, why?" The question stung her.

"How could I ever go to church? I confess every month; sure it's a mortal sin!"

"No sin at all and who'd know?"

"Father Sheridan would ask me; sure, he knows I like you; I told him."

"And he'd condemn it?"

"Oh my! That's why I can come to you, because none of them would even dream that I'd come like this to you. But I love to hold you and hear you talk, and to think I please you makes me so proud and glad."

"Don't you love my kisses best?"

"They make me afraid. Talk to me now; tell me of all the places you've seen. I've been reading of Paris—it must be lovely—wonderful—and the French girls dress so well—oh, I'd love to travel."

Again and again I tried, but the denial was adamant. Molly thrilled and melted under my kissing, but would not consent to what she'd have to confess afterwards to the priest.

A few days later, I made it my business to meet Father Sheridan and found him very intelligent. He was of the old school, had been brought up in St. Omer and had a delightful French tincture of reading and humor, but alas! He was as crazy as any Irish-bred priest on the necessity of chastity. I drew him out on the subject and found him eloquent. At his fingers' tips, he had all the statistics of illegitimacy and was proud of the fact that it was five times less frequent in Ireland than in England; and to my amusement I found it was commoner in Wales than in Scotland. Sheridan would never admit that the Welsh were Christians at all—"all pagans," he'd say, with intense emphasis, "mere savages without a church or a saint!" He was proud of the fact, I found, that it was his duty to denounce a young man and woman from the pulpit if they kept company too long, or with a suspicion of undue intimacy. "They should marry and not burn," was a favorite phrase of his. "The children of young parents are always healthy and strong": it was an obsession with him. Yet he would drink whisky with me till we both had had more than enough.

How do the Irish come to have this insane belief in the necessity and virtue of chastity? It is their unquestioned religious belief that gives it them, yet in the mountains of Bavaria and in parts of the Abruzzi, the peasants are just as religious, and there, too, chastity is highly esteemed, but nothing to be compared to its power in Ireland. I've often wondered why?

To cut a long story short, I used all the knowledge I had with Molly, yet failed completely. I knew that at certain periods women feel more intensely than at others; I found out that three or four times each month Molly was easily excited, especially about the eighth day after her monthlies had ceased. I used every advantage; but nothing gave me victory. One night, I was half-insane, so I promised to do nothing and thus got permission to lie on her, intending if necessary to use a little force. "That's nothing," I repeated, "nothing," as I rubbed my sex on her clitoris; "I'm not going in." But suddenly she took my head in her hands and kissed me. "I trust you, dear; you are too good to take advantage of me," and as I pressed forward, she said quietly, "You know I'd kill myself if anything happened." At once I drew away. I couldn't speak, could hardly think.

"All right!" I cried at last. "You've won because you don't care," and I threw myself away from her.

"Don't care!" she repeated. "I love you, and I'll love you all my life," and as she took me in her arms all my stupid resentment vanished and I set myself to interest her as much as I could.

But with failure in the nightly lists, Ballinasloe soon became intolerable to me. I had long ago exhausted all the beauties of the neighborhood and had come to the conclusion that outside love, the place was as devoid of intellectual interest as a town in western America. The clergyman I couldn't talk to, the lawyers and doctors were all tenth-rate. Some of the younger men were eager to learn and came to the inn in the evening to hear me talk, but I, too, had to *be about my Father's business*.* I went for a trip to Londonderry to study the citadel of Irish Protestantism and to make the final parting with Molly easier. When I returned, I didn't ask her to come to me at night: what was the good? But the night before I went to Belfast she came and I explored with her some of the side-paths of affection and confessed, with all frankness, that since I met Smith I was all ambition—under a vow, so to speak, to develop every faculty I had at any cost. "I am not ambitious,

---

* Such dissonance is typical of Harris, though not even he regularly sets quotations in such exotic contexts.

Molly, of place or power or riches, but of knowledge and wisdom I'm the lover and priest, resolved to let nothing stand in the way."

I explained to her that that was the reason why I had come to Ireland, just as the same desire of knowledge had driven me years before round the world, and would no doubt drive me again. "I don't want happiness even, Molly, nor comfort, though I'll take all I can get of both, but they're not my aim or purpose. I'm wedded to the one quest like a knight of the Holy Grail and my whole life will go to the achievement. Don't ask me why, I don't know. I only know that Smith, my friend and professor in Lawrence, Kansas, lit the sacred fire in me and I'll go on till death. You must not think I don't care for you; I do with all my heart. You're a great woman, heart and soul and body, but my work calls me and I must go."

"I've always felt it," she said quietly, "always felt that you would not stay here or marry anyone here. I understand and I only hope your ambition may make you happy, for without happiness, without love, is there anything worth having in life? I can't believe it, but then I'm only a girl. If you ever thought of coming back, write first. To see you suddenly would stop my heart with joy."

Chapter VIII

How I Met Froude and Won a Place in London and Gave up Writing Poetry!

NOW MY LEHRJAHRE (STUDENT YEARS) were ended, London drew me irresistibly; I hardly know why. It impressed me much more than New York: besides, I feared a return of malaria if I went back to the States; then, too, I had a letter of introduction to Froude* from Carlyle. Why not present it and see what would come of it? My boyish resolution to do every piece of work with all my heart, as well as I could do it, still held, I was sure, its conquering magic. I'd find it as easy to open the oyster of success in London as in New York; easier, I had no doubt. I crossed from Paris to London, took a room in the Grosvenor Hotel, and next morning called in Onslow Gardens. Mr. Froude, I found, was spending the summer at Salcombe in South Devon and was not expected in London for a month or more. I wanted to take his exact address. Accordingly, the servant asked me into the dining-room and brought me writing paper. The furnishing of the room, the pictures here and in the hall made an impression on me of well-to-do comfort and refinement of taste much beyond any impression left on me in New York. I began to feel the truth of what Emerson had said a score of years before: "The Englishman's lot is still the best in the world."

The forty years that have elapsed since, and especially the great war, have changed all this. Life in New York today strikes one as more luxurious than that of London, though still inferior in taste and refinement.

London itself taught me a great deal about the Englishman. It is immense: no limit to its energy: healthy, too, in spite of its wretched climate; well-drained and clean: but it never rises high. One thinks of the East-End, how mean and coarse and grovelling, the narrow streets and cluttering hovels, and the West-End, now comfortable, now pretentious, now primly vulgar—clothed in stucco as in broadcloth. But there are grassy parks and open spaces where one has a glimpse of nature, and here and there too a noble house or fine pointing spire or bold adventurous bridge.

The worst of it is, there is no plan, no general idea directing this indefatigable activity. It is built by beavers and not by men; industry everywhere

* James Anthony Froude (1818–94), the eminent historian so profoundly influenced by Carlyle, whose literary executor he was.

and not intelligence. It depresses the spirit, therefore; its smoke and grime too, are characteristic: no generous ideal: let us all live in fog so long as we eat well and sleep softly. But there is no unnecessary noise; London is the quietest of cities and the methods of transport are excellent and cheap. The industry is efficient, though not artistic.

After the great fire, Wren made out a plan of a new London. His great cathedral, set in a noble space and open to the Thames, was to be the center. Three great boulevards were to run from St. Paul's westward, parallel to the river, each of them 150 feet wide near the cathedral and growing narrower as they passed into the country; every half a mile or so a parish church was to stand in its park-like square of grassy circle; and so the Embankment, the Strand, and Oxford Street could have been developed to high purpose, but no! The builders preferred to build as their fathers had builded, without plan or design, and we have the wretched result: narrow winding streets in the heart of the city, no thought, no soul. London is the meanest of great capitals, with the solitary exception of Berlin; yet, if the English had followed Wren, it might easily have been the noblest.

I went back to the Grosvenor, wondering whether I ought to go to Salcombe or try to get work in London. An accident determined me.

I was in the smoking-room after lunch when a couple of gentlemen drew my attention. The afternoon was wet and they were passing the time by betting on the flies crawling up the window panes. I heard one say, "I'll bet five hundred this one gets higher in two minutes," and then the other: "Done with you and I'll bet a thou mine reaches the top first."

The younger man was nearly drunk, and I soon saw that his older companion sought to confuse him by running three or four different bets at the same time. This idea caused me to watch more carefully, and it soon became clear to me that the older man was cheating the younger. Suddenly, to my surprise I heard him, after a brief dispute, say, "That makes ten thou you owe me—quite enough, too, for such an idiotic game."

The younger man pulled himself together and remarked with the portentous gravity of intoxication: "Five thou, Gerald, at most, and I don't believe you reckoned in the thou I gained with my bluebottle."

"Oh yes, I did," replied the sharper. "Don't you remember: it was at the very outset when I owed you a couple of thousand."

"You're d——d clever, Gerald," retorted the other, as if hesitating, and then with a sudden decision, "I'll give you an I.O.U. this evening." His friend nodded, "All right, old man!"

As the two were leaving the room I called over the waiter. "Who are those gentlemen?" I asked. "The young one, Sir, is Lord C—, son of the Earl of D—; the other isn't staying here. He's a friend and his name's Costello, I believe. Lord C—, Sir, can drink; he's not often drunk like that."

I don't know why, but Lord C— had made so pleasant an impression on me that I resolved to open his eyes, if I could, to the fact that he had won and not lost and ought not to pay £5000, or indeed anything at all.

Accordingly, I sat down, then and there, and wrote an exact accounting of what I had noticed and sent it to Lord C—'s apartment. Next morning I got a note from him, thanking me warmly and asking me to meet him in the smoking-room. We met and I found him curiously generous, willing even to make all sorts of allowances for the so-called friend who had plainly cheated him. On the other hand, I was indignant and advised him to send my letter just as it was to his friend. I was willing to stand by every word. "Very kind of you, I'm sure," said Lord C—. "I think I'll do that. Are you going to stay in London? Would you lunch with me to-day?" I consented and in the course of lunch told him I wanted to go to Salcombe to see Froude. He knew Salcombe and spoke with admiration of the beauties of the Devon coast and indeed of the whole county. "You ought to drive down," he told me. "That is the best way to see our English scenery."

I shrugged my shoulders regretfully. "I'm not rich enough to indulge in such pastime: I must soon get to work."

The next morning I was told that some one wanted to see me at the door. I went there and found a groom with a dog-cart, who handed me a letter from Lord C—, begging me to accept the dog-cart and horse and drive down to Salcombe. "My groom," he added, "knows every foot of the way and I'm not using him for the next month. You've done me a very good turn; I hope you'll allow me to do you one. Only one thing I ask—that you'll not mention anything about the betting episode." But after forty years there can be no harm in recalling it.

Next day, after thanking Lord C— for his splendid present, I set off for Salcombe and about a fortnight later called upon Mr. Froude in his house on a cliff overlooking the bay. I was ushered into a delightful room and gave the servant Carlyle's letter to take to Mr. Froude. In a few moments Froude came in with the letter in his hand. He was tall and slight, of scholarly, ascetic appearance. "An extraordinary letter," he began. "You know what Carlyle says in it?"

"No, I don't," I replied. "I put it in my pocket when he gave it to me, and when I took it out I found it had stuck and I never opened it. I knew it would be friendly and more than fair."

"It's very astonishing," Froude broke in. "Carlyle asks me to help you in your literary ambitions; says he 'expects more considerable things from you than from anyone he has met since parting from Emerson.' I'd be very proud if he had said it about me. Take a seat, won't you, and tell me about your meeting with him. I have always thought him the best brain, the greatest man of our time," and the grey eyes searched me.

"He has been my hero," I said, "since I first read *Latter Day Pamphlets* and *Heroes and Hero Worship* as a cowboy in western America."

"A cowboy!" repeated Froude, as if amazed.

"It was Carlyle's advice," I went on, "that sent me for four years to German universities; and I finished my schooling with a year in Athens."

"How interesting," said Froude, who evidently did not understand that adventures come to the adventurous. We talked for an hour or more, but when he asked me to lunch as a sort of after-thought, I told him I had arranged to drive back to the near-by town and lunch with a friend. On this he assured me that he would return to London in a fortnight or so and soon after give a dinner and invite Chenery,* the editor of *The Times,* and other people of importance in literature to meet me. He would do his best to carry out Carlyle's wishes. I thanked him, of course, warmly, while protesting that I didn't want to give him trouble. He then asked me, had I written anything he could read? I pulled out a small bound book in which I had written in my best copperplate hand a few dozen poems, chiefly sonnets, and gave it to him.

A little later we shook hands and I returned to my inn and next morning set off for London by another road. The English country pleased me hugely, it was so neat and well-kept, but there was nothing grandiose about the scenery—nothing as fine as the Catskills, nothing to compare with the enthralling beauty of eastern France, to say nothing of the Rockies!

Hardly had I left Froude when I realized that I should indeed be a fool if I trusted to his help. "Help yourself, my friend," I kept repeating to myself, "then, if he helps, so much the better; and if he doesn't, it won't matter." I still had a couple of hundred pounds behind me.

When I reached London I sent the groom with the dog-cart and horse back to Lord C—, thanking him for a superb holiday and lovely trip. But I took care the very same day to engage rooms near the British Museum at a pound or so a week, and there I went and unpacked, first telling the Grosvenor Hotel people that I'd call once a week for letters. My acquaintance with Lord C— won me much politeness.

A morning or two later, I saw in one of the papers something about John Morley** and the *Fortnightly Review;* the journal called it, I remember, "the most literary of our reviews." I took down the address of it in Henrietta Street, Covent Garden, and without losing time, went and called about nine o'clock in the morning. To my surprise, the office was a sort of shop, the publishing house of Chapman and Hall. The clerk behind

---

* Thomas Chenery (1826–84), an outstanding philologist and a professor of Arabic at Oxford before he became editor of *The Times* in 1877.

** Viscount Morley of Blackburn (1838–1923). He began writing non-political articles for the conservative *Saturday Review;* in 1867 he became manager of the liberal *Fortnightly Review.* He was appointed editor of the influential *Pall Mall Gazette* in 1880. He was elected an M.P. in 1883 and he entered the House of Lords in 1908. He wrote several classic biographies including *Edward Burke* (1867), *Voltaire* (1782) and *Life of Gladstone* (1903).

the counter told me that Mr. Chapman* usually came in about eleven and if I could wait—I asked for nothing better; so I took a seat and waited.

At about ten-thirty Mr. Chapman came in, a well-made man of five feet ten or so, past the prime of life, with thinning hair and a tendency to stoutness. I got up as soon as I heard his name and said, "I'd like a few minutes with you." He took me up to his room on the first floor and I told him how I had just returned from a visit to Froude, to whom I had taken a letter from Carlyle. He appeared greatly impressed, regretted that he had nothing for me to do; but when I spoke of working for the *Fortnightly*, he said I should come back in the afternoon and see Mr. Escott,** who was the acting editor in place of Mr. John Morley. At four o'clock I turned up and Chapman introduced me to T. H. S. Escott. Escott was a good-looking, personable man, very curious as to how I had come to know Carlyle and what Froude had said to me, but at the end he turned me down flatly.

"I have nothing for you to do, I'm sorry," was his curt dismissal.

"Have you never any translation?" I asked.

"Seldom," he replied, "but I'll bear you in mind!"

"Don't do that," I replied. "Let me come each day and if you've nothing to do, it won't matter. But I'll be on hand if unexpectedly you need a proof read or an article verified or anything."

"As you please," he said rudely, shrugging his shoulders, as he turned away disdainfully—I couldn't but see.

But every morning I was seated in the shop when Chapman came. He used to acknowledge my bow with an embarrassed air. When Escott arrived in the afternoon, he generally went straight up to his back room on the first floor, pretending not even to see me. After about a week Chapman asked me up to his room one day and told me politely that I must see now there was nothing for me to do: would it not be better to try elsewhere rather than wait about? I felt sure Escott had suggested this to him.

I said I hoped I was not bothering him; I would soon have regular work; I'd tell him as soon as I succeeded; meantime, I hoped he would not mind my being on hand.

"No, no!" he hastened to say. "It's for your sake I'm speaking; I only wish I had something for you to do." On this I smiled and went away till the next day, when again I was in my place as before.

Meanwhile I was fitting another string to my bow; I had got to know A. R. Cluer,† now a county court judge, on a railway journey, and almost

---

* Frederic Chapman (1823–95), a publisher of the *Fortnightly Review*, which he founded in 1865. He and his cousin established the firm of Chapman and Hall in 1834, and Chapman had become its head in 1861. Chapman and Hall published the Brownings, Trollope, Meredith, and Dickens.

** Thomas Hay Sweet Escott (?–1924), previously a leader writer for the *Standard*. He wrote several books on politics and several biographies, including one of Lord Randolph Churchill.

† Albert Rowland Cluer (1852–?), barrister, metropolitan police magistrate, 1895–96.

at once we became friends by dint of similarity of taste and interests. He had rooms in the Temple and one day he asked me why I did not try to get work on the *Spectator*. He advised me to ask Escott to give me an introduction to the chief editor, Hutton.* But I would not ask Escott for any favor, and so there and then Cluer went round with me to the *Spectator* office and saw me enter.

When the clerk came, I said, "I want to see Mr. Hutton!"

"Have you an appointment?"

"No," I replied, and at the same time I took out a sovereign and laid it before him. "Tell me where Mr. Hutton is," I said, "and that pound is yours."

"On the second floor," whispered the clerk hastily. "But you won't give me away, will you?"

"No, no," I assured him. "I'll go up and you need never even have seen me." I went out of the shop at once, and up the stairs at the side.

When I got to the second floor I knocked: no answer; a minute or two later I knocked again, and loudly. "Come in!" I heard and in I went. There was a big man seated at a table with his back to me, immersed in some proofs; he was evidently very near-sighted, because his nose was almost touching the manuscripts. I stood a few moments by his left side, quietly taking stock of the room with its bookcases opposite to me, then I coughed loudly. The big man dropped his glasses on the table and turned to me at once, evidently surprised out of politeness.

"Goodness gracious!" he exclaimed, "who are you? How did you come in?"

"My name won't help you much, Mr. Hutton," I replied, smiling, "and I don't want to bother you. I want work, think I can write—"

"We have too many writers," he ejaculated. "Can't find work enough for those we know."

"There's always room at the top," I countered. "Suppose I can do better than any you've got; it'll be to your interest to use me."

"Goodness me!" he exclaimed. "Do you think you can write better than any of us?"

"No, no," I corrected, "but there are some subjects I know better than any Englishman. You're a judge: the first ten lines of an article by me will tell you whether I am merely diseased with conceit or whether I'm really worth using."

"That's true," he said, getting up and going over to the bookcase, "Do you know anything about Russia?"

"I was with General Skobelef at Plevna."

* Richard Holt Hutton (1826–97), one of the proprietors of the *Spectator*, a liberal paper, of which he handled the theological and literary news. He was a friend of Cardinal Newman and of Walter Bagehot, whose works he edited, and he wrote studies of Shelley, Scott, and Browning.

"Goodness me!" he ejaculated again. "Here's a book on Russia and the war that may interest you," and he handed me a volume.

"Have you any special knowledge of the United States?" he went on, still peering at the books.

"I've been through a western university," I replied, "am a member of the American bar, have practiced law."

"Really?" he cried. "Well, here's a book of Freeman* on America that may amuse you. Don't be afraid of telling the truth about it," he went on. "If you disagree with him, say so!"

"Thanks ever so much," I replied. "I'm greatly obliged to you. The chance to show what I can do is all I want," and I went out at once, but not before I had caught a kindly glint in the peering eyes, which showed me that Richard Holt Hutton was really a gentleman who put on a hard abruptness of manner to mask or perhaps to protect his real sweetness of nature.

When I got downstairs I showed the clerk the books as a proof he would not be blamed, and I took pains to thank him again before I rejoined Cluer. When Cluer saw the books and heard that I had talked with Hutton, he exclaimed, "I don't know how you managed it. I won a first class at Oxford and wrote to him, but could not even see him. How did you manage?"

Under a promise of secrecy I told him, and then we talked of the books and what I'd write, but I didn't go straight home and begin the job at once, as Cluer advised.

First of all I sat down and thought. Many days had passed since I returned to London and I had had as yet no hint of success, saw in fact no gleam even of hope. What was I to do? I must win soon!

It struck me almost at once that I ought to know the mark I was aiming at. To win R. H. Hutton, I must know him first; accordingly, next morning I went to the British Museum and asked for all his books. I got a dozen or more ponderous tomes and spent the next two days reading them. At the end of that time I saw the soul of R. H. Hutton before me as a very small entity, a gentle-pious spirit, intensely religious. "He will enjoy a slating of Freeman," I said to myself, "for he knows Freeman to be rude, cocksure and aggressive. I'll give Hutton just what he wants."

I went home and wrote the best stuff I could write on the Russian book, and then, after reading Freeman with great care and finding that indeed he was the very type of an arrogant, pompous pedant who mistook learning for wisdom, I let myself go and wrote an honest but contemptuous review of his book; indeed, there was nothing in it for the soul. I ended my review

---

* Edward Augustus Freeman (1823–92), professor of modern history at Oxford. Harris refers to his *Some Impressions of the United States* (1883). His outstanding work was the *History of the Norman Conquest* (1867–79), in which he maintained that the Germanic nature of English institutions had not been affected by the Norman conquest.

with the remark that "as Malebranche* saw all things in God, so Mr. Freeman sees all things in the stout, broad-bottomed, aggressive Teuton."

I had made another friend in my first week in London who was now to
stand me in good stead, the Reverend John Verschoyle,** then a curate at
Marylebone Church. I don't remember how I met him; but I soon discovered in him one of the most extraordinary literary talents of the time; in
especial a gift for poetry almost comparable to that of Swinburne.

Verschoyle was of good family and had migrated from Trinity College,
Dublin to Cambridge, where at seventeen he had written the Greek verses
for the year book issued by the university; his English verse, too, seemed to
me miraculous—a lyric gift of the highest. Though only an inch or so
taller than I was, he was fifty inches round the chest and prodigiously
strong. I called him a line battle-ship cut down to a frigate. He was
handsome, too, with a high forehead, good features and long, golden
moustache. Of all the men I met in my life, the one that most people would
have selected as likely to do great things, at least in literature; yet he
brought it to nothing and died untimely in middle-age.

He happened to call on me just when I had finished my two reviews and
naturally I gave him them to read. He knew Hutton's works. "A high
churchman," he called him, "who admires Newman prodigiously." At once
he declared that Hutton would certainly take the article on Russia; it was
so new that Russia should show signs of a revolutionary spirit, was so
unexpected, and so forth.

"I wanted your criticism," I insisted. "Please point out any faults: I'm
more at home in German than in English."

He smiled: "Here's a sentence that proves that, I think, and there's
another." Soon we were at it hammer and tongs, but he quickly convinced
me that my half-doubt was amply justified. After he had gone through the
two articles, I had had the best lesson in English I ever got. From that day
on for five years the Bible and Swift never left my bedside, and in those
years I never opened a German book, not even my beloved Heine or
Schopenhauer. It had taken me years to learn German, but it took me twice
as long to cleanse my brain of every trace of the tongue. No writer should
ever try to master two languages. I wrote or rewrote the little essays and
then sent them off to Hutton.

The next day I was back at my post at Chapman's, and when I told
Chapman that I was on the *Spectator* he laughed and said he was delighted;
and a day or two later he called me in and gave me a couple of books he
wanted my opinion on. "Meredith is our reader," he said; "but it takes him

---

* Nicolas Malebranche (1638–1715), a Cartesian French philosopher. He believed
the mind obtained knowledge of matter only through revelation: "God is the source,
the reality, and the place of ideas."

** Reverend John Verschoyle (1853–1915); Harris was fond of him and overestimated his gifts. Curate of Marylebone, he for a time assisted Harris on the
Fortnightly Review.

weeks often to give an opinion and I'd like to know about these books as soon as possible."

My chance had come. I thanked him, went straight home and sat down at once to read and re-read the books. They took me all day and I spent the best part of the night writing my opinion of them. Next morning I went round to Verschoyle with them, who told me the reviews were all right, showed indeed remarkable improvement in my English. "The short sentences strike the right note," he remarked, "but you mustn't let them become stereotyped; you must vary them very often."

I thanked him and took the reviews to Chapman. He was greatly impressed. "I thought you'd keep 'em a week," he said. "I had no wish to hurry you so."

"It's nothing," I replied, "but the one book you could publish with some changes; the other is puerile."

"I agree with you," he said, "and if you take this to the cashier downstairs, he'll give you the two guineas for your opinion."

"No, no," I exclaimed. "I'm heavily in your debt for letting me bother you as I've done. Please use me whenever you can; I'll be only too glad to be of any service." Chapman smiled at me most cordially and from that day on gave me books every week, and asked me my opinion on this or that literary matter almost every day. He must have praised me to Escott too, for one afternoon Escott asked me up to the *Fortnightly* office and gave me a German article he wanted me to read and write an opinion on.

"Shall I translate it?" I asked.

"Only if you find it astonishingly good," he replied. Next day he had my written opinion.

A little later he gave me an Italian article to translate and shortly afterwards, complaining that his work on the *World* took up a lot of his time, he gave me half the *Fortnightly* to correct; and when he found I did this too with the utmost care and speed, he asked me to sit in his room and soon I was playing secretary and factotum there every afternoon.

The importunity that in the Bible won God had been successful too in London.

But though a month had passed since I came from Salcombe, I had heard nothing from Froude, and, stranger still, nothing from the *Spectator*. I could only possess my soul in patience.

Meanwhile I saw Verschoyle nearly every day and one day had a little dispute with him which showed, I think, a difference of nature. We had been discussing a passage in a *Fortnightly* article of mine, when he said: "These prolusions of ours are very interesting but don't lead to any goal."

"Self-improvement is the best of goals," I replied; "but I hate your word 'prolusions.' It's correct enough, but surely a trifle pedantic?"

"The exact word is rarely pedantic," he asserted. "Why not 'prolusion,' rather than 'preparatory exercise?' "

"I can't say," was my answer, "but I want to be understood by the people at once. I would not use 'prolusion' for anything." Verschoyle shrugged his broad shoulders in manifest disagreement.

It was Verschoyle who first introduced me to modern English poetry and to a number of living English poets, notably to a Dr. Westland Marston and his blind son, Phillip.*

They lived in the Euston Road, and though now poor had apparently been well off formerly, and were friends with all the literary men of repute. Verschoyle told me that Phillip Marston had had the most unhappy life. He had been engaged to a very pretty girl, Mary Nesbit (sister of E. Nesbit, afterwards Mrs. Hubert Bland,**) and one morning going to her room to wake her he found her dead. The shock nearly killed him.

A couple of years later, his dearest friend Oliver Maddox Brown,† died almost as suddenly. Three or four years later his sister, Cicely, who had been quite well the day before, was found dead in her bed in the morning. His other sister, Eleanor, died in the following year, 1879; and his most inti-mate friend and fellow-poet, Arthur O'Shaughnessy,†† some two years afterwards. And in 1882 James Thomson,‡ the author of *The City of Dreadful Night,* was taken with a seizure in Phillip's rooms and carried out to a hospital to die; and in the same year, his hero and friend Rossetti died at Birchington. It looked as if fate had picked him out for punishment, and so fear came to me that misfortune often dogs gifted mortals, whereas fortune flees them. Phillip Marston was good-looking with a fine forehead and auburn hair; his eyes seemed quite natural and very expressive. I don't know why, but I agreed almost at once with Verschoyle's estimate that Phil Marston was one of the sweetest and most unselfish of men. We spent the whole afternoon together and before we left Phillip asked me to return when I liked. In a day or two I called again and had some hours with him:

* John Westland Marston (1819–90). Harris assigns the title "doctor" erroneously. A minor playwright; his comedy, *The Favourite of Fortune* (1866), was his most successful work. Prominent in the leading literary circles of London, he was a close friend of Dickens.
Phillip (Bourke) Marston (1850–87). He was blind from the age of three. This affliction, with the loss of relatives and friends as described by Harris, doubtless ac-counts for the morbid strain of his poetry.
** Mrs. Hubert Edith Bland (1858–1924) wrote children's stories, poetry and novels as E. Nisbet. She won fame and fortune in 1899 with the novel *The Story of the Treasure Seekers.* She was an ardent Fabian and published *Ballads and Lyrics of Socialism* in 1908.
† (1855–74). He had an exhibition of his paintings by the age of fourteen, but by then he was also writing poetry, and his interest in writing overshadowed that in painting. The unfinished stories that appeared in his posthumous *Literary Remains* were by all account promising. Frail, he was stricken in 1874 by the gout, and then got blood-poisoning, from which he died.
†† (1844–81) Like Marston and Brown, a minor poet. His first book of poetry, *An Epic of Women* (1870) was his best work. He and Eleanor Marston wrote a book of stories for children, *Toyland* (1875).
‡ (1834–82).

he took to me, he said, because I was almost as hopeless as he was. "Verschoyle," he went on "puzzles me with his Christian belief. I have no belief, none, cannot conceive how any one can cherish any faith in the future, however faint, and I feel that you agree with me."

"Yes, indeed," I replied, and quoted,

> Only a sleep eternal
> In an eternal night!

He bowed his head and said with inexpressible sadness, " 'Dead! All's done with,' as Browning says. There's no hope for the survivors, either, none."

"I am not so sure," I interrupted. "It seems to me that the wisest of men are always the most kindly, and from that fact I draw the hope that in the future, bit by bit, we mortals may get to loving-kindness for each and every man born, and so make this earthly pilgrimage a scented way of inexpressible delights."

"The sweeter you make it," he cried, "the worse it will be to leave it."

"Is that true?" I asked. "Surely, when we have drunk deep of love and life, we shall be able to go to death as one now leaves a table—satisfied."

It was dear Amy Levy,* whom I got to know about this time, who gave perfect expression to my thought, though she herself was as hopeless as Marston:

> The secret of our being, who can tell?
> To praise the gods, and Fate is not my part;
> Evil I see and pain; within my heart
> There is no voice that whispers: "All is well."
> Yet fair are days in summer and more fair
> The growths of human goodness here and there.**

"Beautiful, beautiful," he repeated when I had finished reciting the sextet, "and true; but it does not take us far, does it?"

Phillip Marston was beyond any consolation—pain clothed him as with a garment—but his pity for others and his sympathy with human sorrow was inexhaustible.

A little later he gave me a volume of his poems. "I've written, too, on the eternity of sleep," he said, and in the book I found this sonnet he had written to his love, Mary Nesbit. To me, it seems one of the sincerest and noblest of English elegies, though steeped in sadness.

---

* (1861–89), also a prodigy. Her best works were *Xantippe and Other Poems* and her novel *Reuben Sachs,* a satire on Jewish life. Like the other people just mentioned, her disposition was melancholic and she committed suicide.

** "To Clementine Black," the dedication to *A London Plane-Tree and Other Verses.* The quotation is accurate, except for a few errors in punctuation and the omission of a stanzaic break between the fourth and fifth lines.

It must have been for one of us, my own,
To drink this cup and eat this bitter bread.
Had not my tears upon thy face been shed,
Thy tears had dropped on mine; if I alone
Did not walk now, thy spirit would have known
My loneliness; and did my feet not tread
This weary path and steep, thy feet had bled
For mine, and thy mouth had for mine made moan.
And so it comforts me, yea, not in vain,
To think of thine eternity of sleep;
To know thine eyes are tearless though mine weep;
And when this cup's last bitterness I drain,
One thought shall still its primal sweetness keep—
Thou had'st the peace, and I, the undying pain.

About this time, too, I came to know Miss Mary Robinson* and her
sister, but for some reason or other we did not get on very well. She laughed
at me once over something I had said and chilled me. I was perhaps too
young to realize her value, and soon she married a French professor and
went to Paris to live and I lost sight of her; but now and again since
I have had glimpses of a fine mind and regretted that I had not learned to
know her. I think it was Francis Adams,** the poet of *The Army of the
Night,* who introduced me to the Robinsons. I shall have much to tell of him
later, but now I need only say Verschoyle and the Marstons, Amy Levy,
Miss Robinson and Francis Adams made me aware of the fact that London
at that time, and indeed at all times, thanks to the eternal goodness, is a
nest of singing birds, crowded, indeed, with men and women of talent and
distinction, who moreover are usually devoted to poetry as the noblest of
all the arts.

My chief fault in life and as a critic, as Shaw has felt, is that I have always
been an admirer of great men and never cared greatly for those who fell
short of the highest. Marston interested me as Amy Levy interested me, by
the sheer pathos of their unhappy fate and immitigable suffering, but it was
only later that I came to see that their poetic achievement, too, if not of the
very highest, was of real value and had extraordinary importance.

After his untimely death on the fourteenth of February, 1887, people
talked of poor Marston's drinking habits and how he would sit up at night
till all hours and—the cackle of stupidity! The fools could not even forgive
the blind for trying to turn night into day! If drinking drowned sad, lonely
thoughts, why not drink? I thank dear Phil Marston for hours of sweet com-

---

* (1857–1934). Poet, biographer of Renan, and translator of Euripides. She was
married to James Darmsteter; after his death in 1894 she married Pierre Emile
Duclaux.
** Francis William Lauderdale Adams (1862–1893). The correct title of the book
is *Songs of the Army of the Night* (1888). He also wrote a biographical novel,
Leicesta (1884), and short stories. He married and moved to Australia about 1882,
returning to England in 1890. He then contracted tuberculosis and committed suicide.

panionship and an exquisite, all-embracing sympathy, and England can never forget his noble poetry.

About this time I got a letter one morning that surprised me. My name on the envelope was written in such tiny characters that I could scarcely read it, but when I opened the cover two proofs fell out, *Spectator* proofs at last and a letter in Hutton's tiny script!

"You were right," he began, "your reviews justify you. The one on Freeman is a gem and the Russian one provokes thought and may lead to discussion. I send you proofs of both and should be delighted if you'd call with them when corrected. I want more of your work. Yours truly, R. H. Hutton."

At last the door was forced. I sat as in a charmed trance for some little time, then I opened the proofs and tried to read them as if a stranger had written them. The Russian one was certainly the better of the two, but it was the review of Freeman, aimed at Hutton's head and heart, that had won the prize. Food for thought in that. I began then to say to myself that no one can see above his own head.

As I read the articles I noticed little roughnesses of swing and measure and set myself to correct them on another paper: I wanted to show Verschoyle the virginal proofs and get his opinion. While working in this way the noon post brought me a letter from Froude excusing his long silence, but he wished the dinner in my honor to be a great success and he had to wait till certain people had returned to town. Now, however, he'd be glad to see me on such and such a night and he'd keep my remarkable poems till then. "They have proved to me," he concluded, "that Carlyle's estimate of you was justified."

Nothing could be more flattering, but my discussions with Verschoyle and the reading of his and Marston's poetry had shaken my belief in my qualifications as a lyric poet; still, I had recently written a sonnet or two that I liked greatly and—conceit does not die of one blow.

That afternoon I took the *Spectator* proofs to Verschoyle who, strange to say, agreed with Hutton that the Freeman paper was the better of the two, and he only suggested a single emendation, which I had already jotted down. Clearly his critical gift in prose was not as sure as in verse, or he was not so interested, for I had made some forty corrections.

Next day I took the proofs most scrupulously corrected to Hutton and had a delightful talk with him. "Write on anything you like," he said, "only let me know beforehand what subject you've chosen so that we shan't clash. Let me know always by Monday morning, will you? I like your English, simple, yet rhythmic, but it's your knowledge that's extraordinary. You'll make a name for yourself; I wonder you're not known already. These are not days to hide one's light under a bushel," and he laughed genially.

"On the contrary," I cried, "we put it with large reflectors behind it in front of the tent and pay a barker to praise our illuminating power."

"A barker!" repeated Hutton. "What's that?" and I explained the racy term to him to his delight.

"You Americans!" he repeated. "A barker! What a painting word!"

But I didn't forget that I had still to win his heart, so when a pause came, I remarked quietly, "I wonder, Mr. Hutton, if you could help me to one of my ambitions. I knew Carlyle well, but I also admire Cardinal Newman immensely, though I've never had the joy of meeting him. Would it be too much to ask you for an introduction to him?"

He promised at once to help me. "Though I don't know him intimately," he added reflectively, "still, I can give you a word to him. But how strange that you should admire Newman!"

"The greatest of all the Fathers," I cried enthusiastically. "The sweetest of all the Saints!"

"First rate," exclaimed Hutton. "That might be his epitaph. With that tongue of yours, you don't need any introduction; I'll just cite your words to him, and he'll be glad to see you. 'The greatest of all the Fathers,' " he repeated. "That may indeed be true, but surely St. Francis of Assisi is 'the sweetest of all the Saints?' " I nodded, smiling. Hutton was right, but I felt that I must not outstay my welcome, so I took my leave, knowing I had made a real friend in dear Holt Hutton.

About this time I wrote an article in the *Spectator* which won for me the acquaintance and praise, if not the friendship, of T. P. O'Connor,* M. P., a very clever and agreeable Irishman who stands high among contemporary journalists. He has met most of the famous men of his time, but has hardly ever written of the indicating figures; the second and third rate pleasing him better. So far as I know, he has never even tried to study or understand any great man in the quirks of character or quiddities of nature that constitute the essence of personality. He has written for the many about their gods— Hall Caine and Gosse, Marie Corelli** and Arnold Bennett, Conrad and Gilbert Frankau—and has had his reward in a wide popularity. But in the early eighties he was still young with pleasing manners and the halo about his head of possible achievement.

Now for Froude and his dinner, which had I known it, was to flavor my experience with a sense of laming, paralyzing defeat.

---

* Thomas Power O'Connor (1848–1929). His biography of Disraeli apparently won him notice enough to get him elected to the House of Commons from Selway in 1885 and he was re-elected regularly. He supported Parnell against Gladstone. For a time he was employed by the London office of the *New York Herald*.

** Sir Thomas Henry Hall Caine (1853–1931), a popular novelist. He lived with Dante Gabriel Rossetti from 1881 until Rossetti's death and then wrote his *Recollections of Rossetti* (1882). His *The Eternal City* (1901) sold more than 1,000,000 copies; several of his works were adapted for the stage.

Sir Edmund William Gosse (1848–1929), minor poet, but outstanding literary critic of the times.

Marie Corelli (1855–1924), a pseudonym for Mary MacKay. Her *Barabbas: A Dream of the World's Tragedy* (1893) made her famous; her *Sorrows of Satan* outsold any previous English novel. She considered her critics blasphemers.

Before dinner Froude introduced me to Mr. Chenery, the editor of *The Times,* and at table put me on his left. When the dinner was almost over, he presented me to the score of guests by saying that Carlyle had sent him a letter, asking him to help me in my literary career and praising me in his high way. He (Froude) had read some of my poems and had assured himself that Carlyle's commendation was well deserved; he then read one of my sonnets to let his guests judge. "Mr. Harris," he added, "tells me that he has begun writing for the *Spectator,* and most of us know that Mr. Hutton is a good, if severe, critic."

To say I was pleased is nothing: almost every one drank wine with me or wished me luck with that charming English *bonhomie* which costs so little and is so ingratiating.

As we rose to go to the drawing-room for coffee, I slipped into the hall to get my latest sonnet from my overcoat. I might be asked to read a poem, and I wanted my best. How easily one is flattered to folly at seven and twenty!

When I reached the drawing-room door, I found it nearly closed and a tall man's shoulders almost against it. I did not wish to press rudely in, and as I stood there I heard the big man ask his companion what he thought of the poetry.

"I don't know; why should you ask me?" replied his friend, in a thin voice.

"Because you are a poet and must know," affirmed the tall man.

"If you want my opinion," the weak voice broke in, "I can only say that the sonnet we heard was not bad. It showed good knowledge of verse form, very genuine feeling, but no new singing quality, not a new cadence in it."

"No poet, then?" said the tall man.

"Not in my opinion!" was the reply.

The next moment the pair moved away from the door and I entered; with one glance I convinced myself that my stubborn critic was Austin Dobson,* who assuredly was a judge of the technique of poetry. But the condemnation did not need weighting with authority; it had reached my very heart because I felt it, knew it to be true. "No new singing quality, not a new cadence in it"; no poet then; a trained imitator. I was hot and cold with self-contempt.

Suddenly Mr. Froude called me. "I want to introduce you," he said, "to our best publisher, Mr. Charles Longman, and I'm glad to be able to tell you that he has consented to bring out your poems immediately; and I'll write a preface to them."

Of course I understood that 'good kind Froude,' as Carlyle had called him, was acting out of pure goodness of heart; I knew too that a preface from his pen would shorten my way to fame by at least ten years. But I was too stricken, too cast down to accept such help.

"It's very, very kind of you, Mr. Froude!" I exclaimed, "And I don't

* (1840–1921); he has proved to be a minor poet.

know how to thank you, and Mr. Longman too, but I don't deserve the honor. My verses are not good enough."

"You must allow us to be the judge of that," said Froude, a little huffed, I could see, by my unexpected refusal.

"Oh, please not," I cried. "My verses are not good enough; really, I know; please, please give them back to me!" He lifted his eyebrows and handed me the booklet. I thanked him again, but how I left the room I have no idea. I wanted to be alone, away from all those kind, encouraging, false eyes, to be by myself alone. I was ashamed to the soul by my extravagant self-estimate.

I took a cab home and sat down to read the poems. Some of them were poor and at once I burned them, but after many readings three or four still seemed to me good and I resolved to keep them; but I could not sleep. At last, in a fever, I heard the milkman with his cans and knew it was seven o'clock. I had lost a precious night's sleep. I flung myself out of bed and burnt the last four sonnets, then got into bed again and slept the sleep of the just till past noon. I awoke to the full consciousness that I was not a poet; never again would I even try to write poetry, never. Prose was all I could reach, so I must learn to write prose as well as I could and leave poetry for more gifted singers.

Renewed hope came with physical exercise. After all, I had done a good deal in my first month or so. I had steady work on the *Spectator;* Hutton paid me three pounds for each paper, and I took care to write at least one every week and often two. Escott gave me more and more work on the *Fortnightly,* and after I had told him of Froude's dinner in my honor, he invited me to dine at his home in Brompton and I got to know his wife and pretty daughter. Chapman too invited me to his house in Overton Square, and I began to know quite a number of more or less interesting folk.

Chapter IX

First Love; Hutton, Escott, and the *Evening News*

How DOES LOVE COME FIRST to a man? Romance writers all agree that love comes as a goddess in blinding light, or ravishment of music or charm of scenery, but always crowned, always victorious. Mine is a plain unvarnished tale; love befell me in those first months in London in a most commonplace way, and yet I'll swear with Shakespeare that my love

> . . . was as fair
> As any she belied with false compare.*

I was earning some five or six pounds a week and living quietly in Bloomsbury near the British Museum. I had occasion to call on someone in a boarding-house in the same district who had sent an article to the *Fortnightly*. I was shown into a parlor on the ground floor by the untidy maid and told that the lady would be down soon.

While waiting, a girl was shown in and also asked to wait. She came towards me where I was standing by the window and took my breath. Every detail of her appearance in the strong light is printed in my memory, even the shade of blue of the cloak she was wearing. She was rather tall, some five feet five, and walked singularly well, reminding me of Basque and Spanish girls I had seen, who swam rather than walked—a consequence, I had found out, of taking short even steps from the hips. Her eyes met mine fairly and passed on: long hazel eyes of the best, broad forehead, rather round face, good lips, firm though small chin; a lovely girl, I decided, with a mane of chestnut hair brightened with strands of gold. She was well, though not noticeably dressed, the long blue cloak and her apparent self-possession giving her rather the air of a governess. I resolved to speak to her. "Waiting is weary work," I began with a smile.

"It depends where and with whom," she replied with a touch of coquetry, but without a trace of English accent.

"Are you English?" I blurted out impulsively.

* Sonnet CXXX:

> . . . I think my love as rare
> As any she belied with false compare.

"Half-American, half-English," she answered, smiling. Her smile lit up her face enchantingly; it was like coming from a shuttered room into sunshine.

"My case too," I cried, "only instead of English, you'd have to say half-Welsh."

"Strange," she replied, laughing outright, "in my case, to be exact, you'd have to say half-Irish."

"Let us both keep to our American halves," I said, "then there will be nothing strange in my presenting myself. I am Frank Harris and trying here in London to be a writer."

"And my name is Laura Clapton." A few more questions and in five minutes I found that she was living with her father and mother in Gower Street; her father was a stockbroker and I could call any afternoon. I had time to promise I'd come next day and tell besides how I was working on the *Fortnightly Review* and the *Spectator,* thanks chiefly to my knowledge of various countries and languages.

"I know some foreign languages, too," said Miss Laura.

I was simply delighted to find her accent as good in German, French, Italian and Spanish as it was in English, and her command of the languages extraordinary: "Two years spent with my mother in each country," was her explanation.

Next day I called and was introduced to a little, round-faced, roly-poly of a mother. Very ugly, I thought, with pug nose and small gray-blue eyes, but in spite of face and figure, the little fat woman had an air of dignity, or, it would be truer to say, of imperiousness tinged with temper. When I met Queen Victoria later I was irresistibly reminded of Mrs. Clapton.

When Mr. Clapton came in the same evening, I saw where the daughter had got her good looks. Clapton was a handsome Irishman of perhaps five feet eleven, showing his fifty years in stoutness and greying hair. All his features were excellent, the hazel eyes splendid, and the man's personality genial and attractive. I easily understood how coming to Memphis, Tennessee, at five and twenty, the senator's daughter he met fell promptly in love with him. But he had been unfaithful and the proud southern girl wouldn't forgive him, and had taught her only daughter too to take her side, though in public the family held together. The whole situation was clear that first evening and I took an immediate liking to the good-looking, happy-go-lucky father, who probably out of custom kept up appearances with his unattractive wife for old affection's sake, and the pride he took in his daughter's looks and cleverness. For the daughter was undoubtedly clever and her looks grew on me: moving about in the room, taking off her hat and seating herself, the rhythmic grace of her beautiful figure made itself felt. I think from the beginning the mother disliked me as much as the father liked me. I found that Miss Laura loved the stage, had trained herself, indeed, to be an actress, and was only kept from going on the stage by the mother's insensate vanity and pride of birth. Naturally, I got them theatre tickets and soon became intimate.

A month or so later the father wanted to spend Christmas at Brighton; nothing could have suited me better. I knew Brighton well, so early in the week we went down and stayed at the Albion Hotel. In the mornings we all used to go out walking, but the fat mother soon returned to the hotel with her husband, leaving Laura and myself to our own devices. Two incidents I remember of those first days: I had put some rhetoric into an article in the *Spectator* on Hendrik Conscience,* the Belgian writer, and I read it to Laura one afternoon. "You read wonderfully," she said, "and that prose is lovely. You're going to be a great writer!"

I shook my head. "A good speaker, perhaps," I said, for already I [had] thought of going into the House of Commons.

I didn't believe that I had genius, but I felt sure I could make myself an excellent speaker, and naturally I confided my ambitions to her. She had risen, and as I rose and thrust the paper into my pocket, I repeated passionately the last words of the article. Her eyes were on a level with mine and I suppose the passion in my voice moved her, for her eyes gave themselves to me: the next moment my arms were around her and my lips on hers.

She kissed me naturally, without shyness or reserve. I could not help thinking at once, "She has often given her lips; she's too good-looking to have been left unpursued." The thought gave me boldness. "How beautiful you are," I said putting my arm round her waist.

She smiled but drew back a little. "You flatterer!"

"No, no," I pursued; "not a taint of flattery; I'm so much in earnest that I'm absolutely truthful. Your figure is most beautiful: I love and admire small breasts, just as I admire and love large hips," and I put my hands again on her figure.

"I love your word," she responded, "that you are 'so much in earnest that you are quite truthful,' deep love and truth always go together, don't they?"

"Always," I replied. Her quick ears heard someone coming and she turned away, but the touches had thrilled me, and I could not forbear clasping her waist from behind. She wound herself out of my arms with infinite litheness and with pouting lips and frowning brows reproved my daring, but the finger on her mouth was a warning and her eyes were smiling: she was not really angry at all. The next minute her mother came in.

The situation of the father and mother filled me with pity for the girl; I felt in my bones that the father in especial must have called on her sometimes to help pay the weekly bills. She had been trained in worldly wisdom, yet had kept her spiritual enthusiasms. Her difficulties, which I surmised, endeared her to me.

---

* (1812–83), the progenitor of modern Flemish literature because he wrote in everyday Flemish, as opposed to conventional literary French.

On Christmas Eve we happened to be alone again in the sitting-room. After the first kiss I naturally kissed her whenever I had the chance, and under my kissing and caressing her lips grew hot. But she drew back almost at once. "How strangely you kiss," she said, her eyes thoughtful.

I loved her for her frankness and read it rightly, I think: she was still virgin, but on the point of yielding. I resolved to be worthy of her.

"Laura, dear," I said, "I want to speak to you soul to soul. I love you and want you: give me six months or at most a year more and I shall have won a position in London and money. I've done a good deal in four months; I'll win completely in a year. Give me the year, will you, and I'll ask you to marry me!"

"I love you," she replied, "and trust you. I'll wait, you can be sure," and we kissed again as a sort of consecration—indeed as lovers kiss, whose spirits flow together at meeting of the lips.

The rest of those Christmas holidays can be told rapidly. I felt that Laura did not put much confidence in my assurances of splendid and rapid success. She had heard similar hopes expressed far too often by her father and had found them evaporate [sic]. I first heard the American word from her for such forecasts of hope, "hot air." How was she to know the difference between the gambler and the workman, whose self-confidence was rooted in many and widely different experiences?

I resolved to get back to London as soon as possible, and up to the last day, with the optimism of first love, I hoped to meet Laura there almost every day. On the second of January I paid the hotel bill and was astonished by it; it took nearly all my nest-egg: Clapton had drunk champagne in his bedroom. But what did it matter? I had had the time of my life and a smile from Laura's lips; a glance of approval from her eyes meant more to me than a fortune.

Just before lunch the father asked me to go out with him for a stroll. As soon as we were alone, he began by thanking me for the holiday. "I'd never have let you foot the bill," he began, "but I've had a long run of bad luck in this open stock exchange I founded in London. My partner, I find, has bolted in my absence and taken all the funds, but I only need just a small sum for expenses, a thousand 'll do—"

I would not let him conclude; I wanted to spare him the humiliation of asking. I broke in at once, "I'd let you have it with a heart and a half if I had got it, but the truth is the holiday has brought me, too, to rock-bottom. I must go back and get to work, and I can't even get such a sum quickly. I say to you, as I've said to Laura, give me a year and I'll win."

His look was enough; the splendid long hazel eyes were as hard as buttons. "Never mind," he said, "it doesn't matter." In ten minutes we were back in the hotel and I don't think I got ten words more from him that day. Evidently the father, too, thought me no prize.

When we reached London I drove them first to Gower Street, but their rooms were not ready for them. The father saw the landlady and came down to us in the hall and told us, with feigned indignation, that the hostess had not acted on his wire, but in a couple of hours their old rooms would be ready. "Mr. Harris will perhaps take care of you till then," he added. "I have to see—" The vagueness of the arrangements confirmed my suspicions of Clapton's irresponsibility and increased my sympathy with the queenly girl. Of course, I was only too glad to be of service. I drove the ladies first to my rooms to get rid of my luggage. Though I had not wired, my rooms were all ready, swept and garnished; and the mother and daughter came in and had tea and afterwards I took them to Kettners, a good Bohemian restaurant, for dinner. I left them at eleven o'clock in their rooms and got a long kiss from Laura in the passage; I felt well repaid. As soon as I was alone and rehearsed the happenings of the day, as was my custom, I saw I had no time to lose. "If you want the girl," I said to myself, "you'll have to win a position quickly." Clearly I felt that now both the father and the mother would be linked against me. They might, probably would, turn the cold shoulder and make it unpleasant for me even to call. Besides, I must not lose time and energy courting Laura; this was the determining thought: I must get to work at once and without encumbrance of any kind. That night I wrote to Laura fully, saying I would not see her for three months and telling her why: I would ask her to marry me within the year. She answered, saying she understood and would wait. My choice of her was so absolute that I took it for granted that she had chosen me with the same complete certitude. Yet I felt I must win as soon as possible and win big.

Next morning I went down to Chapman, the publisher. What would he give me for a book on my experiences in western America as a cowboy, etc.? He listened to me and told me he might give £100. "But it's only because I know you," he added. "Usually we expect the author to help us in bringing out his first book." In half an hour I learned a good deal of the practice of publishing and found reason to echo Byron's caustic reply to Murray, who sent him a Bible instead of a check. Byron returned the book with one alteration. He had written in the word: "Now Barrabas was a 'publisher'," instead of the Biblical "robber."

No hope of a fortune through a book. Five days in every week I spent now on this trail, now on that, but London business was better organized than business in the United States at that time and so again and again I found the hoped-for outlet was a blind alley. At length, after nearly a month of disappointments, I went down to the stock exchange and sought for a place as a clerk in a broker's office. I found that only one clerk in each office had the *entrée* to the floor of the House, a privileged position again, to conquer which would cost at least a year's hard work. Besides, except the house of a German-Jew, not a single stockbroker seemed to want my services. But the Jew wanted many German letters written and I was more than willing to do them after hours; but the pay offered was only three pounds a week, and I stood hesitating. On my birthday, the fourteenth of February, I resolved to take Klein's offer and wrote to him that as soon as I had settled some business I'd be round, certainly within a week.

All this time I had been working steadily on the *Spectator* and growing there in influence. On each Saturday and Sunday I wrote two articles that always appeared; indeed, now I could control their position, for one day Hutton had taken me downstairs and introduced me to Meredith Townsend,* his partner, saying that in the holidays, when he (Hutton) was away, he'd be glad if Townsend would use me in his (Hutton's) place.

"He knows half a dozen languages," said Hutton, "and he corrects proofs as carefully as a born reader." Townsend assured me of his interest, and while Hutton was away I got a good deal of editorial work to do on the *Spectator* and came to know Townsend intimately. In many respects he was the complement of Hutton. He had spent many years in the East** and knew China fairly well. As Hutton was profoundly religious, so Townsend cared chiefly for success. Hutton believed with all his soul and mind that mankind was growing in goodness and grace to some divine fulfilment. Townsend was certain that "man in the loomp was bad," as Tennyson's *Northern Farmer* had it, and must come to a bad end. But the two men together fairly filled the English ideal at once sentimental and practical, and so the paper came to power and influence and wealth, notwithstanding the fact that save for a smattering of French, neither editor knew anything of modern Europe or America, nor of modern art and literature. I was really needed by them, and had I started with them a year or two sooner, or continued a year or two longer, I might have brought it to a partnership and the paper to a wider success. But when Hutton wanted to know if twenty-five pounds would satisfy me for the extra editorial work I had done, I smiled and assured him his good word was all I wanted and that I was fully paid with the six pounds a week I made from my articles. I knew how to win, if I didn't know when I would win. However, my chance came, as always, at the last moment.

One day I was in the *Fortnightly* office when Escott, coming up the stairs, met Chapman in the passage between their two rooms. After a word or two of greeting, Escott said loudly, "I think your protégé will get the editorship of the *Evening News*. I gave him a warm letter to Coleridge Kennard,† the banker, who, I understand, foots all the bills."

When he came into the room I had to report to him the results of a mission he had entrusted me with. The topic of the day was "The Housing of

---

* Meredith White Townsend (1831–1911). He was mainly responsible for the international attitude of the *Spectator*. The paper was published at a loss during the American Civil War because it supported the North; but when public sentiment swung that way it became prosperous.

** Townsend had owned and published the *Friend of India,* an influential paper in Serampore during the Mutiny of 1857.

† (1828–90).

the Poor." Lord Salisbury* had written an article in favor of the idea in *The Nineteenth Century* magazine, and Escott, egged on by Joseph Chamberlain,** the Radical leader, had sent Archibald Forbes,† the famous war correspondent, to Hatfield to report on what Lord Salisbury had done on his own estate for the rehousing of his poor. Forbes had sent in a most sensational report. He described houses in the village of Hatfield with vitriol in his pen instead of ink; one dining-room he pictured, I remember, where "feculent filth dripped on the table during meals." The whole paper was a savage attack on Salisbury and his selfish policy. It frightened Escott, and when I pointed out that the antithetical rhetoric really weakened Forbes's case, he asked me, "Would you go down to Hatfield and check Forbes's account," adding, "I have spoken to Mr. Chamberlain about you and your articles in the *Spectator* and he hopes you'll undertake the job."

Of course I went down to Hatfield at once with a proof of Forbes's article in my pocket. In the very first forenoon I found that the house where the "feculent filth dripped" didn't belong to Lord Salisbury at all, but to a leading Radical in the village. At the end of the day I was able to write that Forbes had only visited one house belonging to Lord Salisbury of the thirty he had described.

I then called on Lord Salisbury's agent and told him I had been sent to ascertain the truth: "Would he give it to me?" *Would he?*

He was a thorough-going admirer of Lord Salisbury, whom he described as probably the best landlord in England.

"Lord Salisbury's not rich, you know," he began, "but as soon as he came into the title and property he went over every one of the six hundred houses on the estate: he found four hundred needed rebuilding; we decided that he could only afford to rebuild thirty a year. The same evening he wrote me that he could not accept rent for any of the four hundred houses we had condemned, and when the houses were rebuilt he would only take three per cent of the cost as rental. I'll show you one or two of the houses that are still to be rebuilt," he added. "I shouldn't mind living in them."

I then showed him Archibald Forbes's paper, without disclosing the writer's name. "Lies," he cried indignantly, "all lies and vile libels. If only all noblemen acted to their tenants and dependents as Lord Salisbury does, there would not be a radical in England," and I half-agreed with him.

---

* (1830–1903); Prime Minister 1885–6, 1886–92, 1895–1902. The article actually appeared in the *Quarterly Review,* Oct., 1873. He constantly fought for the improvement of housing; he battled the lack of sanitation and wanted local governments to tear down uninhabitable houses.

** (1836–1914); the father of Neville Chamberlain. His first elective office was as Mayor of Birmingham; he cleared slums and radically improved water and gas service. He was a devoted Radical reformer and harshly critical of the Conservatives in this regard, of whom Salisbury was one. He remained a force in British politics for forty years.

† (1838–1900); the most renowned war correspondent of his day; he was bold in his criticism of military strategy. He wrote the biographies *Napoleon III* (1898), and *Emperor William I* (1889).

Now I reported the whole investigation to Escott and he said, "You must tell Chamberlain about it: he'll be dreadfully disappointed for he had picked Forbes. But I am enormously obliged to you; you must let me pay your expenses, at any rate. I'll get it from Joseph," he added, laughing. "Shall we say twenty pounds?"

"Say nothing," I replied, "but give me a letter recommending me for the editorship of the *Evening News* and we'll call it square."

"With a heart and a half." cried Escott. "I'll give you the best I can write and a tip besides. Get Hutton of the *Spectator* to write too about your editorial qualities and see Lord Folkestone* about the place, for though Kennard pays, Lord Folkestone is really the master. Kennard wants a baronetcy** and Lord Folkestone can get it for him for the asking." Of course I acted on Escott's advice at once. Hutton gave me an excellent letter, declaring that he had used me editorially and hardly knew how to praise me as I deserved. The same evening I sent off all the letters. Two days after I got a note from Lord Folkestone, saying that Mr. Kennard was out of town, but if I'd meet him at the office of the *Evening News* in Whitefriars Street in the morning, he'd show me round and we'd have a talk. Of course I accepted the invitation and left my letter within an hour at Lord Folkestone's house in Ennismore Gardens, then hastened off to Escott at once to find out all about Lord Folkestone.

I found that as soon as his father died, he would be Earl of Radnor with a rent-roll of at least £150,000 a year. "The eldest son's called Lord Folkestone by courtesy, for they own nearly the whole town and this Lord Folkestone married Henry Chaplin's† sister. She's a great musician, has a band of her own made up of young ladies and her only daughter. Radnor is an old man and so Folkestone must soon enter into his kingdom; he's something in the Queen's household," and so forth and so on.

I was soon to know him intimately.

Coincidence has hardly played any part in my life; indeed, one incident about this time is the first occasion in my life when I could use the word. I was returning from Escott's house in Kensington when I asked the cabby to take me by the Strand and Lyceum Theatre, for I was greatly interested then in Irving's productions. As luck would have it, while I was looking at the advertisement, the people were going into the theatre, and, as I turned, a young man jumped out of a four-wheeler and then helped out Laura Clapton and her mother. He was in dress clothes but unmistakably American, thirty years of age perhaps, about middle height, broad and very good-looking. He was evidently much interested in Laura, for he went on talking to her even while helping her mother to alight, and Laura answered him with manifest sympathy.

* (1841–1900), who became in 1889 the fifth Earl of Radnor.
** Ironically, he was granted a peerage but died before it was conferred; it was then granted to his grandson, Sir Coleridge Arthur Fitzroy Kennard (1885–1948).
† Viscount Henry Chaplin (1841–1923).

For a moment—just one wild impulse—I thought of confronting them; then a wave of pride surged over me. As she had not waited even three months, I would not interfere. I drew aside and saw them enter the theatre, rage in my heart.

How far had the acquaintance gone? Not very far, but—

Was Laura, too, that queen among women, a mere spoil of opportunity? Then I would live for my work and nothing else.

But the disappointment was as bitter as death!

Chapter X

Lord Folkestone and the *Evening News*;
Sir Charles Dilke's Story and His Wife's;
Earl Cairns and Miss Fortescue

NEXT MORNING AT TEN O'CLOCK I met Lord Folkestone in the offices of the *Evening News:* a tallish man, slight, very bald, with pointed, white goatee beard and moustache and kindly hazel eyes; handsome and lovable but not strong either in body, mind or character. I hope to insert a photo of him, for he was the first friend I made after Professor Smith; he had charming ways and was something more than a mere gentleman. He met me cordially; thought the commendation of Hutton extraordinary, and Escott's too. He had met Escott.

"Shall we go over the building?" he proposed finally and took me into the machine room downstairs, where three antiquated machines had to be used to turn out thirty thousand copies in an hour. "Only ten thousand are needed," he smiled, thinking the machinery adequate, evidently ignorant of the fact that one Hoe machine would have been twice as efficient as the three at one-half the cost. Then we went up to the fourth floor, where thirty or thirty-five compositors worked to set up some three or four editions daily. After an hour of wandering about, we returned to the office where we had first met.

"There can be no doubt about your qualifications," Lord Folkestone said, "but do you think you can make the paper pay? It is now losing £40,000 a year and Kennard, though rich and a banker, finds that a pull. What hope can you give him?"

I don't know why, but he seemed to me so simple, so sincere, so kindly, that I made up my mind to tell him the whole truth, though it made against me.

"My recommendations, Lord Folkestone," I said, "don't apply to this job at all. I have not the remotest idea how to make a daily paper a success; I've absolutely no experience of such a task. A business man is needed here, not a man of letters, but I've always been successful at whatever I took up, and if you give me the chance I'll make a horse that'll win the Derby or a paper that'll pay. What I ask is one month's experience and then I'll tell you the whole truth. I only beg you in the meantime not to give away my confession of ignorance and inexperience."

"I like you the better for your frankness," he replied cordially, "and you'll have my vote, I can promise you, but Kennard must decide. I've heard that he'll be back tomorrow, so if it suits you, we can meet here tomorrow." And so it was settled.

I found Coleridge Kennard a fussy little person who seemed very anxious to keep the paper strictly Conservative. Because it only cost a ha'penny, people thought it should be radical, but he wanted it to fight communism and all that nonsense: that's why he took it up. But if it couldn't be made to pay, of course he'd have to drop it ultimately. Nobody seemed to know how to make it pay: the advertisements were increasing, but the circulation didn't seem to budge. If instead of selling six or eight thousand a day it sold fifty thousand, the "ads" would come in and it would have to pay. What did I think I could do?

"Give me the paper for one month, Mr. Kennard," I said, "and I'll tell you all about it."

"What conditions?" he asked.

"Your own," I replied. "I shall be perfectly content with whatever you and Lord Folkestone decide. I give you my word I shan't injure the paper."

"Very handsome, I must say," said Kennard. "I think we should accept?" He turned in question to Lord Folkestone.

"Surely," Lord Folkestone nodded, "and for the first time I think we have a chance of making the paper a Derby winner."

In this spirit we shook hands and they introduced me to the heads of departments.

The sub-editors seemed sulky and disappointed: the head machinist, a Scot, too independent; the book-keeper, a Mr. Humphrey, the husband of the brilliant writer, "Madge" of *Truth,* thoroughly kind and eager to help me. I told him before Kennard and Folkestone that I wished to make no changes for the first month; I'd study the field.

As soon as the directors had left, Humphrey gave me the true truth on all points within his knowledge. He thought it nearly impossible to make a cheap Conservative paper pay. There was a manifest contradiction between policy and price; then the machines were worthless and Macdonald not much good and—

Clearly my task would be a difficult one. The chief sub-editor, Abbott, put on a nonchalant air. "Had he any ideas as to how the paper could be made successful?" He did what he was told, he said, and that was all. I went home that night with the latest *Evening News* in my hand and the latest *Echo*, its Radical rival. The *Echo* had a policy, a strictly Liberal policy with less than nothing to offer the workman except cheap contempt for his superiors. My Conservative-Socialist policy must beat it out of the field. The news in both papers was simply taken from the morning papers and the agencies and was as bad in one paper as in the other. It was plain that certain news items should be rewritten and made, after the American fashion, into little stories. I hadn't found the way yet, but I would find it. The lethargy in the whole establishment was appalling. It took an hour to make the stereo-plates for the best machine and often the old rattletrap machine would stop running; and when I went down and interviewed Macdonald, he told me he was the only man who could get the old tin-pot machine to work at all.

The previous editor had never entered the machine-room. I spent an hour every day there and soon one workman struck me, six feet in height and splendidly made, with a strong face. Whenever the machine stopped, Tibbett seemed to know at once what was wrong. When I got him a moment alone I asked him to come to see me upstairs after his work. He came, it seemed to me, reluctantly; bit by bit, by praising him and showing confidence in him and not in Macdonald, he spoke plainly. "Macdonald has got Scotchmen [sic] to work in order to keep his berth; he's no good himself and they are like him. Twelve men in the machine-room; five could do the work and do it better," Tibbett declared. Ten pounds a week, I said to myself, instead of twenty-five, a good saving. I asked Tibbett if I discharged Macdonald and gave him the job whether he'd do it. He seemed reluctant; the cursed *esprit de corps* of the working man made him hesitate, but at length he said he'd do his best, but—but—. Finally he gave me the names of the four men he'd keep.

Next morning I called in Macdonald and discharged him and his brother-in-law together. I gave him a month's salary in lieu of notice, his brother-in-law two weeks, and left the others till the next Saturday.

An hour later there was the devil's own row in the machine-room. The discharged Scots suspected that Tibbett had given the show away and began calling him names. He knocked them down one after the other and they called in the police and had Tibbett arrested for assault and battery. Next day I went to the Police Court and did my best for him, but the stupid magistrate accepted the doctor's statement that the elder Macdonald was seriously injured. His nose, it appeared, was broken, whereas it should only have been put out of joint, and he gave Tibbett a month. His wife was in court and in tears; I cheered her up by telling her I'd have him out in a week, and thanks to Lord Folkestone, who went to the Home Secretary for him, he was let out in the week with a fine of £20 instead of the month's imprisonment. At the end of the week, Tibbett came back and the machines went better than they had ever done. I gave each of his three workmen two pounds weekly and four to Tibbett and a new spirit of utmost endeavour reigned in the machine room. To cut a long story short, I got Tibbett to tell me who was the best man in the casting department—Maltby was his name, the best workman and the most inarticulate man I ever met.

I reduced the expenses there two-thirds, saving another fifteen pounds a week and increasing the efficiency incredibly. At once the time occupied in casting plates for one machine fell from an hour to the best American time of twenty minutes, but Maltby gradually reduced it to twelve minutes with astonishing results, as I shall soon relate.

I began to get lessons on all sides. The war in Egypt was on and one morning, hearing a good deal of noise, I went into the great outer office where the newsboys had assembled for the first edition. They talked loudly and seemed discontented, so I went in among them and asked one for his opinion.

"There's a bloody bill!" cried the youngster disdainfully. He couldn't have been more than twelve, shoving the *Evening News* contents bill in my face. "A bloody bill; how do you expect us to sell papers on that?"

"What's wrong with it?" I asked.

"Nothing right!" was the reply. "Hain't there been a battle and great slaughter? Look at this *Daily Telegraph* bill. There's a real bill for ye; that'll sell paipers! Ours won't!"

Of course I saw the difference at once, so I took the boy critic and a friend of his into my office and with the paper before us sat down to get out a new and sensational bill. Then I sent for the chief sub-editor, Abbott, and showed him the difference. To my amazement he defended his quiet bill. "It's a Conservative paper," he said, "and doesn't shout at you."

The boy critic giggled. "You come out to sell paipers," he cried, "and you'll soon hev' to shout!"

The end of it was that I gave the boy ten shillings and five to his friend and made them promise to come to me each week with the bills, good and bad. Those kids taught me what the London hapenny public wanted and I went home laughing at my own high-brow notions.

The ordinary English public did not want thoughts but sensations. I had begun to edit the paper with the best in me at twenty-eight; I went back in my life, and when I edited it as a boy of fourteen I began to succeed. My obsessions then were kissing and fighting: when I got one or other or both of these interests into every column, the circulation of the paper increased steadily.

I was awakened every morning at seven with breakfast and the papers: I could hardly get up earlier, as the milk did not come till seven. One morning my *Telegraph* told me that there had really been a battle in Egypt and of course the English had won. While driving to the office I cut out and arranged the account in *The Telegraph* and bettered it here and there with reports taken from the *Daily Chronicle* and *The Times*. I was at the office before eight, but no sub-editors came till nearly nine. That didn't matter so much, but the compositors only began to drift in at eight-fifteen. At once I set them to work and by nine I had put the whole paper together, with one short leading article instead of two long ones, and a good bill.

The first edition sold over ten thousand; I told the sub-editors not to be caught napping again and informed the printers that they had all to be present at eight sharp. They promised willingly.

My boy critic was on the job and congratulated me and gave me, incidentally, a new idea. "Some days," he said, "the news of a victory comes into the *Telegraph* between four in the morning, when they go to press, and ten, and then they bring out a speshul edition. My brother works on the *Telegraph;* he's a compositor and he'd give me the first pull of any speshul stuff and I could bring it to you. If your paiper is ready, you could taike the news and be out almost as soon as the *Telegraph*. Then you'd sell; oh my! 'twould be a holy lark!"

I fell in with the idea, told him he should have a sovereign to share with his brother every time he succeeded, and gave him my address: he was to come for me in a cab whenever he got such news. By extra pay I induced three "comps" to come in at six in the morning, and downstairs Maltby and his assistant and Tibbett and his brother were always on hand at the same hour.

One morning the little imp came for me. In half an hour I was in the office and had given the report of a big battle from the *Telegraph* word for word to the comps. They worked like fiends; indeed, the spirit was such that the comp who ought to have gone downstairs with the news called to his two chums to tail on to the rope and jumped into the letter-lift, which would have practically fallen five stories had not the chums clung on to the pulleys at the cost of bleeding fingers. In ten minutes, the *Evening News* was selling on the street, and, as it happened, selling before the *Telegraph*'s special edition. We could have sold hundreds of thousands, had the old machines been able to turn them out. As it was, we sold forty or fifty thousand and Fleet Street learned that a new evening paper was on the job.

About noon that day I had a visitor, Mr. Levi Lawson,* owner of the *Telegraph,* a little, fat, rubicund Jew of fifty or sixty, fuming with anger that his thunder had been stolen. I soon saw that he only suspected that we were out before him, for he informed me that I must never reproduce more than 30 per cent of a *Telegraph* article, even when I published the fact that the account was taken from their columns and gave them full credit. I showed him that I had stated in my preliminary story that the *Telegraph* correspondent was usually the best. That seemed to appease him, and as I knew my zeal had led me too far, I told him that I always meant to give the original purveyor of the news twenty minutes' start.

Just as Lawson was going out, conciliated, in came Lord Folkestone. I introduced Lawson to him and Lawson told him the story, adding, "You've a smart editor in this American; he'll do something." When Folkestone heard the whole story and how the "comp" had risked his life in his eagerness to save half a minute, he had the men up and thanked them and took me off to lunch, saying I must tell the whole story to Lady Folkestone. He confided to me on the way that Lady Folkestone couldn't stand Kennard: "He's not very kindly, you know!"

---

* Correctly, Lionel Lawson, né Lionel Levy (1833–1916). Actually, he was only half-owner. His brother Edward, also a part owner, was made Lord Burnham in 1903.

Lady Folkestone at that time was a large lady of forty-odd, who was as kind and wise as she was big. Henry Chaplin, her brother, the Squire of Lincolnshire, as he was called, was one of those extraordinary characters that only England can produce. Had he been educated, he would have been a great man; he was spoiled by having inherited a great position and fifty or sixty thousand pounds a year. He was handsome, too, tall and largely built, with a leonine aspect. Everyone in the eighties told you how he had fallen desperately in love with a pretty girl, who on the eve of marriage ran away with the Marquis of Hastings.* Chaplin at once went on the turf in opposition to the Marquis; a few years later he got a great horse in Hermit, who burst a blood vessel ten days before the Derby. The Marquis plunged against Hermit: for the first time the Derby was run in a snow storm (God's providence coming in to help righteous indignation) and Hermit won. On settling day the Marquis blew his brains out, or what stood for them, and Chaplin was vindicated. I don't know what became of the lady, but Chaplin went into the House of Commons and soon developed an *ore rotundo* style of rhetoric that sometimes deformed a really keen understanding of life. I knew him as a most lavish spender; he used to order special trains to take his guests to his country house, and his claret was as wonderful as his Comet port. He had read a good deal, too, but he had never forced himself to read anything that did not appeal to him, and so he was far too self-centered in opinion, with curious lacunae of astounding ignorance.

An Englishman through and through, with all the open-handed instincts of a conquering and successful race, and with a deep-rooted love of fair play and surface sentimentalities of all sorts that no one could explain, such as the English taste in men's dress and a genuine indifference to every other art. I have said a lot about Henry Chaplin because his sister was curiously like him in essentials, as generous-kindly and sweet-minded as possible, with at bottom an immense satisfaction in her privileged position. She loved music genuinely, yet when I talked of Wagner's astonishing genius, she seemed to have absolutely no comprehension of it.

Her daughter was tall and pretty, the son, too, a fine specimen so far as looks went, but with no conception of what I had begun to call to myself the first duty, which consists in developing the mind as harmoniously as the body. Such self-development increases one's power enormously, but is as easy and dangerous to overdo as it is easy and dangerous to overdevelop a muscle.

English society I learned to know through the unvarying kindness of the Folkestones: it struck me as superficial always and of the Middle Ages in its continual reference to a Christian, or rather a Pauline, standard of morals, which sat oddly on a vigorous, manly race.

When my month was up I was able to show that I had increased the

* (1855–1920). He married a daughter of Baron Howard of Glossop in 1880. Harris must have the wrong man, for the Marquis did not commit suicide on "settling day."

efficiency of the *Evening News* staff and had saved to boot some five thousand pounds yearly of expenses, while adding nearly as much to the revenue.

Thereupon the directors engaged me for three years as managing director at a salary of a thousand pounds a year and expenses, with a proviso that if I made the paper pay in the time, I should have a fifth of the net profits and an engagement for ten years, or for life, as Kennard suggested.

At once I felt I had won. I could marry now or just go on with the work: why didn't I seek out Laura and marry her? Simply because I had seen her twice at different theatres with the same sturdy, handsome American. The last time, coming out behind her mother, he had taken hold of her bare arm and she had rewarded his lover-like gesture with that smiling gift of herself I knew so well and valued so highly. No, I was not jealous, I said to myself, but I was in no hurry to put my head in the noose. So I worked with all my might at the paper and went out in the evenings. Folkestone had taken me to Poole's, his tailor's, and I was fairly well turned out. I was not a society favorite but already excited some interest, due chiefly to Folkestone's chivalrous backing.

I don't remember exactly how I came to know Arthur Walter* of *The Times,* but we soon became great friends and I spent half my summers at his country house near Finchampstead. Mrs. Walter, too, took me up and was very kind to me, and I came to regard the whole household with real affection. Already I could tell them stories of a London life they knew little or nothing about, the life of the *coulisses.*

Sir Charles Dilke** I got to know intimately through the paper and I may as well tell the story here, for he made me know Chamberlain and the Radical party with fruitful consequences.

A Mr. Crawford,† a man of some position, suddenly filed a petition for divorce and named the Radical baronet, Sir Charles Dilke, as co-respondent. To my astonishment, the mere accusation was like an earthquake: London talked of nothing else. Folkestone gave me the aristocratic view. "Dilke," he said, "was known as a loose fish. The scandal would ruin him with his constitutents, but nobody in society would think any the worse of him." I saw the chance of a journalistic sensation, so I wrote to Dilke at once, saying that if I could do him any good, the *Evening News* would help him to put his case properly before the public. At once he replied, begging me to come to see him in his house in Sloane Street. He met me there next

* (1846–1910). His forebears had founded *The Times* and he became chief proprietor in 1894, when his father died, and remained so until 1908, when *The Times* was made a company.

** (1843–1911); he owned the *Athenaeum,* which his grandfather had purchased. He was a Liberal M.P., and a republican and attacked the Queen by way of criticizing her expenditures. The adultery suit recurred in 1885, and in 1886 he was defeated as a candidate for Parliament. He was returned as a M.P. in 1892 and represented his constituency until he died.

† Donald Crawford, M.P. for Lanark.

326 / *My Life and Loves*

morning with outstretched hands. "Your belief in my innocence," he began, "has been the greatest encouragement to me."

"Good God!" I cried. "Innocent! Like everyone else I thought you guilty; it's the politician I came to help, not the innocent."

At once he smiled, "We can talk then without affectation," and we did. I soon discovered that he took the whole thing far more seriously than I did or than Lord Folkestone. "A verdict against me means ruin to my career in Parliament," he declared.

"But the great Duke of Wellington," I objected, "wrote to Fanny who threatened to publish his letters: 'Dear Fanny, publish and be damned.'"

"An aristocratic society then," replied Dilke, "rather enjoyed a scandal; today the middle classes rule, and adultery to them is as bad as murder."

"Let's make fun of the whole thing," I proposed, "and so lighten the consequences."

"Very kind of you," replied Dilke. "It may help, but it won't save me."

In the next weeks I got to know Dilke well. He was one of the few men I met in London who knew French thoroughly and could speak it as a Frenchman with fluency and a perfect accent, but in spite of this advantage, he knew very little of French literature or art. He lived in politics, and though hard-working, he was not well read, even in English, and anything but brilliant. From time to time I met at his house all sorts of people like Jusserand, now French ambassador at Washington, and Harold Frederic, the brilliant American journalist and writer, and Edward Grey, Dilke's understudy as a minister for foreign affairs; Rhoda Broughton, too, the novelist and a host of others.* For Dilke was a rich man with many intellectual interests and a tinge as I have said, of French culture. He had inherited not only the *Athenaeum* journal from his father, but also miniatures of Keats that I esteemed more highly. This admiration of mine astonished him and he was good enough to offer me a beautiful specimen. "If you would let me give you something for it—" I hesitated.

"What would it be worth?" he asked.

"I'd give you a hundred pounds willingly," I replied.

"Is it worth as much as that?" he exclaimed.

---

* Jean Adrien Antoine Jules Jusserand (1855–1932), ambassador to the United States from 1902 until 1925. He was also a distinguished scholar and wrote *English Wayfaring Life in the Middle Ages* (1889), *Literary History of the English People* (1895), and *Shakespeare in France* (1898).

Harold Frederic (1856–98) became London correspondent for the *New York Times* in 1884 and spent the rest of his life in Europe. He reported the cholera epidemics in Southern France and Italy and showed that the disease came from dirt and bad sewage; he investigated in 1891 the persecution of Jews in Russia. He is best remembered for his good novel, *The Damnation of Theron Ware* (1896).

Edward Grey (1862–1933), parliamentary secretary of the Foreign Office 1892–95; he headed that office 1905–16.

Rhoda Broughton (1840–1920) produced a novel about every two years, e.g., *Goodly Sweetheart* (1872), *Nancy* (1873), *Joan* (1876), *Belinda* (1883), *Doctor Cupid* (1886). She was, for her day, bold in her speech and writing.

"If I had it, I'd not take a thousand for it," I cried.

"Really!" he said, but no longer pressed it on me, for Dilke was anything but generous.

The great question for Dilke in the divorce case was, should he go into the witness box and deny the adultery or not. He never discussed it with me till the trial was on; then at noon one day he called at my office and put the matter before me. Naturally I told him that he must go into the box and deny it. Any gentleman would have to do that for a lady, even if the liaison had been so notorious that his denial would only cause a smile. Thereupon Dilke told me that he had talked the matter over with Joseph Chamberlain in a room in the Law Courts and that Chamberlain had insisted that he mustn't go into the box.

"Dilke," I cried, "it is surely worse than foolish to go to your rival for advice. Chamberlain and Dilke are the two Radical leaders. Fancy Dilke accepting Chamberlain's counsel." Dilke hemmed and hawed and beat about the bush, but at last confessed.

"You see," he said, "my name was often coupled with the name of Mrs. Crawford's mother when I was young in London, and people might be horrified at the idea that I would corrupt my own daughter."

"Good God!" I cried. "That does complicate the affair. But no English judge would allow any question, even in cross-examination, that would tend to discover such a pot of roses."

"It doesn't horrify you?" asked Dilke. "I thought Chamberlain would have a fit when I told him."

"I wouldn't have told him," I said. "But do you think she is your daughter? Is there any likeness, or attraction?"

"No nothing," he replied. "The Greeks, you know, thought nothing of incest. Some indeed say that the highest type of Greek beauty was evolved through the father going with the daughter, the brother with the sister—"

"We can discuss that another time," I said, "and I would like to, because I have some strange facts on it. The consanguinity is supposed to produce greater beauty, but certainly less strength and less intellect; but now I can only beg you to go into the box. If you don't, Stead* and the other Radical journalists will get after you and declare that your abstention is a proof of your guilt. It is probable, too, that the judge will express the same opinion and then the fat would be in the fire. The nonconformist conscience would get on its hind legs and howl."

Everyone remembers that in spite of my good advice, which I urged with all my power, Dilke funked the witness box,** let the case go by default

---

* William Thomas Stead (1849–1912), editor of the *Pall Mall Gazette*. He changed this proper paper into something close to a yellow journal by writing up corruption in government and London criminal life.

** Actually, there were two trials. Dilke did not take the stand in the first trial, but in the second he did and the sordid story of his relations with Mrs. Crawford's mother became public.

against him, and the judge said that his abstention must be taken as a confession: "Every gentleman would repel such an accusation with horror." Yet this righteous judge had heard Mrs. Crawford in the witness box declare that Dilke insisted on bringing a Mrs. Rogerson* to their bed when she was in it, "And Mrs. Rogerson," she added, "was an old woman and Dilke's old flame!" British prudery pretended not to know what this second string to Dilke's bow could possibly mean, but in the best class of society the matter was fully discussed.

While I was defending Dilke as well as I could, John Corlett** of the *Pink 'Un'*, the London paper distinguished for its free speech, came to me and said, "You know Dilke and all about this case of Crawford." I admitted that I knew a good deal about it. "Can't you do something funny on it for me? You know we can sail near the wind, but mustn't make the sails shiver."

An idea came into my head and I gave it to Corlett. "Put in any comment about the case you like," I said, "and then sketch a little palette bed in the simplest of small bedrooms, because that is where Dilke assures me that he sleeps. Put two pillows on the bolster and leave the sketch for the first week with the caption, 'An Exact Reproduction of Sir Charles Dilke's Bedroom!' "

"That won't set the Thames on fire," said Corlett. "Still, the idea has a little piquancy."

"But think what you would be able to do next week," I said, "when you put in great letters that you made one mistake in the picture of Dilke's bedroom last week, that you are happy to be able to rectify it this week. Then reproduce the picture again exactly, putting, however, three pillows on the bolster instead of two."

"I will send you fifty quid for that," said Corlett. "That's the best thing I've heard for a h—l of a while." And he kept his word. I always liked John Corlett. There was no nonsense about him, and he was a first-rate paymaster.

One quality Sir Charles Dilke had of greatness, a quality rare even in England and almost unknown among American politicians: he judged men with astounding impartiality. He knew the House of Commons better than anyone I ever met, with the solitary exception of Lord Hartington,† and I

---

* Mrs. Crawford identified this third person as Fanny Stock, a servant girl, who was unavailable for testimony.

** (1841–1915). Harris errs here: Corlett was proprietor of the *Sporting Times* 1874–1912.

† (1833–1908). He served in the House of Commons for thirty years before he became the eighth Duke of Devonshire. He was a Liberal and second in power only to Gladstone until he broke with Gladstone over Home Rule in 1886. He next broke with the Unionists in 1903, when they prepared to abandon free trade. He came very close three times to being Prime Minister, in 1880, when it seemed Gladstone might retire, in 1886, when he was allied with Salisbury, and in 1887 when Randolph Churchill resigned as chancellor of the Exchequer.

was a fairly good judge of this accomplishment, for from the moment I became editor of the *Evening News,* I began to go to the House of Commons three or four times a week and listen to all the debates from the "Distinguished Strangers' Gallery."

There and in the lobbies I met all sorts and conditions of men from Captain O'Shea and Biggar to Mr. Parnell and Count Herbert Bismarck.*

One incident about Dilke I must not forget to relate. As soon as the result of his trial was made known, Mrs. Mark Pattison,** the widow of the famous rector of Lincoln College, Oxford, cabled to him from India, "I believe in your complete innocence and am returning to marry you at once."

This recalls a story that was hatched in Oxford, I believe, about Mark Pattison, the famous Grecian† and his pretty young blonde wife, who had surrounded herself with a band of young Fellows and scholars, which seemed at variance with the pedantic tone of the elderly head. One day an old friend found Pattison walking in the college garden, lost in thought. "I hope I'm not interrupting," he said, after vainly trying to interest the Rector.

"No, no! my dear fellow," replied Pattison, "but I have ground for thought. My wife tells me that she thinks she's *enceinte,*" and he pursed out his lips in self-satisfaction.

"Good God." cried the friend, "whom do you suspect?"

When we read Mrs. Pattison's cable in the morning paper, Folkestone exclaimed, "Really, I begin to feel sorry for Dilke; his sins are finding him out," and Harold Frederic's word was much the same: "A *bas bleu* on a rake will be something novel even in London."

I never liked Lady Dilke. She was a woman of forty-odd when I first met her, an ordinary stout, short blonde with brown hair, blue eyes, commonplace features and complexion, who was always a pedant—indeed the only blue-stocking I ever met in England. I may give one typical instance of her pedantry and so leave her to rest. When I had made some reputation as a Shakespeare scholar and had declined her invitations for years and years, she wrote to me once, telling me that the French diplomat, M.

* Captain John Augustus O'Shea (1839–1905); an Irish journalist, at this time a special correspondent for the London *Standard.* In *Iron-Bound City* (1886), he relates his experiences in the siege of Paris during the Franco-Prussian War.

Joseph Gillis Biggar (1828–90); a Fenian, born a Presbyterian but a convert to Roman Catholicism in 1877. An ardent Home Ruler, he was elected to Parliament in 1874, and in his obstructionism he was supported by Parnell.

Charles Stewart Parnell. (1846–91). It may be well at this point to recall that Parnell was of English origin and a Protestant; his mother was the daughter of Commodore Charles Stewart of the United States Navy. Winston Churchill gives a brilliant portrait of him in *Great Contemporaries* (London, 1937).

Herbert von Bismarck (1849–1904), the son of the German Chancellor.

** She was a recent widow when she sent this telegram; she and Dilke were married in Paris in 1885.

† (1813–84) Pattison was not a "Grecian"; he wrote on religious subjects.

Jusserand, was a great Shakespearean authority whom I really ought to meet; and "who wishes to meet you," she added. "Won't you therefore dine with us on the—and meet him? Please come at seven and then you can have an hour together before dinner."

I wrote thanking her and turned up at seven sharp; I was eager to see if any Frenchman knew anything at first hand of Shakespeare. Lady Dilke introduced me at once to M. Jusserand in the little off-drawing-room on the first floor and said, "Now I'll leave you two *sommités* of learning to talk and straighten out all difficulties, for you both believe, I think, that Shakespeare was Shakespeare and not Bacon, though I remember once—," and the garrulous lady started off on a long story of how she had once met a Baconian at Lincoln College, "whom even my husband had to respect and this is how he approached the great question—"

Jusserand and I looked at each other and listened with courteous, patient inattention; the lady went on for the whole hour and the dinner-bell found us still listening, neither of us having got in a single word edgeways. To this day I know nothing of Jusserand's views.

From his marriage on, Dilke and I used to lunch together once a week, now in this restaurant, now in that, for many a year, and nine-tenths of what I learned about the House of Commons and English politicians came from him. In fact, it was he who showed me the best side of English Puritanism, its appreciation of conduct and strict observance of all obligations. I always preferred the aristocrat view, at once more generous and looser; but the middle-class semi-religious outlook is perhaps more characteristically English, for it has propagated itself almost exclusively all over the United States and the British colonies.

Dilke taught me where Dickens got his Gradgrind,* the master of facts, "the German paste in the Englishman," I called it. Dilke was well informed in politics and worked up all his speeches in the House with meticulous care. But though he spoke monotonously and without a thrill of any kind, Gladstone, some time before the Crawford divorce case, had solemnly selected Dilke to follow him in the Liberal leadership. Laborious learning is esteemed in England beyond even genius, altogether beyond its value. This is what Goethe meant, I believe, when he spoke of the English as "pedants."

One evening at dinner Dilke corrected Harold Frederic in a little unimportant fact. For some reason or other, Frederic had asserted that only about half the inhabitants of Salt Lake City were Mormons. At once Dilke corrected him: "Ninety per cent, my dear Frederic, and eighty per cent communicants." Harold looked his disgust but said nothing. Afterwards, going home together, he expatiated on this *tic* of Dilke's and arranged with me to catch him. Harold was to get up the number of Copts in Lower Egypt; of course Dilke would pretend to have the figures at his fingers' ends and Frederic would bowl him out. For my part I was charged to find out

* A character in *Hard Times*.

the number of Boers in the Transvaal in comparison with men of other nationalities, and accordingly I got up the figures.

At our next dinner in Sloane Street I turned the talk on Cairo and said how surprised I was at the number of different nationalities there were in that strange land. "I met Copts by the score," I said; at once Dilke fell into the trap.

"Surely," he said, "the Copts in Cairo don't number more than a few hundreds."

"What do you think, Frederic?" I asked across the table, to get the proper audience.

"Copts in Cairo," repeated Frederic. "You can hardly be serious, Dilke; there are some eleven thousand of them."

Dilke was nonplused. "Really, eleven thousand," he kept repeating; "Copts? Really?" He was evidently shocked by the correction.

A few minutes later he committed himself to the statement that there were comparatively few Boers in Johannesburg and thus fell into my hands. I never saw a man so taken aback; accuracy was his fetish and to have it desert him twice in one evening was too much for his equanimity.

I mention these things just to set off a racial peculiarity of the Englishman which, I'm sorry to say, is showing itself almost as prominently in the American, though, I am glad to believe, without the intolerable presumption of the Englishman that knowledge and wisdom are synonymous.

In my first year in the *Evening News* I learned and practiced nearly every journalistic trick. When the annual boat race between Oxford and Cambridge was about to be decided, I found out that the experts usually knew which crew would win. Of course sometimes they are mistaken, but very rarely, and this year they all agreed it was a foregone conclusion for Oxford. Accordingly, on the great morning I had fifty thousand papers printed with "Oxford won" in big letters under the latest preliminary reports of the training, etc. As soon as the telephone message came through that Oxford had won, I let the boys out and this start enabled me to sell all the fifty thousand papers. I did the same thing with race after race on the turf and soon it began to be known that the *Evening News* had the earliest news of the races. I only mention these things to show that I was really working at high pressure day in, day out.

Time and again, luck favored me. One morning the announcement came in that the marriage between Lord Garmoyle* and Miss May Fortescue had been broken off and that the lady was suing for breach of promise. Within ten minutes I had got her address and was off in a hansom to interview her. I found her a very pretty and very intelligent girl who blamed the whole fiasco upon Earl Cairns,** one of the Conservative leaders, who was

---

* Arthur William Cairns (1861–90). He succeeded his father as the second Earl Cairns and in 1887 married Olivia Berens.

** Hugh McAlmont Cairns (1819–85), perhaps the outstanding lawyer of his day

the father of Lord Garmoyle and naturally enough did not wish his only son to marry an undistinguished actress. I gathered from Miss Fortescue that Cairns was a North of Ireland man, a great lawyer, but very religious and prudish, one who still spoke of Sunday as the Sabbath and thought the stage the ante-chamber of hell. When Miss Fortescue saw that I meant to fight for her, she gave me letters both of Lord Cairns and Lord Garmoyle that were very interesting and confessed to me that though she "cared for" Lord Garmoyle, she had put the damages for the breach of promise at ten thousand pounds "because his father will have to pay."

I wrote a two-column article at once, telling the whole story under the title "Beauty and the Peer," exciting all the sympathy possible for Miss Fortescue and throwing all the odium on Earl Cairns. The article caused a tremendous sensation. That a Conservative paper should have printed such an attack upon a Conservative peer and leader was unheard of.

Kennard happened to be in Brighton, but he was told about the article within a couple of hours of its appearance and at once wired to me to stop publishing the story, which he characterized as "obscene!" I went to Lord Folkestone for support and found that he was merely amused. He didn't like Cairns, thought him narrow and bigoted, and encouraged me to go on, while promising to smooth down Kennard's ruffled plumage. Accordingly, I kept on and had a second article next day still more sarcastic. To cut a long story short, Lord Cairns couldn't stand the contemptuous exposure, so paid the ten thousand pounds of damages demanded, and everyone, including Miss Fortescue, gave me and the *Evening News* credit for the victory.

This journalistic triumph doubled the circulation of the paper, increased its advertisements considerably and so gave us all a foretaste of success. I cleaned out the sub-editors' room and put friends of my own in place of the hacks, notably an Australian Irishman named Dr. Rubie; turned out the old leader-writers too and gave their work to Cluer and other friends. The whole place was soon abuzz with life and vigor.

But I had some rebuffs. The office of the *St. James Gazette* was just opposite our office in Whitefriars Street, and when I went out at noon I used to see a dozen of their carts drawn up on one side of the street, while our fifteen or twenty carts were drawn up on the other side—all alike waiting to get the papers and hurry off to distribute them to the various shops all over London. I went into the matter and found that we were paying some six thousand pounds a year for our carts. At once I got an introduction to Greenwood,* the editor of the *St. James*'s, and offered to give his paper, which cost a penny, the benefit of our very much larger distribution at

---

* Frederick Greenwood (1830–1909). He had been with the *Pall Mall Gazette,* but when the owner declared he was going to make it into a Radical paper, Greenwood joined the *St. James Gazette,* which was founded to continue the Conservative policy of the *Pall Mall.* He was a contributor to *Cornhill's* and the *Saturday Review;* he also wrote undistinguished novels.

about half of that his carts cost him. To my astonishment he refused and stuck to his refusal, though it was plainly stupid.

Three years afterwards, when my first stories came out in the *Fortnightly Review,* Greenwood praised them to the skies, and very ingenuously admitted that he had had a prejudice against me because he had heard me called an "American business man" and now regretted his hostility. We became in fact very good friends, and long before he died I grew to esteem and love the man.

Lord Folkestone often got me to call for him at the Carlton Club and there one day he told me a couple of jokes about club life that seemed to me to be amusing. The Carlton Club, as everybody knows, is the official club of the Conservative party, and one day an influential member, recently joined, put up on the notice board a request that the nobleman who had stolen his umbrella would kindly return it immediately. After this notice had been up a week or so, an irascible nobleman went to the secretary and drew his attention to it.

"It is a libel on our order," he said, "and I insist that the name of the nobleman should be given or the notice should be taken down." Hereupon the secretary went and interviewed the member who had put up the notice. "I don't know his name," said the member.

"Why then do you think it is a nobleman?" asked the secretary.

"Well, this club, according to your own statement, is made up of noblemen and gentlemen. No gentleman would steal my umbrella, so it must be a nobleman."

And here is a story of the Athenaeum Club, which in its own way is almost as amusing. The Athenaeum possessed for many years a famous and polite porter, named, I think, Courtney, who could identify hats, umbrellas and walking sticks belonging to members, and was never known to make a mistake. One day a dignified Bishop on his way out was duly handed his things by the janitor.

"This umbrella does not belong to me, Courtney," said the right reverend prelate.

"Possible not, my Lord," replied Courtney, "but it is the one you brought into the club."

Such stories as these abound in London and give a special, distinctive flavor to life in England, and for that reason I shall reproduce some of the best, not forgetting those coined in New York.

Chapter XI

London Life and Humor;
Burnand and Marx

. . . O thou wondrous Mother-age
Make me feel the wild pulsation that I felt before the strife
When I heard my days before me and the tumult of my life.*

LONDON IN THE EARLY EIGHTIES; London after years of solitary study and grim relentless effort; London when you are twenty-eight and have already won a place in its life; London when your mantelpiece has ten times as many invitations as you can accept, and there are two or three pretty girls that attract you; London when everyone you meet is courteous-kind and people of importance are beginning to speak about you; London with the foretaste of success in your mouth while your eyes are open wide to its myriad novelties and wonders; London with its round of receptions and court life, its theatres and shows, its amusements for the body, mind and soul: enchanting hours at a burlesque, prolonged by a boxing-match at the Sporting Club; or an evening in Parliament, where world-famous men discuss important policies; or a quiet morning spent with a poet who will live in English literature with Keats and Shakespeare; or an afternoon with pictures of a master already consecrated by fame. London: who could give even an idea of its varied delights: London the center of civilization, the queen city of the world without a peer in the multitude of its attractions, as superior to Paris as Paris is to New York.

If you have never been intoxicated you have never lived. I have felt myself made better and happier by exquisite wine, keyed up, so to speak, to a more vivid and higher spiritual life, talking better than I ever talked before,

* Tennyson, *Locksley Hall:*

. . . O thou wondrous
Mother-Age!
Make me feel the wild pulsation that I felt before
the strife,
When I heard my days before me, and the tumult of
my life . . .

with an intensified passion that lit all the eyes about me and set souls aflame. But the rapture of such heightened life is only momentary. London made me drunk for years and in memory still the magic of those first years ennobles life for me; and the later pains and sufferings, wrongs and insults, disdains and disappointments, all vanish and are forgotten. I wonder if I can give an idea of what London was to me with the first draught of its intoxicating vintage on my hot lips and the perfumes of it in my greedy nostrils. It's impossible to describe such a variety of attractions, but I'll try, reminding my readers merely that it was my ambition to touch life on many sides.

I had never heard of Frank Burnand,* but one night I dropped in to see his burlesque of *Blue Beard*. The play was worse than absurd, incredibly trivial. Mr. Burnand's hero keeps a note book for jotting down the names and addresses of interesting young women; otherwise he is not much of a monster. His mysterious Blue Chamber contains nothing more terrible than hair-dyes. He is a beardless lad of one-and-twenty; has, however, a blue lock to show; but it's a fraud. His wife and his father-in-law are to lose their heads for discovering his secret; the catastrophe is averted by the timely arrival of troops of young ladies in fantastic martial costumes that reveal most shapely figures.

The dancing and singing, and above all the astonishing plastic beauty of the chorus girls, gave me a foretaste of London, for in Paris the chorus women were usually hags.

Miss Nelly Farren** is the Baron Abomelique de Barbe Bleue and Miss Vaughan, Kate Vaughan,† is Lili, the Baron's bride. Here is the first verse of her song in the second act:

> French language is a bother,
> To learn it I don't care,
> Don't like to hear my mother
> Called by the French a *mère*.
> I like a husband to myself
> But the dear one is my *cher*
> Though I've only got one father
> Yet they swear he is a *père*.

* (1836–1917). He went to Trinity College, Cambridge, to take clerical orders, but converted to Roman Catholicism; he was admitted to the bar in 1862 but he fancied literature and the stage. He became an editor of *Punch* and wrote more than one hundred burlesques of popular dramas.

** (1848–1904), a little short on looks and voice, but a "personality" and the most popular actress in serious drama as well as in burlesque. She also scored in the "boy" parts of Sam Weller in *Bardell vs. Pickwick* and of Leporello in Robert Reece's *Don Giovanni*.

† (1852?–1903), née Catherine Candelon. She too played both in burlesque and serious pieces; two of her great successes were as Lydia Languish in *The Rivals* and as Lady Teazle in *The School for Scandal*. She was also an outstanding dancer and appeared in the ballet *Excelsior* before Queen Victoria in 1885.

Then Kate danced as no one ever danced before or since, with inimitable grace, and the way she picks up her dress and shows dainty ankles and hint of lovely limbs is a poem in itself; and all about her beautiful, smiling girls, in costumes that reveal every charm, sway or turn or dance, as if inspired by her delightful gaiety. In another scene she imitates Sarah Bernhardt and there is infinite humor in her piquant caricature; some one else mimics Irving, and all this in a rain of the most terrible puns and verbal acrobatics ever heard on any stage—an unforgettable evening which made me put Burnand down as one of the men I must get to know as soon as possible, for he was evidently a force to count with, a verbal contortionist, at least, of most extraordinary agility.

I will give one proof of his quality from my memories of ten years or so later, just to give handsome little Frank his proper standing, for he was as kindly pleasant as he was good-looking and witty, and that's saying a good deal.

In the London *New York Herald,* a weekly paper, there had appeared the story of Lord Euston's* arrest, so detailed that it was almost as libelous as the account in the *Star,* the ha' penny Radical evening paper, of which Ernest Parke was the editor. I knew Euston pretty well and he had told me that he meant to make it "hot" for anyone who traduced him. He was a big, well-made fellow of perhaps thirty, some six feet in height and decidedly manly-looking, the last person in the world to be suspected of any abnormal propensities. The story in the *Star* was detailed and libelous: Lord Euston was said to have gone in an ill-famed house in the West Central district; and the account in the Sunday *Herald* was just as damning. On the Monday following, Burnand came to lunch with me in Park Lane and by chance another guest was the Reverend John Verschoyle, whose talent for literature I have already described.

For some reason or other Verschoyle at table had condemned those who married their deceased wife's sister, evidently ignorant of the fact that Burnand had committed this offense against English convention. A little later, after the ladies had left the table, Verschoyle brought the conversation on the article in the *New York Herald* about Lord Euston; he was positive that a Sunday paper, by even mentioning such an affair, had killed itself in London. Burnand remarked, smiling, that he could not agree with such a verdict; surely it was the function of a newspaper to publish "news," and everyone was talking of this incident. But Verschoyle, purity-mad, stuck to his guns. "How could you explain such an 'incident'," he insisted, "to your wife or daughter, if she asked you what it was all about?"

"Very easily," retorted Burnand, still smiling, but with keen antagonism in his sharp enunciation; "I'd say: 'my dear, Lord Euston feels himself above the ordinary law, and having nothing better to do, went to this no-

---

* (1848–1912). In 1878 he married Kate Walsh Smith, who was Kate Cooke of the Variety Theatre; they were divorced in 1878.

torious gambling house to play. He thought the game was going to be poker, but when he found it was baccarat he came away.' "

No wittier explanation could be imagined; even Verschoyle had to try to smile. Curiously enough, in the libel action which Lord Euston brought against the *Star* newspaper, and which resulted in the condemnation of Ernest Parke, the editor, to a year's imprisonment, the explanation of Lord Euston was something like Burnand's excuse for him. He said that someone in the street had given him a card with *poses plastiques* on it; as he was at a loose end that night, he went to the address indicated. When he found that there were no *poses plastiques,* he came away.

One may say that burlesques and wit like Burnand's could also be found in Paris, but the comic humor, plus the physical beauty of the chorus girls, were not to be found there, nor the tragedy. Ernest Parke was a convinced Radical and a man of high character, yet he was sentenced to a year's imprisonment for reproducing, so he told me, a police inspector's statement, and one which in any case did Lord Euston no harm at all. Yet no one in London expostulated or thought of criticizing the judge, though it seemed to me an infamous and vindictive sentence only possible in England. The preposterous penalty discovers a weak and bad side of the aristocratic constitution of English society. The judges almost all come from the upper middle class and invariably, in my experience, toady to aristocratic sentiment. Every judge's wife wants to be a Lady (with a capital, please, printer!), and her husband as a rule gets ennobled the quicker the more he contrives to please his superiors in the hierarchy. If Lord Euston had been Mr. Euston of Clerkenwell, his libeler would have been given a small fine, but not imprisoned, though the imputation even of ordinary immorality would have injured him in purse and public esteem grievously, whereas it could not damage Lord Euston in any way.

And now for a contrast.

It was early in the eighties—I know it was a cold, windy day—that I went up to Haverstock Hill to call upon Dr. Karl Marx at his modest home in Maitland Park Road. We had met some time before, after one of Hyndman's* meetings, and were more or less friends. Hyndman had contradicted something I had said, and when I quoted Engels as on my side, he told me that he knew Engels and spoke German as well as English. Seeing that a large part of the audience was German, I challenged him to reply to me and began speaking in German. When the meeting was over a German came up and congratulated me and asked me would I like to know Karl Marx? I replied that nothing would give me greater pleasure and he took me out

---

* Henry Mayers Hyndman (1842–1921). He was born to a wealthy family, went to Trinity College, Cambridge, and worked under Greenwood on the Conservative *Pall Mall Gazette.* Then he read Marx and he spent the rest of his life and fortune on Socialism. He wrote an extraordinary autobiography, *The Record of an Adventurous Life* (1911) and *Further Reminiscences* (1912).

and introduced me to the famous doctor. He was by no means so famous then as he is now forty years later, though he well deserved to be.

I had read *Das Kapital* some years before. The first book, indeed, all the theoretical part, seemed to be brain-cobwebs loosely spun; but the second book and the whole criticism of the English factory system was one of the most relentless and convincing indictments I had ever seen in print. No one who ignores it should be listened to on social questions. When I had absorbed it, I sent for Marx's other books, *A Life of Lord Palmerston* and *Revelations of the Diplomatic History of the Eighteenth Century*. The *Palmerston* is written by one who had no feeling for character: the hero, an Irishman alive to his finger-tips, is buried under an erudition that prevents one seeing the forest for the trees; but the *Revelations* contain the best picture extant of the progress of Russia from the time she threw off the Tartar yoke to the latter half of the eighteenth century.

In person Marx was broad and short, but strong with a massive head, all framed in white hair; the eyes were still bright blue, by turns thoughtful, meditative and quick-glancing, sharply curious. My German astonished him; where had I got the fluency and the rhetoric? Talking of religious belief, I had said that *der Lauf des menschlichen Gedanker-ganges ist für mich die einzige Offenbarung Gottes* (the course of the progress of human thought is to me the only revelation of God). "*Wunderbar! echt Deutsch!*" Marx exclaimed (peculiarly German), which was the highest form of praise to a German of that time. He met me with critical courtesy, evidently surprised that an Englishman should have read not only *Das Kapital,* but all his contributions to periodicals. I told him I thought his book on the English factory system the most important work on sociology since *The Wealth of Nations* by Adam Smith: on the one hand the advocate of socialism, on the other the individualist, while both forces, I thought, must meet in life and an equilibrium between them must be established. Marx smiled at me, but didn't even attempt to consider the new idea. He made much the same impression on me that Herbert Spencer made twenty years later, but Spencer was contemptuous-angry under contradiction, whereas Karl Marx was inattentively courteous. But both had shut themselves off from hearing anything against his pet theory, one-sided though it was. And just as Herbert Spencer was worth listening to on everything but "the field I've made my own," so was Karl Marx. He was the first to tell me how the French bourgeoisie had massacred thirty thousand communists in Paris in cold blood after the defeat of 1870; but he condemned this bloodshed just as passionately as he condemned the strain of brutality in the anarchist Bakounin.* His deep human pity and sympathy were the best of him, the heart better than the head—and wiser. Much in the same way, Spencer saw that savagery in man was developed and perpetuated in the standing armies of Europe, though wholly at variance with the spirit of

* (1814–76); he believed that the state must be overthrown by violent insurrection, not by peaceable political action.

forgiveness preached from a thousand pulpits. Marx and Spencer, like Carlyle and Ruskin, were of the race of Polyphemus—one-eyed giants; but the latter pair were artists to boot!

Another contrast.

It was about this time that I first met Lord Randolph Churchill's brother, the Duke of Marlborough.* Though he was perhaps ten years older than I was, we became friends through sheer similarity of nature. He too wanted to touch life on many sides. He liked a good dinner and noble wine whether of Burgundy or Moselle, but above all, he loved women and believed with de Maupassant that the pursuit of them was the only entrancing adventure in a man's life. After a dinner at the Cafe Royal one night, he discoursed to me for an hour on the typical beauties of a dozen different races, not excluding the yellow or the black. He had as good a mind as his brother, but nothing like Randolph's genius as a captain or leader of men. I may tell one story of him here, though it took place much later, when I was editing the *Fortnightly Review.* I had met Lady Colin Campbell** in Paris and found that she spoke excellent French and Italian because she had spent her childhood in Florence. Shortly after I was made editor of the *Fortnightly Review*—in 1887 it was, I think—Mrs. Jeune† told me I ought to meet Lady Colin and publish some of her articles. I said I should be very glad to renew acquaintance with so pretty a woman. One day Mrs. Jeune brought about a meeting and told me to go to the back drawing-room where Lady Colin was waiting for me. I went upstairs and opened the door and there was Lady Colin toasting her legs in front of the fire. As soon as I spoke she dropped her skirt, excusing herself on the ground that she had got her feet wet and cold, but the exhibition seemed intentional, the appeal gross. At any rate, it put me off, and I soon found her articles were just as obvious as her tall, lithe figure and great dark eyes and hair. I had rejected one or two of her papers when the Duke asked me to dinner and soon told me, without unnecessarily beating about the bush, that he was in love with Lady Colin and had promised her that I would publish her next paper. I told him I couldn't do it, but he pressed me so earnestly that at length I said, "If you will write me an absolutely frank article, setting forth the sensuous view of life you have often preached to me, I'll accept Lady Colin's contribution blindfold; but I want absolute frankness from you."

He broke in, laughing. "It's a bargain and I am greatly obliged to you; I'll write the article at once and let you have it this week." "Life and Its

* George Charles Churchill, 8th Duke of Marlborough (1849–95). In 1869 he married Albertha Frances Anne, sixth daughter of the First Duke of Abercorn. She had the marriage dissolved in 1883, when the Duke's affair with the Countess of Aylesford was proved in court.
** She obtained a separation from Lord Colin Campbell, 8th Duke of Argyll, for cruelty. She became a widow in 1895 and died in 1911. She wrote *Darrel Blake, A Book of the Running Brook,* and *A Miracle in Rabbits.*
† Wife of Francis Henry Jeune, Baron St. Helier (1843–1905), a distinguished judge.

Pleasures," I soon saw, was frank to indecency. I should have to expurgate it before publishing, but it was sure to cause a huge stir.

I put the article away for some real need and assured the Duke that I would publish it sooner or later. I wish I had kept the paper, but I remember one passage in it which contained his defense. "There are persons," he wrote airily, "who will object to my frank sensuality. I have been asked in astonishment whether I really could see anything to admire in the beautiful knees of a woman. I have no doubt there are little birds who sip a drop or two of clear water at a lake-side and wonder what a healthy frog can find in the succulent ooze that delights his soul. Such prudes, and they are numerous and of both sexes in England, remind me of the witty Frenchman's joke. The talk had come to a discussion of differences between a chimpanzee and a gorilla: 'What animal do you think is the most like a man?' the hostess asked and at once the Frenchman replied, 'An Englishman, Madame, surely.' "

The Duke had as many witty stories at command as anyone I have ever known, and he told them excellently.

He attributed many of them to Travers, the famous wit of New York in the seventies who died alas! without leaving any inheritors of his talent.*

Travers was a real wit without alloy. I have a dozen stories of his which are good and one or two worth preserving. When Fiske and Gould had come together to exploit the finances of the Erie railroad and rob the American people of many millions of dollars, Fiske gave a luncheon party on his yacht and of course, among others, invited Travers. The financier took the wit all over the yacht and finally in the cabin showed him his own portrait painted by Bougereau,** whom he called the most famous French painter, and a portrait of Gould, by some American, hanging near it. "What do you think of 'em?" he asked triumphantly.

"Surely some—something's lacking," stuttered Travers with a puzzled look, for he exaggerated his stutter and pointed his witticisms with an air of bewilderment, just as Lord Plunket† used to do in London.

"Lacking," repeated Fiske; "what do you mean?"

"Mean," ejaculated Travers; "why, that the S-S-S Saviour should b-b-b-be between the two thieves!"

Only one better story than this has come out of America in my time and I'll put it in here to get rid of it. A young American went to a hotel and saw the manager about getting some work; he was hard up, he said, and hungry, and would do almost anything.

The manager put him off on the head waiter, who was slightly colored, but famous for his good manners. He heard the lad's plaint and then, "I guess you'll do your best and work all right, but has you tact?"

* William R. Travers; he died in 1887 in Bermuda.
** William Adolph Bouguereau (1825–1905).
† Sir Horace Curzon Plunket (1854–1932), born in Ireland, educated in England, and a cattleman in the United States.

"Don't know what tact means," said the lad, "but I'll get some if you tell me how!"

"That's it," replied the darky, with a lordly air, "that's it. No one I guess kin tell you what tact is or how to git it, but I'll try to make it clear to you. The other day a lady's bell rang. She was a real beauty from old Verginny and all the waiters wuz busy, so I decided to go up myself and wait on her.

"When I opened the door there she was, right opposite me, in her bath. Yes, in her bath. Of course I drew the door to at once, saying, "Scuse me please, Sir, 'scuse me!' Now the "scuse me' was politeness; but the 'Sir!' That was 'tact.' See! Tact!' "

Chapter XII

Laura, Young Tennyson, Carlo Pellegrini, Paderewski, Mrs. Lynn Linton

I WAS TO MEET MY FATE again and unexpectedly. It was in my second year as editor of the *Evening News* and I was so confident of ultimate success in my business as a journalist that I began to go into society more and more and extend my knowledge of that wonderful pulsing life in London.

One night I went to the Lyceum Theatre. I have forgotten what was on or why I went, but I had seen the whole play and was standing talking to Bram Stoker* by the door when, in the throng of people leaving, I saw Laura Clapton and her fat mother coming down the steps. She smiled radiantly at me and again I was captivated: her height gave her presence, she carried herself superbly—she was the only woman in the world for me. I could tell myself that the oval of her face was a little round, as I knew her fingers were spatulate and ugly, but to me she was more than beautiful. I had seen more perfect women, women, too, of greater distinction, but she seemed made to my desire. She must be marvellously formed, I felt, from the way she moved; and her long hazel eyes, and masses of carelessly coiled chestnut hair, and the quick smile that lit up her face—all charmed me. I went forward at once and greeted her. Her mother was unusually courteous; in the crowd I could only be polite and ask them if they would sup with me at the Criterion, for the Savoy was not known then, as Ritz had not yet come and conquered London and made its restaurants the best in the world.

"Why have you never come to see me?" was her first question.

I could only reply, "It was too dangerous, Laura." The confession pleased her. Shall I ever forget that supper? Not so long as this machine of mine lasts. I was in love for the first time, on my knees in love, humble for the first time, and reverent in the adoration of true love.

I remember the first time I saw the beauty of flowers: I was thirteen and had been invited to Wynnstay. We had luncheon and Lady Watkin Wynn**

* Abraham Stoker (1847–1912), an Irishman who wrote dramatic and literary criticism before he became Irving's manager. He wrote several novels, all of which were of less consequence than his *Personal Reminiscences of Henry Irving* (1906).
** Wife of Sir Watkin Williams-Wynn, (1820–85), 6th baronet of Wynnstay.

afterwards took me into the garden and we walked between two "herbaceous borders," as they're called, rows four and five yards deep of every sort of flower: near the path the small flowers, then higher and higher to very tall plants—a sloping bank of beauty. For the first time I saw the glory of their coloring and the exquisite fragility of the blossoms: my senses were ravished and my eyes flooded with tears!

So, overpowering was the sensation in the theatre: the appearance of Laura took my soul with admiration. But as soon as we were together, the demands of the mother in the cab began to cool me. "Daughter, the window must be shut! Daughter, we mustn't be late: your father—" and so forth. But after all, what did I care; my left foot was touching Laura's and I realized with a thrill that her right foot was on the other side of mine. If I could only put my knee between hers and touch her limbs: I would try as I got up to go out and I did and the goddess responded, or at least did not move away, and her smiling, kindly glance warmed my heart.

The supper was unforgettable, for Laura had followed my work and the subtle flattery enthralled me. "Is May Fortescue really as pretty as you made out?"

"It was surely my cue to make her lovely," I rejoined. Laura nodded with complete understanding. She enjoyed hearing the whole story; she was particularly interested in everything pertaining to the stage.

That evening everything went on velvet. The supper was excellent, the Perrier-Jouet of 1875—the best wine chilled, not iced; and when I drove the mother and daughter home afterwards, while the mother was getting out Laura pressed her lips on mine and I touched her firm hips as she followed her mother. I had arranged too a meeting for the morrow for lunch at Kettner's of Soho in a private room.

I went home drunk with excitement. I had taken rooms in Gray's Inn and when I entered them that night, I resolved to ask Laura to come to them after lunch, for I had bought some Chippendale chairs and some pieces of table silver of the eighteenth century that I wanted her to see.

How did I come to like old English furniture and silver? I had got to know a man in Gray's Inn, one Alfred Tennyson, a son of Frederick Tennyson,* the elder brother of the great poet, and he had taught me to appreciate the recondite beauty in everything one uses. I shall have much to tell of him in later volumes of this autobiography, for, strange to say, he is still my friend here in Nice forty-odd years later. Then he was a model of manliness and vigor; only medium height, but with good features and a splendidly strong figure. His love of poetry was the first bond between us. He was a born actor, too, and mimic; he had always wished to go on the stage—a man of cultivated taste and good company. Here I just wish to acknowledge his quickening influence: I only needed to be shown the right path.

* He collaborated with Alfred in 1827 on *Poems by Two Brothers.*

Very soon I had read all I could find about the two Adam brothers*
who came to London from Scotland and dowered the capital in the latter
half of the eighteenth century with their own miraculous sense of beauty.
The Adelphi off the Strand was named after them: even in their own time
they were highly appreciated. But I was genuinely surprised to find that
almost every age in England had its own ideals of beauty, and that the
silverware of Queen Anne was as fine in its way as that of the Adam
Brothers; and the tables of William and Mary had their own dignity, while
a hall chair of Elizabeth's time showed all the stateliness of courtly manners.
I began to realize that beauty was of all times and infinitely more varied
than I had ever imagined. And if it was of all times, beauty was assuredly
of all countries, showing subtle race-characteristics that delighted the spirit.
What could be finer than the silver and furniture of the First Empire in
France? A sort of reflex of classic grace of form with superabundance of
ornament, as if flowered with pride of conquest. At length I had come into
the very kingdom of man and discovered the proper nourishment for my
spirit. No wonder I was always grateful to Alfred Tennyson, who had
shown me the key, so to speak, of the treasure-house.

It was Alfred Tennyson, too, in his rooms in Gray's Inn, who introduced me to Carlo Pellegrini.** Pellegrini was a little fat Italian from the
Abruzzi and Tennyson's mother was also an Italian, and she had taught
her son sympathy for all those of her race. At any rate, Tennyson knew
Carlo intimately, and in the eighties Carlo was a figure of some note in
London life. He was the chief cartoonist of *Vanity Fair* and signed his
caricatures "Ape." They constituted a new departure in the art: he was
so kindly that his caricatures were never offensive, even to his victims. He
would prowl about the lobby of the House of Commons, taking notes, and
a dozen of his caricatures are among the best likenesses extant. His comrade
Leslie Ward,† who signed "Spy," was nearly as successful. A better drafts-
man, indeed, but content with the outward presentment of a man, not
seeking, as Pellegrini sought, to depict the very soul of the sitter.

Carlo confessed to being a homosexualist, flaunted his vice, indeed, and
was the first to prove to me by example that a perverted taste in sex might
go with a sweet and generous nature. For Carlo Pellegrini was one of
nature's saints. One trait I must give: once every fortnight he went to the
office of *Vanity Fair* in the Strand and drew twenty pounds for his cartoon.
He had only a couple of hundred yards to go before reaching Charing Cross
and usually owed his landlady five pounds; yet he had seldom more than
five pounds left out of the twenty by the time he got to the end of the street.
I have seen him give five pounds to an old prostitute and add a kindly word

---

* Robert (1728–92) and James (1730–94). They were primarily architects, but
also designed furniture.
** (1839–89). He was born in Capua, went to London in 1864, and began working
for *Vanity Fair* in 1869.
† (1851–1922); he also worked for *Vanity Fair*.

to the gift. Sometimes, indeed, he would give away all he had got and then say with a whimsical air of humility, "*Spero che* you will invite me to dine —eh, Frankarris?"

The best thing I can say of the English aristocracy is that this member of it and that remained his friend throughout his career and supplied his needs time and again. Lord Rosebery* was one of his kindliest patrons, my friend Tennyson was another, but it was in the nineties I learned to love him, so I'll keep him for my third volume. Here I only wish to remark that his frank confession of pederasty, of the love of a man for boys and youths, made me think and then question the worth of my instinctive, or rather unreasoned, prejudice. For on reflection I was forced to admit that paederastia was practiced openly and without any condemnation—nay, was even regarded as a semi-religious cult by the most virile and most courageous Greeks, by the Spartans chiefly, at the highest height of their development in the seventh and sixth and fifth centuries before our era. And what was considered honorable by Aeschylus and Sophocles and Plato was not to be condemned lightly by any thinking person. Moreover, the passion was condemned in modern days merely because it was sterile, while ordinary sex-sensuality was permissible because it produced children. But as I practiced Lesbianism, which was certainly sterile, I could not but see that my aversion to paederastia was irrational and illogical, a mere personal peculiarity. Boys might surely inspire as noble a devotion as girls, though for me they had no attraction. I learned, too, from Carlo Pellegrini the entrancing, attractive power of sheer loving-kindness, for in person he was a grotesque caricature of humanity, hardly more than five feet two in height, squat and stout, with a face like a mask of Socrates, and always curiously ill-dressed; yet always and everywhere a gentleman—and to those who knew him, a good deal more.

Next day I was waiting at Kettner's when Laura drove up; I hastened to pay her cab and take her upstairs. She didn't even hesitate as she entered the private room, and she kissed me with unaffected kindliness. There was a subtle change in her; what was it? "Did she love anyone else?" I asked, and she shook her head.

"I waited for you," she said, "but the year ran out and five months more."

"*Mea culpa,*" I rejoined, "*mea maxima culpa,* but forgive me and I'll try to make up—"

After we had lunched and I had locked the door against any chance intrusion of waiter or visitor, she came and sat on my knees and I kissed and embraced her almost at will but—. "What's the matter, Laura? The red of your lips is not uniform; what have you been doing with yourself?"

"Nothing," she replied, with an air of bewilderment. "What do you mean?"

* (1847–1929), Prime Minister 1894–95.

"You've altered," I persisted.

"We all alter in a year and a half," she retorted. But I was not satisfied; once when I kissed the inside of her lips, she drew back questioning.

"How strangely you kiss."

"Does it excite you?" I asked, and a pretty *moue* was all the answer I got in words. But soon under my kissings and caresses her lips grew hot and she did not draw away as she used to do a year and a half before; she gave her lips to me and her eyes too grew long in sensuous abandonment. I stopped, for I wanted to think, and above all, I wanted a memorable gift and not a casual conquest. "I want to show you a lot of things, Laura," I said. "Won't you come to my rooms in Gray's Inn and have a great afternoon? Will you come tomorrow?" And soon we had made an appointment; and after some more skirmishing kisses I took her home.

Laura lunching with me in my rooms in Gray's Inn. The mere thought took my breath, set the pulses in my temples throbbing and parched my mouth. I had already discovered the Cafe Royal, at that time by far the best restaurant in London, thanks to the owner, M. Nichol, a Frenchman, who had come to grief twice in France because he wanted to keep a really good restaurant. But now Nichol was succeeding in London beyond his wildest hopes (London always wants the best) and was indeed already rich. Nichol's daughter married and the son-in-law was charged by Nichol with the purchase of wine for the restaurant. Of course he got a commission on all he purchased, and after five and twenty years was found to have bought and bought with rare judgment more than a million pounds worth of wine beyond what was necessary. In due time I may tell the sequel. But even in 1884 and 1885 the Cafe Royal had the best cellar in the world. Fifteen years later it was the best ever seen on earth.

Already I had got to know Nichol and more than once, being in full sympathy with his ideals, had praised him in the *Evening News*. Consequently, he was always willing to do better than his best for me. So now I ordered the best lunch possible: hors d'oeuvres with caviare from Nijni; a tail piece of cold salmon-trout; and a cold grouse, fresh, not high, though as tender as if it had been kept for weeks, as I shall explain later; and to drink, a glass of Chablis with the fish, two of Haut Brion of 1878 with the grouse, and a bottle of Perrier-Jouet of 1875 to go with the sweet that was indeed a *surprise* covering fragrant wild strawberries.

Nowhere could one have found a better lunch and Laura entered into the spirit of the whole ceremony. She came as the clock struck one and had a new hat and a new dress, and, looking her best, had also her most perfect manners. Did you ever notice how a woman's manners alter with her dress? Dressed in silk she is silky gracious, the queen in the girl conscious of the rustle of the silken petticoat. I had a kiss, of course, and many an embrace as I helped her to take off her wraps. Then I showed her the lunch and expatiated on the tablesilver of the Adam brothers.

When we had finished lunch, the water was boiling and I made the coffee and then we talked interminably, for I was jealously conscious of a change in her and determined to solve the mystery. But she gave me no clue—her reticence was a bad sign, I thought; she would not admit that she had any preferred cavalier in the long year of my absence, though I had seen her twice with the same man. Still, the proof was to come. About four I took her to my bedroom and asked her to undress. "I'm frightened," she said. "You do care for me?"

"I love you," I said, "as I've never loved anyone in my life. I'm yours; do with me what you will!"

"That's a great promise?"

"I'll keep it," I protested.

She accepted smiling: "Go away, sir, and come back in ten minutes."

When I returned I had only pyjamas on, and as I went hastily to the bed I was conscious of absolute reverence: if only the dreadful doubt had not been there, it would have been adoration. As I pushed back the clothes I found she had kept her chemise on. I lifted it up and pushed it round her neck to enjoy the sight of the most beautiful body I had ever seen. But adoring plastic beauty as I do, I could only give a glance to her perfections; the next moment I had touched her sex and soon I was at work: in a minute or two I had come but went on with the slow movement till she could not but respond, and then in spite of her ever-growing excitement, as I continued she showed surprise. "Haven't you finished?" I shook my head and kissed her, tonguing her mouth and reveling in the superb body that gave itself to my every movement. Suddenly her whole frame was shaken by a sort of convulsion; as if against her will, she put her legs about me and hugged me to her. "Stop, please!" she gasped, and I stopped; but when I would begin again, she repeated, "Please," and I withdrew, still holding her in my arms.

A moment later, remembering her fear, I got out of bed and showed her in the next room the *bidet* and syringe. She went in at once, but as she passed me I lifted the chemise and had more than a glimpse of the most perfect hips and legs. She smiled indulgently and turning, kissed me and passed into the dressing-room.

I felt certain now that she had given herself in that d——d year and a half to someone else. She was not a virgin, nor at her first embrace, but she had not been used much. Why? Had she been *enceinte* and got rid of the coming child? That would explain her lips, poor dear girl. If she would trust me and tell me, I would marry her; if not—

When she returned she was all cold; I lifted her into bed, and after taking off her chemise covered her till she got warm, and then bit by bit studied her figure. It was not perfect, but the faults were all merits in my eyes. Her neck was a trifle too short, but her breasts were as small as a girl's of thirteen; her hips were perfect with [an] almost flat belly, long legs and the tiniest, best-kept sex in the world. It was always perfectly clean and sweet. I have never seen one more perfect. The clitoris was just a little mound and the inner lips were glowing crimson. I began to tongue the sensitive spot, and at once she began to move spasmodically. As I touched just below the clitoris, she squirmed violently:

"What are you doing?" she cried, trying to lift my head.

"Wait and see," I replied, "it's even more intense there, the sensation, isn't it?" She nodded breathlessly, and I went on; in a little while she gave herself altogether to my lips and soon began to move convulsively and then: "Oh, Frank, oh! It's too much. I can't stand it, oh, oh, oh!"—she tried to draw away: as I persisted, she said, "I shall scream. I can't stand it— please stop," and as I lifted my head I saw that her love-juice had come down all over her sex. I touched the little clitoris again with my lips but she lifted my head up for a kiss and putting her arms about me strained me to her madly. "Oh you dear, dear, dear! I want you in me, your—, please."

Of course I did as she requested and went on working till her eyes turned up and she grew so pale—I stopped. When she got her breath again—"I would not have believed," she said after a while, "that one could feel so intensely. You took my breath and then my heart was in my throat, choking me—" Those words were my reward. I had learned the way to her supreme moment.

How we dressed I don't know, but passing through the dining-room I found myself desperately hungry and Laura confessed to the same appetite, and once more we set to on the food.

Why was Laura to me different from any other woman? She did not give me as much pleasure as Topsy; indeed, already in my life there had been at least two superior to her in the lists of love, and a couple also who had flattered me more cunningly and given me proofs of a more passionate affection. Her queenly personality, the sheer brains in her, may have accounted for part of the charm. She certainly found memorable words: this first day as we were leaving the bedroom, she stopped, and putting her hands on my shoulders she said, "*Non ti scordare di me*" (Don't forget me), and then, putting her arms round my neck, "We were one, weren't we?" And she kissed me with clinging lips.

And if it wasn't a word that ravished me, it was a gesture of sacred boldness. As she gradually came to understand how her figure delighted me, she cast off shame and showed me that the Swedish exercises she practiced day after day had given her lovely body the most astonishing flexibility. She could stand with her back to a wall and, leaning back, could kiss the wall with her head almost on a level with her hips, her backbone as flexible as a bow. To me she was the most fascinating mistress and companion with a thousand different appeals. To see her in her triumphant nakedness strike an attitude and recite three or four lines, and then take the ultra-modest pose of the Florentine Venus and cover her lovely sex with her hand was a revelation in mischievous coquetry.

But now and then she complained of pains in the lower body, and I became certain that her womb had been inflamed by a willful miscarriage: she had given herself to my American rival. If she had only been frank and told me the whole truth, I'd have forgiven her everything and the last barrier between us would have fallen, but it was not to be. She was still doubtful, perhaps of my success in life, doubtful whether I would go from victory to victory. In the humility of love I wanted to show her the reasons of my success, told her how I had learnt from newsboys, foolishly forgetting that to women ignorant of life, results alone matter: the outward and visible sign is everything to them. It took years for her to learn that I was able to win in life wherever I wished, on the stock exchange even more easily than in journalism. And her mother was always against me, as I learned later. "He can talk, but so can other people," she would say with a side glance at the Irish husband, whose talking was always unsuccessful. But though our immediate surroundings were unfavorable and doubtful, when we were together Laura and I lived golden hours; and now, when I think of her, I recall occasional phrases both of love's sweet spirit and poses of her exquisite body that made me shudder with delight.

Month in, month out, we met in private once at least a week, and once a fortnight or so I took mother and daughter to the theatre and supper afterwards. In that summer I bought a house in Kensington Gore opposite Hyde Park and only a few doors away from the mansion of the Sassoons,* whom I came to know later. This little house gave me a place in London society. I gave occasional dinners and parties in it, helped by Lord Folkestone and the Arthur Walters, and had a very real success. I remember Mrs. Walter once advising me to invite a new pianist who was certain to make a great name for himself, and the first time I met him I arranged an evening for him: a hundred society people came to hear him and went away enthusiastic admirers. It was Paderewski** on his first visit to London, and mine was the first house in which he played.

Of course I would have had Laura there to hear him, but it was difficult for her to go out in the evening without her mother, and I could not stand the mother.

She made herself the centre of every gathering by rudeness, if in no other way, and Laura would not hear a word criticizing her. I remember saying once to her, "You got all your beauty and grace from your father."

She was annoyed immediately. "I got my skin from my mother," she retorted, "and my hair as well and my heart, too, which is a good thing for you, Sir, as you may find out," and she made a face at me of exquisite childishness that enchanted me as much as her loyalty. Girls nearly always prefer their mother to their father: why?

One evening Laura and her mother came to a small evening party I

* Sir Albert Abdallah David Sassoon, (1818–96).
** Paderewski first visited London in 1890; the time here could not have been later than 1885.

gave in Kensington Gore and Mrs. Lynn Linton* was there, who was by way of being a great admirer of mine and a great friend. Laura sang for us: she had been admirably trained by Lamperti of Milan, whom I knew well, but she had only a small voice and her singing was of the drawing-room variety. But afterwards, feeling that she was suffering through the failure of her song. I got her to act a scene from *Phèdre* and she astonished everyone: she was a born actress of the best! Everyone praised her most warmly in spite of the mother's pinched air of disapproval: she was always against Laura's acting. But Mrs. Lynn Linton took me aside and advised me to get rid of the mother: "She's impossible; the girl's a wonder and very good to look at, you Lothario! Or are you going to marry her?"

"Marry," I replied, "sure," for Laura was within hearing.

"Get rid of the mother first," advised Mrs. Lynn Linton. "She's no friend of yours, anyone can see that. How have you offended her?" I shrugged my shoulders; have likes and dislikes any avowable reason?

I found it difficult, not to say impossible, to get any sex-knowledge from Laura. Like most girls with any Irish strain in them, she disliked talking of the matter at all. I asked her, "When did you first come to realize the facts of sex?"

"I don't really know," she'd say. "Girls at school talk: some elder girl tells a younger one this or that and the younger one talks of the new discovery with her chums and so the knowledge comes."

My reverence for her was so extraordinary that although I made up my mind a dozen times to ask her had she ever excited herself as a girl, I never could.

Often, indeed, when I asked her something intimate, she would take me in her arms and kiss me to silence while her eyes danced in amusement; and if I still persisted I'd get some phrase such as, "You have me, Sir, body and soul; what more do you want?"

Once I asked her about dancing. I had grown jealous watching her: she was picked out by the best dancers at every party and the sensuous grace of her movements attracted universal admiration. Not that she exaggerated the sensuous abandonment; on the contrary, it was only indicated now and then. As a dancer she reminded me irresistibly of Kate Vaughan, whom I always thought incomparable, the most graceful dancer I ever saw on any stage. Laura moved with the same easy exquisite rhythm, a poem in motion. But she denied always that the dance excited her sensually. "It's the music I love," she would say, "the rhythm, the swaying harmony of the steps. It's as near intoxication as sense-indulgence."

"But again and again his leg was between yours," I insisted. "You must have felt the thrill." She shrugged her shoulders and would not reply. Again I began. "You know that even your little breasts are very sensitive; as soon

* Mrs. Eliza Lynn Linton (1822–98), an anti-feminist journalist as well as the author of the novels *Joshua Davidson* (1872) and *The Autobiography of Christopher Kirkland* (1885).

as my lips touch them the nipples stand out firm and glowing red and your sex is still quicker to respond. You must feel the man's figure against your most sensitive part. I believe that now and again you take care his figure should touch you: that adds the inimitable thrill now and then to your grace of movement."

At first she seemed to hesitate, then she said thoughtfully, "That seems to me the great difference between the man and the woman in the way of love. From what you say, it is clear that touching a woman's legs or feeling her breast would excite you, even if you didn't care for her, perhaps even if you disliked her; but such a contact doesn't excite a woman in the least, unless she loves the man. And if she loves him as soon as he comes towards her, she's thrilled; when he puts his arms round her, she's shaken with emotion! With us women it's all a question of love; with you men, sensuality takes the place of love and often leads you to cheat yourselves and us."

"That may indeed be the truth," I replied. "In any case, it's the deepest insight I've heard on the matter and I'm infinitely obliged to you for it. Love then intensifies your sensations, whereas it is often the keenness of our sensations that intensifies our love."

"You men, then," she summed up, "have surely the lower and more material nature."

And in my heart I had to admit that she was right.

Whenever we had been long together, her attraction for me was so overpowering that it always excited suspicion in me. I don't know why; I state the fact: I was never sure of her love.

Verses of the old German folksong often came into my mind:

> Sie hat zwei Äuglein, die sind braun
> Heut du Dich!
> Sie werden dich überzwerch anschaun
> Heut du Dich! Heut du Dich!
> Vertrau ihr nicht, sie narret Dich.

> Sie hat ein licht goldfarbenes Haar
> Heut du Dich!
> Und was sie red't das ich nicht wahr,
> Heut du Dich! Heut du Dich!
> Vertrau ihr nicht, sie narret Dich!

(Her beauty's full of contrasts, hazel eyes and golden hair and lovely body: Don't trust her! She's fooling you!)

Chapter XIII

The Prince; General Dickson; English Gluttony; Sir Robert Fowler and Finch Hatton; Ernest Beckett and Mallock; The *Pink 'Un* And Free Speech

IT IS DIFFICULT to talk of English customs in the last quarter of the nineteenth century without comparing them with the morals and modes of life of their ancestors in the last quarter of the eighteenth. In his history of the *Early Life of Fox,* Sir George Trevelyan* paints an astonishing picture of the immoralities of the earlier aristocratic regime. Not only were the leaders of society and parliamentary governors corrupt in a pecuniary sense; not only did they drink to such excess that they were old at forty-five and permanently invalid with gout before middle-age: they gambled like madmen and some sought deliberately to turn their young sons into finished rakes.

I cannot help thinking that it was the hurricane of the French revolution that cleared the air and brought men back to an observance of such laws of morals as are also rules of health. The reform is often attributed to the influence of Queen Victoria, but from 1875 on I never could find the slightest indication or trace of her influence for good. The most striking improvement in aristocratic morality in the last quarter of the nineteenth century was brought about by the loose living Edward, Prince of Wales. Before he and his "Smart Set" came to power in London, it was still usual at dinner parties to allow the ladies to leave the table and go to the drawing-room to gossip while the men drew together and consumed a bottle or two of claret each. It was no longer the custom to get drunk, but to get half-seas over was still fairly usual; and if the ladies disappeared at nine or nine-thirty, it was customary for the men to sit drinking till ten-thirty or eleven. One result was that even men in their thirties knew a good deal about the qualities of fine wine.

It used to be said, and with some truth, that it was English, or rather London, taste that established the prices of the finer vintages of Bordeaux.

* (1838–1928). The correct title of the book is the *Early History of Charles James Fox* (1880).

There can be no doubt at all that it was English taste that taught men and women everywhere to prefer natural Champagne (*brut* or *nature*) to the sweetened and brandied varieties preferred all over the continent, and especially in France. French *gourmets* knew that the firm of Veuve Clicquot had almost a monopoly of Buzet, the finest natural white wine with which to make champagne, but they submitted to having this product sweetened and brandied till it could only be drunk in small quantities, towards the end of dinner with the sweets.

In the seventies the Prince of Wales came to be the acknowledged leader of the "Smart Set." Fortunately for England, he preferred the continental habit of coffee after dinner, black coffee enjoyed with the cigarette. No one who smokes can taste the bouqet of fine claret, and so the cigarette and coffee banished the habit of drinking heavily after dinner.

The Prince too preferred champagne to claret and so the taste in champagne grew keener; and soon the natural wine superseded the doctored French varieties. In the course of a single decade it became the habit in London to join the ladies after having drunk a glass or two of pure champagne during the dinner and a cup of coffee afterwards while smoking a cigarette.

Sobriety became the custom and now a man who drinks to excess would soon find it impossible to discover a house where he would be tolerated. The cigarette, introduced by the Prince of Wales, made London society sober.

In an aristocratic society good customs as well as bad sink down in ever-widening circles like water poured on sand. Gentlemen in England no longer drink to excess and now it is difficult to find a man anywhere who could tell you the year of a great claret or port, whereas in the mid-Victorian era, nine men about town out of ten could have made a fair guess at any known vintage.

The hospitality of the English gentry is deservedly famous; there is nothing like it anywhere else in the world, nothing to be compared to it. Of course I make allowances for the fact that young men are especially wanted at dinners because married people are more difficult to pair off. Besides, the custom of primogeniture that gives everything to the eldest son and drives the younger boys to India or the colonies puts the young men in London at a premium. The fact remains that after my first month as editor of the *Evening News*, I did not dine in my own house half a dozen times in the year, and I had to reject more invitations than I could accept. Nothing was expected of the young man in return: provided he was properly introduced and had decent manners and was now and then amusing or able to tell a good story, he was a *persona grata* everywhere. The kindness was genuine and general and deserves description.

Almost at the beginning of my work in London and when I only knew a few people of position such as Mrs. (afterwards Lady) Jeune, I received an invitation to dinner almost a month ahead from a General Dickson* who, I soon found out, was well-known in London as a prominent member of the Four-in-Hand Club. In the House of Commons I happened to mention him to Agg Gardner** then as now, I believe, the Member for Cheltenham, and he exclaimed, "Dickson! I should think I did know him. One of the best, a rare old boy; gives a very good dinner and usually invites only one lady to half a dozen men. Says that a pretty woman is needed to keep the talk up to a high standard. Of course, you'll go."

When the evening came I went to the house in one of the big West End squares. A couple of old soldiers were acting as footmen in the hall, and scarcely had I taken off my coat when General Dickson in person appeared out of a room to the right and welcomed me cordially. He was a fine-looking man, above middle-height, well set up with broad shoulders. He had good features, too, and his bronzed face was framed by a mass of silver hair.

"I'm glad to see you," he said warmly, giving me a strong handclasp.

"I am delighted to be here," I said, "but I thought myself quite unknown in London. It was therefore doubly kind of you to invite me. I didn't think you'd remember me!"

"I met you at Wolseley's," he said, "and at dinner you said something about beauty that struck me. You said, 'There must be something strange in any excelling beauty.'† Now beauty has passed out of my life, but a good dinner still appeals to me, so I took your phrase and applied it to a dinner—where, mind you, it's equally appropriate. 'There must be something strange in any excelling dinner'. So as I knew I'd have something strange tonight, I thought it only fair to ask you for your opinion of my attempt," and he laughed heartily, pleasantly.

The dinner was very good. There was a pretty, blond woman on the General's right, whose name I forget, though I got to know her fairly well later in London. She played hostess excellently and the service was faultless, too, though all the attendants were evidently old soldiers. The butler, I remember, with silver hair like his master, had the pleasant old custom of announcing the wine he was offering you, 'Chateau Lafitte 1870,' and so on. The dinner was very good, indeed, but no surprise in it till we came to the 'savoury,' when the door at the side opened and a Russian appeared in national costume with a great silver dish. "Milk caviare," our host announced, "sent to me by His Majesty, the Czar, whom I have the honor to know slightly," and he turned smiling to me.

" 'Something strange,' indeed," I cried in response, "for even in Moscow

---

* General Sir Collingwood Dickson (1817–1904). He had a particularly distinguished record in the Crimea.

** James Tynte Agg-Gardner (1846– ?), educated at Harrow and Trinity College, Cambridge.

† Harris was indebted for this *mot* to Francis Bacon.

or Nijni I have never tasted it. I've heard somewhere that it all goes to the Czar."

We all enjoyed the delicacy, though I noticed that the blond mistress of the ceremony did not take any of the cut-up onions which went with the caviare, but contented herself with a squeeze of lemon, and all of us followed her example.

This dinner at General Dickson's taught me that good eating was more studied in London than anywhere else in the world. Agg Gardner knew the General for his table, just as Gardner himself was known to everyone as a *gourmet* and finetaster in both food and wine. He's the head still, I believe of the kitchen committee in the House of Commons.

Strange that we had no word for *gourmet* in English, though we have gormandizer for *gourmand,* and glutton for *goinfre,* and others could be formed as *gutler*—even German has got *Feinschmecker,* but English has no dignified word, I'm afraid, for one who has a fine palate both in food and drink. Even "feaster" has a touch of greed in it instead of discrimination; so I've coined "finetaster," though it's not very good.

But it is only among the better classes that one dines to perfection in London. The best restaurants are no better than the best in Paris or Vienna or Moscow; and the English middle class dine worse than the French middle class because they know nothing of cooking as an art; and the poor live worse and fare harder than any class in Christendom. English liberty and aristocratic harshness result in the degradation of the weak and the wastrel, and alas; often in the martyrdom of the best and most gifted. There are no Davidsons and Middletons,* no despairing suicides of genius in any other country of Christendom, though in this respect America runs England close, for her two greatest, Poe and Whitman, lived in penury and died in utter neglect. "It's needful," we are told, "that offences come, but woe unto him by whom the offence cometh."

The old bad habit of eating and drinking to excess was still rampant in the eighties at city dinners. I remember how astonished I was at my first Lord Mayor's Banquet in 1883. The *Evening News* being Conservative, I was given a good seat at the Lord Mayor's table, nearly opposite him and the chief speakers.

After the first banquet I never missed one for years because of the light these feasts cast on English customs and manners. I will not tell about them in detail, indeed, I couldn't if I would, for my notes only apply to two or three out of a dozen or more. The first thing that struck me was the extraordinary gluttony displayed by seven out of ten of the city magnates. Till that night I had thought that as a matter of courtesy every man in public

* John Davidson (1857–1909). A Nietzschean minor poet, who in *The Testament of John Davidson* (1908) preached that each man should strive to be his true self and that the strongest should rule. He drowned himself.

John Henry Middleton (1846–96). An archaeologist and a recluse. He became famous through his studies of Roman antiquities and was in 1889 appointed director of the Fitzwilliam Museum at Cambridge. He died of an overdose of opiates.

suppressed any signs of greed he might feel, but here greed was flaunted. The man next to me ate like an ogre. I took a spoonful or two of turtle soup and left the two or three floating morsels of green meat. When he had finished his first plateful, which was emptied to the last drop in double quick time, my neighbor, while waiting for a second helping, turned to me. "That's why I like this table," he began, openly licking his lips. "You can have as many helpings as you want."

"Can't you at the other tables?" I asked.

"You can," he admitted, "but here the servants are instructed to be courteous and they all expect a tip. Most people give a bob, but I always give half a crown if the flunkey's attentive. Why do you leave that?" he exclaimed, pointing to the pieces of green meat on my plate. "That's the best part," and he turned his fat, flushed, red face to his second plateful without awaiting my answer. The gluttonous haste of the animal and the noise he made in swallowing each spoonful amused me. In a trice he had cleared the soup-plate and beckoned to the waiter for a third supply. "I'll remember you, my man," he said in a loud whisper to the waiter, "but see that you get me some green fat. I want some Calipash."

"Is that what you call Calipash?" I asked, pointing with a smile to the green gobbets on my plate.

"Of course," he said. "They used to give you Calipash and Calipee with every plateful. I'll bet you don't know the difference between them: well, Calipash comes from the upper shell and Calipee from the lower shell of the turtle. Half these new men," and he swung his hand contemptuously round the table, "don't know the difference between real turtle and mock turtle, but I do."

I couldn't help laughing. "Now you," he went on, "this is your first banquet, I can see. You're either a Member of the 'Ouse or perhaps a journalist. Now, ain't ye?"

"I'm the editor of the Evening News," I replied, "and you've guessed right. This is my first Lord Mayor's Banquet."

"Eat that up," he said, pointing to the green pieces on my plate. "Eat that up; it'll go to your ribs and make a man of you. I gained three pounds at my first banquet, I did, but then I'm six inches taller nor you." He was indeed a man of huge frame.

"No place like this," he went on, "no place in the world," and he emptied another glass of champagne. "The best food and the best drink in God's world and nothing to pay for it, nothing. That's England, this is London, the grandest city on earth, I always say, and I'm proud to belong to it!"

When the first helping of mutton was brought to him, he demanded jelly, and when it was brought he cleared his plate in a twinkling and asked for more.

"Do you know what that is?" he cried, turning again to me. "That's the finest Southdown mutton in the world, three or four years old, if it's a day, and fit for a prince to eat. Fair melts in your mouth, it does. I don't say nuthin' against Welsh mutton, mind ye, or Exmoor, tasty and all that, but give me Southdown. Now that," he added, pointing to the full plate the waiter had brought him, "that's a bellyful; that's cut and come again style!" And he winked approval at the waiter.

To my amazement he had a second and third helping of mutton and went through the rest of the *menu* with the same avidity, getting redder and redder, hotter and hotter all the while. He must have eaten a pound and a half of meat, and he admitted he had drunk three bottles of champagne before the close.

"Doesn't it make you drunk?" I asked.

"Bless you, no," he exclaimed. "If you eat your fill and put a good lining of this mutton round your belly, you can drink as much as you like, or at least I can. Thank God for it," he added solemnly.

In the intervals of the speech-making after the dinner, he confided to me that he was the head, if I remember aright, of the Cordwainer's Company, and invited me in due course to their annual dinner a month later and treated me like a prince.

"You don't eat and drink as you ought to," was his conclusion. "There's no pleasure on earth like it, and unlike all other pleasures, the older you get, the keener your taste!" That was his philosophy. But I found William Smith a kindly host and was not surprised to hear that he stood well with all who knew him. "His word's his bond," they said, "and he's more than kind if you need him. A good fellow is Bill and a true blue Conservative." All in all, a model Englishman.

I remember at a later banquet having a little tub of a man for neighbor. He seemed uncomfortable and I couldn't account for his wrigglings till I saw he had an immense bottle between his legs.

"What's that?" I cried.

"A Jeroboam of Haut Brion '78'," he ejaculated. "The best wine in the world."

"Where on earth did you get that immense bottle?" I enquired. "It's as big as six ordinary bottles."

"No, it ain't," he said. "A magnum is two bottles and this here is four, and a rehoboam is eight, but I can't run to that."

"You don't mean to say," I interrupted, "that you're going to drink four bottles to your own cheek?"

"I don't know about cheek," he retorted angrily, "but thank God I can drink as I like without asking your permission."

"Is it really the best wine in the world?" I queried. "I'd like to taste it! Did you bring it?"

"You can have a glass," the manikin replied, "and I don't offer that to everybody, I can tell you, or there'd be d——d little left for Johnny; but you can have a glass with a heart and a half."

I went on with the bottle of champagne I had ordered till the end of dinner and then reminded my little neighbor of the promised glass.

"I oughtn't to give it you," he grumbled. "You've been smoking and no one can taste the bouquet of fine wine with tobacco smoke in his mouth. But," he added, withholding the bottle, "for God's sake, clean your palate before you taste this wine!"

"How shall I clean my palate?" I asked.

"By eating bread and salt, of course," he said, "but you'll never enjoy the real bouquet and body of wine till you've given up smoking." And as he spoke he poured into his own glass the last drops of the noble Bordeaux. "A great wine," he said, smacking his lips. "The phylloxera ruined the finest vineyards; Chateau Lafitte had to be replanted with American vines. No one will ever again drink a Chateau Lafitte as our fathers knew it, but this Haut Brion is the next best. What do you think I gave for that Jeroboam?"

"I can't imagine," I said. "Perhaps three or four pounds."

He smiled pityingly. "Nearer ten," he replied, "and not easy to get at that! In ten years more it'll be worth double, mark my words. I know what I'm talking about."

A curious little man, I thought to myself when I saw him drinking port and then old cognac with his coffee. "Push coffee, the French call it," he said, tapping his glass of cognac, "and they know what's good."

When the banquet was over he asked me to help him to his carriage, as his legs were drunk. "The only part of me that ever feels the wine," he said grinning. I had nearly to carry him out of the room, but he was violently sick before I got him to his brougham. Evidently, his legs were not the only part of his body to revolt that night.

The way those men ate and drank, gluttonized and guzzled was disgusting, but I had seen German students drink beer till they had to put their fingers down their throats and then go back to the *Kneipe* again, rejoicing in their bestiality. "It's the same race," I said to myself again and again. "The same race with bestiality and brutality as predominant features!"

One evening later I left the hall before the speech-making had begun, and as luck would have it, I met George Wyndham* at the door. "You here!" he cried. "What do you think of English conviviality?"

"English bestiality, you mean," I retorted.

"Bestiality?" he repeated. "I've seen none; what *do* you mean?"

"Come outside," I said and drew him outside the door into the pure air for a minute or so. "Now," I went on, "put your head in when I open the door and you'll understand what I mean!"

As I opened the door the stench was insupportable. "Good God!" cried Wyndham, "Why didn't I notice it before?"

---

* (1863–1913), Balfour's secretary before he became an M.P. from Dover. He wrote on politics for weekly papers and published an edition of Shakespeare's poetry in 1898.

"You're on the right side of the top table," I explained, "and therefore you suffered less than we did."

"Good God!" he repeated. "What a revelation!"

That was the night, I think, when Lord Salisbury, then Prime Minister and chief guest, made a really great speech. He reminded his audience that the previous year, speaking in the same place, he had thought himself able to promise that peace would be maintained in the coming year. "Some might think I was mistaken," he went on, "when they read in this morning's paper of the Black Mountain campaign and other fightings on our northwest frontier in India,* but such frays are not to be called war and hardly constitute a breach of the peace. Seen in true perspective, they are nothing but the wave-breaking in blood-stained foam on the ever advancing tide of English civilization." The fine image was brought out in his most ordinary manner and voice without any attempt at rhetoric and perhaps was the more effective on that account.

But if I wish to give a true picture of the London of my time, I must go further than I've yet gone.

In this year Sir Robert Fowler** was elected Lord Mayor of London for the second time, an almost unique distinction. In view of the attacks that had been made on the city finances and the attempts to democratize the city institutions, it was felt advisable for the great Corporation to put its best foot foremost. Sir Robert Fowler was not only an out-and-out Conservative and a rich man, but also a convinced supporter of all city privileges, and for a wonder a good scholar to boot who had won high university honors. "A Grecian, Sir, of the best!"

I met this gentleman at dinner one night at Sir William Marriott's,† who was M.P. for Brighton and had been made judge-advocate-general; and so had managed to lift his small person and smaller mind to the dignity of ministerial position that ensured, I believe, a life-pension.

I went to Marriott's dinner rather reluctantly; his wife was a washed-out, prim, little woman, kindly but undistinguished, and Marriott himself rather bored me. His dining-room was small and the half dozen city magnates I found assembled rather confirmed my doubts of the entertainment. Suddenly Fowler came in, a large man who must have been five feet ten at least in height and much more in girth.

We were soon at dinner and the way the guests ate and drank and commented on all the edibles and appraised all the wines was a sort of education. One guest held forth on the comparative merits of woodcock and partridge and amused me finally by declaring that a poet had settled the

---

* Salisbury was referring to the Penjdeh incident.

** (1828–91). Salisbury during his first brief tenure as Prime Minister in 1885 made Fowler a baronet. Fowler had taken honors at the University of London in 1848 in classics and literature.

† (1834–1903), who began in politics as a Liberal but turned Conservative in 1884 and was shortly thereafter appointed a judge-advocate-general by Salisbury.

question. "What poet do you mean?" I laughed, for poetry and guzzling were poles apart, I thought.

"I don't know his name," he replied, "but here's the verse," and he began:

> "If the partridge had the woodcock's thigh
> So good a bird could never fly;
> If the woodcock had the partridge breast
> So good a bird was never dressed."

Another *convive* declared that the French knew nothing of champagne except what "we English have taught 'em. I remember when they never thought of preferring one year to another or one special vintage to all others. We taught 'em that Perrier-Jouet 1875 is the best champagne ever seen. The Frenchmen think their blooming Veuve Clicquot's the prime champagne, but they have no palates, they don't know anything about sparkling wines."

I had just taken a spoonful of clear soup when my nostrils were assailed by a pungent, unmistakable odor. I looked at the rubicund little man next to me, but he went on drinking glass after glass of champagne, as if for a wager.

I was on Lady Marriott's left hand, opposite to Sir Robert Fowler, who was of course on her right. By the time we had enjoyed the roast and come to the game, the atmosphere in the room was quite appalling; the partridges, too, were so high that they fell apart when touched. I had never cultivated a taste for rotting meat and so I trifled with my bread and watched the *convives*.

On first sitting down, Sir Robert Fowler had talked a little to Lady Marriott and myself, but after the roast beef had been served he never spoke to us, but ate—like an ogre. Never have I seen a man stuff with such avidity. First he had a helping of beef, then Yorkshire pudding and beef again. After the first mouthful he cried out to his host, "Excellent Scotch beef, my dear Marriott. Where do you get it and how is it kept so perfectly?"

"Secrets of the prison house," replied Marriott, smiling. He knew that once the dinner was finished, the Mayor would forget the whole incident. When I turned to eat I found my huge *vis-à-vis* smacking his lips and hurrying again to his plate, intent on cutting and swallowing huge gobbets of meat while the veins of his forehead stood out like knotted cords and the beads of sweat poured down his great red face!

I looked at Lady Marriott and saw a shrinking in her face corresponding to the disgust I felt. I looked away again to spare her, when suddenly there came a loud unmistakable noise and then an overpowering odor. I stared at the big glutton opposite me, but he had already finished a third plateful of the exquisite Scotch beef and was wiping his forehead in serene unconsciousness of having done anything out of the common. I stole a glance at Lady Marriott; she was as white as a ghost and her first helping of meat still lay untouched upon her plate. The quiet lady avoided my eyes and had evidently made up her mind to endure to the end.

But the atmosphere got worse and worse, the smells stronger and stronger, till I rejoiced every time a servant opened the door, whether to go out or come in. All the guests were eating as if their lives depended on their appetites and Marriott's butler and four men servants were plainly insufficient to supply the imperious desires of his half dozen guests.

I have never in my life seen men gormandize to be compared with those men. And the curious thing was that as course followed course their appetite seemed to increase. Certainly the smell got worse and worse, and when the savory of soft herring roes on toast came on the board, the orgy degenerated into a frenzy.

Another unmistakable explosion and I could not but look again at my hostess. She was as pale as death, and this time her eyes met mine in despairing appeal.

"I'm not very well," she said in a low tone. "I don't think I can see it through!"

"Why should you?" I responded, getting up. "Come upstairs; we'll never be missed!" We got up quietly and left the room and in fact were not missed by anyone. As soon as Lady Marriott breathed the pure air of the hall and stairway she began to revive, while the change taught me how terrible the putrid atmosphere of the dining-room had become. "That's my first City dinner," said Lady Marriott, drawing a long breath as we sat down in the drawing-room, "and I hope devoutly it may be my last. How perfectly awful men can be!"

"So that's Sir Robert Fowler," I said. "The best Lord Mayor, the only scholarly Lord Mayor, London has ever had!"

One story about Fowler must be inserted here, though the incident took place some time later. The Honourable Finch-Hatton,* a son of Lord Winchelsea, had been returned to Parliament as a Conservative. On one of his first nights in the House of Commons he happened to be sitting beside Fowler, who made a long speech in favor of London government and "the great institutions of the greatest City in the world." At the end he said he would not conclude with any proposal till he heard what his opponents had to say in answer to him; he could hardly believe that they had any reasonable reply.

While Fowler was speaking, Finch-Hatton had shown signs of restlessness; towards the end of the speech he had moved some three yards away

---

* Harold Heneage Finch-Hatton (1856–1904). There are many ambiguities here. Harris presumably met Fowler about 1885; "sometime later" would not presumably mean ten years after, or 1895, when Finch-Hatton was first elected to Parliament. Finch-Hatton had been a cattleman and gold prospector in Queensland from 1876 until 1885.

from the baronet. As soon as Fowler sat down, Finch-Hatton sprang up holding his handkerchief to his nose.

"Mr. Speaker," he began, and was at once acknowledged by the Speaker, for it was a maiden speech,* and as such entitled to precedence by the courteous custom of the House. "I know why the Right Honourable Member for the City did not conclude his speech with a proposal; the only way to conclude such a speech appropriately would be with a motion!"

And Finch-Hatton sat down amid the wild cheers and laughter of the whole House after making the wittiest maiden speech on record. The success of the *mot* was so extraordinary that I believe he never again ventured to address the House.

Finch-Hatton had spent half a dozen years as a squatter in Queensland and was said to be the only white man that ever lived who could throw a boomerang as well as a Queensland aborigine. It is certain that no one ever threw a boomerang with such success in the House of Commons, for with one winged word he destroyed the influence of Sir Robert Fowler. As soon as Fowler's name came up afterwards the story of Finch-Hatton's maiden speech was told, too, and wild laughter submerged Fowler's reputation.

But if I have set down these examples of English gluttony and, if you will, of English bestiality, I must also say that in the best English houses you found the best food in the world perfectly served and enjoyed with charming decorum. I often said that the English idea of cooking was the best in the world: it was the aristocratic ideal, the wish to give to every single thing its own peculiar flavor. For example, potatoes are best boiled in their skins; the water should then be drained off and the potatoes allowed to steam a few minutes: then you get a potato at its best. Beef should be roasted before the fire and served lightly cooked; mutton, too, should be roasted, but better done; veal and pork should be well done. Everyone of any position in my time in London knew that grouse lightly roasted and eaten cold with a glass or two of brut champagne made a lunch for the gods.

The French, on the other hand, are usually reputed to be the best gourmets in the world, but I have never eaten a first-rate meal in any French house or restaurant. The French have the democratic idea of cooking and are continually tempted to obliterate all distinctions with a democratic sauce. They will serve you potatoes in twenty ways, all of them appetizing, but none of them giving the true potato flavor. In fact, you don't know half the time what you're eating in France; it's the sauce you taste! Fancy serving a partridge *aux choux:* the whole exquisite flavor of the bird lost, swamped, drowned in the pungent taste and odor of the accursed cabbage! Compare this bourgeois mess with the flavor you get of an English partridge roasted before a fire by a cook who knows the value of the jewel he is asked to set; nothing but boiled rice or the heart of a lettuce with olive oil from Nice should ever be served with the dainty morsel. But then there

---

* Actually, his maiden speech dealt with his experience with Australian land legislation, but there's no doubt that this is the maiden speech he should have made.

are so few cooks in England, and nearly all who merit the name are French.

As I began this chapter with the story of General Dickson's jovial courtesy and excellent dinner, so I must in justice to London end it with the account of a still more memorable feast enjoyed in Ernest Beckett's* (afterwards Lord Grimthorpe's) house in Piccadilly, because it, too, throws light on the consummate *savoir faire* and kindness which enriches English life and distinguishes it above life in any other country.

I had got to know Beckett pretty well towards the end of 1887. He had heard me tell some of the stories I afterwards published and encouraged me by warm praise. He was always pressing me too to go into the House of Commons. "You may write wonderfully," he used to say, "but you'll never write as well as you talk, for you're at least as good an actor as a story teller."

One evening Beckett asked me to dinner; Mallock and Professor Dowden** of Dublin University were the only other guests. I knew both men slightly and had read a good deal of both and especially of Mallock, not only his *New Republic* but all his attacks on socialism in defence of an unrestrained individualism. In spite of his reserved manners and rather slow way of speaking, I had come to feel a genuine esteem for his very considerable abilities. I was glad too to meet Dowden again. His book on Shakespeare I thought piffle; it was all taken from what I had begun to call the Ragbag, the receptacle where the English store all the current ideas about Shakespeare, ideas for the most part completely false and not seldom ridiculously absurd. Nine out of ten English mediocrities are afflicted with the desire to make this God Shakespeare in their own image, and this inexplicable idolatry of themselves has led them into all manner of incongruous misconceptions.

Naturally I had no idea when we sat down to dine that Beckett had arranged the whole affair just to find out whether my knowledge of Shakespeare was really extraordinary or not. Still less did I imagine that Mallock had offered himself as chief inquisitor, so to speak. Towards the end of dinner Beckett turned the conversation deftly enough to Shakespeare and

---

* Correctly, Edmund Becket, Lord Grimthorpe, (1816–1905). He had many talents: he was a successful lawyer, a strong Protestant controversialist, against all ritualism in religion; and he wrote on architecture and mechanics and designed Big Ben.

** William Hurrell Mallock (1849–1923). His *New Republic* (1877) consisted of platonic dialogues, and the participants were drawn from figures such as Jowett, Ruskin, Arnold, and Pater. Mallock tried in this book to demonstrate the impossibility of undogmatic belief. In *Social Equality* he maintained that, because the efforts that produce wealth are unequal, those efforts can be stimulated only by the prospect of unequal rewards. Mallock was a nephew of Froude.

Professor Edward Dowden (1843–1913), of Trinity College, Dublin. Harris refers to *Shakespeare, His Mind and Art* (1875), Dowden's most influential book. He approached Shakespeare from the psychological side, as Harris did, though the emphases differed.

Mallock remarked that though he had only read him casually, carelessly, "like all the world, he had yet noticed that some of Shakespeare's finest expressions—'gems of thought'—were never quoted, indeed, were not even known to most of the professional students." I nodded my agreement.

"Give us an instance!" cried Beckett.

"Well," replied Mallock, "take the phrase, 'frightened out of fear'; could a truth be more splendidly expressed? An epigram unforgettable!"

"You're right," exclaimed Beckett, "and I must confess I don't know where it occurs. Do you, Harris?"

"Enobarbus in *Antony and Cleopatra*," I replied. "Enobarbus is the conscience of the play: the high intellectual judgment of Shakespeare called in, this once, to decide between 'great Caesar' and Shakespeare's *alter ego,* the lover Antony. It's the only time I think that Shakespeare ever used such an abstraction."

"A remarkable *aperçu,*" said Dowden. "I had no idea that you were a Shakespeare lover; surely there are not many in the States?"

"Not many anywhere, I imagine," was my laughing reply.

A moment or two later Mallock began again. "Shakespeare is always being praised for his wonderful character drawing, but I'm often shocked by the way he disdains character. Fancy a clown talking of 'the primrose path!' "

"A clown!" I repeated. "You mean the porter in *Macbeth,* don't you?"

"Of course, the porter!" Mallock replied. "A very clown!"

"Curious," I went on laughing. "I asked because the porter, I believe, doesn't say 'primrose path' but 'primrose way'."

"Are you sure?" exclaimed Mallock. "I could have sworn 'twas 'primrose path'; I think 'path' better than 'way'."

"My memory, too, supports you, Mr. Mallock," Dowden chimed in. "I feel certain it was the 'primrose path'; 'path' is certainly more poetic."

"It is," I replied, "and that's probably why Shakespeare gives 'primrose way' to the sleeper porter and 'primrose path' to Ophelia; you know she warns her brother of the 'primrose path' of dalliance."

"I believe you're right!" exclaimed Mallock. "But what an extraordinary memory you have."

"The man of 'one book,' you know," I laughed, "is always to be dreaded."

"It seems strange that you should have studied Shakespeare with such particularity," Dowden remarked pleasantly. "From some of your writing in the *Spectator,* which our mutual friend Verschoyle has shown me, I thought you rather a social reformer after the style of Henry George."*

"I'm afraid I am," I confessed. "Yet I admit the validity of most of Mr.

---

* (1849–1923), the American economist, who fought for "Single Tax" on land. He believed that the unearned increase on land benefited a few individuals rather than the community; the single tax would relieve labor and capital of taxes and yet provide enough income for all government services.

Mallock's arguments against socialism, though I can't imagine how he can argue against the obvious truth that the land of the people should belong to all the people."

"Why should we care for the people," cried Mallock, "the Great Unwashed. They propagate their kind and die and fill forgotten graves. It is only the great who count; the *hoi polloi* don't matter."

Mallock always put forward the aristocratic creed with even greater ability than Arthur Balfour, yet I thought my view the wiser.

"The physique of the English race is diminishing," I began, "through the poverty of the mass of the people. In 1845 only one hundred and five recruits out of a thousand were under five feet six in height, while in 1887 fifty per cent were below that standard. The girth of chest, too, shows a similar shrinkage."

"That leaves my withers unwrung," scoffed Mallock. "Why should we care particularly about the rag, tag and bobtail of the people?"

"Because your geniuses and great men," I replied, "come from the common mass; the Newtons, Darwins and Shakespeares don't spring from noble loins."

"Nor from the lowest class either," returned Mallock. "From the well-fed, at least."

"The more reason," I retorted, "to give the mass of the people humane conditions of life."

"There we must all be agreed," Beckett broke in. "If the mass of the people were treated as well as the aristocrat treats his servants, all would be well; but the manufacturer treats his workmen, not as servants, but as serfs. 'Hands': the mere word is his condemnation."

The conversation continued on these general lines till suddenly Dowden turned to me.

"One thing you must admit," he said smiling. "Shakespeare took the aristocratic side, was indeed an aristocrat to *his* finger-tips. Surely no great genius was ever so completely indifferent to social reforms or indeed to reforms of any sort. His caricature of Jack Cade* is convincing on that point."

"Quite true!" cried Mallock. "Undeniable, unarguable, indeed."

"Don't say such things," I broke out. "I can't hear them without protest: what age was Shakespeare when he wrote Jack Cade? Think of him fresh from the narrow, brainless life of village Stratford, transplanted into that pulsing many-colored life of London with young aristocrats all about him on the stage. No wonder he sneered at Jack Cade; but ask him twenty years later what he thought of the aristocrats and the harsh misery of ordinary life and you would have got a very different answer! The main truth about Shakespeare, and it's an utterly neglected truth, is that he grew from being

---

* He led a revolt in 1450 against the government and he was executed. The caricature of Cade as a buffoon occurs in *Henry VI*, Part II, Act IV.

an almost ordinary youth into one who stood on the forehead of the time to come, a sacred leader and guide for a thousand years."

"Very interesting," retorted Mallock, "and new, but I want proofs, I'm free to confess, proofs! Where's the Jack Cade in his latest works, or rather, where shall we find Essex and Southampton disdained and Cade treated as a great reformer and martyr to a cause?"

"He's got you there, Harris," exclaimed Dowden.

"Has he? First of all, Mr. Mallock, you'll have to admit that Shakespeare quickly came to see the English aristocrat as he really was. No better or more bitter portrait of the aristocrat exists in any literature than Portia gives of her English suitor in The Merchant of Venice: 'a proper man's picture' but 'a poor dumb show.' He knows no foreign language and his manners, like his clothes, lack all distinction. So much for 'the poor pennyworth!'

"But no Jack Cade on a pedestal, you say. Well, Posthumus was Shakespeare's alter ego, as plainly as Prospero, and what does Posthumus say in prison when he cries to the Gods:

> I know you are more clement than vile men,
> Who of their broken debtors, take a third,
> A sixth, a tenth, letting them thrive again
> On their abatement: that's not my desire . . .*

"What would Shakespeare have said to Chamberlain's Bankruptcy Act, which is the law of England today and for many a year to come? You now take everything from the broken debtor and do not then discharge him, but keep his failure hung over him for years in order to force him to the prison, which the beggared seldom escape. In this we are infinitely viler than Shakespeare's 'vile men.' Shakespeare not a social reformer! If your laws were conceived in the spirit of his maturity, the millenium would be realized. I always put him with Jesus as a thinker." Mallock laughed as at an enormity and I didn't pursue the theme. I had given them pause, which was enough.

We adjourned to the drawing-room for coffee, which was excellent, as the whole meal had been. Beckett ate with the keenest enjoyment, but in strict moderation, and all of us cultivated a similar control. While drinking the coffee Dowden said he hoped I'd write on Shakespeare. "You've certainly given me food for thought," he added courteously.

"And me too," cried Mallock.

When they went away, Beckett kept me and for the life of me I could not understand why, till he suddenly blurted out, "Tant pis if you think worse of me, but I think I owe it to you to tell you the truth. I was talking to Mallock the other day about you, praising your extraordinary scholarship and knowledge of Shakespeare and your genius. He said that genius was difficult to measure, but knowledge was easy; why not let him test your

* Act V, scene 4.

knowledge of Shakespeare; and so I arranged this dinner. If you had come to grief I'd have said nothing, but you came through so brilliantly that I think you ought to know. I hope you're not angry with me?"

"No, no," I replied. "How could I be?"

"I want to be friends," rejoined Beckett warmly. "I want you to regard me as a friend and as a sign of it I wish you'd call me Ernest and let me call you Frank."

"That's dear of you," I responded, and gave him my hand. From that day on Ernest Beckett was a true friend of mine and my affection for him grew till he passed—alas! all too soon, into the eternal silence.

One word more on the freedom of speech used in good society in London in the eighties and nineties of the nineteenth century. It was not so outspoken as the best French or German society, but its rule was very much like the rule of the best Italian or Spanish society: anything was permitted if it was sufficiently funny or witty. In the Prince of Wales' set in especial, it was possible to tell the most *risqué* story, provided always that it was really humorous. And the *Pink 'Un,* or chief sporting paper of the day, edited by John Corlett and printed on pink paper once a week, certainly set a broad example. One instance will prove this. Just before I returned to London the Baroness Burdett Coutts,* a great favorite of the Prince and the Queen for her goodness of heart and many benefactions, though well over sixty years of age, married young Mr. Bartlett,** an American, a good-looking man of six or seven and twenty, and five feet ten in height. Prince Edward, it was said, was asked by the Queen to remonstrate with the old lady. But she met him by saying that she could not make her dear boy unhappy. "He is head over ears in love with me, you know," she said. The Prince could only smile and perhaps repeat the British saying under his breath: "No fool like an old fool."

The week after the marriage Corlett published the announcement in the *Pink 'Un,* and underneath in large letters, this:

AN ARITHMETICAL PROBLEM: How many times does twenty-seven go into sixty-eight and what is there over?

Perhaps nothing except the famous naughty blunder in *The Times* some years later ever caused such widespread merriment.

The tone of English society is the tone of a well-bred man of the world, whereas the tone of American society is the tone of a Puritan grocer.

* Baroness Angela Georgina Burdett Coutts (1814–1906), daughter of Sir Francis Burdett (1770–1844), who married Sophia Coutts of a prominent family of bankers; the Baroness inherited a great part of her grandfather's fortune. She was an avid supporter of the arts; Irving's corpse was viewed by thousands of mourners in her London house.
** William Ashmond-Bartlett (1851–1921). The marriage took place in 1881 and he took her name.

Chapter XIV

Charles Reade; Mary Anderson; Irving; Chamberlain; Hyndman and Burns

IN MY EARLY DAYS in London one event moved me profoundly, the death and burial of Charles Reade.* Somehow or other he had got the name of being bad tempered and quarrelsome and his lovable and great qualities were almost forgotten. Indeed, were it not for the fact that a prominent journalist, George Augustus Sala,** took up the cudgels for his private character and wrote of him as kind-hearted as well as noble-minded, judgment against him would have gone by default. Of course, like all the younger ones, I measured him wholly as a writer and accepted at once every word of Sala's eulogy and went far beyond it. Unlike most Englishmen, I regarded Reade as a far greater writer than Dickens, and indeed had no hesitation in putting *The Cloister and the Hearth* side by side with *Vanity Fair* in my admiration, and perhaps a little higher in my love. Again and again I talked of Reade's masterpiece as the greatest English novel, though the spirit of opposition may have added a tinge of challenge to my passionate superlative.

The announcement of his death reminded me that I might have known him, had I wished. [As at] Rossetti's passing some two years before, my regret was keen and lasting. But I went to his burial and from it learned how careless, or rather how chanceful, is England's sympathy with her great men. True, that Easter Tuesday was a vile day: it rained and the air was raw. He was to be buried too at Willesden, miles away from the center, but there was not a great crowd even at Shepherd's Bush, whence the funeral procession started. A more dismal burial would be hard to imagine. And so I resented even Sala's praise of *It is never too late to mend* as a "magnificent work," and his comparison of Hawes, the governor of the gaol, and Eden the chaplain, as "distinctly original and dramatic characters," with

* (1814–84).
** (1828–95); also a novelist. Harris is speaking of an article that appeared in the *Daily Telegraph*. Sala was a special correspondent for the *Telegraph* in the United States during the Civil War.

the Faust and Mephistopheles and the Gretchen of Goethe. Such overpraise seemed as impertinent-odious as his talking of two Charles Reades: "One a very pugnacious and vituperative old gentleman, always shaking his fist in somebody's face and not infrequently hitting somebody over the head," and "the other Charles Reade I knew and revered as a valiant, upright and withal a charitable and compassionate Christian man, inexhaustible in his pity for suffering, implacable only in his hatred of things shameful and cruel and mean. He was throughout his life a militant man; but his soldiering is over now; there he rests in a peaceful tomb by the side of the Friend whom he loved so long and so deeply."

Only three months before, Tennyson had been made a peer amid universal eulogy; yet here was as great a man put away forever without pomp or circumstance; the ordinary English reader thought more of *Maud* or *The May Queen* than *The Cloister and the Hearth;* still what did it matter? I for one walked through the rain and slush while the gallant Denys, with his "the Devil is dead", went with me and Gerard and Catherine* and the rest of the glorious and ever-living company; and perchance one man's understanding and admiring, passionate love is more than most of us get in this earthly pilgrimage. Surely it is well with dear Charles Reade: I saw his coffin lowered into the grave, but I find it hard to forgive myself. I ought to have seen and known him in order at least to have thanked him for his deathless gift to humanity and the many hours of pure delight I had had with his brave heart and noble spirit.

But now I must say a word or two of other occurrences that throw a certain light on English character and conditions. An American actress, Mary Anderson,** took London by storm. It was said that Lord Lytton† bought a row of the stalls night after night and filled the seats with chosen guests; his admiration surprised everyone who knew him, because he was regarded as an avowed admirer of the *ephebos,* rather than of woman's beauty; but he certainly fell for "our Mary," as some tried to nickname her. This was the Lord Lytton, who in *The New Timon* sneered at Tennyson:

> The jingling medley of purloined conceits,
> Out-babying Wordsworth and out-glittering Keats.††

* Characters in *The Cloister and the Hearth.*
** (1859–1940). Between 1883 and 1889 she spent several seasons in London. In 1890, when she married, she settled in England. She played Rosalind in *As You Like It* at the opening of the Shakespeare Memorial Theatre at Stratford-on-Avon. It was she for whom Wilde wrote *The Duchess of Padua.* She had advanced him $1000, promised him $4000 more if she liked it, and then turned the play down. And she was J. M. Barrie's "dear enemy."
† Lord Edward Robert Bulwer-Lytton (1831–91), viceroy to India (1876–80) and ambassador to France (1887–91). He wrote poems and novels and translated from Serbian under the pseudonym Owen Meredith.
†† These lines are not from *The New Timon.*

And Tennyson's answer was even more savage:

> What profits now to understand
> The merits of a spotless shirt,
> A dapper boot, a little hand,
> If half the little soul is dirt?*

Before Mary Anderson appeared I had called on her and done a sketch of her career for the *Evening News*. She was a tall, graceful, good-looking blonde, but I never dreamed of her huge success. Her mind was as commonplace as her voice. She had no special gift, but on the stage she was beautiful: the foot-lights set her off peculiarly, though she could not act for nuts. To compare her as an actress with Ellen Terry** or even with Ada Rehan† would be ridiculous: she was comparatively inarticulate. Yet her appearances were events; she went from triumph to triumph. Through her success I realized that there are special scenic qualities demanded by the stage. She was very tall and when she came down the stage in white, she dominated it and dwarfed all the other women; in talking she had a slight American accent that would have ruined her as a Shakespearean actress, but by the time she played in *The Winter's Tale* she had shed her twang and spoke fairly; her eyes were a little deep set, her nose perfectly cut: in a room she was just pretty, on the stage a goddess. How much of her success was due to her statuesque grace and how much to Lytton's passionate advocacy can never be known.

Her career taught me how susceptible the English are to mere physical beauty. They rate it in all animals higher than any other race and study it more intimately: shorthorn bull or Berkshire sow, bulldog or greyhound, terrier or mastiff, Southdown ram or Welsh sheep, race-horse or hunter— all are admired for their perfect conformity to type, which argues a most passionate and imaginative understanding of what type is or should be. Were it not for their idiotic Puritanism the English would be the greatest sculptors in the world and world-renowned besides for their extraordinary understanding of every form and type of bodily beauty.

I visited the British Museum with Rodin later to study the figures from the Parthenon. He went into ecstasies over them; they were as sensuous, he declared, as any figures in all plastic art. George Wyndham went with me at another time but he would not be seduced. The Greek feet and ankles were too large and ill-shaped, he argued; the womens' necks, too, and breasts were coarse. He preferred the figures from the Temple of Nike Apteros, and even they had bad faults. At length he asserted that the facial type was too wooden: the nose in a straight line from the forehead was ugly. In fine, the best English type, he insisted, was far finer, lovelier at once and more spiritual than the Greek ideal, and I agreed with him.

---

* From *The New Timon, and the Poets*. Except for errors in punctuation the quotation is accurate.
** (1847–1928).
† (1860–1916), an American actress; she first played in England in 1884.

Europe has learned what natural beauty is from English tourists. Was not Ruskin the first to assert that French trees were far more beautiful than English trees? He did not give the reason, but I may. England is afflicted with a wind from the southwest that blows three hundred odd days each year. Against this attack all trees when young have to stem themselves or they would be uprooted; as it is, they are dwarfed and crooked. And the woodlands of France suffer from the same plague, though much less severely. There are no forests in the world to be compared with the American: in half an hour's drive out of New York up the Hudson one sees more varieties of exquisite and well grown trees than one can find in all France, or even Germany.

And as the trees, so are the men and women: one can find more types of exquisite girlhood and splendid manhood in an hour in New York than one can find in a day in London or a week in Paris or Berlin or Moscow. How is it that American athletes hold all the records? How is it that they can run faster and jump higher than any of the English athletes, though the other day the English were supposed to be supreme in all forms of sport and athletics? In forty years there has not been a single English heavyweight boxer of the first class simply because the mass of the people have been impoverished to a degree that is not yet realized even in England. The physical manhood of the race has been dwarfed by destitution.

But this argument had led me away from my theme. Shortly after my first meeting with Mary Anderson, I saw Tommaso Salvini* as Othello. Salvini had every personal qualification: fine presence and in especial a magnificent and perfectly trained voice, now splendidly sonorous, now sweet, always grateful to the ear. The speech containing the lament, "Othello's occupation gone," was never so superbly rendered: the breaking voice, the tears falling from the convulsed face, the hands even knitting and relaxing, formed an unforgettable picture. Salvini at that moment was Othello and when he suddenly turned on Iago he was terrific; but the famous soliloquy in the bed-chamber before he murders Desdemona was given in far too loud a voice: he would have waked the dead. He had no conception of the complex English passion, that a man can admire, love, even, what he's resolved to destroy, lest "she should sting more men": Shakespeare's own passion, far too complex for the Italian nature. And in *Macbeth* Salvini had no inkling that he was acting the thought-plagued Hamlet. His Macbeth never hesitates, never falters: he has not the "if 'twere done, when 'tis done," and so forth. Yet he was the best Othello I've ever seen.

Why are actors, like politicians, always overpraised? It would take a dozen of the best of them to portray Hamlet to my satisfaction. I should want Irving to look the part, and Forbes-Robertson** to recite some of the

---

* (1829–1915). This Italian was indeed famous for his Othello, which he played to Edwin Booth's Iago in America in 1886.

** (1853–1937). His Hamlet of 1897 was thought by many to be the best of all contemporary performances.

soliloquies, and Terriss* to stab Polonius, and Sarah Bernhardt to send Ophelia to a nunnery with ineffable tenderness; and even then, whom should I get to show the passion of Hamlet's jealousy or the contempt he felt for Kemp,** the clown, who gagged probably and did not say the lines set down for him because he was lifted out of himself by the applause of the groundlings; and worst omission of all, who would impersonate the supreme poet who sings of "the undiscovered country from whose bourne no traveler returns," though he has just been talking to his father's ghost?

It was at a dinner that Arthur Walter gave in his house off Queen's Gate, that I got to know Henry Irving. I had met him before, notably at a supper given by Beerbohm Tree† in the Garrick Club after he had played Shylock at the Lyceum.

I had come from Munich to see his Shylock and compare it with the best Shylock I had ever seen, that of Ernst Possart.†† Irving, having been told by Tree that I had come a thousand miles to see him play, was very gracious and hoped I had liked his impersonation. Naturally, I said, "It was very wonderful, but not Shakespeare's—quite!" Irving insisted on knowing what I meant. Everyone who saw him will remember the scene when Shylock prays to be allowed to go home as a beaten and broken man:

Shy.   I pray you give me leave to go from hence
    I am not well; send the deed after me,
    And I will sign it.
Duke. Get thee gone, but do it.
Gr.   In christening shalt thou have two godfathers:
    Had I been judge, thou shouldst have had ten more,
    To bring thee to the gallows, not the font:
                    (Exit Shylock)

It is the only case, I think, in which our gentle Shakespeare allows a gentleman to insult a beaten man. I was therefore outraged by Irving's conception: he was near the door when Gratiano spoke; at once he turned, walked back to Gratiano, drew himself up, crossing his arms, and scanned him contemptuously from head to foot amid the wild applause of the whole house. When Irving challenged me to explain, I said it seemed to me that if Shylock had treated Gratiano in this way, Gratiano would probably have spat in his face and kicked him off the stage.

"I can't agree with you," retorted Irving dryly. "I think the applause showed I was right in my conception of Shylock as a great tragic figure."

"But Shylock himself tells us," I replied, "that the hero Antonio spat upon his Jewish gaberdine."

* William Terriss (1847–97), an English member of Irving's company.
** One of the Lord Chamberlain's men; at one time a shareholder in the Globe Theatre. He was popular as a clown in Shakespeare's plays; in 1599 he danced from London to Norwich.
† Sir Herbert Beerbohm Tree (1853–1917), actor-manager brother of Max Beerbohm. He took "Tree" for a stage name.
†† (1841–1921), a German Shakespearean actor, director, and producer.

Irving turned away and began talking to someone else. His rudeness annoyed the more because I was reproaching myself for having been too frank.

Long afterwards, when Mounet-Sully* played Hamlet in Paris and Lemaitre,** the great French critic, wanted to know how he compared with Irving, I could not help telling the truth. "Irving," I said, "is the ideal Hamlet for the deaf and Mounet-Sully for the blind!"

But in 1884–85, I met Irving frequently, and Bram Stoker, his manager, always sent me tickets for the Lyceum when I asked for them.

One night I gave a supper party and had Lord Lytton and Harold Frederic, both passionate admirers of Irving; and when we drew together to smoke with the Turkish coffee, Irving talked better than I had ever heard him talk; indeed, till then I had thought him rather inarticulate. I had mentioned, I remember, that Lord Randolph Churchill† had promised to come to "the apotheosis of the God," as he phrased it, but at the last moment had to excuse himself because of an important debate in the House. "Please tell Mr. Irving," he added in his letter, "how I should have liked to describe the prodigious effect of his Mephistopheles made upon me." Of course Irving was delighted and went off at score, speaking in his natural voice and with no trace of his stage mannerisms and mumblings, which I found so insupportable.

"I met Lord Randolph first in 1880 in Dublin," he began. "His father was there as Viceroy and Lord Randolph had gone to live in Dublin. We went across to play a week of Shakespeare and the first night we opened with *Hamlet*. To my surprise, there was no great reception, no special recognition. At the end of the first act Bram Stoker came to me. 'There's someone in the Viceregal box,' he said. 'I think it's Randolph Churchill, the younger son of the Duke.' Now Blandford,†† his elder brother, had made himself notorious a little while before through a very ugly divorce case; but after all, those affairs are private. I shrugged my shoulders therefore. At the end of the next act Bram Stoker came to say that Lord Randolph would like to make my acquaintance and thank me for my wonderful acting, etc. I told him to bring him round, and at the end of the act he brought Lord Randolph to me in my dressing room. He came to me at once with outstretched hands. 'I have to thank you, Mr. Irving,' he began, 'for one of the greatest pleasures of my life, an incomparable evening!' I bowed of course, but he went on. 'I had no idea that *Hamlet* was such a great play.'

* Jean Mounet-Sully (1841–1916). He played the major roles in the plays of Voltaire and Racine with the Comédie Française, but he was especially acclaimed for his Hamlet and Oedipus.
** François Elie Jules Le Maitre (1853–1914), a dramatist and a poet as well as a critic.
† (1849–95). Harris treats him later at length.
†† The eighth duke of Marlborough.

"I stared at him: was he trying to be humorous? I replied dryly: '*Hamlet* is usually supposed to be a great play.'

" 'Really!' he said, 'I hadn't heard of it.' This was too much for me: he was either a fool or trying to pull my leg. I turned away. At once Randolph added in a very courtly way, 'I mustn't take up your time by exposing my ignorances; you are no doubt busy.'

" 'No,' I replied, 'this act is chiefly taken up by the fair Ophelia.'

" 'Really!' he burst out again. 'I think Miss Terry too is wonderful. I mustn't lose a word of what she says.' I smiled and he added, 'I can't go without hoping to meet you again; won't you dine with me on Sunday next in the lodge in Phoenix Park, which my father has been good enough to place at my disposal?'

"His manner, something ingenuous and enthusiastic in his youth, pleased me, and I accepted at once, conscious of a certain sympathy. During the week I was told that he had been in the Viceregal box every night. On the Sunday I went to dine with him a little intrigued: what would he say? He met me in the hall: 'Oh, Mr. Irving,' he began, 'I can't reckon what I owe you: through you I've come to know Shakespeare; what a man he was! Half a dozen of his plays are great plays, and interesting—'

" 'But surely you must have known them before?' I asked. 'Surely at Oxford you must have read some of them, even if in our schooldays the great things get neglected?'

" 'No, no, I assure you,' he replied. 'I never read him at school nor at Oxford. I'm afraid I was very lazy and idle all through, but his *Lear* is a great, great play: I'd love to see you in it; and there's something in the *Antony and Cleopatra* that appeals to me peculiarly. Do you ever play it?'

" 'It's a little difficult to stage,' I answered, and while explaining we took our seats at the table and I found him a first-rate host.

"Lord Randolph made a profound impression on me," Irving went on. "As soon as I realized that he was not posing I said to myself, 'This is a great man, too; unconsciously he thinks that even Shakespeare needs his approval! He makes himself instinctively the measure of all things and of all men and doesn't trouble himself about the opinions or estimates of others.' Afterwards, when they made fun of him in Parliament, as they did at first with silly caricatures of him as an impudent boy, I knew the day would come when they'd have to take him seriously."

I was delighted with the story and with the simple, sincere way Irving told it. I think still it shows intellect in him and an appreciation of greatness that I did not at all expect.

Sometime later Arthur Bourchier,* the actor, told me an amusing story that shows Henry Irving in another light.

---

* (1863–1927), an actor-manager. He joined Lily Langtry's company in 1889 and soon appeared as Jacques in *As You Like It*. He became manager of the Garrick Theatre in 1900; in 1910 he joined Beerbohm Tree in producing several plays of Shakespeare.

"When Benson* at Oxford was drilling his amateur company in Shakespeare and Aeschylus, he asked Irving down once for the opening night of the *Agamemnon*. I was in Benson's company and delighted when he showed me Irving's charming letter of acceptance. He was flattered, he said, by the invitation and would come gladly. We were all on the alert, as you may imagine, on the great night. Well, the performance went without a hitch and afterwards Irving came round on the stage and congratulated Benson in the handsomest way. "A great play," he said, "and a very great actor. I'm delighted to feel, Mr. Benson, that the University, too, has come to enrich the stage. I think you gave the chief things superbly"; and he really spoke simply, as if he meant every word of it, and we drank it all in greedily, as young men do. His praise affected Benson so much that shortly afterwards he confessed, "Your appreciation, Sir, gives me courage"—he began—"I think I shall give the Trilogy."

"Do, my dear fellow," cried Irving, clapping him on the shoulder, "do. It's a part that'll suit you admirably."

"After that," said Bourchier, grinning, "the curtain came down of itself."

I have given this story as well as the others because it illustrates a side of the actor; and now I'll make a further personal confession that tells against myself and puts a certain nobility of Irving in a fair light. In my later years in London I seldom went to the Lyceum and took little stock in Irving's later achievements, though right up to the end of the century his "first nights" were something more than social events.

Irving always gave the impression of being more than an actor: he had a great personality; his marked peculiarities of figure, face and speech set him apart and gave him unique place and distinction. Of the three or four chief personages of the eighties, he was the most singular—more arresting even than Parnell. Randolph Churchill and Gladstone had to be seen in the House of Commons to win full recognition, but Irving, like Disraeli, took the eye everywhere and excited the imagination. As Shylock, even, Irving made everyone else upon the stage appear common, an effect surely not contemplated by the creator of the "Ebrew Jew"! There can be no doubt that his peculiar enunciation and accent on the stage were deliberately adopted in order to increase the effect of his appearance, for in private life he spoke almost like anyone else. His "make-up," in fact, went so far as to include his speech and voice. If we are to believe tradition, Garrick in this was his exact opposite: he was always simple and natural on the stage, we are told, but in private was always acting, always playing a part.

With Goethe, I felt that the the admission of young girls had a more laming effect on the theatre than it had even upon books. "Young girls,"

---

* Sir Francis Robert Benson (1858–1939), also an actor-manager. He founded the Oxford University Dramatic Society and played Clytemnestra in the first production, *Agamemnon*. In 1881 he took the Society to London for one performance of *Romeo and Juliet;* he played Romeo. He directed the Shakespeare festival at Stratford-on-Avon for more than 25 years.

said the great German, "have no business in the theatre; they belong to the cloister and the theatre is for men and women only and the elemental human passions. But as it is impossible to get the maidens and their emasculating influence out of the theatre, I have stopped going to it. I would have to shut my eyes to all the feebleness and foolery, or accept it all, without even trying to improve it, and that's not my role."*

In those first years in London, I had a paltry little spite against Irving: he denied me the advertisement of the Lyceum Theatre on the ground that the *Evening News* was a ha'penny paper; and I thought it mean and shabby of him, and Stoker put the blame on Irving himself. About the same time, I discovered Wilson Barrett's** inordinate ambition to oust Irving from his pride of place. After the Fortescue triumph, I had been introduced to Miss Terry and had flattered her to the top of her bent; and, indeed, I admired her hugely: I thought her far and away the best English actress. Somewhere or other I heard now that Miss Terry's engagement with Irving had run out and that he did not want to increase her salary. At once I flew to Wilson Barrett and induced him to give me a letter offering Ellen Terry double what she was getting with Irving and a percentage in the profits of the Princess's Theatre to boot. I took it to Miss Terry and after reading it she laughed.

"May I keep it?"

"Certainly," I replied. "You would be the chief person in the Princess's." She laughed again. "You tempt cleverly; why?"

"Frankly, because I don't think Irving appreciates you properly." Miss Terry smiled but would not commit herself.

When I announced in the *Evening News* that it was just possible that Miss Terry would soon go to help Wilson Barrett at the Princess's, I had my revenge. In half an hour Bram Stoker was at my office with a flaming contradiction which I refused to insert, saying I had reason to believe that Miss Terry might change her "leading man." I thought Stoker would have had a fit. Away he rushed and in a short while brought Irving back with him, who assured me that Miss Terry had renewed her engagement with him. "It was signed, sealed and delivered."

"I am very glad for your sake," I said, "and will give the news in tomorrow morning's edition," and, I added, "though you may not care for the announcement in a ha'penny paper." Bram Stoker, I saw, understood what I meant, for afterwards the Lyceum advertisement was sent to the *Evening News* without being asked for.

It was a mean and paltry revenge to take, but Bram Stoker had been needlessly curt and disdainful in his initial refusal, and consequently I had

---

* *Conversations with Goethe*, Eckermann, January 29, 1826.

** (1846–1904), another actor-manager; he managed the Court and the Princess's Theatre in London. He played Romeo to the Juliet of Madame Modjesta, who belonged to his company. He brought on a rivalry with Irving through his production of *Hamlet*, but Irving was the victor.

no idea how wrong I had been till some years afterwards, when I assisted at Irving's bankruptcy and the first meeting of his creditors, and learned to my amazement that he had nearly thirty old actresses and actors on his civil list, to whom he gave weekly pensions of from thirty shillings to five pounds. To all the weaker members of his craft that had ever played with him he behaved with a princely generosity: he had filled his great position nobly and I had made it more difficult for him. I was ashamed of myself to suffering.

From that time on I tried to atone to Irving for my forgotten meanness, but I wish to record it here simply as showing that some of our worst deeds are due to want of knowledge and to a too low estimate of our fellow men.

What judges of literature these journalists are! Froude has just published his *Life of Carlyle* and *The Times* compares it with Boswell's *Johnson*. "Carlyle," says *The Times,* "is a greater person than Johnson," and, it adds, "all the reading world will allow that there can be no comparison between Mr. Froude and Boswell"; all of which might be true without establishing the conclusion. The great portraits of the world are not of the greatest persons, nor written by the greatest men, of what life-history would compare with Plato's pictures of Socrates? If the great master of prose and thought had only written one dialogue between Socrates and Xantippe, telling us of their intimate relations and reactions and giving us the woman's and wife's point of view, he might have painted a companion portrait to the *Crito* and the *Phaedo* that would have completed his work.

Carlyle was not as human as Johnson. Let us take one phrase of the great Doctor: he has visited Garrick behind the scenes and breaks out with the confession that "the black legs and snowy bosoms of your actresses, David, excite my amorous propensities." Has he not here painted himself to the life? And then Froude: a better stylist perhaps than Boswell, but without Boswell's intense interest in his subject. What weaknesses has Froude discovered in Carlyle? Why he doesn't even tell us how Carlyle managed to save £30,000. Why didn't Carlyle go to visit Goethe in Weimar? That would have been better than putting bawbee* to bawbee; and when he made his wife jealous, how did he console her and win forgiveness? Froude is interested in literature rather than life, and not in this spirit are great biographies written, or indeed great anything else.

> Erdachtes mag zu denken geben
> Doch nur Erlebtes wird beleben.**

But already everyone was talking of Joseph Chamberlain and his "Unauthorized Programme"† in the *Fortnightly Review,* and of Gladstone

---

* A half-penny.
** Imaginary things may supply food for thought, But only experiences can enliven.
† Chamberlain introduced his independent "programme" during the general election of 1886.

and the mess he had got himself and his government into, partly through his dislike of Chamberlain and of Parnell, who, since the Kilmainham business,* and because of the perpetual unfair attacks in *The Times,* was coming more and more into prominence.

It was in reference to Parnell and his rise that I first said to myself, "Great men, like kites, go up against the wind." But Parnell, thoroughly English as he was and magnificently handsome to boot, certainly the handsomest man in my time in the House of Commons, never succeeded in England, though towards the end he was on the point of succeeding in the House of Commons, a fact which to me deepens the tragedy of his untimely death.

But Chamberlain was the central figure on the political stage. I measured him perhaps harshly on our first meetings. I've told how surprised I was at the noble way Lord Salisbury acted in regard to his tenants' houses at Hatfield, rebuilding as many as he could, year by year, and then fixing a rental not to exceed three per cent on the cost of the building; and above all refusing from the outset to accept any rent at all on the houses he regarded as unfit for habitation.

"Are you sure?" Chamberlain asked me peevishly when I brought him my report. "Can it be that this whole detailed indictment of Archibald Forbes is wrong with any justification?"

Time and again he returned to the charge: "Forbes had no motive, no reason to be unfair: he's supposed to be a great reporter. It's extraordinary, you'll admit that, most extraordinary."

At length I could stand it no longer: he was so petty, so ungenerous to his rival. "It's Salisbury's nobility," I said, "that strikes me as extraordinary. If the Liberal manufacturers and industrial monopolists of England had behaved as well to their workmen as this great landlord had behaved to his tenants, there would be no strikes in England, no trade unions either, no industrial discontent." Chamberlain looked at me with undisguised antagonism in his eyes but said nothing, and soon afterwards I took my leave. One day I waited for him in his dining-room, where there were several Leighton** pictures, and he introduced them to me pompously as, "All by Leighton, the President, you know of our Academy." I nodded and Chamberlain went on, "I gave 2000 pounds for that one."

"Really?" I gasped.

"Yes," he replied, "what do you think it's worth?"

I could not help it; I replied, "I don't know the value of the frame."

It's hardly necessary to say that he didn't want to see me again for many

---

* A treaty was drawn up at Kilmainham in 1882, whereby Parnell and two friends, who had been imprisoned under the Coercion Act, were to be released for abandoning the "no rent to landlords" policy and for abandoning tactics of intimidation.

** Frederic Leighton (1830–96), president of the Royal Academy of Arts. He was a "society" painter, though he apparently served the Assembly well enough as president.

a day. But another incident occurred some time later which explains, I think, my early misjudgment of the man. The gist of Forbes's article appeared in *Truth,* Labouchère's* weekly paper. I asked Escott had he given it to Labouchère but he denied it, saying that it must have been given by Chamberlain himself. I wrote of it as false and foolish and made fun of it in the *Evening News* and Lord Salisbury's agent wrote thanking me for my defence, at the same time telling me that Lord Salisbury had forbidden him to write any correction to the press; and had added finely, "It's impossible for us to praise each other." But my defence of the truth stood me in good stead with Lord Salisbury much later, as I may tell when I come to the Venezuelan difficulty.

Now I had to read Chamberlain's "Unauthorized Programme"** as it appeared month by month in the *Fortnightly Review,* for all this time I was in close touch with Escott and his family. I found it difficult to explain Chamberlain's extraordinary success. He had no idea that Bismarck's work in nationalizing the German railways was the best way of lifting the laboring classes to a higher level; he preferred the old individualistic lenitives: for years he believed in unrestricted free trade; he didn't even know that joint-stock management of industry had every fault of state management and none of its virtues; from a continental point of view he was extraordinarily ignorant; he had read practically nothing and was curiously uneducated.

He had driving force of will and for years I saw little more in him. All this, I think, accounts for Gladstone's dislike of the man, as was shown by the low position he gave the Radical leader when forming his Cabinet in 1886, though Chamberlain was even then absolute master of six seats in Birmingham alone.

Kimberley and Granville,† old worn out war horses, became Indian and Colonial Ministers respectively, whereas Chamberlain had only a minor appointment as head of the Local Government Board.†† This Ministry showed curious weaknesses and justified my sneer that there was "a screw loose in the Cabinet." Everyone knew of course that Chamberlain's great

---

* Henry Du Pré Labouchère (1831–1912), an outstanding journalist, a Radical, and a friend of Bradlaugh's. He founded *Truth* in 1876; the paper indulged in exposés and was frequently sued for libel, though it rarely lost a case.

** Chamberlain wrote eight articles for the *Fortnightly Review* between 1874–1883. He did not introduce the "Unauthorized Programme" until 1885; it proposed free education, improved housing, fair rents, revised taxation, the disestablishment of the Church of England, among other radical measures.

† Kimberley (1826–1902) in 1882 replaced Lord Hartington in the Indian Office; he became foreign secretary under Lord Rosebery in 1894. He was an able public servant, despite Harris' animadversions.

Granville (1815–91), a long-time Liberal leader in the House of Lords. Actually, he was not colonial, but foreign secretary, the last time 1880–85. He served his country well, though others won more recognition in that office.

†† Actually, Chamberlain was made head of the local Government Board in 1882. Queen Victoria was reluctant to have a Radical like Chamberlain in the Cabinet, but she had to yield.

fortune lay in his monopoly of the trade in screws.* But Gladstone should have taken him into his confidence and given him whatever place he wanted, for he was undoubtedly at this time the head of the Radical party and the most influential member of the majority after Gladstone himself. When the Home Rule Bill came before the House, pressed forward, as Randolph Churchill said aptly, by "an old man in a hurry," Gladstone must have realized his blunder in underrating Chamberlain, for Chamberlain and Hartington both resigned, and their resignation, or rather Chamberlain's, made the bill impossible. Gladstone nicknamed the rebels "dissentient Liberals," but the name didn't stick; they soon came to be known as "Liberal-Unionists," and no one could deny that Chamberlain had given up the succession to the leadership of the party rather than sacrifice his principles. But if Gladstone had handled him to the height of his deserving in 1886, some Home Rule Bill would have passed the House and the history of "the distressful country" would have been different.

I could not even account for Chamberlain's extraordinary influence in Birmingham till I made up my mind to go and visit it. Then I was soon convinced; everyone in Birmingham knew his work and spoke in warmest admiration of him. In the very first year he was Mayor, in 1874,** he bought up the gas works on behalf of the Corporation; he increased the efficiency of the services public and private in the most extraordinary way and transferred the growing profits into the pockets of the taxpayers. A year or so later he dealt with the water supply in the same spirit and with even more wonderful results, while showing himself a really democratic English statesman of the best. In the gas business he used all the growth of revenue in relief of the rates, while in the water service he ordained a minimum of profit in order that the continually growing supply should be distributed throughout the community and should especially benefit the poorest classes. In his third term he did even better at a greater personal cost. There were slums in Birmingham of unimaginable foulness, where long continued poverty had festered into disease. One or two facts will give some idea of the situation: infant mortality in the slum was three times as high as in the more decent quarters, the length of life was not one half as long, and the ratio of crime was tenfold higher. Chamberlain conceived the idea of cleansing this Augean stable, and in order to judge him fairly, it must be remembered that his powers were severely limited; and a certain resentment, based on the overgrown love of Englishmen for individual liberty, and hatred of authoritative interference or molly-coddling, made itself felt unpleasantly from the beginning. Yet he triumphed over every

---

* At the age of 18 Chamberlain was employed by Mr. Nettlefold, an uncle, a screw manufacturer. He was successful enough to retire at 38 with a substantial income. It is doubtful that he was a monopolist; the one charge of business ruthlessness made against him was acknowledged to be unfair.

** He first became mayor in 1873, and was re-elected in 1874 and 1875.

difficulty: bolder than Haussmann* in Paris, he drove a great boulevard through the heart of slum-land and called it Corporation Street. Today Corporation Street has the best shops in Birmingham, and he leased out the sites for only seventy years, so that when the leases fall in before the middle of this century, the Birmingham rates will be relieved to the tune of over £100,000 a year.

On my return from Birmingham I couldn't help asking Chamberlain one day how he had managed it. "Your gas and water improvements were easy," I began. "Indeed, in Germany they would be merely usual, but how did you manage your street through slum-land? Didn't some slum owners object to selling and ask extortionate, extravagant prices for their houses?"

"Some," he replied laughing. "Dozens held me up as boldly resolved as highway robbers. But I had various ways of dealing with them. I had obtained powers over more than the slum area, so, if they were determined, I said, 'All right, my friend, I'll alter the direction of my avenue and leave you in the slum you prefer. You'll not profit by my improvement, that's all.' To another I'd say, 'Look here, if you won't come in, I'll leave your tumbled down old shack in the middle of my avenue and I'll take care you don't get permission from the Corporation to rebuild on the site for many a year.' And yet another I'd influence by an appeal to his sense of fair play, and that's very strong in Englishmen. I showed them that I dealt out even-handed justice: no one should profit more than his neighbor, and that finally was my most persuasive argument; but on the whole I had to pay twice or thrice the value of the land to the individual owner."

He told it all with such laughing good humor, showed besides such a rich human sympathy, even with the meanest and most grasping, and such unconquerable resolution to boot, that he won me completely. I had tears in my eyes when he finished and I murmured, "*Well done, good and faithful servant!*"

He took my words up seriously, and putting his hand on my shoulder said, "I love my house here and my ease, but if I could blot out the shameful, criminal poverty of these islands as I have in Birmingham, I'd consent to go penniless into the streets tomorrow. And yet I've no imitators even. The slums of Glasgow are worse than the worst in Birmingham, but no Scot takes the matter in hand and solves it as I have in Birmingham—and more, much more could be done. One spends half one's life before one comes to realize the problem and understands how easy it would be to solve it; and how important! But oh! the time's so short; one can do so little!" And he sighed deeply.

As he sat down again at his writing-table I noticed for the first time his extraordinary likeness to the younger Pitt: I was carried away by sympathy and had to say something. "I'm very glad I went to Birmingham," I began. "I misjudged you; I'm heart-glad to see that a Bismarck is also possible in

---

* Baron Georges Eugene Haussmann (1809–91), a French financier. He handled the funds for the rebuilding of Paris between 1853 and 1871.

England. At any rate, your spirit shows that the problem will be tackled sooner or later and brought to a noble issue."

"That's the hope," he said, smiling. "I'm glad we feel alike on the chief thing," he added.

"I wonder if that's true," I replied. "Your free trade views always make me shudder."

"Aren't you a free-trader?" he exclaimed, in open-mouthed astonishment.

"Indeed, no," I retorted. "Free trade creates your slums, and I admire the despot who transforms them."

He shrugged his shoulders; he was evidently too busy then to embark on a new discussion. "Won't you take a cigar?" he said, holding out the box, and I felt that I was dismissed. But ever afterwards I cherished a profound admiration for the statesman who had turned Birmingham from an ordinary English town into probably the best ordered and healthiest large town in the kingdom. Often afterwards I wished that instead of butting my head against his free trade prepossessions, I had asked him why he didn't found a municipal opera house and theatre in Birmingham and so lift its spiritual life to the level of life in Marseilles or Lyons.

Gladstone's Home Rule bill was defeated because he yielded to small personal prejudice, and yet every Englishman who knew this thought Gladstone a great man; and he commanded a personal reverence greater even than Bismarck in Germany. For my part, I never esteemed him, save as an orator, and at this time had not yet been introduced to him.

All this while the discontent of the working classes in Great Britain, as in Ireland, grew steadily and increased in bitterness. In London it found determined defenders in the Social Democratic Federation. Mr. H. W. Hyndman had started this association a couple of years or so before as a follower more or less convinced of Karl Marx. The first time I heard Bernard Shaw speak was at a meeting of the Federation, but I had left it before he joined and he left it soon afterwards. On a Monday early in February, 1886, the Federation called a meeting in Trafalgar Square which ended in a riot. The mob got out of hand and marched to attack the clubs in Pall Mall and soon proceeded to loot shops in Piccadilly and hold another meeting at Hyde Park Corner. The ringleaders were arrested and tried: they were Hyndman, Williams, Burns and Champion.* Williams and Burns, both workingmen, were bailed out by William Morris, the poet. Hyndman seemed to me an

---

* Jack Williams. Frequent references to him can be found in the literature, but few that reveal anything about him, even his birth and death dates.

John Elliot Burns (1858–1943). He grew up with the labor movement in England. He made it a practice to carry a large red flag at open air meetings; he was acquitted after defending himself with a speech that was reported as "The Man with the Red Flag."

Henry Hyde Champion (1859–1928). After attending Woolwich and serving in the army, he published first editions of Ibsen and Shaw, among others. He defended himself and was acquitted.

ordinary English *bourgeois* with a smattering of German reading: he was above middle height, burly and bearded; Champion, the thin, well-bred officer type with good heart and scant reading; Williams, the ordinary workingman full of class prejudices; and John Burns,* also a workingman, but really intelligent and thoughtful, who afterwards proved himself an excellent minister and resigned with Lord Morley rather than accept the world war. In spite of deficient education, Burns was even then a most interesting man; though hardly middle height, he was sturdy and exceedingly strong and brave. He had read from boyhood and we became great friends about the beginning of the century through the South African War. Burns was an early lover of Carlyle, and the experiences of a workingman's life had not blinded him to the value of individual merit. In many respects he stood on the forehead of the time to come, and if his education had been equal to his desire for knowledge, he would have been among the choicest spirits of the age. Even in 1886 I'm glad to say I rated him far above most of the politicians, though he never reached any originality of thought.

* He was the first working-man Cabinet minister, but, as Harris says, he resigned as president of the Board of Trade when the war began.

Chapter XV

The New Speaker Peel; Lord Randolph Churchill; Col. Burnaby; Wolseley; Graham; Gordon; Joke on Alfred Austin

FROM 1883 ON for thirty years I studied English life and English politics, literature and art as closely as I could. As editor first of the *Evening News* and then of the *Fortnightly Review,* I could meet almost anyone I wanted to meet, and as I made a good deal of money from time to time and soon got the name of giving excellent luncheons, I could meet even people of importance on an even footing. I may as well prove this at once for the benefit of the ordinary American journalist who declares in the *New York World* that all doors were shut in my face and that Balfour* sneered at me. Such a journalist is totally incapable of reading between the lines of plain print.

The incident he refers to is recorded in Mrs. Asquith's** *Autobiography.* "On one occasion," she wrote, "my husband and I went to a lunch given to meet Mr. Frank Harris." She goes on to tell that I monopolized the conversation and that her hero, Arthur Balfour, "scored" off me. I don't recall Balfour's "score"; I never heard him score off anyone; but the fact that the Prime Minister and his wife were asked to meet me shows that I had a very considerable position in London, and I can recall other occasions on which the Asquiths were invited to meet me by more important people.

I have explained such facts in the most modest way by saying that I gave good luncheons and had very interesting people at my table; but the Michael Monohans† and other tenth-rate American critics persist in re-

---

* (1848–1930), Prime Minister 1902–1905. Winston Churchill, in *Great Contemporaries* (rev. ed.; London, 1942), refers to a lunch with Balfour and Harris, during which Balfour "scored" off Harris.

** (1864–1945), the second wife of the Prime Minister. She was impetuous and witty. Jowett called her "the best-educated ill-educated woman that I have ever met." Besides the *Autobiography,* she wrote *Places and Persons* (1925), a record of her travels; *Lay Sermons* (1927); *Octavia* (1927), a novel; *More Memoirs* (1933); and *Off the Record* (1943).

† (1865–1933), an immigrant from Cork who became an American journalist. He is perhaps best remembered for his *Heinrich Heine, Adventurer in Life and Letters* (1910). Monahan reviewed *Contemporary Portraits* in *Forum* (1916) and called Harris a "relatively obscure journalist."

garding me as one of themselves. How did "an obscure journalist," they wonder, come to talk with this and that celebrity on an equality? Perhaps because he was not "obscure," but happened to be an equal, and I emphasize this at the beginning because it redounds to the honor of England, and, indeed, is the chief factor in making English society the most interesting in the world. London recognizes individual ability more quickly and more surely than any other city on earth. Consequently, there is here a diversity of talents not to be found elsewhere and a rich piquancy of varied interests that one seeks in vain in any other capital. Even Vienna and Paris seem dull after London, for in those cities you can always guess whom you will meet from the position of your host and hostess. In one room in London I have seen Prince Edward (afterwards King Edward) talking to Hyndman, the socialist agitator, while Lord Wolseley and Herbert Bismarck listened eagerly intent; at the same time near the fireplace Arthur Balfour, Henry Irving and Theodore Roosevelt hung on the lips of Whistler, who was telling a story.

I remember giving a lunch when I had the old Duke of Cambridge on my right and Russell Lowell, the American ambassador on my left, besides Beerbohm Tree and Willy Grenfell (now Lord Desborough),* John Burns, the firebrand agitator, afterwards an M.P. and minister, the poet George Wyndham and Alfred Russel Wallace, all listening spellbound to the humor and eloquence of Oscar Wilde; and it was the uncle of the Queen** who had asked me to invite him, as he had heard so much of Wilde's genius.

I want to tell of these men and of many others at least as justly renowned in order to give a picture of those crowded days of London in the last decades of the nineteenth and the first of the twentieth century.

As I have said, cherishing the ambition of going into the House of Commons myself, I was at first more eager to know the politicians than the poets. I took pains to be present every evening in the House for several years, until I had learned not only to know the fifty or sixty more prominent members, but also the procedure, traditions and tone of the Assembly. It is often spoken of as unique, ideal and all the rest of it, and the House of Commons must certainly be regarded as the finest deliberative assembly in the world. In the first year or so the circumstance that made the greatest impression on me was the election of Mr. Arthur Peel early in 1884 to the

---

* Duke of Cambridge (1819–1904), first cousin of the Queen, the only male issue of Adolpus Frederich, who was the youngest son of George III. He had in 1840 a morganatic marriage to an actress, Miss Louisa Fairbrother, disregarding the Royal Marriage Act.

James Russell Lowell (1819–91), appointed ambassador to the Court of St. James by President Hayes in 1880.

William Henry Grenfell (1855–1945), a Liberal M.P. on and off until he broke with Gladstone over Home Rule in 1892; he was elected as a Conservative M.P. in 1900. He was a well known sportsman and athlete.

** As noted, the Duke of Cambridge was cousin, not uncle, to Queen Victoria.

Speakership, instead of Mr. Brand, whom I knew, who was retiring as Lord Hampden.* At that time few members even knew anything of Arthur Peel, who was the youngest son of the famous prime minister, and who had been almost undistinguished as a member from Warwick for many years. But the moment he got on his feet to return thanks for his election everyone was thrilled. He was fairly tall, had a good presence, a dark, bearded face set off by a high aquiline nose, an ordinary, baritone voice; yet he had an air of masterful dignity that was impressive; and what he said was noteworthy.

I shall always remember one long sentence, badly constructed, but perfectly natural—the talk of a man thinking aloud and not one reciting a carefully prepared oration—yet carrying in clumsy words a curious sense of authority. "With the support of the House," he said, "I may be permitted," and he paused—"to enforce the unwritten law, the most cherished and inestimable tradition of this House, I mean that personal courtesy, that interchange of chivalry between member and member—compatible with the most effective party debate—which is one of the oldest, and I humbly trust may always be, the most cherished of the traditions of this great Assembly." The sensation was astonishing: everyone felt that he had struck the right note, and had struck it with an almost magical dignity of personal character. From that moment the Speaker held the house in awe. Not his impartiality alone, but his greatness of character was never questioned. Ever afterwards I had a higher opinion of the House of Commons; perhaps among the ruck of silent members whom one didn't know, there might be another Arthur Peel!

I followed the debates more closely than ever and I was able to do this most comfortably through the kindness of Lord Randolph Churchill, whom I came to know well about this time. As soon as he found that I had some difficulty now and then in getting a seat in the "Distinguished Stranger's Gallery," he spoke to the Speaker and to the funny little Master of Arms, Gossett, whom I never saw but in his court dress with little sword, knickers and black silk stockings; and so got me a seat on the floor of the House itself in a sort of pew set apart for the half dozen of the Speaker's friends. There I could hear and see everything, even with my short sight, as if I had been a member.

My first meeting with Lord Randolph Churchill impressed me hugely. He was always represented by *Punch* and the comic papers as a very small man, or even as a boy, in spite of a ferocious upturned moustache. To my astonishment I found he was a good five feet nine or ten inches in height and carried himself bravely. The peculiarity of his face was seldom or

---

* Arthur Peel (1829–1912), Speaker of the House of Commons 1884–95; he had represented Warwick 1865–85. His speech of acceptance was indeed highly admired; he was called by *The Times* "another Peel," a great compliment.
   Henry Robert Brand (1841–1906). He succeeded to the titles Viscount Hampden and Baron Dacre in 1892.

never caricatured; it consisted of a pair of prominent round grey-blue eyes, well deserving the nickname of goggle-eyes. The face was peculiarly expressive of anger or contempt, but a second glace showed that the features were all fairly regular and the shape of the head quite excellent. Altogether a personable man, but when he spoke in the House, he often stood with one hand akimbo on his hip, which, with his thick, upturned, dark moustache, gave him a cocky or cheeky look and led the would-be humorists to treat him as an impudent boy; and he was assuredly lacking in reverence for his elders and supposed leaders in the House of Commons.

At the very beginning he invited me to come one afternoon to the Carlton Club to talk over some incident in the Bradlaugh imbroglio.* I was struck almost at once by the surpassing generalship in the man and by his colossal assurance. Oddly enough, I had come to the meeting without having lunched, and as I knew it was not allowed to give food to a non-member in the Carlton, I mentioned à propos de bottes that I was sharp set. At once he declared that he would have something brought up at once, and when I reminded him of the rule, he shrugged his shoulders, rang, and when the footman came, gave his order with such deliberate curtness that the man was only anxious to get away and do what he was told. I got an excellent lunch and a good bottle of wine in a jiffy: as usual, in England I found that mean rules were made for mean men.

Soon after our first meeting I talked to Randolph of Bradlaugh, for I had formed a high opinion of Bradlaugh's character when he lectured in America. Randolph was proud of an incident that Winston has told excellently in his *Life,* and so I make no apology for reproducing it here.

"On February 21 there was another Bradlaugh scene. The member for Northampton, advancing suddenly to the table, produced a book, said to be a Testament, from his pocket, and duly swore himself upon it, to the consternation of the members. Lord Randolph was the first to recover from the surprise which this act of audacity created. He declared that Mr. Bradlaugh, by the outrage of taking in defiance of the House an oath of a meaningless character upon a book alleged to be a Testament—it might have been the *Fruits of Philosophy*—had vacated his seat and should be treated as if he were dead." In moving for a new writ, he implored the House to act promptly and vindicate its authority. Mr. Gladstone, however, persuaded both sides to put off the decision until the next day. On the 22nd therefore

* Charles Bradlaugh (1833–91), a freethinker, social reformer and Liberal. When, in 1876, in collaboration with Annie Besant, he advocated birth control in a pamphlet, he was very nearly fined and imprisoned. When, upon being elected from Northampton to the House of Commons in 1880, he claimed the right to affirm rather than swear an oath on the Bible, the House refused to seat him. He was re-elected three times more, and by 1882 was willing to take the oath, but on each occasion the House refused him. In 1885 Arthur Peel, the Speaker, allowed no objections to his taking the oath and he was finally seated. He served the House well enough that in 1891, shortly before his death, it expunged from its record all resolutions expelling him.

a debate on privilege ensued. Sir Stafford Northcote merely moved to exclude Mr. Bradlaugh from the precincts of the House, thus modifying Lord Randolph's motion for a new writ. Lord Randolph protested against such a 'milk and water' policy and urged the immediate punishment of the offender. After a long discussion, in which the temper of all parties was inflamed by Mr. Bradlaugh's repeated interruptions, Sir Stafford substituted for his simple motion of exclusion a proposal to expel Mr. Bradlaugh from the House; and this being carried, the seat for Northampton was thereby vacated.

"Lord Randolph seems to have gained much credit in Tory circles for the promptness and energy with which he had acted," his son writes.

Then came the Kilmainham negotiations and Mr. Parnell's release, and on top of all the murder in Phoenix Park of Lord Frederick Cavendish and Mr. Burke.* But alas! Randolph had fallen seriously ill and was out of the fight for half a year. Everyone said that had Randolph been able to head the attack on the Kilmainham Treaty, Gladstone's government would have fallen.

He returned to a triumph. The Liberals had been asked by their Whips not to take part in the discussion on Egypt** and Randolph at once jeered at them "for assisting in the capacity of mutes at the funeral obsequies of free speech." I give this as a proof of his power of speech, though it was his captaincy I always admired, and not his eloquence. Years later, talking with Lord Hartington of Randolph's career, I found that he whom I always regarded as "the conscience of the House of Commons" agreed with me in my estimate of Randolph.

He told me how annoyed Gladstone was with Randolph over the Bradlaugh business. "He doesn't believe in Christianity," said Gladstone, "yet is not ashamed to use the religious prejudices of others to gain some paltry political advantage."

"But at length," said Lord Hartington, "the chiefs of both parties found themselves in one lobby and the majority of the House with Randolph in the other, which convinced me that Randolph was a strategist without an equal. And later no one ever led the House of Commons as he did: he knew the House better than it knew itself. As a Parliamentarian he had no equal, no second, even, in my experience."

* Cavendish (1836–82), chief secretary to the lord-lieutenant of Ireland. Thomas Burke (1829–82), undersecretary for Ireland. They were killed in Phoenix Park, near Dublin, by members of the "Invincibles," a secret society. Burke was marked by the Invincibles for murder; Cavendish, who was not recognized by the killers, died only because he was at Burke's side.

** In 1882, Ahmed Arabi, a fellah officer, led a revolt against the dual control of Egypt by England and France. There was a massacre of Christians at Alexandria in July. By September the revolt had been crushed by British troops under Gen. Wolseley, and the leaders of the revolt, including Arabi, were brought to trial. There was much sympathy for the Egyptians in Parliament: John Bright (1811–89) regarded the bombardment of Alexandria by British warships as "a manifest violation both of international law and of the moral law" and accordingly resigned from the government.

In our first talk I recognized the qualities in Randolph of a great captain, not as clearly as I saw them later, but clearly enough to see in him a reincarnation of the peculiar power of his ancestor, the first Duke. He had, too, at this time an extraordinary geniality and a passionate belief in the efficacy of a series of reforms which I thought merely lenitive, but which he lauded as distinctively English. I shall have much more to say of him later, but here, because it has become the fashion to sneer at him, I wish to put it on record that no one could meet him, as no one could meet Parnell, without recognizing greatness in him. Both of them made a far deeper impression on me than Gladstone, though he was infinitely the most articulate of the two.

In these first years of my editorship I got to know A. M. Broadley,* who wrote for the *World* and made himself prominent as a defender of Arabi Pasha and Egyptian independence. It was Broadley who introduced me to Colonel Burnaby,** who, too, was a whole-hearted partisan of Lord Randolph Churchill. Fred Burnaby was another extraordinary personality, physically, I think, the finest specimen of manhood I've ever seen: over six feet four inches in height and some forty-seven inches around the chest. Stories innumerable were told of his bodily strength and most of them, I believe, were true. When he joined the Horse Guards, some young subalterns got two donkeys through the window into his bedroom. Coming home late one night, Burnaby found them, and taking one under each arm, carried them quietly downstairs. I saw him once take a poker in his hands and bend it. He was good-looking withal: large forehead and chin, straight, heavy nose and really fine, kindly, laughing eyes set well apart, while a heavy dark moustache partially concealed suasive lips. Had I met him fifteen years earlier I might have made a hero of him, for he was intelligent as well as strong; he spoke, too, half a dozen languages and was completely devoid of snobbism or "side." I always felt grateful to him for taking me up as he did. It pleased him that I had read his *Ride to Khiva,* and he told me a story about it that amused me.

On his return to England after his famous "Ride," he was invited to dinner at Windsor to tell the Queen about his adventures. Of course he obeyed the order, got into the train at Waterloo and fell fast asleep, did not change at Weybridge, but went on to Basingstoke, where he woke up. He had then to persuade the station master to make up a special train and send him back to Windsor. "The dearest dinner I ever had in my life," was his humorous comment on the incident.

* (1847–1916), special correspondent for *The Times,* not the *World.* He had been trained in law, so he was equipped to become counsel to Arabi Pasha and the other state prisoners in 1882, of which he wrote in *How We Defended Arabi* (1883).

** Frederick Gustavus Burnaby (1842–85). The feats of strength mentioned by Harris were apparently common talk. Burnaby ran for a seat in the House in 1878 as a Conservative, but was defeated. He contracted a heart and lung disease by 1884, just before he went to the Sudan. *The Ride to Khiva* is an engaging enough story; it was also popular, going through eleven printings in its first year.

We were talking one afternoon about bodily exercise and muscular development when somewhat to my astonishment, Burnaby was all in favor of moderation. "Especially in youth," he said, "we can easily overdo it and develop our muscles at the cost of our vital energy. I don't know how to put it better," he went on, "but I'm sure I'm overdeveloped. I've seen little slips of fellows get the passionate love of fine women, while great athletes are never remarkable as lovers." He spoke with bitterness and I took it as a personal confession, for I had noticed the same truth; and everyone knew later that poor Burnaby's marriage was not happy. Yet Roman ladies and even empresses chose gladiators as lovers: why?

Burnaby came to grief in a way that throws a certain light on the English aristocratic code. One of his brother officers, a captain, I think, had an intrigue with a lady and used to go to meet her at some rooms in the Temple. One day Burnaby on his way to Broadley crossed this officer in the square. Probably he told Broadley jokingly of the *rencontre*. At any rate next week in the *World,* which Broadley wrote for, there appeared a paragraph warning the officer in question not to be caught on his way to N°——in the Temple, as everyone knew the attraction.

The officer called a meeting of his brother officers in the regiment and accused Burnaby of being the tell-tale. Burnaby, essentially truthful, could only say that he did not recall mentioning the fact; but it leaked out that Broadley was the paragraphist and the officers thereupon sent Burnaby, their colonel, to Coventry; and a little later, when Prince Edward was to dine with the regiment, the officers notified Burnaby that if he appeared, no other officer would come to the table. This boycott cut Burnaby to the heart. Before going out to serve in the Sudan with Wolseley's expedition to save Gordon, Burnaby invited me to dinner in his rooms. I had often dined with him before and was always interested. He touched life on a great many more sides than the ordinary English officer; he was well read in three or four literatures and eagerly receptive to all that was fine in art and life. He was an excellent companion, too; told a good story with subtle humor and was essentially large-hearted and generous. In memory I put Fred Burnaby almost with Dick Burton among the noblest men I've known. After the dinner he told me quietly he didn't intend to come back alive. "It seems funny," he remarked in the air, "to be under sentence of death, but within a month or so I shall have entered the great 'Perhaps', as Danton I think called 'the undiscovered country'."

I argued passionately against his decision, told him his life and achievements as a great adventurer loomed bigger in my eyes than the whole corps of officers. "I'd give a wilderness of monkeys and mediocrities," I cried, "for one Burnaby. For God's sake, get hold of yourself and live out a great life to a noble end."

"Perhaps you don't know of the way I'm boycotted?" he asked.

"I've heard of it through Broadley," I replied; but I had heard, too, that

Colonel Ralph Vivian,* who was immensely popular, had turned away from Burnaby markedly a few weeks before in Hyde Park, and I had realized for months past that Burnaby was wounded to the soul.

Now he unburdened his pent-up sorrow.

"Life's a more difficult game than we are apt to imagine in youth," he began. "Who could have a better start than I? Fairly well born with perfect health, great strength, height, too, and not so ugly as a wolf, as the French say; endowed besides, with fair brains, good verbal memory, love of adventure and travel and minded seriously to make the best of all my advantages. At thirty-five invited to Windsor, a personage in society with an uncommon reputation, and the position of a Colonel of the Guards; and at forty through no crime, no fault of my own an outlaw, an outcast." (He spoke with intense bitterness.) "I have no chance of recovery and am the worse off that the outside is still brilliant. Thank God, I know how to die!" And the whole face was transfigured, lit up by indomitable resolution and joyous courage.

"Don't talk like that!" I cried, appalled by the chill of death in the air. "I can't listen to you; it's not worthy of your brains or sense. You have done no intentional wrong," I went on. "Your position is really the revolt of commonplace idiots against a personality, someone of distinction and achievement. It's your business to live it all down, walk through it unheeding. You remember Goethe said, 'When the King rides abroad, the village curs all bark at his horse's heels.' Let 'em bark."

But Burnaby would not be encouraged. "If things were different at home," he sighed, "I might try. But no, I'm a failure, Harris; have come to grief everywhere, so 'one fight more, the best and the last' "; and again the eyes, gladly.

I can't reproach myself. I did all I knew, argued with him, assured him that the highest public opinion would not condemn him; begged him for the sake of all of us who cared for him to play the game out. At length he interrupted me: "The die is cast: I'm going out to the Sudan at the beginning of the week. I'll consider what you've said and I'm infinitely obliged to you for saying it, but each man, my friend, must 'drie his own weird'."**

Tears were in my eyes and my heart was sore as we parted. All the world knows how nobly Burnaby gave his life in the battle of Abou Klea in the Sudan. The Arab rush had broken the British square and the next moment the dervishes would have entered and swept away the formation, when the giant Burnaby hurled himself into the gap in front of his old comrades of the Blues and stemmed the torrent. As the square reformed behind him, Burnaby still fighting, though bleeding from a dozen wounds, went down with an Arab spear through his throat. He had saved a thousand

* (1845–1924). Actually he was in the Scots Guards; he served with distinction in the Egyptian campaign.
** A corruption of *dree one's weird*.

lives and turned disaster into victory. Bennett Burleigh,* the famous war correspondent of the *Telegraph,* wrote to me afterwards that Burnaby saved 'all our lives.'

As I read of his heroic death I cried like a child and then wondered whether his fellow officers were still proud of their idiotic boycott. To me dear Fred Burnaby was the hero of the Sudan, and not Charles Gordon.

I never cared for Chinese Gordon** greatly, perhaps because he was so extolled on all hands, beslobbered with the cheap adulation of those who didn't even know him by sight. I went to interview him for the *Evening News* when he came over from Brussels at Gladstone's behest and was about to start for the Sudan to free the garrisons beleaguered by the forces of the Mahdi. Perhaps because I didn't expect much, I got little or nothing from him. According to Stead and the *Pall Mall Gazette,* he was a "Christian hero . . . Christ's warrior," a blasphemous contradiction in terms only possible in England or America. Charles Gordon was un-English in one respect: there was absolutely no "side" about him; he was transparently simple and sincere. He was good-looking too, with a remarkable forehead, both broad and high. But I discounted large foreheads, for my experience rather justified the German word:

Gross Stirn
Wenig Gehirn,†

though Victor Hugo's praise is apt to infect all of us. Hugo said finely that a large forehead had much the same effect as an expanse of sky in a landscape.

I certainly did not understand Gordon. When I asked him why he gave up his intention to go to the Congo in order to go to Khartoum instead, he smiled, saying the need in the Sudan was more urgent. "He would go to the Congo later," he added, "if God willed." I gathered that he looked on himself as an instrument in God's hands to do whatever he was called upon to do.†† His fatalistic belief seemed to me childish, the result of success and

* (? –1914). He had previously fought in the American Civil War, during which he was twice captured and sentenced to death. He also accompanied Wolseley on the Ashanti expedition. He joined the *Telegraph* in 1882.

** Charles George Gordon (1833–85). He acquired the name "Chinese" from his having taken part in the siege of Peking in 1860 and then having raised a Chinese army to crush the Taiping rebellion. He had been governor of the Sudan in 1877; he was sent in 1884 to suppress a revolt of the Mahdi. He was besieged at Khartoum for ten months while a bewildered government at home wondered what to do. His *Khartoum Diaries* are a vivid record of those trying days. Relief arrived two days after Khartoum had been overcome and Gordon killed. Gladstone's government fell in 1885 partly because of public indignation over his death.

† Large forehead,
  small brain

†† Harris' impression of Gordon very much resembles that of Strachey in *Eminent Victorians.*

much praise working on a poor brain. His conceit or, if you will, his faith, went beyond reason. He had no insight into men or events. As soon as he reached Khartoum he startled Baring* and shocked Gladstone by asking that his old enemy, Zebehr Pasha, the notorious slave-trader, should be sent up from Cairo to help him. Now some of us remembered that Zebehr Pasha's son, Suleiman, got up a rebellion in 1879 in Darfour against Gordon and his lieutenant, Gessi. Gessi beat Suleiman in battle, took him prisoner, and then in cold blood had him executed. Baring was of the opinion that Zebehr would do Gordon harm, and Gladstone's prejudice against the slave-dealer being insuperable, Zebehr was denied to Gordon.

As if to mock his belief in providence, events fought against Gordon from the beginning. Scarcely had he reached Khartoum when the Mahdi's** lieutenant, Osman Digna, took Sinkat by storm and put not only the Egyptian garrison, but every man, woman and child in the place to the sword. No wonder the garrison at Tokar made friends with their savage foe and surrendered on terms, a great many going over, heart and hand, to the enemy. Then Khartoum was threatened and a Christian England forced Gladstone's hand and a military expedition was set on foot to save the savior.

General Wolseley of course led the British forces and he determined, in memory, I imagine, of his Red River Expedition, to go up the Nile instead of taking the short cut by Suakim and Berber. The whole, silly tragi-comedy discovered to me as by a lightning flash all the unspeakable stupidity of government by democracy, which means today by an ill-informed press and a sentimental loud-voiced minority.

Yet amid all the hubbub there came suddenly the voice of an authentic man. One morning *The Times* published a letter from the Mahdi, if I remember rightly, to the English government. It was astoundingly well written and translated into pure Biblical English of the best. I haven't got it, I'm sorry to say, but it made an indelible impression on me as the greatest document published in my time, superior even to the letter Parnell published when Gladstone threw him over in the O'Shea divorce case.†

* Evelyn Baring, (1841–1917). He was made British commissioner of the Egyptian public debt office; in 1879 Baring became British controller-general. He returned to Egypt after Arabi Pasha's revolt in 1883. He served until 1907 as British agent and consul general, and he was eventually the ruler of the country, introducing reforms in finance, administration, and education.
He wanted Egypt to abandon the Sudan when the Mahdi began to show strength, and it was decided that Gordon should head a mission to relieve the Egyptian troops there. Baring agreed to Gordon's appointment only when Gordon was given to understand that he was to evacuate, not hold, the Sudan.
** Mohammed Ahmed Ibn Seyyid Abdullah (1848–85), who had promised to relieve his people of oppressors.
† This was the occasion turned to account by Labouchère in a first-rate pun: he was asked in the smoking-room what he thought of the news that O'Shea had begun his suit, after years of patience. "When I think of O'Shea and Parnell," he said, "I recall the Latin word *otium cum dignitate* pronounced 'osheeum.' " (F.H.)

The Mahdi asked the English why they were coming out against him with horse, foot and artillery? Didn't they know that if they were working with God and for His high purpose, a small force would be invincible? Whereas if their aim was selfish and cruel, no force would be sufficient. Tell me what you want, he said practically, and if it is right and just, you will have no difficulty; on the other hand, if your purpose is secret and evil, you are only ploughing the sand. Addressed really to Gladstone, the wording of the appeal was irresistibly comic; the old Christian rhetor hoist on a petard of his own manufacture.

The whole summer England followed the expedition up the Nile with breathless interest. At length in December, after the victory of Abou Klea, a dash to Khartoum was resolved on. As if to demonstrate the utter worthlessness of his judgment, Gordon sent down a message on 29 December that "Khartoum was all right and could hold out for years."* But Wolseley knew better and early in January, Sir Charles Wilson made his dash for Khartoum; he found the town had already fallen and the Mahdist forces fired on his steamer from the walls. "Gordon a prisoner" was the first report; and then came the truth. Hearing the noise of the Mahdist inrush, Gordon ran out of his palace with drawn sword and was stabbed to death in the entrance to his palace. The whole costly expedition was turned thereby into a fiasco. Were the forces to return and give up the Sudan to the slave-dealer and the Mahdi? Gladstone wished to do this, but aristocratic England could not so easily accept defeat!

As soon as Wolseley returned to England I made it my business to see him, and I was interested to find that his view of men and affairs was not very different from my own. Wolseley was always to me a lightweight: no power of personality, no depth of insight, an ordinary English gentleman with much experience of affairs. By dint of rubbing against abler men than himself he had got a sort of clever woman's *flair* for what was going on above his head; eminently kind and fair-minded, too, with an ambition altogether out of proportion to his capacity. All this and more was illustrated by some stories he told me. I had been asking him about courage and he astonished me by saying that a volunteer army was always better than a conscript army. "One in three of the conscripts," he added, "is sure to be a coward and that minority may bring disaster at almost any time." Somehow or other he convinced me. Then the talk came on Gordon, as most talks did about that time. "Oh you know," he began, "Gordon and I were in the Crimea together, every day side by side for hours in the trench before the Redan."

"Really," I exclaimed. "That must have been interesting!"

"Very interesting," he went on "and an object lesson in that courage we were talking about. Towards the end the trench got within eighty yards or so of the ramparts of the fort and was so shallow and muddy-wet that it

---

* To the contrary, Gordon on December 14 (1884), wrote that if he were not given 200 men within ten days, the town might fall.

did not give us much shelter. At six o'clock each evening we went off duty and others came in our stead. Gerald Graham,* now General Sir Gerald Graham, was the bravest man I ever knew: six feet-odd in height and handsome to boot. Every night as the clock struck Graham used to get up, put his hands in his pockets and stroll off towards his quarters. Soon the Russians remarked this and gathered in the evening on the near rampart for a pot-shot at the big Englishman. As luck would have it, they always missed him. I remonstrated with him again and again. 'It can be only a question of time, Graham,' I said, 'and they'll get you. For God's sake, don't be so foolhardy.' But Graham went on turning himself into a cockshot every evening for weeks and I assure you after ten days or so it was a miracle how he escaped, for some hundreds used to shoot at him and the bullets buzzed like bees."

"You didn't imitate him?" I asked, laughing.

"No, indeed," Wolseley replied seriously. "Even at that time I meant to be Commander-in-Chief of the British Army if I could manage it, and so every evening I crawled along the muddy wet trench for a couple of hundred yards or so on my belly till I was fairly out of range. I thought myself far too valuable to make myself a cockshy."

"And Gordon," I asked, "Gordon was a subaltern with you. How did he act?"

"None of us could make Gordon out at that time," Wolseley replied. "One evening he'd get up, bold as brass, link arms with Graham, and stroll off with him as if the nearest Russian marksman was a thousand miles away. I came to understand bit by bit that it was all a question of his prayers with Gordon. If God had accorded him some sign of approval, he'd stroll away with Graham wholly unconcerned; if, on the other hand, he was left in doubt of the divine guidance, he'd crawl through the mud lower than I thought necessary, and longer. Gordon was a queer fish; but Graham was the bravest of the brave.

"I remember afterwards in the Chinese war meeting Graham by chance," Wolseley continued. "One evening I saw a big man on horseback in the mist and ran across to ask some question. When I reached him I saw it was Graham and in my delight I slapped him on the thigh as I put my question. 'That's all right,' he answered me, 'but please don't slap that thigh: I've just got a bullet in there,' and as I looked at my hand, it was all crimson. Graham paid no more attention to wounds than to danger. You know he got the V.C. I tried time and again to get it but had no luck; life will not give us all our desires."

To my amazement he was disappointed! Fancy a leader of armies wanting the V.C.!

Wolseley was an interesting man, though I think these stories of Gordon and Graham the best I ever got from him. Still, he had led an eventful life

* (1831–99). As Wolseley says, for his bravery at the Redan he won the V.C.

and his memories of the Civil War in America* fascinated me and I shall have to tell them later, for they explain why I worked to get him made Commander-in-Chief and so attain the summit of his ambition. For a good many years we met and dined together half a dozen times every season and he was always an excellent host; and perhaps he enjoyed my cow-punching stories as much as I delighted in his memories of Stonewall Jackson and Robert E. Lee.

It was at Wolseley's house much later when he was the Ranger at Woolwich** that I made a little jest which has been attributed to others. Alfred Austin† had just been appointed Poet Laureate by Lord Salisbury, though he had no more poetry in his composition than a house-fly. He had other merits, however. For years he had written leading articles in the *Standard* and praised Lord Salisbury in and out of season. Accordingly, when Lord Tennyson died, Lord Salisbury appointed Alfred Austin to the post: "Alfred the Little, after Alfred the Great," as some anonymous wit declared. Of course Lord Salisbury should have appointed Swinburne or any one of half a dozen poets greater than this little creature, but no! He appointed his eulogist—a disgraceful outrage on English poetry, the gravity of which he was incapable even of understanding.

I had met Austin often and thought him a mere journalist and place-hunter without talent or personality, but this evening when we met at Wolseley's he treated me with marked condescension. "I've known Mr. Harris," he said, "when he was merely editor of the *Evening News*."

His tone was so high and mighty that I replied, "I hear now that you write poetry as well as prose; which do you intend to use in the future?"

"Oh now," he replied, "I must write a certain amount of poetry."

"Why?" I replied, pretending ignorance.

"Oh, to keep the wolf from the door," he replied, smiling.

"I see," I retorted, "I see, very good: you read your poetry to the wolf, eh?" Austin used to avoid me afterwards, but the word pleased me infinitely, perhaps, because I was seldom witty.

* Wolseley wrote an article for *Blackwood's Magazine* in 1863 on Robert E. Lee and Stonewall Jackson, whom he had met in the U.S. the year before.
** A Royal Military Academy for engineering and artillery.
† (1835–1913).

Chapter XVI

Memories of John Ruskin*

I NEVER MET ANY ONE in my life whose personal appearance disappointed me more than Ruskin's. Until I saw him, I had always believed that a man of great ability showed his genius in some feature or other, but I could find nothing in Ruskin's face or figure that suggested abnormal talent. His appearance was not even prepossessing. He looked shrivelled up and shrunken: though he was perhaps five feet eight or nine in height, he was slight to frailty and stooped; in spite of a prominent, beaked nose, his face too was small, bony-thin and very wrinkled; the grey hair that must once have been reddish was carefully brushed flat; the beard and whiskers were grey, too, and straggling-thin; the eyes were bright, greyish-blue in color, now quick-glancing, now meditative under the thick out-jutting brows; the high aquiline bird-nose was set off by a somewhat receding chin. He looked like some old, unhappy bird, nothing in the face or figure impressive or arresting. His clothes even were old-fashioned: he wore a dark blue frock coat and a very little blue tie; his manner was shy, self-conscious, unassured. I was disappointed to doubting his ability. But as soon as he got excited in speaking his voice carried me away, a thin, high tenor, irresistibly pathetic; it often wailed and sometimes cursed but was always intense; the soul of the man in that singular, musical voice with its noble rhetoric and impassioned moral appeal.

Of course, I knew a great deal about him before I met him, knew he had been a great friend of Carlyle's, knew he was perhaps the most extraordinary master of poetic English prose since Sir Thomas Browne.

I met him first, I think, at the Baroness Burdett Coutts's in Piccadilly. At any rate, wherever it was, my introducer had told Ruskin that I had been a great admirer of Carlyle and that Carlyle had said he expected considerable things from me. This recommendation of Carlyle evidently influenced Ruskin, who treated me from the beginning with caressing kindness.

According to his wish, I called on him, I think, at Morley's Hotel, in Trafalgar Square. It was, I believe, in 1886, but it may have been a year earlier or a year later. I have only disjointed memoranda of our talks. At

* (1819–1900).

first we spoke about Carlyle and I found that Ruskin admired him at least as fervently as I did. At the first pause in the conversation I told him that what he had written on Calais Church always remained with me as perhaps the best piece of description in English, superior even to Carlyle's description of the scene before the battle of Dunbar. "I've so much wanted to know," I confessed, "how you attained such mastery of style so early."

"Poets and imaginative writers are usually precocious, don't you think?" he began with heart-winning courtesy, putting me at once on his own level, in spite of the difference between us in age and position. We talked on that theme for some time, but suddenly he startled me. "I suppose I was precocious," he said, "in many ways. I was in love, I remember, over head and ears in love before I was fifteen."

As I knew he had been divorced from his wife, who declared that the marriage had never been consummated, this astonished me to amazement.

"Really!" I exclaimed, "whom with?"

"A Domecq girl—the daughters of my father's Spanish partner in the wine-business," he explained. "I met them all in Paris when I was fourteen: 'A Southern Cross of Unconceived Stars,' I called them and fell prone in love before Adèle, who was a blonde, a little older than I was. Two or three years later they visited us at Herne Hill, and I remember when I was eighteen or so writing verses on 'her grace, her glory, her smile'; but when I confided to my father that I wanted to marry her, he quickly disillusioned me. 'Your mother would never consent, John,' he said. 'She's a Roman Catholic!'

"I loved my mother and besides was very religious at that time, though not so religious as all that; yet it was soon settled, as life has a trick of settling things. Adèle came to Herne Hill again on a visit in 1839, when I was twenty years of age, but gave me no hope; indeed, I think she did not take me seriously, even; was simply amused and flattered by my devotion. She married the next year, in 1840, and so went out of my life. That affected my health; I was delicate for some years."

Ruskin made an impression on me of a most affectionate, sweet nature; at every meeting he would take my hand and grip it with an intensity of good feeling. At the same time, there was about him a sort of wistful weakness, as of one whose life was full of regrets; and of course I was all agog to find out about his marriage. I had already noticed that if I let him talk, he would soon begin to talk about himself and say things that were of great interest to me. All I had to do was to profess admiration and start him with a question and soon he would become reminiscent and personal— pathetically anxious, I thought, to justify and proclaim himself.

We had been talking, I believe, about Carlyle's deep love for his wife, when Ruskin suddenly told me off hand that he had never been in love at all with his wife, Miss Gray.* When he was about twenty-eight,** he said,

* Euphemia (Effie) Chalmers Gray.
** Actually, Ruskin was twenty-six at the time.

she came to stay with them at Denmark Hill. His mother wanted the match and "She (Miss Gray) was very pleasant and kind, so in April '48 I married her. I had already lost nearly all my religious faith. I went to Normandy with my wife and began *The Seven Lamps of Architecture*.

"When I was a little over thirty, we returned to live in Park Street and I got to know Carlyle and another of your friends, Coventry Patmore* and the Pre-Rafaelites. In 1853 we went to Scotland with Millais** and Millais did my portrait. It was there I discovered that my wife loved Millais. I went to his studio one morning and opened the door quietly, without the faintest suspicion—there they were in each other's arms on the sofa. I was startled and involuntarily stepped back, drawing the door quietly to after me. What was I to do? I was a little shocked but I had never loved her, so there was no pang of pain. I was merely annoyed but I had my dignity to consider. I resolved simply to be more ceremonious than I had been."

I stared my astonishment and Ruskin must have felt it, for he began to explain.

"I did not wish to break off with him. I thought I had no right to. My portrait was not finished and I wanted it finished: I thought it might be one of the great portraits of the world; but I wanted, too, to keep my dignity." I could scarcely help grinning; what had dignity to do with it? But Ruskin went on, "I thought him, and still think, him, a very great master, so I was simply scrupulously polite until the portrait was finished and then he went away. I have no doubt he felt the difference in my manner. I was very cold and reserved and he was not so boisterous as he had been sometimes, or jovial-coarse.

"A little later, my wife left me and brought an action for divorce.† Of course I did not defend it; I had no interest in it. A year later, in 1854, she got her freedom and married Millais. I am rather proud of the fact that, even after this, I wrote enthusiastically about Millais' genius as a painter. Personally they never touched me, never came near me!"

I don't remember how I started him off again, but I think I asked him how he came to admire Turner so early. "I always knew a good deal about painting," he began, "and I was the first, I think, to see Turner's real greatness; I bought many of his works before I was twenty-three. You know I published the first volume of *Modern Painters* when I was twenty-four.

"When Turner died and left his paintings to the nation, I went to see them and found them still in boxes in the cellars of the National Gallery, unappreciated, seemingly—altogether uncared for. I thereupon wrote to Lord Palmerston, I think, the Prime Minister, and told him I should be very proud, indeed, if I were allowed to put Turner's works in order. He put me in communication with the trustees and I was duly appointed, and all through '57 and half through '58 I worked at classifying Turner's pic-

---

* (1823–96), the Pre-Raphaelite poet.
** Sir John Everett Millais (1829–96); a founder of the Pre-Raphaelite movement.
† The marriage was annulled; it had never been consummated.

tures and getting them in order and mounting his water colors. Then came one of the worst blows of my whole life.

"I had always believed that the good and the pure and the beautiful were one, various manifestations of the Divine. Again and again I had associated beauty of color in painting with holiness of life. I knew, of course, that the rule was not invariable: Titian was supposed to have lived a loose life; they even talk about him in connection with his daughter, but it seemed to me like madness, a mere legend, not to be considered. I always cherished the belief that Goodness and Wisdom and Purity and Truth went together with great talent, and Turner was my hero. One day (I think it was in '57) I came across a portfolio filled with painting after painting of Turner's of the most shameful sort—the *pudenda* of women—utterly inexcusable and to me inexplicable.

"I went to work to find out all about it and I ascertained that my hero used to leave his house in Chelsea and go down to Wapping on Friday afternoon and live there until Monday morning with the sailors' women, painting them in every posture of abandonment. What a life! And what a burden it cast upon me! What was I to do?

"For weeks I was in doubt and miserable, though time and again I put myself in tune with the highest, till suddenly it flashed on me that perhaps I had been selected as the one man capable of coming in this matter to a great decision. I took the hundreds of scrofulous sketches and paintings and burnt them where they were, burnt all of them. Don't you think I did right? I am proud of it, proud—" and his lower lip went up over the upper with a curious effect of most obstinate resolution.

I thought it the most extraordinary confession I had ever heard; I remember that it kept me from visiting Ruskin for days and days. In fact, the next time we met he came and called upon me in my little house in Kensington Gore, opposite the Park. I kept away from the Turner question: I felt sure we should quarrel over it, or rather that I should offend him as I had offended other friends with what seemed to me the plain truth. What possible right had he to destroy another man's work, not to speak of the work of one whom he extolled as a heaven-born genius. So I talked of Carlyle and his teaching.

He admitted to me that it was Carlyle who had practically made him a socialist, though "I was already on the road," he added with huge glee. "I found once, you know, that Xenophon, four hundred years before Christ came upon the earth, had talked about 'common fellows in the mart, who were always thinking how they could buy cheapest and sell dearest.' Our modern Gospel!" he added in a tone of triumphant disdain, "Fit only for 'common fellows!' "

"Which do you think your best work?" I asked Ruskin once. "The revelations of art and natural beauty or your sociological books?"

"They form a whole," he replied, pursing out his lower lip in deep thought, "but most people seem to prefer my *Fors—Fors Clavigera*, I mean. Don't you know," he added merrily, "that it was Carlyle who christened my *Fors Clavigera* 'Fors Clavivinegar'?"

Of course I laughed with him, but the jest seemed to me to be poor!

Now and then Ruskin came and spent the evening with me, I remember, in Kensington Gore, but he came oftener to lunch, when we would talk afterwards and I would drive him back to his hotel.

I remember one day telling him how extraordinary it seemed to me that he should have won to such emotion of style without passion.

He turned on me at once. "Why do you say that? I loved more than once passionately: if I had married Adèle, the marriage would have been consummated, I can assure you. But much later, when I was over forty, I fell in love, oh! in love and was consumed as in a flame. Love, love, has been my undoing!" he added in a thin sad voice.

"Really?" I queried, genuinely surprised. "Would you tell me about it?"

After a long pause he told me of going to Ireland and visiting a Mrs. Latouche, and how Rosie, the young daughter of twelve, came down in the evening to greet him, like a fairy in a tiny pink dressing-gown. "She was only a child, but even then so wise and thoughtful, and I was forty-two.

"When she was seventeen, she came to London with her mother and I had wonderful weeks with her at Denmark Hill: she called it 'Edenland.' We met often, especially at Lady Mount Temple's at Broadlands. It was in this very year that I told her I loved her, and with her deep eyes on mine, she asked me to wait until she was of age—'Only three years more,' she said. Of course I spoke to her mother, but she seemed displeased and very reluctant.

"When Rosie was about twenty she was infinitely distressed by my lack of faith. She published a booklet of poems, *Clouds and Light;* she was a most fervent Christian, believing every word of the Master. It was in that very year, I think, that she passed me by, without speaking to me, as Beatrice once passed Dante."

There was intense pathos in his thin voice, something helpless and forlorn in his attitude, in the trembling lower lip and downcast hands, as of one defeated irremediably, that made my heart ache as he spoke.

"My unbelief did me infinite harm with her, loosened the spiritual tie between us, but later I learned the true cause of our separation. Her father (I think Ruskin said) brought her to London and took her to meet Mrs. (afterwards Lady) Millais. My former wife no doubt told her of my asceticism or abstinence, for when after half an hour's talk my darling came downstairs and her father asked her if she now understood his reluctance to sanction our marriage, she said, 'I understand that there are people to whom the body is everything and the soul nothing. Don't talk of it, please; I never want to think of it again!'

"My poor darling! My Rose of Life!"

My notes of all this scene are so fragmentary, mere detached words, only to be explained by the fact that I believed I should never forget the very syllables he used. But alas! The words are all gone and I can only translate, so to speak, my vague impressions into words.* I am not certain of anything, but it seems to me, as well as I can remember, that he told me, too, that in her last illness he was allowed to go to Rosie Latouche and for one whole night hold his love in his arms before she died; or was it that he desired this so intensely that he gave it as his supreme desire? I am uncertain and the fact is not very important.

I am certain of the next thing: that he suddenly started up crying: "There it is! Don't you see the devil?"and he rushed across the room. "The cat!"—and he appeared to pick up a cat. "Open the window," he cried, and I opened the window and he came over and seemed to hurl it out.

"The Devil," he exclaimed, panting. "The Evil One come to tempt me. You saw it! Didn't you?"

I could only reply, "I saw that you seemed to throw something out of the window. But now it's gone," I added, hoping to allay his breathless excitement.

"I'm not well," he broke off suddenly. "Thinking of my dreadful loss and of my darling's death always unmans me: I must not think of it; I dare not. I have been ill every year lately, through thinking of how I lost her, my love. I had an attack of brain fever in '78 and again in '81 and last year again and again. I am getting very old and weak. Forgive me if I wander."

He reminded me of Lear.

His face had gone quite grey and drawn; he filled me with unspeakable pity. What a dreadful, undeserved tragedy! I took him out as if he were a child and drove him back to his hotel. All the while tears were running down his thin, quivering cheeks.

I have never seen any sadder face, except Carlyle's.

I asked him once whether I could get Miss Latouche's poems and he told me that he would let me see his copy. His best poem to her, he said, began, "Rosie, Rosie, Rosie Rare," and I wondered whether he had copied the German lyric:

> Röslein, Röslein, Röslein rot
> Röslein auf der Heide,**

though he knew no German. He dwelt with inexpressible tenderness on the fact that Rosie used to call him "Saint Chrysostom" or "Saint Crumpet," and he always carried in his breast pocket her first letter to him between two thin plates of fine gold.

Ruskin admitted, indeed laid some stress on the fact, that he had lost all belief in what he called derisively "the Jew Jeweler's Heaven"; but at the same time he declared repeatedly that the one thing he was surest of

---

* Nevertheless, what Harris says squares well with fact.
** From a short poem by Goethe, reprinted in Herder's *Volkslieder* in 1779, which is often erroneously supposed to be a traditional folk poem.

in his life was that Rosie's spirit often came to him as "a ministering Angel" and that she was "quite, quite happy."

I remember asking him once about the road at Hinksey, the famous road he had begun to get made at Oxford by the students; he defended it, said that it would be a good thing for all the better classes to learn some handicraft. "Manual labor is good for all of us, even Gladstone," he added laughing, but he did not appear to take much interest in the road. Toynbee* was one of his foremen and Alfred Milner** used to work on the road and Oscar Wilde loved to laugh about it. It was from Oscar, I think, when talking of Ruskin's lectures, that I heard Ruskin's epigram on Naples. It combined, he said, "the vice of Paris, the misery of Dublin, and the vulgarity of New York." But Ruskin had never seen New York and knew nothing of it, just as he knew nothing of the vice of Paris. He was at his best talking of virtues.

I never heard Ruskin lecture, but he told me himself that after some practice he used to trust to the inspiration of the moment for everything, except perhaps the first words and the peroration, which he usualy wrote out and learned by heart. "Sometimes I omitted the summing-up," he added, "just to disappoint the foolish audience."

After all possible qualifications, it is certain that Ruskin had the most extraordinary influence in the university. Strange to say, I got the full impression of it from one of my earliest dinners with Cecil Rhodes. I knew that everyone, even old professors, went to Ruskin's lectures, knew that all the younger men were profoundly moved by his passionate idealism and patriotic fervor; but it was from Rhodes that I came to understand the full effect of Ruskin's extraordinary talent. One can judge of his rhetoric from his inaugural lecture:

> There is a destiny now possible to us, the highest ever set before a nation to be accepted or refused. We are still undegenerate in race; a race mingled of the best northern blood. We are not yet dissolute in temper, but still have the firmness to govern and the grace to obey . . . Will you youths of England make your country again a royal throne of kings; a sceptred isle, for all the world a source of light, a centre of peace; mistress of learning and of the Arts, faithful guardian of time-tried principles, under temptation from fond experiments and licentious desires; and amidst the cruel and clamorous jealousies of the nations, worshipped in her strange valour, of goodwill towards men?

One can imagine the effect of this noble rhetoric on young enthusiastic spirits. Though ordinary professors were never applauded, Ruskin was al-

---

* Arnold Toynbee (1852–83), a tutor in Baliol College. He tried to apply the historical method to economics and did pioneer work in this field, though he died very young. He was also a social reformer, and Toynbee Hill, the first social settlement, was named after him.

** (1854–1925). As high commissioner for South Africa and as governor of the Cape Colony he arranged the assimilation of the Transvaal and the Orange River Colony into the British colonial system. He served in Lloyd George's cabinet during the First World War and in 1920 became colonial secretary.

ways applauded on entering; and sometimes the feeling he called forth was so intense that the students sat spell-bound with bowed heads and dimmed eyes as he folded his notes and went out.

Of course it was his imperialism that endeared him especially to Rhodes; it might have been meant expressly for him.

This is what England must either do, or perish; she must found colonies as fast and as far as she is able, formed of her most energetic and worthiest men; seizing every piece of fruitful waste ground she can set her foot on, and there teaching these her colonists that their chief virtue is fidelity to their country, and that their first aim is to advance the power of England by land and sea . . . You think that an impossible idea. Be it so; refuse to accept it, if you will; but see that you form your own ideal in its stead. All that I ask of you is to have a fixed purpose of some kind for your country and for yourselves, no matter how restricted, so that it be fixed and unselfish.

Among Rhodes's papers after his death was found a note in his handwriting which shows clearly what Ruskin's words had meant to him:

You have many instincts, religion, love, money-making, ambition, art and creation, which from a human point of view I think the best, but if you differ from me, think it over and work with all your soul for that instinct you deem the best. C. J. Rhodes.

It was Ruskin more than any other man who created the empire builder and gave form and purpose to Rhodes's ambition.

Because Rhodes wasn't quite satisfied with English patriotism, he selected Ruskin's last words as the most important. Rhodes had been affected by the Boers as I have been affected by the Americans; he told me often that he could never exclude the Boer from any African empire he might have a hand in forming.

Ruskin as patriot is admirable, though I much prefer some of his writing descriptive of natural beauty, especialy what he says of the Swiss mountains.*

It is only fair to note that Ruskin lived his idealism before expressing it rhetorically. He was all of a piece and transparently frank. He had a great love for Oxford, and I had seen somewhere tht he resigned his Slade Professorship of Fine Arts because he felt himself growing old. "It must have been a source of regret to you," I said to him one day, "that you felt too weak to go on with your famous Oxford lectures."

* Go out, in the spring time, among the meadows that slope from the shores of the Swiss lakes to the roots of their lower mountains. There, mingled with the taller gentians and the white narcissus, the grass grows deep and free; and as you follow the winding mountain paths, beneath arching boughs all veiled and dim with blossom, —paths that for ever droop and rise over the green banks and mounds sweeping down in scented undulation, steep to the blue water, studded here and there with new mown heaps, filling all the air with fainter sweetness,—look up toward the higher hills, where the waves of everlasting green roll silently into their long inlets among the shadows of the pines; and we may perhaps, at last know the meaning of those quiet words of the 147th Psalm, "He maketh grass to grow upon the mountains." (F.H.)

"Too weak," he repeated scornfully. "Weakness had nothing to do with it. The room in which I spoke was always overcrowded and had many inconveniences. It was not well lighted for one thing, so I asked the authorities to provide a decent auditorium for the lectures on art that should mean so much to a well graced university. They replied that they were already in debt and left it at that. Yet the very next day they voted £ 10,000 to erect a laboratory for Dr. Burdon Sanderson to use for his experiments on living animals, and £ 2,000 more to fit up this ante-chamber to Hell with the necessary instruments! Oxford University, too poor to give anything to that love of beauty which does so much to redeem this sordid world, but able to endow vivisection and lavish thousands on instruments of devilish torture!

"My way was clear. I resigned my professorship as a protest and wrote to the vice-chancellor, asking him to read my letter, giving the reasons for my resignation to convocation. But the vice-chancellor had not the grace to answer me or read my letter publicly as I had requested; and when I wrote to the editor of the university paper indignantly, he simply suppressed it; and so the conspiracy of silence triumphed and the London press announced that I had resigned owing to 'advancing years!'

"Oxford preferred the screams of agonizing dumb creatures to anything I could say in praise of the good and beautiful and true! It showed me of what small account I was among men. Perhaps my vanity needed the lesson," he added, sighing "but I lamented the good cause hopelessly lost."

The whole incident is intensely characteristic, showing how England treats its teachers and guides: how differently Paris treated Taine!*

As I got to know Ruskin better and we talked of books at great length, I found his taste often to seek. He lauded Mrs. Browning's poetry to the skies and confessed that he disliked Swinburne; the worst prudery of Puritanism went with his thin blood and lack of virility. And his judgment of painting and painters was almost as faulty, though he thought himself a perfect critic and often declared that it was he who discovered and made the reputation of five great artists "despised until I came: Turner, Tintoret, Luini,** Botticelli and Carpaccio, but they were no greater," he would add, "than Burne-Jones† and Rossetti, my dear boys." The comparison seemed to me inept, so I changed the subject.

Why do I put these vague and inconsecutive memories together? Though he had great influence and was a great name in England for many years, Ruskin did not impress me profoundly, save as a rhetorician: indeed, to me he was not really a man of genius, not a sacred leader of men. He was perverse and purblind, an English Puritan who after he came out of the prison of Puritanism still bore the marks in his soul of subjection to English ideals and subservience to English limitations. All his economics were

* Presumably Harris refers to the election of Taine in 1878 to the French Academy.
** (1481–1532); trained in the school of Leonardo da Vinci.
† Sir Edward Burne-Jones (1833–98).

better put by Carlyle and he injured Whistler,* who was a greater master than his Turner.

In a few weeks of casual meetings I had exhausted him, or felt that he had given all he had to give to me, and his habitual sadness and diseased self-centeredness distressed my youthful optimism.

One morning I asked him cheekily whether he had not been tempted to keep some of Turner's naughty paintings? "They would have been very interesting," I added lamely, feeling him antagonistic.

At once he turned on me. "I've always felt that you don't approve of what I did," he said sharply. "Why don't you speak out? I'm proud of what I did," and his wintry eyes gleamed with challenge.

"Proud!" I repeated. " I think it dreadful to kill a man's work!"

"Perhaps it was the kind of work you would wish to preserve," he snapped; and now I noticed for the first time that when he got angry his lip would curl up on one side and show his canine tooth like a snarl of an angry dog, intensified by the peculiarity that it was only one side of his lip that would lift. He had told me that a dog had bitten him when a boy and split his lip.

"I'm not ashamed to admit that," I continued. "Any attack on puritanical standards and English prudery seems worthful to me; but if a great man had done work I hated, work in praise of war, for instance, or defending cruelty, I would not destroy it. Who am I to condemn part of his soul to death? I hate all final condemnations."

"I did what I felt to be right."

"I'm sure of that," I broke in. "That's the pity of it. The evil men do from high motives is the most pernicious. The being a trustee you took as a challenge to your courage: I understand; but I can only regret it. I'm very sorry."

I had offended him deeply; I knew I had at the time. He never came to me again and before I could make up my mind to go to him I heard that he had left London.

It is painful to me now to recall my stupid frankness, but in essence we were then at opposite poles; yet I ought to have remembered what he did for the English world and what he gave to the English people; and after all no man's gift is perfect. But the truth is, I did not rate Ruskin then so highly as I do today. I had from the beginning the French view of art and artists and felt as they feel, that admiration of beauty is the highest impulse in our humanity. It has since come to be my very soul and in time it has taught me a new ethic. I had no idea then that the English rated artists like acrobats and thought more of a half-educated politician like Chamberlain than of a great painter or sculptor or musician; and so I underrated the originality of Ruskin and had no idea that his constant preoccupation with what is memorable in art and literature, his impassioned admiration of

---

* Ruskin in 1878 made a contemptuous reference to one of Whistler's *Nocturnes*; Whistler sued him for libel and won damages of one farthing.

great work, first astonished and then interested thousands who would never otherwise have come to a comprehension of the artistic ideal. His devotion to art, or, as he would have said, to the beautiful everywhere, lifted thousands of English men and women to a higher understanding of life. Moreover, he enriched English literature with passages of magnificent prose and perhaps the finest descriptions of natural beauty in the language.

Ruskin was to the English a great prophet of the beautiful; art to him was a religion and that view had never suggested itself to them; he taught them to love and admire artists like Turner, Tintoret and Botticelli, and to esteem such great men as benefactors of humanity; he enlarged the English outlook and ennobled it and therefore was a blessing to his people.

I should have been indignant in the eighties with any comparison between him and Carlyle, who to me then was a seer and sacred guide; but Carlyle's deification of force and his disdain for the aesthetic side of life make him appear to me now hardly more valuable than Ruskin. The ordinary English instinct that placed Ruskin side by side with him was nearer right.

In spite of his paltry education and curious limitations, Ruskin was a moral and ennobling influence in England for half a century, and no doubt a stronger influence because at bottom he was bred on the Bible and brought up to revere all English conventions and English ideals.

The end of his life was extremely sad. He went abroad in '88 and '89. In '89 he had an awful illness and he lived almost without mind for another eleven years, dying in 1900.

I do not believe there ever was a sadder life, or, rather, I think he suffered as much as his mind allowed him to suffer; and Carlyle suffered more because he had more intellect, and seeing far more clearly, could not delude himself with the visitations of "a ministering angel." Stripped of the pleasure of love, life is a poor inheritance.

Chapter XVII

Matthew Arnold; Parnell; Oscar Wilde;
The *Morning Mail*; Bottomley

IN MY FIRST YEAR on the *Evening News* I was reaching success and my
employers were more than satisfied with me. I had reduced the loss by
more than one half; indeed, I was able to predict that in my second year
the loss would be down to £15,000 instead of £40,000; and the circulation had risen from eight to twenty thousand daily. I was working as hard
as ever. In the office at eight every morning, I never left it, except for an
hour at lunch, till seven at night; yet I had begun to accept dinner invitations and luncheons on Sunday. Once every week Mrs. Jeune, soon to become Lady Jeune through the knighting of her husband, the well-known
judge, invited me to one of her delightful dinners and receptions where one
met all the celebrities, from the parliamentary leaders to the choice spirits
in art and literature and life.

In the second year, too, I came to know her great rival as a hostess, Lady
Shrewsbury,* who was a little more exclusive. I have told in my life of him
how I met Oscar Wilde at Mrs. Jeune's and the immense impression he
made on me; there, too I met Russell Lowell and Thomas Hardy and a host
of more or less distinguished writers and politicians, some of whom I have
already described in my *Contemporary Portraits*. But here I shall write only
of those who had great influence on me and my development; and among
them I must always rank Pater and Matthew Arnold, especially Arnold, to
whom I was drawn by that love of ideal humanity which explained all his
strictures on English life and English manners.

Matthew Arnold was a delightful companion, full of quaint fancies and
willing, usually, to laugh at himself. I remember telling him of Oscar's jibe
at his niece's, Mrs. Humphrey Ward's,** first novel. He said that "You,
Sir, supplied the 'Literature' and she was determined to contribute the
'Dogma.' " Arnold laughed like a schoolboy. "She's very serious," he said.

* Wife of Charles Henry John, the twentieth Earl of Shrewsbury, (1860–1921),
premier Earl of England.
** Mary Augusta Ward, 1851–1920. She married Thomas Humphrey Ward, fellow
and tutor of Brasenose College, Oxford. Her first novel was *Miss Bretherton* (1884);
she always emphasized the social mission of Christianity.

"I wonder why women are so much more serious than men?" On his return from lecturing in the United States, he told me with humorous enjoyment that most of his success was due to the fact that many people took him for Edwin Arnold.* "Yes, yes," he laughed, "it was *The Light of Asia* that became *The Light of the World* to me and illumined my path. *Thyrsis* was unknown, my poetry unconsidered there. Luckily the trip was successful and relieved me from monetary care; America was very kind to me, though occasionally it chastened my conceit. As you predicted, they invited me to study elocution!"

I heard him once make a speech on "Schools" or "Schooling" somewhere in Westminster: it was all good, but not inspiring, and out of pure mischief I wanted to get to the deepest in him, his shortcomings as a critic. He did not appear to understand French poetry at all deeply. When I praised *La Légende des Siècles* by Hugo to him or the *Sagesse* of Verlaine, he did not seem to care for them, so I talked of Emerson as a great poet like Whitman, but he would not have it. I began by quoting

> So take thy quest through Nature,
> It through thousand natures ply
> Ask on thou clothed Eternity
> Time is the false reply.**

"But is that poetry?" Arnold doubted. "I can't believe it somehow."

"Think of his *Humble Bee*," I cried, "and deny him if you can," and I quoted again,

> Aught unsavory or unclean
> Hath my insect never seen
> But violets and bilberry bells
> Maple sap and daffodels
> Grass with green flag half-mast high;
> Succory to match the sky,
> Columbine with horn of honey
> Scented fern and agrimony
> Clover, catchfly, adder's tongue
> And brier-roses dwelt among,
> All besides was unknown waste
> All was picture as he passed.
> Wiser far than human seer
> Yellow-breeched philosopher.†

"That surely has the true note!"

"It has, it has indeed," Arnold hesitated reluctantly, "but we are all poets at odd moments."

---

* Sir Edwin Arnold (1832–1904). He wrote *The Light of Asia,* a popular epic poem. Arnold was chief editor of the *Daily Telegraph;* his second epic poem, *The Light of the World,* was a popular as well as an artistic failure.
** From *The Sphinx;* the quotation is substantially correct.
† Letter perfect, though some punctuation is lacking.

"Only at odd moments, I should say!" was my reply, for he was merely evading the issue, but he shook his head.

"I think the *Humble Bee* worthy to be ranked with the *Skylark* of Shelley," I went on. "Not for music, of course, but it has homely poetic virtues of its own, and some day it will be known and loved. I seldom praise Emerson," I added, "because he quarreled with Whitman and stood for convention as against freedom of speech."

"I'm afraid that I too am in favor of the conventions," said Arnold. "Speech can easily be too free, can't it?"

"I hate English prudery," I replied, "and English hypocrisy. Life in England is like life in an English Sunday school, with a maiden-lady as a teacher and an atmosphere of deadly dullness. Shall we never get to the larger freedom of Dante, if not that of Goethe?"

"Was Dante ever free in that sense?" asked Arnold.

"Surely," I replied, "some of his humor is the jolly humor of a naughty little boy who puts out his tongue at you and worse."

"Really?" doubted Arnold. "I remember nothing like that in Dante!"

"Here is one verse," and I quoted from the end of the twenty-first canto of the *Inferno:*

> Per l'argine sinistro volta dienno
> Ma prima avea ciascun la lingua stretta
> Co'denti verso lor duca, per cenno:
> Ed egli avea de cul fatto trombetta.

"And he had made a trumpet of his behind!"

"How strange," laughed Arnold. "I never noticed it. I must have read over it! Goethe of course was free, but Goethe put his worst things in *Faust* in asterisks instead of plain words."

"Yet we know from Eckermann," I said, "that Goethe used the plain words and even wrote very naughty plays and poems." Arnold was too English, I think, in feeling to take up the gauntlet.

I tried to get him to write for me for the *Fortnightly Review* and he sent me a poem, a threnody on a favorite dog that has its place in English poetry. He was indeed marvelously gifted, and I always resented the fact that the English had used one of their noblest spirits as an inspector of schools. If Arnold had been honored from thirty to sixty, as he should have been, had men been willing to pay gold to hear him talk on any subject, he would have given us even more than he did. This is to be the chief mystery of life, why men accord so little love and honor to the real guides during their lifetime. Arnold should have been put in a high place and listened to with reverence by the ablest politicians and men of letters, but he was simply disregarded, and how he kept his sunny good humor in the universal indifference was a puzzle to me.

I always felt him superior in range and rightness of thought to any of his contemporaries. There was in him also a depth of melancholy; yet in the intercourse of life he was invariably optimistic. In this, as in many ways, he resembled Anatole France. He had perfect manners, too, like the great Frenchman—met everyone on the pure human level, preferred to talk on high themes, yet used banter charmingly with the barbarians.

He loved to find the best in everyone and gloss over faults, was the first to praise Oscar Wilde to me when everyone condemned him as an eccentric poseur. "A fine intelligence and most wonderful talker," he said. It was because Matthew Arnold seemed to me to reach ideal manhood, was indeed free of faults or mannerisms, that I was always probing to discover his shortcomings.

One day I could not help trying to get to the ultimate of his thought. I used his famous definition of the "Something not ourselves that makes for righteousness" to draw him out. "That 'not ourselves,'" I said, "always seems to me wrong. The only thing in the world that makes for righteousness is the holy spirit of man."

"What about sunsets and flowers and the song of birds?" he replied with a quaint half-smile, "and the music of the spheres. Will you deny them all?"

He had caught me: I could only smile back at him; yet surely the soul of the Divinity is in us men and revealed most completely in our noblest. We cannot read the riddle of nature. Not on the walls of our cell shall the reconciling word be found, but in the heart of man grown tired of bearing:

> The weary weight of this unintelligible world.*

I had just come to think of Matthew Arnold as the most perfect man of letters I had ever met, when the shocking news came that like his father, he had died of heart failure. He sprang over a gate or fence, fell forward and never spoke again. What a tragedy is the untimely end of so great and sweet a nature.

As I came to know it, life in London grew richer and richer to me. Every dinner at Mrs. Jeune's or Lady Shrewsbury's became an event.

And when I mention Mrs. Jeune as hostess, I must not forget the Arthur Walters, who were more than kind to me from the beginning. Every summer from 1884 to 1895 I went to stay more than once at their country place at Finchampstead for weeks at a time. There I met Hurlbert** and Sir Ernest Cassell† and his daughter and other notorious people; and both Arthur and Mrs. Walter became dear to me out of their abounding human kindness.

---

* From *Tintern Abbey:* In which the heavy and the weary weight
           Of all this unintelligible world
           Is lightened.

** William Henry Hurlbert (1827–95); he had until 1883 been chief editor of the *New York Herald.*

† (1852–1926), German-born but naturalized English financier and philanthropist, a close friend of the Prince of Wales. His chief accomplishment was the financing of the irrigation of the Nile.

I tried again and again to get Arthur Walter to see Parnell as he was, but all my efforts were in vain. He was always resolved to regard Parnell as a revolutionary and Irish hater of England.

On the other hand, I had a certain admiration for Parnell and some liking. It was Verschoyle who gave me the first idea of him as a great fighter. He told me a story of his youth in the Shelbourne hotel in Dublin. One day Verschoyle and some of his family were in the hotel and at the next table a tall man was talking what they considered treason. At length Verschoyle's cousin, a notorious athlete and boxer, got up, went over to the next table and said, "If you want to talk treason, you had better get a private room, for I won't listen to it in public."

"Mind your own business," said the tall man, getting up, and the next moment they were hard at it. Verschoyle said, "I was utterly astonished to find that my cousin did not win. The tall man was just as good as he was or a little better. There was the dickens of a fight. When the waiters came in and the police and separated them, we found that the man's name was Parnell, Charles Parnell."

The first time I met Parnell with Mrs. O'Shea was at a dinner given by dear old Justin McCarthy.* It must have been pretty early in Parnell's acquaintance with Mrs. O'Shea, for she was seated opposite to him, and Parnell scarcely ever took his eyes from her face. At this time she seemed to me a sonsy, nice looking woman of thirty-three or thirty-five with pretty face and fine eyes, very vivacious, very talkative, full of good-humored laughter. Now and then, picturing a woman, she exaggerated, I thought, her Irish brogue with some artistry to bring out a characteristic; evidently a lively, clever woman and excellent company. All the while she talked, the dour, silent, handsome man opposite devoured her with his flaming eyes. I remember saying in fun to Justin afterwards, "If she were as much in love with him, as he is with her, it would indeed be a perfect union."

But kindly Justin would not admit the liaison. "He's attracted," he said. "I think we all are. She's an interesting woman." Soon, however, everybody knew that they were lovers and lost in a mutual passion. Parnell was tall and well-made, but he seemed to me too slight to be very strong; but Mrs. O'Shea, whom I questioned on the subject, told me his mere physical strength had astonished her time and again, and she did not dwell on it at all unduly.

Parnell was of the stuff of great men through greatness of character, but as a political leader he was curiously ill-read and ill-informed. Time and again I am compelled to draw attention to the ignorances of English poli-

* (1830–1912), an Irish writer and politician who thought that the best way to right the wrongs of Ireland was to appeal to England's best conscience. He went to London and became a newspaperman. He supported Parnell as an M.P. until Parnell refused to retire temporarily after the O'Shea affair. His best novels were *Dear Lady Disdain* (1875) and *Miss Misanthrope* (1877).

ticians. Even the example of Bismarck and the astounding growth of modern Germany have taught them nothing.

I always felt there was an insane streak in Parnell, though Mrs. O'Shea never hints at such weakness in the two great volumes* she dedicated to their love story. His superstitions showed, I thought, mental weakness. I remember walking with him once to his house to dinner. At the door he stopped and would not enter. Muttering something under his breath, he said, "Do you mind walking a little more before going in?" I didn't mind a scrap, though already we were somewhat late, but after a turn he was still dissatisfied and went on for another stroll. This time he was successful. "I hate four and eight," he said, "but when my last step brings me to the count of nine, I'm happy. Seven, even, will do, but nine's a symbol of real good luck and I can go in rejoicing!" And with a smiling face in he went.

But he knew no economics and had no idea of any remedy for Irish poverty. If he had ever won to complete power in Ireland, he would certainly have disappointed his followers.

In these first two or three years in London something happened of incalculable importance to my whole life, and the lesson came to me without any warning. I had grown accustomed to go on Saturday and Sunday to Lord Folkestone's to lunch, and after lunch Lady Folkestone used to give us coffee in the drawing-room. With the coffee there was always a pretty liqueur decanter full of cognac—really good *fine Champagne*. One day Lord Folkestone came away with me after lunch and said, "I wonder will you forgive me, Frank, if I tell you something purely for your good?"

"I should hope so," I replied. "I can't conceive of anyone telling me something for my good that I'd resent."

"I'm glad to hear you say that," he rejoined. "I'm much older than you know; life has taught me certain things, but I am a bad hand at beating about the bush, so I will tell it you straight off. I noticed yesterday that you drank five or six glasses of cognac with your coffee. Now no one can do that without ruining his constitution. You took enough today to make most people drunk; you showed no sign of it, but it will certainly have its effect. When you consider it, I think you will know it's sheer affection that makes me tell you this."

"I'm sure of it," I said, but I spoke only from my lips, for I was mortally hurt and angry; a little while later we separated and I went on home. I took the affair terribly to heart; I could not but recognize the kindness of Lord Folkestone, the sympathy that had prompted his warning, but my vanity was so great that it hurt me desperately. That evening I came to a saner view. The best thing I can do, I said to myself, is to take the warning to heart. The way to prove that I have self-control is to show it. For one year, then, I won't drink a drop of wine or spirits. I'll stop everything.

Within a week I recognized how right Lord Folkestone had been to warn me. My whole outlook began to alter. I saw many things more quickly

* Cassell & Co., Ltd., London, Toronto, and Melbourne, 1914.

than I had seen them before, and I noticed that not only had I been getting stouter, but that I had been getting more lazy and more self-satisfied.

I began to take exercise and found it at first extremely hard to walk five miles in an hour or to run a quarter of a mile without ill effects, but soon I began to get back to my former strength and health. In three or four months I found out a great many things—found that health of mind and quickness of wit depended, too, on health of body in my case. In three months I began to do my work easier, all work; and as I did away with the drink, the fat literally fell from me. I lost a couple of stone in three or four months and began to walk everywhere instead of driving, and took long walks on Sundays instead of lazy excursions in a carriage.

Before the end of the year I told Lord Folkestone that I owed him more than I owed anyone in the world for his kind warning. "It is eleven months since you warned me," I said, "and I am resolved to go on for another year and drink nothing this next year too."

He was delighted. "You don't know how much better you look," he said. "We have all remarked that you have gone back to the old energy and vigor that you used to have. I am more than glad, but I found it very difficult to tell you. I was so afraid of losing your friendship." I took up his hand and kissed it—one of the few men's hands I have kissed in my life.

Most of this early time in London was brightened by occasional meetings with Oscar Wilde. As I have told in my book about him, I was introduced to him at Mrs. Jeune's; and I was surprised first of all by the kindness of his literary and artistic judgments and then by his wit and humor. "Did I know Frank Miles?"* he asked shortly after we first met. "We are living together; he's one of the finest artists of this time," and nothing would do but we must look out Miles in order that I should be introduced to him then and there.

Frank Miles was at this time, in the early eighties, a very pleasant, handsome, young fellow who made a sympathetic impression on everyone. I went to see them in Chelsea and bought a drawing of Lily Langtry by Miles that I thought wonderful: the same head, life-size, twice—once in profile and the other almost full face.

What has become of it I really don't know. In a year or two I discovered in it Miles's limitations as an artist: it was pretty and well drawn, but hardly more.

Miles declared that he had discovered and immortalized Mrs. Langtry, and at once Oscar stuck in gravely: "A more important discovery than America, in my opinion; indeed, America wasn't even discovered by Columbus: it has since been detected, I understand," and we all laughed. His fun was irresistible.

Partly through the apotheosis of Mrs. Langtry, the Prince of Wales was a frequent visitor in their house; and Miles had commissions from every

---

* (1852–91), another "society" painter; he was known for his studies of the faces of women, as Harris indicates.

pretty woman in society, including the famous Mrs. Cornwallis West.*
What a charming, artistic home it was: Oscar and Miles invited me to tea
and we were waited on by a pretty girl about sixteen years of age, most
fantastically attired, whom they called Miss Sally. Sally Higgs soon became
famous for her rare beauty and was painted by Leighton (afterwards
Lord Leighton) as *Daydreams* and by Marcus Stone,** the Academician,
and a host of others. Sally was astonishingly pretty and charming to boot.
I heard of her often afterwards; a couple of years later she married a boy
just down from Eton, the son of a rich man. The father shipped the boy to
the States and gave Sally a couple of pounds a week as solatium, but she
soon found a rich protector and indeed never had any pecuniary difficulty,
I imagine, in her whole sunny life. Sally, as I soon realized, was a born
Bohemian and not troubled with any so-called moral scruples, though she
was always gay and carefree. She assured me that Miles only liked her
face and "Mr. Wilde says nice things to me and is a perfect gentleman and
that's all."

Miles was the son of a canon and a country rector who made him a good
allowance and at first encouraged his intimacy with Oscar, but later rumors
of Oscar's proclivities reached him, and his first book of poems confirming
the canon's doubts, he insisted that the two friends should part. "My son
must not be contaminated!" Much against his will, as Miles told me, he had
to tell Oscar his father's decision.

Wilde went almost crazy with rage. "D'ye mean that we must part after
years together because your father's a fool?" Miles could only say that he
had no alternative and at once Oscar retorted, "All right, I'll leave the
house at once and never speak to you again," and upstairs he went, packed
his things and left: he was proud to a fault. Sally told me he never returned; and almost immediately Miles's vogue appeared to pass. I saw him
from time to time in London but he quickly dropped out of social life and I
was horrified to hear some years later that he had lost his wits and ended his
days in a mad-house. When I told Oscar he still cherished his anger. "He
had no wits to lose, Frank," he said. "He was an early creation of mine,
like Lily Langtry, and they pass out of one's life as soon as they are
realized." But I always had a soft spot in my heart for Sally, though I
could not but believe that Miles was something more than a mere friend
to her, which shielded her from me.

It was his faculty of enthusiastic praise which distinguished Oscar
Wilde in those first years and made his reputation, as I have said in my
Life of him. Mrs. Langtry I had met in Brighton and taught to skate at the
West Street rink, never dreaming that she would reign in London a year or

---

* Wife of the lord-lieutenant of Denbighshire.
** Marcus Stone (1840–1921). He illustrated books by Dickens and Trollope. He
was elected "Academician," in the Royal Academy in 1877. An "Academician," of
whom there are forty, is a member of the governing body of the Royal Academy,
each appointed by the King.

so later as a peerless beauty. Oscar and Miles discovered her, but it was the Prince of Wales's admiration that gave her position and vogue. Oscar told everyone she was "the loveliest thing that had ever come out of Greece," and when one corrected him with "out of Jersey," he passed it off with "a Jersey Lily, if you please, the perfect type of flower."

Oscar's humor, however, was his extraordinary gift and sprang to show on every occasion. Whenever I meet anyone who knew Oscar Wilde at any period of his life, I am sure to hear a new story of him—some humorous or witty thing he had said.

The other day I saw a man who had met Wilde in New York after his first lecture tour. He told him he hoped it had been a success, and Oscar answered him gravely, but with dancing eyes.

"A great success! My dear man, I had two secretaries, one to answer my letters, the other to send locks of hair to my admirers. I have had to let them both go, poor fellows: the one is in hospital with writer's cramp, and the other is quite bald."*

Oscar and I went together once to Whitechapel to hear Matthew Arnold lecture on Watts's picture, entitled *Life, Death and Judgment*.** "What Puritans Englishmen all are," said Oscar as we came away. "The burden of Arnold's song:

> I slept and dreamed that life was beauty
> I woke and found that life was duty:†

Yet he's a real poet, Frank, an English saint in sidewhiskers!" It was irresistibly comic.

Another time we went to hear Walter Pater lecture; he talked wonderfully but continually fell into a low conversational tone as he read his address. "Speak up. Speak up, please. Louder! We can hear nothing!" resounded through the house time and again.

At length he had finished and came down to join us. Of course we both praised his essay to the skies, and indeed it was exceedingly good from beginning to end, thoughtful and wonderfully phrased; but Pater had been alarmed by the frequent admonitions. "I'm afraid I was not heard perfectly," he said, trying to excuse himself. We reassured him, but he came again to the point. "Was I heard?"

"Overheard now and then," replied Oscar, laughing, "but it was stu-

---

* It is of interest to compare this story with a passage from Wilde's letter of 12 February, 1882, to Mrs. George Lewis: "At Boston I had an immense success; here I expect one. I . . . have a secretary writing autographs all day, and would be bald in a week if I sent the locks of hair I am asked for through the post every morning." (The *Letters of Oscar Wilde*, edited by Rupert Hart-Davis, 1962.)

** George Frederic Watts, (1817–1904). The correct title of the picture is *Time, Death, and Judgment*.

† From *Beauty and Duty*, by Ellen Sturgis Hoopers (1812–1848), a Transcendentalist. In the first line, "dreamt" is the correct spelling.

pendously interesting." "Overheard now and then" was surely the wittiest and most charming description possible.

I have often been asked since to compare Oscar's humor with Shaw's. I have never thought Shaw humorous in conversation. It was on the spur of the moment that Oscar's humor was so extraordinary, and it was this spontaneity that made him so wonderful a companion. Shaw's humor comes from thought and the intellectual angle from which he sees things, a dry light thrown on our human frailties.

If you praised anyone enthusiastically or overpraised him, Oscar's humor took on a keener edge. I remember later praising something Shaw had written about this time, and I added, "The curious thing is, he seems to have no enemies."

"Not prominent enough yet for that, Frank," said Oscar. "Enemies come with success; but then you must admit that none of Shaw's friends like him," and he laughed delightfully. Ah, the dear London days when meeting Wilde had always an effect of sunshine in the mist!

Success came to me in my work and it came, I must confess, through the gambling spirit so powerful in England. I had learned quickly on the *Evening News* that the London public, which wanted to know the results of this or that great horse race, was more easily won than any other public. So I was forced to study the sport which had little attraction for one so dreadfully short-sighted as I was. While interesting myself in it, I came to see that the "starting prices" were the chief factor in the gambling. One day, I think it was in 1885 or 1886, I heard that there was a great dispute about the starting prices. One morning paper, the *Sporting Life,* gave one set of prices and the other, the *Sportsman,* gave a different set. At once I called on one editor and offered to publish his "starting prices" in a special edition of the *Evening News* at eleven or twelve o'clock each morning, giving his paper full credit; indeed, publishing his paper's name above the prices. Of course he was to supply me with "copy" fairly early. He consented at once and gladly, even went out of his way to praise the *Evening News.* On leaving him, I hastened hot-foot to the rival sheet and got that editor, too, to pledge himself to give me the day's "starting prices" as early as possible, if I gave his paper credit for the news. With both editors I signed a contract for, I think, two or three years.

Next morning, when the early edition of the *Evening News* appeared with both starting prices, I was not left long in doubt as to the value of my news. Instead of selling three or four thousand copies, we sold twenty thousand; and in a week this early edition sold more than all the other editions put together; and our advertisement revenue more than doubled itself in a month. I saw that with good machines I could make the paper pay immediately and pay enormously. How was I to get the £15,000, or £20,-000 necessary to equip the paper with proper up-to-date machines?

About this time or a little later I had a great experience. A young fellow came from Birmingham with the idea of founding a halfpenny morning paper. He had only £5,000 but he thought it should be enough, and he came to me to make terms for printing and publishing his offspring. My estimate was by far the cheapest he had had. He was very anxious to know that I would not put the price up on him later. I was greatly interested and said I had thought of starting a morning edition of the *Evening News* and would talk the matter over with him. He took fire at my idea of making each item of news a sort of story in the American fashion, and finally asked me would I help him with the editing. I said I'd be delighted to go in with him, but I did not think £5,000 would go far. He said it ought to go a couple of months and by that time he ought to have a circulation of 50,000; and with a circulation of 50,000, he could get £50,000 more for the venture in Birmingham. "All right," I said, "if you can get the further money, we can get the 50,000 circulation in three months." And so the *Morning Mail* was started; within two months we had 50,000 circulation.

We had already received notice from *The Times* that they had a weekly paper called *The Mail* and that our *Morning Mail* infringed their copyright; and they began an action claiming £20,000 damages. I sent my friend off to Birmingham and went myself to see Arthur Walter of *The Times*. I told him the action was ridiculous—a morning paper, a halfpenny paper in London had neither the shape nor look of the weekly edition of *The Times*, which they called *The Mail*. Arthur Walter told me that he agreed with me, but that his father was very angry over the matter and that he could do nothing. A week later my friend came back from Birmingham and told me that *The Times* action had prevented him getting any money and he would have to close the paper up unless I could finance it.

I spoke to Lord Folkestone about it and soon convinced him that a halfpenny morning paper must beat all the penny papers out of the field. Success and a great fortune were before us, offering themselves, so to speak. He caught fire at the idea of a Conservative morning halfpenny paper that might have a sale of a million and be as influential as *The Times*. He declared he would speak to Lord Salisbury about it; but first, with his inborn loyalty, he thought we ought to propose the scheme to Coleridge Kennard. Accordingly Kennard was brought into counsel.

By this time I had got to know all the Kennard family pretty well. Mrs. Kennard was a tall, fine-looking woman without much individuality, I thought; the son, Hugh, was in the Guards and soon afterwards got married; the daughter, Merry, was charming, both kind and affectionate and very pretty. Hugh confided in me one evening; wanted to know if the *Evening News* could be made a pecuniary success or not. I assured him it could, but would take a year or so. Now I saw him again and set all his doubts at rest, but Coleridge, the father, seemed peevish to me. He didn't want a fortune, he said; he wanted the loss to cease. "It's costing heavily and the hopes you held out," he said to Lord Folkestone, "don't seem likely to be realized!" He soon let me know that his hope was that he might be made a baronet. "I don't care for it for myself especially," he said, "but

I want it for my son and I've spent 70,000 pounds to get it, though I was told at the beginning that 40,000 would more than suffice." I came thus face to face with the fact that every title had its price.

Kennard hated the *Morning Mail* and would not hear of putting up the £20,000 needed for new machinery, so I persuaded Folkestone to go to Lord Salisbury, the leader of the Conservative Party, and put the matter before him, or rather to let me see him. A day or two later Lord Salisbury sent for me and I called on him in Arlington Street and talked to him for an hour. To me it was evident that *The Times* would soon have to reduce its price from threepence to a penny or better still to a halfpenny, for the many must be our masters if they were organized; and I went on to show him by figures that it was only the want of machinery that prevented me from getting a circulation of hundreds of thousands in a month or two. He was interested and put probing questions to me. As a young man he had been poor, and even after his marriage had earned his living as a journalist on the *Saturday Review*, and this vital discipline had made him. But when I told him of my experience in founding the *Morning Mail* and said that I could get a circulation of a million within six months and make a quarter of a million pounds a year out of the paper, he told me that all I had said had been very interesting, but there was an effect of "foreshortening" in all my enthusiasm. He thought it would take many years to get a million circulation; still he would help me. He would ask the Whips to call a meeting of the Conservative party and allow me to address them in the Carlton Club, and if I could get advances from them of the 15,000 or 20,000 pounds I wanted, he would be very glad and more. He said at the end, "I will back the project as far as I can. I think it very possible you will be successful."

In due time I heard from the Whips and one afternoon I went down and talked about the new halfpenny morning paper to three hundred members of the Conservative party in the Carlton Club. They subscribed—at least they put down the moneys they would be willing to be responsible for —and the Whips came to see me, saying they had put down something like 5,000 pounds. I got up at once and said, "That lets me out. I will have nothing to do with the attempt to make bricks without straw; but within ten years some of you will be very sorry that you did not put money in the first halfpenny morning paper proposed to you. When you find in twenty years or so from today a halfpenny paper more influential than *The Times* and making half a million yearly, you will wonder why you did not take a flutter, at least, in it." I was cheered by one or two people, but I was disgusted at the idea that I had put the price as low as I could, and that I had got hardly more than one quarter of what I wanted.

The first Whip came to me and said, "You ought to take the money and come back in six months and they would give you much more. You can get all you want; why throw the handle after the blade?"

"I have come to the parting of the ways," I replied. "I was and am eager to go on with the work, but to go on crippled for a few thousand pounds and to beg and beg and make the plans obvious and expatiate on the proven is not my game; I had rather give it all up. I am going to Rome for six months' holiday."

A big man came to me while I was talking to the Whip and said, "You know you interested me profoundly. My name is Henniker Heaton.* I made my money on a paper in Sydney, Australia, and I think you and I might talk business."

"I shall be delighted," I said, "but it must be very soon, for I am going to Rome unless I get 20,000 pounds down." He said he would come and see me in the office, and he came, and I more or less took to him, but he wanted time to consider the matter and I wasn't going to give him any time. Again and again Walter of *The Times* had told me that if I would take a position on *The Times* he would give it to me; but I had done three years of extremely hard work and in the three years had hardly grown at all intellectually. I wanted some new mental nourishment, wanted to see Rome and study it, and read Ranke and Mommsen** and study them and try to grow a little. For travel and reading were already the bread and meat of my mind.

This idea made Henniker Heaton grin. He thought making money and getting a position was the only thing in the world, and the moment I discovered this in him, I had no more interest in what he said. I went to see Lord Folkestone and after a talk with him I called a meeting of the directors of the *Evening News* and got four months' vacation, and forthwith left for Rome. Oh! I was to blame. Success had come to me too easily in London. I ought to have taken the Whip's advice and gone on with the paper. I should have got all the money I needed and made the *Morning Mail* the success the *Daily Mail* became ten years later, and founded my future on a secure basis of hundreds of thousands of pounds income. But I had won so easily that I took no account of money or the power that money gives, and I went away casually to the most delightful holiday in Rome, which led to my severing my connection not only with the *Morning Mail,* but also the *Evening News,* as I shall tell in due course.

It was in 1887, I think, that a little Jew called Leopold Graham came to the *Evening News* office with some piece of city news. He had no notion of writing and was poorly educated, but he had a smattering of common French phrases and a real understanding of company promoting and

* (1848–1914). He went to Australia at sixteen and married the daughter of Samuel Bennett, who owned the *Australian and County Journal,* published in Sydney. He returned to London in 1884 and was elected as a Conservative to Parliament. He had always been a proponent of penny portage; it is easy to see why a halfpenny paper would attract him.
** Leopold von Ranke (1795–1886), a distinguished German historian who championed objectivity in historical studies and reliance on primary sources.
Theodor Mommsen (1817–1903), German historian and archaeologist of the Roman period.

speculative city business. He interested me at once and we became friendly, if not friends. He told me he was working with Douglas Macrae on the *Financial Times* and there he had met Horatio Bottomley,* whom he described as one of the wiliest men in the city of London. I was interested in the competition between the *Financial Times* and the *Financial News,* directed by the Jew, Harry Marks.** I had got to like Marks; he had had his education as a journalist in New York and was an interesting personality: a man of good height and figure and strong face without marked Jewish features. We became friendly almost at once, though as soon as I took to reading the *News* I saw that Marks had few scruples and many interests.

Macrae made the impression on me of being a harder worker even than Marks, and perhaps a little more scrupulous. I shall never forget how Macrae pressed me one day early in our acquaintance to lunch with him in his office. He could give me a good chop, he said, and a first-rate bottle of "fizz," and as the business we were talking over promised well, I consented. At once he called for "Harmsworth, Alfred Harmsworth,"† and a youth of perhaps twenty or so came into the room, a good-looking fellow whom Macrae commissioned to cook half a dozen chops and to get besides a salad and a Camembert cheese. It was all procured swiftly and deftly put on the table and we lunched fairly well. I hardly noticed Alfred Harmsworth at all.

Bottomley made a far deeper impression on me than any other journalist: he was nearer my own age and Graham had already praised his ability to me enthusiastically—and Ikey was no fool. Bottomley was a trifle shorter even than I was, perhaps five feet four or five, but very broad and even then, when only seven and twenty, threatened to become stout. He had a very large head, well-balanced, too, with good forehead and heavy jaws; the eyes small and grey; the peculiarity of the face a prodigiously long upper lip: he was clean-shaven and his enormous upper lip reminded me at once of the giant Charles Bradlaugh. When I mentioned the fact to Graham afterwards, he replied at once, "Some say he's an illegitimate son of Bradlaugh. In any case, he has the most profound esteem and liking for him, thinks him one of the greatest men of this time."

"He's not far wrong," was my comment. At the time, I was too busy with my own work on the *Evening News* to pay much attention to financial

* (1860–1933), financier, journalist, and M.P. He made and lost several fortunes speculating and was in 1922 convicted of fraudulent conversion. He owned at one time several newspapers, the *Sun* and *John Bull* among them. He died in poverty after being released from jail in 1927.

** (1855–1916). He wrote *Small Change; or lights and shades of New York* (1882), sketches of life in New York as seen by a reporter.

† (1865–1922), later Viscount Northcliffe, who built one of the great newspaper empires of England. In 1894, interestingly enough, he bought the failing *Evening News* for £25,000; in 1908 he became a principal shareholder of *The Times.*

journalism, and some time elapsed before I got to know any of them at all intimately.

In 1888 or '89 Graham told me that Bottomley had bought the Hansard Union and was going to bring out a great company. Everyone knew the name of Hansard as publishers of the debates in Parliament, and like most other people, I had imagined that Hansard had some official status or rights. To my astonishment I learnd that Hansard was merely a printing and publishing firm to which Parliament had given the contract to publish a complete account of its proceedings. Graham made me see that a big public company with this well known name and function would certainly be supported enthusiastically by the investing public. One day Graham brought Bottomley to see me. We lunched together, I think, at the Cafe Royale, and almost at once Bottomley told me of the Hansard Union Company. "An assured success," he declared, and then asked me point blank if I could get Lord Folkestone and Coleridge Kennard to be directors. I told him I'd think it over. Off-hand he said to me, "Get me those two names as directors and I'll give you a cheque for £10,000."

"Big pay," I ejaculated, "and I love big figures. But tell me, what have you paid for all the companies you're going to amalgamate and what is the capitalization?" Without demur and with astonishing exactitude he gave me all the figures. I took notes and afterwards I said, "Practically, you are buying all the businesses for £200,000 and are selling them to the company for a million?"

"I may add a quarter of a million debentures," he rejoined coolly. Needless to say, he added, the quarter of a million alone left him a swinging profit. Next day I put the thing before Folkestone. He said, "If you advise it, Frank, I'll do it: why not?" I told him that in my opinion the venture was overcapitalized and must fail, and he said at once, "That finishes it, Frank, so far as I am concerned; but tell me what Coleridge Kennard says." Coleridge Kennard, when I put the matter before him, said that the capitalization mattered nothing to him: everyone knew that one sold at a profit, if one could. I gave Bottomley Coleridge Kennard's name but refused to take any money for it.

In a couple of years what I foresaw happened. At first the amalgamated companies paid large dividends—if I recollect aright, two in the very first year—and then the whole thing fell into bankruptcy and people spoke of it as "Bottomley's swindle." The failure came too soon, the ruin was too big; it shocked business people. Very soon it was brought before the courts and The Queen vs. Bottomley was the chief event of the day. I went to hear the criminal trial and was never more amused in my life or more interested. It came before Mr. Justice Hawkins,* who was known as the "hanging judge," certainly the severest judge in half a century in London. What chance did Bottomley stand before such a tribunal? I was to learn what brains could do.

* (1817–1907).

At first the case went badly for Bottomley. It was very clear that the business had been overcapitalized and hundreds of thousands of pounds must have gone into Bottomley's pocket. But as soon as he stood up to address the court, all this faded to irrelevance. From the beginning by sheer genius he took the bull by the horns. "I'm glad," he began, "heart-glad that I'm before Mr. Justice 'awkins. He has the name of being a severe judge, but his ability was never questioned; it's his ability I rely on today in my hour of need, his power of getting to the bottom of a complicated business."

From such compliments he went on to a detailed history of the purchase of the various companies. Time and again when he told of acquiring a new company, he drew the attention of the Judge pointedly to the fact that, though the price might seem high, this new business helped to complete and sustain the larger fabric he had in mind. "I want to make my idea clear to you, my Lud!" was the burden of his long, quiet and eminently persuasive exposition. His show of frankness was as wonderful as his detailed knowledge. Before he had finished, even the barristers in the court were won over to admiration: a Q.C.* said, "I've never listened to so complete a statement." One and all forgot that Bottomley had lived for months with every business he had to describe; nothing was astonishing to me, save the point-blank compliments to the Judge he lavished in and out of season. Long before the end of the trial he had converted one of the strongest judges on the bench into his advocate and assistant. Bottomley not only won his case, but turned the judge into his personal friend, who believed not only in his ability but in his integrity. Some time afterwards Mr. Justice Hawkins gave Bottomley the wig and gown he had worn all his life as a Judge. The whole incident is unique in the history of the English bench and proves Bottomley's astounding cleverness as nothing else could. Clearly, he was a man of genius.

But if the lights were high, the shadows were heavy. If he had guided the amalgamated businesses for five years, he might have earned the half million or so he made out of the amalgamation, but to drop his bantling almost as soon as it came to the birth showed cynical contempt, I thought, for public opinion, and indeed for anything but money. Moreover, his long speech at the trial discovered time and again an ignorance of grammar and a cockney incapacity to pronounce the letter *h*, which was astonishing in so able a man. The same Q.C. who had praised his long exposition turned to me at the end with the remark, "A d——d clever outsider!" I always thought that if Bottomley had gone for a couple of years to Germany or to France for hard serious study he might have been one of the masters and guides of the new time, but his ignorance kept his appeal always on a low level and directed it to the all but lowest class.

He wasn't much more ignorant than Lord Randolph Churchill, but Churchill didn't drop his *h*'s, and if he had, the English would have taken it as an amiable eccentricity in the son of a Duke.

* Queen's Counsel.

Look at Horatio Bottomley! What is the characteristic of that short, stout, broad figure, that heavy jowl and double chin? Surely greed. He was greedy of all the sensual pleasures, intensely greedy; even at thirty he ate too much and habitually drank too much. To see him lunching at Romano's with two or three of his intimates, usually subordinates, with a pretty chorus girl on one side and another siren opposite, while the waiter uncorked the fourth or fifth bottle of champagne, was to see the man as he was. He was greedy, too, of power, and vain as a peacock, wanted always to have a paper at his command, and of the half dozen he owned never brought one to success, save *John Bull,* which was a success simply through the blind patriotism excited by the World War.

He went into Parliament, and I remember that he told me once in a moment of expansion that he would yet be Chancellor of the Exchequer. Rhodes a little later made much the same confession to me, and Rhodes had a better chance by far than Bottomley, for he had founded himself upon a great fortune, and though nearly as ignorant as Bottomley, he didn't drop his *h*'s and had all the outward marks of a better class education. I told Rhodes he would hardly succeed, and I didn't disguise from Bottomley that he had no earthly chance. "There are half a dozen men of real ability in the House of Commons," I said, "of ability to be compared to yours; Hicks-Beach,* for example, is of high character and has besides a touch of genius; Balfour has extraordinary charm of person and mind and much reading to boot; Chamberlain, too, has real ability and a great fortune acquired within ordinary rules: these three will all be against you with a savage injustice of antagonism, for they all look on the prizes of a political life as their appanage. On the other side, you have Gladstone, who is an aristocrat at heart, and Dilke ditto, and Parnell, and Redmond, and Healy:** all will be down on you, for you neither represent nor care for their democratic gospel or their personal ambitions. Then there are John Burns and Cunninghame Graham,† who will hate you because of your indifference to ideal causes. In fact, all the leaders of all the parties will turn

---

* Sir Michael Edmond Hicks-Beach (1837–1916), colonial secretary and Irish secretary. His friendship with Churchill hardly favored his political career.

** John Edmond Redmond (1856–1918), a Parnellite who supported Parnell even after the divorce proceedings. Though he was for Home Rule, he was not an extremist, and he was offered, though he declined, a cabinet post in 1915. He did not support the Easter Rebellion, and as a result, in his last years he was opposed to the Sinn Feins, the revolutionary organization.

Timothy Michael Healy (1855–1931). He represented Ireland in the House of Commons 1880–1918, and he was Parnell's secretary until the O'Shea divorce case. He consistently voted in favor of measures that would benefit the Irish. Healy was the first governor-general of the Irish Free State.

† Graham (1852–1936), author, politician, and adventurer. He ranched in the Argentine until he succeeded to the family fortune and he married a Chilean. He was an M.P. from 1886 until 1892, and he was arrested with Hyndman, Burns, Williams, and Champion in the Trafalgar Square riots of 1887. One of the most extraordinary and gifted persons of his time.

the cold shoulder to you, and to get to the top from your stand-point seems to me utterly impossible."

"You think you could do it?"

"I have not so many handicaps," I retorted, "but I'm beginning to doubt whether the driving power of desire is there."

"That's in me," he said smiling, and set his great jaw; and I could not but agree.

Chapter XVIII

The Ebb and Flow of Passion!

ALL THIS WHILE I've said nothing of my love affair with Laura, though it didn't slacken in any way; on the contrary, it grew with indulgence and frequent meetings. My passion for her is the explanation of a great part of my sex-life, so I must tell it here as honestly as I can.

Love, they say, is blind, and if they mean thereby that the secrets of attraction lie too deep for discovery, they are right enough; but love sees many things, virtues as well as faults, unimagined by the ordinary observer.

For years I used to take Laura to lunch twice a week in a private room; why I didn't marry her, I can hardly say. Again and again I was on the point of proposing it when something would come to check me. For example, I met a broker on the stock exchange who put me in one or two good things, while I got certain articles published that did him good. In 1886 already I had made some thousands, and as soon as I had banked it, I told Laura I would give her £10 a week; and of course I paid regularly, often supplementing the weekly sum with a check for £50. Once she asked me for £300. I gave it at once. And then Laura or her mother took it into their hands to go to the United States, and Laura sent me back photos of herself in [a] bathing costume on Long Island that drove me crazy with jealousy and revived all my suspicions. But worse happened!

On their return, while looking for rooms they stayed for a short time in the Charing Cross Hotel. It has always been my custom not only to tip liberally, but to take a personal interest in dependents, and so often I get extraordinary service. One evening I happened to come to the hotel with the news of a play that I knew would interest Laura. I was told by the head-waiter, whom I liked and often had a talk with, that Miss Clapton was in the small salon on the first floor; and he ran up obligingly and when we were at the door, he threw it wide open and turned away. Two persons, a man and a woman, were seated on the sofa opposite; the man must have had his arm round the girl from the startled way they sprang apart: it was Laura and some man who got up and stood waiting while she came over to me. "I *am* surprised!" she said, with that astounding naturalness of the woman. "What good wind blows you here?" I could hardly speak; jealousy seemed to have passed into cold, sardonic hatred: I could not trust myself to speak. I took out the tickets and handed them to her. "Won't you wait for Mother?" she asked, smiling. I wonder I didn't strike her; I turned and went without a word.

I made up my mind then and there that I would never marry her. The mad rage of my jealousy frightened me; had I been married to her and had had the same shock, I might have killed her. All the way home I raged. I never knew who the man was; I never tried to find out: he was indifferent to me; it was her traitorism that counted. I sat down in my house and thought. "Why rage?" I asked myself. "Treat her as your mistress; simply tell her quietly that if you get one more suspicion, you'll never see her again. Let her know it's final. She doesn't want to lose your money and your little gifts: be ruthless."

But no resolve did me any good. Behind my anger, my love moaned crying, "Have I been so careless of you, my darling, that you wanted another affection? What have I failed to do? Love's service all planned and perfect, but not marriage, and Laura's as proud as Lucifer. Marry her tomorrow and she'll be faithful; it's not fair to the girl, this life as a kept mistress." Almost I yielded, but the thought of her mother came between us. I'd have to invite her, be polite at least to her; impossible, and again I saw the man's arm drawn away from Laura's waist! I thought I should go mad.

I got up and rang the bell. Bridget, my servant, came in, and when she brought me the whisky and soda she said, "You don't look well, Sir."

"I don't feel well, Bridget," I said. "I've not eaten."

"Oh, we can get you dinner at once, Sir; there's cold grouse in the larder," and soon I dined while Bridget waited on me. She had lovely Irish eyes and was kindness itself. As she stood by me after helping me to something, I put my arm around her, and nothing loath, our eyes and then our lips met. Soon I found she cared for me and this spontaneous affection did me good, took the unholy rage and bitterness out of me and brought me back to quiet thoughts and sanity. To cut a long story short, I consoled myself with Bridget's affection and fresh prettiness, and the fears of madness all left me not to return for many a day.

Yet next day I was ruthless. Laura had a perfect explanation. "He was a Scot; her mother had invited him to dinner and had then gone up to her room for something and left them together and—"

I smiled. "Don't sit so close together on the sofa next time," I said, "or you'll never see me again. I mean it absolutely: you must make your choice." Laura got furiously angry: what did I suspect; it was a public room: couldn't she sit with a friend? She had manifestly no idea of the storm of rage and hatred she had called to life in me. But conscious of a worse fault in myself, I was willing to forgive and if possible to forget; and I only record the fact in its naked brutality because it's true that I was really frightened of myself, frightened that I should never regain control and so snatched at the nearest way to sanity. But it led me further astray than I had imagined.

What held me to Laura so absolutely?

First of all, of course, there was the immediate attraction of good looks, but I had seen just as beautiful girls who did not attract me deeply. It was Laura's fine intelligence that pleased me so intimately, and especially the fact that her knowledge of languages gave her a cosmopolitan ideal and so allowed her to see the little peculiarities of the people surrounding us in a humorous light. Yet in spite of her amused disdain of English snobbishness and English reverence for mere conventions, she yet regarded the better class of English as the best people in the world, just as I did.

All these threads of attraction and sympathy combined to form a bond which was enormously strengthened by a single strand: she had one of the loveliest figures I've ever seen. I could stand admiring her nudity and studying it by the hour: gradually my passionate admiration took away her shamefacedness and she would strip for me, always, however, treating my adoration as childish. "You must know my figure," she said once, "much better than I know it myself."

"Naturally," I replied, but even now in old age I am at a complete loss and utterly unable to express wherein the infinite attraction consisted.

This love of plastic beauty goes naturally with that adoration of virginity which led me to stray a hundred times in my life and is now as inexplicable to me as it was fifty years ago. Even now a well-made girl's legs of fourteen make the pulses beat in my forehead and bring water into my mouth. After Mrs. Mayhew when I was seventeen, no mature woman who had been enjoyed ever attracted me physically with this intensity. It was the young and untried and with the years the unripe that drew me irresistibly; and once at least a little later I gave myself to the pursuit for months in an orgy of lust. But that's a story for my next volume and is intended to show what wealth can do. Now I can only say that Laura had won me body and mind and soul. For the soul was the chiefest factor in the deathless fascination and it often humbled me. There's a sonnet, entitled *White Heather,* of an almost unknown poet of this time, one Ronald Macfie,* that gives partial expression to this idolatry of love. Here is the sextet:

> O Queen! and I answer the wind in gentle wise,
> Saying that I have chosen as embassy
> This passionless heather, thinking it may devise
> Some white, soft suppliant way towards my plea
> To tell how earth is hallowed by thine eyes,
> How life grows holier in loving thee.**

---

* He was a doctor and wrote books on keeping fit, as well as poetry. This sextet represents his work at its best. Macfie died in 1929.

** The second stanza of the poem. There are a few errors in punctuation, and in the fourth line, "towards" should read "to word."

Laura often found words that affected me like these verses. After enjoying her one golden afternoon and kissing her from mouth to knees, she suddenly took my head in her hands and said to me with a sort of childish gravity, *"Sei tutto il mio ben."*

I've had better bedfellows, mistresses more given to the art of love and far more proficient in arousing maddening sensations, but my instinct on the whole was justified: I loved Laura better than anyone I knew up to that time or for many a year afterwards; esteemed her, too, as more intelligent; and I still think her figure the most beautiful I've ever seen.

It was her mutism that was the barrier between us always, but at long last the heart-talk had to take place. One day she asked me, "If you got a letter reflecting on me, should you mind?"

"What sort of letter?" I asked, and after much probing she confessed it might be a letter of hers that showed "affection—for some one else!"

"Passion, you mean?" I asked.

"Not passion," she replied.

"You may as well tell me everything," I urged, "because the letter, however outspoken, will only confirm my suspicions. I know you were in love with that American and you gave yourself to him. I saw you together."

"No, no!" she cried. "Never as I have to you, never!"

My jealous rage wouldn't take it. "Nonsense!" I cried. "I saw him in the Savoy once put his hand on your bare neck; that's what kept me away from you after the year was up."

Her eyes grew large. "At the Savoy?" she cried. "Mother was with me."

"Yes," I went on pitilessly, "but he was with you often when your mother wasn't there. Why can't you tell the truth? That's the thing that separates us: I can forgive, but you can't be honest! Why not say at once he had you dozens of times. I know more than that."

"Sometimes I think you hate me," she said in a low voice, mournfully. "It's not true: I've never given myself to sex-pleasures as I have with you—never, Frank. You must know that, dear!"

But I was inexorable: I would get the whole truth at last. "Why, you got in the family way with him," I cried, "and he gave you or you took medicine and brought about a miscarriage."

"Oh, oh!" she cried, covering her face with her hands. "You could think that. You're wicked, wicked; that's not love," and she flamed upright before me, "nor the truth." I smiled.

"It isn't the truth," she persisted. "I never had a miscarriage as you say. Disgusting!"

"Call it what you will," I cried. "Your blotched lips showed me you had womb-trouble and inflammation, and as soon as I touched your sex, I knew you were no longer a virgin; but my love was strong enough to forgive you everything, if only you had trusted me enough to tell me the whole truth. You never realized how infinitely I love you."

"You call that love?" she cried. "To try to shame me; oh!"

"More than love," I went on. "To know all and forgive everything and blame myself! I should not have left you a year alone without a word in your equivocal position and with your father and mother. I was to blame, bitterly, and I have taken all the blame to myself, but you should have cared enough to tell the truth, Laura!"

"But if I thought something bad about you," she began, "I couldn't bring it out and hurt you with it. I'd put it away back in my mind and forget it and say to myself, 'That's not Frank, not my love.' I'd deny it to myself and in a month or so, I shouldn't even think of it, much less speak about it.

"Now I'll tell you something, Sir, just to show you the difference of our spirits and what I have had to forgive. When we parted you told me you would let me hear in three months how things were going with you, but certainly within the year. Within the three months I saw you going about with other women, while I refused to go anywhere alone with the American my father had introduced to us, and who wanted me, I could see.

"One evening, six months after our parting, and you had sent me no word, he was taking us all to the Cafe Royale, that I had selected on your recommendation, to dinner, when I saw you coming down the upper flight of stairs with a pretty girl. I found out the stairs led to the private rooms. Ah, how it hurt me! I could scarcely eat, or speak, or even think. I was like one trodden on and numb with pain. While I had been denying ordinary courtesies, you were going with young girls to private rooms. Afterwards for days and days I raged when I thought of it, and then you blame me, and say you'll forgive me, if only I will tell all the truth, and you who began it. What have you to tell? And what have I to forgive?

"Time and again, I've thrust the truth away. I've denied it to myself, and as soon as you came to me I was so glad and proud, so heart-glad that I forgot all your wrongs and insults. I pushed them back in my mind and forgot them. 'They are not my Frank!' I used to say. 'He's wonderful, so strong and wise and he has real passion and affection too.' Oh!"

And the lovely eyes filled with tears: "Men don't love as we women do!"

"Forgive me," I cried, touched in spite of myself. "Forgive me," I repeated. "You were mistaken about the private room, really you were. Till I saw the American caress your bare shoulder I never went to a private room with anyone; indeed, I'm sure I didn't, but I love you for your defence and your half-proud, half-gentle persuasiveness. We won't talk any more about our sins, but you need not be afraid that anything he or anyone else can say will have the smallest effect on me. I love you and I know you, your eyes and sweet soul, and the hard work you've done studying, and your noble loyalty to your mother, and all."

"You darling, darling!" she exclaimed. "Now I believe you love me really, for those are the sort of things that I love about you: your giving money to your sister and her husband, your careless generosity and your wonderful talk. But you're too suspicious, too doubting, you naughty, naughty dear!" And the lovely eyes gave themselves, smiling.

"It's your naughtiness saves you," I responded, "and your wonderful beauty of figure; your little breasts are tiny-perfect, taken with your strong hips and the long limbs and the exquisite triangle with the lips that are red, crimson-red as they should be, and not brown like most, and so sensitive, curling at the edges and pearling with desire."

Suddenly she put her hand over my mouth. "I won't listen," she pouted, wrinkling up her nose—and she looked so adorable that I led her to the sofa and soon got busy kissing, kissing the glowing crimson lips that opened at once to me, and in a minute or two were pearly wet with the white milk of love and ready for my sex.

But in spite of the half-confession, the antagonism between us continued, though it was much less than it had been. I could not get her to give herself with passion, or to let herself go frankly to love's ultimate expression, even when I had reduced her to tears and sobbings of exhaustion. "Please not, boy! Please, no more," was all I could get from her, so that often and often I merely had her and came to please myself and then lay there beside her talking, or threw down the sheets and made her lie on her face so that I could admire the droop of the loins and the strong curve of the bottom. Or else I would pose her sideways so as to bring out the great swell of the hip and the poses would usually end with my burying my head between her legs, trying with lips and tongue and finger and often again with my sex to bring her sensations to ecstasy and if possible to love-speech and love-thanks! Now and again I succeeded, for I had begun to study the times in the month when she was most easily excited. But how is it that so few women ever try to give their lover the utmost sum of pleasure?

One of the most difficult things to find out in the majority of women is the time when they are most easily excited and most apt to the sexual act. Some few are courageous enough to tell their lover when they really want him, but usually he has to find the time and season for himself. With rare courage Dr. Mary Stopes* in the book recently condemned in England out of insane, insular stupidity, has indicated two or three days in each monthly period when the woman is likely to be eager in response. Her experience is different from mine with Laura, chiefly I think because she does not bring the season of the year into the question. Yet again and again I have noticed that spring and autumn are the most propitious seasons, and the two best moments in the month I have found to be just before the period and just when the vitality in the woman's seed is departing, about the eighth or ninth day after the monthly flow has ceased. I may of course be mistaken in this. Pioneers seldom find the best road and the spiritual factors in every human being are infinitely more important than the merely animal.

I may give a proof of this. One day Laura asked me, "Have you helped father recently?"

* Correctly, Marie Carmichael Stopes (1880–1958). Her book, *Contraception: Its Theory, History and Practice,* was published in 1923. She was president of the Society for Constructive Birth Control and Racial Progress.

"What do you mean?" I asked.

"Well, he was hard up a little while ago and bothered mother, and then he got money and got afloat; and yesterday he wanted to know why we never had you now at the house at dinner or for the evening, and I just guessed. Was it you who helped him?" I nodded. "And you never even told me!" she exclaimed. "Sometimes I adore you. I've never known anyone so generous—and not to speak of it, even to me. You make me proud of you and your love," and she put her hand on mine.

"I'm glad," I said, "but why don't you now and then try to give me pleasure in the act?"

"I do," she said, blushing adorably, "but I don't know how to. I've tried to squeeze you, but you ravish me and I can only let myself go and throb in unison. My feelings are overpowering; every fibre in me thrills to you, you great lover."

"There," I said; "that pleases me as much as my gift pleased you."

"Ah," she sighed; "it's the soul we are caught by, while you naughty men are caught by the body."

"By the body's beauty," I responded, laughing, "and by the soul as well."

In my bedroom at Kensington Gore I had a wonderful copy of the well known Titian in the Louvre of a girl lying on her side. Laura one day for fun stretched herself on the bed and took up the exact same pose. She was infinitely better made, slighter everywhere in the body and with more perfect hips and limbs. When she got up and was seated on the bed she suddenly put her foot behind her head, discovering the loveliest curves.

To pay her for her exquisite posturing I tried to amuse her by telling her naughty stories I had chanced to hear. One, I remember, made her laugh heartily. It was the story of a solemn English lady engaging a maid. She had asked all sorts of questions and the maid had withstood the interrogatory with perfect propriety. At length the lady asked, "Oh, Mary, have you been confirmed?" Mary hung her head for a moment, then replied in a low voice, "Yes, Mum, once, but the baby didn't live!" The little play on words had a greater success than far finer stories. Women naturally like best what concerns them most intimately.

Chapter XIX

Boulanger; Rochefort; The Colonial Conference; Jan Hofmeyr; Alfred Deakin; And Cecil Rhodes; The Cardinals Manning and Newman

IT WAS IN 1885 when he was made minister of war by M. Freycinet that General Boulanger began to attract public attention in France.* He seemed to grow in importance with every month, and the noteworthy thing was that set-backs which would have ruined other men made him talked about the more, showing that he fulfilled or satisfied in some degree a deep-seated feeling in the mass of his compatriots. In 1888 there was a senatorial election in the Nord, where he had been elected a Deputy a couple of months before; yet his influence in the senatorial election was negligible—"an extinct volcano," he was called—and sensible people pointed out that he had never given any indication of ability. He seemed to be finished, yet I heard him discussed on all sides in Paris.

The Deputy Laguerre** was his strongest supporter in the Chamber, and Madame Laguerre—Marguerite Durand that was—had been a friend of mine years before when she was an actress in the Théâtre Français. I was always proud of having seen her ability from the beginning. I forget now what play she was acting in, but I remember afterwards she insisted on my telling her how she had acted. At that time I used to go to the Français every night. I shocked her by saying, "You'll never be a great actress; you are too intelligent."

"What do you mean?" she cried. "Surely intelligence is needed in every art?"

* Charles Louis de Saulces de Freycinet (1828–1923), premier for a short while in 1886.

Georges Ernest Jean Marie Boulanger (1837–91). Called "Man on Horseback," as he roused people to demand constitutional changes in government. Fled official accusations of conspiracy (1889).

** Jean Henri Georges La Guerre (1858– ?), the lawyer who defended the anarchist Kropotkin at Lyon in 1883.

"Leave art out of the question," I retorted. "Acting is hardly worthy to be called an art; it is not intelligence that gives fame and popularity to the orator or actor: it's feeling, passion."

"Do you think Sarah Bernhardt has more passion, more feeling than I have?" she asked disdainfully.

"Indeed I don't," I replied, "but she has much less intelligence and she has really an extraordinary organ, her voice. You are supremely occupied with thoughts, ideas, the future of humanity; Sarah cares for none of these things. They handicap you as an actress; you should be a journalist or a propagandist."

"I daresay you're right," she said thoughtfully. Everyone knows how a few years later Marguerite Durand established the first woman's paper in Paris, and though she employed only girls and women on it, yet brought it to success. She married Laguerre but was never a thoroughgoing partisan of Boulanger, as he was. It was in '88 or '89, I think, that there was a great review of troops on the Champs de Mars, and General Boulanger led the column and was acclaimed by the crowd, who went mad in praise of *le brav' General.* He was indeed a brave figure on a horse: he had a good head and handsome face with brown beard and long floating moustache; he was broad, too, and strong, and sat his horse like a centaur. In an hour all Paris seemed to be in the streets: I never saw such enthusiasm; the populace became delirious and a song in favor of the hero sprang from a myriad throats. I then realized how chauvinist the French public is!

Speaking to Madame Laguerre about it, the thought came into my head that the generation after the war of '70 was coming to manhood and aching for revenge, which perhaps explained Boulanger's colossal, astonishing popularity. She would not have it, but said she'd watch and let me know. From another person, too, I heard about Boulanger.

I had known Rochefort* and his paper the *Intransigeant* for some time. He was really an extraordinary personage. I shall never forget his story of how he founded *La Lanterne.* He had got into trouble with Napoleon the Third whom, after Victor Hugo, he used to call "Napoleon le petit," and at length he fled to Brussels. There he resolved to bring out a paper to cast light into the dark places and so called it *La Lanterne.* "But when the first copy was brought to me," he said, "I put it down in utter dejection. There were good things in it, but one thing was lacking: there was no powder in the tail of the rocket, nothing to drive it up and make every one buy it and talk. I sat the whole day beating my brain, trying to excogitate some word that would give it wings. Finally the printer's boy came to the door and I got up in despair: I thought of the state of France, with millions subject to that poor charlatan, and at once the word came. I wrote as the first para-

* Henri Rochefort (1830–1913). Actually, *La Lanterne* was published in Paris in 1868 for eleven editions before Rochefort had to publish it in Brussels. He left France in 1871 in disguise for opposing the government; he returned in 1880 and founded *L'Intransigeant,* a Radical paper. Rochefort fled Paris as did Boulanger.

graph: "France counts thirty-five millions of subjects, not counting the subjects of discontent."

But it was as a lover and critic of art that I really esteemed Henri Rochefort. I had bought my first Barye* from him and from him I heard of the miserable poverty of the great sculptor. "Barye," he said, "was so hard up that he often came to me with the model of a tigress or lion in his pocket and asked outright for help. Sometimes I could not buy his models; I was ashamed to offer so little for such masterpieces. I've bought his things as cheap as fifty francs a piece because I could not spare any more at the time, and now they're worth thousands and will be priceless. He was *le Michelange des fauves,* the Michelangelo of the Cat tribe"—a fine appreciation!

It was Rochefort who took me to see Boulanger in his house in the street Dumont d'Urville, near the Étoile. I was surprised to find Boulanger as short as I was; his torso was fine, but his legs were very short; he looked his best on horseback. With Rochefort he was silent: indeed, I was astounded to see how the clever and witty journalist assumed the lead and kept it. Rochefort was not a man to be content with a second place in any society; he was all nerves and audacity. A thin, slight figure about five feet nine or ten with silver hair bristling up like a brush from his high forehead and his brown eyes flaming, he literally stood over Boulanger and talked without a pause, laughing every now and then at his own phrases. Boulanger made an impression on me of kindliness and perhaps courage, but certainly not of command or dominant will. He was good-looking and of easy, pleasant manners, but not a great man in any sense of the word. When we went away and I spoke of Boulanger's silence, Rochefort said wittily, "The flag does not need to be articulate."

One later story of Rochefort should find its place here just to round off his portrait and explain the great place he held in Paris and the enormous influence he wielded. It was the beginning of the winter after Marchand was forced to retreat from Fashoda.** France was in a fever: nine Frenchmen out of ten were bitterly incensed with the English. Rochefort wrote a leading article in which he asked Queen Victoria not to visit Nice that winter, as had been her custom in those latter years. He began very politely: "France was more than hospitable, more than courteous to women," he said, "and especially to persons of distinguished virtue and position. For these reasons the baser sort of French journalist will assert that you, Madame, are a welcome visitor, but it won't be true; after Fashoda it'll be a lie. We don't want to be reminded of that intolerable humiliation, and

---

* Antoine Louis Barye (1796–1875); his studies of animals were his claim to fame.
** General Jean Baptiste Marchand (1863–1934). He later fought in the Boxer Rebellion and commanded troops in France during the First World War.
   Now called Kodok. The French under Marchand occupied Fashoda in 1898 in a dispute over control of the upper Nile. Kitchener demanded that Marchand retire, which Marchand did for fear of war. The French public was outraged at the withdrawal. In 1899, for yielding claims to the upper Nile, France was ceded part of the Sahara.

especially not by the appearance of *cette vieille calèche qui s'obstine a s'appeler Victoria*" (that old stage-coach that persists in calling itself a Victoria). The word went all over France in an hour and had its effect, though masses of the better class of Frenchmen deplored the gratuitous insult to a harmless old lady.

Rochefort made no secret of his desire to overthrow the Republic in favor of a military despotism, and I believe it was he who told me that the Duchesse d'Uzès* was supplying the Boulangists with funds. At any rate, I got to know it either from him or from Laguerre: one thing was sure; money was forthcoming to any extent.

I shall always be glad that I was in Paris at the end of January, 1889, and was invited by Rochefort to the famous dinner at the Cafe Durand, given in honor of Boulanger's triumph in the election of Paris. The voting was on the 27th of January and the excitement in Paris was incredible. The whole city and every monument in it was placarded with electoral appeals; now and then you read Jacques, but everywhere Boulanger. The posters alone must have cost a fortune: Paris was white with them. The popular newspapers, too, were filled with stories of the hero, everywhere his personality and his achievements; what might not be hoped from him! He was to be president or dictator, head of France, surely, and her army; the savior of the people!

What did all this excitement mean? Even Marguerite Laguerre admitted to me that the thought of *la revanche* was in every French heart, and Boulanger was the selected hero of a new coup d'état. She thought he would be elected and Laguerre put his majority at 25,000; but when the news came in that with half a million votes cast he had a majority of 100,000 (it was afterwards found to be 81,000), Paris went crazy. Even in the Hotel Meurice, where I was staying, there was an air of suppressed excitement. The manager came to see me while I was dressing. "Will there be a revolution?" he wanted to know. When I went out I found the streets crowded and finally took a cab and went round by the Grands Boulevards, as the rue Royale was crammed with people.

Never was there such a dinner: it took place in the big room on the first floor. Everyone will remember that Durand's then was on the corner of the rue Royale, opposite the great Church of the Madeleine. I had been a customer at Durand's for some time; the owner and the waiters knew me and I was ushered upstairs. Already some thirty or forty persons were seated at table. At the end nearest the door *le brav' General*; near him on his right, I think, Comte Dillon,** who as soon as he saw me called out and pointed to the empty chair beside him.

---

* (1847–1933), wife of Emmanuel, 12th Duc d'Uzès. She was a sculptor and a writer (under the pseudonym, "Manuela"), as well as a social leader.
** At one time a stock promoter in the U.S., he was not really a count. He raised great sums for the Boulangist cause, particularly from the Duchesse d'Uzès. He was already in exile when he was condemned for his activities in 1889.

All round the table were journalists and deputies; I had hardly time to congratulate Boulanger when another visitor was being presented to him. I had only just shaken hands with Rochefort when he was dragged off to a conference at the other end of the room. When he returned, he was laughing. "Think of it," he said. "That unfortunate Jacques, our opponent, is dining in the restaurant opposite." Everyone exploded as at the best of jokes. From time to time some new dish was served and we ate; the excitement grew steadily as we drank and the heat became tremendous. At length Rochefort gave the order to open the windows, which all gave on the rue Royale and the great *place*.

Suddenly the cry came to us from the crowd outside: *"Vive Boulanger!"* It was taken up by the thousand voices and carried in a great wave of sound to the Church and far up the Boulevard; and again the air throbbed with the cry: *"Vive Boulanger!"* I went to find Laguerre: he was surrounded; Rochefort: he was perorating. I went to the window: you could have walked across the great open place on the heads of the crowd. I made my way downstairs and the head waiter whom I knew assured me that there were five thousand students in the crowd.

I returned to the dining room. The quietest man in the place was General Boulanger, drinking his coffee calmly at the head of the table. And again the cry went up, thrilling me: *"Vive Boulanger, Vive Boulanger!"* I could not keep still. I went to him and said, "Surely, General, it is time. The hour has struck!"

"What do you mean?" he asked with perfect composure.

"The Elysée Palace is just over there," and I pointed, "hardly quarter of a kilometre to go!"

To my astonishment he shook his head. "What!" I cried. "When are we to start?"

"We have no forces," he replied.

I laughed aloud. "There are five thousand students below there waiting," I cried, and again, as if to give weight to my challenge, came the great wave of sound: *"Vive Boulanger, Vive Boulanger!"*

It affected him. He leant towards me and said, "I'm willing and ready. See Rochefort and Dillon: if they agree, we'll start." I passed behind him round the table and went to Rochefort, still talking; I drew him on one side and said, "Boulanger's ready to go to the Elysée."

Blank surprise came over his face: a moment's thought and then an imperious, *"Non, non! restons dans l'ordre."*

"Order is a first-rate resting place," I said, "but you don't find crowns in it."

"We're not ready," retorted Rochefort. "We've made no preparations!"

"First-rate"; I said, "perhaps the others are equally unprepared. Our force is there in the street ready. Listen!" And again the cry arose: *"Vive Boulanger, Vive Boulanger!"* Rochefort shook his head resolutely and turned away.

Suddenly it came to me: that was why Napoleon the Third had succeeded, because he was ready to try and try again. Had he not failed twice before he finally won? I went back to Boulanger. "What does Rochefort say?" he asked at once and I told him. "But he's wrong," I went on. "That's why Napoleon won. He tried and failed, tried and failed again, but the third time he won. Try! Try again! They can't eat you!"

Le brav' General shook his head. "We've made no preparations," he said, repeating Rochefort's foolish word. And a minute or two later Laguerre had the same answer: "Not prepared"—as if preparation was necessary.

"I can't act against Rochefort," was *le brav' General's* last word.*

"What do you risk?" I cried. "Nothing. They can't punish you for wishing to pay a visit to the President?" He shook his head slowly; he was in doubt. I turned away: kings who daren't crown themselves are not worth crowning.

I went round and shook hands with Rochefort, Laguerre and le Comte Dillon. They were all talking eagerly, hopefully of their chances, of what might happen, no one of them seeing the plain fact that unless they could get an election to sweep France as Paris had been swept that day, they'd never have a better chance than that moment.

I went out into the street, almost at the door was met by a young man who asked, "Is he coming?" I shook my head, grinning as he turned away, evidently disappointed. I hesitated; if they had been Englishmen I'd have asked the young fellow to come up with me and speak to Boulanger himself. But no! They might resent it. I've heard since that Naquet,** the Senator, also advised Boulanger to go to the Elysée that night. It may be true. This is sure: the crowd of students expected the General to do something, to have at least a try for a crown!

His opponents, or one of them, was wiser: it was Mr. Constans,† who had just come into the Government with a speckled reputation from the Far East. Mme. Laguerre's word for him was the best; *ni conscience, ni tête, mais du poing.* He now showed resolution. Scenting the danger, he threatened Boulanger, or sent some false friend to him with the intimation that his arrest had been resolved, and at once Boulanger fled to Brussels. In the summer he came over to London, a damp squib. Everyone saw when he fled from Paris that he had lost his chance. I asked him to dinner in Park Lane and had Wyndham and half a dozen friends to meet him. A witty and pretty Irishwoman insisted that he should talk English to her, and to my surprise he talked quite fairly for a Frenchman, and in answer to my

* Had he moved at this moment, Boulanger indeed might have made himself master of France.
** Alfred Joseph Naquet (1834–1916), a senator from 1883 until 1890, when he resigned to take a seat with the Boulangists in the Chamber of Deputies. He was largely responsible as a senator for legalizing divorce in France in 1886.
† M. Jean Antoine Constans (1833–1913), Minister of the Interior during the Boulangist agitation.

question said that he had been at school in Brighton, "but after thirty years or so one forgets a language."

I dined with him a little later once or twice in Portland Place, but it was depressing and the champagne was appalling, sweet as sugar. His friends, the ubiquitous Rochefort among them, tried a little later to get up a demonstration at the Alexandra Palace and a banquet, but only a few people went out of curiosity; and poor Boulanger issued an immensely long address "to the People, my sole Judge," meaning the people of Paris. But they had already judged and condemned him by default, though he didn't seem to know it.

No one knew or cared how long he stayed in London or when he left it: his bolt was shot. Suddenly, a couple of years later, the news came to us that he had killed himself in Brussels* on the grave of his *bonne amie,* Madame Bonnemain, and so went into the shrouding silence, this poor Antony, who we fancied might have been a Caesar. But greatness was not in him.

Many are called; but few chosen.

The whole incident set me watching. If the French were determined on *la revanche,* interesting things would soon happen, and now as editor of the *Fortnightly Review,* it behooved me to keep in touch with France. But M. Ferry made me alter my opinion. Everyone knows how he made war and annexed Tonquin,** but when I saw him later in Paris and congratulated him on his achievement, he told me it had ruined him. "Even in my own district," he said, "my constituents won't forgive me the lives lost and the cost. The French peasant won't have war: he cares nothing for Alsace-Lorraine. You may take it from me: there'll never be a war of revenge!" But the next generation was of a different spirit; they went in for athletics and practiced bodily exercises even in the army, and Caillaux† told me in 1912 that the chief French generals thought that Russia and France or France and England could easily whip Germany. I didn't share the opinion, but it was impossible not to recognize that there was a new spirit abroad in France, the exact opposite to what M. Ferry had predicted twenty years before.

Now I must recall the chief event to me of this decade, the Colonial Conference of 1887 and my meeting with three men: Cecil Rhodes, Alfred

---

* In 1891. Rochefort, however, returned to France in 1895 to fight against the Dreyfusards and then became editor of *La Patrie.*

** M. Jules François Camille Ferry (1832–93), twice premier, in 1880–81, and in 1883–85.

Or Tonkin (North Viet Nam). A French expedition in Indo-China in 1882 to open up the Red River for trade resulted in a colonial war. The French won Tonquin as a protectorate, but lost it in the 1950's.

† Joseph Marie Auguste Caillaux (1863–1944). He had been Premier in 1911, during negotiations with Germany. He became an opponent of Clemenceau and Clemenceau in 1917 attacked his loyalty. Caillaux was imprisoned for three years and was deprived of his civil rights, which were restored by an Act of the National Assembly in 1924. Harris wrote a study of him in *Latest Contemporary Portraits.*

Deakin and Jan Hofmeyr.* Sir Henry Holland** presided at the meetings of twenty or thirty colonial ministers with a courteous good nature that did not exclude dignity, but it was Jan Hofmeyr, whom I had previously met in Cape Town on my first voyage round the world, that I most wished to see. I wanted to meet him and find out whether my first estimate of him ten years ago or so before was justified. He came to lunch and dined with me; I got to know him really well and considered him from that time on one of the ablest and best men I've ever met. The breadth of view and imperial fairness of his fine Dutch mind taught me to understand and appreciate the best English mind.

I began to see that the English race had high qualities in profusion, and above all a genius for government founded on individual character and a recognition of the real forces in practical life, which did not exclude ideal strivings. Strange to say, though gifted with a singular sense of physical beauty, as I have, I think, shown, the English don't even attempt to foster or develop this, which I regard as their highest endowment. The French establish opera houses and national and municipal schools of music, and subsidize even provincial art galleries and so forth, and the Germans spend money freely, endowing chemical and physical laboratories; but the English and Americans close their eyes to all such spiritual needs. The object of all civilized life is the humanization of man, and it must be admitted that less is done in this direction by England and America than by almost any state in Christendom. Jan Hofmeyr was too much occupied with the possible conflict between Briton and Boer and the pressure of the colored races to care much for national theatres or municipal art schools.

Nor did I talk with him about them, the Dutch caring even less for art than the English. It was Hofmeyr, I think, sturdy, broad, sensible Boer that he was, who introduced me to Cecil Rhodes, but Rhodes at first did not make as good or as deep an impression on me as Alfred Deakin. The Australian seemed more open to ideal influence, and above all, he loved literature as well as politics.

I invited all three to dinner in my little house in Kensington Gore, just opposite Hyde Park. Cecil Rhodes had to go away early and Deakin, too, had an engagement, so that I was soon left alone with Hofmeyr. Hofmeyr spoke slightingly of Deakin while I stuck up for him. At any rate, I concluded, "He's brainier and better read than your Cecil Rhodes!"

"He may be; it's possible," Hofmeyr admitted, "but Cecil Rhodes is

* Cecil Rhodes (1853–1902).
Alfred Deakin (1856–1919), leader of the Liberal Party in Australia in 1885 and later Prime Minister. This conference was called to mark the Golden Jubilee of the Queen's reign.
Jan Hofmeyr (1845–1909), represented the Cape parliament at this conference. He controlled the Afrikander Bond, a political organization, which in 1890 helped Rhodes become premier of Cape Colony.
** Lord Knutsford (1825–1914). Salisbury made him in 1885 financial secretary to the treasury before he became secretary of state for the Colonies.

master of Kimberley and already one of the richest and most powerful men in South Africa. He'll go far and may do big things."

I remember distinctly how shocked I was at this evidence of Hofmeyr's worship of the golden calf. I suppose it was Professor Smith's influence and that of German universities that kept me so naive, though I was over thirty. I had yet to learn how universal the power of money is, and I am sure that my first lesson in world values came that evening from Hofmeyr. In half an hour he showed me the enormous influence Rhodes exercised in the Cape, and indeed all through South Africa because of his great wealth. He summed up, half bitterly, "He has more influence with the Boer leaders than I have, though they have known me all their lives; money is God today and the millionaire rules."

I soon found out how right Hofmeyr was. Dilke, for example, knew all about Cecil Rhodes and told me he'd be glad to meet him with me at any time. "A very able man!" but when I spoke to him of Deakin he was hardly interested, though he knew his name and work. Arthur Walter, too, the son of the manager of *The Times,* spoke of Rhodes with unfeigned respect, though at this time he hadn't met him, whereas my praise of Deakin fell on stopped ears.

Strange to say, Rhodes seemed to like me, perhaps because I knew the Cape and Hofmeyr and felt a great liking for the Boers and was not afraid to proclaim it openly. At any rate, he asked me to lunch and I met some important people in his rooms at the Burlington Hotel, notably Lord Rothschild,* whom I had already met at Dilke's; and on this occasion I noticed that Rhodes cared little for what he ate, though he drank quite as much as was good for him. What I liked about Rhodes from the beginning was his entire absence of "side" or pretence of any sort. I had already settled in my mind the rule, which, however, is subject to important exceptions, that no great or wise man ever gives himself airs. "Side" is a characteristic of the second rate, and when a great man uses it, as Lord Salisbury did occasionally, it is to ward off the pushing or impertinent; still, it is almost always a proof of weakness.

I saw this perfectly exemplified in the Archbishops Manning and Newman.** I had gone to see Manning at Westminster because of an article on the poor of the East End, in whom he professed to be greatly interested. He kept me waiting that first time and then had little knowledge to give me, indeed, had to summon an attendant priest in order to be coached. I shrugged my shoulders and soon rose to go; then he dropped the pontifical air and assured me that he would be much obliged if I sent him whatever I wrote about the East End. From that time on he was perfectly courteous

---

* Sir Nathan Meyer Rothschild (1840–1915), second baronet and first Baron Rothschild of Tring.
** Henry Edward Manning (1808–92). Harris' portrait of him is quite in keeping with that of Lytton Strachey in *Eminent Victorians.*
John Henry Newman (1801–90).

and sympathetic, but I could not but contrast my first impression of him, seated in his great chair and with an attendant priest standing by him, with the perfect simplicity of Newman, who was unaffectedly pleased with my enthusiastic praise of his *Apologia* and almost immediately wanted to know where I stood, what school of thought I favored, what my opinions were on the great themes. When he learned of my utter disbelief, he seemed distressed: I hastened to admit that man's respect for unselfish loving-kindness and indeed for all that is above him showed a touch of the Divine, but Nature red in beak and claw was appalling, and—

Newman nodded gravely. "Doubts are stepping stones to faith," he said, nursing his chin on his hand. "Faith is priceless, wings above the abyss, making us one with the universal soul."

"That reminds me," I said, "of the noblest words in the *Religio Medici:*

There is surely some piece of Divinity in us, something that was before the elements, and owes no homage to the sun.*

"Magnificent!" the old saint cried, his whole face lighting up with a sort of supernal radiance. "Magnificent! Noble words, magnificent; but did you ever read his *Christian Morals* and his *Vulgar and Common Errors?* I like them both."

"No," I replied, "but I'll get them. I love his *Hydriotaphia;* the last chapter of the *Urn Burial* is glorious, full of passages finer even than Bossuet** (Newman nodded smiling); Browne is an enigma to me, a country doctor commanding magical phrases, and yet though as a boy he may have seen Shakespeare, he never mentions him, so far as I know."

"He was a great man, nevertheless," said Newman, "and we are all his debtors. Do you remember one thing he said: 'I love to lose myself in a mystery, to pursue my reason to an *O, altitudo?*' "† I shook my head, and towards the close of our talk he counseled me, smiling, "You should not depreciate memory as you did the other day: it's ungrateful when you can carry about with you in memory's satchel such priceless jewels as that sentence of Browne. Such words enrich life."

I had only said that great verbal memory often hindered one from thinking for oneself, but the memory of great things said greatly do indeed enrich life, as Newman said, and there are few more notable jewels in all English prose than this of Sir Thomas Browne. Whenever I think of Newman and his passionate faith, I am reminded of the great verse:

> . . . Life's truer name
> Is "Onward." No discordance in the roll
> And march of that Eternal Harmony
> To which the stars beat time—
> Only great souls can be so persuaded!

* By Sir Thomas Browne (1605–82). "There is surely a piece of Divinity in us . . . and owes no homage unto the sun."
** (1627–1704), French Jesuit writer and philosopher.
† Also from *Religio Medici.*

Chapter XX

Memories of Guy de Maupassant

IT WAS IN THE EARLY EIGHTIES that Blanche Macchetta, or Roosevelt, as she was before her marriage, made me intimate with Maupassant in Paris.

Blanche was an American who had come abroad to Milan to study singing; she was extraordinarily good-looking, a tall well-made blonde with masses of red-gold hair and classically perfect features. She had deserted music for matrimony, had married an Italian and lived in Italy for years, and yet spoke Italian with a strong American accent and could never learn the past participles of some of the irregular verbs. French she spoke in the same way, but more fluently and with a complete contempt, not only of syntax but also of the gender of substantives. Yet she was an excellent companion, full of life and gaiety, good-tempered and eager always to do anyone a good turn. She wrote a novel in English called *The Copper Queen,* and on the strength of it talked of herself as a *femme de lettres* and artist. She evidently knew Maupassant very well indeed and was much liked by him, for her praise of me made him friendly at once.

His appearance did not suggest talent: he was hardly middle height but markedly strong and handsome; the forehead square and rather high; the nose well cut and almost Grecian; the chin firm without being hard; the eyes well set and in color a greyish-blue; his hair and thick moustache were very dark and he wore besides a little spot of hair on his underlip. His manners were excellent, but at first he seemed reserved and unwilling to talk about himself or his achievements. He had already written *La Maison Tellier,* which I thought a better *Boule de Suif.*

Let no one think my inability to trace De Maupassant's genius in his appearance or manner was peculiar; Frenchmen who had known him for years saw nothing in him, had no inkling of his talent. One day Zola told me that even when the "Medan" stories were being written, no one expected anything from Guy de Maupassant. It was naturally resolved that Zola's story should come first and the other five contributors were to be classed after being read. Maupassant was left to the very last; he read *Boule de Suif.* As soon as he had finished, all the six called out that it was a wonder and hailed him with French enthusiasm as a master-writer.

His reserve at first was almost impenetrable and he wore coat *armour,* as I called it to myself, of many youthful pretences. At one time he told me he was a Norman and had the Norman love of seafaring; at another he confessed that his family came from Lorraine and his name was evidently derived from *mauvais passant.* Now and then he would say he only wrote books to get money to go yachting, and almost in the same breath he would tell how Flaubert corrected his first poems and stories and really taught him how to write, though manifestly he owed little to any teaching. Toward the end he had been so courted by princes that he took on a tincture of snobbism, and, it is said, wore the crown of a marquis inside his hat, though he had no shadow of a right to it, or indeed to the noble *de* which he always used. But at bottom, like most talented Frenchmen, he cared little for titles and constantly preached the nobility and necessity of work and of the daily task; in fact, he admired only the aristocracy of genius and the achievements of artists and men of science.

He dined with me and I told him I wanted to publish his stories in English and would pay for them at the highest French rate. He seemed surprised, but he had need of money and soon sent me stories, some of which I published later in the *Fortnightly Review.*

One winter Dilke lent me his villa at the Cap Brun near Toulon. I invited Percy Ffrench of Monivae,* who had once been British ambassador at Madrid, to pay me a visit, and while he was living with me, we ran across Maupassant in Cannes. Ffrench spoke French as well as English and his praise of me and of my influence in England seemed to affect Maupassant; at any rate, he agreed to come to us on a visit for a few days. He stayed a week or so and I began to know him intimately.

One evening I remember I was praising *L'Héritage* to him. He told me what I had guessed, that the bureau life depicted in the story was taken from his experiences in the Ministry of the Marine in his early days in Paris. I suggested that the ending was too prolonged, that the story ended inevitably with the heroine's condemnation of the girls who proposed to do exactly what she had done. *"Comme ces créatures sont infâmes"* should have been the last word of the tale. He hesitated a little and then, "I believe you're right: that gives snap and emphasis to the irony." After reflecting a little, he asked, "Why don't you write stories?"

"I haven't the art," I replied carelessly, "and I love life more than any transcript of it."

"You couldn't be so good a critic," he went on, "unless you were also a creator. Get to work and we'll have the pleasure of criticizing you in turn."

"I'll think of it," I replied, and indeed from that day on the suggestion never left me. Could I be a writer? I had always known that I could be a good speaker and political thinker, but to write was to measure myself with the greatest; had I genius? If not, I'd be a fool to begin. Suddenly it

* Robert Percy Ffrench of Monivae Castle, County Galway; he died in 1896.

came into my head that I might tell a tale or two and see what effect they'd have. But I didn't take the work seriously for some time; not indeed until the idea of a seat in Parliament became silly to me, but that's another story. The better I knew Maupassant the more I got to like him. He was a typical Frenchman in many ways; kindly, good-humored and fairminded. He liked rowing, was very proud, indeed, of his strength and exceedingly surprised to find that my early English school training and the university life in the U.S.A. had made me, if not stronger, certainly more adroit, than he was. It was from him I first heard the French proverb, *bon animal, bon homme*. His physical vigor was extraordinary; he told, for instance, of rowing all the night through after being the whole day on the Seine. Horseplay always appealed to him, too, even when he happened to be the victim. One morning on the river at Argenteuil, when he rose to take another's place at an oar and stepped on the gunwale of the stout boat to pass on to his thwart, the steersman, seeing the opportunity, threw himself on the gunwale at the exact moment and Maupassant was tossed into the water. "I couldn't help laughing," he said. "It was so perfectly timed."

"Had you a change of clothes?" I asked.

"Oh, no!" he crowed. "I simply rowed hard till I got hot and the clothes dried on me. In those days I never caught cold . . ." It was this abounding physical vigor, I think, that inspired his kindly judgments of his contemporaries and rivals: he found genius even in Bourget.* The only person I ever heard him criticize unfairly was E. de Goncourt: he always spoke derisively of his *écriture artiste*. "The people who have nothing to say are naturally very careful how they say it," was one of his remarks. "It's when the two powers are found together, a deep, true vision of life and a love of words, as in Flaubert, that you get the great master." Goncourt was even more prejudiced; after Maupassant's death he denied vehemently that he was a great writer.

As soon as Maupassant found that I was muscularly very strong, fully his equal indeed, he began to talk of amatory performances. He was curiously vain, like many Frenchmen, and not of his highest powers.

"Most people," he said, "are inclined to think that the lower classes, working men and especially sailors, are better lovers than those who live sedentary lives. I don't believe that; the writer or artist who takes exercise and keeps himself in good health is a better performer in love's list than the navvy or ploughman. It needs brains," was his thesis, "to give another the greatest possible amount of pleasure."

We all three discussed the matter at great length. I told him I thought youth was the chief condition of success, but to our surprise he would not agree to that, and clinched the matter by talking of a dozen consecutive embraces as nothing out of the common. Laughingly, I reminded him of Monsieur Six-fois in Casanova, but he would not accept even that authority.

* Paul Charles Joseph Bourget (1852–1935), a French writer whose novels were largely social tracts.

"Six-fois," he cried contemptuously. "I've done it *six fois* in an hour." I cannot but think that some such statement as this grew into the story told me in Nice in 1923 by my friend George Maurevert,* the writer, that Maupassant, excited by Flaubert's disbelief, went once with a *huissier* as witness to a brothel in Paris and had six girls in an hour. Flaubert was singularly ascetic, yet very much interested in Maupassant's astounding virility.

Believe this story or not as you please, but no one should take it as a libel on Maupassant—still less on contemporary French manners—for Lumbrose tells in his book how Bourget and Maupassant paid a visit to a low brothel in Rome, where Bourget sat in a corner, he says, and was mocked by Maupassant, who went off with a girl.

Time and again Maupassant told me he could go on embracing as long as he wished.

"A dangerous power," I said, thinking he was merely bragging.

"Why dangerous?" he asked.

"Because you could easily get to exhaustion and nervous breakdown," I replied. "But you must be speaking metaphorically."

"Indeed I'm not," he insisted, "and as for exhaustion, I don't know what you mean; I'm as tired after two or three times as I am after twenty."

"Twenty!" I exclaimed, laughing. "Poor Casanova is not in it."

"I've counted twenty and more," Maupassant insisted.

I could do nothing but shrug my shoulders. "Surely you know," he went on after a pause, "that in two or three times you exhaust your stock of semen so that you can go on afterwards without further loss?"

"There would be increased nerve exhaustion, surely," I countered.

"I don't feel it," he answered.

As we separated for the night, Ffrench declared that the whole thing was French braggartism. "They love to show off," he insisted.

But I could not be so sure; Maupassant had made an impression on me of veracity and he was certainly very strong.

On reflection, the idea came to me that perhaps he had begun to care for women very late in life and that in boyhood he had never practiced self-abuse and so had arrears to make up. I determined to ask him when I got a good chance, and a day or two later, when Ffrench happened to be out somewhere and Maupassant and I went for a walk to Toulon, I put the question to him.

"No, no," he replied. "I learned to excite myself by chance. When I was about twelve a sailor one day practiced the art before me, and afterwards, like most healthy boys, I played with myself occasionally. But I did not yield to my desires often."

"Was it religion restrained you?" I asked.

"Oh, dear, no!" he cried. "I was never religious; even as a boy religion was repulsive to me. When I was about sixteen I had a girl, and the delight

* A French journalist who was friendly to Harris to the end.

she gave me cured me of self-abuse. I believe that my experiences were fairly normal, save that I learned from E— that I could go on longer than most men.

"I suppose I am a little out of the common sexually," he resumed, "for I can make my instrument stand whenever I please."

"Really?" I exclaimed, too astonished to think.

"Look at my trousers," he remarked, laughing, and there on the road he showed me that he was telling the truth.

"What an extraordinary power," I cried. "I thought I was abnormal in that way, for I always get excited in a moment, and I have heard men say that they needed some time to get ready for the act; but your power is far beyond anything I have ever seen or heard of."

"That is the worst of it," he remarked quietly. "If you get a reputation, some of them practically offer themselves. But one often meets women who don't care much for the act. I suppose you meet that sort oftener in England, if half one hears is true, than in France. Here the women are generally normal. But it's seldom they feel intensely: however, some do, thank God."

Naturally I spent a great deal of thought on his abnormality.

I soon noticed that he did not admire girls as I did. He seemed to prefer women and to keep to one or two. I half came to the conclusion that he husbanded his powers more than most men. But this he denied absolutely.

"Temptation is there to be yielded to," he declared. "I deny myself nothing that suits or pleases me in life; why should I?"

He was as much given to the pursuit of the unknown as anyone could be. I remember once, when we were talking of hunting big game in America or in Africa, he broke in, declaring that woman is the only game in the wide world worth pursuing. The mere hope of meeting her here or there, in the train going to Cannes or out walking—the Hoped-for One, the Desired— alone gives interest and meaning to life. "The only woman I really love," he went on, with a certain exaltation, "is the Unknown who haunts my imagination—seduction in person, for she possesses all the incompatible perfections I've never yet found in any one woman. She must be intensely sensuous, yet self-controlled; soulful, yet a coquette: to find her, that's the great adventure of life and there's no other."

I was astonished to discover that he was vainer of his amatory performances than even of his stories. "Who knows," he'd say, "whether these tales of mine are going to live or not? It's impossible to tell; you may be among the greatest today but the very next generation may turn away from you. Fame is all chance, the toss of a coin, but love, a new sensation, is something saved from oblivion."

I would not accept this for a moment. "The sensation is fleeting," I cried, "but the desire of fame seems to me the highest characteristic of humanity and in our lifetime we can be certain of enduring reputation and an influence that lives beyond the grave."

Maupassant shook his head, smiling. "*Tout passe;* there is no certainty."

"We know," I went on, "the whole road humanity has traveled for tens of thousands of years. The foetus in the womb shows our progress from the tadpole to the man, and we know the milleniums of growth from the human child to the thinker and poet, the God-man of today. The same process is still going on in each of us; have you become more pitiful than others, larger-hearted, more generous, more sympathetic, more determined to realize the highest in yourself? Put this in your book and it is sure to live with an ever-widening popularity. Goethe was right:

> Wer immer strebend sich bemüht
> Den können wir erlösen.*

"And Rabelais?" he retorted sarcastically, "and Voltaire? How do they fit in your moral Pantheon?"

"Voltaire defended Calas,"** I replied, "and Rabelais would be as easy to praise as Pascal, but your objection has a modicum of truth in it. It is the extraordinary, whether good or evil, that is certain to survive. We remember the name of the Marquis de Sade because of his monstrous, revolting cruelty as surely as that of St. Francis. There's lots of room for skepticism everywhere in life. I was only stating the rule which gives ground enough for hope and encourages to the highest achievement. Three or four of your stories wil be read a thousand years hence."

"We can hardly understand Villon," he retorted, "and the speech of the Ile de France in the twelfth century is another language to us."

"But printing has changed all that," I replied. "It immobilizes language, though it admits the addition of new words and new ideas. Your French will endure as Shakespeare's English endures."

"You don't altogether convince me," Maupassant replied, "though there's a good deal of truth in your arguments; but if you were not a writer yourself, you would not be so interested in fame and posthumous renown."

There he had me and I could only laugh.

A day or two later Ffrench came to tell me how magnificently endowed Maupassant was as a lover. I asked Ffrench whether he thought the abnormality a sign of health.

"Of course," he cried. "Proof of extraordinary strength," but somehow or other I was not so sure.

It was in 1885 or 1886, I think, that he sent me his *Horla*† with an interesting letter.

---

* From *Faust*, II, "Bergschluchten, Wald, Fels und Einöde."
(Whoever strives unceasingly
Him can we redeem.)

** Jean Calas (1698–1762), a French Protestant. One son became a Roman Catholic; another hanged himself in 1761. It was claimed that the second son was strangled to prevent his conversion. Calas was broken alive upon the wheel and a third son was banished. Voltaire pled the case before the Council of State at Versailles. The king and council, after three years, annulled the proceedings, declared Calas innocent, and declared all implication of guilt removed from the family.

† The story, as does *La Peur*, deals with fear and madness.

"Most critics will think I have gone mad," he wrote, "but you'll know better. I'm perfectly sane, but the story interested me strangely: there are so many thoughts in our minds that we cannot explain, fears in us that are instinctive and form, so to speak, the background of our being."

Le Horla made a tremendous impression on me; the title was composed from *le hors-là*, the being not ourselves in life. It was the first of Maupassant's stories which was quite beyond me. I couldn't have written anything like it. And asking myself, "Why?" I came to the conclusion, inspired perhaps by mere vanity, that I was too healthy, too normal, if you will, and that set me thinking.

When next I saw him: "That *Horla* of yours is astonishing," I began. "To fear as you must have feared in order to write that dreadful tale is evidence enough to me that your nerves are all jangled and out of tune."

Maupassant laughed at me. "I've never been in better health," he declared, "never in my life."

I had studied all venereal diseases in Vienna and I had just been reading a new German book on syphilis in which, for the first time, I found the fact stated that it often kills its victims by paralysis between forty and fifty, when the vital forces have begun to decline. Suddenly the thought came into my head and I put the question to Maupassant: "Have you ever had syphilis?"

"All the infantile complaints," he said laughing. "Everyone has it in youth, haven't they? But it's twelve or fifteen years now since I've seen a trace of it. I was completely cured long years ago."

I told him what the German specialist had discovered, but he wouldn't give any credence to it. "I dislike everything German, as you know," he said. "Their science even is exaggerated."

"But the other day," I reasoned, "you complained of pains in your limbs and took a very hot bath; that's not a sign of health."

"Let's go for a long walk," he replied. "You'll soon find I'm not decrepit."

We had our walk and I put my doubts and fears out of mind for the moment, but whenever I though of *Le Horla* I became suspicious. There were chapters, too, in some of his other books which disquieted me.

It was in the spring of 1888, I believe, that I met him at Cannes, where he had come in his yacht *Bel-Ami* from Marseilles. We dined together and he told me that he had had wonderful experiences in Algeria and the north of Africa. He had pushed to Kairouan, the Holy City, it appeared, and admired its wonderful mosque, but he had brought back little, save the fact that each Arab had three or four concubines besides his wife, and that all the women are usually wretchedly unhappy, with jealousy as a sort of continual madness.

He told me of a Jewess who kept a house with her two daughters and said he'd like to write the story of one of them and make her fall in love with a French officer because he took her out driving and was kind to her.

"Any evidence of affection, as apart from passion," he remarked, "has a curious weight, especially with such women. They are far prouder of tenderness than of desire."

"Long novels," he confessed once casually, "are much easier to write than *nouvelles* or *contes*. *Pierre et Jean,* for example, I finished in less than three months and it didn't tire me at all, whereas *La Maison Tellier* cost me more time and a far greater exertion."

Perhaps its was the preference in both writers for the short story that made me always couple Kipling with de Maupassant in my thoughts, but I must admit at once that Kipling was by far the more interesting companion. Draw him out, show him interest, and he could tell a tale by word of mouth as well as he ever wrote one. Unlike most able Frenchmen, Maupassant was not gifted as a talker, perhaps because he never let himself go to the inspiration of the moment; but now and then he would surprise you by width of vision or rightness of judgment, showing a mind, as Meredith said, that had "traveled."

We were all talking of Napoleon one night when I told how he had astonished me. I said once that Jesus had been the first to discover the soul and speak from it and to it, notably in the ineffable *Suffer little children to come unto me.* Years later I found that Napoleon had used the very same phrase: "Jesus discovered the soul."

"I don't like Napoleon," said de Maupassant, "though everyone must admire his intelligence, but I always think Jesus the wisest of men; how he came to such heights of thought in such surroundings is one of the wonders of the world to me. He had no mark upon him of his age; he was for all time."

"It is curious," I agreed, "indeed, almost impossible to frame him in his time. Again and again he speaks for all ages and for all men; but now and then comes the revealing word. Do you remember how the Devil took him up into the high mountain and showed him all the Kingdom of the Earth? It is manifest from that phrase that he thought the world was flat, and if you went high enough you could oversee it all."

"True, true," cried Maupassant. "I hadn't thought of it; yet he leads us all today and we follow humbly and at some distance."

Maupassant was almost as patriotic as Kipling, but not so blinded by the herd-instinct.

"You know," he said to me once, "we Normans and Bretons dislike the English more than the Germans; you are our enemies, it was you who came and sacked our towns and took toll of our wealth. The German is far away from us while you are close, just there across a strip of sea."

"I understand," I replied, "but the English have no fear, no dislike of you. How do you explain that?"

"Curious," he declared. "I think it must be because we were rich and you were poor before the modern industrial era. The rich always fear the poor and they have good reason for their instinctive dread."

The explanation was ingenious and in part true, I imagine.

Very early in our acquaintance, in spite of his alertness of mind and sympathetic, companionable good humor, I began to realize the truth of Taine's word that Maupassant was a sort of *taureau triste,* 'a sad bull.' Maupassant complained at first of his eyes; a year or so later he said that he often went blind for an hour: "A terrifying experience," he called it. About this time he confessed he had tried all the drugs; neuralgia plagued him and he took ether for it—"a temporary relief was better than nothing" —but with his sound good sense, he quickly saw that a drug only deferred the payment while increasing the debt. No wonder Flaubert begged him to be "moderate" in everything, in muscular exertion, in writing even, and especially in yielding to fits of sadness that only left one depressed and drained (*abruti*).

Maupassant loved to ascribe all his malaise to overwork; more than once he boasted to me of having written fifteen hundred pages in one year, to say nothing of articles in the *Gaulois* and the *Gil Blas.* The pages hardly contained more than one hundred and fifty words each, or say two English novels in the year; hard work, but nothing extraordinary, unless one takes into the account his steadily diminishing stock of health, which began to strike me about this time.

One evening I shall always remember. He had had neuralgia in the morning, which had gradually yielded to food and drink, a glass of wonderful port completing the cure. We had been talking of the belief in God when Maupassant turned to the personal factor. "What a strange being is man," he cried, "an imperial intelligence that watches the pains and miseries of its unfortunate fleshy partner. Plainly I note that I am getting steadily worse in health, that my bodily pains are increasing, that my hallucinations are becoming longer, my power of work diminishing. The supreme consolation comes from the certitude that when my state gets too bad, I'll put an end to it. Meanwhile I won't whine, I've had great hours! Ah! Great hours!"

It was in 1889, I think, that I first discovered why he was getting steadily worse in health. He broke an engagement with me, and when we next met a month later, I was still annoyed with him and showed it. To excuse himself, he blurted out that he had had an unexpected visitor from Paris and went on to confess that one's "late loves were the most terrible." "She is exquisitely pretty," he broke in, "perfect physically: a flawless mistress, a perfumed altar of love, and has besides a wealth of passion that I never met before. I can't resist her, and the worst of it is, I can't resist showing off with her and bringing her to wonder. What vain fools we men are and how I pay for the excess afterwards. Really, for a week after an orgy with her I suffer like one of the damned, and even now, though she has been a month gone, I'm a prey to misery (*indicible malaise*). I wish she'd keep away: she drains me, exhausts my vitality, unnerves me."

I thought it my duty to warn him. "You are showing the *surménage* everywhere," I said. "Your skin is leaden, your expression curious, troubled, fearful even. For God's sake, cut out all that orgy business: it's excusable at twenty or thirty but not at forty; it's your test and trial. You'll go under if your mind doesn't master your body. Take Shakespeare's great word to heart: even his Antony would not be 'the bellows and the fan to cool a harlot's lust'; it was doubtless his own confession."

"What a great phrase," cried Maupassant, "the bellows and the fan, great. . . .

"I know all that," he went on, "but then I say to myself, I'm beaten anyhow, growing steadily worse; one more gaudy night will be so much to the good. You can't imagine her myriad seductiveness. She uses a perfume that makes me drunk at first like ether; in an hour it has vanished but the still more intoxicating subtle scent of her body has taken its place; and her bodily beauty, and the ineffable charm of her withholding, and her giving drive me crazy. Never before have I experienced such pleasure or given it.

"Man! she's an aphrodisiac. As soon as my state of depression and misery begins to lighten, I want her. My thoughts turn to her; my mind, my body ache for her. Of course I make all sorts of good resolutions: I will be moderate and restrain myself; but when she is there I feel in me the strength of ten and the desire of conquest, the mad longing to reach an intenser thrill than ever before overpowers me, and her intense response carries me away, and—once more I fall into the depths."

He was assuredly a great lover, one of the most gifted of whom we have any record, and though in talk with me he usually dwelt most on the physical side of the passion, his letters to his mistress show that he was devoted to her spiritually as well, and that she was his heart's mate and complement. There is no greater love story in all literature; it ranks with Shakespeare's Antony and Cleopatra, and some of Maupassant's phrases are as intense as the best of Shakespeare. Surely it deserves to be recorded and given its due importance.

Now who was she, this incomparable mistress?* A Jewess, well off, ten years or so younger than Maupassant and married to a man who would not have forgiven her unfaith had he even suspected it. The lovers had to meet at long intervals and on the sly. Ten years after Maupassant's death she wrote of him and their love in La Grande Revue and it is plain, I think, from those pages, that if Maupassant had told her the effect of their love-orgies on his health, she would not only have refused to be a party to injuring him, but would have sought to help him to self-control.

Her affection for him seems both deep and high; she delights to record all his good qualities: his love and admiration of his mother; his kindness even to shameless beggars; his interest in other men and women, particularly in all curious, uncommon types; his constant desire to be fair and honest. Of course she dwells on his love for her and gives one extract from his letters to her twice. Here it is in French, a superb expression of love's

---

* There are several letters to "Madame X" in the French edition of Maupassant's correspondence, but she is not identified in any way.

humility and that sacred adoration of love that will yet redeem this sordid existence of ours.

Comme je vous aimais! Et comme j'aurais voulu m'agenouiller tout à coup devant vous, m'agenouiller là, dans la poussière, sur le bord du trottoir, et baiser vos belles mains, vos petits pieds, le bas de votre robe, les baiser en pleurant.

It is easy to English it:

"How I love you! How I wished to throw myself on my knees before you, there in the dust of the sidewalk, and kiss your lovely hands, and your little feet, the hem of your dress—kiss them all with hot tears."

This Madame X has more in her than facile appreciation. Maupassant confesses once that he is a "romance-writer, even in his embracings." She adds finely, "I would rather say that he remained a lover even in his romances. . . . And what a wonderful lover he was," she goes on.

Every meeting was a new birth of love, thanks to his genius. Through him I have lived such wonderful enchanting hours that I shudder to think what life would have meant, had I not met and loved him. His letters, and they were many, came at odd moments, most of them were dated at night; often I had only just left him when a letter from him would come, so ardent, so passionate, so tender, that I could hardly refrain from hastening back to him.

Here's the end of one of those love letters that shows, I think, marvelous intensity of feeling, perhaps the most astonishing and convincing expression known to me of the deepest human passion.

A few hours ago, you were there in my arms. Now I'm alone. But you remain with me. All the peculiarities of your personality live in me with such overwhelming unity that I seem to see your voice, to breathe your beauty, to hear the perfume of you . . . I kiss your white hands and my lips dwell on your scarlet mouth . . .

Surely this man reached undream'd of heights!

Some of us knew beforehand that Maupassant was richly affectionate, a born lover if ever there was one, but these golden words are the best proof of his astonishing genius. Alas! His fall was the more appalling.

In 1890 his love recognizes a profound change in him. "He is living," she says, "in a state of spiritual exaltation that brings with it hallucinations." In August he writes from Nice telling her that he needs her: "I am troubled by such strange ideas, oppressed by such mysterious anguish, shaken by such confused sensations that I feel like crying, 'Help, help!'

"The confused echoes of days I have lived torture me now and again, or excite me to a sort of madness"; and then he talks of the wild regrets he feels "for the days that are no more" (*des regrets pour un temps qui fut et qui ne sera plus jamais, jamais*). "I have the feeling," he goes on, "that my end is near and wholly unexpected. Come to me, come!"

It was this appeal, this cry of supreme distress, that brought about her final fatal visit.

Again and again she notes the constant preoccupation of his thought with the idea of death, even at a time when she was filled with a sense of his abounding health and vigor. Towards the end she declares that "his reason never seemed shaken; his sensations had altered, it is true, but not his judgment!"

She is always an advocate of the angel, always sees the best in her lover, and when all is over and long past, further off than far away, her words still ring pathetically sincere; the heart's cry for the golden days, "the days that are no more!"

"Only two years before, how full of life he was, and how strong, and I was young and in love with him. Oh, the sad, painful years I have lived since."

I think no one will deny that if Maupassant had told this woman the truth, she would have helped him to exercise self-restraint. Not once does she dwell on the physical side of their affection. It is the joys of his companionship she recalls, the delights of their spiritual intimacy. It is always he who calls and she who comes.

Maupassant's fate is not so worthy of pity, for he was warned again and again, and we mortals can hardly complain, even of those catastrophes that are unexpected and difficult, if not impossible, to foresee. Even his valet, François, had warned him.

Three or four years before the end Maupassant knew that the path of sense-indulgence for him led directly to madness and untimely death.

He could trace the progress of his malady in body and in mind from Le Horla, in the beginning, to Qui sait with its unholy terror, the last story he ever wrote. Even in his creative work he was warned after every excess and in fifty different ways. First an orgy brought on fits of partial blindness, then acute neuralgic pains and periods of sleeplessness, while his writing showed terrifying fears; and all this disease had to be cured by rest and dieting, baths and frictions, and, above all, by constant change of scene. Then came desperate long-continued depression broken by occasional exaltations and excitements; later still, periods of hallucination, during which his mind wandered and which he recalled afterwards with humiliation and shame; and always, always the indescribable mental agony he spoke of as indicible malaise. Finally he lost control of his limbs, saw phantoms on the highway and was terrified by visions that gave him the certainty of madness, which could only be faced by the fixed resolve to put an end to himself, if the punishments became more than he could bear.

Yet he prayed again and again for the fatal caresses. It is possible that syphilis had weakened his moral fiber; many of us between forty and fifty have come to nervous breakdown and by resolute abstinence, careful exercise and change of scene have won back to health and sanity. But it was the young Maupassant of the boating on the Seine and the heedless insane indulgences with Mimi and Musette that weighted the dice against him.

I once said that it took sheer good fortune for a miracle of genius such as Shakespeare to grow to full height and give the best in him; had it not been for Lord Southampton's gift of a thousand pounds we should never have seen *Hamlet* or *Lear* or *Macbeth* or *The Tempest*. It requires a miracle of genius, and extraordinary bodily strength to boot, in a Frenchman to reach healthful old age as Hugo did and at seventy write on the art and joy of being a grandfather. But Maupassant, like Shakespeare, was first and last a lover, and that's the heaviest of all handicaps.

His valet François* has told us more of the truth about the last stage than any other observer. He noticed at once that Maupassant's inamorata was extremely pretty and beautifully dressed. *"C'est une bourgeoise du plus grand chic; elle a tout à fait le genre de ces grandes dames qui ont été élévées soit aux Oiseaux, soit au Sacre-Coeur. Elle en a gardé les bonnes et rigides manières."* (She's a woman of the greatest distinction, the perfect type of those noble ladies who have been brought up in some famous convent such as the Holy Heart. She has all their charm of manner and their high-bred aloofness.)

As he saw the effect of her intimacy with his master, whom he loved, he grew to hate and dread her visits. Time and again he was tempted to tell the "Vampire," as he called her, to keep away.

On the twentieth of September, 1891, about two o'clock in the afternoon, he heard the bell and at the door found the woman "who had already done my master so much harm. She passed me, as she always did, without speaking, with impassive marble face."

After the catastrophe, he regrets he did not tell her what she was doing and slam the door in her face. He did not know that in August Maupassant had written to her, begging her to come—a piteous last appeal which I have already quoted.

"In the evening Maupassant seemed broken (*accablé*) and didn't speak of the visit. In spite of the constant care, he hadn't recovered a month later. Early in November they went from Paris to Cannes to the Chalet de l'Isere."

Maupassant was still suffering from tortured nerves (*malaise indicible*). On the fifth of December he wrote to his lawyer: "I am so ill that I fear I shall not live more than a few days."

Every two or three days he went across to Nice to lunch with his mother at the villa Les Ravenelles and François went with him to prepare his meal, for he knew exactly how to cook so that his master would get the most nourishment with the least chance of indigestion.

On the twenty-fourth of December he paid his mother a long visit and promised to spend Christmas day with her; he was getting better slowly and wanted above all things to get to work once more and finish a sketch he had begun of Turgenief. He begged his mother to read all Turgenief's novels and send him a page or two on each; she promised she would.

But on Christmas day he put her off: two ladies, two sisters—one married, the other unmarried—had come to see him and he went with them

* Apparently in *Souvenirs sur Guy de Maupassant* (1883–1893).

and spent the day on the island Ste. Marguerite in the Bay of Cannes. We all know who the married one was. François does not tell us anything of this change of plan, but he records that in the afternoon of the twenty-sixth, Maupassant went out for a walk towards Grasse and returned ten minutes later. François was dressing himself but Maupassant called him loudly, imperiously, to tell him that "he had met on the road a shade, a phantom!" "He was evidently," continued François, "the victim of an hallucination and was afraid, though he wouldn't confess it."

"On the twenty-seventh at breakfast he coughed a little and in all seriousness declared that he had swallowed a morsel of sole and it had gone into his lungs and he might die of it."

This day he wrote again to his solicitors that "he was going from bad to worse and believed that he would be dead within a couple of days." As he went out for a sail on his yacht in the afternoon, the sailor Raymond remarked that he could not lift his leg properly to get on board: now he put it too high, and again too low. François remarks that he had already noticed this same symptom of paralytic weakness.

On the first of January Maupassant couldn't shave himself, told François that there was a sort of mist before his eyes; but at breakfast he ate two eggs and drank some tea and feeling better, set off for Nice, as otherwise "my mother will think I'm very ill." François went with him.

Curiously enough the reports of this last day's happenings differ widely. His mother says that they talked the whole afternoon and that she remarked nothing abnormal in him, except a sort of exaltation or subdued excitement. In the middle of dinner alone together (*tête à tête*) he talked wildly (*divaguait*). "In spite of my entreaties, my tears, instead of sleeping there in Les Ravenelles, he would go back to Cannes. I begged him to stay," she says, "went on my knees to him in spite of the weakness of my old bones; he would follow his own plan (*il suivait sa vision obstinée*). I saw him disappear in the night, excited, mad, wandering in mind, going I didn't know where, my poor child" (*Et je vis s'enfoncer dans la nuit . . . exalté, fou, divaguante, allant je ne sais où, mon pauvre enfant*).

Most of this is inexact, a fiction of memory, not fact. François gives us the truth more nearly: he tells us that he prepared Maupassant's *déjeuner* and there were present, besides his mother, his brother's wife, and his niece and his aunt (Madame de Harnois), whom Guy loved greatly. At four o'clock the carriage came for them, and on the way to the station they bought a quantity of white grapes to continue his usual regimen (*cure*). François tells how on reaching home Maupassant changed his clothes, put on a silk shirt to be more comfortable, dined on the wing of a chicken, some chicory, and a soufflé of rice with cream flavored with vanilla, and drank a glass and a half of mineral water.

A little later Maupassant complained of pains in the back. François cured him with *ventouses,* gave him a cup of camomile, and Maupassant went to bed at eleven-thirty. François seated himself in an armchair in the next room and waited till his master should fall asleep. At twelve-thirty François went to his bedroom but left the door open. A moment after the garden bell rang: it was a telegram; but he found Maupassant sleeping with his mouth half open and went back to bed without waking him. He continues. "It was about two-fifteen when I heard a noise. I hurried into the little room at the head of the stairs and found Maupassant standing with his throat cut."

"See what I've done, François," he said. "I've cut my throat; it's a pure case of madness!"

François called Raymond, the strong sailor, to help him, then sent for the doctor and helped to put the poor madman in a strait waistcoat.

In my first sketch of Maupassant, published in the first volume of my *Contemporary Portraits,* I was able to go a little deeper even than François. I reached the Hotel at Antibes early in January, 1892, when all the world was talking of poor Maupassant's breakdown in madness. At once I went across to Nice and from the accounts of eye-witnesses reconstituted the scene at and after the *déjeuner* of the first of January in his mother's villa, Les Ravenelles. During the meal his mind had wandered and so justified his mother's fears and anxieties; after the meal he came out on the little half-moon terrace with the blue sky above and the purple dancing sea in front to mock his agony. I quote here what I wrote at the time.

How desperately he struggled for control; now answering some casual remark of his friends, now breaking out into a cold sweat of dread as he felt the rudder slipping from his hand; called back to sanity again by some laughing remark, or other blessed sound of ordinary life, and then, again, swept off his feet by the icy flood of sliding memory and dreadful thronging imaginings, with the awful knowledge behind knocking at his consciousness that he was already mad, mad —never to be sane again, mad—that the awful despairing effort to hold on to the slippery rock and not to slide down into the abyss was all in vain, that he was slipping, slipping in spite of himself, in spite of bleeding fingers, falling— falling . . .

Hell has no such horror! There in that torture chamber—did it last but a minute—he paid all debts, poor, hounded, haunted creature with wild beseeching eyes, choking in the grip of the foulest spectre that besets humanity . . .

He returned to Cannes by train and at two next morning François heard him ringing and hurried to his bedside, only to find his master streaming with blood and mad, crying wildly, 'Encore un homme au rancart! au rancart!' (Another man on the dust-heap).

Surely this phrase is De Maupassant's, and the remark that François puts in his mouth, "It's a pure case of madness," is only his own later summing up of the situation. "Another man on the dust-heap" is the despairing soul-cry of De Maupassant.

It was found afterwards that De Maupassant had taken out his revolver, but François had already removed the cartridges, so De Maupassant put the revolver down and took up a sort of paper-knife which did not cut deeply enough and injured his face more than his neck.

The doctor got De Maupassant to bed and he slept while François and Raymond watched in the dim light and thought of the irreparable disaster.

In the morning they found the wire from the Jewess, the "Vampire," as François calls her again bitterly, while he wonders whether her evil influence, by means of the telegram Maupassant never saw, could have helped to bring about the supreme catastrophe.

Everyone knows that the great writer got rapidly worse, was taken to Paris to the asylum of Dr. Blanche, became more and more a mere animal till death took him a year and a half later on the third of July, 1893.

Maupassant's life story and tragic end are full of lessons for all artists. What I find in it is the moral I am continually emphasizing, that every power given to us is almost of necessity a handicap and a danger.

It was said of Byron, and is surely no less true of Maupassant, that he "awoke one morning to find himself famous." The publication of *Boule de Suif* put Maupassant in one day among the great masters of the short story. He was praised on all sides as an impeccable artist; it is scarcely to be wondered at that he afterwards neglected self-criticism and hardly ever bettered the workmanship he had shown in that early story. He wrote over two hundred short stories in the next ten years, but perhaps no single tale shows finer artistry.

Again: he was gifted with extraordinary virile power; the consequence was that he got syphilis before he was of age and brought himself to an untimely end because he was determined to show off his prowess as a lover.

When shall we artists and lovers learn that the most highly-powered engines require the strongest brakes?

But how dare I judge him? How inept all criticism appears when I think of his personal charm; the gladness in his eyes when we met; the clasp of his hand; his winged words in the evenings spent side by side; the unforgettable glint when a new thought was struck out; the thousand delights of his alert, clear intelligence; ah, my friend, my dear, dear friend! Gone forever! Guy, swallowed up and lost in the vague vast of uncreated night, lost forever!

I reread his last volume: it begins with a masterpiece: *L'Inutile Beauté;* at the end *Un Cas de Divorce* and *Qui Sait.* And now *Un Cas de Divorce* seems more characteristic to me and more terrible than *Qui Sait,* with deeper words, words wrung from the soul of a great lover—the man's adoration of the beauty of flowers, his passionate love of the orchid with its exquisite roseate flanks and ivory pistils giving forth an intoxicating perfume stronger far and sweeter than the scene of any woman's body.

And he watched the flower fade, wither and die, losing all loveliness, and instead of the seductive perfume, the vile odor of decay.

Chapter XXI

Robert Browning's Funeral; Cecil Rhodes
and Barnato; A Financial Duel;
Actress and Prince at Monte Carlo

EARLY IN DECEMBER, 1889, Smith Elder, the publishers, sent me a copy of *Asolando: Fancies and Facts,* by Robert Browning. I spent the night reading it: good stuff but not a first-rate thing in the booklet. By the bye, where did he get the title? From Asolo, the little place in the hills looking down on Venice and mentioned in *Sordello?* Or perhaps from *asolare:* to wander about? A few days later the news reached us that Browning had died in Venice, aged seventy-seven. For half a dozen years I had had the greatest love and admiration for glorious Robert Browning; indeed, until I met him at Lady Shrewsbury's at lunch, he was, after Carlyle, my hero. I had found a certain likeness between us: his best work was a thinker's and not a singer's; his poetic endowment was not extraordinary. When a youth he had worked through an English dictionary, and I had done the same thing, without knowing that he had set the example, forty years before. My friend Verschoyle had given me a Johnson's dictionary in two huge leather-bound volumes and I had gone through them in a little over a year, putting down in red ink at the bottom of each page all the words that were unfamiliar to me. When this labor was finished I went again through the words in red ink, marking any I had forgotten in blue pencil. Finally, I went through these once more; yet there were still thirty words or so that had not stuck in my memory, but that I did not mind. The mere fact that I had felt the same need as Browning intensified my sympathy for him. Then, too, had he not written to the British public: "Ye who love me not but one day will love"—my feeling from boyhood on, and only now at thirty-odd was I getting near the hope that one day I too should win their liking.

"Glorious Robert Browning," I always called him to myself; but when we met I was disillusioned. I did my best to win him, time and again, and at length. At Lady Jeune's lunch, when he showed his disdain for Lowell, who was fêted and honored, I thought I had won him. When he saw that I too felt nothing but contempt for Lowell's poetry, he thawed to me and we walked across Hyde Park together and he took tea in my little house in Kensington Gore opposite the park. I made up a dinner party soon after with Frederick Harrison,* who was an old friend of his, and Lord and Lady Folkestone; and after the dinner, having primed Lord Folkestone to ask me, I told the company what Browning had meant to me; evidently he was pleased. Harrison afterwards said my praise was too enthusiastic—"overpitched," he called it, but that's a good fault. After this Browning treated me with some cordiality. He came to my house twice or three times but he wouldn't drink, was indeed of an astonishing sobriety. He told me that health came through self-denial; yet he was a little too stout for my ideal of perfect health. He was not as wise in physical things as he thought himself, but he was kindly till I "presumed," I supposed he'd have called it. I tried one day to find out from him where he got the passion of *James Lee's Wife.* I wanted to know whether he had learned the whole gamut of passion from one woman, his wife. At once he drew into himself like a hurt snail and tried to be indignant. I told him Shakespeare was infinitely franker. He quoted the last three lines of his poem to me, beginning with Wordsworth's statement, which he prints in italics.

> . . . *"With this same key*
> *Shakespeare unlocked his heart;* once more!
> Did Shakespeare? If so, the less Shakespeare he."**

Which seemed to me a dire example of the smaller man judging the greater and in itself mere drivel. I undertook to prove to him that Shakespeare had told a good deal even about his own sensual experiences. I cited the sonnet on lust:

> Enjoyed no sooner but despised straight,
> Past reason hunted, and no sooner had
> Past reason hated, as a swallow'd bait
> On purpose laid to make the taker mad.†

"The man who could write that at thirty-five must have been very weak," I began. "It's a confession of weakness: the ordinary healthy man doesn't hate lust after enjoyment; on the contrary—"

But Browning would not discuss or even consider it. "There are things

---

* Correctly, Frederic Harrison (1831–1923), jurist, biographer, and historian. He wrote biographies of Cromwell, William the Silent, Ruskin, and Chatham, as well as *The Meaning of History* (enlarged in 1894) and *Byzantine History in the Early Middle Ages* (1900).
** From "House," from *Pacchiarotto, with Other Poems:*
> Hoity-toity! A street to explore,
> Your house the exception! *'With this same key*
> *Shakespeare unlocked his heart,'* once more!
> Did Shakespeare? If so, the less Shakespeare he!
† Sonnet CXXIX.

that should not be told," he persisted, "things that the public has no right to know"; whereas I was just as sure that all men could learn even from the weaknesses of a great man. Blake knew that

> The errors of a wise man make your rule
> Rather than the perfections of a fool.*

I could not get Browning even to argue or think; he preferred to take my wish to know as an impertinence and we parted in some coldness, though of course as soon as I saw that I could not prevail, I drew back and sought to excuse myself. We met afterwards half a dozen times half casually; he never came to my house again nor had I ever again the chance of a private talk with him.

> And now he was gone
> . . . . . to where on high
> Love weighs the counsel of futurity

Browning—that vivid soul—

> Covered with silence and forgetfulness.

The passing of such men makes life poorer.

When I heard that Browning was to be buried in the Abbey I was heart-glad; an everlasting rest in the great Temple of Silence and Reconciliation was surely due to him. I spoke to Froude about this ceremony on the last day of the dying year and he asked me to go with him. Of course I was only too glad to promise.

It was a foggy, gloomy morning, bleak, too: in the Abbey itself Froude introduced me to Lecky.** I was glad that I had read his *Rationalism* with great interest, for he became friendly when I told him what his phrase for prostitutes—"the sisterhood of sorrow"—had meant to me. "One of the great phrases of our literature," I called it, but I could not help wondering whether with a little loving-kindness the oldest profession could not be made "a sisterhood of joy." But neither he nor Froude would consider it; they called it "a poor French invention," and when I cited what I think the noblest thought in Proudhon,† they still remained entirely unconvinced. Proudhon proposed that the lowest forms of labor, the cleansing of sewers and the most dangerous trades, should be undertaken by the chivalry of youth—a sacred band of volunteers. Men become soldiers, he said, for scant pay and risk their lives for almost nothing. Why not hearten them to take up the vilest and most dangerous work in the same chivalrous spirit? "The sewer brigade would soon win distinction," Proudhon declared, and

---

* From Blake's *Notebook*.

** William Edward Hartpole Lecky (1838–1903). Harris here refers to his *History of the Rise and Fall of the Spirit of Positivism in Europe* (1865).

† Pierre Joseph Proudhon (1809–65). A French Socialist, who considered property and capital as the power of exploiting other men.

in the same way it seemed to me that the sisterhood of sorrow might accept even the degradation of lust as a new distinction!

But they would not have it; the majority of even able men cannot take up a new idea and give it a reasonable hospitality.

While we were talking, the great bell began to toll and the deep tones brought a solemn silence. The whispering was at once hushed.

As I looked about me, I was astonished by the number of well known faces even I with my short sight could distinguish: Meredith and Wolseley and, strange to say, Whistler and Irving and Frederic Harrison, Bret Harte, too, and du Maurier.* The whole space was crowded and the faces gleamed oddly in the grey mist shot through by the gold of a few candles and lamps. Suddenly the organ rang out in Purcell's burial mass and the bier, preceded by choir and clergy, with Browning's son** as chief mourner, was borne to the chancel steps. The papers next day gave a long list of those who followed the coffin, but I could only recognize the fine head of Sir Frederick Leighton.†

The choristers sang a hymn: the young voices brought tears to my eyes and I was not the only one so affected: Huxley's handkerchief was before his eyes as the music ceased.

The coffin was lowered to its place by Chaucer's tomb; the Dean said the benediction and the great organ boomed out the Dead March from *Saul*.

Slowly we all began to move, and when I stood by the grave, great spirits seemed to people the place: Chaucer and Shakespeare, Spenser and Ben Jonson were there, and the great Doctor with his stout figure and reverent soul; and the spirit of Robert Browning met them and words of his seemed to stir the sentient air:

> O lyric love half angel and half bird
> And all a wonder and a wild desire.††

Other lines of his floated into my head, unforgettable lines: the woman's confession in *The Ring and the Book:*

> He was ordained to call and I to come.

And how Browning thanks God that each man has two soul-sides:

> . . . one to face the world with
> One to show a woman when he loves her.

But does the light come after the darkness and will the woman-soul be waiting? Who knows? Who can tell?

* George Louis Palmella Busson Du Maurier (1834–96). Artist, contributor to *Punch*, and author of *Peter Ibbetson* and *Trilby*.
** Robert Barrett Browning (1849–1912), a sculptor; son of the poet.
† Browning wrote an eight-line poem about his painting, *Orpheus and Eurydice*.
†† From *The Ring and the Book:*
    O lyric Love, half-angel and half-bird
    And all a wonder and a wild desire.

Out of the throng in the great church into the foggy great gloom. Even Froude is affected; I hear him whispering: "Soon, soon. He giveth his Beloved sleep," and then aloud: "What a great ceremony!" he went on, "and a great man." I bowed my head.

In the summer of 1888 Rhodes startled English society by giving £10,000 to Parnell on condition that he'd work for the retention of Irish Members in the British House of Commons, for he believed, as he told Parnell, that "Irish Home Rule would lead to Imperial Home Rule." Suddenly it dawned upon English politicians that they must enlarge their views or the ablest men from their own colonies would be against them. I had already helped to found the Imperial Federation League, so I was heart and soul with Rhodes from the beginning. A very notable Englishman, I thought him, without "side" or pose of any sort, using British snobbery with some disdain to forward his own schemes. He spoke of Parnell as "the most reasonable and sensible man I have ever met." People forget many of Rhodes's achievements. In 1887 Lord Salisbury was quite willing to accept Portugal's extravagant claim to a continuous dominion from Angola on the west coast to Mozambique on the east, which would have finally limited England's empire in Africa. Luckily Rhodes had won Sir Hercules Robinson over to his, or rather Bartle-Frere's idea, that England should annex the whole high central plateau of Africa from the Cape to Cairo.* W. H. Smith** was opposed to granting a charter to the Rhodes' Exploration Company till Sir Hercules Robinson talked of "the amateur meddling of irresponsible and ill-advised persons in England." In April, 1889, Lord Gifford, Rhodes, Rudd and Beit applied for a charter and Lord Knutsford† commended the proposal to Lord Salisbury as likely to save the heavy expenses that had been incurred in British Bechuanaland; and Rhodes was informed privately that he would get what he wanted if he put influential persons on his board. Thereupon he got the Duke of Abercorn as Chairman: the Duke got the Prince of Wales's son-in-law, the Duke of Fife, to consent to join the board, and best of all Albert Grey, whom

* Robinson (1824–97); governor of the Cape Colony and high commissioner of South Africa during the Boer War.
Bartle-Frere (1815–84); governor of the Cape Colony and high commissioner for the settlement of native affairs in South Africa 1877–80.
** (1825–91). A Conservative M.P. who at one time defeated John Stuart Mill in the Grosvenor constituency. Smith was first lord of the Admiralty under Disraeli; his being a commoner was sharply criticized; and that criticism was popularly vented in *HMS Pinafore*. Under Salisbury, Smith was secretary of state for war. He succeeded Randolph Churchill as Speaker of the House of Commons.
† Lord Gifford (1849–1911).
Rudd, Rhodes's partner.
Alfred Beit (1853–1906). He emigrated from Germany to South Africa and dealt in diamonds; Rhodes persuaded him to become a British subject. He was one of the great English philanthropists.
Sir Henry Holland.

Courtney called "the Paladin of his generation," and the most distinguished member of the South African Committee.* Though warned by Chamberlain, Albert Grey finally agreed to throw in his lot with Rhodes. The trick was turned and the Chartered Company came into existence.

All through these negotiations I met Rhodes twice or thrice a week and learned to know him intimately, and most of the marked steps of his rise of fortune and power I heard from his own lips. In 1882 his De Beers Company only paid three per cent on the capital of £200,000; in 1888 it paid twenty-five per cent on a capital of over two millions and a quarter. It paid, that is, £6,000 in 1882 and six years later £600,000. Then he told me of his long fight with Barnato** and how at length he incorporated Kimberley Central with De Beers. I shall never forget how summarily he treated it and how differently it all sounded when I heard it from Beit later and then from Barnato and Woolfie Joel.† They went, it appeared, to a final meeting one evening in Kimberley, Rhodes and Beit on one side, Barnato and Woolfie Joel on the other. Beit had made it up with Rhodes to let him do the bargaining: "I'm not a Jew for nothing; I'll get it cheaper than you can!" Rhodes consented.

Barnato and Woolfie were nearing the place when Barnato said suddenly, "What should we get?"

Woolfie said, "Half a million, I hope."

"Bah!" cried Barney, "I'm going to be a millionaire tonight, you'll see. Rhodes doesn't value money," and he smacked his lips.

When the four met, Rhodes, forgetting all that he had promised Beit, began at once, "I hate bargaining: I'll give you, Barnato, more than your holding in Kimberley's worth. I'll give you a cool million cash!"

Beit cried, "Oh my God, my God, Rhodes! You'll ruin us."

Barnato got up at once and reached for his hat: "We may as well go, Woolfie, if they think one million can buy us. I thought we were going to get a square deal," and he turned to the door.

"Sit down, sit down," cried Rhodes. "Here, Beit, you talk to them."

---

* Duke of Abercorn (1838–1913), a leader of the Irish landlords who were against Home Rule. He became president of the British South African Company when Rhodes resigned after the Jameson Raid.

Duke of Fife (1849–1912); the Earl of Fife until he married Louise Victoria Alexandra Dagmar, Princess Royal of Great Britain and Ireland and Duchess of Fife. Not only was the Duke a son-in-law, but he was an intimate of the Prince of Wales.

Albert Grey (1851–1917). Grey became a Liberal M.P. in 1880, but he fell out with Gladstone in 1886 over Home Rule and then lost his seat. He was appointed administrator of Rhodesia after the Jameson Raid.

Leonard Courtney (1832–1918), leader writer on *The Times;* then a professor of political economy at University College; and finally a Liberal M.P. He lost his seat in 1900 when he opposed the Boer War.

** Barnet Isaacs Barnato (1852–97). The "Barnato" was added to Isaacs when he was a comedian in London. He also made his fortune in diamonds in South Africa, and when he merged with Rhodes he became a director in De Beers. When his health failed, he threw himself from a ship.

† A nephew of Barnato's.

The quartette spent the whole night talking, bargaining, disputing, but at length Rhodes and Beit bought Kimberley Central for over five million sterling; yet the amalgamation was a good deal for De Beers and left Rhodes free to make even more out of the gold fields of the Rand than he had made out of diamonds in Kimberley.

When he got the promise of the charter for his exploring company, he went about London with a sheaf of many colored application forms in his breast pocket. Long before this I had introduced him to Arthur Walter of *The Times*.

Strange to say, Arthur Walter did not take to Rhodes at first. "He's a boor," he said. "He forgets common civilities in his haste to push his own ideas."

"True enough," I replied, "but you'll get to like him, Walter; he has no malice in him, nothing petty," and soon my forecast proved true.

On a certain evening Rhodes outstayed Walter and then handed me a colored form. "Write your application for shares in the Chartered Company on that," he said, "and up to a thousand shares you'll get the allotment."

I handed him back the paper, shaking my head; at once he selected another color and pushed it across to me. "That's the biggest I'm giving, Harris; that goes in thousands."

"I don't want it," I said. "I don't gamble."

"Gamble be d——d!" he cried. "This is a certainty: these shares will be dealt in on the stock exchange at a premium of £5; you can make £40,000 in a week by using that form. I'll give you £20,000 for it when you please!"

"No, no, Rhodes," I said. "You mustn't misunderstand me. I believe Chartered Shares will go to a big premium (within a week they went to £8 each), but I like you and what I've done I've done to help you and the cause we both have at heart, and I don't want any pay for it."

He held out his hand to me, saying simply, "I understand, still I wish . . ." I shook my head. "D'ye know there's only one other man in England besides yourself who has refused? Look at this list," and he handed it to me. One of the first names to catch my eye was that of the Duchess of Abercorn; the next that struck me in turning the pages was that of Schradhorst, the brother of the Liberal agitator* who was always against Rhodes's schemes: he was down for 100 shares. "He asked me for 'em," was Rhodes's comment.

"Who's that?" I asked, pointing to a name which had only five shares opposite to it.

"Oh," exclaimed Rhodes after some thought, "that must be the name of the midshipman who took me out in his gig to the flagship in Simon Bay."

We both laughed: from duchess to midshipman, enemy as well as friend, all held out their hands. And Rhodes persisted with me. "You're too care-

* Francis Schradhorst (1840–1900).

less about money, Harris! You'll see; you'll be sorry for it yet. Take £10,000; put it away in Consols and forget it. Before you die, you'll say my advice was the best you've ever had."

Winston Churchill gave me the very same advice twenty years later, said that the money I got him for his *Life* of his father had made him free from care and fear. Rhodes and Winston Churchill were right. I should have taken the money offered me and put it away in Consols and have forgotten about it; I'd have been happier if I had followed their advice.

For a good many years about this time I spent the worst of the winter months in Monte Carlo and at first used to gamble a good deal, though I never lost my head or did myself any serious harm.

One evening at Monte Carlo I became aware that the Prince of Wales was standing just behind me. Almost at the same moment Sir Algernon Borthwick,* whom I knew fairly well, touched my shoulder and bending down told me in a low voice that the Prince wished me to be presented to him. Of course I got up and turned round at once, and the Prince, shaking my hand said, with a strong German accent, "I've heard a great deal about you from my uncle, the Duke of Cambridge. He calls you the best story-teller he has ever met. I hope I may hear you tell some stories one of these days, but now I see you are playing with great luck and I wish you'd put these on for me," and he handed me a bundle of bank notes.

His accent was that of a German Jew and "the" was a stumbling block: "that" was "dat" and "these" "dese." There had been a run of red and I had backed it, so I placed the Prince's pile beside mine and won a couple of times, when I took off a couple of maximums for each of us. I was well inspired, for black won the next *coup* and the Prince was as delighted as a child. What he said about the story-telling came into my head as he stuffed the notes in his pockets. It suddenly occurred to me that probably no one had ever ventured to tell him a naughty story. So I told him a naughty rhyme to his huge amusement.

> Here's to the game of twenty toes,
> It's known all over the town;
> The girls play it with ten toes up
> And the boys with ten toes down.

"Tell me another, tell me another," he cried. So nothing loath, I told him a story that always seemed to me supremely amusing. An old actor found himself one evening on the Thames embankment. Out of work and out at elbows he sat brooding, when one of the female nightbirds sank onto the bench beside him. He made room for her, bowing courteously, so she began to talk, and finally asking him what he was.

"An actor, Madame, merely an old actor. And you?" he added courteously.

* (1830–1908), owner of the *Morning Post*.

"Oh," was the bitter reply. "I'm only a prostitute!"

The broken down actor turned to her earnestly; "Two great professions, Madame, ours, cursed by the competition of amateurs!"

The Prince knit his brow for a moment and then the humor struck him and he laughed heartily.

"Another story, Sir," I began, and told of Lady Hawkins. Sir Henry Hawkins, the famous "hanging" judge, so-called, had married his cook in later life and she used English like a common cockney woman and soon became the notorious Mrs. Malaprop of the last decades of the nineteenth century in London. Sir Henry Hawkins loved beautiful oriental carpets and had got a splendid one for his sitting-room. At a reception once, a young lord complimented Lady Hawkins on the splendid carpet. "I don't know how many men have copulated me upon that carpet," the lady is said to have replied.

The Prince was so delighted and laughed so heartily that I told him the story of the English servant girl who came to her mistress at the end of the first week, saying, "Mum, I'll have to leave."

"Why, Mary," said the mistress, "you've only been here just over a week and we've tried to make it comfortable for you. What's wrong?"

"Well, mum, it's them 'orrid texts in my bedroom. I can't abear 'em."

"Horrid texts, Mary? What texts?" asked the old Puritan lady in astonishment.

"Well, Mum, there's one just over my bed: 'Be ye also ready, for you know not the day nor the hour when the Master cometh.' "

"Well," said the old lady, "what do you object to in that, Mary?"

"Well, mum," said Mary setting her jaw. "I've been ready over a week and he ain't come yet. I can't sleep."

The Prince laughed so consumedly that I continued with old schoolboy "chestnuts" that I should have thought everyone knew. Evidently he had never heard one of them, for he walked up and down the gambling room for half an hour with his arm on my shoulder, shaking with laughter. It was the limericks he seemed to like most; one in especial pleased him so much that he tried to learn it by heart. Here it is.

> There was a young lady at sea
> Who said, "God, how it hurts me to pee."
> "I see," said the Mate,
> "That accounts for the state
> Of the captain, the purser and me."

I noticed that both Lord Hartington and Randolph Churchill were waiting for a chance of speech with the Prince. I told him this and as a sudden thought came into my head, I blurted it out: "Jeanne Granier,* the great French actress is here, Sir, and she's one of the wittiest women in Paris

---

* Future wife of Paul Granier (1843–1904), a French Deputy with an imperialist turn of mind and editor of *Autorité*. She played in *Les Deux Ecoles* in 1902.

and a great story teller. If you'd do me the honor to sup with me tonight at the Grand Hotel, I'd have Granier and we'd try to amuse you."

"I'd love it," he said at once, "but the d——d journalists might talk. Get Lord Randolph Churchill to come too and it'll all be put to his account; more talk about him than me, see?"

"All right, Sir," I said. "Shall we say ten o'clock?"

"Sure, sure!" he replied. "At ten I'll be with you."

On my way to find Jeanne Granier I saw Randolph and he consented to come, but with some unwillingness. "If you don't wish to come," I said, "I can get Lord Hartington, but the worst of it is, he knows no French, while your French is very good."

"That settles it," he said whimsically. "I'll call it a command and come."

I soon found Granier and took her to dinner; she was the best type of French woman and I think we liked each other sincerely. When I told her about the Prince and how I had won him by risqué stories which no one had ever dared to tell him before, she laughed with keen appreciation. "We are all won by the lives we know nothing about," she said. "I'll tell him stories he has never imagined; leave it to me."

We had an excellent dinner and a little before ten made our way to the Grand Hotel. At the very door of the hotel we came across the Prince. It was a wonderful night: the heavens like one deep sapphire set off by the radiance of a full moon. Scarcely had I presented Mlle. Granier to the Prince and he had said how delighted he was to know personally such a queen of the stage, when she struck an attitude and pointing to the moon cried: "*Qu'elle est belle et pâle cette lune-là.*" And then in a man's voice she rejoined, "*Pour belle je n'en sais rien; pour pâle, elle doit bien l'être, elle a passé tant de nuits!*" The Prince laughed, delighted with the witty *innuendo,* and indeed I was surprised by it, till some years afterwards I found that the witty word was from Henri Becque,* the dramatist, who passed almost unnoticed and unknown through life, in spite of possessing a great talent.

When we got upstairs to my rooms Randolph soon put in an appearance, but he didn't add much to the gaiety of the evening. All the burden was carried by Jeanne Granier, who immediately, after a little supper, began telling us stories of her early life on the stage with incomparable verve and humor. She had been on the boards as a child and from ten years of age on had hardly known an evening without being annoyed by the desire of some old man. "What did they do?" asked the prince.

"This manager kissed me, Sir," she said; "that director pinched my bottom (*fesses*) as I passed; the other told me I was pretty and tempting: all of them without exception persecuted me. Yet I liked it all, I must confess, and the bolder they were, the more I liked 'em!" We could not but laugh!

The Prince was rejuvenated, and towards the end Randolph, too, began

* (1837–1889). *La Parisienne* (1885) was his most successful play.

to take an interest in Granier's stories; and really they were excellent and formed a complete intimate picture and chronicle, so to say, of the French stage. The name of Sarah Bernhardt having come up, she recited a witty little verse as an epitaph of the great cabotine:

> Artiste adorée aux deux pôles
> Ci-git Sarah, qui remplissait
> Mieux ses rôles
> Que son corset.

Of course we all talked of Sarah for some time and then went off upon Coquelin, whom I always thought the best actor I had ever seen on any stage. To my amazement Randolph agreed with me; he had seen him in *Le Bourgeois Gentilhomme* and like myself thought him inimitable.

Curiously enough, Granier knew a witty epitaph on him, too, and gave it with astounding *brio* and a shade of malice.

> Ci-gît sous le marbre et le lierre
> Le petit-fils, le digne héritier de Molière:
> Seulement trop modest, au lieu de Poquelin
> Il s'est appelé Coquelin.

I don't know why we all laughed so consumedly or why the hours fled so delightfully, but when we separated it was nearly three o'clock and the Prince thanked me for one of the most charming evenings he had ever spent. He praised Granier, too, to the *n*th and sent her away happy, and even Randolph said that it was a great and memorable night. Before leaving he confessed to me that his inexplicable depression came from losses at the tables. "I must stop gambling," he said. "I have no luck." His luck was out forever, as I shall tell in a later chapter.

It seems to me that it was about this time that the great brewing firm of Guinness turned its business into a limited liability company. The company was brought out by the house of Baring and no one ever saw such a success in company promoting in the city of London. All day long hundreds of people besieged the banking offices and when the doors were shut, some daring spirits put stones in their checks and threw them through the windows, determined to get their applications accepted. The shares went immediately to a large premium and everyone was congratulating Lord Revelstoke* as the head of the great bank. I saw him one afternoon and he admitted to me that Barings had made over a million pounds sterling on the one transaction, and in the one day, a stroke unparalleled, save by some performances of Hooley** some years later.

A day or two afterwards I met Lord Rothschild at dinner at Sir Charles Dilke's, and I was very curious to find out whether the man's ability in any

---

* Edward Charles Baring (1828–1897), who became Baron Revelstoke in 1885. The Baring firm became shaky by 1890 because of loans made to the Argentine government, and it was reorganized into a limited company.
** Ernest Terah Hooley; his *Confessions* was published in 1925.

way matched his great position. I told the story of the Guinness promotion as Lord Revelstoke had told it to me and Lord Rothschild listened with seeming interest. When I had finished he said, "The Guinness promotion was offered to us first but we refused it!"

"That must cause you some regret," I said, "seeing that it was such a success: even Rothschild's must think a million worth putting in their pockets."

"I don't look at it quite in that way," retorted Lord Rothschild. "I go to the House every morning and when I say 'No' to every scheme and enterprise submitted to me, I return home at night carefree and contented. But when I agree to any proposal, I am immediately filled with anxiety. To say 'Yes' is like putting your finger in a machine: the whirring wheels may drag your whole body in after the finger."

"Goodness gracious," I cried, "I never thought of looking at it from that point of view." The great financier seemed to me extra cautious, rather than clever, but he had clever people about him, strange to say, and notably Carl Meyer,* whom I shall tell about in a later volume.

Talking of Lord Rothschild with Dilke later, I found that he agreed with me in my estimate of the gentleman. "When you get to the top of life's pyramid," he said, "caution becomes a virtue, and you have no idea how broad the foundation is laid. The Baron one day took me over the great banking house and showed me in the strong room a million sterling, in sovereigns, that had been put there by his grandfather with the injunction that his father should never touch it, except in case of great emergency. "Wouldn't a draft on the Bank of England," said the son, "be just as good and bring us in thirty thousand a year interest?"

"No," said the grandfather, "there are moments when you need gold if it were for nothing but to give you the sense of security."

I heard later a story of William Waldorf Astor** which bore out the same lesson. I shall probably tell it in my next volume.

---

* (1851–1922), director of the National Bank of Egypt and chairman of the London Committee of De Beers. Harris, however, fails to mention him again.

** (1848–1919), son of John Jacob Astor. He rebelled against his family, entered politics, and was twice defeated running for Congress. President Arthur appointed him Minister to Italy in 1882, and about this time he began to write romances, *Valentino: A Historical Romance of the Sixteen Century in Italy* (1885) and *Sforza, A Story of Milan* (1889). He was revolted by American society, and moved to England and in 1889 became a British subject. In 1890, he inherited $100 million and bought the *Pall Mall Gazette*, the *Pall Mall Magazine*, and *The Observer*. He was made Baron Astor of Hever Castle in 1916 and in 1917 was made a viscount. Harris never mentions Astor again in these volumes.

Chapter XXII

Lord Randolph Churchill*

A GREAT DEAL HAS BEEN WRITTEN about Lord Randolph Churchill by those like Sir Henry Lucy,** who met everyone and knew no one. And Randolph Churchill was not easy to know. The mere outward facts about him and his career have been set forth by his son in two stout volumes, an admirable official Victorian biography distinguished by the remarkable fairness used to explain every incident in his political career, a politician writing of a politician. But of the man himself, his powers, his failing and his quiddities, hardly a soul-revealing word; yet Winston might, nay, probably would have written a real life, had not Randolph been his father, and had he not had his own political career to consider. However, it must be confessed that the sympathy between father and son was very slight. Winston told me once that time and again when he tried to talk seriously on politics, or indeed on anything else, his father snubbed him pitilessly. "He wouldn't listen to me or consider anything I said. There was no companionship with him possible to me and I tried so hard and so often. He was so self-centered no one else existed for him. My mother was everything to me."

So remarkable a personality was Lord Randolph Churchill and such a whispering gallery and sounding board at the same time is London society that it would be almost possible to paint him in his habit as he lived by a series of true anecdotes. Winston enlivened his pages with a couple.

Everyone will remember how as a mere youth Randolph "scored" off Tom Duffield, the Master of the Old Berkshire hounds. In the winter of 1868, when Randolph was not yet twenty years old, he had the ill luck one day to ride very close to the hounds and got himself violently scolded by the irascible old Master: he went off the field at once without replying. But at a hunt dinner shortly afterwards, when he was made chairman by his mother, who was always putting him forward, he was called on to propose the toast of fox hunting, and Mr. Duffield was to respond. Randolph began by declaring himself an enthusiast for all forms of sport. "Fox hunting first,

---

* (1849–95).
** (1843–1924), editor of the *Daily News* and a contributor to *Punch*.

but I've often had good sport after hares. So keen am I that if I can't get fox hunting or hare hunting, I'll go with terriers after rats in a barn; and if I can't get that," he added, pausing, "why, rather than dawdle about indoors, I'd go out with Tom Duffield and the Old Berkshire." A pause of consternation while everybody wondered what would happen; but it was Tom Duffield himself who burst into a peal of good-natured laughter and made of the story a classic.

For years and years, indeed from his entrance into the House till 1886, it was Randolph's courage chiefly that commended him to the House of Commons. It may have been mainly aristocratic *morgue,* but Englishmen liked it none the less on that account.

It is usual for the extremists in a reform party to criticize their more conventional leaders, but this procedure is very unusual among Conservatives. From the beginning Lord Randolph showed this audacity, with a contempt, too, for titular authority that would have been marked, even in a Radical. In 1878 he attacked a Minister, ponderous Sclater-Booth,* in a way that rejoiced the House.

"I don't object," he said, "to the Head of the Local Government Board dealing with such grave questions as the salaries of inspectors of nuisances. But I have the strongest possible objection to his coming down here with all the appearance of a great lawgiver to repair, according to his small ideas and in his little way, breaches in the British Constitution." And then the witty sneer that set the House roaring: "Strange," he went on, as if speaking to himself, "strange, how often we find mediocrity dowered with a double-barreled name!"

Sclater-Booth's harmless little bill introduced the elective principle timidly into County Government. Randolph attacked it as of "brummagem-make," a "most Radical measure, a crowning desertion of Tory principles, a supreme violation of political honesty." Everyone went out of the House comparing this with Disraeli's famous attacks on Peel.

A little later Randolph spoke on Irish education in the most liberal and pro-Irish spirit. Thanks to the years he had passed in Dublin when his father was Viceroy, he knew Ireland and Irish matters better than almost any English politician and so established his reputation for brains as well as audacity. The House always filled to hear him, even more than for any Minister. In spite of the fact that he was still a bad speaker, now too loud, now too low, always dependent on his notes and frequently at a standstill, confused by their volume, he was the greatest attraction in the Chamber; and in the beginning of the Parliament of 1880 the Bradlaugh incident gave him his first real opportunity. He changed his seat to the corner seat below the gangway and at once made himself the head of the new group composed

---

* George Sclater-Booth, Lord Basing (1826–94), who had an undistinguished political career.

of Drummond Wolff,* Gorst** and Arthur Balfour, which he himself christened the "Fourth Party," as Winston relates. For the next seven years Randolph Churchill was incontestably the most sensational figure in the House of Commons, and long before the defeat of Gladstone's government he was recognized as the ablest Conservative in the Chamber. The House of Commons has a very strong schoolboy element in it, and Gladstone's defeat was symbolized to everyone by the fact that hardly were the division figures given to the Opposition Whip, when Randolph jumped up on his corner seat and started all the cheering!

Naturally, he became Leader of the House and Chancellor of the Exchequer in the Conservative Ministry of Lord Salisbury, and here another trait showed itself, his gratitude. Randolph took care that all supporters should be rewarded: Wolff was made a privy counsellor and Gorst an under-secretary of state: honor to the Jew and a salary to the needy.

I remember, after I had got to know and like Lord Randolph, lunching on Sunday at Mrs. Jeune's when he was at the same table. Almost before lunch was finished, Lord Randolph got up and excused himself with "urgent business" and left the room, followed closely by the Conservative Whip. In a few moments, to our astonishment, this gentleman, Winn,† if my memory serves me truly, returned, pale as a ghost and evidently too angry to choose his words. When Mrs. Jeune pleasantly asked him, "Has anything happened," he replied, "A piece of brutal rudeness entirely unprovoked. Yesterday Randolph came to me and said he wanted half an hour's talk. I had to tell him I was too busy then. He asked me to meet him here today, said he'd leave early, begged me to follow his example and we might have half an hour's quiet talk. A little against my habit, I consented; you saw how I followed him; in the hall I asked him, 'Where shall we go for our talk?' He cried, 'Can one never get rid of you and your talks!' and flung out of the house. I was never so insulted in my life!" The poor gentleman seemed almost unable to get over the shock to his dignity; we all commiserated with him while secretly diverted by Randolph's rudeness.

But no one who wishes to win in English political life, not even a Duke's son, can afford to be habitually rude, and especially not to a Whip of his own party. When a day or two later I mentioned the fact to Lord Randolph, he merely grinned. "I had forgotten," he said, "that I asked him to follow

---

* (1830–1908). He was responsible for founding the "Primrose League," named after Disraeli's favorite flower, which turned out to be an effective political organization. When he was defeated for office in 1885, he became a diplomat. He was ambassador to Madrid from 1892 until he returned in 1900.

** Sir John Eldon Gorst (1835–1916). He remained allied with Churchill for but a few years, however. These four men were resourceful critics of Gladstone; they became known as the "Fourth Party" during their efforts to exploit the Bradlaugh incident.

† Roland Winn (1857– ?), educated at Eton, a captain in the Coldstream Guards before he entered Parliament.

me, but he's rather a fool." Still, men intent on gaining and keeping power should learn "to suffer fools gladly," as St. Paul knew.

Another story here that should have found a place before his triumph. He dined with me one night—if I remember rightly, at the short-lived Amphitryon Club—and afterwards he took me with him to a meeting at Paddington, where he was 'billed' to speak. The dinner had been excellent and the Perrier-Jouet of 1875 was, I think, about the best champagne I ever drank. We had a magnum, and for the first and last time in my knowledge of him, Randolph showed himself a little excited, or perhaps I should say, reckless. At any rate, I had never heard him speak so well: in his own constituency, with none but friends and admirers about him, he spoke without notes. Usually he wrote out his speeches and learned them by heart and even then depended on notes for the sequence of subjects and special phrases. This night he talked extemporaneously, and to my astonishment adapted without knowing it a thought in the second part of Goethe's *Faust* to the condition of English politics at that moment. He began by predicting that a general election was at hand, and "which party will win in it, is the question of questions. The Liberals and Mr. Gladstone are very confident; they know that the working classes hold the balance of power; and the Liberal *bourgeoisie* think they are nearer the workmen than the aristocratic Conservatives can possibly be. But my feeling is that this earl or that marquis is much more in sympathy with the working man than the greedy nonconformist butcher or baker or candlestick maker. I want you to seize my point because it explains what I have always meant when I spoke of myself as a Tory-democrat. The best class and the lowest class in England come together naturally: they like and esteem each other; they are not greasy hypocrites talking of morality and frequenting the Sunday school while sanding the sugar; they are united in England in the bonds of a frank immorality."

Naturally I led the cheering, which, however, was curiously feeble and soon died away into half-hearted laughter and much shamefaced grinning. In the pause that followed I looked over the side of the platform to the reporters' table: everyone had dropped his pen or pencil and was waiting for the rest of the speech. Randolph spoke for some time longer and, I thought, with effort, as if to efface the impression of his great and true word.

When we were driving away, he asked me whether he had said anything very dreadful. I sought to reassure him. "The best thing I ever heard or ever expect to hear on an English platform," I said, and I told him what he had said.

At once he took fright. "It's all that d——d champagne," he cried, "but we must see that the phrase doesn't get into *The Times* so that it can be dexterously contradicted or perhaps smothered. You'll help me, won't you?"

Of course I consented, but assured him that the reporters hadn't taken down the phrase. He laughed, but insisted on making assurance doubly sure, so we drove first to *The Times* office; and as good luck would have it, I found Arthur Walter there, who, after hearing everything, sent to the composing room for a "pull" of the report, and to my amusement, the great phrase had been carefully omitted. Next morning I went through all the newspapers: not a single one had thought the truth worth recording. This phrase is still to me the high-water mark of Randolph Churchill's intelligence.

Either a little before or a short time after this occurrence, I was dreadfully disappointed in him. The channel-tunnel scheme had been set on foot and at once I took fire for the idea. A little earlier I had been astonished by the extraordinarily rapid growth both of Antwerp and Hamburg as ports, and I had found out that this was due partly to the fact that freights brought to any British port had to "break cargo" and be transhipped again because there was no channel tunnel which would have allowed trains to run right through to the continent. I made a special study of the question and came to the conclusion that if a tunnel were running, the port of London would soon be once more the first in the world. I couldn't but believe that English common sense would insist on the enterprise being carried out with the briefest possible delay. And there was big money in the gamble. Accordingly, I went to work with pen and word of mouth to convince the English public of its plain self-interest. In ten minutes' talking I persuaded Lord Randolph Churchill, and encouraged by my warm praise of him as a "pioneer," he declared that he would not only vote for the project, but speak for it to boot. On hearing this I felt sure of victory. To cut a long story short, when the debate came on, a new thought entered Randolph Churchill's brain. With a great deal of humor he pictured an English official, the secretary of state for home affairs, hearing that five thousand French troops had seized the tunnel and were coming through to Dover. Ought he or ought he not to blow them all up? "For one," summed up Lord Randolph, "I prefer security to the doubt." The whole picture was idiotic. As I had pointed out to Randolph, no French troops would take such a desperate risk; both ends of the tunnel could be raised above water level, so that they could be easily blown to pieces by a mere gunboat. No general would send troops through such a defile, and if he did, ten to one they'd all have to surrender the next day. But the parliamentary triumph was all Randolph cared for and the whole thing gave me the measure of his insularity. But why, after all, should I blame him, when now, forty years later, the channel tunnel scheme has just been vetoed again by five prime ministers considering the whole question in cold blood, now that airplanes have dropped bombs in London and played havoc with the protection given to England by the sea. At the very moment of writing this, too, I find Winston Churchill defending the construction of a channel tunnel with the very arguments I had used to persuade his father a generation ago. At the moment I was wretchedly disappointed, for I had been fool enough to say that Randolph Churchill would defend the scheme, whereas it was he who damned it altogether. He had made a fool of me and merely grinned when I told him how I had come to grief through believing in his word: from that time on my faith in him was shaken.

He knew more about Ireland, as I have said, than any English member or minister I had come across, and when over the Home Rule Bill of Gladstone he started the slogan, "Ulster will fight and Ulster will be right," I was paralyzed with horror, for I understand the demoniac cleverness of the vile appeal and realized some of the evil consequences. I could not but remonstrate with him. "You are fighting for today," I said, "but tomorrow, with or without Gladstone, Irish Home Rule will come into being and you'll look like Mrs. Partington."*

"Sufficient for the day is the evil thereof" was his cynical answer. He was always the fighting politician out to win personal victories, careless of the evil seed he flung broadcast, with absolutely no vision of an ideal future. I was forced to see that my hopes of him were ill-founded.

We were both at Wadhurst once, the Murietta's place in Sussex, where Madame de Sainturce dispensed a most gracious hospitality. Sir William Gordon Cumming,** I remember, was one of the party, the Sir William who at that time was supposed to be a bosom friend of Prince Edward and gave himself considerable airs because of the royal support. The second day Randolph asked me to come with him to a private room for a talk: he knew that I knew Parnell and Mrs. O'Shea, and he wanted to find out whether it was true that Parnell disguised himself to visit Kitty, and whether that was the explanation of his astonishing changes in appearance. Sometimes Parnell would appear in the House of Commons with a full beard; a week later it was shaved off; now he wore his hair down on his shoulders; next week it was cropped close; and again the top of his head was clean-shaven, as if he had been playing priest.

"What did it all mean?" Randolph wanted to know. I told him the truth as I saw it, that Parnell was one of the strangest human beings I had ever met. He was constantly visiting Mrs. O'Shea in disguise, whether to escape notice or merely because he was superstitious I could never quite determine; thirteen terrified him; he counted the paving stones, and if nine brought him with his right foot to the threshold, he walked in happily; I have known him to walk around for half an hour till a lucky number freed him from fear. To my astonishment, Randolph nodded his head, "I can understand that." I could only stare at him in blank wonder.

While we were talking the door opened and Lady Randolph appeared. Naturally, I got up as she called out, "Randolph," but he sat still. In spite of his ominous silence, she came across to him, "Randolph, I want to talk to you!"

* Who tried to keep the Atlantic Ocean out of her home with a mop.
** (1842–1908).

"Don't you see," he retorted, "that I've come here to be undisturbed?"

"But I want you," she repeated tactlessly.

He sprang to his feet. "Can't I have a moment's peace from you anywhere?" he barked. "Get out and leave me alone!" At once she turned and walked out of the room.

"You ought not to have done that, for my sake," I said.

"Why not?" he cried. "What has it to do with you?"

"Your wife will always hate me," I replied, "for having been the witness of her humiliation. You, she may forgive; me, never."

He laughed like a schoolboy. "Those are the astonishing things in you," he said. "You have an uncanny flair for character and life; but never mind: I'll say you were angry with me for my rudeness and that will make it all right!"

"Say nothing," I retorted. "Let us hope that she may forget the incident, though that's not likely. Ever afterwards Lady Randolph missed no opportunity of showing me that she disliked me cordially. I remember some years later how she got into the express train for the south in Paris and coolly annexed an old man's seat. I spent ten minutes explaining who she was and pacifying the old Frenchman, but she scarcely took the trouble to thank me. She showed her worst side to me almost always and was either imperious or indifferent.

When Lord Randolph became Leader of the House of Commons and Chancellor of the Exchequer, his real greatness came to view at once. The most irresponsible and daring of critics, the type of opposition leader whose *métier* and *raison d'être* was constant attack, frivolous or weighty, took on in one day a new character, a strange unexpected dignity. The metempsychosis astonished everyone: he was not only fair-minded but kind; he would listen to and answer the bore or the fool with dignified courtesy! For the first and only time in the history of the House of Commons, he used his cabinet ministers and party leaders as pawns in a game and treated every debate as a new campaign.

Formerly, ministers used to give their names to the Whips and rise to speak when they chose, without reference to the result as they do today. Randolph Churchill altered all that: in the middle of the debate he thought nothing of asking a cabinet minister to speak later or not to speak at all that night, according to the speeches of the opponents. And it was soon clear that Randolph was a most consummate tactician, using all his lieutenants with uncanny understanding. For instance, there was among the Conservatives a large and voluble Jew named Baron de Worms,* who delighted in spouting shop-soiled commonplaces. At one moment in a debate Randolph sent Baron de Worms a flattering note, telling him he reckoned on him to reply to the Liberal who was then speaking. De Worms nodded, smiling happily, and when his turn came took the floor with pompous fluency. At once Gladstone began to take notes. Shortly after, Randolph whispered to

* (1840–1903).

de Worms to stop: he had given himself away sufficiently and might easily go too far; but de Worms went on till Randolph pulled his coattail violently with a "Sit down, you fool!"

Gladstone got up and made de Worms appear ridiculous. As soon as the Great Debater finished his speech, Randolph rose and deplored the fact that the most eloquent man of the day so often kept the debate on a low level because he loved to expose platitudes. And then he went on to develop new arguments and lift the whole controversy to a higher level. When he sat down everyone in the House admitted that Gladstone had been sharply countered, and not only out-generalled, but put in a secondary place. Till I questioned Randolph afterwards, I had no idea that he had planned the whole attack like a born captain and used poor de Worms as a bait to "draw" Gladstone.

In all the essential qualities of leadership he surprised everyone capable of judging. Gladstone was reported to have said that Lord Randolph was the courtliest man he had ever met and the greatest Conservative since Pitt. In the six weeks after the adjournment, he won golden opinions from all sorts and conditions of men. The best judges, even men as clear slighted as Hartington and Dilke, did not perceive all his qualities till later. After the Bradlaugh debate Hartington said that Randolph knew the House of Commons better than the House knew itself, but Dilke, I think, was the first to see his unique qualities as a director of debate and captain of word warfare. Time and again I quoted Bacon's great word that might have been written expressly about him: "Great men, like the heavenly bodies, move violently to their places and calmly in their places."*

But now and then a spice of the old Randolph delighted the House. A specious motion was made, hiding a cunning trap: Randolph rose. "Surely in vain is the net spread in the sight of any bird," he began and the House howled its appreciation. "Randolph can't be caught napping; he had two eyes"—a score of differently worded eulogies! Everyone in the House seemed lifted to a higher level through his ability. The exact contrary of this took place a few years later when Arthur Balfour became Leader of the House. He persisted in treating members as if they had all come from Connemara and he was still Irish Secretary, and the House resented his insolent impertinences.

When the House met again Lord Randolph's power had grown: he had deposed Gladstone, had won a greater position in the House than Gladstone himself. True, very soon there were rumors of disputes in the Cabinet. "They object to Randolph's budget," we heard, the "they" being Lord George Hamilton for the Navy and W. H. Smith for the Army; but everyone felt that "they" must give in. Then a golden day when one heard that Lord George Hamilton cut down his estimate; there would be peace.

---

* From *Of Great Place*: ". . . and as in nature things move violently to their place, and calmly in their place, so virtue in ambition is violent, in authority settled and calm."

What would Randolph's budget be like? He told me on two or three occasions that he meant to bring in a democratic budget; Gladstone's cry of "Peace, Retrenchment, and Reform" seemed to have got into his blood. In vain I tried to persuade him that the times had changed, that the days of the old ten pound householder who paid all the taxes and therefore loved economy as the chief of virtues had passed away for ever. "The majority of the present-day voters," I asserted, "pay nothing and Englishmen usually prefer freehandedness to economy." He would not even consider it. One evening he told me that "Smith's holding out and won't reduce his estimates and he's backed by Salisbury! Think of the pair," he cried, "old tradesmen both! And both hate me. I'll resign and see what they'll do in front of Gladstone."

"Don't be mad," I cried. "Don't resign, stick to the wheel." Suddenly he told me at dinner that he was going down to Windsor, and when out of ignorance I saw nothing to wonder at in that invitation, he explained to me that in his elder brother's divorce case ten years or so before, he had taken up the cudgels for Blandford against the Queen and had been boycotted by the Court ever since. He was immensely pleased with the Queen's invitation.

When he returned from Windsor, the news of his resignation had preceded him and created an extraordinary sensation: it was whispered with bated breath that he had used the Queen's letter paper to write his resignation to Lord Salisbury, as if Randolph could ever have thought that anyone would imagine he would steal dignity from an invitation to Windsor. Lord George Hamilton went down in the train with him to Windsor and tells us that even then Randolph had made up his mind to resign. In gratitude for some earlier support from *The Times*, Randolph had given that paper the first news and editor Buckle* chastized him very courteously in two whole columns.** The same morning I got a line asking me to come to see him; I went up to Connaught Place with heavy heart about eleven o'clock. The rows of carriages about the house startled me and the house itself was crammed with Tory members of Parliament. I caught Randolph between two rooms. "What d'ye think of it?" he cried, joyously bubbling over. "More than two hundred and fifty Tory members come to attest their allegiance to me: I've won; the 'old gang' will have to give in." But he had reckoned without Salisbury's obstinacy and dislike.

Nothing happened for days and I got another note. Again I went to Connaught Place, empty now, the rooms, and deserted. Randolph came to me. "The rats desert the sinking ship," he began gloomily. "Salisbury has

---

* George Earle Buckle (1854–1935), who succeeded Thomas Chenery as editor, until 1912. He was commissioned to write a *Life of Disraeli* (6 volumes, 1914–20), which has become a classic, and then he was commissioned by King George V to edit the *Letters of Queen Victoria* (6 volumes, 1926–32).

** The only other time this happened was on the publication of Darwin's *Origin of Species* some twenty years before. (F.H.)

cabled Hartington to return from the continent and in a week he'll arrive." "Will Hartington help him?" I asked. "He had a great opinion of you, I know," and I told him how Hartington had praised his leadership of the House to me and how convincing the praise was, because those who praised most highly were the best judges. At first Randolph seemed dejected, but in the course of talk he told me how he had won the Queen at dinner and how she told him she regarded him as a true statesman. "A great woman," he added, "one of the wisest and best of women."

A few days later Hartington arrived; Randolph met him at the railway station and was profoundly impressed. "A noble man," he said afterwards, gravely. "He assured me that he regarded me as a born Conservative leader and would do nothing to embarrass me." A couple of days later he told me in wonderment that Salisbury had offered to serve with or under Hartington and that Hartington had refused: "I must win now; that's Salisbury's last card." But it wasn't. A couple of days later I called upon him; he met me with the exclamation: "I'm dished. Goschen* will be Chancellor; I had forgotten Goschen." He went on to tell me that Mrs. Jeune had suggested it to him. "As soon as she mentioned the name," he said, "I felt struck through the heart. I knew it was all over." And it was. "Old Morality," W. H. Smith, undertook to lead the House and Goschen made himself responsible for the finances and Randolph was out in the cold.

I tried to persuade him that nothing was really lost. "The corner seat below the gangway," I cried, "and your most stinging criticism and in six months 'Old Morality' will be glad to get back to his bookshop, and . . ."

He shook his head to my utter wonder. "I can't," he said. "I am a Conservative; I can't. Ah! If it were Gladstone in power, I'd get to work at once. I can't fight my own side." But he had fought his own side on the Bradlaugh** business six years before; why had he changed? "Why on earth then did you resign?" rose to my lips, but I said nothing.

The tragedy was complete without comment.

One more incident, for the fallen lion was to get more than one kick. Strange it was that from 1880 to his resignation in 1886 everything seemed to favor and help him. After his resignation everything went against him. Astonishingly good luck in a series and then astonishingly bad luck. Yet just at first everything seemed to go well; all through the session of 1887 there were rumors of reconciliation. People were so under the spell of Randolph's consummate leadership and masterful personality that they felt sure he would break out in some new way; he must have something up his sleeve. Then came tidings of a pact with Chamberlain and the mirage of a Center party. As leader of the House, "Old Morality" Smith, without an

---

* George Joachim Goschen (1831–1907), a Liberal but also a unionist, which led him to break with Gladstone over Home Rule in 1885, as Albert Grey and Courtney had done. And he did succeed Churchill as Chancellor of the Exchequer.

** When Sir Stafford Northcote was ready to compromise on the admission of Bradlaugh in the House, the "Fourth Party" opposed him.

"h" to his name, was almost absurd. The rumor grew; then Bright* died and Central Birmingham was vacant. At once I heard through Louis Jennings,** Randolph's best friend and also a good friend of mine, that Randolph, sick of Paddington and villadom, was going to stand for Bright's old seat and make Tory-democracy a reality. But Chamberlain would not hear of such a rival near his throne; he told Hicks-Beach that if Randolph stood for Central Birmingham, the unwritten compact between the Liberal Unionists and the Conservatives would be broken and he would consider himself free to act as he pleased.

Hicks-Beach at first fought for Randolph: he had always the highest opinion of Randolph's genius. When Gladstone fell in 1886, Lord Salisbury called Hicks-Beach with Randolph to determine who should lead the Lower House. Hicks-Beach's claim was older and many would have said better founded; he was a man of high character, great experience and real ability, but he wouldn't hear of any comparison. Randolph, he declared, was the first choice in every way: he must be the Leader and he, Hicks-Beach, would take a place under him. Now he hated to wound Randolph but Chamberlain was inexorable. As Hicks-Beach hesitated, Chamberlain set Lord Hartington to work and Hartington's intervention settled the matter: Randolph must give up the idea of representing Central Birmingham or destroy the coalition. Randolph left the decision to Hicks-Beach and Hicks-Beach told him he must save the party and withdraw. Randolph felt the blow intensely. The news had got out, and to be beaten by Chamberlain, he felt, was humiliating.

Randolph went racing, began to bet heavily and at first made money. People smiled as at the aberrations of a boy.

A year or so later came another blow. The government announced its intention to appoint a Royal Commission to enquire into the accusations of Parnell by *The Times*. Randolph, well informed as always on Irish matters, saw the danger and out of sheer greatness of soul sent to W. H. Smith a protest pointing out the peril, more than hinting, indeed, his opinion that Parnell would be whitewashed. His old colleagues were too stupid to pay any attention to his warning. When the report came before the House early in 1890, Randolph drafted an amendment with Jennings, blaming *The Times* while ignoring the action of the government. Jennings was to introduce the amendment which Randolph promised to support in a speech. The House was thronged: Jennings was in his place waiting to be called on by the Speaker when Randolph got up and began attacking the government in the bitterest words he could find. When he sat down he saw that Jennings

* John Bright (1811–89), the great Radical.
** (1836–1893). A correspondent for *The Times* in America, he became editor of the *New York Times* and saw it through the exposure of the corruption of the Boss Tweed gang. He returned to England, was elected an M.P. in 1885, and became a follower of Churchill. He edited Churchill's *Speeches, With Notes and Introduction* (1889).

was angry and wrote him several little notes, but Jennings was seriously offended and would never speak to Randolph again. The truth is, as his son has said, Randolph was too much of an aristocrat, too self-centered, too imperious and impatiently irritable to be a good friend. He quarreled with almost everyone, notably with Gorst and Matthews,* who owed him much —with everyone, indeed, except Hicks-Beach, Ernest Beckett, afterwards Lord Grimthorpe, his brother-in-law Lord Curzon,** and Wolff, whom he seldom saw.

After the Chamberlain business I saw less of him, but I met him a little later in Monte Carlo and dined with him and had him to dinner more than once, as I shall tell later.

While he played lieutenant to Randolph, I met Louis Jennings frequently and got to like him really; and after the quarrel over the amendment I saw still more of him. He wanted me to take up the *New York Herald* in London and edit it. But I had good reason to distrust Gordon Bennett,† as I may tell later, and so nothing came of Jennings' well meant proposal. But it brought us close together, and in his anger over what he called Randolph's traitorism, we often discussed Randolph and his future. Jennings was an excellent, kind fellow, with brains enough to appreciate Randolph's brains, and dowered besides with perfect unselfish loyalty. Speaking of Randolph once he said, "You know he doesn't like you, don't you?"

"No," I replied. "I thought he rather liked me, not that it matters much: his likings and dislikings are not reasonable."

"He has great charm of manner," said Jennings, "when he likes, and he uses it and reckons on it. But he's done for; we're wasting time talking about him."

"What do you mean?" I cried. "He's in his prime, has twenty years before him and unique parliamentary genius. If he'd give up gambling and playing the fool, he could be Leader of the House and Prime Minister again within a couple of years."

Jennings shook his head: "He's not so strong as you think; in my opinion he's doomed."

"What on earth do you mean?" I exclaimed.

"I oughtn't to tell it, I suppose," he said, "but Randolph told it to me casually enough once when trying to explain a headache and a fit of depression, and it's an interesting story."

Here it is as I heard it from Jennings that evening in Kensington Gore.

"Randolph was not a success at Oxford at first," Jennings began. "He

---

* Henry Matthews (1826–1913). Because of his friendship with Churchill, Matthews was appointed home secretary in 1886 and thereby became the first Catholic since the Emancipation Act to hold a cabinet position. As home secretary, he was severely criticized by Labouchère in *Truth* and by Stead in the *Pall Mall Gazette*.
** (1859–1925). He supported his brother-in-law staunchly. He was viceroy of India from 1898 to 1905, then Conservative leader in the House of Lords. He served as foreign secretary 1919–24.
† James Gordon Bennett (1841–1918), owner of the *New York Herald*.

never studied or read; he rode to hounds at every opportunity and he was always as imperious as the devil. But after all, he was the son of a Duke and Blenheim was near and the best set made up to him, as Englishmen do. He was made a member of the Bullingdon Club, the smartest club in Oxford, and one evening he held forth there on his pet idea that the relationship of master and servant in the home of an English gentlemen was almost ideal. 'Any talent in the child of a butler or gardener,' he said, 'would be noticed by the master, and of course he'd be glad to give the gifted boy an education and opportunity such as his father could not possibly afford. Something like this should be the relationship between the aristocratic class and the workmen in England: that is Tory-democracy as I conceive it.' Of course the youths all cheered him and complimented him and made much of him, and when the party was breaking up, one insisted on a 'stirrup-cup.' He poured out a glass of old brandy and filled it up with champagne and gave it to Randolph to drink. Nothing loath, Randolph drained the cup, and with many good wishes all the youths went out into the night. Randolph assured me that after he had got into the air he remembered nothing more. I must now let Randolph tell his own story."

"Next morning," Randolph began, "I woke up with a dreadful taste in my mouth, and between waking and sleeping was thunder-struck. The paper on the walls was hideous—dirty—and, as I turned in bed, I started up gasping: there was an old woman lying beside me; one thin strand of dirty grey hair was on the pillow. How had I got there? What had happened to bring me to such a den? I slid out of bed and put on shirt and trousers as quietly as I could, but suddenly the old woman in the bed awoke and said, smiling at me, 'Oh, Lovie, you're not going to leave me like that?'

"She had one long yellow tooth in her top jaw that waggled as she spoke. Speechless with horror, I put my hand in my pocket and threw all the money I had loose on the bed. I could not say a word. She was still smiling at me; I put on my waistcoat and coat and fled from the room. 'Lovie, you're not kind!' I heard her say as I closed the door after me. Downstairs I fled in livid terror. In the street I found a hansom and gave the jarvy the address of a doctor I had heard about. As soon as I got to him, he told me he knew my 'brother and . . .' I broke out in wild excitement, 'I want you to examine me at once. I got drunk last night and woke up in bed with an appalling old prostitute. Please examine me and apply some disinfectant.' Well, he went to work and said he could find no sign of any abrasion, but he made up a strong disinfectant and I washed the parts with it; and all the time he kept on trying to console me, I suppose, with cheap commonplaces. 'There isn't much serious disease in Oxford. Of course there should be licensed houses, as in France, and weekly or bi-weekly examination of the inmates. But then we hate grandmotherly legislation in England and really, my dear Lord Randolph, I don't think you have serious cause for alarm.' Cause for alarm, indeed; I hated myself for having been such a fool! At the end I carried away a couple of books on venereal diseases and set at work to devour them. My next week was a nightmare. I made up my mind at once that I deserved gonorrhea for my stupidity. I even prayed to God, as to a maleficent deity, that he might give me that; I deserved that, but no more, no worse: not a chancre, not syphilis!

"There was nothing, not a sign, for a week. I breathed again. Yet I'd have to wait till the twenty-first day before I could be sure that I had escaped syphilis. Syphilis! Think of it, at my age, I, who was so proud of my wisdom. On the fateful day nothing, not a sign. On the next the fool doctor examined me again: 'Nothing, Lord Randolph, nothing! I congratulate you. You've got off, to all appearance, scot-free.'

"A day later I was to dine with Jowett,* the Master of Balliol. It was a Sunday and he had three or four people of importance to meet me. He put me on his left hand; he was always very kind to me, was Jowett. I talked a lot but drank very sparingly. After that first mad excess, I resolved never to take more than two glasses of wine at any dinner and one small glass of liqueur or brandy with my coffee. I wouldn't risk being caught a second time. I was so thankful to God for my immunity that vows of reform were easy.

"In the middle of dinner suddenly I felt a little tickling. Strange! At once I was alarmed, and cold with fear, excused myself and left the room. Outside I asked a footman for the lavatory, went in and looked at myself. Yes! There was a little, round, very red pimple that tickled. I went out and begged the butler to excuse me to the Master. 'I am feeling very ill,' I said, 'and must go home.'

" 'You don't look well,' he replied, and in a minute I was in a hansom and on the way to the doctor's. Luckily he was in and willing to see me. I told him what brought me and showed him the peccant member. At once he took out his most powerful lens and examined me carefully. When he had finished I asked him, 'Well?'

" 'Well,' he said dispassionately, 'we have there a perfect example of a syphilitic sore!' Why I didn't kill him, I don't know.

"Inwardly I raged that I should have been such a fool. I, who prided myself on my brains, I was going to do such great things in the world, to have caught syphilis! I! It was too horrible to think of. Again the fool doctor: 'We must cure it,' he was saying. 'It's incurable,' I retorted; 'all the books admit that.'

" 'No, no,' he purred on. 'Taken in time we can make it innocuous. Mercury is a sovereign remedy, nothing equal to it, though very, very depressing. Have you resolution enough to persevere with it? That's the question.'

" 'You'll see,' I replied. 'Any other advice?'

" 'Absolute abstention from all alcoholic drink,' he said. 'I'll write you out a regimen, and if you follow it, in a year you will be cured and have no further ill effect.'

* Benjamin Jowett (1817–93).

"To cut a long story short, I did what he told me to do, but I was young and heedless and did not stop drinking in moderation and soon got reckless. Damn it, one can't grieve forever. Yet I have had very few symptoms since and before my marriage. The Oxford doctor and a London man said I was quite clear of all weakness and perfectly cured."

I was thrilled by the story: was there another chapter to it? Was this what Jennings meant when he said that Randolph was doomed? What else did he know or fear? I had just found about Maupassant, had begun to attribute his ghastly fears to syphilis. But then Maupassant had taken little or no care to cure himself, while Randolph asserted that he had done everything he was told to do. I could not but ask, "Do you think it has injured Randolph's health?"

"I'm sure of it," Jennings nodded. "He has fits of excessive irritability and depression which I don't like. In spite of what he told me, I don't think he took much care. He laughed at secondary symptoms, but now I hear he's going for a long holiday to South Africa under Beit's auspices and that may cure him. At any rate, his fate no longer concerns me."

A couple more stories and Randolph Churchill's life is told so far as I am concerned. I have already said that I met him in Monte Carlo a good many times in almost successive years. At first he amused me by his childish belief that he could make money gambling at the tables. I told him that at Baden-Baden, Blanc, the proprietor, had only half the odds in his favor and yet had managed to make a great fortune. But he insisted that the power of varying the stake gave the punter an advantage; I was of use to him because I had known Monte Carlo for years, as well as it could be known, croupiers and directors and all. He was childishly self-confident and I found I was wasting my time trying to dissuade him from playing, so I showed him what they call "Labby's system," which is a very slow progression if you lose and therefore less dangerous than most systems, which are usually modifications of the silly doubling game which quickly kills or cures, as your maximum stake is limited.

After several meetings at Monte Carlo Randolph became more friendly to me and talked more frankly with me than he had ever done in the days of his success.

One evening after dinner in the Hotel de Paris we had a really serious talk about politics and I found we were poles apart. I pointed out that just as village communities were superseded by nations, so nations now were in process of being superseded by world empires; already two were being formed, Russia and the United States, which must soon dwarf all nations. The question for England was; would she bring about a union with the colonies and become an English confederation of states with an imperial senate drawn from all her colonies, instead of that potty House of Lords? To my astonishment he got angry. "I know the House of Lords," he exclaimed, "and there's a lot of good sense in it and good feeling and I hate your imperial senate of jumped-up grocers from Ballarat and shopkeepers from Sydney!" I found nothing to say: he lived still in feudal times and his brains were an accident.

I then talked to him of socialism and the part it should play in a well ordered community. Randolph would not have socialism at any price, did not really understand the first word of the modern problem. He would not acknowledge that the prosperity of the working classes in France came from the partition of the land of France during the Revolution. "The comparative prosperity of the French peasants has its drawbacks," he insisted. "Look at their narrow, sordid lives!" he cried, "I prefer England with its wider freedom and one class at least that gets all the best out of life and sets a great example."

After that evening I took little interest in his possible return to power. His want of education maimed him; he could never be a Mazzini, let alone a Bismarck. As he ate and drank and spoke of the well dressed women that came and went, I understood how "illiterate" had come to mean "lewd." I noticed now too for the first time that he was terribly nervous: his hands twitched; he started and shook at every sudden sound. I could only hope that his trip to South Africa would bring him back to health and strength.

He went out in a Donald Currie liner and contributed articles to an English journal, in which he condemned the food and drink as that of a second class lodging house. He was amply justified but he was bitterly attacked for his well founded criticism. All the mercantile world, whose patriotism is mainly self-interest, and their champions in the press, kept on ridiculing him month in month out till they had seriously damaged his reputation with the many. Yet the food on board ship was bad everywhere till Ballin* with the help of Harris established a Ritz restaurant on the *Kaiserin Auguste Victoria* and at once lifted all ocean travel into a higher category of comfort. He was the first to make sea life luxurious.

Randolph came back from South Africa bearded like a pard, a grey-haired old man. Others have told how he tried to regain his place and influence in Parliament and his ghastly failure. The House filled to hear him: he got up and after the first few words began to mumble and hesitate and repeat himself incoherently, while frequent emphatic gestures emphasized the grotesqueness of the exhibition. Balfour sat beside him with his head bent forward, buried in his hands. "Randolph's finished," was the universal verdict. "What's happened to him?" everyone was asking. "Who would have believed it?"

I heard from Beit that Randolph had made money by following his advice and investing in the deep levels; indeed, it is known that when he died he left a great many thousands of pounds to his widow, all derived from this source. Jennings' words recurred to me again and again: "Randolph's doomed," I was soon to learn the reason.

His brother died and at once I announced that I was going to publish in

* Albert Ballin (1857–1918), director-general of the Hamburg-Amerika line.

the *Fortnightly Review* an article on "The Art of Living" by the late Duke. I showed phrases of it to reporters, and as everyone knew the brains and frankness of the Duke, it was easy to work up a tremendous sensation, for indeed the article was almost too outspoken to be published. My readers will remember that I got the article by publishing, at the Duke's request, a paper written by Lady Colin Campbell, who was the Duke's mistress at the time, and a very pretty mistress, too. I only consented to publish her out-pouring on condition that the Duke would write me a perfectly frank paper giving his real views of life and living. He certainly did what I asked: in the paper he declared that women were the only things in life worth winning. "A good dinner and the good talk of able men is interesting, but without women and the pleasure they give, life would be stale, flat and unprofitable, a tale told by an idiot full of sound and fury signifying nothing."

Some years after I had published Lady Colin's paper, the Duke told me that she had insisted on being invited to spend a week at Blenheim by his new wife, formerly the rich Mrs. Hammersley* of New York. The Duchess consented at once in all innocence, and in due course Lady Colin appeared and insisted on flaunting her intimacy with the Duke, whom she always called by his Christian name. In huge glee he told me that the devil of a woman would take him for a walk in the morning alone and keep him till they were late for lunch. "We are such old friends," she said to the Duchess, "and I haven't seen him for so long. You must really forgive us: when we are together time flies."

The Duke said, "My wife is far from being a fool: indeed, no woman is blind in such a case and Lady Colin'll never get another invitation to Blenheim."

That was as much as I knew when I got a letter from Randolph, asking me to come to see him in his mother's house in Grosvenor Street, where he was staying at the time. I went all unsuspecting. I had often had similar notes from him in the past. When he came across the room to shake hands with me, I was appalled by his appearance. In a couple of years he had changed out of character, had become an old man instead of a young one. His face was haggard; his hair greyish and very thin on top; his thick beard, also half-grey, changed him completely. He held himself well, which added dignity, but the old boyish smile had gone. "Sit down, sit down," he said. "We must have a talk! You don't know the Duchess of Marlborough, do you?" he began. "She would like to know you and I think you would be friends. I'm going to bring about a meeting. She's really a remarkable woman and my brother's death has been a dreadful blow to her; she loved him, as good women love us, in spite of our faults. When she read about the article he had written for you and that it was going to be published she was appalled, shocked. She had read the article and hated it, believed it was

* Lillian Warren Hammersley, daughter of Cicero Price, a commodore in the U.S. Navy.

written under the influence of Lady Colin Campbell, whom she disliked, and she burned the article and the proof you had sent him before my brother—and thought it was done with forever. When she saw the announcement that that hateful article was going to appear, she was beside herself. She sent for her solicitors; they told her nothing could be done. Finally she wired for me and I went to see her. I must tell exactly what I said to this poor, grief-stricken woman. 'We have no power,' I said, 'but it was luckly that you sent for me, because I know the editor of the *Fortnightly* well, and I'm sure that as soon as Frank Harris understands the position and your rooted objection, he'll suppress the article. I know him and I can promise for him. Make your mind easy: the article will never appear.' Was I not right, Harris?" he added, getting up and holding out his hand.*

There was a suspicion of the theatre in the appeal, which chilled me a little. It was manifestly prepared, but it was excellently done. Still I hesitated. "You see, I am only a trustee, so to speak," I began. "I don't own the *Review*: this article of the late Duke was bought and paid for at a very high price."

"Of course," Randolph broke in, "it goes without saying that the Duchess will pay whatever's needed, will pay eagerly. That's understood."

"But no money payment will do it," I said, and explained how I had only consented to load the *Review* with Lady Colin's paper because his brother had promised me a contribution so interesting as to atone for the dullness of Lady Colin.

"She was very good-looking," Randolph remarked, "with an extraordinary figure. My brother was a good judge . . ." and he smiled.

"I'm sure you'll see," I went on, "that I can't pleasure you in this matter. I'm not free, you understand . . ."

"I know Frank Harris," he replied. "You can do it, if you will, and I have promised on your behalf. You won't refuse an old friend's last request," and he held out his hand again. As I took his hand and looked at him I felt sick: the deep lines on his face, the heavy gummy bags under his miserable eyes, the shaking hand—it might well be his *last* request!

He misunderstood my silence: he feared it meant refusal. Not knowing he had won, he played his last card. "Come, Harris," he began in the most appealing way, "do what I wish and I'll write you an article on any subject you like in exchange for my brother's! Come, say 'Yes'." A moment later he put his hand over his eyes and sat down heavily. "I have slept badly and I don't feel well today," he went on in trembling, indistinct tones. I could not leave him in doubt a moment longer: he filled me with pity and regret—such an end to such a great career!

* "For reasons you will readily imagine I should be very greatly obliged to you and so would others of [more] importance than I, if you would refrain from inserting in the Fortnightly Review, an article written for that review by my poor brother." (Excerpt of a letter from Randolph Churchill, no date, in catalogue of Charles S. Boesen; found in the Lyngklip Collection in the New York Public Library.)

"It shall be as you wish," I said. He looked at me profoundly, and when he liked, his prominent eyes had something piercing in them. "I was sure of you," he said. "I knew you had only to understand the position to do as we wished! I thank you with all my heart and the Duchess will thank you, too, when she hears the good news. I promised to telegraph her," and he turned towards a side table. Then, bethinking himself, he turned to me, "But what am I to write about for you?" he began. "I'm avoiding all hard tasks, but I'll do my best!"

"Forget it!" I said. "Get well and strong; that's what your friends all want of you and nothing more."

"I'll do my best," he said, "but sometimes I fear the dice are loaded against me."

They were loaded indeed and more heavily than either of us dreamed. The rest of his tragic history is soon told. In the eighties and nineties Sir Henry Thompson, the famous doctor, used to give "octave" dinners, as he called them, from the number of the guests.* He was a good doctor, I believe, and knew a great deal about stricture and the prostate gland, but he was prouder of the fact that he had written two dull novels and had had paintings hung in the Academy exhibitions. He loved to show two or three pictures of Alma Taddema** in his drawing-room, which in itself defines his taste and proscribes his talent. He was kindly, however, and at seventy kindliness is a proof of virtue. His wines, too, were sound without being extraordinary and his guests were often interesting. At one such dinner I remember Randolph was the guest of honor and sat on our host's right. Lord Morris† sat on Thompson's left and I came next, and on my left was Sir Richard Holmes,†† the genial librarian of Windsor. He was kind enough to ask me to come down and pay him a visit and inspect the collection, and I would have accepted eagerly had he not first talked to me of his water color sketches, which also could be seen from time to time gracing the anemic walls of the Academy. The amateur artist, like the amateur writer, is to me almost as boring as the actor or singer.

When we sat down at table I was almost opposite Randolph and could not but notice that he bowed very glumly to Lord Morris, who was on my right, and still more coldly to me. He looked far worse now than when I had seen him in Grosvenor Street only a couple of months before: his face was drawn and his skin leaden grey; there were gleams of hate, anger and fear in his eyes, the dreadful fear of those who have learned how close madness is.

---

* (1820–1904). Not only were there eight guests; the meals were served at eight o'clock and consisted of eight courses. King George V, when Prince of Wales, attended the 300th such dinner.

** Correctly, Sir Lawrence Alma-Tadema (1836–1912), member of the Royal Academy. Irving and Beerbohm Tree employed him as a scene designer.

† (1826–1901). Lord chief justice of Ireland and a Conservative Catholic M.P. who opposed Home Rule.

†† (1835–1911).

The soup had come and gone when I said something about Ireland to Lord Morris, who agreed with me. To my amazement Randolph suddenly broke in angrily. "You know a great deal about Europe, Mr. Harris, and of course all there's to be known about America," he barked at me, "but what do you know about Ireland?"

"I was born in Galway," I replied, "and brought up in the Royal School at Armagh, and one gets from childhood a certain *flair* difficult to acquire in later years."

"Impossible to acquire," chimed in Lord Morris. "No Saxon ever gets it. I knew without asking that you were a native of my dear, distressful country." Lord Morris spoke with a brogue that would bear, but he always showed me a great deal of kindness, perhaps because I learned very early in our acquaintance that he had a foot in both the Irish camps and was one of the very few men whose opinion on Irish matters could be accepted without misgiving. I believe that he was only "scored" off once in his life, and that was by the notorious Father Healy,* a great friend of his. One day Lord Morris was describing a wedding he had witnessed, and carried away by the beauty of the bride, he added, "And there was I with not even a slipper to throw after her."

"Why on earth didn't you throw your brogue?" whipped in Healy, brogue being also the name given to the Irish peasant's stout shoe!

All through the next course Lord Randolph didn't speak a word. As the game was being taken round, the footman noticed that it was not properly cut, so he passed Lord Randolph quickly to get it dispieced at the sideboard. At once Randolph pointing with outstretched hand, squealed out as if in pain, "E-e-e-e-e-e!"

"What is it, Lord Randolph?" asked the host in utter solicitude.

"E-e-e-e!" He repeated the high squeal, while pointing with his finger after the footman. "I want that—e-e-e! Some of that—e-e!"

"It shall be brought back," said Sir Henry. "I'm very glad you like it." The grouse was brought back: Randolph helped himself and began to eat greedily. Suddenly he stopped, put down his knife and fork and glared at each face round the table, apparently suspecting that his strange behavior had been remarked. He was insane, that was clear. From that moment on I could drink but not eat. Randolph Churchill mad! Like Maupassant!

When the table broke up, I asked Holmes had he noticed the incident with the game. "No, I didn't remark anything, but the grouse was excellent," he said. Later I asked Lord Morris had he remarked anything strange in Randolph's behavior. "No," he replied, "except that he seems to be in a d——bad temper. "

"Didn't you notice how he squealed and pointed?" I went on. "He's mad!"

"Was he ever sane?" countered Morris, laughing, and therewith I had to

* Father James Healy (1824–1894). He moved in the best London society. His Saturday dinners were famous, as was his wit.

be content, but ever afterwards I knew I had seen Randolph Churchill in what I called "the malignant monkey stage" of insanity. His shrill prolonged squeal is always in my ears when I think of him.

Years later, after he had returned to London and died there, I happened to be at dinner once, and beside Mrs. Jack Leslie,* his wife's sister. I told her of my experience at Sir Henry Thompson's "octave."

"Randolph was quite mad," she said, "when my sister took him on that last trip round the world. We all knew it. No one but Jenny would have trusted herself to go with him, but she's afraid of nothing and very strong. Yet from things she has let drop, she must have had a trying time with him. Why once, she told me, he drew out a loaded revolver in the cabin and threatened her, but she snatched it from him at once, pushed him back in his berth, and left the cabin, locking the door behind her. Jenny is the bravest woman I ever knew."

No wonder Winston has proved his courage time and again.

One day, some years later, I was at dinner with Lady Randolph, as I always called her, at Lady Cunard's.** I told her something of what Mrs. Jack Leslie had told me and expressed my admiration of her courage in taking Randolph round the world. "At first," she said, "when he was practically a maniac and very strong it was bad enough, but as soon as he became weak and idiotic, I didn't mind."

What an epitaph!

* Léonie Jerome; she married Lieutenant John Leslie in 1884.
** She was an American, née Maud Burke. She married Sir Bache Cunard in 1895; she died in 1948.

Chapter XXIII

A Passionate Experience in Paris:
A French Mistress

IN THIS VOLUME, which contains my memories of De Maupassant, I wish to tell another experience of French life. I was going once from London to Paris: in the train at Calais there was a young German who asked a French fellow traveler something or other and was snubbed for his pains; the Frenchman evidently guessed his nationality from his bad accent and faulty French. Resenting the rudeness, I answered the question, and soon the German and myself became almost friends. When we reached Paris, I told him I was going to the Hotel Meurice, and next day he called on me, lunched with me, and afterwards we drove together to the Bois.

Something ingenuous-youthful in the man interested me: we had hardly got into the Avenue des Acacias when he told me he thought French girls wonderfully attractive. Five minutes afterwards we crossed a victoria in which there was one very pretty girl and an older woman; my German exclaimed that the girl was a beauty and wanted to know if it would be possible to get acquainted with such a star. I told him that nothing was easier: they were a pair of *cocottes,* and if he had a couple of hundred francs to spare he would be well received. I advised him the next time our carriages met to jump into the one with the pretty girl and make hay while the sun shone. He thought this a quite impossible feat, and so the next time we passed, I told him to follow us, and jumped into the carriage myself.

At once the coachman turned down a side road and drove rapidly citywards. I put an arm round each of the women and assured them of our company at dinner at the Cafe Anglais. After a few moments' talk the pretty one whispered to me pertly, "You must make your choice," and as I turned to the older woman, she responded, "You won't regret it if you choose me!" I don't know why, but I immediately withdrew my arm from the waist of the pretty one, saying, "I must be loyal to my friend, who selected you." Five minutes afterwards we drew up at a cafe in the Champs-Elysées and were joined by my German, who could hardly believe his ears when I told him that I was leaving him the pretty and vivacious girl. To cut a long story short, we all dined together in a private room and afterwards conducted the women to their home. My German went upstairs with his inamorata and I went into a large apartment on the first floor. Here, to my astonishment, was a young girl of perhaps twelve who had evidently fallen asleep. As soon as the light was turned on, she sprang to her feet, evidently confused, and hurried to the door. "Don't go," I said, for she was very pretty, but smiling she hurried out. "Your child?" I turned to my companion, who nodded, it seemed to me. This occurrence helped to conform my resolution. "I'm going to sleep on the sofa," I said, "or if you wish it, I'll go to my hotel and you can have the girl with you."

"No, no," replied my companion, whose name was Jeanne d'Alberi. "She never sleeps here, she has her own room, and I am interested in your talk and not a bit sleepy. The theatre is my passion; you've not given me a single kiss," she added, coming over to me and holding up her face.

"I'm not much in the humor for kissing," I said. "I'm sleepy. I think I've drunk too much: that Musigny was potent."

"As you please," she said, and in two minutes had made up a bed for me on the sofa. I pulled off my outer garments, and whilst listening to her splashing in her *cabinet de toilette,* fell fast asleep.

I was awakened suddenly by the acutest pang of pleasure I had ever felt, and found Jeanne on top of me. How she had managed it, I don't know, but the evil was done, if evil there was, and my sensations were too intense to be abandoned. In a moment I had reversed our positions, and was seeking a renewal of the delight, and not in vain: her sex gripped and milked me, with an extraordinary strength and cleverness, such as I had never before imagined possible. Not even with Topsy had I experienced such intensity of pleasure. Taking her in my arms, I kissed her again and again in passionate surprise. "You can kiss me now," she said pouting, "but you didn't believe me when I told you in the victoria to choose me and you would profit by the exchange. My friend has only her pretty face," she added contemptuously.

"You're a wonder!" I exclaimed, and lifting her up I carried her over to the bed. As I laid her down, I lifted her nightie: she was well made from the waist down, but her breasts were flaccid and hung low. Still, one thing was sure. "That wasn't your daughter," I said; "you've never had a child."

She nodded, smiling. "I was lonely," she said simply, "and Lisette was so pretty and so merry that I adopted her years ago, when she was only a year old. I'm old at the game, you see," she added quietly.

I don't know why, but everything Jeanne said increased my interest in her. There was personality and brains in her, though she certainly was anything but pretty, and she not only talked most excellent French, but knew all social customs and observances. When I wished to pay her, she would not accept any money, told me she had no need of anything, and was glad to know me, wanted me as "a friend—and lover," she added, smiling. A day or two later, I gave a lunch at my hotel and had Jules Claretie* of the

* (1840–1913), previously a drama critic for *Figaro* and *Opinion nationale.*

Français, and a famous comic actor from the Palais Royal, and Jeanne, who made a most surprising hostess. Everyone was charmed with her. She found the right word to say to everyone and had more than tact. She told me afterwards she would never forget my kindness in treating her as an equal. Later I found out that she was the daughter of a French general, but had lost father and mother in the same year. A younger sister whom she loved had been disappointed in love and taken to dope and after her death Jeanne had resolved to make money.

She made no secret of the fact that she had two admirers, one a deputy who visited her every fortnight or so and gave her twenty thousand francs a year, the other an old senator who came from time to time, expecting always to find her ready, for he allowed her fifty thousand a year and had given her more than that in one sum. "He's a dear, and I owe him infinite kindness," she said, "and I assure you that when I drove with Adèle in the Bois, it was for her sake, not mine, but I liked your jumping into the carriage and your selection of me."

It was at that lunch, I think, that Claretie told the story of Aimée Desclée which I may reproduce here, as Aimée Desclée was in many ways the most seductive actress I've ever seen on any stage.*

"I knew her," Claretie began, "when I was very young in Paris and had just got a place as dramatic critic on the *Figaro*. I fell in love with her and made up to her, as young men do. One day she told me she wanted to be an actress, to play *Phèdre,* if you please. When I told her she'd have to begin by walking on and could not hope for even a small part for months, she laughed at me and said, that as some men were born generals and not subalterns, so she had no need to serve any apprenticeship. As dramatic critic I knew most of the leaders of the profession, and, strange to say, a few days afterwards I met a man who had taken a theatre and whose leading lady had broken down with bronchitis, if I remember rightly. I told him that I had the very person to take her place and make a great sensation, and I introduced him to Aimée. She made a good impression on him and finally he agreed to produce *Phèdre* and give her her chance.

"The night came, the theatre was filled, and Aimée appeared with worse than stage fright. I never saw such a fiasco. One could hardly hear a word she said and in five minutes, amid the jeers of the audience, she fled from the stage and the curtain came down on an audience half-laughing, half-angry, only to be appeased by getting back their entrance money. It took all my savings!

"Naturally my colleagues on the press made fun of what they called my infatuation. Some assured me that a pretty face did not make a great actress; others hinted that the girl must have hidden charms: in fine, I was ridiculed on all sides.

"I saw nothing more of Aimée, but a year or so later I heard that she had

* (1836–74); since she died when Harris was still in America, where he might have seen her is puzzling.

run away to Italy with a comic actor with whom she was madly in love; then we heard that he had left her in Venice without a sou; and some months afterwards I got a short note from her, asking me to come to see her. There was a curious fascination about her, so I went. When she came into the room I was struck dumb! She had lost all her beauty and grown ten years older. 'What has happened?' I could not but ask.

" 'Like Dante,' she replied, 'I have been in Hell.'

" 'You had a bad time?' I went on stupidly.

"She nodded, and then, 'Do you guess why I've sent for you?' I shook my head. 'I want you to give me another such chance as you gave me before.'

" 'Impossible,' I replied. 'Everyone laughed at me, and now they all know you. I could not if I would.'

" 'Now they won't laugh,' she replied. 'I know the kindness in you for me, know that you will help me, and I assure you of my eternal gratitude. You and I must always be friends,' and she held out both hands to me. Her voice had extraordinary quality and her personality charmed me as ever. I found myself saying, 'I will do my best,' and when she thanked me, smiling with her eyes full of unshed tears, I knew I'd do all I could, and more.

"Strange to say, about a month later a theatrical agent came to me, just as the first had come a couple of years earlier: he had a theatre and a company but the star actress he wanted to boom had gone off to America and left him in the lurch. Did I know of any actress who could play a great part? Without hesitation I took him to Aimée Desclée.

"He knew the whole story of her previous fiasco, but on the way I assured him she had changed, begged him to trust his own judgment, and what I expected happened. He was swept off his balance by her personal magnetism and he staged *Phèdre* for her, only stipulating that no one should know her real name until afterwards.

"Well, we beat the big drum and did all we knew, but the house was almost empty. When Aimée Desclée came on the stage, before she opened her mouth, I thrilled with expectation, and her first words carried us all off our feet. At the end of the first act I went out and sent notes to half a dozen colleagues to come and hear her, but when I returned to the theatre it was full. Paris had already in some magical way got news of the event and in an hour everyone knew that a great actress had been discovered. 'I think,' added Claretie, 'that she was the greatest actress I have ever seen.' "

Claretie told the little story superbly and with strange reticence; yet, to my astonishment, Jeanne heightened the effect. "I heard her a little later in *Froufrou*," she said, "and agree with you. Not only was she a great actress but a great woman. There were tones in her voice that wrung the heart. It was her own soul's suffering that gave her the power: Dumas *fils* was wise to choose her for his heroine."

This lunch taught me that Jeanne in her way was a surprising woman: she was extremely well read, had all the lighter French literature at her fingers' ends, and could find new words to say of Flaubert, and Zola, Daudet and Maupassant even, words that were illuminating. She knew Paris, too, all its heights and depths, was a wonderful companion for a man of letters, and an incomparable mistress.

After a day or two I began to doubt her magic. She never tried to excite me, but whenever I sought her I found the same diabolical power. The French have the word for her: *"Casse Noisettes,"* they call it, or "nut-crackers," a woman's sex with the contractile strength of a hand, and Jeanne knew the exact moment to use it.

I grew more and more infatuated and yet out of fear tried time and again to give her money and tear myself loose, but she would not accept money, though always eager to lunch or dine with me and meet actors, actresses, and men of letters.

One day we had been for a long outing at Fontainebleau, had dined there, and returned. I wanted to kiss her but she turned away. At length I said in pure despite, "I'll have to be getting back to London to my work."

Jeanne looked at me. "I was going to propose something else," she said. "I have a place near Algiers, sunbathed, between the mountains and the sea, wonderful. You could have ponies to ride and could give yourself to writing books and leave that silly journalism once for all."

"I mightn't succeed," I said, "and I have too little money to make the trial."

"I have more money than you think," she remarked quietly. "I have three hundred thousand francs saved and that house and farm and—"

"I can't live on your money," I broke in rudely.

"Why not?" she rejoined. "We could be married and have an almost perfect life."

I started. What a prospect! The intercourse of the past month came back to me. Once I had caught Jeanne by chance when she had just washed her face: she had no eyebrows, she painted them in, and gave her light eyelashes, too, a dark tone with some pigment. Marry her? I laughed to myself and could not help shaking my head.

"I am a fairly good mistress, am I not?" she asked.

"The best possible," I replied. "No one could deny that, and an excellent companion to boot, but I want to see more of life and the world before settling down; and I've always resolved to go round the world every twenty years or so; and I want to learn a couple of new languages and—"

"You could do all that," she insisted. "I should not hinder you. I want to make my house a house beautiful: I want you as husband and companion, but you could always take a winter off or a summer and go round the world, so long as you came back to me; and you would come back, I know you. You want to make a great reputation as a writer and I'm sure you will, but that means years of hard work, carefree years. Think it over." I smiled, but shook my head.

A day or two afterwards she said, "I shall have to send Lisette to school unless we go south together; she's getting to be a big girl and is exquisitely pretty. You should see her in her bath!"

"I'd love to," I said without thinking. The next evening when we came in, Jeanne took me to the next floor and opened the door. There was Lisette in the bath, a model of girlish beauty, astonishingly lithe and lovely. She turned her back on us and snatched a towel hanging near, but Jeanne held it back saying, "Don't be silly, child. Frank won't eat you, and I've told him how pretty and well formed you are."

At this the girl lifted big inscrutable eyes to her and stood at gaze, a most exquisite picture: the breasts just beginning to be marked, the hips a little fuller than a boy's, the feet and hands smaller—a perfect Tanagra statuette in whitest flesh with a roseate glow on the inside of arms and thighs, while the Mount of Venus was just shadowed with down. She stood there waiting, an entrancing maiden figure. I felt my mouth parching, the pulses in my temples beating. What did it mean? Did Jeanne intend—?

The next moment Jeanne lifted the child out of the bath, and covering her with the towel said, "Dry yourself and come down, dear. We're all going to dine soon."

When we were downstairs she asked, "Well, are you going with us to Algiers?"

"Suppose I wanted Lisette?" I asked boldly.

Jeanne shrugged her shoulders. "There are sure to be several Lisettes in your life," she said seriously, "but only one Jeanne, I hope," and she set her eyes on mine.

"You are a wonder," I rejoined, "a marvel!"

Nothing more was said then, but when Lisette came down in her nightie and dressing-gown, Jeanne encouraged her to sit on my knees after dinner, and I seem still to feel the warm imprint of her lithe body on my legs.

When I went back to the Meurice that night I knew I'd have to fight the greatest temptation of my life. Could I fight it?

It was Shakespeare's word that saved me, I verily believe. I could not be "the bellows and the fan to cool a harlot's lust." Yet the temptation was tremendous, for really Jeanne was a most interesting companion and an adorable mistress. I wanted to know why she had selected me. "How does one know why this man pleases you intimately," she asked, "whereas another repels you? You please me physically, interest me mentally, and I know you're hardworking and kind. I think we could have an almost ideal existence, and I'm tired of Paris and lonely, without an object or purpose in life."

"And Lisette?" I asked.

"Oh! the Lisettes are for later," she smiled. "Before she's grown up you'll have found an Arab beauty with even lovelier limbs. It's the artist in you leads you to stray, the attraction of plastic beauty on you. I noticed that at the very beginning, but I can't make my breasts small and round. If I could I would, you may be sure, but I know I can give you more pleasure than any other woman, and so I feel sure you will always come back to me."

It was true, but could I work with Jeanne: that was the doubt. Already I felt more tired than I had been for years. That night I studied my face in the glass and saw that my features had sharpened, and I had lost my healthy color. I was getting grey and worn, and if a month had this result, what would a year effect or ten years? I could not shut my eyes to the truth. I should be played out. I would have one more gaudy, great night; I'd kiss Lisette, too, and feel if she responded, and then for the train to Calais and my work again in London.

And this I did. I gave a big lunch to people of importance in the theatre and in journalism and invited Jeanne and referred everything to her and drew her out, throning her, and afterwards returned to her house to dinner. While she was changing and titivating, I took Lisette in my arms and kissed her with hot lips again and again while feeling her budding breasts, till she put her arms round my neck and kissed me just as warmly; and then I ventured to touch her little half-fledged sex and caress it, till it opened and grew moist and she nestled up to me and whispered: "Oh! how you excite me!"

"Have you ever done it to yourself?" I asked. She nodded with bright dancing eyes. "Often, but I prefer you to touch me." For the first time I heard the truth from a girl and her courage charmed me. I could not help laying her on the sofa, and turning up her clothes: how lovely her limbs were, and how perfect her sex. She was really exquisite, and I took an almost insane pleasure in studying her beauties, and parting the lips of her sex [with] kisses: in a few moments she was all trembling and gasping. She put her hand on my head to stop me. When I lifted her up, she kissed me. "You dear," she said with a strange earnestness, "I want you always. You'll stay with us, won't you?" I kissed her for her sweetness.

When Jeanne came out of the cabinet, we all went into the dining-room, and afterwards Lisette went up to her room after kissing me, and I went to bed with Jeanne, who let me excite her for half an hour; and then mounting me milked me with such artistry that in two minutes she brought me to spasms of sensation, such as I had never experienced before with any other woman. Jeanne was the most perfect mistress I had met up to that time, and in sheer power of giving pleasure hardly to be surpassed by any of western race.

An unforgettable evening, one of the few evenings in my life when I reached both the intensest pang of pleasure with the even higher aesthetic delight of toying with beautiful limbs and awakening new desires in a lovely body and frank honest spirit.

Next day I left Jeanne a letter, thanking her and explaining as well as I could the desire in me to complete my work, and enclosing five thousand francs for her and Lisette, all I could spare. Then I took the train and was in my home in Kensington Gore before nightfall. I had won, but that was about all I could say, and I wasn't proud of myself. For months the temptation was in my flesh, more poignant than at first, till suddenly I heard from the comic actor of the Palais Royale, Monsieur Galipaux, I believe, that Jeanne had left Paris and gone to live in Algiers. "We all miss her," he added.

Since then I've neither seen nor heard of her or Lisette, but she taught me what astonishing quality as lovers some French women possess.

Often since when I've met mad, unreasoning jealousy, the memory of Jeanne has recurred to me. She taught me that a woman can love and delight in giving the most extreme pleasure, and yet be without jealousy of the aesthetic, lighter loves of man. The faithfulness of heart and soul and the spiritual companionship is everything to such a few, rare women.

Chapter XXIV

The Foretaste of Death from 1920 Onward

I HAVE DECIDED AT ONE JUMP to pass over more than a quarter of a century, leaving my maturity to be described later, and so come at once to old age, for there are things to be said that I wish to transcribe with the exact fidelity of a diary.

I had often heard of sixty-three as being "the grand climacteric" of a man's life, but what that really meant I had no idea till I had well passed that age.

Alphonse Daudet has written somewhere that every man of forty has tried at some time or another to have a woman and failed (*fit faux coup*). He even went so far as to assert that the man who denied this, was boasting, or rather lying.

I can honestly say that I had no such experience up to sixty. I had become long before, as I shall tell, a mediocre performer in the lists of love, but had never been shamed by failure. Like the proverbial Scot, I had no lack of vigor, but I too "was nae sae frequent" as I had been. Desire seemed nearly as keen in me at sixty as at forty, but more and more, as I shall relate, it ramped in me at sight of the nudities of girlhood.

I remember one summer afternoon in New York, it seems to me just when short dresses began to come in. A girl of fourteen or fifteen, as I came into the room, hastily sat up on a sofa, while pulling down her dress that had rucked up well above her knees. She was exquisitely made, beautiful limbs in black silk showing a margin of thighs shining like alabaster. I can still feel how my mouth parched at the sight of her bare thighs and how difficult it was for me to speak of ordinary things as if unconcerned. She was still half asleep and I hope I got complete control of my voice before she had smoothed down the bobbed unruly hair that set off her flaming cheeks and angry confused glances.

Time and again in the street I turned to fix in my memory some young girl's legs, trying to trace the subtle hesitating line of budding hips, seeing all the while the gracious triangle in front outlined by soft down of hair just revealing the full lips of the *fica*. Even at forty, earlier still, indeed, as I have related, I had come to love small breasts like half-ripe apples and was put off by every appearance of ripe maturity in a woman. But I found from time to time that this woman or that whom I cared for could give me as keen a thrill as any girl of them all, perhaps indeed keener and more prolonged, the pleasure depending chiefly upon mutual passion. But I'm speaking now of desire and not of the delights of passion, and desire became rampant in me only at the sight of slight half-fledged girlhood.

One experience of my manhood may be told here and will go far to make all the unconscious or semi-conscious lusts manifest. While living in Roehampton and editing the *Saturday Review,* I used to ride nearly every day in Richmond Park. One morning I noticed something move in the high bracken, and riding to the spot, found a keeper kneeling beside a young doe. "What's the matter?" I asked.

"Matter enough," he replied, holding up the two hind legs of the little creature, showing me that they were both broken.

"Here she is, Sir," he went on. "As pretty as a picture, ain't she? Just over a year or so old, the poor little bitch, and she come in heat this autumn and she must go and pick out the biggest and oldest stag in the park and rub her little bottom against him—Didn't you, you poor little bitch!—and of course he mounted her, Sir; and her two little sticks of legs snapped under his weight and I found her lying broken without ever having had any pleasure; and now I've got to put her out of her pain, Sir; and she's so smooth and pretty! Ain't ye?" And he rubbed his hand caressingly along her silky fur.

"Must you kill her?" I asked, "I'd pay to have her legs set."

"No, no," he replied, "it would take too much time and trouble and there's many of them. Poor little bitch must die," and as he stroked her fine head gently, the doe looked up at him with her big eyes drowned in tears.

"Do you really lose many in that way?" I asked.

"Not so many, Sir," he replied. "If she had got over this season, she'd have been strong enough next year to have borne the biggest. It was just her bad luck," he said, "to have been born in the troop of the oldest and heaviest stag in the park."

"Has age anything to do with the attraction?" I asked.

"Surely it has," replied the keepers. "The old stag is always after these little ones, and young does are always willing. I guess it's animal nature," he added, as if regretfully.

"Animal nature," I said to myself as I rode away, "and human nature as well, I fear," with heavy apprehension or presentiment compressing my heart.

Now to my experience. In the early summer of 1920, having passed my sixty-fifth birthday, I was intent on finishing a book of *Portraits* before making a long deferred visit to Chicago. Before leaving New York, a girl called on me to know if I could employ her. I had no need of her, yet she was pretty, provocative, even, but for the first time in my life, I was not moved.

As her slight, graceful figure disappeared, suddenly I realized the wretchedness of my condition in an overwhelming, suffocating wave of bitterness. So this was the end; desire was there but not the driving power. There were ways, I knew, of whipping desire to the standing point, but I didn't care for them. The end of my life had come. God, what a catastrophe! What irremediable, shameful defeat! Then for the first time I began to envy the lot of a woman; after all, she could give herself to the end, on her death bed if she wished, whereas a man went about looking like a man, feeling like a man, but powerless, impotent, disgraced in the very pride and purpose of his manhood.

And then the thought of my work struck me. No new stories had come to me lately: the shaping spirit of imagination had left me with the virile power. Better death than such barrenness of outlook, such a dreadful monotonous desert. Suddenly some lines came to me:

> Dear as remembered kisses after Death,
> Deep as true love and wild with all regret
> Oh, Death in life, the days that are no more!*

As I sat there in the darkening office, tears poured from my eyes. So this is the end!

I crawled home: there, all by myself, I'd be able to plumb the disaster and learn its depth. For the first time in my life, I think, tears were rising in my heart and I was choking with the sense of man's mortality.

> Tears, idle tears; I well know what they mean
> Tears from the depth of some divine despair.

Why "divine"; why not accursed?

> Rise in the heart and gather to the eyes
> When looking at the happy autumn fields
> And thinking of the days that are no more . . .
> Oh! Death in life! the days that are no more!**

I would go home. And then a dreadful incident came back to me. One day, a long time before the World War, Meredith sent me a copy of *Richard Feverel*, all marked with corrections. In his letter he told me that he was setting himself to correct all his books for a final definitive edition. He

---

* Part of the last stanza of "Tears, Idle Tears," a song from *The Princess*, by Tennyson. Harris usually quotes more accurately. The stanza actually runs thus:
> Dear as remembered kisses after death,
> And sweet as those by hopeless fancy feigned
> On lips that are for others; deep as love,
> Deep as first love, and wild with all regret;
> O Death in Life, the days that are no more.

** The first stanza from the same poem more accurately rendered, plus the final line of the poem. The first stanza runs so:
> Tears, idle tears, I know not what they mean,
> Tears from the depth of some divine despair
> Rise in the heart, and gather to the eyes,
> In looking on the happy Autumn-fields,
> And thinking of the days that are no more.

wanted to know what I thought of the changes he had made. "I think you will find them all emendations," he wrote, "but be frank with me, please, for you are almost the only man living whose judgment on such a matter would have weight with me. Morly, too, is a judge, but not of creative work, and as you have always professed a certain liking for *Richard Feverel,* I send that book for your opinion."

Naturally I was touched and sat down to read, feeling sure that the alterations would be all emendations. But the first glances shocked me: he kept preferring the colorless word to the colorful. I went through the job with the utmost care. In some three hundred changes there were three of four I could approve; all the rest were changes for the worse. At once I got my car and drove down to Box Hill.

I came to the little house in the late afternoon and found Meredith had just got back from his donkey drive up the hill. He took me to his working room in the little chalet away from the house and we went at it hammer and tongs. "You've put water in your ink," I cried, "and spoiled some of the finest pages in English. The courtship in the boat, even, you've worsened. For God's sake, stop and leave well, excellent-well, alone!"

At first he would not accept my opinion, so we went through the changes, one after the other. Hours flew by. "How do you explain the fact," he cried at last, "that I'm still unconvinced, that in my heart you've not persuaded me?"

I had to speak out; there was nothing else for it.

"You are getting on," I said. "The creative power is leaving you, I fear. Please, please, forgive my brutal frankness!" I cried, for his face suddenly seemed to turn grey. "You know, you must know how I reverence you and every word of this scene; the greatest love idyll in all literature is dear to me. It's greater than Shakespeare's *Romeo and Juliet.* Don't alter a word, Master, please, not a word! They are all sacred!"

I don't know whether I persuaded him or not; I'm afraid not. As we grow older we grow more obstinate, and he said something once later about finding pleasure in correcting his early work.

But the fact remained fixed in my soul: Meredith had passed the great climacteric; he must have been about sixty-six and he had lost the faculty even of impartial judgment.

Had I lost it too? It seemed probable.

God, the bitterness of this death in life!

The days that are no more!*

From that time on, I began to mention my age, make people guess it, women as well as men, but saw no comprehension, even in thoughtful women. If you are not bald and have no grey hairs—the stigmata of senility —you are all right in their opinion, all right! Oh, God!

---

* Tennyson, *The Princess:*
> Looking on the happy Autumn fields,
> And thinking of the days that are no more.

Yet I soon found that my judgment had not lost its vigor. My virility had decreased, was never prompt to the act as before, but it was still there, and so long as I treasured it, did not spend it, the faculty of judgment was but little changed. My worst fear was groundless: total abstinence was a necessity unless—but that's another story or two.

The want of joy, even the shuddering mistrust of the enfeebled faculties, might be borne without complaint. The general health, however, everyone tells me, begins to suffer: catch a cold and you have rheumatic pains that are slow to cure; eat something that disagrees with you and you are ill not for a few hours, as in maturity, but for days and weeks, don't take exercise enough, or take a little too much, and you suffer like a dog. Nature becomes an importunate creditor who gives you no respite.

I remember years ago visiting Pitt House that stood on the top of Hampstead Heath. I wanted to know why it was called Pitt House: I found that the owner, hearing that Lord Chatham was in bad health, had placed the house at the great statesman's disposal, and ever afterwards it has been known as Pitt House. There the man went who had picked Wolfe and won an empire for Britain after scores of Parliamentary triumphs; there he passed his last days in profound loneliness and black melancholy. Tormented by gout, he used to sit by himself all day long in a little room without even a book, his heavy head upon his hand. He couldn't bear even the presence of his wife, though they had been lovers for many years; he would not even see a servant, but had a hatch cut in the wall so that he could take the meal placed outside on a slide, and, when he chose, push out the platter again and close the hatch against everybody. Think of it: he who had been for long years master of the world, whose rare appearances in the House of Commons had been triumphs, reduced to this condition of despairing solitude! That hatch in the wall was as significant to me as his great speech in defence of the American colonists.

That old age is usually embittered by bad health is true, I think, to most men, but not to me, thank God! I am as well now at nearly seventy as I ever was, better, indeed. I have learned how to keep perfectly well and shut the door in the face of old age and most of its infirmities. Let me, for the benefit of others, tell the story here briefly.

On my third visit to South Africa in the late nineties, I caught black water fever, was deserted on the Chobé river by all my coolies, who thought the spirits had come to take me because I wandered in my speech and talked nonsense loudly. How I won to the sea and civilization in four months of delirium and starvation I shall tell at length when I come to it in the ordinary course. It's enough here to say that on the ship going back to Europe, the inside of my stomach came away in strips and pieces, and when I reached London I found myself a martyr to chronic indigestion. I spent two years going from this celebrated doctor to that all over Europe—in vain. One made me live on grapes and another on vegetables and a third on nothing but meat, but I suffered almost continuously and became as thin as a skeleton.

My own doctor in London brought about the first improvement: he told me to give up smoking. I had smoked to excess all my life, but I stopped at once, though I must admit that no habit was ever so difficult to break off. A year later, if I caught the scent of a really good cigar, the water would come into my mouth, though I soon discovered that by giving up smoking all my food tasted better and fine wines developed flavors I had never before imagined. Had I to live my life again, nothing would induce me to smoke. It is, I think, the worst of all habits, an enemy at once to pleasure and to health. But the indigestion held and made life a misery. Following Schweninger's* advice (he had been Bismarck's doctor), I tried fasting for a fortnight at a time and derived some benefit from it, but not much.

One day my little London doctor advised me to try the stomach pump. The word frightened me, but I found it was only a syphon and not a pump. One had to push an india rubber tube down one's throat, pour a quart or so of warm water into the stomach through a funnel, depress the funnel below one's waist, and the water could come out, carrying with it all the impurities and undigested food. The first time I did it with the help of the doctor and the immediate relief cannot be described. From feeling extremely ill, I was perfectly well in a moment. I had got rid of the peas that the doctor had recommended and I could not help grinning as they came out with the water, proving that his prescription had been bad.

The next day I tried washing out again and soon found that my stomach would not digest bread and butter. No doctor had ever advised me to leave off eating bread and butter, but now the reason was clear. The black water fever had weakened my spleen and so I could not digest starchy things or fats. *In a week the stomach pump gave me a scientific dietary:* I loved coffee, but coffee, I found, was poison to me, for it arrested digestion. Of course I left it off and avoided bread and butter, potatoes, etc., and at once my digestion began to do its work properly. For fifteen or twenty years now I have washed out my stomach nine days out of ten before going to bed, for every now and then I take too much butter or coffee or eat some grease-sodden food in a restaurant; and I find it no more unpleasant to wash out my stomach than to wash my teeth, and it gives me perfect sleep and almost perfect health. But some sufferer may ask, "What do you do if you get indigestion after lunch or after breakfast?" I can only reply that if it is at all painful I wash out immediately; but if it is only slight, I take a dose of an alkaline powder of a Dr. Dubois, a French master who has bettered bicarbonate of soda and all such other lenitives with his alcalinophosphate, which gives instantaneous relief. But the remedy, the infallible and blessed remedy for all ills of digestion, is the stomach pump. Thanks to it, and to strictest moderation in eating and drinking, and total abstinence from

* Ernst Schweninger (1850–1924).

tobacco, I enjoy almost perfect health! I am certainly better now than I have been since I was thirty.

I content myself with a couple of cups of tea in the morning; I make a good meal about one o' the clock; and in the evening take nothing but a vegetable soup and on occasion a morsel of meat or sweet. Now I can drink a small cup of coffee, even with cream, after my lunch and feel no ill effects. Almost seventy, I can run a hundred yards within a couple of seconds as fast as I could at twenty, and I do my little sprint every day.

Perfect health I have won back, but age, though kept at bay, is not to be denied. The worst part of it is that it robs you of hope: you find yourself sighing instead of laughing: the sight of your tomb there just before you on the road is always with you; and since the great adventure of love no longer tempts, one tires of the monotony of work and duties devoid of seduction. Without hope, life becomes stale, flat and unprofitable.

The worst of all is the hopelessness. If you needed money before, there were twenty ways of making it: a little thought and energy and the difficulty was conquered; now, without desire, without joy, without hope, where can you find energy? The mere notion of a crusade fills you with distaste. "Why? What for? What's the good?" come to your lips as the tears rise to your eyes.

Now, too, my memory for names has suddenly become very bad. Often I remember words I want to quote, but for the moment I can't recall the writer's name. Or I go to the shop to buy a book and I've forgotten the author. All this increases my labor and is worse than annoying.

I try to think it balances another weakness of mine which is exceedingly agreeable. All my life long I have forgotten unpleasant events and ordinary people in the strangest way. My wife often says to me, "You remember Mary or Sarah"—a servant who had done this or omitted to do that: I've forgotten her altogether. I remember my wife getting very angry with me in New York once because a second-rate writer followed me to our gate and got me to lend him ten dollars. "Don't you remember," she exclaimed, "how he spoke and wrote against you not six months ago?" I have forgotten the whole occurrence; the petty miseries of life are all overwhelmed in oblivion to me very quickly after they occur, and I count this among the chief blessings of my life. The past to me is all sweet and pleasant, like a lovely landscape sun-veiled.

But the present gets steadily darker; and the future! Whitman's plaint over his *Leaves of Grass* at the very end echoes in my heart.

> Begun in ripen'd youth and steadily pursued,
> Wandering, peering, dallying with all—war,
> peace, day and night absorbing,
> Never even for one brief hour abandoning my
> task,
> I end it here in sickness, poverty and old age.
> I sing of life, yet mind me well of death.*

* "L. of G.'s Purport"; from *Second Annex*, section "Good-Bye My Fancy."

Today shadowy Death dogs my steps, my seated shape, and for years
> Draws sometimes close to me, as face to face.

And yet something, is it what Goethe calls "the sweet custom of living," holds one in life.

I for one cannot accept the solace: with the loss of virility the glamour has gone out of life. One notices that a girl's legs are nothing wonderful; even well formed ones don't thrill and excite as they used to thrill: the magic is almost gone!

Ten years ago I read the announcements of Paris theatres with vivid curiosity; now I would hardly cross the street to witness the bepuffed sensation of the hour.

Nearly all the glamour is gone. Five years ago, I'd take up a book I had just corrected, hot from the press, with intense interest: is there anything new and extraordinary in it? Now I read and the critical sense is extravagantly keen because the glamour has gone, even from my own work. I see plainly that my fourth book of *Portraits* is not so good as the first two; I see that this book of short stories, *Undream'd of Shores* is nothing like so good as its predecessor, *Unpath'd Waters!*

> The skies are discrowned of the sunlight
> The earth dispossessed of the sun.

Why then continue the struggle? Why not make one's quietus with a bare syringe? I have no fear of the undiscovered country. None! Why hesitate? I can't hope to write better at seventy than at sixty; I know that's not likely. Why lag another hour superfluous on the stage? I don't know:

> I pace the earth and breathe the air and feel the sun.*

And there's a certain attraction in it, but very slight: the first hard jolt and I'll go. As it is, my wife's future restrains me more than any other factor: I should grieve her, hurt her? Yet I owe her all kindness!

There's the hypodermic syringe; tomorrow, I'll buy the morphia.

Is there, then, no pleasure in life? Oh yes, one; the greatest, keenest, and wholly without alloy, reading! And in the second line, listening to great music and studying beautiful paintings and new works of art: all pure joy without admixture. I go into my little library and take down a Chaucer: it opens at *The Persones Tale* and in a moment I am in a new world; I read of the Seven Deadly Sins, Pride first, "the rote of all harmes"; for "of this rote springen certain braunches, as ire, envie, accidie or slouthe, avarice or coveitise, glotonie and lecherie . . ."

I have no pride whatever, whether within the heart or without, and none of its branches, in especial "no swelling of herte which is when man rejoyceth him of harme that he hath don"; no trace of any branch, except it be lecherie, though how that pleasant sin can be said to be affiliated to pride, I am at a loss to understand.

* From *Be Still, My Soul, Be Still* by A. E. Housman.

I read first of the "stinking sinne of lecherie that men clepen avoutrie" (adultery) "that is of wedded folk and the avouterers shall bren in helle." My withers are unwrung; I never coveted another man's wife!* But then I read "of lecherie springen divers species, as fornication, betwene man and woman, which ben not maried, and is dedly sinne and ayenst nature." "Ayenst nature?" Why? "Parfay the reson of a man eke telleth him wel that it is dedly sinne; for as moche as God forbad lecherie and Seint Poule. . . ."

Worse follows: "another sinne of lecherie is to bereven a maid of hire maidenhed . . . thilke precious fruit that the book clepeth the hundreth fruit; in Latine hight centesimus fructus," and I smile, for this sweet pleasure is not specially forbidden by "Seint Poule."

Finally I glance at the Wif of Bathes' confession:

> I wol not lie;
> A man shall win us best with flateries
> And with attendance and with besinesse
> Ben we ylimed bothe more and lesse,

or as I learned it at school,

> And with a close attendance and attention
> Are we caught more or less the truth to mention.

Suddenly another great phrase, especialy addressed to women, I believe, catches my eye, warning the fair ones not to dress so as to show the "buttokkes behinde, as it were the hinder part of a she ape in the ful of the mone." Laughing merrily, I resolve not to grieve for the fullness of life or for the full moons I have missed!

Chaucer is but one of many sorcerers who can change the whole world for me and make of heavy, anxious times, joy-brimming, gay hours of amusement and pleasant discourse. And this entertainment I can vary at will; pass from smiling Chaucer to rapt Spenser and hear him telling of

> . . . her angel face
> That made a sunshine in a shady place.**

Thank God! There are hundreds of books I want to read: I must learn Russian and see a new part of God's world; and I've heard of a new Spanish poet from Nicaragua, Rubén Dario,† a love poet of the best, whose prose also is remarkable.

And Arno Holz,†† whom I met in Berlin, has honey at the heart of him;

---

* The reader will remember Mrs. Mayhew in Lawrence.
** Spenser, *The Faerie Queene*, Ib., I, iii, 6.
> Her angel's face,
> As the great eye of Heaven, shined bright,
> And made a sunshine in the shady place.

† (1867–1916).
†† (1863–1929). His early lyric poetry won him a reputation, but his best work was in critical theory. He was a founder of German impressionism.

and Schopenhauer is there, whom I've not listened to for five and twenty years, and so many, many others, thank God. Enough for years! I hate my ignorances: there is Willie Yeats, a compatriot and certainly one of the greatest poets writing in English today, the winner last year of the Nobel prize. And above and beyond them all, Heinrich Heine, whose life I almost wrote and always wished to write—Heine, after Shakespeare, the most lovable of men, "the best of all the humorists," as he said himself, the wisest of moderns, save in his own affairs. I wonder why Heine never wrote any dramas or novels? His keen, impartial vision might have given us wonderful dramas or stories. Why did he never try a novel with that exquisite prose of his, a prose as perfect as Shakespeare's? One of these days I shall give a whole month to Heine, though I know dozens of his poems by heart.

And so I am bathed again in the profound pleasures of the soul, the joys of art and artistic endeavor and accomplishment, that for us moderns just coming of age outweighs all the comforts and solace of religion. Here at last we mortals are on firm ground, with the profound conviction that at length we have come into our inheritance. For by dint of living to the highest in us, as artists should, we men can not only make a new world fairer and more soul-satisfying than any ever pictured in the future by the fanatic, but we can enter into and enjoy our paradise when we will. And love is written over the door in luminous, great letters; and all who care to enter are welcome; and one cannot be too hopeful, for here all desires are realized, all forecasts overpassed.

Now at long last I must take myself seriously to task. Thank God, by taking thought one can add something to one's stature. What is my message to men?

> Men my brothers, men the workers, ever doing something new
> That which they have done but earnest of the things that
> they shall do.*

Partly it is the bold joy in love and frank speech, partly the admiration of great men, and especially of the great benefactors of humanity, of the artists and writers who increase our joys, and of the men of science and healing who diminish our pains. Here in this world is our opportunity: here in these seventy years of earthly life our noble, unique inheritance.

And because of this conviction I loathe wars and the combative, aggressive spirit of the great conquering race, the Anglo-Saxons with their insane, selfish greeds of power and riches. I hate their successes and dread the life they're building with blood for plaster. I want all the armies disbanded and the navies as well and the manufacture of munitions made a criminal offence everywhere.

And I want new armies enrolled: the moneys now spent in offense and defense should be devoted to scientific research; schools of science must be endowed in every town on the most liberal scale, and investigators installed

* Tennyson, *Locksley Hall*. Substitute "reaping" for "doing" in the first line.

for original research and honored as officers. I want schools of music and art too in every city and opera houses and theatres where now are barracks; and above all hospitals instead of our dreadful prisons, and doctors instead of gaolers, nurses instead of executioners. And I want, want, want food and lodging assured to everyone and no questions asked in our poorhouses, which are merely the insurance of the rich against disaster.

My ideals are all human and all within reach, but realized, they would transfigure life.

And if this new ideal is not soon brought into life I am frightened, for the abyss yawns before us. Here is Sir Richard Gregory,* the famous scientist, sounding the alarm in the daily English press of this year 1924. He tells us, "We are on the threshold of developments by which forces will be unloosed and powers acquired far beyond our present imaginings, and if these gifts are misused, mankind must disappear from this planet."

Yet England and America, too, are spending thousands of millions on armies and navies, sets of false teeth that are no good even to bite with, as I told President Harding—to his horror.

What can I do to commend the new Ideal State and the new Ideal Individual? Very little and that little will be effective in measure as I better myself and take the motes out of my own eyes.

> Death closes all; yet something ere the end
> Some work of noble worth may yet be done.**

And so by way of art and letters and belief in a future millenium, on this friendly earth of ours, I reach love of life again and settle down to do the best in me. Can one ever forget that little verse?

> The kiss of the Sun for pardon
> And the song of the birds for mirth—
> One is nearer God's heart in a garden
> Than anywhere else on Earth.†

What do I need after all but a little money to give me security, and even that is not impossible to come by, for my wants are few and I am satisfied with little so long as the spirit is interested and delighted.

And I have been helped by friends again and again. American friends whom I did not even know have sent me moneys and loving encouragement and time and again brought tears to my eyes, sweet tears of gratitude and affection. I can only do my best for them in return, better than my best if possible. And I begin with this humiliating confession.

Shakespeare said that he was more sinned against than sinning. I wish

---

* Probably John Walter Gregory (1864–1932), an explorer and a geologist, who wrote on the future problems of mankind.

** Tennyson, *Ulysses*. Substitute "yet" for "but" in the first line and "note" for "worth" in the second.

† Dorothy Gurney (1858–1932), *God's Garden*. Delete "and" from the second line; otherwise, the quotation is substantially correct.

I could say as much, but I feel that I have sinned against others, at least as deeply as I have been sinned against; and I am not even sure now, as I used to be, that I have been more generous to others than men have been to me.

A few will surely read this, my book, in the spirit in which it was conceived; some will even see what it has cost me.

They talk of making money by an outspoken book: it's absurd. If the book is in English, you lose by writing it; you lose by publishing it; you lose by selling it. In French it is possible to make money by it, but even there it entails loss of prestige. Victor Marguerite, the son of the famous General, was cut out of the Legion of Honor for publishing *La Garçonne* last year, 1923. And a professor, Edmund Gosse, knighted for mediocrity in England, writes about "the brutality of *La Garçonne* and the foul chaos of *Ulysses*," though both Victor Marguerite and James Joyce are children of light, above his understanding.

A year or two ago I was honored on all hands: wherever I came I felt that men and women spoke of me with interest, curiosity at least. Since the first volume of *My Life* appeared, everywhere I feel the unspoken condemnation and see the sneer or the foul, sidelong grin. I have paid dearly for my boldness.

All pathmakers, I say to myself, must suffer, but unjust punishment embitters life: the Horridges in England and the Mayers in America are foul diseases.* Still, my reward is certain, though I shall never see the laurels. Many men and some few women will read me when I am dust and perhaps be a little grateful to me for having burst the fetters and led the way out of the prison of Puritanism into the open air and sunshine of this entrancing world of wonders.

The other day here in Nice, I heard a delightful limerick:

> If the skirts get any shorter
> Said the Flapper with a sob;
> I'll have two more cheeks to powder
> And a lot more hair to bob.

Is there not a laugh in it? And a good laugh is something in this ephemeral life of ours.

---

* Sir Thomas Garder Horridge, (1857–1938). He had some things to his credit. In 1906 in running for the House of Commons he defeated Balfour; in 1907 he won (for a client) a libel suit against the Northcliffe newspapers; and in 1916 he was a judge in the trial of Sir Roger Casement.

Perhaps Julius M. Mayer (1865–1925), Attorney General, State of New York 1905–07; appointed judge of Southern District of New York 1912; appointed U.S. Circuit Judge 1921.

Volume
III

For thilke cause, if that ye rede
I wolde go the middle wey
And write a boke between the twey
Somewhat of lust, somewhat of lore.

"Moral" Gower (1325–1408)

Foreword

Give me the man that on Life's rough sea
Loves to have his sails filled with a lusty wind,
Even till the sail-yards tremble, the masts crack,
And the rapt ship runs on her side so low
That she drinks water while her keel ploughs air.

There is no danger to a man who knows
What life and death is; there's not any law
Exceeds his knowledge, nor is it lawful
That he should stoop to any other law.

*Chapman**

AT LENGTH the oracle has spoken. Mr. Justice Levy** of the Supreme Court in New York has looked into the second volume of *My Life,* and "found it necessary to read but a few passages to arrive at the inevitable conclusion that it is neither literature nor art."

Now who made Levy, with his "inevitable conclusion," a judge of literature and art? He may be a judge of what is legal or illegal; but what does he know of literature or art?

Levy proceeds to declare that my book "is not only obviously and unquestionably obscene, lewd, lascivious, and indecent, but it is filthy, disgusting and utterly revolting," and he adds, not seeing that he is contradicting himself, "I purposely refrain from naming it, as I am averse to

---

* *The Conspiracie and Tragedie of Charles, Duke of Byron,* III, iii, 103–112, by George Chapman (1559–1634):
Give me a spirit that on this life's rough sea
Loves t'have his sails fill'd with a lusty wind,
Even till his sail-yards tremble, his masts crack,
And his rapt ship run on her side so low
That she drinks water, and her keel plows air.
There is no danger to a man that knows
What life and death is; there's not any law
Exceeds his knowledge; neither is it lawful
That he should stoop to any other law.

** Aaron J. Levy (1881–   ), elected to the Supreme Court in 1923 for fourteen years.

enhancing its sale"; but if it is "disgusting and utterly revolting," then surely no sale need be feared. Levy, why play Dogberry* and write yourself down an ass!

But this New York judge has given the police the power to raid private printing establishments without a search warrant and arrest the printers of a book about which nothing is known! "The police," he declares, "do not merit the criticism leveled at them" for exceeding their constitutional powers. "Quite the contrary, they are to be commended," for the book turned out to be obscene. Justice Levy's law is as ridiculous as his view of literature. I can only hope the police may raid his house and arrest him for having in his possession a Bible, the obscene passages in which are known to every schoolboy!

Is there any way of arriving at an impartial and definitive judgment on what should be allowed and what should be forbidden in writing of sexual matters? It will scarcely be denied that there is far less freedom of speech in England and the United States than anywhere else in Christendom, and this Anglo-Saxon prudery is hardly more than a century old. It came with the increase of women readers, coincident with the vast growth in wealth and numbers of English-speaking people since the French Revolution. It is manifestly founded on Puritanism and is supported by the middle classes and has no deeper or more rational sanction. In France, and indeed in every country of Europe, the man of letters today can treat sexual facts as freely as the painter or sculptor treats the nude: it is only in England and the United States that he would be advised to speak of his "little Mary" instead of his stomach.

And since this prudery has come into power, English literature has lost its pride of place. French books and Russian books have taken the position once held by English books. If it were worth the trouble, it would be easy to trace the emasculating effect of this prudery throughout English and American literature; but the main facts are manifest and indisputable.

Let us see what the best Frenchmen have to say about their wider liberty: do they praise or condemn it?

Anatole France,** who died recently, held for a dozen years the foremost place in French literature. He was, by almost universal consent, the foremost man of letters in the world. A book on him has been published lately by Jean Jacques Brousson, who was for many years his secretary. He calls it *Anatole France in Slippers.*† Again and again Anatole France expresses himself on questions of sex with complete freedom.

"A sad prudery reigns over literature; a prudery more stupid, more cruel, more criminal than the Holy Inquisition." (*La triste pudeur règne sur la littérature, la pudeur plus sotte, plus cruelle, que la Sainte Inquisition.*)

And he goes on:

* Character in *Much Ado About Nothing*.
** (1844–1924).
† The English translation appeared in 1925.

"I want Venus from head to foot. Her face is good enough for relations and friends and children, and the husband, but her body must be ready for caresses. For I hope you are not one of those fools who would limit the lover to a kiss on the face, as if she were a holy relic. Lovers can claim all the unedited places and the first editions, if I may so speak . . . (Hark to that, Levy!)

"People praise my learning; I only want to be learned now in the things of love. Love is now my sole and particular study. It is to love that I devote the remains of my continually diminishing power. Why can I not write everything that the little god inspires me with?

"For me now a woman is a book. There is no such thing as a bad book, as I have already told you. Going over its pages, one is sure to find some place that will repay you for your trouble. Page by page, my friends, I love to go over it slowly." And while saying this, "he wet his fingers and made the gesture of caressing some imaginary pages, his eyes sparkling with youth," Brousson adds.

Again and again he returns to this theme: here is his advice to his young secretary:

"Make love now, by night and by day, in winter as in summer. . . . You are in the world for that and the rest of life is nothing but vanity, illusion, waste. There is only one science, love; only one riches, love; only one policy, love. To make love is all the law and the prophets."

It must be remembered that Anatole France, when he complains of the prudery and reticence in literature, is speaking of French literature, the frankest in the world. Again and again Anatole France has written and spoken as frankly as I have written in any page of *My Life,* and yet he complains of French prudery as "stupid, cruel, criminal," and no Judge Levy dares to assail him.

There is another example one should cite. In his last book, published since his death, Paul Verlaine,* perhaps the greatest of French poets, certainly one of the immortals, sings the delights even of unnatural passion, and yet the Upton Sinclairs** will read us Sunday school lectures of what we must say and what leave unsaid in describing normal human desire.

And if the authority of Anatole France and of Verlaine is not enough, I can comfort myself with the saying of Michelangelo: "The great indiscriminating masses always honor what they should despise and love what they should abhor"; or the saying of perhaps the wisest Frenchman: "The value of any work of art can be gauged by the indignation it excites among ordinary folk."

When Rubens was criticized by the Archduke Ferdinand, the governor of the Low Countries, for his bold painting of *The Three Graces,* the great artist answered frankly, "It was in painting the nude that the power of the

---

* (1844–96).
** (1878–   ). He and Harris had friendly correspondence until Sinclair wrote to Harris that he found *My Life and Loves* objectionable.

artist could best be seen" (*c'était au nu qui se voyait le mérite de la peinture*). And this was said at almost the end of his life.

I leave Sinclair to his *Mammonart** and communist tracts, for already the new time is upon us and the new paganism is making its claim felt. The old paganism was emphatic enough: Aristophanes wrote stage scenes that would have made Sinclair shudder, and Plato, "the divine one," as Barrett Browning called him, declared in the fifth book of his *Republic* that the man who condemned women exercising naked was like "unripe fruit" on the tree of life.

And the new paganism, with its creed of self-development, is just as emphatic: we see its first fruits in Anatole France and Verlaine, in *La Garçonne* of Marguerite, in the *Ulysses* of James Joyce, and in this *Life* of mine.

There are other signs of the great awakening that the Sinclairs and Levys know nothing about. In the summer of 1921 in Berlin, I was invited by a society to come to one of their meetings in which men, women and children bathed naked and afterwards sat and talked and even lunched in the open air, clad only in their skins. Of course I went and found two hundred and fifty persons of all ages enjoying themselves naturally. The professor who invited me and his wife beside him and two daughters, one of fifteen and the other of eighteen; we bathed and lunched together, and round us were two hundred others, young and old of both sexes, naked and unashamed. There are, I was assured, over a hundred of these societies in Berlin alone, numbering over one hundred thousand adherents.

As I sat there I became curiously conscious of the fact that the first reformation in religion came from the Germans, and Luther in the sixteenth century was hardly so far in advance of his time as Goethe at the beginning of the nineteenth century. Perhaps these Germans, I said to myself, are again leading the world to a new paganism. One thing is certain. Doctors not only in Germany but all over Europe are preaching sun baths and the immense benefit to be derived from sitting naked for some hours a day in hot sunshine.

Of course, England and America will stick to Puritanism and prudery long after they have abandoned all belief in Christ and his commandment.

My professor and his pretty daughters seemed in no doubt as to the future. One and all declared that the sun bath not only abolished colds and coughs but all sorts of rheumatic aches and pains; the professor declared: "I have never been so well in my life as since I began toasting myself every day in the sun."

But American and English people would naturally ask another question: admitting all the doctors say about the benefit of sun baths, why not take them in private? It does not appear to affect it. The eldest daughter of my professor was engaged to a young chemist, and towards the end of luncheon

---

* An essay on economic interpretation, written in 1925.

he joined us and sat with his betrothed, as Adam might have sat with Eve. Even Germans, well read as they are, do not appear sufficiently to appreciate that in all this they are going back to the old traditions of their race. The chastity of German women surprised the Romans: Tacitus speaks of the German children who ran about the houses naked as when they were born (*nudo et sordido*), and of the girls as well (*eadem juventa*); and a century and a half before Tacitus, Caesar in his Sixth Book describes the primitive custom still more startlingly. "They make no secret of the differences of sex"; he writes, "both sexes bathe together in the rivers, and under their fur wraps and little coverings of skin they are completely naked."*

The mere fact ought to reassure the prudish majority who seem to think that nudity and shamelessness are intimately connected. Of course I shan't convince the Levys; they are beyond reason and beneath humanity; but I may give pause and thought to some who wish to see things as they are. For plainly we are at the parting of the ways. The World War has taught us many things—taught us, as the great American orator put it, to take new mental bearings and so ascertain when and how far we have gone astray.

I am afraid of repeating myself; but I must confess frankly that my use of complete freedom has not helped me in painting women: reticence in sexual matters has become second nature with them; till some woman breaks through the convention there is little to be done; but surely no unprejudiced person will deny that in painting men, freedom of speech is absolutely essential. Let any one try to paint a Maupassant in conventional terms and he must soon see that he can make nothing of him but a conventional lay figure with the soul of him unexpressed. And, as Anatole France says, "All great artists and writers are sensualists, and sensual in proportion to their genius."

Is it possible to say something new on this question, something that will strike people who wish to think fairly?

The other day in my reading I came across this verse of Heine:

> Doch die Kastraten klagten
> Als ich meine Stimm' erhob;
> Sie klagten, und sie sagten:
> Ich sänge viel zu grob.**

> (Ever the eunuchs whimpered
> When I sang out with force,
> They whimpered and they simpered:
> My singing was much too coarse),

and his wit inspired me to try once more to explain from a new angle why freedom of speech should be conceded to the literary artist as it is given to

---

* Chapter XIX.
** Poem 79 of the cycle, *Die Heimkehr, 1823–1824.*

the painter or sculptor, whose revelations are surely more exciting than words can be.

There are two essential desires in man: the one is for food, the other for reproduction. While both are imperious, the one is absolutely necessary, the other, to some extent, adventitious. But while the desire for food is necessary and dominant, it has very little to do with the higher nature, with the mind or soul; whereas the sex-urge is connected with everything sweet and noble in the personality. It is in itself the source of all art; it is so intimately one with the love of the beautiful that it cannot be separated from it. It is the origin of all our affections. It redeems marriage, ennobles fatherhood and motherhood, and is in very truth the root of the soul itself and all its aspirations.

Now if religion had set itself to restrain eating and drinking, and to render immoral all descriptions of feasting or of every possible pleasure of the palate, it would have been, it seems to me, within its right. Doctors tell us that men commonly dig their graves with their teeth. The sad results of too much eating and drinking are seen on all sides: women and men at forty or forty-five go about carrying twenty-five or even fifty or seventy pounds of disgusting fat with them that destroys their health and shortens their lives. Moreover, no one gets anything from eating and drinking but the mere sensuous gratification; they are not connected with any of the higher instincts of our nature. Religion could have condemned indulgence here, it seems to me, in the most stringent way, and been more or less justified.

But instead of that, Christianity, mainly because of Paul and the fact that he was impotent, has attacked the sexual desire and has tried to condemn it root and branch. It doesn't preach moderation here as it should, but total abstinence; and condemns every sexual provocation and all sensuous desires as if they were contrary to human nature, instead of being the very flower of the soul.

If Paul had been a dispeptic or even of weak digestion, instead of being impotent, there is small doubt that he would have condemned any immoderation in eating and drinking, instead of sexual indulgence. And what a difference this would have made in all our lives, and how much more rational ordinary Christian teaching would have been.

Self-indulgence in eating and drinking is simply loathsome and disgusting to all higher natures, and yet it is persisted in by the majority of mankind without let or hindrance. What preacher ever dares to hold the fat members of his congregation up to ridicule, or dreams of telling them that they are not only disgusting, but stupidly immoral and bent on suicide? Indulgence in sex pleasure is much less dangerous to the individual. It is indeed only when indulgence is carried to excess that sexual pleasure can be harmful.

And what I want to know is, why shouldn't one speak just as openly and freely of the pleasures and pains of sexual indulgence as of the pleasures and pains of eating and drinking? Religion, it seems to me, or our duty to our neighbor, has little to do with either of these dominant desires of humanity. In each of them, religion should preach moderation and due regard for the welfare of our neighbor, and nothing more. For the temptation to excess in any sexual desire is only a sign of natural vigor and is therefore closely allied to virtue: as the Bible says, "Out of strength comes forth sweetness."*

Our ordinary convention of speech is simply stupid. I am allowed to talk in any company of the pleasure of eating young partridge, or well-kept pheasant, or high grouse, but I am forbidden to talk in the same way of the pleasures of sexual intercourse. One cannot contrast the thrills of the novice with the delights of the experienced without incurring the condemnation of all and sundry. I can study indigestion and talk of its causes and consequences; I can push my investigations to apoplexy and death; but I must not talk of diseases brought on from sexual promiscuity, nor warn against them. For fifty years now the whole of the prohibitions of society and religion, in this respect, have seemed to me perfectly idiotic. I blame every father and mother for letting boys and girls go into life unschooled and unwarned.

And when in the story of *My Life* I began to treat sex matters freely and honestly, I was overwhelmed by the preposterous condemnation of the English-speaking peoples. Still, behind the storm of cowardly calumny and silly slander on the part of the self-styled critics, I have been encouraged by the testimony of hundreds of men and women who have written, thanking me for my outspokenness. They have all told me what I knew, that frank expression made my life story more interesting and more valuable; for without knowledge of the sexual life of man or woman, one can know little or nothing of the character. And so I begin this third volume of my autobiography, comprising the ten years between 1890 and 1900, with these words of Heinrich Heine, the first of all the moderns.

> Ever the eunuchs whimpered
> When I sang out with force,
> They whimpered and they simpered:
> My singing was much too coarse.

This decade of my life was memorable to me for the discovery of a side of life which I had hitherto almost ignored. I had found out early, at fifteen or sixteen, that if you worked as hard as you could, you came to success everywhere very quickly. So few people do their best that the one who does becomes a marked man almost at once; and thus success leads immediately to large influence. If you choose to save, you can become rich in a few years. But till this later period I had no idea of the speculative part of city life, where fortunes are made in a day by an idea. This knowledge in its complete form came to me through association with Terah Hooley**—the

* Judges 14:14.
** Ernest Terah Hooley (1859– ?).

great speculator of that mid-period in London. As Maupassant and Randolph Churchill were the heroes of my second volume, so Terah Hooley, Cecil Rhodes, Oscar Wilde, and a host of writers and artists were the dominant personalities of this period.

It was asserted by the official receiver in Hooley's bankruptcy that he had made over six million pounds in two years in London; that is why I call him one of the most successful speculators of that time. Rhodes's fortune was even larger and better based and led to all sorts of political influence which I wish to trace as fairly as I can, for I liked both these men and had good reason to like them.

In my first volume travel and study had the chief place and, in my second volume, love and politics; but in this third volume I propose to deal with literature and art and describe my own beginnings as a writer and artist; and when passing thus from things of the will to things of the intellect, I feel that I am rising into serener and purer air, and hope, therefore, to make this third volume more interesting than the earlier ones.

I have always wanted to build Romance in the heart of Reality, making the incidents of my life an Earthly Pilgrimage: of my youth a great adventure; of my manhood a lyric of love; of my maturity the successful quest of El Dorado; and finally, of my old age, a prophetic vision.

And here in this book I wish to admit the reader more closely than ever to the subtle intimacies of my spirit. I want him to realize my tremulous-vague hopes of immortal life; the evidences of my mortality, and the effect of sad-eyed doubtings; the fitful joys of life and love, and the growing spirit of things called inanimate. I want him to meet a thousand instincts and confused desires, and gradually come to know me better than he knows anyone else who has given a record of himself in any literature.

As one gets toward life's term, one is apt to dwell more and more on the supreme value of goodness and loving-kindness. It comes to me often, as if the only things of moment in my life were the kindly things I've done, and the consistent advocacy of forgiveness in my works was the prophylactic against decay—as if goodness were in a very real sense the goal of human life.

It is not altogether then by chance that this third volume should be devoted to some of the best and sweetest souls I have met in this strange crusade of life—Thomson, Meredith, and Burton; I must tell, too, what I owe to Heine, whom I love more even than any of these, though I never met him in the flesh, for Heine left this world in the same month I entered it. All through these years from thirty-five to forty-five the spirit of Jesus came to have ever more and greater influence, not only upon my mind, but also on all my actions.

Chapter I

Mental Self-Discipline

What can we call our own in this world, but our energy, strength and will power? If I could count up all I owe to my great predecessors and contemporaries, there would not be much over.

*Goethe to Eckermann, 1825.**

STRICTLY SPEAKING, one should tell only of one's life that which is symbolic and therefore of universal interest; but it is extremely difficult to draw the line with any precision, and now and then the seemingly trivial accidents of life have a certain deeper meaning of their own; for instance, adventures come to the adventurous, riches to the greedy. I am treating the happenings of my existence as freely as Rousseau treated his: taking memory, for the most part, as artist—but the first pages of his *Confessions* startle me with the extraordinary difference of character between us.

He is full of affection and sentiment even in childhood. As a boy, I certainly loved no one. I liked my eldest brother because when I was about thirteen he began to treat me as an equal and showed me kindness. But the first person I really cared for was Professor Smith of Lawrence, Kansas.

How he managed to discover that there was something more than the ordinary in me the very first time we met, I am at a loss to imagine; it may have been a certain fluency of speech, or an uncommon choice of words.

I remember, on my way up from Texas once, the malarial fever having left me, I was hungry and glad to get down from the stage-coach. Dinner had been laid in a little roadside inn for half a dozen people—but I was the only passenger, and I practically ate the half-dozen dinners!

The motherly woman of the place came in and held up her hands in astonishment. I said, "Of course I will pay you for the six dinners."

"Indeed you won't!" she cried. "You have a right to eat all you can; won't you have another pie?"

I could not help accepting, and took another apple pie. When I was

---

* Thursday, May 12, 1825, *Conversations with Goethe.*

pulling out six dollars to pay, "No, no," she exclaimed, "it is a dollar a head —I know'd at once you was a foreigner!"

"Why do you think I'm a foreigner?" I asked.

"You speak such broken United States!" she replied. I gasped, for already I prided myself on my English speech. Professor Smith was the first to praise me for it.

All my boyhood was informed with a consuming passion to win in life, and to enjoy as much as possible. By living for three years beside Professor Smith, there came to me a passionate desire for growth, a view of the possibility, not of perfection, but of trained and lofty intelligence. From that time on, I read and thought and lived with a purpose, to develop every faculty I had to the uttermost.

A gifted woman writes to me that my first love must have modified my character profoundly. It did nothing of the sort. I never felt what is called love, that is, sexual desire and admiration plus affection, until I was nearly thirty, though desire possessed me incessantly from fourteen on.

In some respects Rousseau was very like me and again very unlike. For instance, he tells us that the true meaning of a scene did not come to him at the time, but hours afterwards he recalled each intonation, each look, each gesture, and realized exactly what each person had thought and felt in his heart. This has been true to me all my life, and I attribute its magic to my excellent memory. How one with a bad memory can reproduce a scene, I am at a loss to imagine. But always, thanks to my exact remembrance, friends and enemies and the indifferent reveal themselves to me in their true colors when I recall their words and looks afterwards.

On another occasion, Rousseau tells us how girls appeal to him according to their fine dress and manners; chambermaids, he says, and shop-girls never attracted him at all: he wanted ladies—cared-for hands, exquisitely dressed hair, pretty shoes, ribbons and laces always won him more than beauty. He knew this preference to be ridiculous, but he could not help feeling it. In my case, the exact reverse was true: it was beauty and youth that attracted me and the dress had absolutely nothing to do with it; even the beauty of face did not affect me as much as a beautful figure, and while still a youth, I was as conscious as a Frenchman of the charm of small wrists and ankles and the deeper significance thereof. I must confess here and now that beauty of line and perfection in form were the soul of my desire from youth to age.

Up to forty, my life was one long effort at self-development. Thanks to the competition in English schools, I wanted, as a boy and youth, to be an extraordinary athlete more than anything else and labored to develop my muscles in every possible way. I read everything I could find on athletics, and questioned my elders every chance I got, while developing myself systematically. With my eldest brother, in the Belfast gymnasium, I practiced assiduously. At fifteen I could pull myself up and chin the bar fifty times; and I shall never forget my joy when I found I could draw myself up with one hand. After prolonged practice with clubs and dumb-bells I could hold out fifty pounds at arms' length, and put up a hundred pounds above my head: I could also walk under a bar and then with a short run, jump it.

But again and again I met someone stronger than myself, or more agile, and at eighteen I put the gloves on with a second-rate professional and got a bad beating. He taught me the most important truth in boxing, that one can hit down very much harder than one can hit up; and that height and length of reach give an enormous advantage. From that day on I realized that I was too small to be a great athlete. My eyes, too, were astigmatic and I was short-sighted; in every physical respect I seemed "cribbed and coffined" to mediocrity. Nature had denied me the crown!

Thanks to this continual exercise, even now, though only five feet six in height, I am broad and strong; nearly forty inches round the chest with fourteen-inch biceps and twelve-inch forearms; stripped I look more like a prize fighter than anything else.

As soon as I learned as a boy of twelve wherein beauty really consisted, I saw that I could have no claim to it; my features were irregular, my eyes only ordinary in size and grey-blue in color, and even my father's sailors always called me "lug-sails" because of my over-large ears. The chief thing about my mug, as Rodin said, was that it had a certain life and energy.

Perhaps the one thing that might be praised in my appearance was my dress: my father, as a naval officer, always advised me to dress as well as possible at all cost. "It is of supreme importance in life," he said, "to be always well dressed; nobody cares where you live or what you eat, but everyone notices your dress." I took his advice to heart, and the public school life taught me the rest. The English of the best class are the best dressed men in the world—they have a supreme sense of the value of appearance.

Strangely enough, Pierre Loti* told me that he had been plagued as a boy with the very same athletic ambition. I met him first in the Palace at Monaco; he was a great friend of the Princess Alice,** who often talked of him. One day I was introduced to him there. He was very small and slight and certainly wore stays, if indeed, he didn't rouge as well; so his confession that he had wanted above all things to be big and an athlete astounded me. We went into the garden together; he was tiny and fully forty, yet to my amazement he insisted on throwing a somersault backwards, and he did it quite perfectly, like a clown, and then went on to show me that the muscles

---

* A pseudonym for Julien Viaud (1850–1923), a French writer of romantic novels; at one time he was an officer in the French Navy.

** (1858–1925), née Alice Heine, a grandniece of Heine, the German poet, the first American Princess of Monaco. Alice at seventeen married le Duc de Richelieu; he died five years later. She had ten million dollars when she married Albert, Prince of Monaco (1848–1922), grandfather of Ranier. Albert inherited his title from Charles III in 1889.

of his arms and legs were like bands of steel. He was of astonishing physical vigor.

"I always wished to be very strong," he said, "till I found out, at about seventeen, that I was too small. It was my admiration of size and strength in a man that made me take a big sailor about with me, even in Paris society, at first, and so gave occasion for much cheap sneering."

Disappointed in my ambition to shine physically, I turned with redoubled energy to the things of the mind; my memory I always knew was very good, indeed: I could read a page of a book slowly and then repeat it almost exactly. I had already learned at school the *Paradise Lost* of Milton in the leisure hours of a school week; later, at about twenty-four, I learned half a dozen Shakespeare plays by heart without any trouble; and mainly to show off, in Athens I learned Demosthenes' oration "On the Crown" in the original Greek from beginning to end.

I had no idea then that one should select with the greatest care everything that one learns by heart in youth; for whatever one learns then sticks in the memory and prevents one from recalling with ease words or passages learned later. Memory has its limitations. I hate to think now that I was fool enough to waste my time and pack some memory drawers with Demosthenes' rhetoric instead of Russian vocables.

My father did even worse for me. He used to give me chapters of the Bible to learn by heart and was delighted to make me spout them before visitors. Often, now, trying to think of something more valuable, I recall some page of the Psalms or even of Chronicles that merely annoys me. One blunders in this world for want of knowledge, and often blunders irretrievably.

I soon found too that a good memory was a handicap to the thinker: to know the thoughts of others prevents one from thinking—to think is a special accomplishment, and has to be specially cultivated.

But no one has shown the way, or indicated, even, the first steps. I found out, however, that denying a thesis and trying to elaborate arguments against it was one way of exercising the mind; so at once I began, in Goethe's phrase, to be the spirit that always denied—*der Geist der stets verneint.*

This practice helped me a good deal, and one trick I discovered which was of even more avail. Before reading a chapter in some book that interested me, I'd write down all my thoughts on the subject, then read the chapter and see how much the author had added to my stock of ideas. This soon taught me many things and above all, made the personalities of the great thinkers plain to me. I found, for instance, that Kant and Schopenhauer were fine minds, as good even as my whilom favorite, Bacon.

Let me give one example of this way of reading. We take up Schopenhauer on *The Art of Literature.* If an intelligent, well read man reads it through, the odds are that he finds nothing wonderful in it, nothing with which he does not agree, and that's the end of the business. But there's a better way to read. I take up a sheet of paper and ask myself what I could write on "Authorship." Because I know Schopenhauer is a first-rate man, I take care to put down on the paper all that life and thought have taught me about the author's work. I revise and revise what I have written, all the while letting my thoughts play about this question, just as if Schopenhauer and I were two competitors and this was the theme given to us by the examiners, which was to determine our respective places in the crucial examination. When you have done this once and then read Schopenhauer's essay, you will appreciate his distinction between those who write for money and those who write because they have thought deeply on some subject and have something original to say. You will probably end where he begins, that writing for money is the mortal disease of literature. You may even share the great pessimist's opinion that "Vermin is the rule everywhere," which is a funny comment on our American belief in democracy.

This way of testing yourself by comparing your ideas with those of a master will not only make you think; but will impress upon you any new thought the author gives you in an extraordinary way. One hour's work of this sort each week will make an incredible difference in your thinking powers and in your knowledge in one short year.

For years I did everything I could think of to better my mind; but whereas the proper exercises for the body and its muscles are fairly well known and classified, there are no such handbooks dealing with the intellect, I just jot down, therefore, the practices I have found most helpful, and among them, this of setting forth what you know of a subject, and then comparing it with what a master has written on the same theme, is the most educative.

Very early in my development I found that travel and the learning of a new language did more for me than even books: each new language, I soon realized, was like a new window opening new views of the world, while enlarging one's conception of life.

But it is excessively dangerous for a writer to learn another language really well. Carlyle told me that he had always regretted that he did not know German as well as English, and advised me to make myself a master of it. So when I went to Germany I studied it assiduously, and not only learnt to speak it as well as I spoke English, but studied its development, learnt Gothic and Old High German and Middle High German, as well as modern German. Besides, I really learnt Latin and Greek through German. The consequence was, when I returned to England my friend Verschoyle pointed out to me that my English style was spoilt by German idioms. I used to say afterwards that it took me three years to learn German and six more years to wash my mind free of it. For I was quite six years in England as a journalist, writing a good deal every day, before I got back to my sure boyish feeling of what was the true English idiom, or the best way to express a new thought in English; and all these years I was afraid to read a German book, nor would I speak a word of German if I could help it. For the characteristic of German is abstract thought, while our English speech is fundamentally poetic.

But a little knowledge of languages does one good. It's like travel: it excites the mind and provokes thought by showing you new views and new limitations of men. Even more than travel, I found that meeting and getting to know men of light and reading was exhilarating, and in the truest sense, inspiring. But I soon found that really great men were extraordinarily rare, and even famous names often covered commonplace natures.

The chief delights of life have come to me from books. I remember reading once of the death of a princess of the Visconti in the early Renaissance, 1420 or thereabouts. She left great possessions in lands, vineyards and jewelry: she did not even trouble to enumerate them, but willed them away in blocks. When she came to her books, however, she bequeathed them one by one to her dearest, adding a word of description or affection to each volume, for they had been her "most treasured possessions"; she had four books in all and she had read every one of them hundreds of times.

That is how books ought to be regarded, but now they are so cheap that we have lost the sense of their inestimable value.

There is a subtle compensation in everything, and the cheapening of books, the vulgarization of knowledge, has a great deal to answer for. We have forgotten how to use books, and they revenge themselves on us.

First of all, reading usually prevents thinking. You want to know how light is transmitted from the sun, let us say. Instead of thinking over the matter, you pick up a book on physics to learn that light is transmitted by the ether at the rate of some fourteen million miles a second.* The ordinary man is satisfied with this farrago of futilities. But the man who has taught himself to think pauses and asks: "What is this ether?" He then learns that the ether is but a name invented to conceal our ignorance. We know nothing about the ether; we take it for granted that light cannot be transmitted through a vacuum. Consequently we have to assume some attenuated form of atmosphere gifted with the power of transmitting light and heat. The whole hypothesis is just as imaginary as that of a personal God and not nearly so uplifting and comforting.

The whole theory of light must be reconsidered. Newton's theory has been accepted on insufficient grounds. We all know that Goethe rejected it and spent fourteen years in evolving a theory of his own. Physicists and men of science rejected Goethe's explanation and most men thought of it as the aberration of a man of genius; but a generation later Schopenhauer, who was certainly an intellect of the first order, examined the whole question and declared that Goethe was right and Newton wrong. But even now our textbooks have hardly done more than fill us to contentment with our ignorance on this important subject.

And so it is with almost everything else; we read a dozen novels hastily, carelessly, for the story alone. We might as well drink quarts of a Tisane

* The figure is obviously in error.

sweetened to please the palate. We get nothing out of our traveling in a foreign country but what we bring with us. It is certain that the more we bring to our reading, the more we get from it.

Schopenhauer saw that there is "no quality of style to be gained by reading writers who possess it. We must have the gifts before we can learn how to use them. And without the gifts, reading teaches us nothing but cold, dry mannerisms, and makes us shallow imitators." Another word of his is better still.

"Be careful," he advises, "to limit your time for reading and devote it exclusively to the works of those great men of all times and countries who overtop the rest of humanity. These alone educate and instruct."

There should be "a tragical history of literature," he adds, "which should tell of the martyrdom of almost all those who really enlightened humanity, of almost all the really great masters of every kind of art: it would show us how, with few exceptions, they were tormented to death without recognition, without followers; how they lived in poverty and misery, while fame, honor, and riches were the lot of the unworthy."

Yet, from intimacy with the greatest, one gets a certain strength and a certain courage, like Browning's here:

> Careless and unperplexed
> When I wage battle next
> What weapon to select, what armour to endue.*

You should find thoughts, too, that Schopenhauer has not found, get outside his mind, so to speak. For example, he does not tell you the chief advantage of authorship. Bacon says that writing makes "an exact man",** but neither Bacon nor Schopenhauer seems to see that writing should teach you how to think, and that no other business is so favorable to mental growth as authorship properly understood: teaching is the best way of learning. Even Schopenhauer is sometimes uninspired. It is not enough to have new things to say, as he believes; you should also say them in the best and most original way, and that is something the German in Schopenhauer prevented him from understanding.

I have praised Schopenhauer so freely that I feel compelled to state one or two of the important points in which I differ from him. For instance, he sneers at those who study personalities; he says, "It is as though the audience in a theatre were to admire a fine scene, and then rush upon the stage to look at the scaffolding that supports it." In this he is mistaken: we should study the development of a great man, if for nothing else, in order to see what helped him in his growth. What was it, for instance, about

---

* From *Rabbi Ben Ezra:*
>   Fearless and unperplexed,
>   When I wage battle next,
>   What weapons to select, what armour to indue.
** From *Of Studies.*

mid-way in his life, say from 1600 or so on, that set Shakespeare to the writing of his great tragedies? He tells you the whole story in his sonnets and in his plays of this period, as I have shown in my book on him.*

And this knowledge is of supreme importance for any complete realization of Shakespeare, but Schopenhauer did not understand the creative intellect. Whenever he talks about novels he is not so sure a guide as when he is talking of philosophies. "Good novelists," he says, "take the general outline of a character from some real person of their acquaintance, and then idealize and complete it to suit their purpose." This is not true of the novelists or dramatists: the creative artist goes differently to work, I believe.

It is perfectly clear, for instance, that Cervantes painted himself in *Don Quixote,* idealized, if you like, a little, but rather by omission of faults than by heightening of idealistic touches. Nor do I imagine that Sancho Panza was taken from any real person of Cervantes' acquaintances; it is to me a generalized portrait of ordinary Spanish characteristics.

And if we go to an even greater imagination, to Shakespeare's, we shall find that he wrote in much the same way. His Hamlet is a portrait of himself, with the omission of his worst fault, which was an overpowering sensuality. His Falstaff, as I have shown elsewhere, is indeed a portrait taken from life, probably from Chettle, the fat man, half-poet, half-wit, a friend of his early days in London. I have proved this, I think, by showing that when the Queen ordered him to picture Falstaff over again and show "the fat Knight" in love, he was unable to find a single new characteristic of his hero; he had to copy his previous work almost word for word. If he had invented the new character, he would have been able to add some new traits at will.

But then I may be asked about the multitude of his other characters, and in order to answer it properly, I should have to take them *seriatim.* But the main truth can be put shortly. Nearly all of the fine lovable characters are partial portraits of himself, and his villains, such as Iago, are really his view of life, as it acts on inferior intelligences. "Put money in your purse. . . . Drown cats and blind puppies"—all Iago's chief sayings might have been put in the mouth of Sancho Panza. They are from the heart of the common Englishman, who is very like the common Spaniard. Shakespeare's expressions are more pregnant, for he was a greater master of language than even Cervantes: but the wicked and hateful purpose of Iago was not sufficiently [motivated] and so he does not live for us as effectively as Sancho.

It was my love of Shakespeare and my study of him that gave me most of what I know, for my study of him taught me to read all other great men, taught me how they grow and how their peculiarities often dwarf them. From this passionate study of Shakespeare I came to see how the high lights of noble feeling and high endeavor were continually shadowed by little snobbisms and pitiful shortcomings.

* *The Man Shakespeare* (London, 1909).

A better lesson, still, I learnt from Shakespeare. As I have told in my book on him, the greatest disappointment in his life came when his beloved Mary Fitton married and left London for good in 1608; and when, in the same year, he got the news of his mother's death. He went back to Stratford and there got to know his daughter Judith. The dramas he wrote afterwards show an astounding growth in beauty of character. He not only forgives his lost love, Mary Fitton, but acknowledges with perfect comprehension all she had taught him, and meant to him. The modesty of his daughter, Judith, too, adds a new tinge of Puritan morality to his judgments of life.

It was Shakespeare's sovereign fairness of mind and nobility of soul [that] first taught me that I ought to modify my native selfishness and pugnacity. Through studying him I came to see gradually that the greater natures and wiser minds owe a certain duty to themselves: we must forgive, he taught me, for little people cannot; and so I came to that modification of the prayer of Jesus, which has been condemned as blasphemous. "Give us this day our daily bread," he says, "and forgive us our trespasses, as we forgive them that trespass against us."

"Give and forgive," I said, "is the true gospel"; and from this time on, with many lapses, due for the most part to selfishness or temper, I tried, in my own life, to realize this striving.

This was my "conversion" to a better life, and it occurred about my fortieth year as a result partly of complete success in material strivings; but more, I am fain to believe, as a natural incident of growth. I came to see that if I would be with the great ones in the future, I too must lead a life of generosity and kindness. It was and is my most profound conviction that all progress in this life comes from gifted individuals, and if we desire the bettering of things or think of this earthly pilgrimage as a slow journeying upward to perfection, we must do our little best to help all the abler men of our time to self-realization and achievement.

Like chooses like in this world, and the natural affinity of the noble is a stronger tie than can easily be imagined. Now, for the first time, I began to live the higher life, as I understood it. And soon new lessons from it began to drift in upon me. I found almost immediately that certain persons, whom I felt to be among the best, now began to seek me out and show me affection. Lord Grimthorpe became a close friend, and charming people in every walk of life began to show me kindness.

"He came to His own, and His own received Him not,"* is one of the few sayings in the New Testament which must be construed in a narrow way: in this world, our own, in the large sense of those like us or on our level, always receive us and treat us with loving-kindness beyond our deserts. If "the way of the transgressor is hard," the way of the heavenly pilgrim becomes the primrose path to the divine life.

It must not be understood that I became a saint, or that ideal strivings

* John 1:11.

dominated me; far from it, alas! Now and then I was hatefully selfish and once, at least, to a woman detestable: she is still living and I cannot confess my meanness without exposing her, but my treatment of her still brings a hot flush of shame to my cheeks. Even wounded vanity, though it may explain, cannot excuse my paltry, detestable conduct. I was as self-centered as ever, and as confirmed an epicurean: a Hellene always, as Heine would have said, and not a Jew, and still less a Saxon; for the Saxons love to accept promissory notes of ecstatic happiness in eternity, whereas the Hellenes are intent on making the best of this present life, and enjoying themselves here below as much as possible.

My worst fault, I think, has always been my impatience: it often gave the impression of bad temper, or cynicism, or worse, for it was backed by an excellent tongue that translated most feelings into words of some piquancy. Consequently, this man spoke of me as truculent and the other as callous and the third as domineering, when in reality I wished to be kind, but was unable to suffer fools gladly. This impatience has grown on me with the years, and as soon as I gave up conducting journals, I limited my intercourse to friends who were always men of brains, and so managed to avoid a myriad occasions of giving offense unnecessarily.

This sharp-tongued impatience was allied to a genuine reverence for greatness of mind or character; but again this reverence brought with it an illimitable disdain for the second-rate or merely popular. I was more than amiable to Huxley or Wallace, to Davidson or Dowson, and correspondingly contemptuous of the numerous mediocrities who are the heroes of the popular press. So I got a reputation for extraordinary conceit and abrupt bad manners.

All the early part of this period I was in love and therefore did not run after new experiences in what the French call *le pays du tendre*. I had an excellent home and troops of friends: I had brought living to a science; I rode every morning in the park, ate and drank in moderation, watched my weight, and by hard exercise kept myself in good condition.

About 1895 I began, little by little, to alter my purpose in life, trying, as far as vanity would let me, to live to the best in me; and when I took control of the *Saturday Review* in that year,* I modified the general method of criticism, as I shall tell; I found it better to praise than to condemn.

Even in this world, loving-kindness is a key to most of the great doors. And though it was in England that I learned this good lesson, strange to say, all the while I worked and thought, England grew smaller to me and more provincial, while America seemed to expand with undreamed of possibilities. But now and again some law case or some presidential or public announcement shamed me to the soul by flaunting some outworn brainless prejudice.

Little by little I turned to France as the motherland of my spirit, though

* Actually, he took it over in 1894.

there were Germans, too, and Italians and Spaniards that quickened and inspired me with enthusiasm similar to my own; cosmopolitan, I called myself from this time on, or perhaps it would suit English and American prejudice better if I invented a new French word and called myself *cosmopolisson.*

Chapter II

Heine

IN CONNECTION with Heine I must begin by relating one event that happened before 1890: I was lunching one day about 1889 with the Princess of Monaco at Claridge's when for some reason or other the talk fell upon Heinrich Heine, the Princess being a grand-niece of the famous poet. I had just been reading some things of his for the hundredth time with huge delight, and curiously enough, a morning or two before in a Vienna paper, I had come across the announcement that the poet's sister was still living and in full possession of all her faculties, though she was nearing ninety.

"Instead of editing a London review," I exclaimed, "I would give anything to go to Germany, get to know Heine's sister, and then write the best life possible of the great poet."

"How could she help you?" asked the Princess.

"It is the first manifestations of a great talent," I said, "that discover the secret, and show the heart. His sister would know his first successes and his first disappointments: all his beginnings; she could recall childish memories throwing light on his growth—unimaginable things—indicating how he came so early to maturity. What he tells of his visit to England as a young man is astounding, his condemnation of English pedantry, snobbishness, and cruelty is extraordinary. 'The figure of justice in England,' he said, 'had a naked sword on her knee, but was quite blind!' "

"Why don't you write his life," asked the Princess, "if you admire him so intensely?"

"It would cost me five thousand pounds to abandon my work here and go abroad for a year," I said, "and I haven't the money to spare."

"I'll give it [to] you," she replied.

"In that case, Madame," I said, "I'll go and do the work without a moment's delay, for Heine's sister is certain to be able to throw new light on a myriad [of] doubtful things, and assuredly she will be able to solve for us the inexplicable tragedy of his life: how did he come to suffer for years in his mattress-grave in Paris and die at six and fifty? Was it syphilis? Or merely sexual self-indulgence? We know he was never very strong; but his sister must have heard the truth, and fancy being in a position to tell the true truth about Heine, the greatest German poet after Goethe; the first of the moderns, as I always call him, because he was a rebel at heart and soul-free of that respect for convention that maimed even Goethe."

The next weeks I spent reading Heine, his *Reisebilder,* his latest poetry and all the books I could get on his life and art; but I heard nothing from the Princess Alice. At length I thought of writing to her, but I couldn't do that. "She may have spoken in haste," I said to myself, "and I should be forcing her perhaps to give me five thousand pounds which she could ill spare." I resolved to put the whole incident out of my mind.

Some time later I read in a German paper of the death of Heine's sister: she was ninety-odd. The very next day I was again lunching with the Princess at Claridge's and I told her of the death. "No one now," I said, "will ever be able to tell the true truth [sic] about Heine's long illness and death."

"I thought you were going to do it," said the Princess.

"I told you, Madame, it would cost five thousand pounds and I couldn't afford it."

"But I said that I would give you the money willingly," was her reply; "why didn't you ask me for it?"

"I was afraid it might embarrass you," I said. "However, it is now too late!"

I should have loved to write Heine's life, infinitely rather than the life of Oscar Wilde, because he was a far greater man and had new and true things to say on the vital problems of modern Europe.

What he has written on Italy and France and Germany constitutes the best criticism in literature, and his *Fragments* on England are almost as penetrating. I have here a personal confession to make. I knew that Heine had only been in England for a few weeks as a young man, and so, half-English as I was, I thought I could afford to neglect what he had written about it. When I went to New York in November, 1914, I was asked to lecture at the German Club, and I selected Heine as my theme; but the committee wanted me to speak on England as well, to say what I really thought of it, so I talked on England for some time. At the end of the evening, a man came over to me and said, "You never quoted the *English Fragments* of Heine, and yet you repeated almost word for word things he had said about the English people."

"How extraordinary," I exclaimed, "to tell you the truth, I [have] never read the *English Fragments,* but I will read them at once."

I found that I had almost used Heine's very words; that my point of view on England and English faults was all but the same as his; but, though he saw all the weaknesses of the people with astonishing clearness and put them in a high light, some of the virtues of that strange folk seemed to have escaped him: for the true Englishman has a deep love for what is fair and large and kindly; he allows himself to maltreat Ireland for hundreds of years, but when his sin is brought home to him, he will give the Irish their freedom in a kindly and generous spirit. After the Civil War in America, eight or nine states contracted debts to England, but England has never called them in nor insisted on repayment; surely there is something nobly generous in such a people. Besides, their high poetry and astounding love of physical beauty should have endeared them to Heine. But Heine's view of English limitations and surface faults is astoundingly acute. It taught me that there was a strange likeness of view between us, and of judgment. Time and again I had been struck by some half-truth pungently expressed, only to find on wider reading that he had seen the other half just as clearly. Much of the piquancy of his writing comes from this peculiarity of his. I went on to read him completely; and the more I read, the more I grew to love and admire him.

The Germans always talk of Goethe and Schiller as their greatest, just as the English foolishly talk of Shakespeare and Milton, without realizing that in *Hyperion* Keats has written far better blank verse than anything ever reached by Milton. And in the same way Heine is a greater poet and a greater prose writer, too, than Schiller, who, like Milton, was rather a rhetorician than a master-singer. Both nations accept the Immortal reluctantly, but console themselves with what is related to them and commonplace.

I love Heine perhaps even more than Goethe, though I recognize that he is inferior to Goethe in philosophic range and deep-thoughted wisdom; he was almost as great a lyric poet as Goethe himself, though Goethe's best lyrics are the finest in all literature—and a far better prose writer. Besides, Goethe was in love with the conventional, whereas Heine was a born rebel, the first, indeed, to voice the revolt of the modern man against all the outworn and irrational forbiddings and prohibitions of our ordinary life.

And how lovable Heine was, and how human-charming, and what a friend of man! Can one ever forget the poem he wrote when Karl Heine, heir of old Solomon Heine, his banker-uncle, who had always allowed him five or six thousand francs a year, wrote to him that he heard he was writing his life and so wished to warn him that if he wrote anything derogatory of the Heines, he would immediately cut off his allowance.

Heine had already written three volumes of what would have been the most interesting autobiography in the world, but how could he continue it if it were to cost his beloved wife the little pension of five thousand francs a year, which would ensure his dear one comparative comfort after his death?

For sweet love's sake, Heine burnt his autobiography and wrote this poem on the incident:

> Wer ein Herz hat und im Herzen
> Liebe trägt, ist überwunden
> Schon zur Hälfte und so lieg' ich
> Jetzt geknebelt und gebunden.

Wenn ich sterbe wird die Zunge
Ausgerissen meiner Leiche
Denn sie fürchten redend käm' ich
Wieder aus dem Schattenreiche.

Stumm verfaulen wird der Todte
In der Gruft und nie verraten
Werd' ich die auf mir verübten
Lächerlichen Freveltaten.*

Was there ever a greater poem written as comment on an actual occurrence?

With rare understanding Heine called himself the best of all the humorists; he is that, and something more, wittier even than Shakespeare, while Goethe, to judge by the scene in Auerbach's Keller in *Faust*, had hardly more humor than a pancake. It is Heine's humor that gilds all his books and makes them unforgettable—a possession of mankind forever. Who can ever forget the verses in the poem entitled *Deutschland,* which he calls "A Winter's Tale," in which he has set forth our modern creed better than anybody else:

Ein neues Lied, ein besseres Lied,
O Freunde, will ich euch dichten:
Wir wollen hier auf Erden schon
Das Himmelreich errichten.

Wir wollen auf Erden glücklich sein,
Und wollen nicht mehr darben;
Verschlemmen soll nicht der faule Bauch,
Was fleissige Hände erwarben.

Es wächst hiernieden Brot genug
Für alle Menschenkinder,
Auch Rosen und Myrten, Schönheit und Lust,
Und Zuckererbsen nicht minder.

* This is poem 67 in *Nachlese, Book II,* "Vermischte Gedichte."
"He who has a heart and in that heart
Harbors love is already halfway overcome,
And so now I lie
Bound and gagged.

When I die, my tongue
Will be cut out of the corpse,
For they fear that talking I might come
Back from the shades

Dumbly the dead man will molder
In the grave, and never reveal
Will I the ridiculous crimes
Committed on me.

Ja, Zuckererbsen für jedermann,
Sobald die Schoten platzen!
Den Himmel überlassen wir
Den Engeln und den Spatzen.

Here for the first time is the modern gospel, complete in essentials and unforgettable in humor. It is indeed "a new song and a better song" that Heine sings to us: "the resolve to found the Kingdom of Heaven here in this world." "We want to be happy on this earth," he says, "and no longer suffer want or allow the lazy belly to consume what industrious hands have created." "There's enough bread for all the children of men," he cries, "and roses and myrtles and beauty and passion besides: ay, and sweet peas to boot—yes, sweet peas for all, and with full content we can leave Heaven to the angels and sparrows."

I would rather have written those four verses than all Schiller.

And in his history of religion, Heine has written our modern faith in prose even more perfectly than in his poetry:

The happier and more beautiful generations who are produced through free choice of love and who come to blossom in a religion of joy will smile sorrowfully over us, their poor ancestors who stupidly controlled ourselves instead of enjoying all the pleasures of this beautiful life, and by denying and killing our passions and desires made ourselves into pale ghosts of real men and women. Yes, I say it boldly, our descendants will be more beautiful and far happier than we are.

This, too, is the heart of my belief and of my hope for the future of mankind, and I have preached it even more boldly than Heine or Whitman and have been punished for it even more savagely.

How wise Heine was and far-sighted!

Think of what he wrote to a friend about Alsace-Lorraine thirty years before the war of 1870 and seventy-five years before the Great War:

I am the friend of the French, as I am the friend of all men who are good and reasonable. Rest quiet, I will never give up the Rhine to the French, and that for the very simple reason that the Rhine belongs to me. Yea, it belongs to me, through inalienable right of birth. I am of the free Rhine, the still freer son; my cradle stood on its banks, and I do not see why the Rhine should belong to any other than the children of the soil.

Alsace and Lorraine can I truly not so lightly incorporate with Germany as you are in the habit of doing, since the people in these countries are deeply attached to France, on account of the rights which they won at the great revolution, on account of those equal laws and free institutions which are very agreeable to the citizen spirit, but which yet leave much to be desired by the stomachs of the masses.

Meanwhile Alsace and Lorraine will again be attached to Germany when we accomplish that which the French have already begun; *when we surpass them in action, as we have already done in thought; when we can exalt ourselves to the last consequence of such thought; when we rout out servility from its last corner of refuge—from heaven; when we free the God who dwells upon earth in hu-*

manity from his state of degradation; when we again restore to their dignity the people disinherited of its happiness, and genius and beauty brought to shame . . .
Yea, not alone Alsace and Lorraine, but all France, all Europe, the whole world shall then fall to our share, the whole world shall become German! I often dream of this mission and universal dominion of Germany when I wander among the oak trees. Such is my patriotism!

Yet Heine poured deathless sarcasm on the worst faults of the German, the wooden, pedantical Prussians with their frozen conceit and on their behinds a coat of arms.

Heine saw life more deeply and fairly than any of his contemporaries:

What will be the end of this agitation to which, as ever, Paris gave the first signal? War, a most frightfully destructive war, which, alas! will call into the arena the two most noble nations of civilization—I mean Germany and France. England, the great sea serpent which can always creep back to its monstrous lair in the ocean; and Russia, which has most secure hiding places in monster pine forests, steppes, and ice-fields—these two would not be quite overthrown by the most decisive defeats; but Germany in such case is threatened with a far worse fate, and even France might have to part with its political existence.
Yet that would only be the first act of the great *extravaganza*—the prelude as it were. The second act is the European, the world revolution, the great duel of the destitute with the aristocracy of wealth, and in that there will be neither talk of nationality, nor of religion. *There will then be only one nation, to wit, the world: and only one faith, to wit, prosperity upon earth . . .*

And then the inevitable twinkle of the eye:

I advise our descendants to come into the world with a very thick skin to their backs.

Heine was just as wise and far-seeing about persons. The best portrait extant of Lassalle, the great socialist, is from Heine's pen, written when Lassalle was only a youth of nineteen.

My friend, Herr Lassalle, is a young man of the most distinguished intellectual gifts, of the most accurate erudition, with the widest range of knowledge, with the most decided quickness of perception which I have yet known; he combines an energy of will and an ability in conduct which excites my astonishment, and, if his sympathy for me does not deceive me, I expect from him the most effective assistance.

I can't help noticing here Heine's extraordinary prophecy of Lassalle's future. "You will do great things in Germany," Heine said to him, "though I fear you will probably be shot by someone."
Heine was always generous in encouragement and lavish in praise of contemporary writers—a rare quality with successful writers; and in the "Romantic School" he has especially praised such young writers "for not having divorced life from literature, and for making politics go hand in hand with science, art, and religion," so that they were all at the same time artists, tribunes, and apostles.

Yea, I repeat the word "apostles," for I know no more distinguishing word. A new faith inspires them with a passion of which the writers of a previous period had no idea. This faith is faith in progress, a faith which springs from knowledge. We have measured the earth, weighed the powers of nature, calculated the resources of industry, and discovered that this earth is large enough for everyone to build therein the hut of his happiness.

It is his deeply moral and true view of life which places Heine forever with the highest, but it is his humor which puts the crown, so to speak, on that gracious smiling face: think of a few phrases taken from his school days:

You have no idea how complicated Latin is! The Romans would certainly never have had sufficient spare time for the conquest of the world if they had had first to learn Latin . . . And geography—I learnt so little of it that later I lost my way in the world (Shakespeare's phrase) . . .

I got on better in natural history. Some of the pictures of apes, asses, kangaroos, etc., remained fixed in my memory; and it happened subsequently very often that a good many people appeared to me at first sight like old acquaintances. . . .

And then later flashes.

When Boerne,* the democrat, observed that if a king had shaken him by the hand he would cut it off, Heine replied, "And I, when his majesty the mob takes my hand—shall wash it."

Speaking of Madame de Stael,** Heine wrote:

"O Woman! we must forgive thee much, for thou lovest much—and many."

With one great magnate of the practical world in Paris, the Baron James de Rothschild,† Heine was on terms of considerable intimacy; he was welcomed in the Rothschild family circle soon after his arrival in Paris, by means of a letter of introduction from his rich Frankfort uncle. The Baron's liking for Heine's society must have been founded on the latter's social qualities, for his intelligence extended only to financial matters, and his acquaintance with art and poetry was of the smallest. Rothschild treated him, he said, *famillionairement;* and one story illustrates their relations.

"You know everything, Heine," said Rothschild one day at dinner; "why is this wine called *Lacryma Christi?*"

"It is called *Lacryma Christi,*" said Heine, "because Christ weeps when rich Jews drink it, while so many poor men are dying of hunger and thirst."

Heine was small in stature and even in youth anything but strong, though Gautier says that at thirty-five in Paris he appeared to be perfectly healthy and had color in his cheeks. Of his first days in Paris, Heine wrote in a continuous state of rapture. "One may regard Paris," he said, "as the

---

* Karl Ludwig Boerne (1786–1837). He was born a Jew with the name Loeb Baruch, but converted to Christianity. He became a journalist and satirized German politics in his *Briefe Aus Paris.*

** (1766–1817), a Romantic literary figure, whose love affairs were known to be varied.

† (1792–1868).

capital of the world; a new form of art, a new religion, a new life coming into being here . . . mighty days are dawning and unknown gods reveal themselves; and at the same time there is everywhere laughing and dancing; everywhere the most cheerful tone of banter prevails and the lightest of jesting . . ."

He wrote a friend: "If any one asks how I find myself here, say 'Like a fish in water,' or, rather, say that when a fish in the sea asks another how he is, the reply is, 'Like Heine in Paris.' "

But the years of his joy and pleasure were few: from '48 till his death in '56, he suffered the long martyrdom of creeping paralysis. Whatever his shortcomings and his sins, Heine paid for them all in those dreadful years of his agony in Paris. Here is a description of him two years before the end by a lady:

He lay on a pile of mattresses, his body wasted so that it seemed no bigger than a child's under the sheet which covered him, the eyes closed, and the face altogether like the most painful and wasted *Ecce Homo* ever painted by some old German painter. . . . When I kissed him, his beard felt like swan's down or a baby's hair, so weak had it grown. and his face seemed to have gained a certain beauty from pain and suffering . . . I never saw a man bear such horrible pain and misery in so perfectly unaffected a manner. He complained of his sufferings and was pleased to see tears in my eyes, and then at once set to work to make me laugh heartily, which pleased him just as much. He neither paraded his anguish nor tried to conceal it, or to put on any stoical airs. He was also far less sarcastic, more hearty, more indulgent, and altogether pleasanter than ever.

All Heine's work appeals to me intensely. He never perhaps reached the highest height of art and created ever-living figures such as Falstaff and Don Quixote: he used mainly his lyrical gift; yet his extraordinary endowment as "the best of all the humorists" gives him rank with the greatest, and he has lent more lightness and grace to German prose than any one else.

Let no one think I am intent on putting Heine higher than he was. In my mind he always comes immediately after Goethe, completing him. Our modern belief, I repeat, has come from Heine, at least was first stated by him; in this respect it is characteristic that he was born with the French Revolution.

Heine understood Christianity on its pathetic side, and if all his sayings and poems on the subject were put together, they would form as illuminating a commentary as Renan's* *Life of Jesus*. A great passage comes to mind in which he speaks of socialism as the religion of the modern world, and "it, too, has its Judases and its Calvarys."

I love to remember that Heine held Jesus in the highest reverence. "Eternal fame," he says, "is due to that symbol of a suffering God, of the Holy One with his crown of thorns, the crucified Christ whose blood like a soothing balsam has healed the wounds of humanity."

* (1823–92); the *Vie de Jésus* was published in 1863.

Heine was far more of a pagan than a Christian: he disliked all stupid conventions so heartily that he leaned perhaps too far away from them; he didn't realize that the chiefest reforming force of our time is just the new commandment which Jesus was the first to formulate. But this is really hyper-criticism, for the synthesis of perfect paganism and pure Christianity is not yet even adumbrated, and it is nearly a century since Heine went silent.

Yet he speaks of Stratford-on-Avon as the "northern Bethlehem," which shows, I think, profound understanding of Shakespeare—the understanding of kinship and kingship.

He was indeed, as he said himself, a "brave soldier in the Liberation War of Humanity," but he was much more than that: I regard him as the best leader we moderns could have had; as a rebel he won to perfect sanity and was able to destroy with his happy humor all the bug-bears, superstitions, conventions, and pruderies that maim and deform our life. If I could only translate him adequately I would make my readers love him as I do. Think of the poem he calls *Enfant Perdu* (A Lost Child); the stanzas bring tears to my eyes:

> Verlorner Posten in dem Freiheitskriege,
> Hielt ich seit dreissig Jahren treulich aus.
> Ich kämpfte ohne Hoffnung, dass ich siege,
> Ich wusste, nie komm' ich gesund nach Haus.

> In jenen Nächten hat Langweil' ergriffen
> Mich oft, auch Furcht—(nur Narren fürchten nichts)—
> Sie zu verscheuchen hab' ich dann gepfiffen
> Die frechen Reime eines Spottgedichts.

>   *   *   *

> Ein Posten ist vakant!—Die Wunden klaffen—
> Der eine fällt, die andern rücken nach—
> Doch fall' ich unbesiegt, und meine Waffen
> Sind nicht gebrochen—Nur mein Herze brach.*

* From Poem XX in the cycle *Lazarus:*

> Last outpost in the war of liberation
> I have loyally occupied for thirty years.
> I fought without hope of victory,
> I knew I would never return in health.

> In those nights, boredom assailed me
> Often, as well as fear (only fools are not afraid)—
> To dissipate it, I then whistled
> The insolent verses of a mocking poem.

> One outpost is vacant:—The wounds gape—
> One falls, the others move up—
> But I fall unconquered, and my weapons
> Are not broken—Only my heart did break.

Such was the courage of the man who died "broken hearted!" And this his creed, which has always been mine. Like Heine, who boasts that all his life he had been a Knight of the Holy Spirit of Truth, I, too, have always loved Truth more than her sisters, Beauty and Goodness; her figure is slighter and less voluptuous; her face, too, less flower-like and round; but the eyes are magnificent, and she is of passion all compact; her kiss—a consecration of sincerity. With her is neither doubt nor fear, and the entire confidence her worship inspires is worth more to her lover than any gift her sisters can bring. Her chosen one must be a fighter who scorns odds; his course is always straight, forward and upward, and on the arduous road he will lose all friends and fellows and the sweet companionship of life; his beloved ones even will desert him. All his days will be days of strife, there is no respite for him, no rest and no reward save in the proud consciousness that he will always be in the forefront of the great battle, and is sure sooner or later to pay the penalty of his devotion, and die on the field unknown and unpraised, bleeding from a hundred wounds.

I admire all the greatest: Shakespeare, Goethe, and Cervantes, but I love Heine: it is under his standard we must all fight for many a year to come till peradventure science gives us a new and higher creed.

Chapter III

Marriage and Politics

I OUGHT TO HAVE BEGUN this volume with my marriage, but it's painful to me to write about it and I must omit many things, for my first wife is still living, and the circumstances and motives of the alliance are not creditable to me. I had been in love with my American girl for six or seven years, as I have told in Volume II of *My Life,* and I had been on the point of marrying her a dozen times. But again and again she had excited my jealousy, once, at least almost to frenzy; and now at a crisis in my life, she went on the Continent with her mother without saying anything to me beforehand, and a friend told me he had seen them on the Channel steamer with a young man in close attendance. I was sick with rage and jealous imaginings. The crisis that I speak of came through my losing the editorship of the *Evening News,* as I shall tell in another chapter.

I had got to know my wife, Mrs. Clayton, a widow, some time before at Mackenzie of Seaforth's in Scotland: he was Lady Jeune's brother. My wife had a house in Park Lane next door to George Wyndham's and often asked me to lunch or dinner. She it was who introduced me to the Duke of Cambridge, who lunched with her at least once a week when he was in London, and to the Vyners, who were intimate friends of hers: Mrs. Vyner, in especial, being also a great friend of the Prince of Wales.

Mrs. Clayton had been married to a rich Yorkshireman of good position: she entertained charmingly and knew everyone. I was delighted to accept her invitations and grew to like her very quickly: she was an excellent companion, not well-read, but intelligent and sympathetic, and we soon became close friends.

Finding me down in the mouth one day, she pressed me for the reason and I told her of Laura. She smiled: "No one who cared for you would go off to the Continent in that way: you had better put Laura out of mind." A little while afterwards she wanted to know why I didn't marry some one and turn my back on all the worries.

"Who would marry me?" I asked. "I'm miserable."

At last I asked her to marry me: she consented, and I was content. Archbishop Plunkett* came across to London and married us within a

* Doubtless William Conyngham Plunket (1828–97), who became Archbishop of Dublin in 1884 (Harris and Mrs. Clayton were married in 1887).

fortnight. We went to Paris, to the Hotel Meurice, and I fell asleep, quite satisfied that I had done very well for myself: my political ambitions, at any rate, would soon be realized.

Next morning I had a rude awakening.

Twenty or thirty people had written to me about my marriage, and among them a couple of girls. When I awoke in the morning I saw my wife crying at the table.

"What's the matter?" I asked.

"Matter!" she exclaimed; "you are a brute. These girls are in love with you and I thought you had no one."

"How dare you open my letters?" I cried, jumping up and going to the table.

But she was furious beyond all manners and I learned, then and there, how much more jealous women are than men. For a long time I could not believe it, but she gradually convinced me of it. If I looked at any woman in the street there was certain to be a row. Time and again she got up in a theatre and walked out, rather than see me stare at some pretty girl, as she said. All this annoyed me the more because I was short-sighted, and could not see anyone distinctly at half a dozen yards.

As soon as I came to realize that she really suffered, I began to school myself, and the schooling went on to the point that I remember when we went into Italy, I used to select a corner in the hotel restaurant and always looked at the bare walls: anything for a quiet life was my motto, and as I had married for selfish reasons, I felt I ought to give full play to my wife's egotism and peculiarities.

I had resolved to make a success of marriage. I was standing for Parliament, for a division of Hackney, and I believed that if I lived properly with my wife I would get into Parliament and soon reach office. I was brought to discount these hopes almost immediately. Two things convinced me. As we were passing through Bologna, on our way to Rome and Sicily, for I wanted to see Rome and Naples again and Palermo and Monreale, I pulled up the blind for some reason or other and looked out of the window, and there, passing in front of me, was Laura with her mother. I thought I should choke; pulses woke in my throat and temples: in one moment I realized that I had bartered happiness for comfort and a pleasant life, that I had blundered badly and would have to pay for the blunder, and pay heavily.

The next incident took place in Rome. Thanks to the English ambassador, I got a young Italian of real ability to read Dante with me. He used to come at ten o'clock each day and read until my wife wished to go for our morning walk, about half-past eleven. One day she came in while I was reading with Signor M. We had just got into a dispute about the meaning of a passage in Dante and I had persuaded him that my view was right. He was a little hurt, and seeing it, I put my hand on his shoulder and said, "You know, I am much older than you, my dear fellow, so you must not mind."

He smiled at me and my wife immediately swept out of the room. I knew something was wrong and as soon as possible finished off the lesson and let my young friend go. When I went into my wife's bedroom I found her almost crazy with rage.

"You caress your friends before my eyes," she cried, "you beast," and she beat my chest with her fists.

I hardly realized what she meant at first, but when it dawned on me, I was furious.

"You are crazy," I said. "No one ever before accused me of that vice: I will never give you another chance. Here ends our marriage." And there it ended.

Her jealousy was almost incredible, and it continued in reference to every one, man or woman, whom I might see and show any liking for. An English friend, a man of good position, with a title and well-off, came to us at Palermo and asked me if I would take him to Monreale and show him the wonders of the church. I said, "Of course"; the row with my wife afterwards lasted for more than a week. Her jealousy was a disease and she suffered agonies through it; but it was also almost always ill-founded, and her mistakes supplied a comic element which often diverted me hugely, in spite of the constant annoyance. For instance, an Irish lady lunched with us one day who was both pretty and intelligent; she talked well and was evidently well-read in both French and English literature. This naturally interested me in her. After lunch I took her to her carriage, and in the brougham sat one of the prettiest girls I have ever seen. "My daughter Katie," said the lady, introducing me; "we call her 'Kitten.'" The girl laughed charmingly. They told me they were driving downtown and so I begged them to give me a lift. I went into the house for my hat, made some excuse to my wife about going to the office, and ran out to join them. For days afterwards my wife went on about this, saying I had behaved shamefully, shown my admiration for the lady too plainly: her knowledge of French books was only a pretext to show off, and so forth. A month later by chance she met me walking in the park with the pretty daughter; of course, my wife turned and went with us to the mother's house; but my wife never seemed to suspect that Kate and I understood each other very well, and at the door, when I refused to go in, she was quite penitent.

"I thought you cared for Mrs. . ." she said as we walked back together to our home. "I think she is clever." She had never even noticed that Kate had been tongue-tied, probably out of nervousness; she suspected the clever woman, yet the girl was to the mother, in my opinion, as a divinity to an ordinary mortal.

We went round Sicily, and came back by Taormina, and my wife was charmed with the natural beauty of the place; she thought it the most entrancing scene in the world; but she cared nothing for the remains of the Greek theatre, which interested me intensely.

After six months of this sort of honeymoon we returned to London and as friends lived together in Park Lane. The six months had done this for me: they convinced me that there was something in the English character that I never could be in sympathy with. The snobbishness, not only of the titled but of gentle-folk of good breeding, began to exasperate me. Lunching in the house in Park Lane with the Duke of Cambridge and half a dozen people of good position taught me that I should always be an outsider, alien to them in imagination and in sympathy. When I went to the House of Commons and took my seat under the gallery I had a confirmation of the same feeling. Everyone now was nicer to me than they had been. I was not only the editor of the *Fortnightly Review,* but I had a house in Park Lane and entertained royalty, and was altogether better worth knowing. I resented the whole thing!

It has happened several times in my life that apparent success has shown me inner failure. As long as I had not won, the struggle obsessed me; but as soon as I saw victory in sight and began to count the spoils, I became discontented, conscious that I was not on the right road. And so now, having won a secure position in the best English life, I found I was out of place. Many factors combined to disillusion me.

I have already told how the English mistake themselves: they believe that they are the most frank and honest race in the world, whereas in reality they are the most cunning, adroit, and unscrupulous diplomatists; their chief quality, as I am always saying, for it came to me with a shock of surprise, is a love of physical beauty in pigs and cattle and barn-yard fowl, as in men and women. They know without the teaching of Montaigne that the only beauty of man is height, and I was rather below the average stature. You may smile at this, gentle reader, but the full significance of it may escape you. In my experience, all the men who have succeeded in England have had height to help them: Kitchener and Buller* were preferred before Roberts, who had more brains in his head than both of them put together, or multiplied by each other. Sir Richard Burton with his six feet was at once accepted as a personality, while little Stanley was treated with scant respect; Parnell, Randolph Churchill, Dilke, Chamberlain, and Hicks Beach were all far above middle height. Tennyson with his noble presence was accepted everywhere, while the far greater poet and man, James Thomson, being small, was altogether ignored. If Swinburne had been tall and strong he would have been Poet Laureate, but his magnificent forehead was spoiled to the English by his low stature. Oscar Wilde owed at least as much of his renown to his great height as to his wit.

I saw that the road to parliamentary success would be hard for me. Englishmen distrust good talkers and have an absolute abhorrence of new ideas. When Cecil Rhodes (another tall man) was praised in *The Times* for his high ideals, my comment was: "True, he had ideals, but his ideals

---

* Sir Redvers Henry Buller (1839–1908). He commanded the British troops in South Africa in 1899. When he failed to relieve the troops at Ladysmith, Lord Roberts replaced him.

were all 'deals' with an 'I' before them." Again, my socialistic leanings were anathema in England: I saw that they had degraded the best men of the common people, but they hated to have a doubt cast on their complacent optimism. True, I had certain advantages: I had had an English education and knew how to dress, my table manners, too, were English of the best; but I was small and self-assured, and worst of all, obsessed by new ideas which ran counter to the interests of the English governing class. Sooner or later on my way to power I should be denounced and betrayed or boycotted. Strange to say, my sense of isolation grew with my success. It became more and more clear to me that I was not on the right road.

This conviction grew with the months. One incident occurs to me. I was doing all I could to make my election in Hackney sure. I was spending three or four thousand a year in the constituency, keeping up the club and speaking every week. The poverty in the district, or rather the destitution of the poor, appalled me; I was resolved to do what I could to better the dreadful conditions of their existence.

When the Parnell scandal came up and Gladstone took sides with his accusers as if he had known nothing before of Parnell's intrigue with Mrs. O'Shea, I went down to Hackney and told the whole truth as I knew it. I said that Gladstone had known of the intrigue with Mrs. O'Shea for years and had smiled over it, and now to pretend to be outraged was a shameful concession to nonconformist prejudice. I made fun of the whole thing and declared that Kitty O'Shea's petticoats could hardly be turned into the oriflamme of English liberty. I was enthusiastically applauded, everyone left in the best of humor, and next day eighty out of the hundred of my committee resigned. They sent me a letter, telling me that making fun of adultery had offended every one of them. There was a notice, too, in several of the daily papers of their resignations, and I saw at once that the matter was serious: my seat was imperiled and one or two of my friends told me I would have to take back what I had said.

Accordingly, I gave a dinner to my committee, sending special letters to the eighty, asking them to be present, and at the end of the dinner I admitted that I had treated the matter too lightly and was sorry; and my eighty critics retracted their resignations and all was pleasant as before. But I had had my lesson. I now knew that if I went into the House of Commons I should have to walk gingerly. I became conscious of the fact that I was walled in on all sides by English middle-class prejudice and mired in shallow Puritanism.

And the roof of snobbishness over me scarcely gave me air to breathe. I began to wonder what was the best way out. I felt as if I were in a prison and must escape. Moreover, Randolph Churchill, who was my chief backer, had already come to grief and would not be able to help me as he had promised. My first wife was a great friend of Lord Abergavenny,* who was known as the "wire-puller" of the Tory party. He had us down to Eridge

* William Nevill (1826–1915).

Castle, his country seat in Kent, and got me to address a Conservative meeting on imperial federation.

I had been one of the first founders of the Imperial Federation League. From away back, I wanted to bring about a confederation of the English colonies, and I saw plainly that the holding by England of India and Egypt worked against this ideal; but when I spoke to influential people about giving up India and Egypt and founding an Imperial Senate to take the place of the House of Lords, and giving political power to the colonies through colonial senators, I found that ninety-nine people out of a hundred thought I was crazy. "Why should we give up Egypt and India," they said, "the twin stars in the English crown?"

"Machiavelli pointed out," I used to say in reply, "that every possession owned by the Romans, but not colonized by Romans, was found to be a weakness in time of war. If you are put to any severe war test, you may find that having to defend India and Egypt will lessen your chances of success. Your heritage in colonies of your own race is surely large enough; why not content yourselves with that? You already possess more than half of the temperate zone."

Lord Abergavenny said to me frankly, "Leave out that talk of Egypt and India and I'll see that you are asked to speak at all the great meetings, and I'll get you a life seat in Parliament to boot."

I felt that it was no use my getting into the House of Commons. I should be like one crying in the wilderness. Besides, I had become conscious of a want of sympathy with all political aims in England: I was half a socialist and absolutely convinced that the awful social inequality in England was altogether wrong, and had already brought about the deterioration of the race. As I have explained in my second volume, I wanted not only the land of England to be nationalized, but also the main joint-stock industries of general utility or public service, such as the railways, gas and water companies, etc., to belong to the public; and I wished the wages given to these millions of State employees to be at least twice as large as the starvation rates of wage usually established. A great lower middle class should be established in England and no one who would work should be unemployed. But these views, held, I believe, by all the best heads, such as Carlyle and Bismarck, found no support in the House of Commons, or, indeed, in any of the governing classes in England. Socialism to them, like atheism, was a word of ill omen. The unrestrained individualism which they praised as liberty seemed to them the only sane doctrine. And the more I lived with the governing caste, and the better I came to know them, the more hopeless I felt. Their aims were not my aims, and my hopes did not appeal to them.

It was gradually borne in upon me that I should have no real career in the House of Commons, that I must be a writer and teacher, and not a framer of policies. But I doubted my own talent. Could I really be a writer? I meant a great one. I would never have given sixpence to have been with the herd, and I thought it utterly impossible for me ever to be with my heroes, Shakespeare, Goethe, and Cervantes. "Sit down and invent a new character like Mephisto or Don Quixote or Falstaff," I said to myself, "and then I would recommend you to take off your coat and write, but if you cannot invent such a character, what is the good of trying to write?" For some years I put off the decision through an acutely painful sense of my own deficiencies.

Modesty is not likely to be ascribed to me. Every idiot who has ever met me talks of my extraordinary conceit. Now, all men are egotists, and all women, too, and I have yet to meet the man or woman who has not an excellent opinion of himself or herself, as the case may be. Nor have I any quarrel with any other man's egotism. I expect it and reckon with it just as certainly as I reckon on the fact that his body casts a shadow. Nay, more, I must even confess that I find egotists peculiarly interesting when they talk about themselves; and this leads me to the truth, that nothing is so interesting as egotism when a man has an ego.

Your ordinary egotist is a bore because he will never talk about himself: he cannot; he has a self to talk about, but he does not know it; he is under the impression that everything that has happened to him in life is interesting and peculiar; whereas the truth is, nearly everything that has happened to him has happened to everybody else and to tell it bores everybody because everyone would prefer to hear himself telling the same thing.

But your egotist who possesses an ego, who is conscious of the divine spark in his nature, tells things that are true of himself and of no one else, unexpected, wonderful things; and thus he becomes enormously interesting, more interesting than Perry and his North Pole, because his vision discovers hitherto unknown vistas, and his outlook makes clear to us heights and depths in ourselves which we had never before realized. His unique and powerful personality is in direct and intimate relation with the center of gravity of the universe, and thus prefigures the future, and when he speaks of himself he is telling of spiritual experiences that will only become commonplace ten thousand years hence.

Perhaps since my revelation of Shakespeare was completed I may have taken myself too seriously, but for years and years of manhood I was too modest. One instance may prove this. I bought a great many of Rodin's sculptures when he wanted money terribly. When he came to England and found that I was known as a writer, he began asking me to let him do my bust. "No, no," I said, "you mustn't waste your time on me. I've done nothing yet that would allow me to use your genius," and when he pressed me, I replied, "I had nothing to do with the making of my mug, so I am not proud of it." At about the same time Bernard Shaw gave him a very large sum to model his head. Shaw was wise in his generation.

Life in London, too, as seen from Park Lane, was infinitely pleasant. One met intelligent, well-bred people, who were more or less interesting, every day, and if I wanted more intelligence than could be found among my wife's friends, I could easily invite Oscar Wilde or Matthew Arnold or Browning, or Davidson or Dowson or Lionel Johnson,* or Dilke or John Burns, and so have the intellectual stimulus I needed. The climate of England, however, was dreadful to me. From November on, for six months it was unendurable, but one could go to Egypt or Constantinople or India or the French Riviera and meet the same people under the same delightful conditions of life. Why should one bother? Life was velvet-shod and sun-lit.

The determining cause of my break with my wife and Park Lane was something different. Without telling me anything about it, my wife sold my bachelor house in Kensington Gore. She said I should not have another establishment to take women to, and in this she was justified; so she accepted the first offer for my house which came to hand, and I thereby lost all sorts of papers, books, photographs and little personal mementos that were exceedingly precious to me. I lost even the photograph Professor Smith, my hero at Kansas University, had given me wtih the splendid encouragement of his dedication. I raged at losing it so foolishly.

I saw that I must make a decisive break. I mustn't go on living simply because the life was pleasant; I must have a higher purpose in it and devote myself to its realization. Could I become a writer? I had a talent for speaking, I told myself, but not for writing.

* (1867–1902), a minor English poet, who is more remembered for his conversion to Catholicism and his support of the *fin-de-siècle* Irish Renaissance than for his poetry.

Chapter IV

Laura in the Last Phases

I HAD BEEN MARRIED A YEAR or more and had returned to London and taken up my ordinary life when one day I got a letter from Laura, asking if she might call on me in my bachelor house in Kensington Gore. I never was so rejoiced in my whole life. My six months' honeymoon had wearied me and the life in Park Lane was simply tiresome, to a degree. I begged her to come at once, and a day or two later Laura came to me in the room where we had met so often. She was as lovely as ever, but at first withdrawn and strangely quiet.

"I wanted to see if you had forgotten me," she said.

"I could as soon forget my own soul," I answered; and our eyes met—hers were inscrutable but slowly turned into a question.

"Then why did you marry?" she exclaimed.

"Why did you lie and go abroad?" I countered.

"My mother's health," she replied.

"Why didn't you tell me?" I attacked.

"I hoped to be back before it would matter to you," she answered.

"Always your mother between us," I said.

"Nothing is altered, then," she went on, "you care for me as much as ever?"

"More, I am afraid," I replied, and it was indeed less than the truth. She was as beautiful to me as ever—more beautiful; in fact, infinitely attractive. Her very faults were dear to me. The worst of it was I could never quite believe in her affection, I don't know why: I never did, either earlier, or then, or later: that was the tragic background of our intimacy.

She assured me that no young man had gone abroad with them and that she cared for no one but me; and I told her how I had seen her with her mother at the station in Bologna, and how terribly it had affected me, making me realize my awful blunder. She put her arms round me at this, and our lips met, and at once hers grew hot.

"Will you come to our room, dear?" I asked.

She nodded her head: "Our room, indeed!" And we went upstairs together. In a few minutes she had undressed, and I lifted her into the bed, taking her chemise off as she lay: her superb form brought heat into my eyes. She was braver than she had been in the past; she made no resistance now, as she often used to make before, and as I began to kiss her, I couldn't but admire the exquisite beauty of her form and sex. Never surely was any one more perfect. For some time I kissed her before she gave any sign of emotion. Then suddenly she called me, "Frank"; and when I lifted myself to answer, she drew me into her arms. "How could you, how could you? You dear, naughty boy! How could you leave me? When I love you more than all the world," and she broke into a flood of tears.

"Why didn't you say so?" I replied. "If you had, I should have been faithful."

"I never felt you cared," she answered, drying her tears, "I even feared you loved your wife till I saw her the other day, then I laughed and wrote to you; I was sure you couldn't love her as you had loved me. Oh, Frank, what hours we have had!"

"The Gods hate human happiness," I said, "that is why I have lost you. But now let us begin again. Come to me on our three holy days—Tuesday, Thursday, and Saturday; tell me what you want frankly and I shall try to meet all your desires."

"They have been pressing me to marry some one," she said; "father has lost money again, but I have refused. If you could help me, it would make it easier."

"I am glad to do it, so glad! I shall give you more than before. Life is going to change and we shall come together yet."

"I love you," she replied, "and only you. I ought to have made that clear, but when we give ourselves, we women, we are apt to think that the man must know we are his and belong to him absolutely, and we are a little ashamed of it."

"You dear," I answered. "I ought to have guessed it; but let us begin again and bring love to a higher perfection."

I had never felt such passionate admiration for any other woman: the beauty of her figure appealed to me intensely, and the mere touch of her firm flesh thrilled me as no one else had ever done. I cannot explain the magnetism, the intensity of the attraction and the passion she inspired in me. Life would have reached its highest through my connection with her if it hadn't been for one thing.

I don't know why, but I was never sure of Laura's love; and that caused in me a curious reflex action: I never tried to give her the greatest sum of pleasure that I possibly could. I often stopped embracing just when she was most passionate, out of a sort of revenge that sprang from hurt vanity.

This passion of vanity is the most cruel master of mankind—a very God. Who that has read them can ever forget Blake's lines:

> Nought loves another as itself
> Nor venerates another so
> Nor is it given unto thought
> A greater than itself to know.*

* From *Songs of Experience,* "A Little Boy Lost."

Why did I doubt Laura's love? I remember once an article appearing in a London paper, putting me among the first writers of the time and declaring that I was a better talker even than Oscar Wilde. It was by Francis Adams, I think. I paid no attention to it, but Laura brought it to me one day in huge excitement wanting to know: "Had I seen it? Who was the writer? Was it true? Had I written a story called *Montes the Matador*—'one of the great stories of the world,' this critic says?"

Her astonishment was so unfeigned that I realized she didn't know me at all. I recalled the fact that at the beginning of our acquaintance, when I told her I would make money within a year or so, she didn't believe me, but went off and grew to care for some one else because she thought I should always be hard up as I was when we first met.

I remember, too, her astonishment when she saw my first articles on Shakespeare. "But how can you be sure," she said, "that he grew as you have depicted him?"

She had not the remotest conception of my intelligence or what I could do in literature; and love is, above everything, I said to myself, divination. One loves because one feels the utmost power of mind, of character, of soul in the beloved. Always I was sure that Laura did not love me, had never loved me; and I punished her for it by my restraints. Yet now and then she reached greatness.

It was after this first reconciliation, just when she had dressed and was standing before the glass, that she found a great word. We had resolved to meet on the next Tuesday. I had given her the latch key to the front door: she suddenly turned and kissed me. "Ah, you bad boy, you have taught me everything, Frank; but not how to do without you."

What could I do but kiss her while tears burnt my eyes. This was the beginning of love's renewal. From that day on we met three times a week for the next three years till my wife sold my bachelor house without my consent and forced us to meet elsewhere.

Even before this, Laura had told me of a rich man who wanted to marry her: he was an invalid, she said, and only wished to secure her in possession of his fortune before he died. I found out later it was partly true: but a certain coolness between us had come again, chiefly through her jealousy. I had a servant who happened to be very pretty: I had never made up to her: devoted to Laura, I scarcely looked at any one else; but one day I was late and found Laura furious.

"Your maid was rude to me," she declared; "you must get rid of her or I won't come again!"

I bowed my head and assured her that next time she should not be bothered. When she went away, I called the maid, and for the first time noticed that she was well made and pretty.

"Why were you rude?" I asked.

"I wasn't rude first," she answered; "but when she was rude, I answered back; do you mind very much?" she went on, coming towards me, with challenging eyes.

"I don't like rudeness," I answered.

What devil is it in a man to make him desire at all times the Unknown, the new? It has never been explained, and never can be explained rationally. It is the primary urge, the keenest desire of the male; and the individual is not responsible for it in the smallest degree. He was fashioned in the far past of time, a creature of unregulated, impassioned desires.

Desires now surged over me in a hot wave, and I took her into my arms and kissed her. Ten minutes later I had stripped her, reveling in the beauty of a slight girlish figure and extraordinary courage. In a quarter of an hour I realized that she was a seductive mistress, endowed with a passion that matched mine, and little cunning ways and turns of speech that pleased me by their cockney originality: she was really, as the French say, "some one!"

"Oh, oh," she cried the first time. "I won't ask you again for more kisses: my heart's in my mouth and flutters there—no, no more—I'm near hysterics! Kiss and part friends! I hope there's nothing to fear?"

"Nothing," I replied; "you can trust me!"

"Then," she cried cheekily as she began to dress, "Kensington Gore is quite a good place to live in."

I recall another scene later. For days she had been thoughtful and gone about heavy-eyed. Suddenly one morning she was her old gay self again; she came laughing into my bedroom with my tea, and when I asked her what had chased away the clouds, she struck an attitude. "You can't guess?" I shook my head.

"I always say," she went on, smiling cheekily, "all's well that end's unwell!"

I couldn't but laugh.

For some time she attended to all my wants and desires with great cleverness, leaving the older housemaid to take her place whenever Laura visited me.

She entertained me with frank stories of her early life. She had been naughty as a girl, she said, especially with one boy, and had given herself at fourteen to her first master, a married solicitor. She loved love, she confessed, and couldn't live without it; but she took everything lightly, and as soon as my passion was satisfied and I knew all her past, I lost interest in her: there was nothing extraordinary in her, either in face or figure or mind, and so I quickly grew to indifference.

At first I found myself putting Laura off more than once to enjoy Sadi— I could not call her "Sarah," though that was her name. But when she saw that I preferred Laura and was really devoted to her, Sadi suddenly left me with a letter, saying that she knew I preferred my "American, though she doesn't love you and will cheat you yet."

Strange creatures, women, to whom love lends a certain intuition!

Early in this year Laura spoke of the Passion Play as given by the peasants at Oberammergau in the Bavarian Alps. I had seen it in 1880 and had greatly admired the way Flunger played the Christ and Lechner the Judas. It would be a great holiday, I thought, so I proposed to take her and her mother for the opening performance in May.

Early in the month we all three went to Munich and stayed at my old hotel, the Vier Jahreszeiten. I was still remembered there and accordingly we were well received, and a couple of days later in the bright sunshine we took the train for Oberau. On the way I told them something about the Passion Play which we were going to see.

It has been played every ten years since 1634 with only two interruptions; an extra presentation in 1815 to celebrate the Great Peace, and another in 1871 to conclude the series interrupted by the Franco-German war. The history of it is almost an epitome of the changes in religious thought of these last centuries.

In the early drama, Lucifer had been one of the leading characters; and in 1740 a monk named Rosner introduced comic incidents and gave Satan many attendant imps and demons, who strutted and gambolled about the stage, making the groundlings grin, until 1800. In consequence of these extravagances, the performance was almost forbidden in 1810; but the play was remodelled and limited to the simple Biblical narrative. In 1840 Pastor Daisenberger revised the text of the play and gave it much of its present reverence and charm.

The railway in 1890 ran as far as the Oberau station, within a short drive of the village: and the drive to the Ettal Monastery was by a new and infinitely more beautiful road than the one I remembered. Oberammergau itself had come to be a most flourishing village. At the dissolution of the Ettal Monastery the land was divided among the neighboring villagers and had made them extremely prosperous: every house showed comfort and well being.

As we drove into Oberammergau I told Laura an amusing experience. In 1880, going early to the first performance of the Passion Play, I suddenly noticed a curiously caparisoned figure standing in the wings, as if about to come on.

"Who is that?" I asked the village magnate who accompanied me.

"That," he said; "oh! that's Adam waiting to be created."

Laura laughed merrily.

The scenery was really splendid; high above us towered the Kopelberg, surmounted by a glittering cross. I had ordered tickets in advance and the proprietor of the Vier Jahreszeiten had secured for us the best accommodation in the inn. But alas, the village innkeeper, reading of a visit by mother, daughter, and one man, gave us one large bedroom with three beds: and when Laura's mother declared that she wouldn't have me in the room, the maid said it was quite easy to put up a *Scheidewand,* and brought in a little screen not three feet high, which shocked the American Puritanism of

Laura's mother so that I thought she would have a fit. I went away and quickly got a couple of rooms at the forester's house.

Everyone knows that the performances at Oberammergau are given in an open-air theatre: that is, the stage and the lower part of the stalls next [to] the stage are in the open air: fortunately there is a cover for the more highly placed spectators, chiefly Americans and English, which protects them both from the sun and rain. The stage is more than quaint: on the left a wide space; on the right a small stage, before which hangs a curtain; further to the right the horse of Annas, the High Priest; on the left, the house of Pilate—the whole outlook framed, so to speak, by green hills and blue sky.

The booming of a cannon tells us that the play is about to begin. You see half of the Old Testament pictures before any of the New; the slaying of Abel, the sacrifice of Isaac, the affliction of Job.

The music, however, was really good and redeemed the trivialities of the first scenes. The orchestra, of course, was in front of the stage. The music, I learned, was written by one Dedler at the beginning of the century, and excellent music it is. It must be admitted that when the curtain drops after each scene, the effect grows in intensity through the harmony of colors and the fine grouping of the figures. All the costumes are taken from old pictures, and the arrangements this year were in the hands of the stage manager of the Munich Court Theatre and Opera-House; and so were all super-excellent, from the children bearing palm branches to the crowd assembled at the entry of Christ into Jerusalem to the singing of hosannas.

I was dreadfully disappointed in the impersonator of Christ, Joseph Maier, but then I had the memory of Flunger, who was a real genius just as the new Judas, one Zwinc, was nothing like as good as Lechner had been ten years before. Maier hadn't the face of Christ; his expression was that of the fighter rather than of the saint; yet, in spite of his bad acting, the agony in Gethsemane set every one in the great audience weeping; and the crucifixion scene must always remain among the imperishable memories of those who saw blood streaming from his hands and feet; then a soldier pierces his side, the last words are uttered, and the great life seems to be finished. After some discussion Joseph of Arimathea begs the body and the disciples, with Mary Magdalene and Mary, the mother of Jesus, bear it away to burial. Then comes the Resurrection and the Ascension, which made no deep impression on me.

The one player who really rose to the height of the drama was a new-comer, one Rosa Lang, who played Mary, the mother of Jesus. She showed superbly the mother's joy and pride in her son, her sorrow at parting, her sympathy with him in affliction, her agony at the foot of the cross.

The idea seemed to occur to no one that this is not at all the way that the mother of Jesus is pictured in the Bible. But of course the usual mother business had to be played at Oberammergau; and thanks to a good actress, the performance was wonderfully effective. Long before the close, Laura and her mother, as well as the five thousand spectators, were sobbing as if their hearts would break.

Strange to say, however, none of us wanted to go back and see the play again the next day. We all preferred to keep the memory of it alive and for some time we went for long drives through the Bavarian highlands. After three or four days, however, Laura's mother thought she would like to see it again, and with much difficulty I got one seat for her; and of course no more could be gotten for love or money, so Laura came and spent the afternoon with me in my room—four hours never to be forgotten.

Who can tell of love-encounters with the same person and intensify interest by bringing something new into each recital? It was love, I suppose, real affection, that made many of our meetings memorable. Here in this bedroom I was surprised by the intensity of her passion; her emotions always seemed to determine her sensations. "You have given me so much," she said, "made the long journey so delightful, and now the unforgettable memory of how the Jesus story was made living and vivid—a part of my being forever. I want to thank you and reward you if I can!"

"Oh, you can," I cried; "let yourself go once with all your heart and I shall be rewarded."

And she did as I asked: for the first time she threw reserve to the winds and met every movement of mine with appropriate response, and finally loved me in turn and showed herself as clever as any French woman in rousing passion to intensity.

And as I began later to kiss her again and excite her, she cried, "I am drained of feeling there, dear; but kiss my breasts, for they burn and throb, and my lips, for I love you."

As we went out two hours later we met the forester's daughter with a girl friend who took Laura in with sidelong appraising glance.

Whenever I think of Laura and the great days we spent together, the superb verses of Baudelaire come back to me:

> The night grew deep between us like a pall,
> And in the dark I guessed your shining eyes,
> And drank your breath, O Sweet, O Honey-gall!
> Your little feet slept on me sister-wise,
> The night grew deep between us like a pall.
>
> I can call back the days desirable,
> And live all bliss again between your knees,
> For where else can I find that magic spell
> Save in your heart and in your Mysteries,
> I can call back the days desirable.*

* Fourth and fifth stanzas of "Le Balcon," from *Les Fleurs du Mal.*

Chapter V

Bismarck and Burton

THE PERIOD THAT BEGAN in 1890 was memorable for many reasons: Sir Richard Burton, one of the greatest of Englishmen, whom I have elsewhere compared with Sir Walter Raleigh, died in October at Trieste, and left life poorer to some of us. Stanley, another explorer, was married to Miss Dorothy Tennant, and almost immediately hideous stories of cruelties perpetrated on the African natives during his last expedition shocked the conscience of England. When they said that Miss Tennant, who was a very charming girl, was going to marry the lion of the season, I said it seemed to me true: "She was about to marry the king of beasts," for Stanley was to me always a force without a conscience. Browning died in December, 1889, and Tennyson a couple of years later. Parnell, too, came to the crisis of his fate about this time, and in France, Renan's death left a sad gap.

But the event that marked the time and gave supreme significance to it was the dismissal of Bismarck. His fall in 1890 shook the world. For nearly thirty years, from 1862 on, Bismarck had dominated Europe. Few remember his beginnings, though he himself has told how

When I first came into office, the king showed me his written abdication. I had first of all to re-establish the royal power, for it was shaken and shattered. I was successful. Yet I am not an absolutist. There is always danger in one-man government. Parliamentary opinion and a free press are necessary to a satisfactory monarchial system. . . .

Universal suffrage was the spirit of the Frankfort Parliament. I adopted it in the Constitution of the North German Confederation and afterwards of the Empire, because it was necessary to counteract the Austrian influence, and it was my aim, therefore, to satisfy all classes.

Bismarck's judgments of his imperial masters are curiously characteristic: while in their service, he spoke well of them. On his tomb Bismarck directed that there should appear these words:

Here rests
Prince Bismarck

Born 1st April, 1815
Died   ——

A faithful German Servant of
Emperor William the First

He wrote: "The old Emperor William* was not a great statesman but a man of sound judgment and a perfect gentleman. He was true to those who worked with him. I was deeply attached to him. The Emperor Frederick, too, was a noble man—a sharp sword, so to speak, with a short blade." But after Bismarck died in 1898 and his *Memoirs* by Busch were published, we got the other side. As he said himself: "I lack altogether the bump of veneration for my fellow men." And so we find what Bismarck really thought of Emperor William the First: "When anything important was going on, he usually began by taking the wrong road, but in the end he always allowed himself to be put straight again. . . . His knowledge of affairs was limited and he was slow in comprehending anything new."

Bismarck found it hard to conceal his contempt for the Crown Prince Frederick.** It even comes out in spiteful little outbursts such as this: "The Crown Prince, like all mediocrities, likes copying, and other occupations of the same sort, such as sealing letters, etc."

And finally Bismarck's opinion of the Kaiser† who dismissed him was written in vitriol even before the final break:

I cannot stand him (Wilhelm the Second) much longer. He wants even to know whom I see, and has spies set to watch those who come in and go out of my office. . . . It comes of an overestimate of himself, and of his inexperience of affairs, that can lead to no good. He is much too conceited: he is simply longing with his whole heart to be rid of me in order that he may govern alone (with his own genius), and be able to cover himself with glory. He does not want the old mentor any longer, but only docile tools. But I cannot make genuflections nor crouch under the table like a dog. He wants to break with Russia, and yet he has not the courage to demand the increase of the army from the Liberals in the Reichstag.

It is interesting to read that in a letter to the Chancellor, the Crown Prince Frederick at Portofino described his eldest son as "inexperienced, extremely boastful and self-conceited."

Bismarck's opinions of his masters are to my mind not only self-revealing but true, and his contemptuous condemnation of Wilhelm the Second has been justified by the result.

Like most of the leading men of the nineteenth century, like Tennyson and Hugo, Gladstone, Salisbury and Parnell, Bismarck was a convinced

---

* (1797–1888).
** (1831–88), only son of William I.
† (1859–1942).

believer, not only in God and divine providence, but also in a life after death; he even believed in apparitions, ghosts, and supernatural signs.

In 1866, just before the war between Prussia and Austria, Bismarck, according to Busch, had been exceedingly cast down: when he was shot at five times and wasn't even grazed, he took it as a sign of divine approbation and was immediately lifted into the happiest humor.

One must think of what Bismarck accomplished even though handicapped by brainless masters! In 1866 he beat Austria and made Prussia the first military power in Europe. He welded many German states into one on the anvil of war, and after 1870 he developed the industries of his people in the most unexpected and successful ways. I have already related how he had profited by the socialist teachings of Lassalle, how in fifty ways he had fostered industry so that every one felt an added incentive to labor and a sure understanding that an extra effort would lead on to fortune. Considering that he was born and bred an outrageous individualist in an aristocratic tradition and yet created a new record as a social reformer, one can only wonder at the profound morality which led him always towards justice. He knew instinctively, as Lincoln knew, that "labor is the superior of capital and deserves much the higher consideration."

His fall was treated excellently in the English press. *Punch* had a famous cartoon on it entitled, "Dropping the Pilot."

But Bismarck was not so great a man, in my opinion, as Sir Richard Burton: in force of character, in daring and in strength, they were not unlike; but Burton had a wider intelligence, a larger mind, and a richer generosity and kindliness of nature.

To me the difference between the fates of Bismarck and Burton gives rise to many reflections. For thirty years Bismarck had supreme power and made Germany the first state in Europe—I had almost said in the world; but England denied Burton almost everything.* Although he had served the foreign office** with extraordinary ability, they refused him even the usual retiring pension.

In my last visit to him in Trieste, I couldn't help asking him how it came about, why the English authorities were so down on him, and he said smiling, "You will laugh if I tell you. I think I blundered in my first talk with Lord Salisbury. He called me 'Burton'; his familiarity encouraged me, and I spoke to him as 'Salisbury.' I saw him wince, and he went back immediately to 'Mr. Burton,' but out of cheek or perversity I kept up the 'Salisbury.' He was so ignorant; he didn't know where Mombassa was; and the idea that I had brought back treaties handing over the whole of Central Africa to Britain merely filled him with dismay. He kept repeating, 'dreadful responsibility—dreadful'; he was in reality, I believe, a very nice old lady." I could not help laughing.

Burton's judgment of Lord Salisbury was justified to me later in a pe-

* But he was knighted in 1886.
** As a consul in South American and European capitals, including Trieste.

culiar way. One evening Teresa, Lady Shrewsbury, after meeting me somewhere at dinner, offered to take me home in her brougham. I thanked her warmly, for she was always interesting, knew everybody, and had a real salon in London.

Arthur Balfour* had been one of the chief personages at the dinner. I asked her what she thought of him. "I know him very slightly," she replied, "but think him very distinguished-looking."

"I'm afraid," I said, "that his outward is the best part of him."

"Strange," she said, "that reminds me that once, driving like this a few years ago with Lady Salisbury, I asked her what she thought of her husband's good-looking nephew. 'Oh, my dear,' she replied, 'he's nothing for us women: I don't believe he has any more temperament than my poor old Bob!'"

So Lord Salisbury was judged by his wife very much as Sir Richard Burton had judged him.

When Burton showed me his translation of *The Arabian Nights* and I saw that he had described every sort of sensuality with the crudest words, I got frightened for him; still, I told him that I would help him so far as I could and put myself at his disposal. I would have liked him to modify some of the bestialities; however, as I have said elsewhere, it wasn't my business to condemn a great man but to help him; and I am proud of the fact that partly through my help he made ten thousand pounds out of the venture. No one could be with Burton for an hour without feeling his extraordinary force of character and the imperial keenness of his intelligence. If England had treated him as she should, he would have given her a glorious empire, the whole central plateau of Africa from the Cape to Cairo, without a war, and no one would be astonished now that I should compare him with Bismarck; but England couldn't use her greatest man of action!

I have never told how we came to know each other intimately. Captain Lovett Cameron,** his lieutenant on several of his African journeys, had introduced me to him; but I was awkward and self-conscious and made some conventional foolish remark that caused Burton to turn from me contemptuously. I confessed my fault to Cameron afterwards, who insisted that the *faux pas* could easily be repaired. "You've no idea how generous-kind Dick is; as soon as he gets to know you, he'll cotton to you," and he fixed a meeting for the morrow in Pall Mall at one of the clubs.

I thought over the meeting and arranged what I'd say. It had suddenly come into my head that Burton knew Lord Lytton† and that they were

* (1848–1930), prime minister, 1902–05, and author of the Balfour Declaration in 1917, which promised the Zionists a home in Palestine.
** (1844–1894). He was sent by the Royal Geographic Society in 1873 to find Livingstone, when Livingstone was already dead. Cameron explored Lake Tanganyika and was the first European to cross Equatorial Africa. He went with Burton to the Gold Coast in 1882, and the two collaborated on a book, *To the Gold Coast for Gold,* in 1883.
† Edward Robert Bulwer Lytton (1831–91), first Earl of Lytton, viceroy of India.

friends. As soon as the three of us met next day, I shot off my bolt. "The other morning," I began, "I walked down Pall Mall just behind two men curiously differentiated in clothes and in person; the one was a little dandy, high heels, yellow kid gloves, tall hat, rouged cheeks—he evidently wore corsets too; the other, a very tall man, swung along with a sombrero on his head and a heavy stick in his hand. I was near enough to hear them talk. The dandy was intent on persuading his companion. "Ah, Dick," he began, "delicacies escape you men of huge appetite; you miss the deathless charm of the androgyne: the figure of the girl of thirteen with sex unexpressed as yet, slim as a boy with breasts scarcely outlined, and narrow hips; but unlike a boy, Dick; no lines or ugly muscles, the knees also are small; everything rounded to rhythmic loveliness—the most seductive creature in all God's world."

"You make me tired, Lytton," cried the big man in a deep tone, "you cotquean, you! Your over-sweet description only shows me that you have never tried the blue-bottomed monkey!"

"First-rate," cried Burton laughing to me, "you have hit off Lytton to the soul, which probably means that my portrait, too, is life-like."

From that hour on the ice was broken between us and we became friends, and I soon found Burton, as Cameron had said, determined unconditionally to forgive all injuries, one of the noblest spirits I have met in this earthly pilgrimage!

It was Burton who discovered the source of the Nile, for on that memorable journey of '58 Speke was merely his lieutenant;* and when they reached Ujiji, on the eastern side of Lake Tanganyika, Burton was the first to proclaim the obvious fact; yet when Speke returned to England and claimed the honor of the discovery, Burton said nothing about the matter; there was in him at all times a real generosity.

Who can forget the verse in which he embodied his stalwart creed?

> Do what thy manhood bids thee do,
> From none but self expect applause:
> He noblest lives and noblest dies
> Who makes and keeps his self-made laws.**

When Burton died, Swinburne wrote for me a long elegy on him in the *Saturday Review,* which ends with this couplet that appealed to me intensely:

* Alan Moorehead in *The White Nile* has done much to clear the air on this matter. Speke discovered on this trip Lake Victoria Nyanza on his own and believed it to be the source of the Nile. He returned to the region in 1860 and traced the Nile out of it, which he reported in his *Journal of the Discovery of the Source of the Nile* (1863). Burton expressed his doubts about Speke's claims, but Speke shot himself hunting the day he was to defend himself before the British Association of Geographers.

** From *The Kasidah of Haji Abdu El-Yazdi,* VIII, 9.

> The royal heart we mourn, the faultless friend
> Burton—a name that lives till fame be dead.*

Like Burton, Bismarck, too, had intimate little messages for me. On the occasion of his seventy-second birthday he said a thing that brought him close to me, for it has been my experience all through my life. "Out of the eight thousand letters of sympathy," he said, "that I have received, a quarter came from women—that pleased me greatly: I regard it as a good sign, for it is my experience that one doesn't reach the female sympathy as easily as the male; besides, women have never liked me: I don't know why; perhaps I couldn't speak nicely enough to them." Yet, if gossip is to be believed, he was more than nice to Pauline Lucca—the great Jewish singer —when she visited Berlin once.

Bismarck made an extraordinary impression on me. I always see him as I saw him first in the Reichstag: he would often sit for hours without speaking or suddenly get up in the middle of a debate and go out, and one felt at once that the Chamber had become common; vitality, distinction, any possibility of the extraordinary had gone out of the atmosphere.

One day, I shall never forget it, though it must be now nearly fifty years ago, he had been baited in the House, and at length, some socialist, I think it was little fiery Bebel,** used the word *wagt* (dare) about his reticence. "The Imperial Chancellor does not tell us whether the edict has come from himself or from the Emperor, *er wagt es nicht zu sagen,*" he added. (He dares not speak out.)

Bismarck started up, his three hairs bristling on his bald head, and stalked out towards his persecutor. "Who says *wagt* to Bismarck?" he jerked out with intense passion. The whole House broke into applause, while the little socialist fairly cowered on his seat as the great man continued. "You can either take it that the project came from His Majesty, the Emperor, and was approved by his Chancellor, or that the project came from the Chancellor and was approved by His Majesty, the Emperor. And whichever you fancy the more probable, you can make it square with what you think is constitutional, exactly as it suits you: *wie Sie wollen.*" The contempt of the corps-student for the little Jew raged in the disdain of voice and manner and words. He strode back to his place and went right on out of the House.

This scene taught me that Bismarck was the most impressive person I had seen up to that time—impressive, of course, chiefly for his courage, but also for his insight. Bit by bit I came to see that he was altogether unscrupulous, determined to make Germany the first country in Europe.

If his voice had been as impressive as his great frame and imperious manner, he would have been simply overwhelming! As it was, it was im-

---

* From *Elegy (1869–91)*. This appeared in the July 1, 1892, issue of the *Fortnightly Review*; Burton had died in 1890.
** August Bebel (1840–1913), an anti-militarist; he helped found the German Social Democratic Party in 1869.

possible to be in his presence and hear him speak without being impressed by his greatness of character.

The only time I met Bismarck to speak to was an event in my life. We had a literary society in Göttingen, his old university. The house he had lived in was shown on the edge of the ramparts; as a corps-student he had fought half a dozen duels, and all successful, thanks chiefly to his great height and length of reach. For some reason or other, the civic authorities in my time passed a law shutting up all drinking places, and all *Kneipen* even (the places where students drank) at one o'clock in the morning. The corps-students objected to this, defied the civic ordinance, and soldiers were ordered out to close the drinking places. At once the corps-students sent a deputation to the Chancellor to beg him to defend their liberties.

Hearing of this, I called on the literary society to do likewise, pointed out that we didn't drink or make night hideous for quiet citizens in the morning hours, and finally three of us were selected to go to Berlin and call upon Bismarck, and see if we could not win him to the cause of freedom. Next day, my friend, von H—, and a man whose name I've completely forgotten, and myself started for Berlin. Von H—, we agreed, was to be the spokesman, and he recited to us an excellent speech.

All went happily at first: I drafted a letter to Prince Bismarck, begging him to hear us for a few minutes as students of his old university. We got a letter from his secretary: the Chancellor would see us at eleven next morning in the Wilhelm Strasse. Needless to say, we were punctual, but when the door opened and Bismarck rose before us at his desk, the courage of my companions oozed away: they both stood bowing like automata with heels together, for all the world as if they had hinges in their backs.

"Begin!" I whispered to von H—, but he bowed again and again, and said nothing. I saw I'd have to speak or be shamed, so I stepped forward and simply said that we had come as members of a literary society; we were not idlers, but students, intent on improving ourselves: we didn't drink or annoy peaceable citizens by howling songs in the small hours, so we hoped he'd order the civic authorities in Göttingen to leave us alone.

"The closing time seems reasonable," Bismarck replied curtly.

"Why shouldn't we talk all night, so long as we don't annoy anyone?" I countered.

"You come into the category of student societies (*Verbindungen*)," he said. "It's difficult to differentiate."

"Good laws shouldn't oppress the well-behaved," I objected. "I'm sure there's a student behind the Chancellor!"

"*Richtig!*" he exclaimed, his face lighting up. "But," the thought came: "the well-behaved don't feel laws as oppressive. You can surely say all you have to say before one o'clock in the morning!"

"Why shouldn't we talk all night if we want to and don't annoy others? As a student Prince Bismarck would not like to have been coerced by soldiers, and we were told that we should be shot down like dogs if we resisted."

"*Richtig!*" he barked again. "The soldiers had their orders—*scharf geladen!*"

"It's mere despotism," I cried, "indefensible and intolerable tyranny; the Gessler hat* sort of thing." He shrugged his shoulders, smiling, and I turned, bowing, and went to the door, for I feared that I had been too bold, while my companions went on bowing like wooden automata. At the door Bismarck called me back: "Are you a German?" he asked.

"An American," I replied.

"So . . ." he interjected, smiling as if at length he understood my boldness. "So! The Declaration of Independence stops at the frontier," and he laughed genially.

When we got outside, my companions congratulated me; but I turned angrily on Von H—: "Had you told me you were going to say nothing, I'd have prepared something: as it was, I was beaten!"

"I would never have believed it," said Von H—, "but I could not have spoken to save my life; the discipline, the pigtail nature—*zopfwesen*—of us Germans since Frederick the Great has got into our blood! But you did splendidly."

"I did very badly," I said.

If I force memory and recount this unimportant little incident, it is just to emphasize the fact that no one I have ever seen in this world had a greater magic of personality than Bismarck—an authentic great man.

No one in Europe at the time realized the disastrous consequences of Bismarck's fall. Every one knew that as far back as '79 he had formed an Austro-German alliance, directed practically against Russia. He was the inspirer too of the French occupation of Tunis in 1881. His object was to create ill feeling between France and Italy, and he succeeded.

In 1882 he won the adhesion of Italy to the alliance and so strengthened Germany against France, as well as against Russia. But even this Triple Alliance did not satisfy him. He knew how to play on imperial rulers. In 1884 he concluded with Russia a secret treaty behind the backs of both his Allies—a treaty by which it was arranged that if Germany or Russia were attacked, the other would come to her ally's assistance.

It was the failure of the Emperor William, and of his Chancellor, the Count von Caprivi,** to renew this secret treaty in 1890 that first weakened Germany's position in Europe.

In 1891 the Russian Government invited a French squadron to Kronstadt —which should surely have warned even the Emperor William of his

---

* When Albert II of Austria was striving to annex the Forest Cantons of Switzerland, one of his officials, a man named Gessler, set the duke's hat on a pole and insisted that the Swiss honor it as they would its owner.

** Graf Georg Leo von Caprivi (1831–1899). He succeeded Bismarck and held office until 1894.

blunder. And in 1893 the Russians sent Admiral Avellane to return the visit to Toulon. Thus the Russian-French alliance was set on foot, if not at once concluded.

Bismarck's diplomacy was more cunning even than that imagined by Machiavelli. French colonial enterprise everywhere, and especially in Africa, was favored by German diplomacy, with the intention of separating France and England. And in this Bismarck's diplomacy continued to be effective after he himself had fallen from power; for the greater part, indeed, of the last decade of the nineteenth century! Fashoda in 1896 almost brought about war between the two countries.

Immediately after the fall of Bismarck, his policy that had made Germany the first of European powers was abandoned. The extraordinary commercial prosperity that had resulted from it continued and blinded the German people to the dangers of the new diplomacy that was, in truth, little more than the erratic impulses of William II. I can never think of William II without recalling the great phrase of Vauvenargues: *Les prospérités des mauvais rois sont fatales aux peuples.*

As soon as I heard of Bismarck's dismissal by the Emperor, I felt sure that William II was a small fish.

"We Germans," said Bismarck later, "fear God and nothing else." He would have been much greater if he had feared God enough to play the game of life quite fairly. He did his best to embroil England with France. His want of moral scruple was his besetting sin.

But, if one can find fault with the inflexible selfish purpose of Bismarck, the policy that succeeded his was devoid of any virtue. William II not only brought France and Russia into a close alliance, but, with inconceivable stupidity, he estranged Italy and exasperated England without winning a single friend, unless, indeed, Turkey could be called a friend.

My private judgment of him, derived chiefly from the Prince of Wales and a casual meeting with the War-lord, as he loved to be called, I will give in due time: but for the moment I can only say that his famous speech, addressed to the Brandenburg Diet in this year, 1892, filled me with unutterable contempt. He talked about God as the "Supreme Lord" and "his unmistakable conviction that He, our former Ally at Rossbach and Dennewitz, will not leave me in the lurch. He has taken such infinite pains with our ancient Brandenburg and our House that we cannot suppose He has done this for no purpose. No; on the contrary, men of Brandenburg, we have a great future before us, and I am leading you towards days of glory."

There was one man in Germany, Maximilian Harden,* who foresaw the ruin of Germany as soon as William II abandoned Bismarck and his successful international policy; perhaps I ought to say a word about him here.

Harden came to Berlin during the Bismarckian era, an ardent admirer of

---

* (1861–1927), a supporter of Bismarck. After Bismarck's fall, his paper, *Die Zukunft*, attacked those advising William II.

Bismarck and the great Chancellor's strictly national theories, a boy of nineteen who had just finished college.

His name then was Max Witkovski—a Jewish boy. A Jew had a hard time of it in Germany in those days. Public recognition seemed impossible. His journalistic career proved to him that a German name would be more advantageous. The English periodicals of the late eighties and early nineties, with their frankness and love of truth, became his ideal of journalism. In vain he tried to persuade publishers to follow the English lead, treating royalty and the aristocracy of birth as boldly as the British.

None could see what good it would do to quarrel openly with those in power. Harden became the pioneer of the new journalism. He started a weekly paper, *Die Zukunft* (The Future). A storm of antagonism arose in all quarters. Harden became the most discussed man in Germany. His paper was read everywhere. He attracted the youth of Germany. The modernists flocked to him; his paper became the mouthpiece of young, rebellious Germany. Never before had such free language been used in a German periodical.

He made enemies galore. Mercilessly he tore down superstitions and showed the inherent weakness of an absolute monarchy. Even his foes read his paper. His circulation became extraordinary for a one-man magazine.

There was rarely a week in which some influential noble or some powerful organization did not start libel suits against the *Zukunft*. Harden hardly ever retracted a statement. He never published an article without proof of its veracity in hand. "Very well," was his eternal answer, "I shall prove and substantiate in court the truth of what I have written." Many of his opponents believed he would not dare to go to court. But he dared. A few sensational libel cases, which he won, left him free to do as he pleased.

He became the most feared publicist in Germany. This is what Harden wrote about William II in 1896:

Germany cannot, in view of the results of the six years since Bismarck's dismissal, refrain from asking their Emperor whether it was indeed necessary to remove, with ruthless hand, the man who raised the Hohenzollern House to a pinnacle, placed the military power of Prussia on a sure basis, founded the German Empire and prepared a future for German influence. . . .

It would be criminal to ignore the dark clouds slowly and threateningly gathering on the German horizon. It would be criminal also to keep silence, seeing that the storm which piled up the clouds blew from the highest point of observation where the greatest serenity of mind ought to prevail.

He dared to publish his famous open letter addressed to William Hohenzollern. The Eulenburg* scandal came as a result. A few suicides among the nobility followed the exposure about the Round Table of the "Most High." Everybody predicted Harden's imprisonment, his trial for *lèse majesté*.

---

* Phillipp Eulenberg (1847–1921), confidential advisor to William II. In 1907 *Die Zukunft* carried a series of exposés of Eulenberg's sexual habits, which ended his public life and injured the prestige of the monarchy.

Nothing happened. He was stronger even than His Imperial Majesty's Court, and everybody knew that he would show little reverence, and still less consideration, for the Kaiser's sacred person. The scandal of the Kaiser's friendship with the notorious Krupp some years later was Harden's complete justification.*

* In 1909 *Vorwärts* ran a series of articles, "Krupp in Capri," which disclosed the sexual side of Krupp's life. Krupp committed suicide. At his funeral, the Kaiser said he repudiated the attacks on Krupp.

Chapter VI

The *Evening News*

IN THE YEARS from 1883 to 1887 I was working sixteen or seventeen hours a day on the *Evening News*. Bit by bit I found out the secret of journalistic success in London, and I may as well tell the story here. First of all, I discovered that the public did not care a row of pins for scholarly or even original leading articles. Arthur Walter praised this part of the *Evening News* very cordially, but I soon found that it had no effect whatever on the circulation. The first thing that gave me the clue to success was the divorce case of Lady Colin Campbell. I had met Lady Colin in Paris and admired, as every one else admired, her tall, superb figure and remarkable brunette beauty. I went to the court chiefly out of curiosity and heard her statement and cross-examination. I then begged the *Evening News* correspondent to give me a verbatim report, for I soon realized that no other paper would treat the case as it deserved. It was full of the most scabrous details. In successive editions that evening, I gave up the whole of the right-hand center page to it, and promised my readers, in the beginning, to give the fullest account possible of the trial. The question was how far I should report the lady's revelations.

I saw Arthur Walter in the evening, and I surprised him by telling him the details of the case; he agreed with me as to what should be published. In *The Times* account next morning, I found that they had drawn the line almost exactly where I had drawn it, though I had told the story at much greater length and made it much more interesting by adding detailed sketches of the chief personages. I pursued the same plan every day of the trial, making a most enthralling human story, as human as I dared in view of English convention.

The circulation of the paper almost doubled in the week, and the whole account attracted so much attention that Edmund Yates* asked me to dinner, and while at dinner invited me to tell him how I had come to such extraordinary success. Everyone, he declared, was reading the *Evening News* for the report of the *cause scandaleuse*. One man, sitting almost opposite me at the table, sniffed again and again at my laughing outspoken-

* (1831–94), owner of the *World*.

ness; it was, I learned afterwards, George Lewis—the famous solicitor.* The next day I received the proof of how envy and malevolence revenge themselves on success. George Lewis indicted the *Evening News* for obscene libel, and almost immediately the case came up before Mr. Justice Denman.** George Lewis read out some of the reports which I had printed and asked that I should be punished. Not wishing to put the paper to any expense, I defended the case in person, and my answer to the accusation was simply to show that I had followed with almost absolute exactness the example set by *The Times,* eliminating every scabrous detail just as *The Times* had eliminated them. "The standard of what is becoming," I said, "varies in every country and every age. I could do no better with a halfpenny paper than keep the limits established by *The Times.* This I have done," and I passed up my account with the account in *The Times* side by side, showing that we often stopped at the same word.

"What have you to say to that?" Mr. Justice Denman asked. My accuser, George Lewis, rose quickly. "I submit," said he, "that it's no answer whatever to the case. I contend that the *Evening News* is guilty of obscene libel, and I ask for a verdict on the strength of these reports."

"But," said Justice Denman, "if you are actuated by a respect for public morality, Mr. Lewis, why don't you select *The Times* rather than the less important *Evening News?*"

"Again, I submit," said Lewis, "that my accusation is unanswered."

Denman smiled and replied, "I give a verdict for the defendant, and wish to express my opinion that the case should never have been brought."

But I had learned my lesson. The fact that the *Evening News* published the longest and most detailed reports had doubled the circulation and brought the paper into the limelight. Now couldn't I go on to make the news pages more interesting? I at once set to work to get a couple of Paris papers, a couple of German papers, and used to glance through them every evening after my work of the day was supposed to have been finished.

As soon as I found either in Berlin, Rome, Madrid or Paris an interesting case, I rewrote it for the *Evening News* and soon saw that this was the road to success. The circulation of the paper rose rapidly, and people of some importance in journalism began to invite me out and show me favor; especially was this the case with Labouchère and Yates, whom I regarded as the two heads of the profession.

I made them both laugh heartily one evening after dinner by telling them of my progress downwards to success. I had edited the *Evening News* at first, I said, at the top of my thought as a scholar and a man of the world of twenty-eight; nobody wanted my opinions, but as I went downwards and began to edit it as I felt at twenty, then at eighteen, then at sixteen, I was

---

* (1833–1911), a great criminal lawyer; it was he who exposed the forgeries of Robert Pigott during the Parnell case.

** George Denman (1819–1896); he perhaps was more gifted as a scholar than as a lawyer, rendering Gray's *Elegy* and Pope's translation of the *Iliad* into Latin.

more successful; but when I got to my tastes at fourteen years of age, I found instantaneous response. "Kissing and fighting," I said, "were the only things I cared for at thirteen or fourteen, and those are the themes the English public desires and enjoys today."

It is to the present hour the true reading of successful popular journalism. Why has the *News of the World* a circulation of over three millions?* Simply because in it you can find most of the suggestive or sensational stories of the week. They have not found out the proper way of increasing their stock and so they are often short of good stories, but the good stories are there to be had always, as I very soon found out when my feet struck the right path.

It was, of course, extremely hard work for me to go through a dozen foreign papers every evening for perhaps a couple of stories, and besides at the best they were foreign stories—not as interesting to the English public as English stories would be. But how, how was I to get English stories?

One day, I was in the sub-editor's room and found that the reporters at all the police courts sent in flimsies with short accounts of what took place in the police courts during the day up to twelve o'clock. One of the stories told of a murder in Clerkenwell. There was no attempt at description: the common reporter had cut the incident down to some eight or ten lines, but beneath it I felt that there was a great human story. I at once jumped into a hansom, ran down to Clerkenwell, got hold of the reporter and made him take me to the scene of the tragedy. The story was appalling and intensely interesting.

A man and wife had lived together till middle age: had brought up a family of three children; comparative success had come through a little tobacco shop they kept, and with success came temptation. The father of forty-five had fallen in love with a girl of fifteen or sixteen who had come to the shop to buy tobacco. He made up to the girl and won her without the knowledge of his wife, who was wholly taken up with the household duties; but the eldest daughter, a girl of fourteen, had quick eyes and noticed that her father was going after the girl. When she saw him kissing her, she went to the mother to tell, feminine jealousy and curiosity blazing. At once the mother revenged herself on the girl. She beat her and called her names in the street until at length the father took his mistress' part and knocked his wife down. Strange to say, her head struck a cartwheel and she died the same night.

The whole story was told in court, but when I retold it in the *Evening News* with the chief details—a description of the jealous daughter and her account of how she had found her father out, and the father's confession —the story had an enormous vogue, and the circulation of the *Evening News* responded to it immediately.

I had found the way to success. Every day the London police courts are filled with love stories and sensational tragedies of all kinds. How to get

* Today, over ten million.

them was the only question. I took six police courts as a nucleus and put an able man in charge of them with these instructions: "Whenever you get any story that promises, go immediately to the police court in question, see the reporter, get all the facts. If there is real interest in the incident, work it up, interview the principals, make a real story of it, and send it in to the paper."

I advised my lieutenant to give a guinea to any police reporter who put him on to a good case. In a month I found the problem was solved. I could fill the six or seven columns of the *Evening News* with sensational stories of London life with the greatest ease.

After some three years' work the circulation of the paper had increased tenfold and it had begun to pay. As I had worked morning, noon and night on it without respite, I got the directors to give me a three months' holiday and went straight to Italy. In Rome I read a good deal of Italian and studied the old Roman remains, and became a friend of Prince Doria. There took place what I called the strangest occurrence in my life, which I may now tell at length.

The undiscovered country from whose bourne no traveler returns has always had a certain fascination for me, as I imagine it has for almost everyone. Long before the discovery of the X-rays had shown that one could see through houses and bodies, I was persuaded that there were more things in heaven and earth than were dreamed of in any philosophy.

The strange attraction of human beings, one to another; the fact that chemical elements only unite according to certain ascertained weights, that gases would mingle, but not become one until an electric spark was passed through them; the myriad analogies in nature suggesting likeness in the eternal disparity; unity in the infinite differences, tormented my curiosity from the time I was twenty. But every time I sought for further knowledge I was met by a blank wall.

I studied spiritualism for six or eight months and was so eloquent about it that the medium admitted me into the secret and showed me all the tricks of his foul trade. I was amused later to find that Browning had had an equally strange experience with "Sludge,"* the medium whom his wife had begun to believe in.

Later still I was surprised to find that Alfred Russel Wallace, a great scientist and the forerunner of Darwin, a transparently honest man, believed absolutely in all sorts of communications with what he called "the spirit world." But my unbelief persisted and persists to this day. Where is the great light?

Still, I had one experience that enormously strengthened Wallace's influence over me in this respect. Desiring complete change and recreation, I took out some Irish horses and hunted regularly on the campagna. It seemed delightful to me to hunt foxes where Paul and Peter had walked, where Caesar and Pompey had marched at the head of their legions, to

* See "Mr. Sludge, 'the Medium,' " from *Dramatis Personae;* the medium was actually an American, Daniel D. Home, whom Browning strongly disliked.

take high wooden fences on a countryside peopled with the ghosts of forgotten worthies. I used to spend some hours every afternoon studying the
antiquities and all the morning galloping across the campagna.

It was the double life that seduced me and gave me absolute health of
both mind and body. Naturally, in the hunting field I got to know nearly all
the Romans of position, and I knew most of the scholars and poets through
my afternoons.

As sometimes happens, there was a blank day in our hunting. The sun
was hot and strong and the dogs could take up no scent at all. The whole
hunt moved from place to place, drawing every spinney blank. Once I
rested beside a sprig of acacia.

I had promised to go to the Dorias to lunch and to talk afterwards to
their guests about the famous picture that was in the Doria galleries, the
so-called *Sacred and Profane Love* by Titian. Every one interested in art
knows the picture. At the left, in a charming Italian landscape, is a beautiful
woman dressed in the utmost splendor of those great Venetian days; and
seated on a round marble well-head, close to, is another woman, quite nude,
wonderfully drawn and painted, realistically realized. Some idiot had christened it *Sacred and Profane Love*. I read it in a different way. It seemed to
me plain that it was a characteristic Renaissance story: a Venetian aristocrat
proud of the beauty of his wife, asked Titian to paint her in all her splendor
of raiment, and at the same time to paint her as he saw her in her nude
loveliness. It was plainly one and the same woman—figure, eyes and hair
unmistakably alike.

Looking forward to the luncheon and the talk, and tired with futile efforts
to find a fox, I broke away from the crowd before noon and rode towards
the city, towards the Porta Pia, along the wonderful road made sacred by
the sufferings of Paul. As I rode into the city, I think by way of the south
gate, I had to slow up and go carefully because of a crowd of three or four
hundred people. When I got through the gate I saw from my horse that the
center of attraction was a veiled woman seated at a plain table drawn up
against the wall. The table was covered with some simple brown cloth. I
said to one on the outskirts of the crowd: "What is it all about?"

"A famous sorceress and soothsayer," he said, "who tells you the future,"
and he crossed himself as he spoke.

Just then a girl went up to the woman, put down some silver, and showed
her hands. I laughed. It seemed strange to me that there in Rome, the city
of a thousand miracles, the heart of a dozen civilizations, this poor cheat
should have won through all the centuries of skepticism.

"A good way of getting rid of small change," I remarked, smiling, and
some Italians echoed me, laughing.

Suddenly the sorceress spoke:

"If that foreigner on the horse would come down and dare the test he
would find that I could tell him new truths. I can unfold the future to him."

"It is the past I would like to know about," I answered. "If you can tell me about the past I'll believe your predictions."

"Come down," she said, "I'll tell you about the past as well as the future."

I looked at my watch and saw that I had half an hour to spare. There was an Italian boy already at my horse's head, promising to hold the cable-tow, so I dismounted and went through the crowd to the sorceress. I offered her a gold coin but she waved it aside. "Do not pay until you are convinced."

I said, "Please understand that I want to know about the past."

"What about the past?" she asked.

"Oh, the most important thing to me in it."

"That's easy," she replied. "Give me both your hands, please. The left one shows what your natural proclivities are, the right how they have been modified by the experiences of your life."

I held out both my hands and stood feeling rather a fool to be wasting my time on such nonsense.

"The most peculiar thing in your life," she said, "up to date, is the love and admiration you had for a man, an American."

"Perhaps you can tell me the man's name," I suggested.

"I will spell it for you," she said, "you begin."

"Begin you—" said I, and she answered, "S-m-i-t-h—Smith."

For a moment I was dumbfounded. How could she know anything about my life in Kansas University?

"What was he like?" I asked.

To my amazement she described him.

"He had a great influence on you," she went on, "made you a student and writer. Am I right?"

"Perfectly right," I said, "but how you got the information I do not know. Whatever you tell me about the future I shall think of and consider ripely."

"The movement of your life," she said, "goes steadily upward, and you will realize all your ambitions. You will win money and fame, and have a very happy and full life. But the curve in later life begins to go down, and I cannot see the end; there is a sea of blood."

"What do you mean," I cried, "blood cause by me?"

"Oh, no, blood over half the world—a sea of blood."

"Am I in it?" I asked.

"I will say no more," she replied. "I oughtn't to tell you anything more."

I laughed. "It is a very dramatic ending. Of course if you think you ought not to tell me, you won't."

"Still you have no belief in it?" she asked, looking at me with sad eyes.

"None," I said, "not a vestige of belief, not in my success nor in the sea of blood."

She nodded her head several times as if in thought and then with a sigh, she said: "I can make you believe it all."

"There I defy you," I laughed. "I do not think I would believe you if it occurred; if in the years to come all you have said turned out to be true, I still should not believe."

"You will leave Rome this evening and go across the seas to England," she cried suddenly.

"Oh, that's a shockingly bad guess," I replied. "I have my rooms in Rome for months: I have horses here and do not intend to leave until spring is changing into summer. Three months at least I shall stay here."

"You will leave Rome this evening," she repeated, "for London. And in the train you will know that the soothsayer spoke truth."

To cut the matter short, I asked her what I owed her.

"What you please," she answered. "Nothing if you do not believe."

I took out a couple of gold coins.

"I believe the first part of what you said," I told her. "It was extraordinary. But nothing like you say is ever going to happen to me."

"Tonight you will know more," she replied.

I bowed and walked through the crowd to my horse and went off to the lunch. I gave my little talk to perhaps a hundred people in the Doria gallery. I had just finished and was being congratulated by the British ambassador and Doria, when a servant came up and said to Doria, "A telegram for Mr. Harris."

With their permission I opened it and found that I was summoned back to London immediately—"Important!" The signature was that of a friend, Lord Folkestone, who would not have sent me such a telegram without absolute need. I showed the telegram to Doria, and, absorbed in the question of what could have happened, I hurried off to my hotel, sent a messenger to get my ticket, packed my clothes, settled my bill and caught the night express to London, getting a sleeping compartment all to myself. An hour later I went into the diner. In glancing out of the window into the gloom I saw that we were just leaving the campagna.

The whole scene of noon came back to me in a flash. Here I was against all probability going to London, as the soothsayer had predicted.

How could she have known? How much truth was there in it all? What did she mean by the "sea of blood" at the end? "A sea of blood," her words were, "a sea of blood over half the world."

A couple of months later I was free again. I returned to Rome and did everything I could think of to find my soothsayer, but in vain. When I inquired of the police, they told me that the soothsayers and similar folk in Rome were legion. Could I give any description?

I never heard of her again. I leave the story now to my readers as a problem. It is the one fact in my life which I am unable to explain in any way.

I must now relate how I lost the editorship of the Evening News. All the while I was in Rome I received weekly statements from the Evening

News and knew that it was going on all right, but without improving under the assistant whom I had picked, an Irishman named Rubie. When I reached England, Lord Folkstone told me that Mr. Kennard. the banker and director who supplied most of the money, had come to have a great opinion of Rubie, my assistant; thought he could do the work quite as well as I could, and, in fact, intended to make a row about my having prolonged my holiday in order to put Rubie in my place as managing editor. I was astonished and amused. I knew that Rubie could not do the paper at all, and I had really worked with all my heart and soul at it, and hadn't taken breathing time or a holiday in the three years.

I meant to take up the whole problem of journalism in a big way when I came back. I wanted to group all the police courts in London in sixes under able heads, and so fill up the whole paper from one end to the other with astonishing stories of London life. I dreamed of a morning paper as well and a million circulation for each; and I would have done it all, but when I came back, I found that success had turned Kennard's head. He would have to pay me a share of the profits; he would always have me as a master in his paper; and as I had prolonged my holiday without leave, I had given him the opportunity he needed. I was to be discharged—decently because of Lord Folkestone—still, to be got rid of.

We had a board meeting at the *Evening News* and Kennard said he wanted to act quite fairly: he thought that I had made the paper successful, and he was quite willing to give me a thousand pounds as a solatium.

One incident is perhaps worth relating here: I brought some friends together who offered Coleridge Kennard some forty thousand pounds for the paper—more than all the money spent on it during my editorship; he refused the offer. I thereupon accepted his offer of a thousand pounds and got up to leave the board room. At this Lord Folkestone rose also, reminded Coleridge Kennard that he had put a good many thousands of pounds in the paper, that he had selected me as editor, and declared now that he was perfectly satisfied with my work. He preferred, he said, to leave the paper with me and lose whatever money he had put into it. In the most charming way, he added, "Come on, Frank, they do not want us," and took me out to his mail-phaeton.

Three months after I left the *Evening News* Kennard met me at the corner of Grosvenor Street and begged me to come back to my old position on the *News*. He told me that the circulation of the paper had fallen off in the most extraordinary way. I smiled at him. "I warned you, Kennard," I said, "that things quickly built up would fall down nearly as quickly, but I am quite happy in the editorship of the *Fortnightly Review* and I will not go back." Two months later Kennard confessed to me that he had sold the *Evening News* for a paltry two thousand five hundred pounds to Harmsworth: he had lost some thirty-eight thousand by discharging me.

Chapter VII

My Pleasures: Driving, Food and Drink, Music and Science

ALL THIS WHILE in London I had one passion: the desire to know and measure all the men of ability in art and literature I could meet. I had, however, a myriad pleasures, among which I must put first the love of horses, of riding and driving, I mean. I still kept up another dozen of athletic amusements; I ran and walked regularly and boxed for at least half an hour each morning, just to keep myself perfectly fit, as I shall explain later.

A London newspaper once published the fact that I was the only editor who drove fine horses tandem down Fleet Street. From 1885 to 1895 or so I had, I think, some of the best driving horses in London. I should like to give the photo of one of them at the end of this chapter;* the mare in question won first prize at the Richmond Horse Show, and was a very beautiful creature—well-formed with high spirit, and in her light American buggy an extraordinary mover; but alas! no picture could do her justice.

All these ten or twelve years in London I had from three to six horses for riding and driving; and I had the carriages built in America simply for lightness and perfection of spring. English carriages are usually very heavy and strong because of the bad old roads of the past, but the good modern road allows one to have lighter carriages, and is therefore better for the horses. I had a mail-phaeton built in New York and sent across which weighed less than four hundred pounds, so that two horses could draw it without feeling its weight, and were therefore free to show perfect paces. I was often stopped by Englishmen in Hyde Park wishing to know where I got the horses and the featherweight phaeton.

In a little portrait I wrote of Cunninghame Graham,** I told of a race we had in Hyde Park one morning, in which I beat his Argentine pony rather easily with an English horse. Graham has written since that he has no

* Photographs mentioned throughout the volumes refer to those included in Harris' original edition.
** In *Contemporary Portraits, Third Series.*

recollection of such a race; perhaps if he had won he would have remembered it.

Whenever I think of horses I cannot but recall Blue Devil, the mare I have told about when I was a cowboy in Texas. She was a wonderful companion! I could throw my hat down and send her back for it: after five miles or more she would go straight to the spot and bring it to me in her mouth. When I was at the University of Lawrence, Kansas, which lies outside the town on a hill, I used to ride her up without bridle or saddle, then dismount and turn her loose, and she would wander about, eating a little grass from time to time, and as soon as I whistled she would come racing to me.

In her honor I must tell that I once made a bet in Lawrence that I could ride one hundred miles on this one horse and walk fifty in twenty-four hours. When it came to the trial, it was a hot July day and I was dreadfully afraid that I had over-rated what Blue Devil could do, so I picked the cool night for her and rode her without a saddle; but about the fiftieth mile she fairly ran away with me just to teach me that she could do what was required of her; and at the hundredth mile, which was completed under eleven hours, she bit me on the shoulder playfully and began to eat her oats as if she had just left the stable; her heart was nearly as big as her body. I almost came to grief walking the fifty miles because one of my boots gave out about the twenty-fifth mile and I had to walk the rest of the distance in my stockings. However, the ride is on record; not a bad achievement for a boy of seventeen!

The English know far more about horses than any other European people, but even in this cult they have been surpassed by the Americans, who first taught them that jockeys should sit as far forward on the withers as possible, and not in the small of the back. Even Fred Archer,* great jockey though he was, was not nearly as good as some American jockeys who came after him and showed their skill on English race courses.

Just in the same way, prize-fighting was further developed in America in ten years' time than in England in a hundred.

I wish the English would understand how their love of tradition limits them in almost everything.

I can't leave this talk about horses without mentioning the advent of the motor-car. It was in the winter of 1895–96 that I went from London as usual to the Riviera, and there saw a motor-car for the first time. A man had brought it to Monte Carlo, and having lost his money, offered it for sale: it was a Georges Richard, seven horse-power, driven by belts. At once I tried it and fell in love with the speed and smoothness of its motion; finally I bought it, giving, I think, fifteen thousand francs for it, or about six hundred pounds.

---

* (1857–1886); he won more than 2000 of the 8000 races he ran. He ruined his health by dieting to maintain his riding weight; eventually he went insane and shot himself.

I used it for almost a month to visit all the beauty spots of the Riviera, and they are numberless and wonderful. When I had drunk my fill of natural beauty, I started over Grasse and Digne to go to Paris. I remember dining late at Grasse and going on by night: we lost first one belt and then another on the road and had to hunt about in the dark for them before we could go on. Still it was evident to me that the motor-car would soon do away with horses: it was the most wonderful mode of traveling that man at that time had discovered.

It took me over a week to reach Paris, and three days to go from Paris to Calais; and when I started out from Dover to go to London, my difficulties began: the very first policeman stopped me and took me to the station; it was there decided that I must have a man to walk in front of the motor with a red flag. I acquiesced apparently, but declared to the police inspector that I would not go beyond four miles an hour and would use all care; and so at last I was allowed to start out for London. On the way I met a gentleman with a pair of horses who turned back at once and began following my motor-car. He asked me numerous questions about it; and the end of it was that he paid me to bring it into his park and let him try it; which I did, and at the finish I sold him the car and went on to London endowed with my new experiences, the chief being the divine beauty of the Riviera, and the new power given to one by the motor-car.

The motor-car enriched life like the discovery of two or three new poets. I always give one instance of its almost magical power. I think I was the first person who ever saw the four great cathedrals of France in one day. I was staying in Amiens, and after a last look at the west door of the cathedral, about seven o'clock in the morning I drove the car to Beauvais and spent some hours with its beauties; thence I drove to Paris. At Paris I just looked at Sainte-Chapelle and went on to Chartres, where I had a late lunch; after lunch and feasting my eyes again on the beauties of the cathedral, I drove on to Rheims and had another great impression.

I suppose the day will come when one will see the four in a morning and fly to Monreale, near Palermo, for lunch, and then from Palermo to the Parthenon of Athens, and so on to the church of San Sofia at Constantinople, the inside of which is one of the wonders of the world.

One other experience I had in the last years of the century which I want to put on record, for it taught me that a machine heavier than air might fly. It was, of course, an American who gave me the experience; I have forgotten his name, although I knew him very well. He talked to me about a flying machine: "The motor-car engine," he said, "was still very heavy," but he felt certain that if speed enough could be got up, it would be possible to fly in an airplane heavier than air. He took me down one day to his place in the country. He had rigged up there a sort of airplane with a motor-car engine and a long set of rails down a fairly steep hill. He told me that the rails were there in order to get sufficient speed in the descent for the airplane to fly; he asked me would I risk a flight with him. I said I should be delighted. We got in; he started the engine; we ran down the slope and to my wonder lifted into the air and went about three hundred yards, crossing a fence in our flight before descending in a grass field. 'Twasn't anything very brilliant, but it taught me, certainly, that man had conquered the air and would yet have a machine to wing the ether like a bird.

Less than twenty years later I went up in an airplane at Nice, but I shall talk about that in another volume.

Now that I am telling about the pleasures of life and living, I want to tell about eating and drinking. I have already noted, I think, in a previous volume, that the English ideal of cooking is the best in the world; it is the aristocratic ideal and consists in the desire to give to each article of food its own especial flavor, whereas French cooking is apt to obliterate all distinctions with a democratic sauce.

The drawback of English cooking is that England has scarcely any cooks, and so it is seldom you find their ideals carried out. In one particular, however, I was always quarreling with English food: you can get the best game in the world in England, but alas, the English always keep it until it is "high," or if you prefer the truth, till it is almost rotten. I remember one Englishman of great position telling me that he always hung grouse till the bird fell of its own weight, drawing out its legs. Professor Mahaffy* in Dublin once told me with huge gusto that he never cared for woodcock till it was represented by a green sauce on his plate. And all this is done, I have been told, in order to make game more tender; but I found out in Scotland once that if you cook game on the day it is shot, before the *rigor mortis* has set in, it is just as tender as if you kept it for a month. I used to take special pains to get my grouse cooked before the *rigor mortis,* and sent down to me from Yorkshire.

I think it was the ladies in England who first told me that my lunches were the best in London because the game was so delightful—not "smelly," they said.

It is possible in London to get the best beef and mutton in the world, and any one who tries Simpson's restaurant in the Strand will soon convince himself of the truth of this assertion. The veal, however, is not nearly so good as it is in France; and of course the average of French cooking is immeasurably higher than the average of English cooking; but I repeat, I have had the best dinners of my life in England.

Ordinarily here in France, at the seaside, one gets fish at the best restaurants that isn't fresh, and when you protest, the *maitre d'hotel* assures you that it is quite fresh; was alive that morning. Now high game is not injurious to the health. Beef and mutton, too, can be kept a long time without being harmful, but stale fish is often deadly; and I therefore want to tell my readers how to distinguish between fresh and stale fish at one glance. When the fish is put before you, you naturally open it; lift the flesh from the backbone;

---

* Sir John Pentland Mahaffy (1839–1919), provost of Trinity College in Dublin, an authority in Greek literature and history, and a social lion.

if the backbone has marked the flesh in the slightest way, it is two or three days old; and if the marks are dark brown, it is probably two weeks old. Yet at the best hotel I had fish of the Mediterranean, and the *arête,* or back bone, had marked the flesh black. No assurance of the *maitre d'hotel* would induce me to touch such fish. French bread, too, that used to be the best in the world, is now tenth-rate, but it is always possible to get sticks of gluten that look and taste like the best bread and are very easy to digest.

Most tinned and canned foods are better done in England than elsewhere, but one especially—*petits pois de Rodel*—prepared in two or three different ways in France, are the best sweet peas I have ever eaten.

Long ago I proposed to make a restaurant that should have rooms given to different schools of cookery: the English room, of course, and the French room, and the Russian room, at least; for these are the three great schools of modern cookery; and the best of them, in my opinion, is the English, so far as the ideal of cooking goes; but New York is beginning to run London very close. You can get nearly as good beefsteak and mutton in New York as in London, and better veal; fish, too, you can get in New York as good, except they have no salmon-trout, and the sole are not quite as good as Dover sole; but you can get better lobsters in New York than anywhere in the world, and deep-sea oysters, too—better than Carlingfords, in spite of British opinion. And as for vegetables and fruits, there is no comparison: the American vegetables and fruits are the best to be found anywhere.

But there is one thing which the French have to perfection, and that is many sorts of wine—the best, I think, in the world. I can get *vin du pays* almost anywhere in France that is light and of excellent flavor, sometimes indeed with a real bouqet, and it is as cheap as mineral water: a franc and a half a bottle, let us say, or two-pence or three-pence in English money, or five cents a bottle. Of course, the best wines, Bordeaux and Burgundy, are much dearer: half a dollar, or a dollar and a half a bottle, according to quality and age; but such luxuries can be omitted when the ordinary wine of the country is absolutely palatable and good. In my time in London champagne was the chief drink, and the English best class knew more about good champagne than the French: they were the first to modify the French habit of adding sugar and brandy to champagne—they have always wanted their wine *nature* or *brut;** and the taste for the best dry champagne in London is far higher than it is in Paris; but Burgundy and Bordeaux, and all the varieties of white and red wines are better understood in France than anywhere else.

My reputation for giving good lunches in London was based on the fact that I knew more about the best qualities and the best years of French wines than most people. I have always had a passionate admiration for Rhine wines, too, and the wines of the Moselle. A long time ago now I once earned

* It will be recalled that Harris discussed champagne in this very manner in the second volume.

my living in London by tasting wines: we used to have an excellent lunch, three or four of us, and the six or eight bottles of wine that we had to taste were brought in after we had enjoyed an excellent beefsteak and had cleaned our palates with bread and salt and olives: then each of us had to give his opinion of the various wines and tell especially which would improve with keeping and so be the better purchase. Most of us could give the year of any special vintage. One man in London knew more about white wine even than I did, but I was a good second, and so I may be allowed to speak on French wines at least with some authority.

I remember making every one at table laugh one day by a comparison between wine and women as the two best things in the world. "Red Bordeaux," I said, "is like the lawful wife: an excellent beverage that goes with every dish and enables one to enjoy one's food, and helps one to live.

"But now and then a man wants a change, and champagne is the most complete and exhilarating change from Bordeaux; it is like the woman of the streets: everybody that can afford it tries it sooner or later, but it has no real attraction. It must be taken in moderation: too much of it is apt to give a bad headache, or worse. Like the woman of the streets, it is always within reach and its price is out of all proportion to its worth.

"Moselle is the girl of fourteen to eighteen: light, quick on the tongue with an exquisite, evanescent perfume, but little body; it may be used constantly and in quantities, but must be taken young.

"If you prefer real fragrance or bouquet, you must go to a wine with more body in it, such as Burgundy, Chambertin or Musigny. Burgundy I always think of as the woman of thirty: it has more body than claret, is richer, more generous, with a finer perfume; but it is very intoxicating and should be used with self-restraint.

"Port is the woman of forty: stronger, richer, sweeter even than Burgundy; much more body in it but less bouquet; it keeps excellently and ripens with age and can only be drunk freely by youth; in maturity, more than a sip of it is apt to be heavy, and if taken every day it is almost certain to give gout. But if you are vigorous and don't fear the consequences, the best wine in the world is crusted Port, half a century old; it is strong with a divine fragrance, heady, intoxicating, but constant use of it is not to be recommended: it affects the health of even its strongest and most passionate admirers and brings them to premature death.

"I prefer the little common wine of France that is light gold in color or rosée with perfect taste, a slight fragrance and no intoxication in half a dozen bottles. Oh, me! Which is a great sigh of regret for the dear dead days and loves desirable!

"Strange," I went on, "the diseases of wine, too, corroborate my comparison. Claret, or the lawful wife, suffers from what the French call *tourné;* if you turn away from her, the wife loses her subtle attraction very easily, and if she turns away from you, look out for storms.

"Burgundy, on the other hand, is apt to become bitter; *amer,* the French call it: the body in it, if kept too warm or not treated properly turns bitter; and champagne is ruined by *graisse,* a sort of viscous ropiness.

"At their best and worst, wines have curious affinities with women. Young men prefer Burgundy because of its sweetness and fire, while old men always choose Moselle because it is harmless, light, has a delicious perfume and no bad effect."

There were many other pleasures in my daily life in Park Lane in those golden years from 1890 to 1900.

I have said nothing of the music in London in the eighties and nineties, but the chief part of it was really all contained in the light operas of Gilbert and Sullivan given at the Savoy Theatre. Their popularity was extraordinary: from *Pinafore, Patience,* and *The Pirates* to *Iolanthe, The Mikado,* and *The Yeomen of the Guard.* I think it was in '81 that D'Oyly Carte opened the Savoy for these operas, and their success was sensational.

I don't know when Gilbert wrote *Bab Ballads,* but he had made the name of "Bab" famous in the comic weekly *Fun* before my time. He had really an extraordinary ironic wit.

I was introduced to him by Beerbohm Tree. He was twenty years older than I was; and, of course, like every one in London, I had already heard a dozen examples of his mordant humor. I remember on one occasion when Tree had been playing Falstaff in the *Merry Wives* for the first time. Gilbert was in the theatre and came round behind the scenes afterwards to assist at Tree's triumph. Again and again Tree tried to get some praise out of Gilbert, but Gilbert put him off with phrases such as: "Your make-up, Tree, is astonishing," as, indeed, it was, Tree being an artist in make-up— a real artist. I still have the great mirror from his dressing-room, in which he painted himself as Svengali and as Bardolph in grease paint on the glass—a marvel of artistic similitude.

Annoyed at length by Gilbert's reiterated praise of his make-up, Tree said: "But, my dear Gilbert, what do you think of my acting?"—wiping his brow at the same time because he had to be enormously padded to mimic the rotundity of Falstaff.

Gilbert could not resist the opportunity for a witty thrust. "I think your skin acts superbly, Tree," was the scathing reply.

On another occasion, when we were all condemning Tree's *Hamlet,* which was really absurd, Gilbert said, "I don't think his *Hamlet* is so bad: it's funny but not vulgar."

He was said to have been a kind and a good friend, and he certainly wrote wonderfully humorous libretti for Sullivan.

For the first time I found that the honors conferred upon the pair were justified. Sullivan was made a baronet in '83, whereas Gilbert was not knighted until 1907. These honors represented very faintly the true values of both men. Sullivan was a charming little fellow: he was never very strong, and he died, I think, with the century.* The Savoy Operas were

* In 1900.

supposed to represent his contribution to popular music, but I was one of the few who thought that his great popularity had really harmed his genius. *The Mikado* was the best and the most popular of the whole series; it is still given frequently in America and England; but *Patience* and *Pinafore* were good, too, and had in them distinct echoes of the *Bab Ballads;* of course, in *Patience,* Gilbert ridiculed the "greenery, yellowy, Grosvenor Gallery, *je ne sais quoi,* young man," which was said to have been an attack upon Oscar Wilde. It may or may not be true, but Gilbert's wit didn't go very deep, whereas the music of Sullivan was of the very first order. One forgets today the splendid *Golden Legend* to remember that the music of *Onward, Christian Soldiers* is his; but he also wrote *The Martyr of Antioch* and *The Light of the World,* and is certainly the first of all English musicians—greater even than Purcell.

He was, too, extraordinarily lovable and kindly. I remember meeting him and asking him to dinner once, I think in '84 or '85, at Monte Carlo; I know it was shortly after he had been made a baronet. He came to dine with me at the Hotel de Paris, and when he came in and saw the table laid for seven or eight people, he said to me: "Do me a favor, Harris; introduce me as Sir Edward Sullivan; of course afterwards you will call me 'Sullivan' without the title, but I want these new people whom I am to meet to know that I am a Baronet." Of course I did as he asked.

I have no way of conveying to my readers the extraordinary boyish sweetness and kindness of the man, but he has remained with me always as a charming memory of a very great musician who kept his child's heart to the last.

The comic-operas at the Savoy Theatre were the most extraordinary theatrical performances that I have ever seen, except those of Wagner in Bayreuth. Everyone connected with the theatre seemed to be first-rate: Barrington was as amusing as Grossmith;* he was tall and big, while Grossmith was very small, tiny indeed. Barrington was a giant in girth and formed a perfect foil to Grossmith, who looked like a gnat. It was in the beginning of the nineties that he started touring with humorous and musical recitals. Grossmith was a sort of elf who could sing with extraordinary speed—the very quality needed to give the patter of Gilbert its full value. The girls, too, were well served in these operas, and they sang wonderfully. Who that heard it could ever forget, *Three Little Maids from School are We?*

It was Dolmetsch,** the Belgian musician, who first taught me what a great musician Sullivan really was; till then I knew nothing of him except as the writer of the comic operas; but Dolmetsch taught me the splendor of

---

* Rutland Barrington (1853–1922). George Grossmith (1847–1902).
** Arnold Dolmetsch (1858–1940), actually a Frenchman. He worked in Boston for Chickering from 1902 until 1909; in 1914 he returned to London and began reviving early English music on the harpsichord and clavichord.

The Golden Legend and the beauty of some of his songs, such as Oh Mistress Mine and Orpheus with His Lute.

Dolmetsch explained many musical problems to me. Of course, everyone knows that he was the first to make the harpsichord and clavichord as in the earlier days, but to hear him play Bach on the instrument that Bach had written his music for was an unforgettable experience: it was like hearing a great sonnet of Shakespeare perfectly recited for the first time.

One cannot speak of music later in London without thinking of Sir Henry Wood* and his conducting of operas: he was as great a conductor, in my opinion, as Toscanini!

I wonder if any one could divine the best experience I had in my life of a quarter of a century in England, the highest spiritual height reached in those colorful years of maturity.

I had run down to Oxford once to see Jowett, and a friend asked me, had I ever heard the boys sing in Magdalen College Chapel; he told me that some one had left a large sum to get the boys perfectly trained, and I know that boys' voices were the most beautiful in the world, so we made an appointment and in due course took our seats.

From the first moment I sat entranced; the boys not only sang divinely, but the music itself was extraordinarily beautiful, and I found out afterwards that it was the best music produced in England in three centuries; a cantata, I think by Purcell, brought tears to my eyes—I had a divine, unforgettable hour with those minstrels of God.

It was then given to me for the first time to catch a glimpse of the highest soul-beauty in the English character, and there is no higher on earth. How the same people who can train those boys to sing such heavenly music should be able to fight the miners and condemn their working-poor to destitution and misery is one of the most hideous puzzles of life to me. They have still in this twentieth century prisons and hospitals side by side; after a Casement** has served them loyally for twenty-five years and been ennobled by and for his services to them, they can murder him in cold blood for his obedience to the highest instincts in him: the poor, purblind creatures could not see that "pardon's the word for all" and forgiveness is nobler than punishment. Yet I still hear those boy voices choiring like young-eyed cherubim!

Curiously enough, I always think of science when music is much in my mind; they are two of my greatest joys, though I don't pretend to know a great deal about them. Still, Wagner to me had a rival in Alfred Russel Wallace, one of the best and wisest of men; and I can't talk of Sullivan as a musician without thinking of William Thomson,† another great and lov-

---

* (1869–1944), at twenty-five years the director of the Wagner Concerts at Queen's Hall in London, and he remained so for fifty years.
** Sir Roger Casement (1864–1916).
† Lord William Thomson Kelvin (1824–1907), known for his work on heat and electricity; he developed the absolute scale of temperature, which is named for him.

able and simply sincere soul who stands with Newton himself and is curiously related to him in his prodigious mastery of mathematics.

Perhaps the greatest scientist of the nineteenth century, and the twentieth has not yet produced his equal, was William Thomson, afterwards Lord Kelvin. His only rival, Helmholtz,* put Kelvin on a pedestal by himself. Every one knows how he made the first Atlantic cable a success;** it was an instrument which he had discovered that sent the first telegram between England and America in '58. He was the first, too, to light his own house with electricity.

In the last days of the century I was introduced to him by Alfred Russel Wallace, and was very much surprised to find that he was lame, the result of a skating accident in youth; but in spite of his lameness he had a wonderful presence—no one could forget the domed head and the kindly, frank eyes and grey beard. Two things I remember him by peculiarly: he talked of Joule† as his master because he was the first to prove that heat was a mode of motion; Kelvin then went on to say that in every transformation of energy from one form to another, a certain proportion changes into heat, and the heat thus produced becomes diffused by radiation. This gradual transformation of energy into heat is perpetually going on and must sooner or later put an end to all life.

Almost before his death his whole theory was thrown overboard. His gloomy predictions of a degeneration of energy, ending in stagnation, are no longer justified. His conception of atoms and atomic energies has been entirely superseded by the electronic view of matter, and we now look forward to an endless and boundless unfolding, not of energy and power alone, but of life itself.

Kelvin was the first, I suppose, to point out that the amount of time now required by the advocates of the Darwinian theory, and upholders of the process of evolution, couldn't be conceded without assuming the existence of a different set of natural laws from those with which we are acquainted. I understood him to speak of Darwinism somewhat contemptuously. He seemed to say: "We know nothing of creation. They talk of life beginning in seething marshes and say this earth has gradually cooled, and is cooling." Kelvin declared positively that if at any time the earth was hotter on the surface by even fifty degrees Fahrenheit than it is now, all life would have been impossible.

I have never known so strenuous a worker. If he had five minutes to wait at any time, he pulled out a little notebook and began to make notes or solve some problem.

---

* Hermann Helmholtz (1821–94), who achieved notable things in thermodynamics, optics, and acoustics.
** He was knighted for this in 1866.
† James Prescott Joule (1818–89); he demonstrated that heat was a form of energy.

The only time I seem to have moved him was when I spoke of the "weary weight of this unintelligible world."*

"Oh, how true," he said, "I want to take that down"; and out came the notebook. "We know nothing," he went on, "and I am much afraid we never shall know anything but appearances; the meaning of it all, the purpose, if purpose there be, is hidden from us; of essentials, we know nothing."

Kelvin always struck me as perfectly simple and unaffected. He made a great fortune; everything he touched seemed to succeed. He lived till over eighty and went through life with perfect simplicity, not a trace of pose or snobbishness—probably in the twenty years from 1890 to 1910, the wisest man in the world.

We are gradually moving away from the attitude of mind engendered by religion to the attitude born of science. Then we accepted statements and believed; now we question all things and doubt.

Will the scientific habit of mind produce as great masterpieces in art and literature as the religious habit? There are no messiahs of science; a Kelvin is superseded almost in his own lifetime; yet the masterpieces of art will surely be built on our emotions and sexual desires, which grow in strength as we grow in health and knowledge of living.

Kelvin knew nothing, I think, of the marvelous discoveries of J. C. Bose** in Calcutta. Bose has proved that plants live and feel as we do, are exhilarated by caffeine and killed by chloroform; he has shown, too, that metals respond to stimuli, are prone to fatigue and react to poisons; in fact, he has extended the realm of life and feeling to infinity.

One result is that we fear and tremble less; but hope and marvel and enjoy more.

* From *Lines composed a few miles above Tintern Abbey:*
    In which the heavy and the weary weight,
    Of all this unintelligible world,
    Is lightened.
** (1858–1937). An Indian physicist and botanist. Besides demonstrating the sensitivity of plants, he studied the reflection and polarization of electric waves.

Chapter VIII

Tennyson and Thomson

In 1892 TWO MEN DIED—Tennyson, the poet, in England, and Renan, the great prose writer, in France. The sensation caused by the death of Tennyson in England was unparalleled: he was treated like a demi-god: on all sides one heard that he was the greatest English poet of the nineteenth century. The *Quarterly Review* affirmed that "no English poet has possessed a more complete command of his genius in its highest form. No crudities of image like those of Byron, nor cloudy word-phantasms such as those of Shelley, nor fanciful affectations like those of Keats, nor versified prose, such as that of Wordsworth, mar his equality of treatment." A well known writer declared that "the marvellous island held nothing more glorious than this man, nothing more holy, wonderful and dear." Swinburne published a threnody on him of lyrical adoration,* and in the press many compared him with Shakespeare. Renan, too, was overpraised by the French, but to nothing like the same extent: they recognized that he was a master of prose, a really great writer, but no Frenchman would have thought of putting him with Montaigne.

Or let us take Victor Hugo, whose life has more points of resemblance with that of Tennyson: he was a greater singer and his genius was far more widely recognized; he was as peculiarly French as Tennyson was English; he, too, lived to a great age and was accorded a public state funeral which was turned into a great ceremony. But there were no such dithyrambs of praise in the French press over Hugo: there was far more measure, more reason; the best heads did not hesitate to qualify their admiration for a great poet and master of musical French.

Tennyson's last day was described by a journalist on the *Pall Mall Gazette* with a fervor of admiration that made him a sacred memory to thousands who had never seen him or read a line of his finer work. I quote the account because it was peculiarly characteristic of English sentiment.

---

* *Threnody*, written October 6, 1892, first published in *The Nineteenth Century* in 1893. On November 13, 1892, Swinburne wrote to his mother: "I have just written some verses on Tennyson's beautiful and enviable death in the arms of Shakespeare, as one may say, reading *my* favorite poem of all just before the end . . ."

The morning yesterday rose in almost unearthly splendour over the hills and valleys on which the windows of Aldworth House look out, where Lord Tennyson lay dying. From the mullioned window of the room where the poet lay, he could look down upon the peaceful fields, the silent hills beyond them, and the sky above, which was a blue so deep and pure as is rarely seen in this country.

Lord Tennyson woke ever and again out of the painless, dreamy state into which he had fallen, and looked out into the silence and the sunlight.

In the afternoon, in one of his waking moments, during which he was always perfectly conscious, he asked for his Shakespeare, and with his own hands turned the leaves till he found *Cymbeline*. His eyes were fixed on the pages, but whether and how much he read no one will ever know, for again he lay in dream or slumber, or let his eyes rest on the scene outside.

As the day advanced a change came over the scene, a change almost awful to those who watched the death-bed. Slowly the sun went down, the blue died out of the sky, and upon the valley below there fell a perfectly white mist. The hills, as our representative was told, put on their purple garments to watch this strange, white stillness; there was not a sound in the air, and, high above, the clear, cloudless sky shone like a pale glittering dome. All nature seemed to be watching, waiting.

Then the stars came out and looked in at the big mullioned window, and those within saw them grow brighter and brighter, until at last a moon—a harvest moon for splendour, though it was an October moon—sailed slowly up and flooded the room with golden light. The bed on which Lord Tennyson lay, now very near to the gate of death, and with his left hand still resting on his Shakespeare, was in deep darkness; the rest of the room lit up with the glory of the night, which poured in through the uncurtained windows. And thus, without pain, without a struggle, the greatest of England's poets passed away.

The idea of the stars growing brighter as the moon rose, and the hills putting on purple while the Lord was dying is pure English, or, perhaps I should say, English journalism. Yet everyone praised the description, and there was no criticism of it.

In every paper, too, one found Carlyle's pen portrait of the poet, which is excellent, though not unduly flattering:

Tennyson is one of the finest looking men in the world. A great shock of rough, dusty hair; bright, laughing hazel eyes; massive aquiline face, most massive yet most delicate; of sallow-brown complexion; almost Indian-looking; clothes cynically loose, free-and-easy; smokes infinite tobacco. His voice is musical, metallic—fit for loud laughter and piercing wail, and all that may lie between speech and speculation free and plenteous. I do not meet in these late decades such company over a pipe! We shall see what he will grow to. He is often unwell; very chaotic—his way is through Chaos and the Bottomless and Pathless; not handy for making out many miles upon.

Carlyle does not even notice that Tennyson was tall and well-made, but he saw distinctly the want of brains in him or he would hardly have emphasized that "chaotic" or shown contempt for his speculative activities. A great part of Tennyson's popularity was undoubtedly due to his Victorian religious belief, for he was an aristocrat by nature and would never even issue a cheap edition of his works. To mention him with Shakespeare, the supremest intellect England has produced, seems to me a crime of *lèse majesté:* he wasn't even a thinker, but a sentimentalist.

I saw Tennyson twice: first in a house in London where he sat enthroned like a god and surrounded by worshipers, male and female. In spite of the incense of unmeasured praise, he said nothing of any value, but I caught a phrase or two that may be worth recording. Speaking of morality, he said, "Moral good is the crown of life. But what value is it," he added, "without immortality? If I knew my life was coming to an end in an hour, should I give anything to a starving beggar? Not a penny, if I didn't believe myself immortal. . . . At the same time, I can't believe in Hell; endless punishment seems stupid to me."

The whole talk appeared to me simply brainless, but he was remarkably handsome, and at the request of his hostess he chanted several stanzas of *Maude* in a fine deep voice that brought out all the music of the verse. But I really formed no definite opinion of him till John Addington Symonds took me with him to Haslemere in this year, 1892. Tennyson then talked of Symonds' *Renaissance in Italy,* which he had been reading with his son Hallam, and the two had a long discussion about Bruno,* in the course of which Tennyson declared that Huxley's belief that we were descended from apes had nothing in it to shock him. "It may be God's way of creation," he said. But soon he got upon Gladstone, whom he recognized as an evil influence. I could not understand why, till he came upon Irish Home Rule, when he asserted that the Irish were more incapable of self-government than any other people in the world. "Really," I interjected, "perhaps better than niggers!" He turned sharply on me: "Niggers are hardly higher in the scale than animals, indeed I prefer dogs—very much."

There was nothing more to be said; all the while I felt I was listening to mere temper, not to intellect, much less genius, which is the intelligence of the heart. Half a dozen men in this last decade of the nineteenth century were his superiors in mind: Matthew Arnold, Browning, Russel Wallace, and Huxley in England, and of course Lord Kelvin; and in France, Hugo, Renan, Flaubert and Taine were altogether on a higher level. Yet he was apotheosized even in his life and before he reached maturity. His semireligious sentimentality and his narrow jingoism were the sources of his astounding popularity in England.

"It is understood," wrote one well-informed critic about him, "that he believed he wrote many of the best and truest things he ever published under the direct influence of higher intelligences, of whose presence he was directly conscious." Writing on March 7th, 1874, to a gentleman who had communicated to him some strange experience which he had had under anaesthetics, Tennyson said, "I have never had any revelations through

---

* Giordano Bruno (1548–1600), a Dominican priest. He fled Venice to escape the Inquisition and taught in England, Germany, and France; when he returned to Venice in 1591 he was burned at the stake. He developed the monadic theory which influenced Leibniz and Spinoza.

anaesthetics, but a kind of waking trance (this for lack of a better name) I have frequently had, quite up from boyhood, when I have been all alone. This has often come upon me through repeating of my own name to myself silently till, all at once, as it were, out of the intensity of the consciousness of individuality, the individuality itself seemed to dissolve and fade away into boundless being, and this not a confused state, but the clearest of the clearest, the surest of the surest, utterly beyond words, where death was an almost laughable impossibility, the loss of personality (if so it were) seeming no extinction, but the only true life."

As if conscious of the significance of the statement thus detailed, he adds:

"I am ashamed of my feeble description. Have I not said the state is utterly beyond words?"

The poet repeating his own name in order to pass from the consciousness of individuality into "boundless being, the only true life" is surely calculated to make one smile. Yet this letter is a prose explanation by the poet of one of the mysterious passages of *In Memoriam*.

> So word by word, and line by line,
> The dead man touch'd me from the past,
> And all at once it seem'd at last
> The living soul was flashed on mine.

> And mine in this was wound and whirl'd
> About empyreal heights of thought,
> And came on that which is and caught
> The deep pulsations of the world.

> Aeolian music measuring out
> The steps of Time—the shocks of Chance—
> The blows of Death. At length my trance
> Was cancell'd, stricken thro' with doubt.

> Vague words! but ah! how hard to frame
> Or ev'n for intellect to reach
> In matter-moulded forms of speech
> Thro' memory that which I became.*

There are many allusions in the *Idylls of the King* and elsewhere in his work to these same visions of the night or of the day, but all confirming the belief in his own immortality, which he sets forth finally in superb verse:

> . . . And he, shall he,
> Man, her last work, who seem'd so fair,
> Such splendid purpose in his eyes,
> Who roll'd the psalm to wintry skies,
> Who built him fanes of fruitless prayer,

* XCIV. The quotation is accurate, except that lines two and three in the last stanza are in reverse order.

Who lov'd, who suffer'd countless ills,
Who battled for the True, the Just,
Be blown about the desert dust,
Or seal'd within the iron hills?*

Curiously enough, Hugo, as we learn from his *Journal de l'Exile,* was even more superstitious than Tennyson: he believed in table-turning and rappings, and in a spirit he called "The White Lady," who made her presence known in the most trivial ways. This superstition seems to belong to the time. In mature manhood, Hugo declares that he never lies down "without a certain terror," and "When I awake in the night, I awake with a shudder! I hear rapping spirits in my room"; and the "White Lady" he calls "an accursed horror." Yet he writes of all this much more reasonably than Tennyson: he says, "The world is still in its infancy: we require ruts and religions; it is doubtful if the average human being has arrived at even a moderate degree of reason: man still has need of written revelation"; and then we get the true reason of his superstition. "All great men have had revelations—all superior minds. Socrates had his familiar genius. Zoroaster, too, and Shakespeare saw phantoms"; and, as if to atone for this nonsense, he adds finely: "In this century I am the first who has spoken not only of the souls of animals, but also of the soul of things. All my life I have constantly said when I saw a tree branch broken or a leaf torn off—'Leave that branch or leaf. Do not disturb the harmony of nature!' "

Another interesting fact about Hugo is that he always refused to publish as his own the poetry he believed was dictated to him by some table-rapping spirit. Here are two verses which Molière is supposed to have dictated to him, though I think them curiously characteristic of Hugo himself:

Quand Molière te dit: Femme, prends tes aiguilles,
Fière pensée, apprends que je te fais honneur,
Toute main qui recoud, dans l'ombre, des guenilles
Brode le manteau du Seigneur.

Ton autre fonction, pensée, est la science,
Pour elle, rien n'est vil et rien n'est importun,
L'homme matériel est le vase; elle est l'anse,
La poésie est le parfum.

The great social movement in favor of the poor and disinherited, which is the glory of the nineteenth century, never touched Tennyson; in this, as indeed in every domain of thought, he was far inferior to Victor Hugo, though in the Frenchman, too, the gift of musical speech could not mask the poverty of new ideas and lack of creative power.

When we think of Victor Hugo's constant appeals to reason and justice in all international disputes, and contrast them with Tennyson's wild rav-

* Also from *In Memoriam,* LV. An intervening stanza is omitted.

ings against Russia or France or Ireland, we are almost compelled to admit that the French habit of mind is higher than the English.

Anecdotes of Victor Hugo are legion, and some of them are very interesting. During the worst days of the siege of Paris, the poet gave away a great deal of money, making use of Madame Paul Meurice*—who did not long survive that terrible time—as his almoner. She told him one day of a poor woman without clothes, food or fuel, whom she thought very deserving. Victor Hugo gave her a hundred francs, which were gratefully accepted. Two days afterwards, Madame Meurice found the woman in the same state of destitution and asked where the hundred francs had gone. She said she had distributed them among famishing mothers and children of her acquaintance; and, as inquiry proved that this was perfectly true, Victor Hugo sent her another hundred francs, on condition that she spend it on her own necessities. This she absolutely refused to do, saying that she would rather not have it at all, so Madame Meurice gave her *carte blanche* to do as she pleased with it. This obstinate woman was no other than Louise Michel,** the Communist, who had already suffered imprisonment and expatriation for her unselfish creed.

I have said nothing about the sex life of either Hugo or Tennyson. That of Hugo is fairly well known, whereas Tennyson's is unknown, even his intimate friends asserting that they knew nothing certainly. I should not think he had ever gone deeply into life anywhere. He was put upon a pedestal too early; he was too fortunate in every way, too highly rewarded. The sacred guides are never so well received; they get prison and hemlock, or the cross, as their reward.

Whenever I recall Tennyson's death and the unmeasured glorification of him in the English press, I am compelled to think of poor James Thomson† and his end.

The poet of *The City of Dreadful Night* died ten years before Tennyson, died in miserable poverty and almost unappreciated; yet, in my opinion, he was as gifted a poet as Tennyson, and far wiser; intellectually, indeed, one of the greatest, a master of prose as well as verse. His life and fate throw a sinister light on English conditions.

In every respect he comes nearer to ideal wisdom than any other modern English poet.

While Tennyson lauds the Crimean War, Thomson condemns it as "a mere selfish haggle, badly begun and meanly finished." He refers to the more recent exploits of English jingoism as "purely iniquitous, battue-wars against tribes of ill-armed savages." He showed sympathy for all the

---

* Wife of the French dramatist (1818–1905), who was literary executor for Hugo.
** (1830–1905), an anarchist. During the Franco-Prussian war she preached aid for the Germans; she was convicted and sent to New Caledonia. When she returned to France she was unchanged, continuing to preach revolution.
† (1834–82).

struggling nationalism of his time, for Italy and Poland and even for the Basques, who had supported the Carlist cause in '73.* Here are his words: "Such was the loyalty of these people, far more noble than ours; for they were giving freely of their substance and their lives, whereas we give chiefly snobbish cringing and insincere adulation, and our rich give the money of the nation in large part wrung from the poor."

Unlike Tennyson, he was devoted to the cause of the people, and fought against every form of privilege and capitalism.

Every Englishman should read his satirical essay on Bumbledom.** He points out that though there is more liberty in England than on the continent in matters affecting political discussion, "the reverse is true as regards questions of morals and sociology, for here the power of Bumble's purse rules our so-called free press and free institutions with a hand heavier than that of any Continental despot."

Thomson knew that there were worse faults of democracy than "political inequalities." "Bumble," he says, "imposes death by starvation."

He tells us in a letter that he used to read and "hugely admired Byron when about fifteen, but when I was sixteen I fell under the domination of Shelley, to whom I have been loyal ever since"—from Byron to Shelley in a year!†

Thomson is really the only Englishman who stands with Heine and Leopardi as a great modern master, and his translations of their poems are the best in English. And Thomson was kindlier and sweeter in all his personal relations than either of them. Even Heine at times distresses one by the contempt he shows for the greatest, such as Goethe. We have no such apology to make for Thomson. He was the most gifted of all his English contemporaries, and he praises the wisest of them enthusiastically. He almost reached perfection, but alas, he sometimes drank too much, is the accusation brought against him, and by Englishmen.

There is the famous reply to a similar accusation brought against General Grant in the Civil War by his detractors. "Tell me what drink he uses," said Lincoln, "and I will send it to the rest of our generals, and then perhaps they, too, will win victories like Grant."

No wonder Thomson let himself drink too much; he could find no market for his work in England, nothing but poverty and neglect. He told me, with that rare power of laughing at himself, which only high genius possesses, that he failed in spite of good resolutions. "You see," he said, "the resolutions were made when I was sober, but after the first glass one is not quite the same who made the resolution, and after the second glass one is still more unlike. If you have been badly nourished, it needs a drink or two,

---

* At which time he was a war correspondent with the Carlists, during the wars of the succession, which lasted from 1833 to 1876.

** *Bumble, Bumbledom, Bumblism* (1865).

† Thomson wrote *Shelley, a Poem,* in 1885, and his pseudonym, Bysshe Vanolis, was in part owed to Shelley.

or three, to bring you to your full vigor, and then one glass more for good fellowship and you're lost!"

One man who knew Thomson even at the end and saw this side of him, that I only caught a glimpse of, wrote:

"I am far from saying that Thomson did not find any happiness in life. His wit and broad fun vied with his varied information and gift of a happy talk in making him a prince of good fellows; and he least of all would be suspected of harboring the worm in his jovial heart.

"But these were the glints of sunshine that made life tolerable; the ever-smouldering fire of unassuageable grief and inextinguishable despair burned the core out of that great heart when the curtain of night hid the play-acting scenes of the day."

After getting to know him fairly well, I met Thomson once by chance coming out of a public house, and I soon found that he was beyond intelligent speech. I turned away too hastily. Yet I cherish more than almost any other memory the memory of my casual meetings with him.

Thomson's essays,* especially on the poets, are far and away the best in English. His view of Tennyson shows the sureness of his judgment, the width of his impartiality:

"Scarcely any other artist in verse of the same rank has ever lived on such scanty revenues of thought (both pure and applied or mixed) as Tennyson. . . . He is continually petty. . . . A great school of the poets is dying out: it will die decently, elegantly, in the full odor of respectability, with our Laureate."

Thomson wrote better of Meredith than even Meredith could write of him:

"His name and various passages in his works reveal Welsh blood, more swift and fiery and imaginative than the English. . . . So with his conversation. The speeches do not follow one another mechanically, adjusted like a smooth pavement for easy walking; they leap and break, resilient and resurgent, like running foam-crested sea-waves, impelled and repelled and crossed by under-currents and great tides and broad breezes; in their restless agitations you must divine the immense life abounding beneath and around and above them."**

Here is what he says of Browning:

"Robert Browning, a really great thinker, a true and splendid genius, though his vigorous and restless talents often overpower and run away with his genius so that some of his creations are left but half-redeemed from chaos."

And then he selects for highest praise his Lazarus in the *Epistle of Karshish, an Arab Physician.*†

---

* *Biographical and Critical Studies* (1896).
** From Thomson's "A Note on George Meredith" (May, 1876).
† *An Epistle, Containing the Strange Medical Experience of Karshish, the Arab Physician.*

Thomson's portrait of Heine gives a better picture of Thomson himself than any one else has given:

In all moods, tender, imaginative, fantastic, humorous, ironical, cynical; in anguish and horror, in weariness and revulsion, longing back to enjoyment, and longing forward to painless rest; through the doleful days, and the dreadful immeasurable sleepless nights, this intense and luminous spirit was enchained and constrained to look down into the vast black void, which undermines our seemingly solid existence . . . and the power of the spell on him, as the power of his spell on us, is increased by the fact that he, thus in Death-in-Life brooding on Death and Life, was no ascetic spiritualist, no self-torturing eremite or hypochondriac monk, but by nature a joyous heathen of richest blood, a Greek, a Persian, as he often proudly proclaimed, a lusty lover of this world and life, an enthusiastic apostle of the rehabilitation of the flesh.

I want finally to put Thomson with the great masters of the nineteenth century. I always think of Blake first as the earliest prophet-seer, then of Wordsworth and Shelley and Keats; but Thomson and Browning stand with these. His friend and biographer, Bertram Dobell,* the poet, says nobly of Thomson that he "was one of the finest and rarest spirits that has ever worn the vestments of mortality." Think of Thomson's final word, which I would put in the forefront of every English Bible, if I could: "England and France are so proudly in the van of civilization that it is impossible for a great poet to live greatly to old age in either of them."

I am not sure that this is true of France; I am quite certain it is profoundly true of England.

Tennyson and Thomson—between these poles you can find England: the one man, supremely endowed with genius for words but the mind of a sentimental schoolboy, was ruined by too great adulation and too many rewards; the other, of far higher mental endowment, bred as a charity orphan, was gradually disheartened by neglect and finally broken by the universal indifference that kept him a pauper.

I know that this judgment will not be accepted readily in England; the English would much rather blame a great man than take any shame to themselves for maltreating him. But one proof occurs to me: in the nineties, more than fifteen years after Thomson's death, H. D. Traill,** one of the first journalists and men of letters of the time, wrote an article in the *Nineteenth Century* on English poets of the Victorian era. He gave a list of sixty-six who were able to speak "the veritable and authentic language of the poet"; he puts Tennyson as the first, mentions even a Mrs. Graham Thomson; but omits James Thomson altogether. Yet, of the two, Tennyson and Thomson—the lord and the outcast—it was the outcast orphan alone

* (1842–1914). He befriended Thomson until Thomson died, and he arranged for the publication of *The City of Dreadful Night;* he is however more famous for his discovery of the works of Thomas Traherne.
** (1842–1900), editor of the *World* and of *Social England.* He was a poet, parodist, and a dramatist as well, and wrote biographies of Sterne, Coleridge, and William II.

that reached the heights. There is no such handicap to genius as praise and money.

> O wretched Earth! God sends thee age by age,
>   In pity of thy wild perpetual moan,
> The saint, the bard, the hero, and the sage:
>   But still the lofty life is led alone,
>   The singer sings as in a tongue unknown,
> The sage's wisdom lamps his single urn;
> Thou wilt not heed or imitate or learn.

Chapter IX

Friends

LONDON IN THE NINETIES! How far away and long ago it all seems, and how shall I describe it? London, to me, is like a woman with wet, draggled dirty skirts (it's always raining in London), and at first you turn from her in disgust, but soon you discover that she has glorious eyes lighting up her pale, wet face. The historic houses, such as Marlborough House, Landsdowne House, Devonshire House and Cadogan House, and a hundred others, are her eyes; and they are simply wonderful treasure-houses of past centuries, with records of each age in gorgeous pictures and books, in tapestries and table silver—all the accessories of good taste and comfortable living.

And if you admire her eyes and tell her so passionately one mid-summer evening, when the sunshine is a golden mist, she will give you her lips and take you to her heart; and you will find in her spirit depths undreamed of, passionate devotions, smiling self-sacrifice and loving, gentle tendance till your eyes dim at the sweet memory of her. And ever afterwards you, the alien and outcast and pariah of this all-hating world, will have a soft heart for London. You will find magic and mystery in her fogs, as Whistler did; and in her gardens some June morning you will wake and find her temperate warmth of desire more enchanting than any tropic heat. London draws me more than any capital, and I have been in most of them, but the sameness of her squares, the destitution of her docks, and, above all, her wretched climate, appall me; and as I grow older I prefer Paris, Berlin or Vienna, where life's contrasts are not so hideous.

Marriage did not mean as much to me as other happenings in my life, and my wife was not, by any means, so important to me or to my mental growth as some of my friends, notably John Addington Symonds, Francis Adams, Grant Allen, and Harold Frederic. In the first ten years of my London life, friends meant more to me than any other influence, and notably such companions as these, who excited me intellectually.

I never could understand why these men did not do some great and ever-memorable work. Symonds was a classic of the best, and master of an excellent prose; knew Italian and French, too, rarely well, and was a student born. He had no hindering English prejudices, regarded sex as lightly as Anatole France himself, and yet he did not write a single masterpiece. Why? He was well-off, too, and gave himself to literature with single-hearted devotion, and yet never reached even Tennyson's place, or Swinburne's.

Grant Allen was in even closer sympathy with his age; learned, too, in science as in literature, and freer in mind than Symonds himself because born in Canada; and yet he could not get beyond *The Woman Who Did.* Why? Again one asks, for it was a ridiculous book as a life's message. And Francis Adams was a larger man, perhaps, than either, though not so well equipped with learning; yet he, too, did nothing of enduring worth.

This fact made it gradually plain to me that intelligence and all round genial culture do not count for fame as much as some extraordinary endowment. It is, as Goethe said, "the extraordinary alone that lives." Swinburne was not comparable with Symonds in wisdom or understanding, or sweetness of character; and yet, because he had written ten pages of wonderful new verse music, he stands higher and is universally admired. The realization of this fact diminished for the first time in me that desire of fame which, so far, had been my driving power.

With these friends I was in constant touch for some important years without a shadow of misunderstanding or disagreement. Francis Adams was really my first good English friend: I met him in Hyde Park. I had been speaking there on socialism and the necessity of introducing some socialistic measures into English life when he came up and spoke to me, and we soon became friends. Shortly afterwards, however, he went to Australia, and I did not see him again for some five years. When he came back our friendship was quickly renewed and I got him to write for me on the *Fortnightly.* He meant a great deal to me, though I was considerably his senior, for he was both frank and sympathetic.

When he came back from Australia he brought with him a wife, not particularly interesting, I thought, but he also brought back a certain weakness of lungs. I managed to help him to go to Egypt. I told him he should live in the desert above Assouan, or in some high place such as Davos Platz, but he did not take my advice and gradually grew worse. He came up the river with me one summer and in the winter stayed with me in London. I found that he was getting more and more hopeless. He spoke of suicide: I begged him not to let his thoughts wander in that direction, assured him that life would be greyer to me without him, and reminded him of his wife. He confessed to me he had tried to kill himself, but his courage had failed him. I told him that courage, like every other virtue, needed practice to become effective; and after he had left me that evening I wrote the little story, *Eatin' Crow,* to show him what I meant. In the morning he read it in manuscript and said: "You may do bigger things, Frank, but you'll never do anything more perfect." He went back to his rooms at Margate, and suddenly I heard he had shot himself, after leaving me a message. His wife, too, wrote me that she had been arrested, so I went immediately to Margate and she told me the whole story.

He was going out for a drive with her when a hemorrhage came on. As he stepped into the carriage, he turned and came back to his room and told her that the blood was from his lungs and that he was dying. He gave her a message for me and then asked for his revolver. As the blood was pouring from his mouth she thought he was dying and bravely gave him the weapon. He put it into his mouth and shot himself; the bullet went through his head into the ceiling. I saw the hole it had made.

In court Mrs. Adams told the whole truth, so the authorities thought she ought to be arrested as an accessory before the fact. But I pleaded with the magistrate, assured him that I knew of her great affection for her husband, and she was set free. I cannot tell here what I lost in Francis Adams—a sort of intellectual conscience and stimulus: the truest and wisest of friends.

Symonds came next in those early days. He had gone to Davos Platz with one lung destroyed and suffering from tuberculosis, but in the vivifying mountain air he quickly gained comparative health; and twice or thrice in summertime he came to London, and once stayed with me in my house in Kensington Gore for some memorable days. We were together every evening and talked the stars down the sky. In sex matters he viewed pederasty with the same tolerance as normal indulgence, and told me how surprised he had been by Whitman's passionate repudiation of abnormal desire.

He showed a certain sympathy with the vice which astonished me, and explained, if it did not justify, Swinburne's later gibe at him on account of his supposed liking for "blue-breeched gondoliers." But Symonds' sympathy was purely intellectual, and I always thought him one of the best of men— full of the milk of human kindness and far nearer ideal manhood than Swinburne or Tennyson.

Grant Allen I have already told about: his influence with me only began when I began to write stories, and lived with me for some time longer.

This is even truer of Harold Frederic, who was, if I remember rightly, the correspondent of the *New York Times*. I met Harold Frederic first at Sir Charles Dilke's and we soon became close friends. I met Sir Edward Grey about the same time in the same house. Frederic had already written several volumes but none yet which corresponded to his ability, none which allowed one to take his measure.

I shall never forget one curious incident that occurred early in our friendship. It took place at a dinner at Dilke's when Harold Frederic sat beside Cecil Rhodes, at that time little known in England.

When most of the guests had departed, Dilke, Frederic and myself came together in our usual way to talk over things.

"Well, Dilke," Frederic began, "that was the first dull dinner I've ever been at in your house. Who was the bloody fool you put me next to? I talked to him on a dozen subjects but could get absolutely nothing out of him."

Both Dilke and I laughed, and on our way home I told Frederic enough about Rhodes to make him modify his condemnation; but he always refused to believe in Rhodes's brains, and in time I came to think that Frederic was probably nearer right in his contemptuous estimate than Dilke or I in our appreciation.

All these years in the nineties Frederic was growing rapidly, but it was primarily the American in him which appealed to me from the first—a power of judging events and persons on their merits, heedless of position or apparent importance.

This was clearly shown to me by his attitude towards the Venezuelan question.* Frederic had taught me to respect President Grover Cleveland who, he thought, was the ablest of American presidents in nearly a hundred years. But Richard Olney** was Secretary of State for foreign affairs and stood with him over the question of the boundaries of Venezuela. I am quite willing to admit that the English government was right in the attitude it took up. Lord Salisbury was about to impose demands on Venezuela by force of arms and Mr. Richard Olney plainly informed him that any such action would be a violation of the Monroe Doctrine. Lord Salisbury had no difficulty in pointing out that this was giving an extension to the Monroe Doctrine that Monroe had never imagined. Mr. Olney retorted that the United States considered itself the best judge of the meaning of the Monroe Doctrine, and almost like a thunder clap on this came a statement from Grover Cleveland, backing up Mr. Olney and plainly stating that armed intervention by England would be regarded as "an unfriendly act" by the United States of America.

I was at that time owner and editor of the *Saturday Review*. I called on Harold Frederic and we both agreed that war was imminent. I wrote an article declaring that in case of war England would cease to exist as a power among the nations, and to run such a risk for a paltry boundary in Venezuela was so absurd as to be criminal stupidity. Lord Salisbury sent for me. He asked me to come and see him in Arlington Street, as he wanted to discuss the article with me. Of course I went next day, and found that he had protected himself by installing Lord Henry Manners,† his secretary, almost between himself and me. He asked me how I had come to my belief in the enormous power of the United States in case of war.

"You don't seem to have a high opinion of Americans except as fighters," he said, "but you surely have an extravagant estimate of their fighting

---

* The Venezuelan Boundary Dispute grew out of the British claims on the common boundary with British Guiana. Venezuela appealed to the U.S., and in 1895, Olney claimed the case should be arbitrated according to the Monroe Doctrine.
** (1835–1917).
† (1852–1925), 8th Duke of Rutland.

strength. Our naval authorities think they could take Washington as they took it before and bombard New York into the bargain."

"Goodness!" I cried. "You frighten me for England when you talk like that."

"Explain yourself," he said. "Why do you feel so convinced of the power of America?"

"First of all," I said, "consider one thing. In the Civil War there were only about sixteen millions of people on the side of the South. Yet, in less than two years, the Southern Navy was wiped out of existence and the Northern Navy was stronger than all the navies of the world put together. In less than two years the Federals had invented every improvement in naval warfare which exists up to this moment. They used rams, big guns, heavy armor plating, and vessels cut down to the water edge so as to show no target and even torpedoes."

"Torpedoes!" exclaimed Lord Salisbury. "Surely you are mistaken."

"In '62 or '63," I replied, "a Southern battleship was blown up in Mobile harbor with a torpedo by Lieutenant Cushing.* The Americans are crazy with the sense of the greatness of their country and the rapidity of its growth. In my opinion they would beat the world in arms today. They are the best organizers of labor in the world, and that is equivalent to being able to produce the best armies and navies."

"You talk persuasively," said Lord Salisbury. "Your view is quite original, but I see your reasons."

The talk went on for a little while, and he asked me when I could come down to Hatfield and have a longer conversation. The end of it was that I went to Hatfield and spoke with great frankness. I told him what I hoped for England was a close Union with her colonies, in order to pave the way for a confederation of all the English-speaking peoples, which might in the future, with the immense power of the United States, put an end to war. It seemed to me as easy to end war as to end dueling.

"A quarrel between England and America," I added, "is to me the worst thing that could be imagined, altogether horrible."

Suddenly I remembered that I had heard Lord Salisbury described as an earnest Christian, so I went on:

"How any Christian could think of the possibility of war between these two peoples is beyond my comprehension. It would be a sin against humanity, for which there would be no forgiveness."

Lord Salisbury suddenly turned away from me, put his hand under his desk, and drew out a sort of shelf, on which there was a glass, I think, of whiskey and soda, and took a drink. "Please forgive me!" he then exclaimed. "Would you like anything to drink?"

I laughed. "No, thank you!"

---

* Lt. William Barker Cushing (1842–74); he became a Union hero for sinking the Confederate *Albemarle* in 1864 at Plymouth, North Carolina.

He looked at me and answered gravely:

"I think in the main you are right: it would be a crime against humanity, against our hopes for man. It is a little difficult," he added, after a pause, "to let Mr. Olney have it all his own way; he is somewhat peremptory and unreasonable."

"As the bigger man," I said, "I hope you will find reason enough in yourself for both." He smiled at me, nodding his head the while.

The whole talk made me realize, as nothing had made me realize before, that my sympathies were with America, even against reason. Lord Salisbury's argument was reasonable; Dick Olney was in the wrong, and yet I was on the side of Dick Olney. I could not make out why till I got Harold Frederic down to stay with me and confided to him one evening, under pledge of secrecy, all that had taken place with Lord Salisbury, and found that we agreed on every point.

From thirty to forty or so Frederic grew as I grew, but owed even less than I did to extraneous influences, for at first I had been greatly influenced by reading foreign languages and so-called scholarship. It was Frederic, indeed, who first showed me how little books and book-learning can add to one's stature, and though George Moore was always there to enforce the lesson, I couldn't honestly say I would willingly divest myself of any fragment of knowledge: Moore's familiarity with modern French literature helped him to a saner view of literary art than he would otherwise have possessed. Moore was always a pleasant acquaintance and interesting companion, rather than friend: I hardly know why.

Early in the nineties, too, I came to know Lionel Johnson and young Crackanthorpe.* I was drawn to them both from the outset: to Crackanthorpe for his gift of story-writing, and especially to Johnson, whose scholarship was worthy of his poetic endowment. Very early in our acquaintance Lionel won my heart by showing that he knew James Thomson and his poetry and was able to appreciate that rare genius. He said to me one day that Thomson's poem on Shelley was the purest piece of Shelleyism in the language. Thomson's prose work had escaped him, but he knew every line of his poetry and treasured it in his heart of hearts. Poor, dear Lionel Johnson, whose whole literary life was even shorter than Thomson's, for he had not long passed thirty when the end came. As in the case of Thomson, they talked of drink; but I have an idea that whenever a ship is highly powered, it should have a strong hull to boot or it cannot last long. Like Thomson, poor Lionel Johnson had a big heart, as well as a first-rate brain, and the little body was not strong enough to house such forces for many years.

> Lonely unto the Lone I go
> Divine to the Divinity.**

* Hubert Crackanthorpe (1870–96). A sketch of him is in *Contemporary Portraits, Second Series*.
** From Lionel Johnson's *The Dark Angel*.

Whenever I think of Lionel Johnson and Crackanthorpe, I am constrained to think of all the poets and men of genius I knew in my London life and the miserable fate of many of them. I have told of Burton, Thomson, Dowson, Davidson, and Middleton; but there were many others like Henry Harland,* some deservedly famous, some inheritors of unfulfilled renown.

But the most startling appearance in these early nineties was certainly Aubrey Beardsley. I know no one in the whole history of art who made such an impression, took up such an independent and peculiar place so early in life.

I came to know him in the late eighties through his sister Mabel, a very charming and pretty girl. She told me that he had been a sort of child-prodigy and had played Bach and Beethoven in public on the piano at ten or twelve.

Beardsley was of pleasant manners and intercourse: his appearance, too, was interesting; a little above average height, but very slight; perfectly self-possessed, though strangely youthful; quite unaffected, but curiously derisive of affectation in others. While still in his teens he used to sneer at Oscar Wilde's poses to his face, though believing to a certain extent in his genius. Of course Oscar was fifteen years his senior and was better read and had already won a high place.

After his success Oscar tried to patronize him, but Beardsley wouldn't have it. "At noontide," he said contemptuously, "Oscar will know that the sun has risen!" Had Oscar's appreciation taken place a year or two earlier it would have made all the difference in their relation, for in a year or less Beardsley passed from pupildom to rare mastery. Today he was imitating Mantegna; six months later he was Beardsley—one of the great modern masters of design.

I introduced him to Whistler. At first Whistler seemed bored and turned over Beardsley's drawings carelessly. Suddenly he stopped and began to study them. A few moments later he looked up. "Wonderful," he said. "You are already a master."

Beardsley burst into tears: poor boy, even then he had hardly reached manhood.

But what is the word of his mystery, the "open sesame" to his heart? More than anyone I have ever known, Beardsley desired immediate fame, recognition of his genius, *now,* as if pricked on with the instinct that he had not long to live. And that demoniac, dominant desire made him sacrifice to sensation, force the note, so to speak, confident always that when he wished he could do great work as it ought to be done—soberly and with reverence.

Beardsley was a little lacking in reverence, that "angel of the world," as

---

* (1861–1905). His first novels, published under the pseudonym Sidney Luska, dealt with the lives of Jewish immigrants in America, where he lived at the time. In 1889 he returned to London and worked for the Bodley Head Press; in 1894 he and Aubrey Beardsley founded the *Yellow Book* magazine.

Shakespeare calls it in *Cymbeline**; but the explanation of his faults to me is always the intense desire of immediate recognition, of fame in the day and hour. I have told elsewhere how he came to mastery in writing in a month or so: it really seemed as if every mode of self-expression was easy to him. His sister Mabel always contended that he was more gifted as a musician than as a draughtsman, and it may well have been true. It was Beardsley's mastery of all forms of art that explained to me the extraordinary achievement of the Keatses and Rimbauds.

There are certain pictures of his that remain as part of my intellectual consciousness. Who can ever forget his Hamlet—the slight, boyish figure with the peering, eager, frightened eyes, trying to grope his way through the depths of a pathless wood; yet this was done in 1892. I can never think of Réjane** save as she appeared to Beardsley, and his Tannhäuser hastening eagerly, breathlessly back to the Venusberg—and these were the conceptions of an unlettered boy of twenty or so, resolved to read all life for himself. Only four years later, he gave us the *Fruit Bearers*, the ponderous satyr leading with his appalling female companion. And finally the *Volpone* series of his ripe maturity—unforgettable. Never was there a more astonishing growth or individuality of talent.

And Beardsley, wonderful as he was, was only one of a dozen. Think of Charles Conder as a colorist, or of Augustus John, that master draughtsman, or Walter Sickert, the painter, or Phil May as a caricaturist; to say nothing of Davidson and William Watson—both master-singers, and a dozen other writers.† All these men of genius seemed to group themselves naturally round Oscar Wilde as a sort of standard-bearer: he stood for years as the representative of art in life which has now become to the intellectuals more important than religion: for no one can deny that the artist and man of letters in the new time has taken the place of the preacher and prophet.

I must confess that the chief influence in my life, in the first years of the nineties, was Oscar Wilde, and in the second rank, Whistler.

Whistler had come to grief before this. Ruskin had talked of one of his paintings as an impudent attempt to throw his paint-box in the face of the English public, and Whistler had brought an action against him, claiming heavy damages. He got one farthing, and the costs practically ruined him.

---

* Act IV, scene 1.
** Gabrielle Réjane (1856–1920), a French actress, of the stature of Sarah Bernhardt.
† Charles Conder (1868–1909); a painter, mostly of landscapes.
Augustus John (1879–1961), one of England's best known painters.
Walter Sickert (1860–1942), a student of Whistler.
Phillip May (1864–1903), a caricaturist; he worked mainly for *Punch*. His books include *Phil May's Sketch Book* (1895), *Phil May's Guttersnipes* (1896), and *Phil May's Winter Annual*.
John Davidson (1857–1909), best known for *Fleet Street Eclogues*.
Sir William Watson (1858–1935). At this time, his poem on Wordsworth's grave made him famous; his political verse kept him from being appointed Poet Laureate.

Bravely, cheerfully, he went abroad to Venice, paint-box in hand, to redeem his fallen fortunes, and did it after middle age with consummate *brio*.

Personally, I always rank Whistler with Rodin and Degas among the greatest artists of my time. I always coupled Degas in my mind with Whistler. Though no two talents could be more different, yet the likeness in some ways between them was most extraordinary. Both were witty and bitter-tongued, sparing neither friend nor foe; both made more money than they needed when money could no longer bring them happiness.

I have given in my sketch* of him twenty instances of Whistler's poisonous tongue. Oscar spoke of him as a wasp with a sting in his tail, and Swinburne's verse lays emphasis on the same quality:

> Fly away, butterfly, back to Japan,
> Tempt not a pinch at the hand of a man,
> And strive not to sting ere you die away.
> So pert and so painted, so proud and so pretty,
> To brush the bright down from your wings were a pity—
> Fly away, butterfly, fly away!**

Let me recall one or two stories of Degas. I was praising Puvis de Chavannes† one day. I had just seen three or four of his great cartoons for some public building and was struck by the suave, idyllic beauty of the landscapes and the Arcadian innocence of the men and women, clothed only in grace.

"He's really another Rafael," I said, "born out of due time."

"There's some truth in that," replied Degas, with curling lip, *"un Rafael du village"* (a village Rafael). I could not help smiling, for the scalpel had touched the weakest spot. There is something provincial in Arcady—it is too far from the center of our struggle today, and our struggle is of intense interest. Degas with his racehorses and jockeys, ballet girls and opera singers, came nearer to us, being of our time and hour.

I recall another story of Degas. He had gone to an exhibition of paintings and suddenly picked out one. "A poor Rembrandt!" he cried, and went over to examine it more nearly because of shortsightedness. "I'm mistaken," he said on getting nearer; "it's a first-rate Forain." Yet Forain†† the caricaturist had always been an admirer and even a disciple of his.

Toward the end of his life Degas was nearly blind and hardly worked at all. He was a solitary and when he accepted an invitation it was always hedged about with conditions, one of which was that there must be no scent, for he hated odors of all kinds. He often said that "love was not a question of skin," as the French proverb has it, "but of smell."

Degas was a relentless skeptic. "I believe in that," he said one day, point-

---

* In *Contemporary Portraits, First Series*.
** "To James McNeill Whistler" (1888).
† (1824–1898), a painter of allegorical subjects such as *War*, *Peace*, and *Work*.
†† Jean Louis Forain (1852–1931). His cartoons satirized the bourgeoisie.

ing to a painting on his easel, "and in nothing else"—a weird, unhappy temperament. He carried his bitterness into his work, whereas Whistler's work is always dedicated to pure beauty. Degas was a realist and supreme draughtsman; Whistler hated reality and was a master colorist. Oddly enough, one would have guessed that Degas, with his sense of line, would have been the great etcher; but it was Whistler who reigned here beyond comparison, save with Rembrandt.

From 1885 on to the catastrophe in 1895, I met Oscar Wilde pretty constantly. He used to lunch with me a couple of times every month, and whenever he brought out a new book, or when some article in the *Fortnightly* attracted him, we would dine together as well and talk half the night. He was, as I have said already, far and away the best talker I have ever met, with the most astounding gift of humor that irradiated all his other qualities. First of all, he was a born story-teller, a better story-teller, by word of mouth, even than Kipling, and with far higher themes, more suggestive, more poetic and symbolical. Often, after telling an exquisite little story, he would drift into portraiture of this or that man he had met: while giving a kindly picture of his subject, he would suddenly illumine it with some humorous, unforgettable word.

The defeat of Oscar Wilde came as a sort of result of the height to which he had climbed. He tasted real success for the first time when his first play was performed, *Lady Windermere's Fan*. It was admirably constructed, and it was just this quality that excited my curiosity. I asked him how he had won to such stagecraft, and he confessed to me quite frankly that he had gone away by himself for a fortnight and studied the construction of half a dozen of the best French and English plays, and from that study had gained the craft. But the parts of his play that won the public were the admirable aphorisms and witty sayings which he strewed about in every scene. I had heard them all before; they had come to him from time to time in conversation, but the effect on the stage to those who had never heard them was really overpowering.

I have pictured him so often, and with such particularity, that I could leave him now to the readers of my *Life* of him, but one is tempted again and again to recall the laughing eyes, the eloquent tenor voice, and the charming phrases.

Speaking of young Raffalovich,* I said that he had come to London apparently to found a salon.

"And he very nearly succeeded," replied Oscar smiling, "he established a saloon."

On another occasion, apropos of some notice in a paper, I remarked, "It is curious to see how thinkers like Matthew Arnold and Herbert Spencer

---

* André Raffalovich (1864–1934), a French- and British-educated Russian of means; he and Wilde were not friendly, apparently because this remark got to Raffalovich.

love to call on titled people, princesses and dutchesses; how inappropriate it all is!"

"Inappropriate, Frank?" cried Oscar. "Surely it is to be expected: doctors must visit the dying."

No afterthought, no art can give any idea of the astounding richness of his verbal humor. One day, walking down by the Houses of Parliament, we came on a meeting of the unemployed who were reinforced by some bands of suffragettes. "Characteristic," I said, in my usual serious way, "one of these days the unemployed will make themselves heard here in Westminster. We are witnessing the beginnings of a social revolution."

"You call it 'characteristic'," said Oscar. "I think it characteristic, too, my dear Frank, to find the unenjoyed united in protest with the unemployed."

No one else ever possessed such humor, both of words and of thoughts. His magnificent gift had conquered even English dullness and he was becoming a social favorite when Nemesis overtook him. One day I heard that the Marquis of Queensbury had insulted him, and then Oscar called on me, as I have narrated in my *Life* of him, and the tragedy began.

Chapter X

Grace

SINCE MATURITY I have always thought of women in three categories: those who love with the head, those who love with the heart, and those who are ruled in love, as in life, by the senses. Fortunately for us men, most women love with all three: head, heart and body; but still an acute student can usually see which of the three powers is in the ascendant.

Those who love with the head are the most dangerous and least attractive: as soon as they find out that their lover or husband has failings or infidelities, they cast about how best to avenge themselves and so punish him. Usually their invention is not long at fault, and woe betide the poor wretch who has to suffer their vindictiveness. The worst tragedies in life come from their malevolence.

The women who love with the heart, on the other hand, are like pearls of great price, and happily they are the most numerous class. Nearly every woman has something of the mother in her, and pity for weakness and loving-kindness beyond reason are always innate in her.

Lastly come those who love by the senses; but men can estimate this category perfectly: the senses are always selfish and seek selfish gratification, and so the sensuous sometimes when piqued or disappointed come to be as harsh and unamiable as those women who have brains and no heart. But, as I have said, most women have all three powers, and we can develop in them the affections we most need by judicious flattery.

My experience has been that girls as a rule never yield willingly to sensual desire, unless it is accompanied with some appeal to the heart or emotion; even some who turn out to be very passionate later do not give themselves readily to the sex-urge.

I want to tell here some experiences at this time which show how all sorts of motive enter into the matter with the girl, whereas the one motive is strong enough as a rule in the man. All through the years from 1890 to 1895, I thought chiefly of Laura and of arranging meetings with her almost exclusively, but in the sex-way I was always inconstant.

I don't know why it was, but from my first months in Paris I had always the feeling that French girls gave themselves more easily to passion than any others. They seemed to know more about it and to give more place to it in their lives than girls of other races; and above all, they were as outspoken about it as English boys, and as a Welsh-Celt I felt a peculiar kinship with the French on that account. When American or English girls are brought up in France, they, too show more understanding of sensuality than those brought up in England or America; the contagion is catching.

All these years I went over to France irregularly every winter: my health was better in Nice than it was anywhere else: I never suffered from my bronchitis there; and of course I stayed in Paris on the way to the Riviera. One day when I was crossing the Channel, it was very rough, indeed, and there was an American lady and a girl on deck together who were very ill— at least the older lady was. I brought the stewardess and tipped her well to take care of the patient; in a few moments the lady said that she would like to go downstairs to the cabin, but the girl preferred to remain on deck. The stewardess and I took Mrs. Sterling down to the ladies' cabin, and I came back to the girl. She seemed about fifteen or sixteen years of age. She had run to the side and been ill once and was still very white. I got her a glass of port wine which brought the color to her cheeks, and with the color all her native courage. "Would you like to walk," I asked, "or would you prefer to lie in the chair?"

"As soon as I stand up," she replied, "I get giddy. I think I had better lie back." So I got her another chair and lifted up her legs onto it before covering them over with the rug.

"What pretty legs you have," I began.

She pulled a face at me and said, "They are like everybody else's, I suppose."

Her gesture amused me.

"Indeed they are not" I said; those were not the days of short dresses, but her dress was short and her legs were beautifully molded. "I believe you wear your dress short," I said, "just to show your lovely legs."

She drew up in the chair at once and said quite angrily, "It isn't true; I hate short dresses. Aunt keeps me in them, but I know when I go back to my mother in New York I shall have long dresses. I am a woman, not a child."

"A very young woman," I remarked to pique her.

"That's all you know about it," she said. "What age do you think I am?"

"About thirteen," I said.

"Oh, you pig," she cried, "I am nearly fifteen."

I had only said thirteen to get her contradiction and so I confessed to her, and then said, "But how long do you want your dresses to be?"

"Down to my ankles."

"Why don't you get long dresses?" I asked.

"My aunt won't let me," she said. "I make her look old already; she says everybody takes her for my mother; she's my mother's younger sister. She loves me and is kind to me, but she wants to keep me in school dresses as long as possible because long dresses would make her look old. But now take your hand away."

"My hand isn't doing any harm, is it?"

"It is, too," she said, "It keeps me nervous, and it has gotten up above my knee. Now, please."

I followed her imperative wish and took my hand away, saying, "You might let me see whether you are a woman or a child."

"You must take my word for it," she said, laughing at me.

"I needn't," I said, and I put my hand on her breast. It was more mature than I had thought, rounded and firm, though still small.

"If you are rude," she said, "I shall go away."

"You won't either," I replied, "because you and I are going to conspire to get you into long dresses."

"Oh," she cried, sitting upright, "how will you do that?"

"Nothing easier," I said, "if you will give me your address in Paris. I am going to the Hotel Meurice in the Rue Rivoli, and either you will come to me or I will go to you; probably it would be better for you to come to me some morning, as the Rue de la Paix is quite close to my hotel and I can take you to Worth or one of the famous dressmakers and get very pretty dresses made for you. Then we will try them on and if they are all right, you must appear in them before your aunt one day and give her no chance of refusing you. She can't put you back in short dresses afterwards."

"Oh," cried Grace, again sitting up in her excitement, "that would be splendid; wouldn't it cost a great deal? Would you really do it?"

"Of course I would," I said. "We will get you the prettiest dresses and hats and everything to match."

"And a mantle," she said, "that makes one look so old. You know I am taller already than my aunt."

"Sure," I said, "and far prettier. Do you know where you will be staying in Paris?"

"Aunt wants me to go to school for one more term," she said, pouting, "but I don't want to go. I learn more French in one night at the theatre than in a week at school, and already I know it a great deal better than she does; in fact, they say I speak it rather well."

"All right," I said, breaking into French, "then we will talk French and you must be like a French girl and not say 'don't' at every moment," and my hand again went under the rug.

She wrinkled up her pretty little nose at me but didn't stop me; evidently the temptation of the dress was working, but as soon as my hand got near the danger point, she said, "Please, be kind; I want to like you, so be good."

I said, "Just one touch and I will."

"Oh, no, please don't," she said.

"Just one touch to make sure you are not cheating."

She smiled, and the next minute I had made sure. But as her face clouded and she drew back looking really hurt, I took my hand away at once and kissed my fingers and thanked her, which brought the smiles back again to her charming face.

If I have not managed to convey the impression of her courage and charm, it is because these qualities at their finest are indescribable: they depend on the eyes and mouth as much as on the varied intonations of the voice, and even on the myriad changes of attitude.

Needless to say, all the way to Paris I took care of the aunt and niece; I brought food and wine into the carriage at Calais and insisted that they should eat, and we all had a very pleasant meal together. The lady told me that she was going to an apartment in the Rue Copernic which I found out was near the Bois, and I arranged to call for them, a few days later, to take them to the theatre.

I said I would find out the best play and call for them on Friday, this being Monday. We became great friends, and accordingly, when we got to Paris, I sent my baggage by a special messenger to the Hotel Meurice, while I drove the aunt and niece in a carriage to the Rue Copernic. When the aunt went in I got the opportunity of telling Grace to come to me on Tuesday or Wednesday, and she said that she would certainly come at eleven o'clock in the morning on one day or the other.

Next morning I got a little note saying she would come on Wednesday, and on the Wednesday at eleven o'clock she came to the hotel. I had everything ready and took her at once to Worth. She had, I believe, one of the pleasantest hours of her life: the woman who fitted her complimented her on her figure, called her "Madame" to her intense delight, and told her it was ridiculous to wear short dresses with her lovely form, and measured her with the utmost particularity, showing off her hips at the same time, with a side glance at me of complete understanding. She did the same thing when she was measuring her bust and recommending a new corset-maker.

"When should the evening dress be tried on?" I asked, for I had ordered a morning dress besides and one for the afternoon.

"They will all be ready this week; if Madame comes on Thursday morning," she said, "I can deliver them by Friday evening; but Madame will have to get the new corsets at once."

Needless to say, I took her round to the corset-maker, but alas! she was not nearly so complacent. She took Grace into a private room to undress her and I was not allowed in until the corset was fitted, fortunately for Grace, unfortunately for me; but the model of the corset was becoming and Grace was enraptured at the idea of going to the theatre in full dress as a woman and not as a child. When I got into the cab to take her home, she kissed me of her own accord very willingly, and when my hand got naughty again she didn't say anything and left her lips on mine.

"You have closed drawers," I said, "you cheat."

She burst out laughing: "I wouldn't have let you put your hand up if I hadn't known that."

"Well," I said, "at any rate, when the new dress comes home, you must

wear the other sort of drawers. You never heard my joke about them?"
"A joke?" she repeated. "No!"

"The English," I said, "talk a great deal about free trade and the freedom of trade with every country in the world, whereas the Americans believe in protection and protective tariffs to favor their own manufacturers."

"I have heard that," she said, "but I don't understand very well what it means. I hate politics!"

"There was once a young fellow in London," I went on, "who made money by selling photographs which showed a good deal of the girls' figures, and so I proposed to him to make two photographs in one and sell them together as 'Free Trade' and 'Protection,' the Free Trade girl with drawers on that were open; the girl labeled Protection had closed drawers such as you wear. The jest caught on and he made a fortune out of it and gave me a thousand pounds for the idea. He sold over a million postcards in a month. 'Free Trade' and 'Protection,' you see."

Grace laughed with all her heart and kissed me.

We parted having arranged that I should come early to take them to the theatre, because we intended to dine before the theatre; Grace assured me she would be ready when I called.

I went to the Rue Copernic about six o'clock, and when I went up to the second floor, Grace admitted me herself in full rig, looking ravishingly pretty. When we went into the sitting-room, the moment the door was closed my right hand went up her clothes to convince myself, and I found that she had adopted Free Trade and was indeed a woman, passionate as well as very pretty. In a minute or two she asked me to stop, but when she kissed me with hot lips I felt able to ask her to come again to the Hotel Meurice next morning; my sitting-room was on the ground floor just by the door on the left and she could come in without being noticed and I would meet her. She promised to come.

We had a great night at the theatre; I took them to see Réjane and they both fell in love with her. The aunt told me when I asked them to supper that I had done quite enough. "I am sure the long dress was your idea," she said. I took all the blame of it and said that they looked like sisters now, which won the aunt's heart.

Next morning Grace came to my hotel.

How am I to describe it, those first hours spent with Grace? When she came into my room, I began to take off her cloak while she laid her hat aside, but when I wanted to undo her dress she resisted. In vain I begged and begged: evidently she had made up her mind before coming in, so at length I gave in and kissed her, saying, "I wanted to see your breasts: I know they are lovely and you won't let me."

"It wouldn't do you any good to see them," she said smiling. "What nice rooms you have here."

"I always have the same," I said, "but never before such a lovely visitor."
Then I opened the door into the bedroom and drew her in. As she looked

around curiously, I put my arms round her legs and, lifting her up, carried her to the bed. The next moment I had thrown up her clothes and buried my face between her thighs.

"What are you doing?" she cried, but as I began kissing love's sweet home and the little red button, involuntarily she opened her thighs and gave herself to the new sensations. As I felt her responding, I drew her nearer to me a little roughly and opened her thighs fully. There never was a more lovely sex, and already the smaller inside lips were all flushed with feeling, while soon pearling love-drops oozed down on my lips.

I kept on, knowing that such a first experience is unforgettable and soon she abandoned herself recklessly, and her hand came down on my head and directed me now higher, now lower, according to her desire.

When the love-play had gone on four or five times and I stood up to rest, she said gravely: "You are a dear and gave me great pleasure, but do you like it?"

"Of course," I said. "Even old Montaigne knew that the pleasure we give the loved one is more than that we get."

"Oh, that's my feeling," she said, "but how am I to give you pleasure?" In answer, I took out my sex. She touched it curiously, drawing back the skin and pushing it forward: "Does that give you pleasure?"

I nodded. "But this," and I put my hand on her sex, "could give me much more; but I don't want to hurt you."

"Why not?" she asked. "I'm not afraid and I'd love to give you pleasure."

"It's only the first time that hurts," I said, "after that we both have the pleasure without pain."

"Is there no danger of a child?" she asked. "I'm ashamed to say that it would not stop me, but I'd like to know."

"No danger," I said, "if I take care."

"I trust you," she said, "my darling," and she gave me her lips.

"Undress," I said, "dear heart; I want to see all your loveliness unveiled, and I'll undress too."

Grace rose without a word and was undressed to her chemise and stockings by the time I had thrown off my clothes. "This naughty chemise," I cried, lifting it up and feasting my eyes on one of the loveliest figures I had ever seen—with small child breasts and great swell of hips and thighs and bottom set off by the smallest waist and perfect small sex—half-fledged—a creature made for love!

I put her on the side of the bed and tried to enter; she was tiny: I could only put in my first finger with difficulty, and even that brought some blood; but by this time my desire was rampant, and she met me by putting up her legs and giving me every opportunity. Soon the head of my sex was in her.

"Does it hurt?" I asked, and Grace's answer was to put arms about my body and legs about my hips and strain me nearer to her.

"One body," she said, "and one soul." The next moment we were coming together and thrilling.

A little pause and I lifted her up and taught her the use of the syringe with warm water, which almost avoids all danger. When I had explained it, she laughed delightedly. After two or three more embraces, she cried that it was getting late and she must get back. As she put on her new corset and the long dress, she exclaimed roguishly: "I deserve the long dress now, don't you think?"

"A dozen of them, you darling," was all I could find to answer. We were in each other's arms all the way to the Rue Copernic. As we entered the house, she turned to me gravely. "An unforgettable afternoon: you are a dear lover and I am proud of having won you."

"And I," I exclaimed, "am humble for the first time in my life—humble with the sense of a greater sweetness than I have deserved. Goodbye, darling, till tomorrow."

"You don't want to see my aunt?"

"No, no!" I said. "I want to keep the memory of you alone and relive every golden moment." Her eyes dwelt on me and she was gone, leaving with me deathless memories and pictures of exquisite loveliness that can never fade.

Why am I able to picture her now after thirty years? I forget nine out of every ten girls I have had in my life: why do I remember the tenth? For something extraordinary either in body or spirit, and Grace is memorable for both—the exquisite girlish figure, the bold self-abandonment, and the divine words of passionate affection! She taught me never to generalize Tennyson's statement in Locksley Hall:

> . . . All her passions matched with mine
> Are as moonlight unto sunlight, and as water unto wine.*

I don't need to tell in detail how I came to know Grace's aunt, Mrs. Sterling, more intimately. It began with her asking me to come to dinner with them and go afterwards to the Theatre Français. We dined at the Grand Hotel and went on to the theatre, and they were both amazed that I was able to go behind the scenes and visit the green room.

I held forth about Nice and its beauties till Mrs. Sterling said she would like to spend a month there, if I would play guide to them. I declared honestly enough that nothing would give me greater pleasure, and so a couple of days later we were all quartered in the Hotel d'Angleterre, which has since become the Hotel Ruhl, at Nice.

I managed that all our rooms should be communicating and I took the middle room, as I said, to protect them. About one o'clock the first night I entered the side-room where Grace was sleeping. I turned up the light, pulled down the bed-clothes and lifted up her chemise: she was ideally beautiful, and the little silky triangle in front deserved all my attention. Scarcely had I begun to kiss her when she awoke:

* . . . and all thy passion, matched with mine,
Are as moonlight unto sunlight, and as water unto wine—

"Frank," she whispered, "I was dreaming of you." In five minutes I had brought her to spasms of pleasure and as her lips were all creaming I threw off my pyjamas and went into her arms. I don't know why, but I never had more poignant sensations; already Grace was an incomparable mistress, taking delight in every movement that could increase the pleasure, and not afraid to take the initiative.

I studied her sex afterwards to find out if possible how she managed to give the ultimate pang of pleasure. Her sex was very small and well-made; the inner lips especially were tiny and used to glow very red with the excitement, but the magic lay in the passionate nature of the girl and her intense desire to do whatever I wished.

Next day I took them to Monte Carlo and showed them the casino and the gambling, but they both disliked the vice for very different reasons. "Greedy old women and nasty old men," said Grace, whereas the aunt noticed the favoritism of the *croupiers* and the *chefs de partie*. We drove home by La Turbie and the Upper Corniche, the famous road made by Augustus Caesar.

At dinner that night Mrs. Sterling let her foot rest against mine. Of course, I had already seen that she was pretty and well-made and still fresh; but forty never appealed to me like fourteen, and I had no wish to change Grace for her aunt. But what was I to do? That night, as I was getting into bed, Mrs. Sterling knocked lightly on my door. I put out the light and crept into bed and pretended to be sleeping. Again the tap, tap! I jumped out of bed. "Who's there?" I cried, while bolting the door into Grace's room, and then went over and half-opened the door into Mrs. Sterling's. She was standing with a dressing-gown about her, halfway between the door and her bed.

"Is there anything the matter?" I said.

"There are such strange noises in this hotel," she said. "Some one knocked at my door and I was scared and knocked at yours."

"First-rate!" I cried, putting my arms round her and kissing her. "You want me?" and I drew her to the bed. She shed her cloak and in a trice I had lifted up her nightie and put her on the bed. She had taken care of herself and had not let herself get too fat, but her figure was nothing like so lovely as that of Grace. Still I had to win her, so I stooped at once to conquer and began kissing her sex. In two minutes she had come three or four times with a hundred "ohs" and "ahs" and sobbing exclamations. "Did your husband ever kiss you there?" I asked.

"Never, never," she said. "He used to have me, but he had always finished before I really began to feel: now you excite me dreadfully and give me intense pleasure besides. Was he right, I wonder—my husband, I mean. He used to say that tall women were so much better than short ones because they were smaller there; do you think it true?"

"I don't really know," I said. "I'm afraid that I don't believe in any general rule."

"But do you like me a little?" she asked. "I know you like Grace; but she's too young, don't you think? Love is only understood in maturity."

What could I say? For answer I began kissing her again and again and when she was fully wound up, I put my sex in and found that she was quite a good performer at the game. But she wearied me as well with her passion as with her praise. She told me she hoped I would stay with her always, and when I said that I'd soon have to be getting back to London to go on with my journalistic work, she begged me to leave it; she was rich, why need I work? She hoped for a child by me: she had always wanted a child—and a deluge of similar hopes and desires.

A length I returned to my room thoroughly disillusioned, and scarcely had I bolted her door and got into bed when I heard a timid "tap" from Grace's side. I hurried over and opened her door. "You were not coming?" she pouted.

"I thought you were tired and sleepy," I said, "but I am glad you tapped." and I carried her to the bed.

Grace was already a wonderful lover. From the beginning she set herself to give one all the pleasure possible and was bold in asking whether this maneuver or that response had been most successful. Accordingly her progress in the art was astoundingly rapid. Already she was such a perfect bedfellow as one only finds twice or thrice in a lifetime. I know that whoever she married later would esteem himself fortunate, and the more experienced he was, the higher he would prize her. The women who complain of their husbands are, I have always found, those who do not know how to heighten delight to ecstasy.

A month later I had a telegram calling me back to London, but I met Grace again later, as I shall tell perhaps in due course. All I can say now is that no one ever had a more perfect mistress than Grace!

Chapter XI

Parnell and Gladstone

IN APRIL, 1886, Mr. Gladstone brought in his Home Rule Bill. The House was so thronged that members sat about on the steps leading up from the floor, and even on the arms of the benches and on each other's knees, while I had to give up my usual seat in the small compartment on the floor of the chamber and be content with a place in the first row of the Distinguished Strangers' Gallery. Herbert Bismarck sat on my left and the Marquis of Breteuil* on my right, yet the visitors that night were so world famous that these men were not even mentioned in next day's papers. Not a seat was vacant in any of the galleries; even that of peers was crammed; every diplomat in London seemed to be present; and cheek by jowl with the black uniform of bishops, Indian princes by the dozen blazing with diamonds, lent a rich Oriental color to the scene.

I had heard Mr. Gladstone often before, and especially on the war in the Sudan a few years earlier, when he had risen, I thought, to great heights, but this performance of the Old Man was none the less remarkable. His head was like that of an old eagle—luminous eyes, rapacious beak and bony jaws; his high white collar seemed to cut off his head of a bird of prey from the thin, small figure in conventional, black evening dress. His voice was a high, clear tenor; his gestures rare, but well chosen; his utterance as fluid as water; but now and then he became strangely impressive through some dramatic pause and slower enunciation, which emphasized, so to say, the choice and music of the rhythmic words.

Though I did not believe in him at all and was, indeed, repelled by the conventional Christian sentimentality he poured out on us when deeply moved, I could not but admit that the old man was singularly eloquent and the best specimen of the Greek rhetor of modern times. Everyone knew that his proposals were a mere resultant of a dozen opposing forces, yet he seemed so passionately sincere and earnest that time and again you might have thought that he was expounding God's law, conveyed to him on Sinai.

* (1848–19 ?), later a Boulangist.

He was a great actor, and as Mr. Foster* once said, could persuade himself of anything and the House of Commons of tragic absurdities.

Herbert Bismarck, a giant of thirty perhaps, with a long Viking-fair moustache and blue eyes, declared at the end that he had never heard so great a speech. And the effect was prodigious; for five minutes the whole House cheered and the people in the galleries sat spell-bound.

A few nights later, Parnell spoke; the House was nothing like full; the galleries more than half empty; the Indian dignitaries conspicuous by their absence; not a bishop nor archbishop to be seen; yet to me the scene was more impressive. There he stood, a tall, thin, erect figure; no reporter had ever said that he was handsome; yet, to my astonishment, he was by far the handsomest man I ever saw in the House of Commons—magnificently good-looking. Just forty years of age, his beard was beginning to grey, but what drew one was the noble profile, the great height, and the strange, blazing eyes in the thin, white face. I could not account for the effect of heat and light in his eyes, till later I noticed that the dark hazel of them was dotted, so to speak, with golden pin heads that in excitement seemed to blaze; the finest eyes that I have ever seen in a human head, except the eyes of Richard Burton.

He began amid Irish cheers, but very quietly in his ordinary voice. I soon noticed that the hands holding his coat were so tense that the knuckles went white; he hadn't a single oratorical trick; he spoke quite naturally, but slowly, as if seeking his words, and soon I began to feel that words to this man stood for deeds. When he spoke of the crimes and coercion of the previous five years, his words seemed to me those of some recording angel; the absence of inflection or passion gave the impression of immutable truth. I remember his very words: they were prophetic; they could be used for the events of thirty years later:

> You have had during these five years—I don't say this to inflame passion—you have had during these five years the suspension of the Habeas Corpus Act; you have had a thousand of your Irish fellow-subjects held in prison without specific charge, many of them for long periods of time, some of them for twenty months, without trial and without any intention of placing them upon trial (I think of all these thousand persons arrested under the Coercion Act of the late Mr. Foster scarcely a dozen were put on their trial); you have had the Arms Act; you have had the suspension of trial by jury—all during the last five years.
>
> You have authorized your police to enter the domicile of any citizen of your fellow subject in Ireland, at any hour of the day or night, and search any part of his domicile, even the beds of the women, without warrant. You have fined the innocent for offenses committed by the guilty; you have taken power to expel aliens from the country; you have revived the curfew law and the blood money of your Norman conquerors; you have manufactured new crimes and

* Either Myles Birket Foster (1825–1899), whose drawings were published in *Punch* and the *Illustrated London News,* or Sir Michael Foster (1836–1907), Liberal MP and professor of physiology at Cambridge. On the introduction by Gladstone of the Home Rule Bill, the second Foster joined the Liberal Unionists and voted with the Conservatives.

offenses, and applied fresh penalties unknown to your law for these crimes and offenses. All this you have done for five years, and all this and much more you will have to do again.

The chill atmosphere of hatred in which he had begun his speech had changed: a good many English members were listening now with all their ears. I felt very much as I had felt when drinking in Bismarck's great speech in the Reichstag five years before, that a great man was talking and the words were prophetic and the place sacred.

Then he spoke of Trevelyan* and himself and I thrilled.

Mr. Trevelyan has said that there is no half-way house between separation and the maintenance of law and order in Ireland by Imperial authority. I say, with just as much sincerity of belief and just as much experience as the right honorable gentleman, that in my judgment there is no half-way house between the concession of legislative autonomy to Ireland and the disenfranchisement of the country and her government as a Crown colony.**

That was the whole problem in a couple of phrases, and I was in no doubts as to who was in the right.

Yet when he sat down the cheering was purely Irish, and the Chief didn't even notice the enthusiasm of his followers.

One day, shortly before I got the editorship of the *Fortnightly Review*, I received a letter, from a man in Dublin, full of curious statements that greatly excited me. I answered him, and in the course of our correspondence I came to see that he was a mine of information about the Irish Party and their doings in Ireland. He stated quite boldly that the Irish Party was responsible for the murder of Lord Frederick Cavendish in Phoenix Park and for most of the subsequent deeds of violence in Ireland. He did not hesitate to implicate Parnell in this knowledge; and so I wrote to him, asking him to come over to London and spend a week with me. He had already told me that he was poor, so I sent him money and asked him to be my guest; and in due time Richard Pigott† came and stayed with me in my house in Kensington Gore.

The very first evening he told me how the knives which had been used in the Phoenix Park murder had been taken from the offices of the Irish Parliamentary Party in Westminster and brought across and distributed to the murderers in Dublin. I was quite willing to believe it all, and my manifest interest seemed to excite him, for he went on expanding the story in every direction. After two or three days I began to doubt him; and at the end of a week I knew that he was drawing on his imagination for his facts and was wholly untrustworthy. At the end I said that I would take the matter into

* Sir George Otto Trevelyan (1838–1928), Secretary for Ireland 1882–84, and noted biographer and historian.
** These quotations, which contain a few minor inaccuracies, are from the House of Commons Debate on the Government of Ireland Bill, June 7, 1886.
† (1828–89). He had in 1881 sold three extreme Irish nationalist papers to Parnell and his followers, when he was no longer trusted by the Fenians and Nationalists.

consideration and would let him know. I did let him know in a day or two that I would have nothing to do with publishing his stories.

A little later *The Times* began publishing its exposure of Parnell, and at length printed a letter purporting to be from Parnell, which plainly implicated him in the Phoenix Park murder. I got a facsimile made of it and reproduced the letter in the *Evening News*. Next day I was out riding to Richmond with Arthur Walter, the son of the owner of *The Times*. He told me, without circumlocution, how glad he was that I had published the letter.

"Why?" I asked. "I published it merely as a piece of news."

"Surely you wouldn't have published it," he said, "if you hadn't believed it."

"I don't believe a word of it," I cried. "I published it as news, on the authority of *The Times*."

"But it is plainly Parnell's handwriting," said Walter.

"In these days," I replied, "handwriting can be photographed and reproduced precisely; it is absurd to trust to similarity in handwriting to prove the authenticity of a letter."

I can't remember whether I told him then or a little later how I had come to know Pigott, but about this time he admitted to me that Pigott was the chief source of *The Times* information, and I warned him against the man.

All the world knows how Parnell brought his action against *The Times* and how Pigott broke down in the witness box and shortly afterwards shot himself in Madrid. But the hatred of Parnell was so pronounced in England that in due time his enemies induced O'Shea to begin his action for divorce and make Parnell the co-respondent. Parnell believed, and said openly, that the result of the case would be to show that he was not guilty of the grave accusation of having brought disunion between husband and wife: it was perfectly well known that the O'Sheas were practically separated before Parnell came upon the scene, but any weapon is good enough to beat a dog with, and so the dispute was given an exaggerated importance by the English press. Gladstone threw up his hands in holy horror and pretended to be shocked at Parnell's sin; I called Gladstone an "old hypocrite" and stated that on more than one occasion he had sent to Mrs. O'Shea for intimate information about Parnell and his views. In her book on Parnell and their mutual love, Mrs. O'Shea tells the plain truth.

For ten years Gladstone had known of the relations between Parnell and myself, and had taken full advantage of the facility this intimacy offered him in keeping in touch with the Irish leader. For ten years! But this was private knowledge. Now it was public knowledge, and an English statesman must always appear on the side of the angels.

So Mr. Gladstone found his religion could at last be useful to his country. Parnell felt no resentment towards Gladstone. He merely said to me, with his grave smile: "That old Spider has nearly all my flies in his web," and, to my indignation against Gladstone, he replied: "You don't make allowances for statecraft. He has the Nonconformist conscience to consider, and you know as well as I do he always loathed me. But these fools who throw me over at his bidding, make me a little sad."*

On the next page she tells of the traitorism of certain members of the Irish Party, when those who owed most to the great Chief turned most currishly against him. Mrs. O'Shea adds, "How long the Irish Party had known of the relations between Parnell and myself need not be here discussed. Some years before certain members of the party opened one of my letters to Parnell."

As I wrote at the time, this traitorism signed the death warrant of Irish Home Rule for a generation at least.

In December, 1890, a vacancy occurred in Kilkenny, and Parnell went over to support his nominee. Miss Katherine Tynan** gives a great picture of the scene before his speech in the rotunda at Dublin.

It was nearly eight-thirty when we heard the bands coming. Then the windows were lit up by the lurid glare of thousands of torches in the street outside. There was a distant roaring like the ocean. The great gathering within waited silently with expectation. Then the cheering began, and we craned our necks and looked on eagerly, and there was the tall, slender, distinguished figure of the Irish leader making its way across the platform. I don't think any words could do justice to his reception. The house rose at him; everywhere around there was a sea of passionate faces, loving, admiring, almost worshipping that silent, pale man. The cheering broke out again and again; there was no quelling it. Mr. Parnell bowed from side to side, sweeping the assemblage with his eagle glance. The people were fairly mad with excitement. I don't think anyone outside Ireland can understand what a charm Mr. Parnell has for the Irish heart; that wonderful personality of his, his proud bearing, his handsome strong face, the distinction of look which marks him more than anyone I have ever seen. All these are irresistible to the artistic Irish. . . .

I said to Dr. Kenny, who was standing by me, "He is the only quiet man here." "Outwardly," said the keen medical man, emphatically. Looking again, one saw the dilated nostrils, the flashing eyes, the passionate face.

When Mr. Parnell came to speak, the passion within him found vent. It was a wonderful speech; not one word of it for oratorical effect, but every word charged with a pregnant message to the people who were listening to him, and the millions who should read him. It was a long speech, lasting nearly an hour, but listened to with intense interest, punctuated by fierce cries against men whom this crisis has made odious, now and then marked in a pause by a deep-drawn moan of delight. It was a great speech—simple, direct, suave—with no device and no artificiality. Mr. Parnell said long ago, in a furious moment in the House of Commons, that he cared nothing for the opinion of the English people. One remembered it now, noting his passionate assurances to his own people, who loved him too well to ask him questions.†

I went across to Ireland for the Kilkenny election. Parnell was stopping in the hotel. In public he wore a bandage over his right eye, saying that

* From Katherine O'Shea's *Charles Stewart Parnell* (London, 1914), pp. 163 ff.
** (1861–1931), an Irish novelist.
† From *Twenty-five Years' Reminiscences* (London, 1913), p. 326. The passage is slightly abridged and contains minor inaccuracies.

some one had thrown quicklime in it and injured it. But when he received Harold Frederic and myself in the inn he had laid aside the bandage and his eye seemed altogether uninjured.

One incident took place then which I shall never forget. Frederic, the American journalist, was a great friend and loyal supporter of Parnell, and the chief therefore talked with us naturally and without pose. But I was shocked by the deep shadows under Parnell's eyes and a look of strain—I had almost said, of wild fear in his eyes. He had been through deep waters!

Suddenly, while we were chatting, there came some noise from outside, and before we could interfere Parnell had whipped outside the window and was standing on the balcony. A funeral was passing down the street in solemn silence. Everyone knows how seriously death is regarded in Ireland. Suddenly Parnell cried at the top of his voice: "There goes the corpse of Pope Hennessy," his opponent in the electoral struggle. In a minute some friends came and helped Frederic to drag him into the room, reminding him that he had forgotten his bandage, which he wore even a week later. The loss of self-control, so marked in so proud and masterful a man, made a deep impression on me. I told Frederic that night that Parnell had serious nerve trouble and would go mad soon if he didn't take care.

Fate was more merciful to him. He returned to his adoring wife at Brighton, but in spite of all her care and devotion, died in her arms in October, 1891, aged just 45. They had been lovers eleven years.

Parnell was a great character, if not a great intellect. But it was natural that England, which couldn't use the far greater man, Burton, couldn't use Charles Parnell. And the whole misery and disunion in Ireland today comes from this fact. Parnell ought to have been an English hero. His love for Mrs. O'Shea was the love of his whole life, and he gave himself to her with the same single-hearted devotion he had vowed in political life to the cause of Ireland.

Almost everyone took for granted that Gladstone was the greatest Englishman of his century, but in my heart I have always regarded him as negligible. His political achievements were merely parochial.

The insane misjudgment of Gladstone reminds me of a dinner I was asked to in London where Mr. Chauncey Depew* was to appear for the first time. Every one was agog to hear the man who came to London with the reputation of being the best after-dinner speaker in America.

After dinner Mr. Depew got up, heralded with fantastic praise and applause, and began a long series of platitudes punctuated with age-worn anecdotes, chestnuts familiar to me in boyhood. He went on interminably while the applause grew fainter and fainter. At length, I said to my *vis-à-vis*, a well-known judge, "Haven't you had enough of this?" He replied, "Enough for a life time," and we both got up and left the room.

* (1834–1928), president of the New York Central Railroad and then a member of the U.S. Senate from 1899–1911. He was defeated in his campaign in 1910 because his name was linked with insurance scandals.

Years later I told this to a young friend from New York, one Allan Dowling.* "I once heard Depew," he said, "in New York, say the most stupid thing conceivable. 'The greatest American I ever met,' he said, 'was undoubtedly Abraham Lincoln; the greatest man was William Gladstone!' " For monumental stupidity, the remark would be hard to beat.

When I told Lord Wolverton,** a great friend of mine, how Chamberlain had cast me off, and the *Fortnightly Review,* because of my views against Free Trade, he immediately proposed that I should see Gladstone and put him in Chamberlain's place. "Then," the banker said, "you can have whatever money you want, and I think you will have a much greater success with Gladstone behind you than you have had with Chamberlain." That I admitted at once. So it was arranged that I should go out to Combe and meet Gladstone and have a talk.

I went out in due course, but I was not impressed much with Gladstone's talk at the dinner. He held forth on every subject that came up, and talked well, but his eagle face and luminous eyes were finer than anything he said. He had read widely, I saw, but it seemed to me that he had thought very little for himself.

At the end of the dinner he went off with an Eton boy and played "Beggar My Neighbor." About ten o'clock the Eton boy went up to bed, and Gladstone came over to half a dozen of us standing in front of the fireplace.

"Did you get much out of the game?" asked his host, Lord Wolverton. "A great deal," said Gladstone. "The boy taught me that four knaves can beat the whole pack."

I could not resist the temptation. "Good God," I interjected, "I should have thought that your experience, Sir, would have shown that one knave was able to do that." He glowered at me and said nothing; he evidently took my jesting remark personally, though I had not so meant it.

Lord Wolverton told me, afterwards, that I had spoiled my chances with Gladstone. I said I thought I should survive, though I did not excuse myself for my foolish repartee.

A little while ago (I am writing in 1926), a Captain Peter Wright got into great trouble for stating that Gladstone was always running after women in the loosest way. The story of course was contradicted by his son, Herbert Gladstone, who is now Lord Gladstone; but Herbert Gladstone's denial should not be taken seriously.

It was common talk in the House of Commons that Gladstone was perpetually after women. It was said, too, that girls used to write him love letters, and that all such letters were brought to Mrs. Gladstone who, after reading them, tore them up, taking care that they shouldn't reach the Grand Old Man.

I distinctly remember Sir Charles Dilke telling me that Gladstone couldn't

* One of the owners of *Partisan Review.*
** (1864–1930).

oppose him because he was known to be still looser himself. But my belief in Gladstone's libertinism was better founded.

But why should I prove it now? An English jury has declared its belief in Mr. Gladstone's goodness: what more is wanted? An Irish M. P., too, Mr. T. P. O'Connor, has asserted that in his judgment Mr. Gladstone knew nothing about Parnell's intrigue with Mrs. O'Shea till the libel suit revealed it, though Mrs. O'Shea, in her book, has stated positively that Gladstone knew all about it years before the scandal. For good reasons I agree with Mrs. O'Shea, and can only regret that Mr. T. P. O'Connor's memory was so strangely subservient to English prejudice.

But, after all, what do the O'Connors matter when the Avorys* sit as judges? The height of the joke was reached when Mr. Justice Avory asserted, from his knowledge of English and Italian, that Lord Milner's** allusion to "Gladstone, as governed by his Seraglio," was quite innocent and conveyed "no hint that such a man was a gross sensualist." Pity that Mr. Justice Avory didn't strengthen his knowledge by a glance at Dr. Johnson's dictionary! Thanks to this judicial freak, Gladstone has received, in correct English fashion, plenary absolution, and thus hypocrisy is justified of its professors, and the sepulchre of English life has enjoyed a new coat of cheap whitewash.

I don't pretend that my opinion has any objective validity; yet, I give it in corroboration of Captain Wright's boldness. But I should never have quarreled with Gladstone without mentioning his judgments, which reveal the essential mediocrity of the man. His heroes were Washington and Burke; the most interesting modern statesmen to him were Lord Randolph Churchill and Parnell. His favorite country after Britain was naturally the United States. Even in his chosen field of words and literary art, all his judgings were mediocre. The modern author he placed highest was Sir Walter Scott; the greatest modern masters of English prose in his opinion were Ruskin and Cardinal Newman; the best biography was Lockhart's† *Life of Scott*. He thought Homer, Dante, Shakespeare, and Goethe the four greatest writers, but he omitted Cervantes altogether, and never seems to have heard of Turgenief. Fancy putting Newman as a writer of prose above Swift or Pater, and fancy a Prime Minister who could write a review article on the genius of Marie Bashkirtseff.††

* Horace Edward Avory (1851–1935).
** (1854–1925), High Commissioner for South Africa and Governor of the Cape Colony from 1879 until 1905. In 1915 he was made a member of the War Cabinet; in 1920 he became Colonial Secretary and headed a commission that advocated Egyptian independence.
† John Gibson Lockhart (1794–1854), a political writer for *Blackwood's*, a novelist, and a biographer. Notable chiefly for his multi-volume biography of Scott (1837–8).
†† Marie Constantinova Bashkirtseff (1860–1884). She began to study singing, but gave it up for painting, and she showed promise before she died of consumption. She is now best known for her *Journal de Marie Bashkirtseff*, published posthumously in 1890.

My quarrel with Gladstone was not so bad as another blunder which I must now relate. In due time I found that my knowledge of Pigott had had a great effect upon Arthur Walter. His father and Mr. MacDonald, the manager of *The Times* had been utterly misled by Pigott, whereas I had got to know him and had soon judged him rightly. The first consequence of *The Times* fiasco was that John Walter practically withdrew from the management of the paper and asked his son Arthur to take his place. Arthur, it seems, after my talk, had told his father that he thought Pigott absolutely untrustworthy. As soon as Arthur Walter got power on *The Times* he sent for me. He had gone down, I remember, to stay with Mrs. Walter at the Hotel Metropole in Brighton. I went down, took a room, put my belongings straight and then went up to him. I found him washing his hands before lunch.

"I sent for you," he said, "because I think now I can offer you the editorship of *The Times*. I believe you would do it greatly, but I wanted to know first of all what you think of Buckle, the present editor, and what you would do with him!"

"I would keep him on as political editor," I replied; "he seems to suit the conservative opinion that is the backbone of *The Times,* and I have so many new things to do that I don't want to make any break with the past that isn't absolutely necessary."

"That's fine of you!" said Arthur Walter, "I suppose you know that Buckle wouldn't give you any place?"

"No one, Walter," I replied, "can see above his own head, and so we must forgive Buckle, but I see little Mr. Buckle perfectly plainly, though he is about six feet high. My idea is to make a general headquarters staff to run *The Times;* to get picked editors on every great subject, a dozen at least, and then fifty contributing editors, the ablest men from every country in Europe."

"Good God," said Walter. "You frighten me; what would it cost?"

"I should give the foreign contributing editors," I said, "about two hundred pounds a year each on their promise immediately to answer by return any questions addressed to them; of course, we would pay for their contributions as well, and I would give the dozen editors in England one thousand pounds a year, plus the honor."

"Even that," he said, "would be an added expense of twenty or thirty thousand pounds a year: how would you cover the loss?"

"I would undertake for that single editorial page," I said, laughing, "to get three columns of advertisements in America and South Africa which would pay the twenty-five thousand pounds a year of new expenses three times over. I would make the leader page in *The Times* the greatest page that has ever been seen in journalism. Every line in it should be on the topmost level of thought! And I would add a financial column which would bring in more cash."

We went in to lunch and I told him more of my ideas, and he was greatly impressed, till I came to the declaration that I would make it a penny paper so as to get over a million circulation. "My father and MacDonald have gone into that," he said, "and they both declare it is absolutely impossible."

"That word shouldn't be in the vocabulary of *The Times*," I said.

But he went on seriously, "You have no idea how carefully they have gone into the whole matter, and it would turn all my father's grey hairs white if he thought that anybody was going to do such a thing."

"You can't afford," I said, "to leave the *Daily Telegraph* with a tenfold greater circulation than that of *The Times*. I assure you the penny paper is necessary, but I won't press it till the success of the other innovations has shown you that I am justified."

He shook his head and begged me to put the idea out of my head. Strange to say, I found that Mrs. Walter was with me in opinion. "If Mr. Harris could get a million circulation for *The Times*," she said, "surely all the advertisements would be immensely more valuable; and by making your own paper, as he says, you might get, if not such good paper as you have now, yet nearly as good at a cheaper rate."

Then for the first time I learned that the paper supply of *The Times* was in the hands of another branch of the family, and they wouldn't consent easily to any great change.

But I committed my great mistake when Walter began to talk of Oscar Wilde. "I hope," he said, "that you wouldn't employ him in any way on *The Times*." I replied that I didn't think he needed any journalistic employment: everything he did was eagerly bought up by the reviews and large publishers.

"I wonder that you go about with him," said Walter. "You are getting a bad name through it."

"Really," I said, "I never heard that his disease was catching. Genius is not infectious."

"In the last six months," Walter went on, "I have received hundreds of letters, signed and anonymous, talking about your connection with him and your perpetual defense of him."

This struck me as extraordinary. I had, then, no idea of the number of anonymous correspondents in London; I learned the vile effects of envy very slowly, for I never felt envious of any one in my life.

"I defend every able man I meet," I said carelessly; "they all have a hard time of it in life and it is a sort of duty to stick up for them."

"As long as you don't employ him," said Walter, "I don't mind, but I thought I ought to tell you that you could do nothing more unpopular than to defend him."

"I always defend my friends," I said.

Walter seemed a little shocked, a little pettish, too, I thought, not to say petty.

About a fortnight later, Walter told me that he had asked Moberly Bell,* their correspondent in Egypt, to come to London to help him. "I couldn't face your innovations, Harris, especially in regard to the price of the paper." I suppose I was too cocksure, and so frightened him.

I record my failures here as openly as my successes. If I had been a little more of a diplomatist I could have won Arthur Walter easily, for he had good brains and a good heart and only wanted the best. I have always blamed myself for my failure.

* (1847–1911). He became manager of *The Times* in 1890 and rapidly repaired the damage done it by its part in the Parnell Commission scandal.

Chapter XII

The *Fortnightly Review*

WHEN I LOST THE *Evening News* in 1887, I saw Arthur Walter on the matter, and soon afterwards had a talk with Frederic Chapman, of Chapman and Hall, publishers of the *Fortnightly Review*. Chapman had told me that Escott, the acting editor of the *Fortnightly Review,* had made trouble with *The Times* by giving them an article which he said was by Gladstone; and when they asked him for the proof, because Gladstone denied it, Escott pretended that he had never made the statement. In consequence, for some months, *The Times* refused to mention the *Fortnightly Review*. Chapman wanted to know if I were appointed editor, would this be made right; Arthur Walter assured him that it would.

I have already told how I came to know Arthur Walter of *The Times;* all through the years from 1885 to 1895 or '96, our intimacy continued. I used to stay with him at his country place near Finchampstead three or four times each summer, and during the winter we met at lunch or dinner once or twice every week. We often spent the evening playing chess: I used to let him win a fair proportion of the games, for success pleased him intensely. I often thought that in the same spirit Gattie, the amateur champion, used now and then to let me win, but not often, for his supremacy forbade it.

Arthur Walter was older than I was and was greatly surprised when he found I was a good Grecian: he himself had won first honors in Mods* at Oxford. He tested my scholarship, I remember, in all sorts of queer ways: for example, he once cited a phrase of Thucydides, which set forth that the whole world was the grave of famous men, and he liked my simple rendering. At another time he showed me the end of a chapter of Tacitus, in which the Roman historian says, *At this time, news came to Rome that fifty thousand Jews, men, women and children, had been put to death in the streets of Syracuse.* "His comment is *Vili damnum.* How do you translate it?" Arthur Walter wanted to know. "A cheap loss?"

"A good riddance," I proposed, and he was delighted. "The exact value," he declared.

---

* The first public examination at Oxford for the B.A. degree, which is conducted by the Moderators.

When Arthur Walter said that he thought me fit for any editorship, even for that of *The Times,* Chapman asked me to call upon him the next day and told me that I could take over the editorship of the *Fortnightly Review* whenever I pleased. Escott was ill at the time; he had broken down in health. I said I would take over the *Review* on condition that the first year's salary went to Escott, as I knew that he was not well off. This was arranged, and I was formally installed as editor of the *Fortnightly Review.*

Shortly afterwards Chapman told me that John Morley wished to see me, and in a minute or two brought him in. Morley had been editor of the *Review* for some fifteen years, was a link with the founders, Lewes* and George Eliot and Herbert Spencer. In popular opinion his editorship was summed up in the fact that he had always spelled God with a small "g." We chatted pleasantly for a few minutes, when he said, "You know, I feel very guilty. I have been, lately, too much of a politician and too little of an editor. In those two boxes over there," and he pointed to two large boxes in the corner of the room, "are the proof of my laziness. In this one," he pointed to one of them, "I put the articles which I didn't feel at all inclined to accept; in that other one, the articles which I could use at any time if I wished to."

At this time Morley must have been forty-five years of age; of spare figure, some five feet ten in height; clean-shaven, with large rudder-nose, firm drawn-in lips of habitual prudent self-restraint; thoughtful, cold grey eyes, large forehead—"A bleak face," I said to myself, seeking for some expressive word. Manifestly, I was not much to his taste. I was as frank and outspoken as he was reserved, and while he had already climbed a good way up the ladder, I thought nothing of the ladder and despised the climbing. Moreover, his gods were not my gods, and he was as unfeignedly proud of his Oxford training as I was contemptuous of all erudition.

It is very difficult, indeed, for men to measure the juniors who are taking their places. We can all see youthful shortcomings and promise is infinitely harder to estimate than performance. Perhaps we could judge them best through their admirations that are not learned or academic and, therefore, in so far original. Morley did not give himself the trouble to see me fairly. But, then, why should he? There were long odds against my being worth knowing, and he was courteous.

I remember he showed me an article with a Greek quotation in it. "I haven't corrected it, Mr. Harris," he said, "nor looked at the accents; I suppose you will do that," courteously giving me credit for sufficient knowledge.

I said something about accents being easy to me after having learned modern Greek in Athens.

"Really," he exclaimed, seemingly surprised, "that must have been an interesting experience. Hasn't the pronunciation changed with the changes in language?"

* George Henry Lewes (1817–1878), the first editor of the *Fortnightly Review.* He is best remembered for his intimacy with George Eliot.

"The scholars all try to pronounce in the old way," I replied. "Lots of professors and students today in the University of Athens plume themselves on speaking classic Greek."

"Astonishing," he exclaimed. "You must tell me about it some day. Very interesting." But the day never came, for if politics soon absorbed him, life and literature absorbed me.

I had been curious about Morley's editorship, and so I went through both boxes, returning nearly all the manuscripts to their owners and excusing myself as hardly responsible for the delay; but in the rejected box I came upon two papers which interested me. The one was by Mrs. Lynn Linton* on "The Modern Girl," which was charmingly written. Of course I wrote to Mrs. Lynn Linton about it, regretting the delay in dealing with it. She came to see me and we became friends at once. I ought to have known her previous work, but as a matter of fact, I didn't. She had married Linton, an engraver of real talent, and he had left her; and she developed a faculty of writing that put her in the front rank of the women of the day. She was kindly, and we remained friends for years, till I took up the habit of going abroad every winter and we gradually lost sight of each other.

The other manuscript which struck me as excellent had a curious title, "The Rediscovery of the Unique," signed by some one totally unknown to me—H. G. Wells! I have already told about it in a portrait of Wells,** and have told, too, of our later connection, when I got him to review stories for me on the *Saturday Review*.

Morley, by his rise to place and power as a politician, enables us to judge how much higher the standard of intellect is in literature than in politics. For Morley was in the first flight of politicians: Secretary for Ireland and afterwards for India, always a considerable figure, though he entered the arena late in life and without the wealth needed for supreme success. In literature, on the other hand, Morley never played a distinguished part. He could not even shine with reflected lustre. In vain he wrote the lives of Cobden and of Gladstone,† with all the advantages of intimate first-hand knowledge and all the assistance gladly proffered by the family and by distinguished contemporaries. His work remains fruitless, academic, jejune, divorced from life, unillumined by genius, unconsecrated by art. A bleak face and a bleak mind!

The truth is, the politician, like the banker or barrister, has only to surpass his living competitors, the best in the day and hour, in order to win supremacy. We cannot compare the Gladstones closely with the Cannings, any more than we can compare the Washingtons with the Lincolns. Men of letters and artists, however, fall into a far higher and more severe competition. Shaw writes a play, Kipling a short story: they easily outstrip most of

---

* Mrs. Eliza Lynn Linton (1822–1898), novelist and journalist. Her "Girls of the Period" articles from the *Saturday Review* were collected and published in 1883.

** In *Contemporary Portraits, Third Series.*

† Of Cobden in 1881, and of Gladstone, four volumes in 1903.

their contemporaries; but Shaw's best play is at once compared with the best of Molière or Shakespeare or Ibsen, and Kipling has to stand comparison with the best of Turgenief or Maupassant, the greatest, not of a generation, but of all time.

Exposed to this higher test as man of letters, Morley failed utterly, in spite of his success as a politician.

Yet it is understood that his life had noble elements in it. His character was much finer than his mind, and he was trusted and esteemed by his political associates in singular measure, in spite of a certain doctrinaire strain of pedantry and outspokenness. Had it not been for his learning, of which they stood in awe, his fellow ministers would probably have called him "Honest John."

When I took over the *Fortnightly Review,* Chapman and Hall were to pay me five hundred pounds a year for editing it and ten per cent of the net profits. If I doubled the circulation, I was to get fifteen per cent of the net profits. I told Chapman I should double the circulation in the first year, and practically did it, but I took nothing out of the *Fortnightly Review.* I used to spend all my salary in paying the contributors more highly, especially the contributors of poetry. It had been customary to pay not more than two pounds a page for any poem, but I gave Matthew Arnold, and Swinburne, too, twenty-five pounds a page, which came out of my salary.

As editor of the *Fortnightly,* I found it very easy at first to get on with Frederic Chapman, but his directors were for the most part stupid, brainless business men. I remember when I wrote my first stories, *Montes the Matador* and *The Modern Idyll*; I brought them to Chapman and asked him to read them. He read them and said they were all right, but when I published *The Modern Idyll* in the *Review,* there was a huge to-do in the press. The *Spectator* condemned the story, passionately. I thought it was Hutton, the chief owner, with his high church prejudices, that had condemned it, but when I went and called upon him, I found it was his partner, Townsend, an utter atheist, who had played critic. He told me he thought the story terrible. A nonconformist dignitary, the Reverend Newman Hall,* I think, wrote, condemning the story root and branch and making a great fuss about it. The end of it was that the directors of the *Fortnightly Review* met together and asked me not to insert any more of my stories in the *Review.* At once I tore up my agreement with them and told them to find another editor as soon as they could.

At the same time Frederic Chapman told Meredith, who was then the reader of novels for Chapman and Hall, of the way the directors had condemned me, and Meredith came up to London to protest. I met him for the first time in Chapman's office—to me a most memorable experience. He was one of the handsomest men I have ever seen, a little above middle height, spare and nervous; a splendid head, all framed in silver hair; but

* Reverend Christopher Newman Hall (1816–1902). Actually, he was a Congregationalist minister.

perhaps because he was very deaf himself, he used to speak very loudly. "We mustn't allow these directors to stand in our light," he cried. "I will talk to them and tell them they have never had as good a story in the *Fortnightly Review* as *Montes*." And he did talk to them to some purpose, for they withdrew their condemnation of my stories and begged me to reconsider my resignation, which I did.

A few months after I had taken over the *Review* I had a dispute with Henry James, which may be worth recording here. Between 1890 and 1905 I used to meet him in London from time to time. I think it was Lady Brooke* of Sarawak who first introduced me to him at a garden party. The Ranee was one of his most devoted admirers; she had a peculiar sense of certain literary values, or perhaps I should say, of certain men of letters. To me James was only a name; I had read none of his works, except some essays or travel-sketches in France, which were mildly interesting to me by virtue of the subject, though commonplace enough in treatment. The book reminded me of a couple of Tauchnitz volumes of sketches in Italy by W. Dean Howells, and ever afterwards I coupled the two men in my mind as absolutely negligible.

I do not attempt to put forth this summary judgment as fair criticism or even as a considered opinion; I give it merely as an instance of my off-hand rejection of any values in literature that did not strike me as of the highest.

Henry James almost immediately confirmed my somewhat contemptuous opinion of his intelligence by praising my predecessor on the *Fortnightly Review* excessively.

"It must have been a privilege," he said, "to follow such an editor. I regard Mr. Morley and Leslie Stephen** as about the first men of letters in England. You agree with me, don't you?"

"Indeed I don't," I cried. "What! With Browning, Swinburne, Tennyson and Arnold living, to say nothing of Meredith?"

"Of course," he broke in, "these poets come first; but I meant to speak of prose writers; men whom the French would call 'men of letters.' "

"It's ridiculous," I persisted, "even to mention such men as Morley and Stephen in the front rank; they are nothing but academic mediocrities; neither of them has ever written a word that can live."

"I'm afraid I cannot agree with you," he rejoined, with courteous distaste.

"Only creative artists are in the front class," I insisted; "Morley and Stephen are only hodmen and incapable of conception."

After this James appeared to avoid me and I had no desire to push the acquaintance. Neither his appearance nor personality attracted me: he was above middle height and inclined to stoutness; a heavy face, the outlines

---

* Wife of Sir Charles Anthony Brooke, 2nd Raja of Sarawak (1829–1917). Her maiden name was Margaret Lili de Wendt.

** (1832–1904), father of Virginia Woolf. He was the first editor of the Dictionary of National Biography, as well as the editor of *Cornhill's*.

obscured by fat; the eyes medium-sized windows, rather observant, perhaps, than reflective; the voice colorless, conventional; manners also conventional. James was always well-dressed, too, in a conventional way. I remember thinking afterwards with some insolence that his well-formed, prominent, rather Jewish-looking nose was the true index of his character. The rudder of the face, I always call the nose; and in James's make-up there was manifestly more steering-power of control than motive power of passion or enthusiasm; not a man to interest me in any degree.

James's so-called obscurity was never an offence to me; indeed, this charge against an author is invariably a spur. After forcing myself once to read and understand Kant, I profess to be able to find a meaning in any book where there is a meaning to be found, and so I set myself to unravel several of James's obscurities. The knots were soon loosed, but alas! I had nothing for my pains. "Much ado about nothing," I said to myself, and tossed the book aside, never again to be re-opened.

The admirers of James, too, I soon discovered, were all people of no importance as judges of literature; would-be geniuses, for the most part, or society women. Consequently, he was soon definitely classed in my estimation—another Howells without a trace of talent, devoted to the painting of commonplace Americans with painstaking industry. But I was fated to be disturbed in this comfortable belief.

One day Max Beerbohm lunched with us and afterwards we went for a walk in Richmond Park. Of a sudden he mentioned a book of Henry James and asked me had I read it.

"Thank God," I replied, "I have always something better to do than waste my time on James."

"You're mistaken, I think," said Max. "He's interesting to me, gets effects through those elaborate sentences that you could hardly get otherwise."

"You don't mean there is any real worth in him," I exclaimed. "I can't believe it; but if you say so, I'll have another look at him. What books of his do you like especially?"

Max mentioned two; I've forgotten what they were; even his praise could not overcome my settled distaste and repugnance. Nevertheless, his opinion remained with me and I record it willingly, though it could never alter my feeling that the man who admires the hodmen cannot be among the masters.

One day someone sent me a thin book of James's, begging me to read it and to give some account of what he thought a master-work. Mindful of Max's appreciation, I sat down and swallowed the draught. It was a story of two children, a little boy and girl, who had been corrupted, if I remember aright, by some teacher or governess. They were a foul pair, carefully presented: lifelike, but not alive, a study in child viciousness—worse than worthless, because not even natural. I never read another line of Henry James.

But one evening I met him, sat opposite to him, indeed, at some big public dinner. After the first greeting I paid no attention to him and talked chiefly to a man at my side, who showed some liking for letters. I don't know how it came about, but the talk fell on Sainte-Beuve. My acquaintance took him for granted as a great critic.

"Not a critic of any value," I declared, "a more over-rated man it would be difficult to find."

"How do you account for it," asked Henry James across the table, "that Arnold and others speak of his judgments with such respect. Who would you put above him as a critic?"

"All the creators," I replied, "but of course Goethe and Balzac, the only critics I take any interest in."

"I never heard Sainte-Beuve run down before," retorted James; "the French writers all admire him."

"I beg your pardon," I replied. "Balzac called him 'Sainte-Beuve le petit,' and as the 'petty Sainte-Beuve' he's destined to be known. The honor of a critic is to pick out the great men among his contemporaries and help them to recognition and to fame. What did Sainte-Beuve do? He denied genius to Victor Hugo and told Balzac that the flood of impurities in his books turned them into sewers; of *La Cousine Bette,* he said, 'Those infamous Marneffes infect the whole work with mephitic odors.' Flaubert he compared with Eugène Sue* and declared that it was a pity he could not write as well as George Sand! The Goncourts, too, and Théophile Gautier and Baudelaire he always disfavored and depreciated. All the great ones of his day came under his ban. The truth is, he was a small man and could only judge fairly those smaller than himself; no one can see above his own head."

"That's *your* judgment," exclaimed James rather rudely.

"Mine today," I shot back, "but everyone's tomorrow. Truth makes converts." In this year, 1926, Sainte-Beuve's posthumous work, *Mes Poisons,* has appeared, fifty years after his death, and even his French admirers have been shocked by his venomous misjudgings.

After Meredith had come to my aid on the *Review,* everything went on merrily for a long time. I thought more of Meredith than a dozen Jameses.

Five or six years later London, and Paris, too, were shocked by bombs thrown in Paris by Henri and Ravachol** I published in the *Fortnightly Review* a personal article on both men, from a friend, praising Henri as one of the sweetest and noblest of human beings. Chapman told me that

---

* (1804–57). A French writer of popular novels.
** Both were anarchists. Ravachol threw bombs at the houses of magistrates who had sentenced persons involved in workingmen's riots near Paris in May, 1891. Emile Henry was a young intellectual who killed eight people with his bombs. They were convicted in 1894, and Henry was sent to the guillotine.

In the *Fortnightly Review* of September 1, 1894, there appeared an article, "Some Anarchist Portraits," by Charles Malato, which treated Henri and Ravachol, among others.

he was shocked, and I became aware about the same time that Oswald Crawfurd,* who had been in the English Embassy at Lisbon, and had now returned and become a great man, was intriguing against me. But I had doubled the circulation of the *Review,* and Walter and others admitted that I was editing it very ably; consequently, I had no fear of my position.

Chapman had become a little difficult to work with. He was naturally a conservative businessman of the old-fashioned English type. He hated poetry and thought it should be paid for at the ordinary rates. When he found that I was giving my salary in payment to his contributors, I fell in his esteem. To give Swinburne fifty pounds for a poem seemed to him monstrous; and when I bought certain articles dearly, he wouldn't have them at any price. And if he disliked art and literature, he hated the social movement of the time with a hatred peculiarly English; he looked upon a socialist as a sort of low thief, and pictured a communist as one who had his hand always in his neighbor's pocket. My defense of Henri and Ravachol shocked him to the soul. And without Chapman's sympathy, I couldn't make of the *Review* what I wanted to make of it. Chapman wouldn't have Davidson's *Ballad of a Nun;* he cut it out of the number when he saw it in proof, though it was paid for; and Bernard Shaw was anathema to him. Gradually, as I grew, my position as editor of the *Fortnightly* became less pleasant to me. I was like a boy whose growth was being hindered by too narrow garments.

One day Chapman wanted to know why I had never asked for the ten per cent arrears of profits that had accumulated for five or six years or more. I told him I did not care anything about the money; he told me the directors thought there should be a settlement and asked me what I would take? I said, "If it is to get rid of me, you must pay me in full. If you are satisfied with me, give me anything you like, I do not care. I am not doing the *Fortnightly Review* for the money." Accordingly, he offered me, I think, about one-third of what I was entitled to, some five hundred pounds, telling me that he had no intention of getting rid of me. I accepted his offer, gave him a full quittance, and two months later the directors gave me notice: at the end of six months they would get another editor. I was shocked! I soon found out that Crawfurd expected to be made editor. I met him one day in the office and told him point blank that if he were appointed editor, I would expose the whole intrigue, and would show how I had been cheated of a thousand pounds. "I do not care who succeeds me in the editorship," I said, "but you shall not profit by the traitorism," and I told Chapman the same thing.

I had never had such a blow in my life. I had never lost a position before that I cared to keep, and at first I was overwhelmed at the idea of being supplanted on the *Fortnightly.* I went up the river to Maidenhead for a sort

* (1834–1909), consul at Oporto, not Lisbon, from 1867 until 1891; he wrote poetry, essays and novels, all quite undistinguished.

of holiday that summer but could not take my thoughts off my humiliation. I had sleepless nights and days of misery and regret. I was really making myself ill and had come to the brink of a nervous breakdown when Willie Grenfell, now Lord Desborough, without knowing of my trouble, took pity on me and began giving me lessons in punting. His companionship and kindness lifted me out of the slough of despond and postponed the evil day.

This was the occasion of my first meeting with Stead,* the famous editor of the *Pall Mall Gazette*. He had recently founded the *Review of Reviews*. He asked me to call on him and wanted to know the reason of my leaving the *Fortnightly*. I told him the facts on his promising to say nothing special about Oswald Crawfurd, who had practically dispossessed me. He promised, and two or three days afterwards sent me an article detailing everything I had said and more. I refused to allow it to appear, and he finally inserted a colorless statement.

Stead was an extraordinary specimen of the lower middle-class type of Englishman—without classical education, without any understanding of any other language or people, save his own. He had a great energy, however, and a very complete realization of all the forces in England, particularly the forces of religious prudishness and nonconformity. In the *Pall Mall Gazette* he got up a crusade against the lust of what he called "The Modern Babylon," and by silly exaggeration managed to get himself into prison for six or eight weeks. He fell foul, too, of Sir Charles Dilke; declared that any one who was unfaithful to his wife was not fit to be in the House of Commons. Of course, I took up arms against him on this point and asserted that Dilke was one of the ablest of our politicians. I wanted to know why Stead would deprive England of his undoubted public services in order to drive him into private life, where he had failed quite lamentably. But Stead stuck to his cursing and got all the powers of nonconformity on his side in order to hound Dilke out of public life.

One incident is so illustrative of English public life and of the effect of ignorant democratic opinion upon even the most eminent statesman, that I must tell it here. Dilke came to see me one day and told me that in the beginning of the row over the divorce suit, he had written to Gladstone, putting himself absolutely in his hands: "If you think it would be good for the Party," he wrote, "I'll give up Parliament and political life altogether; tell me your real wishes and I assure you now, I will honor them."

"Gladstone," he said, "wrote me in reply a most charming letter, saying that he would be very sorry to lose my great ability and that he didn't think, as a leader of the Party, he had any right to play censor of morals. 'At all times,' he added, 'I am proud of your support.' "

A little later Stead got a crowd of women to go to Gladstone and petition him to get rid of Dilke. Thereupon the Great Old Man wrote to Dilke,

---

* (1849–1912). He was imprisoned in 1885 for his attacks on the policy of the government toward white slavery. He was lost on the *Titanic*.

asking him to return his letter, and Dilke told me that he was going to return it.

"If you do," I said, "you will be slung overboard; please say that you value it so much that you couldn't possibly return it, but send him a copy of it."

Gladstone's next reply to the wild women was astonishingly characteristic.

I have lost my notes of it, but I remember high platitudes and his significant refusal to take any action against a colleague; but if Gladstone had had his letter back, I think the G. O. M. would have thrown Dilke to the wolves.

In my mind, I have always compared Stead in England with Bryan in America, and I was rather relieved when he went down in some shipwreck and we were rid of him—just as I was glad that Bryan died during the Dayton trial, a disgrace to American civilization.

There is one bright spot in my memory of Stead: I was talking once to Mrs. Frankau* about him, who was one of the wittiest women in London, and one of the most charming. She told me, laughingly, how she had made up to Stead and encouraged him, till one day he fell on his knees before her and put his arms round her, and she said to herself: "At last!"—when he suddenly told her that he was going to pray that she might always be faithful to her husband. I laughed till I cried at the unexpected foolish appeal.

Stead was regarded in English journalism as a great power for good, though in reality he was an influence from the dark, backward of time and short-sighted in his jingoism, as will appear when I come to the Jameson raid and his persistent defence of Rhodes.

But now I was all at a loose end and suffering for the first time in my life with nerves. I often sat in the corner and cried. I was unable to control myself, could not get better, and was very near an absolute breakdown. And the fatal day when I should be out of work was coming nearer and nearer. Sometimes I began to feel that I should go out of my mind. Neither the exercise in the open air with Willie Grenfell, nor the regular quiet life did me any good. At last, almost in despair, I left Maidenhead and returned to London.

A trifling incident here may be of some value to neuropaths. I had been working hard all the time and late one night had to go home by train. I drove to Waterloo; the porter opened the door to me and I got into the usual carriage. I hadn't asked him whether it was my train or not, but I wanted to ask him, and suddenly found that I couldn't remember my station—blank fear came upon me and the dreadful apprehension washed out all memory. I couldn't even recall my own name: for one moment I was falling into the abyss of despair—without memory life would be impossible!

---

* Julia Frankau, who wrote under the pseudonym, Frank Danby.

I resolved to sleep and settled down in my corner. Just as the train started a man jumped in. "Is this the Richmond train?" he asked. "I was told it was; but I am uncertain."

"Ask the porter," I barked, "and leave me alone."

"Good God!" he cried, and at the next station left the train, evidently thinking he was in the carriage with a madman. This amusement gave me sleep, I think, for I woke up three stations beyond mine; at Richmond I got out and found a cab and told the driver to drive me back to Putney and ring the bell and deposit me at my door and I would pay him double. I curled up in the corner of the cab and fell asleep again, and when I reached my home I was in my right senses with my memory back again; but the fear has always been with me since. Sleep is the best nerve sedative.

For some time nothing seemed to do me any good, but soon an unexpected change came in my fortunes, which had the most salutary influence on my health. I shall tell all about it in another chapter.

It was just when I lost the *Fortnightly,* in the middle of 1895, that the tragedy of Oscar Wilde came to a head.

I have already told the story in my *Life of Wilde* as carefully as I could and in full possession of the facts and notes taken at the time. Bernard Shaw has said that at a lunch with Oscar, at which he was present at the Cafe Royal, I told Oscar the results of his trials beforehand with such astonishing accuracy that Shaw marveled at it later. I really think my years of journalism and the Dilke trial and my personal acquaintance with judges and politicians had taught me to know England and the dominant English opinion very intimately. Oscar, though bred and brought up in it, had no understanding of it at all. He always felt sure he would get off with a minimum sentence. I knew he would get the maximum penalty, and insult and contumely to boot, from the judge and the press. The whole of the English judicial system is loathsome to me in its barbarous harshness; but what I never understood until this trial was that the ordinary English gentleman would behave just as vilely as the judge. For some time before his trial, even Englishmen of a good class who had known him cut Wilde in public, and even before he was condemned, George Alexander* erased his name from the advertisements of his play, while still profiting by keeping the play on the stage. The hatred shown to Oscar Wilde taught me for the first time what Shakespeare meant when he spoke of this "all-hating world." Ladies and gentlemen are ashamed of showing reverence and affection in public, but none of them are ashamed of showing disdain, contempt, and hatred— the little human animal is always proud of exhibiting his worst side out of vanity.

I had no power on the *Fortnightly Review* when Oscar was condemned, and his trial took place just before I got the *Saturday Review,* so I had no organ at my command. I tried to write something suggesting a moderate

* (1858–1918), an actor and producer of Wilde's plays.

sentence, but I couldn't get the article taken anywhere. Here was a brilliant man, one of the best talkers in the world, who had given hundreds of people hours of delightful amusement, and yet everyone seemed glad to show contempt for him; and the judge who went out of his way to insult him was applauded on all hands.

I found out from Ruggles-Brise,* the head of the Prison Commission, that if I could get half a dozen literary men of position to pray the Home Secretary to make Oscar's imprisonment a little easier for him by allowing him to read and to have a light in his cell at night, the petition would be granted. I made the petition as colorless as possible and asked Meredith to sign it, but he would not. I could never understand why. Shaw, too, begged to be excused; but Meredith's refusal really shocked me because I had come to believe him one of the Immortals. But in truth everyone was down on Oscar in the most astonishing way.

A couple of incidents that occurred after he came out of prison, after he had purged his guilt by terrible sufferings, will illustrate just what I mean.

I was dining with Oscar Wilde as my guest at the Cafe Durand one night in Paris, when a certain English lord whom I knew came over to me with a smiling face; as soon as he saw my companion he stopped and exclaimed, "Good God!" and turned abruptly to the door and went out. I happened to be going up in the lift at the Ritz Hotel a day or two later when he came into the lift at the second floor; at once he greeted me saying: "I am so sorry for the other day, Harris, but when I saw whom you were with, I couldn't possibly speak to you: fancy going about with that man in public."

"I know," I said, "there are not many Immortals; I don't wonder you don't want to know them; but why not forget me, too; it would be better, don't you think?" and I turned away and began talking to the lift-man.

Worse still happened to us in Nice. I had taken Oscar to the old Cafe de La Regence and we were dining there when an Englishman came in with a lady. He stopped near the table and stared at Oscar, then took a seat at the next table behind us, saying in a loud voice to his companion:

"Do you know who that is, that infamous Oscar Wilde; fancy his showing himself in public."

Oscar's face blanched; I had already seen that a heavy glass pitcher of water was within the reach of my hand. If the man had said one word more, I would have smashed his face with the pitcher. I turned to him and said: "Your rudeness can be heard; any more of it and you'll be sorry. Now you had better go to another room." Fortunately, at that moment the manager came in, and I appealed to him; he knew me well and told the man he would not be served and asked him to leave the place. The pair had to go. Oscar was trembling from head to foot.

* Sir Evelyn John Ruggles-Brise (1857–1935), a noted prison reformer. He was against housing delinquents with hardened criminals and in 1901 set up Borstal Prison for boys.

"Good God, Frank," he cried, "how dreadful; why do they hate me so; what harm have I ever done them?"

"Think of a London fog," I replied; "it prevents them seeing clearly; don't bother about them: didn't Shakespeare call it this 'all-hating world'?"

Many years later I was to find out what the "all-hating world" could do to show its dislike of me!

Chapter XIII

Prize-Fighting

IN MY SECOND VOLUME I published a long account of the gluttony at the Lord Mayors' banquets in London, and especially of the bestial conduct of the most celebrated mayor that the city of London ever had—Sir Robert Fowler. In the last chapter of this volume I shall tell how the English objected to this and tried to get my books stopped in France through the police.

I have no wish to denigrate the English. When I returned to London in '80–'81, they were kindler to me than the Americans were when I went to New York with an established reputation in 1914. Many individual Englishmen, in the thirty-odd years I spent in London, became dear friends of mine: and one in especial—Ernest Beckett, Lord Grimthorpe—I shall have much to tell about later. He was the best friend, except Professor Smith of Lawrence, that I have met on this earthly pilgrimage, but some Englishmen and English women, too, are friends of mine to this hour. Still, I am resolved, as one of God's spies, to tell the exact truth about them as I see it.

I don't know how I became a member of the National Sporting Club, but I was always greatly interested in athletics. I may here say a word about perfect physical condition to convince the athlete that I know what I am talking about. From thirty to forty in London I had a professional to box with me for half an hour every morning. When I was perfectly fit, my hand used to strike before I consciously saw the opening: as soon as I saw the opening before I struck I knew I was out of condition. The unconscious action should be quicker than the conscious.

In the late eighties and early nineties, I went to the Sporting Club a couple of times a week. Just as I found that my idea of a good dinner was not shared by those who partook of the Lord Mayors' banquets, so I found that my idea of fair play was not that of the majority of the Sporting Club in London.

I remember well one evening in which two lightweights, boys apparently of twenty or twenty-three, were boxing. In the third or fourth round, one of them caught a heavy blow on the chin and staggered about the ring, grasping at the ropes, and missing them, fell down. The referee began the solemn:

"One—two—three—," but before the fatal ten had been announced, the boy had staggered to his feet, only immediately to be knocked down again. I happened to be sitting just below the judge. I got up in my excitement and said, "Oh, please, won't you stop the fight! He has no chance: he may be severely injured by the next blow; please stop it!"

"I have no right to," replied the judge; and a moment later the cry went up, "Knock him out, knock him out!" The victor struck the boy a heavy blow and laid him out on the floor for much more than the count of ten. I couldn't help crying out, "Disgraceful, shameless cruelty." A certain lord near me jumped up and cried, "I don't know you, Sir, and don't want to, but keep your opinions to yourself. We want to see a fight to a finish here and not to be interrupted in the middle by your childish opinions."

I could not help laughing: his indignation was so intense and so sincere. *"Vae victis,"* I said; " 'woe to the beaten, woe to the unsuccessful' should be the motto of Englishmen."

"And a damned good motto, too," exclaimed another man.

Evidently I was at variance with the feeling of the whole club. I spoke to the secretary and got him to take me outside and introduce me to the beaten boy. He was pretty badly hurt but full of courage.

"How did you come to get in the way of that blow on the chin?" I asked.

"I haven't had any work for some time," he said to me, "and I have to keep a mother and sister. I hadn't much to eat this last week so I looked upon this fight as a blessing: it would give me ten shillings even if I were beaten; and if I won I might get ten pounds out of it. If you haven't eaten anything for a couple of days," he went on, "you get light and swimmy-like in the head, and so I got it on the chin—a rare jolt; after that I didn't know much what happened till they helped me out here and gave me a whisky and soda. But now I am going off with ten bob and one of them will get me a beefsteak and then I shall feel better."

I was charmed by the boy's high-spirited pluck, so I said, "Take a ten pound note, too, and make up your mind that you will win the next fight by keeping your chin tucked into your chest: it isn't well to shove it out too much in the open."

"Thank you, Sir," he said laughing, "I'll do my best."

I give this incident simply to expose the dreadful cruelty of the average well-bred Englishman. There is a curious want of chivalry in them, and no compassion for the under-dog. I remember two remarkable incidents exemplifying this that may find a place here.

I was one of those who went down the Seine to see a battle on an island in the river between Sullivan and Charlie Mitchell. While they were putting up the ropes, both the combatants stripped off, and it seemed to me a thousand to one on Sullivan. He must have been five feet eleven in height and was superbly made: the very model of a prize-fighter, though he had become far too fat and had put on a veritable paunch; still the power of him took the breath. For years he had toured America, offering any one five hundred dollars who would stay in the ring with him four rounds; but now he was grown fat and scant of breath, like Hamlet.

Charlie Mitchell, whom I knew very well, was an excellent prize-fighter in what we would call today the light heavyweight division. He was about five feet six in height and very well made; was trained to the hour; and weighed one hundred and sixty pounds or one hundred and sixty-five against the two hundred that Sullivan weighed.

There had been a great deal of rain, and when the men had been in the ring for ten minutes, it was like a mud-puddle and as slippery as a butter-slide. All through the first rounds, Charlie Mitchell, assured of his superior condition, kept away, forcing Sullivan to run after him again and again round the ring. About the fourth round, Sullivan stopped; he was puffing and blowing like a grampus. "Say, Charlie," he bellowed in his deep voice, "is this a prize-fight or a foot-race?"

Everyone burst out laughing. Sullivan had spoken needlessly. In the next round before he got his wind, Charlie met him and had a set-to in the middle of the ring: he ended it by slipping Sullivan's right and hitting him viciously in the stomach with the left, and then, crossing to the chin with his right, knocked the big champion down. "It seems to me it is a prize-fight," said Mitchell coolly; but the heavy blow had taught Sullivan his lesson, and he fought more cautiously for the next half hour or so, till the referee said the fight was over as a draw.

It was curious to note how at once the English spectators changed their attitude and began to pay court to Mitchell.

On the way back to Paris everyone except myself seemed disgusted: the fight should have been fought to a finish, they said. What rot it was to spoil the day with a draw. We had seen some brilliant boxing, and I didn't think the day spoilt at all. It had taught me that Sullivan's day was over.

A little later when the news came through that he had been beaten by Jim Corbett at New Orleans in September, '92, I was not surprised. From all accounts, it was almost a replica of the fight which I had seen with Charlie Mitchell. The first rounds Corbett kept well out of reach, and the crowd jeered at him, while Sullivan kept calling out in his deep bass voice: "Come in and fight." About the third round Corbett went in to fight, and by the end of the fourth round it was seen that the great John Sullivan was beaten. How he ever lasted twenty-five rounds was a wonder! At the beginning of the twenty-first round, Sullivan made a last attempt to turn the tide and rushed at Corbett, but Corbett was too fast and managed to dodge nearly all his blows. This exertion of Sullivan was the last spurt: from that time on, Corbett kept hitting him as he pleased, and finally sent in a terrific right to the chin and Sullivan fell for the full count. On getting to his feet again, he staggered to the ropes, and said, "It is the old story: I am like the pitcher that went to the well once too often," and with the tears running down his face he added, "I have been beaten by a younger and better man, but I thank God he is an American."

John L. Sullivan was a remarkable character, for when he went home beaten and broken and met the treatment usually accorded in this world to the defeated, he gave up drinking and became a temperance lecturer. He made good, too, in this new role, and died fairly well off. In my poor opinion, with the solitary exception of Fitzsimmons, he was the best prize-fighter I have ever seen, and surely at his best, the best prize-fighter in the history of the ring.

Some time later I went to see Slavin fight Jim Smith at Bruges. At first I was in Smith's camp and welcomed his supporters in the hotel at Bruges. Squire Baird, as he was called, was the principal backer of Smith. He was a millionaire, the result of three generations of Scotch [sic] ironmasters. I thought him one of the worst specimens of mankind I had ever seen: foul-mouthed, illiterate; he bragged continuously, but the whole gang did him honor for his wealth.

Next day after some difficulties the ring was pitched and the fight began. The two men seemed fairly well matched: Slavin, a little taller and lighter, but trained to the hour; Smith, strongly made and a good boxer, but clearly suffering from years of good London living. In the first round or two, Slavin took all care, though not afraid to mix it; but after the third round, the fight went all one way; it ended by Slavin knocking Smith down, which surprised the whole crowd of Smith's backers, and most of all, Baird, who kept shouting insults at Slavin from Smith's corner.

Soon afterwards, the crowd of Smith's supporters, drawing the ropes loose, made the way to Smith's corner a sort of lane. Smith stood by his own chair awaiting Slavin's onslaught, and Slavin with rare courage went over to him. As he entered the lane, blows were showered upon him from Smith's supporters, but he nevertheless went through to Smith and knocked him down in his own corner.

The fight was over and ought to have been given to Slavin then and there, but Baird and his gang were not finished with [him]. They raised a cry of "Police" and dragged Smith out of the ring and began sponging him and attending to him, thus giving him time to recover, if recovery were possible. Slavin sat in his corner quietly waiting. When Smith came in again to the ring, Slavin again had to go over to his corner to fight him, and now one of Baird's gang used a knuckle duster, and as Slavin passed, struck him heavily on the ear, cutting him so that the blood poured down his neck and shoulders; but he went on to Smith's corner in spite of a hail of blows from the spectators, and again knocked Smith down. At this the referee, to the surprise of every one, gave the fight as a draw.

Turning to the referee, Slavin exclaimed: "I have come thirteen thousand miles to have a fair fight, and you give it as a draw when the man for three rounds hasn't dared to leave his corner. Look how his supporters hit me and treated me; why in the very first round he wrestled me and shoved his boot nails into my legs"—and he pulled up his short drawers and showed his bleeding thigh. "I didn't even protest," he went on, "I could beat the fellow with one hand. How dare you give it as a draw? There is only one man in the ring!"

The referee replied, "I did it to save you from the brutes on the other side."

"Nonsense," cried Slavin, "turn them all in; I'll take on the whole damned crew." Never was there more splendid Irish courage.

At a word from Baird, his crew ran round to Slavin's corner as if to attack him, but Slavin walked to his chair, paying no more attention to them than if they had been a pack of Sunday school children, and not one dared now to lay a hand on him.

Baird's money had queered the whole fight!

But even before Slavin had spoken, I had left Smith's side and gone across to Slavin's corner, and when Baird came to me afterwards, I took no notice of him and wouldn't speak to him.

I returned to the Sporting Club and told the story and insisted that Squire Baird should be turned out of the club as a disgrace, not only to English sport, but to humanity. And I believe he was turned out. A word of mine about him stuck, I believe: remembering he was a product of Scotch iron-masters and Puritans, I said that the iron had entered into his soul.

A little later a story went about London of his conduct to his mistress, a woman of good breeding, which did him no good. He had bought her, it appeared, and one night he came home with his usual set of drunken prize-fighters and cab-drivers; and when they were all drunk, he rang the bell and sent the maid up for Mrs. L——. The maid came down and said her mistress was in bed. Baird said, "If she doesn't come down, I will go up and fetch her down in her shift." Whereupon the lady had to come down and witness some of the drunken orgy. Next morning she packed up and told Baird she was going to leave him. He went out and in half an hour came back and tried in his rough way to get her to stay. When she wouldn't stay, he took a ball of paper out of his pocket and threw it at her face. She told him what a cur he was to strike a woman; he cried, "Look at it, you fool, before you talk." When she picked it up, she found the ball of paper was made of fifty notes for a thousand pounds each.

The story was told to me by one who had heard Baird tell it. A little later, I believe, Baird died, still a young man, but a dreadful specimen of the evil great wealth can work on a common nature!

A little later I was to meet a much better specimen of the prize-fighter than Slavin, certainly the best character I ever saw in the ring. One day news came to the Sporting Club that Peter Jackson, the colored man, was coming over to London and was spoiling for a fight. I heard from the secretary that Slavin was very eager to meet him, and accordingly they soon met.

I soon got to know Peter Jackson personally and liked his quiet and modest ways. I asked him one day who would win.

"It is a tricky game," he said, "but I don't intend to let Slavin beat me, if I can help it. He is rather a brute. You know I taught him boxing in Australia: one day something or other I said offended him, and he struck me in the face, and we had a set-to. They parted us pretty quickly. But I am not afraid of Slavin and I don't like him, and frankly I don't think he has any chance of beating me."

Charlie Mitchell sized up the fight clearly beforehand. "Slavin," he said, "is a real fighter, and if he starts in at once to mix it, he may get the better of Jackson; but if he boxes with him for the first rounds, he is sure to be beaten; Jackson is about the best boxer I have ever seen—a really fine performer, both in defense and in attack."

The fight bore out Mitchell's prediction to the letter. Slavin boxed the first three or four rounds, and Jackson outboxed him from beginning to end. About the fourth round, Slavin rushed in and struck Jackson heavily about the heart. The round was clearly Slavin's, but the bell saved Jackson.

When they came out again, Slavin tried the same rushing tactics, but Jackson avoided him and kept hitting him in the face and on the chin; and in this round Slavin palpably weakened. From that time on Jackson hit him almost as he wished, and the fight ended pretty quickly with Slavin's complete defeat.

Peter Jackson told me afterwards that the punch which he had got from Slavin over the heart was the heaviest he had ever had in his life.

The colored man, Peter Jackson, like Corbett, was very much of a gentleman: he told me he always hated to knock anyone out, and thought the referee should stop the fight when the complete superiority of one fighter was established. I have said nothing in these memoirs of mine about Corbett, but he was a splendid specimen, and I always believed that his defeat by Fitzsimmons, good as Fitzsimmons was, was due rather to a chance blow, which caught him on the spleen, than to any superiority. Still Fitzsimmons was a marvelous fighter; considering that he never weighed more than one hundred and sixty pounds, the most extraordinary fighter ever seen. It mustn't be forgotten, however, that he had a longer reach than most of the big ones, and blacksmith's fists at the end of enormous arms; he seemed to be built for the ring.

I should perhaps say one word here to explain certain defeats in the prize-ring that are not sufficiently understood. A young man—and prize-fighters should be very young—after training hard for some time and getting into perfect condition, is very apt to discontinue all exercise when the fight is over, and so put on a great deal of fat very quickly. He has been keeping himself fit by the most strenuous exercise, which has developed his appetite as well as his muscles. When he stops training, his appetite continues and immediately fat accumulates, and it accumulates not only round the intestines and abdomen, but round all the muscles, and especially round the main muscle of all, the heart.

It is comparatively easy to take off abdominal fat, but it is extremely difficult and extremely painful to take off fat that has accumulated round the heart. In fact, the moment a man begins seriously to train for this purpose, any prolonged exercise exhausts him and he feels very ill. The heart, lacking its accustomed support, sags, labors, and the man feels faint and sick. For a couple of months, at any rate, the athlete must go on exercising under a constant cloud of sickness and weakness that is apt to bring him to despair. But if he continues, the fat will come off and in a certain time, say six months, he will begin to feel fit and well and strong again, and increasingly fit and strong as time goes on; though in my opinion he will never be quite as good again as he was before the fat accumulated round the heart.

The case of Paget Tomlinson, the famous hurdler, occurs to me. A great natural runner, he had stopped exercising for a year or so, but was called out when Oxford and Cambridge had to meet Harvard and Yale; and though he was still, as he thought, very fit, the clock told him at the beginning of his training that he was nothing like so good as he had been a year or two before. But he trained as a man of brain does train, with perfect method and desperate resolution. He brought himself down to pounds less than he had ever been at the varsity, and persevered through the feeling of disease and sickness, but still the clock would not be conciliated. He got to within half a second of his best time, but could not improve it, and was beaten in the race some three yards by a younger man who had never been out of training.

Now, prize-fighting is a far severer test than a one-hundred-and-twenty yards' sprint over hurdles. How severe it is can be told in almost one sentence. Sharkey and Jeffries had a memorable fight of one hour. In that hour it was found that Sharkey had lost thirteen pounds and Jeffries eleven pounds and a half. These men were both trained to the hour before they went into the ring, and the loss of weight alone shows how tremendous the exertion and strain must have been.

The best way for the fighter, of course, is never to go out of training, strictly to limit what he drinks with his meals, and prevent himself ever going up more than a pound or two; but if he has put on weight, the best way of taking it off is not to go into physical training at once, but to begin by cutting out all drinking with his meals. Half an hour before a meal and two hours afterwards, he should drink nothing. In a month he will be lighter than he ever was, probably even than he was in his first training, and then he can begin by careful exercise and very careful feeding to increase his strength once more and get himself perfectly fit.

Perhaps I should say here too that unfortunately boxing has won such vogue in the last two or three decades that the influence of money has corrupted and degraded the prize-ring. No one can be a champion and be honest; it is almost unthinkable. Big money wants to bet on a certainty: a man cannot be as sure of winning as of losing; hence he will be a better instrument for making money on if he consents to lose than if he wanted to win. The fact is patent, obvious, corroborated by experience everywhere.

Is baseball honest? Is horse-racing honest? Ask a real prize-fighter: "Is prize-fighting honest?" and he'll laugh in your face.

I have only written these recollections of prize-fighters to justify my opinion that the prize-fight is an evil, and boxing one of the lowest forms of athletics. I am very sorry that the French and Germans have taken it up as they have, but fortunately, in the last thirty years, the French have taken up every form of athletics with passionate enthusiasm. I remember thirty years ago seeing some regiments drilling near Toulon; someone had put up a rail about two feet six in height for the men to run and jump over. It was perfectly comic to see how most of the soldiers jumped with both feet together. At the request of the colonel, I went over and showed them how they should jump the rail, taking it in their stride. Thirty years later the ordinary French boy has learned how to jump and how to run, too, while at cycling he is probably as good as any.

The worst evil of boxing came through its increased popularity. As soon as it was taken up in America, the quick Irish-Americans found out that two blows were likely to be decisive; the first blow is an upward stroke catching the chin, which produces a shock on the vertebrae and often results in partial paralysis; the other is the blow on the spleen, which is spoken of as the blow in the pit of the stomach; but when the spleen is really hit, it turns the man sick and he has very little strength for the next ten or fifteen minutes, in spite of perfect training.

I remember one boy in London who had learned the chin blow perfectly; he used always to mix it, at half-arm's length, at about the third round and take whatever punishment he got smiling; but would suddenly flash out either left or right with an upper cut to the chin, which, even if it didn't catch the spot perfectly, was usually sufficient to decide the fight.

It is this knowledge of the weak parts of our frame that has made prize-fighting so intolerably brutal. In my time at the National Sporting Club in London there were two or three old boxers who were still hangers-on at the club, whose heads were all knocked on one side, and faces distorted with partial paralysis, the dreadful debris of human savagery. Wrestling is a far better exercise than prize-fighting and far less likely to injure any of the contestants permanently.

I must not be taken to mean that brutality is chiefly or solely English and German; it is to be found also, though in a less degree, in France and the Latin countries, as well as in northern Europe. I remember once being horrified by seeing *Salammbô** on the films in France. I recalled that Flaubert represented the poor fellow being beaten almost to death by the crowd, including women. The whole brutal exhibition was put on before one with an intense realism, and the crowd delighted in the appalling exhibition. I left the theatre thinking it would take a thousand years to civilize a French crowd; and an Italian crowd is no better, and a Spanish crowd is just as bad.

---

* (1862), historical novel of Carthage by Flaubert, in which the leader of rebel mercenaries suffers a brutal death by running the gauntlet.

I am full of tolerance, I think, for all mortal weaknesses; I can easily forgive all the frailties of the flesh and all the sins of the spirit, with the sole exception of cruelty. Cruelty to man or beast, to rat or snake, seems to me the unforgivable sin, the one utterly loathsome and damnable crime that shows utter degradation, the devil in man.

Of course there are degrees even in this villainy; cruelty to animals adds cowardice to the diabolic.

In Rome once I stopped a peasant who was beating a horse unmercifully: and when I told him he ought to be ashamed of himself, he declared that he would beat the creature as he pleased because it had no soul; and this excuse was urged not once, but twenty times, in favor of sadic [sic] cruelties practiced on dogs and cats. Was it thoughtlessness or want of imagination or something brutal in man's nature? I often asked myself, but never found an answer.

During a winter spent in Spain I got to know and like the Premier, Canovas Del Castillo.* I made him a proposal which I thought interesting; that he should send twenty or thirty of the masterpieces of the Prado Gallery in Madrid to London for the season, especially a dozen paintings of Velasquez, who was then very little known in England. He said at once that if the British government would reciprocate he would do it willingly: the pictures could easily be sent by special train, or on a special warship, or in two or three parcels, so as to diminish the risk of loss. He agreed with me that the international effect of such an exchange could only be inspiring.

When I returned to England I saw Lord Salisbury on the matter, but to my astonishment he held up his hands and wouldn't hear of it, "I am glad I have no power," he said, "it isn't within the range of my duties. You would have to go to the trustees of the National Gallery in order to get the permission, and I don't think they would consent." I sounded one or two of them, but found they all wanted to shelter themselves behind the impossible.

I only mention the matter here because it was one of the many pleasant talks that made me appreciate the Spanish Premier's mind and character. Talking to him once about bull-fighting, to my astonishment he agreed with me that the killing of the horses was shamefully brutal and mere torture.

"Why not stop it?" I asked. "The play of the *chulos* at first and putting in the *banderillas* is extremely fine and interesting with just sufficient danger to make it enthralling; and the killing of the bull with a sword thrust is such an extraordinary feat that every one would wish to have seen it; but the lancers, who on horseback torture the bull to attack the poor old horses and tear them to pieces, constitute a dreadful exhibition."

Canovas finally declared that he would try to stop that part of bull-fighting; and he kept his word. Everyone remembers the result: the mob left the bull-ring hissing and shouting and went after the Premier, who had

* (1828–1897). He was assassinated by an anarchist.

to take refuge in the Royal Palace and then flee out of the back door and get away from Madrid. The thing the Spanish populace most loved was the horrible cruelty and torturing of the poor, broken-down horses.

Before leaving this chapter on prize-fighting and cruelty, I wish to record the most tragic story I have ever heard or read of. When one thinks of tragedy, one recalls unconsciously the tragedy of Socrates, or the still more terrible tragedy of Jesus on the Cross; but once many years ago, while spending a holiday in Venice, an old Venetian told me a story which seemed to me more terrible than these. I have often wanted to use it and have been afraid to, and with the passing of the years the memory became a little vague. But the other day I came across the tale again, told at full length and in its proper historical setting.

It belongs to the time of the five months' siege of Venice by the Austrians, half a century ago now. The story is already passing into oblivion, even among Venetians, but it surely deserves to be revived today. Here it is, word for word:

"The Venetian commanders determined to sever the single link with the mainland, and to blow up the two-and-a-half miles of uniform roading—the work of the oppressors—which bridged the lagoon.

"For some reason the mine did not explode; wherupon a certain Agostino Stefani volunteered to row out in his *sandolo* and set the matter right.

"General Cosenza accepted the bold offer, and in the face of a double fire from the forts of Malghera and San Giuliano, Agostino set out in his light craft.

"He accomplished his task unscathed, but on the return passage over the wide unsheltered stretch of water, the *sandolo* was hit and sunk.

"Agostino was a strong swimmer, but the current was against him, and when a patrol boat at length picked him up, he was exhausted beyond power of articulation.

"Excited crowds on the bank watched his rescue, and suddenly, 'A spy! A spy! A traitor!' was shouted. The reported capture of an Austrian was spread from mouth to mouth. Stones and execrations were hurled at the patrol boat, and suspicion seemed to fly with them and infect the crew, who threw the speechless man back into the water and struck at him with oars and stones. He sank just before General Cosenza's aide-de-camp proclaimed his identity and told of his heroic courage."

What he must have thought before he sank, poor Agostino, with shouts of *"Spione; spione; traditore!"* sounding in his ears!

The benefactor of his fellows—a brave soldier if ever there was one—murdered by those he had fought for, and murdered as a spy and a traitor—*"Spione! traditore!"* ringing as a curse in his death-agony.

Chapter XIV

Queen Victoria and Prince Edward

IT IS IMPOSSIBLE to paint a complete picture of my time without saying something about Queen Victoria and Prince Edward, afterwards King Edward VII. In the preceding volume I have given some personal anecdotes about him and described how his introduction of cigarette smoking after lunch and dinner, immediately the last course was finished, put an end to the custom of heavy drinking which had been usual till his advent. As soon as the upper classes stopped guzzling, the middle classes followed suit, and ever since the revenue from drink has diminished in Britain in curious proportion to the increase of population.

Prince Edward reaped only a small part of the benefit of this change. He had a reputation for loose living and no one wished to think of him as a reformer. Some few knew that he had all the social duties of a sovereign to perform and [a] state to keep up on a small income and with no real power.

It was Edward who changed the traditional policy of Great Britain, which was one of friendly alliance with Germany, into a policy of antagonism to Germany and alliance with France. He was the founder of the *Entente Cordiale* between England and France, and accordingly the first cause, so to speak, of the World War. But in order to exhibit this change of policy in its true light as a complete right-about-face, I must first speak of his mother, Queen Victoria, and describe her influence.

It is difficult to paint a pen portrait of Queen Victoria. First of all, it must be done chiefly from the outside, and secondly, she changed with the years in an astonishing degree. Lord Melbourne, the Prime Minister of her early life, the guide and mentor of her first decisions as a monarch—in fact, the man who trained her—always spoke of her as eminently teachable and docile.

After she married Albert of Saxe-Gotha,* she took her husband as mentor. Her early English education was swallowed up in a German education. She had learnt German as a girl; but now, out of passionate love for her husband, she spoke nothing but German in her home; read chiefly

* Saxe-Coburg and Gotha.

German; took her ideas from her husband; saw life and men through his eyes. She did not love him merely; she grew to idolize him.

A story is told of her early married life which illustrates her devotion. I cannot say how it originated or who was the authority for it; but it became a tradition, one of those stories which are truer than truth, symbol as well as fact.

The husband and wife did not agree about a certain policy. Victoria, still English, was backed up by the Minister whom she was accustomed to trust: at length she said gently to her husband:

"Don't let's argue, dear. I am Queen; I mean the responsibility is mine. You see, don't you?"

"Yes, I see," said Albert, and left the room quietly.

In half an hour she wanted him and was chilled to hear that he had gone out. In an hour she sent again; he was still out.

He did not appear at dinner, and the Queen could not even pretend to eat. Late in the evening she was told he had returned and she waited expectantly; but he kept to his apartment.

At length the Queen could stand it no longer. She went to his room; but the door was locked. She knocked and knocked.

"Albert, Albert!"

"What is it?"

"Oh, let me in; I want to come in."

"I'm sorry, but I've letters to write."

"Let me in, I say; you can do your letters later."

"I want to do them now; please leave me alone."

After begging and begging in vain, the Queen burst into tears.

"Oh, forgive me, I'm so unhappy. I can't bear to quarrel with you. I can't bear it."

That was the literal truth; she could not bear a momentary coldness in the man she worshiped. When two love, the one who loves the least is master; so the Queen became her husband's slave and echo.

Prince Albert's death widowed Victoria—maimed her. For years she found it impossible to take up life without him. Even her duty to her children and the Crown could not draw her from the absorbing anguish of grief; her very reason tottered, for her love was rooted in reverence. Albert was her divinity. To the very end of her life she bowed to his authority.

And when, after many years, she took up life again without him, she seemed changed to everyone. She met her English ministers and advisers from a different standpoint. She felt herself their superior. She not only knew the English view of matters, but also the German view, and this gave her a singular authority. Her confidence in herself, her dignity, her sense of her own importance grew with the years, till she became authoritative. In every difficulty she was accustomed to ask: "How would *he* have acted?" It is on record that on more than one occasion she left her minister and went over to a bust of her husband and asked the stone effigy what she was to do.

Such devotion did not seem ridiculous to her, for love is never contemptible. Besides, there was a great deal of common human nature in her, and it may be well to bring her ordinary qualities first into prominence.

Two stories that can both be vouched for throw, it seems to me, a high light on Queen Victoria's character.

She was a great friend of old Lady Hardwicke's,* and used often to go and have tea with her. Lord Hardwicke** told me once that as a boy he was very curious to know what the two old ladies talked about, and once listened at the door when the Queen was paying an unusually long visit.

It seems that they had sent for fresh tea for the second time, and the two old ladies had consumed an enormous quantity of muffins. They had been talking about their dead husbands, and when the Queen described how her beloved Albert had looked in his court dress when decked out with the Garter for the first time, she burst into tears. "He was so beautiful," she cried, "and had such an elegant shape," and Lady Hardwicke sobbed in sympathy.

"They cried in each other's arms," said he, "and went on crying and drinking tea while swapping stories of their dead husbands."

When the Queen got up she wiped her eyes. "My dear," she sobbed, "I have never enjoyed myself more in my life; a really delightful time—" and Lady Hardwicke mopped her eyes in unison.

"A really delightful time, dear."

When old age came upon her, bringing with it a certain measure of ill health through stoutness, she became irascible and impatient. As a girl even, she was far too broad for her height, and particularly short-necked. In her old age she was very stout, so stout that for ten years before she died, she had to be watched in her sleep continually by one of her women, for fear her head should roll on one side and she should choke, her neck was so short.

There was perpetual scandal in her late middle life about her relations with her Scotch gillie and body servant, John Brown. Even among the officers of her court, there were some who believed in her intimacy with the servant; while there were others equally well informed who would not harbor even a doubt of her virtue.

I remember asking Lord Radnor about it once, who had been in her household for twenty years, and whose daughter had been brought up with the daughters of Prince Edward, but he would not admit the suspicion, though he told me a curious story of the privileges which John Brown† arrogated and the Queen permitted.

On the occasion of a visit from the German Emperor, Lord Radnor had to arrange the reception. He formed up the lords and ladies of the court in

---

* Wife of Charles Philip York (1836–1897), 5th Earl of Hardwicke.
** Albert York, 6th Earl of Hardwicke, godson of the Prince of Wales.
† (1826–83).

two long lines, a sort of lane, in fact, through which the Queen and the German Emperor would pass to the dining-room. Just when he had got everyone in place, John Brown came in and began pushing the lines further back. Lord Radnor told him courteously that he had already arranged the court and that it was all right. John Brown told him he didn't know what he was talking about and pushed him, too, back into the line.

At the moment there was nothing for Lord Radnor to do but submit.

That evening Lord Radnor told the Queen that he had to complain of her servant. The Queen listened impatiently and replied that "It was only John's way; he did not mean any rudeness."

When Lord Radnor insisted that he had been rude, she replied, "You must forgive John. It is his way," adding, with curious naiveté, "he is often short with me."

Brown's apartments were always near those of the Queen.

She sometimes sent for him two or three times in the evening. He would always come down, but he often made her wait, and even neglected to address her as "Madame"; he would just put his head in at the door and say, "Well!" The Queen would say, "I just sent to see if everything was all right." Brown would not even deign to give a word in reply, but went back to his rooms in silence.

Towards the end of his life she gave him a house and piece of ground in her own park at Balmoral, and when he died she set up his statue in the grounds.

One of the first things the Prince of Wales did when he came to the throne was to ask the relatives of Mr. Brown to take the statue away. It is, I believe, still regarded as a precious heirloom in the Brown clan.

In her later life, Victoria left all the ceremonies of royalty to Prince Edward. He had to receive for her and fulfill all the social duties of the monarch, but there his power ended; he was a figure-head and nothing more. She hardly ever attended a court and gave scarcely any dinners, except occasional dinners to royal personages, particularly to her nephew* the German Emperor, and now and then to some German prince; but to the end she kept in her own hands the reins of government. She did not even consult her son about anything or allow him to have any first-hand knowledge of state affairs.

She judged him almost as severely as the German Emperor judged him later. She heard of scandals—stories of his relations with women; she regarded him as *leicht-lebend*—loose, if not dissolute, and there was no weakness she condemned so bitterly. She would never have a divorced woman at her court, and if she received anyone and they afterwards got mixed up in any scandal, she cut out their name relentlessly, even though she had liked them. Looseness of morals was to her the sin that could never be forgiven.

Queen Victoria had all the intolerance of perfect virtue. People she knew

* Her grandson, not her nephew.

and liked and esteemed tried to get her to forgive Colonel Valentine Baker;* pointed out to her how nobly he had acted in not defending himself against the woman who accused him; how he had redeemed his fault, too, by years of high endeavor; how he had shed his blood for the English in Egypt. Nothing could move her. A man should be as pure as a woman, was her creed, and she would tolerate no infringement of it. Her eldest son's lax moral code was a perpetual offense to her.

Up to the very last Queen Victoria was Queen and would brook no interference or advice. Her relations with her ministers for the last thirty years of her life were always on a peculiar footing. She had not only grown more imperious with the years, but wiser. Again and again she had matched her brains with her ministers, and a woman learns rapidly through intercourse with able men; but it was her German husband who had taught her broad-mindedness and given her faith in herself.

This self-confidence grew in the nineties to absurd heights. She wrote several messages to her people which were plain translations from the German.

At a big reception one evening I followed Arthur Balfour up the stairs and a lady, I think the then Duchess of Sutherland,** was chaffing him about the latest Royal message. "Your English," said the lady, "is not so pure as it used to be, my dear Arthur."

"I had nothing to do with it," replied the Prime Minister. "The dear old lady never even showed me the message! I wish she would, but it is difficult now even to hint criticism to her. So I keep quiet; after all it doesn't matter much—"

"Would you like the practice to cease?" I asked him a little later.

"Indeed I should," he answered. "It might lead to an awkward position at almost any time: her ministers are supposed to do these things."

The next week I wrote an article in the *Saturday Review,* entitled "The Queen's English," in which I set forth how this expression came into vogue as expressing how careful her various ministers had been to put only good English into any document which the Queen was supposed to sign. I went on to say that the good custom was being neglected, and I took certain phrases from the latest messages and showed that the bad English of them was due to the fact that they were literal translations from the German.

Yet Arthur Balfour knew no German and was besides a master of good English: it was evident that the Queen herself had written these messages, a custom which, if persisted in, would soon ruin her reputation as a writer of English. "In fact," I summed up, "the Queen's English is now plainly made in Germany."

* (1827–1887). He received Queen Victoria's disapproval for assaulting a girl in a railway carriage and was accordingly dismissed from the army, "Her Majesty having no further occasion for his services."
** Wife of Cromartie Sutherland, 4th Duke of Sutherland (1851–1913).

The exposure put an end to the practice: always afterwards the Queen used to call her ministers to counsel.

Queen Victoria grew to dislike radicalism through her dislike for Gladstone.

"He speaks at me," she said, "as if I were a public meeting."

She loved Disraeli's deference and courtesy, and when he made her Empress of India he won her heart of hearts.

In the South African War she took the English official point of view very strongly while deploring the necessity, as she regarded it, of war; and when her nephew, the German Emperor, sent his famous telegram to Krueger, she wrote to him with her own hand, declaring that he had acted unjustifiably; rated him, indeed, as if he had been a peccant schoolboy. And when he pleaded that he thought her Majesty's ministers had directed the Jameson raid, the old lady replied by declaring that none of her ministers knew anything about it and scolded him sharply for the assumption.

"You have weakened the principle of royalty," she wrote.

It says a good deal for the Kaiser that he apologized humbly and promised never to offend again in the same way.

From this it will be seen that towards the end of her life Queen Victoria's personal influence in the courts of Europe was extraordinary. She was the oldest reigning sovereign, save the Emperor of Austria, and the most secure. Everyone outside of England saw that she had immense power, and yet she was supposed to be a constitutional ruler.

Men of the first capacity as English politicians were astonished at her ability. No two men could have been more unlike than Lord Randolph Churchill and Sir Charles Dilke; yet both spoke of Victoria as the ablest woman they had ever known. Still, her influence was injurious. She strengthened English conservatism and it was already far too strong; she did more than any other person to block the wheels of progress. All her influence during the last twenty years of her life was thrown against reform; she loved the established order and the traditional rule of conduct.

Her foreign policy was bounded by the idea of working in perfect harmony with Germany. She distrusted and disliked France and despised the French. After Fashoda she still passed a couple of months on the French Riviera in the winter, but her relations with the French had been so slight and formal that the difference of feeling between the two races made hardly any impression on her. It was the South African war which got the English thoroughly disliked in France. And the high-handed, not to say, rude way the English acted about Fashoda humiliated French pride and brought the two peoples to the verge of war. I have already told how Rochefort, the greatest of French journalists, wrote in the *Intransigeant* the bitterest attack on Queen Victoria; he even called her "*Cette vieille calèche qui s'obstine à s'appeler Victoria,*" (That old stage coach which persists in calling itself Victoria.)

Prince Edward used to say that he never knew his position till his mother died, and at her death-bed Lord Salisbury spoke to him.

"He had always been cold to me," he said, complainingly, "but when the doctors said, 'The Queen is dead,' Lord Salisbury suddenly altered his tone, his manner, everything. He came to me respectfully; stooped to kiss my hand and hoped that I would believe he would serve me as faithfully as he had tried to serve my mother. I was really touched. Then, for the first time, I realized through his deference what it was to be King of England."

When Edward came to the throne, he brought a new policy into power: so long as Victoria lived, England favored Germany and cold-shouldered France, and the outward visible sign of England's good will was the cession of Heligoland* to Germany.

Of course, Lord Salisbury knew nothing of the value of that island; never dreamed that it could be an outpost of attack on England by airships and a fortress to protect the German navy. He was blissfully ignorant of geography and gasped with astonishment when told once that Zanzibar was an island. But he had served Victoria loyally, and up to the very end of her reign it looked as if the understanding between the two Teutonic peoples was certain to endure for at least another century.

In 1889, when I first knew him, Prince Edward was a typical German in appearance, about five feet eight in height, very heavily built, with dark brown hair and full whiskers, beard and moustache. He was already very stout; but instead of trying to get rid of his fat, or to keep it within bounds, he was much more concerned to conceal it. The trait is characteristic. He dressed with extreme care, and always with the idea that he had a figure. Consequently, his clothes were always a little too tight, and thus drew attention to his rotundity. As is usually the case, his vanity did him harm.

His love of good living and childish self-esteem were his most obvious qualities; they went hand in hand with good humor and a certain *bonhomie* which everyone noticed in him. When threatened by old age, he tried from time to time to diminish his drinking, believing that too much liquid was the cause of his obesity: but he could never be persuaded to cut down his eating. Foolish proverbs, enshrining the stupidity of the past, governed him, or were used by him as justification: "Bread is the staff of life . . . good food never hurt any one," commonplaces appealing to him irresistibly.

The Prince had had every advantage of both German and English training. He spoke English however, with a strong German accent, and continually used bad English through translating literally from the German. In the same way, his French was fairly fluent so long as he kept to the commonplaces of conversation; but as soon as he had to express some unfamiliar thought he was hopelessly at sea, and then his *baragouinage* was that of a South German. Curiously enough, his accent in French and in

---

* The English occupied it in 1807; it was formally ceded by Denmark in 1840; in 1890 it was traded to Germany for Zanzibar.

English was rather like a Bavarian, with an indefinable tang of the Jew. I don't put forward the usual scandalous explanation; I merely note the fact. The Prince's sensualism was as round as his figure, as full-blooded as his body. He gambled whenever he could because of the pleasure it gave him; he smoked incessantly, though the cigarettes plagued him with smoker's cough; but till Nemesis came with the years—ill health and indigestion from want of exercise or from over-eating, which you will—he was generally good humored and kindly disposed: *un bon vivant,* as the French say.

Like the average man, he delighted in popularity. He could not help believing that all desired and sought it, and if they failed, it was because of some shortcoming in them. He could not imagine that anyone would hold himself above the arts which lead to popular applause. When he drove through London, bowing and smiling to cheering crowds, he took it all as a triumph of personal achievement, a final and complete apotheosis.

Edward had all the aristocrat's tastes. He loved horse-racing, was gregarious, hated to be alone, preferred a game of cards to any conversation; in fact, he only talked freely when he went to the opera, where, perhaps, he ought to have been silent. He was a gambler, too, as English aristocrats are gamblers, and his love for cards often got him into difficulties. It has been said by a bitter but keen sighted observer: "King Edward was loved by the English because he had all the aristocratic vices, whereas King George is disliked by them because he has all the middle class virtues."

Early in the nineties I was struck by the story of Father Damien.* There was an echo of the heroic self-sacrifice of St. Paul and the early Christian martyrs in his self-abnegation.

A simple Belgian monk, he had begged to be sent to the South Sea lepers. He made the choice in the spring of lusty manhood, knowing that he would never see his home and his loved ones again, in the full conviction that he, too, must catch the loathsome malady and die piecemeal, rotting for years, and praying in the end for death as a release.

At luncheon one day I happened to have the Vyners: Mrs. Vyner, an intimate friend of the Prince of Wales, was an extraordinary woman; Bob Vyner, her husband, was simply a very rich Yorkshire squire. Mrs. Vyner, without being good-looking, had an extraordinary charm of manner. I remember once saying to her daughter, Lady Alwynne Compton:** "You know, Lady Alwynne, after talking to your mother for some time, one feels a sort of intimate sympathy with her, almost as though it were love."

"The curious part of it is," said Lady Alwynne, "that she is in love with you for the time being; she's extraordinarily sympathetic."

At this luncheon I declared that modern science should turn the sacrifice of Father Damien into a triumph by forming a fund to study leprosy and discover a cure.

* (1840–1889). He died on Moloku in the Hawaiian Islands of leprosy. Robert Louis Stevenson in a tract attacked a clergyman who slandered Damien's work.
** Wife of Charles Compton, 3rd Marquis of Northampton (1816–1877).

"The only worthy memorial to him," I said, "would be to make his self-sacrifice final by eliminating the foul disease from the world."

Mrs. Vyner questioned me closely after lunch and then persuaded me that I should call on Prince Edward and ask him to take the initiative. "I'll speak to the Prince," she said, "and you'll see that he'll take fire at your idea; he's really a good man and eager to help every noble cause."

A day or two afterwards I got a letter from Prince Edward, asking me to come to Marlborough House and explain my scheme about Damien. I went and found Sir Francis Knollys,* the Prince's secretary. I told him I wanted to get up a committee and form a fund, to be called the Damien Fund, to make an end of leprosy in memory of the great hearted man who had given his life for the lepers. "Modern doctors," I said, "will be able to find the microbe of leprosy in six months and so cure the disease." Knollys finally agreed with me and made an appointment with the Prince for the afternoon. When Edward saw me he burst out: "I could hardly believe it was you, Harris! Your naughty stories are wonderful; but what have you to do with leprosy and a fund to cure it?"

"It could be done so easily, Sir," I began. "I'm sure if you'll lend your great influence to the cause, it can be made successful in a year, and one of the vilest diseases that afflict humanity can be done away with."

"All right," cried the Prince. "I'll back you up in every way: see Knollys here and arrange the plan of campaign. I'm with you heartily. We'll have the meetings here." I thanked him cordially for his support.

The chief persons in the kingdom were put on the committee: the preliminaries were settled by Sir Francis Knollys and myself, and a large fund raised. But alas! In spite of all my efforts to keep at least one lay member on the working committee, the whole executive power fell into the hands of the doctors, who each had his own fad to air and his own personality to advertise.

Our first meeting at Marlborough House was a huge success. All the first men in England came to the meeting and some twenty thousand pounds were subscribed in the first half hour. "What should I give?" asked the Duke of Norfolk.**

"You must remember," I said, "that as the first Catholic in the realm, your gift will certainly not be surpassed; the more you give, the more others will give." He gave two thousand pounds, I believe.

While the doctors were disputing in private, strange rumors came to London from the leper settlement in Hawaii. It was said that Father Damien's leprosy had been contracted through his carnal love for some of the female lepers. The wretched story was contradicted, but the slander was

* (1837–1924). He first worked for his father, who was treasurer and comptroller of the royal household; in 1870 he was made Edward's private secretary.
** Henry Fitzalan Howard, 15th Duke of Norfolk (1847–1917), premier Catholic in Britain, and the first Catholic since Sir Thomas More to play a significant part in English public life.

too tasty a morsel to be rejected. The Prince sent for me hot-foot. I found him in a state of great excitement in Marlborough House.

"Here's a pretty kettle of fish!" he cried. "Of course it's not your fault, but this Father Damien must have been a nice person. Fancy choosing lepers—eh? It gives one a shiver. I suppose it's human nature; propinquity, eh?" and he laughed. "We must change the name of our fund, though; what shall we call it?"

"Why change, Sir?" I asked. "That would be to condemn Damien without a trial. I don't believe a word of the vile story."

"Whether you believe it or not," cried the Prince impatiently, "everyone else believes it, and that's the thing I have to consider. Such stories are always believed, and I can't afford to be laughed at like they laugh at Damien. I don't want to be taken for a fool; surely you see that. We may believe what we please, but I have to consider public opinion."

"As you please, Sir," I said, realizing for the first time that in these democratic days Princes, even, are under the hoof of the ignorant despot called opinion. "The name can be changed. 'The Leprosy Fund' is as distinctive a title as 'The Father Damien Fund,' but I regret your decision."

"Oh, come," he exclaimed, restored to complete good humor by my submission. " 'The Leprosy Fund' is excellent. Tell Knollys, will you, that we have changed the title, and take all steps to make it widely known! We must be worldmen, men of the world, I mean, and accept opinion and not be peculiar. It's always foolish to be peculiar; you get laughed at," and so he ran on, expounding his cheap philosophy, the philosophy of the average man and of the street. Fancy a Prince afraid to be peculiar. No wonder Edward was popular; he was always eager to pay the price popularity demands.

The doctors chosen to investigate were appointed by the head of the College of Surgeons, Sir Jonathan Hutchinson,* and the head of the College of Physicians, whose name I forget. But Sir Jonathan Hutchinson took the chief part in the appointments and he was notorious for his belief that leprosy came from the eating of stale fish. This was the theory when he was a youth and studied medicine. It had been completely disproved by the experiments of the Norwegians, who had established the best school and hospital for leprosy in modern Europe, but Sir Jonathan knew nothing of modern research on the subject and insisted on appointing someone who believed or pretended to believe in the stale fish theory. Consequently, the commissioners went to India and returned without achieving anything. They would have been infinitely better advised if they had gone to Norway and profited by the experiments of the Norwegian investigators.

I wanted to use the fund to send two young men to Norway and two to the leper settlement at the Cape of Good Hope, and two more to Calcutta, to study leprosy in all its phases and try to find a cure for it; whereas each of the great doctors had a new theory and a new method to propose. One

* (1828–1913), a renowned ophthalmologist and a leading authority on syphilis.

declared that it was purely contagious; another believed that like syphilis, it could only be propagated through an abrasion of the outer cuticle: not one of them knew anything about the modern researches; they were all full of the conclusions they had formed on the subject after an hour's reading when they were students—one could tell the textbook each of them had used.

I had already noticed that Sir Andrew Clarke* and the other notable medical authorities were opposed to me and my ideas. But they didn't trouble me greatly, as no two of them agreed on any policy. On one point however, they were all at one: as I was not a properly qualified doctor I could know nothing of leprosy, though I had really spent more time on it than all of them put together, and had studied the latest works on it in three or four languages. I found it hopeless to dispute with the doctors, and as soon as the name of the fund was changed I resigned my position as secretary and washed my hands of the whole business, though the Prince and Knollys requested me very kindly to reconsider my decision.

The single experience had taught me several good lessons. For one thing, I began to see the weakness of patronage in England. The Prince could only act in any case through the nominal heads of the profession concerned, and the great London doctors knew nothing about leprosy and cared less. I was convinced that no good would come of the inquiry as directed by them. Progress in science is only made by disinterested, able investigators: one thing was certain; if the money had been subscribed in Germany or in France, a far better use would have been made of it.

In spite of the comparative failure of the scheme, it made the Prince of Wales like me better, and certainly turned Sir Francis Knollys, who was nominally the head of the Prince's household and his most trusted adviser, into a really close friend. When I got to know him I found that he was a lineal descendant of the Sir Francis Knollys, who was the Chamberlain of Queen Elizabeth's Court and made himself a little ridiculous when well advanced in years by falling in love with Mistress Mary Fitton, Shakespeare's love, "the dark lady of the Sonnets," and the mistress of young Lord Pembroke, Shakespeare's patron and friend.

I felt sure this old Sir Francis Knollys was the prototype of Shakespeare's Polonius, and I could give a dozen reasons for my belief.

One day I detailed them to Sir Francis Knollys, who was delighted with the identification, a little to my surprise, for Polonius does not cut a heroic figure in *Hamlet*. I learned to like Knollys with heart and head: he was not only kindly and fair-minded, but absolutely loyal to his friends, and more than anything else I appreciated that loyalty in London, where everybody seems inclined to run his friend down and depreciate even good ideas and unselfish endeavor.

Snobbery is the religion of England. I had always regarded Edmund

---

* (1826–1893), president of the Royal College of Physicians. Mrs. Gladstone was among his patients.

Yates, owner and editor of the weekly paper, *The World,* as a friend of mine, and I had taken care to have him asked to the meetings of the Damien Committee, but now he came out with a long article in *The World,* declaring that I had jumped from Father Damien's shoulders through the window of Marlborough House—the whole article a mere sweat of envy. I never laid any stress on the fact that Prince Edward was kind to me. But to Edmund Yates, who pretended to be my friend, my little social success was much more important than my writing or my friendship. The incident only confirmed my growing belief that most men give themselves much more readily to hatred than to love.

The reasons why the Prince disliked Germany, in spite of his German upbringing, have never yet been told in print. Nevertheless, they are interesting and show how petty slights and foolish misunderstandings may help to cause the greatest wars and deluge Europe with blood.

For many years Prince Edward had been an ardent admirer of Germany and most German institutions.

After the German Emperor began to take up yacht-racing there was a dinner at Cowes, in the early nineties, at which Prince Edward declared that there was no such enviable position in all the world as that of the German Emperor.

"He is the greatest influence in the world," he declared, "for good or evil. Whatever he does is accepted and copied. All his subjects now are taking up yacht-racing because he wishes it and he'll do great things yet, you'll see: to be German Emperor is to be a god on earth."

But when the Kaiser visited England frequently the glamor disappeared and the real difference in the nature of the two men became apparent.

The uncle was prepared to look up to the nephew who wore the crown, but he was not content to be treated with contempt. On the other hand it was perfectly plain that the German Emperor regarded Prince Edward as a fat elderly person who sacrificed the dignity and serious purposes of manhood to the vices and amusements of youth.

I was once at a dinner at Osborne toward the end of Victoria's life which tells the whole story.

By the wish of Victoria the German Emperor was treated with special reverence. The famous gold dinner service even was brought from Windsor to Osborne to do him honor. The Queen would have had even the weather regulated to suit the convenience of her beloved grandson.

The kinship and likeness between grandmother and grandson were extraordinary. They both had the same serious view of life and the same conventional view of morals. All through the dinner the Queen spoke to no one except the German Emperor, who was on her right. There was scarcely any conversation among the other diners.

Occasionally Prince Edward, who sat opposite the Kaiser, ventured a remark, but neither of the sovereigns paid much attention to him.

Grandmother and grandson talked together in excellent German in a low tone at the head of the table, and it took a very bold spirit among the rank and file of the guests even to whisper to his neighbor. The Prince, who sat opposite the German Emperor, was evidently ill at ease; his usual *bonhomie* was blighted. As the meal drew to an end he fidgeted about, looking the picture of discomfort.

Suddenly the Queen got up to go. Everybody stood up and the German Emperor and the Prince accompanied her to the door. When the Queen disappeared there was a sigh of relief. The ice was broken. The air of constraint vanished; every one began to talk. Prince Edward was all smiles. The German Emperor walked back to the table and took his seat again still in profound thought. As Prince Edward seated himself, he asked the Emperor, with a smile, to take the head of the table. The Kaiser did not appear even to hear him, but with clouded brow appeared to be in deep thought: suddenly he pushed back his chair, got up and went hastily out of the room after the Queen, without a word to the Prince, leaving the whole assembly gasping.

Prince Edward flushed; the slight was manifest. He so far forgot himself for the moment as to exclaim: "German manners, I suppose," then went on talking as usual; but the table remained in expectancy; there was a certain embarrassment in the air; the dinner was a failure.

From that time on Prince Edward stood, not with the German Emperor, but opposed to him, and in private did not hesitate to criticize his manners and his want of consideration for others. In fine, he began to look for his nephew's faults and not for his qualities.

A wit at the time summed the whole matter up in the phrase that has more truth than humor in it: "Morals and manners are always at daggers drawn." It was certainly the brainless rudeness of the German Emperor that first made the breach.

When Edward succeeded to the throne, the ever-widening breach became apparent to every one. The German Emperor was not run after nor his visits solicited. When he came to England, he would stay with Lord Lonsdale* or some other friend, but there was no public reception; he came and went unheralded and unwelcomed so far as the court was concerned.

Edward's early experiences as king almost forced him to take a new attitude towards affairs. The Queen had died in the early part of the South African war. King Edward hated the war—was liberal-minded enough to feel that war in one of her colonies was not likely to do England any good; he shared, too, the common feeling that the German Emperor was giving the Boers at least moral support. Every setback in the field made the King more determined to put an end to the war, and as soon as Pretoria was

---

* Hugh Cecil Lowther (1857–1944). His main interests were in sports, and he loved racing and riding to the hounds; and once he sparred with John L. Sullivan and succeeded in knocking him down. The Lowther Belt of the National Sporting Club, the purpose of which was to promote boxing, is named for him.

taken and President Krueger had fled the country, he used all his influence to bring about peace, peace at almost any price.

It will be remembered that peace was made possible at length by the promise of England to give three million pounds to the Boers to rebuild the farm houses that Lord Kitchener had burnt down. That this proposal of Botha's* was accepted was due to King Edward's personal intervention. With the common sense of a man of the world, he saw that fifteen million dollars was a flea bite, not worth talking about. More, as he said, would be spent in a week's war. It was absurd to haggle over such a sum.

As soon as peace was established, everyone felt grateful to the King for having divined the unconscious wishes of his people. He was put on a pedestal; many persons remembered that he had broken the habit of drink in England, and now he had brought about peace in South Africa; almost everyone began to hope that the kindly, good-natured man of the world might be a better ruler than his all too severe and moral mother.

If there was one thing King Edward appreciated and knew all about, it was popular opinion. He soon saw that he had won the confidence of earnest and serious people and at once began to take himself seriously. Everything he did had turned out to be right; why should he not assume the initiative in politics? Not only did he leave the Kaiser uninvited, but he paid a visit to Paris—a state visit—and so pleased the great body of English Liberal opinion, which naturally preferred democratic France to imperial Germany. Then in 1905 he invited the French fleet to Cowes and gave the French admiral and his officers a great banquet at the Royal Yacht Squadron Club when the *Entente Cordiale* was confirmed.

The great banquet that followed in the Guildhall only ratified the agreement, and when Admiral Caillard, driving through London, took off his hat to the statue of Nelson in Trafalgar Square, amid a cheering crowd, everyone felt that at length the two peoples were united in heart and in purpose.

In 1906 French officers from the General Staff came across to London and in consultation with the British military authorities fixed on the place in the north of France where the British army was to assemble if the Germans invaded France. From that time on there was a complete military understanding between the two peoples.

One little incident, as yet unrecorded, did a good deal to change King Edward's dislike of the Kaiser into contempt. It was rumored in London that the Kaiser had fallen in love with a lovely Italian: soon the report became clear and detailed; the lady was a fair, if not a super-subtle, Venetian, the Countess M——.

Whenever the Kaiser went to Italy he met her and spent some time with her.

* Louis Botha (1862–1919). He commanded the South African troops at Ladysmith and Colenso and became commander of the Transvaal army in 1900. After the war, he favored co-operation with the British.

The scandal delighted King Edward. Eagerly he asked anyone who might know:

"Is it true? Do you know her? Is she really lovely? Are they devoted to each other?"

Question on question.

"Well, Sir," came the reply, "it is true at least that the Kaiser visits her whenever he can, spends every moment of free time with her: it is true that countless photographs of him all autographed are all over her rooms; and——"

"Tell me," cried King Edward, "is he taken in uniform or in mufti?"

"In both, Sir," was the reply.

"Then he loves her," was the King's comment. "It is true. Oh, those moralists; they are always the worst——" and he laughed delightedly.

This discovery increased his self-assurance in the most extraordinary degree; he began to speak of himself as a diplomat, and French nobles, like the Marquis de Breteuil, and French politicians of all kinds flattered and praised him to the top of his bent.

Many streams added volume to the great current: the King's personal preference for the French over the Germans was the most obvious force; then came the influence of liberal England; but the main river was the individual rivalry of Germany, now challenging England in the most vital way.

Early in King Edward's reign people began to notice that the production of German steel was exceeding that of English steel; that German industries were competing on an even footing in neutral markets with English industries—beginning, indeed, to oust the English products from one market after another.

Experts went to visit Germany and came back praising German methods and German education; bodies of workingmen returned to eulogize German state socialism. Statesmanship, as understood in England, could not follow the rising tide of rivalry with approval. The *Entente Cordiale* with France was confirmed in form, and hardly had British politicians arrived at an understanding with Delcassé when the possibility of war with Germany was mooted.

Each year saw the bonds uniting England to France strengthened. The German Kaiser's visit to Morocco fanned the embers of suspicion, dislike and trade-jealousy to a flame. What had the Germans to do in Morocco? Why did the French stand it? The English press began asking: "Isn't it about time that we taught the Germans their place?"

The storm clouds blew over, but a year or two later came the visit of the German cruiser *Panther* to Agadir, and everyone saw that events were ripening to a catastrophe. The Prime Minister of France, Monsieur Caillaux, told Sir Edward Grey that he would break off negotiations with Germany without ceremony if Sir Edward Grey would assure him of British support in case of war. Sir Edward Grey recommended him to wait, declared that England would support France in case France was attacked, but begged him to let the occasion be a German aggression. "We must carry the opinion of neutral nations with us," he said again and again, and finally, "Wait; the time is not yet ripe."

When Monsieur Caillaux consulted his Russian allies, they answered still more plainly that Russia was not ready—had not yet recovered from the war with Japan. But all the while the storm clouds grew heavier—the ill feeling between the peoples more pronounced.

King Edward never saw the storm break that he had done so much to conjure up, but after his death forces he had set in motion went on acting, and when Russia was ready the storm burst.

Chapter XV

Prince Edward

I HAVE OMITTED one or two incidents in the chapter on Prince Edward which I think I must relate now. When I was giving up my position on the Damien Fund Committee, which had become the Leprosy Fund, the Prince said, "I find you too serious, Harris. What I really want are some more of your naughty stories; why not come up and dine tomorrow night and tell me some?"

Of course I went and told him a round dozen of humorous stories which he had never heard before and which amused him infinitely, whether they were old or new: I only remember one or two in particular. I told him the old chestnut about the first time the Prince de Joinville met the famous actress Rachel:* he passed her his card after writing on it: *"Quand? Où? Combien?"* (When? Where? How much?)

Rachel replied: *"Ce soir; Chez moi; Rien."* (This evening; my house; nothing.)

To my astonishment, Prince Edward liked it so much that he tried to memorize it.

The second was better. There is a story told in New York of the friendship between an Englishman and an American who were out together one day on Long Island: they came upon a pretty girl fishing in a very, very shallow little brook.

"What are you fishing for there?" exclaimed the Englishman, "There are no fish in that shallow brook; what can you hope to catch?"

She swung round on the rock she was sitting on and said cheekily: "Perhaps a man."

"In that case," laughed the American, "you shouldn't sit on the bait."

The girl tossed her head, evidently not appreciating the freedom; and the pair went away. Half an hour later the Englishman burst out laughing. "I didn't see your joke at first," he said.

"Joke?" said the American; "it was pretty plain."

* (1821–1858), of the Comédie Française; acclaimed for her Phèdre. She toured the U.S. in 1885.

"I didn't think so," said the Englishman. "How could you know she had worms?"

I remember telling the Prince of the gormandizing habits of the English city folk and of the smells made at the Lord Mayor's banquet, corrupting the whole atmosphere of the great hall. He laughed but said it was a pity to tell anything against one's own country; he would rather forget it. And the story of Fowler, the famous Lord Mayor who made it impossible for Lady Marriott, at her own table, to sit out the dinner, seemed to him appalling. He hoped I would never mention it. "We should forget what's unpleasant in life," was his guiding rule.

"But sir," I said, "there are similar instances in France, though they are treated more lightly."

"Really?" he asked in some excitement. "Tell me one."

"There is a story told," I said, "of Monseigneur Dupanloup, Bishop of Orleans, who was supposed to be one of the wittiest men of his time. He was at dinner once with a lady who made a peculiar little noise and then proceeded to shuffle with her feet on the parquet so as to cover the indiscretion with similar sounds.

" 'Oh, Madame,' said the witty Bishop, 'please don't trouble to find a rhyme; it is not important.' "

The Prince laughed but did not prize the witty word at its real worth.

There are two stories about the Prince himself which are really funnier and which should find a place here.

For several years in London he was really in love with a lady who had a title and who was extremely pretty and on his own level in love of life and humor. He asked her to meet him after the theatre one night and had borrowed the house of his aide-de-camp, a Mr. T. W. The aide-de-camp, in giving him the key, told him that supper would be laid out and that all the servants would be sent away so that he might feel completely at ease. The lady had said she could only make herself free after the opera; and after the opera she drove to Mr. T. W.'s house and found the Prince fishing in the gutter: he had dropped the key and couldn't find it again.

The lady had driven up in a hansom, and she finally persuaded the Prince to get in with her and drive about for an hour or so; at the end of the drive, he took her to the corner of the square in which she lived; they both got down, and the Prince handed the cabby a shilling. Immediately the cabby hopped off his box in wild wrath crying, "What's this? What's the bloomin' bob for?"

The Prince said, "Your fare, my man!"

"Fare," cried the cabby, "for two hours driving and ten miles!"

The lady, having seized the situation, took out her purse hastily and gave the cabby two sovereigns.

When he saw that the pieces were gold, his manner changed. "Thank you, mum," said he, "thank you kindly. I know'd you was a lady as soon as I seed you. But where did you pick 'im up?"

No one was so delighted with this story as the Prince, who told it with huge gusto. I give the story as an exemplification of the extraordinary ignorance of common things shown by some of the privileged. The Prince told me that he had always heard that a shilling was the price paid to cabmen, and he thought that was the cabman's fare, for two hours' work.

The other story is perhaps a little more risky. A later flame of the Prince, when he became King, had a very pretty daughter about thirteen. The Prince, calling one day, happened to see the pretty girl and spoke enthusiastically about her to the mother. The mother said she would go and bring her in; and she went out and told her daughter that she was going to present her to the King and she must be very careful not to offend him in any way. "If he wants to kiss you, let him kiss you," she said. "What does it matter?"

In a few moments she brought the beschooled child in and presented her to the King and he began talking to the girl; the mother made some excuse and went out of the room. A quarter of an hour later she came back and found the girl alone: the King had left. "Well, what happened?" she asked.

"Nothing," said the girl. "I don't like him much, he paws one about so."

"Did he kiss you?" said the mother.

"Oh yes," replied the girl, "he kissed me; he put his hands on me; pulled me down and made me sit on his knee; he said I was beautiful and charming; I tried to smile, but I don't care much for him—fat old man—he looked at me so funnily."

"But why did he go away?" the mother asked.

"I don't know," said the girl. "He suddenly put me down and got up saying, 'Oh, I'm coming,' and hurried out of the room; but, mother he hasn't come yet!"

"That's all right," said the lady, "you have been a very good girl."

This incident was supposed to be the reason why the lady received over a hundred thousand pounds from the King.

I must tell another story to show him in a better light. A certain banker's wife who had been a great friend of the Prince's got into difficulties. Her husband's bank was on the point of failing, and the husband told his wife that she would have to ask the Prince for the five hundred thousand pounds which had been advanced to him; so she wrote to the Prince, begging him to come and see her. He came, and she told him all that had happened and her dreadful difficulty.

"Don't you distress yourself," he said. "Of course I will get the money at once. If my friend Baron Hirsch* calls, please see him: I think he will make it right."

The next day Baron Hirsch called and saw the lady and said he wanted to give her a cheque for five hundred thousand pounds, plus interest. When she thanked him, he said, "If you would receive me sometimes and regard

* Baron Maurice de Hirsch (1831–1896), a financier and philanthropist, born in Munich, who made his fortune in Balkan railways. He contributed $50 million to the colonization of the Argentine for Russian Jews.

me as a friend, I would write this cheque for a million just to make the figures round, you know, as you say in England."

Every woman is inclined to prefer round figures and so the lady smiled and was delighted, and the cheque was made out for a million.

When the lady told me the story, she added: "The Prince, you know, is really good and kind: he called two or three days afterwards to ask me to tell my husband how much he had been helped by the loan and to assure me that if he could do anything for me at any time, he would be eager to do it. He is a great gentleman."

There was a Mr. X of good position in London in the nineties, who made himself conspicuous by his devotion to the Prince's wife. People said all sorts of things and hinted at worse, but the association was strictly platonic: everyone knew that the Princess was impeccable, a heroine after Tennyson's model:

> Faultily faultless, perfectly regular, icily fair.*

Those who knew asserted that as a signal favor he was now and then permitted to hold the Princess' hand while extolling the loveliness of nature.

But for some reason or other, perhaps from the uneasy sense of dignity which everyone ascribed to him, the Prince rather resented the way his wife's name was coupled with that of Mr. X.

At Wadhurst once the Prince and Mr. X were both present at a garden party. The day was perfect, the park lovely. In the great tent, equipped with small tables, a most perfect luncheon was served. Afterwards a Spanish girl danced, as only a Spaniard can dance, with satanic vigor and impudence, spiced with provocative glance and bold gesture. She was applauded and encored again and again and was followed by an Indian nautch girl, whose challenge was not of spirit and defiant gesture, but of yielding and languor and deliberate revealing of round limb and lithe grace of form.

Everything that day seemed perfect. It would have been hard to imagine a better luncheon or more lovely surroundings, and the hostess had brought just the people together who suited each other. The Spanish dancer broke up the English restraint and set pulses beating; the nautch girl deepened the note. As usual in England, the loosening of bonds led to innocent fun: a pretty girl took a scarf and gave an astonishing imitation of Alma; another, I think a daughter of the house, forthwith beat the *gitana,* dancing with infinite spirit and go; everyone was standing in groups, talking, chattering, laughing. The footmen had cleared away the tables almost as silently as spirits; the Prince was the center of a gay circle.

Suddenly someone threw an orange at a friend; it was caught and returned like lightning, thrown and returned again, but this time badly aimed, it struck the Prince on the shoulder. He turned around, his smile gone,

---

* From Tennyson's *Maud,* Part I, 2:
> Faultily faultless, icily regular, splendidly null,
> Dead perfection, no more.

picked up the orange and then dashed it at Mr. X, who was standing opposite to him and could not possibly have been the guilty one.

The insult was so plainly intentional that Mr. X started forward as if to avenge it when one of the men standing by caught him, whirled him round and led him immediately out of the tent.

But the Prince had marked the gesture and was so infuriated that he exclaimed:

"That man must leave the house or I shall," and he went in search of his hostess.

The Marchesa sought to pacify him; but he held to his resolve and the hostess had nothing to do but tell Mr. X of the Prince's decision. He behaved perfectly.

"I'm so sorry, Marchesa," he exclaimed, "but really if I offended, it was quite involuntarily. I hope you know I would do nothing consciously in your house that you would object to. I've already packed and will get up to London by the evening train.

"Now, please don't fash yourself. It'll all blow over and I am, as always, infinitely indebted to you for having allowed me to come."

He was so handsome and so submissive that he quite won his hostess, who always afterwards took his part.

I do not give this as a proof that the Prince was jealous. He had no reason to be and he knew it, though like most loose livers he was inclined to be suspicious and did not believe much in any virtue. Still of his wife he felt perfectly sure. He often used to say that she was perfect save for one fault, and that annoyed him beyond measure.

The Princess was always late—incurably unpunctual, and the Prince, believing that "punctuality is the politeness of princes," loved to be exact to the minute; used to boast that he was never late in his life.

When they were going to any function he was always ready ahead of time and ten minutes before the start would send up to the Princess to warn her. The reply would come back, "I shall be ready dear." But she never was ready. The hour would strike. The gentlemen-in-waiting would all be on the *qui vive*. The Prince would grow impatient and send up again. Reassuring answers would be returned, but no Princess. The Prince would fume and fret and threaten to go on alone and finally, twenty minutes late, the Princess would sail in with her stereotyped smile and amiable manners, as if unconscious of anything wrong. But the Prince could never forgive the perpetual waiting. He often said it was like a pea in one's boot—intolerable. And when annoyed by waiting he sometimes criticized her bitterly; one day he was told she was dressing her hair and would be down soon. As the maid disappeared he cried: "Hair indeed; she has no more hair than her brother and he's as bald as an oyster." Another time I praised her smile. "Yes," replied the Prince, "her smile's the best part of her fortune; it has made her popular and it is easy for her to smile for she can hear nothing: she's as deaf as a post."

Some English aristocrats could never forgive Edward's loose morals. There was a certain Duke who would not meet the Prince, even when he had invited himself to dine with the Duchess. "Is the Duke really ill?" I asked his wife on one such occasion. "Dear no!" she replied. "He's locked in the w.c. on the third floor, with a novel, and will not appear till the Prince has gone. We all say he's ill."

When he was on the Riviera, Edward usually lived at Cannes. Mrs. Vyner, who was the queen of the English colony there, had always been one of his special favorites. And no one wondered at it, for Mrs. Vyner had the genius of charming, sympathetic manners. He disliked the Prince of Monaco, who was serious and a friend of the German Emperor, whom he loathed. Yet he frequently ran over to Monte Carlo to have a fling at the tables, and at one visit there he met Lady Brougham in one of the gambling rooms. As every one knows, she had a lovely villa at Cannes, and in fact her husband's father* was the person who really brought Cannes into notice and made it the favorite winter resort of the best English set.

Lady Brougham was a delightfully pretty and vivacious woman, always beautifully gowned and up-to-date in the sense that she would be furious if the date were not tomorrow rather than yesterday. Her husband was a large, heavy, pompous person with unfeigned reverence for what he regarded as principles, which were usually mere conventions: he took himself seriously; I always thought of him as a sort of English Chadband.** When Prince Edward met Lady Brougham that evening in the rooms of Monte Carlo, he said to her after a few moments' talk, "Dear Lady Brougham, I should like to dine with you next Sunday evening. May I?"

"How kind of you," exclaimed the lady. "We should be only too proud."

"All right," he said, "I will write you," meaning he would send her a list of people he would wish to meet him, "and we'll have a little game of 'bac' afterwards, eh?"

Lady Brougham professed herself delighted and they parted. As soon as she could find him, she told Lord Brougham the Prince was going to dine with them on the next Sunday, but when she mentioned the little "bac" afterwards, Lord Brougham put down his large flat foot decisively.

"I cannot have any gambling in my house on Sunday; it is against my principles."

"Nonsense," cried his wife, "don't be disagreeable; your principles are only bearishness."

"No, no," he said, and his long upper lip came down and his jaws set in the way she had learned thoroughly to dislike. "I draw the line at gambling on Sunday nights. I cannot allow it."

He stuck to his guns till at last his wife, unnerved and disgusted, cried,

---

* Henry Brougham, first Baron Brougham and Vaux (1778–1868). When Parliament was not in session, he resided at Cannes, where he was finally buried.
** A character in *Bleak House*.

"Then you must tell the Prince so yourself, for I won't, and then we shall never be on his 'list.' I think it is beastly of you."

The pompous person went off nevertheless to beard the Prince. When the Prince saw him, he cried in his German accent, "Oh, Lord Brougham, I have just met your charming wife and she was good enough to say I might dine with you next Sunday."

"Surely, Sir," replied Lord Brougham, bowing, "we would be delighted, but my wife tells me that you want to play baccarat afterwards. It will be Sunday, Sir."

"Does that make any difference?" asked the Prince.

"Yes," said Lord Brougham, blurting out the unpleasant truth, "it is against my principles to have gambling in my house on Sunday."

The Prince looked at him quietly. "I am very sorry, Lord Brougham; in that case there will not be any 'bac.' I shall write to Lady Brougham. I would not hurt your principles for anything."

"I hope, Sir," began Lord Brougham, again pompously, but the Prince bowed slightly and turned away. He had had enough of the large gentleman's principles.

Next morning Lady Brougham received a little note from him which ran thus:

Dear Lady Brougham:
I am sorry but I shall not be able to dine with you on Sunday next as I must really go to Mentone to pay a duty visit.
I hope I have caused you no inconvenience. I should hate to do that for *you* are always charming to me.

Yours sincerely,
Edward.

"There," said the lady, flouncing into her husband's room about twelve o'clock next day, "that is what comes of your silly principles. I wish all your principles were at the bottom of the sea. They make life not worth living."

But Lord Brougham was full of self-content till he found that a good many people who gave zest to life did not care to meet him after they had heard the story; in fact, he began to wish that his principles had not been so rigid when it was too late, for one peculiarity of Edward was that he never forgot or forgave a slight to his dignity. His vanity was at least as imperious as Lord Brougham's principles. From that time to the day of his death he never dined in the Villa Eleonore.

Edward was most generous and kindly so long as things went in accord with his wishes. At a reception by the Vyners one night, the Prince walked up and down the room with his arm on my shoulder while I told him one or two new stories. Suddenly I said to him, "You know, Sir, I mustn't accept any more of your kind invitations as commands because I must get to work; I must withdraw from all this London life and try to make myself a writer."

"A little gaiety will do you good from time to time," he replied.

"No, Sir," I said. "Please believe what I say; I must get to work."

He seemed huffed, greatly put out. "You are the first," he said, "who ever spoke to me like that."

"It is my necessity, Sir," I said, "that drives me to work. I shall always be proud of your kindness to me."

"A strange way of showing it," he said, and turned away.

Once later at Monte Carlo I was talking to Madame Tosti, the wife of the well know London musician,* when the Prince came directly across the room to speak to us. I don't know why, but I felt sure he meant to be rude to me, so I took the bull by the horns and copied Beau Brummel's famous word to King George. "Now I leave you," I said to the lady, "to your stout friend." And I turned away, but I could see that the Prince was furious.

I must end these stories of the Prince with the wittiest thing I had ever said. One night he went to the house of the Duchess of Buccleuch,** whose husband didn't like him because he thought him a loose liver. The Prince was in extraordinarily good form and won everyone—really found a kindly and appropriate word for twenty or thirty people, one after the other. I told him his success had been as astonishing as Caesar's at the battle of Zela, when he afterwards wrote to his friend Amantius, *"Veni, vidi, vici"* (I came, I saw, I conquered). "Of course," I went on, "that's not what Caesar really said; what he really said was, 'I saw, I conquered, and—I came!'" The Prince laughed heartily. "You are incorrigible," he said. So I was encouraged to tell him the famous witticism of Degas. Some one spoke condemning Minette or Mimi, as it is often called in French, meaning the kissing of the woman's sex. Degas replied with the old saying: *"Quelle triste vieillesse vous vous préparez!"* (What a dreary old age you are making for yourself!)

The Prince pretended not to understand what I meant, and when it was explained, thought the practice unmanly.

To atone, I told him another story which pleased him a little more. A married woman took her young sister of twelve for the first time to the theatre. The child sat entranced, though the play was a poor melodrama to the third act, when the hero asks the heroine to marry him: she will not; again he asks her and she refuses. "If you refuse again," he cried, "I'll make you my paramour!" At once the little cockney girl exclaimed, "'Ark at the swine!"

Then I told him another story which pleased him better. "At the end of one of my lectures in New York," I began, "a man in the audience rose and evidently as a joke said:

* Sir Francesco Paolo Tosti (1846–1916), singing master to the royal family and a professor at the Royal Academy of Music.
** Wife of the 6th Duke of Buccleuch (1831–1914), and daughter of the Duke of Abercorn. Before her marriage she was Mistress of the Robes to Queen Victoria. She died in 1912.

" 'The lecturer spoke of "virgin" once or twice; would he be kind enough to tell us just what he means by "virgin"?'

" 'Certainly,' I replied, 'the meaning is plain; "vir," as everyone knows, is Latin for a man, while "gin" is good old English for a trap; virgin is therefore a mantrap.'

"Everyone laughed and a lady in the hall rose and kept up the game.

" 'I believed,' she said, 'that all traps were usually open and afterwards closed, while the reverse seems to be the case with the mantrap.'

"The laughter grew and finally a man got up: 'I have another objection,' he said. 'Traps are always easy to enter and hard to get out of, whereas this trap is hard to enter and easy to get out of.' "

The Prince, laughing, said, "You made those two answers up, Harris, I'm sure."

"I give you my word," I replied, "that the definition was all I invented."

Volume

IV

Chapter I

How I Began to Write

IT WAS THE CONFLICT with my committee in Hackney over Parnell and his treatment by Gladstone that brought me to the parting of the ways. The Venezuela affair, the Damien incident, and my dislike of a lazy, aimless life, however luxurious, helped to decide me. Was I to continue to fool about London and waste myself on little committees, or should I give up my candidature for the House of Commons in Hackney and go abroad and try to become a writer? A long spell of bad weather in November, unceasing fog and rain, determined me. I packed up and went off to the Riviera. In a week I was installed at the Hotel of Cap d'Antibes with Mr. Sella as host, who gave me two excellent rooms on the first floor. I found that Grant Allen and his wife were staying in the hotel. I had known him for some time, but now I met him more intimately and soon confided to him that I had made a new start and was going to try to write some short stories.

Every night he and his wife came up to my sitting-room after dinner and I told them the stories before I wrote them. I told them the story of *The Sheriff and His Partner,* of *Montes, the Matador* and *A Modern Idyll* on three successive nights. They praised them all enthusiastically, and when they went away I sat down to write out the stories, one story each night. When I had finished all three I sent them off to the *Fortnightly Review* to be set up, and asked for proofs to be returned to me at once. I remember I spent two nights on the *Modern Idyll,* and afterwards worked on the proofs, while *Montes* came perfectly on the first attempt. I was so excited with hope and fear that I went to Monte Carlo to while away the time till I could hope to get my stories back in print.

In a week or so I returned and went to my room and read the three stories. I saw that the story of *The Sheriff and His Partner* was spoilt by letting the facts dominate; real life is seldom artistic; I thought *Montes, the Matador* very much the better. I remember saying to myself that I had done what I intended, given the Spaniard his real place as an heroic man of action. I confess I thought it was better than the *Carmen* of Prosper Merimée, which, up to that time, I had regarded as the best Spanish story. But I preferred *A Modern Idyll* to either of the other two. There was in it a Sophoclean irony that appealed to me intensely. When the Deacon insisted on paying in order to keep the clergyman who was his wife's lover in the same town, I was hugely delighted: I felt sure it was good work.

I gave the three stories to Grant Allen and he agreed with me that *Montes, the Matador* and *A Modern Idyll* were much better than *The Sheriff and His Partner*. I began to work on other short stories. A fortnight later Grant Allen came and told me that he had a letter from Meredith about my stories. He had sent *Montes* and *A Modern Idyll* to him and asked his opinion on them. We both regarded Meredith as the highest literary judge in England at that time. Meredith did not care so much for *A Modern Idyll:* "The story was too subacid," he thought, but he praised *Montes* to the skies. To my delight, he said it was better than *Carmen* in every way; I had given even the bulls individuality, he said, whereas Merimée had dismissed them as brutes and had been content to give life to the one woman. Meredith ended his criticism with the words, "If there is any hand in England can do better than *Montes,* I don't know it."

I have always thought of that letter as my knighting. And I really cared nothing afterwards for anyone's opinion of my work. Curiously enough, when I sat down to write a longer story, *Elder Conklin,* I found it very difficult, and the worst of it was that I didn't seem able to judge it properly. I suddenly remembered that Horace tells us that he couldn't judge his poetry for nine years—*novem annos,* and I found later, when a book of my stories was printed, that I could not judge them even to my own satisfaction till five or six years had elapsed after they were written. Really, an author is like a mother: her latest baby seems to her the most perfect, just as his latest story or play seems to the author the best he has done.

I sent out my first stories to three or four English magazines; although I was the editor of the *Fortnightly Review,* they were every one returned to me with thanks: only one editor even asked me to send him some other work, telling me that he didn't think that the English public cared for stories about bull-fighting. This amused me, so I turned *A Modern Idyll* and *Montes, the Matador* into my best French and sent them off to the *Revue des Deux Mondes* in Paris. Ferdinand Brunetière,* at that time editor of the *Revue,* was called "The Door of the French Academy." He wrote me immediately a charming letter, saying that it was the first time that he had ever received two masterpieces in one letter, but he went on to tell me that my French was faulty and that he hoped I would let him correct the worst passages. I was only too delighted. As soon as the stories appeared in the *Revue des Deux Mondes,* they were praised in the English press, and at once the same editors who had rejected them wrote, asking me for some more stories. In this way I was brought to realize how low is the standard of criticism in England. The English editors always regarded me as an American, and had pleasure in trying to put me in what they thought was my place.

* (1849–1906); also a literary critic who developed a theory of the evolution of literary forms.

Talking one day to Meredith of the low standard of English literary criticism, he turned on me and said, "It is so true: I have never once been criticized in England at all fairly."

"Good God," I cried, "not even your poetry?"

"Well," he said, "my poetry has been treated a little better than my prose. Your ordinary editor feels that he knows nothing about poetry because he doesn't care for it, so he leaves it for an expert to judge; but he thinks he can judge a story as well as any one living, and so he has no hesitancy in telling me that my forte is not story-writing, and that *Richard Feverel* is not to his taste."

"I'll repair the omission," I said, "for I look upon you as only second to the very greatest, to my heroes: Shakespeare, Goethe, and Cervantes."

"Strange," he said, turning away, perhaps to hide his emotion, "that is what I have sometimes thought of myself, but I never hoped to hear it said."

"I shall say it and loudly," I declared. And so I tried my best to get Matthew Arnold and Browning to write the truth about Meredith, but they both made excuses. Browning told me that "praise of the living always seems tainted." Why, I couldn't imagine, but my scheme fell through. Yet, think of what Meredith did in superb poetry, and of *Richard Feverel,* that great love idyll in prose; and how difficult it is to win mastery in both arts, or, indeed, in either. I often think of William Watson's noble epigram: *

> Forget not, brother singer, that though Prose
> Can never be too truthful nor too wise,
> Song is not Truth—not Wisdom—but the Rose
> Upon Truth's lips, the light in Wisdom's eyes!

Here I cannot but recall a funny incident which occurred a little earlier. I had gone up to Paris and had my usual sitting-room in the Hotel Meurice; one day when I came in I found George Moore** waiting for me. He naturally had picked up the little stories which were lying in print on the table and had read them.

"Where did you get these stories, Harris?" he asked. "I don't care for the *Montes;* it is too romantic; I hate bulls and bullfighting; but *The Sheriff and His Partner* is very good, and *A Modern Idyll* is a masterpiece. I might have done it myself. Who is the writer? Whoever he is, he ought to be proud of himself."

"I wrote 'em all, Moore," I said.

"You!" he cried in astonishment. "Where did you learn to write stories?"

"They are my first fruits," I replied, laughingly.

---

* (1858–1936). This is the entire poem, entitled *To* —; the quotation is accurate except for minor errors in punctuation.

** (1852–1933). An Irish writer who lived in London and then in Paris, where he was influenced by Zola and wrote "realistic" novels such as *Esther Waters* (1894). Arnold Bennett acknowledged a debt to him in *A Mummer's Wife.* His memoirs were published in several volumes between 1886 and 1914.

"Good God!" he cried. "It must make you feel very conceited."

"On the contrary," I said, "it has made me feel very humble. I am not sure that *A Modern Idyll* is better than Balzac's *Chef d'Oeuvre Inconnu* or his *Autre Étude de Femme*."

"Good gracious!" cried Moore. "You surely didn't think you could write better than Balzac straight off, did you?"

"Certainly I did," I replied, "or I'd never have begun."

A little later Moore wrote to me, asking for permission to turn the *Modern Idyll* into a play, and I believe he did it with Arthur Symons, under the title of *The Curate's Call*,* or something of that sort. It had little interest for me.

I wanted to know whether I could do a long novel. Above all, I wanted to know how I was to render the portrait of Shakespeare and his life that was in my mind. But the joy in me already was rampant. I knew that, like Saul, I had gone out to find my father's asses and had found a kingdom. I was drunk with the hope that I might really be a great writer, as Carlyle said, "One of that strange race called Immortal."

Immediately I took the matter seriously to heart. I returned to London and sought counsel from the wisest, but got little or nothing for my pains, till it suddenly came to me that I ought to increase my vocabulary as much as possible; and when I told this to my friend, Verschoyle, he agreed with me and sent me an early edition of Johnson's great dictionary. I put in two years' work at it, as I have already related in detail.

The worst of it was that at first I had no guide as to how I should use the larger vocabulary which I had acquired, till one day I came across the words of Julius Caesar, who, according to Aulus Gellius,** advised all writers "to avoid, as the seaman avoids a rock, any word that isn't well known and commonly used" (*ut tamquam scopolum sic vitas inauditum et insolens verbum*).

The simplest speech is the best in prose. It was Joubert, I think, who called simplicity "the varnish of the great masters."

Meredith advised me to read English prose exclusively for some time, till I got free of the obsession of German, and accordingly I read *Gulliver's Travels,* Donne's *Sermons,* and Dryden's *Prefaces,* and soaked myself in their rhythms and cadences. I read, too, Froude's *Short Stories on Great Subjects,* and learnt pages of Pater and of the Bible. Above all, while writing a good deal of journalism, I forced myself every day to write one or two sentences as carefully as possible: now I chopped them up into short sentences and then wrote them all as one long phrase, studying the different effects; now I began with the logical beginning and afterwards began at the end; in short, I studied day by day for some years the structure of our English speech.

* *The Minister's Call.*
** A second-century jurist. His twenty-volume *Nostes Atticus* is invaluable because of its quotations from works now lost to us.

I don't think I got much from it all; still, reading the masters taught me their peculiarities, and was in itself good discipline; and thus in time I learned that the half is greater than the whole. As Goethe said: *"In der Beschränkung zeigt sich erst der Meister."**

I am not inclined to lay much stress on style or mere verbal excellence: a conception may be as great in sandstone as in marble, in putty as in bronze. Of course, I prefer the marble and bronze to sand and putty, but the conception is, after all, the chief thing.

I came to love English words, too, for their bold, naked exposures, for the pulsing, painting heat in them, and their shrill shrieks of pain; for the hot rhetoric, too, drawn from the childhood of the race, and the high poetry embalming man's dreams of the future and the ultimate triumph of beauty and goodness and truth.

Words to me often possess individual life and the evocative magic of personality:

> Gilding pale streams with heavenly alchemy**

is to me a revelation of Shakespeare's soul; and when I read

> All the soft luxury
> That nestled in his arms,†

I see Fanny Brawne atoning to Keats for her brainlessness by her soft, luxuriant nestling.

What a beautiful word "mouth" is! and what a dreadful, ill-sounding brute is "logic"; how stiff is "right," and how stupid "honest"; one word always amuses me—the word "wanton"; English lexicographers can find no derivation for it, and so they have suggested that it means "want one," as if any loose woman ever would want only one! The idiocy of the professors could scarcely find a more perfect illustration. I could go on forever; think of the beauty of Keats's:

> There is a budding morrow in midnight,††

or of Shakespeare's supreme verse:

> Not mine own fears, nor the prophetic soul
> Of the wide world dreaming on things to come.‡

One should remember, too, that Hamlet exclaims: "Oh my prophetic soul!"‡‡

I think I was the first to point out that even Shakespeare had favorite

---

* From *Sonett: Natur und Kunst*: "The master reveals himself in his restraint."
** *Sonnet XXXIII.*
† From *Calidore, A Fragment.*
†† *To Homer* (Sonnet).
‡ *Sonnet CVII.*
‡‡ Act I, scene 5.

words, such as "gild," that he used in and out of season; even the greatest of men have a peculiar vocabulary, and the limitations of speech mark limitations of memory and of mind. The style changes with the growth of the man. Shakespeare sloughs off his early euphuism, becomes in middle life very fluid, intensely articulate, reaching even to simplicity, and then in age packed sentences into words, deep thoughts into an epithet—a most remarkable growth.

I am not likely to underrate the magic of words, and English writers are apt to be more articulate than Americans of the same mental caliber. Lowell noticed this, but found no explanation for it, whereas I believe the reason is that all English writers love poetry more than Americans do and start their literary career by trying to write verse. This practice soon gives a large vocabulary and a keen sense of the value of the painting epithet and of rhythm.

Some of my correspondents have asked me to tell them what in my judgment are the best pages in English prose: I think Swift perhaps the best model of all; but there is hardly a finer passage in English literature than Pater's page on the Mona Lisa:

The presence that thus so strangely rose beside the waters is expressive of what in the ways of a thousand years men had come to desire. Hers is the head upon which all 'the ends of the world are come,' and the eyelids are a little weary. It is a beauty wrought out from within upon the flesh, the deposit, little cell by cell of strange thoughts and fantastic reveries and exquisite passions. Set it for a moment beside one of those white Greek goddesses or beautiful women of antiquity, and how they would be troubled by this beauty, into which the soul with all its maladies has passed. All the thoughts and experience of the world have etched and moulded there, in that which they have of power to refine and make expressive the outward form, the animalism of Greece, the lust of Rome, the mysticism of the middle age with its spiritual ambition and imaginative loves, the return of the Pagan world, the sins of the Borgias.*

And Ruskin's page on Calais Church is almost as fine. I thrill when he speaks of

the large neglect, the noble unsightliness of it; the record of its years written so visibly, yet without sign of weakness or decay; its stern wasteness and gloom eaten away by the Channel winds, and overgrown with the bitter sea grasses. . . . as some old fisherman beaten grey by storm, yet drawing his daily nets.

The last chapter of Ecclesiastes and Paul's words on Faith, Hope, and Charity are even higher.

There are prose writers like Carlyle and Heine of an incomparable splendor of achievement. No one surely has ever read the first page or the last volume of Carlyle's *French Revolution* and come away without being deeply affected by the experience. Yet Carlyle was not as great as Cervantes.

* From "Leonardo da Vinci"; there are two minor errors in syntax and a few discrepancies in punctuation.

The greatest page in Cervantes, however, as I often say, I have never seen quoted: it is near the end of the second part of *Don Quixote,* written shortly before his death, when he was well over three score years of age.

There comes a cloud upon the plain, and the Don immediately takes it for the paynim host who have come out to fight him. Sancho Panza, the squire, says it smells badly and may well be the pagans, so skins up a tree to be safe. Don Quixote lays his lance in rest and spurs out to combat. A little while later he is flung to the ground and trampled on; and when the wild mob has passed, Sancho comes down the tree, goes over to the knight and is rejoiced to find that he is not killed, not even wounded seriously; only bruised and cut and dirtied.

"What was it?" asked the Knight. "What a terrible charge!"

"It was indeed," said Sancho, "a crowd of swine were being driven to market; but as you are not wounded seriously, it doesn't matter."

"I am wounded to the soul," cried the Don; "to go out to do noble deeds and be trampled on by the swine;—that's the last insult, the final disaster. Take me home; my fighting is over and done."

And so the noble idealist went to his long rest after being trampled on by swine!

With the exception of some sayings of Jesus, and especially the story of "The Woman Taken in Adultery," there is nothing greater in prose than this page of Cervantes.

My experiences of poetry, too, perhaps deserve to be recalled. I have already described in the preceding volume how I gave up writing poetry, but with the years my love for poetry has grown if possible more intense.

In London it used to amuse Colonel John Hay, when he was American ambassador there, to hear me recite his *Jim Bludso:*

> He weren't no saint,—but at jedgment
> I'd run my chance with Jim,
> 'Longside of some pious gentlemen
> That wouldn't shake hands with him.
> He seen his duty, a dead-sure thing,—
> And went for it thar and then;
> And Christ ain't a-going to be too hard
> On a man that died for men.

But I always preferred even to that fine poem the *Prayer of the Romans:*

> We lift our souls to Thee, O Lord
> Of Liberty and of Light!
> Let not earth's kings pollute the work
> That was done in their despite.
> Let not Thy light be darkened
> In the shade of a sordid crown,
> Nor Piedmont swine devour the fruit
> Thou shook'st with an earthquake down. . . .

Let the People come to their birthright,
And crosier and crown pass away,
Like phantasms that flit o'er the marshes
At the glance of the clean white day.*

This work of Hay, with some of Emerson and *The Prayer of Columbus* of Whitman constitute, I think, the greatest American poetry; but the best English poetry of the nineteenth century is finer still.

I sometimes wonder whether accidents are not providential. We have almost driven God out of the universe and installed law in his stead; but curious chances and coincidences often remind us that there are more things between heaven and earth than are dreamt of in our philosophy.

In the first volume I declared that any originality of thought I may possess is due in the first case to the fact that, when a cowboy on the trail some fifty years ago, I had no books and by the camp fire at night had to answer the obstinate questionings of sense and outward things without any help from the choice and master spirits of my time. I was forced to think because I could not read.

In the second volume I described how the second happy chance of my life willed it that all my education took place in the United States, in France and Germany, and that when I came to English literature I read and studied without preconceived English ideas. My Shakespeare book is one result of this foreign education; but all my views of English literature are untinged by English prepossessions and English prejudices.

I can still recall vividly the shock it gave me to find William Rossetti putting Shelley above Keats. Writing of the graves of the two poets in the Protestant cemetery in Rome, he first mentions Keats, and the slab of marble covering his remains with its pathetic inscription: "Here lies one whose name is writ in water"; and, he adds, "A few paces further on and you come to a still more sacred grave, the grave of the world-worn and wave-worn Shelley, the divinest of the demi-gods."

"Ass, ass!" I cried, throwing the book down in an outburst of rage. But I found this judgment of Rossetti was the ordinary and accepted English judgment, and I had to take myself in hand and force myself to rationalize my overwhelming and almost instinctive prepossession in favor of Keats. I knew hundreds of verses of Shelley by heart, but one has only to read his *Skylark* and then Keats's *Nightingale* in order to realize how immeasurably superior was John Keats. And the *Skylark* is about the best of Shelley's work, whereas Keats, in the *Ode to a Grecian Urn* and *La Belle Dame Sans Merci,* has reached higher heights. All one winter in Rome, every Sunday morning, I used to lay flowers on the unhonored grave of Keats; the grave of Shelley was always covered by unknown admirers.

"Keats is with Shakespeare," I cried to myself, indignant, and Shakespeare himself had never done anything at twenty-six to be compared with

* In the seventh line, "Piedmont" should read "pampered."

Keats. His best is the best poetry in English, except here and there some divine verse of Shakespeare.

In one of my earliest essays of poetic criticism in England I made this declaration of faith and was immediately attacked for it on all hands.

"You will come to my opinion," was my retort, "in a little time." And two or three days afterwards I showed my chief critic a letter from Lord Tennyson in which he said: "How glad I am to see this opinion which I have held for thirty years at length finding its way into print. Keats sings from the very heart of poetry and I am glad you have said it."

A little later Matthew Arnold expressed the same opinion:

"No one else in English poetry, save Shakespeare, has in expression quite the fascinating felicity of Keats, his perfection of loveliness. 'I think,' he said humbly, 'I shall be among the English poets after my death.' He is; he is with Shakespeare."*

But Matthew Arnold's reasoning does not seem to me conclusive. He says:

"Notwithstanding his short term and imperfect experience, by virtue of his feeling for beauty and of his perception of the vital connection of beauty with truth, Keats accomplished so much in poetry that in one of the great modes by which poetry interprets, in the faculty of naturalistic interpretation, in what we call natural magic, he ranks with Shakespeare."**

Though Keats has once or twice reached magical interpretation of nature. only to be compared with that of Shakespeare or Blake, no one has yet noticed that in manifold richness of rhythm and in the dying fall of new cadences, the blank verse of Keats in *Hyperion* surpasses even the "organ tones" of Milton.

I could, if I would, give a dozen passages to prove that, to me at least, Keats and not Shelley was the "divinest of the demi-gods." Yet England almost let him starve. It was thirty-seven years after his death before Keats's poems were reprinted in England, and it took fifty-odd years for him to reach his proper place, side by side with Shakespeare and Blake.

Think of his sonnet *On Seeing the Elgin Marbles:*

> My spirit is too weak—mortality
> Weighs heavily on me like unwilling sleep,
> And each imagin'd pinnacle and steep
> Of godlike hardship, tells me I must die
> Like a sick Eagle looking at the sky.†

And his *Ode to a Nightingale:*

> Fade far away, dissolve, and quite forget
> What thou among the leaves has never known,
> The weariness, the fever, and the fret
> Here, where men sit and hear each other groan . . . ††

* From "John Keats," *Essays in Criticism, Second Series.*
** *Ibid.*
† In the third line the word is "imagined."
†† In the second line, "has" should read "hast."

> Thou wast not born for death, immortal Bird!
> No hungry generations tread thee down;
> The voice I hear this passing night was heard
> In ancient days by emperor and clown:
> Perhaps the self-same song that found a path
> Through the sad heart of Ruth, when, sick for home,
> She stood in tears amid the alien corn;
> The same that oft-times hath
> Charm'd magic casements, opening on the foam
> Of perilous seas, in faery lands forlorn.*

The dying cadences of these lines are the finest in English verse. Think, too, of the lines in his last sonnet:

> The moving waters at their priestlike task
> Of pure ablution round earth's human shores.**

Who would have dared to say then that this half-educated, consumptive lad had written purer English than Shakespeare himself and finer blank verse than Milton, and considering his years, stands without a peer in the Pantheon of Humanity?

No wonder Shelley wrote of him, Shelley who was gifted in every way, well-born, well-bred, well-taught, yet able to keep his personal divine inspiration through all the vicissitudes of life:

> . . . Till the future dare
> Forget the past, his name and fate shall be,
> An echo and a Light unto Eternity.†
> .. . . till the Future dares
> Forget the Past, his fate and name shall be
> An echo and a light unto eternity.

I have said little of Shelley, but he was a divine poet and some of his verses are always with me:

> Music, when soft voices die,
> Vibrates in the memory;
> Odours, when sweet violets sicken,
> Live within the sense they quicken.
>
> Rose leaves, when the rose is dead,
> Are heap'd for the belovèd's bed;
> And so thy thoughts, when thou are gone,
> Love itself shall slumber on.††

It was Keats who enforced the lesson which Shakespeare was the first to teach me, that poetry at its best is on the topmost height of thought, either lighting the feet of struggling humanity or encouraging men and

---

* In the next to last line, "charm'd" should read "charmed."
** From *Bright Star!*
† From *Adonais:*
†† In the next to last line, "are" should read "art."

women on the upward way, or by sheer beauty attuning them to the humane ideal.

After Keats came Thomson and Tennyson, of whom I have already written; and the next one who had a great effect upon me was Robert Browning. I have done a sort of portrait of him and have devoted several pages to him already in this *Life* of mine, but here I wish to say one or two things more.

I couldn't understand why he was not more widely appreciated in England. Every cultivated man or woman knew poems of his wife, Mrs. Barrett Browning—and she has written some fine poetry—yet, Robert Browning was supposed to be difficult and obscure, though I never could see any difficulty or obscurity. He was one of the bravest souls, and one of the most optimistic that I have ever met.

Think of the verses in *Rabbi Ben Ezra:*

> Not on the vulgar mass
> Called 'work,' must sentence pass,
> Things done, that took the eye and had the price;
> O'er which, from level stand,
> The low world laid its hand,
> Found straightway to its mind, could value in a trice:

> But all, the world's coarse thumb
> And finger failed to plumb,
> So passed in making up the main account;
> All instincts immature,
> All purposes unsure,
> That weighed not as his work, yet swelled the man's amount:

> Thoughts hardly to be packed
> Into a narrow act,
> Fancies that broke thro' language and escaped;
> All I could never be,
> All, men ignored in me,
> This, I was worth to God, whose wheel the pitcher shaped.*

Browning often spoke to me of the way he had been neglected and his work mis-seen, but always with a happy cheerfulness, as if it didn't matter. I remember one story he used to tell, that John Stuart Mill came across some of his early work, I think *Bells and Pomegranates,* and wrote to Browning, asking him, would he like him to review it in Tait's Magazine, which was then the chief literary organ. Of course Browning said he would be delighted and was very grateful.

Mill thereupon wrote to the editor, and the editor replied that of course he would be very glad to accept anything from the pen of Stuart Mill, but not a review of *Bells and Pomegranates,* because that had already been re-

---

* The quotation is almost letter-perfect.

viewed in a previous number of the magazine. Browning thereupon sent for the previous number of the magazine and found that the review in question was short if not sweet:

Bells and Pomegranates, by Robert Browning: *Balderdash.*

"It depended, you see," said Browning, "on what looked like the merest accident, whether the work of a new and as yet almost unknown writer should receive an eulogistic review from the pen of the first literary and philosophic critic of his day—a review which would have rendered him most powerful help, exactly at the time when it was most needed—or whether he should only receive one insolent epithet from some nameless nobody. I consider," he added, "that this so-called 'review' retarded any recognition of me by twenty years' delay."

There are many things in life which I can never hope to understand, but the vagaries of popularity are to me among the most incomprehensible of mysteries. As I have said in another place, had I been asked who was the artist most certain to be popular in England, where the love of beauty is almost a religion, I should have said, Whistler, who never did anything which hadn't a touch of beauty in it, who was devoted to beauty, more even than to sublimity. But no, the English mocked him and wouldn't have him for twenty years. And it was Ruskin, who was transparently honest and filled with the same enthusiasm for beauty, who did Whistler the greatest injury.

In the same way, if I had been asked beforehand the poet who would most appeal to Englishmen, with their manful courage and optimistic view of life, I should have said Robert Browning; and Robert Browning went through life almost unknown to the end! Meredith, I think it is, who wrote of

> A song seraphically free
> From taint of personality.*

But it was just the inevitable touch of personality that endeared Robert Browning to me.

It was in the early nineties that I came across a verse that started me on a new quest:

> To see a world in a grain of sand,
> And a heaven in a wild flower;
> Hold infinity in the palm of your hand,
> And eternity in an hour.**

I was so startled that I had to get Blake at once, and I simply devoured him. For months I used to annoy every one by reciting verses of his and declaring that he was the greatest spirit born in England since Shakespeare died.

His *Garden of Love* appealed to me intensely:

* From *The Lark Ascending.*
** From *Auguries of Innocence;* except for omissions of initial capitals on some words, Harris is accurate.

> I went to the Garden of Love
> And saw what I never had seen;
> A Chapel was built in the midst,
> Where I used to play on the green.
>
> And the gates of this Chapel were shut
> And 'Thou shalt not' writ over the door;
> So I turned to the Garden of Love
> That so many sweet flowers bore.
>
> And I saw it was filled with graves,
> And tombstones where flowers should be;
> And priests in black gowns were walking their rounds.
> And binding with briars my joys and desires.

I have already quoted dozens of Blake's verses in my books; again and again he gives expression to the very spirit of Jesus, and the greatest lines of natural magic in all English poetry are his.

> ... Let the west wind sleep on
> The lake: speak silence with thy glimmering eyes
> And wash the dusk with silver.*

His finest verses always make me feel that there will be greater men born into the world than any we know of.

As Blake himself wrote, his deepest words will

> ... still go on
> Till the heavens and earth are gone.
>
> For above Time's troubled fountains,
> On the great Atlantic mountains,
> In my golden house on high,
> There they shine eternally.**

Talking once with Oscar Wilde and another friend, the topic came up of undiscovered beauties of high poetry. "That's the best of winning a great reputation," said Oscar; "everything you do well is sure to be known."

"I don't agree with you," I objected; "the finest things, even in Shakespeare, are unknown."

Oscar laughed. "Come, come! A wild paradox," he expostulated.

"You have read the sonnets," I went on; "well, I don't believe you know the finest line in them."

"Nonsense," he exclaimed impatiently, "everyone knows Shakespeare's best. Why Wordsworth has gone through all the sonnets, pointing out the best and after that, there's no gleaning."

---

* From *To The Evening Star*; in the first line substitute "thy" for "the."
** From *Poem from MSS*, written about 1810. Five lines have been omitted between the 2nd and 3rd lines quoted. Harris has neglected to use capitalization in most of the nouns.

"I don't believe that Wordsworth could see the best for himself," I retorted. "Your English moralizers like Wordsworth and Milton all have blind spots in them."

"Not in poetry," persisted Oscar. "But what is your line?"

"My line," I said, "is finer than anything in Sophocles, more purely Greek, and curiously enough, it is in praise of beauty and is simply divine; 'beauty,' Shakespears says, 'Whose action is no stronger than a flower.' "

"Divine, indeed!" cried Oscar. "But where does it come?"

I recited the verse. He was evidenty puzzled a little at having overlooked the jewel for he said, "I'll let you know tomorrow whether Wordworth has missed that sonnet or not; I feel sure its very simplicity would have struck him."

Next day he came to me laughing.

"Frank, it's absolutely astounding; you're right; Wordsworth quotes the very next sonnet, the 66th, but omits the 65th; it's incredible!"

"It was to be foreseen," I insisted. "I knew he'd miss the best, because in Shakespeare's dramatic writings the miracles of wisdom and insight are invariably declared by the learned commentators to be from some other hand; some inferior collaborator has touched the zenith Shakespeare couldn't reach. At least that's my experience."

"You must really write your book on Shakespeare," said Oscar seriously; "it will do you all the good in the world. Fancy a western cowboy," he laughed delightedly, "teaching Oxford how to discover new beauties in Shakespeare. It'll make your reputation in England," he added.

"Once I hoped so," I replied, "now I doubt. Swinburne discovered Blake for the English, but no one reads him, and James Thomson is still unknown. No, it takes time and more generations than one to separate the sinners from the saints."

"Well, Frank, the sinners are more amusing—eh?"

There is another sonnet of Shakespeare's that comes from the same height of inspiration—a personal sonnet:

> That time of year thou mayest in me behold,
>   When yellow leaves, or none, or few, do hang
> Upon those boughs, which shake against the cold
>   Bare, ruin'd choirs where late the sweet birds sang.*

Here, too, I am intimately pleased by the profound art of the verse; line after line of simple iambics, and then the discord in the last line that makes the melody harmonious—"Bare, ruin'd choirs"—and then the music taken up again—"where late the sweet birds sang."

Of course there are other great sonnets in English, for example Wordsworth's sonnet on *Toussaint l'Ouverture* has the finest sextet to be found anywhere:

---

* *Sonnet LXXIII*; except for punctuation, Harris is accurate.

> Thou hast left behind
> Powers that will work for thee; air, earth and skies;
> There's not a breathing of the common wind
> That will forget thee; thou hast great allies;
> Thy friends are exultations, agonies,
> And love, and man's unconquerable mind.

And I often think the sextet of Lord Alfred Douglas' sonnet about himself and his death is worthy to rank even with this:

> For in the smoke of that last holocaust,
> When to the regions of unsounded air
> That which is deathless still aspires and tends,
> Whither my helpless soul shall we be tossed?
> To what disaster of malign Despair,
> Or terror of unfathomable ends?*

That "terror of unfathomable ends" is as sublime as anything in Dante. But I can't say I like the sonnet in English; in Italian it's easy, for Italian is full of rhymes; but English is poor in rhymes, and a perfect sonnet in English is in my opinion almost impossible. Yet at its best it's like a fugue by Bach, beyond praise, as in two or three of Shakespeare's and two or three of Wordsworth's, and a couple of Keats's.

When I began writing on Shakespeare in the *Saturday Review,* Theodore Watts,** Swinburne's friend and housemate and the critic of the *Athenaeum,* was very much interested and wrote to me. We met several times and he was frankly astonished that I cared so much for poetry. He had evidently always thought of me as an American who could hardly grapple with such high things.

One evening at the Cafe Royal I tempted him with some rare Musigny, soft to the palate as velvet and of an exquisite lingering bouquet. It unlocked the tongue of "the little sick walrus," as I used to call him to myself and other ribald juniors, and he began to swell in self-praise.

"Shakespeare's sonnets are no true sonnets," he insisted. "He neither knew nor perhaps cared for the true sonnet form; but Rossetti knew it and so do I. Do you know the sonnet I wrote on—"

"No," I replied. "Won't you recite it to me?" I added for courtesy's sake.

"I will if I can remember it," he replied, and at once began to recite verses that were good enough technically but without any inspiration or touch of beauty. I listened patiently and nodded my head at the close, as if in mute admiration, the truth being that I hate to tell flattering lies about high things. Watts seemed to sense my coldness and was piqued by it, for at length he took his courage in both hands and said solemnly: "Rossetti said that was the most perfect sonnet in English!"

"Really!" I cried, startled out of all politeness, for I knew Rossetti's

---

* The last lines of *Dies Amara Valde.*
** Theodore Dunton-Watts (1832–1914); he lived with Swinburne the last thirty years of Swinburne's life.

keenness of mind and reverence for good work, and such a judgment shocked me.

But Watts repeated the phrase, nodding his head the while like a mandarin.

While he was speaking, it came to me that possibly Rossetti had said, "The most perfect sonnet," meaning simply in verse-form, and wishing above all things to praise a genial, ingratiating, but commonplace creature. And once started on this disdainful way, suddenly a thought struck me, and though it was dreadfully rude, I thought Watts was probably too intoxicated to notice it, and so I resolved to say the thing.

Everybody knows that Theodore Watts was a solicitor and practiced law for a good many years before he went over to literature. Now the usual fee of a solicitor or attorney in England is six shillings and eight pence.

"Oh, I see what Rossetti meant," I cried.

"What's that?" interjected Watts suspiciously.

"Well, you were sure, weren't you, to make the form perfect?" I queried.

"What do you mean?" he asked.

"I mean," I replied, "that you had had such a lot of practice beforehand in sixes and eights."

He glared at me and then snuffled. I really feared he was going to cry and felt a little ashamed of myself. Shortly afterwards we parted; I think it was the end of our attempt at friendly relations. Afterwards we just bowed and left it at that. That the sick walrus should think of matching himself with the greatest of the world's poets seemed to me worse than absurd. I reminded myself of Shakespeare's verses:

> . . . These our actors,
> As I foretold you, were all spirits and
> Are melted into air, into thin air:
> And, like the baseless fabric of this vision,
> The cloud-capp'd towers, the gorgeous palaces,
> The solemn temples, the great globe itself,
> Yea, all which it inherit, shall dissolve
> And, like this insubstantial pageant faded,
> Leave not a rack behind. We are such stuff
> As dreams are made of, and our little life
> Is rounded with a sleep. Sir, I am vex'd;
> Bear with my weakness; my old brain is troubled:
> Be not disturb'd with my infirmity:
> If you be pleased, retire into my cell
> And there repose: a turn or two I'll walk,
> To still my beating mind.*

"My beating mind"—the most tell-tale phrase in all Shakespeare.

Goethe, too, reached the highest height of poetry in Gretchen's appeal to the Madonna:

* From *The Tempest*, Act IV, scene 1.

Ach neige,
Du Schmerzenreiche,
Dein Antlitz gnädig meiner Not!

Das Schwert im Herzen,
Mit tausend Schmerzen
Blickst auf zu deines Sohnes Tod.

Wer fühlet,
Wie wühlet
Der Schmerz mir im Gebein?
Was mein armes Herz hier banget,
Was es zittert, was verlanget,
Weisst nur du, nur du allein!

Ich bin, ach! kaum alleine,
Ich wein, ich wein, ich weine,
Das Herz zerbricht in mir.
Wohin ich immer gehe
Wie weh, wie weh, wie wehe
Wird mir im Busen hier!*

After that I feel inclined to quote here the earliest English poem that I know of, which is really fine:

What if Art be slowe,
Sweetlie let it growe,
As groweth tender grasse,
'Neath God's smalle rain.
But of shoutyng, strivyng, crying,
        roaryng, fightyng,
Waxeth nought save dust aloft,
Upon the plaine.

* Oh bend,
  You sorrow-filled one.
  Your countenance mercifully to my anguish!

Sword in the heart,
With a thousand sorrows,
You look upon your son's death.

Who can feel
How it rages,
The sorrow in my bones?
What my poor heart fears here,
What makes it tremble, what it desires,
Only you know, you alone.

I am, oh, scarce alone.
I weep, I weep, I weep,
My heart breaks within me.
Wherever I may go,
How heavy, heavy, heavy
Grows my heart here.

I went to New York in 1914 when the World War came on, determined to make my way to China and Japan and spend three or four years in getting to know the languages, art and literature of those countries; for personal reasons I didn't go, so my life is maimed, and my life work, which I had thought I would make perfect, must be completed by some one else. Therefore I end with Browning's word in *Andrea del Sarto:*

"And thus we half-men struggle."

This always goes in my mind with the end of that great poem:

... What would one have?
In heaven, perhaps, new chances, one more chance—
Four great walls in the New Jerusalem,
Meted on each side by the angel's reed,
For Leonard, Rafael, Agnolo and me
To cover—the three first without a wife,
While I have mine! So—still they overcome
Because there's still Lucrezia,—as I choose.

"Again the Cousin's whistle! Go, my Love."

Chapter II

The *Saturday Review*

UP TO THIS TIME, I have said very little about my financial position. I must now make this omission good. From the time of taking over the *Evening News* in the early eighties, I had got into touch with finance in London. I not only knew the editors of the financial papers, but was a friend of both the owners, Macrae of the *Financial Times* and Harry Marks of the *Financial News,* and through my knowledge of South Africa and sympathy with the people, I had come into close relations with a good many of the South African financiers.

I had known Cecil Rhodes ever since the Colonial Conference in '87, as I have already narrated, and through him I came to know Alfred Beit, who somewhat later made himself, through the success of the gold mines of Johannesburg, one of the most important financiers in the world. About the same time I became friendly with Albert Ochs, who was the head of the famous diamond buying house of Hatton Gardens. He had a brother, James Ochs, who conducted the Paris business, and another younger brother of less importance; but Albert Ochs, in many respects, was very like Beit—a first-rate financial head. He had inherited half a million or so from his father in the diamond business, and while keeping on the old established trade in diamonds, bought an interest in certain gold mines in Johannesburg, and so came into the wider field of international finance.

We soon became intimate; I really liked Albert Ochs, and trusted him. I had made money with him more than once by getting articles in favor of his enterprises in all sorts of papers. Later I tried time and again to bring him into a union with Beit and Rhodes, which he infinitely desired, but that's another story to be told later.

Beit seemed to dislike Ochs, and one day told me a humorous story to account for his prejudice against him.

Beit and Wernher,* it appears, used to lunch together at the Holborn Restaurant, and one day Beit noticed that old Ochs, Albert's father, had got a seat at the next table and seemed to be listening attentively to the

* Sir Julius Charles Wernher (1850–1912), who also made his fortune in South Africa in diamonds. He, with Beit and Rhodes, consolidated to form De Beers.

private talk that went on between himself and Wernher. At this time Beit and Wernher, too, were diamond brokers in Hatton Gardens; in fact, in time, through Rhodes's help, they took over the whole business from Kimberley and ousted all competitors, including Ochs.

When Wernher went out, old Ochs bowed very politely to Beit and asked, "Would you mind if I come and sit with you? I'm alone."

Beit said, "I'm going very soon, but if you would care to sit here, come." Ochs came over and took Wernher's vacant seat; Beit sat and talked with him wondering what he wanted.

Suddenly Ochs said, "Is Mr. Wernher coming back?"

"No, I do not think so," Beit replied. "He has had to go off on private business."

"Oh," said Ochs, "then may I help myself to some of the potatoes he has left?" And as soon as Beit said, "Yes," he harpooned one or two of the cold potatoes and began to eat them. "Then I understood," said Beit, "that he had not come in the hope of finding out any secret, but simply, millionaire like, to realize a small economy." It was this story, I think, that first gave me the idea of my saying, "Means and meanness go together"; for a little later still I found the same characteristic just as fully developed in Alfred Beit, as I may tell in due course.

My friendship with Albert Ochs and Beit showed me a good deal of the inside of finance, and I knew that they would let me have the money to buy a paper as soon as I put a fair proposition before them.

One day in London I heard casually that the *Saturday Review* had just been sold to the son-in-law of the man who made Stephen's Ink. I had gone after the *Saturday* years before and was assured by Mr. Beresford Hope* himself that if the sale of it were ever mooted, I should have the first refusal. Now, some years after his death, I found it had been sold by his children for a paltry thousand pounds. I went down at once to the office and saw the owner, Lewis Edmunds, Q.C.,** who knew no more about literature than he knew about skyscrapers. He told me that the paper was not for sale, but he would be willing to consider an offer. At once I said, "All right, I will give you a pound for every reader of the *Saturday Review,* taking the average of the last three weeks. I will pay you ten per cent down and the balance within a fortnight."

"Will you take our figures for the sales?" he asked.

"Certainly," I replied. Forthwith he rang a bell and ordered the old book-keeper who came in to say what the average sales had been for the last three weeks. In ten minutes the figures were on the table. The average sales were 5,600. At once I gave him my check for five hundred and sixty and a promise to pay the remainder within a fortnight, against his written undertaking to hand me over the journal—and I went out of the office the probable owner of the *Saturday Review.*

* (1820–1887).
** (1860– ?); he became Queen's Counsel in 1895.

When I thought the matter over I realized that I possibly hadn't more than five hundred pounds in the bank, and so went out to get an extra hundred. I went to one friend after another and failed: A. was not in; B. was away on a holiday; C. would have to consult his wife as to the matter; but at last late in the evening I fell across Brandon Thomas,* the actor and playwright, and told him why I had come. He said, "I will lend you one thousand pounds on condition I may have a sixth-share in the venture." I gave him the undertaking, and a couple of years afterwards he got five thousand pounds for his sixth-share.

The purchase of the *Saturday Review* put me on my feet in every sense. Just as everyone had found that the step from the *Evening News* to the *Fortnightly Review* was a step up for me, so from the *Fortnightly Review* to the ownership and editorship of the *Saturday Review* was again a big step up. The losing of the *Fortnightly Review* did me good: it made me resolve to edit the *Saturday Review* as well as I could. So I sat down to plan the ablest possibly weekly: first of all, the staff must be better than the best hitherto.

I thought I had fewer prejudices than most men, and a better understanding of greatness than any editor in London, and so I set myself to pick the ablest. To my friend Runciman** I had promised the place of musical critic and my assistant. The first man I wrote to was George Bernard Shaw. He was at that time writing musical articles on the *World* for four pounds a week. I wrote to him that music was not the forte of the man who had written *Widowers' Houses* and begged him to come to the *Saturday Review* and write articles on the theatre—for he was a born dramatist—and I would pay him double what he was getting.

I had in Shaw the ablest possible lieutenant—though with his communistic views, he was a peculiar man to put as first lieutenant on the conservative *Saturday Review*. Then I asked H. G. Wells to take over the reviewing of novels in the *Saturday,* and when he, too, accepted, I felt that I had made real progress.

Finally, I got D. S. McColl,† who has since become the head of the Tate Gallery, to do the art criticism. McColl was one of the first in England, I think, to understand Cézanne as well as Monet and Manet; and I think I heard from his lips first of all the name of Gaugin mentioned with understanding: all through the next four years on the *Saturday* he tried to teach the English public the new development of French art which has since led the world.

* (1856–1914), the author of *Charley's Aunt* (1892).
** John F. Runciman (1866–1916).
† Dugald Sutherland MacColl (1859–1948), art editor for the *Spectator* (1890–96) and then for the *Saturday Review* until 1906. He was made Keeper of the Tate Gallery in 1909. His *Nineteenth-Century Art* (1902) was one of the first sound books on the French impressionists.

As a master of science, I picked Dr. Chalmers Mitchell,* who is now, I believe, the head of the Zoological Society. It is enough to say that Chalmers Mitchell deserved the position or any other post, for he was not only a student of science of real ability, but he wrote charmingly to boot. Always, in my mind, I thought of him as a younger Huxley; yet Huxley lives in the history of science, and I am not sure that Chalmers Mitchell has done anything which entitles him to immortality; but he certainly was one of the most notable contributors to the *Saturday Review* in my time, besides being of a charming, pleasant nature with the critical habit very strongly developed. Chalmers Mitchell was above middle height with spare, well-kept body and fine expressive face—a notable personality.

A little later I got Cunninghame Graham.** I have left him to the last because I have always thought of him as an amateur of genius. He was picturesquely handsome and always well dressed. I came to believe that his physical advantages and his wealth alone prevented him from being one of the great writers. He has written one or two of the best short stories in English, notably *Un Monsieur;* and surely his travel sketches in the Argentine and elsewhere are among the best extant.

The next thing to do was to outline the policy. The *Saturday Review* had been called the *Saturday Reviler* and was evilly notorious as the most poisonous critic of all lost and all new causes. I told my contributors from the beginning that I wanted to change this character radically. I wanted the *Saturday Review* to become known as the finder of stars and not the finder of faults; and at once I refused to give pride and place to merely fault-finding articles, though these too are necessary when dealing with be-puffed mediocrities.

One instance will do as well as fifty. One day I picked up a new book by a new author. *Almayer's Folly,* by Joseph Conrad. I had not seen the name before, but a glance at the first page told me that the man was a writer. At about the same time a Mr. Low† came in (a brother of Sydney Low), a very able writer. I threw him the book and said: "There seems to be good stuff in that."

He took it with him and in a few days sent me a murderous review. I got another copy of the book and read it. After reading it, I sent the review back to Low, saying it was altogether wrong: Joseph Conrad was a good

---

* Sir Peter Chalmers Mitchell (1864–1945), secretary to the Zoological Society of London from 1903 until 1935. His best known book is his biography of T. H. Huxley (1900).

** Robert Bontine Cunninghame Graham (1852–1936). He went to the Argentine in 1869, became a rancher, and married a Chilean poet. He inherited his family estates in 1883 and returned home. He was elected an MP in 1886 and was among those arrested in 1887 during the Trafalgar Square riots, with Hyndman, Burns, Champion, etc. Cunninghame Graham was a capable essayist and writer of short stories. Harris gives a winning sketch of him in *Contemporary Portraits, Third Series.*

† (1857–1932), editor of the *St. James Gazette.*

writer and as a newcomer should be praised and not condemned, standing, as he did, high above the ordinary!

Then I sent the book to H. G. Wells.

After a week or two Wells blew in boisterously. "What a book," he cried, throwing it down on the table. "Thanks very much for sending it to me. That sort of stuff makes one's task as a reviewer pleasant, but I am afraid you will think my review far too long and far too eulogistic. I have written pages about Conrad, not columns, and I have praised him to the skies. Will you stand it?"

"First-rate," I cried, "just what I had hoped from you. I sent the book to a man who crabbed it. After all, a great reviewer should be a star-finder and not a fault-finder."

For some reason or other, I never met Conrad until the autumn of 1910, fifteen years later. Talking one day with Austin Harrison of the *English Review,* Conrad's name came up and I asked: "How does he look? What age is he? Has he any foreign accent? Is he a great personality?" —a stream of questons.

Harrison declared that Conrad knew me, always spoke warmly of me, and ended by proposing that we should motor down to his cottage in Kent. We did so the very next Sunday.

Conrad met us most cordially, was eager to record that the review in the *Saturday Review* had given him reputation. I had thought from his photograph that his forehead was high and domed, but it was rather low and sloped back quickly. He was a little above middle height and appeared more the student than a sea-captain. Both he and his wife were homely, hospitable folk, without a trace of affectation. But Harrison's presence prevented any intimacy of talk, and the nearest I got to Conrad was when I asked him for a recent book, *The Mirror of the Sea.* He stipulated that I should send him my latest in exchange, and under the dedication to me he wrote the first and last verses of Baudelaire's magnificent poem comparing man to the sea. He repeated the last line:

O lutteurs éternels, o frères implacables,*

with a note of bitter sadness I thought characteristic. His French, I noticed, was impeccable.

Since then I have read most of Conrad's books, but I have never rated him at all as highly as Wells did.

What a crew of talent to get together on one paper before they were at all appreciated elsewhere. Wells and Shaw, Chalmers Mitchell, D. S. McColl, and Cunninghame Graham. I think the best staff ever seen on any weekly paper in the world; and that on a paper which was practically bankrupt when I took it over; and yet all these men remained with me for the three or four years of my editorship.

Wells impressed me as about the best mind that I had met in my many

---

* The last line of "L'Homme et la mer," from *Les Fleurs du Mal.*

years in England: a handsome body and fine head. I had hoped extraordinary things from him, but the Great War seems to have shaken him, and his latest attempt to write a natural history of the earth chilled me. A history of humanity to the present time in which Shakespeare is not mentioned and Jesus is dismissed in a page carelessly, if not with contempt, shocks me. Yet as Browning said,

> Thus we half-men struggle.

I can hardly mention Wells at this time without speaking of Bernard Shaw: I had known Shaw before I took over the *Fortnightly*. I had heard him speak in the East End and had thought his communism shallow, for it left out individualism, which is at least as important a force. But after getting him to work for me as dramatic critic on the *Saturday*, I met him almost every week. I saw at once that he had a good mind: one of the best of his time indeed; but somehow or other his extremely slight body and his vegetarianism became to me typical of the man.

His plays, too, are all full of Shaw. In one play Shaw assumes a dozen different names; but the characters are all Shaw. His is an acute intelligence, delighting in reasoning and argument, but never going deep, seldom indeed reaching creation of any value. When I think of Bernard Shaw, I am always reminded of Vauvenargues' fine word: "All great thoughts come from the heart."* All Shaw's thoughts come from the head.

The other day I was amused by a criticism of Shaw by a Mr. James Agate** who is, I believe, the dramatic critic of the *Sunday Times*. He lays it down that Mr. Shaw is not able to create a human being. "All the Shavian creations," he says "are like Martians or Selenites or other fantastic creatures with enormous brains and no bodies and consequently no appetites." Yet he goes on to assert that "There [are] more fundamental brains in any single play of Shaw's than in the whole of Shakespeare's output." To me this is worse than fantastic silliness. But I remember that Shaw, many years ago, told me, and he has written it somewhere, that it humiliated him to compare his brains with Shakespeare's; I told him roundly I could give him a dozen instances where Shakespeare has used more brains in two or three lines than is to be found in all Shaw's work. He challenged me for an instance, and I gave him one: Shakespeare's Cleopatra is with Antony in Egypt, and Antony goes to meet Caesar. Cleopatra feels instinctively that no one can fight Caesar successfully; dreading Caesar's power, she fled from Actium; but at the end of the day Antony returns in triumph and says that he has beaten Caesar to his camp; he cries to her

> . . . leap thou, attire and all,
> Through proof of harness to my heart, and there
> Ride on the pants triumphing!

---

* *Réflexions et maximes*, 127.
** (1877–1947), theatre critic on the *Sunday Times* from 1923 until his death.

And her reply is

> Lord of Lords!
> O infinite virtue, comest thou smiling from
> The world's great snare uncaught?*

She knows that in spite of her beauty and cleverness and her position as queen, she has been caught in the world's great snare: she knows that it would require "infinite virtue" to be successful—and all this realization of life is packed into a couple of lines. Shaw would not admit the extraordinary virtue of the passage.

Nothing to me is clearer than the fact that the highest mental effort is the creative intelligence; the greatest minds in the world are those that have created new world-figures:

> Forms more real than living Man,
> Nurslings of Immortality.**

Shakespeare has given us Hamlet and Cleopatra, and better still Falstaff; Goethe, Mephistopheles, and better still, Gretchen; Cervantes, Don Quixote and Sancho Panza; and Turgenief, Bazarof. No one ranks with these few creators of ever-living generic figures.

Yet it is unfair to say that Shaw has not created any character: he has given himself in twenty characters as a sharp witted man who sees things chiefly from the ludicrous side because he is not greatly gifted with body or heart. Someone has said that "to the heart, life is a tragedy; and to the mind, it is a comedy." Shaw sees it usually as a comedy, but his *Cleopatra* exists for me, and the characters in *Candida* are something more than reproductions of his own personality; but to compare his mental faculties with the great ones is simply silly. He has done nothing comparable to Swift's best work, to say nothing of Shakespeare's.

In my portrait of Shaw I have spoken of his kindness to me at some length. Here I wish to add that in America, too, when I asked him to write for my magazine *Pearson's* in New York, and begged him to tell me what I should have to pay him, he wrote me that Hearst was giving him five thousand dollars for everything he wrote, but that it was enough to know that I wanted him to write for me, to continue writing for me, for I had done him a great deal of good by giving him the pride of place on the *Saturday Review*.

He told a friend of mine the other day that he never felt any reverence for any one; and this amused me greatly, for it is a peculiarly Shavian trait. How could he feel reverence for any one, when the only person he really knows is Shaw; yet he is an admirable journalist, and in many ways a good and kindly man, and I enjoyed my intercourse with him on the *Saturday*.

How good any real power is! Some of Shaw's sayings have delighted me.

---

* Act IV, scene 8.
** From Shelley's *Prometheus Unbound*, I, line 747.

In the beginning of the war, when nearly every one had lost his head, Shaw spoke of "the British bull dog masquerading as an angel of peace"; and later he spoke of the "one hundred per cent American as ninety-nine per cent village idiot." Village idiot! I could have kissed him for the word.

I see that the *Saturday Review* has published an account of its editors and contributors on its seventy-fifth birthday. On my staff it left out Wells, Chalmers Mitchell, and D. S. McColl; and had the grotesque impudence to put a little Jew named Baumann to write about me as an editor. Baumann naturally began by saying that I had begged him to write for the *Saturday Review*, which is not the fact. A mutual friend, Lord Grimthorpe, begged me to help the little man; and I think I took a couple of articles from him, but he was never on the staff and never was able to rise to the ordinary level.

There is no such certain test of greatness as the dislike and denigration of the mediocre!

The *Saturday Review*, as I remodelled it, met with a good deal of opposition at first. Officious people by the score wrote to me, condemning Bernard Shaw as an illiterate socialist, and Wells as a sort of Jules Verne. But the circulation began to lift at once, and I was very glad of it, for very soon I came to loggerheads with the Oxford University Press.

They had published some book or other, and Professor Churton Collins brought me a review of it, in which he pointed out that in this book, issued by the University Press, there were some three hundred grave errors of fact. I published his review and immediately there was a terrible to-do; the exposure was shocking. The University Press wrote to me curtly that they wished to withdraw their advertisements. They had engaged space in the *Saturday Review* for some three years beforehand and, of course, they paid their bill regularly at the end of each year. I wrote to the University Press that if they had had any regard for truth, they would have written thanking me and my reviewer, but as they wished to enroll themselves among the powers of darkness and ignorance, I would allow them to withdraw their advertisements, which they accordingly did.

Shortly afterwards I got a notice from Longman's, complaining of a review of a Greek book they had published. The review was written by the first authority in England, Sir Richard Jebb.* Longman's wrote that it was evidently written by some ignoramus, and as the Oxford University Press had severed their connection with the *Saturday Review*, the house of Longman would also like to withdraw their advertisements.

I had been thunderstruck at the unconscionable impudence of the Oxford University Press, but when I got Longman's letter as well, I went to see him. I knew him through Froude's introduction, who prized him highly. I therefore called upon Charles Longman, who told me he was sure the review was written by some incapable and envious person. I had got

---

* (1841–1905), regius professor of Greek at Cambridge; his nine-volume work on Sophocles is a classic.

Professor Jebb's permission to tell him that he had written it, so at length I told Longman, in confidence, the critic's name; and we parted, apparently good friends, Longman saying he would reconsider the whole thing. A week after he wrote that I had changed the whole character of the *Review* and he agreed with the University Press, on the whole, and would like to withdraw his advertisements.

Their example was followed by several other publishers. In every case I gave the fools the permission to withdraw their advertisements, and at the end of a month or two saw myself face to face with the revenue of the *Saturday Review* diminished by three or four thousand pounds a year— the small profit I had managed to create turned into a heavy loss. What was to be done?

I went into the city and saw Alfred Beit, head of the great house of South African Mines. I pointed out to him that the *Saturday Review* went to all the best houses in England. I asked him to give me the balance sheet and yearly report of all his companies as an advertisement and I would write a note, if not an article, on each company when he sent me the balance sheet, the advertisement to cost fifty guineas. I came out of his office with his promise and the names of fifty-odd companies, so I had made up a good part of my loss in an hour.

I went to Barnato's, saw Woolfie Joel, and got a dozen of his companies on the same terms. I then went on to J. B. Robinson* and got eight of his companies. In short, in that one day's work in the city I had filled the gap in my revenue made by the withdrawals of the English publishing houses, and had increased the yearly revenue of the *Saturday Review* by two thousand a year. I knew I could reckon on Cecil Rhodes's help to boot.

That was the reason, I think, why the book reviews of the *Saturday Review* from '94 on became famous for their truth, which is so much disliked by most English and American reviews.

I mentioned the whole incident just to teach people what sort of pressure is exercised by Mr. Bumble, the publisher, on his true critic. Bumble wants praise and nothing else.

Curiously enough, a little later I had a somewhat similar experience with an insurance company. I got one of the ablest insurance critics in the world to write an article on the methods of a certain company and their balance sheet—and the company wrote, withdrawing its advertisement. I thereupon let my critic loose on all the faults of their work, and the consequence was that five or six of the best insurance companies wrote to me that they would like to advertise in the *Saturday Review*. For the one advertisement I lost I gained several better ones. This brought me to the conclusion that the business men of England are more honest and clear-minded than those who deal with literature and publishing.

There is something in art and literature which seems to corrupt the

---

* Sir Joseph Benjamin Robinson (1840–1929), a South African mine owner.

ordinary business mind. I think the corrupting influence lies in the extraordinary difference of values, which no ordinary man can foresee or explain. A publisher gets two books, both to his mind fairly well written and interesting; when he publishes them he finds that the worse one catches on and he sells 100,000 copies, whereas the other is a dead loss. He has given, let us say, a hundred pounds for each of them. "A" that he liked best is the failure, and "B" the success. A little later, he gets another book like "B" and finds that it is a complete failure—and so he makes up his mind that the only thing he wants to pay for is eulogy; and he prays for success because he is unable to deserve or merit it, or even to know how it should be gained.

I had one other curious experience with the *Saturday Review*—I found that a certain number of the best class of business people would only advertise if it had a cover on. The cost of putting a good green cover on it would only be some fifty pounds a week, whereas I could get over two hundred a week for the advertisements. I immediately put the cover on and got the advertisements, thereby improving not only the looks, but the revenue of the *Review*.

After I had bought the *Saturday Review,* I went and had a talk with Ochs, and he told me he would help me and outlined the proposition he thought suitable. I should form a company with a capital of about thirty thousand pounds that would take over and own the paper, and this I did, but I put also an addendum to his proposal, constituting five hundred deferred shares that would take no profits, but would control the appointment of the editor and staff. As I held all these five hundred shares myself, I thereby gave myself complete control of the paper. When I asked Albert Ochs for the five thousand pounds that I had to pay for the *Saturday Review,* he gave me four thousand pounds against shares and thought I ought to find the other thousand easily.

Now, what was the financial position of the *Saturday Review* when I took it over? The paper was losing money, roughly fifty or sixty pounds a week. Its circulation that once had been thirty or forty thousand had shrunk year by year, till now it was only five or six thousand a week. The income from the sales was less than a hundred pounds a week, and the income from advertisements that had been a thousand pounds a week had diminished to one hundred and fifty pounds or less.

The pay, however, of contributors, had rather increased than diminished, and everyone now expected at least three pounds for writing a column or two. By paying my staff, Shaw, Wells, McColl, Runciman and Chalmers Mitchell much more than the ordinary price, I had further increased my difficulties; but at the same time I knew dozens of young Oxford men at the bar and in journalism who were willing indeed to review books for the *Saturday Review* for nothing, on condition of getting the books; so instead of my contributors costing me over two hundred pounds a week, I got them down to under a hundred and so turned a loss of fifty or sixty pounds into a profit of thirty or forty pounds. The advertisement revenue I soon increased greatly, as I have told, so that the paper was clearing easily one hundred and fifty pounds a week.

I think I have explained sufficiently the financial position. I had 25,000 shares that I could sell very readily if I wanted money, and I had besides 500 deferred shares that ensured me the continuance of my position.

At this time or a little later I sold 5,000 shares to Beit for cash, and 2,000 or 3,000 more to other people who wanted an oar in the boat, and so made myself secure from the monetary point of view for some years to come.

I had only run the *Saturday Review* a short time when the Jameson Raid in the Transvaal shocked the world and necessitated on my part a prolonged absence from England.

Chapter III

The Jameson Raid*—Rhodes and Chamberlain

SCARCELY HAD I GOT the *Saturday Review* and taken the first steps to make it successful when the Jameson Raid took place, nominally in obedience to a call for help and protection from the English women and children in Johannesburg. I knew South Africa too well to be deluded for a moment by this shallow pretext. At once I denounced the raid and everyone who defended it. I soon found its defenders were numerous and could make their voices heard in a hundred journals from *The Times* down.

I saw Beit about it, and Ochs, Woolfie Joel, too, and others, and came very soon upon the proofs that the raid was instigated by Rhodes for selfish interests and would set South Africa in a blaze.

Information reached me that the raiders had been assembled at Pitsani by Rhodes, and everybody in South Africa knew that their real object was not to succor the Outlanders in Johannesburg, but to overthrow the government in Pretoria.

English opinion on the Jameson Raid and its ignoble end was rather undecided till the German Kaiser sent his famous telegram to Krueger, in which he practically told Krueger that if he wanted help he would give it to him. This inconceivably stupid act not only consolidated English opinion in favor of Jameson, but was the very beginning of that dislike of Germany and condemnation of the German Kaiser which later led to the Great War. Even the British Government resented the insult; it mobilized a part of the fleet and, I believe, called ships away from the Mediterranean to the North Sea. It is not too much to say that the English dislike of the Germans dates from that idiotic telegram.

After the Kaiser's telegram, I saw Arthur Walter, but found him a hot partisan of the Jameson Raiders with ears closed to any reason. At first, as I have told, he didn't like Rhodes, but Moberly Bell soon inoculated him

* Sir Leander Starr Jameson (1853–1917), administrator for the South Africa Company. In 1895, when hostilities between the Boers and Outlanders occurred in Johannesburg, Jameson moved with 500 troops to the relief of the Outlanders. He was overwhelmed by the Boers at Krugersdorp and surrendered on January 2, 1896. Jameson was handed over to the British and was sentenced to a short term in prison. By 1900, however, he was elected to the Cape Legislative Assembly, and he became Premier of the Cape Colony in 1904.

with the pan-English patriotic enthusiasm which suited his innate conservatism.

I had thought that the loss of the American colonies would have taught the English people that interference, even with their own kin thousands of miles away, was ill-advised and apt to be dangerous. But in London in 1895 I found nine men out of ten convinced that it was necessary to "teach the Boers a lesson and put Krueger in his place." That brutal unreason was so wide spread and intense that I resolved to go to South Africa in order the better to combat this old hereditary madness.

It all reminds me that Englishmen have not grown much in one hundred and fifty years. Didn't Benjamin Franklin write to Lord Kames,* somewhere about 1760, that "the foundations of the future grandeur and stability of British Empire lie in America, and though, like other foundations, they are low and little now, they are nevertheless, broad and strong to support the greatest political structure that human wisdom ever yet erected"? And it was due to Franklin that at the Treaty of Paris in 1763 Guadeloupe was restored to France, while Canada remained with England, though popular English opinion at the time wished rather to retain "the valuable sugar-islands of Guadeloupe" and give Canada to France.

If England had only the sense to profit by Franklin's foresight instead of jeering at him and insulting him, how different the course of world history would have been! As it is, Britain owes her chief possession in North America to his wisdom. In the same way, in 1896, I found that practically the whole of British opinion, as well in England as in South Africa, was totally and lamentably perverse. I must now return to my own story.

There was no time to lose if I was to do any good, so I took ship at once and was in Cape Town before mid-January, 1896, leaving Runciman in charge of the *Saturday Review* as my assistant, after having begged him, on any doubtful question, to take counsel with my old friend, the Reverend John Verschoyle.

The first person I wanted to see in South Africa was Jan Hofmeyr, then Rhodes; but curiously enough the day I arrived, Sir James Sivewright** came to lunch at the same hotel, and as soon as he heard of me, came up, introduced himself and gave me the benefit of his unrivaled knowledge of South Africa. When he realized that I wanted the truth and was prepared to accept it, he let himself go freely. He spoke of Hofmeyr with affection and of Rhodes with pity. I soon found him one of the wisest and best informed of counselors. I asked him about Governor General Sir Hercules Robinson,† whom I knew and liked. "Alas!" said Sivewright. "He's too wedded to Rhodes; but he's honest and capable."

* (1696–1782), Scottish philosopher.
** (1848–1916), general manager of South African Telegraphs 1877–85, Commissioner of Crown Lands and Public Works in the Cape Colony 1890, and Commissioner of Public Works 1896–8.
† (1824–97).

At length we came to the Jameson Raid and the famous telegram from the women in Johannesburg, asking for Jameson's help. "That telegram," said Sivewright, "was written in Rhodes's office in Cape Town and sent from there to *The Times*." I was horrified, but he gave me the proofs of what he alleged.

My first day in Cape Town had been astonishingly fruitful. At once I wrote an article and some notes for the *Saturday Review* and then, out of my affection for Arthur Walter, I wrote to him, giving chapter and verse for my belief, and begging him to modify the attitude of *The Times*. A little later Cecil Rhodes told me he knew I was working against him through Walter, and after that I let *The Times* take care of itself.

After the raid, Rhodes went up to Kimberley and the British element made his railway journey a sort of triumphal progress, but the more thoughtful spirits all condemned him. On his return to Cape Town he prepared to go back to England at once.

I had several interesting talks with him, and because he had been jolted, so to speak, out of his ordinary self-centered optimistic attitude, I came to know him better than ever before. I found he had gone entirely astray.

"What on earth could you hope to win by the raid?" I asked at length.

"I don't admit I had anything to do with it," Rhodes replied.

"Let us leave that," I answered, "but what could Dr. Jim* hope to win by it? Suppose he had got into Johannesburg; next day it would have been surrounded by five thousand Boers and in a week would have had to surrender."

"In a week a great deal might happen," said Rhodes sententiously.

"I understand," I replied. "Hercules Robinson would probably have gone north and consulted Krueger to play fair, but neither in war nor peace could your raiders have gained anything. It was an idiotic move."

"And suppose Chamberlain had taken a hand in the game?" Rhodes went on.

"You mean to say?" I cried; he nodded—

"Worse and worse," I countered; "that would have meant war, a race war in South Africa with fifty thousand Boer settlers and eighty thousand English loafers; you would have needed one hundred thousand British soldiers. Rhodes, you could not want that!"

"Krueger would have given in," he said.

"You know better," I cried, "you know Krueger would never give in and his Boers would back him to the last."

"Evidently you know South Africa better than I do," was his final fling.

"I am appealing," I said, "to Rhodes sober, the Rhodes I knew years ago, who taught me a good deal about South Africa and the Boer stubbornness."

"Well," he said smiling, "the end is not yet; don't condemn me before the end."

To that I nodded my head.

* Jameson.

This talk was only preliminary; I wanted to know Rhodes better: his real view of life and what he wanted to do in it. At length, one evening, I came to an understanding of his peculiar view of the world.

He had already spoken to me of Ruskin, who had influenced him profoundly through a lecture at Oxford; and he had come to believe that the Darwinian theory of evolution was the most probable explanation of the world, that it is the law of some supreme being, rather than the result of blind forces. God, he thought, was obviously trying to produce a type of humanity the best fitted to bring peace, liberty, and justice into the world, and thus make, as Heine said, "A Kingdom of God on this earth." One race to him seemed to approach God's ideal type—his own, the Anglo-Saxon. He knew no language but English, and that only imperfectly, and so was easily convinced of the superiority of the Anglo-Saxon character. God's purpose, to him, was to make the Anglo-Saxon race predominant.

As an ideal, it seemed to me grotesque. The races of the world to me were like flowers in a garden, and I would cherish every variety for its own especial excellence; far from being too numerous, they were not numerous enough, and there was not enough variety. The French seemed to be dropping into the second class, according to the judgment of force and numbers, but how could humanity afford to lose the French ideal of life? The French had done more for abstract justice in their social relations and more, too, for the ideal in art than any other race; we couldn't afford to lose the French. Yet, there are only forty millions of French people, whereas there are already nearly two hundred millions of Anglo-Saxons, and soon there will be a thousand millions, and yet what mistakes they make! Would not the consciousness of power make them increasingly intolerant?

I couldn't influence Rhodes; he talked to me repeatedly of Bartle Frere's idea: the English should possess Africa from the Cape to Cairo. "They already own more than one-half of the Temperate Zone," I said; "isn't that enough for them? And they don't know how to use it."

Still, I had already come to see that the vast central plateau of Africa from the Cape to Cairo was the most magnificent possession in the world, finer far than even the North American colonies that England had thrown away. Was it the chance of insular position, or really some superiority in the race, that had given one empire after the other into their possession? On the surface, it was merely the greed of the aristocratic English class to get ever more land into their power. But their continual extraordinary growth perhaps shows some spiritual ascendency. I should like to believe it, though I later found certain special virtues in the attempts at German colonization.

One day at dinner I ventured on a jest which distressed Rhodes dreadfully. I said I could understand God, in His youth, falling in love with the Jews, an extremely attractive race, but in His old age to fall in love with the Anglo-Saxon was a proof of senility that I could hardly forgive Him. Rhodes cried out at once: "You say things, Harris, that hurt."

"I would like to shock your idolatry of the English," I cried; "fancy the race that loves commerce and wealth more than any other and yet refuses for a century to adopt the metric system in weights and measures and coinage! Harold Frederic used always to talk of the stupid Britons."

"The masters of the world," Rhodes retorted.

"Nonsense," I replied. "The Americans are already far stronger and more reasonable."

We parted friends but disagreed profoundly.

Rhodes was completely uneducated, ignorant, indeed, to a degree that was painful; an almost blind force from which as much might be feared as hoped. Yet perhaps of his want of education, he was in most intimate sympathy with the intense patriotism and imperial ideas of the English governing class, and he was rich enough to advance his views in a hundred ways; money, to him, was chiefly a means to an end.

After much talk with Sivewright, I called on Jan Hofmeyr, who greeted me with the old kindness. "Very glad you've come out," he said; "now there's some chance of making the truth known." He did not conceal his profound disappointment with Rhodes. "Another Briton," he said, "whom we had taken for a great Afrikander," and he added, with rare prescience, "he may do worse for us yet! He's really madder than Oom Paul"* We talked for hours day after day and at length, when I had to say "Goodbye," he gave me a letter to Chief Justice Kotzé** at Pretoria, whom he praised cordially: "He will give you pure wine to drink on almost every South African subject."

From Sivewright and Jan Hofmeyr I got the truth about the raid and then called on Sir Hercules Robinson, the Governor General. He was before all an official, and an English official at that, but he had a certain understanding of South Africa and the best South African opinion; and though he sympathized with Rhodes's imperial ambitions, he would never defend such an outrage as the raid.

He seemed to have aged a good deal in the three or four years since I had seen him in London. I noticed signs of nervousness in him that I had not expected. He astonished me almost at once by saying: "We are still friends, are we not?"

"Of course; always," I replied warmly.

"People have been saying," he went on, "that you were sent out by Chamberlain, but that can hardly be true. He would surely have let me know. Still, he is capable even of that, I suppose."

His words and tone set me marveling. But for the moment I could not occupy myself with his opinion of Chamberlain. I noted that he was a good deal irritated and left it at that.

---

* Krueger.
** Sir John Gilbert Kotzé (1849–1940). He ran against Krueger for the presidency of the South African Republic in 1893 but was defeated. In 1898, just before the Boer war, Krueger dismissed Kotzé as Chief Justice over an interpretation of the constitution.

"No," I replied, "no, I have nothing to do with Mr. Chamberlain. I imagine he would hardly be likely to send me as an agent."

"I am glad of that," said Hercules Robinson. "We can then be on the old footing, can't we?"

I nodded.

"Why didn't you come to see me at once?"

"To tell you the truth," I answered frankly, " I wanted to see Jan Hofmeyr, wanted certain information before I came. I had to get clear in my own mind about the raid and Rhodes's complicity in it, and I didn't think it would be fair to question you in your position—I, your friend."

"You have found out all you wanted to know?"

"I have found out that you were all in it," I replied, thinking the challenge would excite him. "Rhodes planned it of course, but you winked at it."

"Winked at it," he repeated hotly; "you are mistaken: it isn't true."

"Oh, no," I laughed. "I was saying, 'winked' at it to be very diplomatic and polite. You knew all about it."

"Indeed, I did not," he took me up. "What put that into your head?"

"Come," I said gravely. "Surely you won't maintain that an armed force could have lain weeks on the border without your knowing it."

"But I assure you," he said, "you are mistaken. I knew nothing of the raid."

"I should like to take your word," I persisted, "but it is impossible. I have absolute proof."

"Proof?" he cried. "That's impossible. You must explain: you must see that your statement is—is—dishonoring. I have assured Krueger on my honor that it isn't true; he accepted my assurance, so must you."

I shook my head. "I'm afraid I can't."

"But I can explain everything," he went on. "For the first time in my experience the Colonial Office acted over my head. If you must know the whole truth, Chamberlain withdrew the political officer who was on the border; Chamberlain said he would deal with the matters connected with Jameson directly. I shrugged my shoulders, and let it pass. It was all a part, I thought, of his new method of doing business. He has his own peculiar methods," he concluded bitterly.

New light began to drift in on me; at least a hitherto unthought of suspicion.

"But you saw Rhodes on the matter," I ventured. "He must have told you at any rate that Jameson's forces were there to bring a little pressure on Krueger; he must have talked to you about the reform agitation he had helped to get up in Johannesburg."

"I shouldn't have listened to such nonsense for a moment," cried Robinson. "The way to get things out of Krueger is to behave straightforwardly with him."

"Rhodes got something out of him over the Drifts business by threatening war."

"That was different," Robinson admitted reluctantly. "Krueger felt he was in the wrong there. But now I hope you understand that I had no complicity in that shameful, stupid raid."

I had resolved to continue, so I persisted.

"I told you I had proofs," I replied. "You have destroyed one supposition, but the proofs remain."

"Proofs?" he said, in an anxious, irritated tone of voice. "There are none; there can't be any, Harris."

"Indubitable proofs," I repeated.

"It's impossible," he exclaimed. "Treat me like a friend. I tell you on my word of honor I knew nothing of the raid."

"I am sorry," I replied, "but if you want me to deal like a friend with you, I can only say I can't believe it."

"Good God," he cried, getting up from the desk and walking about the room. "This is maddening. Speak plainly, lay your proofs before me, and I will undertake to demolish every one of them."

"If I show you proofs that you can't demolish," I said, "will you deal fairly by me and tell me all you really know, and what I want to know?"

"Certainly," he exclaimed. "I give you my promise; I have nothing to conceal."

"All right," I cried, "I will give you the proofs one after another. Here is the first."

Sir Hercules Robinson's face was a study in conflicting emotions as I went on.

"When you first got news on the Sunday morning that Jameson had crossed the frontier, you wired to him to return, and you wired to Krueger saying that you had ordered Jameson to return, and that the raid was not authorized by Her Majesty's Government."

"Yes," Robinson broke in sharply, "that's what I did."

"You must have expected an answer in two hours," I went on. "If not an answer from Jameson, certainly an answer from Krueger."

"Of course," replied Robinson, "and I got a reply from Krueger."

"Pardon me for contradicting you," I replied, "but you did not. You got from Krueger a mere statement that Jameson had crossed the border at a certain hour with an armed force. You must have known from that telegram that President Krueger hadn't had your telegram."

"No," replied Robinson, "I see what you mean, but we were all very much excited and nervous, and I drew no such inference. The first thing I did was to send to Rhodes to ask if he knew anything about Jameson's act. I wanted to consult with him."

"I suppose he was not to be seen?" I said.

"That's true," said Robinson. "But how did you know?"

"Easy to be guessed," I replied carelessly.

"Rhodes returned no reply to any of my messages: in fact, he wouldn't see my messengers," Robinson went on.

"But at ten o'clock," I insisted, "you had a call from Jan Hofmeyr. He asked you to send out a proclamation, a public proclamation declaring that Her Majesty's Government had nothing to do with the raid, and that you had recalled Jameson by wire. You would not do this."

"I didn't see the necessity of it," Hercules Robinson answered. "I had wired to Jameson, and I had wired to Krueger, and I considered that enough. Krueger knew that the raid was unauthorized, and that was the main point."

"But Krueger did not know it," I replied, "and you must have known that he didn't know."

"What do you mean?" cried Robinson. "I knew nothing at all of it." And then he added, as if to himself, "When I was up at Pretoria, Krueger never said that to me."

"Outsiders see most of the game," I went on. "Let us go back to that Saturday. You have an exciting morning, but you get your lunch, and after lunch at about, I suppose, three-thirty o'clock, you get another wire from Krueger repeating his news, amplifying it, saying that Jameson had crossed the frontier with Maxim guns, and asking you what you are going to do. Now you must have known that he hadn't yet got your first telegram."

"No, I didn't know," said Robinson. "It all passed in the hurry and excitement of the moment."

"But why didn't you duplicate your telegram to him," I asked, "saying that the raid was not authorized, and that you would order Jameson's return?"

"I did," he said.

"No, you didn't," I replied, "not at once, that is. Later that afternoon," I went on, "or rather that evening, you got a telegram from Krueger again giving you the news, and insisting on a reply."

"You are right," Robinson broke in, "I remember now; it was that last telegram that I answered. But how did you know all this?"

"How I know doesn't matter," I replied. "The point is, I am giving you facts. You must have taken great care that the second telegram of yours, after you had received three from Krueger, each of which showed that he had not received your first wire; I say, you must have taken extraordinary care to see that the second telegram reached him at once."

"It must have reached him in an hour," said Robinson carelessly, "just as the first must."

"You would be surprised to know," I replied, "that it didn't reach him at all that night, nor till far on in the next day. You left Krueger to his Hollander counselors for a day and a half without any word from you."

"Good God!" cried Robinson. "It can't be true; yet it would explain his attitude to me at first. But how can it be? It's absurd."

"Send and find out when your telegrams went," I urged. "You must have a book of telegrams, where times and everything are entered?"

"Of course, of course," he cried. "That is all in the hands of the Imperial Secretary, Sir Graham Bower.* I will ring for him."

He rang, and when a man came, sent him to ask Sir Graham Bower to come at once. Two minutes later Sir Graham Bower appeared: an ordinary dark man, unimportant looking, smiling, I thought, a little nervously, a set smile.

"Oh! Bower," broke out Robinson, "Harris has a most extraordinary tale. Pardon me, I must introduce you. This is Sir Graham Bower, the Imperial Secretary, and this is a friend of mine, Frank Harris, the editor of the *Saturday Review* whom we have talked about."

We bowed and shook hands.

"Bower," Robinson broke in again, "Harris has brought a most extraordinary story that on the Sunday morning when we got the first news of the raid, my telegram to Krueger, telling him we had wired ordering Jameson to return, and that the raid was not authorized by Her Majesty's Government, never went off. I don't know how he knows, but that is what he says."

"No, no," I broke in. "I say that it didn't reach Pretoria that day, and not till well on in the next day."

"Nonsense," cried Robinson. "Please get the telegraph book, Bower, and prove it to Harris."

Bower turned and went out of the room, still with the same smile on his face. I felt sure then he was playing a part. I thought I had found the villain of the piece, but waited for the proof. Meanwhile Robinson and I stood together in tense expectation.

In two minutes Bower returned with a large book in his hand.

"The telegram," he said, "I find, went off at twelve-thirty."

"Twelve-thirty!" cried Robinson. "You must be mistaken. That is hours after I sent it."

"It went off in the usual way," Bower remarked, with studied carelessness.

"Usual way!" said Robinson, looking at him. "But it was of the first importance."

"There was a great deal of excitement and running to and fro," he said.

"I know, I know," said Robinson. "I sent you to Rhodes—but still, Bower—twelve-thirty."

A thought came to me, and I drew the bow at a venture.

"But you have a special form," I said, "for telegrams from power to power, a special form of telegram that takes precedence over all others. Why was this telegram sent as an ordinary telegram, and not on your special form?"

* (1848–1933), Imperial Secretary to the High Commissioner for South Africa 1884–97.

I had hardly begun to speak when Bower's face changed expression. I knew I had guessed right.

"Of course it went on the proper form," cried Robinson. "There can be no doubt of it, can there, Bower? You can prove it."

I smiled. Bower said very lightly, too lightly, "I suppose so."

"But think, Bower," Robinson went on, "think what it means."

"I can't be sure. I'm not sure," replied Bower.

"Not sure," cried Robinson, turning on him, "not sure! But you can't realize what it means, man. Harris here says that we got a second telegram from Krueger in the afternoon, telling us of the raid again and asking us what we were going to do. We believed, or I believed, that my first telegram had already reached him, telling him that we disavowed the raid, and had ordered Jameson to return. Harris says that when we got that second telegram we must have known that Krueger hadn't got my first telegram; and Harris is right. I should have drawn that inference; I remember it struck me at the time as curious that Krueger should merely repeat the news. Then came Krueger's third telegram, and of course Harris insists again it must have made me see that Krueger had not received my first telegram. We answered it, and now Harris says that both these telegrams of mine, official telegrams, must have been sent as ordinary telegrams, for Krueger didn't get even the first of them in the day; Krueger got no word from us till the Monday afternoon, Harris asserts."

"I can only tell Mr. Harris," said Bower, "that the whole place was in a state of the intensest excitement. I went twice or three times to Rhodes and couldn't see him; visitors called at every moment, Hofmeyr and others, who had to be seen: everyone was running about."

"All the more reason," I said, "for sending such important telegrams on the specal official forms."

"My God!" said Robinson, putting his hands to his head. "My God! That's what Krueger's cold reception of me meant."

There could be no doubt about the matter. Hercules Robinson was blameless in the affair. He had been kept out of it. Rhodes had found a surer tool in the Imperial Secretary, Sir Graham Bower.

I rubbed the point in decisively.

"Your message," I said, "the telegram of the High Commissioner, the most important telegram ever sent from this office, went as an ordinary telegram, and instead of taking precedence, followed some hundreds of others in ordinary sequence to Pretoria; and Krueger sat in council all day, sending message after message to you, and getting no reply, but getting wire after wire from country districts to the effect that Jameson was pushing on towards his capital as hard as he could. Can you expect Krueger to trust the English after this? All that day, all that night, the old man waited, and half the next day before you gave him the chance to act."

"Good God!" said Robinson.

"You don't want me any more, Sir?" asked Graham Bower, pointedly, and left the room.

"What's to be done now?" cried Hercules Robinson, falling into his seat. "What's to be done? But how did you know all this? How have you in a few days found out more than I knew, I with such power and experience, and living at the center?"

A little later I went up to Johannesburg, and while there was asked to go and see the President by Chief Justice Kotzé of the High Court. I went across one day to Pretoria. It is like a town set in a saucer with low hills ringing it round; a town of squat Dutch houses set amid trees and little noisy rivulets of water running down the sides of the streets—everywhere the chatter of children and childish games, and quiet home life. And in the strange little provincial town, two or three magnificent public buildings that represent fairly enough the obstinate patriotism of the Boer.

I was invited to call upon the President at six o'clock in the morning, but I declared that if I got up at that hour I should be at my worst, and I wanted to be at my best. When the President heard that I never got up before the day was well aired, he invited me to come and have coffee with him, and so I called upon him in the early afternoon, called with Chief Justice Kotzé, who was kind enough to offer to act as interpreter. The house was an ordinary Boer house, the reception-room an ordinary Boer parlor with wax flowers, colored worsted mats and a huge Bible as its chief ornaments, unless I include the enormous spittoon, which was used at every moment by the master. I hardly dare to describe the coffee. For providing this coffee Krueger got eight hundred a year besides his salary of eight thousand pounds, and I should think that for eight pounds he could make enough of it to float a battleship. It was the vilest liquid I had ever attempted to drink; a very disagreeable decoction of Gregory powder in half-warm milk. I took one sip and left it at that.

I told about the interview in its main lines in the *Saturday Review* at that time, and gave the best portrait I could of the village Cromwell called Paul Krueger. Every one is familiar with his likeness to a great gorilla, his porky baboon face, and small piggy grey eyes, but no portrait could give an impression of the massive strength, the power, and restrained passion of the man. He must have been fifty-four inches round the chest, and when seated looked like a Hercules. The worst fault in his gigantic figure was the shortness of his legs. Strange to say, he is one of the few men who has grown greater in my memory, and this in spite of all the fumblings and failings of his later years. Had he been trained, had he had any education or reading, Paul Krueger would have been one of the greatest of men. As it was, he was one of the most remarkable.

Krueger was suspicious, as the ignorant always are, self-centered like most strong-willed, successful men, but not devoid of heart and conscience. His treatment of the Outlanders in Johannesburg was simply insane. Some eighty thousand of them had made Johannesburg the greatest gold-mining industry in the world; they paid more than nine-tenths of the state taxes. Instead of getting just enough to live on—a few hundreds a year—from his twenty thousand Boer burghers, Krueger was now a rich man. The Outlanders had turned the Transvaal from a bankrupt state into the wealthiest in South Africa, with a revenue of three millions sterling a year: yet in 1894 he had made it impossible for them to obtain a vote in a country to which they contributed practically the whole revenue. They had no control even over the affairs of the city they had founded and built up. Krueger still treated Johannesburg as a mining camp under his own mining commissioner.

Dutch was taught in the schools, and not English. Though denied all rights of citizenship and treated as aliens, the Outlanders were nevertheless liable to be impressed for service in native wars. Krueger's iniquities were surely unparalleled. He had given foreigners a concession for the manufacture of dynamite, which was imported into the country by monopolists, and sold at such a price to the mines that it practically imposed a tax of half a million pounds a year on the industry. Another lot of adventurers got the concession for carrying coal along the Rand, which they did at the highest possible rate; another group owned a liquor concession which corrupted the natives.

The curious thing was that Krueger's treatment of the Outlanders was no worse than his treatment of the Boers in the Cape. He wouldn't allow the Transvaal to enter the Customs Union; and pigs, cattle, and coal from the Cape could be imported only on payment of fantastic duties. The spirit of his policy was shown in one act. When the Transvaal railway management proposed to put up the rate from the Vaal above six-pence a ton in order to kill the Cape traffic, Krueger asked them to make it a shilling; and when the traders left the railway at the Free State border and carried their goods over the short stretch to Johannesburg in bullock-wagons, Krueger proclaimed that the Vaal Drifts, which they had to cross, would be closed to them.

This last piece of despotism brought a new force into the field. In 1895 Joseph Chamberlain had made himself the Minister of the Colonies; and although he had no liking for Rhodes, still, when Rhodes appealed to him, he took his view and described President Krueger's act about the Drifts as one "almost of hostility," and declared his willingness to back up his protest by force. Reluctantly, Krueger saw he had gone too far and threw open the Drifts. Then the raid took place, which blotted out even the memory of most of the President's stupidities and threw the onus of flagrant wrong doing upon Rhodes.

Early in the interview Krueger asked me point blank whether I believed, like Hercules Robinson, that Chamberlain didn't know about the raid. I said, "I couldn't tell: there was no proof. I felt certain the Cabinet didn't know it, and could hardly believe that Mr. Chamberlain would act as dictator in such a matter."

"The Cabinet didn't know of it?" questioned Krueger. "You are sure?"
"As sure as I can be of such a thing," I replied.

In the back of my mind was the feeling that Chamberlain must have known all about it, may have talked even to Mr. Balfour about it, but I wanted to say rather less than more of what I believed out of patriotic feeling, and so I maintained the possibility of Chamberlain's innocence.

Krueger turned on me sharply.

"You know that Rhodes planned it, paid for it, directed it?" he barked.

"Surely," I replied. "He confessed as much in Cape Town to Jan Hofmeyr, and I have wired that home to my paper."

"So," he cried, "you admit that Rhodes was a scoundrel?"

"Worse," I replied quietly, "a blundering idiot, to think that five hundred men could beat the Boers."

The great burly man sprang erect, while his little grey eyes snapped in the fat pork face. He looked like a maddened baboon.

"Four hundred boys," he shouted. "Do you know what I would have done with them?"

"No," I said smiling, "I should like to know."

"What I proposed in council," he roared, glaring at me, "was to lead each by the ear to the border and kick their bottoms back into Bechuanaland."

"Why didn't you do it?" I cried, shouting with laughter. "Oh, my goodness! What a pity you didn't do it and enrich history with a unique scene. The most genial proposal I ever heard. That is what ought to have been done with them: impudence should always be met with contempt."

My delighted acceptance of his proposal brought the old man to good humor at once, but he was still suspicious.

"Do you know," he went on, "that one of Jameson's lieutenants, a leader of the raid, an officer in your army, too, told the Bechuanaland police that the raid was looked upon favorably by the government?"

"But the police," I said, "didn't believe him. If the police had come in as raiders, then the complicity of the government would be difficult to deny."

"Hercules Robinson is honest," said Krueger, as if to himself, "good, too, but getting old and weak: thinks it clever to speak with two tongues. But we shall soon know."

"Know what?" I asked.

"Know whether your government, whether Chamberlain and Rhodes were agreed."

"How will time help you?" I asked, wondering.

The old man went into a long explanation which the Chief Justice translated, telling me that notebooks, and telegrams had been found upon the battlefield, and that they had all been decoded, and established the complicity of Rhodes and Beit in the raid up to the hilt. I was told I might go and see the telegrams, and I did see them all the next day, some time early in February, the same telegrams that were published in *The Times* in May, and caused a sensation.

But Krueger was not to be diverted for long from the main point.

"We shall soon know," he repeated, "whether Chamberlain was behind Rhodes or not."

"How?" I asked.

"Well," he said, "it is clear that the English people were behind him. Look how they cheer the raiders, and how they talk of them as heroes. But if they punish them that will be clear, and if they punish Rhodes, then I shall know that Chamberlain and the government were not behind him."

There was such menace in the old man's voice and manner, such rage of anger, that I tried to show him the other side.

"Difficult," I said "to punish Rhodes. How would you have him punished?"

"Oh," he cried, "I don't want him punished in money or in person. He was made a Privy Councillor. Let them take that away from him: anything to show their disapproval, and I shall be content. I want to believe that the English government is honest, as it was when Gladstone was there."

I could not help but admit that that might be done, should be done.

"If it is not done," cried the old man, "I shall know what to do."

"What?" I asked.

He growled and glared, and didn't answer, but one night after dinner Kotzé told me that Chamberlain had asked Krueger to come to London and state his case, saying that he would be treated with perfect fairness. I knew that Chamberlain disliked Rhodes, personally, and had never forgiven him for giving ten thousand pounds to Parnell, and when Kotzé told me all this, I said to him that I thought I ought to see the President again; and he arranged for the meeting immediately and undertook as before to act as interpreter between us.

This last interview with Krueger seemed to me very important: first of all, I thanked him for letting Leyds* show me the telegrams that proved that the Jameson Raiders were on their way to overthrow the Transvaal government, and I got the President's permission to publish the telegrams as I wished. I then alluded to the trial of the chief raiders and said I hoped that no capital punishment would be inflicted. "It would be ridiculous," I said, "to punish the servants with death and let the master go free." Krueger nodded agreement. "President," I added, "as we agree on so much, I want to persuade you to go to London as Chamberlain desires. You will give him the parliamentary triumph which he wants, and in return he will give you a free hand against Rhodes. You needn't fear for the independence of the Transvaal if you do this: it will be insured for our time at least."

"Why should I go to London?" he broke in.

"Policy," I said, "nothing else. Chamberlain is much more dangerous

* Willem Johannes Leyds (1859–1940), State Secretary for the South African Republic, 1893–1897, and Minister Plenipotentiary, 1898–1902.

than Rhodes: if you get Chamberlain on your side, you need fear nothing for the next twenty years."

"Do you mean," he said, "that otherwise the English would come and try to take the Transvaal again?"

"I have no right to speak for them," I said, "but I am frightened; Englishmen don't believe that forty or fifty thousand Boers should be allowed to play despots and deprive one hundred thousand Englishmen of political rights in the country which they have made wealthy. You will have to judge the matter, Mr. President," I added, "but Chamberlain is strong either as a friend or an enemy, and I always remember what Ben Franklin, one of the wisest of Americans, said: 'There never was a good war or a bad peace.' "

"We have a better friend than Chamberlain," he said. "You forget that we have the Almighty God, and He has freed the Transvaal once for all."

"I can only tell you," I said, "how I think the game should be played; I am no one, you are one of the protagonists."

"I am glad to have met you," was his concluding speech to me; "for the first time I have met an Englishman who tells me what he considers the exact truth. I hope you will put our case plainly before the public, and I don't say I won't take your advice about Chamberlain, though I dislike the idea of going to London. I have grown old," he barked, "and am tired, and I got nothing in London before."

"There is much to get there now," were my last words, "and you would win Chamberlain easily."

Delighted with my praise, the old man said, "As soon as I heard of the raid I got out my rifle and put on my old *velt-schoon;* I was going to lead my burghers against Jameson, but—" he pointed to Kotzé, "he and the others persuaded me not to go."

Whatever Krueger was, he was a great old fighter! It was his courage and combativeness which led him to his ruin. I remember saying to Kotzé when we came away: "Unless Krueger goes to London and gives Chamberlain his parliamentary triumph, he will be sorry for it. There is a great text in the Bible; I wonder if you know it: 'If thou hadst known, at least in this thy day, *the things which belong unto thy peace!* but now they are hid from thine eyes!' "

Of course Kotzé understood. When we parted I told him that I would send the telegrams to the *Saturday Review* to be published—but I must pass over that story in silence, for it reminded me of the worldly wisdom of Dante's phrase:

> Degli amici guarda mi Dio
> Degli memici mi guardo Io

"God save me from my friends; my enemies I'll take care of myself."

In the days that followed, and after my return to England, I saw plainly enough how Krueger's suspicions must be strengthened to certainty. The raiders were received in London by cheering crowds: the leaders, who were punished by short terms of imprisonment, were let out even before the term had been served. Rhodes was regarded everywhere as a hero, and even the commission that was set on foot to bring the truth to light contented itself with finding out little or nothing, and with rewarding instead of punishing the villain.

One scene from that commission I must give because it is of historic interest; it was the only real attempt made to cross-examine Rhodes before the commission, and it established not only his complicity, but threw a more sinister light on the whole conspiracy; and established finally, in my mind, the guilty complicity of Joseph Chamberlain.

The chairman of the commission was a Mr. Jackson, whom I had known as Financial Secretary to the Treasury.* I had met him at dinners and had had long talks with him, and had learned to appreciate his fairmindedness and good sense. He gave me a desk to myself, apart from the pressmen's desk in the room where the sittings were held. It was well in front, where I could see and hear everything.

From the beginning it was evident that it was a white-washing commission. Everyone paid the most extravagant deference to Rhodes, a deference which often called forth from him expressions of amused contempt. Chamberlain bowed when he addressed a question to him. Sir Richard Webster** was proud to help him to brandy and soda like a waiter. The idea of a millionaire as a criminal in England was too ludicrous for words. Even Labouchère lost all his pert impudence when questioning him. Indeed, poor Labby was at a loss: he was only half-informed, and Rhodes's advocates on the commission, and especially Chamberlain, could do what they pleased with him.

But there was one man on the commission equal to his task, Sir William Vernon Harcourt.† He had studied his brief, had made himself familiar with the facts, seemed quietly determined to get at the truth. When he took Rhodes in hand, the relative proportions of the two men became plain at once. Rhodes began to lose his self-confidence, hesitated, hectored. Sir William Vernon Harcourt apologized, used great courtesy, never insisted, but returned with new questions. Again and again Chamberlain interfered to turn the attack, but Sir W. Vernon Harcourt was not to be denied or diverted from the main points; he smiled at Chamberlain and went on pushing in probe after probe in deadly fashion.

Rhodes and his supporters in the press had been putting forward the notion that the agitation in Johannesburg was a real reform movement, whereas Sir William Vernon Harcourt evidently believed that the cosmopolitan Jew financiers directing the mines in Johannesburg didn't even wish

* William L. Jackson; he represented Leeds in Parliament in 1893 and 1896.
** (1842–1915), Lord Chief Justice of England. He took part in the Venezuelan Boundary Dispute.
† (1827–1904), Solicitor-General 1873–74, Home Secretary 1880–85, and Chancellor of the Exchequer 1886, 1892–95; an authority on international law.

to become citizens of the Transvaal Republic. He had already made it pretty plain that it was a fictitious and carefully fomented agitation. Rhodes, on the other hand, asserted that Jameson had gone in to assist the reformers and to keep order.

Sir William Vernon Harcourt went on to the morning before the raid and read a telegram from Jameson to Woolff in Johannesburg: "Meet me as arranged before you left on Tuesday night, which will enable us to decide which is the best destination."

"Can you explain to me, Mr. Rhodes, what is the meaning of those words, 'which is the best destination'? " Thus daintily Sir William Vernon Harcourt placed the bomb upon the table.

Rhodes pretended indignation.

"No, I certainly could not; you see, Woolff was at Johannesburg: Jameson telegraphed from Pitsani. I should say the 'best destination' means the best route."

Sir William Harcourt smiled.

"That is not the ordinary meaning of destination. Was it proposed that Dr. Jameson, instead of going to Johannesburg, should go to Pretoria direct? Have you ever heard that, Mr. Rhodes?"

The bomb had exploded, the tension in the room was extraordinary: members craned forward and held their breath so as not to miss a word.

Rhodes hesitated, and then:

"I don't think I could have heard. I couldn't be sure. No," he added, "all I understood was that he would go to Johannesburg if required by the people of Johannesburg."

Again Sir William Harcourt insisted.

"Was there such a proposal? I ask because this is very important."

Mr. Rhodes turned and replied sulkily, fighting desperately for time. "I don't see the importance of it."

Sir William Harcourt, though interrupted by Mr. Pope,* one of the opposing counsel, persisted quietly;

"I am putting a most important question. Was it ever discussed between you and Dr. Jameson whether or not he should go direct to Pretoria and attack President Krueger's Government, instead of going to Johannesburg?"

Mr. Rhodes fumbled: "I really couldn't answer that definitely; it might have been said." Then, catching at a straw, "Ask Dr. Jameson."

"You are an even more important person than Dr. Jameson. I really must ask you."

"I have given you my answer; I cannot remember; I don't see the importance of it."

Sir William Vernon Harcourt: "There is a very important difference between going to assist an insurrection in Johannesburg and going to make an attack direct upon the government of Pretoria."

* Samuel Pope (1826–1901).

Rhodes admitted the proposal may have been discussed, though he couldn't remember it.

Thus Sir William Harcourt by his questions had brought out the fact which, indeed, was contained in a telegram of Jameson, that the objective of the raid was not decided when the doctor started; that Jameson had it in mind not to go to Johannesburg at all, but to make a dash for Eirene, the place where the Boers stored their arms and ammunition about seven miles from Pretoria, and thus attack Krueger's government at the heart and directly.

Everyone expected Sir William Harcourt to pursue his interrogatory on the morrow, but he did not, and I was deeply disappointed. The commission broke off for the day and the point was never touched on again.

For the life of me, I couldn't fathom the situation or guess the secret. I found it out afterwards, however, from Dilke, the best informed Member of Parliament. He told me what I have already explained in Chapter XIV,* that when the German Emperor congratulated Krueger on having defeated the raid, Queen Victoria reproved him sharply and declared that he seemed to be trying to make her government responsible for it, whereas none of her ministers knew anything about the raid. The German Emperor apologized humbly for his mistake.

"But when the South African Committee stirred the whole matter up again," Dilke said, "a Conservative statesman called upon Sir William Vernon Harcourt and told him about the Queen's letter to the German Emperor, and his reply; and when he had recited the facts, the Conservative went on to point out that if Sir William Vernon Harcourt pursued his questions and demonstrated the complicity of Chamberlain, or, indeed, rendered Chamberlain's complicity probable, he would be proving the Queen to have told what was not the truth to the German Emperor. He left it to Sir William Vernon Harcourt's sense of what was fit and becoming whether he would continue his interrogatory or not. Sir William Vernon Harcourt thereupon abandoned his plan, and gave up the victory he might have won over Chamberlain."

The committee condemned severely Sir Graham Bower, the Imperial Secretary, who had betrayed his superior, Sir Hercules Robinson, but Chamberlain gave him a governorship at once. Thus is traitorism rewarded in England.

Much the same thing happened with Robinson. He made two or three distinct charges against Chamberlain, and on my way home in April, '96, at Cape Town, he gave me chapter and verse for these accusations, but begged me not to say anything about them till he had returned to London and seen me, as he intended to make them in person against Chamberlain.

When he came back I wrote to him, saying that I was ready to see him at any time he might wish, and he replied that he would give me an im-

* Of Volume III.

mediate appointment. Then he wrote again, putting me off in a letter with a very changed tone; and when I pressed him, he wrote saying he was very ill, too ill to see any one, although he had seen the Colonial Office and Chamberlain in the meantime. Suddenly he was made Lord Rosmead and nothing more was heard of his accusation against Chamberlain. The English often close mouths with titles.

Chapter IV

African Adventures and Health

I MUST TELL of some of my African adventures which took place shortly after I passed my fortieth birthday.

Africa—what gaudy memories the mere word calls to life: that first evening in the desert south of Biskra, with the grave Arabs sitting round, listening to the story-teller shaping the age-old tale to a new ending, acting the characters the while, mimicking villain and hero, slave and ruler, and with a magic of personality, making the drama live before our eyes.

Or that long ride up Table Mountain with Cecil Rhodes. I still see him standing—a greater Cortez—with his back to the Pacific, starting towards Cairo, six thousand miles away, dreaming of the immense central plateau, three times as large as the United States, as one empire.

That great central plateau where the air is light and dry, like champagne, and mere breathing's a joy; where the blessed sun reigns all through the long day, and the earth grows odorous under the hot embrace, and the sweat dries on the naked back in selvages of salt like the ripples on a sandy beach, while the night is cool and refreshing as the yellow moon comes up over the black forest and turns the camp into fairyland, while sweet airs breathe sleep on weary limbs.

And the freedom of it! Not the freedom of London: freedom to do as others do, dress as others dress, and speak as others speak, parroting phrases that were half lies when first coined, and smearing unctuous sentimentalities on dagger points; no, not that! Africa's freedom is of the wild and waste places of the earth, where one can be a man and can think his own thoughts and speak truth and live truth and stretch yokeless neck and free arms in God's sunlight.

Towards the end of February, 1896, I came to the conclusion that I understood South Africa, and as Rhodes was still absent in London, I determined to make my way up the country, at any rate as far as the Victoria Falls on the Zambesi, which I had always wanted to compare with Niagara. Accordingly, I organized an expedition and set off with one hundred and fifty carriers. I had as lieutenants two Boers, brothers, whom I had met in the Free State, and so long as they were with me, everything went fairly well. But their cruelty to the Negro carriers was almost diabolic, and one day, when the elder brother kicked a Negro and broke his leg and wanted to leave him to die in misery, I revolted. The end of it was that I paid them both for the entire trip and said "Goodbye" to them. We parted good friends, and the elder brother told me to keep my eyes skinned and see that the Negroes always boiled the drinking water or I'd get fever and come to grief. He turned out to be right. I thought kindness would be as efficacious as cruelty, but I was mistaken.

Still, I won through to the Zambesi, and one sunlit morning, for the first time, the great Victoria Falls that dwarf Niagara, burst on me, robed in rainbow mists, as if to hide the depths, while the great Zambesi stretched away to the right, a silver pathway to the far-off sea. The solitude, the scenery, the great river, and the falls, the wild animals of all sorts, and above all, the sense of living in the world as it was a hundred thousand years ago, made this experience the chief event in my life, separating the future from the past and giving me a new starting point.

I was two or three days exploring the falls from every point of view, and at night had divine rest in my tent. A day's journey away, fifteen miles or so north of the falls, and perhaps five hundred feet higher, I could still hear the roar and seemed to feel the earth quake.

This trek fagged us all out; the road was bad and the heat intolerable. The hundred and twenty or thirty Negro bearers I had with me put down their loads and threw themselves on the ground, careless of tsetse fly or mosquito, eager only to sleep and rest, even before eating. It was with difficulty that I got my personal servants to put up even my bell-tent. The big one they professed they could not find; three or four of the bearers, it appeared, had not yet come up. At last the tent was fixed and my mattress put down in it. My little table and stool were brought out and they gave me something to eat, fish and deer's meat, washed down with good whisky and water.

I had had the tent placed, as usual, fifty or sixty yards away from the camp of my carriers. The Negroes had not even cut thorn bushes as a Zareeba or fence to protect themselves. Sleep was the one thing we all wanted.

Though within the tropics, we were some thousands of feet above the sea level, so the air was quite cool at night, though the sun in the daytime was scorching. After my meal, I told the head man he could go and sleep. I went into my tent, put on pyjamas and lay down. The tent was small and the cool air so delicious that I left the flap open. In the evening air it waved a little, the elastic that held the square of it back being a little worn. Lying down on my mattress in front of the opening, I could see the great purple vault of sky, and on the right, the edge of the wood, perhaps a hundred yards away.

In a minute I was asleep, plunged into the dreamless slumber of absolute bodily exhaustion.

Suddenly I was annoyed by a noise. I was pulled out of my dreamless sleep by a repetition of it. Very cross, I tried to blink open my eyes. At first I could hardly see anything.

Again the flip! What was the noise?

At the camp everything was in deepest peace and silence. The mosquito netting was all around my head and my hands were gloved. I could hear the insects humming.

Again the flip! At length I was wide awake, more than awake.

The flap of the tent had closed and then opened again. And again the sound. The flap of the tent, three-quarters closed for a moment, was then pulled back by the elastic. I could have reached it by stretching out my hand, but I was now too full of anxious curiosity.

What could it be that made the flap of the tent go back and forth so regularly?

Suddenly my curiosity was steeped in fear. I did not know why. Instead of getting up and stepping out to see what caused the flap to act so strangely, I put my head to the ground and peered underneath the tent.

Gradually my eyes became accustomed to the dark and I soon could see outlines a bit more clearly.

There was something there against the sky, and as I looked along it I saw a tail with a tuft on the end of it.

What could it be?

All of a sudden the flap of the tent was driven to again and then pulled back by the elastic. I peered more closely at the object, made out the outline, and realized the whole affair.

It was a full grown lion, lying on the ground playing with the flap of my tent, like a big cat. He had evidently crept up to the tent, probably attracted by my odor, seen the flap moving a little in the wind, and struck it with his paw. It went and came back again, and after a moment or two he had struck it once more.

A lion playing with the flap of my tent, two feet from me!

Quickly I drew up my Westley Richards rifle that was always loaded at my side, and lay down to try to get an exact line on his head and ear.

Then I thought: Why should I kill him? The big cat was really doing no harm. The something cat-like, childish, in his play made me smile. This feeling of pity and friendliness probably saved my life, for just as I was hesitating—G-r-r-r-m—I heard a long, rumbling sort of moan to the left, and as I looked out through the tent, I saw distinctly the outline against the sky, perhaps four yards away, of another lion, or rather a lioness, as she had no mane.

How many were there?

I had seen a dozen together before then. They might be all around my little tent, for all I knew. One blow of one of their paws would carry the tent away and leave me exposed in the center.

It was perhaps wiser to keep quiet and await developments. The lioness moved a few feet forward and then stretched herself, yawning. I could see her as distinctly as possible, not ten feet away now.

Suddenly my lion at the flap joined her, stood opposite her for a moment, then turned his head slowly towards the flap and my humble person.

Again the rifle went to my shoulder, and I wondered, looking straight at the lion, whether he saw me as plainly as I saw him. Then I reflected that against the black of the tent he could not see me at all. That was my solitary advantage over him. Both beasts were uneasy, curiously watchful, especially the lioness.

Suddenly a sound came from the camp, and her head went round at once, turned towards the sound. The next moment she crouched down close to the ground and moved stealthily out of my limited field of vision.

The sound was repeated. Probably a Negro had got up for something in the camp, for at the second sound the lion turned, and walked slowly out of my vision after his mate.

I found it quite impossible to sleep. I tried to, but the proximity of the big beasts was too disquieting. I found myself listening, on the thin edge of expectancy, with nerves stretched for every sound.

I grew more and more wakeful. Again and again I peered along the ground, but could see nothing.

The lions had either gone to the woods or to the camp. I could not tell which. No sign of them.

Suddenly, I began to see the trees on the right more distinctly. The night was over. Two minutes afterwards long arrows of light: it was day.

I went outside and clapped my hands. A couple of headmen came to me and I pointed to the ground by the flap. They read the signs quite plainly— "big lion"; and when I pointed a few feet away, they found the spoor of the lioness and followed it down to where the pair had gone into the wood.

The marks of a half-grown cub were with the lioness.

I told them what had happened, that the lion had been playing with the flap, and I still hear their "Woo-oof" of wonderment.

The second day of our trek I fell ill with malaria, which soon developed into blackwater fever. I treated myself with big doses of quinine and arsenic and went on, but the third day I must have been given another drink of ordinary unboiled river water.

I found it almost impossible to get the Negroes to boil the water: they told me lie after lie. That evening my temperature was over 105°. I had learned, with Bilroth in Vienna, that at 105° the fever begins to feed on the heart itself, and one must at all costs diminish the fever, even with ice-packs. But I had no ice, and that day and the next, in spite of large doses of quinine and arsenic, my temperature continued very high. For two or three days I was out of my mind and raved in delirium. My head man, a big Negro, told me with tears that the men said the spirits who spoke through me were determined to take me; and one morning I found that no one answered my call. Fortunately, the evening before I [had] wanted some tins of soup, and my Negro kept bringing me tins of sardines, which I tossed in the corner of the tent; in the morning, when I awoke and rang my bell, no one answered; and when I crawled on hands and knees outside the tent, I found the camp deserted and my medicine chest broken in pieces and strewn all over the ground. I was deserted by the carriers who had smashed up my medicine chest before going, believing that all my power was to be found in the medicines.

There was further evidence that kindness was not understood by the ordinary Negro. I had made it a rule from the beginning to keep my tent fifty yards from their encampment, and I soon found it necessary to make a further order: that they should go about their private business one hundred yards from the ordinary encampment; now, when they thought I was about to die and they were resolved to steal all my belongings and bolt, they had been dirty first all over the place as a sign of contempt, I suppose.

At any rate, here I was in the wilderness with nothing but my rifle and revolver and a knife and perhaps twenty cartridges in the belt around my waist, and nothing to eat, and so weak that I couldn't stand. I said to myself at once: "This is the end; the sooner I put a bullet through my head the better. No use writing anything; it would never be seen. If any white people come to the place and find my dead body, my rifle will tell them the tale. Had I anything to say of any value to anybody?" I decided that I had not. I took up the rifle to end it all, when suddenly my eye caught sight of the five or six tins of sardines which I had tossed the night before into the corner of the tent.

Six boxes of sardines and one of soup meant life for a good while, and after all I was quite close to the Zambesi, to the river that ran to the sea and to civilization, say, six hundred miles away. If I had been well, twenty miles a day would have gotten me to the sea in a month, but even ill, surely I might do it in two months! I tied my most necessary things into a bundle, took several boxes of matches and a little tin kettle, strapped the whole on my back, and two mornings after I came again to the Zambesi. I determined to stick to the river and look for a canoe: some dug-out or canoe might be abandoned and I might have the luck to find it.

Next morning I began to make my way to the sea: at first the fever was very high, but I kept on taking daily doses of quinine and nightly doses of arsenic. But alas! I had only the one package, picked from the box which had been by my bedside: I had to be content with small doses.

Perhaps the hard exercise or the starvation did me good: in two or three days I reckoned I had made about fifteen miles down the river, and I was certainly stronger, so I took my first meal of three sardines. All the afternoon I was ill, and the next day could scarcely crawl. Wherever I saw the semblance of a path through the reeds to the river I looked out for a canoe, but for many days I saw nothing, except some hippos in the river and deer in the distance. The less I ate, however, the less fever I had. But the weakness persisted, my legs seemed to have no bones in them, and half an hour's walk tired me out. What I suffered, I can never tell. I couldn't have made much more than sixty or seventy miles in the month; and it was a month before I found a canoe, three days after I had wolfed my last sardine.

But the dug-out was salvation, and as I lay in it, I realized that I should now be able to make fifty or sixty miles a day; one lucky shot would give me food, and the current would bring me to civilization in ten days or a fortnight: the mere hope gave me new life. In an hour I had made a couple of rude paddles and had waded through the reeds and pushed into the full stream. No more painful walking or crawling—thank God!

Luck held with me. That day, or the next, I saw a small hippo standing on the bank. I took most careful aim and fired and he fell to the shot; in a few dozen strokes I was into the bank and beside him: he was dead—the bullet had gone clean through his head just behind the eye. Once only in my life did I feel more of a murderer, but necessity is the first law, so I opened his mouth and cut out his tongue, and went down the river half a mile with it before I lit a little fire and boiled it in my kettle, boiled and boiled and boiled it till it was more than cooked; and I had my first real meal in five or six weeks. It was the turning point—my fever got less from day to day and I slept interminably; one thing only bothered me: my beard grew inordinately and there were some grey hairs in it—there were not many—I could still count them, and I was over forty—but I resented their appearance and swore to myself that I wouldn't mount the white feather until I was over sixty, if I could ever get out of Africa.

I have nothing more to recount of any interest till I got to the first Portuguese settlement, and there I had an amusing experience. I secured my canoe on the bank but I couldn't make up my mind to leave the kettle and a few odds and ends, so I carried them with me. As soon as I got into the street of the little village, every one I came across had a good look at me and then bolted incontinently: children, women, men—everybody. As I passed a barbershop, I thought I would make myself decent before trying to get anything in a restaurant. The barber was shaving a man, but as soon as he saw me he dropped his razor and shot into the back room; the man, half-shaved, got up, indignant, but after one look at me, he slipped out into the street and disappeared; so I went over and looked at myself in the glass. Never was there such an appearance: nose and eyes and a long ill-grown beard on the face of a corpse—I had never seen any human face so thin, and my dirty shirt and clothes, and the kettle in one hand, and all my belongings in the other; I don't wonder that the people fled. I knocked at the inner room and the barber ventured out as soon as he saw the gold sovereign —I had a good deal of money about me. In a little while he cut off my beard and shaved me, but even then my face frightened me: it was emaciated, a skeleton-face. I asked the barber for a restaurant and he pointed on down the street to one, and in five minutes I was seated at a table with a beefsteak in front of me. I ate very little because I was afraid of indigestion, and with good reason: in an hour I had thrown up most of what I had eaten; and I was back in the restaurant to try something else, till I saw it was useless. My stomach had been ruined by the berries and leaves I had eaten: I could digest scarcely anything; meanwhile, half the town came to the restaurant to see me.

In spite of the heat, I bought an overcoat which covered my rags, and got a room for the night in a decent hotel and had a long hot bath: it seemed impossible to get clean. Before going to bed, I saw the doctor, who was a Portuguese and knew some English. He told me to eat only soup and brought me little arsenic pills that did me a great deal of good. What I weighed then I have no idea, but a month later on the German steamer taking me up the coast, I weighed less than eighty pounds, although my normal weight was then about one hundred and sixty.

I must explain why I didn't get stouter. Only on the first day was I able to eat and digest a little food. On the second day everything disagreed with me; I had acute spasm after spasm of indigestion. I tried everything, but my stomach was hopelessly enfeebled, partly by the berries and partly by the other indigestible things I had eaten. If any reader wants to know the best thing I had in weeks—it was a small snake, the head of which I cut off and then boiled the body; and the worst thing I ever attempted to eat was a caterpillar; there was a certain red berry which really poisoned me, but the taste of the caterpillar will live with me as long as I live: it was disgusting.

The doctor on the German liner tried everything to help my digestion, but nothing did me any good. In Germany, Schweninger made me believe that a fast of ten or fourteen days would bring my stomach into good order. I tried the fast and prolonged it till I found my legs failing on going down some stairs; then I began to drink milk and afterwards vegetable soup, and so brought myself gradually to a normal diet. But as soon as I began to eat solids again, I had unbearable indigestion.

Schweninger taught me nothing except the science of getting thin, which he had proved on Bismarck: his discovery was that drinking with one's meals alone makes fat. If you drink nothing for half an hour before your meals and for two hours after, you will lose weight at the rate of a couple of pounds a day, after the first day or two. By following this regimen, Bismarck, when already old, lost some sixty pounds and came to better health. Later I, too, tried this cure and found it efficacious. Since then, whenever I want to bring my weight down to normal, I simply follow Schweninger's regimen for a few days.

When I found that I could get no relief from Schweninger, nor, for that matter, from doctors all over Europe, I returned to London. That summer a well-known specialist told me to put my house in order, for I had only a short time to live. He said, "I cannot hear your heart, and," pointing to some steps on the other side of the road, "if you ran up those steps it would probably kill you." The Princess of Monaco had brought me to him, and so when we got out into the street, I ran up and down the steps three times as hard as I could, and laughed with her afterwards.

A year later, in passing the doctor's house, I went in to call on him. After examining me carefully, he told me that my heart was in perfect condition, my arteries like those of a boy; and he wondered why I had come to him. When I referred him to his prediction, he turned my case up in his diary and said he had written that my heart was almost inaudible, weaker than any woman's. He begged me to tell him what I had done and how I had brought about the change.

I have already explained that it was my house doctor in London who first made me acquainted with the stomach pump. It taught me what I could digest and what I ought to shun, thus giving me a complete and scientific dietary. As I made it a rule to leave off everything that disagreed with me I soon came to almost perfect health.

Of course, every now and then I sinned a little. If, inspired by company, I drank a little more than I should, the washing out of my stomach cured the evil and gave me perfect rest. If I ate a little too much starch or oil, and the first water of the purging was colored or impure, I gave my stomach another bath, but always went to bed with my stomach as clean as my mouth.

One fact I may give here, which doctors and scientists may seek to explain. After some years of careful dieting I found that I could eat and digest little bread or even butter. Of course, I would only eat the butter or bread at lunch, but sometimes a slight pain in my forehead a couple of hours afterwards taught me that I had indulged too freely: the pain passed away and I took my usual light dinner. Four hours or so later I would wash my stomach out and suddenly the butter, eaten at lunch twelve hours before, would appear. The stomach had allowed all the rest of the lunch and dinner to pass on into the intestines, but had retained the butter to be washed out in due course.

This fact has made me almost believe that the individual cells of the stomach are semi-rational in some sort, and will act in the interests of the general health.

One other factor should be mentioned in connection with the stomach pump, and that is the intestinal bath of warm water, which is taken once or twice a week to regulate the bowels and keep them healthy.

But even the most careful dietary did not bring perfect health without regular exercise. From boyhood on I had exercised pretty carefully both morning and evening. I recognized early that indigestion in adults usually comes from the fact that they do not move the middle part of the body enough. The child is always bending and stooping, and so exercises the abdomen; but the adult keeps the stomach and bowels almost quiescent. I found that exercising this part of the body was better for health than developing the muscles of the arms and legs and chest. And so for many years my exercises were all taken with a view to bettering my digestion.

I may note here that I was nearly forty before I had the first attack of indigestion; it was really the dreadful experience on the Zambesi that ruined my stomach. As I grew in years from forty on I found that exercise could easily be too violent: I began to leave off the heavy clubs and large dumbbells I had loved to use in youth.

Strangers, and even those who know me, are continually surprised and astonished at my almost perfect physical health and a comparative youthfulness of appearance that goes with it. When I explain that my health is due to study of the body and to careful observance of the rules which are conducive to healthy living, they all beg me to publish some of the facts.

Very few people realize how completely it is within the power of a fairly strong man to make himself perfectly healthy. After my breakdown in health in 1896, I began, as I have said, to study health and digestion in every way possible. In the autumn of this year, I found I was growing bald: a bald spot had appeared on the top of my head. I immediately set myself to think out a remedy. Advancing years, of course, was the real cause, and my spell of ill health; but now that I had regained my health, what was I to do to get rid of the baldness? It seemed to me that the bald spot came chiefly through the use of the hat, which prevented the hairs being blown about and the roots of them exercised; accordingly, I thought of a substitute and I began to scratch my head so as to excite the hairs surrounding the bald spot. In a little while I found that I was right, because the hairs came back and the baldness gradually disappeared: six months did the trick and I have had no trouble since.

In much the same way, later still, I found my eyes tiring with much reading and writing. I went to the best oculists and got glasses which helped me a little, but soon again, in spite of the glasses, I began to suffer. I had always been short-sighted from astigmatism, but I saw well near at hand, and up to about fifty could read for ten or twelve hours a day without noticing any fatigue; now, after four or five hours reading or writing, my eyes used to get blurred for minutes together; I had to put the book down and wait. These weak spells grew more and more frequent at an alarming rate, I went to the oculists, but found they were just as ignorant as the doctors: one recommended different glasses, but no change helped me; another told me that I should be very proud of being able to read two hours at a stretch without suffering. In fact, I got no satisfaction from any of the so-called specialists; whereupon I took the matter up for myself. "You are suffering," I said, "because your eyes move mechanically up and down a page and so grow tired." Thereupon I began to exercise my eyes every morning, casting them from one end of the room all over it to the other, for a quarter of an hour a day. At the end of a month I threw away all my reading glasses and now find that at over seventy I can read or write twelve or fourteen hours a day without trouble, just as I could as a boy. A change of work is almost as good a rest for the eyes as for the other parts of the body.

I am often asked where I get my knowledge of the body. As a German student fifty years ago, I heard of the celebrated doctor Bilroth in Vienna, and went there and studied under him. I would rather at that time have been a doctor than anything else. There were two sacred orders of mankind to me always: those who diminish pain and those who increase pleasure. I didn't think my self good enough to be a writer or scientist and so give enjoyment, but I did think I could be a great doctor; I soon found that I was taking the science much more seriously than the ordinary students or doctors or even professors.

I could give dozens of shocking instances of the careless indifference to human suffering, not only of the students and doctors, but also of the nurses; but I will simply give the final one, which made me leave the university. I came into the operating-room one day and found that a doctor had just carried out the difficult operation of cutting a cancer from a woman's breast. The room was half-filled with students, which astonished me, and I asked what was the occasion? I was told the doctor had bet a fairly large sum that he would cut the cancer out and finish the operation in a certain number of minutes; I think it was fifteen. I was horrified when he turned around and smiling remarked that he had won. When I looked at the patient I suddenly saw a small trickle of blood on her breast. I pointed and said to the doctor: "You have been too hasty." His face changed: he had immediately to take the stitches out, open up the wound again and tie up the artery, which he had forgotten or overlooked because of the constant application of the ice-bag. By the time the breast was open, the blood was already spurting from the artery; and as he took it up to tie it, the woman made a slight movement and was dead.

"It might have happened to any one," he remarked.

"You are a brute," I cried, "and should be charged with worse than murder." I left the room or I would have struck him. I spoke of it to the superiors, which all the students resented, but the superiors consoled me and themselves with the fact that she was a poor woman and really couldn't expect such treatment as was given to those who paid.

The whole incident, coming on top of fifty lesser experiences, made me see that I would always be at odds with the whole of the profession and that I might as well give up my wish to be a surgeon, so I left Vienna and went on to Greece.

Before I leave this question of health, I must say just one thing: the wisest of French proverbs is *une fois n'est pas coutume*—(once is not a habit), which, being interpreted, means that you can do a great many things once which, if you attempted to do frequently, would bring you to utter grief. I have known the time that a drinking bout did me real good, but if I had continued it every night for a week I should have been a pitiable object; and so there are many things one can eat once in a while which one can't eat every day. *Une fois n'est pas coutume* is a great rule of physical health.

Chapter V

Dark Beauties

THIS TREK to the Zambesi was the most extraordinary adventure of my life. It altered my whole conception of life. Up to that year, about my fortieth, I had always tried to believe in a Divinity

> . . . that shapes our ends,
> Rough-hew them how we will.*

Now I began to put the comma after "rough" instead of after "ends."

As soon as we got into Bechuanaland to the north-east of the Transvaal, Negro tribes, men and women, came constantly to visit us; they begged bright cloths from us and knives, and naturally my Boers, who knew them intimately, had provided me with all sorts of things with which to barter for furs, etc. I soon found that the younger of the brothers was fond of gratifying his lust with any young Negro girl who took his fancy, and I had to acknowledge that the girls were anything but reserved. Karl was a fine, big man, fully six feet in height and perhaps thirty years of age, and his brother was even bigger and burlier, perhaps ten years older, and altogether more brutal: we always spoke of him as the "Doctor."

One morning, I remember, we were late in starting and some of the Negro leaders were laughing because Karl was not ready, having been occupied with a Negro girl in his tent. As soon as the "Doctor" learned this, he strode to the tent, and tearing up the fastenings, overthrew it and exposed his brother, half-dressed, who was packing his valise. The young Negro girl who had been helping him started up when the tent fell, and smiling, held out her hands to the "Doctor." Red with rage, he caught her by the left breast and flung her from him. She shrieked and began to cry: Karl expostulated with him; but I was furious.

"I want you to know once for all," I cried, "that I won't have these colored people ill-treated."

"*Bestie!*" he replied.

"They may be beasts, in your opinion," I went on, "but I insist that they

* *Hamlet,* Act V, scene 2.

shall be treated decently. To kiss a girl first and then maltreat her is shameful! And I won't stand for it!"

Karl nodded agreement with me while the "Doctor" went off muttering and scowling.

It was Karl who gave me at our next stopping place a lesson in Negro morality. A small tribe had come to our camp to beg: he and I got out some colored stuffs and showed them to the women and girls, who went crazy with delight. One of the prettiest of them and best formed, a girl of perhaps fifteen, took up a piece of bright blue. She was, of course, naked, except the little apron that half-covered her nudity. Karl at once threw the cloth about her shoulders: she laughed gleefully and strutted about with it; he went over and kissed her, saying she could have it. At once she threw her arms about him and then, saying something, lifted her apron.

"What does she say?" I asked.

"That she's ready for a man!" said Karl.

"What does she mean?" I asked, and Karl set himself to explain to me a custom which I found was almost universal.

"As soon as half a dozen girls in a tribe reach puberty," Karl said, "they are taken by a couple of old women to the nearest stream. There the old crones, with great ceremony, break the girls' maidenheads and then declare them fit and ready, in a week or so, to give pleasure to men and bear children."

The whole affair seemed astonishing to me: I had always imagined that the maidenhead was a result, or at least an indication, of the proprietary instinct of the male, and if it were thus gradually developed by natural selection, why do away with it in such a coarse way? But Karl assured me that the girls were all delighted to be rid of it and free to devote themselves to the higher uses of maturity.

After a month's trekking we were visited one evening by a tribe which possessed a young girl almost completely white. The heads of the tribe assured Karl that she was the product of a white missionary, who fifteen years ago had journeyed far, far to the north across the great river.

Some time later I told Stanley the story and wondered whether by a new sort of paper-chase, he had tracked Livingstone by parti-colored offspring across Africa. But Stanley had no sense of humor and seemed to resent the imputation. Still, I must record one fact in regard to this girl: she was extraordinarily proud of her white blood and begged Karl to find her some white man to whom she might give herself and so have done with colored men forever. Curiously enough, though of sufficient age, she had refused to submit to the ministry of the old colored women and therefore still preserved her maidenhead. She wanted white children, she declared, and would never yield herself to a Negro.

It was the Doctor who undertook to content her desire and was gratefully accepted, though I always thought there was more than a little Negro blood in his veins; still, he was at least half-white.

In the course of the next month or so we came upon three similar instances, and in every case the same insensate pride in the mulatto. It grew to be a joke with us that we were following in the missionary's footsteps!

When we were nearing the Zambesi, we spent a whole day trekking through a dense forest, and there towards midday discovered a troop of baboons. The Doctor happened to be a little ahead of us, and almost at once a huge female baboon picked him out and began, with unmistakable gestures, to show him that he had taken her fancy and that she was more than willing to be his love. Naturally the incident amused me highly and I induced the brothers to let the game go on. To cut a long story short, that female kept close to the Doctor to the edge of the forest and beyond it. The grotesque obscenity of the exhibition, the unmistakable passion of the animal, gave me a new understanding of the intimate ties that bind us men to our simian ancestors.

> However we brazen it out
> We men are a little breed.*

I never took any part in the nightly orgies that went on between the members of our caravan and the girls of the various tribes that visited us to beg and to barter. I was content with my Kodak to take snapshots of the prettiest girls and the finest young men, and here I made some remarkable discoveries. None of the girls objected to stand for me, and not one hesitated to take off the little apron of hide they usually wore; but underneath the apron there was a small covering, perhaps two fingers broad, which they all objected to removing. They regarded their sex as ugly and would not willingly expose it.

Another curious fact: I soon found that these girls did not recognize themselves in their photos. One of our leaders was a Negro with perfectly white hair. When we showed the girls this Negro and his photoed likeness, they all exclaimed with delight: they could recognize him, but not themselves. I have often noticed that a dog does not recognize his likeness in a glass; perhaps it needs a certain amount of intelligence to know even what we look like.

Some of these young colored girls had very beautiful figures: it is usually thought that their calves are too thin and their breasts too flaccid. Naturally, taking into consideration their early maturity, they soon show these signs of age, but from ten to fifteen they are often perfectly made.

Why didn't they tempt me? I can't say; the half-white girls appealed to me much more; but the pure Negro type left me completely unmoved.

I loved to take their photographs in the most lascivious attitudes, enjoyed draping them in a pretty piece of stuff and thus bringing out their ever-present coquetry; but when they sought to excite me, I would slap their bottoms and turn away. I never could understand the attraction they pos-

* From Tennyson's *Maud,* Part I: iv. "However we may brave it out, we men are a little breed."

sessed for most white men. I had known the fact from my varsity days in Lawrence, Kansas, where all my comrades used to hunt regularly in the Negro quarter; but even then I never went with them, not out of any moral scruple, but simply because the black girl, however well made, did not excite in me what Dr. Johnson called his "amorous propensities."

Yet I was told by Karl and the Doctor that the Negro girls were far more passionate than the white ones. "There is no comparison," Karl used to declare; "Negro girls, and boys, too, feel the sex thrill far more intensely than any whites."

It may be true. I have seen Parisian cocottes making heroes of Negro lovers; they have told me time and again just what Karl asserted; but it is not only the vigor of the Negro, but also the size of his sex which causes him to be so esteemed by the French prostitutes. On the other hand, the Negro girl, too, is far larger than the white and that certainly detracts from the man's pleasure. Besides, the mousey smell is always present, and that was enough to choke my desire. But the want of intelligence is the chief deterrent; for Hindu girls are often very dark and have the mousey odor, yet their brains or higher spiritual understanding make them eminently desirable.

Yet my virtue was destined to suffer one defeat. One evening, a girl we had met, who was almost completely white, was encouraged by Karl to come nude to my bed. I was tossing about asleep in the night when she came and laid down beside me, or rather on me. The heat of her body had excited me before I even awoke, and before I was fully conscious I was enjoying her. I felt no disappointment when I saw her: I have seen Italian girls with darker skins and coarser features; but I cannot say that she gave me any extraordinary thrill. Yet, she did her best and the game of love to her was the best game in the world. She delighted in teaching me all the Swahili terms for the sex and for sensual pleasures. And when I used them she would scream with enjoyment.

This girl was rather intelligent, and so I asked her about sexual perversions. She seemed to think there was nothing in them, that naturally all human beings took what pleasure they could get whenever they could get it. There was no shadow of moral law in the matter. She even told me that most of the colored girls didn't know how to kiss until they were taught and were quite astonished at any extension of kissing.

I would have forgotten all about this girl, had she not begged me to take her with me on my expedition. I could not do this, but some bright cloths and beads soon consoled her for my defection, and one day I saw her making up to the big Doctor, which at once chased away any lingering scruples I may have had.

I have been asked to write on sexual perversions; but I have no personal experiences of them, being wholly taken up with the normal desires of the man for the woman; but once in New York I received a letter from a girl in Toronto which bears every mark of truth in its frank lesbianism. I found out afterwards that the explanation of this girl's perversion was to be found in the constant physical pursuit of her, when still a mere child, by her father. I give the letter here textually.

Mother opens the door when I ring the home bell. It is sad and pleasant to greet her. We stand talking for a minute in the hall.
"Is *he* there?" Mother knows to whom I refer.
"Yes." She hesitates; then wifelike, pleadingly: "Be nice to him."
I promise.
The children greet me hilariously and I wonder what to say to them. Children always embarrass me.
The father obtrudes himself with weighty tenderness:
"Why doesn't my elf come and kiss me?"
He is fatter, greyer, more dissolute. Only eyes and forehead still partly survive the wreck. I grit my teeth and appear to kiss him willingly, angry with myself that I cannot prevent my flesh from suffering at the contact. His breath is unpleasant with the odor of whiskey and cheese. It revives a vivid childhood scene:
Fresh from the woods, fragrance of earth and leaves clinging to her, a mist of poetry in her brain from something she had been writing or reading, I see the child that was me, darting into the house at tea-time.
"Streak-of-lightning! Come and give your dad a kiss!"
The child goes obediently to be kissed, resentful only at having her thoughts disturbed. Cheese and whiskey! She is horribly disgusted. How could anyone with such a breath want to kiss her? Then I see her breaking away, racing into the garden and burying her head in the flowers.
My first distaste for my father was certainly an aesthetic distaste, which soon became disgust.
"Cold as ever!" he complains because I get away from him as soon as I can. "All brain; no heart whatever." Mother smiles; she knows me better.
He reaches for his whiskey: "Have a drink: it'll warm your chilly blood."
"No, thank you. Not so early in the morning; I haven't eaten yet."
Mother rescues me with breakfast.
"He's drinking too much," she remarks unhappily.
I had never blamed him for drinking, like mother continually did. But I could not help despising him for not being strong enough to make it serve him.
There is little but the unhappy in the handful of news mother unfolds to me during breakfast. Most of it hangs about the man of the family.
"He has been more ill than well lately. I can't help thinking he will not live long . . . and all these children . . . five of them under fifteen!" Helplessly: "I don't know what it will mean."
I do.
I see a scale balancing—mother, children—writing, the poetry, my own life—and my heart is breaking with resentment.

I try to put the black thoughts in chains, since they are far too evilly vigorous to banish. After all, I came here to link hands with love.
I go to the telephone and call Louise's number. No answer. She must be out, although nine-thirty is early for her. There is nothing to do but fill an hour with futile occupations. Later I make another attempt, but still she is not there.
At noon I telephone Louise's number again. This time her husband answers:

"She is spending the holidays at St. Agathe . . . won't be back till Monday."
I do not know what I feel, but something terribly more than disappointment.
Streets drabber than ever, and rain drizzling down.

I want to put Montreal behind me at once, but a berth for Sunday night is
already reserved and I haven't money to get another. All I can do is to stay.
Defiance begins to possess me. Since I must remain, I'll enjoy it. I go immediately to a telephone and call Marguerite. Before I left Montreal for New York
she displayed a great deal of love for me. I had tried to meet it with sympathy;
certainly always did respond with pleasure and passion, for she is beautiful, very
much the artist (musically), and fascinating.

I recognize her voice at the other end of the wire.

"Marguerite! *C'est Sapho qui parle.*"

"*Oh, ma chère!* What happiness. Where are you? I must see you at once! Will
you come here?"

The French enthusiasm, the voice vibrating with unmistakable delight, are
wine to me. In spite of her insistence that we must meet at once—"*immédiatement! immédiatement!*" she repeats—we finally agree to see each other that
evening at a friend's studio.

I go again into the street with a little of the greyness lifted. How mysteriously
heartening is pleasure, and the thought of pleasure.

Night, and the indestructible magic of passion in the veins and the mist of a
spring evening dimming the lights that are softer than most city lights. The
ancient buildings have become more characterful. They are not splendid and
blatant like New York's concrete monsters.

I run up the old staircase to the studio. It is early and the hostess is not yet
there, but I enter. In Montreal we leave our studios unlocked, or the key in
some accessible corner. The familiar studio, full of the pictures I had watched
being painted, is another pleasure. Someone had freed incense or sandalwood
perfume in the room.

I am stretched on a sofa with a cigarette, trying not to think of Louise,
whom I had loved more than once in this place, when someone knocks at the
door. I open it and find the woman from the adjoining studio standing there,
like a Baccante, with a decanter of red wine in her left hand. She wears a
transparent kimona and rather disarranged hair. I am glad enough to see her.
We had been friends once upon a time.

"I saw you come in," she explained, putting the decanter down on a table.
I motion towards it:

"What's that for?"

"Oh! You've forgotten since you lived in that desert across the border!"

It was plain to me that she had not "forgotten." She seemed to have been
practicing well that very day. She poured wine for both of us, then reclining
so that her kimona became very vague about the shoulder, began immediately
to tell me, French fashion, about her lover—the latest.

In my last few years in Montreal, everyone seemed to come to me with confessions. I became a sort of repository for the troubles of the artistic tribe, and
at one time had locked in my memory the intimate secrets and misdeeds of
about one-half of Montreal's *quartier-latin*. They came to me with everything
from confessions of rape—even murder, once—to the tiniest sins of the spirit.
Why they trusted me, I do not know. I felt quite at home when Davila, nicknamed "Devil," called "Dev" for handiness, immediately unfolded an intrigue
for me.

She departed when Regina, mistress of the studio, arrived at eight o'clock. Regina greeted me with a maidenly kiss on the cheek. Regina is an artist, two or three years my senior, although she appears to be younger. She has not the brains nor the curiosity about life ever to be a great painter. Her claims to the title of artist lie chiefly in a vivid, almost virile color sense, and a careful technique. Her claims to my admiration are far more numerous. Her type is oriental; coloring richly dark; magnificent, slow-burning eyes; features that would be heavy but for the life that shines through, as though they were transparent; figure a little too full, but redeemed by the firmness of unused youth; hard, not too large breasts; and beautiful hands.

I draw her to my side on the couch and begin talking about her pictures. There is a lot to criticize in the latest.

"It is difficult to realize, looking at you," I tell her, "but love, even passion, is lacking in your work. How do you keep it out?"

"I don't know. I have not ever really loved."

I had guessed that much, but I merely say:

"Why don't you?"

"I have not yet found anyone I want to fall in love with."

That is an attitude I am not in sympathy with.

I rarely await Fate's sweet pleasure. So I tell her:

"Love is worth the loving regardless of that. The perfection is in the artist and the art itself, not in the instrument, is it not so?"

She seemed troubled about it. "Men do not inspire me," hesitatingly, "My lips are loath to meet theirs as my brush is to paint them. No. They do not inspire me in the least."

Woman always waits to be inspired! Well—Marguerite is not due for an hour and this little creature is very seductive. I take both her hands and kiss them. I love beautiful hands.

"Perhaps I can inspire you."

She smiles uncertainly, but I draw her towards me and kiss her mouth; her eyes, and throat; then the mouth again. It grows warm, and the little nipples of her breasts harden under my fingers. I have never caressed such a sensitive skin. It burns and trembles wherever it is touched, and I am surprised that so responsive a body should be innocent of love. She does not seem to wish that it should remain innocent, tempting me with the most beautiful abandon, that I would willingly meet with all my passion; but Fate, unusually malicious, intervenes with footsteps on the stairs. It is quite certain they belong to Marguerite, whom I had forgotten. Regina hears them, too, and hot, restraining hands creep and cling round me. I cannot help feeling sorry for her. A final kiss that neither of us wants to end, and she lets me go.

Pulling a screen around the couch to give Regina time to arrange her things—for something besides, Marguerite's eyes harbor a dash of green!—I reach the door just as the knock comes. Nothing can restrain the exuberance of Marguerite's greeting. For Regina's sake, I am glad of the screen.

Marguerite is pale, more lithe, more tiger-like, than when I last saw her, and even then I would run my hands over her body and ask how she managed to hide the stripes! The yellow-green eyes are pure tiger. Her clothes are chosen with the absolute art that only the French seem to possess.

Regina, looking self-possessed enough, even to my eye, comes from behind the screen and takes Marguerite's wraps. Before we are seated others arrive.

Conversation and wine carry the evening swiftly to midnight. Marguerite, passion apparently making her impatient, whispers to me several times to leave and go home with her. I am eager enough to go, but the moods of her impatience interest me to watch. It is not kind, perhaps, but a dash of pain is good seasoning for pleasure—makes it more vital, aggressive.

A little later I get Regina into a corner, tell her I am about to leave, and ask if I may see her tomorrow, before I depart for New York. She consents, of course, her large eyes kissing me; then says impulsively:

"I wish you could stay longer. I would love to do a head of you with just the expression you had when—we were together on the couch."

"So! I did inspire you?" I kiss the beautiful hand, hoping Marguerite does not see, and leave her.

Marguerite and I go decorously enough downstairs, but outside the air, the everlasting moon, the desertedness of the streets, are too much for us. We embrace the minute the policeman at the corner turns his back.

Marguerite and I are perfectly in accord about one important detail of love—we believe that the surroundings should harmonize with the passion; so she, quite naturally, immediately dims the lights when we enter her home, puts glowing charcoal in the incense burner, and pours liqueur—appropriately perverse little glasses; then, forgetting everything, apparently, but her need of love, sinks down beside me, where I recline on the rug and receives my kisses on her flung-back throat and face.

The foolish clothes that interrupt my lips! I unfasten them and slip them off; my own as well. The couch is more comfortable than the rug. I raise her and we stand against each other, embrace, kiss—the perfect kiss of completely meeting bodies. It creates desire too keen to be borne. Perspiration dampens her skin and mine. The perfume she has put on her body, not sweet but something insidiously acrid of eastern origin, fills my head with a hot mist. We sway to the couch and lie for a minute, bound by our burning arms, breasts crushed together.

I release myself and begin to weave a mesh of kisses over her: the eyes, the hair, the perfect mouth, the breasts that have no shadow of fault, past the tiny coiling navel where the skin is increasingly sensitive, so quivering more with every kiss. (I always want to call a woman I love a harp.) At last the kiss that seals them all! Her body is convulsed with the intensity of the sensation. Stressful little moans come from her throat blended with endearing names. Her hands caress me frantically. We draw closer together. Her mouth finds my sensitive places. Incredible pleasure. Somewhere in my mind there is this thought: What a beautiful piece of work a sculptor who dared would make of this perverse intertwining of two figures in lesbic passion! Both bodies are fair enough, firm and young and supple-muscled. It must have been done by the ancients.

Cool rills of perspiration create separate tiny thrills where they traverse the skin. The quivering of her limbs, the bitter salts of her body on my tongue and lips, the sweet pressure and motion of her mouth, shake me into a scarlet blindness. The mounting sensations make me think of melodies I have heard, growing and growing to a crescendo and ending with the sudden silence that symbolizes the crisis.

We seem to flutter down from a far height and lie exquisitely quivering with the pleasure of perfect passion.

I raise myself a little and, gently now, lay little kisses along the limbs, the hips, upward over the breasts, across the throat back to the lips and grateful eyes. She is still—like a marble girl. I barely know her until she circles me with her arms and whispers, "Lover! Sweet, little burning lover!"

I can think of no name to call her that would harmonize with the reverence that fills me for her beauty and the intensity of the pleasures we have enjoyed. I kneel beside her and kiss her hands.

It seems to be almost a law that we love those who respond to us and worship all that gives us pleasure—pleasure in its very widest sense.

Vice—! The thought amuses me. There are only *vicious people*.

Marguerite rises, goes and pours out something, then returning, crouches beside me, and holds up one of her little glasses to my lips with enchanting grace.

Then we go and lie on the bed, she bringing Verlaine for me to read to her, while she strokes my body, resting her cheek against one of my breasts.

If the spirit of Verlaine lurked anywhere in the room, I am certain there was approval in its nebulous heart.

And Regina on the morrow—Regina!

Chapter VI

Barnato, Beit, and Hooley

'Tis a very good world to live in,
To lend or to spend or to give in;
But to beg or to borrow or get a man's own,
'Tis the very worst world that ever was known.

IT WAS THROUGH MY SOJOURN in South Africa in 1896 that I came to know the world of modern finance, where millions sometimes are made or lost in a day by speculation. It was in Johannesburg that I first got acquainted with this characteristic of the time.

Long before meeting him, I had heard of Barney Barnato: every one in the Rand Club knew the sturdy little middle-aged man, who was said to be worth twenty millions and was considered by many to be the true rival of Rhodes and Beit. Ten or twelve years before he had landed in Kimberley with the proverbial five pound note. How had he made such a fortune in so short a time? His presence and speech were against him; he was commonly dressed and spoke like an uneducated Cockney, dropped his "h's" and made grammatical howlers in almost every sentence. Rhodes after all was "someone," while Barnato was plainly a rank "outsider," to use the ordinary English phrase.

It was said of Barney that in early days at Kimberley he had got a living by showing off as a fighter: he would put a square of carpet on the ground and bet that no one could stand up to him on it for five minutes. One rough miner after the other used to take on the job, but they soon found that little Barnato was really hard to beat, and they usually lost thir money and took a good deal of punishment into the bargain.

Barnato soon bought claim after claim in Kimberley, and working as he had fought, with all his heart, quickly became one of the richest men in the camp. From the beginning he was inconceivably mean: he never paid for a drink—always pretended that he had no loose cash about him. A story was told of him that always seemed to me to paint him to the life. Going to the Kimberley races once, he answered some jest made at his expense by saying that he would bet he could make a thousand pounds before the evening. Several people bet with him. When he got to the race course, Barnato went up to a woman who was selling lemonade and drinks and asked her how

much she expected to make during the day. She said, "Perhaps ten pounds."
"I'll give you twenty," he said, "for your stock, and five for yourself—is
it a deal?"

The woman consented and Barnato began to sell her stock, and he did
it with such humor and such understanding of almost every miner who
came up that he soon had a great crowd about him and sold out at fabulous
prices, getting higher and higher sums toward the end of the day; and
finally achieved his aim and made his clear thousand pounds, besides the
bets he had also won.

His common cockney English endeared him to the ordinary miner, but
his knowledge of life and men was extraordinary; his energy extraordinary,
too, as was his self-confidence. I have told the story how Rhodes and Beit
bought him out at Kimberley; but Barnato soon established himself in
Johannesburg as one of the great mine owners and made another huge
fortune. Yet he only gambled when he was sure to win. I was once at a
game of baccarat in his house where nearly a quarter of a million changed
hands in two hours while Barney, having shed his boots, dozed on a sofa
in the room.

I remember his telling me once that he was worth twenty-five millions.
"My boy," he added, "I have made three millions in one day." I always
thought that that was the day when he sold his claims in Kimberley to
Rhodes and Beit.

I am giving no portrait of him, and yet I liked Barney Barnato, for he
was really likable in spite of his meanness about petty sums. He told me
one day how he had given one hundred pounds for his first claim in the
diamond mine of Kimberley: he worked day and night at it with his niggers,
and when he got down, a month later, to the blue ground where the stones
were found, he made ten thousand pounds in the first hour. "Thirty good
diamonds," he said. "I could hardly believe my ears when I was offered
eight thousand pounds for them; but I didn't sell them till I got the round
ten thousand—about half their real worth, I should think."

"The week after, I bought three adjoining claims and since then my bank
balance has grown pretty rapidly; I'm not complaining. I remember on my
first day on the carpet in Kimberley, I had to fight like a wildcat with a big
miner, and all for five quid—a change, eh?"

Every one knows how Barney Barnato bucked against the falling market
in Johannesburg, brought about by Rhodes's schemes. He was said to have
lost a million. I met him once near the end when he told me how Rhodes
and Beit had kept him out and how he had bought on a falling market and
lost his money. "My dear Barney," I said, "one of these days you will make
another fortune. What's a million to you?"

"A million!" he snarled, "A million to me—it's ten hundred thousand
pounds, you—!" There was something mad in his glare. It suddenly came
to me that Barney had worn his mind out, and when he hurried into an
inner room, muttering to himself, I felt sure that if he didn't soon win to

self-control, he would come to grief. I perhaps read Barney correctly because I, too, had suffered from nerves and knew how essential it was to cure them. I may say here that constant change of scene and companionship, and the determination to take life easy for awhile are the best cures; but poor Barnato stuck to his work till the last.

A little later, on his way to England, he threw himself off the steamer into the sea; his body was recovered and brought to Southampton.

Woolfie Joel, his nephew, told me that Barney had worn himself out. Woolfie Joel had many of the fine qualities that Barney Barnato lacked. He hadn't the genius of his uncle, but he was far better educated and of a generous and kindly nature. I always had a great liking for Woolfie Joel.

It is the development of a man, the growth of him, that is of supreme interest to his fellows: whoever can tell this story is sure of hearers; but how much more sure when the story is that of the master of millions in a day when all would be rich if they could.

It was in Alfred Beit's house in Park Lane in '97 or '98 that I put him to the question. We were seated in the room which was at once a sort of rockery and palm garden: a room of brown rocks and green ferns and tesselated pavement—an abode of grateful, dim coolness and shuttered silence, silence made noticeable, as it were, framed off by the vague hum of the outside world.

We had been talking of Kimberley and his early days there and his first successes, and I was eager to learn how, even in the race for wealth, he had outstripped a man like Barney Barnato, who had reached Kimberley years before him, and who had never cared for anything in his life but money, and had sought it night and day with the meanness of avarice which collects pennies and saves crusts; or, better still, which dines sumptuously at someone else's expense, inspired by the insane Jew greed which finds a sensual delight in the mention of gold and silver, and diamonds and pearls, and rubies—above all, rubies, hued like pigeon's blood, and more precious than a thousand times their weight in refined gold. In spite of his savage greed and oriental garishness, Barney Barnato had a touch of genius in him, and wasn't easily beaten at his own game.

In person Beit was not very remarkable: he was short—shorter even than Barney Barnato—and plump; in later days the plumpness became fat. But even in his prime he seemed to have "run to head"; the great round ball appeared too large for the little body and small limbs; but it was excellently well-shaped, the forehead very broad, and high-domed to reverence and idealism, like a poet's; the rest of the face was not so good; the nose fairly large, but slightly beaked, not noticeably fleshy—a good rudder; the chin rather weak than strong—no great courage or resolution anywhere. After the forehead the eyes and mouth were the two noteworthy features: the eyes prominent, large, brown, the glance at once thoughtful and keen; the mouth coarse and ill-cut, the lower lip particularly heavy. It reminded me of Rhodes's face; but Rhodes's mouth was coarser and more cruel than Beit's;

his nose, too, larger and more beaked; his chin and jaw much more massive —altogether a stronger face, though not so intellectually alert.

Beit's manner was nervous, hesitating: he had a tiny dark moustache and a curious trick of twirling at it with the right hand, though he seldom touched it; the embarrassed nervousness of a student, rather than the assurance of a man of affairs accustomed to deal with men; but the nervousness was chiefly superficial, due perhaps to weak health, for as soon as he began to talk business he came to perfect self-possession.

Beit did not seem to wish to talk of Barney Barnato; he admitted his gifts, but evidently did not like him. But if Beit disliked being compared with Barnato, nothing flattered him more than to be compared with Rhodes. He had a profound and pathetic admiration for Rhodes, the admiration which only a born idealist could keep through many years of intimate companionship. And in connection with Rhodes, he had no disinclination to talk about himself; the phrase of Goethe, paraphrased at the beginning of this portrait, seemed to touch him.

"Yes," he said, "that's the good time of a man's life, if he only knew it, the *Entwicklungsperiode.*"

"It is the beginning," I went on, "that is supremely interesting; how from nothing you won the first fifty thousand pounds, that interests everyone; but how afterwards you turned the fifty thousand into twenty millions is much less interesting."

"Well," said Beit, "I was one of the poor Beits of Hamburg; my father found it difficult even to pay for my schooling, and you know that is cheap enough in Germany; I had to leave before I had gone through the *Realschule*. Of course, in Hamburg at that time everyone was talking about the discovery of diamonds in South Africa, and so, after helping my father for a little time, he made up his mind to send me to Amsterdam to learn all about diamonds. I went there and spent two years, and in that time got to know a good deal about diamonds."

"Of course," I interjected, "in that time you must also have learnt Dutch."

"No," replied Beit; "no. I just did my work, and wasted my spare time like other young men. A little later my father had some interest with the house of Jules Porges in Paris, and I was sent out by him to Kimberley. I got my passage money and three hundred pounds for the first year. When I reached Kimberley, I found that very few people knew anything about diamonds; they bought and sold at haphazard, and a great many of them really believed that the Cape diamonds were of a very inferior quality. Of course, I saw at once that some of the Cape stones were as good as any in the world; and I saw, too, that the buyers protected themselves against their own ignorance by offering for them one-tenth part of what each stone was worth in Europe. It was plain that if one had a little money there was a fortune to be made, and I remember I wrote to Porges, offering to give up my position and pay him back my passage money if he woud let me off my engagement to work for him for a year; but he would not let me off, so I went on working.

"I wrote to my father frequently, long letters, telling him all about Kimberley; how incredibly rich the ground was; how easy it was to make money with a little capital; and I begged him to send me as much as he could get together by the end of the year, and I promised him to return whatever money he lent me with good interest within a year.

"Before the end of my time with Porges, my father got together a couple of thousand pounds and sent it to me; but I did not use it in buying diamonds, as I should have done if he had sent it to me in the first six months. Kimberley was growing so fast that the demand for houses was extraordinary, so I bought a bit of land and put up twelve or thirteen offices, corrugated iron shanties, of which I kept one for myself. I let out these twelve or thirteen shanties, and I got eighteen hundred pounds a month for them."

"Eighteen hundred pounds a month!" I said. "How long did that continue?"

"For years and years," said Beit. "Twelve or thirteen years, I think, and then the pit had grown so large that my ground was wanted, and I sold the ground on which the shanties were built for a fair sum—I think it was about two hundred and sixty thouand pounds. I got something for the dwellings, too, I think," and he laughed. "Not a bad speculation!"

"No," I said, "indeed; that solves the question of how you came from poverty to riches."

While getting a subscription once for a charity, I came across a curious trait in his character—he seemed to over-estimate the value of small sums of money. If you spoke to him of two or three pounds, or twenty-two or twenty-three, he was always eager to show you how thirty shillings could do in the one case, and how it was possible to attain the desired end with half the amount in the other. But the moment you spoke in thousands, he seemed to treat them as counters. He would jump from five thousand to fifty thousand as if there were no intervening figures. The truth was, of course, that Beit had learned the value of small sums of money when he was young and poor in Hamburg and Amsterdam, and no one knew better than he did how much could be done with a pound. But when you talked in thousands you were speaking to Beit the millionaire, who made fifty thousand in an afternoon, and did not attach precise importance to either sum.

Beit went into the Jameson Raid at Rhodes's request, but he protested against every stage of that mad and stupid enterprise. Indeed, the story of Jameson's Raid would only show that Beit was intensely loyal to Rhodes, even when he believed him to be entirely in the wrong. Beit was a good type of business man. He had an instinctive aversion to politics and raidings, and was chiefly interested in such enterprises as could be shown in a profit and loss account.

But there was another side of his nature: like many Jews, he had a real love and understanding of music; and he admired pictures and bronzes, too, though he was anything but a good judge of them. At bottom Beit was a sentimentalist, and did not count or reckon when his feelings were really touched. This was the fine side of the man, the side through which Rhodes used him, the side which, by contrast with his love of money, showed the breadth and height of his humanity. Of all the millionaires I had chanced to meet, Beit was the best. He had a great deal of the milk of human kindness in him, quick and deep sympathies, too, sympathies even with poverty, perhaps through his own early struggles; and if any plan of a social utopia had been brought forward in his time, no one would have detected its weakness more quickly that Beit, no one would have seen its good points more clearly or been more willing to help it to accomplishment.

After Cecil Rhodes's death, I had written an article about him and about his will, in which I declared that posthumous benefactions seemed to me no proof of benevolence because they lacked the savor of sacrifice, and, to use Bacon's phrase, "were but the painted sepulchre of alms." Beit expressed his astonishment at this criticism, and thought there was a great deal of unselfish nobility shown in Rhodes's will, and added that he only hoped to make as good use of whatever he might possess when he died. Indeed, when Beit died in 1906, he left over two million pounds to charity.

It was in the late summer of 1896, after my return from South Africa, that A. M. Broadley called on me one day in the office of the *Saturday Review* and brought a new interest into my life. I had known Broadley for a good many years and had long been convinced of his business ability, as well as his journalistic skill. He told me that he was making a good deal of money with Ernest Terah Hooley, whom I had just heard of as the successful promotor of the Dunlop Company. Broadley offered to bring me up to see him, suggesting that I should find it to my profit to help him in his financial schemes. Nothing loath, I went with Broadley and was introduced to Hooley at the Midland Grand Hotel. To my surprise, I learned that the financier had taken the whole of the first floor of the Midland Grand Hotel for his offices. I don't know how many rooms there were, but I believe there were certainly fifty; and from ten o'clock in the morning until six at night, almost every room was filled with people who had axes to grind. Hooley flitted from room to room, always good humored and decisively quick in dealing with the most heterogeneous projects.

At one moment he was discussing the raising of a loan of sixteen millions with Li Hung Chang on the security of the Chinese customs, and with him was Sir Robert Hart,* the Englishman who knew more about China than any other living westerner. In Hooley's private room, one would meet Arthur du Cros** who had more to do with the successful Dunlop promotion

---

* (1835–1911); Inspector of Maritime Affairs in Peking.
** (1871–?), managing director and deputy chairman of the Dunlop Rubber Company.

than any other member of his family, and who afterwards became a member of Parliament and was knighted, I believe, for this achievement: an alert, intelligent man, a good organizer, but intensely combative. In another room a nobleman who had come to sell Hooley the Prince's yacht *Britannia;* in still another room, a persuasive Spaniard, who appeared with the news that sugar had been made from sea water, and all he wanted was a million for the discovery. From room to room went Hooley, a rather tall, well-made man with black hair, black beard, black moustache, a long beaked Jewish nose, and long half-closed Jewish eyes, well dressed and always polite without a particle of "side," too earnestly busy to show any conceit. He told me at once that Broadley had been very useful to him and he hoped that I should be. I replied that I was quite willing to follow my friend Broadley's lead; and after two minutes' talk Hooley hurried away to another room.

From that time on I went up to the Midland Grand Hotel practically twice a week, and soon became conversant with Hooley's financial methods and with many of Hooley's ideas. He certainly knew more about the value of land in England than any one I had ever seen, and he had a perfectly open mind for any and every scheme, and was most easy of access. In his bankruptcy two years afterwards, the official receiver proved that Hooley had made over six millions of hard cash in just these two years. Hooley himself always said that he had made a million and a half over the Dunlop promotion alone. His astounding success can only be explained by the fact that he was lifted on the most astonishing wave of prosperity that perhaps has ever been known in any country—never in my thirty years of residence has London known so prosperous a period; and Hooley was an optimist to the fingers' tips, suited perfectly to the time, without a suspicion that there could be a change in feeling or a slump in finance.

When I got to know him pretty well, I found to my amazement that he had a man named Martin Rucker for a partner, who never helped him in any way; and it was months before I learned that Rucker had been a bicycle agent and had put some money in with Hooley at the very beginning and had remained with him as a sort of deadweight ever afterwards. It was he, in fact, who brought about Hooley's first fall.

I soon got the idea that the best companies to promote would be those which had spent most in advertising in the past and were therefore widely known. I put this idea to Hooley, and he accepted it at once. "You ought to turn Bovril into a company," I said, "because every one knows of it and it would go like wildfire; and Schweppe's soda water, too."

"Go to it," said Hooley; "get me an option on any such concern, bring it to me, and you can count on a fair deal."

I immediately went to work to get to know the owners of Bovril: it was really in the hand of one person, a Mr. Johnson, I think. Coming from Hooley, I was admirably received and soon found that the company was making something over a hundred thousand pounds a year, and that they wanted a good deal over a million for it. I went with the news to Hooley, who told me to go ahead if the figures were correct. I returned and began to bargain; the seller wanted about a million and a half, and I wanted to bring him to a million and a quarter. We had practically decided on a million and three hundred and fifty thousand pounds, when one day he laughed at me and told me that he had accepted an offer of two millions that day, that it was all settled and that Hooley was the purchaser. I drove immediately to the Midland Grand Hotel to see Hooley and found it was all true.

"You were too slow, my boy," he said, "much too slow: another man told me he could get it for two millions and I told him to put it through, and I gave him a check as deposit."

"You have done me out of the ten percent which you promised me," I said, "because I was trying to get it under a million and a half, and it was practically settled."

"Don't talk like that:" cried Hooley, "do you wish to show your brains? In that room there are twenty financiers, all rich men; you know more about Bovril than almost any one; you have been at it over a fortnight; go in and persuade them that two millions is a fair price and I will give you ten thousand at once. Is it a deal?"

"I'll do my best," I said.

Hooley opened the door and introduced me to a crowded room with the words, "Frank Harris has been looking into Bovril for a month, knows all about it, and is prepared to show you that two millions is a low price for it." A large man thrust himself forward at once, whom I afterwards knew as Nocton, a very able solicitor. "Have we the figures correct," he said, "that Bovril has never made one hundred and fifty thousand pounds in a year? If so, it ought to be capitalized at about a million and a half at the very outside. Why should two millions be given for it?"

"The growth of the business in the last five years," I said, "since they began to advertise widely, has been most extraordinary: the income has more than doubled, has practically grown from fifty thousand a year to one hundred and forty thousand; it is only fair to suppose that it will grow in the same proportion in the next five years, and even more, for as a Hooley promotion it will be advertised everywhere and should therefore be cheap at three millions. Besides, it has no competitors and it has become a household name in Great Britain. Given a proper prospectus, every one will take shares in Bovril."

"You are evidently the man to write it," said Nocton. And from that time we were friends, for Hooley backed up the idea at once.

I got away as soon as possible, seeing that I was not wanted. In ten minutes Hooley came to me in another room. "You have done the trick, my boy; a cool million has been subscribed on my terms, and I owe you ten thousand. Will you have it in cash or shares?"

"Half cash, half shares," I said.

"Good for you," he said, and then and there wrote me a check for five thousand pounds and a note to say that I should have five thousand shares when the Bovril promotion was completed. While he was writing, another thought came into my head: "Why not let me sketch out the prospectus, as Nocton suggested?"

"You are trenching on Broadley's domain," he said, "and I have almost promised it to someone else: still, there is five thousand pounds in it—go to it—if your argument is the best, you will probably get it."

"Thanks," I said, and away I went.

The greater part of my scheme appeared later as the Bovril prospectus. I had taken pains to study the law and to keep within it in every particular.

I won't attempt to describe all my further financial ventures with Hooley; it is enough to say that I took a small part in several of his promotions, like the rest of his supporters. I would put in, say, five thousand pounds in cash, on condition that I got ten thousand in cash or shares if the deal came off successfully. I remember particularly taking such a share in the Schweppe promotion, which was not one of his great successes, and he left some three thousand pounds unpaid to me.

His failure was astonishingly sudden. Martin Rucker, his partner, wanted to buy an estate and become a country gentleman, and finally settled with Hooley for a million pounds cash for his half share. Hooley gave him the million cash, although Broadley and I both protested that it was madness to strip himself of so great a sum in cash; but Hooley was not to be argued with or persuaded. He gave the million and Rucker was seen no more. But almost immediately the financial tide which had so far been on the flow began to ebb. Hooley involved himself in Manchester in the Trafford Park scheme, and suddenly became in need of cash: the banks, as usual scenting necessity, drew in their credits, and Hooley, though several times a millionaire on paper, was soon in financial difficulty.

He explained all this to Broadley and myself at some length, and it occurred to me that I might be able to interest Beit in his schemes and so float Hooley over his difficulty. I went to Beit and talked the Trafford Park scheme at some length. It was really a great enterprise: Beit, seeing it, at once promised his support on conditions. "We will go in as partners," he said, "on an even footing; I will put up five hundred thousand pounds and so must Hooley, and the scheme shall be developed by him, and we will divide afterwards."

Greatly excited, I hurried back to Hooley and told him how I had succeeded; he too was delighted. We were to meet Beit on the following Monday for lunch at the Savoy Hotel, and the provisional partnership would then be concluded. But on the Thursday Hooley came to me and told me that he could only raise three hundred and fifty thousand pounds in cash, that his banks had refused him the other one hundred and fifty thousand, and therefore he would put up shares for double the amount. I begged him not to alter the agreement in any way; I felt certain that as soon as the cooperation was whispered, a dozen of Beit's friends would be dead against his participation with Hooley.

Hooley went again to the banks and returned to me on the Saturday saying, "It is impossible; I can put up four hundred thousand, but the last one hundred thousand must be made up by shares."

I begged him to use every effort, and he said that he had—it was impossible, so I went to the lunch with Beit alone to tell him Hooley's latest decision. The moment I described his position, Beit said, "That settles it; my partner has been terribly against the whole business. Wernher won't hear of Hooley, and now as I can get out without breaking my word, I won't go on."

I went back and told Hooley and found him in a strange mood. He didn't care what happened; it didn't matter, for they couldn't take away his ability to make money. The Trafford Park scheme was the best in the world; he would work it through somehow: Beit's aid was not so important.

"Beit," I said, "could put ten millions cash on the table if he wanted to; with his backing, you would have been the strongest financial force in England, that is to say, in the world today. I am very sorry."

A little later Hooley announced coolly that he was going into bankruptcy. "It seems to me to be pure madness," I said to Broadley. But Hooley went on like a naughty child, who, having wet one toe by chance, would wade into the gutter to his neck. He made himself a bankrupt and shortly afterwards was sent to Brixton Prison for a year, apparently to teach him that to lose six million in England was a crime.

Of course, he often exaggerated and talked wildly; it was part of the optimistic nature of the man and a consequence of his astonishing success; but I don't believe that Hooley ever tried to cheat any one dishonorably (sic) in his life. I have done business with a great many men in London, and think Hooley as honest, perhaps even more honorable, than most of the men I have worked with.

When he came out of prison, I met him by chance in the Strand and of course held out my hand and greeted him as of old. "You know," he said, "I have just come out of Brixton?"

"Yes," I replied, "but that doesn't alter my opinion of you. When will you dine with me?"

He was very much obliged to me, he said, but he was going back to Risley Park, which he had settled on his wife after his Dunlop success. He told me that I was one of the few people who hadn't altered to him. Away he went, and I have not seen him since, though I understand that his book describing his career has been a best seller.*

One curious thing happened which tinged my liking for Hooley with a shade of doubt. Broadley declared that he was not fair to us, and I found out that that was the case. When I sent my claim in for the three thousand

* Published in 1925.

pounds unpaid over Schweppe's to the official receiver, I got a letter from him that made me gasp. He asked me to define the debt and how it had been incurred. I told him that I had put up five thousand pounds in the Schweppe promotion on Hooley's undertaking to pay ten thousand cash or shares, as I might decide after the promotion. I had received seven thousand in cash and no more. The official receiver answered me, saying that he was very sorry to question my word, but could I get any proof that I had put up the five thousand pounds. I went at once to my bank—Coutts's—got the original check endorsed by Hooley and took it to the official receiver in person and asked him for an explanation; I thought his request extraordinary. The moment he saw the check his manner altered; he became cordial. "You have no idea," he said. "I have got claims from a dozen journalists, but no one else except yourself helped Hooley with the cash. Here is Mr. So and So who is asking for twenty thousand, yet he never advanced a penny. Please forgive me if I thought that you were like the rest, claiming money without having risked any."

The thought came to me afterwards that Hooley had misrepresented me, as Broadley said; but I imagine that it was only because he classed all journalists together in a lump. He was careless, but not malevolent.

For some reason or other the *Daily Mail* was always against me, and in this matter of Hooley's bankruptcy it more than hinted that I was trying to get money without having done anything for it. Curiously enough, the result of the investigation of the official receiver cleared me and established the fact that the *Daily Mail* correspondent was one of those who had claimed money without having given any *quid pro quo*. Harry Marks, too, of the *Financial News,* was astonished to hear that I had put up money with Hooley.

"I am claiming twenty thousand pounds from his estate," he said, "but I never gave him any money. He never asked me for it."

Hooley's example taught me the value of company promoting, and I resolved sooner or later to market the twenty-odd thousand shares I still possessed in the *Saturday Review.*

Chapter VII

The South African War: Milner and Chamberlain;
Kitchener and Roberts

ALL THESE YEARS, '97 and '98, in which I had sketched out my Shakespeare book and written half a dozen new stories, I had come more and more to feel that I must do my own work and that the drudgery of journalism was interfering with the real business of my life. The public spirit of the time, too, didn't please me. It was evident to me that Chamberlain was seeking to establish British authority, or as he would have said, British supremacy, in South Africa. At length came the news that Alfred Milner* was appointed by Chamberlain as Governor General, and was to be sent out to the Cape with full authority.

Ever since Harold Frederic introduced me to Alfred Milner, when we were all in the thirties, I had thought of him as the most perfect example of a modern German in mind that I had ever seen. Both in defects and in qualities, he was characteristically German and not English. For the German trusts reason and knows thoroughly what he has learned, while the best Englishman has a subconscious belief that there are instincts higher than reason, and he has never learned anything deeply enough to feel that he knows it as a master. These immature spiritual antennae are what makes the Englishman the tragic creature he often is in practical life, and the lovable person he is at his best; and their absence gives the German his supremacy in the present and forecasts perhaps his comparative failure in the future.

Now Harold Frederic was a great friend of Milner, and he had told me a good deal about him and his imperialistic views. I became a little anxious and saw Beit on the matter, but he assured me there was nothing important afoot, and at the same time he wanted to know why I had not asked him to take any shares in the *Saturday Review*. I told him he could take five thousand whenever he pleased; and he took five thousand and gave me his check; others took shares too, especially when a dividend of five per cent was declared on the capital. I was on easy street as regards money, but still

* (1854–1925).

a little doubtful of the political situation, when Harold Frederic came and said he was giving a big dinner at the Savoy Hotel to Milner on his appointment to South Africa, and asked me to speak at the dinner. I said I should be glad to.

Harold Frederic in his speech talked of Milner and himself as only a man of genius could talk. He spoke first of Milner's generous recognition of other men; how he had pressed work upon him and praised his writing enthusiastically; he gave this as a sign of kindness of heart, whereas in Milner it was merely the efficiency of the bureaucrat. Then he spoke of Milner's career.

"From the first," he said, "at Oxford, even, the English had picked Milner out for a high position.* He had had a German training and had won besides all sorts of scholastic honors at Oxford. We all knew when he arrived in London and became Stead's assistant on the *Pall Mall Gazette* that he was sure to come to honor, and all of us are glad now to congratulate him," for he's a jolly good fellow, and so forth.

Milner said little or nothing, did not commit himself in any way, whereas I spoke with perfect frankness. I said that the Englishman who went out to South Africa with power and who brought the Boers and British to mutual trust and harmony would do great work; but such a heaven-sent diplomatist would have to show sympathy with the Boers from the very outset. The English, of course, would trust him; he should make it his first object to win the confidence of the Boers, who were naturally suspicious. The British Empire extended north of the Transvaal over the whole central plateau of Africa to Nairobi or to Khartoum, or, if you wished, to Cairo; surely from the Transvaal border to Khartoum was enough for British colonization in the next two hundred years.

"There," I went on, "was the most fruitful land in the world, and the best climate in the world; and I think a great colonizing effort should be made, for all the unemployed in Britain might be established on that magnificent plateau and thus extend and consolidate the greatest empire on earth. The first essential to success," I insisted, "was to win the Boers by treating them fairly. They were not anti-English; they were, in spite of the war of 1880 and in spite of the Jameson Raid, inclined to be pro-English; and as soon as Krueger died the English colonists in the Transvaal would be accorded full citizen rights. The Boers would do this so much the quicker if the land to the north of the Transvaal were settled up by Englishmen. Why shouldn't the next colonial Governor be the Moses of this new Exodus? On the other hand, if the new Governor quarreled with the Boers and excited that dislike which lay so near ignorance, he might have a war on his hands that would sow evil broadcast and would retard the development, not only of South Africa, but also of Great Britain."

I did my very best in this sense. A good many people applauded me, but after the dinner, when Harold Frederic and I strolled together to the

* He had won a fellowship at New College.

Liberal Club and I congratulated him on one of the best speeches I had ever heard, he said: "My dear Harris, I never made a good speech before in my life, and you usually talk well, but tonight I thought you were at your worst; you showed such distrust of Milner. I assure you, he's a Radical and a good fellow."

"I don't believe he's a Radical; he's a German and he'll fail ruinously in South Africa. He'll bring war. You've only to look at him; he frightens me."

Lord Desborough* came to me afterwards and said that he agreed with a good many of my ideas, but he wished that I could really meet Milner because Milner was a prince of good fellows and absolutely fair-minded. Finally he invited me to lunch with him at Willis' rooms; and I lunched there a week later with Milner and Lord Desborough.

It was at this time the fashionable rendezvous for lunch in London, and I noticed that three or four people, whom I had known socially, treated me with marked coldness. I was put down as a lover of the Boers, and a good many of the governing class disliked my attitude intensely. Man after man came out and bowed to Milner and Desborough in the pleasantest way, while contenting themselves with the merest nod to me. After lunch Milner went away and Desborough remarked to me that he had never known Milner so cautious: "He didn't speak his mind or give us even an inkling of what he thought." But I still believed that it was absolutely impossible for any English governor to be mad enough to make war with the Boers. "After all," I said to Lord Desborough, "they are the real colonists in South Africa; except the gold hunters in Johannesburg and the diamond diggers in Kimberley, there are no Englishmen outside of Natal and the Cape. Will Milner go in for colonization and make for himself a deathless reputation, or will he proceed to quarrel with the Boers?" I knew at the bottom of my heart that Krueger would quarrel with any one: was indeed as combative as a bull-terrier.

Desborough could tell me nothing, except that he hoped for the best; still, he felt pretty sure that Milner would do what Chamberlain wished and always act in the best interests of England. We had to leave it at that.

In due time Milner went out to South Africa, and in my mind's eye I saw a meeting between him and President Krueger.

Milner tall, thin, with shaven, stony face, calm, direct regard and immaculate attire, the type of clean, intelligent efficiency; and Oom Paul, huddled in his armchair, looking like a sick gorilla with a fringe of thick, dirty hair under his heavy animal face, and small hot eyes glinting out under the bushy brows: the one man ignorant to the point of believing the world to be flat, the other intelligent and equipped with all the learning of the schools; and yet Krueger a great heart and great man, and Milner small and thin, proud of easily holding his emotions in leash to his reason. I dreaded the clash, for behind Milner was all the power of Britain, and yet Krueger

* Willie Grenfell.

was right: "We Boers hold South Africa; you can't get rid of us; it is foolish to bully your bedfellow."

Milner's first speech at Graaf Reinet taught me all that I wished to know about him, and more. The gist of his speech, I shall never forget, and I don't care to look out the words. "The Boers," he began, "talk about their loyalty: I see no merit in this; I should think they would be loyal; they live in perfect peace, protected by the might of England, by her armies and navies; loyalty is a cheap price to pay for such complete security." And so he went on, as if love were a thing to be bought and affection had a price. He had no conception whatever that the ordinary Boer never dreamed of any attack from the outside and would have laughed at the idea. The whole speech was a British challenge; still, at first nothing seemed to come of it, and I gradually settled down into the hope that no decisive issue would arise in my time.

I then went into one of the bad speculations of my life. I had got to know the two managers of the Savoy Hotel, Ellis and Cesari, very well indeed. They had made a success of the Savoy Hotel, and as soon as Cesari knew that I came to the French Riviera nearly every winter, he told me that he could make a marvelous success of a hotel at Monte Carlo. Next winter I came down and saw some hotels which were for sale. I didn't care for any of them, but when I spoke to the Princess of Monaco about it, she said she would be delighted to make any hotel I took a success so far as it lay in her power; and so I told Cesari that if he could find a good hotel as an investment I might take a hand in it, for I had already bought a good deal of property on the Cap d'Estel between Monte Carlo and Eze, and would be glad to develop a hotel or reserve on it.

The next winter, Cesari came out and soon told me that he had discovered a wonderful hotel. I went to Monte Carlo and saw it, didn't think much of it, but allowed myself to be persuaded. Cesari played me false, spent some thousands of pounds on the furnishings of the hotel, and some thousands of pounds more on wine, and the first season was fairly successful. Unluckily for me, about this time one of De Lara's* brothers took an interest in a hotel in Monte Carlo, and Princess Alice went continually to that hotel and left me in the lurch, saying that her husband didn't wish her to come to my place. This only made me the more obstinate, and I determined to build a reserve; I got estimates for ten thousand pounds, set the men to work under Cesari's supervision, but as my bad luck would have it, the managership of a great hotel in Paris was offered to Cesari, and he left me practically without notice.

At the crucial moment I suddenly found myself called away to South Africa again. Milner was pushing matters to an extremity. I went out and saw to my horror that he had brought it almost to war. I returned to Lon-

---

* Brothers of Isadore de Lara (1858–1935), a composer and also a friend of Albert of Monaco, whom Albert favored over Harris.

don, determined to see Chamberlain in order to try to save England from what I regarded as a catastrophe.

I wrote to Chamberlain and asked him to give me an hour of his time; and he was good enough to consent. He had altered in many ways since we parted over the policy of the *Fortnightly Review*. He had given up his belief in Free Trade and had come to see that a closer union of England and her colonies was only to be achieved by "Fair Trade," but as soon as I spoke of South Africa I found that he disagreed with me. The English Empire, he thought, must be founded on justice, strict justice; and Krueger and his Boers were unjust to the English settlers in Johannesburg, who had made the Transvaal the richest state in South Africa and yet were denied any rights of citizenship. I learned from him that he meant to force the Boers and Krueger to act justly. I tried to argue with him as I have argued in these pages, but nothing I could say had any effect. It all seemed sun-clear to him, whereas I knew that the use of force must lead to a South African war, which could have nothing but evil results. I did my very best; I went so far as to plead with him that he might assure Krueger that England would guarantee the independence of the Transvaal on condition that he gave rights of citizenship to the Johannesburgers; but the more I pleaded, the more I felt that it was all in vain; Chamberlain's mind was made up. He had the best of the verbal argument, and power to boot; and Krueger would have to give in. I was perfectly certain that Krueger would never give in.

A little while later Lord Hardwicke came to me and wanted to know whether I would sell the *Saturday Review*. I said that I had no objection. There were only about ten or twelve thousand shares which hadn't been taken up, besides the reserved shares—the few hundreds reserved for me. I asked him did he wish to get control in order to change the editorship, or was he willing to keep me on as editor. He said that he didn't think there was any wish to change me; so the end of it was that I sold him the ten or twelve thousand shares, which gave him, or rather Beit and Rhodes, the control of the *Saturday Review*.

Some months later, Hardwicke told me that "they wanted to treat me fairly, but the policy of the *Review* in regard to South Africa must be modified to suit Chamberlain and Rhodes; would I do it, or would I resign?"

"It's a perfect *impasse*," I said. "You have got the voting power on everything except the vote for the editor and his assistants, and that is controlled by the five hundred shares which I possess and will not part with."

A few weeks passed and he came to me and asked me if I would please put a price on those five hundred shares. I had already had thirty thousand pounds out of the *Saturday Review* for the five thousand I had put in it, and I had come to see that it was necessary for me to give all my time to writing. Still, I did not want to lose the *Saturday*, so I put the prohibitive price of ten thousand pounds on the five hundred reserved shares; to my astonishment he came to me a little later with his check for ten thousand pounds. I could do nothing but resign myself, which I did the more easily as it freed me to do my own work as a writer, and particularly the work on Shakespeare that I was anxious to complete.

I went away immediately to the South of France and began to work seriously at the "Shakespeare." It was nearly twenty years since I had discovered him in his works; in all these years I had read him again and again for various qualities to make sure that my version of him was the correct one. The work was entrancing to me, but difficult. I had continually to be on my guard not to ascribe any of my own failings to him; fortunately for me, the differences in character and development were so marked it was not impossible to picture him in almost every trait.

In this summer of '99 I got the first rough sketch of the book down on paper. In reading it through, I was delighted with the portrait, when suddenly the papers told me that Milner had met President Krueger in South Africa and had failed utterly to come to any understanding with him, and thereupon Milner had sent a telegram to Chamberlain, which filled me with fear: it was the special pleading of an advocate, an advocate, too, who cared nothing for the Boers or South African opinion. I saw at once that Milner had adopted Chamberlain's position from one end to the other.

Now for the first time I felt how wrong I had been to give up the *Saturday Review;* and, it began to dawn upon me, it was because Rhodes and Chamberlain were determined to push the matter to war that Beit and Hardwicke had bought control of the *Saturday.* Chamberlain began to send troops to South Africa, and then another voice, and a great one, made itself heard distinctly.

At this very time, the greatest living woman writer, Olive Schreiner,* wrote an impassioned article (afterwards published under the title *Words in Season*), pleading for fair play to the Dutch and for a policy of conciliation, just as I had pleaded.

It didn't seem possible that England would attempt to use force against the Transvaal, but I was frightened as Olive Schreiner was, and month by month the fear grew. One thing was certain: Chamberlain and Milner could make war if they wished, and it grew plainer and plainer that they meant to; they pushed Krueger to concession after concession, then declared them all worthless; and in the meantime English troops kept pouring into Natal and Cape Town. The old gorilla had to fight. War! The shame and horror of it ate into my very heart.

Almost the last thing I wrote in the *Saturday Review* was a prediction that if the English made war in South Africa, it would last for years and cost them two hundred millions of money and would alter none of the essential conditions. In fact, it would be at best labor and lives lost, the

* (1855–1920); she wrote the first South African novel of any literary merit, *The Story of a South African Farm* (1883), which was published under the pseudonym "Ralph Ivan." She fought hard for women's rights, as well as for the Boers.

most brainless adventure that England ever engaged in. Years afterwards some London paper reproduced this prediction of mine as extraordinarily correct, and I remember Winston Churchill asking me one day how I had come to be so right.

"I wasn't right," I replied, "the war cost England more than a thousand millions."

"What do you mean?" he asked in astonishment.

"When you speak of what it cost," I said, "you reckon up the money paid out, but you don't count the financial consequences. Consols before the war were 114; after the war they were 94 or 5: there was a loss of twenty points of some eight hundred millions of money; but if you lost one hundred and fifty millions on Consols, you lost two hundred millions on your railroads, and a proportionate sum on all the other industries. That ineffably stupid, brainless war cost over a thousand millions of English money, and nothing, less than nothing, was gained by it. You won contempt and hatred in South Africa and gained nothing, not even fighting fame. Campbell-Bannerman* was quite right in giving back their independence to the Boers: it was the only thing to do; but even that didn't atone for the atrocious bloodshed and wanton loss."

The mere attempt to coerce Krueger showed such manifest stupidity that it forced me to doubt the English race, doubt whether they had political wisdom enough to carry out a great policy and be worthy of their astounding birthright.

Instead of beginning to settle up the great plateau of Africa from the north of the Transvaal to the Zamesi, they spent a thousand millions in ruining their prestige in Africa and bringing mourning into thousands of homes for no reason. But even Olive Schreiner could not stop Chamberlain from sending British soldiers into Natal to bring pressure on Krueger, and Milner went on talking and telegraphing rabid nonsense to excite the combative English feeling; and at length came the war.

By this time I had finished the first draft of my book on Shakespeare and was back in England; before even the war was declared, I went to see Lord Wolseley, who had been a friend of mine for a great many years. It was at the end of the summer before the war was declared that I asked him in his room in the War Office whether there was going to be war. He told me it was practically decided. I said, "How terrible! What a dreadful calamity!"

He sprang up from the table. "We are making no mistake this time," he said. "I'll send out an army corps and bring it to a quick ending."

"You don't really think," I said, "that an army corps will be sufficient?"

"There are not more than forty or fifty thousand Boers," he said. "I reckon that forty or fifty thousand British soldiers should be enough for them, and more than enough."

"You don't know the country," I said, "nor the Boers: two army corps, four, five army corps will not be enough."

* (1836–1908); Prime Minister, 1905–08.

He lifted his hands in amused deprecation. "You don't know our English soldiers," he said; "at any rate, Buller* is going out; he knows the Boers."

"Buller!" I cried, and as soon as possible I went away. The next day I went and called on Buller and had a talk with him. I had known him, too, for many years, and had always looked upon him as a big foolish person, only to be tolerated because of his charming wife, Lady Audrey; but in this conversation, Buller surpassed himself.

"What are your tactics?" I asked. "Where are you going to land?"

"Oh, I suppose it will be Durban," he said; "the nearest way to the Transvaal is through Natal."

"But all Cape Colony will be seething," I said, "on the other side of you. The young Boers there will be able to go up through the Free State to the aid of their cousins in the Transvaal. What is your policy?"

"There is only one policy in war," replied Buller. "Get alongside the other fellow and give him hell."

"But suppose he won't let you get alongside of him," I said.

"There is never any difficulty," he said, "if you want to fight."

A few months later I read of a scene that came vividly before me as pictured in the London papers—Buller with an army of thirty thousand men brought to a standstill by the shooting of two or three thousand Boers hidden on the other side of a river. He sent out artillery and soon the sharpshooting Boers had killed every one of the gunners and then sent a force across the river to take the British guns and dump them in the river; it was done without loss: Buller with a force outnumbering the Boers ten to one beaten to a standstill by sharp-shooters who could use cover!

It was in late December or early January, after the war had begun, that Lord Desborough asked me to lunch at the Bath Club, and at the beginning of the lunch he said: "I have asked Harris to come here because he was the only person to predict that the British forces would have many defeats. When Chamberlain asked for a credit of ten millions and everyone said that the war wouldn't last three weeks, no one except Harris saw that after three months we should need a credit of a hundred millions and should feel dreadfully disappointed at the outcome."

'Twas just after Spion Kop, I remember, when Buller had tried to occupy the little mountain and a couple of thousand men he sent up were beaten by a few hundred Boers so that they had to be withdrawn the same day. *The Times* had just published a dispatch of Buller, in which he said that he had retreated from Spion Kop without losing a gun or an ammunition wagon. An army general at Grenfell's lunch started the talk by declaring that that was a splendid message of Buller—that he retreated from Spion Kop without losing a gun or ammunition wagon.

"Or," I added interrupting, "a moment's time."

Everyone laughed; but the general got very red. When Grenfell pressed

---

* Sir Henry Redvers Buller (1839–1908). He was eventually, in the face of his failures, succeeded by Roberts as commander-in-chief in the Boer War.

me for my opinion, I said, "I am sorry to say that I think the English will win; the Boers have made as bad blunders as the English: they have been led away by the memory of '80–81 and by Buller's attack, and have gone to fight in Natal; they should have left only a small force on the frontier and gone down into Cape Colony to get recruits, where they could have got a hundred thousand men of their own race to help them. Because they have not done this, they will be beaten. The next English general will land in Cape Town and go up through Cape Colony, and in a month or so the whole aspect of the war will have changed.

"But nothing alters the fact that the war is the worst one that the English have ever been engaged in, except, indeed, their terrible defeat in the Argentine,* which no one seems to remember. But this is even worse, for South Africa was already practically Anglicized, made English in sentiment from one end of the country to the other.

"I remember spending an evening with General Cronjé,** who was a typical Boer, but his daughters would talk of nothing except of the dramas on the London stage and how they longed to go for a night to Covent Garden to hear Grand Opera."

I must have spoken with intense bitterness because at the end of the lunch Lord Desborough, in saying "Good-bye" to me, said: "I am afraid, Harris, we must part; when you speak against England as you do, it is like speaking against my mother; I cannot bear it. I am sorry, but we mustn't meet again."

I realized then that I was completely out of touch with the English, and as the gloomy days went on, I came to be more and more isolated.

I don't know how to express what I felt about that inexcusable war and my detestation of the men who brought it about. I think everyone who reads what I have written about Joseph Chamberlain and Alfred Milner must admit that I have treated them more than fairly, with sympathy, indeed, and a desire, above all, to omit no good feature of character, no gift of intellect. But they worked together to bring about the South African war, and afterwards I always said and felt that they were viler than any criminal, two of those whom Dante meant when he said they were hated of God and of His enemies.

After the war, Chamberlain invited me to dinner and I replied, regretting that I couldn't accept. He met me a day or two afterwards in the lobby of the House of Commons and came up to me, smiling.

"Your letter rather surprised me," he said. "I thought we were friends and that you would tell me when you would be free, in case you had an engagement."

I replied, "I am very sorry, Mr. Chamberlain, but I can only see you as

---

* A reference to a British attack on Buenos Aires in 1806, in which the British took the city, only to lose it the next year.
** Piet Cronjé (1835–1911), a Boer general. Eventually he surrendered to Roberts at Paardeberg.

the maker of the war in South Africa and I cannot meet you with any decent, friendly feeling. I think it a horrible thing to have done. I mustn't speak about it or I should be insulting, and I have no wish to insult you."

"I am sorry," he replied, "but I did what I regarded as my duty."

I said, "I know, but the word 'duty' is worse than prostituted," and I hurried away.

Milner, too, I saw afterwards, met in fact at a certain house, but when he spoke to me I went past him as if I hadn't seen or heard him. I was told afterwards that both Chamberlain and Milner spoke of me as a "savage without manners," but there are higher laws than those of manners.

Swinburne wrote a shameful sonnet in August, 1899, which was printed in *The Times* in defense of the war. He speaks of the Boers as "dogs, agape with jaws afoam," and ends with

Strike, England, and strike home.*

Meanwhile, Lord Roberts had taken over the commander-in-chiefship and the whole war had altered. I did not know Roberts at all well. Years before, he had invited Sir Charles Dilke to pay him a visit on the northwest frontier of India and see what he had done with the British forces in Afghanistan. Dilke asked me to go with him and at first I consented eagerly, but when I talked it over with Wolseley, he persuaded me that I was wrong: he told me that Roberts had nothing in him at all—was a little fighting Irishman under the thumb of his wife, Lady Roberts; he was sure I should only be losing my time. I could see no reason for Wolseley's condemnation, for I had always found him fair minded: I took his advice in this instance and told Dilke I couldn't go with him; and so I missed Roberts. Towards the end of the year 1899 a story was told me which led me to think that I would have to alter my opinion about him.

When it became plain that Buller could do nothing except make a fool of himself in South Africa, and lead his troops to defeat and disaster, the Defense Committee under Lord Hartington got together to consider matters, and for some unknown reason they all agreed that Roberts ought to be sent out; but the Secretary of State for War objected. "We passed Roberts over," he said, "who was the senior, and sent out Buller. How can we go back to Roberts now? How can one confess such a blunder?"

"Quite easily," said Lord Hartington; "tell Roberts that we made fools of ourselves and we are sorry for it and beg him to come to our help; say that England wants him."

The moment the War Secretary broached the matter to Roberts, he exclaimed, "At last, at last!"

The Secretary of War asked him what he meant. He replied, "You know they sent me out in '80, but when I got to Cape Town I found that Gladstone had just made peace after the bitter defeat of Majuba. The news sent me down to my cabin crying with rage—to make peace after such a defeat!

* From *The Transvaal* (October 9, 1899).

But when I thought it over I felt certain that if I lived long enough my time would come, so I resolved to give up drinking and smoking and live as long as I could for the chance of redeeming our name; that's why I said, 'At last.' "

"I wanted to apologize," said the Secretary, "for passing you over and sending Buller out."

"No apology needed," said Roberts, "I have my chance at last. I will do the work; you can tell them so."

One day I read in the paper that Roberts when to church on Sunday at Cape Town, and I must confess this gave me a shock, till a friend told me the story that I have just told here. At any rate, Roberts went forward through Cape Colony and through the Free State to the Transvaal and led his troops against the chief force of the Boers under General Cronjé and won a complete victory—almost without loss. One word in the account made the victory clear to me: the correspondent said that Roberts, holding the Boers in front, made a flank attack.

When he returned to England a couple of years later, I got to know him, and asked him, had I been right in my thought about his tactics.

He said, "Quite right. The Boers had come from all parts of a country three times as big as England: the Boers from the north of the Transvaal couldn't possibly know anything about the Boers from the south, so when they were on the battlefield I knew that there could be no cohesion among them; and at the same time, I realized perfectly that they were far better shots than the troops of my army, so I protected my front with a cross fire of artillery while attacking their flanks, and at once saw I was justified; the Boers began to retreat; successive flank attacks broke up the whole organization, and my artillery turned the retreat into a rout."

The bringing of two or three hundred thousand English soldiers up through Cape Colony and the Free State held Cape Colony to quietude, and the brains of Lord Roberts did the rest. The defeat and retreat of Cronjé was the turning point of the war.

People still talk of Kitchener as if he had been the equal of Roberts, and I have heard the victory in South Africa attributed to his generalship, so I must tell what I think of Kitchener. I had met him first when I was in Cairo fifteen-odd years before. I had gone out partly to cure bronchitis and partly to get an understanding of Egypt. I met Sir Evelyn Baring, now Lord Cromer, in Cairo; and he introduced me to his assistant, who was a far abler man, Gerald Portal,* afterwards Sir Gerald Portal, who died all too soon for England.

Gerald Portal came and lunched and dined with me at Shepheard's Hotel, and took me to the English Club; and at the English Club one day he asked me whether I knew Kitchener; I shook my head. "The Chief," he

---

* (1858–94). He died of malaria caught on an expedition to East Africa in 1893. He had become famous for a mission to Abyssinia in 1887; when he became Consul General at Zanzibar, he persuaded the Sultan to stop the slave trade.

said, "Sir Evelyn Baring, thinks a great deal of him, but I couldn't form such a high opinion about him: he was so silent."

"I remember," I said, "my father telling me that the only way for a man of no family and no wealth to get on in the English army or navy was either by servility or silence. He added that I was incapable of both. Perhaps Kitchener's trying silence!"

"I will go to Suakim," I added, "if you will give me a letter to him. I will see Kitchener and let you know what I think of him."

I had already engaged in Cairo a Levantine Jew intepreter; he spoke English nearly as well as I did, and boasted that he spoke perfect Arabic; it seemed to me he knew nearly every known tongue, for his modern Greek was better than mine, and his Italian perfect.

In due time I went to Suakim and called on Kitchener and was invited by him to dinner. There were a couple of sheiks at the table, and from time to time Kitchener spoke to them in Arabic. His French was not good, though I had understood that he had passed some years as a young man in France. This surprised me so much that I asked him whether he knew Arabic.

"I am pretty useful at it," he said.

When I got home I told my secretary what Kitchener had said. He burst out: "I know Kitchener; I met him in Cyprus, worked for him: he knows no Arabic, not he! He knows nothing: he's a mere ignorant bluff. I tell you what to do. I'll teach you two or three Arabic proverbs; you shoot them off at dinner: the sheiks will understand, but Kitchener won't."

He insisted so vehemently and so contemptuously about Kitchener's ignorance that I resolved to put it to the test, for his manner at the dinner had not impressed me; he had gotten his reputation through silence and not through wisdom, in my opinion. So I spent an hour learning two or three Arabic sentences till my secretary told me that I pronounced them perfectly. The next night, dining again with Kitchener, I took the opportunity and shot off the wittiest of them. The sheiks burst out laughing and answered me in Arabic, and I grinned as if I understood what was said. Kitchener turned to me and said, "You know Arabic?"

"Oh, I am not useful at it," I replied. But I noticed that after that he used no more Arabic.

I came away from Suakim with the one word for Portal which I gave him the first day at lunch. "No one," I said, "ever was so great a soldier as Kitchener looks."

Some months later I found that Portal shared my contemptuous opinion of Kitchener's ability. And the South African war only confirmed my opinion. As soon as Roberts left South Africa, the war under Kitchener dragged on. He founded a system of blockhouses, hoping to surround the Boers. I said his blockhouses were made for blockheads and predicted that he would achieve nothing with them; and he did achieve nothing, except waste of a huge sum.

When I got to know Lord Roberts after the war and came to a high appreciation of his soldier's insight, I wanted to get his opinion of Kitchener, and he gave it to me without circumlocution.

"You know," he said, "after beating Cronjé by flank attacks, I sent Kitchener after him to round the Boers up and bring them to surrender. He had seen how I conducted the fight: I didn't dream of telling him anything about it; he must have understood, I supposed. The next news I got was that he pursued Cronjé and his beaten force of four or five thousand men and attacked them at Paardeberg. He attacked them in front and lost twelve hundred men in an hour and had to draw off beaten. I almost cried when I heard it. When I came up I found the Boers by the river and immediately began a cross fire of artillery. The cross fire was deadly; the Boers took shelter in the river bed and there I left them, keeping always a cross fire of artillery ready at all the points they could get out. When they attempted to come out, they were met by heavy artillery fire. Five days afterwards, they all surrendered with a loss to us of under twenty men. I don't want to say anything against Kitchener: he can't even see what is before his eyes; he can't even learn: he is a fool."

I said, "Did you tell them that at the Council of Defense?"

"No, no," said the little man laughing. "It wasn't my business to tell them. I knew that when I got Cronjé's force I had broken the back of the Boers in South Africa, and even Kitchener couldn't utterly spoil the work done."

But the South African war dragged on under Kitchener till the Boers were brought to submission with a promise of three or four millions to rebuild their houses, and shortly afterwards Campbell-Bannerman was wise enough to give them their liberty again and leave them in power in the Transvaal. Today, from one end to the other, thanks to this piece of belated wisdom, the Transvaal is as English as it was before the ineffably stupid Boer war.

Chapter VIII

San Remo

I MUST NOW TELL the greatest amatory experience of my life. I had made a great deal of money with Hooley, and was besides tormented with the wish to complete at any cost my book on Shakespeare. I had done some chapters in the *Saturday Review,* and Shaw, among others, had praised them highly. It was and is my belief that Shakespeare has been mis-seen and misunderstood by all the commentators. Ordinary men are always accustomed to make their gods in their own image, and so the English had formed a Shakespeare who loved his wife and yet was a paiderast; who had made money at his business and retired to enjoy his leisure as a country gentleman in village Stratford after living through the bitter despair of *Timon,* and the madness of *Lear:* "O, let me not be mad, Sweet Heaven . . . I would not be mad!"

The only particle of truth in the fancy portrait has been contributed by Tyler, who, inspired by Wordsworth's saying that in the sonnets Shakespeare "unlocked his heart," proved that the sonnets showed that Shakespeare, about 1596, had fallen in love with a maid-of-honor named Mary Fitton and had been in love with her, as he said himself about 1600, for three years. I came to Tyler's aid by proving that this episode had been dragged into three different plays of the same period, and I went on to show that this love episode had practically been the great love of Shakespeare's life, and had lasted from 1596 to 1608. I proved also that though he disliked his wife, he was perfectly normal; that his fortune rested on the gift of Lord Southampton to him of a thousand pounds when he came of age in 1596; and that so far from having increased his wealth and been a prudent husbandman, he had never cared for "rascal counters," and died leaving barely one year's income, probably after the drinking-bout of tradition, in which he had drunk perhaps a little too much, for, to use his own words, he had "poor, unhappy brains for drinking": a too highly powered ship for the frail hull! Does he not talk in *The Tempest* of walking to "still his beating mind"?

All this and more I wanted to set forth, but was it possible to bring such a totally new conception of Shakespeare into life, and so to prove it that it would be accepted? I hated the English climate in the winter, and so I set off in an October fog for the Riviera; and I don't know why, but I went through Nice to San Remo. At San Remo, the hotel life quickly tired me, and I went about looking for a villa. I discovered a beautiful villa with views over both the mountains and the sea and a great garden; but alas, it was for sale and not for hire, the gardener told me.

This gardener deserves a word or two of description. He was a rather small man, perhaps forty-five or fifty years of age, a slight, strong figure, with an extraordinarily handsome head, set off by quite white moustaches— the suggestion of age being completely contradicted by the clearness of the skin and the brightness of his eyes. Ten thousand pounds was wanted for the villa, but the gardener told me that if I bought it, I could always sell it for as much as I paid for it, or more. I took this assertion with a grain of salt, but the end of it was that the gardener amused me so much that I bought the villa and went to live in it.

I ordered my days at once for work and for the first week or two did work ten or twelve hours a day, but one memorable afternoon I came upon the gardener, whom I had taken into my service, reading Dante, if you please, in the garden. I had a talk with him and found that he knew not only Dante, but Ariosto, and Leopardi, and Carducci,* and was a real student of Italian literature. I passed a great afternoon with him, and resolved whenever I was tired in the future to come out and talk with him.

Two or three days afterwards I was overworked again, and I went out to him and he said: "You know, when I saw you at first, I thought we should have a great time together here; that you would love life and love; and here you are writing, writing, writing, morning, noon and night—wearing yourself out without any care for beauty or for pleasure."

"I like both," I said, "but I came here to work; still, I shouldn't mind having some distractions if they were possible; but what is possible here?"

"Everything," he replied. "I have been putting myself in your place: if I were rich, wouldn't I enjoy myself in this villa!"

"What would you do?" I asked.

"Well," he said, "I would give prizes for the prettiest girls, say one hundred francs for the first; fifty francs for the second; and twenty-five as consolation prizes if five or six girls came."

"What good would that do?" I asked. "You wouldn't get young girls that way, and you certainly wouldn't get their love."

"Wouldn't I!" he cried. "First of all, in order to see who was the prettiest, they would have to strip, wouldn't they? And the girl who is once naked before you is not apt to refuse you anything."

I had come to a sort of *impasse* in my work; I saw that the whole assumption that Shakespeare had been a boy lover, drawn from the sonnets, was

---

* Giosué Carducci (1835–1907), an Italian poet; awarded the Nobel prize in 1906.

probably false, but since Hallam* it was held by every one in England, and every one, too, in Germany, so prone are men always to believe the worst, especially of their betters—the great leaders of humanity.

Heinemann, the publisher, had asked me for my book on Shakespeare before I left England, but as soon as I wrote him that I was going to disprove Shakespeare's abnormal tastes, he told me that he had found every authority in England was against me and therefore he dared not publish my book. Just when I was making up my mind to set forth my conviction, came this proposal of my gardener. I had worked very hard for years on the *Saturday Review* and in South Africa, and I thought I deserved a little recreation; so I said to the gardener, "Go to it. I don't want any scandal, but if you can get the girls through the prizes, I will put up the money cheerfully and will invite you to play master of ceremonies."

"This is Tuesday," he said. "I think next Sunday would be about the best day."

"As you please," I replied.

One Sunday, having given a *congé* to my cook and waiting-maid, I walked about to await my new guests, the cook having laid out a good *déjeuner* wth champagne on the table in the dining-room. About eleven o'clock a couple of girls fluttered in, and my gardener conducted them into two bedrooms and told them to make themselves pretty and we would all lunch at half-past twelve. In half an hour five girls were assembled. He put them all into different rooms and went from room to room, telling them that they must undress and get ready for inspection. There was much giggling and some exclamations, but apparently no revolt. In ten minutes he came to me and asked me, was I ready for inspection?

"Certainly," I said; and we went to the first room. A girl's head looked out from under the clothes: she had got into bed. But my gardener knew better than to humor her: he went over and threw down the bed clothes, and there she was completely nude. "Stand up, stand up," he said, "you are worth looking at!"

And indeed she was. Nothing loath, she stood on the bed as directed and lent herself to the examination. She was a very pretty girl of twenty or twenty-one; and at length, to encourage her, he took her in his arms and kissed her. I followed suit and found her flesh perfectly firm and everything all right, except that her feet were rather dirty; whereupon my gardener said, "That's easily remedied." We promised her a prize and told her that we would return when she had washed and put on her clothes and made herself as pretty as possible; and he led me into the next room.

The girl in this one was sitting on the bed, half-undressed, but she was very slight and much younger, and evidently very much excited, because she glowered at us as if she hated us. The moment we came into the room she went for the gardener, telling him that if she had known it was

* Henry Hallam (1777–1859), English historian and father of Arthur Hallam, subject of Tennyson's *In Memoriam*.

required to be naked, she wouldn't have come near us. The gardener kissed her at once and told her not to be frightened, that she was pretty sure of winning a prize, and she need not undress. And we went on to the third room.

There I had one of the surprises of my life: a girl stood on the rug near the bed with the color coming and going in her cheeks; she was in her shirt, but with her dress held round her hips. She, too, said she didn't want to strip—she would rather go home.

"But nothing has happened to you," said the gardener. "Surely a couple of men to admire you isn't going to make you angry; and that frown doesn't suit your loveliness at all."

In two or three minutes the wily Italian had dissipated her anger and she began to smile, and suddenly, shrugging her shoulders, she put down the dress and then at once stood up at his request, trying to laugh. She had one of the loveliest figures and faces that I ever saw in my life. Her breasts were small, but beautifully rounded and strangely firm; her hips, too, and bottom were as firm as marble, but a little slight. Her face was lit up with a pair of great hazel eyes and her mouth, though a little large, was perfectly formed: her smile won me. I told the gardener that I didn't want to see any more girls, that I was quite content, and he encouraged me to kiss and talk to her while he went into the next room to see the next applicant.

As soon as the gardener left the room, my beauty, whose name was Flora, began questioning me: "Why do you choose me? You are the owner, aren't you?"

I could only nod. I had sense enough to say, "Partly for your beauty, but also because I like you, your ways, your courage."

"But," she went on, "real liking does not grow as quickly as that, or just by the view of a body and legs."

"Pardon me," I rejoined, "but passion, desire in a man comes first: it's for the woman to transform it into enduring affection. You like me a little because I admire and desire you; it's for me by kindness and sympathy to turn that liking into love; so kiss me and don't let us waste time arguing. Can you kiss?"

"Of course I can," she said, "every one can!"

"That's not true," I retorted. "The majority of virgins can't kiss at all, and I believe you're a virgin."

"I am," she replied; "but you'll not find many in this crowd."

"Kiss me," I went on, taking her in my arms and kissing her till I found response in hot lips. As she used her tongue, she asked roguishly, "Well, Sir, can I kiss?"

"Yes," I replied, "and now I'll kiss you," and I laid her on the bed and buried my face between her legs.

She was a virgin, I discovered, and yet peculiarly quick to respond to passion: an astonishing mistress! She didn't hide from me the fact that, like most school girls in Italy, as in France, she had been accustomed to provoke her own sensuality by listening to naughty stories and by touching herself ever since puberty. But what kept her from giving herself freely was her fear of the possible consequences. My assurances seemed to have convinced her, for suddenly she started up and danced round me in her fascinating nudity. "Shall I have a prize?"

"The first," I cried.

"*Carissimo mio,*" and she kissed me a dozen times. "I'll be whatever you want and cover you with love."

Our talk had gone on for perhaps half an hour, when a knock came at the door, and the gardener came in to find us both quite happy and, I think, intimately pleased with each other. He said, "The other two you had better see or they will be disappointed, but I think you have picked the prettiest."

"I am quite content," I replied, "to rest on your approval of them."

But my self-willed beauty said, "Let us go and see them; I will go with you," and we went into the next room, said a few flattering things, and went on to the fifth room, where there was a girl who said she wouldn't undress.

"At any rate," said the gardener, "the matter is settled; we can all go in and have lunch, and then my master will give the prizes."

We had a great lunch, all helping each other and ourselves, and when the champagne was opened, every one seemed to enjoy the feast infinitely. But when the prize giving came, I was ashamed, hating to give one less than the other, so I called the gardener to one side and told him my reluctance. "Nothing easier," he said. "I have made you out to be a great English lord. Go into that bedroom on the right and I will send them in one by one. If I were you, I would give the two first prizes and I will give the consolation stakes."

"Splendid," I said, "but give me a reasonable half-hour before sending in the second one." Flora came in and got her first prize, kissed me, and offered herself to my desire by opening the bed. Then for some reason or other a good idea came into my head.

I put up my hands. "That's for later, I hope," I exclaimed. "It means affection, and you don't care for me yet; perhaps you will with time, and if you don't, I'll forgive you. There's no compulsion here."

"How good of you," she exclaimed. "Just for saying that I want to kiss you, *caro mio* (you dear)," and she threw her arms round my neck and gave me a long kiss.

Naturally, I improved the occasion, and turned the kiss into an embrace by putting my hands up her dress on her sex. After I had touched her for a minute or so, she trembled and came, and as I put my arms round her and kissed her, she kissed me passionately in return. "*Carissimo mio,*" she murmured, and hid her glowing cheek on my neck. While she was putting her dress in order before the glass, she began talking quickly: "You know, I hope this isn't the only time. I want to come back without any prize, for I like you and you have been kind to me. I was frightened at first—you must forget all that; you will, won't you? *Cuore mio;* I'll find new love names for you," and she did.

"But why did you want to see us all naked," she went on, "we're all alike, aren't we?"

"No, indeed," I cried, "you are all different."

"But you can't love one because her breasts are smaller than another's. No woman would care for such a thing. I love your voice and what you say and your eyes, but not your legs: fancy!" and she laughed aloud.

Finally she said, "When may I come again? soon, please!"

"Surely," I replied, "when will you come? I want your photograph."

"Any day you like," Flora said. And we fixed the meeting for Tuesday. She went off delighted.

The next girl who came in was the young girl, the second we saw, who had not undressed and who had declared that she wouldn't have come if she had known the conditions. At once she said to me: "I don't mind undressing for you: I know you now," and in a trice she had pulled her things off: she was very pretty. I afterwards photographed her in the swing in the garden. But she was nothing astonishing, just a very pretty and well-made girl of sixteen. Her name, she told me, was Yolande; she lived with an aunt. I may have more to tell of her later, though her quick temper made me avoid her.

When I gave her the second prize of seventy-five francs, she said, "You are giving me the second prize; if I had been nicer you perhaps would have given me the first."

Her frankness amused me. "Does it make much difference to you, the difference between seventy-five and one hundred francs?"

She nodded her head: "It will make a difference to my dress," she said. "I want pretty underthings"—and she curled up her nose.

"Well," I replied, "say nothing about it, and take another twenty-five francs." At once she threw her arms around my neck and kissed me, and then, "May I come back?"

"Sure, sure," I replied.

"May I bring some one else?"

"Any one you please," I said.

That is about all I remember of the first séance, except that the beauty, Flora, whom I have tried to describe, did not leave the villa till long after dinner.

When I talked with my gardener of the event afterwards, he told me that he had preferred the youngest of all, whom I had not seen. "Clara," he said, "was the prettiest of the lot." As I told him I thought her too thin for beauty and too young to be mentally attractive, he promised to show me her nudity the next Sunday. I wanted to know about the next Sunday. "Will you be able to get three or four new girls?"

"Good God," he exclaimed, "twenty, if you like! These girls will whisper it all about and you may be sure you will have an ever increasing number. This villa is going to get a good name if you continue!"

"I will continue weekly," I said, "but if there are likely to be more girls, I might bring a friend over from Monte Carlo, who happens to be there and who is really an English lord."

"By all means," he said; "the more, the merrier."

Accordingly, I sent a telegram to my friend, Ernest — asking him to come and spend a happy weekend with me. In due time he came. And it was well that he did come, for the second week showed me that the gardener was wiser and knew his country people better than I did: at least twenty girls came to win prizes, girls of all ages from fifteen to thirty. My gardener proposed that he should weed them out to six or seven, giving them consolation prizes without stripping them. Both Ernest and I were quite content, but we wanted to see his choice, and we were astonished by the ability with which he made his selection: practically, we had to agree with him. Twelve or fourteen girls were sent home with twenty-five francs each, without any further attempt at discrimination; and our inspection began without making me waver in my allegiance to Flora.

It was in these first weeks at San Remo that I began to discover that the body was not so important in love or in passion as the mind and character. I had no slightest desire to leave my beauty for any of the newer queens; and I didn't want her to strip, even for Ernest's inspection, although she was willing to. But I had become her lover now, and love desires exclusive possession.

The third meeting had a new termination. Another young Englishman, named George —, a friend of Ernest, had fallen in love with one the week before. We had the three queens, as we called them, to dinner, as well as to lunch. After dinner the gardener appeared with one, and declared that if our girls would strip, he would show that his was the prettiest of the lot. None of the three girls minded: they were all willing, so we had another contest; but we resolved to give the winner of this contest two hundred francs. I don't believe that the famous choice of Paris, with the three queens of Heaven before him, ever showed such beauties. I must try to describe them. Of two of them I have photographs, which I must not reproduce; and the third, my queen, I have already described. It is for my readers to use their imaginations. And I cannot even give the photo of the gardener's choice, for she wasn't a bit more than fourteen years of age. When we made fun of him about this, he said philosophically, "I am older than you men, and I have noticed that the older we get the younger we like the girls." On this we all burst out laughing. My readers may compare the four beauties for themselves.

This was the first time in my life that I ever studied the sex of women; and it was the gardener who brought it about. We had decided that all our three beauties were lovelier than his, when he challenged us to a new test.

"What do we desire most in a girl?" he asked: "surely a small and well-made sex. Well, I'll bet Clara has the smallest and best sex of the lot."

Ernest at once declared that the gardener was right; so we asked our beauties to submit to his examination. They laughed at us but yielded to the general wish. Clara won, as the gardener predicted; my Flora was second; Ernest's beauty, third; and George's fourth. But all had to admit that from the outside Flora's sex was the most perfectly formed.

We found that the chief centre of pleasure, as a rule, was the clitoris and that almost in proportion to its size; sometimes it was not distinguishable, but in the three beauties it was normal, whereas in Clara it was abnormally developed—fully an inch long. The inner lips too, in her case, were very heavy; and when the gardener told us that he had brought her twice to fainting, we had to agree with him that she felt more acutely than any of the rest.

Flora, however, disdained the test and said that she felt more at something said, at a beautiful thought or fine deed than she ever felt by mere sexual excitement.

One day Ernest and George went to Monte Carlo and brought over two more friends. The gardener was overjoyed, for as the girls increased, so his tips increased, and his amusement, too, I think. But from now on, our Sundays occasionally developed into orgies; that is, we wandered about, selecting now this and now that girl, instead of remaining faithful to the queens; but usually, as soon as the newcomers went away, we returned to our old allegiances. But from the outset I limited my time for amusement to two days a week: Wednesdays and Sundays; all the other days I spent working.

I shall never forget one occasion when we all went down bathing in a state of nature—half a dozen girls and four men. After the bath, we all came up and lay about on the grass and soon the lovely girlforms seduced the men, and the scene turned to embracing, which the beauty and abandon of the girls made memorable.

This life continued for five or six weeks, till one Thursday I was interrupted by the gardener, who came and asked me to come down to see a cousin of Clara's, Adriana. I found a very lovely girl with reddish fair hair and grey eyes: quite different in looks from the ordinary Italian. I could reproduce the likeness of her that a painter-friend, Rousselet,* developed later from a photograph. But she was certainly one of the most beautiful beings I have ever seen in my life, and curiously enough, she seemed at first as sweet and sympathetic and passionate as she was lovely. I took to her at once and, strange to say, even Flora liked her. She told us she was an orphan and seemed always grateful for any kindness: when Flora told her she liked her and was not jealous, "How could you be jealous?" said Adriana. "You are too lovely to know what envy means."

Flora kissed her, saying: "My dear, I don't know whether it is wisdom in you or goodness, but you are certainly wonderful."

* Probably Ernest Rousselot, the still-life painter.

We had been at these games more than half the summer when Ernest proposed we should vary the procedure by letting the girls select their favorites. No sooner proposed than done. We gave them prizes and asked them to apportion them: at once they established one purse and gave us all an equal prize; but they determined, too, who was the first favorite, and who the second, and so on.

I had no reason to complain of the result; but I was at a loss to know why I was chosen so frequently: was it due to a hint of the gardener, or simply to the fact that I was known to be the owner of the villa? I never could quite determine, but I was chosen so often that the game became monotonous; and when I was left out, Ernest was the winner, though George was far better looking than either of us, and at least ten years younger.

At length we hit on a new game: one Sunday about fifty girls had come, so Ernest proposed that our four beauties should select the prettiest four of the newcomers, while we men stood round and studied their feminine choice. We soon found it was impossible to know why this or that girl was chosen, but assuredly the prettiest were seldom, if ever, successful; nevertheless, the four selected were soon initiated.

One day there came a new development: three mothers had brought their girls, and George proposed we should get the mothers to select the most beautiful four to throne it at our lunch. To my delight, Flora was selected, and an excellent selection made from the others.

Every week, I had almost said, every Wednesday and every Sunday, there was something new: we constantly drove in George's carriage, or Ernest's, or both, either into the mountains or along the coast. George had discovered a wonderful, lonely, little bay for bathing, almost uninhabited, and we used to go there frequently, and half a dozen of us would bathe together; then the meals, especially the dinners, were always feasts which often ended in some droll invention.

The curious part of my personal adventure was the changes in the character of Adriana. It was almost indescribable; from being all sympathy and sweetness, she began, I think, through jealousy, to become more and more imperious.

"You know," she began one day, when she had come of her own accord to see me, "your Flora is engaged to be married; as soon as I saw her, I knew she wouldn't go begging long; she's pretty, though you must know her legs are thin. But perhaps you like thin legs?"

"You are the best made of them all," I began, "please let me see you, and don't bother about any one else."

"If I'm the only one," she replied, pouting; "I can't bear to be second—"

"Make yourself the first:" I said, "it's up to you: be sweeter than Flora, more passionate than Clara, and you'll win—"

"Clara," she cried, "is nothing but a little prostitute, like her mother before her; she's quite common—"

I couldn't help provoking her. "The gardener swears," I said, "that she has the smallest sex in the whole country and is besides the most passionate of all of you—"

"I hate these comparisons," cried Adriana. "They degrade one to the level of the mere animal; surely there's more to me than round limbs and a small sex? I'd give anything, everything to love, but to mere desire— nothing—"

"Desire," I remarked, "is the door to love and the guide; physical beauty can be seen and measured, so to speak, whereas affection and devotion need time to be appreciated. Do you know," I added warningly, "jealousy is no proof of affection; on the contrary, I think jealous people are usually hardhearted: pride is their master passion, not affection."

"Oh; I'm proud," she cried, "I admit it, but I think if you cared for me and me alone, I would do anything for you whatever you wished."

I turned the talk by admiring her arms and bust, for I didn't wish to change Flora; and, lovely though Adriana was, I resented her imperiousness; but her body was too perfect and I ended by making her feel and enjoy her.

"Did I please you?" she asked afterwards.

"More than ever," I said.

"You see," she cried; "may I come tomorrow?"

"Oh, you know," I said, "I have to work; I would like you to come, but not before Saturday."

"Then you will have Flora on Wednesday," she said pouting.

"No," I replied, to get rid of her, "I promise I'll have no one until you come again."

She kissed me, and there the matter ended for the time. But she soon made herself impossible by her exactions.

It was the advent into our company of one Frenchman, whom I shall call by his Christian name, Jean, who brought us to an acquaintance with new sensualities. He chose again a girl, Rosa, and declared that by whipping her bottom he could bring her to a passion of desire and soon the whippings, just to redden the skin, became more or less general among us: from time to time we all tried it; and strange to say the girls were most partial to it— the sufferers, so to speak, though the suffering plainly was very slight and soon lost in pleasure. On more than one occasion the whippings became general, and nothing prettier could be imagined than three or four girls being excited in this way. Generally it was one of the girls who did the whipping; it was curious how much rougher they were than the men; it showed us all very plainly that women think less of small pains than men do.

Another thing Jean did was to send to Paris and get half a dozen instruments resembling the sex of men in stiff Indian rubber; and these, too, we found could be used to excite our beauties to a hitherto unknown extent.

We all agreed finally that the sensuality of women lasted much longer than that of men, and women needed much more exciting. But Jean's greatest achievement was altogether new to most of us. He heard the gardener one day bragging of his mistress because she had the smallest sex.

"Of course," said Jean, "you know that you can make any girl's sex as small as you like."

We showed astonishment and he went on: "There are three or four injections which will contract the sex as much as you please, contract it so that you cannot enter easily the sex of a woman who has had a child: it's ridiculous to talk of a small sex as a beauty when anyone can have it."

In the next week or ten days we had all tried his injections of alum water and found that his remedy was in every case infallible; but still we preferred those who were naturally small.

Ernest told us that he had had a similar experience in the East, I think in Java, and I had to admit that I had learned about it in India.

Jean, too, would not be fettered for a moment to any girl, but every Wednesday and every Sunday chose a new partner; and he used to amuse us all infinitely with his stories of how he treated them and how he enjoyed them. One day when Jean had been bragging of his performances, one of his mistresses suddenly interrupted him by saying, "The only way one can ever get you to go twice is by whipping you," and we all laughed, for Jean was distinctly younger than any of us except George, and we hitherto had taken his bragging, more or less, to be the truth.

Looking back over that wonderful summer, I consider my most valuable experiences to be the stories the girls told of themselves: the sex experiences in girlhood of Flora and Adriana taught me a great deal, for they both were normal. I am sure Flora's confessions were perfectly truthful and, though Adriana concealed a good deal usually, she now and then revealed herself very completely. This is what Flora told me: but I'll keep these revelations for another chapter.

Chapter IX

The Girls' Confessions

Flora

"YOU ASK ME to strip my mind; well, I'll try," Flora began, "and if I omit anything, you must just question me, for I want to please you, you dear!

"Ever since I can remember, I have revelled in certain kinds of—may I call them, naked thoughts. Even as young as seven I must have been lewd —this is stripping myself with a vengeance. I remember I had measles at school, and a doctor whose pet I was attended me. He was very good-looking. I suppose he was a hero to me—anyway, I distinctly remember the sensation he caused me by undressing and touching me. That may be ordinary enough, but I used to dream about it, think about it, delight in it. Is that natural? I've never told any one—they wouldn't understand—so I don't know whether it is usual or not.

"And later at nine years of age or so, a girl much older than myself made me much worse. Of course, she used me to gratify her sensations, but it was very bad for me. She put my hand on her and told me to rub. I think I must have been really depraved, for later two other girls got very intimate with me, but this time I was the ring-leader. I can hardly say what we didn't do—you will understand. This at the age of nine and ten, and they say boys are more depraved than girls! I don't believe it. From that you can have some idea what I am like now.

"My dreams lead to sensations. I just revel in passions that have no outlet whatever, unless I satisfy them myself. And often I do that. That's one side of me.

"I wish to God those of my sex weren't such hypocrites. Even my best friend, with whom I discuss all sorts of things, chiefly men and women, often seems thoroughly disgusted and tells me seriously I'm getting very immoral. She was saying the other day that she had dreamt she was walking naked and alone down the main street, and she thought everyone had had that dream more or less frequently. I said I had never dreamt I was naked and *alone* anywhere! That it was wasting a splendid sensation. She was really annoyed.

"Then there were two other girls; they were about the same age as myself, thirteen and fourteen. They were sisters and very wild; I mean undisciplined. I didn't like them at all, they were too rude and bold and very mean. Still they served a purpose. They used to strip and put me in bed and one of them rubbed vaseline or some sort of grease between my legs, and the other looked on till her turn came. The sensation of being looked at was almost as good as the one of being rubbed. I must have been a cunning little devil, because I certainly wasn't able to analyze the why and the wherefore of it at all; I just knew I liked it.

"And then came older girls; when I was about fifteen, a girl took me up to her room and locked the door; it was a sort of wardrobe room—small and pitch dark. I was old enough to realize then just what I was doing. She put my hand on her sex and I touched her as well as I could. I know I liked doing it. Naturally she was fully developed and somehow that was an added enjoyment for me. It did me harm in that I used to brood over it, gloat over it, enjoy my lewd thoughts—well, fifteen is too young for that, especially as I didn't need encouraging."

"But why shouldn't you be encouraged?" I couldn't help asking.

"I was already too much inclined that way," she replied.

"So much the better," I went on; "I can't understand the implied condemnation."

"Nor can I," she rejoined. "It's merely habit, the customary way of thinking and speaking.

"You want to know everything: are girls' desires as vagrant as those of men? Yes, and quite as strong, I think; when, as a young girl, a man attracted me, a complete stranger—or showed me he wanted me, in the tram or anywhere, I used to cross my legs and press my thighs together and squeeze my sex till I came just as if I had used my hand; often I was all wet. There, you have the truth!

"Why did I come here? Naturally, I hoped to win a first prize, but really that was not my chief motive. The gardener said there was a young goodlooking Englishman in the villa who would be very nice to me; the money was only the hope we all used to excuse ourselves. We pretended to be seeking the money, but in truth we were seeking lover and love—new emotions.

"When the gardener left me in the bedroom that first morning, I noticed how fine the sheets were and the pretty pictures in the room: 'When will he come?' I asked myself; 'What will he do?' And my heart was in my mouth.

"Before you came in that first time to see me, the hope of you set all my pulses throbbing. I threw myself on the bed and thought about it, and thinking gradually brought about the feeling that demands satisfaction, so I satisfied it by touching myself—waiting for you: you dear, you!

"I've told you nothing about men, you say; but really, I had no experiences to speak of till I came here. My mother was always warning me of the consequences and the risk of having a child was always present.

"I often saw men in the town I could have liked, but we lived right out in the country, and till your gardener came and talked to me and assured me there was no risk and a great deal of fun, I never gave myself to any man: you are first, and you know it, don't you, dear?

"One young fellow used to come out last summer from the town and we used to take long walks, and he said he loved me and was always touching my breasts and trying to excite me in fifty ways; but when I mentioned marriage, he sheered off. Men want pleasure and no ties and I don't blame them. If I were a man, I'd do the same: it's we women run the risk; but not with you, dear.

"Oh, now, often I can feel those slow long kisses of yours on my breasts and—I close my eyes and give myself to you: love is the best thing in the world, but how am I to love when you go away and the great days are ended? Oh, I wish my life could end with them: I have had the best of life."

"Don't say that," I cried. "The best of your life is still to come, and I shall not be gone forever."

And then the love play began again and went on till we were called out to lunch, and we found a feast that deserves to be described at length, but I am afraid of tiring my readers.

Though I liked Flora immensely, I often made fun of her coldness. She used to resent this, saying, "You do not know me!"

One day she found me with Adriana, and that evening she asked me: "Do you go with her because she's passionate?"

I nodded my head: it's useless to try to explain to a woman the attraction of novelty.

The next day, to my astonishment, Flora surpassed herself: she really used her sex as an instrument and gave me intense thrills.

As I cried out, "Enough dear!" she triumphed.

"Am I better than your Adriana?"

"Much better," I replied, "but why don't you act like that always?"

"I don't know!" she replied. "It's due to a sort of reserve I can't explain, but you mustn't believe with the gardener that Clara or Adriana or any of them feel more than I do. A man may be proud of liking the act; a woman is always ashamed to confess it or show it!"

The year after I had left San Remo, Flora wrote to me at the Hotel de Paris at Monte Carlo. She told me that all her life since I had gone away was stale and flat. If I didn't want her any more, she would prefer to kill herself: she could not endure her dull, uneventful existence. The letter was some months old, but I raced over to San Remo at once to make things right if possible. Naturally, I first sought out my gardener. He was astonished. "She has just been married," he cried, when I showed him the letter, "and well married; he's rich. I'll tell you all about it tomorrow."

It turned out to be as he had said: my Flora had married, and married exceedingly well, and when I sought her out, she didn't hesitate to tell me that half her success had come from the apprenticeship she had gone through with us Englishmen. "You taught me to love, Sir," she said, "and it was your teaching mainly that made it easy for me later to excite love without feeling it much. Yet my husband is a dear fellow, and I think I shall be happy with him: you don't mind?" she asked, smiling archly the while.

"Mind! Of course not!" And I said to myself, "Another ship come safely to port."

Adriana

Adriana's account was very like that of Flora's in the early years, but at first she was more outspoken.

"Passion—I'm made of it, a colt—wild, crazy, untamed colt—quick, rashly impulsive, savage—and yet I've emotion enough in me—high poetry; the violin, 'flame in the skies of sunset'—all bring tears to my eyes: the rippling of a stream, the green foliage of trees, books and pictures—a deep sweet world.

"Of course, it was an older girl who first taught me sensuality; I don't really think she ever touched me. It was quite a one-sided affair, but what I did to her gave me quite a little pleasure of my own. Of course, I didn't know what she did it for. I liked it and that was all that mattered to me.

"I had a governess just before I went to school. I can't remember, but, anyway, she's the only female, barring the first I mentioned, who made me aware of her passion. She would insist on bathing me. I knew that was funny, as none of the others had wished to. But she banged on the door the first night, and when I admitted her, she came over to me and slowly took away the towel covering me. I felt ashamed—her eyes made me feel so—her look made me blush—it also began to make me feel strangely pleased, with that feeling of pleasure we all experience, I think, when we are looked at. Well, every week she bathed me and I became fully aware of her feelings towards me once behind the bathroom door. And I loved it. She would lift me out of the bath and lay me across her knees and the delightful sensation of being devoured by her greedy eyes made me open my legs —for her to rub me.

"From twelve to fourteen I was at school and developed a passion for one of the seniors. And while I would have been thrilled at a single touch of her fingers even on my hand, she never took even the very slightest notice of me. The sight of her thrilled me, and if she passed me and I felt her brush against me, it set my heart beating. But that sort of hero worship is very common at school.

"Another girl of my own age one night surprised me by asking me to accompany her into the bathroom. I went along wondering. She locked the door and then in a somewhat shamefaced fashion, asked me to touch her. I did, and she touched me. Both of us were highly excited, but we were interrupted, and somehow we never tried anything further afterwards.

"You ask me about exciting myself. I was doing it constantly from ten or eleven on. About thirteen I got quite thin and pale, and my mother told me one evening how a young girl friend of hers had ruined her health by touching her sex and so warned me. After that, I used to do it every Saturday night. Then I had an orgy, once a week; it was splendid. I used to think of some man who had attracted me or shown that he wanted me and I'd begin.

"One day in the tram a common man came in and threw himself down opposite me. Of a sudden I noticed that his trousers were unbuttoned and I saw his sex: it made me angry at first; he was so dirty and common. But as I stole glances at it, it excited me fearfully; I crossed my legs and squeezed my sex and at once I came. I could not help it: when I got out I was all streaming—wet to my knees.

"You ask me about my feelings. I have only to wait a very short time before I come, usually. But it all depends on the state of my mind. If there is not a good (I should say bad) atmosphere, it takes long, but if I feel really passionate—almost lewd—a minute will do it. And I can do it again perhaps three times, but that's the limit. My legs give way under me after that—so I judge I've had the best of myself; anyway I couldn't do more than that consecutively.

"No one thrill is ever exactly like the last; you soon learn to differentiate. Of course, they all recur, but never one after the other—and sometimes my favorite thrill comes most seldom; it is when all my muscles stiffen and grow rigid; it may not occur for days, even weeks."

Naturally, I went to work at once to bring on the rigid paroxysm in Adriana and found no difficulty. "You could not do it again," she said, but in ten minutes I proved that I could bring about the rigid orgasm as often as I liked. In fact, once after bringing on the paroxysm three or four times, she burst out crying and laughing in a sort of wild hysteria that took me hours to quiet.

"I love you," she said to me, "and that's why I can't control myself. But why do you want any one else? I'll give you all myself, more than any one else can, you dear! But you must be faithful!"

"When are you most passionate?" I asked, and she replied:

"I have not noticed that I am more passionate at certain times—at least orthodox times—than others. I know it is so, or should be so, but everything to me depends on my mind and emotion.

"Did I tell you of any man having me? She wouldn't, I'm sure, your Flora, but I will. I was ony sixteen and my folks got me work in the office in an hotel. He was the manager and married: I knew his wife, and his eldest daughter was older than I was. He was very kind to me from the beginning. I saw he desired me, of course.

"One fête day, three years ago, every one was in the street; but he had given me some work and I didn't like to leave it. In the middle of the procession he came to the door and sent me to fetch his fountain pen from his bedroom on the fourth floor. Of course I went, and while I was searching for his pen, he came into the room and had locked the door before I knew or guessed anything. He took me almost by force; he put his hands up my clothes and lifted me on to the bed; and while I was saying I'd cry out, he hurt me so that I shrieked; but he went on. Afterwards he kissed me and told me all sorts of sweet things, but I never put myself in his power again. I had a terrible dread for two weeks and then I feared the pain for years more. One day a girl told me I'd not suffer again.

"Then a boy came. I was tempted by his virginity, but I didn't yield; then last year a young visitor at the hotel made love to me—he didn't hurt, and I enjoyed it ecstatically, for I really liked him, and he had such dear pleasing ways: he was always bringing me flowers, and he would kiss my hands, and was always telling me how pretty I was and how much he loved my eyes: he was a dear!

"But now I've fallen in love with you with my whole soul and body passionately; and that's what makes me wild with jealousy. Flora is always boasting that you like her best, and I can't believe it, but I hate to hear her. I could strike the slut. But you do go with her, and I go home and cry half the night. Why can't you love me alone or love me best? Then I wouldn't care. But always to be second, to find that Flora is preferred to me: it's driving me crazy."

Of course I kissed her, smiling, and she said: "Promise you'll only go with me for this next week, and I'll give my very soul to you; promise! You'll see how sweet I can be—promise! I'll say all the naughty words and do all the naughty things: I want to! There! Do you hear that; I'll do more than you imagine, you dear, you!"

I promised and kept my word, but after that week Adriana never came back again, and so we lost the loveliest figure of all. In her, jealousy was stronger than passion, as it is in many, many women.

Clara

It was the gardener again who brought me to the chief discovery. He told me that Clara had no reticences and would tell me anything, so one day I got him to bring her and questioned her. She said:

"What is there to tell? It's the same thing over and over again, only it gets better and better all the time, different to (sic) most things in life. I don't know when I began. I don't think I was more than seven, but almost immediately I noticed that I didn't care for girls touching me; I only wanted boys, and I was very curious about them, though I pretended not to be.

"One boy, five or six years older than I was, when I was about ten, told me all about it and suited the action to the word. He hurt me a little, but the pleasure, even at the beginning, was greater than the pain, and so I went on with anyone I liked; and I liked a good many.

"I got very careful about thirteen because I knew what the consequences might be, and I made up my mind only to go with a man I really cared for. I don't know why I fell in love, but I did when I was about fifteen, with a gentleman who was good-looking and had charming manners. He spoke to me in the street, took me for a drive, kissed me and put his hand all over me. I didn't mind. He really was charming but when he took me up to his bedroom in his hotel, I told him I was frightened; but he assured me that I'd run no risk with him, and he kept his word. Yet, that sort of half-pleasure didn't content me, so I was very glad, indeed, when your gardener came; and since then I have been as happy as a bird!

"You want to know whether I have touched myself. Sure; all girls have. If they say they haven't, they lie; the silly fools. Why shouldn't we have pleasure when it's so easy?

"I remember my father took me once to the picture gallery in Genoa. I loved the pictures; but one had a young man in it who looked right at me. I got off next morning and went back to the gallery to my pictured lover. I could not help it; I sat down on the bench opposite to him and crossed my legs and squeezed my sex till I was wet. And when I went to bed that night I thought of him, and his lovely limbs and his great eyes, and I touched myself with my hand pretending it was him till I came again and again, and at last got so wild I just had to stop or I'd have screamed—but lots of girls are like that.

"I think I was one of the few who let a boy have me time and again. I could not resist: the truth is, I wanted him as much as he wanted me, and when an older man came after me, it was worse: I could not refuse him, and I felt more with him than with any boy, till I came here, and the great games began. Oh, I love them all; and I've always been taken with you since you gave me the first prize when I had only won the second. You great sweet!"

Naturally, after this we had a long kissing match that ended in a new rendezvous, which was repeated frequently, for I found Clara in many respects the most delightful of all the girls. She had really no reticences, and loved to show her sex and to talk about her intense sensations in the crudest terms; but she never invented or beautified anything, and this simplicity of truth in her was most attractive. When, for example, she said, "When you have me I feel the thrills running all down my thighs to the knees," she was plainly describing an immediate personal experience, and when she told me that merely hearing my voice in the villa made her sex open and shut, I could be sure it was the truth. And bit by bit this truth of reciprocated sensation grew on me, till I, too, was won by the novelty of the emotion. Clara was the most wonderful mistress of them all; though the youngest.

I have spoken here only of pleasant occurrences; and it is interesting or amusing incidents that I remember best in my past life; but towards the end of the summer there was a good deal of trouble with some of the girls. It began with the defection of Adriana; as if encouraged by her jealousy, others felt inclined to follow her example and make conditions.

The three queens, and Clara in especial, remained fairly constant to the end, but Jean and his girls were a constant source of trouble. He would change in the same day, and that always led to remonstrances or angry scenes. Finally, both Ernest and George had to go back to England, and I was ashamed of having let the summer pass without completing my work.

When I returned later to San Remo to see Flora, I found that Clara, too, had got well married. She explained it by saying that widows always found husbands easier than girls, knowing more of what men wanted.

A word here about the difference between the jealousy of man and that of woman.

The jealousy of woman: If the man went with another woman because he loved her, the woman would weep, but forgive him. Love is all powerful to her. But if the man went with another girl out of mere passion, even if he didn't care for her, the woman would be furious: she sees the act—it is an unpardonable traitorism.

The jealousy of man is just the contrary: If the woman went with another man, and gave herself to a passing fancy, the man would be hurt, but would forgive her easily. But if the woman gave herself to some one out of love, the man would be furious and too angry to forgive.

Chapter X

Celebrities of the Nineties

I WANT TO GIVE as fair and large a picture as I can of this third period of my life—the last decade of the nineteenth century. Casanova is often praised for having given a good picture of his age, yet he has painted no great man of his time, no writer of the first rank, no artist, no statesman, with the solitary exception of Frederick the Great, whom he hardly does more than mention.

In this *Life* of mine I have tried to picture my growth of character and mind and soul as faithfully as I can, and to complete this history by putting in the foreground, so to speak, the great men and deeds which characterized the age. In my first volume I tried to paint Whitman, Emerson, Carlyle, and others; and in my second volume Skobelef, Ruskin, Randolph Churchill and Maupassant. In this volume I have given sketches of many artists and writers, and I wish to complete the picture with further memories of my contemporaries.

I met Zola and talked with him a dozen times before I ventured to differ with him on any subject. He thought his later books, *Lourdes* and *Rome,* his best books, whereas I felt that *L'Assommoir, La Terre, Germinal* and *Nana* were far better, to say nothing of *Page d'Amour, Le Rêve* and *La Faute de l'Abbé Mouret,* which I thought at least as good. *Lourdes* and *Paris* and the rest were all to me lifeless, machine-made things that had never grown.

I tried to make him see that Balzac's latest tales, *La Cousine Bette* and *Cousin Pons,* seemed to me manufactured and mechanical in comparison with *Père Goriot* or *La Recherche de l'Absolu,* or *Eugénie Grandet,* and in truth many of the earlier works, such as *Le Curé de Tours.*

Zola would not agree with me. He regarded *Cousine Bette* and *Cousin Pons* as the best things Balzac had ever written.

I remember when he came over to London once, he could talk of nothing but the quiet of the place, the strange peace that reigned in the streets. "What a great city," he said, "here, there is no noise." He wanted to know why *La Terre* was regarded as pornographic, which incensed him very much. "If they knew, how much worse life is," he cried, "they would stop talking such nonsense." And with that sentiment I was in complete agreement.

I got more pleasure from a side of Zola that is almost unknown. I knew that as a young man he had been an art critic of a Paris paper; I think it was *Le Figaro;* and he interested me enormously when he talked about the modern schools of painting. He was the first person I ever heard say that Cézanne was one of the greatest masters that ever lived. George Moore praised Manet, Monet, and Degas, but said little or nothing about Cézanne, though he was the greatest of the lot, the true head of the school. Zola let out the secret one day when he told me that he had been at school with Cézanne and that when Cézanne came to Paris, he, Zola, was almost the first person whom Cézanne called upon and interested in his work.

It is strange that Zola never wrote any book about painting, and when I asked him why he did not, he told me that it was not his art, that he felt as an outsider to it. But his love of painting and of artistic things generally was seen in his house, which was filled with old furniture and quaint decorations.

I cannot help thinking that Zola might have given us as good a book on modern French art, as Fromentin* gave us on the art of Holland, and such a volume would be, as Thucydides called his book, "a possession forever."

Zola, though one of the heads of the time, had a peculiarly uninteresting outward. He was a little below ordinary height, but strongly built and rather stout. His hair and beard and walk showed strength, but there was nothing distinctive about his face: an ordinary round face with thick nose and ordinary lips that might have passed in any crowd. He had not even the distinction of ugliness; his pale face, coarse lips and brown beard were merely commonplace.

I was astonished to find that Alphonse Daudet had a very high opinion of Zola. "Have you ever seen his notes," he said, "on any book he is going to write? It is extraordinary, the way he gets up his subject, studies every part of it. I suppose he knew more about Lourdes when he wrote about it than any one living. He went down and spent a month in the place."

Yet Zola used to interest me by saying that too much knowledge is as dangerous as too little. You had to know enough to see all the peculiarities of a place or a theme, but the moment you knew so much about it, that its resemblance to other places struck you rather than its differences, you had done too much work. "For my part," Daudet added, "I write without any notes, trusting to the idiosyncracy of the characters to develop the plot and, in fact, I trust to what people call inspiration, which is probably another name for laziness, rather than to study."

In striking contrast to Zola, Daudet was picturesque, very good-looking indeed: he wore his hair long, but his nose was well-cut, his eyes large, the shape of his face excellent.

* Eugène Fromentin (1820–76), French painter and art critic. Harris refers to his *Maitres d'autrefois* (1876).

I happened to see Daudet again after Turgenief's letters had been published, and I found him strangely angry. He resented Turgenief's criticism as if it had been a personal offence. "We all treated him as one of ourselves," he kept repeating, "and here he talks of us as if Zola and Flaubert and the rest of us were pigmies and he alone was the great writer and artist."

I wanted to see whether I could get a new word out of him, so I said: "Well, you know, some of us think that in Bazarof, Turgenief has depicted the one new character added to European literature since the Mephistopheles of Goethe."

"Good God," cried Daudet, "but is not Madame Bovary a character, and Zola's Lantier? I cannot understand such criticism."

To insist would have been surely rude, yet to some of us Madame Bovary is poor stuff and Lantier poorer still in comparison with Bazarof. Bazarof is the model of the realist for all time, deeper than Tartuffe or Le Misanthrope, and they are both greater creations than Madame Bovary or Lantier.

Daudet's novels were better than his criticism.

I don't know why, but Daudet often reminded me of W. E. Henley.*
I met Henley first at dinner at Sidney Low's house, who had followed Greenwood as editor of the *St. James Gazette*. Henley was then editing the *Scots Observer,* which he later removed to London as the *National Observer.*

Seated at the table, Henley was a great big man with broad shoulders, looking at least six feet in height, with an immense leonine head, full golden beard, large blue eyes and good features, a handsome and striking personality.

Almost immediately we came to some difference about the relative value of the play and the novel. I spoke of the novel as the most complex and therefore the highest form of art, and he replied: "That's nonsense," so rudely that I retorted: "Let us wait until the ladies go and then we'll continue the argument." Too surprised to find words, Henley grunted "Hmph!" But after the ladies had left the table, he turned on me and said: "Now I would like to know why you think the novel a higher form of art than a play, or for that matter, a poem?"

"It can include poems," I retorted, "as Goethe showed, and it has all the powers of a play and many that the play lacks."

Henley grunted again: "I don't see that mere assertion proves anything!"

"The dramatic presentation of character," I went on, "is, of course, the best for simple characters, but suppose you want to make a complex character. Suppose, for instance, you want to show your readers a man of great courage, who for some reason or other, (a weakness of heredity, drink, let us say, or some hereditary murder) is a coward at night: the spectators would not understand what you meant. You have to put in the finer qualifying shades of character by explanations. This you can do in the novel,

* (1849–1903); he was a considerable critic and editor, as well as a writer.

and that's why I said that the novel was the largest form of art, a more complex form even than the play."

To my astonishment, Henley replied quite frankly: "I never thought of it, but I believe you are right"; and we became, to a certain extent, friends.

When he afterwards laid down the law about poetry, I did not contradict him, and when he asked me whether I agreed with him or not, I told him I only believed in criticizing the art that I myself practiced, and not being a poet, I never disputed with poets about their mystery.

When we got up to join the ladies, I was horrified. Henley's legs were all twisted, and instead of being a man of six feet and over, he was only middle height. My host told me that from his poems in hospital, it was pretty clear that syphilis had turned him from a giant into a cripple.*

I remember some later meetings with Henley; once when he sent me his *Song of the Sword* for the *Fortnightly Review,* which I should have liked to publish, but Chapman, the managing director, would not hear of it. "Free verse," he said, "is neither poetry nor prose," and he begged me not to have anything to do with it.

Henley was not a great man, but a very interesting one. He thought it his duty to edit every contribution sent him, and he did edit every word, every phrase, weighed every comma and colon, until the whole of his paper was steeped in his own style, so that it often seemed as if it were all written by one man.

My chief object, when I got a paper of my own, the *Saturday Review,* was the antipodes of his. I encouraged everybody to express himself as personally as possible, and the more he differed with me, as a rule, the more I liked his work. I do not see how one could have got Bernard Shaw, H. G. Wells, McColl, Chalmers Mitchell and Cunninghame Graham to do their best on any other terms.

What then was Henley's success? He got together a band of youthful admirers who wrote for him and afterwards became known as journalists. I don't remember one man of real ability in Henley's crowd; not one, so far as I recollect, made a great name for himself in the future. But success in the day and hour he had in abundance and admirers, such as the Right Hon. George Wyndham, who always called Henley a remarkable poet, mainly I used to think, because Henley's poetry, second rate as it was, was better than his own.

There was another figure whom I got to know very well in the nineties, an infinitely more gifted man than Henley in another art: Auguste Rodin. I have done a portrait of him, but here I wish to add a few more words.

At our very first meeting I noticed that he had no venom in him and no exclusions. He was of the race of the great masters, easily moved to enthusiasm, without a particle of envy in his composition. He accepted life as it was, lived it to the fullest, and had few regrets. The only trace of bitterness I ever saw in him came to the surface when an American millionaire

* It is generally accounted that Henley was crippled by some form of tuberculosis.

offered him ten thousand dollars for a portrait-head, provided he would finish it in a week.

"I explained to him," said Rodin, relating the incident, "that in such a short time I could do nothing more than a likeness. I should not be able to understand the soul of him, much less find out how best to suggest it through his features; but he declared that a likeness was all he wanted, and so"—and he threw up his hand—*"ma foi,* I said, 'Yes.' " He swung round a moment later as if the thought had stung him: "Fifty thousand francs in a week. Ah, had I had those fifty thousand in a year when I did my 'man with the broken nose,' I'd have done a dozen types that now—"

There was an inexpressible sadness in his voice, and well there might be. "A dozen types," I said to myself, "all swallowed up and lost 'in the vague womb of uncreated night.' "

Rodin died during the World War, leaving twenty or thirty great portraits of his contemporaries, from Henley and Shaw to Rochefort, Hugo and Balzac, to say nothing of a dozen groups and figures that can never be forgotten. His *Thinker* is finer than the Medician figure of Michelangelo; his *Baiser,* his *Nymph and Satyr,* his *Succube,* are all examples of bronze turned into flesh by virtue of an incomparable craftsmanship and the urge of an astonishing sensuality that could lend even to marble the pulsing thrills of life.

I can still see a little female figure, perhaps half-life size, that stood for some years in the center of the salon in his little villa at Meudon. I christened it *La Parisienne,* and he adopted the name at once joyfully, and indeed it might have stood as a personification of the gay capital—the only city in the world where artists feel at home. There was a certain perversity in its frank beauty that was exquisitely characteristic. The hips were slight, the limbs slight, too, with something of the divine awkwardness of girlhood; but the breasts stood out round and firm, defiantly provocative; the nose, too, was tip-tilted, cheeky; the face, one would swear, smiling with a gay challenge.

Madame Rodin, I remember, regaled us with some *petits fours* that were very good, and some desperate coffee which made me wonder why it was not called chicory honestly, as it should have been. The little old woman served the Master like a servant at once and mother for half a century; then, conscious of his immense debt to her loving care, and anxious to make tardy amends, Rodin married her. I think so much of her humble devotion that I do not believe the new dignity affected her much: yet I may be mistaken in this, for she died a month or so afterwards, and a little later Rodin, as if unable to bear the separation after so many years of companionship, followed her into the silent land.

I remember meeting Rostand in Paris in 1898. He was then at the height of his vogue. *Cyrano de Bergerac* had been brought out by Madame Bernhardt in 1897, when he was just 27 years of age. There have been few such triumphs: the play ran 400 nights in Paris and nearly as long in Berlin in

Fulda's translation.* Petersburg and Madrid, Belgrade even, went crazy over it, and dozens of companies played it all over the United States.

Rostand met me like a prince might meet a small unknown boy. I have never seen any Frenchman put on such airs. He was a little over average height and dressed with a touch of eccentricity all in black; a big black satin stock, showing only a narrow white edge of collar, seemed to hold up his head, and he held it very high. His face was pale; his features regular; his dark eyes rather large and long—a handsome face with an air of haughty disdain—the French word *morgue* exactly expressed it. Though Marcel Schwob** (who introduced me) spoke of me as a master and mentioned that my stories had appeared in *La Revue des Deux Mondes,* Rostand contented himself with a slight bow, while his eyebrows lifted with an air of patient inattention. I had prepared a compliment, but I kept it to myself and turned aside abruptly. I didn't think much of Cyrano, and Rostand's other work seemed to me negligible, while the airs he gave himself were inexcusable in so young a man. No great man ever plays *grand seigneur* without some extraordinary good reason.

Nothing was talked about but his plays; he was asked about his method of work. He gave ordinary facts with the air of a God letting new truths drop from Sinai. It seemed that like most of us the period of gestation in him was long, the parturition hurried. "I read and think a great deal," he said, "till it's all clear and then write incessantly." A well bred murmur of admiration greeted the oracle. It was quite certain that no really great man could have won such popularity so early. I went away as soon as I decently could.

Rostand was born rich; success came at twenty with his first book *Les Musardies,* and his wealth enabled him to screen himself off from anything harsh or true, spoiled in fact a great theatrical talent.

Once later I was destined to meet him. I had taken Oscar Wilde to dine at Maire's restaurant, intending to go afterwards to Antoine's theatre close by. Rostand was already at table when we entered. I hardly knew whether to bow to him or not. To my surprise he rose and bowed more than politely —cordially.

Thus encouraged, I went over to him and shot off the compliment I had prepared months before. He laughed delightedly, and when I introduced Oscar, he showed a kindly human side I had scarcely expected. During the dinner he kept up an intermittent conversation from table to table, and was really charming, attributing the success of his play mainly to the incomparable acting.

Oscar took the ball on the hop, and told of seeing Coquelin at a dress rehearsal. The great actor, it appeared, was doubtful whether he should add

* Ludwig Fulda (1862–1932); he was posthumously awarded the cross of the French Legion of Honor for his translations of French plays.
** (1867–1905), French novelist and translator of Shakespeare and Defoe; Wilde dedicated *Salome* to him.

to his already prominent nose; "It is mine and Cyrano's," he exclaimed, "why alter it?"

"They may say," interjected Oscar with an air of deep meditation, "that you play the part so well because it is your own story; I think I'd increase the nose."

"You're right," replied Coquelin gravely. "I must remain the artist, the artist always, above *my* creation."

Oscar told the story superbly, mimicking air and manner and throwing into high relief the actor's vanity: "My creation."

Rostand enjoyed the tale ingenuously, and the talk turning on noses, I could not help reciting the witty remark made about Baron Hirsch.* Some one said: "You'd hardly believe he was a Jew were it not for his nose." "True," replied the listener, "God forgives and the world forgets, but the nose remains."

Suddenly we found it was time to go if we would not lose part of the play, and then Rostand told us that he also wanted to see *Poil de Carotte* (Carrots!), I think it was, with Madame Nau in the title part, so we turned down the boulevard together and went to our seats like old friends.

On reflection, Rostand seemed to me a richly endowed romantic nature, dwarfed by wealth and wanting the spur of desperate incentive. But he came at the psychological moment. The second generation since the great defeat was growing up and full of the old Gallic vanity and the courage which was resolved to act and not to talk. The French youths all took up athletics, went in for boxing, even; left realism for romance and began to affirm, instead of denying. The romance of daring was in the air and Rostand gave it a voice. In almost everything he was a herald of the new time; his family life was very happy; in fine, in spite of surface faults, he was a good representative of the new France. It is almost symbolical to me that he should have been born in 1870, in the year of disaster, and died in 1919, in the assurance of victory.

I have written a good deal about Meredith and tried to give a true picture of him as one of the greatest writers of the time and a charming personality.

Shortly after I took over the *Saturday Review,* he came up to London to undergo an operation, and I met him again and was of course as cordial as I could be, but I could never forgive him for having refused his name to the petition in favor of Oscar Wilde. Up to that time, I used to go down to Boxhill to spend some hours with him nearly every week. Afterwards I only met him on rare occasion by chance. His operation seemed to have weakened him a good deal, for afterwards he took to riding about in a little carriage which he drove himself, and almost ceased to walk. I excused myself for not seeing him more often by telling him that I spent fully six months of every year in the south of France, whereas he preferred Boxhill and the Sussex Downs.

* (1831–96), a financier from Munich; he made his fortune in Balkan railroads.

It was on one of these visits to Nice that I got to know Maeterlinck* and Georgette Le Blanc** whom I regarded as his wife. Maeterlinck was an interesting personality, but I never got much out of him beyond what any one could get from his books. He never seemed able to reveal new sides of himself in talk.

I remember he asked me once why I didn't review his translation of the *Macbeth,* which he had sent to me. I told him I would if he liked, but I didn't think his knowledge of English was sufficient; however, I promised to do my best. Later, in London, remembering the promise, I picked up his translation; I looked at one line in it: "After life's fitful fever he sleeps well," and I found Maeterlinck had translated it: *"Après les convulsions fiévreuses de la vie il dort bien."* I saw at once that he had taken "fitful" to mean full of fits, as "painful" is full of pain, and had no conception that it simply meant intermittent. Therefore I sent a friend to the British Museum, who brought me back the information that of the one hundred translations of *Macbeth* in French, about eighty-five had followed François Victor Hugo in this misrendering of "fitful"; and the other had left it out altogether: *"Aprés le fièvre de la vie il dort bien."*

I sent this to Maeterlinck, thinking he would laugh over the matter, but when I met him again in Nice the next year, he and Georgette came and lunched with us and he broached the subject at once by saying that the translations of Shakespeare were quite impossible. I tried to agree with him by saying that of course it took an equal poet to try to translate from one language into the other adequately.

But he would have it that Shakespeare was quite impossible, and he gave an example from *Hamlet* where Ophelia says:

> Here's rosemary—that's for remembrance;
> Here are pansies—that's for thoughts . . .

"The first sentence can be translated," he said, "but the second can't, because in French the word for pansies is almost the same as the word for thoughts; you cannot say, *'Voila des pensées—c'est pour penser.'* "

"Oh," I retorted, "I think it quite possible. Picture the scene to yourself: Ophelia is speaking before the King and Queen and she knows, with a woman's divination, that the Queen is the real culprit, so she says, *'Voila des pensées,'* and then, looking at the Queen, adds, stuttering, *'c'est pour penser.'* "

Francis Carco,† who was also at the lunch, applauded me for the thought, but Maeterlinck pretended not to understand.

---

* (1862–1949), Belgian playwright.
** She was already a famous actress and was kind to Maeterlinck before he became a successful dramatist. She lived with him from 1901 until 1918, when she was displaced by a younger woman.
† A pseudonym of Francis Carcopino-Tusoli (1886–1958), a French writer. This meeting obviously took place after the nineties, during which Carco had barely reached his teens.

Really, whenever Frenchmen translate from English, they are apt to come to grief. The other day I saw that one of them had translated "Love's last shift" into *"La dernière chemise de l'amour."*

I knew Albert, Prince of Monaco, fairly well for more than a quarter of a century. The *New York Times* gave a column article to him while he was visiting America shortly before his death; it said that "he belonged to the Grimaldis of Genoa . . . one of the most ancient houses of Europe"; described him as "a wise old man of the world, honorably distinguished as a savant; an enlightened ruler . . . sagacious and experienced," and God knows what besides. Now, Albert of Monaco was not a Grimaldi at all, but a Matignon* of little Breton squire stock, and his "wisdom and enlightenment" were low cunning.**

One incident will give a better picture of this Princelet than pages of word painting. When I first knew him he was always talking of his dislike of "the gambling house" of Monte Carlo, which gave him his princely revenue and paid besides all the expenses of his three miles long and half a mile wide kingdom. Every one staying in the palace was requested not to visit or even enter "the gambling house," and the Prince was continually complaining that his father had given M. Blanc a lease of the place till 1907, or else "I'd shut it up tomorrow. I hate the corruptions of it. It is really wrong for a father so to bind and fetter a son; I loathe the place," so he used to preach.

It seemed to me that the Prince protested too much; in any case, surely he need not have accepted "the wages of sin," had he had not been so inclined. But bit by bit his protests affected me; I came to believe in his honesty.

For there was a side to the Prince which pleased me. He was a sportsman. He had a great country house at Marchais on the borders of Lorraine; it had at one time belonged to the Ducs de Guise and was set, a great house, in the midst of marshes.

There was most excellent shooting to be had in the swamps of Marchais; wild geese and ducks by the myriad flocked there from the north in cold weather, and wild swans, too, and the woods were well stocked with pheasants and rabbits and hares.

But there were other amenities at Marchais. So long as the Princess Alice ruled there, the food was excellent and there used to be wonderful music in the evenings.

One met at Marchais all the literary geniuses and the leaders of French thought: Bourget and Loti, Saint-Saëns and Sarah Bernhardt. In Marchais, more than in any other French house, one touched life at many points.

* The Goyon-Matignons, succeeding the Grimaldis by marriage, adopted the name Grimaldi.

** Actually, Albert took exception to Princess Alice's friendship with Harris and forbade her to visit Harris' hotel in Monte Carlo, which she had promised to patronize, and it was mainly for this reason that Harris' hotel venture failed.

Naturally, I was delighted to go to Marchais and spend long days with the Prince shooting. I have been awakened at four o'clock in the morning with the news that wild swans had just come in and in ten minutes I was up and dressed. Before we started out I had a cup or two of delicious hot coffee and such eggs and bacon, preserves and bread as one seldom finds. Then down in the cold night to ride six or seven miles to the ground, and when there to crawl for perhaps another mile on one's stomach between straw fences to the huts, out of which one could watch the great swans sailing the water and shoot them, if one wanted to. Then as day dawned we would take this wood for pheasants, and that stubbled plain for red-legged partridge, and so fleet the day in healthy exercise. Then home to a hot bath and a superb dinner with super-excellent French wine and coffee, and a great evening with good music by Tosti* or De Lara, or a talk in a quiet room with a member of the Institute or the Academy.

Who could resist the seduction! One evening the Prince assured me that he meant to shut up the "tripot" or "den," as he called it, at Monte Carlo as soon as he had the right, and begged me to preach this in the British press, so as not to surprise people when it took place.

"I want to avoid complaints," he said, "and the leaders of English life are powerful in France."

Naturally, I did my best for his high purpose.

I knew the "gambling house" at Monte Carlo extremely well: I had spent a good many winters at the Principality, and it was apparent to me that the way to give tone and importance to the whole place was by founding a special Sporting Club which should have all the best visitors as members, especially the best English and French and Americans. One day I outlined this scheme to the Prince of Monaco, saying that if he decided that he had to leave the "gambling house" as it was, the way to improve it would be by establishing a high class Sporting Club in close connection with it.

He asked me to make out the whole scheme. I told him it would cost some time and labor: and he wanted to know how he should reward me. "Very simple," I said, "you can make me a permanent secretary at a decent salary."

"Certainly," he exclaimed enthusiastically. "You help me: make out the whole constitution and articles of the club, print them and let me have them, and you shall be permanent secretary at a salary, say, of a thousand pounds a year, and of course lodgings in the club." I said that would suit me excellently; I made out the whole thing—constitution, articles and all—and submitted it to him. He told me it was exactly what he wanted.

A little later it was rumored that the Prince of Monaco had concluded a treaty with Monsieur Camille Blanc, the chief shareholder in the "gambling

* Sir Francesco Paolo Tosti (1846–1916), an Italian composer who took out British papers and was knighted in 1908.

house," and had given him fresh extension of his lease, on condition of receiving some millions of francs.

One night in London I mentioned the matter to one of the kings of finance; he laughed outright.

"So you're the culprit," he cried; "that's a jolly good one on you."

"Why?" I asked. "What are you laughing at?"

"I'm laughing," he said, "because that wily fox, the Prince of Monaco, got you for nothing to frighten M. Blanc so that he has concluded a new contract for fifty years to come on most favorable terms."

I knew intuitively that I had been done by the fox. But I had been cheated, I found, more completely than I had even imagined. The Prince of Monaco sold the whole idea of the Sporting Club, as constituted by me, to Camille Blanc, and got another large sum for it, taking care not to encumber the deal with a permament secretary, and so cheated me.

There were two sides to Prince Albert, as to most men: he really loved science and prosecuted his deep sea fishing in the interests of science; at the same time he married an immensely rich heiress, and he sold the future of Monte Carlo to Camille Blanc, after getting the highest possible from the financier by publishing his resolve to shut the "tripot" as soon as the lease was out.

Verily, *The children of this world are wiser in their generation than the children of Light!**

* Luke, 16:8.

Chapter XI

Jesus, the Christ

OPINION IS SLOWLY COMING to the conviction that Jesus of Nazareth is the greatest spirit in recorded time. Very early they proclaimed him divine, and now for nearly two thousand years all sorts and conditions of men have studied him and talked of him. But very few, so far as I know, have even tried to see him as he was. He was so sweet and so great that even after twenty centuries the jury of his peers has not yet been formed, nor the final verdict pronounced. As I have loved him without adoring him, I contribute here my voice to the final decision, and describe besides how I came to my belief, and the effect it had upon my conduct.

In my portrait of Renan, I have told how, towards the end of the century, Sir Charles Dilke had given me an introduction to him, and Dilke was one of the few Englishmen who spoke French as well as he spoke English: his commendation therefore had some weight. At first, Renan received me with great kindness and almost immediately began to ask me how his *Life of Jesus* was appreciated in England. I said that it was regarded as the best life—much better than Strauss's:* but again and again he came back to the matter with a desire of praise which seemed almost childish to me, and an invincible disdain of any criticism, however well founded, which sometimes provoked me.

Every time I came to Paris for some years, I went to see him, and after a couple of visits he began to treat me with a sort of condescension, which was really due to the fact that I had never told him fully what was in my mind about his work. At length I resolved to do this.

One day, I have forgotten how, he provoked me and I said to him:

"Master, what was the ordinary language that Jesus spoke?"

"Aramaic," he replied, "the common Jewish dialect of Hebrew."

"I have always hoped," I said, "that he spoke Greek ordinarily, though of course it may have been Latin."

"Oh no," said Renan, "he only spoke one language; he was quite uneducated, so far as we know."

* David Friedrich Strauss (1808–74), a German theologian. His *Das Leben Jesu* treated the gospels as history and interpreted Biblical history as myth.

"What does it mean," I said, "when on the cross he cries, *'Eloi, Eloi, Lama Sabachthani?'* That's Aramaic, isn't it?"

"Yes," said Renan, "surely."

"Then they go on to say in the Bible, 'which being interpreted means, "My God, my God, why hast Thou forsaken me?" ' It is surely plain from this that he usually spoke another language, which did not need to be interpreted, and that here on the Cross in his mortal anguish, he fell into the language of his childhood, and they therefore translated it."

"I see your inference," cried Renan; "strange that I had never thought of that before; where did you get the idea?"

I smiled, but it almost made me tell him that I had gotten hardly anything from his *Life of Jesus,* often as I had looked into it.

There are many little touches in the Bible which seem to make the Master plain to me. If I had another life to live, I would learn Aramaic and Hebrew and try to do what Renan failed to do: give a real portrait of the greatest man who ever wore flesh.

When his mother and father left him as a boy, and finding that he was not with them, returned to Jerusalem and discovered that he had been in the synagogue, he said to them: "Wist thou not that I must be about my Father's business?" This and the remark afterwards that his mother kept all such sayings in her heart seemed to reveal him to me as extraordinary, even in boyhood.

It has always seemed strange to me that Jesus called his disciples, and as many as twelve. Most able men have two or three who cherish their sayings and love to be with them, but we have no record of their selection by the teacher: usually it is the disciples who choose. The story seems to me a little difficult to understand because it is very unusual, and so far as I can discover, not symbolic.

A little later Jesus will not see his mother or his brethren, nor acknowledge the claims of kinship. There is a possible, even a likely explanation of this: when he engaged his disciples and began his independent career, he first went back to Nazareth, we are told, but his assumption of authority annoyed the people and "filled them with wrath." "Is not this Joseph's son?" they asked. "And have we not his brothers and sisters here with us?" And he had to hide from the indignation of the people.

We are told expressly: "Neither did his brethren believe in him." His friends and kinsmen, indeed, appear to have shielded him by saying, "He is beside himself"; and their excuse, I imagine, so wounded him that later he refused to see them, declaring that "Whosoever shall do the will of God, the same is my brother, and my sister and mother."

Again, later, we have the estrangement from his mother in a more pronounced form. "A certain woman of the company," according to St. Luke, "lifted up her voice and said unto him: 'Blessed the womb that bore thee and the paps which thou has sucked!' But he said: 'Yea, rather, blessed they that hear the word of God and keep it.' "

It is extremely difficult to see him through the mist cast about him by his biographers. He begins his Sermon on the Mount with a series of aphorisms such as young men of talent are accustomed to make, some of them intensely characteristic: "Blessed are the meek: for they shall inherit the earth"—surely the strangest prediction ever made to the children of men!

And later, the encouragement:

Blessed are ye, when men shall revile you, and persecute you, and shall say all manner of evil against you.

Rejoice, and be exceeding glad: for great is your reward in heaven: for so persecuted they the prophets which were before you.

Then the most beautiful of all:

Blessed are the pure in heart: for they shall see God.

But after these superb phrases, which seem to show us the very spirit of the young prophet, come verses which one cannot understand at all:

Agree with thine adversary quickly, whilst thou art in the way with him; lest at any time the adversary deliver thee to the judge, and the judge deliver thee to the officer, and thou be cast into prison.

Verily I say unto thee, thou shalt by no means come out thence, till thou hast paid the uttermost farthing.

This childish morality, based on fear, is out of tune with the rest of the chapter; it was perhaps some youthful expression of submission to authority. Jesus returns to the theme again toward the end of the chapter, and lifts it to new heights:

Ye have heard that it hath been said, thou shalt love thy neighbour and hate thine enemy.

But I say unto you, Love your enemies, bless them that curse you, do good to them that hate you, and pray for them which despitefully use you, and persecute you.

And again the ineffable word which remains as a commandment:

Be ye therefore perfect, even as your Father which is in heaven is perfect.

But the point which first made him clear to me was the revelation of his physical weakness. Why did he fall under the cross? Most men would find it easy enough to carry the cross, which was of dried wood and wasn't very heavy. The first time I saw one was in the Russo-Turkish war of '76–77, when the Turks had crucified some of their opponents; these crosses one could have carried a long time without any difficulty, with one end over one's shoulder and the other trailing on the ground.

But the chief proof of his weakness is that he is said to have died on the cross within a few hours; at this, we are told, "Pilate marvelled"—and well he might, for most men can endure the torture of the cross for days; and it was to convince themselves that he was really dead that a soldier put the spear into his side and "forthwith came there out blood and water."

Now if he were dead, he must have been dead for some time, the time at least necessary for someone to go to Jerusalem and see Pilate and return again to Calvary with the order to test the apparent death. If he were dead for a couple of hours, surely nothing would come out of a wound save a little moisture; I therefore draw the conclusion that he had fainted merely and afterwards came to, and through the care of the women who loved him, was able to show himself to his disciples; but the crucifixion had broken him, and the dreadful doubt—"My God, my God, why hast thou forsaken me?"—and soon afterwards he died.

As I told Renan, I disliked his insistence on the personal beauty of Jesus. Mohammed was said by every one to be astonishingly good-looking, with splendid eyes, but no disciple at the time seems to have said anything like this of Jesus. What took them was that "he spoke as never man spoke"; and although his face must have been transfigured by his emotion, still it was the message and not the face of the messenger which struck every one as most important.

Best of all his sayings, I love the story of the woman taken in adultery, the greatest story in the world, if I may judge it.

It is only recorded by John: was he the beloved disciple because he would recall the highest word?

Jesus had said time and again that he had come to fulfill the law of Moses and not to change it; and now the Jews brought him a woman "taken in adultery, *in the very act*," and said: "Moses commanded that such should be stoned, but what sayest thou?"

Jesus was caught in a flagrant contradiction; he had always said that he had come to fulfill the law, so now to gain time for thought, he stooped and with his finger wrote upon the ground, "*as though he heard them not.*"

And then he took counsel with his own soul and answered divinely: "He that is without sin among you, let him first cast a stone at her."

And the Jews were so honest that "being convicted by their own conscience," they went out, one by one.

When Jesus had lifted up himself, and saw none but the woman, he said unto her, "Woman, where are those thine accusers? Hath no man condemned thee?"

She said, "No man, Lord!"

And Jesus said unto her, "Neither do I condemn thee: go, and sin no more."

Now what does this "Neither do I condemn thee!" mean, save that he, too, was not without sin?

The puzzling things in the Gospel narrative are the contradictions in spirit: think of that verse in St. Luke: "But those mine enemies, which would not that I should reign over them, bring hither, and slay them before me." And in almost every one of the Gospels there is some dreadful contradiction of this sort which brings one near doubt. For example, Mark tells us in his first chapter how Jesus came from Nazareth and was baptized of John in Jordan, and the heavens opened and the Spirit like a dove descended upon him. And there came a voice from heaven saying: "Thou art my beloved Son in whom I am well pleased."

Afterwards, John was cast into prison, and while there, if we can believe Matthew, he heard of the works of Christ and sent two of his disciples to ask him: "Art thou he that should come or do we look for another?" In other words: "Art thou the Messiah?"

But how extraordinary, for when John baptized Jesus, he must have seen the heavens opened and the spirit in the form of a dove descending and heard the voice saying: "Thou art my beloved Son." How then could John doubt?

Even the prayer Jesus taught his disciples hardly reaches his highest: "Give us this day our daily bread. Forgive us our trespasses as we forgive *those* who trespass against us. And lead us not into temptation." I should prefer simply: "Give and forgive."

Why then believe at all in the existence of Jesus? Why not accept the conclusion of Mr. Robertson* and others, and, I am told, the great majority of Rabbis, who think that he never existed?

First of all, it is my conviction that every great movement in the world comes from a great man. I cannot believe that the verses: "Love your enemies . . ." and "Be ye therefore perfect . . ." ever came as a part of ordinary belief: such words are the very perfume, so to speak, of an extraordinary and noble nature.

Besides this, there are the two almost contemporary records: the one in Josephus and the other in Tacitus. The one in Josephus has been tampered with in the interest of so-called Christianity, but the fact that it was inserted already testifies to a personality: and the phrase in Tacitus: "*quidam Jesu,*" confessing contempt—"a certain fellow called Jesus"—is purely Roman, and comes from the same man who thought the murder of fifty thousand Jews, men, women, and children, in the streets of Syracuse "a good riddance."

Beyond all doubt Jesus lived and died as his disciples tell us, and what consolation there is for all of us in his ultimate triumph. Here is a poor Jew, known only to a few fishermen in a small and despised province of the Roman Empire, speaking a dialect that was only understood by a handful of sectaries, and condemned when between thirty and forty years of age to a shameful death.

No record of what he said or did for fifty years after his crucifixion, and then nothing but fragmentary memories of three or four unlettered followers. Yet, by virtue of half a dozen sentences and a couple of little parables

* John MacKinnon Robertson (1856–93), Shakespeare scholar and free-thinker; among his books are *Short History of Miracles* and a *History of Free Thought in the Nineteenth Century.*

—how can one help recalling here the Prodigal Son with its message of pure affection—he has come to be a leader and teacher of hundreds of millions of the most intelligent peoples in the world—in some sort, their idol and God.

Is it not plain from this one example that the Good is imperishable and Divine and must ultimately conquer even in this world?

For two thousand years, now, Christianity has been preached to us as an ideal; even the ministers of the gospel have regarded its teaching as impracticable, and from St. Paul down, one and all have sought to mix some hard alloy of conventional morality with the golden evangel of Jesus, in order to give it currency among men.

I wish to go a step further, to push the light a space on into the all-encircling night. In the Sermon on the Mount, Jesus stated his belief once for all:

I say unto you, love your enemies, bless them that curse you, do good to them that hate you, and pray for them which despitefully use you and persecute you.

And this is put aside as a counsel of perfection. It seems to me the impartial statement of scientific truth.

Jesus gave no reason for his gospel; did not attempt to prove it, save to the soul by its own virtue. For many centuries the saying was a stumbling block even to the wisest, but when it came to Shakespeare, he saw its everlasting truth and found a reason for it and so added a coping stone to the divine Temple of Humanity. The passage is in *Timon of Athens:*

> He's truly valiant that can wisely suffer
> The worst that man can breathe, and make his wrongs
> His outsides, to wear them like his raiment, carelessly,
> And ne'er prefer his injuries to his heart,
> To bring it into danger.*

In other words, if we nurse hatreds we are doing ourselves harm: we must love our enemies, for if we hate them we prefer our injuries to our heart's well being and bring it into danger.

Shakespeare did not go further than this; he saw that a man should take wrongs done to him lightly and for his own sake should not cherish resentment. It was a great step forward; but there is still a truth behind, which Shakespeare, the most articulate of men, would surely have expressed, had he seen. It is by the heart we grow; hatred injures the heart; dries up the sympathies; impoverishes the blood, so to speak; stops all growth.

This further truth was revealed to me by my art. I found that till I loved a man I could not understand him, could not see him as he saw himself, and so could not depict him fairly. But as soon as I began to like him, I began to make excuses for his faults, and when I grew to care for him really, I saw that he had no need even to be excused. Hatred gives nothing but the

* Act III, scene 5.

shadows in the portrait: you can make a likeness with shadows alone; but if you want to reveal a man's soul fully, to make a work of art, you must know the best in the man and use high lights as well; and these you can only get from loving comprehension.

The road up for all of us is sympathy. How fine the Greek word "sympathy" is, and what a lesson it teaches of the divinity of pain; it means literally "to suffer with." We mortals grow near one another by "suffering with" one another, and so come by pain to love and through love to comprehension. Shelley's word is forever true:

> They learn in suffering what they teach in song.*

The French proverb, "*tout comprendre est tout pardonner*" (to understand all is to pardon all), does not go far enough. If we understand a man perfectly, there is no need to pardon, for we are then above forgiveness, even beyond good and evil; we see why and how he acted.

And this effort to love our enemy, and so come to see him as he sees himself, is soul-enriching in a thousand ways. First of all, the getting rid of an enemy is exhilarating and delightful. Then every new friend is an acquisition more precious by far than any great portrait to a collector in his gallery; and when we have forced ourselves to annex several of these rich prizes that we had no title to and money could not buy, we begin to see that this is no alien or difficult world, and not dangerous at all. The woods that seemed so dark and threatening to our childhood, now show us shady nooks and gay green glades and pleasant avenues sun-kissed. Love is the guide; and the good magician, Love.

A new commandment I give unto you: that ye love one another.

This is the scientific law of life, the end, if not the beginning, of all human morality!

I was about forty before I came to understand its supreme significance. It influenced me in my conduct of the *Saturday Review,* as I have stated, in my desire to get the best men to work with me, careless of their opinions, and to set them, so far as possible, to praise and not to blame.

The message of Jesus has, I think, influenced my life more and more with every year I have lived since, but still I hardly dare call myself a Christian, because I also believe in the pagan view of life. Who can doubt that it is the first duty of man to develop all his faculties to the uttermost, and to enjoy all the beauties and pleasures of life so far as he can without injuring others? The doctrine of love for others only supplements and crowns this primary creed.

It seems plain to me that the intense spirituality of Christ's teaching has had an unexpected result in increasing sensuality and the sensuous expres-

* From *Julian and Maddalo,* line 544.

sion of affection. Was it the love of the Magdalen—which, everyone knows, was the heart of the religious enthusiasm of the Middle Ages—which intensified and in some sense ennobled passion, or was this exaltation of the woman who had "loved much" also a result of increasing sensualism—probably at once both cause and consequence?

It cannot be denied that the growth of sensuality is the chief note of all the centuries since. It is embodied to me in the coming to honor of the kiss. Naturally, the kiss in the beginning was a purely maternal act: it is unknown to the Yellow and Negro races, who rub noses instead; in early Sanskrit literature, too, the kiss was always maternal or filial. The kiss seems to have been unknown as a token of love even to the ancient Greeks: there is no mention of a kiss in the love scenes of Homer; and among the ancient Romans, the kiss was a mere salutation.

It is possible that the Jews were somewhat more advanced; St. Paul advises his followers to greet one another "with an holy kiss," and there seems to me to be a strange confession in that "holy."

However that may be, the kiss in our time has become even more than a token of love: I cannot but recall Shakespeare's deathless lines to his dark lady:

> Of many thousand kisses, the poor last
> I lay upon thy lips.*

Saint-Beuve, in one of his rare flashes of insight, says: *"Nous sommes tous aujourd'hui fils d'une littérature sensuelle"* (We are all today children of a sensual literature).

It is curious to me that even the greatest have done so little to justify the new commandment of Jesus, to love one another.

Even Cervantes is silent on the matter: his Don Quixote will fight windmills, but is not Quixotic enough to preach the doctrine of love to his neighbor; nor does Goethe; and yet what can be plainer than the fact that unless this gospel of Jesus is learned and put to practice, the generations of men will cease to exist?

A scientist in London wrote me the other day that already they had under control five or six of the original elements. "When we have control of a dozen," he added, "a man will go about with power enough in his waistcoat pocket to destroy a whole city like London or New York." It seems to me possible that men may win power before goodness, and the race may then come to an untimely end. If not, its survival will be in great part due to the divine spirit of Jesus.

While passing this chapter through the press, news came to me of the recently discovered version of Josephus in the Russian language. This manuscript of "The Jewish War" was found in Esthonia some twenty years ago; it is of supreme interest because it throws new light on the life of

---

* *Antony and Cleopatra*, IV, 15.

Christ, and even records events which are not to be found in the Greek text of the Gospels.

The original of Josephus' work was written in Aramaic or Hebrew (as is to be inferred from one passage), and the best scholars are now beginning to see that the newly found text was taken from this version; and that certain allusions to the history of Jesus were omitted by the writer from his Greek translation in order not to offend his Roman patrons. Here are some of the most interesting passages from the Russian manuscript:

At this time arises a man, if one may call him a man, who by his nature and behavior showed himself as if more than human. His works were wonderful, and he worked wonders, strange and powerful. Thus it is possible for me to call him a man; through looking at him in every way, I would also not call him an angel. And all he did, he did by word and command; as if by some inner power. Some said of him that our first law-giver had risen from the dead and showed forth much healing power. Others considered that he was sent of God. But he opposed altogether the Law; and did not hold the Sabbath according to ancestral custom. Yet he did nothing overtly criminal; but by word he influenced all. And many out of the people followed him and received his teaching. And many souls wavered, wondering whether by it the Jewish tribes could free themselves from Roman hands. Now it was a habit of his to stay much on the Mount of Olives in face of the city. And also there he manifested his healing powers to the people. And there gathered to him "Slaves" a hundred and fifty, and many from among the Folk. When they saw his power that all was as he willed by means of the word, they besought him that "he would enter the city and cut down the Roman soldiers and Pilate, and rule over us." But that he scorned.

And thereafter, when the Jewish leaders got to know of it, they assembled themselves with the high priests and said: "We are powerless and weak to stand against the Romans. But as also the bow is bent, we will go and tell Pilate what we have heard, and we will be untroubled; lest if he hear it from others, we be robbed of our goods and ourselves cut down and our children scattered." And they went and told Pilate. And he sent and had many of the people struck down.

And as for the wonder-worker, he had him brought before him. And when he had tried him, he perceived that he was a doer of good and not of wrong; neither a rebel, nor a striver after political power, and he set him free. He had given heed to his perturbed wife.

And he went again to his accustomed place and did his customary works. And at once again more people gathered to him, so that his works were more celebrated than ever; the Scribes became filled with envy and gave thirty talents to Pilate that he should kill him. And after he had taken, he consented that they should themselves carry out their purpose. And they took him and crucified him according to Imperial Law.

It was only natural that Josephus, when he turned his story written in Aramaic into Greek, should omit this bribing of Pilate, which would surely have offended the Romans. After most careful consideration, I regard this account as a wonderful addition to the Gospel story as we have it. It does not represent Jesus as divine; in fact it gives an almost modern view of the rarest spirit that has ever steered humanity.

Chapter XII

The End of the Century

THE LAST YEARS OF THIS CENTURY were dignified by an extraordinary proposal, which has been allowed to fall into complete oblivion: the Tsar Nicolas II sent in August, 1898, to all European rulers and to the United States, a proposal to bring about a great conference in order to ensure peace among the nations and put an end to the constantly increasing armaments that were impoverishing Europe. The Tsar's words were:

"The maintenance of general peace and a possible reduction of the excessive armaments which weigh upon all nations, present themselves, in the existing conditions of the whole world, as the ideal towards which the endeavors of all governments should be directed."

The difficulties in reaching any agreement were of necessity great, but did not appear at first to be insurmountable. The conference met: all the nations sent of their wisest. The president was M. de Staal, Germany sent Count Munster, England Sir Julian Pauncefote, America the Hon. Andrew D. White, Italy Count Nigra, France Leon Bourgeois, Spain the Duke of Tetuan, China sent Yang Yu, Persia her poet, Riza Khan, Servia the celebrated writer, Miyatovich.* The young Queen of Holland put the great palace of the Hague at the disposition of the delegates. Alas! Even before the Congress met, signs of disagreement arose.

A little dispute between Lord Salisbury and Dick Olney of the United States put the chief difficulty in a nutshell. Suppose the conference condemned a war and a certain nation or nations began hostilities. How could the conference get power to enforce its decision? Plainly, the difficulty had

---

* Sir Julian Pauncefote (1828–1902), Minister and then Ambassador to the U.S. from 1889 until his death. He kept relations with the U.S. friendly during the Spanish-American War; he was senior delegate to the First Hague Conference and helped set up a permanent tribunal of arbitration.

Andrew White (1832–1918), the first president of Cornell University. He was ambassador to Germany 1897–9, and chairman of the American delegation to the First Hague Conference. He persuaded Andrew Carnegie to build the Palace of Justice at the Hague.

Leon Bourgeois (1851–1925), Premier of France 1895–6 and a delegate to the First Hague Conference; later he was a proponent of the League of Nations. He won the Nobel Peace Prize in 1920.

to be met in some way or other, yet, though the talk went on for months, it all came to nothing. But the peace proposal and the conference cast a certain grim light upon the murder later in Siberia of the Tsar and his whole family by his unruly subjects.

The year 1899 was to me extraordinarily painful. I have already told how my work in South Africa had taken away my attention from investments in Monte Carlo and Nice, which I had neglected and which therefore turned out very badly. I lost thirty or forty thousand pounds and had to find some new way of making money. Suddenly in this mood I went back from the Riviera and stayed a short time in Paris.

On one of my earlier hurried visits to Paris I met Whistler, who took me to lunch at his house in the Rue du Bac. He talked to me passionately of his quarrel with Sir William Eden,* which arose about the price to be paid for the portrait he had done of Lady Eden. He read to me his newest pamphlet: "The Baronet and the Butterfly."

I had already written in the *Saturday Review* in Whistler's favor in the dispute with Sir William Eden because I thought it petty of a man as rich as Eden to quarrel over a hundred pounds with a great artist; but now I noticed a malevolence in Whistler that amazed me.

I have told in my *Life of Wilde* how I had dined with Whistler in London and told him that Oscar was engaged in prison in writing a new work, a very important drama; and I simply recorded the fact that my story called forth "a stinging gibe at Oscar's expense."

I may now recount Whistler's word. "Oscar writing a new work," he said, "a great romantic drama; we must find a name for it. I have it" he cried; "it must be known as *The Bugger's Opera.*"

If Whistler had been more kindly, he would have been a greater man. In full maturity of talent he dissipated himself in squabbles and quarrels which had really no meaning or importance.

Of course, I always took care to meet Oscar whenever I was in Paris; at this time he was hard up and I had to promise him money.

I must now tell perhaps the most characteristic piece of humor that I ever heard from him. He called on me one morning and found me reading the Bible.

"Wonderful book, Frank," he said.

"A fairy tale of religion," I said, "the development of a national conscience."

"Not quite that, Frank," he said gravely, "it's its truth that impresses me."

"Truth?" I questioned.

"Yes, Frank," and the fine eyes laughed. "It begins, you know, with a man and a woman in a garden and naturally it ends with Revelations."

I was delighted with the word; and of course had to try to equal it, so I told him the story of my old friend Marix. I was astonished one day at

* (1849–1915); Sir Anthony Eden's father.

Volume Four / 815

meeting him coming out of a private room of the Cafe Royal, for at that time, even, he was quite grey and must have been seventy years of age.

"My boy," he said, "I have just been with the prettiest girl in London, and had a great time."

"Come, come, Marix," I said, "you are too old to brag."

"Oh, you unbeliever," he said, "don't you know the English proverb: 'Many a good tune comes from an old fiddle?' "

"That's true," I said, "but even the English have never been foolish enough to say that the good tune comes from an old bow (beau)."

In one of these talks, Oscar told me a scene from a play he had thought of writing, in which the wife, who was also the mistress of the house, has gone up to her private sitting-room to rest: she is lying down behind the screen with a "migraine," when her husband comes in with the woman he is in love with at the moment. In the middle of their love-making, which the wife can't help overhearing, a knock comes at the door and they hear outside the voice of the husband of the lady, who demands admission. The scene is resolved by the lady of the house getting up from behind the screen and opening the door, and thus saving the guilty couple.

It occurred to me that I had a story about a Mr. and Mrs. Daventry in my head, which would suit this scene. I finally bought the right to use it for a hundred pounds from Oscar. He asked me fifty pounds for the scene and I gave it to him, and I told him I would give him fifty pounds more if he would write the first act. He promised, but did not keep his word. I went back to London and wrote the play, *Mr. and Mrs. Daventry,* in four or five days, and took it to Mrs. Patrick Campbell, who accepted it at once. I only made one condition—that Mr. Daventry should be played by Fred Kerr,* whom I regarded as one of the best character actors on the English stage.

As Oscar would not write the first act, I wrote it and did it badly, and I rewrote it for the fiftieth night when I had had a little stage experience. Afterwards Oscar twitted me about my purchase, saying I had bought the great scene from the *Lady Teazle* of Sheridan without recognizing it.

When the play was put on at first, it had a very bad press: the London papers all told me that I had written a French play better suited for Paris than for London; and I found Mrs. Campbell, the next day, in despair because of the unfavorable notices. I cheered her up by telling her that I would pay all the expenses of the play for a half-share in it.

"If you can afford to do that," she said, "I can afford to risk it."

"This bad press," I said, "will make the play."

Clement Scott,* the most influential critic of the time, tried to damn the play out of personal dislike for me and gave one phrase in the play astonishing notoriety. People talked in the play of the "English vice" till at

---

* (1858–1933). He became manager of the Vaudeville Theatre in London in 1895; he played his first movie role in 1930 in *Raffles.* His memoirs, *Recollections of a Defective Memory,* appeared in 1931.
** (1841–1904); critic for the *Daily Telegraph.*

length the protagonist, Mr. Daventry, turns round and asks: "Is there such a thing, Lady Hillington, as an English vice? What is the peculiarly English vice?"

"Oh," retorted the clever woman, "I thought every one knew that, Mr. Daventry; the English vice is adultery with home comforts."

That brought all the best class of London society in streams to the theatre, and created such an excitement that about the fiftieth night the censor interfered and cut the phrase out. I went to see him. "Why do this?" I asked. "Surely the phrase is harmless enough, and true to boot."

"Oh, I am delighted with it" he replied, "I tell it every night. I wish you could tell me as good a one about the French. Couldn't you tell me what the French vice is?"

"Quite easily," I replied. "You know that in all the apartment houses in Paris they have a notice '*eau et gaz à tous les étages*' (water and gas on every floor). Well, you know the word *garce,* meaning a naughty flapper, is pronounced very much like *gaz,* so I say '*eau et garces à tous les étages*' that is the French vice."

He roared with laughter and thanked me, and this word of mine had almost as great a success, told by him in private, as anything in the play: but in the middle of the success, when I was receiving some hundreds of pounds a week from the play, Queen Victoria died, and the period of mourning stopped all plays in London for a fortnight; but after the period of mourning had passed my play was the only play, I believe, revived in that season, and it ran for fifty or sixty more nights—until Mrs. Patrick Campbell got rid of Fred Kerr, whom I had picked to play the protagonist, Mr. Daventry, and so spoilt the whole cast.

The success emboldened me to write other plays and I wrote three or four, notably one *Shakespeare and His Love,* and one entitled *The Bucket Shop.**

The one on Shakespeare was immediately taken by Beerbohm Tree, who gave me five hundred pounds in advance for it and promised to open his season with it; but in the meantime he found that his daughter Viola had some talent and wished to go on the stage; and he therefore rejected my play for another because, as he said, he couldn't make love to his own daughter on the stage, whereas Shakespeare in my play was the lover personified. So I withdrew the play and it was never given in London. A year or so later I wrote *The Bucket Shop* and the Stage Society asked me to allow them to give a representation of it. The success was so great that the society, with my consent, put it on for a second performance, when again the house was crowded.

I found such difficulty, however, with actors and actresses that I resolved to return to writing stories: each actor and actress seems to be firmly convinced that his or her part is greater than the whole, and they will deform the whole at any moment for a personal success in the part. Besides, I

* The former, in 1910 and the latter, probably in 1911.

made more money on the stock exchange than I could make at either play-writing or book-writing, and so I resolved to write merely the books that pleased me, careless of what the monetary outcome might be.

When I had done a number of short stories, some which later appeared in my book *The Veils of Isis** I began to see that the art of narration was still in its infancy. I saw that though the French were masters of the art of story-writing, there wasn't a single story in French, long or short, which I considered at all perfectly designed.

My practice taught me that the most important thing in a story is the speed of narration; no one wants his reader to skip passages or to feel that this or that part is too long. Most writers think that they can avoid being tedious by jumping from one part of the story to another; but this habit is apt to distract attention. The true art consists in so graduating the speed of the narration that the reader feels that he is being carried along faster and faster to an inevitable conclusion, much as if he were caught in the rapids of Niagara above the falls. And in order to be able to graduate the speed, the introduction of the characters should be deliberate and slow in exact proportion to the length of the story. For as soon as the characters are all known to the readers and the trend of the story is indicated, then the pace should begin to quicken, and chapter by chapter the speed should increase and should be felt to be increasing, so that skipping or tedium should be absolutely impossible. I can understand using telegraphese at the end of a story to prevent any suspicion of dragging.

In time, with a great deal of practice, I learned many things about the art of story-writing, which I shall perhaps tell about in a future volume.

In the meantime, I had no journal; the South African war was going on, English defeats growing more and more frequent, every one disappointed and dejected. A sad close to a wonderful period! My old enemy, bronchitis, had seized me in October and I couldn't shake it off. I was in bed with it in a little country house I had outside London when I read of Oscar Wilde's death. The world went greyer to me.

The news from the front continued to get worse and worse. It seemed to me that the South African war marked the decadence of England. I thought and said it showed a lack of understanding, a lack of all high qualities of heart as well as of head, so grave that I couldn't see any possibility of England standing in the future side by side with the United States. The English had spent a thousand millions of money on that unspeakably silly South African war, whereas, if they had spent half that sum in settling up the central plateau of Africa, even from the north of the Transvaal to the Zambesi with their own unemployed, they might have laid the foundations of a greater empire than even the one they had lost in North America.

Now, after many years, I wonder still whether it is too late for them to

---

* New York, 1915; a collection of short stories, almost all of which were published the year before in *The Yellow Ticket and other Stories*.

recover, but their policy since the Great War is exactly the same as it was in the South African War—a policy of petty grocers much more intent on getting than on giving—and greedy of small immediate gains. Fancy disputing with the miners about an eight hours' day. The miner has to go to his work and return and wash from head to foot in warm water, and on the average this costs him, at least, two hours more; ten hours a day of meanest labor for eight hours pay is bad enough for anyone. The workers in England are always vilely treated.

Another evil is that the aristocrat always supports the employers and exploiters of labor as against the workingmen, although his conduct to his own servants and dependents is usually excellent; consequently, the strife in England between the employer and the workman becomes keener and keener: the employer wishes to pay as little as he can, and naturally under these circumstances, the workman tries to do as little as he can. The chief result is that though the mining conditions in England are more favorable than they are anywhere else in the world, for in South Wales and elsewhere they have coal quite close to the sea, yet coal can be produced in America and shipped from Virginia, four hundred miles to the sea, and sold to compete with English prices in the London markets. The English employers continually seek to make their money by grinding the workmen, instead of using their own brains in new labor saving appliances and inventions—and now in this year, 1927, they are bringing in a law to make a general strike criminal and so reduce the workmen to practical slavery. Nothing has been done in twenty years to develop the central plateau of Africa—the noblest field for colonization in the world! I harp on this because of its extraordinary importance: I wish all good things for England, for I know well her chivalrous and honorable side, enskied by beauty and sainted by noble deeds, a side realized in her poetry, the finest in the world's literature. But if she ever wins again to financial power it will be through her colonies, and she possesses no colony that can compare with that Central African plateau.

But if England doesn't care to use her power wisely, what must be said of America? The United States Government has never even shown an inkling of its highest function. Already she is by far the strongest power in the world, strong enough to disband her army and navy and make the chief navies of the world a mere police force and insurance against piracy and privateering; and the money she now spends on armaments could be used to spiritualize her people. By putting an end to war, she may inaugurate that reign of peace upon earth and universal good will to men which is, so to speak, the first recognition by the soul of the new commandment given to us by Christ.

The money rewards of work are far larger in America than anywhere else in the world, and so artists and thinkers and writers of all sorts are swept into the struggle for money and carried away by success. Of course, this fact should have led the governors to increase at any cost the spiritualization of the people. Conservatories of music and opera houses should have been founded by the state in every city of fifty-thousand inhabitants. Long ago America should have had municipal theatres, too, as well as municipal opera houses, and even municipal schools of chemistry and physics for original research, after the German fashion, but nothing of this sort has been done.

America, I am afraid, is becoming more and more a mere weapon of the rich to plunder the poor. Yet something great in America drew me always; my love of Professor Smith, who had been my earliest teacher in Kansas, taught me that there was an ideal there higher than anywhere else on earth, because kinder. Every revelation of English snobbishness led me back to the democratic feeling in America with intense pleasure. I always knew that all snobbishness was a love of unreal superiorities, and always loathed the vice; as Emerson said, it dwarfs the dignity of manhood, and prevents one feeling at home with the best in every country.

Let me tell a story to show this. When I was a student in Lawrence, Kansas, there was a wastrel in the town who pretended to have been a pal of Ulysses Grant, the President. This wastrel was always hanging round the bar of the Eldridge House, or some other saloon, and if he had ever met you in any company always called you afterwards by your Christian name and proposed a drink. His tipple was what he called port wine, a most awful concoction of sugar, logwood and raw alcohol that had no more relation to Oporto than the wastrel had to civilization.

I have forgotten his name, but we youths were more or less interested in him and his stories. He told us how President Grant in his youth used to drink a great deal more than was good for him. We often wondered whether he was telling the truth or merely inventing.

Suddenly, it was announced that President Grant was coming to Lawrence. He was to dine at the Eldridge House on a certain day, accompanied by the governor and two or three senators and the mayor of the town.

We boys thought our time had come, so we got the old wastrel, primed him up with a drink or two of his port wine, and took him to the Eldridge House five minutes before the President was expected to arrive.

In due course the President's carriage drew up at the entrance. The governor got out, helped the President out, and the mayor and various other dignitaries brought up the rear. Just as Grant got to the door of the hotel in the full glare of the light, we pushed the old wastrel forward in front of him, and he stood with a deprecating smile, holding out his hand, saying, "Ulysses, Ulysses."

Grant's grim face did not relax. He looked at the human wreck with sharp, little gray-blue eyes, taking him all in, the dirty thread-bare clothes, frayed trousers, shabby boots and hat—everything—but not a gleam of recognition.

The wastrel was ludicrous—pathetic. "You hain't forgot Hap," he said, grinning.

Suddenly Grant's hard face changed. "Are you So and So?" he said.

"Sure," quavered the wastrel, "sure. I knew you'd remember me."

"Of course I do," said the President, holding out his hand; "of course I do. Yet it is twenty or more years since I saw you. You must come in and dine."

The wastrel's face quivered like jelly and he looked down at his clothes and hands.

"What matter?" Grant went on heartily. "Come right in; these gentlemen will forgive your dress." And in they all went, to our amazement, the President and the drunken wastrel in the lead.

It was said afterwards that no one had ever heard Grant talk so much as at that dinner. He spoke on three or four different occasions to the wastrel—a thing unheard of. But when we boys turned away, I remember it struck me that there was something noble in Grant's recognition and cordiality—something unthinkable almost to the European.

I remember trying once to persuade Arthur Balfour, after telling him this incident, that this feeling of equality, this generosity, was the strong mortar that clamped the American people together with a grip firmer even than the Roman mortar which was stronger than the stone itself.

America suffers from an exaggerated and almost insane individualism, yet there is slowly growing up an ideal of mutual help that may yet redeem all the races of men.

The slow rate of human progress is what distresses one. It has taken a thousand years for us to get rid of Hell and devils and to distrust prisons and punishments, but now that we believe in sympathy and affection, our progress will be more rapid. It is money now that separates us one from another: greed must be conquered, and case-hardened selfishness, too, by a new sense, a truly Christian sense, of mutual loving-kindness; and so we shall get rid of war and its insane stupidity and cruelty. My quarrel with President Wilson was that he might have done this easily, but any American president could do it in a single term, and win for himself and his land an immortality of renown.

This new ideal was born in the wonderful nineteenth century, the century that has enlarged and enriched life in so many ways.

In 1870, one-third of the globe was unexplored, unknown; as soon as the dark continent was charted and the poles discovered, man took the depths of the sea for his park and the limitless fields of the air for his playground. The X-Rays, too, and wireless telegraphy have multiplied our spiritual possessions and added, so to speak, the imaginative touch to our new powers. Railways were first used in the late thirties and then in the nineties motor cars to make travel easy and delightful. Instead of having only theatres to amuse us, we have astounding cinema shows as well and can sit in our rooms and listen to the greatest singers in the last half century, or hear the greatest modern actors; statesmen, too, long dead, will make their best speeches for us as if still alive.

And in spite of all our petty squabbles and cowardly selfishness, the pace quickens from year to year; in spite of the World War and poison gasses and infamous blockades that ruined women and children, we have made more progress in science in the last ten years than in any previous decade. We have just begun to understand the infinite power of the atom and are now studying to harness it to our needs. And soon the forces of nature will be enslaved and free us all from the curse of working to supply bodily wants, and so we can turn the whole world into an enchanted place, for we begin to see that everything is possible and wonders indescribable will yet be realized by the awakened spirit of man.

This is my faith, the faith that guides me and directs, and I hope that those who read me may be inspired by it. I believe unshakeably in the holy spirit of man; in his infinite perfectibility; in the divine impulse in him to grow, not only in knowledge, or even in wisdom, but in goodness, in consideration for others, in loving-kindness and gentle pity, and all the sweet offices of love. Paul preached Faith, Hope, and Love, but he had no faith such as we have, no hope so well-founded as ours. Think of what we have done in the last hundred years, and forecast, if you will, the transcendent future. Tennyson's words recur to me:

> For I looked into the future far as human eye could see,
> Saw the wonders of the world and all the rapture that would be.*

* From *Locksley Hall:*
> For I dipt into the future, far as human eye could
> see,
> Saw the Vision of the world, and all the wonder that
> would be;

Chapter XIII

Sex and Self-Restraint

LIKE HEINE, I have always been puzzled by the sex restraints and prohibitions in men and women, and annoyed by their prudery in confessing their practices and desires. As I have told elsewhere in this volume, I studied medicine in Vienna when I was only twenty-three and devoted especial attention to all sex questions; and some friends now request me to tell what I know of these matters, for they interest everyone.

I was in doubt whether or not to do this when I received an anonymous letter from a girl in America, who, plainly to me, is telling the story of her own experiences, and very sad they are. If the girl had had a little more knowledge, she might have escaped the worst of her suffering, and so I place what little knowledge I have gained at the disposal of men and women who may need and desire it. She begins:

This is the woman's side of your volume two (the writer not having seen volume one). Not that this is meant to be a sermon—nor that "the writer" doesn't believe in frankness and in truth; (on the contrary, "the writer" has suffered much because others objected to truth instead of dissimulation).

A young girl born in a Roman Catholic community, where the Blessed Virgin Mary is a great patron, where virginity is considered a priceless jewel. The girl with a bright mind, anxious to learn, easily surpassing classmates, liking to "think"—beginning to think about Catholic dogmas, until that culminated long afterwards in leaving the Church. Born poor, the girl had enough to do to work in order to be able to study, to go to a "select" (it happened) preparatory school, business school, Roman Catholic College, then a larger, leading women's college. Never had an opportunity to meet boys as social equals. Consequently had an idealized version of mankind in her mind. A good-looking girl, not of the "pretty" type, she did attract men, and it was a new land of not-known possibilities to her. However, she never met "eligible" people, nor naturally was she very "eligible" to "worthwhile" people, having no background but herself, no money but what she earned, etc.

Full of energy, enthusiasm, zeal for service, etc., after college, (during the senior year, met an impecunious, brilliant young man, who loved her ardently, brilliantly, youthfully, and exploringly, with much interchange of brilliant correspondence, exploring ideas, etc.—he was an irresponsible intellectual hero—the girl wanted strength and daring in every way in a man—a break, and the boy died of the flu).

Another plunge into an unknown group: uneducated, very young girl-nurses thrown into a knowledge of sex and bestiality. Our girl read up on surgery, watched operations, etc., got to know the "wise and kindly" older house-physician, a good surgeon, kindly and sometimes untiring. And this older house-physician had your view of sex, Frank Harris; and every virgin was an attraction to him, and no harm was ever done a girl (in his estimation) unless she were made pregnant, and of course he never did that. He was a pleasant kindly man, and new minds, with to-her-new experiences always interested "our girl." He gave lectures on anatomy to the half-fledged nurses with no education, which gave him a delightful opportunity to instill veiledly and very sinuously the idea that the sex organs must be used or they atrophy. He knew so much of what a virgin did not know, that when he showed strong emotion at the girl's telling him she was leaving the next day or so, he did persuade her to let him "have" her, after he had soothed her conscience by asking her to marry him; she with her zeal for service, thought of getting him to be a missionary, or such, with her. So the next night they registered as Mr. and Mrs.— in a small New York hotel he knew.

It was an anatomical experiment to her with a dear friend. When he wanted her to play with his "sex", she loved and fondled his dear head instead. It was a new knowledge to her that when she stroked his nude back, his "sex" throbbed with each stroke as he asked her to hold it. And he—afterwards—having kissed her with seeming reverence, deeply, lovingly on the mouth as she lay there, in the morning, insisted on putting a ten dollar note in her dress, when she said, surprisedly, "Why, darling, why don't you get me some dear little remembrance if you must." He had explained to her as a friend that servant girls "pick up" ten dollars or so a night from a pick-up on the street, and it helps out their income! And the unsuspecting "kid" (and she was over twenty-one) never dreamed he was a very loose liver.

That ended it for the man, or any man—n'est ce pas? Not so with any woman, or this woman. As you know, sex in woman is very close to deep friendship and tenderness, and not a passing thing. They wrote. His idea was to have her spend week-ends with him as often as possible. With the education she had had—just that, with no idea of further responsibility—a life in common, interchange of ideal, and so on, was very cheapening. When a friend at the hospital (the only one not of the "cheap" gang of loose-nurses) wrote her that the Doctor had said in a class the reason he had not married was that he could not be faithful to any one woman—the girl wrote a letter to end the thing. And the Doctor did not come back!

Just before that, the girl had her first experience in "loving up." "Loving up" was a term new to her used by the hospital nurses. The friend, above-mentioned, had asked her to join her in a party, three men and three girls, to take a ride in a big limousine. One man had the car, the other two were brothers, one of the girls was an ex-patient of hers. She dressed up "our girl" in some attractive clothes of her sister's, and rouged her, and "our girl" seemed to be very stunning and captivated the heart of her ex-patient's brother. It was a new experience to her, to be made physical love to, with long-drawn-out kisses and a very new thing to have a man put her hand on his "sex" and to find it a hard big thing! and to have him try to put his hand up her clothes! And it frightened her then, and later when he tried to get her again.

The girl took a course in a religious university and met a young British Presbyterian Minister of Scotch-Irish descent, that year. Said young man seemed rather sophisticated to her, and she was distant to him, didn't quite like the daring look in his eye. They talked a lot however; afterwards when he seemed to know so much more about the course (a radical current events course) he was invited to tea one day to finish a long talk in which he tried to find out all he could about her. He asked her to a dinner and dance afterwards, which was new and strange to "our girl." Since it happened that there was a surprise party on at home (at the training school—a beautiful place architecturally to live in by the way) she could not go, and surreptitiously slipped out to tell him at the corner she could not. However, she asked him later to go with her to a Tammany Hall ball, as a sociological experiment. He was marvelously dressed up in a skirted coat, smart cane, etc.—very handsome and gay and full of pep. She had gone to a movie with him once, and after it, walked in the park with him where he lightly jumped over a bench and did other physical strength stunts to her surprise. They ran a race together, and when he outstripped her, he ran backwards, and then caught her swiftly and turned her around, and lifted her (a big girl) high up in the air and carried her! All much to her surprise, and thrilling, too; he being, of course, a good man of high ideals, being a practicing Minister as well as a student!

They danced at the ball, and he was very, very passionate, to her surprise. During a wait on the balcony between dances, he said sophisticated little things, and then a glance of their eyes suddenly met, said "I love you" to each other—strangely disturbing to the girl! They went home soon after—he said, "It's getting too warm."

Then they stopped at a Chinese restaurant to get her some Chinese candy; but domineeringly he went to a table and said to her, "Sit there; come over here beside me." They had food; he ate ravenously. He flirted, and she was new at flirting. She toyed with sugar and said nonentities. He looked all around the place to see he was unobserved (she wore a large hat) and kissed her on the cheek, and to her very susceptible self, it seemed very insufficient. Then they left to go home. Just outside of the door, upstairs on the landing, he caught her and kissed her most thoroughly, and she felt his sex getting close, close to hers (and he a Minister!) and herself being hugged as only a strong man could hug. To her amazement, he did not say: "Will you marry me?" When they reached the street (a Chinaman coming up had made them part at last) she said, "What made you do that?" He said, (to her disappointment) "Oh, I am very passionate." They took a last bus, sat on the top—the only ones—and he finally took her on his lap and tried (as you say) to put a naughty hand up her dress, and she seemed a willing victim, and so he stopped. And he said, "We must not see so much of each other since we fall so hard for each other."

Again—to a man that ended the matter. To a girl it seemed to mean the beginning of a deeper friendship. You don't seem to understand what that may leave in a girl's mind of sorrow and disappointment.

Suddenly another married man, a Jew, met her, offered to teach her how to write, made love to her, tried to make her his mistress, never did succeed in getting her to go away with him. The unsophisticated girl went with him to his office in the building of the . . . School. He told her later he had asked her only in order to make love to her.

Our girl was almost killed with mere loneliness. One day on going into town she wore her new suit (quite attention-attracting), missed the train and took the trolley, having only a ten dollar bill (her month's wages) in her pocket. Her seat-partner paid her fare and started to talk to her about the loneliness of a traveling man, district manager, etc., etc., of a shooting stall in Canada, etc. Finally he asked her to have dinner with him that evening. The lonely girl did. He talked liberally, of trial marriage, etc. Our lonely girl was susceptible to comradeship but not to trial marriage. He asked her to get another girl for another man. She got a girl and the girl's own man-friend—one she rarely saw; the four went to a new thing—a night restaurant roof garden where she saw astonishing things—little girls (very young) displaying their sex from the rear suddenly. It disturbed her; she pitied them, having studied children and loved them; they were such young girls and so ignorant looking. However, her newfound friend was a hospitable, big-talking passionate person. He rushed her along on the street, he tore along to her friend's apartment, the friend gave the key, and persuaded the girl to let his sex touch hers. That one performance may have given her gonorrhea! He asked to come out next day. He tried to get her to come to the hotel but she did not.

During the week some man-friend of his called her up saying the man had left her telephone number and address and had asked him to call her up. This humiliated the girl and she hung up the receiver, and was very, very miserable.

The following Saturday she went to the station to take a train into a college club meeting (she hadn't money enough to join the college club, but this was a group meeting). On the way before she reached the station, a beautiful car stopped and the beautifully gotten up uniformed chauffeur said respectfully: "Can't I give you a lift?" Parched in life at the awful estate place, she who had never taken a "lift" accepted, sat beside the person and was amused at his respectful awed talking to her, calling her "ma'am" telling of his travels over the world in the car for his young and wealthy master. The master sounded interesting. He said how lonely it was to ride around without a companion. He seemed to be having to do that for some reason or other. It was hot summer time and the breeze in hiding was grateful to "our girl." He said he would be glad to put his own car at her service any time she wished. He asked her if she would go to a beautiful place she had heard of but never seen. She wasn't sure so he asked her please to call him up. The next day she did and couldn't get him. The "house" evidently answered and said he was a servant and in the stable. However in the p. m. at the end of the lane leading to the beautiful estate where our girl languished, was a tin-canny car and the chauffeur; and with a text book on botany under her arm, our girl got in.

It was a beautiful ride, a beautiful place; the chauffeur was respectful! There was no one else who wanted our girl's companionship. On the way back he stopped the car on a woody place, laid out a newspaper and asked her to sit down. He put his initials on a tree, a place he used to visit as a boy, he said. He did not put the date so the girl offered to put on the date. As she had her arms raised, he suddenly kissed her! To her it seemed to say that he was lonely, and that was a weak spot in her. Enlarging the thing from him and her to a world more or less of lonely human beings (and she had been suffering the pangs of solitariness in the midst of people) she felt sorry—felt pity. He carried her (as said, she was not a slight thing) across a foot-path, and (there is no beauty to be described) used her for his pleasure like an animal, used her regardless of her *pain*. She was down-and-out with lack of hope (and yet a strange undirect insatiable ambition to be something was always in her); she went "home" (to the old maid—the only home she had); he wrote her an illiterate note meant to be kindly.

She wrote to the psycho-analyst Dr. (man) [sic] and told him some symptoms; he wrote to her that she should be examined for he felt sure she had gonorrhea. Alone in a strange city with no one in whom she could confide; she searched for a woman doctor, found none, finally went to the head of a social agency to whom one of the journalists had written much. She went not for charity but for advice. He was kind, got her a woman Doctor who finally had her go to a hospital where they regarded her as an outcast, had her eat on tin dishes in an off-porch, the nurses promiscuously spilled lysol on the floor here and there—the girl was wretched, miserable, alone; she wrote to the woman Doctor and the doctor took her away (the hospital said they would not have her) in the women's college hospital—after a night spent with a nurse, secured for forty dollars a week—(an ignorant, old inefficient Irish body R. C. who sang R. C. hymns) at a children's bureau house filled with bedbugs and with the girl paying food expenses. The nurse had nothing to do and did less, almost douched her with clear lysol by mistake instead of potassium permanganate— the only reason it didn't happen was because our girl saw it first!

The girl went through a great deal of spiritual discomfort, and mental distress with nobody doing the slightest to change conditions at all in the future. Finally when able she hunted herself another job, and got one for another social agency as secretary to a female director; gave herself completely to the work, which was to help school-children; labored enthusiastically, industriously at less than she was worth "for the good of the cause" month by month paid off the accumulated debt, realized that much as she loved children and companionship evidently she was a fool in that line and marriage was not for her. She was in the hospital a month, undergoing treatment—infection was at the cervix, had not yet reached into the uterus—and the treatment was to prevent it doing so.

She was pronounced cured but went to the doctor (the celebrated woman surgeon who took her over to the hospital: she was killed later in an auto accident) a youthful woman doctor successor (former helper) each month to make sure. After a year or more she took a course or two at a school of social work and there had one instructor who seemed very efficient, thorough, etc.

To make a long story short, they fell deeply, permanently, desperately, soul-stirringly in love. And he was married to his first cousin (his mother's sister's daughter) both Jews, had two children, a girl and a boy; "Was no longer," (he said, swearing the truth) "married to the woman, lived daily, hourly in mind and soul with 'our girl'; planned to marry her!" They seemed to be perfectly mated in every way. He seemed to become younger—he was ten years older than she. However, like all men, this man seems to be a coward from the heel up. I omit all the heart-rending details, of his waving back and forth, of their not being sure that she was pregnant (the doctor said she could not become pregnant for a year) and upon a thorough examination (when later events showed that she had been three months pregnant) said she was not pregnant. Eventually after much pain and sorrow at the defection of the adored one, the baby came.

Our girl had been in the valley of humiliation and death of spirit and even loving the man, decided she was not after "the past" worthy unless—so in all honesty, truthfulness and sincerity, she told him before even their "marriage" was consummated so that he could retreat if he wished to. Everything was talked over frankly and they reverenced and respected each other.

So therefore (he lied like a devil) he went back to his cousin and the girl paid all the bills of suffering, humiliation and anguish, always asking her to pity him, that he would never again be happy, that he loved only her, etc., etc., that he was poor (the girl did the economizing; he did the spending while talking of poverty), if he had money (he had a salary of $7,500 a year) it would all be different.

Meanwhile other men thinking our girl a widow are perfectly willing to offer themselves as lovers, provided it cost them nothing much in the way of responsibility, and they can get a "beautiful thrill" out of a most beautiful experience, and she has learned that men can be sudden and tempestuous and bold and brutal, and they can be sly and cunning and long-time-patient with that goal in view, and they can be devilishly unjust and mean and wicked when they don't get what they want—always talking nicely about "beauty" in such intimacy.

The head of the Children's Bureau, mentioned before, came to the front again, killed the man's love for his child, took him under his wing, to bring him back to his "holy family," told a lot of dirty, cowardly, fiendish, impossible lies about the girl (he said if the thing became known it would hurt social work in his city, so the man must be saved, regardless). And the man's megalomaniac wife had just had a miscarriage while the man does not pay for the support of his daughter by his beloved!

Our girl is supporting her child among many obstacles and hardships and can't run the risk of having a government put her in jail for writing to you. Hence the anonymity.

You seem not to care much about children, or the next generation in your second volume, nor how you may be injuring a dear and beautiful girl-child in your quest for your own pleasure.

I liked your "Contemporary Portraits" and your "The Man Shakespeare" very much. And I liked a great deal of your "Life."

This letter appears to me to be an authentic human document, revealing curiously the average woman's point of view; it bears the imprint of reality on every page, partly because of its contempt of English usage in its ignorance of grammar; but it is quite exceptional in pain and suffering; not once does "the girl" describe, or even mention, the joys of sexual intercourse, and if she had few of the pleasures, she had assuredly more than a fair share of the suffering. Finally, she gave herself out of love to a married man; she had a child by him, and was brutally abandoned—a sad, sad story.

I have enjoyed all the pleasures I could in life, while always seeking to do as much good as possible and as little harm to the girl or woman-partner. I believe that, with one exception, I have not done much harm to any one.

The reason why girls don't give themselves freely is the fear of getting a child: they are usually too ignorant or too trusting to feel the fear of getting some disease, though it is this fear which obsesses and scares the man; but the dread of becoming *enceinte* is even less founded: with a little care that catastrophe can be avoided. As a rule the man covers his sex with a French letter or else covers the neck of the woman's womb with a pessary; but both of these diminish the enjoyment and are not so sure as they might be, for the French letters sometimes burst, and the pessary falls off occasionally, and the result is that pregnancy may take place.

The method suggested in the Bible in the story of Onan is the one I think best: when Onan got excited, he withdrew his sex, and we are told that "he spilled his seed on the ground." I found out in Vienna that as a rule one needs only to do this after the first orgasm: in ordinary cases, there is little or no danger in the second or in following consecutive embraces. And usually this self-restraint is worth practicing on the part of the man since it gives almost complete security to the girl.

But if the girl is caught and pregnancy results, to get rid of the foetus and bring on the monthly period is comparatively easy in the first two months, especially easy at the end of the first month: a dose of ergot usually suffices. Indeed, I have known jumping down two or three stairs to bring about the desired result; but as a rule, the girl does not act energetically this first month, and the difficulty is enormously increased by leaving the matter for two months; but it is still easy to bring it about the second month, and without much danger of inflammation or consequent illness; the third, fourth, and fifth months are excessively dangerous, and abortion then should be carried out by a skilled hand, for as soon as the foetus adheres to the side of the womb, it is not easy to get rid of; even when a miscarriage is brought about, one must take care to remove all the filaments attached to the side of the womb with a silver spoon, of course perfectly disinfected; a skilled hand is needed in this case. In the sixth, seventh, eight, and ninth months, abortion is comparatively easy, but there is life in the child.

We had in Vienna a method of bringing about abortion, especially at the end of the first, or even the second month, which had no ill effects; we made a pointed pencil of certain ingredients which swell with the heat of the body; this pencil would be introduced slowly and carefully into the neck of the womb; as soon as it began to swell, the abortion was begun: nature then made its own effort and got rid of the intruding semen.

Of course, in all cases in which the girl seeks to bring about abortion she ought, if possible, to have the advice and skilled assistance of a good doctor; and in spite of the insane legal prohibitions, it is not difficult to find such help.

I am now going to complete this chapter by giving a personal experience which may have a certain interest as revealing the depths over which ordinary life is built.

When I first went to Berlin as a student, nearly fifty years ago, now, I went out looking for rooms not too far from the university and near the great avenue, Unter den Linden. I soon found two excellent rooms and a bathroom on the third floor, which were let by a nice looking woman of about forty or forty-five. "Who will attend to me?" I asked, for the price was rather high. "Either I myself or my daughter," said the woman, and going to the door she called, "Kätchen!" A pretty girl of sixteen or so came running and bowed to me smiling. "All right," I said, "I'll take the rooms and move in this afternoon." In a few hours I came in and the mother and daughter helped me to arrange everything and make myself comfortable. The woman brought me my coffee in the morning at eight o'clock, got my bath ready and went away. I was perfectly content, and even better satisfied when, after a couple of mornings, Kätchen brought me my coffee, arranged the bath, chatting to me the while.

Everything went perfectly for about a month: Kätchen and I had become great friends and I had already taught her that kissing sweetened service. To do her justice, she seemed eager to profit by the teaching, but at the same time showed a fear of being caught, I thought by her mother; and that seemed to me extraordinary.

One Sunday morning she hurried away and the mother came in her stead. "Where's Kätchen?" I asked.

"Her father's there," the woman replied, "and he doesn't like her to serve anyone."

"Send your younger daughter, Lisabeth!" I said cheekily, and the woman, as if scared, answered, "Oh, that would be worse!"

"Why worse?" I went on. "I won't eat her, and surely your husband can't want the three girls to attend to him."

"Please, please, Sir," she cried, "don't speak so loud. He might hear and then our good times would be over."

"Over?" I questioned. "Is he such a brute?"

"Oh, Sir," she cried with tears in her voice, "forgive me! I'll tell you everything tomorrow. Now I must go," and away she hurried, evidently in extreme excitement or fear.

The next morning in came the mother again, and she told me the father was very suspicious and had told her that I was too young for Kätchen to wait upon me. "Nonsense!" I cried. "I want Kätchen to come out with me to the theatre."

"Oh, Sir, please not!" cried the mother passionately. "Then he'd be sure to know and he'd be furious. Be content with me for a week or so and he may forget—and I'll send Kätchen to you again."

"All right;" I said, "it's idiotic," but I had a good deal of work to do and wasn't sorry to be forced to get on with it.

Three or four days more elapsed and Kätchen brought me my coffee again and sat on my bed talking with me. I had my arm round her pretty, slim waist and was kissing her, when a knock came on the door and a man's voice called her loudly. She sprang from the bed with white face and frightened eyes and vanished.

I got up, bathed and dressed quickly, and then rang to have the breakfast things taken away. The mother came in; evidently she had been crying. "Please, please Sir, take care," she said. "He's in one of his mad rages: he came back from work on purpose to catch Kätchen. Oh, Sir, take care and don't go out till noon."

"I'm going out very soon," I said, carelessly, "and shan't put it off for anyone."

"I pray you go very quietly," she said in a low voice. "We all want you to stay."

"I don't understand," I said, feeling bewildered, for there were not many students who could pay what I was paying.

"Nobody could understand," she cried, "how unhappy I am. Please Sir," she added imploringly.

"All right," I said, laughing to reassure her. "I'll slip out like a mouse and return just as quietly—"

"Please come back before six," she said. I promised and went.

That evening I got back about five and saw the mother. I asked for Kätchen. The mother said, "I'll send her, Sir, but please let her go soon; he comes home from work soon after six."

Kätchen came and was more loving than before, though manifestly on the *qui vive,* listening for every sound. Before six, even, she kissed me and said she'd have to go and I took her to the door; there the kissing began again and lasted, I suppose, longer than we thought, for just as I opened the door that gave on the passage to her room, there was a man at the bottom of the short flight of stairs; he sprang up them as the girl ran into the door to the right leading to her apartment. The man came straight to me. He was about my height and sturdily built, plainly a man of forty-five at least, or fifty.

"You can leave this house tomorrow," he said in a low hoarse voice.

"Who are you to give me orders?" I asked.

"I'm the master here," he replied, "and I tell you, you had better go."

"My month's only beginning," I replied, "and I want the usual notice."

"If you don't go tomorrow," he said, "you'll be carried out—"

"You're a fool to threaten," I said. "To go soon would be to prove that I was afraid of you and I'm not."

"If you had more sense, you would be," he replied.

"Get out of my way," I retorted, "I'm going."

"You go," he said, "and don't come back."

As he didn't move I pushed him slightly. He at once seized my right arm and struck savagely at my face.

As a trained athlete, I had already weighed the possibilities; as he pulled my arm I went with it to destroy his balance. As he struck I threw my head aside and my left foot behind him. The next moment he over-balanced, and slipping back to recover himself, slipped on the stairs and went with a crash to the bottom and lay still.

At once the neighboring door opened and the mother and Kätchen rushed out. I had already sprung down and lifted the man; his nose was bleeding, but his head was not seriously hurt. He would be quit for a painful bruise and a headache, and so I informed the woman, who seemed scared to death. With her help, I carried him into his bedroom, and on the way saw the two younger daughters: Lisabeth, whom I knew slightly, an ordinary girl of thirteen or so, and Marie a pretty child of ten, who, to my surprise, stared while Kätchen wept.

That evening I got a letter from the mother, asking me to go, saying the

Father threatened to kill me, and she was frightened. "Pray, pray, go," she ended. "I don't want any money, dear Mr. Harris, and forgive me."

Next morning she came in with my breakfast. "He's gone to work," she said, "in a silent, black rage; he says if you don't go, he'll kill you. Please, dear Mr. Harris, do go. You'll easily get other rooms."

"I won't go a foot," I said, "and tell him if he tries to kill me, he'll get badly hurt. I thought I had taught him that." To my wonder she broke into a storm of tears.

"I'm the most unhappy creature in the world. I wish he'd kill me."

"Don't cry," I said, "of course, if you really want it I'll go, but—"

She seized my hand and kissed it, wetting it with tears. "I'll tell you everything," she said. "I owe it to you. I don't know how to begin. I loved my husband and at first was very happy with him. He has lots of good qualities. He works hard and he thinks of his home, but I don't know how to tell it. One day, when Kätchen was about twelve, she came to me and said her father kissed her funnily and since then—Oh, I can't tell you. He took her into my bed! Oh, it is dreadful! Fancy, in my bed. I know I can trust you not to tell anybody, but I am the most unhappy woman in all the world. My dear children, ruined by their father! Was ever anyone so unhappy! What am I to do? If I had told you at first, it might have made all the difference, but I couldn't bear to. But now forgive us and forget us. Oh, I am so—miserable."

I comforted her as best I could. I was horror stricken and filled with disgust for the man. Perhaps a point of envy sharpened my hatred of him. It ended by my saying, "I'll go within a week and I will write it so that you can show it to him, but I must get a place and I can't get one in a moment. In a week or so I'll be gone."

Strange, the fact that her father had used her killed my liking for Kätchen.

But Lisabeth more than filled her place. One morning Lisabeth came in with my coffee. "Oh, I'm glad you've come," I said. "What good wind blew *you* in?"

"They're all crying," she said. "Father's been raging; but I wouldn't care what he said."

"Suppose I ask you for a kiss," I said, smiling and holding out my hand, "would you be afraid to give it?"

"Not I," she cried, coming to my side at once and giving me not one kiss, but a dozen. "You see," she said, sitting on the edge of my bed, "Father has scared them, but he can't scare me and he knows it. He tried to kiss me the other day, but I wouldn't have it."

"Go to mother," I said, "or Kate, but leave me alone."

"There he is now!" she exclaimed, and at that moment the father's voice was heard in peremptory tone.

"Lisabeth, you're wanted."

"I'm not either," she replied cheekily; "you go away!" And to my astonishment he went off grumbling.

Lisabeth appealed to me and came to me in my new lodging, and I gave her dresses and trinkets as soon as I found that she was perfectly free of her father's influence. "I never liked him," she said to me once. "As soon as I saw how he made mother suffer, I was through with him. Kate can stand him, but I can't."

I found Lisabeth an engaging practical mistress. Although so young, she reckoned everything in cash. "I want a purse," she used to say, "and when I've ten thousand marks in it, I'll feel safer." And before she was fifteen she had the ten thousand marks. She was very well made, but had not nearly so pretty a face as her sister Kate; yet, in worldly wisdom, was a hundred years ahead of her.

For some reason or other, I didn't get a place in a week, but I told the woman I had seen one that would do and it would be free in two or three days. I hadn't seen Kätchen in the meantime. One afternoon I had been out, and I had given the order to send for my things in the morning to transfer them to my new lodging. At that time it was very difficult to get two rooms and a bathroom without getting a whole apartment, and I had been lucky to find a good one. In the evening I went out for a walk. I meant to go up Unter den Linden, through the great arch and into the Tiergarten: I went and had my walk and returned. Coming back under the arch, I noticed the light of one of the hotels shining into the darkness and looked away. For some reason or other, a few seconds later, when I was in the middle of the arch and complete darkness, I looked again and saw quite close to me a flash! For a moment I didn't know what it was and stopped. The next second I knew it was a big knife—like a carving knife—and I stepped to the right just in time, for the man rushed at me and stabbed. My side step was just right, and as his knife came down, I struck him under the jaw as hard as I could and he went down like a log. In a second I had picked up the knife and saw that the man was Kätchen's father. I was furious. His face was all distorted by his hatred and by my blow. His nose was bleeding and he looked a sorry sight, but the danger made me furious. I couldn't help it—I drew back and hit him as hard as ever I could, and down he went again. This time he lay still and I had to drag him by the legs out into the light. As he lay there, I kicked him two or three times and thought of calling the police. Thinking of his unhappy wife and children, I thought he had perhaps had punishment enough for once, so I lifted him up and sat him against the arch. In a few minutes he came to himself.

"You damn fool," I said, "you had better get home and behave better to your wife and children. It is lucky for you that I had given the order to leave your house, or I'd break every bone in your body. You murderous cur."

"You go," he muttered, "or I'll kill you, you damned Englishman."

"It's lucky for you," I said, "that I'm going to sleep somewhere else tonight, but the police ought to be notified about you."

He got up on his feet and was evidently pretty shaky. "I'm taking the knife," I said, "just as a memento."

"I sharpened it for you," said he, glaring at me.

As I went down Unter den Linden, it really seemed to me as if the man was mad. There was madness in his distorted face and in his growling voice. "His wife will have to patch up his eye, and his jaw will prevent his eating for a few days," I thought. But as I grew cooler, I suddenly noticed that I had taken the skin off the knuckles of both hands and they were smarting. What insanity! I could still see the woman's face and hear her voice: "I'm so unhappy! No one in the world is so miserable. To have my dear little children ruined by their father!"

In my experience, incest is infinitely commoner among the Germanic peoples than it is among the Latins or Slavs. It is curious that in spite of the poverty and the fact that in some homes large families have to live in one room, incest is almost unknown among the Celts. But then I am of the opinion that the Irish and Scotch and even the Welsh Celts are far more moral in the highest sense of the word than their English neighbors.

Several of my men correspondents in America and in England have asked me to say something about venereal diseases, especially to tell them whether syphilis is curable. I am going to tell elsewhere how I met Ehrlich* at the medical congress in London, I think, in 1913. He was the discoverer of salvarsan, or as he called it later "606." I was one of the few who could talk German to him, so we became real pals. Since his death a good deal of doubt has been cast on the efficacy of "606"; but the best knowledge of today justifies me in saying that diligently used and followed by treatment with mercury, it can cure syphilis; cure it so completely that there isn't a trace in the blood, and that even subsequent offspring are perfectly healthy.

Ehrlich, as I shall tell in my portrait of him, was one of the great benefactors of humanity.**

Gonorrhea is much more common and much more easily cured: a great deal of rest, and unlimited drinks of strong barley water, and no sign of wine, spirits or beer, should bring about a complete cure in a month, but during the month it is very distressing, very painful, very dirty, and there is always danger of worse developments if it isn't taken seriously.

One little story may find a place here. I remember a young friend of mine who had caught syphilis in New York and who showed me a loaded revolver with which he intended to kill the woman who had infected him. I laughed at him. "The poor girl may not even have known she was ill," I said. "Don't be a fool; take my advice and always blame yourself for the mishaps of life, and no one else."

---

* (1854–1915); co-winner of the Nobel prize for medicine in 1908.
** That "portrait" appears neither in this volume nor in *Contemporary Portraits*.

Chapter XIV

The Prosecution of *My Life*

Be still, be still, my soul; it is but for a season:
Let us endure an hour and see injustice done.*

IN THE SECOND VOLUME I promised that I would end this volume with an account of my life up to date, and so now I must tell what has befallen me in this past year, 1926.

I was astonished one day here in Nice to get a citation to appear before a Judge Bensa, to answer a charge of *"outrage aux bonnes moeurs"*—an outrage on good morals; and the Judge informed me that the outrage in question was the publication of the second volume of *My Life*.

"Why not the first volume?" I asked.

"Oh, because that was published in Germany; we have nothing to do with it; but this volume was printed in France, so we must take note of it."

"My crime, then," I said, "is that I wished to benefit French printers and to give them work; for if I had published the second volume in Germany or Italy, I should not have been molested."

He shrugged his shoulders. "Have you sold the book in France?" was the next question.

"It was 'privately printed,'" I said, "as you can see. I didn't anticipate any sale in France and therefore I did not trouble to get the book into the shops; but later, here and there, a book-seller whom I know has told me that he has been asked for a copy of *My Life* by Americans or Englishmen who wished to complete their sets of my books, and so I have given these book-sellers copies to sell, always on condition that they should not be exhibited in the windows or held for ordinary sale. The sale in France has therefore been very restricted: certainly in all, I have not sold fifty copies. It has never been *mise en vente* (exposed for sale)."

The Judge took note of this, but said it didn't matter whether I sold thirty, or three, or three thousand; it was the fact of the sale that was important. I bowed, of course, to this judicial reasoning.

* From A. E. Housman's *Be Still, My Soul, Be Still.*

At first my advocate, Maître Gassin, told me that the case would certainly not come before any court. It was ridiculous, he thought, to make the printing of a book in France a crime, when nothing was done with the book printed in Germany and brought into France by the thousands; but the second or third time I saw him, I found that he regarded the case much more seriously.

"We are not rich in France," he said, "and I felt they would never spend the two or three thousand francs in getting your book translated, but I have seen the authorities, and they tell me that the prosecution has been started from Paris, and the money for the translation of the book has been paid. You have got some enemy or enemies in Paris who are making their influence felt."

I had already obtained from M. Bensa, the judge, a note of the pages which were objected to in the second volume of *My Life:* some forty in all out of four hundred, and among these marked forty were three or four pages together. The moment I looked them out, I found that one of them was my description of English gormandizing at the Lord Mayor's banquets in the city of London, and another dealt with the conduct of Sir Robert Fowler, who was twice Lord Mayor, and his gluttony and disgusting behavior at Sir William Marriott's table when Lady Marriott had to leave the room.

Now this episode is merely revolting, and I had put it in simply because I thought it a duty to give as complete a record of my life as I could, and the habit of over-eating and over-drinking reigns in England all through the middle classes. I have told how Prince Edward put a stop to it in the best class by introducing the habit of going at once to coffee and cigarettes after dinner, instead of guzzling bottle after bottle of Burgundy or claret, which was the custom of the upper classes till he came.

Again I found that anything I had told of Prince Edward's liking for naughty stories and for witty limericks had also got me into trouble, and was marked down as offensive. Another passage especially objected to was the account of how Lord Randolph Churchill became infected with disease.

From these indications it seemed to me that the persecution came from the English Foreign Office; and this inference I have since found to be correct. The publicity given by the prosecution will certainly add to the sale of the book, which accordingly is now about to appear in several other European languages.

Yet the prosecution was annoying if only for the cost; and just because the accusation seemed ridiculous, I became anxious. I had once tasted prison through contempt of the English Judge Horridge by commenting on the conduct of a case which never came to trial, just because the whole thing was ridiculous. I was punished without a shadow of reason. Now I was to be punished again, just for telling some truths about England and Englishmen in a foreign country. The case, I am told, won't come on for some months, but I dread it most because of the unreason in the charge.

Here for example is a book, *La Garçonne* of Marguerite, which tells of love between men and boys, and girls with girls, yet this book has sold five hundred thousand copies in France, and the author has not been brought before any court except the court of the Legion of Honor. Verlaine, too, the great poet, has given to the world posthumously a book of poems adorned with the lewdest illustrations, and all singing the praise of unnatural vices.

Finally, I have before me a copy of a publisher's circular, issued expressly as from the *Libraire du Ministère des Affaires Etrangères,* with the sanction therefore of the Office of Foreign Affairs in Paris, wherein I find exposed for sale at low prices Le Marquis de Sade, *Gamiani, Les Mémoires de Suzon* in French, and *The Pearl* in English—all frankly pornographic works.

My offense is after all nothing but the description of the normal love of man for woman; and I am to be punished for twenty pages in 400 and for selling thirty or forty volumes in France, every one of which, I believe, has been sold to Englishmen or Americans. My crime is that I have given work to French printers rather than to German or Italian printers. Yet my advocate, Maître Gassin, tells me that the matter is serious and being pursued with fiendish earnestness.

One fact I must record here. As soon as news of my prosecution got into the press, all the French writers whom I know, notably Barbusse, Morand, Willy Bréal, Davray, De Richter, Maurevert, and others, wrote in my favor, expressing their contempt for such persecution.* Every French author of note appears to be on my side and all agree with the great phrase of Vauvenargues: *"Ce qui n'offense pas la société, n'est pas du ressort de la justice"* (That which does not offend society, has nothing to do with justice).

But no English or American writer has taken up the cudgels for me or written one word in my defense. Far from that, not a single English or American writer has even considered the book fairly or tried to see any merit in it, and while English journals have usually taken the indecency for admitted, American journals, such as the *New York World* and the *Nation,* have covered me with cheap insults. All this, of course, was to be expected. But I may be permitted to believe that the genial conduct of the French writers shows a higher level of understanding and a nobler humanity.

*Henri Barbusse (1873–1935). His novel, *Le Feu* (1916), which was about the first World War, won him the Prix Goncourt.

Paul Morand (1888–   ). He made his reputation with two novels, *Ouvert la Nuit* (1922) and *Fermé la Nuit* (1923).

Michel Jules Alfred Bréal (1832–1915), French philologist.

Henry D. Davray (1873–   ), French journalist; he translated Meredith, Wells, Bennett, and Conrad.

Jean Paul De Richter (1847–1937), art critic and historian.

George Maurevert, French journalist who was friendly to Harris to the end.

A previous experience substantiates this belief. I was in Paris when Zola published his *Nana,* which described the life of a courtesan in Paris. The book came as a shock to every reader in the city. Not only did it sell over fifty thousand copies in the first week, but the day after it appeared, everyone who counted had read it and could talk of nothing else.

"This is the limit" was the one remark that went uncontradicted. Not only was the book outspoken, but it was indubitably salacious and unspeakably suggestive and provocative. Serious people at once began to talk of prosecution. And with this in mind I hurried to call on Daudet, Dumas fils and others.

Daudet received me with his usual kindness.

"I regret the book," he said. "I am sorry that Zola wrote it; it will give French literature a worse name than it has already in Europe, and, really, the stigma will be deserved. Zola has gone too far this time. I have only glanced at the book, but there are pages in it that are more provocative than the youthful indiscretions of Mirabeau or Gustave Droz."*

"Then you would be in favor of prosecution?" I asked.

"Of course not," Daudet cried. "How can you imagine such a thing? Zola is a great writer. He must be allowed license that one would never accord to an ordinary penman. There will be no prosecution. We would all unite against that at once. No ordinary magistrate could sit in judgment on Emile Zola. But I am sorry he published the book. It can only damage his reputation."

"Yet everybody says that it will add greatly to his bank balance," I ventured.

Daudet held up his hands.

"Zola assuredly did not care for that aspect of it," he replied.

Dumas and the others agreed with Daudet, and *Nana* was left unpursued.

What will be the outcome of the prosecution of my book, I am unable even to guess. I can only abide the issue. Meanwhile I often catch myself reciting what Matthew Arnold called *My Last Word:*

Let the long contention cease,
Geese are swans and swans are geese;
Let them have it as they will
Thou are tired, best be still.

They out-talked thee, jeered thee, cursed thee,
Better men fared thus before thee
Fired their ringing shot and passed
Hotly charged, though broke at last.

* Honoré Gabriel, Marquis de Mirabeau (1749–91), the revolutionary; he wrote *Erotica biblion,* as well as *Ma Conversion* and *Essai sur lettres de cachet* during his imprisonment (1777–80).
Gustave Droz (1832–95), the novelist; author of *Monsieur, Madame, et Bébé* (1866), *Entre nous* (1867), *Les Étangs* (1876), and *L'Enfant* (1885).

> Charge once more and then be dumb;
> Let the victors when they come,
> When the forts of folly fall
> Find thy body by the wall.*

Let me now for a moment talk of old age again. I said in my second volume that old age had little to recommend it, but I find a good many authorities against me on the matter.

And many friends have reproached me for the sadness of the last chapter in my previous volume, which I wrote when I was about seventy. A dozen, at least, have written to me, asking me whether there were no consolations peculiar to old age. There may be many, but not for the man who after seventy still feels young. Fortenelle** at the age of ninety-five, was asked which were the twenty years of his life that he regretted the most; he replied that he regretted none of them, but that nevertheless the period he would wish to relive, the period in which he had been happiest, was from fifty-five to seventy-five. "At fifty-five," he said, "one's fortune is made; one's reputation established; one is well considered by the many, honored perhaps by the few. Moreover, one sees things as they are; most of one's passions are cooled and calmed; one has reached the goal of one's career; done what one could for society; and one has then fewer enemies, or perhaps one should say fewer envious people, because one's merit is generally recognized."

Buffon,† too, at seventy years of age, declares that the philosopher can only regard old age as a foolish prejudice; and he goes on to paint a picture of senile pleasures.

"Every day," he says, "that I get up in good health, have I not the full

*THE LAST WORD
Creep into thy narrow bed,
Creep, and let no more be said!
Vain thy onset! all stands fast.
Thou thyself must break at last.

Let the long contention cease!
Geese are swans, and swans are geese.
Let them have it how they will!
Thou art tired; best be still.

They out-talked thee, hissed thee, tore thee?
Better men fared thus before thee;
Fired their ringing shot and passed,
Hotly charged—and sank at last.

Charge once more, then, and be dumb!
Let the victors, when they come,
When the forts of folly fall,
Find thy body by the wall!
** (1657–1757), the French writer; he died in Paris at 100.
† (1707–88).

enjoyment of the day as much as ever I had? If I order my appetites, my desires, my hopes according to the dictates of wisdom and reason, am I not as happy as I ever could have been; and the thought of the past and its pleasures, which seem to give some regrets to old fools, affords me, on the contrary a joyful memory of charming pictures, precious recollections of pleasurable incidents; and these pictures and memories are free of taint and perfectly pure and bring to the soul only an agreeable emotion. The restlessness, the disappointments, the mistakes which accompany the pleasures of youth have all disappeared in age, and every regret should disappear with them, for what is regret, after all, but the last quiver of that foolish personal vanity which refuses to grow old."

There is a good deal of truth in all this, but not, as I say about myself, for the man who after seventy still feels young. To him, old age is like poverty; its blessings must be sought in their rarity. Bernard Shaw writes me that he is "a ruin and that all the pre-seventy in him is dead." All the pre-seventy and the pre-fifty are nearly as much alive in me as they were twenty years ago. The keenest regret I have is that I haven't money enough to go around the world for the third time and see it all again and tell of the changes which fifty years have shown in it. I should have thought some paper would be willing to pay for my account of this journey, but no one offers to, and my autobiography and my works of the last four or five years have brought me in less than any single year's work of my whole life.

I had no idea, when I determined to write my life frankly, that I should be punished as I have been for my outspokenness. I knew, of course, that most of the foolish and all the envious would declare that I was writing pornography in my old age; they would say "Harris was always dirty, you know; filthy minded." I knew the popular verdict beforehand and smiled at it, but I had no idea that this Anglo-Saxon condemnation would injure the sale of my other books as it has. I used to receive ten thousand dollars a year from them; the publication of the first volume of *My Life* cut this income down to less than a thousand dollars yearly, and injured in like degree the sale value of anything I may write. Moreover, this condemnation keeps me from returning to London or New York and beginning life again if I wanted to, utilizing my knowledge of the stock exchange to rebuild my fortune.

Thirty odd years ago my friend, Burton, published his *Arabian Nights,* which was freer, not to say viler, than anything I have ever written, and the books went through the post freely, and he made ten thousand pounds out of the publication. But now England has copied America in one of its worst acts: every one knows that if you send an obscene book through the post in America, you can be had up and punished as if you had published the book. But this execrable law, which allows a foolish official to judge the great innovators on the same level as the corrupters, has now been adopted by England. Twenty-five or thirty years ago she had better sense. Nevertheless, an English translation of Brantôme* is now being published and freely distributed in England; but the best English lawyers assure me that I could not hope for any leniency.

I remember in the prosecution of Mrs. Besant** and Bradlaugh the judge stated that if the book was a dear book, it was not to be condemned like a cheap book, which might fall into the hands of boys and girls. This sane English compromise now has been tossed aside and the public prosecutor can proceed against any one for sending an obscene or indecent book through the mails, just as in America, even if one put a price on it, as I do, that should prevent it falling into the hands of any except those who really want it. But now that aristocratic England has taken on the livery of democratic America, there is no room for the man who uses English as his mother tongue to warn or to guide his fellows frankly. "God's spies" are punished as if they were the devil's minions.

I don't think I have committed any violation even of these idiotic laws, but I am assured that I should find scant justice in America at the hands of the Justices Levys and Mayers; and just as little perhaps in London at the hands of the Horridges.

He who wishes to give a true record of his life is almost compelled to leave out the most interesting incidents of it. But some amusing ones, the brave soul may still record.

Heine has left on record how he was treated by the vile swarm of Suabian critics, but none of them ever attacked him as venomously as I have been attacked in America. I want to give some specimens of it. Here is an editorial article in the *Evening World* of New York, of August 23, 1926: it is headed:

THE CASE OF FRANK HARRIS

At the autumn assizes at Nice, Frank Harris, the writer, will face charges of offending public morals, and possible imprisonment. Many years ago, he was a figure of some importance in the literary life of London. Editor of an important periodical, he associated on terms of more or less intimacy with many of the most distinguished writers of England and France. In those days the only thing scandalous about him was his insufferable egotism. His connection with Oscar Wilde led to the writing of a biography of the dramatist which has much merit. In later life he has distinguished himself in the writing of entertaining character studies of literary and political celebrities, albeit he is charged with taking liberties with the truth.

Then, old, world-weary, broken in health, he wrote the first volume of an autobiography, published first in Germany, which was disgusting in its frankness and its crudity. The attempt to circulate this nauseating collection of dirty stories in America led to some arrests.

---

* Pierre Brantôme (1535–1614), a French soldier and courtier. He wrote racy memoirs, such as *Vies des dames illustres* and *Vies des dames gallantes*.

** Annie Besant (1847–1933); about 1870 she was associated with Bradlaugh and wrote a pamphlet with him which advocated birth control; republication of the pamphlet in 1876 resulted in a sentence of imprisonment for six months and a fine of £200, but the sentence was successfully appealed.

It appeared that the disgust of even his well-wishers taught him nothing, for his arrest in France follows the publication of the second volume. Always a sensualist, it is impossible to believe that he presented himself in undress from any motive other than a desire for money. Having put himself in the class of street-walkers, he is entitled to no sympathy. The Frank Harris of years ago died long ago, and it is his cadaver that has been writing recently. The odor proves it.

This editorial is a mere collection of slanderous lies: so far am I from being broken in health that I never enjoyed better health in my life, and in this very August walked over twenty miles one day without feeling even tired. I was never arrested in France—that is another invention of the *Evening World*. Before I began writing *My Life*, I knew that frank speech would not bring me in any money; but even "street-walkers" would have my sympathy: with Anatole France, I believe that they will be set above Queens in the Kingdom of Heaven. Instructed by the English Foreign Office, the French authorities found thirty pages to object to in four hundred and thirty—a slightly larger proportion than Whitman's; but hardly enough to make an honest man talk of a book as a "nauseating collection of dirty stories."

No decent journal in the world, except in New York, would have allowed an anonymous and cowardly slanderer to write such an editorial—a mere tissue of foul lies and fouler insults. Nor does this stand alone. The *Saturday Review of Literature*, the most widely circulated literary organ in the states, in its issue of February 13, 1926, gives more than a page to an outpouring of similar lies and abuse. And, worse still, Upton Sinclair, the author of *The Jungle*, which I have praised, wrote to me that "I think it is the vilest book I have ever laid eyes on: I think it is absolutely inexcusable . . . I regard the book as a poisonous one."

I put all this silly abuse on record just to comfort those of God's spies who come after me and who will no doubt be persecuted by the brainless and envious as I have been.

I have been asked what I mean by the term "God's Spies!"

Whoever will be one of "God's Spies," as Shakespeare called them, must spend years by himself in some solitude of desert or city, resolutely stripping himself of the time-garment of his own paltry ego, alone with the stars and night winds, giving himself to thoughts that torture, to a wrestling with the Angel that baffles and exhausts. But at length the travail of his soul is rewarded; suddenly, without warning, the Spirit that made the world uses him as a mouthpiece and speaks through him. In an ecstasy of humility and pride—"a reed shaken by the wind"—he receives the message. Years later, when he gives the gospel to the world, he finds that men mock and jeer at him, tell him he is crazy, or worse still, declare they know the fellow, and ascribe to him their own lusts and knaveries. No one believes him or will listen, and when he realizes his own loneliness, his heart turns to water, and he himself begins to doubt his inspiration. That is the lowest hell. Then, in his misery and despair, comes one man who accepts his message as authentic-true; one man who shows in the very words of his praise that he, too, has seen the Beatific Vision, has listened to the Divine voice. At once the prophet is saved: the sun irradiates his icy dungeon; the desert blossoms like a rose; his solitude sings with choirs invisible. Such a disciple is spoken of ever afterwards as the beloved and set apart and above all others.

Fortunately for me, I have found several such disciples: Esar Levine, Ben Rebkuhn, Raymond Thomson and [Einar] Lyngklip.* These young Americans came to my lectures in New York and offered me their services. For years now they have helped me in all the ways of affection, suffered even fines and imprisonment for me—and no man hath greater love than this! Esar Levine has helped me a great deal with this volume, for he knows all my writing better than I do. And now other Americans, Thomson and Lyngklip, come to me in the same sweet spirit. I think the world will soon recognize—for they are all still in the twenties—that the friendship of these men is to me a title of honor.

As I told at the end of the second volume of *My Life,* my chief pleasures in life are still those derived from literature and art and the intercourse with wise and loving friends. I get as much pleasure, too, from a good dinner, in spite of using strict moderation, as I ever did, and more I think than ever from a beautiful sunset or exquisite sky and mountain and sea effects; but most of all from my work, and from the resolute purpose to make each book better than the previous one at the cost of multitudinous revisions.

And now a word from my heart about my deepest belief. I have told how, as a schoolboy, just before taking my first Communion, I had come to doubt the accepted revealed religion; but still, in a vague way, I believed in a good, if somewhat ineffective, purpose in life, and for thirty years cherished a vague belief in a God and his goodness and in human progress. But between fifty and sixty when I first read Fabre** and came to realize the senseless cruelties that dominate the animal and insect world, I began to doubt, and I soon lost sight of any upward way in the horror-haunted chaos. Doubts soon took shape and meaning. A hundred organs are given to man for pain, and one for pleasure: he has thirty feet of intestine, all for suffering, where one would suffice; and worse still, pain is never in any relation to welfare, has in it no warning, even; one suffers more from a toothache than from a mortal wound. If there is a creator, he is malevolent, rather than kind.

I disliked the word "atheist," and felt with Huxley that "agnostic" was a truer description of my mental state: for if the idea of a personal God had altogether vanished from my consciousness, I still believed in a slow and

---

* Levine, a writer and anthologist resident in New York.

Rebkuhn, now a publisher of magazines in New York.

Thomson, died about 1940; he was once employed by Consolidated Edison of New York.

Lyngklip died in the 1940's; he left his collection of Harrisiana to the New York Public Library.

** Jean Henri Fabre (1823–1915), entomologist.

gradual unfolding of a higher and nobler social life for men on this earth. Again and again I came back to Goethe's word:

Uns zu verewigen
Sind wir ja da!*

Men at least should grow in goodness and loving-kindness, should put an end, not only to war and pestilence, but also to poverty, destitution and disease, and so create for themselves a Paradise on this earth, and turn the pilgrimage of life first into a Crusade where every cross should be wreathed with roses, and at length into a sacred struggle worth of God himself to put an end to all suffering and make of existence a hymn of highest achievement.

The truth is, man must be his own God in the highest sense and must create not only a Heaven for men but for insects and plants, too, for all life, especially the so-called lower forms of it—a triumphal chant of joy-crowned endeavor.

The trees, even the humblest plants, we know struggle upward to the light; surely they should be helped—all difficulties and disorders should be incentives to the divine shaping spirit of man.

Yet Whitman praised death, "beneficent death." "Hateful death!" I cry. I hate it, as Goethe hated it, at least for the choice and master spirits. Who will make good the loss? It is irreparable for me. Death!

I prefer Browning's word here to Whitman's; it's truer. Death he calls "The Arch-fear;"** I often think of it as an ocean; in the great flood another wave sinks and nothing is changed—except to the wave and the other waves near at hand!

With death before him, how any thinking man can believe in an omnipotent and beneficent God, I cannot imagine. I am not thinking now of cruelty, though it is the primary law of His creation, but simply of death that comes to all of us, no matter whether we have lived nobly or vilely. How easy it would have been for a benevolent deity to give a second life of youthful vigor to every man or woman who had lived in the main to the highest in him, and how such a reward would have quickened virtue and discouraged vice and made of man's life a sacred progress to all the heights. But as it is, death comes! And even before death, his dread heralds, decaying strength, failing faculties, loss of memory and of joy, the sunlight even drained of warmth. And we children of an hour quarrel and dispute and show greed and envy while the days shorten to the inevitable end. How could Whitman praise death!

But after all, what does death matter? It is hideous and terrible, if you will; but few can tell when the curtain will fall and the play for them be finished. And meanwhile one's work remains. A, B, and C look at it and

* To eternalize ourselves,
  That is our mission.
** From *Prospice:* Where he stands, the Arch Fear in a visible form,
  Yet the strong man must go.

shrug indifferent shoulders and the years pass and one seems forgotten. Suddenly, some one comes who is interested. "Strange," he says, "how did this work escape praise?" And he begins to praise it, and others follow him, wondering where this new teacher should be placed.

Sometimes, as in the case of Shakespeare, the recognition has to wait three hundred years. What matter? It was a century before anyone dreamed of placing Heine with Goethe: what do the years matter? Sooner or later we are judged by our peers and the judgment is unchangeable. I wait for my peers, welcoming them.

"He has written naughty passages," says one, and my friend replies, "so did Shakespeare in 'Hamlet' and with less provocation." "His life is the fullest ever lived," says my disciple, and they all realize that a supreme word has been spoken and that such a man is among the great forever.

Volume
V

Foreword

IN THE FOURTH VOLUME of *My Life* I have told how the French judicial authorities, though egged on by the British government, refused to prosecute me on account of the publication in France of my second volume. The Judge, M. Bensa, ordered a *non-lieu,* declaring that there was no ground for a prosecution.

As soon as the question of a prosecution was mooted, a dozen Frenchmen of importance in letters wrote me at once, protesting against the idea and declaring their intention to stand by me to any extent. One well known writer indeed offered to translate all the boldest passages and have them published in a great French review. This result seemed to increase the malice of the English government to fever heat. A little while later I got letters from friends in England, to whom I had sent copies of my books, telling me that they had been visited by police inspectors who produced photographed copies of my letters and copies of their replies, proving that they had received my books and demanding that these obscene books should be delivered over to the authorities at once or my friends would be prosecuted for possessing them. In this way they have not only killed the sale of *My Life* in England but all my other books as well.

Now all this is against law and surely in defiance of justice. What right has any English government to open private letters and photograph them and use them for such a purpose? But the present English government with Joynson Hicks (mediocrity again distinguished by a double-barrelled name) as the Minister, went further even than this. One of my friends replied to the police inspector that he had only received an expurgated copy of the book, which was the fact, but the police inspector told him that the whole book was obscene, and especially the passage about Lord Mayor Fowler.

In order to satisfy myself that the English government's prosecution was wholly political and not of morals, I sent a day or two afterwards to a London publisher for a copy of Brantôme translated literally from the French. The book came safely through the English post. The English government sees nothing reprehensible in Brantôme's lecherous descriptions, nothing either in Rabelais or Chaucer or Shakespeare, or Wycherley, but they object to have the bestiality of the Lord Mayors' Banquets of our days published to the world. And the English government will go to any length of illegality or iniquity in order to save its face and reputation of its officials.

The English government has not changed much in the last hundred years; the oligarchy is still all powerful and punishes its critics and enemies with more venom than Russian Tsardom.

The English believe to a certain extent in political liberty but real liberty of speech and thought is nowhere so detested as in England, where the conventional is adored. The other day I came across in my papers the story of Ernest Jones,* the poet and Chartist of the middle of the nineteenth century. He had written notable books both in prose and poetry and had won a considerable position in literary circles. I have already said somewhere or other that the English aristocracy regards a poet with much the same good humored contempt it has for an acrobat: it was thirty years after his death before Keat's masterwork could be republished. But anyone who dares to write against the English oligarchy or in favor of equality of rights before God and the law is regarded by the English ruling class as an enemy, to be suppressed at all costs.

In the revolutionary fervor of 1848 Jones spoke in favor of the people. At once he was tried and sentenced to two years imprisonment. He had already married the daughter of a Member of Parliament, but that only aggravated his offence in the eyes of the English rulers. One of my most valued possessions is the letter written in Jones' own hand to a friend, telling how he was treated in prison and afterwards. I quote from it now, for in almost every particular his persecution shows the same spiteful malevolence as has been shown to me. Under a date in 1855, Jones, after praising the press for its generous appreciation of his work, writes:

"About that time I became involved in the political excitement of 1848, and for a speech delivered in January of that year, was arrested, and imprisoned in Westminster Prison for two years and one week, in *solitary* confinement, on the *silent system* without books, pen, ink or paper for the first 19 months,— locked for *fourteen* days in a dark cell on *bread and water during the height of the cholera* in 1849,—not allowed during that terrible time to hear whether my wife and children were alive or dead!—allowed to exchange a letter with my wife only four times per year and to see her only four times per year for 20 minutes each time, in presence of a turnkey. When I once wrote to Sir George Grey,** I was not allowed to write that time to my wife" (Unequaled petty meanness!); "when I once saw Sir J. Walmesley, George Thompson and O'Connor,† I was not allowed that quarter to see my wife; when I had heard that she was dangerously ill, I was not allowed to hear how she progressed—and

* (1819–69); a fervent Chartist who refused a bequest of £2000 a year which stipulated that he leave that political reform organization.
** (1799–1882); then home secretary. He acted with great vigor during the Chartist disturbances.
† Feargus O'Connor (1794–1885); the Irish Chartist.

I myself was reduced to such a state of weakness, that I was obliged at one time to *drag* myself across the cell if I wanted to move across it. My day cell had unglazed windows all the winter thro'—my night cell a grating opening at once on the air, of one and half feet square! All this was proved in Parliament when Lord Dudley Stuart brought my case forward, and my petition and the evidence were printed by order of the House.

"*In prison,* I wrote (by stealth, on *smuggled paper*) "The New World", "The Painter of Florence", and a number of minor pieces. "The Painter of Florence" is the poem now published under the name of "The Cost of Glory". "The New World", having no ink, I chiefly *wrote with my blood.*

"But what a change with the press as soon as this time of imprisonment had expired!—(Everyone else was released 6 months before his time—I alone was kept in the full 2 years and a week.) The press would no longer notice my writings! I am a Barrister—my practice at once ceased."

I give this instance of the paltry malevolence and petty meanness of the English governing class three quarters of a century ago simply to show that in character it has not altered. It is not freedom of language in sex matters that it objects to; but criticism of its Lord Mayors and Ministers must be suppressed at all costs. And this English governing class, while the most powerful in any nation, is astoundingly illiterate and ignorant. In all the centuries it has never produced an artist or writer or thinker of the first class, not even a word of high appreciation of genius, much less a deed favoring it; it is in my opinion the vilest influence in the world to-day, lower even than the hundred per cent American who forgives Coolidge for making war on Nicaragua in defiance of the Constitution—that hundred per cent American who is, according to Bernard Shaw, "ninety-nine per cent village idiot." But the American idiot at least is kindly minded, ever disposed to forgiveness and generosity, while the English aristocrat is even more hidebound and bitter than the Prussian lieutenant. The other day the English Conservative Government tried to turn all workmen into slaves by making it criminal to engage in a general strike. As the American is now rather apt to be taken in by English pretences of affection, I have written this warning to put him on his guard against the most selfish oligarchy in the world.

In my own case it seemed to me evident that when I began to write the story of *My Life* good readers would readily understand and forgive, even if they did not approve my freedom of speech and the recital of amorous engagements. "Surely," I said to myself, "they will see that I wrote twenty volumes wholly conventional and did not begin *My Life* till I was sixty-five years of age, when the blood has cooled." Fair-minded Americans would say, I thought, "If Harris affronts criticism at long last by freedom of speech, it is plainly because he regards it as a duty. We shall do well to try to see things with his eyes, for there is no seductive heightening of sensation nor any attempt to exaggerate sexual pleasure in any description." But alas! almost without exception the so-called critics fell upon me with every species of insult. Really, I begin to think that the large public is utterly beneath consideration. Why should one do his best for such earthworms? But after all, one does it for oneself and for the future.

Before I complete this preface I must draw attention to one or two mistakes that I have made in the third installment of *My Life*.

After telling how the French men of letters stood by me and helped me, I said that no English or American writer had acted in the same way. I was clearly wrong; Dreiser came at once very nobly to my aid, in spite of the fact that he had previously resented some criticism of mine. Isaac Goldberg* too wrote in my favor at once, and Haldeman-Julius** published his defence. I was clearly mistaken in saying that no American had come to my help. I was astonished at my own blunder, so I went back to my notes and found that I had said that no English writer had come to my assistance, but my secretary had elaborated it into "English or American writer," and I had passed the amplification in proof without noticing it. How could such a thing happen, I may be asked. Well, the book was printed here in France, and French printers make such blunders that I always read their proof sheets for faults in language rather than in sense.

I owe this apology to the American friends, notably Dreiser, Mencken, Viereck,† Goldberg, Haldeman-Julius and others who stood by me fearlessly.

Another, though minor point. I have been criticized in England for saying that in spite of the dreadful growing power of Puritanism in his time, Shakespeare plainly showed again and again that if allowed, he would have written at least as freely as Chaucer. When challenged to prove this assertion, I gave the conversation in *Hamlet,* in which Prince Hamlet, talking to his maiden love Ophelia before the whole court and within earshot of his mother, uses smutty expressions again and again. It is impossible to believe that any prince, much less a pink of courtesy such as Hamlet, could have offended the elementary laws of decency in such a way unless the personal feeling of the poet had blinded him to probability and good manners.

In some previous part of *My Life* I have said that I would later write about sexuality as understood in India, China and Japan. A good many friends have written to me, asking why I did not keep this promise. I hope to make ample amends in this volume. But I should like just to say here that the sexuality in Japan is perhaps more marked than in any other country on earth. I have already given somewhere, I think in a volume of "Essays," a short account of Japanese morality as exemplified by ten or twelve of their commandments, which are merely laws of health; one of

---

* (1887–1938); he wrote reviews for Haldeman-Julius.

** Emanuel Haldeman-Julius (1889– ?); author, editor and publisher, particularly of *The Little Blue Books.* One small booklet, *Frank Harris and Haldeman-Julius* (1950), by Albert Mordell, explains Harris' debt to him.

† George Sylvester Viereck (1884–   ), German-born author and editor of several periodicals, including *American Monthly,* 1914–27. Like Harris, he was pro-German. Sentenced to prison in 1942 for not registering as an enemy agent, he was released in 1947.

them insists on the necessity of taking a hot bath every day. But here I can go deeper.

Everyone knows how flowers are esteemed in Japan. Whenever they put a picture or kakemono on the walls of a room, they don't regard the decoration as complete without the addition of flowers. To the Japanese flowers have not only a spiritual, but a sexual interest. The front of a leaf is regarded as male, while the reverse of it is considered feminine. In much the same way the forms of flowers are sexualized: buds are regarded as masculine while full blown flowers and especially those that have passed their prime are regarded as feminine. The Japanese will often marry buds and full blown flowers by putting them side by side in a way as self-revealing to them as any picture. Even the color of flowers has sexual significance, ay, even the direction of the twigs: those sprouting to the right are masculine while those to the left are feminine. And the difference between water plants and land flowers is also sexualized very distinctly.

No one, so far as I know, has yet noticed this tendency of the Japanese mind. The truth is the Japanese sexualize everything; plants and trees and even rocks and stones. A waterfall to them must be either masculine or feminine and the peculiarity that causes the distinction is universally recognized. I well remember one day a Japanese friend pointed to a waterfall, saying, "How splendid it is, what strength in the rush of water and courage in that leap into the unknown: splendid manliness!" When I laughed and asked for an explanation of his words, he pointed to a little fall quite near that slid down quietly, almost shaded by bushes. "There," he said, "you have the maiden. Some find it more beautiful, but I prefer the force and courage of the male."

It would be fair to say that everything in nature is sexualized by the Japanese. For example, the south is masculine while the north is feminine.

In my little "essay" on Japanese morals I said that their commandments were perhaps more valuable and certainly more reasonable than the so-called Jewish Commandments. This comparison made the London *Spectator* extremely angry: it even went so far as to say that all such writing should be boycotted. I wonder what the ordinary Englishman will say to my further probings into the sex-feeling of the Japanese. When I come to it, I shall have to tell how frankly the Japanese masters regard sex. Their greatest poets and greatest painters have written books and painted pictures which English Puritans would regard as worse than pornography, and could they know the work of Hokusai in its entirety, it would give them fits, or be completely neglected.

As usual, I feel called upon in this preliminary chapter to say something of my own health and habits. Last winter in my seventy-first year I caught a severe attack of influenza. I had worked very hard for over a year at the third installment of *My Life* which had run into two volumes, and in the same time I had brought together two volumes of *Portraits* and half finished a couple of novels. Run down through overwork and less than my usual amount of exercise in the open air, the virulent disease took me at a disadvantage.

After nearly a month of fever and sleeplessness I became convalescent, and realizing that my neglect of walking-exercise was the principal cause of my illness, I went to work at once, took good long walks morning and afternoon, varied by little sprints of running. In a week I was feeling my old self again, when one morning I noticed that the veins in my right leg were standing up in knots and that the leg was greatly swollen. I went at once to the doctor. As soon as he saw my leg he cried, "Phlebitis! You must stop walking and keep that leg up the greater part of the day."

"But my general health will suffer," I said; "I get indigestion when I don't take exercise."

"Better that," he said, "than lose your leg; it's serious; you have been playing with a loaded revolver. Stop walking for six months."

I followed the doctor's instructions, laid myself up for six months practically and took little exercise. The leg got better but soon my digestion began to trouble me and I found I had to eat less and less. Within two or three months, however, I came to fair general health. Naturally in this period of forced inaction I had been reading more than ever and suddenly my eyes began to trouble me again after fifteen years of peace. I went to the oculist, but he could only give me glasses for reading and for seeing at a distance, just the same as I had had twenty years before; but the blur in my eyes continued and it became painful to read for more than half a dozen hour a day. I have told in a previous volume how I cured my eyes twenty years ago by exercising them for a quarter of an hour in the morning and the same time at night. I exercised my eyes over the whole horizon instead of limiting them to a book, and after a month or so the exercise did me so much good that I was able to discard my glasses.

Now I began the same remedy, but it had not the same good effect. I found that I had to curtail my reading to half a dozen hours a day and the glasses did not help me in the smallest degree, though the oculist insisted that my eyes were first-rate. I must just look on the blur as a concomitant of old age.

At the same time I have been plagued by a worse disability. In this year I have lost a great part of my verbal memory. For the life of me I cannot remember names; I can recall verses of poetry and phrases, but I cannot remember who wrote them. This simply doubles the labor of writing. Apparently life is telling me that my working time is nearly over. The worst of it is that all this has come to me since the publication of *My Life* has brought me from comparative wealth to poverty; my income has shrunk and shrunk till now the two ends do not meet.

It is perhaps well that "the night cometh wherein no man can work."*

Yet my purpose holds and my resolve to complete my task at all costs: unexpected help came to me this last year through the extraordinary sale

* John, 9:4.

of the first two volumes of *My Life* when published in Germany; perhaps the next volumes will be equally successful; and it amuses me to know that it was the announcement of the British prosecution that gave me my chief advertisement. So the Joynson Hickses subserve better purposes than they have in view.

Who shall say where the influences in life end that make for good? We move about in a world not realized, but one piece of doggerel verse is often in my mind:

> In the life of strife and struggle
> Two things stand like stone:
> Kindness in another's trouble—
> Courage in your own.*

Help may come to the brave soul when least expected.

* From *Ye Wearie Wayfarer*, Fytte 8, by Adam Lindsay Gordon (1833–70):
> Life is mostly froth and bubble,
> Two things stand like stone, etc.

Chapter I

I AM NOT CONTENT with what I have written in *My Life:* I might have done it better. I am obsessed by the desire to make each chapter of this volume memorable by some new thought.

I think I have done this in my foreword. The curious sexuality of the Japanese has never before been told, so far as I know. And now I am minded to dignify this first chapter even more notably.

The other refers to 1900 and the following years and at once I am struck by the fact that with the new century a new era dawned. In 1890 Bismarck fell from power and soon a new Europe came into existence; in 1899 Gladstone died; in January Queen Victoria passed away after the longest reign in English history. Then came the end of the South African war and Lord Salisbury gave up his position as Prime Minister; and his chief lieutenants such as Hicks Beach retired with him. In 1902 Cecil Rhodes died, the last and perhaps the greatest of empire builders.

In 1900 Oscar Wilde passed away in Paris and the so-called Reinsurance Treaty between Russia and Germany was allowed to lapse by the German Kaiser. But it was the Jameson raid and the Kaiser's extraordinary letter to Krueger* in 1896, and later the South African war and the death of Cecil Rhodes, that made the greatest impression on me at this time, though my sale of *The Saturday Review* and my change of residence to Nice in order to devote myself to writing and especially to finishing *The Man Shakespeare* were of profound influence on my private life.

Now in 1927 as I take up pen to write about the beginning of the twentieth century, I feel that my time is short; I have passed the three score years and ten allotted to man and if possible I must do better than my best quickly.

Huxley says somewhere:

"The soul of the struggle is: have you done your work, given all there was in you to give, conveyed the message entrusted to you as perfectly as you could? If so death is merely the seal. One's work is there and awaits the final judgment."

* The Kaiser sent a telegram of encouragement to Krueger after the Jameson Raid.

With every word of this I agree.

The first thing that struck me in the new century was the flight of the Brazilian Santos-Dumont* in a dirigible air-ship in 1901. After innumerable attempts he solved the problem by circling over Paris and rounding the Eiffel tower.

In 1906 he made the first perfectly successful flight in an airplane driven by a motor at Bagatelle in the Bois de Boulogne. Of course between 1901 and 1906 we heard of the experiments and the exploits of the Wright brothers in America; but nothing can take away from Santos Dumont the honor of having been the first to wing the air in a machine-driven plane. It seemed to all of us an exploit lifting the spirit and worthy of the new century. But at the same time we were all disturbed by the insane action of the German Emperor. His disgraceful message to Krueger in 1896 was still in all minds and the well informed knew in 1898, in 1899 and again in 1905 that the puffed-up fool was on the point of sending ultimatums to London or threats of war and had again and again refused to accept England's offers of peace and amity. In 1911 we learned on good authority that his foreign secretary was ready to declare war on France.

The conquest of the air on the one hand and this criminal vaporing and threatening on the other were the chief characteristics of the first years of the new century.

Thinking of all that, I recalled one day a phrase of Lincoln that made an extraordinary impression on me. "It seems to me sometimes," he said "as if life were an obscene jest." This shocked me at once as one of the great phrases of the world. That Lincoln, a pious soul, if ever there was one, should have risen to this height of insight and perfection of phrase enthralled me. To the devout and kindly spirit, life in its purposeless cruelty must often seem to be a wretched jest. But Lincoln made of the end of his life a great hymn of courage and love: why should I not make of my last years a worthy verse or two?

> O fear not in a world like this
> And thou shalt know ere long
> Know how sublime a thing it is
> To suffer and be strong.

To the woman-soul life must often seem an obscene jest; but the spirit of man should turn the jest into a crusade and make of the "obscenity" which is only want of understanding, a consecration and sacred joy.

I began these [thoughts] with the great word of Lincoln for to me it cuts off the first half of my life up to forty-five or so from the remainder. Till about the beginning of the century I had tried to believe in God and some transcendant purpose in life, had much the same optimistic dream as Whitman cherished, but gradually learnt from Fabre and others that all such

* Alberto Santos-Dumont (1873–1932).

hopes are worse than vain. How can one imagine a soul or purpose in a world governed by mechanical laws, where cruelty is the rule and beauty and love mere accidents; a world where goodness is rare and sporadic and hate and evil all but universal; a world where well-being could be insured to all, yet where poverty and prostitution are the chief features; a world in fine where the most civilized people, while calling themselves Christian, wage a diabolic war for four years for no purpose at a cost of thirty million lives. Stupidity and malevolence are the twin rulers of human destiny and there is no hope for the future save in the soul of man, and even there high purpose is fitful and often dwarfed by animal necessities.

Possessed with this dreadful understanding, I dedicated myself to the writer's craft: I was making enough money to live with ease; the world was before me, I could travel all over it and study and enjoy myself without stint; yet I chose deliberately to concentrate myself on work and devote all my energies to a labor from which I could hope neither money nor honor. I knew that if I did the best in me, first-rate work, I should find but few readers: the better the work, the fewer; yet I was resolved to do all I knew, come what come might.

Before the beginning of the century I had sold *The Saturday Review* to a company headed by Lord Hardwicke,* and gone abroad to Nice to write my interpretation of Shakespeare. Perhaps the most intimate things I did not write—it was Wagner and the way he was hated in Munich as an old man that gave me the clue. I remember wishing to give a dinner in his honor at the Vierjahresseiten Hotel where I was a welcome guest. I told the manager what I wanted, but he astonished me by saying, "Surely you will take a private room."

"Private room," I repeated. "Why?"

He grinned. "Everybody knows Wagner's relation to the young King. Everyone knows they are lovers."

"You must be mad," I cried. "What! A young king chooses a man more than double his age?"

"Well," he said sulkily, "I can only say what everyone believes, and we know that the King is spending our money foolishly on this old communist and musician."

"You must be crazy," I said. But I found on all sides a dislike of Wagner that I could not understand. When walking with him in the street, people I knew used to pretend that they did not see me. And the fact of the universal contempt is not to be denied, [for] when the King proposed to build a theatre for him in Munich, the people showed such bitter opposition that the project had to be given up; and a little later I learned from Wagner himself that the King told him that he could not protect him even in his own capital; and so Wagner had to leave Munich!

---

* And financed by Rhodes, who was very uncomfortable about Harris' exposure of his part in the Boer War.

It was this strange dislike of this extraordinary genius that made me understand a fact or two in Shakespeare's life which are not generally appreciated. When living towards the end of his life in Stratford as a "retired country gentleman," according to English commentators, his chief friend was the village usurer, we are told, a person who was certainly not *persona grata* to the better classes. And when Shakespeare left his home and went to London for a visit, we are informed that his daughter used to get some clergyman to stay in his room. I feel convinced it was in some sort [a means] to atone for her father's evil reputation.

The man in those days who made his money by a theatre was to the growing mass of Puritans hardly better than the keeper of a brothel. It was the hatred shown to Wagner that first taught me how Shakespeare too must have suffered: nine men out of ten hate and vilify genius. And the higher the genius the worse he is apt to fare: Socrates had a painless death, but Jesus was crucified; the noblest has the worst fate.

I did not wish to emphasize this fact in my book on Shakespeare. I knew that I had already said enough to be disliked in England and I did not wish to worsen my chance of being read fairly. But now that I have been finally outlawed by the English authorities, I am free to tell the whole truth. Towards the end of his life in 1614 and 1615, Shakespeare was no doubt generally looked down on in his native village, and the better classes gave him the cold shoulder. Had he been distinguished as Wagner was by the favor of the monarch, he would have been welcomed with a great reception in Stratford, and even the Lucys would no doubt have forgotten their old grudge and have paid him marked honor. But towards the end Shakespeare had no sponsor in the privileged classes: Lord Pembroke, having injured him by stealing his love, Mary Fitton, had transferred his patronage to Ben Jonson, his rival. Small wonder that Shakespeare, left lonely in his old age, centered his affection on his youngest daughter and immortalized her sweetness and innocence in three plays: Perdita, the lost one; Marina, found at length; and Miranda, born to be admired. Poor Shakespeare! idealist to the end.

I made up my mind to paint a true portrait of Shakespeare and so do away for ever with the silly effigy of him throned as an English hero by generations of critics and commentators who could not see him if they would, having no clue in themselves to his nature.

I set to work then in the thorough fashion taught me in German universities: time and again, to make sure of a single trait in his character, I would read over again every word he had written. The book as it stands cost me nearly ten years of labor: I took it up in 1898 and didn't finish it till 1907. In these ten years I did much other work, stories and portraits, but Shakespeare was always in the forefront of my mind.

Let me give one little incident: on page 386 I had written that Shakespeare's "passion for Mary Fitton lasted some twelve years." One night

Professor Tyrrell* of Dublin, a dear friend of mine, having come to London to see me, insisted on discussing this. "I wonder where you got that 'dozen years,' he asked, "for in the sonnets Shakespeare himself speaks of his love as having lasted 'three years'."

"Yes," I replied, "but he wrote that sonnet in 1600; he met Mary Fitton first in 1597 but his passion continued from his pictures of her as Rosaline in 'Romeo and Juliet' and her portrait later as Rosaline in 'Love's Labour's Lost' down to his last portrait of her in Cleopatra, first published about 1608, for that was the year when Mary Fitton married and left London for good; and in that same year Shakespeare too left London and retired to Stratford. He pictures his 'dark gypsy' in Cleopatra even more cunningly than in the two Rosalines or in the 'Dark Lady' of the sonnets, though Plutarch had only told him that she was a 'fair Greek'."

"How well you know him," cried Tyrrell, "even Dowden admits that; but twelve years of passion is a long time!"

"Mary Fitton," I said, "was sent away from Court by Queen Elizabeth about 1600 or so; she returned in 1605 and stayed till 1608. In those five years of her absence from London Shakespeare wrote all his great tragedies."

When we separated for the night I felt sure that Shakespeare somewhere or other had alluded to those twelve years of his passion, so I took up his last plays and in an hour found the unmistakable allusion in *The Tempest*. Ariel I had always represented to myself as "the shaping spirit of his imagination," but Sycorax to me was nothing but a witch, yet I came upon the phrase wholly unexpected that Sycorax imprisoned Ariel for "a dozen years" because Ariel was

> a spirit too delicate
> To act her earthy and abhorr'd Commands—**

Shakespeare's soul rebelling against passion's thralldom.

It is only an indication, if you will, but all the while in *The Tempest* this "twelve years" recurs, during which Shakespeare's beloved spirit Ariel was subject to the "earthy commands" of the foul witch without rhyme or reason.

Next morning I showed Tyrrell the passage and he agreed with me as to its significance: Shakespeare's love lasted from 1597 to 1608.

After my Shakespeare book was finished I found that Arnold Bennett was praising my earlier work beyond measure in London under a *nom de plume*. I went across to Paris and called on him in Fontainebleau to thank him. "Why don't you write more?" he asked; so I told him of my book on Shakespeare and that nobody wanted to publish it. He wished to see it so I sent him a copy. He answered me by writing that "unless the professors

* Robert Yelverton Tyrrell (1844–1914), classical scholar, co-editor of a commentary on the *Correspondence of Cicero* (7 vols., 1879–1900).
** *The Tempest*, Act I, scene 2.

can point out blunders that I don't see, it's the best work that has ever been done on Shakespeare, and I can get it published at once."

This he did: Shaw praised the book whole-heartedly, Middleton Murry* too, and others of the best, but I never made the price of printing out of the book.

Many years before, I had discovered Nice and thought it not only the best climate in Europe, but altogether a charming place of abode. The best class of English and Americans frequent Nice and all the French writers too of the best come there in the winter, the intellectual heads of the world. The surrounding country is astonishingly beautiful, so I made up my mind to settle in Nice and go on with my writing. This I did and in the next ten years I wrote three or four volumes of short stories and several volumes of *Portraits*—all the while enjoying a sunlit and carefree life, going to London for months at a time to edit *Vanity Fair*** and other magazines: always however, returning to my beloved Nice for the winter which there had no terrors for me. I never had bronchitis, my old ailment, in Nice or indeed any other disease, and could work there ten hours a day without undue fatigue.

Some may wonder why I left Nice time and again to take up journalism in London. First of all, the pleasant easy-going life in Nice didn't give me the stuff for new stories or portraits like the stirring life in London; then too the extraordinary conduct of the Kaiser kept me on tenterhooks. His letter to Krueger had alienated English feeling towards him and his later actions tended still further to exasperate the proudest race on earth.

From the dismissal of Bismarck in 1890 till the World War in 1914, the chief figure in Europe was Kaiser Wilhelm the Second. I have already told of meeting him with Edward, Prince of Wales, and of how astonished I was by his rude authoritativeness.

Whoever wants to realize all the tragedy of the World War has only to read the book of Emil Ludwig† entitled *Kaiser Wilhelm II*. It is not a great biography but it is a most damning indictment. Ludwig shows that the Emperor really thought he could make himself the protector of Krueger and the Transvaal even at the cost of war with England. He did not see that he could not have landed a single German soldier in the Transvaal against the will of the English. When he began building his battle-fleet avowedly to match the English, he did not see that the English would be forced to keep the upper-hand in sea power; and if they left anything to chance, they would certainly be supported in the last resort by the enormous power and wealth of the United States.

For years he built upon the support of Russia and the personal friend-

---

* (1889–1957); writer and critic, husband of Katherine Mansfield.
** 1907–10. Harris edited *The Candid Friend* (a weekly), 1901–02; the *Automobile Review*, the *Motorist and Traveler*, and a revived *Candid Friend*, 1905–06; *Hearth and Home* (a weekly), 1911–12; *Modern Society* (a weekly), 1913–14; and in the U.S., *Pearson's*, 1916–22.
† (1861–1948).

ship of the Tsar "Nicky," though Bülow* convinced him that Russia had entered into a close alliance with France.

In all history we have no record of so brainless a ruler. And yet Kaiser Wilhelm had a certain mental intelligence and charm of intercourse. He was by nature an actor, greedy of popular applause. I think of the charming letter he wrote to his grandmother Queen Victoria when he was forty years of age:

How incredible it must seem to you that the tiny weeny little brat you so often had in your arms, and dear Grandpapa swung about in his napkin, has now reached the forties, just the half of your prosperous successful life. . . . It is to be hoped you are not ill-pleased with your queer and impetuous colleague.

And then think of his defiance:

When Metternich frankly declared in July 1908 that the English Ministers were all for peace and only wanted a reciprocal diminution in the Navy Estimates, the Emperor was infuriated and wrote in the margin: "A veiled threat! We will suffer no dictation! Ambassador has exceeded his instructions!" Further: "It must be made clear to him that an arrangement with England at the expense of the fleet is no desire of mine. It is a piece of boundless impudence, a mortal insult to the German people and their Emperor: it must be imperatively and finally discountenanced. . . . The Law will be carried out to the last fraction; whether Britain likes it or not is nothing to us: If they want war, let them begin it—we are not afraid! . . . I must beg that the Ambassador will henceforth take no notice whatever of this kind of vapouring!"

"Thus the Emperor having taken in the Reichstag so that the dogs would have to pay" assumed the pose of the All-Highest!

Those who have read this book of Ludwig on the Kaiser will have to admit that Wilhelm was the chief cause of the World War.

One curious fact should be recorded here. Ludwig traces his growth in conceit in a marvelous way: very early Ballin** wrote about Bülow: "Bülow is utterly ruining the Emperor; with his perpetual adulation, he is making him overestimate himself beyond all reason."

And the tide of flattery mounted steadily: in 1912 Lamprecht,† Germany's leading historian wrote of the Kaiser: "His is a personality of primitive potency, of irresistible authority, for which . . . the whole domain of emotion and experience is perpetually opened anew, as for the soul of a creative artist . . . Self-reliance, fixity of purpose, ever directed to the loftiest aims—those are the distinguishing marks of the Imperial personality."

And the Kaiser sucked it all in for Gospel; he wrote: "My subjects

---

* Prince Bernhard Heinrich von Bülow (1849–1929); German Chancellor 1900–1909.
** Albert Ballin (1857–1918); head of the Hamburg-Amerika line and a close adviser of the Kaiser.
† Karl Gotthard Lamprecht (1856–1915).

should always do what I tell them; but they will think for themselves and that's what makes all the trouble."

Again and again too Ludwig gives proof of the Kaiser's cowardice: he calls it "poltroonery," but worst of all was his instability and his curious belief in the divine rights of monarchs. Really, it seems to one reading this long exposure as if a King had to be specially designed by the Almighty in order to insure Germany's defeat in the World War.

The Kaiser made the navy which brought him the enmity of England, [but] when Tirpitz* in December, 1914 wanted to use it to blockade England, the Kaiser would not allow it, though the English Admiral, Sir Percy Scott,** admitted afterwards that had the German fleet been used then as Tirpitz wanted, "England would have been forced to sue for peace in a month to avoid famine."

The Kaiser not only provoked the war, but took care so to wage it that he must lose it. The war had altered England's position too; her insularity was no longer a protection, and though she did not seem to realize it, she had lost her pride of place to the United States, both as a world power and in business. And yet this was the country that, thanks to Sir Austin Chamberlain† in 1927, refused to diminish the number of her cruisers and so spurred the American government on to increase the United States Navy, as if in immediate fear of war.

Of course, the first and most necessary reform of our time is to do away with armaments altogether, for it is the armaments that bring about the wars. The United States, confident in its unique strength and impregnable position, should have been the first to inaugurate the new policy; but their politicians are mere children. England, too, should have taken up the duty, but instead spends more on her armaments today than she did before the World War, and so the vile and insane competition goes on. If we did away with armaments, we could put an end also to poverty. The cost of the World War was more than enough to have abolished all poverty in Europe for a hundred years.

In less than a century, the average length of human life has been increased over ten years and perfect health is now as common at fifty as it used to be at thirty. From day to day, life is growing more wonderful and more enjoyable. Here and there a seer or prophet has appeared who proves that the twin evils of our civilization—poverty and prostitution—could easily be conquered and life changed to a paradise. Fancy! Already one can sit in one's own room in Paris or London or New York and listen to the opera in any capital, and soon we shall not only hear the voices but at the

* (1849–1930); German admiral.
** (1853–1924).
† (1863–1937); a son of Joseph Chamberlain and half-brother to Neville Chamberlain; foreign secretary 1924–29. He shared the Nobel Peace Prize in 1924 (with Charles G. Dawes) for negotiating the Locarno Pact.

same time see the singers. We have annihilated distance, given ourselves ears and eyes to enjoy all the best in the world.

I have been asked to give my mature views on religious subjects. One friend asks, "Can you or any sane man believe in God or Providence?"

In view of almost universal pain and suffering with extinction at the end of our life, it seems to me impossible to believe in the goodness of any God. By "God" indeed we are beginning to note a life-force that comes to highest consciousness in the best men. If we mean by a belief in "Providence" the strong conviction that throughout all time an unbroken order has reigned in the universe, I cherish the belief; but to me it does not altogether exclude chance. Providence to me is an anthropomorphic rendering of the faith in evolution. It is true, I think, that one can hardly find a trace of a moral purpose in nature—*that* is a product of man's intelligence and does him the greatest credit. But it too has been evolved according to law.

The hope of the world is in creative evolution; but when will the powerful personalities begin to act in concert and play the part of gods in developing the Kingdom of Man? When shall we begin deliberately to remodel life? Who will be the great-hearted leader into the Promised Land? The age is ripe for a new departure. When we have put an end to war and poverty, the next step must be to abolish prisons and found in their place hospitals with doctors and nurses as the only jailors. For theft and murder and indeed all wrong-doing come from a diseased mentality and should be treated as a malady with patient loving-kindness.

Chapter II

IT WAS MY INTENTION to fill this chapter with a full-length "Portrait" of Cecil Rhodes as a contrast in political wisdom to the almost unique stupidity of the German Kaiser. But on riper thought that is not needed: it will be enough, I think, to relieve out one or two points and so contrast the methods and thoughts of an empire builder with the ways of an empire destroyer.

As early as 1887 at the Colonial Conference in London, Rhodes had outlined the true colonial policy of England in the future. There was no snobbishness in him and he saw that the despotism of the aristocratic class was out of keeping with modern ideas. He told me once that if there had been any brains in English rulers, the seat of government would have been settled for five years in Washington and then five years in London. To him "The British Constitution" was an absurd anachronism and should be remodelled on the lines of the American Union with federal self-governing colonies as the constituent states.

Rhodes had lots of faults but there was greatness in him, and in the main he seemed to gravitate to what was right. He made dreadful mistakes: he could not believe that Krueger would fight and here he sinned against the light for he was the only man in South Africa of any position who held that view. He believed too that the English would beat the Boers easily and again he found himself mistaken. But he was the ablest exponent of the true imperialism.

At the beginning of the century when the war was practically over, he addressed a meeting of the South African League in Cape Town and his words deserve to be remembered.

The Dutch are not beaten; what is beaten is Kruegerism, a corrupt and evil government, no more Dutch in essence than English. No! The Dutch are as vigorous and unconquered today as they have ever been; the country is still as much theirs as it is yours, and you will have to live and work with them hereafter as in the past. Remember that when you go back to your homes in the towns or in the up-country farms and villages: let there be no vaunting words, no vulgar triumph over your Dutch neighbours; make them feel that the bitterness is past and that the need of co-operation is greater than ever; teach your children to remember when they go to their village school that the little Dutch boys and girls they find sitting on the same benches with them are as much part of the South African nation as they are themselves, and that as they learn the same lessons together now, so hereafter they must work together as comrades for a common object—the good of South Africa.

In the three or four years of the war he had changed physically to an astonishing extent: he had become puffy-faced and bloated, but his high purposes held. His first will had been made when he was a youth of 24. In his final will of 1899 he published his resolve to found a great educational scheme to apply to all the English-speaking portions of the world. He gave scholarships to young Americans, Germans and others to enable them to study in Oxford.

It is not time yet to judge of the full effect of these "Rhodes scholarships," but that they have done good is perfectly certain.

Curiously enough, he founded his ideas of the scholar after the provisions in All Souls college in Oxford where it speaks of *bene natus, bene vestitus et mediocriter doctus.* Rhodes did not know enough Latin to write the phrase correctly: he wrote "*moderate doctus.*"

His private life no one knew much about. He had a secretary once who told me stories of his erotic tendencies, worthy of Oscar Wilde; but I never believed in them whole-heartedly. Rhodes always seemed to me to be lacking in virility; political ideas engrossed his attention, when really good erotic tales scarcely induced him to listen. And in Cape Town, where he was well known, his reputation in this respect was never even assailed.

The end of his life was tragic: he had drunk too much for years, eaten too much too and the heart began to give way. The Princess Radziwill* had been connected with him in some way and had forged his name to a number of bills of exchange. He had to go to Cape Town to defend himself. He gave his evidence practically on his death bed, but his last home was chosen for him carefully by Dr. Jameson, who brought him to a little cottage at Muizesberg near the sea shore, where he could look out over the great ocean and get the cool breezes. They rigged up a sort of cable over his bed and here he used to hang when his heart fluttered and the breathing became difficult. His old friends all wrote to him affectionately. Hofmeyr was the first to send him a message of reconciliation and daily cables came from friends in London.

Dying, Rhodes reached his true height. "Everything in the world is too short:" he said one day, "life and fame and achievements, everything is too short," and just before his death on March 26th, 1902, he was heard to say, "So little done, so much to do," which might well be his epitaph.

I feel that I ought to tell something about Rhodes's greatest rival Paul Krueger, the President of the Transvaal, though in statecraft he was no

---

* Princess Catherine Radziwill (1854–1941), a Russian who used the pseudonym, Count Paul Vàssili, for her writing, which included *Behind the Veil of the Russian Court, Confessions of the Czarina,* and *The Taint of the Romanovs.*

match for Rhodes. It was said that when a young man he was the greatest athlete in the country. He was just six feet in height, and was, it was said, an extraordinary runner, and possessed besides of extraordinary strength.

It was Sir James Sivewright who told me that on one occasion Krueger ran a foot-race against the pick of Kaffir braves. There were large prizes of good cattle. It was a long day's run across country past certain well known landmarks—amongst others his own father's house. Young Krueger soon distanced all his pursuers, and when he reached his father's house he was so far ahead that he went in and had some coffee. His father, however, was so angry with him for running across country without his rifle that he very nearly gave his son a flogging. But he made the boy take a light rifle with him when he left to finish his race.

On sped young Krueger, the Kaffir braves toiling after him as well as they could. They threw away their impediments as their muscles weakened; their path became strewn with shields, spears, clubs, and even the bangles they wore on their legs and arms. But in spite of it all, Paul Krueger kept far ahead of them.

His speed on foot was so extraordinary that it was commonly said that he could outrun a horse, and I believe that on one occasion he did in a long day; but in time the myth faculty came into play and a long day was altered to half a mile, and it was usually said that Krueger ran faster than a horse can gallop for half a mile, which, of course, was utterly impossible. But in twelve hours he did, I believe, surpass a horse.

Another story equally strange was told me. Krueger had been chasing buffalo and his horse had brought him close up to his victim. Suddenly the huge beast put his foot into a hole and fell head over heels into a swamp. Krueger was on top of it in a moment, horse, rider and buffalo all rolling pell-mell in the same soft ground. Krueger was the first to collect his wits. He sprang at the head of the buffalo, seized both its horns in his hands, and while the beast lay upon its side, twisted its neck so as to force its nose under water; and thus, after a struggle, Krueger killed the buffalo, drowning it by sheer strength. I had heard this story already in Cape Town, but would not believe it until I had the President's corroboration of this extraordinary feat.

It was the same Sivewright, the Minister of Public Works in the Cape Colony, who told me that he once called upon Krueger with a certain English duke, who was by no means conceited, but was somewhat deficient in diplomacy. The conversation, as I recall it, ran about as follows. Of course it was conducted by means of an interpreter.

Duke: "Tell the President that I am the Duke—— and have come to pay my respects to him."

Krueger gave a grunt signifying welcome.

Duke, after a long pause: "Tell him that I am a member of the English Parliament."

Krueger gave another grunt, puffing his pipe.

Duke, after a still longer pause: "And—you might tell him that I am—er—a member of the House of Lords—a Lord—you know."

Krueger puffed as before and nodded his head, with another grunt. Then, turning, [he] said gruffly, "Tell the Englishman that I was a cattle-herder."

There was no snobbishness in Krueger, but great obstinacy and he was as combative as a bull-terrier. I told him that he had better give in to Chamberlain and give the Englishman the pride of a victory in words. "Or else," I said, "you may be sure there will be war, which will help no one."

Krueger said, "You may be right, but the issue is in the hands of God. I can only do what I regard as right, and the issue is not so certain as you think. We Boers are hard to beat." He afterwards sent for me, saying that I was the only Englishman he had met who told him the truth. It would have been easy for Chamberlain to manage Krueger, as it was easy for Krueger to placate Chamberlain, but, alas! They preferred to fight, and I cannot but admit that the chief wrong was Chamberlain's. The consciousness of power leads usually to provocative bullying. The struggle cost poor Krueger his life.

Some months later than Rhodes, in this same year 1902, a greater man, Emile Zola, died in Paris. He and his wife were discovered one morning asphyxiated in their bed—a mere accident putting an end to a very laborious, brave and noble life. I knew Zola fairly well, [but] not nearly so intimately as I knew Rhodes; but he was much more articulate and lived habitually on a higher level of thought than the South African statesman. For example, I remember him saying once, "*L'homme de génie n'a jamais d'esprit,*" which is perhaps a little too sweeping a generalization, but certainly discovers a truth which is not frequently present, even to good minds. Its true explanation is to be found in a saying of Lincoln: "Wit laughs *at* everybody, humour laughs *with* everybody."

I remember asking Zola once about his beginnings. He told me how he had worked to get his Bachelor of Arts degree, had spent dozens of hours on Latin and Greek and gone into the examination with some hope—only to find himself rejected for his weakness in French! Zola began his literary career with poetry, but it did not catch on; then he tried stories, *Contes à Ninon,* I believe, but they did not sell. Even after he had outlined the *Rougon-Macquart* series he told a friend, "We'll never be popular." This when he was thirty; before he was forty, he was a "best-seller," not only in France, but internationally.

When Zola paid his first visit to London, I went about with him once or twice, and after practically his first walk he began to praise London: "A wonderful city, the most entrancing capital in the world because the quietest." I had to recognize the truth of the remark, yet I had never heard it mentioned before. But think of it and you'll admit the profound though obvious truth that London is not more memorable for fogs and rain than for its strange quietude.

Zola had a fine mind. Even in Paris he was condemned for his freedom of speech and his obsession with matters of sex, but those who wrote like this seem to have forgotten his early works such as *Le Rêve* and *La Faute de l'Abbé Mouret,* in which he showed himself to be purely a romance writer, an idealist, and not a realist at all. But his so-called realistic books such as *Nana, L'Assommoir* and *La Terre* would also be easy to defend: he wanted to give a true picture of life as he saw it, and he has certainly done so. The fault is that he has given us no portrait of the reformer or of any leader of men, but the work he did was good work and well done.

I have always been appalled by the misjudgments in life. A friend has just reminded me that Matthew Arnold, the best of English critics, writing on Wordsworth shortly before his death, declared that most probably Byron and Wordsworth would finally come to be regarded as the masters of English poetry at the beginning of the twentieth century. What, not Keats, or Shelley, but Byron and Wordsworth: Byron who, I used to say, never wrote a line of poetry in his life and Wordsworth certainly could not carry Byron into the Holy of Holies. It is not only in England and America that such gross misjudgments are possible; in all countries one notices misvaluations, due for the most part to patriotic peculiarities.

The other day I came across the statement by a Russian of talent that "Tolstoi was of course the greatest Russian writer, but Dostoievsky was the most peculiarly Russian and would always be the most esteemed." Nothing said of Turgenief who is the greatest of all the Russians and the only master-artist of them all. I would rather have written *Fathers and Sons* than all Dostoievsky.

In the mid-eighties in London I knew and liked Andrew Lang. A Scot, he had won high honors at Oxford and had everything in his favor: he was rather tall, good-looking and of pleasant frank address; a good writer too, and his contributions were widely read; finally, he became a Member of the Royal Academy. When I was appointed editor of the *Fortnightly Review,* I asked Lang to lunch and had a long talk. He adjured me to get two men at once on my staff, Robert Louis Stevenson, "a man of undoubted genius," he called him, and Rider Haggard, "the best story-teller in English." I was flabbergasted, but when he insisted I told him I was more interested in a word of Swinburne on poetry than in all R.L.S. would or could write in a month; and as for Rider Haggard, well, in the words of a satirist who came later, I should be glad

> When the Rudyards cease from Kipling
> And the Haggards Ride no more.*

Whenever I'm tired with ordinary life and ordinary ideas, I always turn or try to turn to the charm of poetry or high thoughts in prose. Suddenly

---

* Last two lines of *To R. K.,* an amusing poem by James Kenneth Stephen (1859–92).

now there come to me some verses which please me infinitely, but for the life of me I can't recall who wrote them or where they come from:

> And I, who with expectant eyes
> Have fared across the star-lit foam,
> See through my dreams a new Sun rise
> To conquer unachieved skies,
> And bring the dreamer home.*

That "unachieved skies" is a masterpiece of singing, and of course my dear friend Richard Middleton was the poet.

In my first volume of *Portraits* I wrote of both him and Davidson and blamed the English Government and the English people for letting such singers starve while ennobling mediocrities and millionaires and wasting a thousand million sterling on the idiotic South African War. A little while later I got a couple of anonymous letters asking me why I myself did nothing for the poets whose value to humanity I seemed to appreciate so highly? I thank my stars I am able to take up the glove thus thrown down to me. Let me deal first with the case of Davidson, as he was prior in the matter of time. I had just discovered how hard up he was, and had offered him money which his pride made it hard for him to accept. Worrying over the matter, I went to the Savoy Hotel to lunch, and I had hardly made myself comfortable when Mr. Asquith and a friend came in and took seats at a table some fifteen yards away. "There's my chance," I thought, "why should not Asquith give Davidson a pension and so help him really?" Half an hour afterwards, his friend went out leaving Asquith alone.

At once I took my courage in both hands and went over and spoke to him.

"I have a strange request to make to you," I said. "There's a real poet half starving in London and I think you ought to put him on the pension list. He is too proud to take money from me, but you could make him prouder by helping him; he has children too and deserves help: his name is John Davidson."

"I never heard of him," said Mr. Asquith.

"Let me quote you a verse or two of his," I cried, and forthwith recited the verses:

> My feet are heavy now, but on I go,
> My head erect beneath the tragic years.
> The way is steep, but I would have it so;
> And dusty, but I lay the dust with tears,
> Though none can see me weep: alone I climb—
> The rugged path that leads me out of time—
> Out of time and out of all,
> Singing yet in sun and rain,
> "Heel and toe from dawn to dusk,
> Round the world and home again."

* From *The New Dawn* by Middleton (1882–1911).

"Very fine indeed," cried Mr. Asquith with immediate appreciation, "very fine and inspiring."

"He has done great things," I cried, "things certain to live in English literature." And I quoted another verse:

> Farewell the hope that mocked, farewell despair
> That went before me still and made the pace;
> The earth is full of graves, and mine was there
> Before my life began, my resting place;
> And I shall seek it out and with the dead
> Lie down forever, all my sayings said;
> Deeds all done, and songs all sung,
> While others chant in sun and rain,
> "Heel and toe from dawn to dusk,
> Round the world, and home again!"*

"Give me his name and address," said Mr. Asquith, "and I will see what can be done."

Naturally the same day I sent the Prime Minister a short sketch of Davidson's life and a volume of his poems, with some of the best marked.

A little later Davidson's name appeared on the pension list for one hundred pounds a year.

I mention the matter here chiefly in honor of Mr. Asquith. It is through ignorance that the best in England is left unrewarded: no one could have been quicker than Mr. Asquith to appreciate poetic genius, no one more eager to reward it.

But the help came late and was insufficient in amount to save Davidson. Fancy, twelve hundred pounds a year is the whole sum set apart yearly by Great Britain to assist poets and artists and their dependents: twelve thousand a year or one hundred and twenty thousand would not be too much to pay to lift genius above misery.

I have told the story of Davidson here, for when he killed himself a little later, his despair put me on my guard; and when a year or so afterwards I came to realize Middleton's straitened circumstances and his curious fatalism, I was determined to save him from a similar fate. I gave him work on *Vanity Fair* and paid him largely besides for his contributions, whether in prose or poetry, though he always led me to believe that his people were well off and that he had no immediate need of money. But I was twenty or twenty-five years older than Middleton, and it is usually only men of the same generation who are completely frank with each other. Middleton did not confide in me about his illness—probably he was ashamed to tell to an older man what was the result of youthful folly—but he did confess to me once that he wanted to leave England and do serious poetic work.

At once I told him I had a little place in Nice where he could go and

---

* The last stanzas of "The Last Journey," from *The Testament of John Davidson*, quite accurately quoted.

spend the winter in the most perfect surroundings. "Perpetual sunshine," I said, "and rare loveliness of mountain and sea, and it will cost you nothing; go there and do your best, and we will all be proud of the result."

He thanked me warmly and said he would think it over. A few days later when I again praised Nice, he confided to me that he had not the money for the journey. I gave him twenty pounds and begged him to go at once, saying I had already written to the servants to take all care of him.

A couple of days later he went to Brussels and left me a little penciled note, saying there was a girl in Brussels whom he wanted to see again and he hoped I would not blame him for preferring beauty and Brussels to Nice. In reply I wrote him that I had wished to please, not constrain him, and hoped if I could do anything for him in Brussels he would let me know. A month later his sister and his friend Savage came to tell me how Middleton had taken his life in Brussels.

Difficult to save these poets, but in these two instances I cannot blame myself. At least in the case of Middleton I had done my very best.

The age in which we live is peculiarly unsuited to high genius, being at once materialistic and skeptical; and the friction between thin skin and this rude "all-hating world" is most painful in youth. Davidson should have got through: he was about fifty and had still great songs to give us and no crushing needs to distract him. He said to me once when I spoke to him in this sense that there was no hope of anything *new*, nothing to inspire soul or body. "I have lived," he added dully, "and that is all that can be said." It is a poor philosophy, but who can supply the spring of life that has run dry? But Middleton was not thirty, had not given of his best, and yet he too turned away from life's game, saying a "broken and a contrite spirit Thou wilt not despise."

When I read his verses again I understood him better:

> So here's an end, I ask forgetfulness
> Now that my little store of hours is spent,
> And heart to laugh upon my punishment—
> Dear God, what means a poet more or less?*

But, oh, how I wish that he had been able to recall an earlier mood:

> We are more rich than kings,
> Or any men that be,
> While down eternity
> We beat with shadowy wings.**

Middleton's death, coming so soon after Davidson's, saddened me to the very soul, and even now when I think of these gifted spirits who made life richer for me, my eyes grow dim with tears. Yet there is some consolation which another poet has voiced:

---

* Last stanza of *Lament for Lilian.*
** Third stanza of *The Happy Cruise.*

If he missed
World's honors, and world's plaudits, and the wage
Of the world's deft lacqueys, still his lips were kissed
Daily by those high angels who assuage
The thirstings of the poets—for he was
Born unto singing—and a burden lay
Mightily on him, and he moaned because
He could not rightly utter to the day
What God taught in the night. Sometimes, nathless,
Power fell upon him, and bright tongues of flame,
And blessings reached him from poor souls in stress;
And benedictions from black pits of shame,
And children's love, and old men's prayer,
And a Great Hand that led him unawares.

So he died rich. And if his eyes were blurred
With big films—silence! he is in his grave,
Greatly he suffered; greatly, too, he erred;
Yet broke his heart in trying to be brave.
Nor did he wait till Freedom had become
The popular shibboleth of courtier's lips;
He smote for her when God Himself seemed dumb
And all His arching skies were in eclipse.

Dowson up to 1900 and Davidson and Middleton for the next ten years were the companions of my spirit. I hardly know why, but Dowson was nearer to me always than even Davidson. Certain cadences of his lived with me as intimately as any English poetry. I suppose between us there must have been some kinship of soul, and yet we were antipodes in a hundred respects: he could never resist drink or the enticements of passion; I could and did scorn both for years at a time in the longing for a perfected manhood. And yet how his words appealed to me, not only the greatest, but some of the most careless.

Too tired to mock or weep
The world that I have missed,
Love, in your heaven let me sleep
An hour or two, before I keep
My unperturbed tryst.*

Just love and desire and nothing more; but what better things are there in life than just these?

* This quotation is really the third stanza of Middleton's *The Last Hope.*

Chapter III

EARLY IN THE CENTURY when I was about 45, I made up my mind to go round the world again as I had done twenty odd years before and study those parts of it, India, China and Japan, which I had rather scamped before. By this time I had got a fairly complete knowledge of my own nature and had won out of love for it, though I knew none wiser and none so kindly. I realized distinctly that I liked the figures of girls from twelve to sixteen more than I ought to like them. The girlish form before the characteristics of sex became predominant attracted me intensely.

A friend one evening in London advised me to visit India, assuring me that my peculiarity was there dominant, that often girls were married before puberty; nay, that girls of ten often bore children, were mothers before being women. I started for India then, determined to see all there was to be seen and to indulge myself whenever the temptation became overpowering.

Going through the Red Sea in September the heat was terrific; the women passengers for the most part chose to sleep on deck in armchairs and their clothing grew slighter and slighter. I had got to know a Mrs. Wilson and her daughter of fifteen going out to join the father, a civil servant in Bombay. Mrs. Wilson was pretty, well read, and enthusiastic about my writings; the girl, Winnie, was far prettier with slight half-formed figure and the loveliest dark brown eyes—almost a perfect beauty, I thought her, with her girlish outlines and entrancing face. How to win her? Naturally I began by paying her attention and dispensing compliments of all sorts at every moment. I found she loved music, so I talked to her of Wagner and Liszt by the half hour at a time; and one day I started the thesis that perfect beauty such as hers must be the outward and visible sign of a perfect soul. "You must live up to it," I said, "and in ten years you will be famous. You will make all men, and not merely one, adore you. We all long for perfection and alas! never find it—it is the passion of the soul."

We soon became friends, till one day I remember Mrs. Wilson took me to task. "You are turning Winnie's head," she said, "and it really isn't fair of you."

"I shall do her no harm, I promise you," I said. "I only tell her she must make her spirit as perfect as her face."

"She is pretty, isn't she?" said the mother. "And now she's really sweeter than ever." "A charming girl," we both agreed. All the while I was thinking how to win her: chance favored me twice running.

Our cabins were on the same floor and once I heard Winnie complaining that she had to wait for her bath. I called the steward, gave him a liberal tip and asked him to speed up the stewardess and get her to tell me when the bath was ready. In a quarter of an hour the stewardess told me that the "young lady's bath was ready." I gave her a good tip and begged her to keep hot towels for the girl when she emerged; she promised eagerly, showing that tips of gold coin were scarce. I went along, tapped at the door and told Winnie that her bath was ready, disguising my voice as I spoke. Then I fled back to my room.

In five minutes the fat stewardess came to me. "If you'd like to see her," she said in a whisper, "I can show her to you."

"Really?" I cried. "I'd like nothing better," and followed her to the adjacent bathroom, where through a knothole one had a complete view of the bath and the pretty bather. "Go in," I whispered to the stewardess after feasting my eyes for a while, "go in and help her to dry herself and show me all her beauties, even the most secret—everything. I'll pay properly."

The stewardess smiled, nothing loath, went in, soaped Winnie's back, keeping her front towards my knot-hole, and then, after putting a big towel about her shoulders, made her put up one leg at a time to get [her] foot dried. As Winnie stood with her foot on the edge of the bath I thought I had never seen anything lovelier. The blood burned in my cheeks, and as curve after subtle curve was revealed, I grew wild with [the] desire to touch and kiss. The stewardess played her part to perfection. While she dried the right leg, she drew it apart so that the whole sex was discovered, and just as I thought I could stand no more, she began patting the sex itself very gently with the towel, before helping Winnie out of the bath and beginning to dry the other leg.

"You have never been touched there," she said to the girl, and suited the action to the word.

"No, indeed," said Winnie. "Mamma took me away from school because one of the mistresses liked me too much."

"Oh well," said the stewardess, "one of these days some man will have a treat, for I never saw a prettier form, never." And she was right, for now I noticed that Winnie's breasts were superlative: round, small, wide-apart and high up, as Chaucer wished them—perfection perfected.

"The gentleman who ordered your bath," the clever stewardess went on, "is in love with you, I guess."

"Really?" exclaimed Winnie, flushing a little.

"We all like him," said the stewardess, "he's the best on board. Take my advice; be nice to him; you won't regret it; he's a real good sort, we know."

This time I was sure Winnie flushed with pleasure. "I like him too," she said simply and began looking for her bath-robe.

In two minutes I was back in my room. As she passed I opened the door. "Had a good bath?" I asked, smiling.

"Excellent," said Winnie, passing with the bath-towel still about her. I drew a piece of the neck open.

"I wish I could see your figure," I cried. "I'm sure you are lovely." Her brows frowned a little, so I just stooped and kissed her hand and she ran on.

While I was thinking it all over, reliving the scene, I recalled a little black spot like a wart upon her right buttock. Suddenly it occurred to me I could use this knowledge to break down her modesty. I resolved to try on the morrow. Of course I rewarded the stewardess as soon as we met, and she told me without beating about the bush that there was a girl in the steerage at least as pretty as Winnie. "Shall I bring her up and give her a bath, Sir? She'd be glad to come any day, I'm sure."

"All right," I said, "there's no hurry for a day or two. I'll let you know," and with a smile of understanding, I went back to my cabin.

Next day, while walking the deck with Winnie, I told her I had had a great dream. "You came to me," I said, "just as you were after the bath, but without your *peignoir,* and I saw you as you are." She pouted half in unbelief, half in disdain. "If I tell you something about yourself that you don't know," I went on, "will you believe me and show yourself to me as in my dream?"

"I won't promise," she said, "but I want to hear what you saw."

"You have a little black mole there," I went on, touching the right side of her hip, "and I want to see it, it's so cute!"

"I haven't," she cried.

"Look," I said, "when you undress to-night and you'll see I'm right."

After lunch we were seated in the shade when she suddenly said, "You're right, there is a mole. I looked. I was curious. But how did you dream so exactly? That puzzles me."

"Great affection," I began as if musing, "has strange powers. I saw you, your little breasts and your figure—all of it, every hair as clearly as if you were undressed before me now. Some day you'll let me see you, won't you?"

"I don't know," she replied. "You're a strange man," she mused, "but you interest me greatly. Why do you want to see me?"

"Your beauty holds me; you surely know that."

"Men are funny creatures," she began. "If I could dream like you do, I'd want to see your heart, to know whether you really care for me, but I don't think the figure important."

"Love is not born full-grown," I replied. "It has to be won!"

"How, tell me how!" she cried.

"Chiefly by giving," I answered. "Surely you know that," and so the talk went on.

Next morning as she came from the bath, I met her as before, and when she smiled at me I drew her resolutely into my cabin and closed the door. "Show me," I said, "please." I drew her bathrobe from her neck. Luckily it slipped from her hand and fell right open.

I had one good look, but Winnie at once pulled it together crying, "That's unkind. I don't like that. Please let me go." She spoke angrily, so I opened the door with "I'm sorry," and let her go, a little disappointed.

Five minutes afterwards the stewardess knocked at my door and I gave her another sovereign almost mechanically. "Thank you, Sir, many thanks," she said and lingered. "Might I say something?" she asked.

"Certainly," I replied. "What is it?"

"Those young things," she went on, "give themselves airs; they know nothing really. Take my advice, Sir. Leave Miss Winnie alone for a day or two; let her see you with Ethel Dodge of the second cabin, and she'll soon repent and change. Nothing like a bit of jealousy to make a girl kind," she smiled. "Miss Winnie there thinks you belong to her, must do whatever she wishes, you are hers—once she sees you like another girl and the other likes you, she'll alter her tune, believe me."

"I believe you," I cried," but when can I see Miss Dodge?"

"Tomorrow, Sir," she said. "I've given her a bath and told her you were paying and she wants to thank you. She has a prettier figure than Miss Wilson, if I'm a judge, fuller and rounder; but you can see for yourself, if you like," she added. "I'll tap at your door tomorrow early and the knothole is still there," and she laughed.

"You are a wonder," I said. "All right then, I'll expect you about eight tomorrow morning and I'll tell you what I think of Miss Dodge."

"Let her come to your cabin afterwards to thank you," said the cunning stewardess, "and let Miss Wilson hear you together. I'll give her a hint that she'll lose you if she doesn't take care and you'll have no more trouble."

"You are a magician," I cried. "Conduct the campaign as you think best and take this for your pains," and I gave her a five pound note.

"Thank you, thank you," she cried.

"That's only the beginning," I said, "if you succeed. You know we've only a few more days."

"You'll have 'em both, Sir, before that, trust me. I know gals!" And she vanished, smiling with gladness.

The next morning I saw Ethel Dodge through the knothole. She was so attractive that I wanted her to come to my cabin as she came from the bath. The stewardess introduced me and Ethel seemed willing to be friends. She was pretty and well made, but nothing like so lovely as Winnie. She wanted money, however, was indeed going out to be married to a sergeant. She confessed at once that she loved love and was not averse to earning money on her voyage. While we were talking as the best of friends, I heard the stewardess tap lightly on the door, and whoever was passing must have heard us laugh. I gave Ethel more than she hoped and she plainly told me she was at my service always, for she liked me greatly. "No nonsense about you, that's what I like," said Ethel. I hardly knew what she meant.

When I met Winnie on deck half an hour later, she was very cold, so I merely bowed and smiled and passed on. A little later, while I was pacing the deck, she stopped me and spoke. "I suppose you're proud of your new conquest?" she said.

"No," I replied, "I've made no conquest new or old."

"Yet I heard you both laughing in your room as I passed," she replied.

"Possibly," I said, "but that proves nothing."

"You probably took off her bathrobe," Winnie said passionately.

"I didn't even want to," I answered.

"I wish I could believe that," she cried with intense feeling in voice and look. As luck would have it, we had reached the forecastle and were clean out of sight and hearing—alone. I put my arm round her waist, drew her to me strongly and kissed her lips. While my mouth was on hers, her arms went round my neck and she cried, "Then you do love me best."

"You alone," I cried passionately. "Promise that you'll come tomorrow morning and you'll find me waiting, longing for you."

"I'll come," she said, all her soul in her eyes. "You don't know how I suffered this morning when I heard your two voices; and that stewardess had just told me how Miss this and that were after you. Oh, Frank, be good to me. I love you more than I can say, you dear!" And our lips clung together in a long kiss.

The next morning I was at the knothole when Winnie was bathing and I noticed that she was very reserved with the stewardess. I augured happiness from her reserve. I therefore hastened back to my cabin and of course met her at the door. I drew her over to my bed and without a word took off her bathrobe and lifted her on to the bed. I saw at once she was very nervous and afraid, so I laid down with her after covering us both with the quilt, and began to kiss her and talk just to reassure her. When I saw that I had succeeded, I let my hands stray; then I began kissing her breasts while praising their beauty, and soon my right hand began caressing her sex. Even this first time she was far more responsive than I had dared to hope. But when in a moment she clung to me kissing me, I said: "You must fear nothing with me. I hate giving pain or putting you in any danger; just trust me and you'll find I'll lead you from delight to ecstasy." The next moment I had pushed up the quilt and my lips were on her sex. In a moment or two her hands had come down on my head by way partly of caress, partly to guide me to the center of pleasure. In a quarter of an hour she was hysterical with sensation, sobbing with delight. "Well," I said, taking her in my arms, "are you content to trust me now?"

She nodded, while her great brown eyes thanked me, "But, but . . ."

"But what?" I asked.

"Does that give *you* pleasure?" she replied.

"You darling," I cried, "that is like you to want to give me delight. That's for a later lesson," I went on, "when you are as sure of me as of yourself."

"You don't need to wait," she said saucily. "I'm more than sure that I have the dearest, best lover in the world."

"Do you know how long we've been here?" I asked a little later. "It's after ten and your mother may come to see after you."

"Really?" she cried. "Oh, I must get up," and as she got up I kissed the wart that had helped me to such delight and caressed her lovely body. A moment later she had gone and I began to dress.

The stewardess came in the evening for her reward and I gave her another tenner and talked to her of her protégée, Miss Ethel, who liked me sincerely, it appeared, and was quite willing to be my lover. I found the stewardess very wise indeed and eager to help me in every way. We had a long talk and at the end she told me more of India and Hindoo girls than I could have learned in a hundred books.

"If you like young girls, Sir," she began, "India is the happy hunting ground for you. They are nearly all married by eleven and I've known girls of nine pregnant. India is a terrible place for girls. They are often married before they are women, and the midwives who attend them in confinement are a fearful set, dirty and cruel and ignorant.

"Then, you know, when the husband of fifty or sixty dies, there is nothing for the girl widow to do but become a prostitute. And the diseases, you never saw anything like them. You might say that every girl has gonorrhea and four out of ten syphilis. It's appalling."

"I like girlish figures," I said, "but what you tell me will keep me quiet."

"You're in luck to have me with you," she broke out. "I know Bombay and the bazaar like my pocket; I can get you whatever you want and I'll take care there are no evil consequences. You can rely on me."

"I do," I replied sincerely. "I regard it as a great piece of luck to have met you."

"I have done nothing yet," she resumed, "but in Bombay I can be of the greatest service to you." And on this understanding we parted for the moment.

That night Winnie came to my cabin.

"I mustn't stay long," she began. "Mother might find out."

"Just do what you wish," I replied, taking her in my arms and kissing her. "We can always have our hour in the morning," and I lifted her into the bed. How shall I describe her? Let my reader think of a Tanagra statuette in warm flesh and blood. After kissing her mouth and then her neck and breasts, I went down to the sacred spot and soon found that love's instrument responded far more passionately than the first time. I kept on kissing for perhaps quarter of an hour, till she began to shake convulsively and try to lift my head. At once I got up and went to her mouth, but could not help seeing on the way that her little sex was now quite open, round and red.

"Take me," she said, "I want to make you enjoy as I do; I want us both to go mad together."

At once I put my sex in her hand and she directed it to the entrance. "If it hurts too much," I said, "stop me. I can't bear to give you pain."

And indeed this has been a characteristic of me during practically all my life; rape is almost unthinkable to me. I always prefer to leave a good deal to the initiative of the woman. If she loves you, she will endure a good deal of suffering to give you pleasure.

Naturally as entering was difficult, I wet the head of my sex with saliva at first and afterwards, as that was insufficient, with cold cream. In a few moments the head penetrated and Winnie caught her breath. I knew the moment to be rough had come, so I pushed with all my might, and to my astonishment Winnie, instead of flinching, responded bravely and my sex went in till our hairs met. Afraid of hurting, I kept quiet, but Winnie soon began to squirm, and so inspired, I went on with the great game while Winnie wound her legs about mine. In a few moments we were both bathed in exquisite mutual delight.

"Do you love me?" was her first question. "Am I a good lover?" her next.

"Better than imagination," I said. "You are a divine mistress and lover but now I must teach you how to avoid consequences."

As we got up I had first to sponge away the blood on her lovely thighs and then I showed her the syringe.

"It does not give complete safety," I said, "but it's always very useful and at first is usually enough. Next time we'll take other measures, for you are much more passionate than I had imagined and that increases the risk."

"I'd love to have a child of yours," she remarked, "and I'm sure you would not leave me to suffer alone."

"Surely not," I responded, "but prudence is a good counsellor and we want to know each other better before."

"How could we know each other better, you funny man?" she asked with that spice of sly humor I was soon to recognize as one of her most endearing traits.

"Wait," I went on, "at any rate till you feel no pain but only pleasure. Pain, I think, always does harm, might harm you."

After another bout or two of kissing and caressing Winnie resolved to get back to her room and I went with her till she sent me back with an imperious hand-kiss.

In my bed I relived every moment again and again, dwelt on every incident, every word and movement of Winnie's, till suddenly I saw the light in the port and knew it was morning. Then I fell into [a] deep sleep and awoke about eight and forthwith thought of the bath and the knothole. But alas! Winnie was not there nor the stewardess for the moment. However, I knew I should see the stewardess some time in the afternoon and I wanted another talk, for she interested me and I had no idea yet how she had won to her knowledge of India, which I felt to be extraordinary.

That afternoon I found that Mrs. Redfern, the stewardess, was not unwilling to talk of her past experiences. She had been ten years in Bombay as the wife of a non-commissioned officer who later got a post under the government. After her husband died she did some nursing and so grew to know Indian conditions from the inside. She told me that the life of most of the girl-wives was appalling; three out of every six died in their first confinement through the unsanitary conditions and fearful dirt of the mid-wives. And the children of these children were almost invariably undersized weaklings. She had hardly ever met a wife of some years standing who was not diseased, but she assured me she could easily find a child-widow who was perfectly well and would please the most fastidious. I told her I would take her as my guide and guardian.

Once or twice she came back to her belief that Ethel would be a very attractive mistress and here I must make a confession. Since I had had Winnie and the novelty was worn off, I often found myself desiring Ethel's more opulent beauties. What devil is it in men that makes them desire the untried? I cared for Winnie, esteemed her more than I could ever esteem Ethel, knew too that she was incomparably prettier, and yet I commenced to desire Ethel in spite of all reason.

That same evening Mrs. Redfern caught me in my cabin and proposed that Ethel should come to me that night.

"Not in this cabin," I said, thinking Winnie might come.

"I'll put her two doors away, in number seventeen," she replied, "and if you wish to visit her, the door will not be locked against you."

I laughed, but asked her to put Ethel off for a night or so, then gave Mrs. Redfern another gold tip and went my way.

In my cabin late that evening I hesitated. If Winnie had come I'd have been content; why didn't she? I could not guess, but I waited, seeing always the heavier hips and more luscious mouth of Ethel. At eleven Winnie came but she was ill: through the intense excitement, she said, her monthlies had come on long before time. I kissed her and consoled her and accompanied her back to her room. The next night, when I knew Winnie would not come, I went to number seventeen, opened the door and turned on the light. Ethel was in bed awaiting me. I locked the door and she drew back the clothes. Her nightie was in the way; I drew it up, and as I did so, she stretched out her arms and I was struck by the thick tufts of dark hair.

I found Ethel quite as passionate as Winnie, but in a more selfish way. Excited fully, she thought more of her pleasure than of yours, while Winnie had always her lover's delight in mind. She was of far commoner clay; she would not talk of her sensations, thought I too must wish to forget all about the act as soon as it was over.

The last night before reaching Bombay Winnie came to me and we had a long intimate talk and arranged meetings in Bombay. She could not do without me, she said, and begged me to be nice to her father so that we might meet easily. I swore I would be as pleasant as I could be, and next day I saw her and her mother safely to their carriage.

I went to the hotel recommended by Mrs. Redfern, who also took up her abode there. The second evening she brought me a girl of twelve—a widow —rather pretty but childish. Her sex was naturally very small but she had little response to passion in her; she seemed afraid to complain and didn't enjoy [it] greatly. She was happy for the first time when I paid her. Mrs. Redfern could only say, "Better luck next time," but the better luck seldom materialized. Time and again she brought pretty children but we could not talk and there was an awkwardness over the whole affair; several of them had all their hairs taken off which seemed to increase their youthfulness. The experience cured me of my liking for the immature. For even the best of them never gave me the thrill I had experienced with older girls. The sex was often very small, but it had not the gripping, pumping power of the mature woman. Some of the older women, especially in France, used all the contractive power of their sex and the spasmodic movement of the hips up to the navel to increase the throe of pleasure. A woman from twenty on, gifted with passion and in love with you, gives more pleasure than almost any girl.

It is strange that nearly everywhere women think that the whole act of love on their part is summed up in surrender. To excite the man, to give him the utmost thrill of pleasure, to respond at least to his desire passionately, never seems to occur to the average woman anywhere, except in Japan frequently, sometimes in China, and often in that Garden of India, Ceylon. But with the girl-children in India proper there is rarely any response, and Mrs. Redfern confessed to me that nearly all the older girls of seventeen to twenty were diseased or had had some disease.

I didn't mind much for the second day Winnie came to my rooms and found me in and we had another long talk. She seemed as charming as ever and declared that next day she would be well again.

It has appeared to me on ripe reflexion that I have not done enough to portray each of the girls I had love-duets with. I am resolved in this volume at least to try and give their view of life and the love episodes.

It seems to me as if I had differentiated them better perhaps in the first volume than in the subsequent ones, for in some way or other the freshness of youth made them more vivid to me. But some women in maturity made a deathless impression on me and I do not want to pass them over without outlining their very souls; for some of them were kindlier, more loving and more generous than could be imagined, at least by me, and these surely deserve to be saved from oblivion.

I remember one in especial in the south of France, who gave herself to me so simply, so easily, that I did not at all realize that she was possessed —in utter ignorance of sexual things—by the very spirit of love. She was of good family and I soon found that her abandonment was so complete that it was almost certain to lead to pregnancy and this frightened me. I knew and esteemed her mother and father and I was not free at the time, nor could I hope to free myself in any reasonable time, so I drew away from her the more resolutely because my passion grew so intense that I knew if I gave way to it, the result would be disaster.

Years later I met her; she had married and was happy; yet there was between us an instinctive sympathy, an attachment of heart and mind and soul that fills me with reverence for the spirit of pure love in her. She was so wise and yet so enthusiastic, so capable of devotion and yet free of all superstition. And when she told me that her yielding at first was wholly free of sensuality, that all she wanted was to please and content and if possible delight me, I remembered little things that convinced me the confession was wholly true. She had not weighed consequences, nor thought of disgrace: it was enough for her to love and to give herself to love, body and soul. I never met a nobler nature. And many years later when we met again, she showed me a generosity and a desire to help me in every way that filled me with shame of my unworthiness. There are some women nobler than men and thank God I have met one or two of them that have heightened my estimate of the possibilities of human goodness and E . . . was the best of them all.

Chapter IV

HALF A DOZEN FRIENDS who have read the first three installments of *My Life* have begged me in the Fourth* to talk of those formative influences which have meant most to me and had the profoundest effect upon my work. Now, I cannot say that anything outside myself has ever had any influence on my work. But my mind itself, my very soul, has been excited and affected by this poet and that prose-writer. The artist, whether in words, or colors, or form, or thought has always influenced me profoundly, and I am more than willing now to pay my tribute of thanks to some I have not yet portrayed.

Perhaps the wisest man I have met in my life was Alfred Russel Wallace, the scientist who wrote of the survival of the fittest some time before Darwin. Dr. Wallace's pamphlet was so similar to Darwin's work that even some of its phrases appeared as titles in Darwin's MS. He was indeed the first to interpret the evolution of the world as Darwin afterwards interpreted it. It must be recorded in his honor that as soon as Darwin's book came out on the *Origin of Species* in 1859, Wallace hailed him as the chief of the school, and declared at once that the theory would be known as Darwinism, though he himself had promulgated it years before. When I asked him how he came to this unexampled generosity, he smiled in his kindly way and said, "You could not talk of Wallacesism, but you could talk of Darwinism. Besides, to be serious, Darwin had done all the spade work which I had neglected, thought unnecessary."

One more word in Wallace's honor. As soon as Henry George** came to England he attended his meetings, and wrote, and spoke in favor of land nationalization; though he was well off, he proclaimed himself a socialist and declared that England was guilty, for though the richest of countries, it was the home of the worst poverty in the world. I was surprised and glad to find that the wisest of men was also the kindliest and the best.

* Originally there were only four volumes to *My Life*, but Harris early decided to publish Vol. III as vols. III and IV. Hence he refers to this present volume forgetfully as "Fourth."
** (1839–97); American economist who wanted to abolish poverty through a "single tax" on land.

The first time I met Wallace was in the office of the *Fortnightly Review*. He and Frederic Chapman, the head of the publishing house, had been boys at school together in the West of England: I got them out to dinner, set them talking, and so by means of his schoolboy memories made Wallace's more intimate acquaintance.

Later he used to come and see me whenever he was in London. We used to lunch together and spend the afternoon playing innumerable games of chess. He was not a great player; but a good amateur—careful, not brilliant.

I came to have the most sincere admiration for him as a man of rare genius. He was tall, I should say about six feet in height, and well, though loosely made. A fine face framed in silver hair; the features regular, well balanced; the eyes super-excellent, the light in them, the kindly radiance of genius. Wallace had all the candor of a child and met everyone with amiability and gentle courtesy. He would discuss any subject, and while defending his own views with eminent ability, would listen to diametrically opposed opinons with a certain sympathy. A very simple and great nature.

It is by the heart we grow, and Wallace kept himself so sincere, so kindly, that he grew in wisdom to the very end of his life instead of stopping, as most men and women stop growing mentally, almost before their bodily growth is completed. A quarter of a century ago he was quite conscious, to use his own words, that "the materialistic mind of his youth and early manhood was being slowly molded into a socialistic, spiritualistic, and theistic mind." He had crossed that desert of skepticism which I speak of sometimes as stretching from Luther to Voltaire, and had entered the Promised Land of Faith and Hope. He believed devoutly in God, in a constantly acting mind of almost unimaginable grandeur and prescience.

I may be inclined to overrate Wallace because I found myself in agreement with him on many points, though I could never accept his view of God or what he used to call "the chief article of my belief"—the faith in a life after death. I came late to an appointment one day and found him in my smoking-room waiting for me. His face was transfigured, smiling in a sort of ecstasy. I excused myself to him and said I was sorry.

"It is no matter," he said, "I have been listening to celestial harmonies."

"Really?" I queried. "What do you mean?"

"Don't you hear violins?" he said. "I can hear them distinctly; one was playing on my knee just as you came in."

I stared at him in amazement but he was perfectly sincere. He held up his hand. "Listen," he said.

I listened, but heard nothing.

"You will hear them," he went on, "one of these days, for all who love them hear them."

"What do you mean exactly?" I asked. "Can you recall musical passages with such vividness that you really hear them again, as a great musician I once knew could recall music?"

"O, no, no," he said quietly. "I am not a musician, indeed, until I became a spiritualist I did not care much about music. I was listening to the music of the spheres, supernal harmonies." And his face was like that of an angel, his eyes shining with a sort of unearthly happiness.

Afterwards, of course, we had long discussions on the matter. He believed devoutly, simply, in a life after death, in this life indeed as a mere moment in the life of the spirit, and he insisted that personal identity would be preserved beyond the grave. I could not follow him in this though I admired the spiritual beauty of the creed and its incalculable effect upon life and conduct. Still, I could not help playing Thomas, and can only affirm that whenever he called up spiritual phenomena before me I was unable to witness the manifestations. I gave myself to the experiments again and again, but never could catch the faintest glimpse of the undiscovered country that he assured me lies beyond this life.

Yet who shall say that Wallace was not right? No more simple, sincere, and noble soul has lived in these times.

I remember going down to stay with him once in the country. One evening we had company, I should think twenty people in all, ladies and gentlemen. I went to my room after dinner to write a letter, and when I came down to the drawing-room, I found the whole company assembled and everyone very quiet. I said to a girl near the door: "What is it?"

"We are listening," she said, "to heavenly music. Don't you hear it?"

"No," I replied, "I hear nothing. What is the music like?"

"Indescribable," she said, "sweeter than Mozart."

In a pause later I crossed the room and spoke to an old lady. "Do you hear the music, Madam?" I asked.

"Of course," she said.

"And what is it like?" I went on.

"Entrancing, like the best of Mozart."

I was flabbergasted. For half an hour they all listened to music that I could not hear, and were delighted with harmonies beyond my ken.

If the Order of Merit had any meaning, the name of Wallace would have figured in the list when the Order was first created, instead of the names of some generals and admirals whose services to man never spread beyond the quarter-deck or mess-room table.

Part of his belief is of permanent value: he was the first to point out that man is the center of the universe.

"There is no reason to believe," he says,

that the stars are infinite in number. The increased size and power of the telescope, and that powerful engine of research the photographic plate, alike lead to the same conclusion—namely, that we are piercing to the outer elements of the starry system. The total number of visible stars from the first to the ninth magnitude is about two hundred thousand. If they increased in number on to the seventeenth magnitude at the same rate that they increase from the first to the ninth, there ought to be 1,400,000,000 stars visible through the best telescope, instead of which there are not more than 100,000,000. As our instruments reach further and further into space they find a continuous diminution in the number of stars, thus indicating the approach of the outer elements of the stellar universe. If the universe is not infinite, but has limits, where is its centre?

He sums up his conclusions as follows:

The three startling facts—that we *are* in the centre of a cluster of suns, and that that cluster *is* situated not only precisely in the *plane* of the Galaxy, but also *centrally* in that plane, can hardly now be looked upon as chance coincidences without any significance in relation to the culminating fact that the planet so situated *has* developed humanity.

Of course the relation here pointed out *may* be a true relation of cause and effect, and yet have arisen as the result of one in a thousand million chances occuring during almost infinite time. But, on the other hand, those thinkers may be right who, holding that the universe is a manifestation of Mind, and that the orderly development of Living Souls supplied an adequate reason why such an universe should have been called into existence, believe that we ourselves are its sole and sufficient result, and that nowhere else than near the central position in the universe which we occupy could that result have been attained.

Wallace distinguishes between the struggle of existence *per se*

and the struggle for spiritual intellectual and moral existence. Evolution can account for the land-grabber, the company promoter and the sweater; but, if it fails to account for the devotion of the patriot, the enthusiasm of the artist, the constancy of the martyr, the resolute search of the scientific worker after Nature's secret, it has not explained the whole mystery of humanity.

Wallace goes on to speak of Spiritualism. He holds that "proof of the existence of the soul beyond the grave is already established. The study of the spiritual nature of man," he says,

is coming more and more to the front of human inquiry. The proper study of mankind is man, and if you leave out the spiritual nature of man you are not studying men at all. I prefer the term spiritualism. I am a spiritualist, and I am not in the least frightened of the name!

Wallace did not believe that everything not made by man must have been made by God. His cosmogony was spacious and found room for other intelligences than those of humanity and deity. We are compassed about, he believed, by an infinity of beings as numerous as the stars, and the vast universe is peopled with as many grades of intelligence as the forms of life with which this little earth is peopled. To deny spiritual phenomena, because some of them appear to be beneath the dignity of Godhead, seemed to this patient and courageous investigator an act of folly, a confession too miraculous for his investigation, and in his philosophy there was no impossible and no preternatural.

Alfred Russel Wallace was too great to be seen or understood by any of the kings, or ministers, or courtiers; his work and his fame, his noble wisdom and simple life belong to humanity—are indeed, as Thucydides said of himself, part of the possession of men forever. He was too noble even to be mourned at death; the best of him lives on in those he influenced, his memory an inspiration.

I reproduce here the portrait of him as I knew him.

As soon as I returned to London in 1880–81, after my student-time in Germany and Greece, I came to know William Morris.* He did not affect me deeply, seemed a smaller Wallace to me, though his work both in verse and decoration was always individual and good. But [that] he knew Dante Gabriel Rossetti** and everything Rossetti did, whether in poetry or painting, touched me nearly.

Strange to say, Rossetti's work as a painter appealed to me even more deeply than his poetry. Naturally, too, I had read all about his wife† and his sister†† that could be found out. I cannot explain the impression he made upon me better than by reproducing here his face of Lucy Rossetti:‡ it is informed, it seems to me, by the very spirit of pure love. It is evidently capable, too, of passion; but the mark of it is the curious amalgam of affection, devotion and sympathy that women know as the soul of love. And yet, women, strange to say, don't admire Rossetti as much as [do] men. And Rossetti's vision of young Swinburne too interested me and I reproduce it, though very different from the Swinburne of fifteen years later, whom I knew; still, in its way, a masterpiece.

From the moment I saw Rossetti's *Ecce Ancilla Domini,* I was carried off my feet and hoped for nothing better than to get to know the master. For this reason, as soon as I met William Morris at some socialist meeting, I got introduced to him and soon led him on to speak of Rossetti. Of course, I told him how I should like to meet the master and at once, in the very kindest way, he promised to bring about a meeting as soon as possible, though he warned me that Rossetti was not as strong as he used to be and indeed had left London for a time for his health's sake. It appeared that he suffered from insomnia, the "beating mind" that Shakespeare, too, deplored. And this in spite of the fact that Rossetti, Morris said, was short and stout and strong. The explanation, I suppose, is that he did not take exercise enough and gave himself too much to headwork.

A little while later Morris told me that Rossetti had gone to Birchington-on-Sea for [a] rest, and when I proposed that we should run down and call upon him, Morris offered to give me a letter to the poet, but told me he had too much to do to accompany me, to my lasting, bitter regret. I thought it better then to wait till Rossetti came up to London [but] suddenly the news came that he was dead. Born in 1828, he had passed away in 1882.

* (1834–96).
** (1828–82).
† Elizabeth Siddal, the model for many of his pictures. She died two years after the marriage from an overdose of laudanum.
†† Christina Rossetti (1830–94).
‡ Elizabeth.

Morris told me that he was most affectionate—"without an enemy in the world" were his words—and a charming lovable companion. I knew him as one whose impassioned vision had reached my heart and I mourned for him as one mourns for those rare kindred spirits, who love what we love and desire what we desire.

I do not want to overrate Rossetti. I can see plainly enough that his technical power as a poet was far superior to his skill of hand as a painter; his draughtmanship sometimes leaves a good deal to be desired, and even his palette was not as rich as that of the great masters. But there was what one critic has well called the "re-birth of wonder" in all his work; to him the world was an enchanted place and his women were all heroines of the spirit. They appealed to me peculiarly, while his extraordinary admiration of Dante seemed to me to resemble my passion for Shakespeare. My life was poorer to me because I had not met or spoken to this master of romance.

The other day, Karin Michaelis,* the Danish author, wrote me that "the only thing she thanked God for (if, indeed, he was worth mentioning) was that he had made her capable of enthusiastic admiration." The phrase appealed to me intensely: it is by our passionate admirations that we grow.

I had had all too few of them in my life. Shakespeare, of course, was always there, the lord of my admiration; and after him I learned most from Coleridge and Blake and Keats, in English. But no painter, save Rembrandt, appealed to me like Rossetti and his weakness of hand seemed to increase, in some strange way, my liking for his spirit. *Dante's Dream* and *Dante sketching Beatrice* held for me the very essence of romance.

Some friends have asked me to give them my opinion of English prose writers and above all to say which of them I like best. I think that Swift has written the best English prose and with his best work stand the prefaces of Dryden. Swift, in his simplicity and clearness, has given the very spirit of English prose, but of course there are passages of Ruskin and of Pater which reach higher heights of feeling than anything in Swift.

Every now and then a new book brings me to wonder. Some four years ago, when it was first published by Boni and Liveright of New York, I received *The Holy Tree* by Gerald O'Donovan and was carried off my feet. After finishing it, I wrote some reviews of it, declaring that it held more of the spirit of true love than any book I had ever read. But my praise seemed lost in the void and was not taken up by anybody.

The other day I opened the book again to see if my praise had been overstrained and almost came to the conclusion that the book must have been written by a woman and an Irish woman at that: it is super-excellent. My schooldays in Ireland had taught me that there was far more affection, far more pure love, in Ireland than in England, and this belief solves a problem that has tormented many minds. It is known that Cromwell's soldiers,

* (1872–   ); pro-German during World War I, she wrote novels dealing with social matters and war.

planted here and there in Ireland in order to represent English ideas, were converted to the Irish view very quickly. In a single generation the Ironsides became more Irish than the Irish.

I have explained this to myself by the power there is of love and affection in Ireland and here, for the first time in my life, I find a book which gives me this spirit of love in its very essence, and gives it as a readable story; to me an entrancing book. Boni and Liveright, the publishers, tell me that all they know about Gerald O'Donovan is that he was an Irish priest who had a various and adventurous life and later worked for Lord Northcliffe in London.

And now, I must tell of another "find." It is more than fifteen years now, since I first wrote of David Graham Phillips as the first of American novelists, the only one indeed, to hold his own with Fielding and Thackeray, endowed with an even deeper knowledge of the human heart than any other writer in English.* My praise, repeated time and again, found no echo in the world of journalism either in America or in England, and once more I was forced to admit that the number of persons able to recognize a master or a masterpiece is extremely limited. There are hardly half a dozen in the hundred and fifty millions of English readers.

The other day I asked my friends in New York to send me any of Phillips' works I had not got, and they sent me two—the one *The Reign of Gilt,* and the other, *George Helm. The Reign of Gilt* is one of Phillips' worst works. It is at once argumentative and thin, certainly not worth reading. The other, *George Helm,* is one of Phillips' very best, an undoubted masterpiece. It is simply the story of a common man of great character, called George Helm, who falls in love with a girl of the best class and finally wins her, in spite of himself and her. It is one of the best love stories I have ever read and I have never seen a word of praise of it, in any print.

Why doesn't some English publisher get the right of publishing the seven best of Phillips' works? There is certainly money to be made in publishing *The Hungry Heart, The Grain of Dust, The Husband's Story, The Price She Paid.* There is a deeper understanding of character, especially of feminine character, in these books than I have ever found anywhere else. I would rather compare Phillips to Turgenief than to any English writer. D. H. Lawrence has since surpassed even Phillips in *Lady Chatterley's Lover,* but I shall deal later with that masterpiece of passion.

* (1867–1911). Harris was overly enthusiastic about both Phillips and O'Donovan, who were very minor novelists at best.

Chapter V

I WAS MORE INTERESTED in Meredith than in any other man of my time. I thought him one of the greatest of men, worthy to stand with Shakespeare and Wordsworth. I knew him first just as I first knew Alfred Russel Wallace, through my connection with *The Fortnightly Review* and Mr. Chapman. He was one of the handsomest of men, just above middle height, slight and strong of figure with a superb head and face; the head all outlined in greying hair, but excellently shaped and the face noble: straight nose, incomparable blue eyes, now laughing, now pathetic, excellent mouth and chin—in fine a very good looking man, sane at once and strong. I have told elsewhere how Grant Allen sent him one of my earliest stories *Montes, the Matador* and how he praised it as better than the *Carmen* of Mérimée because I had given even the bulls individuality: and he ended his praise with the words, "if there is any hand in England that can do better, I don't know it." As I have said somewhere, I regarded that judgment as my knighting. No contempt touched me afterwards; Meredith to me already stood among the greatest; indeed, I could never make out why, with all his gifts, he had not done a masterpiece.

Born in 1828, he brought out his first book of *Poems* in 1851, and I think he was always more of a poet than a prose-writer. But good as his best poetry is: even *Love in the Valley* has stanzas I can never forget and *Modern Love* with the entrancing "Margaret's Bridal Eve" is greater still; and just in the same way *Richard Feverel* comes near being the best conventional love-story in the language; and the later *Diana of the Crossways* is at least as admirable. Yet neither in poetry nor in prose has Meredith reached the highest or given his full measure.

The reason always escaped me. When I knew him first about 1885 he was the reader for Chapman and Hall and made his £500 or £600 a year out of this easily enough while his books added perhaps as much more to his income. He had a house on Box Hill in Surrey and lived like a modest country gentleman; nothing in his circumstances hindered him from reaching Cervantes or Shakespeare.

And his conversation was astonishing; he touched every thing that came up from the highest stand-point; he praised the Irish as if he had been bred in Ireland and the Welsh as the highest of the Celtic stock; once indeed he went so far as to suggest merrily that the English should invade France in order to get some French women to enlarge their matter of fact narrowness of mind. He was in favor of the Boers too, and a passionate advocate of women's suffrage; he wanted feminine influence in government as in the home; and once he went so far as to advocate the making of Britain into one state of the American Union, "the Eastern Star in the Banner of the Republic," as he said, for he was profoundly convinced that the British were dropping back, were indeed no longer leaders in the world-race. Their fatal lack of imagination," he said, "dwarfs them." In fine, in every question he was an unprejudiced and most interesting guide.

And every man he mentioned lived unforgettably in his judgments: who can ever forget his criticism of Tennyson's "dandiacal Fluting"; "The great length of his mild fluency: the yards of linen-drapery for the delight of women." And then "The praises of the book shut me away from my fellows," and the superb return: "To be sure there is the magnificent Lucretius." Then he sees Irving as Romeo: "No love-play but a pageant with a quaint figure ranting about"; and his judgment of Gladstone: "This valiant, prodigiously gifted, in many respects admirable old man, is, I fear me, very much an actor." And finally he touches the height in a letter to his son.

Don't think that the obscenities mentioned in the Bible do harm to children. The Bible is outspoken upon facts, and rightly. It is because the world is pruriently and stupidly shamefaced that it cannot come in contact with the Bible without convulsions.

Look for the truth in everything and follow it, and you will then be living justly before God. Let nothing flout your sense of a Supreme Being, and be certain that your understanding wavers whenever you chance to doubt that he leads to good. We grow to good as surely as the plant grows to the light. The school has only to look through history for a scientific assurance of it. And do not lose the habit of praying to the unseen Divinity. Prayer for worldly goods is worse then fruitless, but prayer for strength of soul is that passion of the soul which catches the gift it seeks.

To an acquaintance he writes protesting against the charge of cynicism.

None of my writings can be said to show a want of faith in humanity, or of sympathy with the weaker, or that I do not read the right meaning of strength. And it is not only women of the flesh, but also women in the soul whom I esteem, believe in, and would aid to development.

I once pressed him for his views of women and found him as wise as Goethe. "We learn the best from those we love," he said. "We have doubled Seraglio Point, but have not yet rounded Cape Turk—the Turkish idea is very strong in the male breast."

Personally I must always speak of Meredith as the most interesting of companions. We agreed in almost everything but the flashes of his humor made his conversation entrancing. I still regard him with Russel Wallace as the wisest men I've ever met; but Wallace's belief in another and larger life after death shut him away from me, while Meredith's love of nature and his delight in nature-studies all appealed to me. I remember how I met him for the last time in his little pony-chaise on Box Hill shortly before his death.

"People talk about me," he said, "as if I were an old man. I don't feel old in the least. On the contrary," he went on, in his humorous sardonic fashion, "I do not believe in growing old, and I do not see any reason why we should ever die. I take as keen an interest in the movement of life as ever, I enter into the intrigues of parties with the same keen interest as of old. I have seen the illusion of it all, but it does not dull the zest with which I enter into it, and I hold more firmly than ever my faith in the constant advancement of the race. My eyes are as good as ever they were, only for small print I need to use spectacles. It is only in my legs that I feel weaker. I can no longer walk, which is a great privation to me. I used to be a keen walker; I preferred walking to riding; it sent the blood coursing to the brain; and besides, when I walked I could go through woods and footpaths which I could not have done if I had ridden. Now I can only walk about my own garden. It is a question of nerves. If I touch anything, however, slightly, I am afraid that I shall fall—that is my only loss. My walking days are over."

He did not need to go beyond his garden to be in the midst of the Garden of the Gods. As a young man he wrote in *Love in a Valley,*

> When the westering sun is leaving the valley in gloom
> Lovely are the curves of the white owl sweeping
> Wavy in the dusk lit by one large star
> Lone on the fir-branch, his rattle note unvaried,
> Brooding o'er the gloom, spins the brown eve-jar.
> Darker grows the valley, more and more forgetting:
> So were it with me if forgetting could be willed.*

There in the midst of all living, singing, flowering things, he lived alone and marvelled that people thought him lonely. His wife had been dead for many years. His daughter was married and lived between Box Hill and Leatherhead. His son, who was in London, came to see him every fortnight.

"I do not feel in the least lonely," he told me. "I have my books and my thoughts, and besides, I am never lonely, with nature and the birds and beasts and insects, and the woods and the trees, in which I find a constant companionship."

And on this occasion he went deeper than ever before:

"I see," he said, "the revelation of God to man in the history of the world, and in the individual experience of each of us in the progressive triumph of God, and [in] the working of the law by which wrong works out its own destruction. I cannot resist the conviction that there is something

---

* The quotation is accurate, except for a few errors in punctuation.

more in the world than nature. Nature is blind. Her law works without regard to individuals. She cares only for the type. To her, life and death are the same. Ceaselessly she works, pressing ever for the improvement of the type. If man should fail her, she will create some other being; but that she has failed with man I am loath to admit, nor do I see any evidence of it. It would be good for us," he added thoughtfully, "if we were to take a lesson from nature in this respect, and cease to be so wrapped up in individuals, to allow our interests to go out to the race. We should all attain more happiness, especially if we ceased to care so exclusively for the individual I. Happiness is usually a negative thing. Happiness is the absence of unhappiness."

In this passage I think Meredith reaches the highest: "There is something more (and higher) in the world than nature." I put on record the farthest reaches of Meredith's faith, which I too share. To me this life is all that man knows of can reckon upon; but it is surely in love and spirit-growth a gift incomparable and higher than what we know as nature. It is the Wallaces and the Merediths who have made it divine to me and perchance in my time I have made it more worthful to certain of younger companions.

Of the two I have always felt myself nearer to Meredith than to any other man I have known personally.

Chapter VI

MRS. REDFERN WAS NOT SATISFIED with failure, or perhaps the ordinary failures did not bring her in money enough. In any case she was resolved to win my vagrant fancy, if it was at all possible. Soon after her first unfortunate introductions in Bombay she began talking to me of a wonderful girl who was quite independent but now at sixteen would soon have to choose a lover or a husband.

"Some go much longer," I objected.

"Not in this climate," she said. "When a girl of sixteen sees girls of ten and twelve already given up to love, her chastity begins to trouble her, I can assure you. But I want to be certain that you will give this girl the best reception, for she is a peach."

She interested me and we soon decided on an afternoon. I arranged the sitting-room with flowers and fruit and wine, and really, when Mrs. Redfern came in with her "protégée" I was astonished. The girl was dressed in English fashion and yet was surely too dark to be English; still she spoke English without accent. But I could not help asking her, "Are you English?"

"Half English," she said, and I learned later that her father was an English officer, while her mother was an Indian of good family. Her name was May and she deserved it. She was certainly very pretty and her gentle and sympathetic manners increased the effect of her beauty. Mrs. Redfern stripped the girl before me and made me notice that the hairs everywhere had been taken off; indeed she seemed quite in love with the girl herself. She kissed her body passionately and told me that she was a *Padmini*, or lotus-girl, and when I asked what that meant, she would have it that the girl's *Yoni* was like the bud of a lotus-flower; and her *Kama-salila* or love-juice had the perfume of a lily that was just opening. She became as lyrical in her praise as if she had been the lover, and indeed the girl's body deserved her eulogy. The only fault to be found was that the skin was rather dark; but she had no trace of the mousey odor that Indian women usually exude.

I soon said "Good-bye" to Mrs. Redfern and a little later convinced myself that May, though not a virgin, was well disposed towards me through the extravagant eulogy of Mrs. Redfern. I resolved to do my best to please her. I therefore played with her till she lost all fear and began to give herself to desire. And when I had enjoyed her and given her pleasure to the full, I drew her out about her life and found it had been very lonely. A noncommissioned officer, an Indian and his wife, had been given charge of her by her father, who had settled a small pension on her; and so she had lived between the two contrasting civilizations, so to speak, understanding both but not loving either. The Indian, she said, was kinder than the English but had no notion of sex-morality. I found out that she had been brought up in a temple as a bride of the god Brahma and had been taught all love-ways and arts by the priests; in fact, she had only given [in] to Mrs. Redfern hoping that I would take care of her, or at least free her from the temple service. Of course, I promised to do what I could, and with Mrs. Redfern's help found that the task was not difficult. The English father had put the pension in the girl's control after her sixteenth year. I soon got her into Mrs. Redfern's care, who had a real affection for her.

For over a month I lived between Winnie and May and was more than content with my lot. Winnie was much stronger and more resolute, but May was more sensuous and her yielding and gentleness were inexpressibly touching. When I disappointed her, the big eyes filled with tears, whereas Winnie would get angry and tear her passion to tatters. Still, they both gave me intense pleasure. I often thought of bringing them together. Before this idea was realized Mrs. Redfern brought out a new project.

She was naturally eager to earn all the money she could get, so one day she made a great to-do of something she hoped to bring that would astonish me. "It's only to be had in the best houses," she declared.

"What is it?" I wanted to know.

"They call it the hedgehog," she replied, "but that tells you nothing. If I can get one for you, you will have to admit that India has taught you one thing worth knowing.

A few days later she drew out a "hedgehog" and showed it to me: it was a silver ring with a number of very tiny fine feathers brought in all round it. The ring was not closed and Mrs. Redfern slipped it over my thumb and said, "There; if you use that, you will make all the girls crazy for you."

"Really," I exclaimed, "you mean if I put it on, it will give them more pleasure?"

"You try," she exclaimed. "Don't tell them; but try and you will soon see that I've made you a wonder-worker."

"All right," I said, "I'm much obliged to you, and if you turn out to be a good prophet, I'll be liberal."

"I'm sure you will," she smiled, "but if you would try it the second time and not the first, I would feel even surer."

"Why the second time?" I asked.

"You know perfectly well," she exclaimed laughing, "you know that nine girls out of ten feel more the second time than they do the first, and if you use my tickler when they are already thrilling, you will have wonderful results."

"I'll try it this very evening," I said, "and tomorrow I will let you know all about it."

"All right," she replied, "that will suit me and meantime I'm after another instrument that will surprise you still more and make every girl crazy for you."

"First rate," I laughed, "thanks to you I think I shall learn something from India.

"The greatest country in the world," she said, solemnly, "for love-tools, or foods, or excitants: they know more here about sex-sensations and how to vivify and intensify them than anywhere else. Try my tickler and you will see."

That evening Winnie was coming to spend a couple of hours with me. At first she seemed less passionate than usual, but after half an hour or so of love's dalliance, when I thought she had reached the height of feeling, I slipped on the ring and began the final essay.

In a moment I knew that Mrs. Redfern was justified. Almost at once Winnie spread herself feverishly and soon for the first time began to move her body uncontrollably and utter strange sounds, now whimpering, now gasping, "Oh! I can't stand it; oh! stop, please, or I shall go mad! Oh! Oh! Oh!"

I too had finished, so I removed the tickler and soon Winnie was all questions. "Why did you never make me feel so intensely before? I did not feel particularly naughty tonight, but you made me lose all self-control; I never enjoyed so keenly. Oh, you wonder, Frank. I'm all yours, you know, but now you've made me crazy. How did you do it so wonderfully?"

Of course, I kept my secret. Then began for me with Winnie an astonishing series of experiences. Passion provokes passion, and when one gives intense pleasure one is summoned to try again. And again and again I tried and each time with some new thrill of delight. I have heard her cry, "Oh, you are in me and that is paradise for me. My womb opens to you, and at the same time you excite me, tease me so, that I could bite you. When I am all yours you make me feel most intensely: I cannot explain."

At the same time I noticed that as her passion increased, so her love grew: she became more and more devoted to me and would wait for hours for me to see her. Indeed it was this trait of absolute devotion that led to our separation.

I was resolved now to try the tickler as soon as possible with May. Somehow or other I felt sure that May's response would be extraordinary, for though I had not yet brought her to lose control, I knew she was passionately endowed. Her kisses promised much, and after a few kisses she used to tremble from head to foot. I resolved to use the tickler at the proper time. I would beg her to come soon and have a gorgeous night.

Next day I gave Mrs. Redfern fifty pounds and asked her to bring May that night. She could not, she told me; she would have to give a couple of day's notice and think of an excuse if I wanted her for the whole night. I did and so it was arranged. On the evening settled I was ready. But at first May disappointed me. I had excited her before I put on the silver ring but she did not respond to its use as quickly as Winnie, nor as passionately. Yet to my astonishment she guessed what the instrument was like; the priests had educated her sexually to complete understanding. She told me that when a woman was pregnant this instrument was never used, as it was supposed to excite too intensely. But when I gave her a new dress or a new hat, I found enthusiastic response in her. May was much [more] susceptible to gratitude than to passion.

What curious differences there are in women: Winnie took all such gifts as a matter of course, but responded to a new touch of sensuality as a violin to the bow. I always said that Winnie won me so completely that I never learned India thoroughly: she so obsessed me that I could spare no time for anyone else or any other thing.

But alas! her devotion made her people think. Her father had her followed once to my hotel and at length her mother came to me and begged me for the girl's sake to go away and leave her, or she would never get married; and finally I consented and went on to Burma.

There in Rangoon began for me a new series of experiences which forced me to the conclusion that the Burmese half-caste girl is one of the most fascinating in God's world, as she is certainly one of the prettiest and best formed. She is cheap too: they are all sold at from thirteen to sixteen by their parents and seldom cost even twenty pounds. But I had been wearied of passion with Winnie and Japan called to me and China, and my time for traveling was limited, so I resolved to go on, but not before I had noticed all through the East the custom practiced by the Englishman and the American, of living with native women and having half-breed children. The Eurasian girl or boy in Burma is often an excellent specimen, not only physically but mentally, but the girl's lot is almost always unhappy and often tragic.

Chapter VII

Can Personal Immortality Be Proven?

IN MY QUARTER OF A CENTURY in London there were at least two men of conspicuous ability who came to the front by proclaiming the certainty of a life after death. The one was a Mr. Sinnett* who preached in a new Magazine entitled "Broad Views." "I know people," he said boldly, "who not only remember their past lives, but are in a position, if it were worth while, to write a complete diary of every day of those ante-natal lives. For all persons the faculty in due course of time will come."

Every soul now being born into the world, Mr. Sinnett insisted, went out of the world from 1,500 to 2,000 years ago. We are therefore all contemporaries of the Apostles and the Caesars, and the ante-natal autobiographies of some of us ought to be worth reading. Dr. Anna Kingsford** believed she was a re-incarnation of Plato, and Mrs. Besant is said to be Hypatia come to life again; but these are mere assertions.

Mr. Sinnett sets forth

what happens to the soul after the death of the body. The experiences that come on first when a human soul is emancipated from the prison of the flesh are not of a very exalted order. As consciousness fades from the physical vehicle, it carries with it the fine sheath of astral matter which has interpenetrated the coarser physical vehicle during life, and in this ethereal but still quite material envelope, it exists for a time in the region commonly called the astral plane.

On the astral plane the soul, in a vehicle of consciousness which is insusceptible to heat or cold, incapable of fatigue, subject to no waste, and, therefore, superior to the necessity of taking food, continues an existence for a variable period which in many of its aspects is so like the life just abandoned that uninstructed people who pass over, constantly find it impossible to believe that they are what is called dead. But the state of things, though, as it grows familiar, and as the field of view is enlarged, may be agreeable enough, and may be associated with the renewal of friendships and affections interrupted for a time by death, is not the state of things that corresponds to the Heaven of religious teaching. . . .

* Alfred Percy Sinnett (1840–1921); he wrote several books on the occult and on the growth of the soul.

** (1846–88); she was successively the wife of a Protestant clergyman, a Catholic convert, an anti-vivisectionist, an M.D., a vegetarian, and a theosophist.

Nothing that has ever been said from the religious point of view concerning the blissful condition of the soul in Heaven involves any exaggeration. On the contrary, the basic fact connected with existence on the plane of nature corresponding to the Heaven of theology is bliss, absolute, complete and unalloyed.

But surely the methods of nature provide for all cases, and not merely for those of the spiritual aristocracy. What are we to think of the condition in Heaven of, let us say, a drunken coalheaver, whose earthly life has been anything but meritorious. Mr. Sinnett might reply that even in such a man's life there may have been some little gleams of a spiritual feeling, something resembling love for a woman or a child.

Mr. Sinnett concludes by declaring that this theory of his "is no 'theory' at all, but a living fact of consciousness." Still to most of us as yet it is only a theory and hardly even plausible.

Plainly the whole hypothesis depends on the ante-natal biographers and they are conspicuous by their absence.

The second person to preach eternal life was a Frederic Myers,* who was much more scientific than Sinnett, if I may be forgiven for using such a word about either of these dreamers. His book on *Human Personality and Its Survival of Bodily Death* is, he tells us, the result of thirty years' close study and serious thought.

Myers declares that "messages of the departing and departed have actually proved: a) Survival pure and simple; the persistence of the spirit's life as a structural law of the universe; the inalienable heritage of each several soul. b) In the second place," he says, "these messages prove that between the spiritual and the material worlds an avenue of communication does, in fact, exist; that which we call the despatch and the receipt of telepathic messages, or the utterance and the answer of prayer and supplication. c) In the third place, they prove that the surviving spirit retains, at least in some measure, the memories and the loves of earth. Without this persistence of love and memory should we be in truth the *same?*" Finally, he declares that "every element of individual wisdom, virtue, [and] love, develops in infinite evolution towards an ever-highering hope; towards Him who is at once thine innermost Self and thine ever unattainable Desire."

But all this is founded on the slightest basis, is indeed mere assertion. The whole theory is as fantastic and absurd as that of Sinnett. It only shows the intense human desire to live again after this life, but after thousands of years of study we have not the slightest proof of any such existence.

A little later there was much stronger testimony: Sir Oliver Lodge** succeeded Frederic Myers as President of the Society for Psychical Research and a few years later as head of the British Association he made some startling statements which his position in science rendered extremely

* (1843–1903); a school inspector, poet, and essayist, and a founder of the Society for Psychical Research. The book Harris refers to was published in 1903.

** (1851–1940); a pioneer in the development of radio who was also devoted to psychical research.

important. He stated boldly that "Personality persists beyond bodily death." M. Bergson* made as positive an assertion to the same effect only a short time before in an address to the Society for Psychical Research. But Lodge went further and his words carried weight. He said: "The evidence to my mind goes to prove that discarnate intelligence, under certain conditions, may interact with us on the material side, thus indirectly coming within our scientific ken; and that gradually we may hope to attain some understanding of the nature of a larger, perhaps aetherial, existence and of the conditions regulating intercourse across the chasm. A body of responsible investigators has even now landed on the treacherous but promising shores of a new continent. Yes, there is more to say than that. The methods of science are not the only way, though they are our way, of being piloted to truth. *Uno itinere non potest pervenire ad tam grande secretum.*"

He was asked if he could tell of his investigations. "Not yet," he answered. "One must wait a little longer; but I am convinced that those on the other side are trying to speak to us, and that they are doing all in their power to help us."

And he went on: "When the time comes in which men not only think or hope that they survive death, but when they *know it,* know it is a fact of life, then many of our problems will solve themselves. For it is inconceivable that men thus convinced of Immortality should lack the spirit of fellowship; inconceivable, surely, that they should depress each other, struggling for material enjoyments which entail suffering on their fellow-creatures. One believes, as Christ believed, that Brotherhood among men absolutely depends upon faith in a divine Fatherhood; the whole labour of Christ's teaching was to persuade men to believe in the existence of a God in order that they might live on the earth as the sons of one Father. Because we have ceased to believe in Immortality, because we have grown to be incurious about life after death, life here and now has assumed the dangerous characteristics which are at present troubling the politicians. Social existence is organised almost entirely on an animal basis; struggle for existence is still one of our main conditions; the dignity of life tends to disappear more and more with the stability of the social order; men are not now so concerned about *character,* about real values, as about money and enjoyment. This is why I regard the labour of psychical research as so well worth while; it is a labour which ought to result in restoring to mankind a sense of Infinity— that sense of the greatness, the grandeur, and the dignity of existence without which poetry must perish, the imagination wither, and the human species sink into a miserable condition of animal degradation."

These are weighty words: no such dignified pronouncement has been made in our time and yet, though I should like to believe that "personality persists after death," and though I believe that all manner of good would come from the faith, I cannot believe. I often wish I could.

I find myself in closer agreement with Maeterlinck, who wrote a series

* Henri Bergson (1859–1941); French philosopher.

of articles on "Life after Death" in *The Fortnightly Review* during 1913. He begins by declaring that he has "no reluctance to admit the survival and the intervention of the dead, but it is for the spirit, or for those who make use of its name, first to prove that the dead really exist."

And he sums up: "The spiritualists follow the tracks of our dead for a few seconds, in a world where seconds no longer count; and then they abandon them in the darkness."

He goes on: "The fact remains that this inability to go even a few years beyond the life after death detracts greatly from the interest of their experiments and revelations; at best, it is but a short space gained; and it is not by this juggling on the threshold that our fate is decided. I am ready to go through what may befall me in the short interval filled by those revelations, as I am even now going through what befalls me in my life. My destiny does not lie there, nor my home. The facts reported may be genuine and proved; but what is even much more certain is that the dead, if they survive, have not a great deal to teach us, whether because, at the moment when they can speak to us, they have nothing to tell us, or because, at the moment when they might have something to reveal to us they are no longer able to do so, but withdraw for ever and lose sight of us in the immensity which they are exploring."

Even Maeterlinck here seems to believe more than I can credit.

It is true that Alfred Russel Wallace believed devoutly in a life after death and believed too, as I have told, that there was continual communication between the dead and the living. But I strained ears in vain and remained at long last a confirmed skeptic. Meredith, too, another wise man, believed in a Divine Providence and the gradual disappearance from this life of all that was maimed or wrong. I could hardly rise to that height of faith. Wise men, I saw, were instruments of good in life and might yet lift this earthly life to a high plane of enjoyment and spiritual growth; but even this appeared to me doubtful, and I could find no trace of a God in nature and no hope of a life after death for man. Skepticism was rooted in my nature.

Small wonder that Professor Metchnekoff,* one of the greatest of modern scientists, declares that "since the awakening of the scientific spirit in Europe it has been recognized that the promise of a future life has no basis of fact to support it. The modern study of the functions of the mind has shown beyond all question that these are dependent on the functions of the body, in particular of those of the central nervous system."

I cannot understand why we hesitate to explain life according to our present knowledge. There is no trace of an omnipotent or all-good God to be found anywhere in Life; but there is everywhere in animals, as in insects, in birds as in fishes, abounding evidence of a creative impulse, an impulse that is the chief source of our bodily pleasures and is at the same

* Ilya Metchnekoff (1845–1916); shared a Nobel prize in 1908 with Ehrlich for his work in immunology.

time the soul, so to speak, of all our highest spiritual joys. To deny this universal creative impulse would be as ridiculous, it seems to me, as to talk of goodness in creation.

There are two other facts that appear to consort better with our wishes. We seem to be able to trace hierarchy in living creatures and it is fairly plain that the tenure of life corresponds roughly to this hierarchy, that is, the highest or most complicated creatures live the longest. Furthermore the highest in the hierarchy, men and women, are also the kindliest, the most unselfish; in short, the most moral or rather the only ones in whom morality can be said to exist.

We have then in life an universal creative impulse and this impulse satisfies itself in producing higher and higher creatures; or, if you will, more and more complex creatures, and these creatures in proportion to their complexity live longer than the others and finally develop a morality of kindness and unselfishness which the other creatures know little or nothing about.

There is a certain order in the universe, a rude imperfect order, if you will, but order nevertheless—order and law.

And strange to say, in this cosmos ruled by law, there are continued revelations of pure beauty; now a sunset or sunrise; again a coast-line framing a dark blue ocean transfigured by silvery moonlight; or a mountain gorge with pine-clad heights and shadowy depths holding a little rivulet; or simply a superb man's figure or the soul-glow in a girl's eyes—beauty everywhere, as if produced by chance—purposeless without order of any kind or law that we can detect.

Now is the creative impulse to stop and be satisfied with men and women? That is a question we cannot answer from experience. Some say the creative impulse is committed by its very nature to an endless succession of cycles. I see no reason to believe this; rather, I believe that the best men will sooner or later get together and transform this world of ours into an earthly paradise by making men and women better and wiser than we can easily imagine them to-day. It seems so simple to begin by abolishing war and doing away with armies and navies while spending the money thus saved on the education and development of the many. We could thus put an end to poverty and know nothing more of the millionaire or the starving child, and every foot of progress upward would make the next step easier, the good result more certain. The heaven dreamed of by "God's spies" can be realized here on this earth and in man's lifetime if we set ourselves to the work.

One cannot resist the question: are we tending to this goal or are we merely taking our wishes for the spirit and purpose of the universe? Even so, it may be that our unselfish desires are themselves prophetic of the future.

It looks as if the creative impulse we have found everywhere in life is working out its own fulfilment. How else can we explain the fact that the best men centuries after their death are selected out and adored as Gods, their teaching even becoming our example and inspiration?

In truth we men are called and chosen to a purpose higher than our consciousness, and the creative impulse, if not God, is at least a conscious striving to reach the highest. And we must cooperate with this impulse and do our best to make this life worth living for all and so turn men and women into ideals and this earthly pilgrimage of ours into a sacred achievement.

Chapter VIII

I HAVE OFTEN BEEN ASKED why on my African travels I was so cold in regard to the native women. I have seen Zulu girls and Swahili girls too with superb figures, and statues in ebony appeal to me as keenly as statues in ivory; how then could I live among Negroes on the most familiar terms without ever yielding to passion? I have no reasonable explanation to give, except that the colored races did not appeal to me, and when a colored girl made an appeal and half seduced me, the first touches were apt to cure my nascent desire.

The sex in the Negro, male or female, is far larger than in Europeans, and the black takes far longer to excite. The more developed the mind, the quicker is the response to passion; in fine, the Negro seemed to me in every respect inferior to the white. Of course if I had cared for any of the Negresses, it would have been easy to amend the physical disproportion—injections of alum would soon have reduced the size of the girl's sex—but nothing would better the slower nervous sensibility or lift the lower race to the European level of intellect and feeling.

In Central Africa the Negresses often compare the white lover to a cock: "scarcely has he begun till it's all over"; whereas the Negro was likened to a dog that prolonged the spasm indefinitely. All through Africa I found colored girls preferred their own stock, and often quadroons admitted that they preferred full-blown Negroes to any other lovers. Naturally in all this I am thinking merely of the act: the white lover uses mind and heart to win his beloved and often produces deeper emotion by a word or thought than by any deed; whereas the Negro suitor wastes hardly a moment in preliminary flatteries or appeals. It may be taken as certain that the genital sensitiveness of the pure Negro is nothing like so great as that of the white man. For these reasons and a host of similar ones, among which the chief was the mousey odor of the colored race, I was almost immune to temptation all the time I spent in Africa.

Of course, the disabilities were less in the case of quadroons and octoroons; but whenever I noticed colored blood I was chilled. Negresses and half-castes alike seemed to dislike all side-shows; kisses even were only tolerated and sodomy was universally condemned. Yet I often took pleasure in watching colored girls and women performing either with Boers or with their own sort. Their jealousies and passions were a constant source of interest to me.

Again and again I have been amused by the vagaries of modesty. I found more than one tribe in Central Africa in which the women and girls went completely nude in front, while covering their behinds sedulously, very much as Egyptian and Arab women when surprised by men lift up their solitary garment to conceal their eyes while exposing the sex. The natives of Tasmania move about, even among the white race, in their nudity seemingly unconcerned; but when they sit down with men, they take care to put their right heel so that it conceals their sex.

In Constantinople the women continually took all their hair off and were no more ashamed of their nudity than of their bare hands. I did not find these differences in India, though modesty was never very marked, while in China it was conspicuous by its absence. In China sensuality was studied more perhaps than anywhere else in the world.

In Shanghai I first learned that various poisons and aliments are supposed to increase desire or intensify sensation, but I cannot say that I found any of them efficacious. Indeed, I came in time to explain their use by the curious insensitiveness of Chinese women. First of all I was told that to smoke opium had the double effect of quickening the sensation and prolonging it. But I smoked the 20 pipes prescribed again and again without attaining either objective. Then someone told me I should have tried cocaine but I found that just as inoperative. Finally an English doctor who had lived for years in Pekin vaunted the benefits of ether, and in this case I am bound to say that I too could trace a distinct stimulation of desire; but this good result was off-set by the evil effect of the intoxicant itself. For a couple of days afterwards I felt sick and out of sorts. In fine, no poison seems to be worth recommending.

And the exciting food and drinks were to me just as disappointing.

It is possible to increase the size of the man's organ as it is easy to diminish the size of the woman's, but no increase of pleasure can be reckoned on save by the sadist.

In Pekin one day I was shown an apparatus which deserves description as it was intended to give pleasure to Chinese women. It consists of an oblong ball or rather a kind of egg in silver or ivory, the size of a small fowl's egg. The Chinese screw off the top of the egg and fill it half full of mercury, then screw it up again and grease it carefully.

The woman puts it into her sex and stretches herself on a rocking-chair, giving it a swinging movement to and fro. This rocking provokes the alternative moving of the mercury to one end and the other of the egg, making it slide about in the canal and producing a special sort of sexual excitement. The oblong end helps the slipping out of the apparatus when the woman gets up.

I had such an egg for a long time in my possession, in fact I had several of them, but I have given them all away. Several times I tried them and found they acted marvelously.

I went to China full of hope: I came away more disappointed than I can say. I looked upon Lao-Tse as one of the greatest of thinkers; I knew that here and there were wonderful works of art; I felt sure that I should meet men and women on the topmost levels of life; and if I must confess it, I was certain that some woman at least would give me unforgettable hours. Well, on my second visit to China I spent nearly a year in the country: I never met a great man, no Rabindranath Tagore,* and no woman that could find a place in my picture gallery.

Yet here and there I was brought to admiration: I got to know a man in the north of China who had the most wonderful carpets in the world. One he showed me which I must describe. It was some three centuries old, all deep blue and straw color with an astonishing depth of texture and coloring, and across the centre of the blue a hesitating path, perhaps a foot broad, where the blue was worn down to pale amber; and when I asked him what it meant, he replied simply, "That was the way to the Lord's chair worn by innumerable feet in three hundred years."

Now and then too, but rarely, I came across some word or thought worthy of Lao-Tse himself. I remember well how my friend who owned the carpets told me once that China was the most moral country in the world. "Time and again," he said, "we have been assaulted and invaded. We always drive the intruder back, but we never take possession of his country in revenge as the European nations do. Believe me, we Chinese are the only people who are above revenge."

It seemed to me a great word.

A hundred times I was astonished by the coldness of Chinese girls and women. They would give themselves easily enough, as simply indeed as the Indian of the bazaar, but they did not even pretend to feel any pleasure, much less indulge in any orgasm. After a few months I began to regard them with complete indifference. When I picked one out because of her eyes or mouth or complexion, I felt sure I was going to be disappointed, and in every case my fears were justified. Of course, I did not know the language and so the indifference of the women is partly explained; but still I cannot but regard them as the coldest of the children of Eve.

Some of them were beautiful—as a rule the eyes were funny and there were few faces that would seem to a European ideally lovely, but now and then even that happened, and far more frequently the figures were perfectly formed even according to our Western standards. But passion, real sensual feeling, was rarer than loveliness of face; still now and then I found that too and in most unlikely surroundings.

I remember once going home with a pretty woman in Pekin. She spoke a few words of English and paralyzed me by asking for her "little present"

* (1861–1941); awarded the 1913 Nobel Prize for Literature.

first. Shrugging my shoulders, I gave her a couple of pounds which seemed to please her greatly and put me even more on my guard. I made up my mind to take all care and use a French letter, but when we came to the bedroom I was astonished to find a girl-child of twelve or thirteen in the bed. "My daughter," said the woman, "she is too young to know anything. You don't mind?"

"No," I said, but after an hour or so of sleeplessness I found the girl looking at me with wide, smiling eyes. As soon as our glances met, she came nearer to me, and as I stretched out my hand, she put it against her breasts. Naturally I turned to her and found to my astonishment an extraordinary mistress, passionate at once and devoted, who apparently had mastered the whole art of love; for she not only gave herself with complete abandon, but sought at the same time to excite her lover to the utmost and give him every possible thrill. She spoke English too far better than her mother and I soon came to the conclusion that the whole sexual nature had been abnormally developed by her mother's practices. When I offered her money she did not wish to take it, but wanted to know my hotel and the number of my room and whether she might come there next day and at what hour. Of course, I fixed a time and was at the door waiting for her. And all the months I was in Pekin I used to see her nearly every day; she convinced me that passion and devotion, the very soul of love, was not unknown in China.

Strange to say, she wanted a child, but there I could not agree. "If you had a child," I said, "I should be tied to Pekin always and I must go away."

"Then you don't love me," was her reply.

"Oh, yes I do," I answered, but always felt she had the best of the argument. One day she told me she was fourteen and her mother had asked her for money. Naturally, I gave it with both hands. She was an adorable mistress. One evening she wanted to know if I would like her better if she took all the hairs off as most women did. I said, "No."

I liked her better as she was, but she went on earnestly, "I have the salve and will use it, if you say so. You know, there is nothing I would not do to keep your love—nothing!"

Parting from her was the hardest task I had in all my travels.

Fortunately I found an old banker who gave her from me a yearly pension, and three years afterwards she married an American; and I had a letter from her in due course, declaring that she was very happy and about to have a child.

Before going to Japan I stayed for a couple of months with an English friend and his wife in Hong-Kong, but the residence there made little or no impression on me. They told me I should find nothing worth while in Japan, but in that they were not soothsayers. Still for the time being they gave me rest and change and I was in need of both.

I write of all these things quite frankly because I believe that Puritanism is not only dead but deserved to die, and I feel sure that bodily pleasure of all sorts will be more and more sought after in the future. We are coming to a new understanding of life and its joys, just as we are reaching a deeper realization of our duty to our neighbor. We are developing an intensified paganism or the cult of the body at the same time that we are extending the new commandment given to us by the Christ. We really should seek to help and benefit our fellow-man in every way, just as we naturally seek to get all possible pleasure out of life. The reconciliation of the two creeds in a higher synthesis will possibly be the religion of the future.

Chapter IX

MY PROOF that the South African War had cost Great Britain over 1,000 millions of money and had worsened our relations with South Africa made me many enemies in England, but all the evil effects of war have seldom been adequately or carefully stated. Let me give here some new facts.

In 1901, the commission of police in London reported that in the twelve months during which Lord Kitchener was looting and burning and devastating South Africa, the criminal classes were carrying on similar operations in the heart of the empire. In a single twelve months burglaries in London rose fifty per cent. Forgeries also showed a similar increase; house-breaking rose twenty-two per cent, and shop-breaking fifteen per cent. As with crime, so with drunkenness. The number of convictions for drunkenness in the five years from 1897 to 1901 showed an increase of fifty per cent in London over the convictions for the five years from 1892 to 1896. The increase of vagrancy was even more appalling. In 1901 the number of vagrants relieved at the workhouse showed an increase of twenty per cent, and in 1901 the number was actually one hundred per cent higher than the figure at which it stood ten years before.

The tide of pauperism, which had been steadily ebbing during the Liberal régime of peace, turned completely. In 1900 there was one pauper for forty-two of the population, in 1901, one in forty, and in November 1902, one in 38.4. Not less ominous is the tale told in the *Labour Gazette* as to the increase in the number of unemployed. When the war began the percentage reported as unemployed by the trades unions was little more than 2.5. In November 1902 the percentage had doubled. The poverty in England chiefly due to the English ruling classes was intensified through this purposeless war. Here I will use another authority:

In 1904 Montague Crackenthorpe* in an article in *The Nineteenth Century* gave some figures which deserve to be widely known. He proved that "nine hundred and twenty-nine out of every thousand persons in the Kingdom die in poverty, and one of every four in London dies supported by

* (1832–1915).

public charity. Eight millions of people in the United Kingdom are on the edge of starvation, and twenty millions are not comfortable."

Such facts should be known to every man, but not one Englishman in ten thousand cares to note them, and not one in ten million attempts to understand their profound significance, much less dream of a remedy. Meanwhile Crackenthorpe sets over against this mass of human misery "murderous English sports"; "bubble" companies; gambling in all classes; £600 a year spent by the ordinary society woman on petticoats, gloves, shoes and boots alone. He sums up: "The worship of wealth in England reaches a point beyond anything that has been seen before."

Perhaps the worst of all is the true statement: "The people of England have come to look on starvation and suffering which they call distress as part of the social order. Chronic starvation is regarded as a matter of course."

I cannot help adding a table showing the cost of armaments in each of these first years of the century:

France	£38,400,000
Germany	£38,000,000
United States	£38,300,000
Russia	£43,000,000
Italy	£15,700,000

Great Britain spent £69,000,000, the heaviest outlay of the kind in the world.

The South African war was made by England as if to justify the dastardly Jameson Raid, and it was well perhaps that she should pay for it, but the wrongs she committed in South Africa were beyond belief.

In the South African war, Chamberlain made the mistake of choosing the worst possible lieutenant. Lord Milner was all for fighting until the Boers surrendered unconditionally. He armed scores of thousands of blacks. He closed the gates of the concentration camps against the miserable women and children whose homes he had burned and let loose his armed savages upon the helpless wanderers. A little further pressure and these methods of barbarism would, he believed, result in unconditional surrender.

But, thank God, the King was wiser; he was sick and tired of the war. We had drained the empire of our last resources in recruits. The Peace of Vereeniging* was the result. Peace was made on terms despite Lord Milner, but as the execution of the terms was left to him, the Boers maintain that the difference was chiefly on paper. Surrender on terms is all very well, but if the terms are not executed, and no means exist whereby they can be enforced, such surrender is practically unconditional.

Sometime after the South African war, I met Joseph Chamberlain in the lobby of the House of Commons, and he came over to me in the friendliest way and wanted to know why I had refused his last invitation to dinner. I

* In 1902.

said that the dreadful South African war was the cause of my coldness. "I thought you would be the greatest English statesman," I said, "but you had the bad luck to choose Milner, and the two of you have written one of the worst pages in all English history."

"I did what I thought my duty," he said. "Milner went beyond all my orders, but now it is all over and done with."

"Not to me," I said. "That war marks the beginning of the fall of the English Empire."

"I am sorry," he said and turned away. But now, a quarter of a century later, I see no reason to modify my opinion, though Campbell Bannerman by his wise concessions to the Boers did much to blot out the worst results of the Chamberlain-Milner rule; and, of course, the World War had still more disastrous consequences. Thanks to this last blunder, Britain lost the leadership of the nations and can never again regain it, in spite of the wonderful opportunity which still exists for her in Africa.

Very few realize that Africa is made up of three zones: the first all along the ocean, unhealthy save in the north and south; but go three hundred miles inland and you come to a land lifted from 1250 to 2500 feet above the sea, a plateau which is healthy and sunbaked; go inland another hundred miles and you come to the centre tableland, lifted from 3000 to 5000 feet above the level of the sea.

This central plateau is perhaps the healthiest and most interesting portion of the known world. And the English now own the whole of it from Khartoum to the Cape. If they would spend one hundred millions yearly in transporting their unemployed to this central plateau and keeping them a reasonable time decently, they would retrieve all their losses of the World War in two or three generations and form a central African empire healthier and more fruitful than the United States.

One man, and so far as I know only one, understood this: Mr. Abe Bailey* was born and bred in South Africa. He understood what might be done. He has farms in the north of Cape Colony, near Colesberg; they extend for an area of about 200,000 acres. When I met him, years ago, he had about 3000 acres in cultivation. He contemplated an extension of the cultivated area to 15,000 acres. By far the greatest part of his holding consisted of Karroo.

"The Karroo," said Mr. Bailey, "is the best soil in the world and is capable of the greatest development."

"I thought it a wilderness," I said.

"It is a wilderness of untold wealth," he replied. "It only requires intelligent cultivation to make South Africa one of the greatest farming countries in the world."

"But you have no water in the Karroo."

"That is where you make your mistake," said Mr. Bailey. "I have bored

---

* (1864–1940); financier and friend of Rhodes. He was imprisoned for alleged complicity in the Jameson Raid.

ninety-three times in the various parts of my farms and have struck water every time except once. Sometimes it was only fourteen feet below the surface, and the deepest boring we found necessary to make was 135 feet. In some instances the water rises to the surface by itself, but as a rule it has to be pumped up by windmills. We have about ninety windmills on our farm. There is plenty of wind, and with their aid all my cattle can be watered where they are pastured.

"I hope before long to have fifteen thousand acres under lucerne. We take five or six crops off it every year, and after I had fed all my stock last year we had six hundred and fifty tons of lucerne hay left on hand. It is marvelous what lucerne will do. I estimate the value of my lucerne at £7 an acre—not bad for land which I bought seven years ago at 17 shillings an acre."

"Don't you exhaust the soil?" I asked.

"Not at all. The lucerne grows up by itself. When once the land is laid down under lucerne, it continues to grow year after year; supply it with water and you have an unfailing supply of fodder for your stock."

"What stock does your farm carry?"

"I am rather proud of the variety of my stock. Mine is the only farm in the whole world on which you will find sheep, cattle, horses, Angora goats, and ostriches, all doing well, and all the best of their kind."

"Do you think there is much land in South Africa that could be made as profitable as your farm?"

"I think," replied Mr. Bailey, "I have got the pick of the bunch, but there are millions of acres that are almost as good, with any number of spruits running to waste, and square miles of Karroo which are quite waterless for want of the windmill. I think," added Mr. Bailey, "my farm has demonstrated in practical fashion that South Africa can be made one of the richest farming countries in the world. But you must have (1) brains in the management; (2) windmills to raise water for your stock; (3) dams to secure the irrigation of the flat land on either side of the spruit; (4) lucerne with which to fodder your stock in winter time, and (5) you must raise nothing but the best stock. If you stick to these five rules you will not go far wrong."

If the English had given Abe Bailey power, he might have made an Eldorado of South Africa.

But you have British statesmen like Asquith and Grey, who will make a World War without fear or doubt or hesitation, but no one who will attempt at small cost to build up a world empire. Yet the central plateau of Africa is sure to become a world empire in the near future, for the climate is not only healthful, but the country is astoundingly attractive and rich as well, sunbaked and life-giving all the year round, without being too hot even in summer and on the equator.

The great event of January, 1906, was the overwhelming defeat of the party that made the South African War. The great event of February was the re-establishment at Westminster of a Parliament which in every sense represented the heart of the nation. For years Parliament had been sinking in public esteem. In the last years of the Balfour ministry it had come to be treated with contempt. Now all that was changed. Westminster was alive again. Even the peers showed symptoms of a new life.

The King's speech, which was of considerable length, contained the welcome announcement that responsible government was to be established this year in both the Transvaal and the Orange Free State, in the confident expectation that "the grant of free institutions will be followed by an increased prosperity and of loyalty to the empire."

And best of all, the Chinese laborers in the Transvaal, or slaves as they really were, were to be sent home again at the cost of the British government. In the division of the question of Chinese labor, the government majority rose to 325.

And so Milnerism was finally killed. His speech in the House of Commons was his death-song. In it the tyrant stood confessed—a tyrant whose one ideal of government was to use racial supremacy as his sole instrument. There was no longer any disguise. Naked and unashamed, Milnerism stood revealed before our eyes.

No wonder Lord Milner is miserable. To have been directly responsible for the slaughter of 25,000 fighting men, and for the doing to death of 5,000 women and 20,000 helpless infants, would have been a terrible burden to bear, even if the end had justified the means. But Lord Milner, in the frankest fashion admitted his failure:

"Just now the Transvaal—indeed, all South Africa—is under a cloud. It has cost us great sacrifice. The compensations which we expected, and reasonably expected, have not come."

Seldom has there been a more signal and instantaneous manifestation of the magic influence of justice and sympathy than in the rally of the whole Boer nation to his Majesty's ministers the moment they showed that they intended to keep faith with his Afrikander subjects. General De Wet* even carried this so far as to deprecate making any representations to the new government until time had been given them to see what they would do of their own free will. The Boers have helped British Liberals by making it exceedingly clear and plain what are the actual needs of the country.

Campbell Bannerman was wise enough to do all they wanted and thus won for himself and the Liberal party undying honor. The aristocracy and Milnerism had come to much the same grief in South Africa at the end of the nineteenth century as their predecessors achieved in the United States at the end of the eighteenth.

* Christian De Wet (1854–1922); he first won recognition in the Transvaal War of 1881–2, and he wrote a book on the Boer War. He was captured during the South African uprising in 1914 and was imprisoned for six months.

Chapter X

MY FIRST VISIT to Japan, more than fifty years ago now, was one of intense enjoyment. I was interested almost at once as I have never been interested anywhere else. Almost immediately I grasped the main fact that the people were freer of morality than even the French. I meant to stay a month and stayed nearly six. I went all up the inland sea and began, I think, to understand that great people in most of its idiosyncracies. I had good help: an English Captain who soon became a friend, owned the chief English paper in Japan, and he was never tired of putting me right.

The first thing that struck me wherever I went in Japan was the astonishing politeness and courtesy of the people. To enter either an hotel or an inn was a real pleasure. Everyone seemed glad to see you and the little waitresses were smiling with pleasure and delighted to do whatever they could for you.

All through the country I had the same experience: everywhere courtesy was present to a degree unknown in Europe. Of course, I soon learned that this courtesy was developed in the home, where everyone bowed to age. The grandfather and the grandmother were most respected, then came the father and the mother, and then the children. And the children obeyed the same law: the eldest girl or boy came into the room first, the others followed in order of age—an astonishingly courteous people to whom deference is a pleasure.

The Japanese language, too, is full of ceremonial phrases which are impossible to translate into any European tongue. They are the politest race in the world and perhaps the most amiable.

Many scenes stand out still in my memory. I remember in an up-country town my jinricksha was stopped by some naked girls and women who came out of a bathing place; they all wanted to see if I was white all over, and I could only laugh and let them convince themselves. The crowd increased to half a hundred, and they were of all ages and all absolutely nude. When I touched the breasts of a pretty girl she seemed pleased and the whole crowd laughed as at a good joke.

Bit by bit I came to understand that there was not a trace of sexual modesty in Japan from one end to the other; most of the women even did not understand what Europeans mean by the concept.

Every foreigner is naturally eager to see géishas dancing, but he is astonished at first to find how modest and how graceful the dances are, more like those of ancient Greece perhaps than any I can think of.

The *géisha ya* are places where the dancing girls are trained and let out day or evening to tea-houses or private parties; they are generally managed by women. Little girls are taken into these houses and trained, not only in the art of dancing, but are also taught singing and *samisen* playing and all the etiquette of entertaining guests. The géisha is always willing to become the mistress of any foreigner who may desire her or from whom she can expect a fair sum of money; but in Japan she is not therefore looked down upon as she would be in Europe. The géishas are the pleasantest part of Japanese entertainments; as soon as the dainty girls enter the room, sometimes in gold or scarlet, or both, and dance before you, imitating leaves driven by the wind, all the guests wake up; or the girls will play warriors and copy the warlike gestures of old heroes; and then suddenly they give up pretences and come and sit beside their temporary employers, laughing, jesting and drinking.

Soon the foreigner finds out that the géishas are really dancers and that the prostitute or *jörö* is of a lower class altogether. Every city in Japan has its *jöröya* or licensed quarter of prostitution. The supervision is rigid and immediately one can recognize the *obi* or sash, tied in front instead of behind as a badge. But even these women are not looked down upon in Japan as they are in Europe. Many of them are sold in childhood to the keeper of the houses and there trained for the work. A few have sacrificed themselves freely for those they love, and many romances are written about the virtuous jörö who has sacrificed herself for her loved one and who finds a lover willing and eager to make her again a respectable wife and a mother of decent children.

There are theatres for men and theatres for women, but the two sexes never play on the same stage, I don't know why. The performances last all day from eight or nine in the morning till eight or nine in the evening; they were not especially interesting to me. But the most peculiar and important Japanese entertainment is the fortune-teller. Of course they have most influence with the lowest class, but they are consulted on important occasions by all classes. A marriage, an illness, a journey, are all alike subjects for the fortune-teller. Just in proportion as there is little belief in the supernatural in life, so men and women tend to become more superstitious.

The freedom in Japan is very interesting. I remember being asked by a court official to stay with him and study Japanese manners in his house. My friend, the captain, advised me to accept and I did so. The first evening my host told me in his broken English that his wife would be too old to be attractive to me, while his daughters were too young; but he would send me a pretty girl to entertain me in the night. I laughed, never thinking he meant what he said. But when I got to my bedroom, I found a pretty maid awaiting me, who as soon as I entered began to undress. She was too pretty to be sent away, and I had recognized her at once as the most charming of the servants who had waited on us. My friend, the captain, laughed when I told him and said that nothing was more usual.

It is undoubtedly the system of concubinage that degrades the whole status of women in Japan. The emperor, in accordance with the old Chinese code, was allowed twelve concubines or *mékaké*, while the samurai are allowed two. All men of the higher class are allowed to introduce these mékaké into their families, and naturally these concubines, though beneath the wife in position, are often more beloved than the wife herself. In the lower classes the wife often protests and maintains her exclusive rights, but the wife of the nobleman is not powerful enough. Consequently the position of the wife of the noble in Japan is usually unhappy and often tragic. By a recent law no child of a concubine can inherit a legal title, and this may do much to establish the higher class woman in a securer position.

Not once but a dozen times up country I came upon some woman or girl taking a bath: never did I see the slightest trace of embarrassment, much less of what we would call modesty. The girl or woman would get out of the hot bath and proceed to dry herself with her little blue towel just as if there was no man within ten miles of her. At the same time, I have heard Japanese ladies speak scornfully of the low-necked dresses worn by English and American ladies at court. Who can explain the thousand eccentricities of manners?

In many respects I found life in Japan much saner than life in Europe, but in one respect there was no comparison. If you took a géisha as a mistress and asked her whether she was healthy or not, you could rely on her answer; especially if you treated her fairly, you could usually trust her to tell you the exact truth as she knew it. Consequently there was less danger of foul venereal disease in Japan than in Europe. Besides, there was less danger of getting a child: every géisha knew how to prepare some little wad of oiled paper which she introduced into the vagina and so made pregnancy practically impossible. In Europe the wise mistress uses a wad of cotton wool with a small string attached, but [the] Japanese way is just as efficacious.

In many ways I came to regard Japan as the France of the East, not only in the disdain of ordinary modesty, but also in love of art and appreciation of artists and writers. Besides, just as there is an heroic soul behind all the flighty heedlessness of French character, so there is an extraordinary heroism in Japan that every now and then astonishes the observer. A wife injures her husband or a soldier makes some blunder that brings ruin on others; forthwith the woman or man recognizes his fault and does justice by taking his own life.

I shall never forget one of my first days in Japan or one of my last. I was invited by my friend, Captain B., to a festive evening. He had brought together a special corps of géishas and they were attended by *mousmées* who came and sat with us while the géishas danced. The little mousmée who came to me was the prettiest of the whole lot and I suppose I showed her that I admired her. At any rate, the dance was not half over when her hand began to stray, and from light touches she soon went on to bolder demonstrations of desire. At length I said to her, "Later," one of the few Japanese words I knew. She pouted and then laughed with enjoyment, nodding her head.

When the géishas finished their dance and came back to sit with us, I said to my host, "Is it possible for me to keep the little mousmée?"

"Sure," he replied, and with a word or two made my resolve known. Never did I see such gratitude in any human face as the little mousmée showed to me there. I was sure that for some reason or other her self-pride at being preferred to the more important géishas was inordinately pleased, and I felt sure that I should be rewarded. And I was. As soon as we were alone together in the bedroom, she began to show a mixture of affection and passion impossible to describe. She was pretty and beautifully formed and had evidently learned all the tricks of [the] love-trade—a strange little mistress, who was also clever enough to cease exciting me when she thought I was satisfied. Her body—a perfect instrument of love.

When I began again to make love to her, she threw away restraint and became astonishing. But all the while the self-restraint was underneath, so to speak, and both in her passion and her self-control she made the night memorable to me. I have always known since that there were Japanese maidens as lovely as the loveliest of any other race and gifted besides with a zest of love and passion that one usually finds only in France.

When Captain B. and I met in the morning, I told him all my feelings and gave him a ten pound note to convey my satisfaction to my little friend. To my wonder and his the money was refused and the mousmée told me with a brave glance that she would always be willing to welcome me without money and without price. Captain B. declared that it was the first time in all his twenty years' acquaintance with Japan that such a thing had happened.

About a week later I received a letter from the mousmée saying that she cared for me and if I wished she would come and be my servant till I left Japan. I thank God I had sense enough to accept her offer, and most of what happened to me afterwards was due to her guidance and will be told in a later chapter.

Chapter XI

Maurice Maeterlinck, Wells, Frederic Howe, and Sir John Gorst

I HAVE KNOWN Maeterlinck for more than a quarter of a century. When I first met him, Georgette LeBlanc was living with him as his wife; she was most sympathetic. It was Georgette LeBlanc who told me how she had met him first, I think in Brussels or in Bruges, and at once had fallen desperately in love with him and told him so; love on both sides consummated in marriage, as I understood. Before meeting Maeterlinck I had a great admiration for his early work; everything he did interested me, and in my mind he always stood as one of the world-figures of our time.

In 1906 he wrote an extraordinary article on "Our Morality," wherein he expounded the view that I have put forth again and again in these pages. "Christianity," he said, "is dead and the inhibitions of Christianity, including chastity, must disappear with it." He faces the issue boldly:

"Already we have thrown off a number of constraints which were assuredly hurtful, but which at least kept up the activity of our inner life. We are no longer chaste, since we have recognized that the work of the flesh, cursed for twenty centuries, is natural and lawful."

Maeterlinck shrugs his shoulders at those who are afraid that the practice of a lofty and noble morality will perish in an environment that obeys other laws. He says:

"Those who assure us that the moral ideal must disappear because the religions are disappearing, are strangely mistaken. It was not the religions that formed this ideal, but the ideal that gave birth to the religions. . . . There is nothing as yet to be changed in our old Aryan ideal of justice, conscientiousness, courage, kindness and honor. We have only to draw nearer to it, to clasp it more closely, to realize it more effectively; and, before going beyond it, we have still a long and noble road to travel beneath the stars."

He is equally confident that virtue in this life stands in no need of support drawn from beyond the tomb.

This is plain enough, but Maeterlinck does not stop there.

He maintains that "what constitutes the essence of morality is the sincere and strong wish to form within ourselves a powerful idea of justice and love which always rises above that formed by the clearest and most generous portions of our intelligence. Its sources must be sought," he declares in noble words, "not in the precepts of religions, but in imagination and the mystic summit of our reason. Do and say what we may, we have never been, we are not yet, a sort of purely logical animal. There is in us, above the reasoning portion of our reason, a whole region which answers to something different which is preparing for the surprises of the future, which is awaiting the events of the unknown."

This part of our intelligence, he calls "imagination or mystic reason."

Maeterlinck adjures the rationalist and materialist to "leave us a few fancy virtues. Allow a little space for our fraternal sentiments. It is very possible that these virtues and these sentiments, which are not strictly indispensable to the just man of to-day, are the roots of all that will blossom when man shall have accomplished the hardest stage of the struggle for life."

And here he reaches the highest height of thought. "Also we must keep a few sumptuary virtues in reserve, in order to replace those which we abandon as useless, for our conscience has need of exercise and nourishment. . . . Our ideal no longer asks to create saints, virgins, martyrs; but even though it takes another road, the spiritual road must remain intact, and is still necessary to the man who wishes to go further than simple justice. It is beyond that simple justice that the morality begins of those who hope in the future. It is in this perhaps fairy-like, but not chimerical part of our conscience that we must acclimatize ourselves and take pleasure. It is still reasonable to persuade ourselves that in so doing we are no dupes."

Since writing this, Maeterlinck has written a masterpiece on "Bees,"* but as much of the knowledge was taken from Fabre, I don't think so much of the book. But the other day he wrote another masterpiece on the "Ants"— a book no one should miss.

But alas, for some reason or other he has parted company with Georgette and is now living with a young girl whom Georgette was foolish enough to bring into the house. I liked Georgette so much that after she left, I did not pursue my acquaintance with Maeterlinck. Probably I was wrong; but such breaks damage friendship.

Whenever I think of Maeterlinck, Wells comes into my head. He has always seemed to me about the best brain in England and his constant advocacy of socialism has interested me profoundly. In the *Grand Magazine* for September 1907 he pointed out that "in land and housing, railways, food, drink, and coal, there is a strong case for the substitution of collective control for the private ownership methods of the present time." He insists that "private ownership is only a phase in human development necessary and serviceable in its time, but not final." He maintains that "the idea of the

* 1901.

private ownership of things and the rights of owners is enormously and mischievously exaggerated in the contemporary world. The conception of private property has been extended to land, to material, to the values and resources accumulated by past generations, to a vast variety of things that are properly the inheritance of the whole race. As a result of this, there is an enormous obstructional waste of human energy and an entire loss of opportunity and freedom for the mass of mankind; progress is retarded, there is a vast amount of avoidable wretchedness, cruelty and injustice."

And he sums up:

"The socialist holds that the community as a whole should be inalienably the owner and administrator of the land, of all raw materials, of all values and resources accumulated from the past, and that all private property must be of a terminable nature, reverting to the community and subject to the general welfare."

This statement, though true, does not contain all the truth; it never seems to occur to Wells that order in the universe is kept by the interaction of two forces, the centripetal or socialistic, and the centrifugal or individualistic. Every department of life that the individual can control should be left to him, for he stands for initiative and progress; but all the departments of life and public service, which he can only control through joint-stock companies or with others, should be given over to state control, such as railways, gas and water companies; and, of course, the land must belong to all.

Goethe was the first to state the truth: In the fragment of a play on *Prometheus,* Epimetheus asks, "What then is thine?" And Prometheus answers:

> The sphere that my activity can fill;
> No more, no less.

Wells sees nothing in individualism and goes on to preach that the spirit of gain must give way to the spirit of service. The present dominance of the spirit of gain leads, he says, to "the apotheosis of the Rockefeller type," and he analyzes the more than dubious methods by which great fortunes are made. He says wisely: "All the beauty of life is chilled and crippled by the predominance of the spirit of gain."

To me it seems that Maeterlinck is probably the greater man. The evils of English life where unrestrained individual greed is at its very worst has limited Wells's thinking, whereas Maeterlinck lives beyond the present and forecasts the ideal of the future.

Curiously enough, Wells never seems to see the chief evil in English life, which is assuredly the dominance of the aristocracy. So far as I know he has never mentioned the widespread corruption due to this ruling class. Fortunately one American, a Mr. Frederic Howe,* has shown himself wiser.

---

* (1867–1940), lawyer, political scientist, and reformer; he was an authority on municipal government.

He says England is still feudal to the core:

> Above are the landed gentry, below are forty millions of workers. The class which governs, governs in its own interests. Corruption under the form of law flourishes in the British Parliament. The British Government is really merged in the economic interest of the aristocracy.
>
> *Robbery of tenants, railways, cities.* By an ancient valuation the land tax is still only six million dollars yearly. Were the land of Great Britain revalued periodically as is the land of every American state, the aristocracy which controls the government would pay nearly two hundred million dollars a year instead of six million dollars.

Mr. Howe is amazed at the way in which the local rates are assessed against the tenant and paid by the occupier; the landlord pays nothing, or next to nothing. So thrift is actually punished. The taxation of land values is still ignored by Parliament. "Its members are making use of the trust reposed in them to increase their own revenues through tax evasions by hundreds of millions of dollars each year."

He is also indignant at the way in which the landed gentry rob the railways. Parliament, composed of the landed gentry, exacts from the railway companies exorbitant prices for the land they have to purchase. He quotes, with horror, the case of the Borough of Marylebone, which "wished to buy the electric installation of a private company for three million dollars. The private company demanded four million dollars. The matter was submitted to arbitration and the referees decided that the Council must pay 6½ million dollars and 2½ million dollars additional expenses. The real worth of the plant was under three millions, and the ratepayers had to pay nine million dollars."

Mr. Howe maintains that "it is the same interested class in Parliament that approves of extortion from cities desiring to purchase the water and gas and other monopolies."

> Thus Sheffield paid 1,463,000 dollars for an electric lighting plant whose value was but 605,700 dollars. Birmingham paid over 2,000,000 dollars for a system whose value was but 1,065,000 dollars. The city of Liverpool paid 3,000,000 dollars for the franchises of the steel railways. But the metropolis of London was the worst sufferer. It paid 205,790,000 dollars for the eight private water companies which it purchased in 1905. The total value of the property was estimated to be but 121,662,000 dollars; while the companies claimed that they should be allowed 247,895,000 dollars.

Finally Mr. Howe maintains that "judged by the American standard of honesty, Congress is a more honorable body than Parliament. Englishmen submit to being plundered; Americans rebel. Great Britain takes it as a matter of course that in the last Parliament 229 members of the House of Commons held between them 673 directorships in corporations, while 108 Peers were on the boards of 367 companies."

A class plundering a nation. So Mr. Howe describes the arrangement by which the landlords of Great Britain regard the Government as theirs by divine sanction. He criticizes the social eminence of the country families:

In their local sphere they are supreme. This worship of a class, a class for centuries identified with the land, is the controlling fact in the life of Great Britain. It is woven into all legislation. It dominates society. It ramifies into jurisprudence. It supports the Church. It explains the poverty of the millions and the luxurious wealth of the few. It corrupts the professions and public opinion. It enervates the Army and the Church. It has undermined the physical stamina of the people. It has created a servility on the part of those who form the middle and lower classes—found nowhere else in Europe. It is this control by the few hundred thousand at the top that is impoverishing the nation. For the privileges of the few have become an exhausting burden on the many.

This is doleful reading, and a more doleful prospect is held out by Mr. Howe:

Viewed in a large perspective, Great Britain has reached a condition not dissimilar from that of Rome in the declining days of the Republic, when the Senate, enriched by the plunder of public lands, dispossessed the people from the soil and drove them to the cities, there to subsist on public aid. Like the privileged orders of the old régime in France, those who rule Great Britain have made use of their power for the creation of special privileges.

Sir John Gorst, the Conservative veteran, contributed to the *North American Review* in 1905 a weighty indictment of the British governing classes. It is entitled "Physical Degeneration in Great Britain." He said:

These investigations leave no doubt that in the poorer districts of Great Britain and Ireland, a large proportion of the children—the exact proportion there is no evidence to determine—is growing up so deteriorated by starvation and from insufficient and improper food, that they can never become normal citizens, that they will be the seed-bed of disease and crime, and that as long as they live they must remain a burden on society.

The report, he adds, occasioned general alarm:

It was discussed at Town Councils and Education Committees and in public meetings of every sort. But when Parliament met in 1905, it proved that the only people who had paid no attention were the Government. All Departments disclaimed having taken any step to consider or carry out its recommendations, and the Board of Education, when hard pressed, appointed another committee of junior officials to subvert, if they could, some of its conclusions.

And Sir John Gorst summed up:

The deterioration is allowed to go on unheeded under the eyes of public authorities although the legal right of all children to be well fed and properly cared for is undoubted. In many schools the condition of ailing children is actually aggravated. Fresh air and fresh water are not provided; sight and hearing are injured by exercises or discipline; lessons, driven into children starving or exhausted by labour, addle their feeble brains. For the neglect of the physical condition of the poor and their children, the rich indeed must pay a terrible penalty. Consumption has its seed-bed among the starving scholars, and the contagion strikes rich and poor alike.

Chapter XII

Ellen Terry and Sarah Bernhardt;
Lord Grey, Rochefort and Rudyard Kipling;
Marcelin Berthelot

I HAVE WRITTEN LITTLE about the greatest English and French actresses of my time; little about Ellen Terry, whom I love, and little about Sarah Bernhardt, who for twenty years was the idol of civilized Europe. No two women could be more dissimilar: whatever height Ellen Terry reached as an actress, she was before and above everything a woman; whereas Sarah was always a *cabotine* pure and simple, even when she was most a woman. I knew both women pretty intimately, though Sarah was far nearer to me than Ellen.

Ellen Terry was the best actress in half a dozen of Shakespeare's plays that I have ever seen. She made even Ophelia interesting.

Very early in her career I noticed that she talked on the stage, now giving directions to some other actress, now criticizing even Irving. She was the acme of naturalness even on the stage, or rather the stage was the true scene of her life and triumphs. And now she is eighty-odd years old and just as charming and attractive as ever.

Her first marriage with the great painter Watts* took place when she was sixteen. Watts was thirty years older. She sat for him in a dozen characters and he painted her magnificently; but what caused the rupture between them, he never told, and she was almost as reticent—though once she admitted that she "never loved Watts," which perhaps was confession enough. "He was charming," she said, "and I loved the pictures he made of me, but I never cared for him."

The first time I saw Sarah was in 1878, I think, in the Comédie Française. After the play I went behind the scene with Marguerite Durand and she introduced me to Sarah. Sarah treated me with very mild interest, but it was written that I should know her better.

I had met the Damalas** in Athens; they were all staying at the Hotel

---

* George Frederick Watts (1817–1904); they parted in a year.
** Sarah Bernhardt married Jacques Damala in 1882.

d'Athènes just opposite the Royal Palace, where I also had a room. The son was in the Corps de Pages; the sister had married a Scot, and deserted by him, was living with her mother. They had all come from Marseilles and were as good looking a trio as one could meet in a day's walk. I have told how I became intimate with the girl through the looseness of the mother, and when the son threw up the page business and went to Paris, I applauded him.

Six months later we met in Paris, where he soon became the accredited admirer of Sarah Bernhardt. He was one of the handsomest men I have ever seen and Sarah fell for him to a degree that was almost incredible. I have told how she got him to act on her stage and took him on one of her journeys through Eastern Europe. In Trieste, I think it was, she noticed that he was deceiving her with a young actress in her company and at once blackguarded him before the whole troop. Damala heard her to the end in silence, and then said simply: "Madame, you will never again have the opportunity of calling me names." His ideal was always the perfect gentleman: he left that same evening for Paris. Without him she could not continue her tour and returned to Paris disconsolate and begged me to bring about a meeting with the only man she had ever loved. I did what she wished, but Damala would not go back to her. "A great talent," he said to me, "but a small nature and a foul tongue."

It was almost her epitaph. I never thought her as great an actress as Ellen Terry, and certainly never comparable to the Duse.

In these years in London between the beginning of the century and the Great War, there were many men of ability that one ought to write about. First and foremost of course Sir Edward Grey, and then Abe Bailey and Barney Barnato, and J. B. Robinson. Grey, of course, was an English aristocrat, whereas the other three were South African millionaires. The first time I met Grey was at dinner at Sir Charles Dilke's. Dilke had a high opinion of him; Grey was good-looking, above medium height, slightly but well built, with a mind that seemed very receptive. In reality, he had no measure of those that talked to him; he accepted Dilke's opinions of South Africa as readily as mine, and when Harold Frederic talked to him of the United States, he accepted some things and rejected others, according to his original conceptions. Consequently he learned nothing valuable. He listened most pleasantly, but I soon found out that he had learned nothing except an argument or two to defend his original view. Grey has one of the closed minds of the world and it is almost as bad as to have no mind at all. I rate him now below almost any of his contemporaries in position.

Abe Bailey was a Transvaal millionaire whom I have already written about, and Barney Barnato had not only made one fortune in Kimberley, but another and larger one in Johannesburg. I have told how he lost a million or so bucking against Rhodes and Beit, and how he finally threw himself overboard on the steamer returning to England and perished miserably. But Abe Bailey was better balanced, if not so rich; he resolved to make a second home in London and now for more than 25 years has been an important figure there.

J. B. Robinson, too, pursued the same course, though for one reason or another he was disliked by most of his fellows. Since the beginning of the century he has been a resident in Park Lane and is strong and well, though he was over fifty years of age in 1900, a slight weakness of hearing being his chief physical defect. Robinson, curiously enough, was about the first man to find and buy diamonds in Kimberley, and also was the first to discover and exploit the gold mines of the Rand. He can tell the romantic story of South Africa's wealth better than any other man, but it is now quite well-known.

None of these people impressed me like Henri Rochefort in Paris. He was really an extraordinary person full of wit and venom. I have already told how after Fashoda, when he heard that Queen Victoria intended to pass the winter in Nice for her health, he wrote in his paper *L'Intransigeant* that she had better stay at home. She was not wanted in France, he said, "that old stagecoach that persists in calling itself Victoria." He came to see me and spent a month or so with me in London. I found him kindly to those he knew, but he held nine out of ten men in disdain. For fifty-odd years he had fought as a journalist in Paris, "the noblest profession," he said, "when not the lowest," and now in 1912 for the first time he had to rest.

"I'll soon be at work again," he said, "my old teeth can still bite." But a little later in his eighty-third year he went out and in June 1913 all Paris followed his remains to the grave. There was Clemenceau whom he had called "a loathsome leper," and Briand, "the moulting vulture," and Jaurès,* his pet aversion, "the decaying turnip."

Was his influence good or bad? Distinctly bad, I should say, but Paris forgave him everything because of his wit, as London has forgiven everything to Kipling because of his hidebound patriotism.

Very few people now remember the noble letter in which George Russell** "AE," scourged Kipling for what he had written about Ireland. Of course, the trouncing was well deserved. Kipling had written against the Irish, just as he has written a dastardly story against the Russians, whom he regarded as dangerous to England; and when France in 1906 pushed forward at Fashoda into what was regarded as British Africa, Kipling wrote against the French furiously; and in the World War he coolly declared that no German should be allowed to survive. Why he fell foul of Ireland, I cannot recall, but Russell's letter will witness forever against him in literature. It begins:

I speak to you, brother, because you have spoken to me, or rather, you have spoken for me. I am a native of Ulster. So far back as I can trace the faith of my forefathers, they held the faith for whose free observance you are afraid.

* Jean Jaurès (1859–1914); he founded the Socialist paper, *L'Humanité*.
** (1867–1935).

You have Irish blood in you. I have heard, indeed, Ireland is your mother's land, and you may, perhaps, have some knowledge of the Irish sentiment. You have offended against one of our noblest literary traditions in the manner in which you have published your thoughts.

I would not reason with you but that I know there is something truly great and noble in you, and there have been hours when the immortal in you secured your immortality in literature, when you ceased to see life with that hard cinematograph eye of yours and saw with the eyes of the spirit, and power and tenderness and insight were mixed in magical tales. Surely you were far from the innermost when, for the first time, I think, you wrote of your mother's land and my countrymen.

I have lived all my life in Ireland holding a different faith from that held by the majority. I know Ireland as few Irishmen know it, county by county, for I travelled all over Ireland for years, and, Ulster man as I am, and proud of the Ulster people, I resent the crowning of Ulster with all the virtues and the dismissal of other Irishmen as "thieves and robbers." I resent the cruelty with which you, a stranger, speak of the most lovable and kindly people I know.

You are not even accurate in your history when you speak of Ulster's traditions and the blood our forefathers spilt. Over a century ago Ulster was the strong and fast place of rebellion, and it was in Ulster that the Volunteers stood beside their cannon and wrung the gift of political freedom for the Irish parliament. You are blundering in your blame. You speak of Irish greed in I know not what connection, unless you speak of the war waged over the land; and yet you ought to know that both parties in England have by act after act confessed the absolute justice and rightness of that agitation, Unionist no less than Liberal, and both boast of their share in answering the Irish appeal. They are both proud today of what they did. They made inquiry into wrong and redressed it.

But you, it seems, can only feel angry that intolerable conditions imposed by your laws were not borne in patience and silence. For what party do you speak? When an Irishman has a grievance you smite him. How differently you would have written of Runnymede and the valiant men of England who rebelled whenever they thought fit. You would have made heroes out of them.

Have you no soul left, after admiring the rebels in your own history, to sympathize with other rebels suffering deeper wrongs? Can you not see deeper into the motive for rebellion than the hireling reporter who is sent to make up a case for the paper of a party?

The best in Ulster, the best Unionists in Ireland, will not be grateful to you for libelling their countrymen in your verse. For, let the truth be known, the mass of Irish Unionists are much more in love with Ireland than with England. They think Irish Nationalists are mistaken, and they fight with them, and they use harsh words, and all the time they believe Irishmen of any party are better in the sight of God than Englishmen. They think Ireland is the best country in the world, and they hate to hear Irish people spoken of as "murderers and greedy scoundrels."

Murderers! Why, there is more murder done in any four English shires in a year than in the whole of the four provinces of Ireland. Greedy! The nation never accepted a bribe, or took it as an equivalent or payment for an ideal, and what bribe would not have been offered to Ireland if it had been willing to foreswear its traditions?

I am a person whose whole being goes into a blaze at the thought of oppression of faith, and yet I think my Catholic countrymen infinitely more tolerant than those who hold the faith I was born in. I am a heretic judged by their standards, a heretic who has written and made public his heresies, and I have never suffered in friendship or found by my heresies an obstacle in life.

I set my knowledge, the knowledge of a lifetime, against your ignorance, and I say you have used your genius to do Ireland and its people a wrong. You have intervened in a quarrel of which you do not know the merits like any brawling bully who passes and only takes sides to use his strength. If there was a high court of poetry, and those in power jealous of the noble name of poet and that none should use it save those who were truly knights of the Holy Ghost, they would hack the golden spurs from your heels and turn you out of court.

You had the ear of the world and you poisoned it with prejudice and ignorance. You had the power of song, and you have always used it on behalf of the strong against the weak. You have smitten with all your might at creatures who are frail on earth but mighty in the heavens, at generosity, at truth, at justice, and Heavens have withheld vision and power and beauty from you, for this your verse is only a shallow newspaper article made to rhyme.

One of the noblest letters ever written; but it did not hinder Kipling from getting the Nobel prize, though he has done more to stir up hate between the nations than any other living man. I have told of meeting him casually many years ago now when he first returned from India, but this letter of "AE" is the final judgment on him.

I cannot resist the temptation to write of an even greater man, a noble Frenchman, Marcelin Berthelot,* one who, I think, touched the zenith of humanity. His father was described by Renan as an accomplished physician, and a man of admirable charity and devotion: "Living in a populous district, he treated most of his patients gratuitously, and lived and died poor." At the close of a brilliant college career, Marcelin chose science. He soon became friends with Renan, and the friendship seems to have been ideal. His great contributions to human progress lay in chemical synthesis, thermochemistry and agricultural chemistry. His synthetic chemistry created acetylene and a whole series of hydrocarbons.

He never would consent to derive the slightest personal benefit from any of his discoveries, but always relinquished the profit to the community at large.

He was, nevertheless, constantly urged to fill his pockets. Owing to his first researches on *carburette d'hydrogène,* he discovered an improvement in the manufacture of gas for lighting purposes which constituted for Paris alone a saving of several hundred millions of francs to the gas company. He immediately made his discovery public without deriving any personal advantage from it.

Important manufacturers, such as the millionaire Menier,** often came to him with proposals of partnership, or tried to buy some of his processes for the synthetic manufacture of organic compounds. The brewers of

* (1827–1907); he had charge of the defenses of Paris in 1870 and was foreign minister, 1895–96.
** Emile Justin Menier (1826–81); chocolate manufacturer.

northern France once offered him two million francs if he would give them the monopoly of one of his discoveries. Enormous fortunes have been made out of one single item of his scientific treatises. His researches on explosives led to smokeless powder and would have accumulated riches for him equal to those of Nobel.

Germany owes the greater part of her wonderful modern industrial development to the introduction to science of Berthelot's revolutionary synthetic method.

In the course of his long career he never took out a single patent, and always relinquished to humanity the benefit of his discoveries. "The scientist," he said, "ought to make the possession of truth his only riches."

He wrote in 1895: "It is now half a century since I attained the age of manhood, and I have faithfully lived up to the ideal dream of justice and truth which dazzled my youth. . . . I have always had the will to achieve what I thought morally the best for myself, my country, and humanity."

While perpetually engaged in his chemical researches he still took part in public life. He became a senator, a minister of public instruction, minister of foreign affairs, and a pioneer of the *entente cordiale*.

His private life was just as beautiful. His wife was thus described at the time of her wedding by the brothers De Goncourt:

"A singular beauty, never to be forgotten; a beauty, intelligent, profound, magnetic, a beauty of soul and thought resembling one of Edgar Poe's creations of the other world. The hair parted, and standing away from the head, gave the appearance of a halo; a prominent calm forehead . . . large eyes full of light, encircled by a dark ring, and the musical voice of an ephebe."

For forty-five years husband and wife lived side by side; they were not separated for a day. In the closest union of heart and thought their affection was never veiled by the slightest cloud.

The loss of her grandson in a railway accident was Madame Berthelot's death-blow. The first attack of heart disease she got over, but at the close of 1906 her husband saw that nothing could stop it. Then this old man of eighty was to be seen watching night and day at the bedside of his dear patient, measuring hour by hour the diminution of her vital forces at the same time as he noted the deep inroads made in his own organism by the keen anguish which he suffered. The patient retained her admirable serenity until the last hour, and her last words were said to her daughter: "What will become of him when I am gone?"

A few minutes later one of his sons, who had followed him into the room, heard him heave a deep and harrowing sigh; he took his hand to say a few tender words of consolation to him, but the arm dropped inactive. Through the sad blow, that great heart was broken.

Madame Berthelot was buried with her husband in the Pantheon, the first time that this supreme honor was rendered to a woman.

Had his life been spared, Berthelot would, a friend says, probably have astonished the world by his observations on trees as regulators of electricity and as possible media of electrical communication, and on the world-wide disasters which the clearing off of forests to make paper is likely to occasion. His walks in the forests of Meudon opened to him new and original views on the harmonies of creation.

Berthelot was a charming lecturer, charming from every point of view—artistic expression, voice, enunciation, and appearance.

There was often a rhythm in his sentences which caught the ear and helped the memory to retain them. His knowledge of Greek and Latin was deep, and he thought the classics an invaluable mental discipline.

His son, Philippe Berthelot, is now in the Foreign Office at Paris and many of us foreigners who live in France have reason to be grateful to him. He too lives quite simply but is naturally proud of his father's extraordinary character and noble achievements. I often think of Marcelin Berthelot as an ideal; he is the first man of whom I have said this: he was as unselfish and sweet natured as Debs, with a thousand times his powers and temptations. We are apt to think of Frenchmen as resembling Rochefort; it is well to be reminded sometimes that there are Frenchmen such as Marcelin Berthelot.

Chapter XIII

THE NOTE OF ALL THE FIRST YEARS of the new century was the change in feeling between England and Germany. The feeling in England towards Germany [had grown] steadily worse ever since the Kaiser's letter backing up Krueger in 1896, and every word of braggadocio of the German Emperor about the growth of the German fleet intensified the bitterness in England.

Curiously enough, almost all the chief London journalists worked persistently to increase the bad feeling. Colonel Maxse and his friends in the *National Review* let no opportunity pass unused, and Mr. Strachey and his staff in *The Spectator* were just as venomous; Sir Rowland Blennerhasset, too, in *The Fortnightly*; Dr. Dillon in *The Contemporary;* and Mr. Arnold White as a free lance did all they could to fan the flame of hatred.*

In June, 1913 the Kaiser celebrated the twenty-fifth anniversary of his ascension to the throne. The assemblage of kings and princes and all the notables of Germany gave a truly imperial color to the proceedings, and the military pageant was very impressive. The unparalleled expansion of German commerce and manufacture owed something to his encouragement. In not a few departments German science had won to the first place in the world. The population had increased from forty-two to sixty-six millions. The birth-rate, though decreasing, averaged thirty-one per 1,000 against twenty-six in England and ten in France. Agriculture had prospered greatly and now supplied Germany with ninety-five per cent of her necessary food, though prices had risen considerably. The German railways totaled 60,000 kilometers, 230,000 ships passed in and out of her harbors annually, and the commerce of Hamburg was exceeded only by that of London. In the production of sugar Germany stood first with two million tons yearly, and potash was almost exclusively a German possession. More important still, in the production of iron Germany was second only to the United States, in that of coal she took third place after the United States and England. It was stated in the Reichstag that if the recent growth of trade could be

---

* Colonel Maxse (1864–1932); John St. Loe Strachey (1860–1927); Sir Rowland Blennerhasset (1832–1907); Emile Joseph Dillon (1854–1933); Arnold White (1848–1925)

maintained, Germany in this respect would surpass England in ten years and occupy the first place.

In the same month of June, 1913 President Poincaré* was asked to pay a visit to England and was feted everywhere as "a friend and ally." Of course, it was a formal visit to King George, yet Poincaré was the chief figure at the great review of English battleships at Portsmouth. Several papers lauded the late King Edward for having brought about the first good understanding with France.

Meanwhile peace conferences followed each other as if in derision and at the end of August, 1913, a great Palace of Peace, due to the liberality of Andrew Carnegie, was opened at the Hague. It was the first universally recognized temple of peace and was praised on all hands in the press as a time mark of "visible history." First the Hague Peace Conference of 1899 and now this "pledge of peace universal and eternal," as the magazines called it: twenty years ago a dream and now "a permanent Palace of Peace to express the unity of the entire race." Mr. Van Swinderen, the head of the permanent Board of Arbitration, in his speech accepting the custody of the magnificent building said, "No international controversies were so serious that they could not be settled peaceably if both parties desired it." Meanwhile it was asserted openly by the representatives of labor that the previous peace conference had been a failure chiefly because no one cared to propose that merchant ships should be immune in all wars.

The second Hague Conference, held in 1907, had proposed that the third should be held in 1915 and that each nation should prepare a committee and charge it to make the proposals considered necessary; but in 1913 neither Russia nor England appointed such a committee. Clearly a pledge of universal and eternal peace needed better ratification than a splendid temple. But Stead, the founder of the *Review of Reviews* and *The War on War,* the great apostle of peace, had unfortunately gone down with the *Titanic* in 1912, and there was no one in England to take his place or work for peace as he had worked. One result was that in 1913–14, when the British expenditure on the army and navy had risen to £75,000,000, the expenditure on the Peace Conference was nil.

When I first began to hear things that led me to believe a world war was possible, I could not credit them. Grey, I said to myself, is too sensible and France has too much to fear; but Germany was always there with her brainless, provoking Kaiser. Still, I made up my mind that there was nothing serious to fear till the spring of 1914, when I was imprisoned by Judge Horridge for contempt of court. Never was there a more unjust verdict. In the journal I had founded, *Modern Society,* an article had appeared commenting on Lord Fitzwilliam's divorce case,** but I was not the editor and

* (1860–1934).
** Fitzwilliam was a correspondent in the divorce case of a Mrs. Leslie Melville; his attorney asked for contempt charges against Harris in January, 1913.

had gone myself to the south of England to write my book on Oscar Wilde and never even saw the article before it was published. For the first time the managing director of a company was held responsible in sheer malice as if he had been the editor. The judge's clerk told me I would be forgiven if I apologized; but I had nothing to apologize for and therefore refused.

I was not a criminal and was only imprisoned by order of the judge and could be let out at any moment. I was therefore treated better than even the first class misdemeanants, but I can never describe how dreadful to me the prison was. Fixed hours for everything: at seven o'clock the light went out and you had to pass the hours till seven next morning in complete darkness. To get hot water to shave was impossible, even if you paid the keepers, and thanks to my wife, who brought me in money, I paid them lavishly, so lavishly that one day the cook came up to know what I would like to eat for lunch. But he could not make bad meat into good meat, or bad mutton into palatable mutton, and when I stopped eating altogether because of the dreadful attacks of indigestion, the doctor came in and found me fainting one day and told me that if I would not eat, I should be forcibly fed. I asked him to let me have hot water to wash my stomach out. He told me he had nothing to do with that. I suffered like a beaten dog every day. Prison in England is for healthy people, but for those with indigestion, it is a perfect hell.

Then the man in the next cell to me kept crying and groaning half the night. If the Horridges could be sent to prison for a week before being appointed, prison life would soon be bettered. But at the end of the week I was told that if I apologized I would be freed; I refused again to apologize. Still my friends did a good deal for me. Lord Grimthorpe and others went to the Home Secretary and declared that my punishment was disgraceful and must be stopped, and at the end of the month Mr. Justice Horridge sent his own doctor to me to see if I was indeed ill. The doctor reported that he would not answer for my life if I were imprisoned for another week and so I was set free.

An amusing incident signalized my deliverance. I had tipped all the keepers and attendants so well that when I went out at ten o'clock in the morning to leave the prison, they all took different parcels of mine to carry for me, half a dozen of them, when suddenly the governor of the prison arrived screaming with rage. "What are you doing here?" he shouted at one keeper.

"Oh," said the one addressed, "I brought his hatbox."

"And you, what are you doing?"

"I brought his coat." Another had brought my rug. The governor was furious with rage and said that one more prisoner, such as I was, would turn the prison upside down. My wife and I stood there laughing.

The prison and my rage at being unjustly punished had broken my health. Horridge and his novel idea of punishing a managing director as if he had been the editor, nearly killed me: I was fifty-eight years of age;

the prison fare had ruined my digestion. I came out very ill indeed and the kindness my friends showed me only increased my dislike of England and most English attributes. I came down to the south of France and there in brilliant sunshine soon began to get better; by the summer I was well again. But now war was in the air and I resolved not to return to England, but go to New York and begin a new life there. With only a few dollars in my pocket I set off; my wife preferred to return to London and await results.

I have often been asked how I managed to succeed in America and succeed so quickly. The story is simple, but I may tell it here. I only knew really one man in New York, but he was both powerful and kindly— Otto H. Kahn.*

In my first days in New York I did a good deal of thinking. I was at the St. Regis Hotel which I had puffed when I visited New York three or four years before. I had then become friends with Mr. Hahn the proprietor, and he was now very nice to me. I asked him to my room one day and put the case before him: would he let me stay at the hotel as I was staying, for three months, and then I would be able to pay him everything. If he could not give me credit, I would have to leave. He told me very nicely that he could not give me three months' credit, so I left next day and went into lodgings on Riverside Drive.

There I sat down and wrote a short article on railroads and sent it to the heads of three railways, including the Union Pacific. I began by saying that there were several great railroads in the world: one of the greatest was the Canadian Pacific that went from Quebec to the Pacific; a still greater railway was the railway that ran across Europe from Calais and across Asia to Vladivostok; but a still greater railway was the Union Pacific that ran from New York to San Francisco because it had done a great deal to bring about the union of the American states. But the greatest of all railways was the Paris-Lyon-Méditerranée. You could embark in Paris and in a few hours be in Dijon, the capital of the old kingdom of Burgundy; or you could remain in your seat all night and get up at Fréjus, in the middle of the civilization of old Rome. The Paris-Lyon-Méditerranée is the greatest railroad in the world because it crosses not only countries but centuries, and annihilates not space only but time.

I sent this little note to the heads of three American railways and asked them if they wanted an advertisement agent who could do new advertisements for them, and whether they would employ me. I told them I wanted a large sum per month, and I gave this little paragraph as a specimen of my work. I was employed by two of them at once, by the Union Pacific and by the Chesapeake and Ohio, and I went down to stay at White Sulphur in Virginia to study the road, being assured of a good reception in the hotel. I must also add that Otto Kahn was kind enough to write both to the Union Pacific and the Chesapeake and Ohio, recommending me.

* (1867–1934); American banker and art patron.

Some time later I got to know Arthur Little,* who was the printer and practically the owner of *Pearson's Magazine*. He was not only kindly but wise and soon put me in the magazine as editor. Of course, I gave up my position on the railways and went back to my old work.

At first, I was very successful with *Pearson's*; the circulation rose rapidly and for nearly a year it looked as if I could make a great magazine out of it. But later came bad times. The Germans had entered France and were beating the French and the English together. They had also in a year practically crushed Russia. The idea was in the air that America should go to the help of the Allies and prevent Germany winning an undeserved victory. I have told the whole story of how America declared war on April the 6th, 1917. I was against the war passionately; I wanted America to force a peace, a "peace without victory," as Wilson had said, which she could have done quite easily. But Wilson was not the man for the job, and so the war dragged on, sacrificing every month more than a million lives. To me it was all horrible and I protested against it in *Pearson's* again and again. That soon got me the dislike of the authorities at Washington and A. S. Burleson, the Postmaster General, held up *Pearson's Magazine* again and again in the post for weeks at a time. When I went to Washington and asked why he did it, he told me that it was on information he had received that it was seditious and against the interests of America. I pointed out that he had been mistaken six times running, but got no satisfaction from the fool. Finally he held up the magazine for twenty-seven days and that practically ruined the circulation. A.S.S. Burleson, as I called him to his face, was too strong for me. Instead of making twenty-five thousand dollars a year, I began to lose money, and soon the position became intolerable to me.

But in 1918 the war ended, as I had predicted it would, and I began to lecture in my bureau on Fifth Avenue in New York, and made some money. But I had to give up my hopes of a great and significant journalistic success, thanks to the enmity of the government at Washington. One little incident will show how far Wilson's spite went.

Suddenly, in 1919, I was asked to produce my naturalization papers. When I told the official that I could not, he said, "Oh, it must be done if you wish to be treated like an American citizen; otherwise you might be turned out of the country." I felt the threat and explained, "I was admitted to the bar in Lawrence, Kansas in 1875 or 1876, and I could not be admitted to the Bar and practice law without being a citizen." He said he had to refer the whole case to Washington. I proved that I was admitted to the bar in Lawrence, Kansas, as I had said, but after two or three days the official came and told me that it was not sufficient, and the government would not regard me as a citizen. I answered, "I have no wish to vote; I only want to remain quietly here."

But he said, "You had better make yourself a citizen, *if you can.*" That

* (1873–1943).

seemed to me significant. Accordingly, I took all the necessary steps and was again accepted as an American citizen in 1919 and so put an end to the petty annoyances of Wilson's government and A. S. Burleson.

One word more to show the idiocy of war. Considerable commotion was excited in June, 1905 by the publication of Sir W. Butler's* report on the clever contrivance by which, after the South African war was over, millions of pounds' worth of stores were sold by the British government to contractors at a low price and immediately bought back by the government from the same contractors at a very high price. Hay, for instance, was sold at eleven shillings per one hundred pounds and bought back at seventeen shillings. As there was no need to have sold it at all—otherwise it would not have been bought back again—this transaction represents an ingenious contrivance to put six shillings for every one hundred pounds of hay sold into somebody's pocket at the expense of the British taxpayer. The hopeless state of confusion into which ministers had allowed everything to slide in South Africa is shown by the fact that they were quite unable to say what had been lost by sheer dishonesty, or whether, as Mr. Balfour wished to make out, England had actually made money on the transactions. Jingo finance is a mere affair of blindman's buff. The War Office at first objected to selling the stores by contract, then gave way. It first demanded monthly returns of sales, and then allowed month after month to pass without any returns being made. Meanwhile, contractors got rich, hand over fist. Ministers obstinately turned a deaf ear to the warnings of the Liberal leader, and instead of exposing, did all they could to hush up the scandal. Fortunately, the auditor-general, an official independent of the executive, brought the matter before the public accounts committee. By this means General Butler's report came to be published. Otherwise everything would have been hushed up "in the best interests of the army."

* (1838–1910); a British general.

Chapter XIV

AND NOW I MUST WRITE of my little mousmée in Japan who came to me of her own accord as secretary and companion. She taught me all I know of Japan and a good deal of girls' nature to boot. First of all she showed me that the position of women in Japan among the better classes was far lower than I had ever supposed it; she assured me that the boy-child in the family was everything and that the girl had to do what she was told; and if she married, the inferiority was only intensified. Whatever her husband did was good, and if his will ran counter to hers in anything, she had simply to give in or be broken. She taught me that the Japanese wife was everything to her husband, not only a mistress but a valet as well. She takes care of his clothing, brings it to him in the morning and helps to put it on, and must put away with care whatever he takes off. In the poorer families all the washing, sewing and mending is done by the wife. Every Japanese woman (excepting those of the highest rank) knows how to sew, and makes not only her own garments, and those of her children, but her husband's as well.

It is the wife who gets up first in the morning, wakes the servants and prepares the breakfast. As soon as she puts out the *andon,* which is the only night light used in Japanese houses and is merely a piece of wick floating in a saucer of vegtable oil, she opens the sliding doors, lets in a flood of light, and soon completes her own hasty toilette.

Certainly a Japanese man is lucky in having all the little things in life attended to by his thoughtful wife—a good, considerate, careful body-servant, always on hand to bear for him all the trifling worries and cares.

The husband once started on his daily rounds, the wife settles down to the work of the house. Her sphere is within her home, and though, unlike other Asiatic women, she goes without restraint alone through the streets, she does not concern herself with the great world. Yet she is not barred out from all intercourse with the outer world, for there are sometimes great dinner parties, given perhaps at home, when she must appear as hostess, side by side with her husband, and share with him the duty of entertaining the guests.

So rigid are the requirements of Japanese hospitality that no guest is ever allowed to leave a house without having been pressed to partake of food, if it be only tea and cake. Even tradesmen or messengers who come to the house must be offered tea, and if carpenters, gardeners, or workmen of any kind are employed about the house, tea must be served in the middle of the afternoon with a light lunch, and tea sent out to them often during their day's work. If a guest arrives in jinriksha, not only the guest, but the jinriksha men must be supplied with refreshments. All these things involve much thought and care on the part of the lady of the house.

Among the daily tasks of the housewife, one, and by no means the least of her duties, is to receive, duly acknowledge, and return in suitable manner, the presents received in the family. Presents are not confined to special seasons. Children visiting in the family are always given toys, and for this purpose a stock is kept on hand. The present giving culminates at the close of the year, when all friends and acquaintances exchange gifts of more or less value, according to their feelings and means. Should there be any one who has been especially kind, and to whom return should be made, this is the time to do it.

The Japanese mother takes great delight and comfort in her children, and the right directions of their habits and manners is her constant thought and care. She seems to govern them entirely by gentle admonition, and the severest chiding that is given them is always in a pleasant voice, and accompanied by a smiling face. Even with plenty of servants, the mother performs for her children nearly all the duties often delegated to nurses in other countries.

From my mousmée I learned everything connected with sex. She taught me that sex-modesty, as we understand it, is utterly unknown in Japan and China too. She brought me to the *géisha-ya* or the establishments where dancing girls are trained before they are let out by the day or evening to tea-houses or private parties. She herself had been trained in one of these from the age of seven by the woman proprietor, and she was one of the best dancers I have ever seen. She taught me that though most of the theatres are for men actors, there [are] also theatres with only women performers, but curiously enough there are no theatres where men and women play together on one stage.

She took me to her professional story-tellers or *hanashika,* just as she took me too to favorite spots near Tokyo to see the famous cherry blossoms in April and May. Thousands of visitors crowd to Uyeno Park for the cherry and peach blossoms, to Kameido for the plum and wisteria, and to Oji for its famous maple trees. A prize fight near London, or a horse race, would hardly attract a larger crowd and would scarcely be more educative. The little mousmée made me understand gradually that Japanese civilization was higher than the English save in the one essential of religion.

Through the knowledge of Japan I learned what Christianity with its care for the individual soul had done for women.

The moment we spoke of sex things (I have forgotten to say that my little mousmée talked a little English) her revelations became extraordinary. I asked her one of the first days how she had lost her virginity, and she told me that one of the school-mistresses had made up to her when she was ten and had soon kissed all her virginity away. She told me never to go with anyone in the Yoshiwara: if I wanted anyone she would soon find out if they were healthy or not and let me know.

"But there," she said, "you are rich. You can have a lovely girl whenever you like without danger; why run any risk?"

At length, shamefaced, I said, "Could you find me one?" "A dozen," she replied laughing, "more seductive than I am."

And in the long run she brought me a girl exquisitely pretty and amiable; but no better than herself, and strange to say, she was resolved to witness the sacrifice. From that moment on I fell for the mousmée herself, and though I was perhaps unfaithful once or twice, for the greater part of my stay in Japan I contented myself with my little friend. I notice that again and again I call her "little"; but she was not little for a Jap and beautifully made to boot.

There was nothing in the way of sex she did not know. She delighted in showing herself to me and was not averse to explaining that when she liked a man, her sex thrilled and plagued her all day long. "Do you never touch it?" I asked.

"What good would that do?" she replied. "When I touch it myself I feel almost nothing, but when you touch it, I go nearly mad." I soon found that her sex was very small; but she assured me that this was a mere question of race. "The Chinese," she said "are far larger than the Japanese." But passion, she always insisted, was a question of temperament and not of the bodily organs; and in time I came to agree with her. "Often," she said, "you make me feel so intensely that my womb comes down to meet you and the inside of my thighs quivers and is sensitive for hours afterwards. I shall be so unhappy when you go away. I would rather die than live and yet I know that you will not, cannot stay here much longer. What am I to do when I can see you no more?"

What was I to say or do? To the best of my ability I consoled her. But before I went she had introduced to me one of the most charming girls I have ever met. She was not one of the prettiest, though her figure was superb, but her face was hardly more than piquant and interesting. But she was full of tricks and whimsies of all sorts. The first time we met when I kissed her she told me she thought it "disgusting"; kissing was a dirty Western custom; but she had no other reservations and showed an individuality of feeling that fascinated me. The next time we met she would not have me talk passion at any price. "I don't want to feel," she said. "I would rather talk. But my friend would always rather feel. Oh, don't say 'no.' That is only a pose; we two know each other."

I soon found she was right; her friend wanted to feel far more than talk.

The mousmée's friend told me curious things. She never wished to give herself until a man said or did something that won her, and after that there was no resistance. "For instance, as you were going away," she said, "you kissed my friend's hand and the courtesy and gentleness woke desire in me."

Shortly afterwards I took her into the bedroom. She stripped herself without a word, but when I had kissed her a little while she grew wild. "I want everything," she said, but when she got it she came back to the kissing. "I had no idea," she cried, "that this means more to girls, excites us more than anything else. You have no idea what it means to me. I feel as if I were going mad. Have you done it to any other girl?"

"To many," I replied. "Some respond as you do, but the majority are comparatively cold."

"Oh, pshaw!" she exclaimed. "You kiss them and let them touch you at the same time and they won't want anything better in life or get anything better."

One day I said to her, "I want you to feel as much as you can. You are so beautifully made. I want you to reach the ultimate: tell me how."

"Begin slowly," she said, "and keep on till I tell you to stop." And so I did. After a quarter of an hour kissing her sex, she began to sigh and squirm and at length she cried: "Stop, stop! I can't stand any more! I'm getting hysterical now and that frightens me!"

My chief pleasure has always been in giving pleasure to girls, for the spasm of delight of a man is too quickly over and brings with it an extraordinary weakness and tiredness that does not disappear for some time, whereas the girl feels no exhaustion whatever.

When I think of the devotion of that mousmée, I am always astonished. She loved me, yet never showed any sex jealousy. On one of the first occasions she brought a pretty geisha to me, saying, "She is famous, but I don't think you'll care for her." Then she got her to lie down and exposed her sex. "You see," she said, parting the lips, "she's not very small and she takes a long time to excite."

"How do you know that?" I asked.

"Because I tried before bothering you with her; but she wanted to come, thinking, I suppose, her eyes would win you." And the girl's eyes were indeed very pretty.

Another time she brought me another mousmée. "Look at her," she cried, "she's worth it. Her sex is smaller than mine. Look," and she showed me her nudity, "and with a touch she is all aflame. Now I'll leave you together, for perhaps she and I together will be able to keep you in Kioto. For you know," and she nestled up to me, "I am beginning to be sure that you really care for me, you're always so kind to me, you dear!"

When I finally left Japan, I gave the mousmée enough to make her independent. Taken all in all, she was one of the best endowed and most charming women I have ever met; to her friend, too, I was more than generous, according to Japanese standards.

A friend who has just read this volume of *My Life* tells me that one omission surprises him. "Why have you written nothing of the scenery and nothing about the great temples or works of art in India, China and Japan?" he asked. "I had thought you would have given us deathless impressions of them, but there is not one word! Why?"

"I am afraid Bernard Shaw's criticism of me is finally correct," I said. "He wrote, you know, that if I were as good a critic of the second rate and third rate as I was of the first rate, I should be the greatest critic that ever lived. So it is with me about scenery and about great works of art. I remember the first time I saw the cathedral of Chartres: I stood before it for hours and cried like a child."

It was one of the great moments of my life. The cathedrals at Amiens and at Beauvais impressed me, too, but Chartres had a sort of personal appeal, as if the maker was full of emotion in his own creation. The cathedral at Reims, too, made a great impression on me. I have seen them a hundred times since and always with the same admiration. But nothing in India, China or Japan gave me an emotion like this. Even Strasbourg or Cologne, or Mon Reale did not appeal to me in the same way, I don't know why.

I can only say that Chartres seemed to me like a hymn of joy in stone— and I must make another sad confession. I was next impressed by one or two of the great buildings in America. I think if you saw one of those buildings put in an open place you would be enormously impressed by it, in spite of its utilitarian ugliness; there is something magnificently grandiose in it that moves the soul.

But, you will say, the scenery, at least in India, might have been described. It is true, I thought Cashmere as beautiful as Switzerland, and the Himalayan mountains were wonderful again and again. But I have never described Switzerland, so why should I describe Cashmere?

It is only the strange or the ineffable that really appeals to me. The Inland Lakes in Japan I could talk about for hours. They are not only very beautiful in themselves, but always mixed up with little views of the charming, courteous, naughty people, who have no morality but live beautifully.

What is the good of word-pictures of places? I have always the feeling it is impossible to give scenery by words. One speaks of a hillside covered with golden gorse, or of a great cliff, or of snow peaks in the further distance; but to conjure up the beautiful scene is beyond the power of the word.

I know nothing of natural beauty that was astonishing in China, and the chief Chinese cities I wish rather to forget than to remember. Japan is the only land in all the East that touched my heart, and its beauties, as I said, are always connected with the charming people.

But all that is probably my limitation. I am sure that if Ruskin had seen one tenth part of what I have seen, he would have given wonderful pictures in words. But I think more of one extraordinary person and find more wonders in one soul and heart like that of Meredith or Dowson than in a thousand scenes belauded in all the guide books. One phrase of Meredith, his laughter, the light in his eyes, as he recited his own poetry gave me unforgettable emotions. Think of a verse like this by Dowson:

> I should be glad of loneliness,
> And hours that go on broken wings,
> A thirsty body, a tired heart,
> And the unchanging ache of things,
> If I could make a single song
> As lovely and as full of light,
> As hushed and brief as a falling star,
> On a winter night.

Chapter XV

Friends in America

IT WAS ON MONDAY, AUGUST 3RD, 1914, that Sir Edward Grey made his great pronouncement in the House of Commons. It appeared from it that on Sunday, the previous day, he had assured France that "in case of any attack upon her unprotected northern and western coasts, the British fleet would give all the protection in its power." He then went on to speak of the necessity of supporting Belgium. At his side sat Asquith, Lloyd George and Winston Churchill, and after his speech the House broke up cheering!

It all seemed to me worse than absurd. Everyone knew that it was the industrial growth of Germany that was the real cause of the enmity between England and Germany, exacerbated, no doubt, by the creation of the German fleet and the idiotic assertions of the Kaiser that he meant it as a counterpoise to the English naval power. But was there sufficient reason for war in all that? Would it not have been wiser for England to develop her industries by giving her work-people better conditions of living? War seemed to me the one unforgivable offense, an outrage on the spirit of good, a crime against humanity.

But war it was nevertheless, a world war without necessity or adequate reason. And soon I was to learn on the best authority that if Germany had known England intended to take sides against her, the war would never have been made. As I have said elsewhere, as soon as the Kaiser knew that England would be among the enemies, he did his uttermost at the last moment to avoid the war. Alas! The die was already cast, and it was crass ignorance of this sort that cost the lives of some thirty millions of human beings and retarded the development of Europe by more than a century, and put a pause to the humanization of man in society.

One day I learned that Le Clos—President Poincaré's house at Campigny —had been shelled in two bombardments. If only the same thing could have happened to Grey's house or Asquith's, I should have chortled. War should be confined to the half dozen men who are responsible for it and then no one would grieve greatly; but that the Kaiser and Grey should be able to sentence millions to an untimely death seems to me worse than madness.

As I have told, I went to New York at the outbreak of the World War and soon found remunerative work. In a year the editorship of *Pearson's Magazine* was offered to me by Arthur Little and at once I got to my real work. No one could have been kinder to me than Little, and as soon as my wife came out and joined me, and we made our home in Washington Square, I was perfectly content.

True, I wanted to go to China and Japan and learn those languages, but after all a man can't do everything in one short life, and I soon made up my mind to make *Pearson's* the best magazine in the United States. I certainly made it better till the beginning of 1917, when I first realized that President Wilson was going to lead the United States into the World War. It seemed insensate stupidity to me that the very man who was the first to talk nobly of "peace without victory" as the ideal, should now wish for victory and war. In every number of the magazine I remonstrated, and as soon as Burleson was made Secretary for the Post Office I found he was injuring the circulation of *Pearson's* in every possible way, legally and illegally. By holding the magazine in the post, pretending to examine it for sedition, he reduced the circulation from 120,000 to 20,000, and that spelt ruin to me.

But I was not conquered even then. Immediately I began to lecture in my shop on Fifth Avenue and at once was making as much money as *Pearson's* had made before. But this doubled my work and the injustice of the government persecution burned in me.

Gradually my thoughts turned away from America. This winter too I caught pleurisy in New York, and I began to long for the milder climate of Nice. "Why kick against the pricks?" I asked myself, and when Wilson led the United States into the World War, I made up my mind to return to France as soon as I could conveniently.

But I had gained in the United States much more than a few thousand dollars. I had won the friendship of Colonel Arthur Little, who afterwards in a hundred ways showed me tireless affection. I have written a portrait of Arthur Little in which I tried to do him justice.

And strangely enough, I had won also the affection of another man, whom I have not yet written about anywhere: J. Wilson Hart. It came about in this way. I was trying to find out why the circulation of *Pearson's* did not increase as it should have increased. I got an introduction to the head of the American News Company and went to see him; he told me little or nothing. But he said the head of the circulation department was a Mr. Hart who would be able to explain everything to me. Accordingly I went into Mr. Hart's room and saw him. Almost immediately I was struck by a sort of English accent. He at once told me he was pure American and not English at all. He explained to me almost everything that I was doing from a popular point of view. "This article," he said, "will do you good; that one will do you harm. You know you are carelessly outspoken and that is always a handicap." Almost at once I got to like his frankness and his understanding, and I asked him if he would come to lunch one day. He came, and we had a long talk, and he asked me to his house too. I began through him to understand the under-currents of American life.

American life is much less prejudiced than English life, but it, too, has its peculiarities. From the moment I gave Hart my first books to read we became real friends and remained friends, I am glad to say, through all the years since. There is no one for whom I have deeper affection or in whom I place more implicit trust. He is really, like Arthur Little, a prince among men, and he and his wife brightened the last days of our stay in New York in a hundred different ways.

Meanwhile it had come into my head to write the story of *My Life*. Time and again I had been shocked by the idiotic prudery of English and American publishers. Once I had sold a book of *Portraits* to Methuen in London. In it I told how I asked Browning once whether he had got the passion of *James Lee's Wife* from his own wife. He told me I had no business to ask that. "It's interesting," I retorted.

"But Shakespeare would never have told you," he replied.

"Of course, he would and he did," I said, and I quoted two or three passages. Browning shook his head and would not confess.

Methuen begged me to cut this passage out of the book. "Everyone," he said, "knows that a gentleman gets all his knowledge of passion from his wife."

"Idiocy," I cried, "sheer idiocy!" But I found American publishers just as unintelligent and quite as prudish.

So gradually the idea grew in me to fight the whole of this prudery and write *My Life* as freely as possible. It was impossible to do this in the United States; no one would have dared to print, much less publish it, and so the idea grew in me to return to Europe.

This project was fostered by the shameful peace in 1918 and the infamous Treaty of Versailles by which, in spite of Wilson's promises, beaten Germany and her allies were cheated and plundered in every possible way and eastern Europe mutilated. A little while later I returned to Europe and, leaving my wife in Nice, went to Berlin to publish the first volume of *My Life and Loves*.

I had no difficulty of any sort and soon found the life in Berlin as interesting as that of Paris. I came to know Gerhart Hauptmann* and other notable writers and illustrators including Grosz.** And the German printers were just as good as English printers. But alas! I made one blunder. An American friend wanted to know one day why I never put any nude pictures in my book. "If you did this," he said, "I could sell five thousand copies of the book in Chicago and send you back nearly fifty thousand dollars." He knew some one too who would supply the pictures, and in a weak moment I yielded. Later I learned that the whole five thousand copies

---

* (1862–1946); German dramatist and novelist.
** George Grosz (1893–   ); after attacking German militarism, he fled to the U.S. in 1932.

were seized in Chicago, and I never got a cent from them. Worse still, the postal authorities also seized some five hundred copies of my book on Oscar Wilde in two volumes, and I got nothing out of the whole shipment. Less than nothing in fact, as I shall now explain. When the English postal authorities seize a book as obscene they burn it or, at least, you are not troubled with it any more; but the American postal authorities confiscated *My Life* and then sold the copies against me. I got several undoubted proofs of this shameful fraud.

In 1920 many thousand copies of Casanova were openly sold in the United States and in Great Britain, but Frank Harris' works were coolly confiscated. Such anomalies in the practice of law are worse than criminal. However, I laughed over them all at the time and they still amuse me. But one thing did not amuse me. After publishing the first volume of *My Life*, I learned that a law had been passed in the U.S. and afterwards adopted in England to the effect that sending any obscene books through the mail was equivalent to publishing them, and such action would be punished by the infliction of a year's imprisonment and up to five thouand dollars fine. Now, some friends had sent copies of my book to America to their friends, and so it seemed to me that I might fall under the whip of this law. But all that I shall discuss in another chapter. Prohibition to enter England never bothered me in the slightest degree. I had no wish to go back there. But possible trouble on entering America was punishment to me as I shall tell.

Chapter XVI

IT IS VERY DIFFICULT for me to write this chapter. I hate accusing my own people of crimes, but now and then it is an imperative duty, an obligation of conscience. These accusations shame me to the soul.

In 1919 Secretary of War Baker* promised to punish the officers who were found guilty of brutalities to soldiers in prison camps in France. "It is not too late," he declared, "to punish any officer or enlisted man still in the service."

It was not too late to punish, but it was too late to prevent atrocious cruelties which stain the name of America, and which it was Secretary Baker's obvious duty to prevent at all costs.

For over two years he had been listening to the reports of courts-martial, confirming or mitigating, and revising them. He ought to have learned his work. "There have been three hundred and fifty thousand condemnations by courts-martial in these United States": I am quoting the daily papers. Dozens of soldiers and conscientious objectors have been sentenced to ten and twenty years' imprisonment for offenses that nowhere else in the civilized world would have been punished with more than one or two years. Secretary Baker sympathized with medieval cruelty or he'd have revised the first of these atrocious sentences. Dozens of men have been tortured till they went mad in prison or committed suicide or died in agony, but Secretary Baker has gone about eating, drinking and talking platitudes, while callously neglecting his chief duty. He has allowed these myriad crimes, these devilish atrocities to be perpetrated under this rule all these months without doing anything to prevent them.

The story of the martyrdom of the three Hofer brothers, who belonged to the religious sect of the Mennonites, will always in my mind be associated with Mr. Secretary Baker.

These men were objectors to war services on religious grounds. Though married, they were taken from their home in South Dakota to Camp Lewis and treated worse than dogs on the way. Their beards were clipped with clippers to make them ridiculous, and they were cursed by the various

* Newton D. Baker (1871–1937).

guards, just to show them what our brand of Christianity means. After two months in close confinement they were court-martialed and sentenced to *thirty-seven years' imprisonment* which, however, was reduced by the commander to *twenty years*.

They were sent to Alcatraz prison in San Francisco Bay, fettered at the ankles and wrists. Here they were put in solitary dungeons below ground in darkness, filth and stench. For four and half days they received no food. They had to sleep on the wet concrete floor, without a blanket. During the next one and a half days they were manacled by the wrists to the bars of their cell, so high that they could hardly touch the floor with their feet. David, the one discharged man now at home, says he still feels the effects in his sides.

When they were taken out of the "hole" at the end of the week, they were covered with scurvy eruptions, insect-bitten, and with arms so swollen that they could not get the sleeves of their jackets over them.

They had been beaten with clubs in the dungeons by their soldier guards so unmercifully that when taken out, Michael fell down unconscious. Did Secretary Baker approve of this? If he didn't, he ought to have taken care that the brutality was never repeated.

The torturing at Alcatraz prison lasted for four months. Then they were transferred to Fort Leavenworth, chained two and two. The journey lasted four days and nights.

At Leavenworth they were driven through the streets and prodded with bayonets as if they had been swine. They were manacled nine hours a day and given only a bread and water diet. Two of the brothers, Joseph and Michael, died under the torturing. Joseph's wife, Marie, almost forced her way to her husband's corpse, and found that he had already been laid in the coffin and was now clad in the military uniform which he had died rather than put on.

Is there any doubt as to who was the better man, the brothers Hofer who went through martyrdom to death for their noble belief, or Secretary Baker, who was responsible for their murder?

After the facts had been brought before the Secretary of State again and again, month after month, day after day, at long-last, on December 6, 1918, nearly a month after the war was ended, Secretary Baker found time to issue an order prohibiting cruel corporal punishment, and the further handcuffing of prisoners to the bars of their dungeons, etc. Secretary Baker then knew such torturing was being practiced, knew too that it was illegal. Five days later, however, Jacob Wipf, who had been confined with the Hofer brothers, was still handcuffed to the bars of his cell for nine hours a day. A monster petition for the release of conscientious objectors was laid before the Secretary of War and further relief was given to the tortured prisoners.

On January 27, 1919, one hundred and thirteen conscientious objectors were discharged from the barracks at Fort Leavenworth in pursuance of an order of Secretary Baker, dated December 2. It took nearly two months to execute an order of this conscientious Secretary, and even then Jacob Wipf was not released. He was only set free on April 13, 1919.

Senator Norris of Nebraska, who had been a judge before he became Senator, said, "The Mennonites are the best people on earth. I have never seen one of them in a court. If everybody were as good as they, there would be no need of courts and prisons."

That is why two out of the three brothers were tortured to death by Secretary Baker, who, however, now says to console us that there is lots of time to punish officers guilty of cruelties.

Secretary Baker could have got good army opinion on these matters, had he wished. The other day Major Harry S. Barrett told a newspaper correspondent at Baltimore that the Kaiser was never such an autocrat as the commissioned officers in the U.S. Army. He said:

At Camp McClellan, where Maryland men were trained for nine months, they lived in a hell. There one's life was not one's own. Such a thing as justice did not exist either for the National Guardsmen or their officers.

Courts-martial were the order of the day, and for even infinitesimal breaches of discipline the lives of men who had freely offered their services for their country were irreparably ruined.

President Wilson chooses his lieutenants characteristically: Burleson and Baker, Burleson who declares that he always acted justly and Baker who is responsible for the torture of hundreds and the murder of dozens of innocent and good men, but who smiles and says it is not too late yet to punish the guilty. Burleson and Baker.

He goes on:

Punishments (by courts-martial) are not only grossly harsh, as compared with the penalties imposed for like offenses by our criminal courts, but they also differ so widely that we find the same offense punished in one court-martial by twenty-five years in the penitentiary and in another by six months' confinement in disciplinary barracks.

A boy overstaying his leave, or yielding to a natural impulse to go home for Christmas, is charged not with absence without leave, but with desertion.

Of course Mr. Secretary Baker is primarily responsible for these atrocities which shame all of us who call ourselves Americans. In spite of being informed again and again of the facts he did nothing till the complaints were brought to the ears of the President, who shortly before leaving for France told Secretary Baker that the torturing should cease. Secretary Baker thereupon issued an order forbidding manacling and some other of the most cruel practices.

He was pressed to amnesty all conscientious objectors at Christmas, but he did nothing till the scandal became intolerable; and then reluctantly— I use the word most advisedly—he released one hundred and thirteen objectors who were illegally confined. There are still three hundred men in Leavenworth military prison alone who should be freed.

Now as the state does not compensate the victims of its blunders as the British do, Mr. Secretary Baker's conduct appears to me beyond excuse.

Here are some facts which may bring home to American men and women the atrocities daily practiced in our prisons on men of the highest character.

It must be understood that I am quoting from a pamphlet entitled, "What happens in Military Prisons," published with a name-list of the persons responsible at Room 1505, 116 South Michigan Avenue, Chicago and vouched for by the statements of a dozen of the conscientious objectors themselves. I also quote from newspapers such as the *World* and *The Literary Digest*.

The crimes (sic) for which the objectors are punished are of many sorts: "Soldier No. 12,135 overdrew his bank account $2 on a $40 cheque. He reimbursed the bank, but the court-martial gave him six years."

In no civilized country would this mistake incur even blame. Mr. Secretary Baker may regard this as a record.

Soldier No. 13,005 took $4,000 from a canteen cash register, pleaded guilty, and was sentenced to a year. He was not obliged to return the money.

Another soldier was given 25 years for overstaying a 48 hours leave by 25 minutes.

This would seem idiotic even in comic opera.

Here are some extracts from the pamphlets which are borne out by affidavits:

Camp Funston, Kansas, Saturday, September 14, Colonel Barnes, the Provost Marshal, called at the Guard House. He ordered us to stand at "attention," and when we refused to comply, he proceeded to kick the legs of the men. . . .

Monday, September 16. We were again placed upon bread and water diet. . . . Between September 7 and 22 we had only two days of regular rations.

Monday, September 23. We were ordered to stand at "attention" by the incoming "officer of the day" and upon refusal we were told that we would be taken out every two hours during the night. This was done.

Friday, September 27. Again, while exercising, the men were grossly maltreated. The bayonet was applied to all of us—Larsen receiving a scar.

At midnight we were suddenly and unexpectedly roused by the sergeant of the guard and ordered to take a cold shower. We were then violently dragged into the shower-room and held underneath the spray, night clothes and all, until thoroughly exhausted. The "Officer of the Day" was present and directed the proceedings.

Another cold shower was administered to us in the afternoon. At 8 P.M. the "Officer of the Day," a captain, and the sergeant of the guard ordered all to undress in the squadron and prepare for a cold shower, the third that day. We were marched to the toilet in a body. The captain himself brought forth scrubbrushes, used ordinarily for cleaning toilet seats and brooms used for sweeping, and ordered that we scrub each other with them. Franklin refused to use the filthy brush. He was seized and roughly thrown to the cement floor, dragged back and forth and viciously belabored until thoroughly exhausted. He was then placed under the cold spray and left there until he collapsed.

Colonel Barnes, the Provost Marshal, called while some of the objectors were taking their enforced exercise. He ordered them to stand at "attention." When they refused he beat them vigorously with his heavy riding crop over the ankles. He deprecated the ruining of his tick, and implied that the only reason he did not brain Shotkin was that "he was not worth the trouble."

Eight more pages filled with similiar atrocities.

The *World* tells of torturing in Alcatraz Island, the notorious California prison, a dungeon on the level of the sea. We quote from their report. No martyr roll can show nobler witnesses:

> The four men were handcuffed by the wrists to an iron bar whose level barely allowed their feet to touch the floor. Guards stripped them of their civilian clothing down to underwear. Blankets or covering of any kind were refused them and they lived in shivering fear of the cold and damp of the cell: . . .
>
> For full 36 hours, these quiet heroes remained "strung up" as it is called. Not a bite of food of any sort was furnished them and but one glass of water. They suffered—chilled to the bone, nearly naked, hungering and thirsting—and with pain and fatigue torturing their every nerve. To add to their torments, guards came to them during this 36-hour period and beat them brutally with clubs. Yet never once did they think of accepting the easy way out by succumbing to the military will.
>
> For the rest of the five-day period they were exempt from this "hanging up," but the other features of the punishment remained in force. They were without clothing. The cell was damp and musty. They were allowed but a single glass of water each 24 hours, and not a morsel of food for the full five days. The dungeon contained no bed and their rest was taken on the water-soaked floor. Washing and toilet facilities were entirely lacking and thus they were forced to live there close to the filth of their own excrement. Frequently the sentries came in to manhandle the victims.
>
> Full of the horror and pain of it all, these four protestants against war gradually became physically weaker and weaker. They felt the "death by inches" close upon them. Sanity remained to them only by the sturdiest effort of will.
>
> At last the authorities, fearing the consequences of their action, released them from this ordeal. They emerged from the dungeon broken in health, and barely managing to walk. Upon reaching the light and fresh air of the upper prison, they were found to have contracted scurvy. . . .
>
> The four men were then sent to Fort Leavenworth where, of course, the cells are much better. Again they were put in solitary confinement. In their weakened condition they contracted pneumonia from sleeping on the bare cement floor. In ten days, two of them were dead. This is how we punish conscientious opinion in the United States in the twentieth century!

And finally, to pile horrors on horror's head, we reproduce the following almost incredible testimony from Fort Oglethorpe, testimony which is, we understand, in the hands of Congressman Dent.

> A captain ordered a conscientious objector placed waist deep in the feces of a latrine pit, and ordered a sergeant to splash filth over him. He was pulled out by fellow prisoners.
>
> A Polish deserter was brought to Fort Oglethorpe suffering from jaundice. He was given no food or medical attention for two days. He was ordered to work by a provost sergeant, but collapsed when he attempted to stand. Lieu-

tenant Massey, the prison official, ordered a guard with a bayonet to force him out. He was jabbed four times and fainted. A little later he died.

The great majority of these prisoners were religious fanatics: nearly all of them endured to the end and some of them won the martyr's crown.

Two of them defy oblivion even in these smug days: one was hanging up by the wrists when he was informed that he had won the Carnegie prize for saving a girl's life at the risk of his own; the other, being ordered into the trenches in France, went "over the top" into "No Man's Land" of his own free will gaily, and brought back wounded soldiers through the rain of bullets.

> How long, O Lord, how long
> Shall Thy handmaid linger?
> She who shall right the wrong
> And make the oppressed strong
> Sweet morrow bring her!
> Hasten her over the Sea!
> Bring her to men and to me!
> O Slave pray still on thy knee
> Freedom's ahead!

The Official answer

The War Department, Washington, D.C.

The Editor PEARSON'S MAGAZINE.

May 10, 1919.

Dear Sir,

The article which appears in your magazine for March, 1919 concerning "The Torturing of Conscientious Objectors," has been referred to this office. It is inevitable, in an army of nearly four million men, gathered with the intention of defending their country from the foreign foe, full of enthusiasm and eagerness to do their utmost in their country's cause, that certain members of this great body, upon meeting other men who profess conscientious scruples against sharing the distress and hardships of the soldier's life, should be totally unable to comprehend such an attitude and should treat them roughly. Such occurrences, however, have been the rare exceptions and not, as your article implies, the general rule. They have not occurred simultaneously, but have been scattered over a period of nearly two years, and in every case where the charges have been in any degree justified, prompt remedial action has been taken, and punishment accorded to those responsible for the conditions. Your article is, in effect, a collection of all charges made at any time with reference to brutal treatment of soldiers of this type, regardless of whether the charges were later definitely disproved, or that if there were any justification therefor, the conditions were promptly remedied; and as such it conveys a false and unjustifiable impression.

Very truly yours,
(Signed) F. P. KEPPEL
Third Assistant Secretary
of War

In my many years of journalism in Great Britain and France, I have again and again had to deal with government officials and their answers to all sorts of charges; but I have never seen so weak an answer as this of Mr. Keppel. Consider first the accusation. In *Pearson's* for March I stated that:

American officers have again and again brutally mishandled conscientious objectors; have frequently beaten defenseless men with whips; have ordered them to be douched with cold water from a power-hose till they fainted; have had them awakened every two hours during the night; had them hung up by their wrists to the bars of their cells for nine hours a day; had them jabbed with bayonets; and have continued these practices and worse till some of their victims died.

Mr. Secretary Baker has dismissed commissioned officers from our army for such cruelties, thus admitting the truth of the accusation.

I went on to say that I had read these charges continually in the *World* and other New York papers and had taken no action in the matter till I saw that Mr. George T. Page, the president of the American Bar Association, had condemned our military laws and our system and methods of administering military justice as "unworthy of the name of law and justice." Then and not until then I formulated the charges as above with a double object: first, to win a general amnesty for all conscientious objectors and secondly, to put an end once for all to all military sentences and to all courts-martial.

In other words, my objects were purely benevolent. I didn't want the officers who had sinned to be punished; I wanted a radically bad system abolished and the victims of the system set at liberty.

Now how does the American War Office, in the person of Mr. Keppel, answer? He says that the cases of "rough treatment" were "inevitable"; were, besides, "the rare exception"; that "in every case prompt remedial action" has been taken and that, seemingly because my article does not admit this, it conveys "a false and unjustifiable impression."

The first part of this answer fills me as an American with almost intolerable shame. Fancy a highly placed government official palliating the torturing of defenseless men as "rough treatment"; and when they died of the "rough treatment," Mr. Keppel shrugs his shoulders and comforts himself with the phrase "that it was inevitable." No, Sir, it was not inevitable, thank God.

Over two thousand conscientious objectors were sentenced in England to various terms of imprisonment: in no case, I believe, was a longer sentence given than two years; in no single case was torturing such as took place in our prisons even alleged. No British officers jabbed defenseless men with bayonets, or beat them with clubs, or kicked them, or did them to death. Such cruelty did not take place in Britain; in America, the land of Lincoln, Mr. Keppel declares it was "inevitable."

I do not believe him; I will not believe him; I regard his defense as a vile slander on my countrymen.

If Mr. Baker had dealt with the first case that occurred, as he should have dealt with it by discharging the officer from the army and setting the victims free, there would have been no second case. It was inevitable that such instances of cruelty should multiply and abound when no attempt was made to punish the offense or restrain the offender.

Think of the shame Mr. Keppel puts upon us Americans. He sees clearly that the passion of the soldier comes from the desire to defend one's country from a foreign foe; but our passion was nothing to that felt in Great Britain. No Zeppelins came over our towns, dropping bombs that destroyed women and children; no submarines blew up our passenger-ships on our coasts, hurrying hundreds of innocent people to a terrible death; we were in no dread of invasion. We had no excuse for passionate anger and the madness of revenge; no blinded officers were being led about our streets; yet it was "inevitable" that we should practice cruelty in cold blood, whereas the British could be humane, even when exasperated by most atrocious injury.

Mr. Keppel has altogether too low an opinion of us Americans. Had Mr. Baker learned the lesson of Lincoln's life and cut down to two years or to one year the first sentence of ten or twenty years passed by an American military court on a conscientious objector, the shame of such sentences would not now be burning in our cheeks.

Mr. Keppel staggers from blunder to blunder in his letter. He says, "Such occurrences were the rare exception" and is not ashamed to add that my "article is in effect a collection of all charges made at any time."

Will it be news to him that I did not quote one whole page in all of the pamphlet entitled, "What Happens in Military Prisons," and left a dozen other pages filled with details of other torturings altogether unmentioned; that I quoted only part of one article in the *World,* leaving a dozen others unused? How dare he say that my article "is in effect a collection of all charges made at any time," when he must know, when he ought to know, when it is his bounden duty to know, that my article did not contain a tenth or a twentieth part of the charges that were made at that time.

I am sorry his disingenuousness compels me to say that such outrages were not the rare exceptions, that the majority of imprisoned conscientious objectors, so far as I have been able to learn, have complained and still complain of atrocious cruelty and ill-treatment.

Mr. Keppel sums up his case for the War Department by asserting that "in every case where the charges have been in any degree justified, prompt remedial action has been taken and punishment accorded to those responsible."

"What "prompt remedial action" is there for murder? What "prompt remedial action" can be offered to a mother who has had a son done to death in such a way?

I am glad, however, that Mr. Keppel makes his ineffable blunder, for in making it he draws attention to one of the worst lacunae in American justice. In one of my articles on the night court in New York, I drew attention to this flaw; but no one in authority saw any personal advantage in correcting it, so it remains to this day, a disgrace to our judicial system.

When a woman is accused before a London magistrate of soliciting men, of being in fact a prostitute, and manages to clear herself of the charge, the magistrate always accords a sum of money from the poor-box to atone for the wrong done her.

This practice of compensation has become a principle of English justice. For instance, a suffragette was sent to prison in Brixton in 1913. She slipped when in prison and broke her ankle. The prison doctor saw her and said it was nothing; she should go on walking. Her month ran out and she was discharged. A competent London doctor examined her and found that her ankle-bone had been broken; through not having been reset, one leg was permanently shorter than the other. The matter was brought to the notice of the Home Secretary, who happened to be Mr. Winston Churchill. He naturally exonerated the doctor from all blame, but accorded to the woman five hundred pounds, or twenty-five hundred dollars, for the injury she had sustained.

Now such action I should call "remedial," though it was hardly prompt. In cases of death through a mistake of the court or of the prison authorities, thousands of pounds have been paid to surviving relatives in Great Britain. This is true remedial action. Has Washington taken any such remedial action in any one of the cases of torturing conscientious objectors?

I hope Mr. Keppel will be able to answer me in the affirmative and repeat his pleasing phrase that "in every case prompt remedial action has been taken," in which case I for one shall forgive him, though punishment has not "in every case," or indeed, in any case, been "accorded to those responsible for the conditions."

I even go further (so anxious am I to ignore mistakes and forget punishment so long as I can make reform operative and good triumphant) and hereby promise that if Mr. Keppel will now introduce this reform and see to it that such prompt remedial action is taken in even one case so as to form a precedent, I for my part will from now on refrain from badgering him with his past misadventures and will hold his name, besides, in grateful memory.

Chapter XVII

MANY FRIENDS HAVE ASKED ME to write about my own books: how came I to write *Montes* and *Unpath'd Waters* and my book on Shakespeare, and so forth and so on. All the earlier years of the century I spent on my Shakespeare. Early in life I had read Professor Dowden and other commentators on him and was astounded by their blindness and stupidity. Then came Tyler's book on the Sonnets, which was the final word to Shaw and to a great many others, but not to me. Tyler took it that when Shakespeare in a sonnet speaks of his love for Mary Fitton as lasting three years, that settled the question; and indeed the love began in 1597 and continued to the writing of the sonnet in 1600.

Sir Sidney Lee* has informed the world that Shakespeare's sonnets were mere "poetical exercises" and the story told in them had nothing to do with his life.

But I knew that Shakespeare had written the story of the sonnets in three plays of that time and so the truth of the story was established. Besides, Mary Fitton was sent home to Cheshire by Elizabeth in 1601 and did not return till 1605, and in these five years Shakespeare wrote all his deepest tragedies. It was easy for me to see that "false Cressida" was a later picture of his dark-eyed girl and that "Cleopatra," completed in 1608, was another full length portrait; and that in fact his love lasted twelve years and not three. The best of his life was given to his love of Mary Fitton, and after 1608, when she finally married and left London, he soon retired to Stratford, his work done. When in his last plays he speaks of her, it is with tender affection, as in the fifth act of *Cymbeline,* or in the *Winter's Tale* in those magical lines:

> Thus your verse
> Flowed with her beauty once,

or in high appreciation, as in the speeches of Enobarbus in *Antony and Cleopatra.*

* (1859–1926); noted English scholar, editor of the *Dictionary of National Biography*.

It was Shaw who first advised me to tell all I know of Shakespeare, but I rather fear I have hurt the book as a work of art by telling too much. Yet one little fact has come to me even in this last year, which is full of significance. Of course, I always believed that the Mr. W. H. to whom Shakespeare dedicated the Sonnets was William Herbert, afterwards Lord Pembroke, and that he was the "false friend" whom Shakespeare had sent to plead his cause with the Maid-of-Honor, Mary Fitton. It was Herbert, too, who won the girl for himself and got her with child. But the new facts I have found are illuminating.

It is known that on June 16th, 1600, Herbert and Mary Fitton attended a masque at Blackfriars.

On February 5th, 1601, Mary Fitton proved with child by Herbert, who refused to marry her.

By March 25th their child was still-born.

Now, if flushed with her success in the masque, Mary had yielded to Herbert on that 16th June 1600, the child normally would have been born about March 25th, so that it works out very closely.

In the years of leisure from 1900 to 1914, which I won through selling the *Saturday Review,* I did much of my best work. Of course, the Shakespeare work always came first; but I also wrote *The Women of Shakespeare* and the play *Shakespeare and his Love*; *The Bomb,* too, falls in this period, and most of my best short stories: *Montes the Matador, Unpath'd Waters, The Veils of Isis, Great Days.* Then, too, I completed the first sketch of my *Oscar Wilde.*

While working steadily on my Shakespeare, I kept writing short stories and portraits, and I may say here that the stories always came to me as a whole, complete from the first line to the last. The portraits, on the other hand, were more tricky. Now and then the personality made the portrait, as in the case of Wagner and Dowson, but time and again I had to use now memory, now wit, in order to get a likeness that might be life-worthy. Mencken says my portraits are far better than my stories, but that only shows his personal predilection. I know my stories are my best work. But curiously enough, my short stories are better than my long ones, whereas no short portrait is equal to the one in two volumes I painted of Oscar Wilde. For the forty years of my career as a writer, I have sought perfection and time and again have done my best. My autobiography is sure of long life, but before I lay down the pen finally, I want to create one generic figure that will rank with Hamlet and Falstaff, with Don Quixote and Sancho Panza. I have chosen a jealous woman as my prototype and hope to render her in a three-act play astonishingly, for I have always found women infinitely more jealous than men. Who ever saw a man jealous of his son and his son's affection? But I have known women so jealous of their daughters that they went nearly crazy with rage and hate. And not one form of jealousy is peculiarly feminine, but several. The mother is jealous of her child's love of a man, jealous of the girl herself, jealous of the affection the girl shows to others—jealousy is the woman's passion. And it is very curious that the sensual animal love of a man is never so cursed by jealousy as the higher, more spiritually responsive: she is cursed with the lowest form of spiteful denigration, just as the loveliness of her body is often deformed by immense breasts or buttocks. This work I hope to finish in this summer of 1928.

There is one long novel of mine, *The Bomb,* which pleases me in every respect, and I believe *The Bomb* will be read and enjoyed when its author is no longer among the living.

Montes the Matador, [which] some regard as my best story, was written after a visit to Spain. Naturally, loving Spain, I studied the bull-ring and have, I think, the unique honor among foreigners of twice taking part in the proceedings. I had learned all about cows and bulls as a cowboy on the Texas-Mexican frontier, and while in Spain I found the story of a man who stood with legs and arms tied together on a table covered with a red cloth to await the bull's onset. I knew that one could jump as far with his legs tied together as if they were free, and so I offered to try this feat and was accepted in the bull-ring. I never had so much applause in my life and never earned it so easily. I made up my mind to write *Montes* as a sort of corrective to the *Carmen.* Spanish men seemed to me quite as fine as Spanish women, and I thought I could beat *Carmen.* When Meredith said I had succeeded I was mightily uplifted and never afterwards troubled greatly about what Tom, Dick or Harry said of my work. Meredith to me was among the immortals and his praise was conclusive.

I am often asked why I now write no more stories. I have written two or three more, notably *Beyond Good and Evil,* and *A Last Kindness,* and several plays, especially *A New Commandment* and *The Bucket Shop;* but in the last five or six years the shaping spirit of imagination seems to have left me. I can write as good a portrait tomorrow as any I have done, but a short story must come to me of itself to be any good—these are born, not made.

After all, I have done enough: half a dozen of the best short stories in English; and more than a dozen of the best "portraits" of my contemporaries; the best book of criticism to be found anywhere—*The Man Shakespeare*; the best biography, *The Life and Confessions of Oscar Wilde*; and I dare to believe the best autobiography ever written, *My Life*; to say nothing of such books as *The Bomb* and *Great Days*; and such plays as *Mr. and Mrs. Daventry,* which ran one hundred and sixty nights in London.

And now I want to do the fifth volume of *My Life* and a long novel, *Pantopia, or the Undiscovered Country,* and then I shall have finished.

Meanwhile my life is not unpleasant: lying in my bed of a morning, the servant comes in to open the blinds and lets in a flood of golden sunshine. Then she brings me my tea and the papers; I settle down to an hour of pure enjoyment. Later there is a walk with my wife to the old Roman Arena at Cimiez with gorgeous views over the mountains and sea; then return home and lunch and after lunch a nap; then the newest book in German or Italian or French. About three we drive into the mountains and about five home again and new books till dinner at seven-thirty; and then my own writing to revise or books again till bedtime. What a good life!

Another day some friends call and there is always the attraction of the unknown or partially known. Twice a week I go to the theatre or opera, and twice a week to this or that cinema. With the cinema I am nearly always disappointed; it is strange to me that people should produce such bad shows. The best I have seen lately is one on Napoleon that covered three nights, and yet the man who wrote it evidently knew little or nothing of his subject. A friend, too, has just sent me a play on Shakespeare by Clemence Dane,* bepuffed in all the English papers, yet it is the worst play on Shakespeare I have seen. It is not only demonstrably false in a hundred particulars, but it is written without the smallest comprehension of the man—a wretched cheap production.

Why is it that I have not done as well here in Nice between 1921 and 1928 as I did in the first years of the century. I think the truth is that ever since I produced the first volume of my Autobiography and so diminished the income from my other works, I have been more or less care stricken. I have always lived comfortably, and suddenly to find my income diminished by more than nine-tenths is not pleasant and forces me to think of ways and means more than of stories or plays.

Yet I hope still to be able to finish all my work. And these last ten years have not been unproductive; not only have I completed four long installments of my autobiography, but I have also done the fifth and sixth volumes of *Portraits* and a book of *Essays*. Now I want to get my life of Shakespeare on the films, and also *Montes* and perchance *The Magic Glasses*.

The film producers, as I have said, in all countries are astoundingly ignorant and stupid, otherwise they would have done my life of Shakespeare long before *The Four Horsemen* that made Ibañez rich. But all new arts are plagued by a want of artists: the artistic faculty is the highest in man and accordingly the rarest. Has not Maugham just told us how he offered work after work cheaply to the film producers and no one would take any of them, whereas now he commands ten times the price he asked ten years ago and gets it without difficulty? Even in Germany they are prodigiously stupid: fancy producing at vast expense a film on Napoleon that lasts for three performances and shows nothing of the character of the protagonist. The poor old fool who wrote it did not even know that he ought particularly to have studied the school years of Napoleon in order to get a glimpse of his soul.

* The pseudonym of Winifred Ashton; the play was *Will Shakespeare*.

Chapter XVIII

The Peace Crime and the Criminals:
Portraits of the Peacemakers

> Go, soul, the body's guest
> Upon a thankless errand;
> Fear not to touch the best
> The truth shall be thy warrant.
>
> *Sir Walter Raleigh*

FOR MONTHS AND MONTHS I was absorbed in trying to divine what took place at the Peace Conference and how so foul and poisonous a brew was concocted by the four head cooks, and now Maynard Keynes,* an Englishman, tells us in this book the whole truth or as much of it as is necessary for us to know. He's a Cambridge don, a student of economics who was present at all the meetings of the Big Four as the representative of the British Treasury.

Nevertheless, the difficulties of his task and the mastery he shows in accomplishing it must not be underrated. Think of the Boer War and the shameful way it was mistold by Conan Doyle;** recall this war and the so-called histories of it, which for the most part are sensational tales spiced with hateful atrocities and foolish paeans invented to intensify patriotic conceit, and consider this book, which tells the truth luminously and nothing but the truth about Clemenceau and Lloyd George and Wilson.

Read for example the pages where Keynes describes Lloyd George's clap-trap electoral appeals at the end of 1918 and the astounding damning conclusion:

He (Lloyd George) had pledged himself and his government to make the demands of a helpless enemy inconsistent with solemn engagements on our part, on the faith of which this enemy had laid down his arms.

---

* (1883–1946); the English economist. The book is *The Economic Consequences of the Peace.*
** (1859–1930); Doyle served as a physician during the Boer War. A pamphlet of his, "The War in South Africa," which presented the British case in that war, and which won him a knighthood, is what Harris refers to.

There are few episodes in history which posterity will have less reason to condone, —a war ostensibly waged in defense of the sanctity of international engagements ending in a definite breach of one of the most sacred possible of such engagements on the part of the victorious champions of these ideals.

As an honorable gentleman, Keynes adds the note:

Only after the most painful consideration have I written these words. The almost complete absence of protest from the leading statesman of England makes one feel that one must have made some mistake. But I believe that I know all the facts, and I can discover no such mistake.

It will hardly help his career to have told the Prime Minister that even General Elections should be fought "on lines of prudent generosity instead of imbecile greed."

Again and again he proves to the hilt that Mr. Lloyd George and the other allied governments acted dishonorably to the beaten Germans, and brainlessly to boot.

It may be postulated at once that Mr. Maynard Keynes will never again be asked to represent the British Treasury at any important conference. Even now he has had to draw what consolation he could from a mere C.B., yet he has written a superb book, while Conan Doyle got a knighthood for writing a series of infamous libels and patriotic falsehoods.

But Keynes, if one can read him rightly from this one book, will care very little what Lloyd George may do for him or to him, or what Sir Eric Geddes* may think about him. He knew that the truth needed telling and he told it—another of the Knights of the Holy Spirit!—who has proven against his will the want of honor and of conscience among the rulers of England.

Clemenceau Painted to the Life

A great feat if you think of it: this young man of thirty-seven daring to measure and depict men of great position, with reputations established in the world, and show them in their futile conceits, senseless greeds, and childish revenges.

He has pictured the biggest of them, Clemenceau, in a great phrase: "He had one illusion—France, and one disillusion—mankind, including Frenchmen, and his colleagues not least."

Keynes proceeds to tell us that the "Tiger's" hatred of Germany was insensate; but he does not forget to add in a note that "he was by far the most eminent member of the Council of Four," and that "he alone amongst the four could speak and understand both French and English." Curiously ill-educated these democratic leaders!

* (1875–1937), member of the war cabinet in 1918.

On another occasion he ranks Clemenceau with Mr. Balfour far above the President as "exquisitely cultivated gentlemen."

His pen-portrait of Clemenceau ranks with the best ever done:

> The figure and bearing of Clemenceau are universally familiar. At the Council of Four he wore a square-tailed coat of very good thick, black broadcloth, and on his hands, which were never uncovered, grey suede gloves; his boots were of thick black leather, very good, but of a country style, and sometimes fastened in front, curiously, by a buckle instead of lace. . . .
>
> He carried no papers and no portfolio, and was unattended by any personal secretary, though French ministers and officials would be present. . . . His walk, his hand, and his voice were not lacking in vigor, but he bore nevertheless, especially after the attempt upon his life, the aspect of a very old man conserving his strength for important occasions. He spoke seldom, leaving the initial statement of the French case to his ministers or officials; he closed his eyes often and sat back in his chair with an impassive face of parchment, his grey gloved hands clasped in front of him.
>
> A short sentence, decisive or cynical, was generally sufficient; a question, and unqualified abandonment of his ministers, whose face would not be saved, or a display of obstinacy reinforced by a few words in a piquantly delivered English.
>
> But speech and passion were not lacking when they were wanted, and the sudden outburst of words, often followed by a fit of deep coughing from the chest, produced their impression rather by force and surprise than by persuasion.

But it is Keynes's picture of Wilson that American readers will look for, and they will certainly not be disappointed. This portrait is full length, and Keynes paints Wilson not only in his habit as he lived, but he reveals fold on fold and corner after corner of his little soul as only a master-artist could discover them.

Wilson's True Portrait

I shall be forgiven for quoting Keynes at length:

> When President Wilson left Washington in 1918, he enjoyed a prestige and a moral influence through the world unequalled in history. . . . The enemy peoples trusted him to carry out the compact he had made with them; and the allied people acknowledged him not as a victor only, but almost as a prophet.
>
> In addition to this moral influence the realities of power were in his hands. The American armies were at the height of their numbers, discipline, and equipment. Europe was in complete dependence on the food supplies of the United States; and financially she was even more absolutely at their mercy. Europe already not only owed the United States more than she could pay; but only a large measure of further assistance could save her from starvation and bankruptcy. Never had a philosopher held such weapons wherewith to bind the princes of this world. . . .
>
> With what curiosity, anxiety, we sought a glimpse of the features and bearing of the man of destiny. . . .

The collapse of the President has been one of the decisive moral events of history. . . . The disillusion was so complete, that some of those who had trusted most, hardly dared speak of it. Could it be true? they asked of those who returned from Paris. Was the Treaty really as bad as it seemed? What had happened to the President? What weakness or what misfortune had led to so extraordinary, so unlooked for a betrayal?

The Great Betrayal

Keynes calls it "a betrayal" because:

The nature of the contract between Germany and the Allies resulting from this exchange of documents (at the Armistice) is plain and unequivocal. The terms of the peace are to be in accordance with the addresses of the President, and the purpose of the Peace Conference is "to discuss the details of their application." The circumstances of the contract were of an unusually solemn and binding character; for one of the conditions of it was that Germany should agree to Armistice terms which were to be such as would leave herself helpless. Germany having rendered herself helpless in reliance on the contract, the honor of the allies was peculiarly involved in fulfilling their part and, if there were ambiguities, in not using their position to take advantage of them.

Now what were the terms of the contract:

The Fourteen Points: (3). "The removal, so far as possible, of all economic barriers and the establishment of an equality of trade conditions among all the nations consenting to the peace and associating themselves for its maintenance."
(4). "Adequate guarantees given and taken that national armaments will be reduced to the lowest point consistent with domestic safety. . . .
There shall be no annexations, no contributions, no punitive damages. . . .
Self-determination—

A solemn contract, Keynes reiterates, "lost in the morass of Paris, the spirit of it altogether, the letter in parts ignored and in other parts distorted."

The German commentators had little difficulty in showing that the draft treaty constituted a breach of engagements and of international morality comparable with their own offense in the invasion of Belgium.

And again: "The quality which chiefly distinguishes this transaction from all its historical predecessors, is its insincerity."
And this "betrayal," this "insincerity," was, in the main, Wilson's. And the explanation is to be found in his mind and character.
It becomes necessary for me to sum up the gist of one hundred pages in one; my readers will follow Keynes's voyage of discovery into the intricacies of Wilson's soul.

The President was not a hero or a prophet; he was not even a philosopher; but a generously intentioned man, with many of the weaknesses of other human beings, and lacking their dominating intellectual equipment which would have been necessary to cope with the subtle and dangerous spellbinders. His temperament was not primarily that of the student or the scholar. . . .

This blind and deaf Don Quixote was entering a cavern where the swift and glittering blade was in the hands of the adversary.

And then the truth in a flash!

Wilson, "The Old Presbyterian"

"The clue once found was illuminating. The President was like a Nonconformist minister, perhaps a Presbyterian. His thought and his temperament were essentially theological not intellectual."

Besides, the man's mind was second-rate:

In fact the President had thought out nothing; when it came to practice his ideas were nebulous and incomplete. He had no plan, no scheme, no constructive ideas whatever for clothing with the flesh of life, the commandments which he had thundered from the White House. . . .

He had not only no proposals in detail, but he was in many respects, perhaps inevitably, ill-informed as to European conditions. And not only was he ill-informed—that was true of Mr. Lloyd George also—but his mind was slow and unadaptable.

And the summing up:

"There can seldom have been a statesman of the first rank more incompetent than the President."

And this verdict is repeated time and again:

"His mind was too slow and unresourceful to be ready with any alternatives. . . . He was far too slow-minded and bewildered."

And again a further ray of light:

He did not remedy these defects by seeking aid from the collective wisdom of his lieutenants. . . .

And this was due to the abnormal reserve of his nature which did not allow near him any one who aspired to moral equality or the continuous exercise of influence.

O shades of Lansing and Bryan and House!

In fine, Wilson had met men "much abler than himself" and he was "foolishly and unfortunately sensitive to the suggestion of being a Pro-German."

At length Keynes takes us to where the spellbinders have learned the Presbyterian temperament of their adversary and proceed to lead him by the nose whither they please—a masterpiece of description.

Having decided that some concessions were unavoidable, Wilson might have sought by firmness and address and the use of the financial power of the United States to secure as much as he could of the substance, even at some sacrifice of the letter. But the President was not capable of so clear an understanding with himself as this implied. He was too conscientious. Although compromises were now necessary, he remained a man of principle and the Fourteen Points a contract absolutely binding upon him. He would do nothing that was not honorable; he would do nothing that was not just and right; he would do nothing that was contrary to his great profession of faith. . . .

Then began the weaving of the web of sophistry and Jesuitical exegesis that was finally to clothe with insincerity the language and substance of the whole Treaty. . . .

The subtlest sophisters and most hypocritical draftsmen were set to work, and produced many ingenious exercises which might have deceived a cleverer man than the President.

Thus instead of saying that German-Austria is prohibited from uniting with Germany except by leave of France (which would be inconsistent with the principle of self determination), the Treaty with delicate draftsmanship states that 'Germany acknowledges and will respect strictly the independence of Austria.' . . .

Thus instead of giving Danzig to Poland, the Treaty established Danzig as a 'Free' City, but includes this 'Free' City within the Polish Customs frontier. . . .

Thus the Saar Valley, which has been German for a thousand years, the Saar Valley, where only a hundred Frenchmen can be found among the 600,000 Germans, is given to France.

And finally the dreadful indictment:

Thus it was that Clemenceau brought to success what had seemed to be, a few months before, the extraordinary and impossible proposal that the Germans should not be heard. If only the President had not been so conscientious, if only he had not concealed from himself what he had been doing, even at the last moment he was in a position to have recovered lost ground and to have achieved some very considerable successes. But the President was set. His arms and legs had been spliced by the surgeons to a certain posture, and they must be broken again before they could be altered. To his horror, Mr. Lloyd George, desiring at the last moment all the moderation he dared, discovered that he could not in five days persuade the President of error in what it had taken five months to prove to him to be just and right.

After all, it was harder to de-bamboozle this old Presbyterian than it had been to bamboozle him; for the former involved his belief in and respect for himself.

Thus in the last act the President stood for stubbornness and a refusal of conciliations.

This is the last touch of consummate irony: "It was harder to de-bamboozle the old Presbyterian than it had been to bamboozle him" because the former involved his self-esteem.

So the curtain is drawn on Wilson's ludicrous conceit. In all history there is no more contemptible figure and hardly one more pathetic.

Another Judgment

Sometime in 1889 or 1890 I was sitting in the office of *The Fortnightly Review* when a Dr. Dillon* was announced, and a slight dark man with Celtic cocked nose and irregular features, sharp eyes and large bald forehead, made his appearance. He wished to write about Russia, he said, and in the course of conversation let out the fact that he had been a professor in a Russian university for some years: Kiev, if I'm not mistaken. I soon found he was one of those Irishmen who are by nature scholars without being pedantic or unduly imaginative; a poised reflective intelligence neither very deep nor very passionate. After an hour's talk I agreed to take a series of articles from him and in the next month or so received his first paper.

I hadn't read twenty lines when I saw that Dillon could write, was eminently articulate indeed, and on occasion, happily rhetorical without reaching new heights.

At the very outset Dillon proved himself a born journalist, splendidly equipped and a master of his instrument, though the instrument was neither very large or unduly subtle.

He told me he didn't wish to sign the papers with his own name; what did I think of E. B. Lanin?

"Born in Dublin?" I enquired, and he laughingly admitted the soft impeachment, for Eblana is Russian for Dublin.

The papers created a certain stir and the next thing I heard was that Dillon was engaged as Special Correspondent by the *Daily Telegraph* and was about to set out for the Near East.

From time to time since I have read and enjoyed his work.

Now comes this book of his, *The Inside Story of the Peace Conference*. It arrived at the same time as Keynes's book so that I was in doubt which book to prefer.

And now that I've read both, my *a priori* guess is more than justified. Keynes's book belongs to literature; indeed, there are pages in it that should not readily die; the picture of Clemenceau is worthy of being compared to a portrait of Clarendon, if not of Carlyle, and Carlyle himself has given us no full length picture of an obstinate, obfuscated, conscientious and conceited Puritan such as Woodrow Wilson.

It is true, after the first hundred pages or so of brilliant portraiture, Keynes's book falls off and drags the reader through a morass of economic detail, only to prove what was self-evident to all impartial thinkers from the beginning, that the so-called reparations and indemnities of the peace treaty are iniquitous and impossible to carry out. The greater part of central Europe and much of eastern Europe has been utterly ruined, partly by the war, but more by the infamous blockade and the prolonged negotiations of

* Emile Joseph Dillon (1854-1933).

the Armistice. As Count Brockdorf-Rantzau* said in May, 1919, "Those who sign this treaty will sign the death sentence of many millions of German men, women and children." Keynes adds, "I know of no adequate answer to these words." And the chief remedy he proposes to cancel all inter-allied indebtedness will do little to repair the mischief already set on foot.

Even if these United States went into the work of rehabilitation with the same contempt for money and sacrifice they showed in prosecuting the war, the ruin would still be wide spread and the suffering appalling. But America is already wearied of altruistic effort, has besides, her own troubles, political and economic, and the vast mass of her population is indifferent to European strugglings, in truth contemptuous of them. Austria and Poland, and in lesser degree Germany, are going to lose millions of women and children by starvation and the diseases consequent on malnutrition, because the 'Little Three' know nothing of the international problems they were suddenly called upon to solve.

Here is where Dillon's book comes in to complete the sad predictions of Keynes. For Dillon knows eastern Europe and Russia intimately, and for thirty years past. He speaks four or five languages fluently and could have been trusted as an envoy or as one of God's spies to go to Moscow or Warsaw or Vienna and bring back the facts of the situation. But Wilson sent out well-intentioned ignoramuses to inform him, and when they came back with unpleasant revelations he refused to hear them in order to protect his own complacent conceit. Lloyd George was unconscious of his own boundless ignorance and Clemenceau was content to ignore all suffering that wasn't French.

The result is that it must be two or three generations at least before Europe recovers from the ruin caused by the infamous prolongation of the British blockade and by the brainless iniquity of those whom Dillon calls "the Wreckers of Versailles." The whole lamentable outcome is foreshadowed and predicted by Dillon with considerable lucidity.

He starts naturally by explaining that Paris was chosen as the place for the Peace Conference in deference to the French desire. Geneva would have been infinitely preferable; accordingly, he hired a house there, only a month later to relinquish it. He sees plainly that the choice of Paris was a terrible initial blunder.

In judging the three or four representatives of the great states, Dr. Dillon is in practical agreement with Mr. Keynes. He says somewhat harsher things about Mr. Lloyd George than even Mr. Keynes did. He begins by telling us that a "good war leader can be a poor peace negotiator." He goes on to call the English Prime Minister "a word weaving trimmer," and declares that he was "guided by no sound knowledge" and was "utterly devoid of the ballast of principle." He proceeds to make fun of Lloyd George's ignorance

---

* (1869–1928); he resigned as foreign minister of Germany, rather than accept the terms of the Versailles Treaty.

of ordinary geography. " 'What is that place Rumania is so anxious to get?' George asked once, meaning Transylvania."

Dillon's judgment of Clemenceau is practically the same as that of Keynes, though not so well expressed. Senor Orlando,* on the other hand, he appears to hold in high esteem.

It is curious that his condemnation of Wilson is even more whole-hearted than Mr. Keynes's!

He says that his coming to Europe "might have become a turning point in the world's history had he transformed his authority and prestige into the driving-requisite to embody his beneficent scheme." But he "wasted the opportunity for lack of moral courage." He calls him another Moses. He explains his failure by saying roundly that he was "cowed by obstacles which his will lacked the strength to surmount." He delights in recording that Mr. Wilson's own correspondent on the *George Washington* set forth his intentions in these words:

"The President sails for Europe to uphold American ideals and literally to fight for his Fourteen Points. The President, at the peace table, will insist on the freedom of the seas and a general disarmament. . . . The seas, he holds, ought to be guarded by the whole world. . . ."

[But:]

The announcement of Mr. Wilson's militant championship brought him a wireless message from London to the effect that the Freedom of the Seas at all events, must be struck out of his program if he wished to do business with Britain. And without a fight or remonstrance the President struck it out. The Fourteen Points, too, were not discussed at the Conference.

The Peace Conference

Dr. Dillon records the fact of the Peace treaty at length. He sums it up by declaring that "from the rank soil of secrecy, repression, and unveracity sprang noxious weeds." He scorns "the idea of separating Vienna from South Moravia, the source of its cereal supplies, situated at a distance of only thirty-six miles, which transformed the Austrian capital into a head without a body." But the "eminent anatomists," he sneeringly adds, played even worse tricks.

We should like to learn with more precision how you conceive the Society of Nations? When you insist on the independence of Belgium, or Serbia, or Poland, twenty or twenty-five millions of people, you surely mean that the masses of the people are everywhere to take over the administration of the country. But it is odd that you did not also require the emancipation of Ireland, of Egypt, of India, and the Phillippines, who amount to nearly 400 millions of souls.

* Vittorio Emanuele Orlando (1860–1952); Premier of Italy 1917–19.

He tells the story of Prinkipo, and attributes the silly proposal to Mr. Wilson, and notes that it ended in comedy.

Finally Dr. Dillon declares that the treaty is a tissue of absurdities and the League of Nations utterly unpractical. The peace treaty, he says, is worse than "the infamous treaty of Brest-Litovsk; no such bitter draught of disappointment was swallowed by the nations since the world first had political history. . . ."

"Freedom of the Seas" became British supremacy of the seas. . . . "Abolition of War" means, as British and American and French generals and admirals have since told their respective fellow-citizens, thorough preparation for the next war. . . . "Open covenants openly arrived at" signify secret conclaves and conspirative deliberations carried on in impenetrable secrecy. . . . "The Self-determination of all peoples" finds its limits in the rights of every great power to hold minor nationalities in thrall.

And he sums up: "Mr. Wilson has discharged the functions of gravedigger to the idea of a pacific society of nations."

Chapter XIX

Last Word

THE MOST IMPORTANT THING in our life to-day is the extraordinary change and transformation brought about by science. I am not thinking chiefly of the airplane or the motor car, but of other changes. The other night I sat in my room in Nice and listened to an opera given in Madrid; half an hour later we heard *Thais* as rendered in the opera house in Paris. And some hours afterwards we heard a "first night" at the Metropolitan in New York; and afterwards I could distinctly hear the thanks of the impresario and recognized his voice.

Still more wonderful is it to sit in your room in the south of France and see as in a glass the finish of the Derby.* Soon events all over the world will be seen in every household. Imagination is staggered by this increase in knowledge, but still it is not very important to the mental or soul growth. And it certainly will do little or nothing to increase goodness in the individual.

It all makes, however, for the solidarity of men and tends to reduce the chance of war. There is progress everywhere, though partial and slight; but meanwhile poverty continues and crimes of all sorts, and it is difficult to be very hopeful.

Of all who have written on this subject, Wells seems to me to have come nearest to what I regard as the heart of truth. He speaks of a "world-mending" movement and says:

It is a movement that aims ultimately to make life nobler and finer, to render the conditions of life better, and great multitudes of people happier and more free and worthy than they are at the present time . . .
One perceives something that goes on, that is constantly working to bring order out of chaos, beauty out of confusion, justice, kindliness out of cruelty and inconsiderate pressure.

And he goes on:

In the matter of thoughtless and instinctive cruelty—and that is a very fundamental matter—mankind mends steadily. I wonder and doubt if in the whole world at any time before this an aged, ill-clad woman, or a palpable cripple

* Harris here must be speaking of seeing the Derby on film.

could have moved among a crowd of low-class children so free from combined or even isolated insult as such a one would be to-day if caught in the rush from a London board school.

Then, for all our sins, I am sure the sense of justice is quicker and more nearly universal than ever before. Certain grave social evils, too, that once seemed innate in humanity have gone—gone so effectively that we cannot now imagine ourselves subjected to them. The cruelties and insecurities of private war, the duel and overt slavery, for example, have altogether ceased, and in all Western Europe and America chronic local famines and pestilence come no more.

It would be difficult to deny all this or indeed any part of it; yet there is another and gloomier side to the picture. The old codes of morality are moribund. The Ten Commandments command only a very qualified assent; the Christian religion as a real inspiration of practical life and conduct is dead; the social conventions and Mrs. Grundy* remain, feebly galling and officious.

Before the war of 1914, wars were usually finished in a few months and with inconsiderable loss. The World War lasted four years, cost thirty millions of lives and incalculable sums of money. Moreover, it has positively worsened the condition of eastern Europe and the whole thing was meaningless and brainless.

The world-mending movement is very slow and partial and it seems certain that the ideal of all sensible men and women will take many centuries to come into being.

Knowledge comes but wisdom lingers,**

and all we can do is just to labor unceasingly to bring the better time nearer.

This, too, is the main object of this book—strange as it may seem to the ordinary philistine who is inclined to condemn whatever is new and to prefer his prejudices to any hopes.

Perhaps it might be possible to regard Goethe's ideal as shown in his *Prometheus* as the highest yet delineated by men. Prometheus is the rebel who defies Zeus, and similarly man must sometimes rebel against the conditions that would dwarf him and hinder the growth of his individuality; he must be a fighter even against the gods, and in his struggle he must prove strong and unyielding, and yet such a disposition should not be a permanent trait of his character.

To get the whole of Goethe one would have to add another character, such as Ganymede to the *Prometheus*. The humanity of such a man teaches him to be tender and pliable, to be full of concession and compromise; he must be courageous and warlike at the same time, kind-hearted and a peacemaker. He must be animated with the spirit of independence and yet be

* See *Speed the Plough*, by Thomas Morton (1764–1838): "Always ding, dinging Dame Grundy into my ears—What will Mrs. Grundy say? What will Mrs. Grundy think?"
** From *Locksley Hall*.

possessed of reverence and regard for order. He must be a doubter and yet have faith.

The more complex the ideal, the more difficult it is to realize and we begin to see that in the nature of things progress must be partial and slow.

But time is longer than we formerly had any conception of. We have recently learned of a civilization many centuries before the Christian era, in which women—it appears—played a high part. In the island of Crete, from 3500 years before our era to 1500 B.C., there existed an extraordinary society, more modern in many respects than that of Greece or Rome.

Dr. Hall* has written a book about it in which he declares it is the most wonderful archaeological discovery of our time. Sir Arthur Evans** and other English investigators have shown from the evidence of the frescoes that women then lived on a practical equality with men. How and why this Cretan empire fell is still obscure; the language those islanders spoke is yet to be deciphered. Still, there can be no doubt that they handed down to Athens a remarkable legacy of beauty and an extraordinary aesthetic sense.

It is plain, too, that the civilization of Egypt had reached a high level earlier still; in fact, we are only just beginning to learn of civilized societies that preceded ours by thousands of years. We men decay and die, but time is practically eternal.

* Harry Reginald Holland Hall (1837–1930); he wrote on art and archaeology.
** (1851–1941); he made noteworthy archaeological discoveries in Crete.

Index

Index